BAG
of
BONES

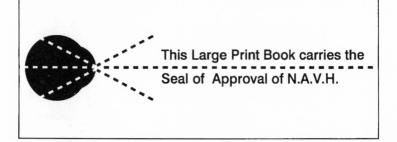

This Large Print Book carries the
Seal of Approval of N.A.V.H.

STEPHEN KING

BAG of BONES

Thorndike Press • Thorndike, Maine

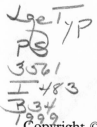

Copyright © 1998 by Stephen King

Acknowledgments may be found on page 899.

Published in 1999 by arrangement with Scribner, an imprint of Simon & Schuster, Inc.

Thorndike Large Print ® Basic Series.

The tree indicium is a trademark of Thorndike Press.

The text of this Large Print edition is unabridged. Other aspects of the book may vary from the original edition.

Set in 16 pt. Plantin by Minnie B. Raven.

Printed in the United States on permanent paper.

Library of Congress Cataloging in Publication Data

King, Stephen, 1947–
    Bag of bones / Stephen King.
      p. cm.
    ISBN 0-7862-1720-0 (lg. print : hc : alk. paper)
    ISBN 0-7862-1721-9 (lg. print : sc : alk. paper)
    1. Large type books. I. Title.
  [PS3561.I483B34 1999]
   813'.54—dc21
                                    98-31495

This is for Naomi.
Still.

Yes, Bartleby, stay there behind your screen, thought I; I shall persecute you no more; you are harmless and noiseless as any of these old chairs; in short, I never feel so private as when I know you are here.

"Bartleby,"
HERMAN MELVILLE

Last night I dreamt I went to Manderley again . . . As I stood there, hushed and still, I could swear that the house was not an empty shell but lived and breathed as it had lived before.

Rebecca,
DAPHNE DU MAURIER

Mars is heaven.
RAY BRADBURY

Author's Note

To some extent, this novel deals with the legal aspects of child custody in the State of Maine. I asked for help in understanding this subject from my friend Warren Silver, who is a fine attorney. Warren guided me carefully, and along the way he also told me about a quaint old device called the Stenomask, which I immediately appropriated for my own fell purposes. If I've made procedural mistakes in the story which follows, blame me, not my legal resource. Warren also asked me — rather plaintively — if I could maybe put a "good" lawyer in my book. All I can say is that I did my best in that regard.

Thanks to my son Owen for technical support in Woodstock, New York, and to my friend (and fellow Rock Bottom Remainder) Ridley Pearson for technical support in Ketchum, Idaho. Thanks to Pam Dorman for her sympathetic and perceptive reading of the first draft. Thanks to Chuck Verrill for a monumental editing job — your personal best, Chuck. Thanks to Susan Moldow, Nan Graham, Jack Romanos, and Carolyn Reidy at Scribner for care and feeding. And thanks to Tabby, who was there for me again when things got hard. I love you, hon.

S.K.

Chapter 1

On a very hot day in August of 1994, my wife told me she was going down to the Derry Rite Aid to pick up a refill on her sinus medicine prescription — this is stuff you can buy over the counter these days, I believe. I'd finished my writing for the day and offered to pick it up for her. She said thanks, but she wanted to get a piece of fish at the supermarket next door anyway; two birds with one stone and all of that. She blew a kiss at me off the palm of her hand and went out. The next time I saw her, she was on TV. That's how you identify the dead here in Derry — no walking down a subterranean corridor with green tiles on the walls and long fluorescent bars overhead, no naked body rolling out of a chilly drawer on casters; you just go into an office marked private and look at a TV screen and say yep or nope.

The Rite Aid and the Shopwell are less than a mile from our house, in a little neighborhood strip mall which also supports a video store, a used-book store named Spread It Around (they do a very brisk business in my old paperbacks), a Radio Shack, and a Fast Foto. It's on Up-Mile Hill, at the intersection of Witcham and Jackson.

She parked in front of Blockbuster Video,

went into the drugstore, and did business with Mr. Joe Wyzer, who was the druggist in those days; he has since moved on to the Rite Aid in Bangor. At the checkout she picked up one of those little chocolates with marshmallow inside, this one in the shape of a mouse. I found it later, in her purse. I unwrapped it and ate it myself, sitting at the kitchen table with the contents of her red handbag spread out in front of me, and it was like taking Communion. When it was gone except for the taste of chocolate on my tongue and in my throat, I burst into tears. I sat there in the litter of her Kleenex and makeup and keys and half-finished rolls of Certs and cried with my hands over my eyes, the way a kid cries.

The sinus inhaler was in a Rite Aid bag. It had cost twelve dollars and eighteen cents. There was something else in the bag, too — an item which had cost twenty-two-fifty. I looked at this other item for a long time, seeing it but not understanding it. I was surprised, maybe even stunned, but the idea that Johanna Arlen Noonan might have been leading another life, one I knew nothing about, never crossed my mind. Not then.

Jo left the register, walked out into the bright, hammering sun again, swapping her regular glasses for her prescription sunglasses as she did, and just as she stepped from beneath the drugstore's slight over-hang (I am imagining a little here, I sup-pose, crossing over into the country of the novelist a little, but not by much; only by inches, and you can trust me on that), there was that shrewish howl of locked tires on pavement that means there's going to be ei-ther an accident or a very close call.

This time it happened — the sort of acci-dent which happened at that stupid X-shaped intersection at least once a week, it seemed. A 1989 Toyota was pulling out of the shopping-center parking lot and turning left onto Jackson Street. Behind the wheel was Mrs. Esther Easterling of Barrett's Or-chards. She was accompanied by her friend Mrs. Irene Deorsey, also of Barrett's Or-chards, who had shopped the video store without finding anything she wanted to rent. Too much violence, Irene said. Both women were cigarette widows.

Esther could hardly have missed the or-ange Public Works dump truck coming down the hill; although she denied this to the police, to the newspaper, and to me when I talked to her some two months later, I think it likely that she just forgot to look. As my own mother (another cigarette widow) used to say, "The two most common ailments of the elderly are ar-thritis and forgetfulness. They can be held

11

responsible for neither."

Driving the Public Works truck was William Fraker, of Old Cape. Mr. Fraker was thirty-eight years old on the day of my wife's death, driving with his shirt off and thinking how badly he wanted a cool shower and a cold beer, not necessarily in that order. He and three other men had spent eight hours putting down asphalt patch out on the Harris Avenue Extension near the airport, a hot job on a hot day, and Bill Fraker said yeah, he might have been going a little too fast — maybe forty in a thirty-mile-an-hour zone. He was eager to get back to the garage, sign off on the truck, and get behind the wheel of his own F-150, which had air conditioning. Also, the dump truck's brakes, while good enough to pass inspection, were a long way from tip-top condition. Fraker hit them as soon as he saw the Toyota pull out in front of him (he hit his horn, as well), but it was too late. He heard screaming tires — his own, and Esther's as she belatedly realized her danger — and saw her face for just a moment.

"That was the worst part, somehow," he told me as we sat on his porch, drinking beers — it was October by then, and although the sun was warm on our faces, we were both wearing sweaters. "You know how high up you sit in one of those dump trucks?"

I nodded.

12

"Well, she was looking up to see me — craning up, you'd say — and the sun was full in her face. I could see how old she was. I remember thinking, 'Holy shit, she's gonna break like glass if I can't stop.' But old people are tough, more often than not. They can surprise you. I mean, look at how it turned out, both those old biddies still alive, and your wife . . ."

He stopped then, bright red color dashing into his cheeks, making him look like a boy who has been laughed at in the schoolyard by girls who have noticed his fly is un-zipped. It was comical, but if I'd smiled, it only would have confused him.

"Mr. Noonan, I'm sorry. My mouth just sort of ran away with me."

"It's all right," I told him. "I'm over the worst of it, anyway." That was a lie, but it put us back on track.

"Anyway," he said, "we hit. There was a loud bang, and a crumping sound when the driver's side of the car caved in. Breaking glass, too. I was thrown against the wheel hard enough so I couldn't draw a breath without it hurting for a week or more, and I had a big bruise right here." He drew an arc on his chest just below the collarbones. "I banged my head on the windshield hard enough to crack the glass, but all I got up there was a little purple knob . . . no bleeding, not even a headache. My wife says

13

I've just got a naturally thick skull. I saw the woman driving the Toyota, Mrs. Easterling, thrown across the console between the front bucket seats. Then we were finally stopped, all tangled together in the middle of the street, and I got out to see how bad they were. I tell you, I expected to find them both dead."

Neither of them was dead, neither of them was even unconscious, although Mrs. Easterling had three broken ribs and a dislocated hip. Mrs. Deorsey, who had been a seat away from the impact, suffered a concussion when she rapped her head on her window. That was all; she was "treated and released at Home Hospital," as the *Derry News* always puts it in such cases.

My wife, the former Johanna Arlen of Malden, Massachusetts, saw it all from where she stood outside the drugstore, with her purse slung over her shoulder and her prescription bag in one hand. Like Bill Fraker, she must have thought the occupants of the Toyota were either dead or seriously hurt. The sound of the collision had been a hollow, authoritative bang which rolled through the hot afternoon air like a bowling ball down an alley. The sound of breaking glass edged it like jagged lace. The two vehicles were tangled violently together in the middle of Jackson Street, the dirty orange truck looming over the pale-blue im-

14

waited on her not fifteen minutes before.

"Mrs. Noonan?" he asked, forgetting all about the compress for the dazed but apparently not too badly hurt Irene Deorsey. "Mrs. Noonan, are you all right?" Knowing already (or so I suspect; perhaps I am wrong) that she was not.

He turned her over. It took both hands to do it, and even then he had to work hard, kneeling and pushing and lifting there in the parking lot with the heat baking down from above and then bouncing back up from the asphalt. Dead people put on weight, it seems to me; both in their flesh and in our minds, they put on weight.

There were red marks on her face. When I identified her I could see them clearly even on the video monitor. I started to ask the assistant medical examiner what they were, but then I knew. Late August, hot pavement, elementary, my dear Watson. My wife died getting a sunburn.

Wyzer got up, saw that the ambulance had arrived, and ran toward it. He pushed his way through the crowd and grabbed one of the attendants as he got out from behind the wheel. "There's a woman over there," Wyzer said, pointing toward the parking lot.

"Guy, we've got two women right here, and a man as well," the attendant said. He tried to pull away, but Wyzer held on.

"Never mind them right now," he said.

"They're basically okay. The woman over there isn't."

The woman over there was dead, and I'm pretty sure Joe Wyzer knew it . . . but he had his priorities straight. Give him that. And he was convincing enough to get both paramedics moving away from the tangle of truck and Toyota, in spite of Esther Easterling's cries of pain and the rumbles of protest from the Greek chorus.

When they got to my wife, one of the paramedics was quick to confirm what Joe Wyzer had already suspected. "Holy shit," the other one said. "What happened to her?"

"Heart, most likely," the first one said. "She got excited and it just blew out on her."

But it wasn't her heart. The autopsy revealed a brain aneurysm which she might have been living with, all unknown, for as long as five years. As she sprinted across the parking lot toward the accident, that weak vessel in her cerebral cortex had blown like a tire, drowning her control-centers in blood and killing her. Death had probably not been instantaneous, the assistant medical examiner told me, but it had still come swiftly enough . . . and she wouldn't have suffered. Just one big black nova, all sensation and thought gone even before she hit the pavement.

"Can I help you in any way, Mr. Noonan?" the assistant ME asked, turning me gently away from the still face and closed eyes on the video monitor. "Do you have questions? I'll answer them if I can."

"Just one," I said. I told him what she'd purchased in the drugstore just before she died. Then I asked my question.

The days leading up to the funeral and the funeral itself are dreamlike in my memory — the clearest memory I have is of eating Jo's chocolate mouse and crying . . . crying mostly, I think, because I knew how soon the taste of it would be gone. I had one other crying fit a few days after we buried her, and I will tell you about that one shortly.

I was glad for the arrival of Jo's family, and particularly for the arrival of her oldest brother, Frank. It was Frank Arlen — fifty, red-cheeked, portly, and with a head of lush dark hair — who organized the arrangements . . . who wound up actually *dickering* with the funeral director.

"I can't believe you did that," I said later, as we sat in a booth at Jack's Pub, drinking beers.

"He was trying to stick it to you, Mikey," he said. "I hate guys like that." He reached into his back pocket, brought out a handkerchief, and wiped absently at his cheeks with it. He hadn't broken down — none of the Arlens broke down, at least not when I was with them — but Frank had leaked steadily all day; he looked like a man suffering from severe conjunctivitis.

There had been six Arlen sibs in all, Jo the youngest and the only girl. She had been the pet of her big brothers. I suspect that if I'd had anything to do with her death, the five of them would have torn me apart with their bare hands. As it was, they formed a protective shield around me instead, and that was good. I suppose I might have muddled through without them, but I don't know how. I was thirty-six, remember. You don't expect to have to bury your wife when you're thirty-six and she herself is two years younger. Death was the last thing on our minds.

"If a guy gets caught taking your stereo out of your car, they call it theft and put him in jail," Frank said. The Arlens had come from Massachusetts, and I could still hear Malden in Frank's voice — *caught* was *coowat, car* was *cah, call* was *caul.* "If the same guy is trying to sell a grieving husband a three-thousand-dollar casket for forty-five hundred dollars, they call it business and ask him to speak at the Rotary Club luncheon. Greedy asshole, I fed him his lunch, didn't I?"

"Yes. You did."

"You okay, Mikey?"

"I'm okay."

"Sincerely okay?"

"How the fuck should I know?" I asked him, loud enough to turn some heads in a nearby booth. And then: "She was pregnant."

His face grew very still. "*What?*"

I struggled to keep my voice down. "Pregnant. Six or seven weeks, according to the . . . you know, the autopsy. Did you know? Did she tell you?"

"No! Christ, no!" But there was a funny look on his face, as if she had told him *something*. "I knew you were trying, of course . . . she said you had a low sperm count and it might take a little while, but the doctor thought you guys'd probably . . . sooner or later you'd probably . . ." He trailed off, looking down at his hands. "They can tell that, huh? They check for that?"

"They can tell. As for checking, I don't know if they do it automatically or not. I asked."

"Why?"

"She didn't just buy sinus medicine before she died. She also bought one of those home pregnancy-testing kits."

"You had no idea? No clue?"

I shook my head.

He reached across the table and squeezed my shoulder. "She wanted to be sure, that's all. You know that, don't you?"

A refill on my sinus medicine and a piece of fish, she'd said. Looking like always. A woman off to run a couple of errands. We had been trying to have a kid for eight years, but she had looked just like always.

"Sure," I said, patting Frank's hand. "Sure, big guy. I know."

It was the Arlens — led by Frank — who handled Johanna's sendoff. As the writer of the family, I was assigned the obituary. My brother came up from Virginia with my mom and my aunt and was allowed to tend the guest-book at the viewings. My mother — almost completely ga-ga at the age of sixty-six, although the doctors refused to call it Alzheimer's — lived in Memphis with her sister, two years younger and only slightly less wonky. They were in charge of cutting the cake and the pies at the funeral reception.

Everything else was arranged by the Arlens, from the viewing hours to the components of the funeral ceremony. Frank and Victor, the second-youngest brother, spoke brief tributes. Jo's dad offered a prayer for his daughter's soul. And at the end, Pete Breedlove, the boy who cut our grass in the summer and raked our yard in the fall, brought everyone to tears by singing "Blessed Assurance," which Frank said had been Jo's favorite hymn as a girl. How Frank found Pete and persuaded him to sing at the funeral is something I never found out.

We got through it — the afternoon and evening viewings on Tuesday, the funeral service on Wednesday morning, then the little pray-over at Fairlawn Cemetery. What I remember most was thinking how hot it was, how lost I felt without having Jo to talk to, and that I wished I had bought a new pair of shoes. Jo would have pestered me to death about the ones I was wearing, if she had been there.

Later on I talked to my brother, Sid, told him we *had* to do something about our mother and Aunt Francine before the two of them disappeared completely into the Twilight Zone. They were too young for a nursing home; what did Sid advise?

He advised something, but I'll be damned if I know what it was. I agreed to it, I remember that, but not what it was. Later that day, Siddy, our mom, and our aunt climbed back into Siddy's rental car for the drive to Boston, where they would spend the night and then grab the Southern Crescent the following day. My brother is happy enough to chaperone the old folks, but he doesn't fly, even if the tickets are on me. He claims there are no breakdown lanes in the sky if the engine quits.

Most of the Arlens left the next day. Once more it was dog-hot, the sun glaring out of a white-haze sky and lying on everything like melted brass. They stood in front of our house — which had become solely my house by then — with three taxis lined up at the curb behind them, big galoots hugging one another amid the litter of tote-bags and saying their goodbyes in those foggy Massachusetts accents.

Frank stayed another day. We picked a big bunch of flowers behind the house — not those ghastly-smelling hothouse things whose aroma I always associate with death and organ-music but real flowers, the kind Jo liked best — and stuck them in a couple of coffee cans I found in the back pantry. We went out to Fairlawn and put them on the new grave. Then we just sat there for awhile under the beating sun.

"She was always just the sweetest thing in my life," Frank said at last in a strange, muffled voice. "We took care of Jo when we were kids. Us guys. No one messed with Jo, I'll tell you. Anyone tried, we'd feed em their lunch."

"She told me a lot of stories."

"Good ones?"

"Yeah, real good."

"I'm going to miss her so much."

"Me, too," I said. "Frank . . . listen . . . I know you were her favorite brother. She never called you, maybe just to say that she missed a period or was feeling whoopsy in the morning? You can tell me. I won't be pissed."

"But she didn't. Honest to God. *Was* she whoopsy in the morning?"

"Not that I saw." And that was just it. I hadn't seen *anything*. Of course I'd been writing, and when I write I pretty much trance out. But she knew where I went in those trances. She could have found me and shaken me fully awake. Why hadn't she? Why would she hide good news? Not wanting to tell me until she was sure was plausible . . . but it somehow wasn't Jo.

"Was it a boy or a girl?" he asked.

"A girl."

We'd had names picked out and waiting for most of our marriage. A boy would have been Andrew. Our daughter would have been Kia. Kia Jane Noonan.

Frank, divorced six years and on his own, had been staying with me. On our way back to the house he said, "I worry about you, Mikey. You haven't got much family to fall back on at a time like this, and what you do have is far away."

"I'll be all right," I said.

He nodded. "That's what we say, anyway, isn't it?"

"We?"

"Guys. 'I'll be all right.' And if we're not, we try to make sure no one knows it." He looked at me, eyes still leaking, handkerchief in one big sunburned hand. "If you're not all right, Mikey, and you don't want to call your brother — I saw the way you looked at him — let me be your brother. For Jo's sake if not your own."

"Okay," I said, respecting and appreciating the offer, also knowing I would do no such thing. I don't call people for help. It's not because of the way I was raised, at least I don't think so; it's the way I was made. Johanna once said that if I was drowning at Dark Score Lake, where we have a summer home, I would die silently fifty feet out from the public beach rather than yell for help. It's not a question of love or affection. I can give those and I can take them. I feel pain like anyone else. I need to touch and be touched. But if someone asks me, "Are you all right?" I can't answer no. I can't say help me.

A couple of hours later Frank left for the southern end of the state. When he opened the car door, I was touched to see that the taped book he was listening to was one of mine. He hugged me, then surprised me with a kiss on the mouth, a good hard smack. "If you need to talk, call," he said. "And if you need to be with someone, just come."

I nodded.

"And be careful."

That startled me. The combination of heat and grief had made me feel as if I had been living in a dream for the last few days, but that got through.

"Careful of what?"

"I don't know," he said. "I don't know, Mikey." Then he got into his car — he was so big and it was so little that he looked as if he were wearing it — and drove away. The sun was going down by then. Do you know how the sun looks at the end of a hot day in August, all orange and somehow *squashed,* as if an invisible hand were pushing down on the top of it and at any moment it might just pop like an overfilled mosquito and splatter all over the horizon? It was like that. In the east, where it was already dark, thunder was rumbling. But there was no rain that night, only a dark that came down as thick and stifling as a blanket. All the same, I slipped in front of the word processor and wrote for an hour or so. It went pretty well, as I remember. And you know, even when it doesn't, it passes the time.

My second crying fit came three or four days after the funeral. That sense of being in a dream persisted — I walked, I talked, I answered the phone, I worked on my book, which had been about eighty per cent complete when Jo died — but all the time there was this clear sense of disconnection, a feeling that everything was going on at a distance from the real me, that I was more or less phoning it in.

Denise Breedlove, Pete's mother, called and asked if I wouldn't like her to bring a couple of her friends over one day the following week and give the big old Edwardian pile I now lived in alone — rolling around in it like the last pea in a restaurant-sized can — a good stem-to-stern cleaning. They would do it, she said, for a hundred dollars split even among the three of them, and mostly because it wasn't good for me to go on without it. There had to be a scrubbing after a death, she said, even if the death didn't happen in the house itself.

I told her it was a fine idea, but I would pay her and the women she brought a hundred dollars each for six hours' work. At the end of the six hours, I wanted the job done. And if it wasn't, I told her, it would be done, anyway.

"Mr. Noonan, that's far too much," she said.

"Maybe and maybe not, but it's what I'm paying," I said. "Will you do it?"

She said she would, of course she would.

Perhaps predictably, I found myself going through the house on the evening before they came, doing a pre-cleaning inspection. I guess I didn't want the women (two of whom would be complete strangers to me) finding anything that would embarrass them or me: a pair of Johanna's silk panties stuffed down behind the sofa cushions, perhaps ("We are often overcome on the sofa, Michael," she said to me once, "have you noticed?"), or beer cans under the loveseat on the sunporch, maybe even an unflushed toilet. In truth, I can't tell you any one thing I was looking for; that sense of operating in a dream still held firm control over my mind. The clearest thoughts I had during those days were either about the end of the novel I was writing (the psychotic killer had lured my heroine to a high-rise building and meant to push her off the roof) or about the Norco Home Pregnancy Test Jo had bought on the day she died. Sinus prescription, she had said. Piece of fish for supper, she had said. And her eyes had shown me nothing else I needed to look at twice.

Near the end of my "pre-cleaning," I looked under our bed and saw an open paperback on Jo's side. She hadn't been dead long, but few household lands are so dusty as the Kingdom of Underbed, and the light-gray coating I saw on the book when I brought it out made me think of Johanna's face and hands in her coffin — Jo in the Kingdom of Underground. Did it get dusty inside a coffin? Surely not, but —

I pushed the thought away. It pretended to go, but all day long it kept creeping back, like Tolstoy's white bear.

Johanna and I had both been English majors at the University of Maine, and like many others, I reckon, we fell in love to the sound of Shakespeare and the Tilbury Town cynicism of Edwin Arlington Robinson. Yet the writer who had bound us closest together was no college-friendly poet or essayist but W. Somerset Maugham, that elderly globetrotting novelist-playwright with the reptile's face (always obscured by cigarette smoke in his photographs, it seems) and the romantic's heart. So it did not surprise me much to find that the book under the bed was *The Moon and Sixpence*. I had read it myself as a late teenager, not once but twice, identifying passionately with the character of Charles Strickland. (It was writing I wanted to do in the South Seas, of course, not painting.)

She had been using a playing card from some defunct deck as her place-marker, and as I opened the book, I thought of something she had said when I was first getting to know her. In Twentieth-Century British Lit, this had been, probably in 1980. Johanna Arlen had been a fiery little sophomore. I was a senior, picking up the Twentieth-Century Brits simply because I had time on my hands that last semester.

"A hundred years from now," she had said, "the shame of the mid-twentieth-century literary critics will be that they embraced Lawrence and ignored Maugham." This was greeted with contemptuously good-natured laughter (they all knew *Women in Love* was one of the greatest damn books ever written), but I didn't laugh. I fell in love.

The playing card marked pages 102 and 103 — Dirk Stroeve has just discovered that his wife has left him for Strickland, Maugham's version of Paul Gauguin. The narrator tries to buck Stroeve up. *My dear fellow, don't be unhappy. She'll come back . . .*

"Easy for you to say," I murmured to the room which now belonged just to me.

I turned the page and read this: *Strickland's injurious calm robbed Stroeve of his self-control. Blind rage seized him, and without knowing what he was doing he flung himself on Strickland. Strickland was taken by surprise and he staggered, but he was very strong, even after his illness, and in a moment, he did not exactly know how, Stroeve found himself on the floor.*

"You funny little man," said Strickland.

It occurred to me that Jo was never going to turn the page and hear Strickland call the pathetic Stroeve a funny little man. In a moment of brilliant epiphany I have never forgotten — how could I? it was one of the worst moments of my life — I understood it wasn't a mistake that would be rectified, or a dream from which I would awaken. Johanna was dead.

My strength was robbed by grief. If the bed hadn't been there, I would have fallen to the floor. We weep from our eyes, it's all we can do, but on that evening I felt as if every pore of my body were weeping, every crack and cranny. I sat there on her side of the bed, with her dusty paperback copy of *The Moon and Sixpence* in my hand, and I wailed. I think it was surprise as much as pain; in spite of the corpse I had seen and identified on a high-resolution video monitor, in spite of the funeral and Pete Breedlove singing "Blessed Assurance" in his high, sweet tenor voice, in spite of the graveside service with its ashes to ashes and dust to dust, I hadn't really believed it. The Penguin paperback did for me what the big gray coffin had not: it insisted she was dead.

You funny little man, said Strickland.

I lay back on our bed, crossed my forearms over my face, and cried myself to sleep that way as children do when they're unhappy. I had an awful dream. In it I woke up, saw the paperback of *The Moon and Sixpence* still lying on the coverlet beside me, and decided to put it back under the bed where I had found it. You know how confused dreams are — logic like Dalí clocks gone so soft they lie over the branches of trees like throw-rugs.

I put the playing-card bookmark back between pages 102 and 103 — a turn of the index finger away from *You funny little man, said Strickland* now and forever — and rolled onto my side, hanging my head over the edge of the bed, meaning to put the book back exactly where I had found it.

Jo was lying there amid the dust-kitties. A strand of cobweb hung down from the bottom of the box spring and caressed her cheek like a feather. Her red hair looked dull, but her eyes were dark and alert and baleful in her white face. And when she spoke, I knew that death had driven her insane.

"Give me that," she hissed. "It's my dust-catcher." She snatched it out of my hand before I could offer it to her. For a moment our fingers touched, and hers were as cold as twigs after a frost. She opened the book to her place, the playing card fluttering out, and placed Somerset Maugham over her face — a shroud of words. As she crossed her hands on her bosom and lay still, I realized she was wearing the blue dress I had buried her in. She had come out of her grave to hide under our bed.

I awoke with a muffled cry and a painful jerk that almost tumbled me off the side of the bed. I hadn't been asleep long — the tears were still damp on my cheeks, and my eyelids had that funny stretched feel they get after a bout of weeping. The dream had been so vivid that I had to roll on my side, hang my head down, and peer under the bed, sure she would be there with the book over her face, that she would reach out with her cold fingers to touch me.

There was nothing there, of course — dreams are just dreams. Nevertheless, I spent the rest of the night on the couch in my study. It was the right choice, I guess, because there were no more dreams that night. Only the nothingness of good sleep.

Chapter 2

I never suffered from writer's block during the ten years of my marriage, and did not suffer it immediately after Johanna's death. I was in fact so unfamiliar with the condition that it had pretty well set in before I knew anything out of the ordinary was going on. I think this was because in my heart I believed that such conditions only affected "literary" types of the sort who are discussed, deconstructed, and sometimes dismissed in the *New York Review of Books*.

My writing career and my marriage covered almost exactly the same span. I finished the first draft of my first novel, *Being Two*, not long after Jo and I became officially engaged (I popped an opal ring on the third finger of her left hand, a hundred and ten bucks at Day's Jewellers, and quite a bit more than I could afford at the time . . . but Johanna seemed utterly thrilled with it), and I finished my last novel, *All the Way from the Top*, about a month after she was declared dead. This was the one about the psychotic killer with the love of high places. It was published in the fall of 1995. I have published other novels since then — a paradox I can explain — but I don't think there'll be a Michael Noonan novel on any list in the foreseeable future. I know what writer's block is now, all right. I know more about it than I ever wanted to.

When I hesitantly showed Jo the first draft of *Being Two,* she read it in one evening, curled up in her favorite chair, wearing nothing but panties and a tee-shirt with the Maine black bear on the front, drinking glass after glass of iced tea. I went out to the garage (we were renting a house in Bangor with another couple on as shaky financial ground as we were . . . and no, Jo and I weren't quite married at that point, although as far as I know, that opal ring never left her finger) and puttered aimlessly, feeling like a guy in a *New Yorker* cartoon — one of those about funny fellows in the delivery waiting room. As I remember, I fucked up a so-simple-a-child-can-do-it birdhouse kit and almost cut off the index finger of my left hand. Every twenty minutes or so I'd go back inside and peek at Jo. If she noticed, she gave no sign. I took that as hopeful.

I was sitting on the back stoop, looking up at the stars and smoking, when she came out, sat down beside me, and put her hand on the back of my neck.

"Well?" I said.

"It's good," she said. "Now why don't you come inside and do me?" And before I

36

could answer, the panties she had been wearing dropped in my lap in a little whisper of nylon.

Afterward, lying in bed and eating oranges (a vice we later outgrew), I asked her: "Good as in publishable?"

"Well," she said, "I don't know anything about the glamorous world of publishing, but I've been reading for pleasure all my life — *Curious George* was my first love, if you want to know —"

"I don't."

She leaned over and popped an orange segment into my mouth, her breast warm and provocative against my arm. "— and I read this with great pleasure. My prediction is that your career as a reporter for the *Derry News* is never going to survive its rookie stage. I think I'm going to be a novelist's wife."

Her words thrilled me — actually brought goosebumps out on my arms. No, she didn't know anything about the glamorous world of publishing, but if she believed, I believed . . . and belief turned out to be the right course. I got an agent through my old creative-writing teacher (who read my novel and damned it with faint praise, seeing its commercial qualities as a kind of heresy, I think), and the agent sold *Being Two* to Random House, the first publisher to see it.

Jo was right about my career as a reporter, as well. I spent four months covering flower shows, drag races, and bean suppers at about a hundred a week before my first check from Random House came in — $27,000, after the agent's commission had been deducted. I wasn't in the newsroom long enough to get even that first minor bump in salary, but they had a going-away party for me just the same. At Jack's Pub, this was, now that I think of it. There was a banner hung over the tables in the back room which said GOOD LUCK MIKE — WRITE ON! Later, when we got home, Johanna said that if envy was acid, there would have been nothing left of me but my belt-buckle and three teeth.

Later, in bed with the lights out — the last orange eaten and the last cigarette shared — I said, "No one's ever going to confuse it with *Look Homeward, Angel*, are they?" My book, I meant. She knew it, just as she knew I had been fairly depressed by my old creative-writing teacher's response to *Two*.

"You aren't going to pull a lot of frustrated-artist crap on me, are you?" she asked, getting up on one elbow. "If you are, I wish you'd tell me now, so I can pick up one of those do-it-yourself divorce kits first thing in the morning."

I was amused, but also a little hurt. "Did you see that first press release from Random

House?" I knew she had. "They're just about calling me V. C. Andrews with a prick, for God's sake."

"Well," she said, lightly grabbing the object in question, "you *do* have a prick. As far as what they're calling you . . . Mike, when I was in third grade, Patty Banning used to call me a booger-hooker. But I wasn't."

"Perception is everything."

"Bullshit." She was still holding my dick and now gave it a formidable squeeze that hurt a little and felt absolutely wonderful at the same time. That crazy old trouser mouse never really cared what it got in those days, as long as there was a lot of it. "*Happiness* is everything. Are you happy when you write, Mike?"

"Sure." It was what she knew, anyway.

"And does your conscience bother you when you write?"

"When I write, there's nothing I'd rather do except this," I said, and rolled on top of her.

"Oh dear," she said in that prissy little voice that always cracked me up. "There's a penis between us."

And as we made love, I realized a wonderful thing or two: that she had meant it when she said she really liked my book (hell, I'd known she liked it just from the way she sat in the wing chair reading it, with a lock of hair falling over her brow and her bare legs tucked beneath her), and that I didn't need to be ashamed of what I had written . . . not in her eyes, at least. And one other wonderful thing: her perception, joined with my own to make the true binocular vision nothing but marriage allows, was the only perception that mattered.

Thank God she was a Maugham fan.

I was V. C. Andrews with a prick for ten years . . . fourteen, if you add in the post-Johanna years. The first five were with Random; then my agent got a huge offer from Putnam and I jumped.

You've seen my name on a lot of bestseller lists . . . if, that is, your Sunday paper carries a list that goes up to fifteen instead of just listing the top ten. I was never a Clancy, Ludlum, or Grisham, but I moved a fair number of hardcovers (V. C. Andrews never did, Harold Oblowski, my agent, told me once; the lady was pretty much a paperback phenomenon) and once got as high as number five on the *Times* list . . . that was with my second book, *The Red-Shirt Man*. Ironically, one of the books that kept me from going higher was *Steel Machine*, by Thad Beaumont (writing as George Stark). The Beaumonts had a summer place in Castle Rock back in those days, not even fifty miles south of our place on Dark Score Lake. Thad's dead now. Suicide. I don't know if it had anything to do with writer's block or not.

I stood just outside the magic circle of the mega-bestsellers, but I never minded that. We owned two homes by the time I was thirty-one: the lovely old Edwardian in Derry and, in western Maine, a lakeside log home almost big enough to be called a lodge — that was Sara Laughs, so called by the locals for nearly a century. And we owned both places free and clear at a time of life when many couples consider themselves lucky just to have fought their way to mortgage approval on a starter home. We were healthy, faithful, and with our fun-bones still fully attached. I wasn't Thomas Wolfe (not even Tom Wolfe or Tobias Wolff), but I was being paid to do what I loved, and there's no gig on earth better than that; it's like a license to steal.

I was what midlist fiction used to be in the forties: critically ignored, genre-oriented (in my case the genre was Lovely Young Woman on Her Own Meets Fascinating Stranger), but well compensated and with the kind of shabby acceptance accorded to state-sanctioned whorehouses in Nevada, the feeling seeming to be that some outlet for the baser instincts should be provided and someone had to do That Sort of Thing. I did That Sort of Thing enthusiastically (and sometimes with Jo's enthusiastic connivance, if I came to a particularly problematic plot crossroads), and at some point around the time of George Bush's election, our accountant told us we were millionaires.

We weren't rich enough to own a jet (Grisham) or a pro football team (Clancy), but by the standards of Derry, Maine, we were quite rolling in it. We made love thousands of times, saw thousands of movies, read thousands of books (Jo storing hers under her side of the bed at the end of the day, more often than not). And perhaps the greatest blessing was that we never knew how short the time was.

More than once I wondered if breaking the ritual is what led to the writer's block. In the daytime, I could dismiss this as supernatural twaddle but at night that was harder to do. At night your thoughts have an unpleasant way of slipping their collars and running free. And if you've spent most of your adult life making fictions, I'm sure those collars are even looser and the dogs less eager to wear them. Was it Shaw or Oscar Wilde who said a writer was a man who had taught his mind to misbehave?

And is it really so far-fetched to think that breaking the ritual might have played a part in my sudden and unexpected (unexpected by me, at least) silence? When you make your daily bread in the land of make-believe, the line between what is and what seems to be is much finer. Painters sometimes refuse to paint without wearing a certain hat, and baseball players who are hitting well won't change their socks.

The ritual started with the second book, which was the only one I remember being nervous about — I suppose I'd absorbed a fair amount of that sophomore-jinx stuff; the idea that one hit might only be a fluke. I remember an American Lit lecturer's once saying that of modern American writers, only Harper Lee had found a foolproof way of avoiding the second-book blues.

When I reached the end of *The Red-Shirt Man*, I stopped just short of finishing. The Edwardian on Benton Street in Derry was still two years in the future at that point, but we had purchased Sara Laughs, the place on Dark Score (not anywhere near as furnished as it later became, and Jo's studio not yet built, but nice), and that's where we were.

I pushed back from my typewriter — I was still clinging to my old IBM Selectric in those days — and went into the kitchen. It was mid-September, most of the summer people were gone, and the crying of the loons on the lake sounded inexpressibly lovely. The sun was going down, and the lake itself had become a still and heatless plate of fire. This is one of the most vivid memories I have, so clear I sometimes feel I could step right into it and live it all again. What things, if any, would I do differently? I sometimes wonder about that.

Early that evening I had put a bottle of Taittinger and two flutes in the fridge. Now I took them out, put them on a tin tray that was usually employed to transport pitchers of iced tea or Kool-Aid from the kitchen to the deck, and carried it before me into the living room.

Johanna was deep in her ratty old easy chair, reading a book (not Maugham that night but William Denbrough, one of her contemporary favorites). "Ooo," she said, looking up and marking her place. "Champagne, what's the occasion?" As if, you understand, she didn't know.

"I'm done," I said. *"Mon livre est tout fini."*

"Well," she said, smiling and taking one of the flutes as I bent down to her with the tray, "then *that's* all right, isn't it?"

I realize now that the essence of the ritual — the part that was alive and powerful, like the one true magic word in a mouthful of gibberish — was that phrase. We almost always had champagne, and she almost always came into the office with me afterward for the other thing, but not always.

Once, five years or so before she died, she was in Ireland, vacationing with a girlfriend, when I finished a book. I drank the champagne by myself that time, and entered the last line by myself as well (by then I was using a Macintosh which did a billion different things and which I used for only one) and never lost a minute's sleep over it. But I called her at the inn where she and her friend Bryn were staying; I told her I had finished, and listened as she said the words I'd called to hear — words that slipped into an Irish telephone line, travelled to a microwave transmitter, rose like a prayer to some satellite, and then came back down to my ear: "Well, then *that's* all right, isn't it?"

This custom began, as I say, after the second book. When we'd each had a glass of champagne and a refill, I took her into the office, where a single sheet of paper still stuck out of my forest-green Selectric. On the lake, one last loon cried down dark, that call that always sounds to me like something rusty turning slowly in the wind.

"I thought you said you were done," she said.

"Everything but the last line," I said. "The book, such as it is, is dedicated to you, and I want you to put down the last bit."

She didn't laugh or protest or get gushy, just looked at me to see if I really meant it. I nodded that I did, and she sat in my chair. She had been swimming earlier, and her hair was pulled back and threaded through a white elastic thing. It was wet, and two shades darker red than usual. I touched it. It was like touching damp silk.

"Paragraph indent?" she asked, as seriously as a girl from the steno pool about to take dictation from the big boss.

"No," I said, "this continues." And then I spoke the line I'd been holding in my head ever since I got up to pour the champagne. " 'He slipped the chain over her head, and then the two of them walked down the steps to where the car was parked.' "

She typed it, then looked around and up at me expectantly. "That's it," I said. "You can write The End, I guess."

Jo hit the RETURN button twice, centered the carriage, and typed The End under the last line of prose, the IBM's Courier type ball (my favorite) spinning out the letters in their obedient dance.

"What's the chain he slips over her head?" she asked me.

"You'll have to read the book to find out."

With her sitting in my desk chair and me standing beside her, she was in perfect position to put her face where she did. When she spoke, her lips moved against the most sensitive part of me. There were a pair of cotton shorts between us and that was all.

"Ve haff vays off making you talk," she said.

"I'll just bet you do," I said.

I at least made a stab at the ritual on the

day I finished *All the Way from the Top*. It felt hollow, form from which the magical substance had departed, but I'd expected that. I didn't do it out of superstition but out of respect and love. A kind of memorial, if you will. Or, if you will, Johanna's real funeral service, finally taking place a month after she was in the ground.

It was the last third of September, and still hot — the hottest late summer I can remember. All during that final sad push on the book, I kept thinking how much I missed her . . . but that never slowed me down. And here's something else: hot as it was in Derry, so hot I usually worked in nothing but a pair of boxer shorts, I never once thought of going to our place at the lake. It was as if my memory of Sara Laughs had been entirely wiped from my mind. Perhaps that was because by the time I finished *Top*, that truth was finally sinking in. She wasn't just in Ireland this time.

My office at the lake is tiny, but has a view. The office in Derry is long, book-lined, and windowless. On this particular evening, the overhead fans — there are three of them — were on and paddling at the soupy air. I came in dressed in shorts, a tee-shirt, and rubber thong sandals, carrying a tin Coke tray with the bottle of champagne and the two chilled glasses on it. At the far end of that railroad-car room, under an eave so steep I'd had to almost crouch so as not to bang my head when I got up (over the years I'd also had to withstand Jo's protests that I'd picked the absolute worst place in the room for a workstation), the screen of my Macintosh glowed with words.

I thought I was probably inviting another storm of grief — maybe the worst storm — but I went ahead anyway . . . and our emotions always surprise us, don't they? There was no weeping and wailing that night; I guess all that was out of my system. Instead there was a deep and wretched sense of loss — the empty chair where she used to like to sit and read, the empty table where she would always set her glass too close to the edge.

I poured a glass of champagne, let the foam settle, then picked it up. "I'm done, Jo," I said as I sat there beneath the paddling fans. "So *that's* all right, isn't it?"

There was no response. In light of all that came later, I think that's worth repeating — there was no response. I didn't sense, as I later did, that I was not alone in a room which appeared empty.

I drank the champagne, put the glass back on the Coke tray, then filled the other one. I took it over to the Mac and sat down where Johanna would have been sitting, if not for everyone's favorite loving God. No weeping

48

and wailing, but my eyes prickled with tears. The words on the screen were these:

```
today wasn't so bad, she sup-
posed. She crossed the grass to
her car, and laughed when she
saw the white square of paper
under the windshield. Cam
Delancey, who refused to be
discouraged, or to take no for
an answer, had invited her to
another of his Thursday-night
wine-tasting parties. She took
the paper, started to tear it
up, then changed her mind and
stuck it in the hip pocket of
her jeans, instead.
```

"No paragraph indent," I said, "this continues." Then I keyboarded the line I'd been holding in my head ever since I got up to get the champagne. `There was a whole world out there; Cam Delancey's wine-tasting was as good a place to start as any.`

I stopped, looking at the little flashing cursor. The tears were still prickling at the corners of my eyes, but I repeat that there were no cold drafts around my ankles, no spectral fingers at the nape of my neck. I hit RETURN twice. I clicked on CENTER. I typed The End below the last line of prose, and then I toasted the screen with what should have been Jo's glass of champagne.

"Here's to you, babe," I said. "I wish you were here. I miss you like hell." My voice wavered a little on that last word, but didn't break. I drank the Taittinger, saved my final line of copy, transferred the whole works to floppy disks, then backed them up. And except for notes, grocery lists, and checks, that was the last writing I did for four years.

Chapter 3

My publisher didn't know, my editor Debra Weinstock didn't know, my agent Harold Oblowski didn't know. Frank Arlen didn't know, either, although on more than one occasion I had been tempted to tell him. *Let me be your brother. For Jo's sake if not your own,* he told me on the day he went back to his printing business and mostly solitary life in the southern Maine town of Sanford. I had never expected to take him up on that, and didn't — not in the elemental cry-for-help way he might have been thinking about — but I phoned him every couple of weeks or so. Guy-talk, you know — *How's it going, Not too bad, cold as a witch's tit, Yeah, here, too, You want to go down to Boston if I can get Bruins tickets, Maybe next year, pretty busy right now, Yeah, I know how that is, seeya, Mikey, Okay, Frank, keep your wee-wee in the teepee.* Guy-talk.

I'm pretty sure that once or twice he asked me if I was working on a new book, and I think I said —

Oh, fuck it — that's a lie, okay? One so ingrown that now I'm even telling it to myself. He asked, all right, and I always said yeah, I was working on a new book, it was going good, real good. I was tempted more than once to tell him *I can't write two paragraphs without going into total mental and physical doglock — my heartbeat doubles, then triples, I get short of breath and then start to pant, my eyes feel like they're going to pop out of my head and hang there on my cheeks. I'm like a claustrophobe in a sinking submarine. That's how it's going, thanks for asking,* but I never did. I don't call for help. I *can't* call for help. I think I told you that.

From my admittedly prejudiced standpoint, successful novelists — even modestly successful novelists — have got the best gig in the creative arts. It's true that people buy more CDs than books, go to more movies, and watch a *lot* more TV. But the arc of productivity is longer for novelists, perhaps because readers are a little brighter than fans of the non-written arts, and thus have marginally longer memories. David Soul of *Starsky and Hutch* is God knows where, same with that peculiar white rapper Vanilla Ice, but in 1994, Herman Wouk, James Michener, and Norman Mailer were all still around; talk about when dinosaurs walked the earth.

Arthur Hailey was writing a new book (that was the rumor, anyway, and it turned out to be true), Thomas Harris could take seven years between Lecters and still produce bestsellers, and although not heard from in almost forty years, J. D. Salinger was still a hot topic in English classes and informal coffee-house literary groups. Readers have a loyalty that cannot be matched anywhere else in the creative arts, which explains why so many writers who have run out of gas can keep coasting anyway, propelled onto the bestseller lists by the magic words AUTHOR OF on the covers of their books.

What the publisher wants in return, especially from an author who can be counted on to sell 500,000 or so copies of each novel in hardcover and a million more in paperback, is perfectly simple: a book a year. That, the wallahs in New York have determined, is the optimum. Three hundred and eighty pages bound by string or glue every twelve months, a beginning, a middle, and an end, continuing main character like Kinsey Millhone or Kay Scarpetta optional but very much preferred. Readers love continuing characters; it's like coming back to family.

Less than a book a year and you're screwing up the publisher's investment in you, hampering your business manager's ability to continue floating all of your credit cards, and jeopardizing your agent's ability to pay his shrink on time. Also, there's always *some* fan attrition when you take too long. Can't be helped. Just as, if you publish too much, there are readers who'll say,

"Phew, I've had enough of this guy for awhile, it's all starting to taste like beans."

I tell you all this so you'll understand how I could spend four years using my computer as the world's most expensive Scrabble board, and no one ever suspected. Writer's block? What writer's block? We don't got no steenkin writer's block. How could anyone think such a thing when there was a new Michael Noonan suspense novel appearing each fall just like clockwork, perfect for your late-summer pleasure reading, folks, and by the way, don't forget that the holidays are coming and that all your relatives would also probably enjoy the new Noonan, which can be had at Borders at a thirty per cent discount, oy vay, such a deal.

The secret is simple, and I am not the only popular novelist in America who knows it — if the rumors are correct, Danielle Steel (to name just one) has been using the Noonan Formula for decades. You see, although I have published a book a year starting with *Being Two* in 1984, I wrote *two* books in four of those ten years, publishing one and ratholing the other.

I don't remember ever talking about this with Jo, and since she never asked, I always assumed she understood what I was doing: saving up nuts. It wasn't writer's block I was thinking of, though. Shit, I was just having fun.

By February of 1995, after crashing and burning with at least two good ideas (that particular function — the *Eureka!* thing — has never stopped, which creates its own special version of hell), I could no longer deny the obvious: I was in the worst sort of trouble a writer can get into, barring Alzheimer's or a cataclysmic stroke. Still, I had four cardboard manuscript boxes in the big safe-deposit box I keep up at Fidelity Union. They were marked *Promise, Threat, Darcy,* and *Top.* Around Valentine's Day, my agent called, moderately nervous — I usually delivered my latest masterpiece to him by January, and here it was already half-past February. They would have to crash production to get this year's Mike Noonan out in time for the annual Christmas buying orgy. Was everything all right?

This was my first chance to say things were a country mile from all right, but Mr. Harold Oblowski of 225 Park Avenue wasn't the sort of man you said such things to. He was a fine agent, both liked and loathed in publishing circles (sometimes by the same people at the same time), but he didn't adapt well to bad news from the dark and oil-streaked levels where the goods were actually produced. He would have freaked and been on the next plane to Derry, ready to give me creative mouth-to-mouth, adamant in his resolve not to leave until he had yanked me out of my fugue. No, I liked Harold right where he was, in his thirty-eighth-floor office with its kickass view of the East Side.

I told him what a coincidence, Harold, you calling on the very day I finished the new one, gosharooty, how 'bout that, I'll send it out FedEx, you'll have it tomorrow. Harold assured me solemnly that there was no coincidence about it, that where his writers were concerned, he was telepathic. Then he congratulated me and hung up. Two hours later I received his bouquet — every bit as fulsome and silky as one of his Jimmy Hollywood ascots.

After putting the flowers in the dining room, where I rarely went since Jo died, I went down to Fidelity Union. I used my key, the bank manager used his, and soon enough I was on my way to FedEx with the manuscript of *All the Way from the Top*. I took the most recent book because it was the one closest to the front of the box, that's all. In November it was published just in time for the Christmas rush. I dedicated it to the memory of my late, beloved wife, Johanna. It went to number eleven on the *Times* bestseller list, and everyone went home happy. Even me. Because things would get better, wouldn't they? No one had *terminal* writer's block, did they (well, with the possible exception of Harper Lee)?

All I had to do was relax, as the chorus girl said to the archbishop. And thank God I'd been a good squirrel and saved up my nuts.

I was still optimistic the following year when I drove down to the Federal Express office with *Threatening Behavior*. That one was written in the fall of 1991, and had been one of Jo's favorites. Optimism had faded quite a little bit by March of 1997, when I drove through a wet snowstorm with *Darcy's Admirer*, although when people asked me how it was going ("Writing any good books lately?" is the existential way most seem to phrase the question), I still answered good, fine, yeah, writing lots of good books lately, they're pouring out of me like shit out of a cow's ass.

After Harold had read *Darcy* and pronounced it my best ever, a bestseller which was also *serious,* I hesitantly broached the idea of taking a year off. He responded immediately with the question I detest above all others: was I all right? Sure, I told him, fine as freckles, just thinking about easing off a little.

There followed one of those patented Harold Oblowski silences, which were meant to convey that you were being a terrific asshole, but because Harold liked you so much, he was trying to think of the gentlest possible way of telling you so. This is a wonderful trick, but one I saw through about six years ago. Actually, it was Jo who saw through it. "He's only pretending compassion," she said. "Actually, he's like a cop in one of those old *film noir* movies, keeping his mouth shut so you'll blunder ahead and end up confessing to everything."

This time I kept my mouth shut — just switched the phone from my right ear to my left, and rocked back a little further in my office chair. When I did, my eye fell on the framed photograph over my computer — Sara Laughs, our place on Dark Score Lake. I hadn't been there in eons, and for a moment I consciously wondered why.

Then Harold's voice — cautious, comforting, the voice of a sane man trying to talk a lunatic out of what he hopes will be no more than a passing delusion — was back in my ear. "That might not be a good idea, Mike — not at this stage of your career."

"This isn't a stage," I said. "I peaked in 1991 — since then, my sales haven't really gone up or down. This is a *plateau*, Harold."

"Yes," he said, "and writers who've reached that steady state really only have two choices in terms of sales — they can continue as they are, or they can go down."

So I go down, I thought of saying . . . but didn't. I didn't want Harold to know exactly how deep this went, or how shaky the ground under me was. I didn't want him to

58

know that I was now having heart palpitations — yes, I mean this literally — almost every time I opened the Word Six program on my computer and looked at the blank screen and flashing cursor.

"Yeah," I said. "Okay. Message received."

"You're sure you're all right?"

"Does the book read like I'm wrong, Harold?"

"Hell, no — it's a helluva yarn. Your personal best, I told you. A great read but also fucking *serious shit*. If Saul Bellow wrote romantic suspense fiction, this is what he'd write. But . . . you're not having any trouble with the next one, are you? I know you're still missing Jo, hell, we all are —"

"No," I said. "No trouble at all."

Another of those long silences ensued. I endured it. At last Harold said, "Grisham could afford to take a year off. Clancy could. Thomas Harris, the long silences are a part of his mystique. But where you are, life is even tougher than at the very top, Mike. There are five writers for every one of those spots down on the list, and you know who they are — hell, they're your neighbors three months a year. Some are going up, the way Patricia Cornwell went up with her last two books, some are going down, and some are staying steady, like you. If Tom Clancy were to go on hiatus for five years and then bring Jack Ryan back, he'd come back strong, no argument. If *you* go on hiatus for five years, maybe you don't come back at all. My advice is —"

"Make hay while the sun shines."

"Took the words right out of my mouth."

We talked a little more, then said our goodbyes. I leaned back further in my office chair — not all the way to the tipover point but close — and looked at the photo of our western Maine retreat. Sara Laughs, sort of like the title of that hoary old Hall and Oates ballad. Jo had loved it more, true enough, but only by a little, so why had I been staying away? Bill Dean, the caretaker, took down the storm shutters every spring and put them back up every fall, drained the pipes in the fall and made sure the pump was running in the spring, checked the generator and took care to see that all the maintenance tags were current, anchored the swimming float fifty yards or so off our little lick of beach after each Memorial Day.

Bill had the chimney cleaned in the early summer of '96, although there hadn't been a fire in the fireplace for two years or more. I paid him quarterly, as is the custom with caretakers in that part of the world; Bill Dean, an old Yankee from a long line of them, cashed my checks and didn't ask why I never used my place anymore. I'd only been down two or three times since Jo died, and not a single overnight. Good thing Bill didn't ask, because I don't know what answer I would have given him. I hadn't even really thought about Sara Laughs until my conversation with Harold.

Thinking of Harold, I looked away from the photo and back at the phone. Imagined saying to him, *So I go down, so what? The world comes to an end? Please. It isn't as if I had a wife and family to support — the wife died in a drugstore parking lot, if you please (or even if you don't please), and the kid we wanted so badly and tried for so long went with her. I don't crave the fame, either — if writers who fill the lower slots on the Times bestseller list can be said to be famous — and I don't fall asleep dreaming of book club sales. So why? Why does it even bother me?*

But that last one I *could* answer. Because it felt like giving up. Because without my wife *and* my work, I was a superfluous man living alone in a big house that was all paid for, doing nothing but the newspaper crossword over lunch.

I pushed on with what passed for my life. I forgot about Sara Laughs (or some part of me that didn't want to go there buried the idea) and spent another sweltering, miserable summer in Derry. I put a cruciverbalist program on my PowerBook and began making my own crossword puzzles. I took an interim appointment on the local YMCA's board of directors and judged the Summer Arts Competition in Waterville. I did a series of TV ads for the local homeless shelter, which was staggering toward bankruptcy, then served on *that* board for awhile. (At one public meeting of this latter board a woman called me a friend of degenerates, to which I replied, "Thanks! I needed that." This resulted in a loud outburst of applause which I still don't understand.) I tried some one-on-one counselling and gave it up after five appointments, deciding that the counsellor's problems were far worse than mine. I sponsored an Asian child and bowled with a league.

Sometimes I tried to write, and every time I did, I locked up. Once, when I tried to force a sentence or two (any sentence or two, just as long as they came fresh-baked out of my own head), I had to grab the wastebasket and vomit into it. I vomited until I thought it was going to kill me . . . and I did have to literally crawl away from the desk and the computer, pulling myself across the deep-pile rug on my hands and knees. By the time I got to the other side of the room, it was better. I could even look back over my shoulder at the VDT screen. I just couldn't get near it. Later that day, I approached it with my eyes shut and turned it off.

More and more often during those

late-summer days I thought of Dennison Carville, the creative-writing teacher who'd helped me connect with Harold and who had damned *Being Two* with such faint praise. Carville once said something I never forgot, attributing it to Thomas Hardy, the Victorian novelist and poet. Perhaps Hardy *did* say it, but I've never found it repeated, not in *Bartlett's*, not in the Hardy biography I read between the publications of *All the Way from the Top* and *Threatening Behavior*. I have an idea Carville may have made it up himself and then attributed it to Hardy in order to give it more weight. It's a ploy I have used myself from time to time, I'm ashamed to say.

In any case, I thought about this quote more and more as I struggled with the panic in my body and the frozen feeling in my head, that awful *locked-up* feeling. It seemed to sum up my despair and my growing certainty that I would never be able to write again (what a tragedy, V. C. Andrews with a prick felled by writer's block). It was this quote that suggested any effort I made to better my situation might be meaningless even if it succeeded.

According to gloomy old Dennison Carville, the aspiring novelist should understand from the outset that fiction's goals were forever beyond his reach, that the job was an exercise in futility. "Compared to the dullest human being actually walking about on the face of the earth and casting his shadow there," Hardy supposedly said, "the most brilliantly drawn character in a novel is but a bag of bones." I understood because that was what I felt like in those interminable, dissembling days: a bag of bones.

Last night I dreamt I went to Manderley again.

If there is any more beautiful and haunting first line in English fiction, I've never read it. And it was a line I had cause to think of a lot during the fall of 1997 and the winter of 1998. I didn't dream of Manderley, of course, but of Sara Laughs, which Jo sometimes called "the hideout." A fair enough description, I guess, for a place so far up in the western Maine woods that it's not really even in a town at all, but in an unincorporated area designated on state maps as TR-90.

The last of these dreams was a nightmare, but until that one they had a kind of surreal simplicity. They were dreams I'd awake from wanting to turn on the bedroom light so I could reconfirm my place in reality before going back to sleep. You know how the air feels before a thunderstorm, how everything gets still and colors seem to stand out with the brilliance of things seen during a high fever? My winter dreams of Sara Laughs were like that, each leaving me with a feeling that was not quite sickness. *I've dreamt again of Manderley,* I would think sometimes, and sometimes I would lie in bed with the light on, listening to the wind outside, looking into the bedroom's shadowy corners, and thinking that Rebecca de Winter hadn't drowned in a bay but in Dark Score Lake. That she had gone down, gurgling and flailing, her strange black eyes full of water, while the loons cried out indifferently in the twilight. Sometimes I would get up and drink a glass of water. Sometimes I just turned off the light after I was once more sure of where I was, rolled over on my side again, and went back to sleep.

In the daytime I rarely thought of Sara Laughs at all, and it was only much later that I realized something is badly out of whack when there is such a dichotomy between a person's waking and sleeping lives.

I think that Harold Oblowski's call in October of 1997 was what kicked off the dreams. Harold's ostensible reason for calling was to congratulate me on the impending release of *Darcy's Admirer*, which was entertaining as hell and which also contained some *extremely thought-provoking shit*. I suspected he had at least one other item on his agenda — Harold usually does — and I was right. He'd had lunch with Debra Weinstock, my editor, the day before, and they had gotten talking about the fall of 1998.

"Looks crowded," he said, meaning the fall lists, meaning specifically the *fiction* half of the fall lists. "And there are some surprise additions. Dean Koontz —"

"I thought he usually published in January," I said.

"He does, but Debra hears this one may be delayed. He wants to add a section, or something. Also there's a Harold Robbins, *The Predators* —"

"Big deal."

"Robbins still has his fans, Mike, still has his fans. As you yourself have pointed out on more than one occasion, fiction writers have a long arc."

"Uh-huh." I switched the telephone to the other ear and leaned back in my chair. I caught a glimpse of the framed Sara Laughs photo over my desk when I did. I would be visiting it at greater length and proximity that night in my dreams, although I didn't know that then; all I knew then was that I wished like almighty fuck that Harold Oblowski would hurry up and get to the point.

"I sense impatience, Michael my boy," Harold said. "Did I catch you at your desk? Are you writing?"

"Just finished for the day," I said. "I am thinking about lunch, however."

"I'll be quick," he promised, "but hang with me, this is important. There may be as many as five other writers that we didn't expect publishing next fall: Ken Follett . . . it's supposed to be his best since *Eye of the Needle* . . . Belva Plain . . . John Jakes . . ."

"None of those guys plays tennis on my court," I said, although I knew that was not exactly Harold's point; Harold's point was that there are only fifteen slots on the *Times* list.

"How about Jean Auel, finally publishing the next of her sex-among-the-cave-people epics?"

I sat up. "Jean Auel? Really?"

"Well . . . not a hundred per cent, but it looks good. Last but not least is a new Mary Higgins Clark. I know what tennis court she plays on, and so do you."

If I'd gotten that sort of news six or seven years earlier, when I'd felt I had a great deal more to protect, I would have been frothing; Mary Higgins Clark *did* play on the same court, shared exactly the same audience, and so far our publishing schedules had been arranged to keep us out of each other's way . . . which was to my benefit rather than hers, let me assure you. Going nose to nose, she would cream me. As the late Jim Croce so wisely observed, you don't tug on Superman's cape, you don't spit into the wind, you don't pull the mask off that old Lone

Ranger, and you don't mess around with Mary Higgins Clark. Not if you're Michael Noonan, anyway.

"How did this happen?" I asked.

I don't think my tone was particularly ominous, but Harold replied in the nervous, stumbling-all-over-his-own-words fashion of a man who suspects he may be fired or even beheaded for bearing evil tidings.

"I don't know. She just happened to get an extra idea this year, I guess. That does happen, I've been told."

As a fellow who had taken his share of double-dips I knew it did, so I simply asked Harold what he wanted. It seemed the quickest and easiest way to get him to relinquish the phone. The answer was no surprise; what he and Debra *both* wanted — not to mention all the rest of my Putnam pals — was a book they could publish in late summer of '98, thus getting in front of Ms. Clark and the rest of the competition by a couple of months. Then, in November, the Putnam sales reps would give the novel a healthy second push, with the Christmas season in mind.

"So they *say*," I replied. Like most novelists (and in this regard the successful are no different from the unsuccessful, indicating there might be some merit to the idea as well as the usual free-floating paranoia), I never trusted publishers' promises.

"I think you can believe them on this, Mike — *Darcy's Admirer* was the last book of your old contract, remember." Harold sounded almost sprightly at the thought of forthcoming contract negotiations with Debra Weinstock and Phyllis Grann at Putnam. "The big thing is they still like you. They'd like you even more, I think, if they saw pages with your name on them before Thanksgiving."

"They want me to give them the next book in November? Next *month?*" I injected what I hoped was the right note of incredulity into my voice, just as if I hadn't had *Helen's Promise* in a safe-deposit box for almost eleven years. It had been the first nut I had stored; it was now the only nut I had left.

"No, no, you could have until January fifteenth, at least," he said, trying to sound magnanimous. I found myself wondering where he and Debra had gotten their lunch. Some fly place, I would have bet my life on that. Maybe Four Seasons. Johanna always used to call that place Frankie Valli and the Four Seasons. "It means they'd have to crash production, *seriously* crash it, but they're willing to do that. The real question is whether or not *you* could crash production."

"I think I could, but it'll cost em," I said. "Tell them to think of it as being like same-day service on your dry-cleaning."

"Oh what a rotten shame for them!" Harold sounded as if he were maybe jacking off and had reached the point where Old Faithful splurts and everybody snaps their Instamatics.

"How much do you think —"

"A surcharge tacked on to the advance is probably the way to go," he said. "They'll get pouty of course, claim that the move is in your interest, too. *Primarily* in your interest, even. But based on the extra-work argument . . . the midnight oil you'll have to burn . . ."

"The mental agony of creation . . . the pangs of premature birth . . ."

"Right . . . right . . . I think a ten per cent surcharge sounds about right." He spoke judiciously, like a man trying to be just as damned fair as he possibly could. Myself, I was wondering how many women would induce birth a month or so early if they got paid two or three hundred grand extra for doing so. Probably some questions are best left unanswered.

And in my case, what difference did it make? The goddam thing was written, wasn't it?

"Well, see if you can make the deal," I said.

"Yes, but I don't think we want to be talking about just a single book here, okay? I think —"

"Harold, what I want right now is to eat some lunch."

"You sound a little tense, Michael. Is everything —"

"Everything is fine. Talk to them about just one book, with a sweetener for speeding up production at my end. Okay?"

"Okay," he said after one of his most significant pauses. "But I hope this doesn't mean that you won't entertain a three- or four-book contract later on. Make hay while the sun shines, remember. It's the motto of champions."

"Cross each bridge when you come to it is the motto of champions," I said, and that night I dreamt I went to Sara Laughs again.

In that dream — in all the dreams I had that fall and winter — I am walking up the lane to the lodge. The lane is a two-mile loop through the woods with ends opening onto Route 68. It has a number at either end (Lane Forty-two, if it matters) in case you have to call in a fire, but no name. Nor did Jo and I ever give it one, not even between ourselves. It is narrow, really just a double rut with timothy and witchgrass growing on the crown. When you drive in, you can hear that grass whispering like low voices against the undercarriage of your car or truck.

I don't drive in the dream, though. I never

drive. In these dreams I walk.

The trees huddle in close on either side of the lane. The darkening sky overhead is little more than a slot. Soon I will be able to see the first peeping stars. Sunset is past. Crickets chirr. Loons cry on the lake. Small things — chipmunks, probably, or the occasional squirrel — rustle in the woods.

Now I come to a dirt driveway sloping down the hill on my right. It is our driveway, marked with a little wooden sign which reads SARA LAUGHS. I stand at the head of it, but I don't go down. Below is the lodge. It's all logs and added-on wings, with a deck jutting out behind. Fourteen rooms in all, a ridiculous number of rooms. It should look ugly and awkward, but somehow it does not. There is a brave-dowager quality to Sara, the look of a lady pressing resolutely on toward her hundredth year, still taking pretty good strides in spite of her arthritic hips and gimpy old knees.

The central section is the oldest, dating back to 1900 or so. Other sections were added in the thirties, forties, and sixties. Once it was a hunting lodge; for a brief period in the early seventies it was home to a small commune of transcendental hippies. These were lease or rental deals; the owners from the late forties until 1984 were the Hingermans, Darren and Marie . . . then Marie alone when Darren died in 1971. The only visible addition from our period of ownership is the tiny DSS dish mounted on the central roofpeak. That was Johanna's idea, and she never really got a chance to enjoy it.

Beyond the house, the lake glimmers in the afterglow of sunset. The driveway, I see, is carpeted with brown pine needles and littered with fallen branches. The bushes which grow on either side of it have run wild, reaching out to one another like lovers across the narrowed gap which separates them. If you brought a car down here, the branches would scrape and squeal unpleasantly against its sides. Below, I see, there's moss growing on the logs of the main house, and three large sunflowers with faces like searchlights have grown up through the boards of the little driveway-side stoop. The overall feeling is not neglect, exactly, but *forgottenness*.

There is a breath of breeze, and its coldness on my skin makes me realize that I have been sweating. I can smell pine — a smell which is both sour and clean at the same time — and the faint but somehow tremendous smell of the lake. Dark Score is one of the cleanest, deepest lakes in Maine. It was bigger until the late thirties, Marie Hingerman told us; that was when Western Maine Electric, working hand in hand with the mills and paper operations around

Rumford, had gotten state approval to dam the Gessa River. Marie also showed us some charming photographs of white-frocked ladies and vested gentlemen in canoes — these snaps were from the time of the First World War, she said, and pointed to one of the young women, frozen forever on the rim of the Jazz Age with a dripping paddle upraised. "That's my mother," she said, "and the man she's threatening with the paddle is my father."

Loons crying, their voices like loss. Now I can see Venus in the darkening sky. Star light, star bright, wish I may, wish I might . . . in these dreams I always wish for Johanna.

With my wish made, I try to walk down the driveway. Of course I do. It's my house, isn't it? Where else would I go but my house, now that it's getting dark and now that the stealthy rustling in the woods seems both closer and somehow more purposeful? Where else *can* I go? It's dark, and it will be frightening to go into that dark place alone (suppose Sara resents having been left so long alone? suppose she's angry?), but I must. If the electricity's off, I'll light one of the hurricane lamps we keep in a kitchen cabinet.

Except I can't go down. My legs won't move. It's as if my body knows something about the house down there that my brain does not. The breeze rises again, chilling gooseflesh out onto my skin, and I wonder what I have done to get myself all sweaty like this. Have I been running? And if so, what have I been running toward? Or from?

My hair is sweaty, too; it lies on my brow in an unpleasantly heavy clump. I raise my hand to brush it away and see there is a shallow cut, fairly recent, running across the back, just beyond the knuckles. Sometimes this cut is on my right hand, sometimes it's on the left. I think, *If this is a dream, the details are good.* Always that same thought: *If this is a dream, the details are good.* It's the absolute truth. They are a novelist's details . . . but in dreams, perhaps everyone is a novelist. How is one to know?

Now Sara Laughs is only a dark hulk down below, and I realize I don't want to go down there, anyway. I am a man who has trained his mind to misbehave, and I can imagine too many things waiting for me inside. A rabid raccoon crouched in a corner of the kitchen. Bats in the bathroom — if disturbed they'll crowd the air around my cringing face, squeaking and fluttering against my cheeks with their dusty wings. Even one of William Denbrough's famous Creatures from Beyond the Universe, now hiding under the porch and watching me approach with glittering, pus-rimmed eyes.

"Well, I can't stay up here," I say, but my

legs won't move, and it seems I *will* be staying up here, where the driveway meets the lane; that I will be staying up here, like it or not.

Now the rustling in the woods behind me sounds not like small animals (most of them would by then be nested or burrowed for the night, anyway) but approaching footsteps. I try to turn and see, but I can't even do that . . .

. . . and that was where I usually woke up. The first thing I always did was to turn over, establishing my return to reality by demonstrating to myself that my body would once more obey my mind. Sometimes — most times, actually — I would find myself thinking *Manderley, I have dreamt again of Manderley.* There was something creepy about this (there's something creepy about any repeating dream, I think, about knowing your subconscious is digging obsessively at some object that won't be dislodged), but I would be lying if I didn't add that some part of me enjoyed the breathless summer calm in which the dream always wrapped me, and that part also enjoyed the sadness and foreboding I felt when I awoke. There was an exotic strangeness to the dream that was missing from my waking life, now that the road leading out of my imagination was so effectively blocked.

The only time I remember being really

frightened (and I must tell you I don't completely trust any of these memories, because for so long they didn't seem to exist at all) was when I awoke one night speaking quite clearly into the dark of my bedroom: "Something's behind me, don't let it get me, something in the woods, please don't let it get me." It wasn't the words themselves that frightened me so much as the tone in which they were spoken. It was the voice of a man on the raw edge of panic, and hardly seemed like my own voice at all.

Two days before Christmas of 1997, I once more drove down to Fidelity Union, where once more the bank manager escorted me to my safe-deposit box in the fluorescent-lit catacombs. As we walked down the stairs, he assured me (for the dozenth time, at least) that his wife was a *huge* fan of my work, she'd read all my books, couldn't get enough. For the dozenth time (at least) I replied that now I must get *him* in my clutches. He responded with his usual chuckle. I thought of this oft-repeated exchange as Banker's Communion.

Mr. Quinlan inserted his key in Slot A and turned it. Then, as discreetly as a pimp who has conveyed a customer to a whore's crib, he left. I inserted my own key in Slot B, turned it, and opened the drawer. It looked very vast now. The one remaining manuscript box seemed almost to quail in the far corner, like an abandoned puppy who somehow knows his sibs have been taken off and gassed. *Promise* was scrawled across the top in fat black letters. I could barely remember what the goddam story was about.

I snatched that time-traveller from the eighties and slammed the safe-deposit box shut. Nothing left in there now but dust. *Give me that,* Jo had hissed in my dream — it was the first time I'd thought of that one in years. *Give me that, it's my dust-catcher.*

"Mr. Quinlan, I'm finished," I called. My voice sounded rough and unsteady to my own ears, but Quinlan seemed to sense nothing wrong . . . or perhaps he was just being discreet. I can't have been the only customer, after all, who found his or her visits to this financial version of Forest Lawn emotionally distressful.

"I'm really going to read one of your books," he said, dropping an involuntary little glance at the box I was holding (I suppose I could have brought a briefcase to put it in, but on those expeditions I never did). "In fact, I think I'll put it on my list of New Year's resolutions."

"You do that," I said. "You just do that, Mr. Quinlan."

"Mark," he said. "Please." He'd said this before, too.

I had composed two letters, which I slipped into the manuscript box before setting out for Federal Express. Both had been written on my computer, which my body would let me use as long as I chose the Note Pad function. It was only opening Word Six that caused the storms to start. I never tried to compose a novel using the Note Pad function, understanding that if I did, I'd likely lose that option, too . . . not to mention my ability to play Scrabble and do crosswords on the machine. I had tried a couple of times to compose longhand, with spectacular lack of success. The problem wasn't what I had once heard described as "screen shyness"; I had proved that to myself.

One of the notes was to Harold, the other to Debra Weinstock, and both said pretty much the same thing: here's the new book, *Helen's Promise*, hope you like it as much as I do, if it seems a little rough it's because I had to work a lot of extra hours to finish it this soon, Merry Christmas, Happy Hanukkah, Erin Go Bragh, trick or treat, hope someone gives you a fucking pony.

I stood for almost an hour in a line of shuffling, bitter-eyed late mailers (Christmas is such a carefree, low-pressure time — that's one of the things I love about it), with *Helen's Promise* under my left arm and a paperback copy of Nelson DeMille's *The*

Charm School in my right hand. I read almost fifty pages before entrusting my final unpublished novel to a harried-looking clerk. When I wished her a Merry Christmas she shuddered and said nothing.

Chapter 4

The phone was ringing when I walked in my front door. It was Frank Arlen, asking me if I'd like to join him for Christmas. Join *them,* as a matter of fact; all of his brothers and their families were coming.

I opened my mouth to say no — the last thing on earth I needed was a crazed Irish Christmas with everybody drinking whiskey and waxing sentimental about Jo while perhaps two dozen snotcaked rugrats crawled around the floor — and heard myself saying I'd come.

Frank sounded as surprised as I felt, but honestly delighted. "Fantastic!" he cried. "When can you get here?"

I was in the hall, my galoshes dripping on the tile, and from where I was standing I could look through the arch and into the living room. There was no Christmas tree; I hadn't bothered with one since Jo died. The room looked both ghastly and much too big to me . . . a roller rink furnished in Early American.

"I've been out running errands," I said. "How about I throw some underwear in a bag, get back into the car, and come south while the heater's still blowing warm air?"

"Tremendous," Frank said without a moment's hesitation. "We can have us a sane bachelor evening before the Sons and Daughters of East Malden start arriving. I'm pouring you a drink as soon as I get off the telephone."

"Then I guess I better get rolling," I said.

That was hands down the best holiday since Johanna died. The only good holiday, I guess. For four days I was an honorary Arlen. I drank too much, toasted Johanna's memory too many times . . . and knew, somehow, that she'd be pleased to know I was doing it. Two babies spit up on me, one dog got into bed with me in the middle of the night, and Nicky Arlen's sister-in-law made a bleary pass at me on the night after Christmas, when she caught me alone in the kitchen making a turkey sandwich. I kissed her because she clearly wanted to be kissed, and an adventurous (or perhaps "mischievous" is the word I want) hand groped me for a moment in a place where no one other than myself had groped in almost three and a half years. It was a shock, but not an entirely unpleasant one.

It went no further — in a houseful of Arlens and with Susy Donahue not quite officially divorced yet (like me, she was an honorary Arlen that Christmas), it hardly could have done — but I decided it was time to leave . . . unless, that was, I wanted to go driving at high speed down a narrow street that most likely ended in a brick wall. I left on the twenty-seventh, very glad that I had come, and I gave Frank a fierce good-bye hug as we stood by my car. For four days I hadn't thought at all about how there was now only dust in my safe-deposit box at Fidelity Union, and for four nights I had slept straight through until eight in the morning, sometimes waking up with a sour stomach and a hangover headache, but never once in the middle of the night with the thought *Manderley, I have dreamt again of Manderley* going through my mind. I got back to Derry feeling refreshed and renewed.

The first day of 1998 dawned clear and cold and still and beautiful. I got up, showered, then stood at the bedroom window, drinking coffee. It suddenly occurred to me — with all the simple, powerful reality of ideas like up is over your head and down is under your feet — that I could write now. It was a new year, something had changed, and I could write now if I wanted to. The rock had rolled away.

I went into the study, sat down at the computer, and turned it on. My heart was beating normally, there was no sweat on my forehead or the back of my neck, and my hands were warm. I pulled down the main menu, the one you get when you click on the apple, and there was my old pal Word Six. I clicked on it. The pen-and-parchment logo came up, and when it did I suddenly couldn't breathe. It was as if iron bands had been clamped around my chest.

I pushed back from the desk, gagging and clawing at the round neck of the sweatshirt I was wearing. The wheels of my office chair caught on a little throw rug — one of Jo's finds in the last year of her life — and I tipped right over backward. My head banged the floor and I saw a fountain of bright sparks go whizzing across my field of vision. I suppose I was lucky not to black out, but I think my real luck on New Year's Morning of 1998 was that I tipped over the way I did. If I'd only pushed back from the desk so that I was still looking at the logo — and at the hideous blank screen which followed it — I think I might have choked to death.

When I staggered to my feet, I was at least able to breathe. My throat felt the size of a straw, and each inhale made a weird screaming sound, but I was breathing. I lurched into the bathroom and threw up in the basin with such force that vomit splashed the mirror. I grayed out and my knees buckled. This time it was my brow I struck, thunking it against the lip of the basin, and although the back of my head didn't bleed (there was a very respectable lump there by noon, though), my forehead did, a little. This latter bump also left a purple mark, which I of course lied about, telling folks who asked that I'd run into the bathroom door in the middle of the night, silly me, that'll teach a fella to get up at two A.M. without turning on a lamp.

When I regained complete consciousness (if there is such a state), I was curled on the floor. I got up, disinfected the cut on my forehead, and sat on the lip of the tub with my head lowered to my knees until I felt confident enough to stand up. I sat there for fifteen minutes, I guess, and in that space of time I decided that barring some miracle, my career was over. Harold would scream in pain and Debra would moan in disbelief, but what could they do? Send out the Publication Police? Threaten me with the Book-of-the-Month-Club Gestapo? Even if they could, what difference would it make? You couldn't get sap out of a brick or blood out of a stone. Barring some miraculous recovery, my life as a writer was over.

And if it is? I asked myself. *What's on for the back forty, Mike? You can play a lot of Scrabble in forty years, go on a lot of Crossword Cruises, drink a lot of whiskey. But is that enough? What else are you going to put on your back forty?*

I didn't want to think about that, not then. The next forty years could take care of themselves; I would be happy just to get through New Year's Day of 1998.

When I felt I had myself under control, I went back into my study, shuffled to the computer with my eyes resolutely on my feet, felt around for the right button, and turned off the machine. You can damage the program shutting down like that without putting it away, but under the circumstances, I hardly thought it mattered.

That night I once again dreamed I was walking at twilight on Lane Forty-two, which leads to Sara Laughs; once more I wished on the evening star as the loons cried on the lake, and once more I sensed something in the woods behind me, edging ever closer. It seemed my Christmas holiday was over.

That was a hard, cold winter, lots of snow and in February a flu epidemic that did for an awful lot of Derry's old folks. It took them the way a hard wind will take old trees after an ice storm. It missed me completely. I hadn't so much as a case of the sniffles that winter.

In March, I flew to Providence and took part in Will Weng's New England Crossword Challenge. I placed fourth and won fifty bucks. I framed the uncashed check and hung it in the living room. Once upon a time, most of my framed Certificates of Triumph (Jo's phrase; all the good phrases are Jo's phrases, it seems to me) went up on my office walls, but by March of 1998, I wasn't going in there very much. When I wanted to play Scrabble against the computer or do a tourney-level crossword puzzle, I used the PowerBook and sat at the kitchen table.

I remember sitting there one day, opening the PowerBook's main menu, going down to the crossword puzzles . . . then dropping the cursor two or three items further, until it had highlighted my old pal, Word Six.

What swept over me then wasn't frustration or impotent, balked fury (I'd experienced a lot of both since finishing *All the Way from the Top*), but sadness and simple longing. Looking at the Word Six icon was suddenly like looking at the pictures of Jo I kept in my wallet. Studying those, I'd sometimes think that I would sell my immortal soul in order to have her back again . . . and on that day in March, I thought I would sell my soul to be able to write a story again.

Go on and try it, then, a voice whispered. *Maybe things have changed.*

Except that nothing had changed, and I knew it. So instead of opening Word Six, I moved it across to the trash barrel in the lower right-hand corner of the screen, and dropped it in. Goodbye, old pal.

Debra Weinstock called a lot that winter, mostly with good news. Early in March she reported that *Helen's Promise* had been picked as one half of the Literary Guild's main selection for August, the other half being a legal thriller by Steve Martini, another veteran of the eight-to-fifteen segment of the *Times* bestseller list. And my British publisher, Debra said, loved *Helen,* was sure it would be my "breakthrough book." (My British sales had always lagged.)

"*Promise* is sort of a new direction for you," Debra said. "Wouldn't you say?"

"I kind of thought it was," I confessed, and wondered how Debbie would respond if I told her my new-direction book had been written almost a dozen years ago.

"It's got . . . I don't know . . . a kind of *maturity.*"

"Thanks."

"Mike? I think the connection's going. You sound muffled."

Sure I did. I was biting down on the side of my hand to keep from howling with laughter. Now, cautiously, I took it out of my mouth and examined the bite-marks. "Better?"

"Yes, lots. So what's the new one about? Give me a hint."

"You know the answer to that one, kiddo."

Debra laughed. " 'You'll have to read the book to find out, Josephine,' " she said. "Right?"

"Yessum."

"Well, keep it coming. Your pals at Putnam are crazy about the way you're taking it to the next level."

I said goodbye, I hung up the telephone, and then I laughed wildly for about ten minutes. Laughed until I was crying. That's me, though. Always taking it to the next level.

During this period I also agreed to do a phone interview with a *Newsweek* writer who was putting together a piece on The New American Gothic (whatever that was, other than a phrase which might sell a few magazines), and to sit for a *Publishers Weekly* interview which would appear just before publication of *Helen's Promise*. I agreed to these because they both sounded softball, the sort of interviews you could do over the phone while you read your mail. And Debra was delighted because I ordinarily say no to all the publicity. I hate that part of the job and always have, especially the hell of the live TV chat-show, where nobody's ever read your goddam book and the first question is always "Where in the world do you get those wacky ideas?" The publicity process is like going to a sushi bar where you're the sushi, and it was great to get past it this time with the feeling that I'd been able to give Debra some good news she could take to her bosses. "Yes," she could say, "he's still being a booger about publicity, but I got him to do a couple of things."

All through this my dreams of Sara Laughs were going on — not every night but every second or third night, with me never thinking of them in the daytime. I did my crosswords, I bought myself an acoustic steel guitar and started learning how to play it (I was never going to be invited to tour with Patty Loveless or Alan Jackson, however), I scanned each day's bloated obituaries in the *Derry News* for names that I knew. I was pretty much dozing on my feet, in other words.

What brought all this to an end was a call from Harold Oblowski not more than three days after Debra's book-club call. It was storming outside — a vicious snow-changing-over-to-sleet event that proved to be the last and biggest blast of the winter. By mid-evening the power would be off all over Derry, but when Harold called at five P.M., things were just getting cranked up.

"I just had a very good conversation with your editor," Harold said. "A very enlightening, very *energizing* conversation. Just got off the phone, in fact."

"Oh?"

"Oh indeed. There's a feeling at Putnam, Michael, that this latest book of yours may have a positive effect on your sales position in the market. It's very strong."

"Yes," I said, "I'm taking it to the next level."

"Huh?"

"I'm just blabbing, Harold. Go on."

"Well . . . Helen Nearing's a great lead character, and Skate is your best villain ever."

I said nothing.

"Debra raised the possibility of making *Helen's Promise* the opener of a three-book contract. A very *lucrative* three-book contract. All without any prompting from me. Three is one more than any publisher has wanted to commit to 'til now. I mentioned nine million dollars, three million per book, in other words, expecting her to laugh . . . but an agent has to start *somewhere,* and I always choose the highest ground I can find. I think I must have Roman military officers somewhere back in my family tree."

Ethiopian rug-merchants, more like it, I thought, but didn't say. I felt the way you do when the dentist has gone a little heavy on the Novocain and flooded your lips and tongue as well as your bad tooth and the patch of gum surrounding it. If I tried to talk, I'd probably only flap and spread spit. Harold was almost purring. A three-book contract for the new, mature Michael Noonan. Tall tickets, baby.

This time I didn't feel like laughing. This time I felt like screaming. Harold went on, happy and oblivious. Harold didn't know the bookberry tree had died. Harold didn't know the new Mike Noonan had cataclysmic shortness of breath and projectile-vomiting fits every time he tried to write.

"You want to hear how she came back to me, Michael?"

"Lay it on me."

"She said, 'Well, nine's obviously high, but it's as good a place to start as any. We feel this new book is a big step forward for him.' This is extraordinary. *Extraordinary.* Now, I haven't given anything away, wanted to talk to you first, of course, but I think we're looking at seven-point-five, minimum. In fact —"

"No."

He paused a moment. Long enough for me to realize I was gripping the phone so hard it hurt my hand. I had to make a conscious effort to relax my grip. "Mike, if you'll just hear me out —"

"I don't need to hear you out. I don't want to talk about a new contract."

"Pardon me for disagreeing, but there'll never be a better time. Think about it, for Christ's sake. We're talking top dollar here. If you wait until after *Helen's Promise* is published, I can't guarantee that the same offer —"

"I know you can't," I said. "I don't want guarantees, I don't want offers, *I don't want to talk contract.*"

"You don't need to shout, Mike, I can hear you."

Had I been shouting? Yes, I suppose I had been.

"Are you dissatisfied with Putnam? I think Debra would be very distressed to hear that. I also think Phyllis Grann would do damned near anything to address any concerns you might have."

Are you sleeping with Debra, Harold? I thought, and all at once it seemed like the most logical idea in the world — that dumpy, fiftyish, balding little Harold Oblowski was making it with my blonde, aristocratic, Smith-educated editor. *Are you sleeping with her, do you talk about my future while you're lying in bed together in a room at the Plaza? Are the pair of you trying to figure how many golden eggs you can get out of this tired old goose before you finally wring its neck and turn it into pâté? Is that what you're up to?*

"Harold, I can't talk about this now, and I *won't* talk about this now."

"What's wrong? Why are you so upset? I thought you'd be pleased. Hell, I thought you'd be over the fucking moon."

"There's nothing wrong. It's just a bad time for me to talk long-term contract. You'll have to pardon me, Harold. I have something coming out of the oven."

"Can we at least discuss this next w—"

"*No,*" I said, and hung up. I think it was the first time in my adult life that I'd hung up on someone who wasn't a telephone salesman.

I had nothing coming out of the oven, of course, and I was too upset to even think about putting something in. I went into the living room instead, poured myself a short whiskey, and sat down in front of the TV. I sat there for almost four hours, looking at everything and seeing nothing. Outside, the storm continued cranking up. Tomorrow there would be trees down all over Derry and the world would look like an ice sculpture.

At quarter past nine the power went out, came back on for thirty seconds or so, then went out and stayed out. I took this as a suggestion to stop thinking about Harold's useless contract and how Jo would have chortled at the idea of nine million dollars. I got up, unplugged the blacked-out TV so it wouldn't come blaring on at two in the morning (I needn't have worried; the power was off in Derry for nearly two days), and went upstairs. I dropped my clothes at the foot of the bed, crawled in without even bothering to brush my teeth, and was asleep in less than five minutes. I don't know how long after that it was that the nightmare came.

It was the last dream I had in what I now

think of as my "Manderley series," the culminating dream. It was made even worse, I suppose, by the unrelievable blackness to which I awoke.

It started like the others. I'm walking up the lane, listening to the crickets and the loons, looking mostly at the darkening slot of sky overhead. I reach the driveway, and here something *has* changed; someone has put a little sticker on the SARA LAUGHS sign. I lean closer and see it's a radio station sticker. WBLM, it says. 102.9, PORTLAND'S ROCK AND ROLL BLIMP.

From the sticker I look back up into the sky, and there is Venus. I wish on her as I always do, I wish for Johanna with the dank and vaguely tremendous smell of the lake in my nose.

Something lumbers in the woods, rattling old leaves and breaking a branch. It sounds big.

Better get down there, a voice in my head tells me. *Something has taken out a contract on you, Michael. A three-book contract, and that's the worst kind.*

I can't move, I can never move, I can only stand here. I've got walker's block.

But that's just talk. I *can* walk. This time I *can* walk. I am delighted. I have had a major breakthrough. In the dream I think *This changes everything! This changes everything!*

Down the driveway I walk, deeper and

deeper into the clean but sour smell of pine, stepping over some of the fallen branches, kicking others out of the way. I raise my hand to brush the damp hair off my forehead and see the little scratch running across the back of it. I stop to look at it, curious.

No time for that, the dream-voice says. *Get down there. You've got a book to write.*

I can't write, I reply. *That part's over. I'm on the back forty now.*

No, the voice says. There is something relentless about it that scares me. *You had writer's* walk, *not writer's* block, *and as you can see, it's gone. Now hurry up and get down there.*

I'm afraid, I tell the voice.

Afraid of what?

Well . . . what if Mrs. Danvers is down there?

The voice doesn't answer. It knows I'm not afraid of Rebecca de Winter's housekeeper, she's just a character in an old book, nothing but a bag of bones. So I begin walking again. I have no choice, it seems, but at every step my terror increases, and by the time I'm halfway down to the shadowy sprawling bulk of the log house, fear has sunk into my bones like fever. Something is wrong here, something is all twisted up.

I'll run away, I think. *I'll run back the way I came, like the gingerbread man I'll run, run all the way back to Derry, if that's what it takes, and I'll never come here anymore.*

Except I can hear slobbering breath behind me in the growing gloom, and padding footsteps. The thing in the woods is now the thing in the driveway. It's right behind me. If I turn around the sight of it will knock the sanity out of my head in a single roundhouse slap. Something with red eyes, something slumped and hungry.

The house is my only hope of safety.

I walk on. The crowding bushes clutch like hands. In the light of a rising moon (the moon has never risen before in this dream, but I have never stayed in it this long before), the rustling leaves look like sardonic faces. I see winking eyes and smiling mouths. Below me are the black windows of the house and I know that there will be no power when I get inside, the storm has knocked the power out, I will flick the lightswitch up and down, up and down, until something reaches out and takes my wrist and pulls me like a lover deeper into the dark.

I am three quarters of the way down the driveway now. I can see the railroad-tie steps leading down to the lake, and I can see the float out there on the water, a black square in a track of moonlight. Bill Dean has put it out. I can also see an oblong something lying at the place where the driveway ends at the stoop. There has never been such an object before. What can it be?

Another two or three steps, and I know. It's a coffin, the one Frank Arlen dickered for . . . because, he said, the mortician was trying to stick it to me. It's Jo's coffin, and lying on its side with the top partway open, enough for me to see it's empty.

I think I want to scream. I think I mean to turn around and run back up the driveway — I will take my chances with the thing behind me. But before I can, the back door of Sara Laughs opens, and a terrible figure comes darting out into the growing darkness. It is human, this figure, and yet it's not. It is a crumpled white thing with baggy arms upraised. There is no face where its face should be, and yet it is shrieking in a glottal, loonlike voice. It must be Johanna. She was able to escape her coffin, but not her winding shroud. She is all tangled up in it.

How hideously *speedy* this creature is! It doesn't drift as one imagines ghosts drifting, but *races* across the stoop toward the driveway. It has been waiting down here during all the dreams when I had been frozen, and now that I have finally been able to walk down, it means to have me. I'll scream when it wraps me in its silk arms, and I will scream when I smell its rotting, bug-raddled flesh and see its dark staring eyes through the fine weave of the cloth. I will scream as the sanity leaves my mind forever. I will scream . . . but there is no one out here to hear me. Only the loons will hear me. I have come again to Manderley, and this time I will never leave.

The shrieking white thing reached for me and I woke up on the floor of my bedroom, crying out in a cracked, horrified voice and slamming my head repeatedly against something. How long before I finally realized I was no longer asleep, that I wasn't at Sara Laughs? How long before I realized that I had fallen out of bed at some point and had crawled across the room in my sleep, that I was on my hands and knees in a corner, butting my head against the place where the walls came together, doing it over and over again like a lunatic in an asylum?

I didn't know, couldn't with the power out and the bedside clock dead. I know that at first I couldn't move out of the corner because it felt safer than the wider room would have done, and I know that for a long time the dream's force held me even after I woke up (mostly, I imagine, because I couldn't turn on a light and dispel its power). I was afraid that if I crawled out of my corner, the white thing would burst out of my bathroom, shrieking its dead shriek, eager to finish what it had started. I know I was shivering all over, and that I was cold and wet from the waist down, because my bladder had let go.

I stayed there in the corner, gasping and wet, staring into the darkness, wondering if you could have a nightmare powerful enough in its imagery to drive you insane. I thought then (and think now) that I almost found out on that night in March.

Finally I felt able to leave the corner. Halfway across the floor I pulled off my wet pajama pants, and when I did that, I got disoriented. What followed was a miserable and surreal five minutes in which I crawled aimlessly back and forth in my familiar bedroom, bumping into stuff and moaning each time I hit something with a blind, flailing hand. Each thing I touched at first seemed like that awful white thing. Nothing I touched felt like anything I knew. With the reassuring green numerals of the bedside clock gone and my sense of direction temporarily lost, I could have been crawling around a mosque in Addis Ababa.

At last I ran shoulder-first into the bed. I stood up, yanked the pillowcase off the extra pillow, and wiped my groin and upper legs with it. Then I crawled back into bed, pulled the blankets up, and lay there shivering, listening to the steady tick of sleet on the windows.

There was no sleep for me the rest of that night, and the dream didn't fade as dreams usually do upon waking. I lay on my side, the shivers slowly subsiding, thinking of her coffin there in the driveway, thinking that it made a kind of mad sense — Jo had loved Sara, and if she were to haunt anyplace, it would be there. But why would she want to hurt me? Why would my Jo ever want to hurt me? I could think of no reason.

Somehow the time passed, and there came a moment when I realized that the air had turned a dark shade of gray; the shapes of the furniture loomed in it like sentinels in fog. That was a little better. That was more like it. I would light the kitchen woodstove, I decided, and make strong coffee. Begin the work of getting this behind me.

I swung my legs out of bed and raised my hand to brush my sweat-damp hair off my forehead. I froze with the hand in front of my eyes. I must have scraped it while I was crawling, disoriented, in the dark and trying to find my way back to bed. There was a shallow, clotted cut across the back, just below the knuckles.

Chapter 5

Once, when I was sixteen, a plane went supersonic directly over my head. I was walking in the woods when it happened, thinking of some story I was going to write, perhaps, or how great it would be if Doreen Fournier weakened some Friday night and let me take off her panties while we were parked at the end of Cushman Road.

In any case I was travelling far roads in my own mind, and when that boom went off, I was caught totally by surprise. I went flat on the leafy ground with my hands over my head and my heart drumming crazily, sure I'd reached the end of my life (and while I was still a virgin). In my forty years, that was the only thing which equalled the final dream of the "Manderley series" for utter terror.

I lay on the ground, waiting for the hammer to fall, and when thirty seconds or so passed and no hammer *did* fall, I began to realize it had just been some jet-jockey from the Brunswick Naval Air Station, too eager to wait until he was out over the Atlantic before going to Mach 1. But, holy shit, who ever could have guessed that it would be so *loud?*

I got slowly to my feet and as I stood

there with my heart finally slowing down, I realized I wasn't the only thing that had been scared witless by that sudden clear-sky boom. For the first time in my memory, the little patch of woods behind our house in Prout's Neck was entirely silent. I stood there in a dusty bar of sunlight, crumbled leaves all over my tee-shirt and jeans, holding my breath, listening. I had never heard a silence like it. Even on a cold day in January, the woods would have been full of conversation.

At last a finch sang. There were two or three seconds of silence, and then a jay replied. Another two or three seconds went by, and then a crow added his two cents' worth. A woodpecker began to hammer for grubs. A chipmunk bumbled through some underbrush on my left. A minute after I had stood up, the woods were fully alive with little noises again; it was back to business as usual, and I continued with my own. I never forgot that unexpected boom, though, or the deathly silence which followed it.

I thought of that June day often in the wake of the nightmare, and there was nothing so remarkable in that. Things had changed, somehow, or *could* change . . . but first comes silence while we assure ourselves that we are still unhurt and that the danger — if there was danger — is gone.

Derry was shut down for most of the following week, anyway. Ice and high winds caused a great deal of damage during the storm, and a sudden twenty-degree plunge in the temperature afterward made the digging out hard and the cleanup slow. Added to that, the atmosphere after a March storm is always dour and pessimistic; we get them up this way every year (and two or three in April for good measure, if we're not lucky), but we never seem to expect them. Every time we get clouted, we take it personally.

On a day toward the end of that week, the weather finally started to break. I took advantage, going out for a cup of coffee and a mid-morning pastry at the little restaurant three doors down from the Rite Aid where Johanna did her last errand. I was sipping and chewing and working the newspaper crossword when someone asked, "Could I share your booth, Mr. Noonan? It's pretty crowded in here today."

I looked up and saw an old man that I knew but couldn't quite place.

"Ralph Roberts," he said. "I volunteer down at the Red Cross. Me and my wife, Lois."

"Oh, okay, sure," I said. I give blood at the Red Cross every six weeks or so. Ralph Roberts was one of the old parties who passed out juice and cookies afterward, telling you not to get up or make any sudden movements if you felt woozy. "Please, sit down."

He looked at my paper, folded open to the crossword and lying in a patch of sun, as he slid into the booth. "Don't you find that doing the crossword in the *Derry News* is sort of like striking out the pitcher in a baseball game?" he asked.

I laughed and nodded. "I do it for the same reason folks climb Mount Everest, Mr. Roberts . . . because it's there. Only with the *News* crossword, no one ever falls off."

"Call me Ralph. Please."

"Okay. And I'm Mike."

"Good." He grinned, revealing teeth that were crooked and a little yellow, but all his own. "I like getting to the first names. It's like being able to take off your tie. Was quite a little cap of wind we had, wasn't it?"

"Yes," I said, "but it's warming up nicely now." The thermometer had made one of its nimble March leaps, climbing from twenty-five degrees the night before to fifty that morning. Better than the rise in air-temperature, the sun was warm again on your face. It was that warmth that had coaxed me out of the house.

"Spring'll get here, I guess. Some years it gets a little lost, but it always seems to find its way back home." He sipped his coffee, then set the cup down. "Haven't seen you at the Red Cross lately."

"I'm recycling," I said, but that was a fib; I'd come eligible to give another pint two weeks ago. The reminder card was up on the refrigerator. It had just slipped my mind. "Next week, for sure."

"I only mention it because I know you're an A, and we can always use that."

"Save me a couch."

"Count on it. Everything going all right? I only ask because you look tired. If it's insomnia, I can sympathize, believe me."

He *did* have the look of an insomniac, I thought — too wide around the eyes, somehow. But he was also a man in his mid- to late seventies, and I don't think anyone gets that far without showing it. Stick around a little while, and life maybe only jabs at your cheeks and eyes. Stick around a long while and you end up looking like Jake La Motta after a hard fifteen.

I opened my mouth to say what I always do when someone asks me if I'm all right, then wondered why I always felt I had to pull that tiresome Marlboro Man shit, just who I was trying to fool. What did I think would happen if I told the guy who gave me a chocolate-chip cookie down at the Red Cross after the nurse took the needle out of my arm that I wasn't feeling a hundred per cent? Earthquakes? Fire and flood? Shit.

"No," I said, "I really haven't been feeling so great, Ralph."

"Flu? It's been going around."

"Nah. The flu missed me this time, actually. And I've been sleeping all right." Which was true — there had been no recurrence of the Sara Laughs dream in either the normal or the high-octane version. "I think I've just got the blues."

"Well, you ought to take a vacation," he said, then sipped his coffee. When he looked up at me again, he frowned and set his cup down. "What? Is something wrong?"

No, I thought of saying. *You were just the first bird to sing into the silence, Ralph, that's all.*

"No, nothing wrong," I said, and then, because I sort of wanted to see how the words tasted coming out of my own mouth, I repeated them. "A vacation."

"Ayuh," he said, smiling. "People do it all the time."

People do it all the time. He was right about that; even people who couldn't strictly afford to went on vacation. When they got tired. When they got all balled up in their own shit. When the world was too much with them, getting and spending.

I could certainly afford a vacation, and I could certainly take the time off from work — *what* work, ha-ha? — and yet I'd needed the Red Cross cookie-man to point out what should have been self-evident to a college-educated guy like me: that I hadn't been on an actual vacation since Jo and I had gone to Bermuda, the winter before she died. My particular grindstone was no longer turning, but I had kept my nose to it all the same. It wasn't until that summer, when I read Ralph Roberts's obituary in the *News* (he was struck by a car), that I fully realized how much I owed him. That advice was better than any glass of orange juice I ever got after giving blood, let me tell you.

When I left the restaurant, I didn't go home but tramped over half of the damned town, the section of newspaper with the partly completed crossword puzzle in it clamped under one arm. I walked until I was chilled in spite of the warming temperatures. I didn't think about anything, and yet I thought about everything. It was a special kind of thinking, the sort I'd always done when I was getting close to writing a book, and although I hadn't thought that way in years, I fell into it easily and naturally, as if I had never been away.

It's like some guys with a big truck have pulled up in your driveway and are moving things into your basement. I can't explain it any better than that. You can't see what these things are because they're all wrapped up in padded quilts, but you don't need to see them. It's furniture, everything you need to make your house a home, make it just right, just the way you wanted it.

When the guys have hopped back into their truck and driven away, you go down to the basement and walk around (the way I went walking around Derry that late morning, slopping up hill and down dale in my old galoshes), touching a padded curve here, a padded angle there. Is this one a sofa? Is that one a dresser? It doesn't matter. Everything is here, the movers didn't forget a thing, and although you'll have to get it all upstairs yourself (straining your poor old back in the process, more often than not), that's okay. The important thing is that the delivery was complete.

This time I thought — hoped — the delivery truck had brought the stuff I needed for the back forty: the years I might have to spend in a No Writing Zone. To the cellar door they had come, and they had knocked politely, and when after several months there was still no answer, they had finally fetched a battering ram. *HEY BUDDY, HOPE THE NOISE DIDN'T SCARE YOU TOO BAD, SORRY ABOUT THE DOOR!*

I didn't care about the door; I cared about the furniture. Any pieces broken or missing? I didn't think so. I thought all I had to do was get it upstairs, pull off the furniture pads, and put it where it belonged.

On my way back home, I passed The Shade, Derry's charming little revival movie house, which has prospered in spite of (or perhaps because of) the video revolution. This month they were showing classic SF from the fifties, but April was dedicated to Humphrey Bogart, Jo's all-time favorite. I stood under the marquee for several moments, studying one of the Coming Attractions posters. Then I went home, picked a travel agent pretty much at random from the phone book, and told the guy I wanted to go to Key Largo. Key *West,* you mean, the guy said. No, I told him, I mean Key Largo, just like in the movie with Bogie and Bacall. Three weeks. Then I rethought that. I was wealthy, I was on my own, and I was retired. What was this "three weeks" shit? Make it six, I said. Find me a cottage or something. Going to be expensive, he said. I told him I didn't care. When I came back to Derry, it would be spring.

In the meantime, I had some furniture to unwrap.

I was enchanted with Key Largo for the first month and bored out of my mind for the last two weeks. I stayed, though, because boredom is good. People with a high tolerance for boredom can get a lot of thinking done. I ate about a billion shrimp, drank about a thousand margaritas, and read twenty-three John D. MacDonald novels by actual count. I burned, peeled, and finally tanned. I bought a long-billed cap with

PARROTHEAD printed on it in bright green thread. I walked the same stretch of beach until I knew everybody by first name. And I unwrapped furniture. A lot of it I didn't like, but there was no doubt that it all fit the house.

I thought about Jo and our life together. I thought about saying to her that no one was ever going to confuse *Being Two* with *Look Homeward, Angel*. *"You aren't going to pull a lot of frustrated-artist crap on me, are you, Noonan?"* she had replied . . . and during my time on Key Largo, those words kept coming back, always in Jo's voice: crap, frustrated-artist crap, all that fucking schoolboy frustrated-artist crap.

I thought about Jo in her long red woods apron, coming to me with a hatful of black trumpet mushrooms, laughing and triumphant: *"Nobody on the TR eats better than the Noonans tonight!"* she'd cried. I thought of her painting her toenails, bent over between her own thighs in the way only women doing that particular piece of business can manage. I thought of her throwing a book at me because I laughed at some new haircut. I thought of her trying to learn how to play a breakdown on her banjo and of how she looked braless in a thin sweater. I thought of her crying and laughing and angry. I thought of her telling me it was crap, all that frustrated-artist crap.

111

And I thought about the dreams, especially the culminating dream. I could do that easily, because it never faded as the more ordinary ones do. The final Sara Laughs dream and my very first wet dream (coming upon a girl lying naked in a hammock and eating a plum) are the only two that remain perfectly clear to me, year after year; the rest are either hazy fragments or completely forgotten.

There were a great many clear details to the Sara dreams — the loons, the crickets, the evening star and my wish upon it, just to name a few — but I thought most of those things were just verisimilitude. Scene-setting, if you will. As such, they could be dismissed from my considerations. That left three major elements, three large pieces of furniture to be unwrapped.

As I sat on the beach, watching the sun go down between my sandy toes, I didn't think you had to be a shrink to see how those three things went together.

In the Sara dreams, the major elements were the woods behind me, the house below me, and Michael Noonan himself, frozen in the middle. It's getting dark and there's danger in the woods. It will be frightening to go to the house below, perhaps because it's been empty so long, but I never doubt I must go there; scary or not, it's the only shelter I have. Except I can't do it. I can't move. I've got writer's walk.

In the nightmare I am finally able to go toward shelter, only the shelter proves false. Proves more dangerous than I had ever expected in my . . . well, yes, in my wildest dreams. My dead wife rushes out, screaming and still tangled in her shroud, to attack me. Even five weeks later and almost three thousand miles from Derry, remembering that speedy white thing with its baggy arms would make me shiver and look back over my shoulder.

But *was* it Johanna? I didn't really know, did I? The thing was all wrapped up. The coffin looked like the one in which she had been buried, true, but that might just be misdirection.

Writer's *walk,* writer's *block.*

I can't write, I told the voice in the dream. The voice says I can. The voice says the writer's block is gone, and I believe it because the writer's *walk* is gone, I'm finally headed down the driveway, going to shelter. I'm afraid, though. Even before the shapeless white thing makes its appearance, I'm terrified. I say it's Mrs. Danvers I'm afraid of, but that's just my dreaming mind getting Sara Laughs and Manderley all mixed up. I'm afraid of —

"I'm afraid of writing," I heard myself saying out loud. "I'm afraid to even try."

This was the night before I finally flew

back to Maine, and I was half-past sober, going on drunk. By the end of my vacation, I was drinking a lot of evenings. "It's not the block that scares me, it's *undoing* the block. I'm really fucked, boys and girls. I'm fucked big-time."

Fucked or not, I had an idea I'd finally reached the heart of the matter. I was afraid of undoing the block, maybe afraid of picking up the strands of my life and going on without Jo. Yet some deep part of my mind believed I must do it; that's what the menacing noises behind me in the woods were about. And belief counts for a lot. Too much, maybe, especially if you're imaginative. When an imaginative person gets into mental trouble, the line between seeming and being has a way of disappearing.

Things in the woods, yes, sir. I had one of them right there in my hand as I was thinking these things. I lifted my drink, holding it toward the western sky so that the setting sun seemed to be burning in the glass. I was drinking a lot, and maybe that was okay on Key Largo — hell, people were supposed to drink a lot on vacation, it was almost the law — but I'd been drinking too much even before I left. The kind of drinking that could get out of hand in no time at all. The kind that could get a man in trouble.

Things in the woods, and the potentially

safe place guarded by a scary bugbear that was not my wife, but perhaps my wife's memory. It made sense, because Sara Laughs had always been Jo's favorite place on earth. That thought led to another, one that made me swing my legs over the side of the chaise I'd been reclining on and sit up in excitement. Sara Laughs had also been the place where the ritual had begun . . . champagne, last line, and the all-important benediction: *Well, then,* that's *all right, isn't it?*

Did I want things to be all right again? Did I truly want that? A month or a year before I mightn't have been sure, but now I was. The answer was yes. I wanted to move on — let go of my dead wife, rehab my heart, move on. But to do that, I'd have to go back.

Back to the log house. Back to Sara Laughs.

"Yeah," I said, and my body broke out in gooseflesh. "Yeah, you got it."

So why not?

The question made me feel as stupid as Ralph Roberts's observation that I needed a vacation. If I needed to go back to Sara Laughs now that my vacation was over, indeed why not? It might be a little scary the first night or two, a hangover from my final dream, but just being there might dissolve the dream faster.

And (this last thought I allowed in only

one humble corner of my conscious mind) something *might* happen with my writing. It wasn't likely . . . but it wasn't impossible, either. *Barring a miracle,* hadn't that been my thought on New Year's Day as I sat on the rim of the tub, holding a damp washcloth to the cut on my forehead? Yes. *Barring a miracle.* Sometimes blind people fall down, knock their heads, and regain their sight. Sometimes maybe cripples are able to throw their crutches away when they get to the top of the church steps.

I had eight or nine months before Harold and Debra started really bugging me for the next novel. I decided to spend the time at Sara Laughs. It would take me a little while to tie things up in Derry, and awhile for Bill Dean to get the house on the lake ready for a year-round resident, but I could be down there by the Fourth of July, easily. I decided that was a good date to shoot for, not just the birthday of our country, but pretty much the end of bug season in western Maine.

By the day I packed up my vacation gear (the John D. MacDonald paperbacks I left for the cabin's next inhabitant), shaved a week's worth of stubble off a face so tanned it no longer looked like my own to me, and flew back to Maine, I was decided: I'd go back to the place my subconscious mind had identified as shelter against the deepening dark; I'd go back even though my mind had also suggested that doing so would not be without risks. I would not go back expecting Sara to be Lourdes . . . but I would allow myself to hope, and when I saw the evening star peeping out over the lake for the first time, I would allow myself to wish on it.

Only one thing didn't fit into my neat deconstruction of the Sara dreams, and because I couldn't explain it, I tried to ignore it. I didn't have much luck, though; part of me was still a writer, I guess, and a writer is a man who has taught his mind to misbehave.

It was the cut on the back of my hand. That cut had been in all the dreams, I would swear it had . . . and then it had actually appeared. You didn't get that sort of shit in the works of Dr. Freud; stuff like that was strictly for the Psychic Friends hotline.

It was a coincidence, that's all, I thought as my plane started its descent. I was in seat A-2 (the nice thing about flying up front is that if the plane goes down, you're first to the crash site) and looking at pine forests as we slipped along the glidepath toward Bangor International Airport. The snow was gone for another year; I had vacationed it to death. *Only coincidence. How many times have you cut your hands in your life? I mean, they're*

117

always out front, aren't they, waving them-
selves around? Practically begging for it.

All that should have rung true, and yet
somehow it didn't, quite. It should have, but
. . . well . . .

It was the boys in the basement. They
were the ones who didn't buy it. The boys in
the basement didn't buy it at all.

At that point there was a thump as the
737 touched down, and I put the whole line
of thought out of my mind.

One afternoon shortly after arriving back
home, I rummaged the closets until I found
the shoeboxes containing Jo's old photographs. I sorted them, then studied my way
through the ones of Dark Score Lake. There
were a staggering number of these, but because Johanna was the shutterbug, there
weren't many with her in them. I found one,
though, that I remembered taking in 1990
or '91.

Sometimes even an untalented photographer can take a good picture — if seven
hundred monkeys spent seven hundred
years bashing away at seven hundred
typewriters, and all that — and this was
good. In it Jo was standing on the float with
the sun going down red-gold behind her.
She was just out of the water, dripping wet,
wearing a two-piece swimming suit, gray
with red piping. I had caught her laughing

and brushing her soaked hair back from her forehead and temples. Her nipples were very prominent against the cups of her halter. She looked like an actress on a movie poster for one of those guilty-pleasure B-pictures about monsters at Party Beach or a serial killer stalking the campus.

I was sucker-punched by a sudden powerful lust for her. I wanted her upstairs just as she was in that photograph, with strands of her hair pasted to her cheeks and that wet bathing suit clinging to her. I wanted to suck her nipples through the halter top, taste the cloth and feel their hardness through it. I wanted to suck water out of the cotton like milk, then yank the bottom of her suit off and fuck her until we both exploded.

Hands shaking a little, I put the photograph aside, with some others I liked (although there were no others I liked in quite that same way). I had a huge hard-on, one of those ones that feel like stone covered with skin. Get one of those and until it goes away you are good for nothing.

The quickest way to solve a problem like that when there's no woman around willing to help you solve it is to masturbate, but that time the idea never even crossed my mind. Instead I walked restlessly through the upstairs rooms of my house with my fists opening and closing and what looked like a hood ornament stuffed down the front of my jeans.

Anger may be a normal stage of the grieving process — I've read that it is — but I was never angry at Johanna in the wake of her death until the day I found that picture. Then, wow. There I was, walking around with a boner that just wouldn't quit, *furious* with her. Stupid bitch, why had she been running on one of the hottest days of the year? Stupid, inconsiderate bitch to leave me alone like this, not even able to work.

I sat down on the stairs and wondered what I should do. A drink was what I should do, I decided, and then maybe another drink to scratch the first one's back. I actually got up before deciding that wasn't a very good idea at all.

I went into my office instead, turned on the computer, and did a crossword puzzle. That night when I went to bed, I thought of looking at the picture of Jo in her bathing suit again. I decided that was almost as bad an idea as a few drinks when I was feeling angry and depressed. *But I'll have the dream tonight,* I thought as I turned off the light. *I'll have the dream for sure.*

I didn't, though. My dreams of Sara Laughs seemed to be finished.

A week's thought made the idea of at least summering at the lake seem better than ever. So, on a Saturday afternoon in early May when I calculated that any self-respecting Maine caretaker would be home watching the Red Sox, I called Bill Dean and told him I'd be at my lake place from the Fourth of July or so . . . and that if things went as I hoped, I'd be spending the fall and winter there as well.

"Well, that's good," he said. "That's real good news. A lot of folks down here've missed you, Mike. Quite a few that want to condole with you about your wife, don't you know."

Was there the faintest note of reproach in his voice, or was that just my imagination? Certainly Jo and I had cast a shadow in the area; we had made significant contributions to the little library which served the Motton–Kashwakamak–Castle View area, and Jo had headed the successful fund drive to get an area bookmobile up and running. In addition to that, she had been part of a ladies' sewing circle (afghans were her specialty), and a member in good standing of the Castle County Crafts Co-op. Visits to the sick . . . helping out with the annual volunteer fire department blood drive . . . womaning a booth during Summerfest in Castle Rock . . . and stuff like that was only where she had started. She didn't do it in any ostentatious Lady Bountiful way, either, but unobtrusively and humbly, with her head lowered (often to hide a rather sharp smile, I should add — my Jo had a Biercean sense of humor). Christ, I thought, maybe old Bill had a right to sound reproachful.

"People miss her," I said.

"Ayuh, they do."

"I still miss her a lot myself. I think that's why I've stayed away from the lake. That's where a lot of our good times were."

"I s'pose so. But it'll be damned good to see you down this way. I'll get busy. The place is all right — you could move into it this afternoon, if you was a mind — but when a house has stood empty the way Sara has, it gets stale."

"I know."

"I'll get Brenda Meserve to clean the whole shebang from top to bottom. Same gal you always had, don't you know."

"Brenda's a little old for comprehensive spring cleaning, isn't she?" The lady in question was about sixty-five, stout, kind, and gleefully vulgar. She was especially fond of jokes about the travelling salesman who spent the night like a rabbit, jumping from hole to hole. No Mrs. Danvers she.

"Ladies like Brenda Meserve never get too old to oversee the festivities," Bill said. "She'll get two or three girls to do the vacuuming and heavy lifting. Set you back maybe three hundred dollars. Sound all right?"

"Like a bargain."

"The well needs to be tested, and the gennie, too, although I'm sure both of em's okay. I seen a hornet's nest by Jo's old studio that I want to smoke before the woods get dry. Oh, and the roof of the old house — you know, the middle piece — needs to be reshingled. I shoulda talked to you about that last year, but with you not using the place, I let her slide. You stand good for that, too?"

"Yes, up to ten grand. Beyond that, call me."

"If we have to go over ten, I'll smile and kiss a pig."

"Try to have it all done before I get down there, okay?"

"Coss. You'll want your privacy, I know that . . . just so long's you know you won't get any right away. We was shocked when she went so young; all of us were. Shocked and sad. She was a dear." From a Yankee mouth, that word rhymes with *Leah*.

"Thank you, Bill." I felt tears prickle my eyes. Grief is like a drunken houseguest, always coming back for one more goodbye hug. "Thanks for saying."

"You'll get your share of carrot-cakes, chummy." He laughed, but a little doubtfully, as if afraid he was committing an impropriety.

"I can eat a lot of carrot-cake," I said,

"and if folks overdo it, well, hasn't Kenny Auster still got that big Irish wolfhound?"

"Yuh, that thing'd eat cake til he busted!" Bill cried in high good humor. He cackled until he was coughing. I waited, smiling a little myself. "Blueberry, he calls that dog, damned if I know why. Ain't he the gormiest thing!" I assumed he meant the dog and not the dog's master. Kenny Auster, not much more than five feet tall and neatly made, was the opposite of gormy, that peculiar Maine adjective that means clumsy, awkward, and clay-footed.

I suddenly realized that I missed these people — Bill and Brenda and Buddy Jellison and Kenny Auster and all the others who lived year-round at the lake. I even missed Blueberry, the Irish wolfhound, who trotted everywhere with his head up just as if he had half a brain in it and long strands of saliva depending from his jaws.

"I've also got to get down there and clean up the winter blowdown," Bill said. He sounded embarrassed. "It ain't bad this year — that last big storm was all snow over our way, thank God — but there's still a fair amount of happy crappy I ain't got to yet. I shoulda put it behind me long before now. You not using the place ain't an excuse. I been cashing your checks." There was something amusing about listening to the grizzled old fart beating his breast; Jo would have kicked her feet and giggled, I'm quite sure.

"If everything's right and running by July Fourth, Bill, I'll be happy."

"You'll be happy as a clam in a mudflat, then. That's a promise." Bill sounded as happy as a clam in a mudflat himself, and I was glad. "Gointer come down and write a book by the water? Like in the old days? Not that the last couple ain't been fine, my wife couldn't put that last one down, but —"

"I don't know," I said, which was the truth. And then an idea struck me. "Bill, would you do me a favor before you clean up the driveway and turn Brenda Meserve loose?"

"Happy to if I can," he said, so I told him what I wanted.

Four days later, I got a little package with this laconic return address: DEAN/GEN DELIV/TR-90 (DARK SCORE). I opened it and shook out twenty photographs which had been taken with one of those little cameras you use once and then throw away.

Bill had filled out the roll with various views of the house, most conveying that subtle air of neglect a place gets when it's not used enough . . . even a place that's caretook (to use Bill's word) gets that neglected feel after awhile.

I barely glanced at these. The first four were the ones I wanted, and I lined them up on the kitchen table, where the strong sunlight would fall directly on them. Bill had taken these from the top of the driveway, pointing the disposable camera down at the sprawl of Sara Laughs. I could see the moss which had grown not only on the logs of the main house, but on the logs of the north and south wings, as well. I could see the litter of fallen branches and the drifts of pine needles on the driveway. Bill must have been tempted to clear all that away before taking his snaps, but he hadn't. I'd told him exactly what I wanted — "warts and all" was the phrase I had used — and Bill had given it to me.

The bushes on either side of the driveway had thickened a lot since Jo and I had spent any significant amount of time at the lake; they hadn't exactly run wild, but yes, some of the longer branches did seem to yearn toward each other across the asphalt like separated lovers.

Yet what my eye came back to again and again was the stoop at the foot of the driveway. The other resemblances between the photographs and my dreams of Sara Laughs might only be coincidental (or the writer's often surprisingly practical imagination at work), but I could explain the sunflowers growing out through the boards of the stoop no more than I had been able to explain the cut on the back of my hand.

I turned one of the photos over. On the back, in a spidery script, Bill had written: *These fellows are way early . . . and trespassing!*

I flipped back to the picture side. Three sunflowers, growing up through the boards of the stoop. Not two, not four, but three large sunflowers with faces like searchlights.

Just like the ones in my dream.

Chapter 6

On July 3rd of 1998, I threw two suitcases and my PowerBook in the trunk of my mid-sized Chevrolet, started to back down the driveway, then stopped and went into the house again. It felt empty and somehow forlorn, like a faithful lover who has been dropped and cannot understand why. The furniture wasn't covered and the power was still on (I understood that The Great Lake Experiment might turn out to be a swift and total failure), but 14 Benton Street felt deserted, all the same. Rooms too full of furniture to echo still did when I walked through them, and everywhere there seemed to be too much dusty light.

In my study, the VDT was hooded like an executioner against the dust. I knelt before it and opened one of the desk drawers. Inside were four reams of paper. I took one, started away with it under my arm, then had a second thought and turned back. I had put that provocative photo of Jo in her swimsuit in the wide center drawer. Now I took it, tore the paper wrapping from the end of the ream of paper, and slid the photo halfway in, like a bookmark. If I *did* perchance begin to write again, and if the writing marched, I would meet Johanna right around page two hundred and fifty.

I left the house, locked the back door, got into my car, and drove away. I have never been back.

I'd been tempted to go down to the lake and check out the work — which turned out to be quite a bit more extensive than Bill Dean had originally expected — on several occasions. What kept me away was a feeling, never quite articulated by my conscious mind but still very powerful, that I wasn't supposed to do it that way; that when I next came to Sara, it should be to unpack and stay.

Bill hired out Kenny Auster to shingle the roof, and got Kenny's cousin, Timmy Larribee, to "scrape the old girl down," a cleansing process akin to pot-scrubbing that is sometimes employed with log homes. Bill also had a plumber in to check out the pipes, and got my okay to replace some of the older plumbing and the well-pump.

Bill fussed about all these expenses over the telephone; I let him. When it comes to fifth- or sixth-generation Yankees and the expenditure of money, you might as well just stand back and let them get it out of their systems. Laying out the green just seems wrong to a Yankee, somehow, like petting in public. As for myself, I didn't mind the outgo a bit. I live frugally, for the most part, not out of any moral code but because my imagination, very lively in most other respects, doesn't work very well on the subject of money. My idea of a spree is three days in Boston, a Red Sox game, a trip to Tower Records and Video, plus a visit to the Wordsworth bookstore in Cambridge. Living like that doesn't make much of a dent in the interest, let alone the principal; I had a good money manager down in Waterville, and on the day I locked the door of the Derry house and headed west to TR-90, I was worth slightly over five million dollars. Not much compared to Bill Gates, but big numbers for this area, and I could afford to be cheerful about the high cost of house repairs.

That was a strange late spring and early summer for me. What I did mostly was wait, close up my town affairs, talk to Bill Dean when he called with the latest round of problems, and try not to think. I did the *Publishers Weekly* interview, and when the interviewer asked me if I'd had any trouble getting back to work "in the wake of my bereavement," I said no with an absolutely straight face. Why not? It was true. My troubles hadn't started until I'd finished *All the Way from the Top*; until then, I had been going on like gangbusters.

In mid-June, I met Frank Arlen for lunch at the Starlite Cafe. The Starlite is in

Lewiston, which is the geographical mid-point between his town and mine. Over dessert (the Starlite's famous strawberry short-cake), Frank asked if I was seeing anyone. I looked at him with surprise.

"What are you gaping at?" he asked, his face registering one of the nine hundred un-named emotions — this one of those somewhere between amusement and irritation. "I certainly wouldn't think of it as two-timing Jo. She'll have been dead four years come August."

"No," I said. "I'm not seeing anybody."

He looked at me silently. I looked back for a few seconds, then started fiddling my spoon through the whipped cream on top of my shortcake. The biscuits were still warm from the oven, and the cream was melting. It made me think of that silly old song about how someone left the cake out in the rain.

"*Have* you seen anybody, Mike?"

"I'm not sure that's any business of yours."

"Oh for Christ's sake. On your vacation? Did you —"

I made myself look up from the melting whipped cream. "No," I said. "I did not."

He was silent for another moment or two. I thought he was getting ready to move on to another topic. That would have been fine with me. Instead, he came right out and asked me if I had been laid at all since Johanna died. He would have accepted a lie on that subject even if he didn't entirely believe it — men lie about sex all the time. But I told the truth . . . and with a certain perverse pleasure.

"No."

"Not a single time?"

"Not a single time."

"What about a massage parlor? You know, to at least get a —"

"No."

He sat there tapping his spoon against the rim of the bowl with his dessert in it. He hadn't taken a single bite. He was looking at me as though I were some new and oogy specimen of bug. I didn't like it much, but I suppose I understood it.

I had been close to what is these days called "a relationship" on two occasions, neither of them on Key Largo, where I had observed roughly two thousand pretty women walking around dressed in only a stitch and a promise. Once it had been a red-haired waitress, Kelli, at a restaurant out on the Extension where I often had lunch. After awhile we got talking, joking around, and then there started to be some of that eye-contact, you know the kind I'm talking about, looks that go on just a little too long. I started to notice her legs, and the way her uniform pulled against her hip when she turned, and she noticed me noticing.

And there was a woman at Nu You, the place where I used to work out. A tall woman who favored pink jog-bras and black bike shorts. Quite yummy. Also, I liked the stuff she brought to read while she pedalled one of the stationary bikes on those endless aerobic trips to nowhere — not *Mademoiselle* or *Cosmo*, but novels by people like John Irving and Ellen Gilchrist. I like people who read actual books, and not just because I once wrote them myself. Book-readers are just as willing as anyone else to start out with the weather, but as a general rule they can actually go on from there.

The name of the blonde in the pink tops and black shorts was Adria Bundy. We started talking about books as we pedalled side by side ever deeper into nowhere, and there came a point where I was spotting her one or two mornings a week in the weight room. There's something oddly intimate about spotting. The prone position of the lifter is part of it, I suppose (especially when the lifter is a woman), but not all or even most of it. Mostly it's the dependence factor. Although it hardly ever comes to that point, the lifter is trusting the spotter with his or her life. And, at some point in the winter of 1996, those looks started as she lay on the bench and I stood over her, looking into her upside-down face. The ones that go on just a little too long.

Kelli was around thirty, Adria perhaps a little younger. Kelli was divorced, Adria never married. In neither case would I have been robbing the cradle, and I think either would have been happy to go to bed with me on a provisional basis. Kind of a honey-bump test-drive. Yet what I did in Kelli's case was to find a different restaurant to eat my lunch at, and when the YMCA sent me a free exercise-tryout offer, I took them up on it and just never went back to Nu You. I remember walking past Adria Bundy one day on the street six months or so after I made the change, and although I said hi, I made sure not to see her puzzled, slightly hurt gaze.

In a purely physical way I wanted them both (in fact, I seem to remember a dream in which I *had* them both, in the same bed and at the same time), and yet I wanted neither. Part of it was my inability to write — my life was quite fucked up enough, thank you, without adding any additional complications. Part of it was the work involved in making sure that the woman who is returning your glances is interested in you and not your rather extravagant bank account.

Most of it, I think, was that there was just too much Jo still in my head and heart. There was no room for anyone else, even

after four years. It was sorrow like choles-
terol, and if you think that's funny or weird,
be grateful.

"What about friends?" Frank asked, at
last beginning to eat his strawberry short-
cake. "You've got friends you see, don't
you?"

"Yes," I said. "Plenty of friends." Which
was a lie, but I *did* have lots of crosswords to
do, lots of books to read, and lots of movies
to watch on my VCR at night; I could practically recite the FBI warning about unlawful copying by heart. When it came to
real live people, the only ones I called when
I got ready to leave Derry were my doctor
and my dentist, and most of the mail I sent
out that June consisted of change-of-address
cards to magazines like *Harper's* and *National Geographic*.

"Frank," I said, "you sound like a Jewish
mother."

"Sometimes when I'm with you I *feel* like
a Jewish mother," he said. "One who believes in the curative powers of baked potatoes instead of matzo balls. You look better
than you have in a long time, finally put on
some weight, I think —"

"Too much."

"Bullshit, you looked like Ichabod Crane
when you came for Christmas. Also, you've
got some sun on your face and arms."

"I've been walking a lot."

135

"So you look better . . . except for your eyes. Sometimes you get this look in your eyes, and I worry about you every time I see it. I think Jo would be glad *someone's* worrying."

"What look is that?" I asked.

"Your basic thousand-yard stare. Want the truth? You look like someone who's caught on something and can't get loose."

I left Derry at three-thirty, stopped in Rumford for supper, then drove slowly on through the rising hills of western Maine as the sun lowered. I had planned my times of departure and arrival carefully, if not quite consciously, and as I passed out of Motton and into the unincorporated township of TR-90, I became aware of the heavy way my heart was beating. There was sweat on my face and arms in spite of the car's air conditioning. Nothing on the radio sounded right, all the music like screaming, and I turned it off.

I was scared, and had good reason to be. Even setting aside the peculiar cross-pollination between the dreams and things in the real world (as I was able to do quite easily, dismissing the cut on my hand and the sunflowers growing through the boards of the back stoop as either coincidence or so much psychic fluff), I had reason to be scared. Because they hadn't been ordinary dreams, and my decision to go back to the lake after all this time hadn't been an ordinary decision. I didn't feel like a modern *fin-de-millénaire* man on a spiritual quest to face his fears (I'm okay, you're okay, let's all have an emotional circle-jerk while William Ackerman plays softly in the background); I felt more like some crazy Old Testament prophet going out into the desert to live on locusts and alkali water because God had summoned him in a dream.

I was in trouble, my life was a moderate-going-on-severe mess, and not being able to write was only part of it. I wasn't raping kids or running around Times Square preaching conspiracy theories through a bullhorn, but I was in trouble just the same. I had lost my place in things and couldn't find it again. No surprise there; after all, life's not a book. What I was engaging in on that hot July evening was self-induced shock therapy, and give me at least this much credit — I knew it.

You come to Dark Score this way: I-95 from Derry to Newport; Route 2 from Newport to Bethel (with a stop in Rumford, which used to stink like hell's front porch until the paper-driven economy pretty much ground to a halt during Reagan's second term); Route 5 from Bethel to Waterford. Then you take Route 68, the old County Road, across Castle View, through Motton (where downtown consists of a converted barn which sells videos, beer, and second-hand rifles), and then past the sign which reads TR-90 and the one reading GAME WARDEN IS BEST ASSISTANCE IN EMERGENCY, DIAL 1-800-555-GAME OR *72 ON CELLULAR PHONE. To this, in spray paint, someone has added FUCK THE EAGLES.

Five miles past that sign, you come to a narrow lane on the right, marked only by a square of tin with the faded number 42 on it. Above this, like umlauts, are a couple of .22 holes.

I turned into this lane just about when I had expected to — it was 7:16 P.M., EDT, by the clock on the Chevrolet's dashboard.

And the feeling was coming home.

I drove in two tenths of a mile by the odometer, listening to the grass which crowned the lane whickering against the undercarriage of my car, listening to the occasional branch which scraped across the roof or knocked on the passenger side like a fist. At last I parked and turned the engine off. I got out, walked to the rear of the car, lay down on my belly, and began pulling all of the grass which touched the Chevy's hot exhaust system. It had been a dry summer, and it was best to take precautions. I had come at this exact hour in order to replicate my dreams, hoping for some further insight into them or for an idea of what to do next. What I had not come to do was start a forest fire.

Once this was done I stood up and looked around. The crickets sang, as they had in my dreams, and the trees huddled close on either side of the lane, as they always did in my dreams. Overhead, the sky was a fading strip of blue.

I set off, walking up the righthand wheel-rut. Jo and I had had one neighbor at this end of the road, old Lars Washburn, but now Lars's driveway was overgrown with juniper bushes and blocked by a rusty length of chain. Nailed to a tree on the left of the chain was NO TRESPASSING. Nailed to one on the right was NEXT CENTURY REAL ESTATE, and a local number. The words were faded and hard to read in the growing gloom.

I walked on, once more conscious of my heavily beating heart and of the way the mosquitoes were buzzing around my face and arms. Their peak season was past, but I was sweating a lot, and that's a smell they like. It must remind them of blood.

Just how scared was I as I approached Sara Laughs? I don't remember. I suspect that fright, like pain, is one of those things that slip our minds once they have passed. What I *do* remember is a feeling I'd had before when I was down here, especially when

I was walking this road by myself. It was a sense that reality was thin. I think it *is* thin, you know, thin as lake ice after a thaw, and we fill our lives with noise and light and motion to hide that thinness from ourselves. But in places like Lane Forty-two, you find that all the smoke and mirrors have been removed. What's left is the sound of crickets and the sight of green leaves darkening toward black; branches that make shapes like faces; the sound of your heart in your chest, the beat of the blood against the backs of your eyes, and the look of the sky as the day's blue blood runs out of its cheek.

What comes in when daylight leaves is a kind of certainty: that beneath the skin there is a secret, some mystery both black and bright. You feel this mystery in every breath, you see it in every shadow, you expect to plunge into it at every turn of a step. It is here; you slip across it on a kind of breathless curve like a skater turning for home.

I stopped for a moment about half a mile south of where I'd left the car, and still half a mile north of the driveway. Here the road curves sharply, and on the right is an open field which slants steeply down toward the lake. Tidwell's Meadow is what the locals call it, or sometimes the Old Camp. It was here that Sara Tidwell and her curious tribe built their cabins, at least according to Marie Hingerman (and once, when I asked

Bill Dean, he agreed this was the place . . . although he didn't seem interested in continuing the conversation, which struck me at the time as a bit odd).

I stood there for a moment, looking down at the north end of Dark Score. The water was glassy and calm, still candy-colored in the afterglow of sunset, without a single ripple or a single small craft to be seen. The boat-people would all be down at the marina or at Warrington's Sunset Bar by now, I guessed, eating lobster rolls and drinking big mixed drinks. Later a few of them, buzzed on speed and martinis, would go bolting up and down the lake by moonlight. I wondered if I would be around to hear them. I thought there was a fair chance that by then I'd be on my way back to Derry, either terrified by what I'd found or disillusioned because I had found nothing at all.

"You funny little man, said Strickland."

I didn't know I was going to speak until the words were out of my mouth, and why those words in particular I had no idea. I remembered my dream of Jo under the bed and shuddered. A mosquito whined in my ear. I slapped it and walked on.

In the end, my arrival at the head of the driveway was almost too perfectly timed, the sense of having re-entered my dream almost too complete. Even the balloons tied to the SARA LAUGHS sign (one white and one blue, both with *WELCOME BACK MIKE!* carefully printed on them in black ink) and floating against the ever-darkening backdrop of the trees seemed to intensify the déjà vu I had quite deliberately induced, for no two dreams are exactly the same, are they? Things conceived by minds and made by hands can never be quite the same, even when they try their best to be identical, because we're never the same from day to day or even moment to moment.

I walked to the sign, feeling the mystery of this place at twilight. I squeezed down on the board, feeling its rough reality, and then I ran the ball of my thumb over the letters, daring the splinters and reading with my skin like a blind man reading braille: *S* and *A* and *R* and *A*; *L* and *A* and *U* and *G* and *H* and *S*.

The driveway had been cleared of fallen needles and blown-down branches, but Dark Score glimmered a fading rose just as it had in my dreams, and the sprawled hulk of the house was the same. Bill had thoughtfully left the light over the back stoop burning, and the sunflowers growing through the boards had long since been cut down, but everything else was the same.

I looked overhead, at the slot of sky over the lane. Nothing . . . I waited . . . and nothing . . . waiting still . . . and then there it was, right where the center of my gaze had been trained. At one moment there was only the fading sky (with indigo just starting to rise up from the edges like an infusion of ink), and at the next Venus was glowing there, bright and steady. People talk about watching the stars come out, and I suppose some people do, but I think that was the only time in my life that I actually saw one appear. I wished on it, too, but this time it was real time, and I did not wish for Jo.

"Help me," I said, looking at the star. I would have said more, but I didn't know what to say. I didn't know what kind of help I needed.

That's enough, a voice in my mind said uneasily. *That's enough, now. Go on back and get your car.*

Except that wasn't the plan. The plan was to go down the driveway, just as I had in the final dream, the nightmare. The plan was to prove to myself that there was no shroud-wrapped monster lurking in the shadows of the big old log house down there. The plan was pretty much based on that bit of New Age wisdom which says the word "fear" stands for Face Everything And Recover. But, as I stood there and looked down at that spark of porch light (it looked very small in the growing darkness), it occurred to me that there's another bit of wisdom, one not quite so good-morning-starshine, which suggests fear is actually an acronym for Fuck Everything And Run. Standing there by myself in the woods as the light left the sky, that seemed like the smarter interpretation, no two ways about it.

I looked down and was a little amused to see that I had taken one of the balloons — untied it without even noticing as I thought things over. It floated serenely up from my hand at the end of its string, the words printed on it now impossible to read in the growing dark.

Maybe it's all moot, anyway; maybe I won't be able to move. Maybe that old devil writer's walk has got hold of me again, and I'll just stand here like a statue until someone comes along and hauls me away.

But this was real time in the real world, and in the real world there was no such thing as writer's walk. I opened my hand. As the string I'd been holding floated free, I walked under the rising balloon and started down the driveway. Foot followed foot, pretty much as they had ever since I'd first learned this trick back in 1959. I went deeper and deeper into the clean but sour smell of pine, and once I caught myself taking an extra-big step, avoiding a fallen branch that had been in the dream but wasn't here in reality.

My heart was still thudding hard, and sweat was still pouring out of me, oiling my skin and drawing mosquitoes. I raised a hand to brush the hair off my brow, then stopped, holding it splay-fingered out in front of my eyes. I put the other one next to it. Neither was marked; there wasn't even a shadow of scar from the cut I'd given myself while crawling around my bedroom during the ice storm.

"I'm all right," I said. "I'm all right."

You funny little man, said Strickland, a voice answered. It wasn't mine, wasn't Jo's; it was the UFO voice that had narrated my nightmare, the one which had driven me on even when I wanted to stop. The voice of some outsider.

I started walking again. I was better than halfway down the driveway now. I had reached the point where, in the dream, I told the voice that I was afraid of Mrs. Danvers.

"I'm afraid of Mrs. D.," I said, trying the words aloud in the growing dark. "What if the bad old housekeeper's down there?"

A loon cried on the lake, but the voice didn't answer. I suppose it didn't have to. There *was* no Mrs. Danvers, she was only a bag of bones in an old book, and the voice knew it.

I began walking again. I passed the big pine that Jo had once banged into in our Jeep, trying to back up the driveway. How she had sworn! Like a sailor! I had managed to keep a straight face until she got to "Fuck a duck," and then I'd lost it, leaning against the side of the Jeep with the heels of my hands pressed against my temples, howling until tears rolled down my cheeks, and Jo glaring hot blue sparks at me the whole time.

I could see the mark about three feet up on the trunk of the tree, the white seeming to float above the dark bark in the gloom. It was just here that the unease which pervaded the other dreams had skewed into something far worse. Even before the shrouded thing had come bursting out of the house, I had felt something was all wrong, all twisted up; I had felt that somehow the house itself had gone insane. It was at this point, passing the old scarred pine, that I had wanted to run like the gingerbread man.

I didn't feel that now. I was afraid, yes, but not in terror. There was nothing behind me, for one thing, no sound of slobbering breath. The worst thing a man was likely to come upon in these woods was an irritated moose. Or, I supposed, if he was really unlucky, a pissed-off bear.

In the dream there had been a moon at least three quarters full, but there was no moon in the sky above me that night. Nor would there be; in glancing over the weather page in that morning's *Derry News*, I had

146

noticed that the moon was new.

Even the most powerful déjà vu is fragile, and at the thought of that moonless sky, mine broke. The sensation of reliving my nightmare departed so abruptly that I even wondered why I had done this, what I had hoped to prove or accomplish. Now I'd have to go all the way back down the dark lane to retrieve my car.

All right, but I'd do it with a flashlight from the house. One of them would surely still be just inside the —

A series of jagged explosions ran themselves off on the far side of the lake, the last loud enough to echo against the hills. I stopped, drawing in a quick breath. Moments before, those unexpected bangs probably would have sent me running back up the driveway in a panic, but now I had only that brief, startled moment. It was firecrackers, of course, the last one — the loudest one — maybe an M-80. Tomorrow was the Fourth of July, and across the lake kids were celebrating early, as kids are wont to do.

I walked on. The bushes still reached like hands, but they had been pruned back and their reach wasn't very threatening. I didn't have to worry about the power being out, either; I was now close enough to the back stoop to see moths fluttering around the light Bill Dean had left on for me. Even if the power *had* been out (in the western part of the state a lot of the lines are still above ground, and it goes out a lot), the gennie would have kicked in automatically.

Yet I was awed by how much of my dream was actually here, even with the powerful sense of repetition — of *reliving* — departed. Jo's planters were where they'd always been, flanking the path which leads down to Sara's little lick of beach; I suppose Brenda Meserve had found them stacked in the cellar and had had one of her crew set them out again. Nothing was growing in them yet, but I suspected that stuff would be soon. And even without the moon of my dream, I could see the black square on the water, standing about fifty yards offshore. The swimming float.

No oblong shape lying overturned in front of the stoop, though; no coffin. Still, my heart was beating hard again, and I think if more firecrackers had gone off on the Kashwakamak side of the lake just then, I might have screamed.

You funny little man, said Strickland.

Give me that, it's my dust-catcher.

What if death drives us insane? What if we survive, but it drives us insane? What then?

I had reached the point where, in my nightmare, the door banged open and that white shape came hurtling out with its wrapped arms upraised. I took one more step and then stopped, hearing the harsh sound of my respiration as I drew each breath down my throat and then pushed it back out over the dry floor of my tongue. There was no sense of déjà vu, but for a moment I thought the shape would appear anyway — here in the real world, in real time. I stood waiting for it with my sweaty hands clenched. I drew in another dry breath, and this time I held it.

The soft lap of water against the shore.

A breeze that patted my face and rattled the bushes.

A loon cried out on the lake; moths battered the stoop light.

No shroud-monster threw open the door, and through the big windows to the left and right of the door, I could see nothing moving, white or otherwise. There was a note above the knob, probably from Bill, and that was it. I let out my breath in a rush and walked the rest of the way down the driveway to Sara Laughs.

The note was indeed from Bill Dean. It said that Brenda had done some shopping for me; the supermarket receipt was on the kitchen table, and I would find the pantry well stocked with canned goods. She'd gone easy with the perishables, but there was milk, butter, half-and-half, and hamburger, that staple of single-guy cuisine.

I will see you next Mon., Bill had written. *If I had my druthers I'd be here to say hello in person but the good wife says it's our turn to do the holiday trotting and so we are going down to Virginia (hot!!) to spend the 4th with her sister. If you need anything or run into problems . . .*

He had jotted his sister-in-law's phone number in Virginia as well as Butch Wiggins's number in town, which locals just call "the TR," as in "Me and mother got tired of Bethel and moved our trailer over to the TR." There were other numbers, as well — the plumber, the electrician, Brenda Meserve, even the TV guy over in Harrison who had repositioned the DSS dish for maximum reception. Bill was taking no chances. I turned the note over, imagining a final P.S.: *Say, Mike, if nuclear war should break out before me and Yvette get back from Virginia —*

Something moved behind me.

I whirled on my heels, the note dropping from my hand. It fluttered to the boards of the back stoop like a larger, whiter version of the moths banging the bulb overhead. In that instant I was sure it would be the shroud-thing, an insane revenant in my wife's decaying body, *Give me my dust-catcher, give it to me, how dare you come down here and disturb my rest, how dare you come to Manderley again, and now that you're here, how will you ever get away? Into the mystery with you, you silly little man. Into the mystery with you.*

Nothing there. It had just been the breeze again, stirring the bushes around a little . . . except I had felt no breeze against my sweaty skin, not that time.

"Well it must have been, there's nothing there," I said.

The sound of your voice when you're alone can be either scary or reassuring. That time it was the latter. I bent over, picked up Bill's note, and stuffed it into my back pocket. Then I rummaged out my keyring. I stood under the stoop light in the big, swooping shadows of the lightstruck moths, picking through my keys until I found the one I wanted. It had a funny disused look, and as I rubbed my thumb along its serrated edge, I wondered again why I hadn't come down here — except for a couple of quick broad daylight errands — in all the months and years since Jo had died. Surely if she had been alive, she would have insisted —

But then a peculiar realization came to me: it wasn't just a matter of *since Jo died*. It was easy to think of it that way — never once during my six weeks on Key Largo had I thought of it any other way — but now, actually standing here in the shadows of the dancing moths (it was like standing under some weird organic disco ball) and listening to the loons out on the lake, I remembered that although Johanna had died in August of 1994, she had died in Derry. It had been miserably hot in the city . . . so why had we been there? Why hadn't we been sitting out on our shady deck on the lake side of the house, drinking iced tea in our bathing suits, watching the boats go back and forth and commenting on the form of the various water-skiers? What had she been doing in that damned Rite Aid parking lot to begin with, when during any other August we would have been miles from there?

Nor was that all. We usually stayed at Sara until the end of September — it was a peaceful, pretty time, as warm as summer. But in '93 we'd left with August only a week gone. I knew, because I could remember Johanna going to New York with me later that month, some kind of publishing deal and the usual attendant publicity crap. It had been dog-hot in Manhattan, the hydrants spraying in the East Village and the uptown streets sizzling. On one night of that trip we'd seen *The Phantom of the Opera*. Near the end Jo had leaned over to me and whispered, "Oh fuck! The Phantom is snivelling again!" I had spent the rest of the show trying to keep from bursting into wild peals of laughter. Jo could be evil that way.

Why had she come with me that August? Jo didn't like New York even in April or October, when it's sort of pretty. I didn't know.

I couldn't remember. All I was sure of was that she had never been back to Sara Laughs after early August of 1993 . . . and before long I wasn't even sure of that.

I slipped the key into the lock and turned it. I'd go inside, flip on the kitchen overheads, grab a flashlight, and go back for the car. If I didn't, some drunk guy with a cottage at the far south end of the lane would come in too fast, rear-end my Chevy, and sue me for a billion dollars.

The house had been aired out and didn't smell a bit musty; instead of still, stale air, there was a faint and pleasing aroma of pine. I reached for the light inside the door, and then, somewhere in the blackness of the house, a child began to sob. My hand froze where it was and my flesh went cold. I didn't panic, exactly, but all rational thought left my mind. It was weeping, a child's weeping, but I hadn't a clue as to where it was coming from.

Then it began to fade. Not to grow softer but to *fade*, as if someone had picked that kid up and was carrying it away down some long corridor . . . not that any such corridor existed in Sara Laughs. Even the one running through the middle of the house, connecting the central section to the two wings, isn't really long.

Fading . . . faded . . . almost gone.

I stood in the dark with my cold skin crawling and my hand on the lightswitch. Part of me wanted to boogie, to just go flying out of there as fast as my little legs could carry me, running like the gingerbread man. Another part, however — the rational part — was already reasserting itself.

I flicked the switch, the part that wanted to run saying forget it, it won't work, it's the dream, stupid, it's your dream coming true. But it *did* work. The foyer light came on in a shadow-dispelling rush, revealing Jo's lumpy little pottery collection to the left and the bookcase to the right, stuff I hadn't looked at in four years or more, but still here and still the same. On a middle shelf of the bookcase I could see the three early Elmore Leonard novels — *Swag*, *The Big Bounce*, and *Mr. Majestyk* — that I had put aside against a spell of rainy weather; you have to be ready for rain when you're at camp. Without a good book, even two days of rain in the woods can be enough to drive you bonkers.

There was a final whisper of weeping, then silence. In it, I could hear ticking from the kitchen. The clock by the stove, one of Jo's rare lapses into bad taste, is Felix the Cat with big eyes that shift from side to side as his pendulum tail flicks back and forth. I think it's been in every cheap horror movie ever made.

"Who's here?" I called. I took a step toward the kitchen, just a dim space floating beyond the foyer, then stopped. In the dark the house was a cavern. The sound of the weeping could have come from anywhere. Including my own imagination. "Is someone here?"

No answer . . . but I didn't think the sound had been in my head. If it had been, writer's block was the least of my worries.

Standing on the bookcase to the left of the Elmore Leonards was a long-barrelled flashlight, the kind that holds eight D-cells and will temporarily blind you if someone shines it directly into your eyes. I grasped it, and until it nearly slipped through my hand I hadn't really realized how heavily I was sweating, or how scared I was. I juggled it, heart beating hard, half-expecting that creepy sobbing to begin again, half-expecting the shroud-thing to come floating out of the black living room with its shapeless arms raised; some old hack of a politician back from the grave and ready to give it another shot. Vote the straight Resurrection ticket, brethren, and you will be saved.

I got control of the light and turned it on. It shot a bright straight beam into the living room, picking out the moosehead over the fieldstone fireplace; it shone in the head's glass eyes like two lights burning under water. I saw the old cane-and-bamboo chairs;

the old couch; the scarred dining-room table you had to balance by shimming one leg with a folded playing card or a couple of beer coasters; I saw no ghosts; I decided this was a seriously fucked-up carnival just the same. In the words of the immortal Cole Porter, let's call the whole thing off. If I headed east as soon as I got back to my car, I could be in Derry by midnight. Sleeping in my own bed.

I turned out the foyer light and stood with the flash drawing its line across the dark. I listened to the tick of that stupid cat-clock, which Bill must have set going, and to the familiar chugging cycle of the refrigerator. As I listened to them, I realized that I had never expected to hear either sound again. As for the crying . . .

Had there *been* crying? Had there really?

Yes. Crying or *something*. Just what now seemed moot. What seemed germane was that coming here had been a dangerous idea and a stupid course of action for a man who has taught his mind to misbehave. As I stood in the foyer with no light but the flash and the glow falling in the windows from the bulb over the back stoop, I realized that the line between what I knew was real and what I knew was only my imagination had pretty much disappeared.

I left the house, checked to make sure the door was locked, and walked back up the driveway, swinging the flashlight beam from side to side like a pendulum — like the tail of old Felix the Krazy Kat in the kitchen. It occurred to me, as I struck north along the lane, that I would have to make up some sort of story for Bill Dean. It wouldn't do to say, "Well, Bill, I got down there and heard a kid bawling in my locked house, and it scared me so bad I turned into the ginger-bread man and ran back to Derry. I'll send you the flashlight I took; put it back on the shelf next to the paperbacks, would you?" That wasn't any good because the story would get around and people would say, "Not surprised. Wrote too many books, probably. Work like that has got to soften a man's head. Now he's scared of his own shadow. Occupational hazard."

Even if I never came down here again in my life, I didn't want to leave people on the TR with that opinion of me, that half-contemptuous, see-what-you-get-for-thinking-too-much attitude. It's one a lot of folks seem to have about people who live by their imaginations.

I'd tell Bill I got sick. In a way it was true. Or no . . . better to tell him someone *else* got sick . . . a friend . . . someone in Derry I'd been seeing . . . a lady-friend, perhaps. "Bill, this friend of mine, this *lady*-friend of mine got sick, you see, and so . . ."

I stopped suddenly, the light shining on

the front of my car. I had walked the mile in the dark without noticing many of the sounds in the woods, and dismissing even the bigger of them as deer settling down for the night. I hadn't turned around to see if the shroud-thing (or maybe some spectral crying child) was following me. I had gotten involved in making up a story and then embellishing it, doing it in my head instead of on paper this time but going down all the same well-known paths. I had gotten so involved that I had neglected to be afraid. My heartbeat was back to normal, the sweat was drying on my skin, and the mosquitoes had stopped whining in my ears. And as I stood there, a thought occurred to me. It was as if my mind had been waiting patiently for me to calm down enough so it could remind me of some essential fact.

The pipes. Bill had gotten my go-ahead to replace most of the old stuff, and the plumber had done so. Very recently he'd done so.

"Air in the pipes," I said, running the beam of the eight-cell flashlight over the grille of my Chevrolet. "That's what I heard."

I waited to see if the deeper part of my mind would call this a stupid, rationalizing lie. It didn't . . . because, I suppose, it realized it could be true. Airy pipes can sound like people talking, dogs barking, or children crying. Perhaps the plumber had bled them and the sound had been something else . . . but perhaps he hadn't. The question was whether or not I was going to jump in my car, back two tenths of a mile to the highway, and then return to Derry, all on the basis of a sound I had heard for ten seconds (maybe only five), and while in an excited, stressful state of mind.

I decided the answer was no. It might take only one more peculiar thing to turn me around — probably gibbering like a character on *Tales from the Crypt* — but the sound I'd heard in the foyer wasn't enough. Not when making a go of it at Sara Laughs might mean so much.

I hear voices in my head, and have for as long as I can remember. I don't know if that's part of the necessary equipment for being a writer or not; I've never asked another one. I never felt the need to, because I know all the voices I hear are versions of me. Still, they often seem like very real versions of other people, and none is more real to me — or more familiar — than Jo's voice. Now that voice came, sounding interested, amused in an ironic but gentle way . . . and approving.

Going to fight, Mike?

"Yeah," I said, standing there in the dark and picking out gleams of chrome with my flashlight. "Think so, babe."

Well, then — that's *all right, isn't it?*

Yes. It was. I got into my car, started it up, and drove slowly down the lane. And when I got to the driveway, I turned in.

There was no crying the second time I entered the house. I walked slowly through the downstairs, keeping the flashlight in my hand until I had turned on every light I could find; if there were people still boating on the north end of the lake, old Sara probably looked like some weird Spielbergian flying saucer hovering above them.

I think houses live their own lives along a time-stream that's different from the ones upon which their owners float, one that's slower. In a house, especially an old one, the past is closer. In my life Johanna had been dead nearly four years, but to Sara, she was much nearer than that. It wasn't until I was actually inside, with all the lights on and the flash returned to its spot on the bookshelf, that I realized how much I had been dreading my arrival. Of having my grief reawakened by signs of Johanna's interrupted life. A book with a corner turned down on the table at one end of the sofa, where Jo had liked to recline in her nightgown, reading and eating plums; the cardboard cannister of Quaker Oats, which was all she ever wanted for breakfast, on a shelf in the pantry; her old green robe hung on the back of the bathroom door in the south wing, which Bill Dean still called "the new wing," although it had been built before we ever saw Sara Laughs.

Brenda Meserve had done a good job — a humane job — of removing these signs and signals, but she couldn't get them all. Jo's hardcover set of Sayers's Peter Wimsey novels still held pride of place at the center of the living-room bookcase. Jo had always called the moosehead over the fireplace Bunter, and once, for no reason I could remember (certainly it seemed a very un-Bunterlike accessory), she had hung a bell around the moose's hairy neck. It hung there still, on a red velvet ribbon. Mrs. Meserve might have puzzled over that bell, wondering whether to leave it up or take it down, not knowing that when Jo and I made love on the living-room couch (and yes, we were often overcome there), we referred to the act as "ringing Bunter's bell." Brenda Meserve had done her best, but any good marriage is secret territory, a necessary white space on society's map. What others don't know about it is what makes it yours.

I walked around, touching things, looking at things, seeing them new. Jo seemed everywhere to me, and after a little while I dropped into one of the old cane chairs in front of the TV. The cushion wheezed under me, and I could hear Jo saying, "Well *excuse* yourself, Michael!"

I put my face in my hands and cried. I suppose it was the last of my mourning, but that made it no easier to bear. I cried until I thought something inside me would break if I didn't stop. When it finally let me go, my face was drenched, I had the hiccups, and I thought I had never felt so tired in my life. I felt strained all over my body — partly from the walking I'd done, I suppose, but mostly just from the tension of getting here . . . and deciding to stay here. To fight. That weird phantom crying I'd heard when I first stepped into the place, although it seemed very distant now, hadn't helped.

I washed my face at the kitchen sink, rubbing away the tears with the heels of my hands and clearing my clogged nose. Then I carried my suitcases down to the guest bedroom in the north wing. I had no intention of sleeping in the south wing, in the master bedroom where I had last slept with Jo.

That was a choice Brenda Meserve had foreseen. There was a bouquet of fresh wildflowers on the bureau, and a card: WELCOME BACK, MR. NOONAN. If I hadn't been emotionally exhausted, I suppose looking at that message, in Mrs. Meserve's spiky copperplate handwriting, would have brought on another fit of the weeps. I put my face in the flowers and breathed deeply. They smelled good, like sunshine. Then I took off my clothes, leaving them where they dropped, and turned back the coverlet on the bed. Fresh sheets, fresh pillowcases; same old Noonan sliding between the former and dropping his head onto the latter.

I lay there with the bedside lamp on, looking up at the shadows on the ceiling, almost unable to believe I was in this place and this bed. There had been no shroud-thing to greet me, of course . . . but I had an idea it might well find me in my dreams.

Sometimes — for me, at least — there's a transitional bump between waking and sleeping. Not that night. I slipped away without knowing it, and woke the next morning with sunlight shining in through the window and the bedside lamp still on. There had been no dreams that I could remember, only a vague sensation that I had awakened sometime briefly in the night and heard a bell ringing, very thin and far away.

Chapter 7

The little girl — actually she wasn't much more than a baby — came walking up the middle of Route 68, dressed in a red bathing suit, yellow plastic flip-flops, and a Boston Red Sox baseball cap turned around backward. I had just driven past the Lakeview General Store and Dickie Brooks's All-Purpose Garage, and the speed limit there drops from fifty-five to thirty-five. Thank God I was obeying it that day, otherwise I might have killed her.

It was my first day back. I'd gotten up late and spent most of the morning walking in the woods which run along the lakeshore, seeing what was the same and what had changed. The water looked a little lower and there were fewer boats than I would have expected, especially on summer's biggest holiday, but otherwise I might never have been away. I even seemed to be slapping at the same bugs.

Around eleven my stomach alerted me to the fact that I'd skipped breakfast. I decided a trip to the Village Cafe was in order. The restaurant at Warrington's was trendier by far, but I'd be stared at there. The Village Cafe would be better — if it was still doing business. Buddy Jellison was an ill-tempered fuck, but he had always been the best fry-cook in western Maine and what my stomach wanted was a big greasy Village-burger.

Now this little girl, walking straight up the white line and looking like a majorette leading an invisible parade.

At thirty-five miles per I saw her in plenty of time, but this road was busy in the summer, and very few people bothered creeping through the reduced-speed zone. There were only a dozen Castle County police cruisers, after all, and not many of them bothered with the TR unless they were specifically called there.

I pulled over to the shoulder, put the Chevy in PARK, and was out before the dust had even begun to settle. The day was muggy and close and still, the clouds seeming low enough to touch. The kid — a little blondie with a snub nose and scabbed knees — stood on the white line as if it were a tightrope and watched me approach with no more fear than a fawn.

"Hi," she said. "I go beach. Mummy 'on't take me and I'm mad as hell." She stamped her foot to show she knew as well as anybody what mad as hell was all about. Three or four was my guess. Well-spoken in her fashion and cute as hell, but still no more than three or four.

"Well, the beach is a good place to go on

the Fourth, all right," I said, "but —"

"Fourth of July and fireworks *too,*" she agreed, making "too" sound exotic and sweet, like a word in Vietnamese.

"— but if you try to walk there on the highway, you're more apt to wind up in Castle Rock Hospital."

I decided I wasn't going to stand there playing Mister Rogers with her in the middle of Route 68, not with a curve only fifty yards to the south and a car apt to come wheeling around it at sixty miles an hour at any time. I could hear a motor, actually, and it was revving hard.

I picked the kid up and carried her over to where my car was idling, and although she seemed perfectly content to be carried and not frightened a bit, I felt like Chester the Molester the second I had my arm locked under her bottom. I was very aware that anyone sitting around in the combined office and waiting room of Brooksie's Garage could look out and see me. This is one of the strange midlife realities of my generation: we can't touch a child who isn't our own without fearing others will see something lecherous in our touching . . . or without thinking, way down deep in the sewers of our psyches, that there probably *is* something lecherous in it. I got her out of the road, though. I did that much. Let the Marching Mothers of Western Maine come after me and do their worst.

"You take me beach?" the little girl asked. She was bright-eyed, smiling. I figured that she'd probably be pregnant by the time she was twelve, especially given the cool way she was wearing her baseball cap. "Got your suitie?"

"Actually I think I left my suitie at home. Don't you hate that? Honey, where's your mom?"

As if in direct answer to my question, the car I'd heard came busting out of a road on the near side of the curve. It was a Jeep Scout with mud splashed high up on both sides. The motor was growling like something up a tree and pissed off about it. A woman's head was poked out the side window. Little cutie's mom must have been too scared to sit down; she was driving in a mad crouch, and if a car *had* been coming around that particular curve in Route 68 when she pulled out, my friend in the red bathing suit would likely have become an orphan on the spot.

The Scout fishtailed, the head dropped back down inside the cab, and there was a grinding as the driver upshifted, trying to take her old heap from zero to sixty in maybe nine seconds. If pure terror could have done the job, I'm sure she would have succeeded.

"That's Mattie," the girl in the bathing

suit said. "I'm mad at her. I'm running away to have a Fourth at the beach. If she's mad I go to my white nana."

I had no idea what she was talking about, but it *did* cross my mind that Miss Bosox of 1998 could have her Fourth at the beach; I would settle for a fifth of something whole-grain at home. Meanwhile, I was waving the arm not under the kid's butt back and forth over my head, and hard enough to blow around wisps of the girl's fine blonde hair.

"Hey!" I shouted. "Hey, lady! I got her!"

The Scout sped by, still accelerating and still sounding pissed off about it. The ex-haust was blowing clouds of blue smoke. There was a further hideous grinding from the Scout's old transmission. It was like some crazy version of *Let's Make a Deal*: "Mattie, you've succeeded in getting into second gear — would you like to quit and take the Maytag washer, or do you want to try for third?"

I did the only thing I could think of, which was to step out onto the road, turn toward the Jeep, which was now speeding away from me (the smell of the oil was thick and acrid), and hold the kid up high over my head, hoping Mattie would see us in her rearview mirror. I no longer felt like Chester the Molester; now I felt like a cruel auc-tioneer in a Disney cartoon, offering the cutest li'l piglet in the litter to the highest bidder. It worked, though. The Scout's mudcaked taillights came on and there was a demonic howling as the badly used brakes locked. Right in front of Brooksie's, this was. If there *were* any old-timers in for a good Fourth of July gossip, they would now have plenty to gossip about. I thought they would especially enjoy the part where Mom screamed at me to unhand her baby. When you return to your summer home after a long absence, it's always nice to get off on the right foot.

The backup lights flared and the Jeep began reversing down the road at a good twenty miles an hour. Now the transmission sounded not pissed off but panicky — please, it was saying, please stop, you're killing me. The Scout's rear end wagged from side to side like the tail of a happy dog. I watched it coming at me, hypnotized — now in the northbound lane, now across the white line and into the southbound lane, now overcorrecting so that the lefthand tires spumed dust off the shoulder.

"Mattie go fast," my new girlfriend said in a conversational, isn't-this-interesting voice. She had one arm slung around my neck; we were chums, by God.

But what the kid said woke me up. Mattie go fast, all right, *too* fast. Mattie would, more likely than not, clean out the rear end of my Chevrolet. And if I just stood here,

169

Baby Snooks and I were apt to end up as toothpaste between the two vehicles.

I backed the length of my car, keeping my eyes fixed on the Jeep and yelling, "Slow down, Mattie! Slow down!"

Cutie-pie liked that. "S'yo down!" she yelled, starting to laugh. "S'yo down, you old Mattie, s'yo down!"

The brakes screamed in fresh agony. The Jeep took one last walloping, unhappy jerk backward as Mattie stopped without benefit of the clutch. That final lunge took the Scout's rear bumper so close to the rear bumper of my Chevy that you could have bridged the gap with a cigarette. The smell of oil in the air was huge and furry. The kid was waving a hand in front of her face and coughing theatrically.

The driver's door flew open; Mattie Devore flew out like a circus acrobat shot from a cannon, if you can imagine a circus acrobat dressed in old paisley shorts and a cotton smock top. My first thought was that the little girl's big sister had been baby-sitting her, that Mattie and Mummy were two different people. I knew that little kids often spend a period of their development calling their parents by their first names, but this pale-cheeked blonde girl looked all of twelve, fourteen at the outside. I decided her mad handling of the Scout hadn't been terror for her child (or not *just* terror) but total automotive inexperience.

There was something else, too, okay? Another assumption that I made. The muddy four-wheel-drive, the baggy paisley shorts, the smock that all but screamed Kmart, the long yellow hair held back with those little red elastics, and most of all the inattention that allows the three-year-old in your care to go wandering off in the first place . . . all those things said trailer-trash to me. I know how that sounds, but I had some basis for it. Also, I'm Irish, goddammit. My ancestors were trailer-trash when the trailers were still horse-drawn caravans.

"Stinky-phew!" the little girl said, still waving a pudgy hand at the air in front of her face. "Scoutie *stink!"*

Where Scoutie's bathing suitie? I thought, and then my new girlfriend was snatched out of my arms. Now that she was closer, my idea that Mattie was the bathing beauty's sister took a hit. Mattie wouldn't be middle-aged until well into the next century, but she wasn't twelve or fourteen, either. I now guessed twenty, maybe a year younger. When she snatched the baby away, I saw the wedding ring on her left hand. I also saw the dark circles under her eyes, gray skin dusting to purple. She was young, but I thought it was a mother's terror and exhaustion I was looking at.

I expected her to swat the tot, because that's how trailer-trash moms react to being tired and scared. When she did, I would stop her, one way or another — distract her into turning her anger on me, if that was what it took. There was nothing very noble in this, I should add; all I really wanted to do was to postpone the fanny-whacking, shoulder-shaking, and in-your-face shouting to a time and place where I wouldn't have to watch it. It was my first day back in town; I didn't want to spend any of it watching an inattentive slut abuse her child.

Instead of shaking her and shouting "Where did you think you were going, you little bitch?" Mattie first hugged the child (who hugged back enthusiastically, showing absolutely no sign of fear) and then covered her face with kisses.

"Why did you do that?" she cried. "What was in your head? When I couldn't find you, I died."

Mattie burst into tears. The child in the bathing suit looked at her with an expression of surprise so big and complete it would have been comical under other circumstances. Then her own face crumpled up. I stood back, watched them crying and hugging, and felt ashamed of my preconceptions.

A car went by and slowed down. An elderly couple — Ma and Pa Kettle on their way to the store for that holiday box of Grape-Nuts — gawked out. I gave them an impatient wave with both hands, the kind that says what are *you* staring at, go on, put an egg in your shoe and beat it. They sped up, but I didn't see an out-of-state license plate, as I'd hoped I might. This version of Ma and Pa were locals, and the story would be fleeting its rounds soon enough: Mattie the teenage bride and her little bundle of joy (said bundle undoubtedly conceived in the back seat of a car or the bed of a pickup truck some months before the legitimizing ceremony), bawling their eyes out at the side of the road. With a stranger. No, not exactly a stranger. Mike Noonan, the writer fella from upstate.

"I wanted to go to the beach and *suh-suh-swim!*" the little girl wept, and now it was "swim" that sounded exotic — the Vietnamese word for "ecstasy," perhaps.

"I said I'd take you this afternoon." Mattie was still sniffing, but getting herself under control. "Don't do that again, little guy, please don't you ever do that again, Mommy was so scared."

"I won't," the kid said. "I really won't." Still crying, she hugged the older girl tight, laying her head against the side of Mattie's neck. Her baseball cap fell off. I picked it up, beginning to feel very much like an outsider here. I poked the blue-and-red cap at

173

Mattie's hand until her fingers closed on it.

I decided I also felt pretty good about the way things had turned out, and maybe I had a right to. I've presented the incident as if it was amusing, and it was, but it was the sort of amusing you never see until later. When it was happening, it was terrifying. Suppose there had been a truck coming from the other direction? Coming around that curve, and coming too fast?

A vehicle *did* come around it, a pickup of the type no tourist ever drives. Two more locals gawked their way by.

"Ma'am?" I said. "Mattie? I think I'd better get going. Glad your little girl is all right." The minute it was out, I felt an almost irresistible urge to laugh. I could picture me drawling this speech to Mattie (a name that belonged in a movie like *The Unforgiven* or *True Grit* if any name ever did) with my thumbs hooked into the belt of my chaps and my Stetson pushed back to reveal my noble brow. I felt an insane urge to add, "You're right purty, ma'am, ain't you the new schoolmarm?"

She turned to me and I saw that she *was* right purty. Even with circles under her eyes and her blonde hair sticking off in gobs to either side of her head. And I thought she was doing okay for a girl probably not yet old enough to buy a drink in a bar. At least she hadn't belted the baby.

"Thank you so much," she said. "Was she right *in* the road?" Say she wasn't, her eyes begged. At least say she was walking along the shoulder.

"Well —"

"I walked on the line," the girl said, pointing. "It's like the crossmock." Her voice took on a faintly righteous tone. "Crossmock is safe."

Mattie's cheeks, already white, turned whiter. I didn't like seeing her that way, and didn't like to think of her driving home that way, especially with a kid.

"Where do you live, Mrs. — ?"

"Devore," she said. "I'm Mattie Devore." She shifted the child and put out her hand. I shook it. The morning was warm, and it was going to be hot by mid-afternoon — beach weather for sure — but the fingers I touched were icy. "We live just there."

She pointed to the intersection the Scout had shot out of, and I could see — surprise, surprise — a doublewide trailer set off in a grove of pines about two hundred feet up the little feeder road. Wasp Hill Road, I re-called. It ran about half a mile from Route 68 to the water — what was known as the Middle Bay. Ah yes, doc, it's all coming back to me now. I'm once more riding the Dark Score range. Saving little kids is my specialty.

Still, I was relieved to see that she lived

close by — less than a quarter of a mile from the place where our respective vehicles were parked with their tails almost touching — and when I thought about it, it stood to reason. A child as young as the bathing beauty couldn't have walked far . . . although this one had already demonstrated a fair degree of determination. I thought Mother's haggard look was even more suggestive of the daughter's will. I was glad I was too old to be one of her future boyfriends; she would have them jumping through hoops all through high school and college. Hoops of fire, likely.

Well, the high-school part, anyway. Girls from the doublewide side of town did not, as a general rule, go to college unless there was a juco or a voke-tech handy. And she would only have them jumping until the right boy (or more likely the wrong one) came sweeping around the Great Curve of Life and ran her down in the highway, her all the while unaware that the white line and the crossmock were two different things. Then the whole cycle would repeat itself.

Christ almighty, Noonan, quit it, I told myself. *She's three years old and you've already got her with three kids of her own, two with ringworm and one retarded.*

"Thank you *so* much," Mattie repeated.

"That's okay," I said, and snubbed the little girl's nose. Although her cheeks were still wet with tears, she grinned at me sunnily enough in response. "This is a very verbal little girl."

"Very verbal, and very willful." Now Mattie did give her child a little shake, but the kid showed no fear, no sign that shaking or hitting was the order of most days. On the contrary, her smile widened. Her mother smiled back. And yes — once you got past the slopped-together look of her, she was most extraordinarily pretty. Put her in a tennis dress at the Castle Rock Country Club (where she'd likely never go in her life, except maybe as a maid or a waitress), and she would maybe be more than pretty. A young Grace Kelly, perhaps.

Then she looked back at me, her eyes very wide and grave.

"Mr. Noonan, I'm not a bad mother," she said.

I felt a start at my name coming from her mouth, but it was only momentary. She was the right age, after all, and my books were probably better for her than spending her afternoons in front of *General Hospital* and *One Life to Live*. A little, anyway.

"We had an argument about when we were going to the beach. I wanted to hang out the clothes, have lunch, and go this afternoon. Kyra wanted —" She broke off. "What? What did I say?"

"Her name is Kia? Did —" Before I could

177

say anything else, the most extraordinary thing happened: my mouth was full of water. So full I felt a moment's panic, like someone who is swimming in the ocean and swallows a wave-wash. Only this wasn't a salt taste; it was cold and fresh, with a faint metal tang like blood.

I turned my head aside and spat. I expected a gush of liquid to pour out of my mouth — the sort of gush you sometimes get when commencing artificial respiration on a near-drowning victim. What came out instead was what usually comes out when you spit on a hot day: a little white pellet. And that sensation was gone even before the little white pellet struck the dirt of the shoulder. In an instant, as if it had never been there.

"That man spitted," the girl said matter-of-factly.

"Sorry," I said. I was also bewildered. What in God's name had *that* been about? "I guess I had a little delayed reaction."

Mattie looked concerned, as though I were eighty instead of forty. I thought that maybe to a girl her age, forty *is* eighty. "Do you want to come up to the house? I'll give you a glass of water."

"No, I'm fine now."

"All right. Mr. Noonan . . . all I mean is that nothing like this has ever happened to me before. I was hanging sheets . . . she was

178

inside watching a *Mighty Mouse* cartoon on the VCR . . . then, when I went in to get more pins . . ." She looked at the girl, who was no longer smiling. It was starting to get through to her now. Her eyes were big, and ready to fill with tears. "She was gone. I thought for a minute I'd die of fear."

Now the kid's mouth began to tremble, and her eyes filled up right on schedule. She began to weep. Mattie stroked her hair, soothing the small head until it lay against the Kmart smock top.

"That's all right, Ki," she said. "It turned out okay this time, but you can't go out in the road. It's dangerous. Little things get run over in the road, and you're a little thing. The most precious little thing in the world."

She cried harder. It was the exhausted sound of a child who needed a nap before any more adventures, to the beach or anywhere else.

"Kia bad, Kia bad," she sobbed against her mother's neck.

"No, honey, only three," Mattie said, and if I had harbored any further thoughts about her being a bad mother, they melted away then. Or perhaps they'd already gone — after all, the kid was round, comely, well-kept, and unbruised.

On one level, those things registered. On another I was trying to cope with the strange thing that had just happened, and the equally strange thing I thought I was hearing — that the little girl I had carried off the white line had the name we had planned to give our child, if our child turned out to be a girl.

"Kia," I said. Marvelled, really. As if my touch might break her, I tentatively stroked the back of her head. Her hair was sun-warm and fine.

"No," Mattie said. "That's the best she can say it now. *Kyra*, not Kia. It's from the Greek. It means ladylike." She shifted, a little self-conscious. "I picked it out of a baby-name book. While I was pregnant, I kind of went Oprah. Better than going postal, I guess."

"It's a lovely name," I said. "And I don't think you're a bad mom."

What went through my mind right then was a story Frank Arlen had told over a meal at Christmas — it had been about Petie, the youngest brother, and Frank had had the whole table in stitches. Even Petie, who claimed not to remember a bit of the incident, laughed until tears streamed down his cheeks.

One Easter, Frank said, when Petie was about five, their folks had gotten them up for an Easter-egg hunt. The two parents had hidden over a hundred colored hard-boiled eggs around the house the evening before, after getting the kids over to their grandparents'. A high old Easter morning was had by all, at least until Johanna looked up from the patio, where she was counting her share of the spoils, and shrieked. There was Petie, crawling gaily around on the second-floor overhang at the back of the house, not six feet from the drop to the concrete patio.

Mr. Arlen had rescued Petie while the rest of the family stood below, holding hands, frozen with horror and fascination. Mrs. Arlen had repeated the Hail Mary over and over ("so fast she sounded like one of the Chipmunks on that old 'Witch Doctor' record," Frank had said, laughing harder than ever) until her husband had disappeared back into the open bedroom window with Petie in his arms. Then she had swooned to the pavement, breaking her nose. When asked for an explanation, Petie had told them he'd wanted to check the rain-gutter for eggs.

I suppose every family has at least one story like that; the survival of the world's Peties and Kyras is a convincing argument — in the minds of parents, anyway — for the existence of God.

"I was so scared," Mattie said, now looking fourteen again. Fifteen at most.

"But it's over," I said. "And Kyra's not going to go walking in the road anymore. Are you, Kyra?"

She shook her head against her mother's shoulder without raising it. I had an idea she'd probably be asleep before Mattie got her back to the good old doublewide.

"You don't know how bizarre this is for me," Mattie said. "One of my favorite writers comes out of nowhere and saves my kid. I knew you had a place on the TR, that big old log house everyone calls Sara Laughs, but folks say you don't come here anymore since your wife died."

"For a long time I didn't," I said. "If Sara was a marriage instead of a house, you'd call this a trial reconciliation."

She smiled fleetingly, then looked grave again. "I want to ask you for something. A favor."

"Ask away."

"Don't talk about this. It's not a good time for Ki and me."

"Why not?"

She bit her lip and seemed to consider answering the question — one I might not have asked, given an extra moment to consider — and then shook her head. "It's just not. And I'd be so grateful if you didn't talk about what just happened in town. More grateful than you'll ever know."

"No problem."

"You mean it?"

"Sure. I'm basically a summer person who hasn't been around for awhile . . .

which means I don't have many folks to talk to, anyway." There was Bill Dean, of course, but I could keep quiet around him. Not that he wouldn't know. If this little lady thought the locals weren't going to find out about her daughter's attempt to get to the beach by shank's mare, she was fooling herself. "I think we've been noticed already, though. Take a look up at Brooksie's Garage. Peek, don't stare."

She did, and sighed. Two old men were standing on the tarmac where there had been gas pumps once upon a time. One was very likely Brooksie himself; I thought I could see the remnants of the flyaway red hair which had always made him look like a downeast version of Bozo the Clown. The other, old enough to make Brooksie look like a wee slip of a lad, was leaning on a gold-headed cane in a way that was queerly vulpine.

"I can't do anything about them," she said, sounding depressed. "*Nobody* can do anything about them. I guess I should count myself lucky it's a holiday and there's only two of them."

"Besides," I added, "they probably didn't see much." Which ignored two things: first, that half a dozen cars and pick-em-ups had gone by while we had been standing here, and second, that whatever Brooksie and his elderly friend hadn't seen, they would be more than happy to make up.

On Mattie's shoulder, Kyra gave a ladylike snore. Mattie glanced at her and gave her a smile full of rue and love. "I'm sorry we had to meet under circumstances that make me look like such a dope, because I really am a big fan. They say at the bookstore in Castle Rock that you've got a new one coming out this summer."

I nodded. "It's called *Helen's Promise*."

She grinned. "Good title."

"Thanks. You better get your buddy back home before she breaks your arm."

"Yeah."

There are people in this world who have a knack for asking embarrassing, awkward questions without meaning to — it's like a talent for walking into doors. I am one of that tribe, and as I walked with her toward the passenger side of the Scout, I found a good one. And yet it was hard to blame myself too enthusiastically. I had seen the wedding ring on her hand, after all.

"Will you tell your husband?"

Her smile stayed on, but it paled somehow. And tightened. If it were possible to delete a spoken question the way you can delete a line of type when you're writing a story, I would have done it.

"He died last August."

"Mattie, I'm sorry. Open mouth, insert foot."

"You couldn't know. A girl my age isn't even supposed to be married, is she? And if she is, her husband's supposed to be in the army, or something."

There was a pink baby-seat — also Kmart, I guessed — on the passenger side of the Scout. Mattie tried to boost Kyra in, but I could see she was struggling. I stepped forward to help her, and for just a moment, as I reached past her to grab a plump leg, the back of my hand brushed her breast. She couldn't step back unless she wanted to risk Kyra's slithering out of the seat and onto the floor, but I could feel her recording the touch. My husband's dead, not a threat, so the big-deal writer thinks it's okay to cop a little feel on a hot summer morning. And what can I say? Mr. Big Deal came along and hauled my kid out of the road, maybe saved her life.

No, Mattie, I may be forty going on a hundred, but I was not copping a feel. Except I couldn't say that; it would only make things worse. I felt my cheeks flush a little.

"How old *are* you?" I asked, when we had the baby squared away and were back at a safe distance.

She gave me a look. Tired or not, she had it together again. "Old enough to know the situation I'm in." She held out her hand. "Thanks again, Mr. Noonan. God sent you along at the right time."

"Nah, God just told me I needed a hamburger at the Village Cafe," I said. "Or maybe it was His opposite number. Please say Buddy's still doing business at the same old stand."

She smiled. It warmed her face back up again, and I was happy to see it. "He'll still be there when Ki's kids are old enough to try buying beer with fake IDs. Unless someone wanders in off the road and asks for something like shrimp tetrazzini. If that happened he'd probably drop dead of a heart attack."

"Yeah. Well, when I get copies of the new book, I'll drop one off."

The smile continued to hang in there, but now it shaded toward caution. "You don't need to do that, Mr. Noonan."

"No, but I will. My agent gets me fifty comps. I find that as I get older, they go further."

Perhaps she heard more in my voice than I had meant to put there — people do sometimes, I guess.

"All right. I'll look forward to it."

I took another look at the baby, sleeping in that queerly casual way they have — her head tilted over on her shoulder, her lovely little lips pursed and blowing a bubble. Their skin is what kills me — so fine and perfect there seem to be no pores at all. Her Sox hat was askew. Mattie watched me reach in and readjust it so the visor's shade fell across her closed eyes.

"Kyra," I said.

Mattie nodded. "Ladylike."

"Kia is an African name," I said. "It means 'season's beginning.' " I left her then, giving her a little wave as I headed back to the driver's side of the Chevy. I could feel her curious eyes on me, and I had the oddest feeling that I was going to cry.

That feeling stayed with me long after the two of them were out of sight; was still with me when I got to the Village Cafe. I pulled into the dirt parking lot to the left of the off-brand gas pumps and just sat there for a little while, thinking about Jo and about a home pregnancy-testing kit which had cost twenty-two-fifty. A little secret she'd wanted to keep until she was absolutely sure. That must have been it; what else could it have been?

"Kia," I said. "Season's beginning." But that made me feel like crying again, so I got out of the car and slammed the door hard behind me, as if I could keep the sadness inside that way.

Chapter 8

Buddy Jellison was just the same, all right —
same dirty cooks' whites and splotchy white
apron, same black hair under a paper cap
stained with either beef-blood or strawberry
juice. Even, from the look, the same oat-
meal-cookie crumbs caught in his ragged
mustache. He was maybe fifty-five and
maybe seventy, which in some genetically favored men seems to be still within the farthest borders of middle age. He was huge
and shambly — probably six-four, three hundred pounds — and just as full of grace, wit,
and *joie de vivre* as he had been four years before.

"You want a menu or do you remember?"
he grunted, as if I'd last been in yesterday.

"You still make the Villageburger De-
luxe?"

"Does a crow still shit in the pine tops?"
Pale eyes regarding me. No condolences,
which was fine by me.

"Most likely. I'll have one with everything
— a Villageburger, not a crow — plus a
chocolate frappe. Good to see you again."

I offered my hand. He looked surprised
but touched it with his own. Unlike the
whites, the apron, and the hat, the hand was
clean. Even the nails were clean. "Yuh," he

said, then turned to the sallow woman chopping onions beside the grill. "Village-burger, Audrey," he said. "Drag it through the garden."

I'm ordinarily a sit-at-the-counter kind of guy, but that day I took a booth near the cooler and waited for Buddy to yell that it was ready — Audrey short-orders, but she doesn't waitress. I wanted to think, and Buddy's was a good place to do it. There were a couple of locals eating sandwiches and drinking sodas straight from the can, but that was about it; people with summer cottages would have to be starving to eat at the Village Cafe, and even then you'd likely have to haul them through the door kicking and screaming. The floor was faded green linoleum with a rolling topography of hills and valleys. Like Buddy's uniform, it was none too clean (the summer people who came in probably failed to notice his hands). The woodwork was greasy and dark. Above it, where the plaster started, there were a number of bumper-stickers — Buddy's idea of decoration.

HORN BROKEN — WATCH FOR FINGER.

WIFE AND DOG MISSING. REWARD FOR DOG.

THERE'S NO TOWN DRUNK HERE, WE ALL TAKE TURNS.

Humor is almost always anger with its makeup on, I think, but in little towns the

189

makeup tends to be thin. Three overhead fans paddled apathetically at the hot air, and to the left of the soft-drink cooler were two dangling strips of flypaper, both liberally stippled with wildlife, some of it still struggling feebly. If you could look at those and still eat, your digestion was probably doing okay.

I thought about a similarity of names which was surely, *had* to be, a coincidence. I thought about a young, pretty girl who had become a mother at sixteen or seventeen and a widow at nineteen or twenty. I thought about inadvertently touching her breast, and how the world judged men in their forties who suddenly discovered the fascinating world of young women and their accessories. Most of all I thought of the queer thing that had happened to me when Mattie had told me the kid's name — that sense that my mouth and throat were suddenly flooded with cold, mineral-tangy water. That *rush*.

When my burger was ready, Buddy had to call twice. When I went over to get it, he said: "You back to stay or to clear out?"

"Why?" I asked. "Did you miss me, Buddy?"

"Nup," he said, "but at least you're from in-state. Did you know that 'Massachusetts' is Piscataqua for 'asshole'?"

"You're as funny as ever," I said.

190

"Yuh. I'm goin on fuckin Letterman. Explain to him why God gave seagulls wings."

"Why was that, Buddy?"

"So they could beat the fuckin Frenchmen to the dump."

I got a newspaper from the rack and a straw for my frappe. Then I detoured to the pay phone and, tucking my paper under my arm, opened the phone book. You could actually walk around with it if you wanted; it wasn't tethered to the phone. Who, after all, would want to steal a Castle County telephone directory?

There were over twenty Devores, which didn't surprise me very much — it's one of those names, like Pelkey or Bowie or Toothaker, that you kept coming across if you lived down here. I imagine it's the same everywhere — some families breed more and travel less, that's all.

There was a Devore listing for "RD Wsp Hll Rd," but it wasn't for a Mattie, Mathilda, Martha, or M. It was for Lance. I looked at the front of the phone book and saw it was a 1997 model, printed and mailed while Mattie's husband was still in the land of the living. Okay . . . but there was something else about that name. Devore, Devore, let us now praise famous Devores; wherefore art thou Devore? But it wouldn't come, whatever it was.

I ate my burger, drank my liquefied ice

cream, and tried not to look at what was caught on the flypaper.

While I was waiting for the sallow, silent Audrey to give me my change (you could still eat all week in the Village Cafe for fifty dollars . . . if your blood-vessels could stand it, that was), I read the sticker pasted to the cash register. It was another Buddy Jellison special: CYBERSPACE SCARED ME SO BAD I DOWNLOADED IN MY PANTS. This didn't exactly convulse me with mirth, but it *did* provide the key for solving one of the day's mysteries: why the name Devore had seemed not just familiar but evocative.

I was financially well off, rich by the standards of many. There was at least one person with ties to the TR, however, who was rich by the standards of everybody, and filthy rich by the standards of most year-round residents of the lakes region. If, that was, he was still eating, breathing, and walking around.

"Audrey, is Max Devore still alive?"

She gave me a little smile. "Oh, ayuh. But we don't see him in here too often."

That got the laugh out of me that all of Buddy's joke stickers hadn't been able to elicit. Audrey, who had always been yellowish and who now looked like a candidate for a liver transplant, snickered herself. Buddy gave us a librarian's prim glare from the far end of the counter, where he was reading a flyer about the holiday NASCAR race at Oxford Plains.

I drove back the way I had come. A big hamburger is a bad meal to eat in the middle of a hot day; it leaves you feeling sleepy and heavy-witted. All I wanted was to go home (I'd been there less than twenty-four hours and was already thinking of it as home), flop on the bed in the north bedroom under the revolving fan, and sleep for a couple of hours.

When I passed Wasp Hill Road, I slowed down. The laundry was hanging listlessly on the lines, and there was a scatter of toys in the front yard, but the Scout was gone. Mattie and Kyra had donned their suities, I imagined, and headed on down to the public beachie. I'd liked them both, and quite a lot. Mattie's short-lived marriage had probably hooked her somehow to Max Devore . . . but looking at the rusty doublewide trailer with its dirt driveway and balding front yard, remembering Mattie's baggy shorts and Kmart smock top, I had to doubt that the hook was a strong one.

Before retiring to Palm Springs in the late eighties, Maxwell William Devore had been a driving force in the computer revolution. It's primarily a young people's revolution, but Devore did okay for a golden oldie — knew the playing-field and understood the

193

rules. He started when memory was stored on magnetic tape instead of in computer chips and a warehouse-sized cruncher called UNIVAC was state-of-the-art. He was fluent in COBOL and spoke FORTRAN like a native. As the field expanded beyond his ability to keep up, expanded to the point where it began to define the world, he bought the talent he needed to keep growing.

His company, Visions, had created scanning programs which could upload hard copy onto floppy disks almost instantaneously; it created graphic-imaging programs which had become the industry standard; it created Pixel Easel, which allowed laptop users to mouse-paint . . . to actually fingerpaint, if their gadget came equipped with what Jo had called "the clitoral cursor." Devore had invented none of this later stuff, but he'd understood that it *could* be invented and had hired people to do it. He held dozens of patents and co-held hundreds more. He was supposedly worth something like six hundred million dollars, depending on how technology stocks were doing on any given day.

On the TR he was reputed to be crusty and unpleasant. No surprise there; to a Nazarene, can any good thing come out of Nazareth? And folks said he was eccentric, of course. Listen to the old-timers who remember the rich and successful in their salad days (and all the old-timers claim they do), and you'll hear that they ate the wallpaper, fucked the dog, and showed up at church suppers wearing nothing but their pee-stained BVDs. Even if all that was true in Devore's case, and even if he was Scrooge McDuck in the bargain, I doubted that he'd allow two of his closer relatives to live in a doublewide trailer.

I drove up the lane above the lake, then paused at the head of my driveway, looking at the sign there: SARA LAUGHS burned into a length of varnished board nailed to a handy tree. It's the way they do things down here. Looking at it brought back the last dream of the Manderley series. In that dream someone had slapped a radio-station sticker on the sign, the way you're always seeing stickers slapped on turnpike toll-collection baskets in the exact-change lanes.

I got out of my car, went to the sign, and studied it. No sticker. The sunflowers had been down there, growing out of the stoop — I had a photo in my suitcase that proved it — but there was no radio-station sticker on the house sign. Proving exactly what? Come on, Noonan, get a grip.

I started back to the car — the door was open, the Beach Boys spilling out of the speakers — then changed my mind and went back to the sign again. In the dream, the sticker had been pasted just above the RA of SARA and the LAU of LAUGHS. I touched my fingers to that spot and thought they came away feeling slightly sticky. Of course that could have been the feel of varnish on a hot day. Or my imagination.

I drove down to the house, parked, set the emergency brake (on the slopes around Dark Score and the dozen or so other lakes in western Maine, you always set your brake), and listened to the rest of "Don't Worry, Baby," which I've always thought was the best of the Beach Boys' songs, great not in spite of the sappy lyrics but because of them. *If you knew how much I love you, baby,* Brian Wilson sings, *nothing could go wrong with you.* And oh folks, wouldn't that be a world.

I sat there listening and looked at the cabinet set against the right side of the stoop. We kept our garbage in there to foil the neighborhood raccoons. Even cans with snap-down lids won't always do that; if the coons are hungry enough, they somehow manage the lids with their clever little hands.

You're not going to do what you're thinking of doing, I told myself. *I mean . . . are you?*

It seemed I was — or that I was at least going to have a go. When the Beach Boys gave way to Rare Earth, I got out of the car, opened the storage cabinet, and pulled out two plastic garbage cans. There was a guy named Stan Proulx who came down to yank the trash twice a week (or there was four years ago, I reminded myself), one of Bill Dean's farflung network of part-timers working for cash off the books, but I didn't think Stan would have been down to collect the current accumulation of swill because of the holiday, and I was right. There were two plastic garbage bags in each can. I hauled them out (cursing myself for a fool even while I was doing it) and untwisted the yellow ties.

I really don't think I was so obsessed that I would have dumped a bunch of wet garbage out on my stoop if it had come to that (of course I'll never know for sure, and maybe that's for the best), but it didn't. No one had lived in the house for four years, remember, and it's occupancy that produces garbage — everything from coffee-grounds to used sanitary napkins. The stuff in these bags was dry trash swept together and carted out by Brenda Meserve's cleaning crew.

There were nine vacuum-cleaner disposal bags containing forty-eight months of dust, dirt, and dead flies. There were wads of paper towels, some smelling of aromatic furniture polish and others of the sharper but still pleasant aroma of Windex. There was a moldy mattress pad and a silk jacket which had that unmistakable dined-upon-by-moths look. The jacket certainly caused me no regrets; a mistake of my young manhood, it looked like something from the Beatles' "I Am the Walrus" era. Goo-goo-joob, baby.

There was a box filled with broken glass . . . another filled with unrecognizable (and presumably out-of-date) plumbing fixtures . . . a torn and filthy square of carpet . . . done-to-death dishtowels, faded and ragged . . . the old oven-gloves I'd used when cooking burgers and chicken on the barbecue . . .

The sticker was in a twist at the bottom of the second bag. I'd known I would find it — from the moment I'd felt that faintly tacky patch on the sign, I'd known — but I'd needed to see it for myself. The same way old Doubting Thomas had needed to get the blood under his fingernails, I suppose.

I placed my find on a board of the sunwarmed stoop and smoothed it out with my hand. It was shredded around the edges. I guessed Bill had probably used a putty-knife to scrape it off. He hadn't wanted Mr. Noonan to come back to the lake after four years and discover some beered-up kid had slapped a radio-station sticker on his driveway sign. Gorry, no, 't'wouldn't be proper, deah. So off it had come and into the trash it had gone and here it was again,

198

another piece of my nightmare unearthed and not much the worse for wear. I ran my fingers over it. WBLM, 102.9, PORTLAND'S ROCK AND ROLL BLIMP.

I told myself I didn't have to be afraid. That it meant nothing, just as all the rest of it meant nothing. Then I got the broom out of the cabinet, swept all the trash together, and dumped it back in the plastic bags. The sticker went in with the rest.

I went inside meaning to shower the dust and grime away, then spied my own bathing suitie, still lying in one of my open suitcases, and decided to go swimming instead. The suit was a jolly number, covered with spouting whales, that I had purchased in Key Largo. I thought my pal in the Bosox cap would have approved. I checked my watch and saw that I had finished my Villageburger forty-five minutes ago. Close enough for government work, *kemo sabe,* especially after engaging in an energetic game of Trash-Bag Treasure Hunt.

I pulled on my suit and walked down the railroad-tie steps which lead from Sara to the water. My flip-flops snapped and flapped. A few late mosquitoes hummed. The lake gleamed in front of me, still and inviting under that low humid sky. Running north and south along its edge, bordering the entire east side of the lake, was a right-of-way path (it's called "common property" in the deeds) which folks on the TR simply call The Street. If one were to turn left onto The Street at the foot of my steps, one could walk all the way down to the Dark Score Marina, passing Warrington's and Buddy Jellison's scuzzy little eatery on the way . . . not to mention four dozen summer cottages, discreetly tucked into sloping groves of spruce and pine. Turn right and you could walk to Halo Bay, although it would take you a day to do it with The Street overgrown the way it is now.

I stood there for a moment on the path, then ran forward and leaped into the water. Even as I flew through the air with the greatest of ease, it occurred to me that the last time I had jumped in like this, I had been holding my wife's hand.

Touching down was almost a catastrophe. The water was cold enough to remind me that I was forty, not fourteen, and for a moment my heart stopped dead in my chest. As Dark Score Lake closed over my head, I felt quite sure that I wasn't going to come up alive. I'd be found drifting face-down between the swimming float and my little stretch of The Street, a victim of cold water and a greasy Villageburger. They'd carve Your Mother Always Said To Wait At Least An Hour on my tombstone.

Then my feet landed in the stones and

slimy weedstuff growing along the bottom, my heart kick-started, and I shoved upward like a guy planning to slam-dunk home the last score of a close basketball game. As I returned to the air, I gasped. Water went in my mouth and I coughed it back out, patting one hand against my chest in an effort to encourage my heart — come on, baby, keep going, you can do it.

I came back down standing waist-deep in the lake and with my mouth full of that cold taste — lakewater with an undertinge of minerals, the kind you'd have to correct for when you washed your clothes. It was exactly what I had tasted while standing on the shoulder of Route 68. It was what I had tasted when Mattie Devore told me her daughter's name.

I made a psychological connection, that's all. From the similarity of the names to my dead wife to this lake. Which —

"Which I have tasted a time or two before," I said out loud. As if to underline the fact, I scooped up a palmful of water — some of the cleanest and clearest in the state, according to the analysis reports I and all the other members of the so-called Western Lakes Association get each year — and drank it down. There was no revelation, no sudden weird flashes in my head. It was just Dark Score, first in my mouth and then in my stomach.

I swam out to the float, climbed the three-rung ladder on the side, and flopped on the hot boards, feeling suddenly very glad I had come. In spite of everything. Tomorrow I would start putting together some sort of life down here . . . trying to, anyway. For now it was enough to be lying with my head in the crook of one arm, on the verge of a doze, confident that the day's adventures were over.

As it happened, that was not quite true.

During our first summer on the TR, Jo and I discovered it was possible to see the Castle Rock fireworks show from the deck overlooking the lake. I remembered this just as it was drawing down toward dark, and thought that this year I would spend that time in the living room, watching a movie on the video player. Reliving all the Fourth of July twilights we had spent out there, drinking beer and laughing as the big ones went off, would be a bad idea. I was lonely enough without that, lonely in a way of which I had not been conscious in Derry. Then I wondered what I had come down here for, if not to finally face Johanna's memory — all of it — and put it to loving rest. Certainly the possibility of writing again had never seemed more distant than it did that night.

There was no beer — I'd forgotten to get

a sixpack either at the General Store or at the Village Cafe — but there was soda, courtesy of Brenda Meserve. I got a can of Pepsi and settled in to watch the lightshow, hoping it wouldn't hurt too much. Hoping, I supposed, that I wouldn't cry. Not that I was kidding myself; there were more tears here, all right. I'd just have to get through them.

The first explosion of the night had just gone off — a spangly burst of blue with the bang travelling far behind — when the phone rang. It made me jump as the faint explosion from Castle Rock had not. I decided it was probably Bill Dean, calling long-distance to see if I was settling in all right.

In the summer before Jo died, we'd gotten a wireless phone so we could prowl the downstairs while we talked, a thing we both liked to do. I went through the sliding glass door into the living room, punched the pickup button, and said, "Hello, this is Mike," as I went back to my deck-chair and sat down. Far across the lake, exploding below the low clouds hanging over Castle View, were green and yellow starbursts, followed by soundless flashes that would eventually reach me as noise.

For a moment there was nothing from the phone, and then a man's raspy voice — an elderly voice but not Bill Dean's — said,

"Noonan? Mr. Noonan?"

"Yes?" A huge spangle of gold lit up the west, shivering the low clouds with brief filigree. It made me think of the award shows you see on television, all those beautiful women in shining dresses.

"Devore."

"Yes?" I said again, cautiously.

"Max Devore."

We don't see him in here too often, Audrey had said. I had taken that for Yankee wit, but apparently she'd been serious. Wonders never ceased.

Okay, what next? I was at a total loss for conversational gambits. I thought of asking him how he'd gotten my number, which was unlisted, but what would be the point? When you were worth over half a billion dollars — if this really was *the* Max Devore I was talking to — you could get any old unlisted number you wanted.

I settled for saying yes again, this time without the little uptilt at the end.

Another silence followed. When I broke it and began asking questions, he would be in charge of the conversation . . . if we could be said to be having a conversation at that point. A good gambit, but I had the advantage of my long association with Harold Oblowski to fall back on — Harold, master of the pregnant pause. I sat tight, cunning little cordless phone to my ear, and watched the show in the west. Red bursting into blue, green into gold; unseen women walked the clouds in glowing award-show evening dresses.

"I understand you met my daughter-in-law today," he said at last. He sounded annoyed.

"I may have done," I said, trying not to sound surprised. "May I ask why you're calling, Mr. Devore?"

"I understand there was an incident."

White lights danced in the sky — they could have been exploding spacecraft. Then, trailing after, the bangs. *I've discovered the secret of time travel,* I thought. *It's an auditory phenomenon.*

My hand was holding the phone far too tightly, and I made it relax. Maxwell Devore. Half a billion dollars. Not in Palm Springs, as I had supposed, but close — right here on the TR, if the characteristic underhum on the line could be trusted.

"I'm concerned for my granddaughter." His voice was raspier than ever. He was angry, and it showed — this was a man who hadn't had to conceal his emotions in a lot of years. "I understand my daughter-in-law's attention wandered again. It wanders often."

Now half a dozen colored starbursts lit the night, blooming like flowers in an old Disney nature film. I could imagine the crowds gathered on Castle View sitting cross-legged on their blankets, eating ice cream cones and drinking beer and all going *Oooooh* at the same time. That's what makes any successful work of art, I think — everybody goes *Oooooh* at the same time.

You're scared of this guy, aren't you? Jo asked. *Okay, maybe you're right to be scared. A man who feels he can be angry whenever he wants to at whoever he wants to . . . that's a man who can be dangerous.*

Then Mattie's voice: *Mr. Noonan, I'm not a bad mother. Nothing like this has ever happened to me before.*

Of course that's what most bad mothers say in such circumstances, I imagined . . . but I had believed her.

Also, goddammit, my number was unlisted. I had been sitting here with a soda, watching the fireworks, bothering nobody, and this guy had —

"Mr. Devore, I don't have any idea what —"

"Don't give me that, with all due respect don't give me that, Mr. Noonan, you were seen talking to them." He sounded as I imagine Joe McCarthy sounded to those poor schmucks who ended up being branded dirty commies when they came before his committee.

Be careful, Mike, Jo said. *Beware of Maxwell's silver hammer.*

"I did see and speak to a woman and a little girl this morning," I said. "I presume they're the ones you're talking about."

"No, you saw a *toddler* walking on the road alone," he said. "And then you saw a woman chasing after her. My daughter-in-law, in that old thing she drives. The child could have been run down. Why are you protecting that young woman, Mr. Noonan? Did she promise you something? You're certainly doing the child no favors, I can tell you that much."

She promised to take me back to her trailer and then take me around the world, I thought of saying. *She promised to keep her mouth open the whole time if I'd keep mine shut — is that what you want to hear?*

Yes, Jo said. *Very likely that is what he wants to hear. Very likely what he wants to believe. Don't let him provoke you into a burst of your sophomore sarcasm, Mike — you could regret it.*

Why was I bothering to protect Mattie Devore, anyway? I didn't know. Didn't have the slightest idea of what I might be getting into here, for that matter. I only knew that she had looked tired, and the child hadn't been bruised or frightened or sullen.

"There *was* a car. An old Jeep."

"That's more like it." Satisfaction. And sharp interest. Greed, almost. "What did —"

"I guess I assumed they came in the car together," I said. There was a certain giddy pleasure in discovering my capacity for invention had not deserted me — I felt like a pitcher who can no longer do it in front of a crowd, but who can still throw a pretty good slider in the old back yard. "The little girl might have had some daisies." All the careful qualifications, as if I were testifying in court instead of sitting on my deck. Harold would have been proud. Well, no. Harold would have been horrified that I was having such a conversation at all.

"I think I assumed they were picking wildflowers. My memory of the incident isn't all that clear, unfortunately. I'm a writer, Mr. Devore, and when I'm driving I often drift off into my own private —"

"You're lying." The anger was right out in the open now, bright and pulsing like a boil. As I had suspected, it hadn't taken much effort to escort this guy past the social niceties.

"Mr. Devore. The computer Devore, I assume?"

"You assume correctly."

Jo always grew cooler in tone and expression as her not inconsiderable temper grew hotter. Now I heard myself emulating her in a way that was frankly eerie. "Mr. Devore, I'm not accustomed to being called in the evening by men I don't know, nor do I intend to prolong the conversation when a man who does so calls me a liar. Good evening, sir."

"If everything was fine, then why did you stop?"

"I've been away from the TR for some time, and I wanted to know if the Village Cafe was still open. Oh, by the way — I don't know where you got my telephone number, but I know where you can put it. Good night."

I broke the connection with my thumb and then just looked at the phone, as if I had never seen such a gadget in my life. The hand holding it was trembling. My heart was beating hard; I could feel it in my neck and wrists as well as my chest. I wondered if I could have told Devore to stick my phone number up his ass if I hadn't had a few million rattling around in the bank myself.

The Battle of the Titans, dear, Jo said in her cool voice. *And all over a teenage girl in a trailer. She didn't even have any breasts to speak of.*

I laughed out loud. War of the Titans? Hardly. Some old robber baron from the turn of the century had said, "These days a man with a million dollars thinks he's rich." Devore would likely have the same opinion of me, and in the wider scheme of things he would be right.

Now the western sky was alight with unnatural, pulsing color. It was the finale.

"What was that all about?" I asked.

No answer; only a loon calling across the lake. Protesting all the unaccustomed noise in the sky, as likely as not.

I got up, went inside, and put the phone back in its charging cradle, realizing as I did that I was expecting it to ring again, expecting Devore to start spouting movie clichés: *If you get in my way I'll* and *I'm warning you, friend, not to* and *Let me give you a piece of good advice before you.*

The phone didn't ring. I poured the rest of my soda down my gullet, which was understandably dry, and decided to go to bed. At least there hadn't been any weeping and wailing out there on the deck; Devore had pulled me out of myself. In a weird way, I was grateful to him.

I went into the north bedroom, undressed, and lay down. I thought about the little girl, Kyra, and the mother who could have been her older sister. Devore was pissed at Mattie, that much was clear, and if I was a financial nonentity to the guy, what must she be to him? And what kind of resources would she have if he had taken against her? That was a pretty nasty thought, actually, and it was the one I fell asleep on.

I got up three hours later to eliminate the can of soda I had unwisely downed before retiring, and as I stood before the bowl, pissing with one eye open, I heard the sobbing again. A child somewhere in the dark, lost and frightened . . . or perhaps just *pretending* to be lost and frightened.

"Don't," I said. I was standing naked before the toilet bowl, my back alive with gooseflesh. "Please don't start up with this shit, it's scary."

The crying dwindled as it had before, seeming to diminish like something carried down a tunnel. I went back to bed, turned on my side, and closed my eyes.

"It was a dream," I said. "Just another Manderley dream."

I knew better, but I also knew I was going back to sleep, and right then that seemed like the important thing. As I drifted off, I thought in a voice that was purely my own: *She is alive. Sara is alive.*

And I understood something, too: she belonged to me. I had reclaimed her. For good or ill, I had come home.

Chapter 9

At nine o'clock the following morning I filled a squeeze-bottle with grapefruit juice and set out for a good long walk south along The Street. The day was bright and already hot. It was also silent — the kind of silence you experience only after a Saturday holiday, I think, one composed of equal parts holiness and hangover. I could see two or three fishermen parked far out on the lake, but not a single power boat burred, not a single gaggle of kids shouted and splashed. I passed half a dozen cottages on the slope above me, and although all of them were likely inhabited at this time of year, the only signs of life I saw were bathing suits hung over the deck rail at the Passendales' and a half-deflated fluorescent-green seahorse on the Batchelders' stub of a dock.

But did the Passendales' little gray cottage still belong to the Passendales? Did the Batchelders' amusing circular summer-camp with its Cinerama picture-window pointing at the lake and the mountains beyond still belong to the Batchelders? No way of telling, of course. Four years can bring a lot of changes.

I walked and made no effort to think — an old trick from my writing days. Work your body, rest your mind, let the boys in the basement do their jobs. I made my way past camps where Jo and I had once had drinks and barbecues and attended the occasional card-party, I soaked up the silence like a sponge, I drank my juice, I armed sweat off my forehead, and I waited to see what thoughts might come.

The first was an odd realization: that the crying child in the night seemed somehow more real than the call from Max Devore. Had I actually been phoned by a rich and obviously bad-tempered techno-mogul on my first full evening back on the TR? Had said mogul actually called me a liar at one point? (I was, considering the tale I had told, but that was beside the point.) I knew it had happened, but it was actually easier to believe in The Ghost of Dark Score Lake, known around some campfires as The Mysterious Crying Kiddie.

My next thought — this was just before I finished my juice — was that I should call Mattie Devore and tell her what had happened. I decided it was a natural impulse but probably a bad idea. I was too old to believe in such simplicities as The Damsel in Distress Versus The Wicked Stepfather . . . or, in this case, Father-in-Law. I had my own fish to fry this summer, and I didn't want to complicate my job by getting into a potentially ugly dispute between Mr. Computer and Ms. Doublewide. Devore had rubbed my fur the wrong way — and vigorously — but that probably wasn't personal, only something he did as a matter of course. Hey, some guys snap bra-straps. Did I want to get in his face on this? No. I did not. I had saved Little Miss Red Sox, I had gotten myself an inadvertent feel of Mom's small but pleasantly firm breast, I had learned that Kyra was Greek for ladylike. Any more than that would be gluttony, by God.

I stopped at that point, feet as well as brain, realizing I'd walked all the way to Warrington's, a vast barnboard structure which locals sometimes called the country club. It was, sort of — there was a six-hole golf course, a stable and riding trails, a restaurant, a bar, and lodging for perhaps three dozen in the main building and the eight or nine satellite cabins. There was even a two-lane bowling alley, although you and your competition had to take turns setting up the pins. Warrington's had been built around the beginning of World War I. That made it younger than Sara Laughs, but not by much.

A long dock led out to a smaller building called The Sunset Bar. It was there that Warrington's summer guests would gather for drinks at the end of the day (and some for Bloody Marys at the beginning). And when I glanced out that way, I realized I was no longer alone. There was a woman standing on the porch to the left of the floating bar's door, watching me.

She gave me a pretty good jump. My nerves weren't in their best condition right then, and that probably had something to do with it . . . but I think she would have given me a jump in any case. Part of it was her stillness. Part was her extraordinary thinness. Most of it was her face. Have you ever seen that Edvard Munch drawing, *The Cry*? Well, if you imagine that screaming face at rest, mouth closed and eyes watchful, you'll have a pretty good image of the woman standing at the end of the dock with one long-fingered hand resting on the rail. Although I must tell you that my first thought was not *Edvard Munch* but *Mrs. Danvers*.

She looked about seventy and was wearing black shorts over a black tank bathing suit. The combination looked strangely formal, a variation on the ever-popular little black cocktail dress. Her skin was cream-white, except above her nearly flat bosom and along her bony shoulders. There it swam with large brown age-spots. Her face was a wedge featuring prominent skull-like cheekbones and an unlined lamp of brow. Beneath that bulge, her eyes were lost in sockets of shadow. White hair hung scant and lank around her ears and down to the prominent shelf of her jaw.

God, she's thin, I thought. *She's nothing but a bag of —*

A shudder twisted through me at that. It was a strong one, as if someone were spinning a wire in my flesh. I didn't want her to notice it — what a way to start a summer day, by revolting a guy so badly that he stood there shaking and grimacing in front of you — so I raised my hand and waved. I tried to smile, as well. Hello there, lady standing out by the floating bar. Hello there, you old bag of bones, you scared the living shit out of me but it doesn't take much these days and I forgive you. How the fuck ya doin? I wondered if my smile looked as much like a grimace to her as it felt to me.

She didn't wave back.

Feeling quite a bit like a fool — THERE'S NO VILLAGE IDIOT HERE, WE ALL TAKE TURNS — I ended my wave in a kind of half-assed salute and headed back the way I'd come. Five steps and I had to look over my shoulder; the sensation of her watching me was so strong it was like a hand pressing between my shoulderblades.

The dock where she'd been was completely deserted. I squinted my eyes, at first sure she must have just retreated deeper into the shadow thrown by the little *boozehaus,* but she was gone. As if she had been a ghost herself.

She stepped into the bar, hon, Jo said. *You know that, don't you? I mean . . . you* do *know it, right?*

"Right, right," I murmured, setting off north along The Street toward home. "Of course I do. Where else?" Except it didn't seem to me that there had been time; it didn't seem to me that she could have stepped in, even in her bare feet, without me hearing her. Not on such a quiet morning.

Jo again: *Perhaps she's stealthy.*

"Yes," I murmured. I did a lot of talking out loud before that summer was over. "Yes, perhaps she is. Perhaps she's stealthy." Sure. Like Mrs. Danvers.

I stopped again and looked back, but the right-of-way path had followed the lake around a little bit of curve, and I could no longer see either Warrington's or The Sunset Bar. And really, I thought, that was just as well.

On my way back, I tried to list the oddities which had preceded and then surrounded my return to Sara Laughs: the repeating dreams; the sunflowers; the radio-station sticker; the weeping in the night. I supposed that my encounter with Mattie and Kyra, plus the follow-up phone-call from Mr. Pixel Easel, also qualified as passing strange . . . but not in the same way as a child you heard sobbing in the night.

217

And what about the fact that we had been in Derry instead of on Dark Score when Johanna died? Did that qualify for the list? I didn't know. I couldn't even remember why that was. In the fall and winter of 1993 I'd been fiddling with a screenplay for *The Red-Shirt Man*. In February of '94 I got going on *All the Way from the Top*, and that absorbed most of my attention. Besides, deciding to go west to the TR, west to Sara . . .

"That was Jo's job," I told the day, and as soon as I heard the words I understood how true they were. We'd both loved the old girl, but saying "Hey Irish, let's get our asses over to the TR for a few days" had been Jo's job. She might say it any time . . . except in the year before her death she hadn't said it once. And I had never thought to say it for her. Had somehow forgotten all about Sara Laughs, it seemed, even when summer came around. Was it possible to be that absorbed in a writing project? It didn't seem likely . . . but what other explanation was there?

Something was very wrong with this picture, but I didn't know what it was. Not from nothin.

That made me think of Sara Tidwell, and the lyrics to one of her songs. She had never been recorded, but I owned the Blind Lemon Jefferson version of this particular tune. One verse went:

It ain't nuthin but a barn-dance sugar
It ain't nuthin but a round-and-round
Let me kiss you on your sweet lips sugar
You the good thing that I found.

I loved that song, and had always wondered how it would have sounded coming out of a woman's mouth instead of from that whiskey-voiced old troubadour. Out of Sara Tidwell's mouth. I bet she sang sweet. And boy, I bet she could swing it.

I had gotten back to my own place again. I looked around, saw no one in the immediate vicinity (although I could now hear the day's first ski-boat burring away downwater), stripped to my underpants, and swam out to the float. I didn't climb it, only lay beside it holding onto the ladder with one hand and lazily kicking my feet. It was nice enough, but what was I going to do with the rest of the day?

I decided to spend it cleaning my work area on the second floor. When that was done, maybe I'd go out and look around in Jo's studio. If I didn't lose my courage, that was.

I swam back, kicking easily along, raising my head in and out of water which flowed along my body like cool silk. I felt like an otter. I was most of the way to the shore when I raised my dripping face and saw a woman standing on The Street, watching me. She was as thin as the one I'd seen down at Warrington's . . . but this one was green. Green and pointing north along the path like a dryad in some old legend.

I gasped, swallowed water, coughed it back out. I stood up in chest-deep water and wiped my streaming eyes. Then I laughed (albeit a little doubtfully). The woman was green because she was a birch growing a little to the north of where my set of railroad-tie steps ended at The Street. And even with my eyes clear of water, there was something creepy about how the leaves around the ivory-streaked-with-black trunk almost made a peering face. The air was perfectly still and so the face was perfectly still (as still as the face of the woman in the black shorts and bathing suit had been), but on a breezy day it would seem to smile or frown . . . or perhaps to laugh. Behind it there grew a sickly pine. One bare branch jutted off to the north. It was this I had mistaken for a skinny arm and a bony, pointing hand.

It wasn't the first time I'd spooked myself like that. I see things, that's all. Write enough stories and every shadow on the floor looks like a footprint, every line in the dirt like a secret message. Which did not, of course, ease the task of deciding what was really peculiar at Sara Laughs and what was peculiar only because my *mind* was peculiar.

I glanced around, saw I still had this part of the lake to myself (although not for much longer; the bee-buzz of the first power boat had been joined by a second and third), and stripped off my soggy underpants. I wrung them out, put them on top of my shorts and tee-shirt, and walked naked up the rail-road-tie steps with my clothes held against my chest. I pretended I was Bunter, bringing breakfast and the morning paper to Lord Peter Wimsey. By the time I got back inside the house I was grinning like a fool.

The second floor was stifling in spite of the open windows, and I saw why as soon as I got to the top of the stairs. Jo and I had shared space up here, she on the left (only a little room, really just a cubby, which was all she needed with the studio north of the house), me on the right. At the far end of the hall was the grilled snout of the monster air-conditioning unit we'd bought the year after we bought the lodge. Looking at it, I realized I had missed its characteristic hum without even being aware of it. There was a sign taped to it which said, *Mr. Noonan: Broken. Blows hot air when you turn it on & sounds full of broken glass. Dean says the part it needs is promised from Western Auto in Castle Rock. I'll believe it when I see it. B. Meserve.*

I grinned at that last — it was Mrs. M. right down to the ground — and then tried the switch. Machinery often responds favorably when it senses a penis-equipped human in the vicinity, Jo used to claim, but not this time. I listened to the air conditioner grind for five seconds or so, then snapped it off. "Damn thing shit the bed," as TR folks like to say. And until it was fixed, I wouldn't even be doing crossword puzzles up here.

I looked in my office just the same, as curious about what I might feel as about what I might find. The answer was next to nothing. There was the desk where I had finished *The Red-Shirt Man*, thus proving to myself that the first time wasn't a fluke; there was the photo of Richard Nixon, arms raised, flashing the double V-for-Victory sign, with the caption WOULD YOU BUY A USED CAR FROM THIS MAN? running beneath; there was the rag rug Jo had hooked for me a winter or two before she had discovered the wonderful world of afghans and pretty much gave up hooking.

It wasn't quite the office of a stranger, but every item (most of all, the weirdly empty surface of the desk) said that it *was* the work-space of an earlier-generation Mike Noonan. Men's lives, I had read once, are usually defined by two primary forces: work and marriage. In my life the marriage was over and the career on what appeared to be permanent hiatus. Given that, it didn't seem strange to me that now the space where I'd spent so many days, usually in a state of real happiness as I made up various imaginary lives, seemed to mean nothing. It was like looking at the office of an employee who had been fired . . . or who had died suddenly.

I started to leave, then had an idea. The filing cabinet in the corner was crammed with papers — bank statements (most eight or ten years out of date), correspondence (mostly never answered), a few story fragments — but I didn't find what I was looking for. I moved on to the closet, where the temperature had to be at least a hundred and ten degrees, and in a cardboard box which Mrs. M. had marked GADGETS, I unearthed it — a Sanyo Memo-Scriber Debra Weinstock gave me at the conclusion of our work on the first of the Putnam books. It could be set to turn itself on when you started to talk; it dropped into its PAUSE mode when you stopped to think.

I never asked Debra if the thing just caught her eye and she thought, "Why, I'll bet any self-respecting popular novelist would enjoy owning one of these babies," or if it was something a little more specific . . . some sort of hint, perhaps? Verbalize those little faxes from your subconscious while they're still fresh, Noonan? I hadn't known then and didn't now. But I had it, a genuine pro-quality dictating-machine, and there were at least a dozen cassette tapes in my car, home dubs I'd made to listen to while driving. I would insert one in the Memo-Scriber tonight, slide the volume control as high as it would go, and put the machine in its dictate mode. Then, if the noise I'd heard at least twice now repeated itself, I would have it on tape. I could play it for Bill Dean and ask him what *he* thought it was.

What if I hear the sobbing child tonight and the machine never kicks on?

"Well then, I'll know something else," I told the empty, sunlit office. I was standing there in the doorway with the Memo-Scriber under my arm, looking at the empty desk and sweating like a pig. "Or at least suspect it."

Jo's nook across the hall made my office seem crowded and homey by comparison. Never overfull, it was now nothing but a square room–shaped space. The rug was gone, her photos were gone, even the desk was gone. This looked like a do-it-yourself project which had been abandoned after ninety per cent of the work had been done. Jo had been scrubbed out of it — *scraped* out of it — and I felt a moment's unreasonable anger at Brenda Meserve. I thought of what my mother usually said when I'd done something on my own initiative of which she disapproved: "You took a little too much on y'self, didn't you?" That was my feeling

224

about Jo's little bit of office: that in emptying it to the walls this way, Mrs. Meserve had taken a little too much on herself.

Maybe it wasn't Mrs. M. who cleaned it out, the UFO voice said. *Maybe Jo did it herself. Ever think of that, sport?*

"That's stupid," I said. "Why would she? I hardly think she had a premonition of her own death. Considering she'd just bought —"

But I didn't want to say it. Not out loud. It seemed like a bad idea somehow.

I turned to leave the room, and a sudden sigh of cool air, amazing in that heat, rushed past the sides of my face. Not my body; just my face. It was the most extraordinary sensation, like hands patting briefly but gently at my cheeks and forehead. At the same time there was a sighing in my ears . . . except that's not quite right. It was a susurrus that went *past* my ears, like a whispered message spoken in a hurry.

I turned, expecting to see the curtains over the room's window in motion . . . but they hung perfectly straight.

"Jo?" I said, and hearing her name made me shiver so violently that I almost dropped the Memo-Scriber. "Jo, was that you?"

Nothing. No phantom hands patting my skin, no motion from the curtains . . . which there certainly would have been if there had been an actual draft. All was quiet. There was only a tall man with a sweaty face and a tape-recorder under his arm standing in the doorway of a bare room . . . but that was when I first began to really believe that I wasn't alone in Sara Laughs.

So what? I asked myself. *Even if it should be true, so what? Ghosts can't hurt anyone.*

That's what I thought then.

When I visited Jo's studio (her *air-conditioned* studio) after lunch, I felt quite a lot better about Brenda Meserve — she hadn't taken too much on herself after all. The few items I especially remembered from Jo's little office — the framed square of her first afghan, the green rag rug, her framed poster depicting the wildflowers of Maine — had been put out here, along with almost everything else I remembered. It was as if Mrs. M. had sent a message — *I can't ease your pain or shorten your sadness, and I can't prevent the wounds that coming back here may re-open, but I can put all the stuff that may hurt you in one place, so you won't be stumbling over it unexpected or unprepared. I can do that much.*

Out here were no bare walls; out here the walls jostled with my wife's spirit and creativity. There were knitted things (some serious, many whimsical), batik squares, rag dolls popping out of what she called "my baby collages," an abstract desert painting made from strips of yellow, black, and orange silk, her flower photographs, even, on top of her bookshelf, what appeared to be a construction-in-progress, a head of Sara Laughs herself. It was made out of toothpicks and lollipop sticks.

In one corner was her little loom and a wooden cabinet with a sign reading JO'S KNITTING STUFF! NO TRESPASSING! hung over the pull-knob. In another was the banjo she had tried to learn and then given up on, saying it hurt her fingers too much. In a third was a kayak paddle and a pair of Rollerblades with scuffed toes and little purple pompoms on the tips of the laces.

The thing which caught and held my eye was sitting on the old rolltop desk in the center of the room. During the many good summers, falls, and winter weekends we had spent here, that desktop would have been littered with spools of thread, skeins of yarn, pincushions, sketches, maybe a book about the Spanish Civil War or famous American dogs. Johanna could be aggravating, at least to me, because she imposed no real system or order on what she did. She could also be daunting, even overwhelming at times. She was a brilliant scatterbrain, and her desk had always reflected that.

But not now. It was possible to think that Mrs. M. had cleared the litter from the top of it and plunked down what was now there,

227

but impossible to believe. Why would she? It made no sense.

The object was covered with a gray plastic hood. I reached out to touch it, and my hand faltered an inch or two short as a memory of an old dream

(give me that it's my dust-catcher)

slipped across my mind much as that queer draft had slipped across my face. Then it was gone, and I pulled the plastic cover off. Underneath it was my old green IBM Selectric, which I hadn't seen or thought of in years. I leaned closer, knowing that the typewriter ball would be Courier — my old favorite — even before I saw it.

What in God's name was my old typewriter doing out here?

Johanna painted (although not very well), she took photographs (very good ones indeed) and sometimes sold them, she knitted, she crocheted, she wove and dyed cloth, she could play eight or ten basic chords on the guitar. She *could* write, of course; most English majors can, which is why they become English majors. Did she demonstrate any blazing degree of literary creativity? No. After a few experiments with poetry as an undergrad, she gave up that particular branch of the arts as a bad job. *You write for both of us, Mike,* she had said once. *That's all yours; I'll just take a little taste of everything else.* Given the quality of her poems as opposed to the quality of her silks, photographs, and knitted art, I thought that was probably wise.

But here was my old IBM. Why?

"Letters," I said. "She found it down cellar or something, and rescued it to write letters on."

Except that wasn't Jo. She showed me most of her letters, often urging me to write little postscripts of my own, guilt-tripping me with that old saying about how the shoemaker's kids always go barefoot ("and the writer's friends would never hear from him if it weren't for Alexander Graham Bell," she was apt to add). I hadn't seen a typed personal letter from my wife in all the time we'd been married — if nothing else, she would have considered it shitty etiquette. She *could* type, producing mistake-free business letters slowly yet methodically, but she always used my desktop computer or her own PowerBook for those chores.

"What were you up to, hon?" I asked, then began to investigate her desk drawers.

Brenda Meserve had made an effort with these, but Jo's fundamental nature had defeated her. Surface order (spools of thread segregated by color, for instance) quickly gave way to Jo's old dear jumble. I found enough of her in those drawers to hurt my heart with a hundred unexpected memories, but I found no paperwork which had been typed on my old IBM, with or without the Courier ball. Not so much as a single page.

When I was finished with my hunt, I leaned back in my chair (*her* chair) and looked at the little framed photo on her desk, one I couldn't remember ever having seen before. Jo had most likely printed it herself (the original might have come out of some local's attic) and then hand-tinted the result. The final product looked like a wanted poster colorized by Ted Turner.

I picked it up and ran the ball of my thumb over the glass facing, bemused. Sara Tidwell, the turn-of-the-century blues shouter whose last known port of call had been right here in TR-90. When she and her folks — some of them friends, most of them relatives — had left the TR, they had gone on to Castle Rock for a little while . . . then had simply disappeared, like a cloud over the horizon or mist on a summer morning.

She was smiling just a little in the picture, but the smile was hard to read. Her eyes were half-closed. The string of her guitar — not a strap but a string — was visible over one shoulder. In the background I could see a black man wearing a derby at a killer angle (one thing about musicians: they really know how to wear hats) and standing beside what appeared to be a washtub bass.

Jo had tinted Sara's skin to a *café-au-lait* shade, maybe based on other pictures she'd seen (there are quite a few knocking around, most showing Sara with her head thrown back and her hair hanging almost to her waist as she bellows out her famous carefree yell of a laugh), although none would have been in color. Not at the turn of the century. Sara Tidwell hadn't just left her mark in old photographs, either. I recalled Dickie Brooks, owner of the All-Purpose Garage, once telling me that his father claimed to have won a teddybear at the Castle County Fair's shooting-pitch, and to have given it to Sara Tidwell. She had rewarded him, Dickie said, with a kiss. According to Dickie the old man never forgot it, said it was the best kiss of his life . . . although I doubt if he said it in his wife's hearing.

In this photo she was only smiling. Sara Tidwell, known as Sara Laughs. Never recorded, but her songs had lived just the same. One of them, "Walk Me Baby," bears a remarkable resemblance to "Walk This Way," by Aerosmith. Today the lady would be known as an African-American. In 1984, when Johanna and I bought the lodge and consequently got interested in her, she would have been known as a Black. In her own time she would have been called a Negress or a darkie or possibly an octoroon. And a nigger, of course. There would have been plenty of folks free with that one. And did I believe that she had kissed Dickie

231

Brooks's father — a white man — in front of half of Castle County? No, I did not. Still, who could say for sure? No one. That was the entrancing thing about the past.

"It ain't nuthin but a barn-dance sugar," I sang, putting the picture back on the desk. "It ain't nuthin but a round-and-round."

I picked up the typewriter cover, then decided to leave it off. As I stood, my eyes went back to Sara, standing there with her eyes closed and the string which served her as a guitar strap visible over one shoulder. Something in her face and smile had always struck me as familiar, and suddenly it came to me. She looked oddly like Robert Johnson, whose primitive licks hid behind the chords of almost every Led Zeppelin and Yardbirds song ever recorded. Who, according to the legend, had gone down to the crossroads and sold his soul to Satan for seven years of fast living, high-tension liquor, and streetlife babies. And for a jukejoint brand of immortality, of course. Which he had gotten. Robert Johnson, supposedly poisoned over a woman.

In the late afternoon I went down to the store and saw a good-looking piece of flounder in the cold-case. It looked like supper to me. I bought a bottle of white wine to go with it, and while I was waiting my turn at the cash register, a trembling old man's voice spoke up behind me. "See you made a new friend yes'ty." The Yankee accent was so thick that it sounded almost like a joke . . . except the accent itself is only part of it; mostly, I've come to believe, it's that singsong tone — real Mainers all sound like auctioneers.

I turned and saw the geezer who had been standing out on the garage tarmac the day before, watching along with Dickie Brooks as I got to know Kyra, Mattie, and Scoutie. He still had the gold-headed cane, and I now recognized it. Sometime in the 1950s, the *Boston Post* had donated one of those canes to every county in the New England states. They were given to the oldest residents and passed along from old fart to old fart. And the joke of it was that the *Post* had gone toes-up years ago.

"Actually two new friends," I replied, trying to dredge up his name. I couldn't, but I remembered him from when Jo had been alive, holding down one of the overstuffed chairs in Dickie's waiting room, discussing weather and politics, politics and weather, as the hammers whanged and the air-compressor chugged. A regular. And if something happened out there on Highway 68, eye-God, he was there to see it.

"I hear Mattie Devore can be quite a dear," he said — *heah, Devoah, deah* — and one of his crusty eyelids drooped. I have seen a fair number of salacious winks in my time, but none that was a patch on the one tipped me by that old man with the gold-headed cane. I felt a strong urge to knock his waxy beak of a nose off. The sound of it parting company from his face would be like the crack of a dead branch broken over a bent knee.

"Do you hear a lot, old-timer?" I asked.

"Oh, ayuh!" he said. His lips — dark as strips of liver — parted in a grin. His gums swarmed with white patches. He had a couple of yellow teeth still planted in the top one, and a couple more on the bottom. "And she gut that little one — cunnin, she is! Ayuh!"

"Cunnin as a cat a-runnin," I agreed.

He blinked at me, a little surprised to hear such an old one out of my presumably new-fangled mouth, and then that reprehensible grin widened. "Her don't mind her, though," he said. "Baby gut the run of the place, don'tcha know."

I became aware — better belated than never — that half a dozen people were watching and listening to us. "That wasn't my impression," I said, raising my voice a bit. "No, that wasn't my impression at all."

He only grinned . . . that old man's grin that says *Oh, ayuh, deah; I know one worth two of that.*

I left the store feeling worried for Mattie Devore. Too many people were minding her business, it seemed to me.

When I got home, I took my bottle of wine into the kitchen — it could chill while I got the barbecue going out on the deck. I reached for the fridge door, then paused. Perhaps as many as four dozen little magnets had been scattered randomly across the front — vegetables, fruits, plastic letters and numbers, even a good selection of the California Raisins — but they weren't random anymore. Now they formed a circle on the front of the refrigerator. Someone had been in here. Someone had come in and . . .

Rearranged the magnets on the fridge? If so, that was a burglar who needed to do some heavy remedial work. I touched one of them — gingerly, with just the tip of my finger. Then, suddenly angry with myself, I reached out and spread them again, doing it with enough force to knock a couple to the floor. I didn't pick them up.

That night, before going to bed, I placed the Memo-Scriber on the table beneath Bunter the Great Stuffed Moose, turning it on and putting it in the DICTATE mode. Then I slipped in one of my old home-dubbed cassettes, zeroed the counter, and went to bed, where I slept without dreams or other interruption for eight hours.

★ ★ ★

The next morning, Monday, was the sort of day the tourists come to Maine for — the air so sunny-clean that the hills across the lake seemed to be under subtle magnification. Mount Washington, New England's highest, floated in the farthest distance.

I put on the coffee, then went into the living room, whistling. All my imaginings of the last few days seemed silly this morning. Then the whistle died away. The Memo-Scriber's counter, set to 000 when I went to bed, was now at 012.

I rewound it, hesitated with my finger over the PLAY button, told myself (in Jo's voice) not to be a fool, and pushed it.

"Oh Mike," a voice whispered — mourned, almost — on the tape, and I found myself having to press the heel of one hand to my mouth to hold back a scream. It was what I had heard in Jo's office when the draft rushed past the sides of my face . . . only now the words were slowed down just enough for me to understand them. *"Oh Mike,"* it said again. There was a faint click. The machine had shut down for some length of time. And then, once more, spoken in the living room as I had slept in the north wing: *"Oh Mike."*

Then it was gone.

236

Chapter 10

Around nine o'clock, a pickup came down the driveway and parked behind my Chevrolet. The truck was new — a Dodge Ram so clean and chrome-shiny it looked as if the ten-day plates had just come off that morning — but it was the same shade of off-white as the last one and the sign on the driver's door was the one I remembered: WILLIAM "BILL" DEAN CAMP CHECKING CARETAKING LIGHT CARPENTRY, plus his telephone number. I went out on the back stoop to meet him, coffee cup in my hand.

"Mike!" Bill cried, climbing down from behind the wheel. Yankee men don't hug — that's a truism you can put right up there with tough guys don't dance and real men don't eat quiche — but Bill pumped my hand almost hard enough to slop coffee from a cup that was three-quarters empty, and gave me a hearty clap on the back. His grin revealed a splendidly blatant set of false teeth — the kind which used to be called Roebuckers, because you got them from the catalogue. It occurred to me in passing that my ancient interlocutor from the Lakeview General Store could have used a pair. It certainly would have improved mealtimes for the nosy old fuck. "Mike, you're a sight for sore eyes!"

"Good to see you, too," I said, grinning. Nor was it a false grin; I felt all right. Things with the power to scare the living shit out of you on a thundery midnight in most cases seem only interesting in the bright light of a summer morning. "You're looking well, my friend."

It was true. Bill was four years older and a little grayer around the edges, but otherwise the same. Sixty-five? Seventy? It didn't matter. There was no waxy look of ill health about him, and none of the falling-away in the face, principally around the eyes and in the cheeks, that I associate with encroaching infirmity.

"So're you," he said, letting go of my hand. "We was all so sorry about Jo, Mike. Folks in town thought the world of her. It was a shock, with her so young. My wife asked if I'd give you her condolences special. Jo made her an afghan the year she had the pneumonia, and Yvette ain't never forgot it."

"Thanks," I said, and my voice wasn't quite my own for a moment or two. It seemed that on the TR my wife was hardly dead at all. "And thank Yvette, too."

"Yuh. Everythin okay with the house? Other'n the air conditioner, I mean. Buggardly thing! Them at the Western Auto promised me that part last week, and now they're saying maybe not until August first."

"It's okay. I've got my PowerBook. If I want to use it, the kitchen table will do fine for a desk." And I *would* want to use it — so many crosswords, so little time.

"Got your hot water okay?"

"All that's fine, but there is one problem."

I stopped. How did you tell your caretaker you thought your house was haunted? Probably there was no good way; probably the best thing to do was to go at it head-on. I had questions, but I didn't want just to nibble around the edges of the subject and be coy. For one thing, Bill would sense it. He might have bought his false teeth out of a catalogue, but he wasn't stupid.

"What's on your mind, Mike? Shoot."

"I don't know how you're going to take this, but —"

He smiled in the way of a man who suddenly understands and held up his hand. "Guess maybe I know already."

"You do?" I felt an enormous sense of relief and I could hardly wait to find out what he had experienced in Sara, perhaps while checking for dead lightbulbs or making sure the roof was holding the snow all right. "What did *you* hear?"

"Mostly what Royce Merrill and Dickie Brooks have been telling," he said. "Beyond that, I don't know much. Me and mother's been in Virginia, remember. Only got back last night around eight o'clock. Still, it's the big topic down to the store."

For a moment I remained so fixed on Sara Laughs that I had no idea what he was talking about. All I could think was that folks were gossiping about the strange noises in my house. Then the name Royce Merrill clicked and everything else clicked with it. Merrill was the elderly possum with the gold-headed cane and the salacious wink. Old Four-Teeth. My caretaker wasn't talking about ghostly noises; he was talking about Mattie Devore.

"Let's get you a cup of coffee," I said. "I need you to tell me what I'm stepping in here."

When we were seated on the deck, me with fresh coffee and Bill with a cup of tea ("Coffee burns me at both ends these days," he said), I asked him first to tell me the Royce Merrill–Dickie Brooks version of my encounter with Mattie and Kyra.

It turned out to be better than I had expected. Both old men had seen me standing at the side of the road with the little girl in my arms, and they had observed my Chevy parked halfway into the ditch with the driver's-side door open, but apparently neither of them had seen Kyra using the white line of Route 68 as a tightrope. As if to compensate for this, however, Royce claimed that Mattie had given me a big my hero hug and a kiss on the mouth.

"Did he get the part about how I grabbed her by the ass and slipped her some tongue?" I asked.

Bill grinned. "Royce's imagination ain't stretched that far since he was fifty or so, and that was forty or more year ago."

"I never touched her." Well . . . there had been that moment when the back of my hand went sliding along the curve of her breast, but that had been inadvertent, whatever the young lady herself might think about it.

"Shite, you don't need to tell me that," he said. *"But . . ."*

He said that *but* the way my mother always had, letting it trail off on its own, like the tail of some ill-omened kite.

"But what?"

"You'd do well to keep your distance from her," he said. "She's nice enough — almost a town girl, don't you know — but she's trouble." He paused. "No, that ain't quite fair to her. She's *in* trouble."

"The old man wants custody of the baby, doesn't he?"

Bill set his teacup down on the deck rail and looked at me with his eyebrows raised. Reflections from the lake ran up his cheek in ripples, giving him an exotic look. "How'd you know?"

"Guesswork, but of the educated variety.

Her father-in-law called me Saturday night during the fireworks. And while he never came right out and stated his purpose, I doubt if Max Devore came all the way back to TR-90 in western Maine to repo his daughter-in-law's Jeep and trailer. So what's the story, Bill?"

For several moments he only looked at me. It was almost the look of a man who knows you have contracted a serious disease and isn't sure how much he ought to tell you. Being looked at that way made me profoundly uneasy. It also made me feel that I might be putting Bill Dean on the spot. Devore had roots here, after all. And, as much as Bill might like me, I didn't. Jo and I were from away. It could have been worse — it could have been Massachusetts or New York — but Derry, although in Maine, was still away.

"Bill? I could use a little navigational help if you —"

"You want to stay out of his way," he said. His easy smile was gone. "The man's mad."

For a moment I thought Bill only meant Devore was pissed off at me, and then I took another look at his face. No, I decided, he didn't mean pissed off; he had used the word "mad" in the most literal way.

"Mad how?" I asked. "Mad like Charles Manson? Like Hannibal Lecter? How?"

"Say like Howard Hughes," he said. "Ever

242

read any of the stories about him? The lengths he'd go to to get the things he wanted? It didn't matter if it was a special kind of hot dog they only sold in L.A. or an airplane designer he wanted to steal from Lockheed or McDonnell-Douglas, he had to have what he wanted, and he wouldn't rest until it was under his hand. Devore is the same way. He always was — even as a boy he was willful, according to the stories you hear in town.

"My own dad had one he used to tell. He said little Max Devore broke into Scant Larribee's tack-shed one winter because he wanted the Flexible Flyer Scant give his boy Scooter for Christmas. Back around 1923, this would have been. Devore cut both his hands on broken glass, Dad said, but he got the sled. They found him near midnight, sliding down Sugar Maple Hill, holding his hands up to his chest when he went down. He'd bled all over his mittens and his snowsuit. There's other stories you'll hear about Maxie Devore as a kid — if you ask you'll hear fifty different ones — and some may even be true. That one about the sled *is* true, though. I'd bet the farm on it. Because my father didn't lie. It was against his religion."

"Baptist?"

"Nosir, Yankee."

"1923 was many moons ago, Bill. Sometimes people change."

"Ayuh, but mostly they don't. I haven't seen Devore since he come back and moved into Warrington's, so I can't say for sure, but I've heard things that make me think that if he *has* changed, it's for the worse. He didn't come all the way across the country 'cause he wanted a vacation. He wants the *kid*. To him she's just another version of Scooter Larribee's Flexible Flyer. And my strong advice to you is that you don't want to be the window-glass between him and her."

I sipped my coffee and looked out at the lake. Bill gave me time to think, scraping one of his workboots across a splatter of birdshit on the boards while I did it. Crowshit, I reckoned; only crows crap in such long and exuberant splatters.

One thing seemed absolutely sure: Mattie Devore was roughly nine miles up Shit Creek with no paddle. I'm not the cynic I was at twenty — is anyone? — but I wasn't naive enough or idealistic enough to believe the law would protect Ms. Doublewide against Mr. Computer . . . not if Mr. Computer decided to play dirty. As a boy he'd taken the sled he wanted and gone sliding by himself at midnight, bleeding hands not a concern. And as a man? An old man who had been getting every sled he wanted for the last forty years or so?

"What's the story with Mattie, Bill? Tell me."

It didn't take him long. Country stories are, by and large, simple stories. Which isn't to say they're not often interesting.

Mattie Devore had started life as Mattie Stanchfield, not quite from the TR but from just over the line in Motton. Her father had been a logger, her mother a home beautician (which made it, in a ghastly way, the perfect country marriage). There were three kids. When Dave Stanchfield missed a curve over in Lovell and drove a fully loaded pulptruck into Kewadin Pond, his widow "kinda lost heart," as they say. She died soon after. There had been no insurance, other than what Stanchfield had been obliged to carry on his Jimmy and his skidder.

Talk about your Brothers Grimm, huh? Subtract the Fisher-Price toys behind the house, the two pole hairdryers in the basement beauty salon, the old rustbucket Toyota in the driveway, and you were right there: *Once upon a time there lived a poor widow and her three children.*

Mattie is the princess of the piece — poor but beautiful (that she *was* beautiful I could personally testify). Now enter the prince. In this case he's a gangly stuttering redhead named Lance Devore. The child of Max Devore's sunset years. When Lance met

Mattie, he was twenty-one. She had just turned seventeen. The meeting took place at Warrington's, where Mattie had landed a summer job as a waitress.

Lance Devore was staying across the lake on the Upper Bay, but on Tuesday nights there were pickup softball games at Warrington's, the townies against the summer folks, and he usually canoed across to play. Softball is a great thing for the Lance Devores of the world; when you're standing at the plate with a bat in your hands, it doesn't matter if you're gangly. And it sure doesn't matter if you stutter.

"He confused em quite considerable over to Warrington's," Bill said. "They didn't know which team he belonged on — the Locals or the Aways. Lance didn't care; either side was fine with him. Some weeks he'd play for one, some weeks t'other. Either one was more than happy to have him, too, as he could hit a ton and field like an angel. They'd put him at first base a lot because he was tall, but he was really wasted there. At second or shortstop . . . my! He'd jump and twirl around like that guy Noriega."

"You might mean Nureyev," I said.

He shrugged. "Point is, he was somethin to see. And folks liked him. He fit in. It's mostly young folks that play, you know, and to them it's how you do, not who you are. Besides, a lot of em don't know Max Devore from a hole in the ground."

"Unless they read the *Wall Street Journal* and the computer magazines," I said. "In those, you run across the name Devore about as often as you run across the name of God in the Bible."

"No foolin?"

"Well, I guess that in the computer magazines God is more often spelled Gates, but you know what I mean."

"I s'pose. But even so, it's been sixty-five years since Max Devore spent any real time on the TR. You know what happened when he left, don't you?"

"No, why would I?"

He looked at me, surprised. Then a kind of veil seemed to fall over his eyes. He blinked and it cleared. "Tell you another time — it ain't no secret — but I need to be over to the Harrimans' by eleven to check their sump-pump. Don't want to get sidetracked. Point I was tryin to make is just this: Lance Devore was accepted as a nice young fella who could hit a softball three hundred and fifty feet into the trees if he struck it just right. There was no one old enough to hold his old man against him — not at Warrington's on Tuesday nights, there wasn't — and no one held it against him that his family had dough, either. Hell, there are lots of wealthy people here in the summer. You know that. None worth as

247

much as Max Devore, but bein rich is only a matter of degree."

That wasn't true, and I had just enough money to know it. Wealth is like the Richter scale — once you pass a certain point, the jumps from one level to the next aren't double or triple but some amazing and ruinous multiple you don't even want to think about. Fitzgerald had it straight, although I guess he didn't believe his own insight: the very rich *are* different from you and me. I thought of telling Bill that, and decided to keep my mouth shut. He had a sump-pump to fix.

Kyra's parents met over a keg of beer stuck in a mudhole. Mattie was running the usual Tuesday-night keg out to the softball field from the main building on a handcart. She'd gotten it most of the way from the restaurant wing with no trouble, but there had been heavy rain earlier in the week, and the cart finally bogged down in a soft spot. Lance's team was up, and Lance was sitting at the end of the bench, waiting his turn to hit. He saw the girl in the white shorts and blue Warrington's polo shirt struggling with the bogged handcart, and got up to help her. Three weeks later they were inseparable and Mattie was pregnant; ten weeks later they were married; thirty-seven months later, Lance Devore was in a coffin, done with softball and cold beer on a summer evening, done with what he called "woodsing," done with fatherhood, done with love for the beautiful princess. Just another early finish, hold the happily-ever-after.

Bill Dean didn't describe their meeting in any detail; he only said, "They met at the field — she was runnin out the beer and he helped her out of a boghole when she got her handcart stuck."

Mattie never said much about that part of it, so I don't know much. Except I do . . . and although some of the details might be wrong, I'd bet you a dollar to a hundred I got most of them right. That was my summer for knowing things I had no business knowing.

It's hot, for one thing — '94 is the hottest summer of the decade and July is the hottest month of the summer. President Clinton is being upstaged by Newt and the Republicans. Folks are saying old Slick Willie may not even run for a second term. Boris Yeltsin is reputed to be either dying of heart disease or in a dry-out clinic. The Red Sox are looking better than they have any right to. In Derry, Johanna Arlen Noonan is maybe starting to feel a little whoopsy in the morning. If so, she does not speak of it to her husband.

I see Mattie in her blue polo shirt with her

name sewn in white script above her left breast. Her white shorts make a pleasing contrast to her tanned legs. I also see her wearing a blue gimme cap with the red *W* for Warrington's above the long bill. Her pretty dark-blonde hair is pulled through the hole at the back of the cap and falls to the collar of her shirt. I see her trying to yank the handcart out of the mud without upsetting the keg of beer. Her head is down; the shadow thrown by the bill of the cap obscures all of her face but her mouth and small set chin.

"Luh-let m-me h-h-help," Lance says, and she looks up. The shadow cast by the cap's bill falls away, he sees her big blue eyes — the ones she'll pass on to their daughter. One look into those eyes and the war is over without a single shot fired; he belongs to her as surely as any young man ever belonged to any young woman.

The rest, as they say around here, was just courtin.

The old man had three children, but Lance was the only one he seemed to care about. ("Daughter's crazier'n a shithouse mouse," Bill said matter-of-factly. "In some laughin academy in California. Think I heard she caught her a cancer, too.") The fact that Lance had no interest in computers and software actually seemed to please his father. He had another son who was capable of running the business. In another way, however, Lance Devore's older half-brother wasn't capable at all: there would be no grandchildren from that one.

"Rump-wrangler," Bill said. "Understand there's a lot of that goin around out there in California."

There was a fair amount of it going around on the TR, too, I imagined, but thought it not my place to offer sexual instruction to my caretaker.

Lance Devore had been attending Reed College in Oregon, majoring in forestry — the kind of guy who falls in love with green flannel pants, red suspenders, and the sight of condors at dawn. A Brothers Grimm woodcutter, in fact, once you got past the academic jargon. In the summer between his junior and senior years, his father had summoned him to the family compound in Palm Springs, and had presented him with a boxy lawyer's suitcase crammed with maps, aerial photos, and legal papers. These had little order that Lance could see, but I doubt that he cared. Imagine a comic-book collector given a crate crammed with rare old copies of *Donald Duck*. Imagine a movie collector given the rough cut of a never-released film starring Humphrey Bogart and Marilyn Monroe. Then imagine this avid young forester realizing that his father owned not just acres or square miles in

251

the vast unincorporated forests of western Maine, but entire *realms*.

Although Max Devore had left the TR in 1933, he'd kept a lively interest in the area where he'd grown up, subscribing to area newspapers and getting magazines such as *Down East* and the *Maine Times*. In the early eighties, he had begun to buy long columns of land just east of the Maine–New Hampshire border. God knew there had been plenty for sale; the paper companies which owned most of it had fallen into a recessionary pit, and many had become convinced that their New England holdings and operations would be the best place to begin retrenching. So this land, stolen from the Indians and clear-cut ruthlessly in the twenties and fifties, came into Max Devore's hands. He might have bought it just because it was there, a good bargain he could afford to take advantage of. He might have bought it as a way of demonstrating to himself that he had really survived his childhood; had, in point of fact, triumphed over it.

Or he might have bought it as a toy for his beloved younger son. In the years when Devore was making his major land purchases in western Maine, Lance would have been just a kid . . . but old enough for a perceptive father to see where his interests were tending.

Devore asked Lance to spend the summer

of 1994 surveying purchases which were, for the most part, already ten years old. He wanted the boy to put the paperwork in order, but he wanted more than that — he wanted Lance to make sense of it. It wasn't a land-use recommendation he was looking for, exactly, although I guess he would have listened if Lance had wanted to make one; he simply wanted a sense of what he had purchased. Would Lance take a summer in western Maine trying to find out what *his* sense of it was? At a salary of two or three thousand dollars a month?

I imagine Lance's reply was a more polite version of Buddy Jellison's "Does a crow shit in the pine tops?"

The kid arrived in June of 1994 and set up shop in a tent on the far side of Dark Score Lake. He was due back at Reed in late August. Instead, though, he decided to take a year's leave of absence. His father wasn't pleased. His father smelled what he called "girl trouble."

"Yeah, but it's a damned long sniff from California to Maine," Bill Dean said, leaning against the driver's door of his truck with his sunburned arms folded. "He had someone a lot closer than Palm Springs doin his sniffin for him."

"What are you talking about?" I asked.

" 'Bout *talk*. People do it for free, and most are willing to do even more if they're paid."

253

"People like Royce Merrill?"

"Royce might be one," he agreed, "but he wouldn't be the only one. Times around here don't go between bad and good; if you're a local, they mostly go between bad and worse. So when a guy like Max Devore sends a guy out with a supply of fifty- and hundred-dollar bills . . ."

"Was it someone local? A lawyer?"

Not a lawyer; a real-estate broker named Richard Osgood ("a greasy kind of fella" was Bill Dean's judgment of him) who denned and did business in Motton. Eventually Osgood *had* hired a lawyer from Castle Rock. The greasy fella's initial job, when the summer of '94 ended and Lance Devore remained on the TR, was to find out what the hell was going on and put a stop to it.

"And then?" I asked.

Bill glanced at his watch, glanced at the sky, then centered his gaze on me. He gave a funny little shrug, as if to say, "We're both men of the world, in a quiet and settled sort of way — you don't need to ask a silly question like that."

"Then Lance Devore and Mattie Stanchfield got married in the Grace Baptist Church right up there on Highway 68. There were tales made the rounds about what Osgood might've done to keep it from comin off — I heard he even tried to bribe

254

Reverend Gooch into refusin to hitch em, but I think that's stupid, they just would have gone someplace else. 'Sides, I don't see much sense in repeating what I don't know for sure."

Bill unfolded an arm and began to tick items off on the leathery fingers of his right hand.

"They got married in the middle of September, 1994, I know that." Out popped the thumb. "People looked around with some curiosity to see if the groom's father would put in an appearance, but he never did." Out popped the forefinger. Added to the thumb, it made a pistol. "Mattie had a baby in April of '95, making the kiddie a dight premature . . . but not enough to matter. I seen it in the store with my own eyes when it wasn't a week old, and it was just the right size." Out with the second finger. "I don't know that Lance Devore's old man absolutely refused to help em financially, but I *do* know they were living in that trailer down below Dickie's Garage, and that makes me think they were havin a pretty hard skate."

"Devore put on the choke-chain," I said. "It's what a guy used to getting his own way would do . . . but if he loved the boy the way you seem to think, he might have come around."

"Maybe, maybe not." He glanced at his watch again. "Let me finish up quick and get out of your sunshine . . . but you ought to hear one more little story, because it really shows how the land lies.

"In July of last year, less'n a month before he died, Lance Devore shows up at the post-office counter in the Lakeview General. He's got a manila envelope he wants to send, but first he needs to show Carla DeCinces what's inside. She said he was all fluffed out, like daddies sometimes get over their kids when they're small."

I nodded, amused at the idea of skinny, stuttery Lance Devore all fluffed out. But I could see it in my mind's eye, and the image was also sort of sweet.

"It was a studio pitcher they'd gotten taken over in the Rock. Showed the kid . . . what's her name? Kayla?"

"Kyra."

"Ayuh, they call em anything these days, don't they? It showed Kyra sittin in a big leather chair, with a pair of joke spectacles on her little snub of a nose, lookin at one of the aerial photos of the woods over across the lake in TR-100 or TR-110 — part of what the old man had picked up, anyway. Carla said the baby had a surprised look on her face, as if she hadn't suspected there could be so much woods in the whole world. Said it was *awful* cunnin, she did."

"Cunnin as a cat a-runnin," I murmured.

"And the envelope — Registered, Express

Mail — was addressed to Maxwell Devore, in Palm Springs, California."

"Leading you to deduce that the old man either thawed enough to ask for a picture of his only grandchild, or that Lance Devore thought a picture *might* thaw him."

Bill nodded, looking as pleased as a parent whose child has managed a difficult sum. "Don't know if it did," he said. "Wasn't enough time to tell, one way or the other. Lance had bought one of those little satellite dishes, like what you've got here. There was a bad storm the day he put it up — hail, high wind, blowdowns along the lakeshore, lots of lightnin. That was along toward evening. Lance put his dish up in the afternoon, all done and safe, except around the time the storm commenced he remembered he'd left his socket wrench on the trailer roof. He went up to get it so it wouldn't get all wet n rusty —"

"He was struck by lightning? Jesus, Bill!"

"Lightnin struck, all right, but it hit across the way. You go past the place where Wasp Hill Road runs into 68 and you'll see the stump of the tree that stroke knocked over. Lance was comin down the ladder with his socket wrench when it hit. If you've never had a lightnin bolt tear right over your head, you don't know how scary it is — it's like havin a drunk driver veer across into your lane, headed right for you, and then swing back onto his own side just in time. Close lightnin makes your hair stand up — makes your damned *prick* stand up. It's apt to play the radio on your steel fillins, it makes your ears hum, and it makes the air taste roasted. Lance fell off the ladder. If he had time to think anything before he hit the ground, I bet he thought he *was* electrocuted. Poor boy. He loved the TR, but it wasn't lucky for him."

"Broke his neck?"

"Ayuh. With all the thunder, Mattie never heard him fall or yell or anything. She looked out a minute or two later when it started to hail and he still wasn't in. And there he was, layin on the ground and lookin up into the friggin hail with his eyes open."

Bill looked at his watch one final time, then swung open the door to his truck. "The old man wouldn't come for their weddin, but he came for his son's funeral and he's been here ever since. He didn't want nawthin to do with the young woman —"

"But he wants the kid," I said. It was no more than what I already knew, but I felt a sinking in the pit of my stomach just the same. *Don't talk about this,* Mattie had asked me on the morning of the Fourth. *It's not a good time for Ki and me.* "How far along in the process has he gotten?"

258

"On the third turn and headin into the home stretch, I sh'd say. There'll be a hearin in Castle County Superior Court, maybe later this month, maybe next. The judge could rule then to hand the girl over, or put it off until fall. I don't think it matters which, because the one thing that's never goin to happen on God's green earth is a rulin in favor of the mother. One way or another, that little girl is goin to grow up in California."

Put that way, it gave me a very nasty little chill.

Bill slid behind the wheel of his truck. "Stay out of it, Mike," he said. "Stay away from Mattie Devore and her daughter. And if you get called to court on account of seein the two of em on Saturday, smile a lot and say as little as you can."

"Max Devore's charging that she's unfit to raise the child."

"Ayuh."

"Bill, I *saw* the child, and she's fine."

He grinned again, but this time there was no amusement in it. " 'Magine she is. But that's not the point. Stay clear of their business, old boy. It's my job to tell you that; with Jo gone, I guess I'm the only caretaker you got." He slammed the door of his Ram, started the engine, reached for the gearshift, then dropped his hand again as something else occurred to him. "If you get a chance, you ought to look for the owls."

"What owls?"

"There's a couple of plastic owls around here someplace. They might be in y'basement or out in Jo's studio. They come in by mail-order the fall before she passed on."

"The fall of 1993?"

"Ayuh."

"That can't be right." We hadn't used Sara in the fall of 1993.

" 'Tis, though. I was down here puttin on the storm doors when Jo showed up. We had us a natter, and then the UPS truck come. I lugged the box into the entry and had a coffee — I was still drinkin it then — while she took the owls out of the carton and showed em off to me. Gorry, but they looked real! She left not ten minutes after. It was like she'd come down to do that errand special, although why anyone'd drive all the way from Derry to take delivery of a couple of plastic owls I don't know."

"When in the fall was it, Bill? Do you remember?"

"Second week of November," he said promptly. "Me n the wife went up to Lewiston later that afternoon, to 'Vette's sister's. It was her birthday. On our way back we stopped at the Castle Rock Agway so 'Vette could get her Thanksgiving turkey." He looked at me curiously. "You really didn't know about them owls?"

"No."

"That's a touch peculiar, wouldn't you say?"

"Maybe she told me and I forgot," I said. "I guess it doesn't matter much now in any case." Yet it seemed to matter. It was a small thing, but it seemed to matter. "Why would Jo want a couple of plastic owls to begin with?"

"To keep the crows from shittin up the woodwork, like they're doing out on your deck. Crows see those plastic owls, they veer off."

I burst out laughing in spite of my puzzlement . . . or perhaps because of it. "Yeah? That really works?"

"Ayuh, long's you move em every now and then so the crows don't get suspicious. Crows are just about the smartest birds going, you know. You look for those owls, save yourself a lot of mess."

"I will," I said. Plastic owls to scare the crows away — it was exactly the sort of knowledge Jo would come by (she was like a crow herself in that way, picking up glittery pieces of information that happened to catch her interest) and act upon without bothering to tell me. All at once I was lonely for her again — missing her like hell.

"Good. Some day when I've got more time, we'll walk the place all the way around. Woods too, if you want. I think you'll be satisfied."

"I'm sure I will. Where's Devore staying?"

The bushy eyebrows went up. "Warrington's. Him and you's practically neighbors. I thought you must know."

I remembered the woman I'd seen — black bathing-suit and black shorts somehow combining to give her an exotic cocktail-party look — and nodded. "I met his wife."

Bill laughed heartily enough at that to feel in need of his handkerchief. He fished it off the dashboard (a blue paisley thing the size of a football pennant) and wiped his eyes.

"What's so funny?" I asked.

"Skinny woman? White hair? Face sort of like a kid's Halloween mask?"

It was my turn to laugh. "That's her."

"She ain't his wife, she's his whatdoyoucallit, personal assistant. Rogette Whitmore is her name." He pronounced it ro-GET, with a hard *G*. "Devore's wives're all dead. The last one twenty years."

"What kind of name is Rogette? French?"

"California," he said, and shrugged as if that one word explained everything. "There's people in town scared of her."

"Is that so?"

"Ayuh." Bill hesitated, then added with one of those smiles we put on when we want others to know that *we* know we're saying

262

something silly: "Brenda Meserve says she's a witch."

"And the two of them have been staying at Warrington's almost a year?"

"Ayuh. The Whitmore woman comes n goes, but mostly she's been here. Thinkin in town is that they'll stay until the custody case is finished off, then all go back to California on Devore's private jet. Leave Osgood to sell Warrington's, and —"

"Sell it? What do you mean, *sell* it?"

"I thought you must know," Bill said, dropping his gearshift into drive. "When old Hugh Emerson told Devore they closed the lodge after Thanksgiving, Devore told him he had no intention of moving. Said he was comfortable right where he was and meant to stay put."

"He bought the place." I had been by turns surprised, amused, and angered over the last twenty minutes, but never exactly dumbfounded. Now I was. "He bought Warrington's Lodge so he wouldn't have to move to Lookout Rock Hotel over in Castle View, or rent a house."

"Ayuh, so he did. Nine buildins, includin the main lodge and The Sunset Bar; twelve acres of woods, a six-hole golf course, and five hundred feet of shorefront on The Street. Plus a two-lane bowlin alley and a softball field. Four and a quarter million. His friend Osgood did the deal and Devore paid with a personal check. I wonder how he found room for all those zeros. See you, Mike."

With that he backed up the driveway, leaving me to stand on the stoop, looking after him with my mouth open.

Plastic owls.

Bill had told me roughly two dozen interesting things in between peeks at his watch, but the one which stayed on top of the pile was the fact (and I did accept it as a fact; he had been too positive for me not to) that Jo had come down here to take delivery on a couple of plastic goddam owls.

Had she told me?

She might have. I didn't remember her doing so, and it seemed to me that I would have, but Jo used to claim that when I got in the zone it was no good to tell me anything; stuff went in one ear and out the other. Sometimes she'd pin little notes — errands to run, calls to make — to my shirt, as if I were a first-grader. But wouldn't I recall if she'd said "I'm going down to Sara, hon, UPS is delivering something I want to receive personally, interested in keeping a lady company?" Hell wouldn't I have *gone?* I always liked an excuse to go to the TR. Except I'd been working on that screenplay . . . and maybe pushing it a little . . . notes pinned to the sleeve of my shirt . . . *If you go*

out when you're finished, we need milk and or-
ange juice . . .

I inspected what little was left of Jo's vegetable garden with the July sun beating down
on my neck and thought about owls, the
plastic goddam owls. Suppose Jo *had* told
me she was coming down here to Sara
Laughs? Suppose I had declined almost
without hearing the offer because I was in
the writing zone? Even if you granted those
things, there was another question: why had
she felt the need to come down here personally when she could have just called
someone and asked them to meet the delivery truck? Kenny Auster would have been
happy to do it, ditto Mrs. M. And Bill Dean,
our caretaker, had actually been here. This
led to other questions — one was why she
hadn't just had UPS deliver the damned
things to Derry — and finally I decided I
couldn't live without actually seeing a bona
fide plastic owl for myself. Maybe, I
thought, going back to the house, I'd put
one on the roof of my Chevy when it was
parked in the driveway. Forestall future
bombing runs.

I paused in the entry, struck by a sudden
idea, and called Ward Hankins, the guy in
Waterville who handles my taxes and my
few non-writing-related business affairs.

"Mike," he said heartily. "How's the
lake?"

"The lake's cool and the weather's hot, just the way we like it," I said. "Ward, you keep all the records we send you for five years, don't you? Just in case IRS decides to give us some grief?"

"Five is accepted practice," he said, "but I hold your stuff for seven — in the eyes of the tax boys, you're a mighty fat pigeon."

Better a fat pigeon than a plastic owl, I thought but didn't say. What I said was "That includes desk calendars, right? Mine and Jo's, up until she died?"

"You bet. Since neither of you kept diaries, it was the best way to cross-reference receipts and claimed expenses with —"

"Could you find Jo's desk calendar for 1993 and see what she had going in the second week of November?"

"I'd be happy to. What in particular are you looking for?"

For a moment I saw myself sitting at my kitchen table in Derry on my first night as a widower, holding up a box with the words Norco Home Pregnancy Test printed on the side. Exactly what *was* I looking for at this late date? Considering that I had loved the lady and she was almost four years in her grave, what *was* I looking for? Besides trouble, that was?

"I'm looking for two plastic owls," I said. Ward probably thought I was talking to him, but I'm not sure I was. "I know that sounds weird, but it's what I'm doing. Can you call me back?"

"Within the hour."

"Good man," I said, and hung up.

Now for the actual owls themselves. Where was the most likely spot to store two such interesting artifacts?

My eyes went to the cellar door. Elementary, my dear Watson.

The cellar stairs were dark and mildly dank. As I stood on the landing groping for the lightswitch, the door banged shut behind me with such force that I cried out in surprise. There was no breeze, no draft, the day was perfectly still, but the door banged shut just the same. Or was sucked shut.

I stood in the dark at the top of the stairs, feeling for the lightswitch, smelling that oozy smell that even good concrete foundations get after awhile if there is no proper airing-out. It was cold, much colder than it had been on the other side of the door. I wasn't alone and I knew it. I was afraid, I'd be a liar to say I wasn't . . . but I was also fascinated. Something was with me. *Something was in here with me.*

I dropped my hand away from the wall where the switch was and just stood with my arms at my sides. Some time passed. I don't know how much. My heart was beating furiously in my chest; I could feel it in my temples. It was cold. "Hello?" I asked.

Nothing in response. I could hear the faint, irregular drip of water as condensation fell from one of the pipes down below, I could hear my own breathing, and faintly — far away, in another world where the sun was out — I could hear the triumphant caw of a crow. Perhaps it had just dropped a load on the hood of my car. *I really need an owl,* I thought. *In fact, I don't know how I ever got along without one.*

"Hello?" I asked again. "Can you talk?"

Nothing.

I wet my lips. I should have felt silly, perhaps, standing there in the dark and calling to the ghosts. But I didn't. Not a bit. The damp had been replaced by a coldness I could feel, and I had company. Oh, yes. "Can you tap, then? If you can shut the door, you must be able to tap."

I stood there and listened to the soft, isolated drips from the pipes. There was nothing else. I was reaching out for the lightswitch again when there was a soft thud from not far below me. The cellar of Sara Laughs is high, and the upper three feet of the concrete — the part which lies against the ground's frost-belt — had been insulated with big silver-backed panels of Insu-Gard. The sound that I heard was, I am quite sure, a fist striking against one of these.

Just a fist hitting a square of insulation, but every gut and muscle of my body seemed to come unwound. My hair stood up. My eyesockets seemed to be expanding and my eyeballs contracting, as if my head were trying to turn into a skull. Every inch of my skin broke out in gooseflesh. Something was in here with me. Very likely something dead. I could no longer have turned on the light if I'd wanted to. I no longer had the strength to raise my arm.

I tried to talk, and at last, in a husky whisper I hardly recognized, I said: "Are you really there?"

Thud.

"Who are you?" I could still do no better than that husky whisper, the voice of a man giving last instructions to his family as he lies on his deathbed. This time there was nothing from below.

I tried to think, and what came to my struggling mind was Tony Curtis as Harry Houdini in some old movie. According to the film, Houdini had been the Diogenes of the Ouija board circuit, a guy who spent his spare time just looking for an honest medium. He'd attended one séance where the dead communicated by —

"Tap once for yes, twice for no," I said. "Can you do that?"

Thud.

It was on the stairs below me . . . but not

too far below. Five steps down, six or seven at most. Not quite close enough to touch if I should reach out and wave my hand in the black basement air . . . a thing I could imagine, but not actually imagine doing.

"Are you . . ." My voice trailed off. There was simply no strength in my diaphragm. Chilly air lay on my chest like a flatiron. I gathered all my will and tried again. "Are you Jo?"

Thud. That soft fist on the insulation. A pause, and then: *Thud-thud.*

Yes and no.

Then, with no idea why I was asking such an inane question: "Are the owls down here?"

Thud-thud.

"Do you know where they are?"

Thud.

"Should I look for them?"

Thud! Very hard.

Why did she want them? I could ask, but the thing on the stairs had no way to an—

Hot fingers touched my eyes and I almost screamed before realizing it was sweat. I raised my hands in the dark and wiped the heels of them up my face to the hairline. They skidded as if on oil. Cold or not, I was all but bathing in my own sweat.

"Are you Lance Devore?"

Thud-thud, at once.

"Is it safe for me at Sara? Am I safe?"

270

Thud. A pause. And I *knew* it was a pause, that the thing on the stairs wasn't finished. Then: *Thud-thud.* Yes, I was safe. No, I wasn't safe.

I had regained marginal control of my arm. I reached out, felt along the wall, and found the lightswitch. I settled my fingers on it. Now the sweat on my face felt as if it were turning to ice.

"Are you the person who cries in the night?" I asked.

Thud-thud from below me, and between the two thuds, I flicked the switch. The cellar globes came on. So did a brilliant hanging bulb — at least a hundred and twenty-five watts — over the landing. There was no time for anyone to hide, let alone get away, and no one there to try, either. Also, Mrs. Meserve — admirable in so many ways — had neglected to sweep the cellar stairs. When I went down to where I estimated the thudding sounds had been coming from, I left tracks in the light dust. But mine were the only ones.

I blew out breath in front of me and could see it. So it *had* been cold, still *was* cold . . . but it was warming up fast. I blew out another breath and could see just a hint of fog. A third exhale and there was nothing.

I ran my palm over one of the insulated squares. Smooth. I pushed a finger at it, and although I didn't push with any real force, my finger left a dimple in the silvery surface. Easy as pie. If someone had been thumping a fist down here, this stuff should be pitted, the thin silver skin perhaps even broken to reveal the pink fill underneath. But all the squares were smooth.

"Are you still there?" I asked.

No response, and yet I had a sense that my visitor *was* still there. Somewhere.

"I hope I didn't offend you by turning on the light," I said, and now I did feel slightly odd, standing on my cellar stairs and talking out loud, sermonizing to the spiders. "I wanted to see you if I could." I had no idea if that was true or not.

Suddenly — so suddenly I almost lost my balance and tumbled down the stairs — I whirled around, convinced the shroud-creature was behind me, that it had been the thing knocking, *it*, no polite M. R. James ghost but a horror from around the rim of the universe.

There was nothing.

I turned around again, took two or three deep, steadying breaths, and then went the rest of the way down the cellar stairs. Beneath them was a perfectly serviceable canoe, complete with paddle. In the corner was the gas stove we'd replaced after buying the place; also the claw-foot tub Jo had wanted (over my objections) to turn into a planter. I found a trunk filled with vaguely recalled table-linen, a box of mildewy cassette tapes (groups like the Delfonics, Funkadelic, and .38 Special), several cartons of old dishes. There was a life down here, but ultimately not a very interesting one. Unlike the life I'd sensed in Jo's studio, this one hadn't been cut short but evolved out of, shed like old skin, and that was all right. Was, in fact, the natural order of things.

There was a photo album on a shelf of knickknacks and I took it down, both curious and wary. No bombshells this time, however; nearly all the pix were landscape shots of Sara Laughs as it had been when we bought it. I found a picture of Jo in bellbottoms, though (her hair parted in the middle and white lipstick on her mouth), and one of Michael Noonan wearing a flowered shirt and muttonchop sideburns that made me cringe (the bachelor Mike in the photo was a Barry White kind of guy I didn't want to recognize and yet did).

I found Jo's old broken treadmill, a rake I'd want if I was still around here come fall, a snowblower I'd want even more if I was around come winter, and several cans of paint. What I didn't find was any plastic owls. My insulation-thumping friend had been right.

Upstairs the telephone started ringing.

I hurried to answer it, going out through the cellar door and *then* reaching back in to

273

flick off the lightswitch. This amused me and at the same time seemed like perfectly normal behavior . . . just as being careful not to step on sidewalk cracks had seemed like perfectly normal behavior to me when I was a kid. And even if it wasn't normal, what did it matter? I'd only been back at Sara for three days, but already I'd postulated Noonan's First Law of Eccentricity: when you're on your own, strange behavior really doesn't seem strange at all.

I snagged the cordless. "Hello?"

"Hi, Mike. It's Ward."

"That was quick."

"The file-room's just a short walk down the hall," he said. "Easy as pie. There's only one thing on Jo's calendar for the second week of November in 1993. It says 'S-Ks of Maine, Freep, 11 A.M.' That's on Tuesday the sixteenth. Does it help?"

"Yes," I said. "Thank you, Ward. It helps a lot."

I broke the connection and put the phone back in its cradle. Yes, it helped. S-Ks of Maine was Soup Kitchens of Maine. Jo had been on their board of directors from 1992 until her death. Freep was Freeport. It must have been a board meeting. They had probably discussed plans for feeding the homeless on Thanksgiving . . . and then Jo had driven the seventy or so miles to the TR in order to take delivery of two plastic owls. It didn't answer all the questions, but aren't there always questions in the wake of a loved one's death? And no statute of limitations on when they come up.

The UFO voice spoke up then. *While you're right here by the phone, it said, why not call Bonnie Amudson? Say hi, see how she's doing?*

Jo had been on four different boards during the nineties, all of them doing charitable work. Her friend Bonnie had persuaded her onto the Soup Kitchens board when a seat fell vacant. They had gone to a lot of the meetings together. Not the one in November of 1993, presumably, and Bonnie could hardly be expected to remember that one particular meeting almost five years later . . . but if she'd saved her old minutes-of-the-meeting sheets . . .

Exactly what the fuck was I thinking of? Calling Bonnie, making nice, then asking her to check her December 1993 minutes? Was I going to ask her if the attendance report had my wife absent from the November meeting? Was I going to ask if maybe Jo had seemed different that last year of her life? And when Bonnie asked me why I wanted to know, what would I say?

Give me that, Jo had snarled in my dream of her. In the dream she hadn't looked like Jo at all, she'd looked like some other woman, maybe like the one in the Book of Proverbs, the strange woman whose lips were as honey but whose heart was full of gall and wormwood. A strange woman with fingers as cold as twigs after a frost. *Give me that, it's my dust-catcher.*

I went to the cellar door and touched the knob. I turned it . . . then let it go. I didn't want to look down there into the dark, didn't want to risk the chance that something might start thumping again. It was better to leave that door shut. What I wanted was something cold to drink. I went into the kitchen, reached for the fridge door, then stopped. The magnets were back in a circle again, but this time four letters and one number had been pulled into the center and lined up there. They spelled a single lower-case word:

```
hello
```

There was something here. Even back in broad daylight I had no doubt of that. I'd asked if it was safe for me to be here and had received a mixed message . . . but that didn't matter. If I left Sara now, there was nowhere to go. I had a key to the house in Derry, but matters had to be resolved here. I knew that, too.

"Hello," I said, and opened the fridge to get a soda. "Whoever or whatever you are, hello."

Chapter 11

I woke in the early hours of the following morning convinced that there was someone in the north bedroom with me. I sat up against the pillows, rubbed my eyes, and saw a dark, shouldery shape standing between me and the window.

"Who are you?" I asked, thinking that it wouldn't reply in words; it would, instead, thump on the wall. Once for yes, twice for no — what's on your mind, Houdini? But the figure standing by the window made no reply at all. I groped up, found the string hanging from the light over the bed, and yanked it. My mouth was turned down in a grimace, my midsection tensed so tight it felt as if bullets would have bounced off.

"Oh shit," I said. "Fuck me til I cry."

Dangling from a hanger I'd hooked over the curtain rod was my old suede jacket. I'd parked it there while unpacking and had then forgotten to store it away in the closet. I tried to laugh and couldn't. At three in the morning it just didn't seem that funny.

I turned off the light and lay back down with my eyes open, waiting for Bunter's bell to ring or the childish sobbing to start. I was still listening when I fell asleep.

★ ★ ★

Seven hours or so later, as I was getting ready to go out to Jo's studio and see if the plastic owls were in the storage area, where I hadn't checked the day before, a late-model Ford rolled down my driveway and stopped nose to nose with my Chevy. I had gotten as far as the short path between the house and the studio, but now I came back. The day was hot and breathless, and I was wearing nothing but a pair of cut-off jeans and plastic flip-flops on my feet.

Jo always claimed that the Cleveland style of dressing divided itself naturally into two subgenres: Full Cleveland and Cleveland Casual. My visitor that Tuesday morning was wearing Cleveland Casual — you had your Hawaiian shirt with pineapples and monkeys, your tan slacks from Banana Republic, your white loafers. Socks are optional, but white footgear is a necessary part of the Cleveland look, as is at least one piece of gaudy gold jewelry. This fellow was totally okay in the latter department: he had a Rolex on one wrist and a gold-link chain around his neck. The tail of his shirt was out, and there was a suspicious lump at the back. It was either a gun or a beeper and looked too big to be a beeper. I glanced at the car again. Blackwall tires. And on the dashboard, oh look at this, a covered blue bubble. The better to creep up on you unsuspected, Gramma.

"Michael Noonan?" He was handsome in a way that would be attractive to certain women — the kind who cringe when anybody in their immediate vicinity raises his voice, the kind who rarely call the police when things go wrong at home because, on some miserable secret level, they believe they deserve things to go wrong at home. Wrong things that result in black eyes, dislocated elbows, the occasional cigarette burn on the booby. These are women who more often than not call their husbands or lovers daddy, as in "Can I bring you a beer, daddy?" or "Did you have a hard day at work, daddy?"

"Yes, I'm Michael Noonan. How can I help you?"

This version of daddy turned, bent, and grabbed something from the litter of paperwork on the passenger side of the front seat. Beneath the dash, a two-way radio squawked once, briefly, and fell silent. He turned back to me with a long, buff-colored folder in one hand. Held it out. "This is yours."

When I didn't take it, he stepped forward and tried to poke it into one of my palms, which would presumably cause me to close my fingers in a kind of reflex. Instead I raised both hands to shoulder-level, as if he had just told me to put em up, Muggsy.

He looked at me patiently, his face as Irish as the Arlen brothers' but without the Arlen look of kindness, openness, and curiosity. What was there in place of those things was a species of sour amusement, as if he'd seen all of the world's pissier behavior, most of it twice. One of his eyebrows had been split open a long time ago, and his cheeks had that reddish windburned look that indicates either ruddy good health or a deep interest in grain-alcohol products. He looked like he could knock you into the gutter and then sit on you to keep you there. I been good, daddy, get off me, don't be mean.

"Don't make this tough. You're gonna take service of this and we both know it, so don't make this tough."

"Show me some ID first."

He sighed, rolled his eyes, then reached into one of his shirt pockets. He brought out a leather folder and flipped it open. There was a badge and a photo ID. My new friend was George Footman, Deputy Sheriff, Castle County. The photo was flat and shadowless, like something an assault victim would see in a mugbook.

"Okay?" he asked.

I took the buff-backed document when he held it out again. He stood there, broadcasting that sense of curdled amusement as I scanned it. I had been subpoenaed to appear in the Castle Rock office of Elmer

Durgin, Attorney-at-Law, at ten o'clock on the morning of July 10, 1998 — Friday, in other words. Said Elmer Durgin had been appointed guardian *ad litem* of Kyra Elizabeth Devore, a minor child. He would take a deposition from me concerning any knowledge I might have of Kyra Elizabeth Devore in regard to her well-being. This deposition would be taken on behalf of Castle County Superior Court and Judge Noble Rancourt. A stenographer would be present. I was assured that this was the court's depo, and nothing to do with either `Plaintiff` or `Defendant`.

Footman said, "It's my job to remind you of the penalties should you fail —"

"Thanks, but let's just assume you told me all about those, okay? I'll be there." I made shooing gestures at his car. I felt deeply disgusted . . . and I felt *interfered with*. I had never been served with a process before, and I didn't care for it.

He went back to his car, started to swing in, then stopped with one hairy arm hung over the top of the open door. His Rolex gleamed in the hazy sunlight.

"Let me give you a piece of advice," he said, and that was enough to tell me anything else I needed to know about the guy. "Don't fuck with Mr. Devore."

"Or he'll squash me like a bug," I said.

"Huh?"

"Your actual lines are, 'Let me give you a piece of advice — don't fuck with Mr. Devore or he'll squash you like a bug.' "

I could see by his expression — half past perplexed, going on angry — that he had meant to say something very much like that. Obviously we'd seen the same movies, including all those in which Robert De Niro plays a psycho. Then his face cleared.

"Oh sure, you're the writer," he said.

"That's what they tell me."

"You can say stuff like that 'cause you're a writer."

"Well, it's a free country, isn't it?"

"Ain't you a smartass, now."

"How long have you been working for Max Devore, Deputy? And does the County Sheriff's office know you're moonlighting?"

"They know. It's not a problem. *You're* the one that might have the problem, Mr. Smartass Writer."

I decided it was time to quit this before we descended to the kaka-poopie stage of name-calling.

"Get out of my driveway, please, Deputy."

He looked at me a moment longer, obviously searching for that perfect capper line and not finding it. He needed a Mr. Smartass Writer to help him, that was all. "I'll be looking for you on Friday," he said.

"Does that mean you're going to buy me lunch? Don't worry, I'm a fairly cheap date."

His reddish cheeks darkened a degree further, and I could see what they were going to look like when he was sixty, if he didn't lay off the firewater in the meantime. He got back into his Ford and reversed up my driveway hard enough to make his tires holler. I stood where I was, watching him go. Once he was headed back out Lane Forty-two to the highway, I went into the house. It occurred to me that Deputy Footman's extracurricular job must pay well, if he could afford a Rolex. On the other hand, maybe it was a knockoff.

Settle down, Michael, Jo's voice advised. *The red rag is gone now, no one's waving anything in front of you, so just settle —*

I shut her voice out. I didn't want to settle down; I wanted to settle *up*. I had been *interfered with*.

I walked over to the hall desk where Jo and I had always kept our pending documents (and our desk calendars, now that I thought about it), and tacked the summons to the bulletin board by one corner of its buff-colored jacket. With that much accomplished, I raised my fist in front of my eyes, looked at the wedding ring on it for a moment, then slammed it against the wall beside the bookcase. I did it hard enough to make an entire row of paperbacks jump. I thought about Mattie Devore's baggy shorts and Kmart smock, then about her father-in-law paying four and a quarter million dollars for Warrington's. Writing a personal god-damned check. I thought about Bill Dean saying that one way or another, that little girl was going to grow up in California.

I walked back and forth through the house, still simmering, and finally ended up in front of the fridge. The circle of magnets was the same, but the letters inside had changed. Instead of

hello

they now read

help r

"Helper?" I said, and as soon as I heard the word out loud, I understood. The letters on the fridge consisted of only a single alphabet (no, not even that, I saw; *g* and *x* had been lost someplace), and I'd have to get more. If the front of my Kenmore was going to become a Ouija board, I'd need a good supply of letters. Especially vowels. In the meantime, I moved the *h* and the *e* in front of the *r*. Now the message read

lp her

I scattered the circle of fruit and vegetable magnets with my palm, spread the letters, and resumed pacing. I had made a decision not to get between Devore and his daughter-in-law, but I'd wound up between them anyway. A deputy in Cleveland clothing had shown up in my driveway, complicating a life that already had its problems . . . and scaring me a little in the bargain. But at least it was a fear of something I could see and understand. All at once I decided I wanted to do more with the summer than worry about ghosts, crying kids, and what my wife had been up to four or five years ago . . . if, in fact, she had been up to anything. I couldn't write books, but that didn't mean I had to pick scabs.

Help her.

I decided I would at least try.

"Harold Oblowski Literary Agency."

"Come to Belize with me, Nola," I said. "I need you. We'll make beautiful love at midnight, when the full moon turns the beach to a bone."

"Hello, Mr. Noonan," she said. No sense of humor had Nola. No sense of romance, either. In some ways that made her perfect for the Oblowski Agency. "Would you like to speak to Harold?"

"If he's in."

"He is. Please hold."

One nice thing about being a bestselling author — even one whose books only appear, as a general rule, on lists that go to fifteen — is that your agent almost always happens to be in. Another is if he's vacationing on Nantucket, he'll be in to you there. A third is that the time you spend on hold is usually quite short.

"Mike!" he cried. "How's the lake? I thought about you all weekend!"

Yeah, I thought, *and pigs will whistle.*

"Things are fine in general but shitty in one particular, Harold. I need to talk to a lawyer. I thought first about calling Ward Hankins for a recommendation, but then I decided I wanted somebody a little more high-powered than Ward was likely to know. Someone with filed teeth and a taste for human flesh would be nice."

This time Harold didn't bother with the long-pause routine. "What's up, Mike? Are you in trouble?"

Thump once for yes, twice for no, I thought, and for one wild moment thought of actually doing just that. I remembered finishing Christy Brown's memoir, *Down All the Days,* and wondering what it would be like to write an entire book with the pen grasped between the toes of your left foot. Now I wondered what it would be like to go through eternity with no way to communicate but rapping on the cellar wall. And even then only certain people would be able to hear and understand you . . . and only those certain people at certain times.

Jo, was it you? And if it was, why did you answer both ways?

"Mike? Are you there?"

"Yes. This isn't really my trouble, Harold, so cool your jets. I do have a problem, though. Your main guy is Goldacre, right?"

"Right. I'll call him right aw—"

"But he deals primarily with contracts law." I was thinking out loud now, and when I paused, Harold didn't fill it. Sometimes he's an all-right guy. Most times, really. "Call him for me anyway, would you? Tell him I need to talk to an attorney with a good working knowledge of child-custody law. Have him put me in touch with the best one who's free to take a case immediately. One who can be in court with me Friday, if that's necessary."

"Is it paternity?" he asked, sounding both respectful and afraid.

"No, *custody.*" I thought about telling him to get the whole story from the Lawyer to Be Named Later, but Harold deserved better . . . and would demand to hear my version sooner or later anyway, no matter what the lawyer told him. I gave him an account of my Fourth of July morning and its aftermath. I stuck with the Devores, mentioning nothing about voices, crying children, or thumps in the dark. Harold only interrupted once, and that was when he realized who the villain of the piece was.

"You're asking for trouble," he said. "You know that, don't you?"

"I'm in for a certain measure of it in any case," I said. "I've decided I want to dish out a little as well, that's all."

"You will not have the peace and quiet that a writer needs to do his best work," Harold said in an amusingly prim voice. I wondered what the reaction would be if I said that was okay, I hadn't written anything more riveting than a grocery list since Jo died, and maybe this would stir me up a little. But I didn't. Never let em see you sweat, the Noonan clan's motto. Someone should carve DON'T WORRY I'M FINE on the door of the family crypt.

Then I thought: *help r.*

"That young woman needs a friend," I said, "and Jo would have wanted me to be one to her. Jo didn't like it when the little folks got stepped on."

"You think?"

"Yeah."

"Okay, I'll see who I can find. And Mike . . . do you want me to come up on Friday for this depo?"

"No." It came out sounding needlessly abrupt and was followed by a silence that seemed not calculated but hurt. "Listen, Harold, my caretaker said the actual custody hearing is scheduled soon. If it happens and you still want to come up, I'll give you a call. I can always use your moral support — you know that."

"In my case it's *im*moral support," he replied, but he sounded cheery again.

We said goodbye. I walked back to the fridge and looked at the magnets. They were still scattered hell to breakfast, and that was sort of a relief. Even the spirits must have to rest sometimes.

I took the cordless phone, went out onto the deck, and plonked down in the chair where I'd been on the night of the Fourth, when Devore called. Even after my visit from "daddy," I could still hardly believe that conversation. Devore had called me a liar; I had told him to stick my telephone number up his ass. We were off to a great start as neighbors.

I pulled the chair a little closer to the edge of the deck, which dropped a giddy forty feet or so to the slope between Sara's backside and the lake. I looked for the green woman I'd seen while swimming, telling myself not to be a dope — things like that you can see only from one angle, stand even ten feet off to one side or the other and there's nothing to look at. But this was apparently a case of the exception's proving the rule. I was both amused and a little uneasy to realize that the birch down there by The Street looked like a woman from the land side as well as from the lake. Some of it was due to the pine just behind it — that bare branch jutting off to the north like a bony pointing arm — but not all of it. From back here the birch's white limbs and narrow leaves still made a woman's shape, and when the wind shook the lower levels of the tree, the green and silver swirled like long skirts.

I had said no to Harold's well-meant offer to come up almost before it was fully articulated, and as I looked at the tree-woman, rather ghostly in her own right, I knew why: Harold was loud, Harold was insensitive to nuance, Harold might frighten off whatever was here. I didn't want that. I was scared, yes — standing on those dark cellar stairs and listening to the thumps from just below me, I had been fucking terrified — but I had also felt fully alive for the first time in years. I was touching something in Sara that was entirely beyond my experience, and it fascinated me.

The cordless phone rang in my lap, making me jump. I grabbed it, expecting Max Devore or perhaps Footman, his overgolded minion. It turned out to be a lawyer named John Storrow, who sounded as if he might have graduated from law school fairly recently — like last week. Still, he worked for the firm of Avery, McLain, and Bernstein on Park Avenue, and Park

Avenue is a pretty good address for a lawyer, even one who still has a few of his milk-teeth. If Henry Goldacre said Storrow was good, he probably was. And his specialty was custody law.

"Now tell me what's happening up there," he said when the introductions were over and the background had been sketched in.

I did my best, feeling my spirits rise a little as the tale wound on. There's something oddly comforting about talking to a legal guy once the billable-hours clock has started running; you have passed the magical point at which *a* lawyer becomes *your* lawyer. Your lawyer is warm, your lawyer is sympathetic, your lawyer makes notes on a yellow pad and nods in all the right places. Most of the questions your lawyer asks are questions you can answer. And if you can't, your lawyer will help you find a way to do so, by God. Your lawyer is always on your side. Your enemies are his enemies. To him you are never shit but always Shinola.

When I had finished, John Storrow said: "Wow. I'm surprised the papers haven't gotten hold of this."

"That never occurred to me." But I could see his point. The Devore family saga wasn't for the *New York Times* or *Boston Globe*, probably not even for the *Derry News*, but in weekly supermarket tabs like the *National Enquirer* or *Inside View*, it would fit like a glove — instead of the girl, King Kong decides to snatch the girl's innocent child and carry it with him to the top of the Empire State Building. Oh, eek, unhand that baby, you brute. It wasn't front-page stuff, no blood or celebrity morgue shots, but as a page nine shouter it would do nicely. In my mind I composed a headline blaring over side-by-side pix of Warrington's Lodge and Mattie's rusty doublewide: **COMPU-KING LIVES IN SPLENDOR AS HE TRIES TO TAKE YOUNG BEAUTY'S ONLY CHILD.** Probably too long, I decided. I wasn't writing anymore and still I needed an editor. That was pretty sad when you stopped to think about it.

"Perhaps at some point we'll see that they do get the story," Storrow said in a musing tone. I realized that this was a man I could grow attached to, at least in my present angry mood. He grew brisker. "Who'm I representing here, Mr. Noonan? You or the young lady? I vote for the young lady."

"The young lady doesn't even know I've called you. She may think I've taken a bit too much on myself. She may, in fact, give me the rough side of her tongue."

"Why would she do that?"

"Because she's a Yankee — a *Maine* Yankee, the worst kind. On a given day, they can make the Irish look logical."

"Perhaps, but she's the one with the target

pinned to her shirt. I suggest that you call and tell her that."

I promised I would. It wasn't a hard promise to make, either. I'd known I'd have to be in touch with her ever since I had accepted the summons from Deputy Footman. "And who stands for Michael Noonan come Friday morning?"

Storrow laughed dryly. "I'll find someone local to do that. He'll go into this Durgin's office with you, sit quietly with his briefcase on his lap, and listen. I may be in town by that point — I won't know until I talk to Ms. Devore — but I won't be in Durgin's office. When the custody hearing comes around, though, you'll see my face in the place."

"All right, good. Call me with the name of my new lawyer. My other new lawyer."

"Uh-huh. In the meantime, talk to the young lady. Get me a job."

"I'll try."

"Also try to stay visible if you're with her," he said. "If we give the bad guys room to get nasty, they'll get nasty. There's nothing like that between you, is there? Nothing nasty? Sorry to have to ask, but I *do* have to ask."

"No," I said. "It's been quite some time since I've been up to anything nasty with anyone."

"I'm tempted to commiserate, Mr. Noonan,

but under the circumstances —"

"Mike. Make it Mike."

"Good. I like that. And I'm John. People are going to talk about your involvement anyway. You know that, don't you?"

"Sure. People know I can afford you. They'll speculate about how *she* can afford *me*. Pretty young widow, middle-aged widower. Sex would seem the most likely."

"You're a realist."

"I don't really think I am, but I know a hawk from a handsaw."

"I hope you do, because the ride could get rough. This is an extremely rich man we're going up against." Yet he didn't sound scared. He sounded almost . . . *greedy*. He sounded the way part of me had felt when I saw that the magnets on the fridge were back in a circle.

"I know he is."

"In court that won't matter a whole helluva lot, because there's a certain amount of money on the other side. Also, the judge is going to be very aware that this one is a powderkeg. That can be useful."

"What's the best thing we've got going for us?" I asked this thinking of Kyra's rosy, unmarked face and her complete lack of fear in the presence of her mother. I asked it thinking John would reply that the charges were clearly unfounded. I thought wrong.

"The best thing? Devore's age. He's got to

be older than God."

"Based on what I've heard over the weekend, I think he must be eighty-five. That would make God older."

"Yeah, but as a potential dad he makes Tony Randall look like a teenager," John said, and now he sounded positively gloating. "Think of it, Michael — the kid graduates from high school the year Gramps turns one hundred. Also there's a chance the old man's overreached himself. Do you know what a guardian *ad litem* is?"

"No."

"Essentially it's a lawyer the court appoints to protect the interests of the child. A fee for the service comes out of court costs, but it's a pittance. Most people who agree to serve as guardian *ad litem* have strictly altruistic motives . . . but not all of them. In any case, the *ad litem* puts his own spin on the case. Judges don't have to take the guy's advice, but they almost always do. It makes a judge look stupid to reject the advice of his own appointee, and the thing a judge hates above all others is looking stupid."

"Devore will have his own lawyer?"

John laughed. "How about half a dozen at the actual custody hearing?"

"Are you serious?"

"The guy is eighty-five. That's too old for Ferraris, too old for bungee jumping in Tibet, and too old for whores unless he's a mighty man. What does that leave for him to spend his money on?"

"Lawyers," I said bleakly.

"Yep."

"And Mattie Devore? What does she get?"

"Thanks to you, she gets me," John Storrow said. "It's like a John Grisham novel, isn't it? Pure gold. Meantime, I'm interested in Durgin, the *ad litem*. If Devore hasn't been expecting any real trouble, he may have been unwise enough to put temptation in Durgin's way. And Durgin may have been stupid enough to succumb. Hey, who knows what we might find?"

But I was a turn back. "She gets you," I said. "Thanks to me. And if I wasn't here to stick in my oar? What would she get then?"

"*Bubkes.* That's Yiddish. It means —"

"I know what it means," I said. "That's incredible."

"Nope, just American justice. You know the lady with the scales? The one who stands outside most city courthouses?"

"Uh-huh."

"Slap some handcuffs on that broad's wrists and some tape over her mouth to go along with the blindfold, rape her and roll her in the mud. You like that image? I don't, but it's a fair representation of how the law works in custody cases where the plaintiff is rich and the defendant is poor. And sexual equality has actually made it worse, because while mothers still tend to be poor, they are no longer seen as the automatic choice for custody."

"Mattie Devore's got to have you, doesn't she?"

"Yes," John said simply. "Call me tomorrow and tell me that she will."

"I hope I can do that."

"So do I. And listen — there's one more thing."

"What?"

"You lied to Devore on the telephone."

"Bullshit!"

"Nope, nope, I hate to contradict my sister's favorite author, but you did and you know it. You told Devore that mother and child were out together, the kid was picking flowers, everything was fine. You put everything in there except Bambi and Thumper."

I was sitting up straight in my deck-chair now. I felt sandbagged. I also felt that my own cleverness had been overlooked. "Hey, no, think again. I never came out and *said* anything. I told him I assumed. I used the word more than once. I remember that very clearly."

"Uh-huh, and if he was taping your conversation, you'll get a chance to actually count how many times you used it."

At first I didn't answer. I was thinking back to the conversation I'd had with him, remembering the underhum on the phone line, the characteristic underhum I remembered from all my previous summers at Sara Laughs. Had that steady low *mmmmm* been even more noticeable on Saturday night?

"I guess maybe there could be a tape," I said reluctantly.

"Uh-huh. And if Devore's lawyer gets it to the *ad litem,* how do you think you'll sound?"

"Careful," I said. "Maybe like a man with something to hide."

"Or a man spinning yarns. And you're good at that, aren't you? After all, it's what you do for a living. At the custody hearing, Devore's lawyer is apt to mention that. If he then produces one of the people who passed you shortly after Mattie arrived on the scene . . . a person who testifies that the young lady seemed upset and flustered . . . how do you think you'll sound then?"

"Like a liar," I said, and then: "Ah, fuck."

"Fear not, Mike. Be of good cheer."

"What should I do?"

"Spike their guns before they can fire them. Tell Durgin exactly what happened. Get it in the depo. Emphasize the fact that the little girl thought she was walking safely. Make sure you get in that 'crossmock' thing. I love that."

"Then if they have a tape they'll play it and I'll look like a story-changing schmuck."

"I don't think so. You weren't a sworn

298

witness when you talked to Devore, were you? There you were, sitting out on your deck and minding your own business, watching the fireworks show. Out of the blue this grouchy old asshole calls you. Starts ranting. Didn't even give him your number, did you?"

"No."

"Your *unlisted* number."

"No."

"And while he *said* he was Maxwell Devore, he could have been anyone, right?"

"Right."

"He could have been the Shah of Iran."

"No, the Shah's dead."

"The Shah's out, then. But he could have been a nosy neighbor . . . or a prankster."

"Yes."

"And you said what you said with all those possibilities in mind. But now that you're part of an official court proceeding, you're telling the whole truth and nothing but."

"You bet." That good *my-lawyer* feeling had deserted me for a bit, but it was back full-force now.

"You can't do better than the truth, Mike," he said solemnly. "Except maybe in a few cases, and this isn't one. Are we clear on that?"

"Yes."

"All right, we're done. I want to hear from

either you or Mattie Devore around elevenish tomorrow. It ought to be her."

"I'll try."

"If she really balks, you know what to do, don't you?"

"I think so. Thanks, John."

"One way or another, we'll talk very soon," he said, and hung up.

I sat where I was for awhile. Once I pushed the button which opened the line on the cordless phone, then pushed it again to close it. I had to talk to Mattie, but I wasn't quite ready yet. I decided to take a walk instead.

If she really balks, you know what to do, don't you?

Of course. Remind her that she couldn't afford to be proud. That she couldn't afford to go all Yankee, refusing charity from Michael Noonan, author of *Being Two*, *The Red-Shirt Man*, and the soon-to-be-published *Helen's Promise*. Remind her that she could have her pride or her daughter, but likely not both.

Hey, Mattie, pick one.

I walked almost to the end of the lane, stopping at Tidwell's Meadow with its pretty view down to the cup of the lake and across to the White Mountains. The water dreamed under a hazy sky, looking gray when you tipped your head one way, blue when you tipped it the other. That sense of mystery was very much with me. That sense of Manderley.

Over forty black people had settled here at the turn of the century — lit here for awhile, anyway — according to Marie Hingerman (also according to *A History of Castle County and Castle Rock,* a weighty tome published in 1977, the county's bicentennial year). Pretty special black people, too: most of them related, most of them talented, most of them part of a musical group which had first been called The Red-Top Boys and then Sara Tidwell and the Red-Top Boys. They had bought the meadow and a good-sized tract of lakeside land from a man named Douglas Day. The money had been saved up over a period of ten years, according to Sonny Tidwell, who did the dickering (as a Red-Top, Son Tidwell had played what was then known as "chicken-scratch guitar").

There had been a vast uproar about it in town, and even a meeting to protest "the advent of these darkies, which come in a Horde." Things had settled down and turned out okay, as things have a way of doing, more often than not. The shanty town most locals had expected on Day's Hill (for so Tidwell's Meadow was called in 1900, when Son Tidwell bought the land on behalf of his extensive clan) had never appeared. Instead, a number of neat white cabins sprang up, surrounding a larger building that might have been intended as a group meeting place, a rehearsal area, or perhaps, at some point, a performance hall.

Sara and the Red-Top Boys (sometimes there was a Red-Top Girl in there, as well; membership in the band was fluid, changing with every performance) played around western Maine for over a year, maybe closer to two years. In towns all up and down the Western Line — Farmington, Skowhegan, Bridgton, Gates Falls, Castle Rock, Motton, Fryeburg — you'll still come across their old show-posters at barn bazaars and junk-atoriums. Sara and the Red-Tops were great favorites on the circuit, and they got along all right at home on the TR, too, which never surprised me. At the end of the day Robert Frost — that utilitarian and often unpleasant poet — was right: in the northeastern three we really do believe that good fences make good neighbors. We squawk and then keep a miserly peace, the kind with gimlet eyes and a tucked-down mouth. "They pay their bills," we say. "I ain't never had to shoot one a their dogs," we say. "They keep themselves to themselves," we say, as if isolation were a virtue. And, of course, the defining virtue: "They don't take charity."

And at some point, Sara Tidwell became Sara Laughs.

In the end, though, TR-90 mustn't have been what they wanted, because after playing a county fair or two in the late summer of 1901, the clan moved on. Their neat little cabins provided summer-rental income for the Day family until 1933, when they burned in the summer fires which charred the east and north sides of the lake. End of story.

Except for her music, that was. Her music had lived.

I got up from the rock I had been sitting on, stretched my arms and my back, and walked back down the lane, singing one of her songs as I went.

Chapter 12

During my hike back down the lane to the house, I tried to think about nothing at all. My first editor used to say that eighty-five per cent of what goes on in a novelist's head is none of his business, a sentiment I've never believed should be restricted to just writers. So-called higher thought is, by and large, highly overrated. When trouble comes and steps have to be taken, I find it's generally better to just stand aside and let the boys in the basement do their work. That's blue-collar labor down there, non-union guys with lots of muscles and tattoos. Instinct is their specialty, and they refer problems upstairs for actual cogitation only as a last resort.

When I tried to call Mattie Devore, an extremely peculiar thing happened — one that had nothing at all to do with spooks, as far as I could tell. Instead of an open-hum line when I pushed the cordless's ON button, I got silence. Then, just as I was thinking I must have left the phone in the north bedroom off the hook, I realized it wasn't *complete* silence. Distant as a radio transmission from deep space, cheerful and quacky as an animated duck, some guy with a fair amount of Brooklyn in his voice was singing: "He followed her to school one day, school one day, school one day. Followed her to school one day, which was against the rule . . ."

I opened my mouth to ask who was there, but before I could, a woman's voice said "Hello?" She sounded perplexed and doubtful.

"Mattie?" In my confusion it never occurred to me to call her something more formal, like Ms. or Mrs. Devore. Nor did it seem odd that I should know who it was, based on a single word, even though our only previous conversation had been relatively brief. Maybe the guys in the basement recognized the background music and made the connection to Kyra.

"Mr. Noonan?" She sounded more bewildered than ever. "The phone never even rang!"

"I must have picked mine up just as your call was going through," I said. "That happens from time to time." But how many times, I wondered, did it happen when the person calling you was the one you yourself had been planning to call? Maybe quite often, actually. Telepathy or coincidence? Live or Memorex? Either way, it seemed almost magical. I looked across the long, low living room, into the glassy eyes of Bunter the moose, and thought: *Yes, but maybe this is a magic place now.*

"I suppose," she said doubtfully. "I apologize about calling in the first place — it's a presumption. Your number's unlisted, I know."

Oh, don't worry about that, I thought. *Everyone's got this old number by now. In fact, I'm thinking about putting it in the Yellow Pages.*

"I got it from your file at the library," she went on, sounding embarrassed. "That's where I work." In the background, "Mary Had a Little Lamb" had given way to "The Farmer in the Dell."

"It's quite all right," I said. "Especially since you're the person I was picking up the phone to call."

"Me? Why?"

"Ladies first."

She gave a brief, nervous laugh. "I wanted to invite you to dinner. That is, Ki and I want to invite you to dinner. I should have done it before now. You were awfully good to us the other day. Will you come?"

"Yes," I said with no hesitation at all. "With thanks. We've got some things to talk about, anyway."

There was a pause. In the background, the mouse was taking the cheese. As a kid I used to think all these things happened in a vast gray factory called The Hi-Ho Dairy-O.

"Mattie? Still there?"

"He's dragged you into it, hasn't he? That

awful old man." Now her voice sounded not nervous but somehow dead.

"Well, yes and no. You could argue that fate dragged me into it, or coincidence, or God. I wasn't there that morning because of Max Devore; I was chasing the elusive Villageburger."

She didn't laugh, but her voice brightened a little, and I was glad. People who talk in that dead, affectless way are, by and large, frightened people. Sometimes people who have been outright terrorized. "I'm still sorry for dragging you into my trouble." I had an idea she might start to wonder who was dragging whom after I pitched her on John Storrow, and was glad it was a discussion I wouldn't have to have with her on the phone.

"In any case, I'd love to come to dinner. When?"

"Would this evening be too soon?"

"Absolutely not."

"That's wonderful. We have to eat early, though, so my little guy doesn't fall asleep in her dessert. Is six okay?"

"Yes."

"Ki will be excited. We don't have much company."

"She hasn't been wandering again, has she?"

I thought she might be offended. Instead, this time she *did* laugh. "God, no. All the fuss on Saturday scared her. Now she comes in to tell me if she's switching from the swing in the side yard to the sandbox in back. She's talked about you a lot, though. She calls you 'that tall guy who carrot me.' I think she's worried you might be mad at her."

"Tell her I'm not," I said. "No, check that. I'll tell her myself. Can I bring anything?"

"Bottle of wine?" she asked, a little doubtfully. "Or maybe that's pretentious — I was only going to cook hamburgers on the grill and make potato salad."

"I'll bring an unpretentious bottle."

"Thank you," she said. "This is sort of exciting. We never have company."

I was horrified to find myself on the verge of saying that I thought it was sort of exciting, too, my first date in four years and all. "Thanks so much for thinking of me."

As I hung up I remembered John Storrow advising me to try and stay visible with her, not to hand over any extra grist for the town gossip mill. If she was barbecuing, we'd probably be out where people could see we had our clothes on . . . for most of the evening, anyway. She would, however, likely do the polite thing at some point and invite me inside. I would then do the polite thing and go. Admire her velvet Elvis painting on the wall, or her commemorative plates from the Franklin Mint, or whatever she had going in the way of trailer decoration; I'd let Kyra show me her bedroom and exclaim with wonder over her excellent assortment of stuffed animals and her favorite dolly, if that was required. There are all sorts of priorities in life. Some your lawyer can understand, but I suspect there are quite a few he can't.

"Am I handling this right, Bunter?" I asked the stuffed moose. "Bellow once for yes, twice for no."

I was halfway down the hall leading to the north wing, thinking of nothing but a cool shower, when from behind me, very soft, came a brief ring of the bell around Bunter's neck. I stopped, head cocked, my shirt held in one hand, waiting for the bell to ring again. It didn't. After a minute, I went the rest of the way to the bathroom and flipped on the shower.

The Lakeview General had a pretty good selection of wines tucked away in one corner — not much local demand for it, maybe, but the tourists probably bought a fair quantity — and I selected a bottle of Mondavi red. It was probably a bit more expensive than Mattie had had in mind, but I could peel the price-sticker off and hope she wouldn't know the difference. There was a line at the checkout, mostly folks with damp tee-shirts pulled on over their bathing suits and sand from the public beach sticking to their legs.

While I was waiting my turn, my eye happened on the impulse items which are always stocked near the counter. Among them were several plastic bags labeled MAGNA-BET, each bag showing a cartoon refrigerator with the message BACK SOON stuck to it. According to the written info, there were two sets of consonants in each Magnabet, PLUS EXTRA VOWELS. I grabbed two sets . . . then added a third, thinking that Mattie Devore's kid was probably just the right age for such an item.

Kyra saw me pulling into the weedy dooryard, jumped off the slumpy little swingset beside the trailer, bolted to her mother, and hid behind her. When I approached the hibachi which had been set up beside the cinderblock front steps, the child who'd spoken to me so fearlessly on Saturday was just a peeking blue eye and a chubby hand grasping a fold of her mother's sundress below the hip.

Two hours brought considerable changes, however. As twilight deepened, Kyra sat on my lap in the trailer's living room, listening carefully — if with growing wooziness — as I read her the ever-enthralling story of Cinderella. The couch we were on was a shade of brown which can by law only be sold in discount stores, and extremely lumpy into the bargain, but I still felt ashamed of my casual preconceptions about what I would find inside this trailer. On the wall above and behind us there was an Edward Hopper print — that one of a lonely lunch counter late at night — and across the room, over the small Formica-topped table in the kitchen nook, was one of Vincent van Gogh's *Sunflowers* series. Even more than the Hopper, it looked at home in Mattie Devore's doublewide. I have no idea why that should have been true, but it was.

"Glass slipper will cut her footie," Ki said in a muzzy, considering way.

"No way," I said. "Slipper-glass was specially made in the Kingdom of Grimoire. Smooth and unbreakable, as long as you didn't sing high C while wearing them."

"I get a pair?"

"Sorry, Ki," I said, "no one knows how to make slipper-glass anymore. It's a lost art, like Toledo steel." It was hot in the trailer and she was hot against my shirt, where her upper body lay, but I wouldn't have changed it. Having a kid on my lap was pretty great. Outside, her mother was singing and gathering up dishes from the card table we'd used for our picnic. Hearing her sing was also pretty great.

"Go on, go on," Kyra said, pointing to the picture of Cinderella scrubbing the floor. The little girl peeking nervously around her

311

mother's leg was gone; the angry I'm-going-to-the-damn-beach girl of Saturday morning was gone; here was only a sleepy kid who was pretty and bright and trusting. "Before I can't hold it anymore."

"Do you need to go pee-pee?"

"No," she said, looking at me with some disdain. "Besides, that's you-rinating. Peas are what you eat with meatloaf, that's what Mattie says. And I already went. But if you don't go fast on the story, I'll fall to sleep."

"You can't hurry stories with magic in them, Ki."

"Well go as fast as you can."

"Okay." I turned the page. Here was Cinderella, trying to be a good sport, waving goodbye to her asshole sisters as they went off to the ball dressed like starlets at a disco. " 'No sooner had Cinderella said goodbye to Tammy Faye and Vanna —' "

"Those are the sisters' names?"

"The ones I made up for them, yes. Is that okay?"

"Sure." She settled more comfortably on my lap and dropped her head against my chest again.

" 'No sooner had Cinderella said goodbye to Tammy Faye and Vanna than a bright light suddenly appeared in the corner of the kitchen. Stepping out of it was a beautiful lady in a silver gown. The jewels in her hair glowed like stars.' "

"Fairy godmother," Kyra said matter-of-factly.

"Yes."

Mattie came in carrying the remaining half-bottle of Mondavi and the blackened barbecue implements. Her sundress was bright red. On her feet she wore low-topped sneakers so white that they seemed to flash in the gloom. Her hair was tied back and although she still wasn't the gorgeous country-club babe I had briefly envisioned, she was very pretty. Now she looked at Kyra, looked at me, raised her eyebrows, made a lifting gesture with her arms. I shook my head, sending back a message that neither of us was ready quite yet.

I resumed reading while Mattie went to work scrubbing her few cooking tools. She was still humming. By the time she had finished with the spatula, Ki's body had taken on an additional relaxation which I recognized at once — she'd conked out, and hard. I closed the *Little Golden Treasury of Fairy Tales* and put it on the coffee-table beside a couple of other stacked books — whatever Mattie was reading, I presumed. I looked up, saw her looking back at me from the kitchen, and flicked her the V-for-Victory sign. "Noonan, the winner by a technical knockout in the eighth round," I said.

Mattie dried her hands on a dishtowel and came over. "Give her to me."

I stood up with Kyra in my arms instead. "I'll carry. Where?"

She pointed. "On the left."

I carried the baby down the hallway, which was narrow enough so I had to be careful not to bump her feet on one side or the top of her head on the other. At the end of the hall was the bathroom, stringently clean. On the right was a closed door which led, I assumed, into the bedroom Mattie had once shared with Lance Devore and where she now slept alone. If there was a boyfriend who overnighted even some of the time, Mattie had done a good job of erasing his presence from the trailer.

I slid carefully through the door on the left and looked at the little bed with its ruffled coverlet of cabbage roses, the table with the dollhouse on it, the picture of the Emerald City on one wall, the sign (done in shiny stick-on letters) on another one that read CASA KYRA. Devore wanted to take her away from here, a place where nothing was wrong — where, to the contrary, everything was perfectly right. Casa Kyra was the room of a little girl who was growing up okay.

"Put her on the bed and then go pour yourself another glass of wine," Mattie said. "I'll zip her into her pj's and join you. I know we've got stuff to talk about."

"Okay." I put her down, then bent a little

farther, meaning to plant a kiss on her nose. I almost thought better of it, then did it anyway. When I left, Mattie was smiling, so I guess it was okay.

I poured myself a little more wine, walked back into the scrap of living room with it, and looked at the two books beside Ki's fairy-tale collection. I'm always curious about what people are reading; the only better insight into them is the contents of their medicine cabinets, and rummaging through your host's drugs and nostrums is frowned upon by the better class.

The books were different enough to qualify as schizoid. One, with a playing-card bookmark about three quarters of the way through, was the paperback edition of Richard North Patterson's *Silent Witness*. I applauded her taste; Patterson and DeMille are probably the best of the current popular novelists. The other, a hardcover tome of some weight, was *The Collected Short Works of Herman Melville*. About as far from Richard North Patterson as you could get. According to the faded purple ink stamped on the thickness of the pages, this volume belonged to Four Lakes Community Library. That was a lovely little stone building about five miles south of Dark Score Lake, where Route 68 passes off the TR and into Motton. Where Mattie worked, presumably.

I opened to her bookmark, another playing card, and saw she was reading "Bartleby."

"I don't understand that," she said from behind me, startling me so badly that I almost dropped the books. "I like it — it's a good enough story — but I haven't the slightest idea what it means. The other one, now, I've even figured out who did it."

"It's a strange pair to read in tandem," I said, putting them back down.

"The Patterson I'm reading for pleasure," Mattie said. She went into the kitchen, looked briefly (and with some longing, I thought) at the bottle of wine, then opened the fridge and took out a pitcher of Kool-Aid. On the fridge door were words her daughter had already assembled from her Magnabet bag: KI and MATTIE and HOHO (Santa Claus, I presumed). "Well, I'm reading them both for pleasure, I guess, but we're due to discuss 'Bartleby' in this little group I'm a part of. We meet Thursday nights at the library. I've still got about ten pages to go."

"A readers' circle."

"Uh-huh. Mrs. Briggs leads. She formed it long before I was born. She's the head librarian at Four Lakes, you know."

"I do. Lindy Briggs is my caretaker's sister-in-law."

Mattie smiled. "Small world, isn't it?"

"No, it's a big world but a small town."

She started to lean back against the counter with her glass of Kool-Aid, then thought better of it. "Why don't we go outside and sit? That way anyone passing can see that we're still dressed and that we don't have anything on inside-out."

I looked at her, startled. She looked back with a kind of cynical good humor. It wasn't an expression that looked particularly at home on her face.

"I may only be twenty-one, but I'm not stupid," she said. "He's watching me. I know it, and you probably do, too. On another night I might be tempted to say fuck him if he can't take a joke, but it's cooler out there and the smoke from the hibachi will keep the worst of the bugs away. Have I shocked you? If so, I'm sorry."

"You haven't." She had, a little. "No need to apologize."

We carried our drinks down the not-quite-steady cinderblock steps and sat side-by-side in a couple of lawn-chairs. To the left of us the coals in the hibachi glowed soft rose in the growing gloom. Mattie leaned back, placed the cold curve of her glass briefly against her forehead, then drank most of what was left, the ice cubes sliding against her teeth with a click and a rattle. Crickets hummed in the woods behind the trailer and across the road. Farther up Highway 68, I could see the bright white fluorescents over the gas island at the Lakeview General. The seat of my chair was a little baggy, the interwoven straps a little frayed, and the old girl canted pretty severely to the left, but there was still no place I'd rather have been sitting just then. This evening had turned out to be a quiet little miracle . . . at least, so far. We still had John Storrow to get to.

"I'm glad you came on a Tuesday," she said. "Tuesday nights are hard for me. I'm always thinking of the ballgame down at Warrington's. The guys'll be picking up the gear by now — the bats and bases and catcher's mask — and putting it back in the storage cabinet behind home plate. Drinking their last beers and smoking their last cigarettes. That's where I met my husband, you know. I'm sure you've been told all that by now."

I couldn't see her face clearly, but I could hear the faint tinge of bitterness which had crept into her voice, and guessed she was still wearing the cynical expression. It was too old for her, but I thought she'd come by it honestly enough. Although if she didn't watch out, it would take root and grow.

"I heard a version from Bill, yes — Lindy's brother-in-law."

"Oh ayuh — our story's on retail. You can get it at the store, or the Village Cafe, or at that old blabbermouth's garage . . . which my father-in-law rescued from Western Savings, by the way. He stepped in just before the bank could foreclose. Now Dickie Brooks and his cronies think Max Devore is walking talking Jesus. I hope you got a fairer version from Mr. Dean than you'd get at the All-Purpose. You must've, or you wouldn't have risked eating hamburgers with Jezebel."

I wanted to get away from that, if I could — her anger was understandable but useless. Of course it was easier for me to see that; it wasn't my kid who had been turned into the handkerchief tied at the center of a tug-of-war rope. "They still play softball at Warrington's? Even though Devore bought the place?"

"Yes indeed. He goes down to the field in his motorized wheelchair every Tuesday evening and watches. There are other things he's done since he came back here that are just attempts to buy the town's good opinion, but I think he genuinely loves the softball games. The Whitmore woman goes, too. Brings an extra oxygen tank along in a little red wheelbarrow with a whitewall tire on the front. She keeps a fielder's mitt in there, too, in case any foul pops come up over the backstop to where he sits. He caught one near the start of the season, I heard, and got a standing O from the players and the folks who come to watch."

"Going to the games puts him in touch with his son, you think?"

Mattie smiled grimly. "I don't think Lance so much as crosses his mind, not when he's at the ballfield. They play hard at Warrington's — slide into home with their feet up, jump into the puckerbrush for the flyballs, curse each other when they do something wrong — and that's what old Max Devore enjoys, that's why he never misses a Tuesday-evening game. He likes to watch them slide and get up bleeding."

"Is that how Lance played?"

She thought about it carefully. "He played hard, but he wasn't crazed. He was there just for the fun of it. We all were. We women — shit, really just us girls, Barney Therriault's wife, Cindy, was only sixteen — we'd stand behind the backstop on the first-base side, smoking cigarettes or waving punks to keep the bugs away, cheering our guys when they did something good, laughing when they did something stupid. We'd swap sodas or share a can of beer. I'd admire Helen Geary's twins and she'd kiss Ki under the chin until Ki giggled. Sometimes we'd go down to the Village Cafe afterward and Buddy'd make us pizzas, losers pay. All friends again, you know, after the game. We'd sit there laughing and yelling and blowing straw-wrappers around, some of the guys half-loaded but nobody mean. In those days they got all the mean out on the ballfield. And you know what? None of them come to see me. Not Helen Geary, who was my best friend. Not Richie Lattimore, who was Lance's best friend — the two of them would talk about rocks and birds and the kinds of trees there were across the lake for hours on end. They came to the funeral, and for a little while after, and then . . . you know what it was like? When I was a kid, our well dried up. For awhile you'd get a trickle when you turned on the tap, but then there was just air. Just air." The cynicism was gone and there was only hurt in her voice. "I saw Helen at Christmas, and we promised to get together for the twins' birthday, but we never did. I think she's scared to come near me."

"Because of the old man?"

"Who else? But that's okay, life goes on." She sat up, drank the rest of her Kool-Aid, and set the glass aside. "What about you, Mike? Did you come back to write a book? Are you going to name the TR?" This was a local *bon mot* that I remembered with an almost painful twinge of nostalgia. Locals with great plans were said to be bent on naming the TR.

"No," I said, and then astonished myself by saying: "I don't do that anymore."

I think I expected her to leap to her feet,

overturning her chair and uttering a sharp cry of horrified denial. All of which says a good deal about me, I suppose, and none of it flattering.

"You've retired?" she asked, sounding calm and remarkably unhorrified. "Or is it writer's block?"

"Well, it's certainly not *chosen* retirement." I realized the conversation had taken a rather amusing turn. I'd come primarily to sell her on John Storrow — to shove John Storrow down her throat, if that was what it took — and instead I was for the first time discussing my inability to work. For the first time with anyone.

"So it's a block."

"I used to think so, but now I'm not so sure. I think novelists may come equipped with a certain number of stories to tell — they're built into the software. And when they're gone, they're gone."

"I doubt that," she said. "Maybe you'll write now that you're down here. Maybe that's part of the reason you came back."

"Maybe you're right."

"Are you scared?"

"Sometimes. Mostly about what I'll do for the rest of my life. I'm no good at boats in bottles, and my wife was the one with the green thumb."

"I'm scared, too," she said. "Scared a lot. All the time now, it seems like."

"That he'll win his custody case? Mattie, that's what I —"

"The custody case is only part of it," she said. "I'm scared just to be here, on the TR. It started early this summer, long after I knew Devore meant to get Ki away from me if he could. And it's getting worse. In a way it's like watching thunderheads gather over New Hampshire and then come piling across the lake. I can't put it any better than that, except . . ." She shifted, crossing her legs and then bending forward to pull the skirt of her dress against the line of her shin, as if she were cold. "Except that I've woken up several times lately, sure that I wasn't in the bedroom alone. Once when I was sure I wasn't in the *bed* alone. Sometimes it's just a feeling — like a headache, only in your nerves — and sometimes I think I can hear whispering, or crying. I made a cake one night — about two weeks ago, this was — and forgot to put the flour away. The next morning the cannister was overturned, and the flour was spilled on the counter. Someone had written 'hello' in it. I thought at first it was Ki, but she said she didn't do it. Besides, it wasn't her printing, hers is all straggly. I don't know if she could even write hello. Hi, maybe, but . . . Mike, you don't think he could be sending someone around to try and freak me out, do you? I mean that's just stupid, right?"

"I don't know," I said. I thought of something thumping the insulation in the dark as I stood on the stairs. I thought of hello printed with magnets on my refrigerator door, and a child sobbing in the dark. My skin felt more than cold; it felt numb. A headache in the nerves, that was good, that was exactly how you felt when something reached around the wall of the real world and touched you on the nape of the neck.

"Maybe it's ghosts," she said, and smiled in an uncertain way that was more frightened than amused.

I opened my mouth to tell her about what had been happening at Sara Laughs, then closed it again. There was a clear choice to be made here: either we could be sidetracked into a discussion of the paranormal, or we could come back to the visible world. The one where Max Devore was trying to steal himself a kid.

"Yeah," I said. "The spirits are about to speak."

"I wish I could see your face better. There was something on it just then. What?"

"I don't know," I said. "But right now I think we'd better talk about Kyra. Okay?"

"Okay." In the faint glow of the hibachi I could see her settling herself in her chair, as if to take a blow.

"I've been subpoenaed to give a deposition in Castle Rock on Friday. Before Elmer

Durgin, who is Kyra's guardian *ad litem* —"

"That pompous little toad isn't Ki's anything!" she burst out. "He's in my father-in-law's hip pocket, just like Dickie Osgood, old Max's pet real-estate guy! Dickie and Elmer Durgin drink together down at The Mellow Tiger, or at least they did until this business really got going. Then someone probably told them it would look bad, and they stopped."

"The papers were served by a deputy named George Footman."

"Just one more of the usual suspects," Mattie said in a thin voice. "Dickie Osgood's a snake, but George Footman's a junkyard dog. He's been suspended off the cops twice. Once more and he can work for Max Devore full-time."

"Well, he scared me. I tried not to show it, but he did. And people who scare me make me angry. I called my agent in New York and then hired a lawyer. One who makes a specialty of child-custody cases."

I tried to see how she was taking this and couldn't, although we were sitting fairly close together. But she still had that set look, like a woman who expects to take some hard blows. Or perhaps for Mattie the blows had already started to fall.

Slowly, not allowing myself to rush, I went through my conversation with John Storrow. I emphasized what Storrow had said about sexual equality — that it was apt to be a negative force in her case, making it easier for Judge Rancourt to take Kyra away. I also came down hard on the fact that Devore could have all the lawyers he wanted — not to mention sympathetic witnesses, with Richard Osgood running around the TR and spreading Devore's dough — but that the court wasn't obligated to treat her to so much as an ice cream cone. I finished by telling her that John wanted to talk to one of us tomorrow at eleven, and that it should be her. Then I waited. The silence spun out, broken only by crickets and the faint revving of some kid's unmuffled truck. Up Route 68, the white fluorescents went out as the Lakeview Market finished another day of summer trade. I didn't like Mattie's quiet; it seemed like the prelude to an explosion. A *Yankee* explosion. I held my peace and waited for her to ask me what gave me the right to meddle in her business.

When she finally spoke, her voice was low and defeated. It hurt to hear her sounding that way, but like the cynical look on her face earlier, it wasn't surprising. And I hardened myself against it as best I could. Hey, Mattie, tough old world. Pick one.

"Why would you do this?" she asked. "Why would you hire an expensive New York lawyer to take my case? That *is* what you're offering, isn't it? It's got to be, because *I* sure can't hire him. I got thirty thousand dollars' insurance money when Lance died, and was lucky to get that. It was a policy he bought from one of his Warrington's friends, almost as a joke, but without it I would have lost the trailer last winter. They may love Dickie Brooks at Western Savings, but they don't give a rat's ass for Mattie Stanchfield Devore. After taxes I make about a hundred a week at the library. So you're offering to pay. Right?"

"Right."

"Why? You don't even know us."

"Because . . ." I trailed off. I seem to remember wanting Jo to step in at that point, asking my mind to supply her voice, which I could then pass on to Mattie in my own. But Jo didn't come. I was flying solo.

"Because now I do nothing that makes a difference," I said at last, and once again the words astonished me. "And I *do* know you. I've eaten your food, I've read Ki a story and had her fall asleep in my lap . . . and maybe I saved her life the other day when I grabbed her out of the road. We'll never know for sure, but maybe I did. You know what the Chinese say about something like that?"

I didn't expect an answer, the question was more rhetorical than real, but she surprised me. Not for the last time, either. "That if you save someone's life, you're responsible for them."

"Yes. It's also about what's fair and what's right, but I think mostly it's about wanting to be part of something where I make a difference. I look back on the four years since my wife died, and there's nothing there. Not even a book where Marjorie the shy typist meets a handsome stranger."

She sat thinking this over, watching as a fully loaded pulptruck snored past on the highway, its headlights glaring and its load of logs swaying from side to side like the hips of an overweight woman. "Don't you *root* for us," she said at last. She spoke in a low, unexpectedly fierce voice. "Don't you root for us like he roots for his team-of-the-week down at the softball field. I need help and I know it, but I won't have that. I *can't* have it. We're not a game, Ki and me. You understand?"

"Perfectly."

"You know what people in town will say, don't you?"

"Yes."

"I'm a lucky girl, don't you think? First I marry the son of an extremely rich man, and after *he* dies, I fall under the protective wing of another rich guy. Next I'll probably move in with Donald Trump."

"Cut it out."

"I'd probably believe it myself, if I were on the other side. But I wonder if anyone

328

notices that lucky Mattie is still living in a Modair trailer and can't afford health insurance. Or that her kid got most of her vaccinations from the County Nurse. My parents died when I was fifteen. I have a brother and a sister, but they're both a lot older and both out of state. My parents were drunks — not physically abusive, but there was plenty of the other kinds. It was like growing up in a . . . a roach motel. My dad was a pulper, my mom was a bourbon beautician whose one ambition was to own a Mary Kay pink Cadillac. He drowned in Kewadin Pond. She drowned in her own vomit about six months later. How do you like it so far?"

"Not very much. I'm sorry."

"After Mom's funeral my brother, Hugh, offered to take me back to Rhode Island, but I could tell his wife wasn't exactly nuts about having a fifteen-year-old join the family, and I can't say that I blamed her. Also, I'd just made the jv cheering squad. That seems like supreme diddlyshit now, but it was a very big deal then."

Of course it had been a big deal, especially to the child of alcoholics. The only one still living at home. Being that last child, watching as the disease really digs its claws in, can be one of the world's loneliest jobs. Last one out of the sacred ginmill please turn off the lights.

"I ended up going to live with my aunt Florence, just two miles down the road. It took us about three weeks to discover we didn't like each other very much, but we made it work for two years. Then, between my junior and senior years, I got a summer job at Warrington's and met Lance. When he asked me to marry him, Aunt Flo refused to give permission. When I told her I was pregnant, she emancipated me so I didn't need it."

"You dropped out of school?"

She grimaced, nodded. "I didn't want to spend six months having people watch me swell up like a balloon. Lance supported me. He said I could take the equivalency test. I did last year. It was easy. And now Ki and I are on our own. Even if my aunt agreed to help me, what could she do? She works in the Castle Rock Gore-Tex factory and makes about sixteen thousand dollars a year."

I nodded again, thinking that my last check for French royalties had been about that. My last *quarterly* check. Then I remembered something Ki had told me on the day I met her.

"When I was carrying Kyra out of the road, she said that if you were mad, she'd go to her white nana. If your folks are dead, who did she —" Except I didn't really have to ask; I only had to make one or two simple connections. "Rogette Whitmore's the white nana? Devore's assistant? But that means . . ."

"That Ki's been with them. Yes, you bet. Until late last month, I allowed her to visit her grandpa — and Rogette by association, of course — quite often. Once or twice a week, and sometimes for an overnight. She likes her 'whita poppa' — at least she did at first — and she absolutely adores that creepy woman." I thought Mattie shivered in the gloom, although the night was still very warm.

"Devore called to say he was coming east for Lance's funeral and to ask if he could see his granddaughter while he was here. Nice as pie, he was, just as if he'd never tried to buy me off when Lance told him we were going to get married."

"Did he?"

"Uh-huh. The first offer was a hundred thousand. That was in August of 1994, after Lance called him to say we were getting married in mid-September. I kept quiet about it. A week later, the offer went up to two hundred thousand."

"For what, precisely?"

"To remove my bitch-hooks and relocate with no forwarding address. This time I did tell Lance, and he hit the roof. Called his old man and said we were going to be married whether he liked it or not. Told him that if he ever wanted to see his grandchild, he had better cut the shit and behave."

With another parent, I thought, that was probably the most reasonable response Lance Devore could have made. I respected him for it. The only problem was that he wasn't dealing with a reasonable man; he was dealing with the fellow who, as a child, had stolen Scooter Larribee's new sled.

"These offers were made by Devore himself, over the telephone. Both when Lance wasn't around. Then, about ten days before the wedding, I had a visit from Dickie Osgood. I was to make a call to a number in Delaware, and when I did . . ." Mattie shook her head. "You wouldn't believe it. It's like something out of one of your books."

"May I guess?"

"If you want."

"He tried to buy the child. He tried to buy Kyra."

Her eyes widened. A scantling moon had come up and I could see that look of surprise well enough.

"How much?" I asked. "I'm curious. How much for you to give birth, leave Devore's grandchild with Lance, then scat?"

"Two million dollars," she whispered. "Deposited in the bank of my choice, as long as it was west of the Mississippi and I signed an agreement to stay away from her — and from Lance — until at least April twentieth, 2016."

"The year Ki turns twenty-one."

"Yes."

"And Osgood doesn't know any of the details, so Devore's skirts remain clean here in town."

"Uh-huh. And the two million was only the start. There was to be an additional million on Ki's fifth, tenth, fifteenth, and twentieth birthdays." She shook her head in a disbelieving way. "The linoleum keeps bubbling up in the kitchen, the showerhead keeps falling into the tub, and the whole damn rig cants to the east these days, but I could have been the six-million-dollar woman."

Did you ever consider taking the offer, Mattie? I wondered . . . but that was a question I'd never ask, a sign of curiosity so unseemly it deserved no satisfaction.

"Did you tell Lance?"

"I tried not to. He was already furious with his father, and I didn't want to make it worse. I didn't want that much hate at the start of our marriage, no matter how good the reasons for hating might be . . . and I didn't want Lance to . . . later on with me, you know . . ." She raised her hands, then dropped them back on her thighs. The gesture was both weary and oddly endearing.

"You didn't want Lance turning on you ten years later and saying 'You came between me and my father, you bitch.'"

"Something like that. But in the end, I couldn't keep it to myself. I was just this kid from the sticks, didn't own a pair of pantyhose until I was eleven, wore my hair in nothing but braids or a ponytail until I was thirteen, thought the whole state of New York was New York City . . . and this guy . . . this *phantom father* . . . had offered me *six million bucks*. It terrified me. I had dreams about him coming in the night like a troll and stealing my baby out of her crib. He'd come wriggling through the window like a snake . . ."

"Dragging his oxygen tank behind him, no doubt."

She smiled. "I didn't know about the oxygen then. Or Rogette Whitmore, either. All I'm trying to say is that I was only seventeen and not good at keeping secrets." I had to restrain my own smile at the way she said this — as if decades of experience now lay between that naive, frightened child and this mature woman with the mail-order diploma.

"Lance was angry."

"So angry he replied to his father by e-mail instead of calling. He stuttered, you see, and the more upset he was, the worse his stutter became. A phone conversation would have been impossible."

Now, at last, I thought I had a clear picture. Lance Devore had written his father an unthinkable letter — unthinkable, that was, if you happened to be Max Devore. The letter said that Lance didn't want to hear from his father again, and Mattie didn't, either. He wouldn't be welcome in their home (the Modair trailer wasn't quite the humble woodcutter's cottage of a Brothers Grimm tale, but it was close enough for kissing). He wouldn't be welcome to visit following the birth of their baby, and if he had the gall to send the child a present then or later, it would be returned. Stay out of my life, Dad. This time you've gone too far to forgive.

There are undoubtedly diplomatic ways of handling an offended child, some wise and some crafty . . . but ask yourself this: would a diplomatic father have gotten himself into such a situation to begin with? Would a man with even minimal insight into human nature have offered his son's fiancée a bounty (one so enormous it probably had little real sense or meaning to her) to give up her first-born child? And he'd offered this devil's bargain to a girl-woman of seventeen, an age when the romantic view of life is at absolute high tide. If nothing else, Devore should have waited awhile before making his final offer. You could argue that he didn't know if he *had* awhile, but it wouldn't be a persuasive argument. I thought Mattie was right — deep in that wrinkled old prune which served him as a heart, Max Devore thought he was going to live forever.

335

In the end, he hadn't been able to restrain himself. There was the sled he wanted, the sled he just had to have, on the other side of the window. All he had to do was break the glass and take it. He'd been doing it all his life, and so he had reacted to his son's e-mail not craftily, as a man of his years and abilities should have done, but furiously, as the child would have done if the glass in the shed window had proved immune to his hammering fists. Lance didn't want him meddling? Fine! Lance could live with his backwoods Daisy Mae in a tent or a trailer or a goddamned cowbarn. He could give up the cushy surveying job, as well, and find real employment. See how the other half lived!

In other words, you can't quit on me, son. You're fired.

"We didn't fall into each other's arms at the funeral," Mattie said, "don't get that idea. But he was decent to me — which I didn't expect — and I tried to be decent to him. He offered me a stipend, which I refused. I was afraid there might be legal ramifications."

"I doubt it, but I like your caution. What happened when he saw Kyra for the first time, Mattie? Do you remember?"

"I'll never forget it." She reached into the pocket of her dress, found a battered pack of cigarettes, and shook one out. She looked at

336

it with a mixture of greed and disgust. "I quit these because Lance said we couldn't really afford them, and I knew he was right. But the habit creeps back. I only smoke a pack a week, and I know damned well even that's too much, but sometimes I need the comfort. Do you want one?"

I shook my head. She lit up, and in the momentary flare of the match, her face was way past pretty. What had the old man made of *her?* I wondered.

"He met his granddaughter for the first time beside a hearse," Mattie said. "We were at Dakin's Funeral Home in Motton. It was the 'viewing.' Do you know about that?"

"Oh yes," I said, thinking of Jo.

"The casket was closed but they still call it a viewing. Weird. I came out to have a cigarette. I told Ki to sit on the funeral parlor steps so she wouldn't get the smoke, and I went a little way down the walk. This big gray limo pulled up. I'd never seen anything like it before, except on TV. I knew who it was right away. I put my cigarettes back in my purse and told Ki to come. She toddled down the walk and took hold of my hand. The limo door opened, and Rogette Whitmore got out. She had an oxygen mask in one hand, but he didn't need it, at least not then. He got out after her. A tall man — not as tall as you, Mike, but tall — wearing a gray suit and black shoes as shiny as mirrors."

She paused, thinking. Her cigarette rose briefly to her mouth, then went back down to the arm of her chair, a red firefly in the weak moonlight.

"At first he didn't say anything. The woman tried to take his arm and help him climb the three or four steps from the road to the walk, but he shook her off. He got to where we were standing under his own power, although I could hear him wheezing way down deep in his chest. It was the sound a machine makes when it needs oil. I don't know how much he can walk now, but it's probably not much. Those few steps pretty well did him in, and that was almost a year ago. He looked at me for a second or two, then bent forward with his big, bony old hands on his knees. He looked at Kyra and she looked up at him."

Yes. I could see it . . . except not in color, not in an image like a photograph. I saw it as a woodcut, just one more harsh illustration from *Grimm's Fairy Tales*. The little girl looks up wide-eyed at the rich old man — once a boy who went triumphantly sliding on a stolen sled, now at the other end of his life and just one more bag of bones. In my imagining, Ki was wearing a hooded jacket and Devore's grandpa mask was slightly askew, allowing me to see the tufted wolf-pelt beneath. What big eyes you have, Grandpa, what a big nose you have,

Grandpa, what big teeth you have, too.

"He picked her up. I don't know how much effort it cost him, but he did. And — the oddest thing — Ki *let* herself be picked up. He was a complete stranger to her, and old people always seem to scare little children, but she let him pick her up. 'Do you know who I am?' he asked her. She shook her head, but the way she was looking at him . . . it was as if she *almost* knew. Do you think that's possible?"

"Yes."

"He said, 'I'm your grandpa.' And I almost grabbed her back, Mike, because I had this crazy idea . . . I don't know . . ."

"That he was going to eat her up?"

Her cigarette paused in front of her mouth. Her eyes were round. "How do you know that? How *can* you know that?"

"Because in my mind's eye it looks like a fairy tale. Little Red Riding Hood and the Old Gray Wolf. What did he do then?"

"Ate her up with his eyes. Since then he's taught her to play checkers and Candyland and box-dots. She's only three, but he's taught her to add and subtract. She has her own room at Warrington's and her own little computer in it, and God knows what he's taught her to do with that . . . but that first time he only looked at her. It was the hungriest look I've ever seen in my life.

"And she looked back. It couldn't have

been more than ten or twenty seconds, but it seemed like forever. Then he tried to hand her back to me. He'd used up all his strength, though, and if I hadn't been right there to take her, I think he would have dropped her on the cement walk.

"He staggered a little, and Rogette Whitmore put an arm around him. That was when he took the oxygen mask from her — there was a little air-bottle attached to it on an elastic — and put it over his mouth and nose. A couple of deep breaths and he seemed more or less all right again. He gave it back to Rogette and really seemed to see me for the first time. He said, 'I've been a fool, haven't I?' I said, 'Yes, sir, I think you have.' He gave me a look, very black, when I said that. I think if he'd been even five years younger, he might have hit me for it."

"But he wasn't and he didn't."

"No. He said, 'I want to go inside. Will you help me do that?' I said I would. We went up the mortuary steps with Rogette on one side of him, me on the other, and Kyra walking along behind. I felt sort of like a harem girl. It wasn't a very nice feeling. When we got into the vestibule, he sat down to catch his breath and take a little more oxygen. Rogette turned to Kyra. I think that woman's got a scary face, it reminds me of some painting or other —"

"*The Cry*? The one by Munch?"

"I'm pretty sure that's the one." She dropped her cigarette — she'd smoked it all the way down to the filter — and stepped on it, grinding it into the bony, rock-riddled ground with one white sneaker. "But Ki wasn't scared of her a bit. Not then, not later. She bent down to Kyra and said, 'What rhymes with lady?' and Kyra said 'Shady!' right off. Even at two she loved rhymes. Rogette reached into her purse and brought out a Hershey's Kiss. Ki looked at me to see if she had permission and I said, 'All right, but just one, and I don't want to see any of it on your dress.' Ki popped it into her mouth and smiled at Rogette as if they'd been friends since forever.

"By then Devore had his breath back, but he looked tired — the most tired man I've ever seen. He reminded me of something in the Bible, about how in the days of our old age we say we have no pleasure in them. My heart kind of broke for him. Maybe he saw it, because he reached for my hand. He said, 'Don't shut me out.' And at that moment I could see Lance in his face. I started to cry. I said, 'I won't unless you make me.' "

I could see them there in the funeral home's foyer, him sitting, her standing, the little girl looking on in wide-eyed puzzlement as she sucked the sweet Hershey's Kiss. Canned organ music in the background. Poor old Max Devore had been crafty enough on the day of his son's viewing, I thought. Don't shut me out, indeed.

I tried to buy you off and when that didn't work I upped the stakes and tried to buy the baby. When that also failed, I told my son that you and he and my grandchild could choke on the dirt of your own decision. In a way, I'm the reason he was where he was when he fell and broke his neck, but don't shut me out, Mattie, I'm just a poor old geezer, so don't shut me out.

"I was stupid, wasn't I?"

"You expected him to be better than he was. If that makes you stupid, Mattie, the world could use more of it."

"I *did* have my doubts," she said. "It's why I wouldn't take any of his money, and by last October he'd quit asking. But I let him see her. I suppose, yeah, part of it was the idea there might be something in it for Ki later on, but I honestly didn't think about that so much. Mostly it was him being her only blood link to her father. I wanted her to enjoy that the way any kid enjoys having a grandparent. What I didn't want was for her to be infected by all the crap that went on before Lance died.

"At first it seemed to be working. Then, little by little, things changed. I realized that Ki didn't like her 'white poppa' so much, for one thing. Her feelings about Rogette are the same, but Max Devore's started to make her nervous in some way I don't understand and she can't explain. I asked her once if he'd ever touched her anywhere that made her feel funny. I showed her the places I meant, and she said no. I believe her, but . . . he said something or did something. I'm almost sure of it."

"Could be no more than the sound of his breathing getting worse," I said. "That alone might be enough to scare a child. Or maybe he had some kind of spell while she was there. What about you, Mattie?"

"Well . . . one day in February Lindy Briggs told me that George Footman had been in to check the fire extinguishers and the smoke detectors in the library. He also asked if Lindy had found any beer cans or liquor bottles in the trash lately. Or cigarette butts that were obviously homemade."

"Roaches, in other words."

"Uh-huh. And Dickie Osgood has been visiting my old friends, I hear. Chatting. Panning for gold. Digging the dirt."

"Is there any to dig?"

"Not much, thank God."

I hoped she was right, and I hoped that if there was stuff she wasn't telling me, John Storrow would get it out of her.

"But through all this you let Ki go on seeing him."

"What would pulling the plug on the visits have accomplished? And I thought that allowing them to go on would at least keep him from speeding up any plans he might have."

That, I thought, made a lonely kind of sense.

"Then, in the spring, I started to get some extremely creepy, scary feelings."

"Creepy how? Scary how?"

"I don't know." She took out her cigarettes, looked at them, then stuffed the pack back in her pocket. "It wasn't just that my father-in-law was looking for dirty laundry in my closets, either. It was Ki. I started to worry about Ki all the time she was with him . . . with *them*. Rogette would come in the BMW they'd bought or leased, and Ki would be sitting out on the steps waiting for her. With her bag of toys if it was a day-visit, with her little pink Minnie Mouse suitcase if it was an overnight. And she'd always come back with one more thing than she left with. My father-in-law's a great believer in presents. Before popping her into the car, Rogette would give me that cold little smile of hers and say, 'Seven o'clock then, we'll give her supper' or 'Eight o'clock then, and a nice hot breakfast before she leaves.' I'd say okay, and then Rogette would reach into her bag and hold out a Hershey's Kiss to Ki just the way you'd hold a biscuit out to a dog to make it shake hands. She'd say a word and Kyra would rhyme it. Rogette would toss her her treat — woof-woof, good dog, I always used to think — and off they'd go. Come seven in the evening or eight in the morning, the BMW would pull in right where your car's parked now. You could set your clock by the woman. But I got worried."

"That they might get tired of the legal process and just snatch her?" This seemed to me a reasonable concern — so reasonable I could hardly believe Mattie had ever let her little girl go to the old man in the first place. In custody cases, as in the rest of life, possession tends to be nine tenths of the law, and if Mattie was telling the truth about her past and present, a custody hearing was apt to turn into a tiresome production even for the rich Mr. Devore. Snatching might, in the end, look like a more efficient solution.

"Not exactly," she said. "I guess it's the logical thing, but that wasn't really it. I just got afraid. There was nothing I could put my finger on. It would get to be quarter past six in the evening and I'd think, 'This time that white-haired bitch isn't going to bring her back. This time she's going to . . .' "

I waited. When nothing came I said, "Going to what?"

"I told you, I don't know," she said. "But I've been afraid for Ki since spring. By the time June came around, I couldn't stand it anymore, and I put a stop to the visits.

Kyra's been off-and-on pissed at me ever since. I'm pretty sure that's most of what that Fourth of July escapade was about. She doesn't talk about her grandfather very much, but she's always popping out with 'What do you think the white nana's doing now, Mattie?' or 'Do you think the white nana would like my new dress?' Or she'll run up to me and say 'Sing, ring, king, thing,' and ask for a treat."

"What was the reaction from Devore?"

"Complete fury. He called again and again, first asking what was wrong, then making threats."

"Physical threats?"

"Custody threats. He was going to take her away, when he was finished with me I'd stand before the whole world as an unfit mother, I didn't have a chance, my only hope was to relent and *let me see my grand-daughter, goddammit.*"

I nodded. " 'Please don't shut me out' doesn't sound like the guy who called while I was watching the fireworks, but that does."

"I've also gotten calls from Dickie Osgood, and a number of other locals," she said. "Including Lance's old friend Richie Lattimore. Richie said I wasn't being true to Lance's memory."

"What about George Footman?"

"He cruises by once in awhile. Lets me know he's watching. He hasn't called or stopped in. You asked about physical threats — just seeing Footman's cruiser on my road feels like a physical threat to me. He scares me. But these days it seems as if everything does."

"Even though Kyra's visits have stopped."

"Even though. It feels . . . thundery. Like something's going to happen. And every day that feeling seems to get stronger."

"John Storrow's number," I said. "Do you want it?"

She sat quietly, looking into her lap. Then she raised her head and nodded. "Give it to me. And thank you. From the bottom of my heart."

I had the number on a pink memo-slip in my front pocket. She grasped it but did not immediately take it. Our fingers were touching, and she was looking at me with disconcerting steadiness. It was as if she knew more about my motives than I did myself.

"What can I do to repay you?" she asked, and there it was.

"Tell Storrow everything you've told me." I let go of the pink slip and stood up. "That'll do just fine. And now I have to get along. Will you call and tell me how you made out with him?"

"Of course."

We walked to my car. I turned to her when we got there. For a moment I thought she was going to put her arms around me and hug me, a thank-you gesture that might have led anywhere in our current mood — one so heightened it was almost melodramatic. But it was a melodramatic situation, a fairy tale where there's good and bad and a lot of repressed sex running under both.

Then headlights appeared over the brow of the hill where the market stood and swept past the All-Purpose Garage. They moved toward us, brightening. Mattie stood back and actually put her hands behind her, like a child who has been scolded. The car passed, leaving us in the dark again . . . but the moment had passed, too. If there had been a moment.

"Thanks for dinner," I said. "It was wonderful."

"Thanks for the lawyer, I'm sure he'll be wonderful, too," she said, and we both laughed. The electricity went out of the air. "He spoke of you once, you know. Devore."

I looked at her in surprise. "I'm amazed he even knew who I was. Before this, I mean."

"He knows, all right. He spoke of you with what I think was genuine affection."

"You're kidding. You must be."

"I'm not. He said that your great-grand-father and his great-grandfather worked the same camps and were neighbors when they weren't in the woods — I think he said not far from where Boyd's Marina is now. 'They shit in the same pit,' is the way he put it. Charming, huh? He said he guessed that if a couple of loggers from the TR could produce millionaires, the system was working the way it was supposed to. 'Even if it took three generations to do it,' he said. At the time I took it as a veiled criticism of Lance."

"It's ridiculous, however he meant it," I said. "My family is from the coast. Prout's Neck. Other side of the state. My dad was a fisherman and so was his father before him. My great-grandfather, too. They trapped lobsters and threw nets, they didn't cut trees." All that was true, and yet my mind tried to fix on something. Some memory connected to what she was saying. Perhaps if I slept on it, it would come back to me.

"Could he have been talking about someone in your wife's family?"

"Nope. There are Arlens in Maine — they're a big family — but most are still in Massachusetts. They do all sorts of things now, but if you go back to the eighteen-eighties, the majority would have been quarrymen and stonecutters in the Malden–Lynn area. Devore was pulling your leg, Mattie." But even then I suppose I knew he wasn't. He might have gotten some part of the story wrong — even the sharpest guys begin to lose the edge of their recollection by the time they turn eighty-five — but Max

Devore wasn't much of a leg-puller. I had an image of unseen cables stretching beneath the surface of the earth here on the TR — stretching in all directions, unseen but very powerful.

My hand was resting on top of my car door, and now she touched it briefly. "Can I ask you one other question before you go? It's stupid, I warn you."

"Go ahead. Stupid questions are a specialty of mine."

"Do you have any idea at *all* what that 'Bartleby' story is about?"

I wanted to laugh, but there was enough moonlight for me to see she was serious, and that I'd hurt her feelings if I did. She was a member of Lindy Briggs's readers' circle (where I had once spoken in the late eighties), probably the youngest by at least twenty years, and she was afraid of appearing stupid.

"I have to speak first next time," she said, "and I'd like to give more than just a summary of the story so they know I've read it. I've thought about it until my head aches, and I just don't see. I doubt if it's one of those stories where everything comes magically clear in the last few pages, either. And I feel like I *should* see — that it's right there in front of me."

That made me think of the cables again — cables running in every direction, a subcutaneous webwork connecting people and places. You couldn't see them, but you could feel them. Especially if you tried to get away. Meanwhile Mattie was waiting, looking at me with hope and anxiety.

"Okay, listen up, school's in session," I said.

"I am. Believe me."

"Most critics think *Huckleberry Finn* is the first modern American novel, and that's fair enough, but if 'Bartleby' were a hundred pages longer, I think I'd put my money there. Do you know what a scrivener was?"

"A secretary?"

"That's too grand. A copyist. Sort of like Bob Cratchit in *A Christmas Carol.* Only Dickens gives Bob a past and a family life. Melville gives Bartleby neither. He's the first existential character in American fiction, a guy with no ties . . . no ties to, you know . . ."

A couple of loggers who could produce millionaires. They shit in the same pit.

"Mike?"

"What?"

"Are you okay?"

"Sure." I focused my mind as best I could. "Bartleby is tied to life only by work. In that way he's a twentieth-century American type, not much different from Sloan Wilson's Man in the Gray Flannel Suit, or — in the dark version — Michael Corleone

351

in *The Godfather*. But then Bartleby begins to question even work, the god of middle-class American males."

She looked excited now, and I thought it was a shame she'd missed her last year of high school. For her and also for her teachers. "That's why he starts saying 'I prefer not to'?"

"Yes. Think of Bartleby as a . . . a hot-air balloon. Only one rope still tethers him to the earth, and that rope is his scrivening. We can measure the rot in that last rope by the steadily increasing number of things Bartleby prefers not to do. Finally the rope breaks and Bartleby floats away. It's a goddam disturbing story, isn't it?"

"One night I dreamed about him," she said. "I opened the trailer door and there he was, sitting on the steps in his old black suit. Thin. Not much hair. I said, 'Will you move, please? I have to go out and hang the clothes now.' And he said, 'I prefer not to.' Yes, I guess you could call it disturbing."

"Then it still works," I said, and got into my car. "Call me. Tell me how it goes with John Storrow."

"I will. And anything I can do to repay, just ask."

Just ask. How young did you have to be, how beautifully ignorant, to issue that kind of blank check?

My window was open. I reached through

it and squeezed her hand. She squeezed back, and hard.

"You miss your wife a lot, don't you?" she said.

"It shows?"

"Sometimes." She was no longer squeezing, but she was still holding my hand. "When you were reading to Ki, you looked both happy and sad at the same time. I only saw her once, your wife, but I thought she was very beautiful."

I had been thinking about the touch of our hands, concentrating on that. Now I forgot about it entirely. "When did you see her? And where? Do you remember?"

She smiled as if those were very silly questions. "I remember. It was at the ballfield, on the night I met my husband."

Very slowly I withdrew my hand from hers. So far as I knew, neither Jo nor I had been near TR-90 all that summer of '94 . . . but what I knew was apparently wrong. Jo had been down on a Tuesday in early July. She had even gone to the softball game.

"Are you sure it was Jo?" I asked.

Mattie was looking off toward the road. It wasn't my wife she was thinking about; I would have bet the house and lot on it — either house, either lot. It was Lance. Maybe that was good. If she was thinking about him, she probably wouldn't look too closely at me, and I didn't think I had much control of my expression just then. She might have seen more on my face than I wanted to show.

"Yes," she said. "I was standing with Jenna McCoy and Helen Geary — this was after Lance helped me with a keg of beer I got stuck in the mud and then asked if I was going for pizza with the rest of them after the game — and Jenna said, 'Look, it's Mrs. Noonan,' and Helen said, 'She's the writer's wife, Mattie, isn't that a cool blouse?' The blouse was all covered with blue roses."

I remembered it very well. Jo liked it because it was a joke — there *are* no blue roses, not in nature and not in cultivation. Once when she was wearing it she had thrown her arms extravagantly around my neck, swooned her hips forward against mine, and cried that she was my blue rose and I must stroke her until she turned pink. Remembering that hurt, and badly.

"She was over on the third-base side, behind the chickenwire screen," Mattie said, "with some guy who was wearing an old brown jacket with patches on the elbows. They were laughing together over something, and then she turned her head a little and looked right at me." She was quiet for a moment, standing there beside my car in her red dress. She raised her hair off the back of her neck, held it, then let it drop again. "Right *at* me. Really seeing me. And she had a look about her . . . she'd just been laughing but this look was sad, somehow. It was as if she knew me. Then the guy put his arm around her waist and they walked away."

Silence except for the crickets and the far-off drone of a truck. Mattie only stood there for a moment, as if dreaming with her eyes open, and then she felt something and looked back at me.

"Is something wrong?"

"No. Except who was this guy with his arm around my wife?"

She laughed a little uncertainly. "Well I doubt if he was her boyfriend, you know. He was quite a bit older. Fifty, at least." *So what?* I thought. I myself was forty, but that didn't mean I had missed the way Mattie moved inside her dress, or lifted her hair from the nape of her neck. "I mean . . . you're kidding, right?"

"I don't really know. There's a lot of things I don't know these days, it seems. But the lady's dead in any case, so how can it matter?"

Mattie was looking distressed. "If I put my foot in something, Mike, I'm sorry."

"Who *was* the man? Do you know?"

She shook her head. "I thought he was a summer person — there was that feeling about him, maybe just because he was wearing a jacket on a hot summer evening

— but if he was, he wasn't staying at Warrington's. I knew most of them."

"And they walked off together?"

"Yes." Sounding reluctant.

"Toward the parking lot?"

"Yes." More reluctant still. And this time she was lying. I knew it with a queer certainty that went far beyond intuition; it was almost like mind-reading.

I reached through the window and took her hand again. "You said if I could think of anything you could do to repay me, to just ask. I'm asking. Tell me the truth, Mattie."

She bit her lip, looking down at my hand lying over hers. Then she looked up at my face. "He was a burly guy. The old sportcoat made him look a little like a college professor, but he could have been a carpenter for all I know. His hair was black. He had a tan. They had a laugh together, a good one, and then she looked at me and the laugh went out of her face. After that he put an arm around her and they walked away." She paused. "Not toward the parking lot, though. Toward The Street."

The Street. From there they could have walked north along the edge of the lake until they came to Sara Laughs. And then? Who knew?

"She never told me she came down here that summer," I said.

Mattie seemed to try several responses

and find none of them to her liking. I gave her her hand back. It was time for me to go. In fact I had started to wish I'd left five minutes sooner.

"Mike, I'm sure —"

"No," I said. "You're not. Neither am I. But I loved her a lot and I'm going to try and let this go. It probably signifies nothing, and besides — what else can I do? Thanks for dinner."

"You're welcome." Mattie looked so much like crying that I picked her hand up again and kissed the back of it. "I feel like a dope."

"You're not a dope," I said.

I gave her hand another kiss, then drove away. And that was my date, the first one in four years.

Driving home I thought of an old saying about how one person can never truly know another. It's easy to give that idea lip service, but it's a jolt — as horrible and unexpected as severe air turbulence on a previously calm airline flight — to discover it's a literal fact in one's own life. I kept remembering our visit to a fertility doc after we'd been trying to make a baby for almost two years with no success. The doctor had told us I had a low sperm count — not disastrously low, but down enough to account for Jo's failure to conceive.

"If you want a kid, you'll likely have one without any special help," the doc had said. "Both the odds and time are still on your side. It could happen tomorrow or it could happen four years from now. Will you ever fill the house with babies? Probably not. But you might have two, and you'll almost certainly have one if you keep doing the thing that makes them." She had grinned. "Remember, the pleasure is in the journey."

There had been a lot of pleasure, all right, many ringings of Bunter's bell, but there had been no baby. Then Johanna had died running across a shopping-center parking lot on a hot day, and one of the items in her bag had been a Norco Home Pregnancy Test which she had not told me she had intended to buy. No more than she'd told me she had bought a couple of plastic owls to keep the crows from shitting on the lakeside deck.

What else hadn't she told me?

"Stop," I muttered. "For Christ's sake stop thinking about it."

But I couldn't.

When I got back to Sara, the fruit and vegetable magnets on the refrigerator were in a circle again. Three letters had been clustered in the middle:

g d
o

I moved the *o* up to where I thought it belonged, making "god" or maybe an abridged version of "good." Which meant exactly what? "I could speculate about that, but I prefer not to," I told the empty house. I looked at Bunter the moose, willing the bell around his moth-eaten neck to ring. When it didn't, I opened my two new Magnabet packages and stuck the letters on the fridge door, spreading them out. Then I went down to the north wing, undressed, and brushed my teeth.

As I bared my fangs for the mirror in a sudsy cartoon scowl, I considered calling Ward Hankins again tomorrow morning. I could tell him that my search for the elusive plastic owls had progressed from November of 1993 to July of 1994. What meetings had Jo put on her calendar for that month? What excuses to be out of Derry? And once I had finished with Ward, I could tackle Jo's friend Bonnie Amudson, ask her if anything had been going on with Jo in the last summer of her life.

Let her rest in peace, why don't you? It was the UFO voice. *What good will it do you to do otherwise? Assume she popped over to the TR after one of her board meetings, maybe just on a whim, met an old friend, took him back to the house for a bite of dinner.* Just *dinner.*

And never told me? I asked the UFO voice, spitting out a mouthful of toothpaste and then rinsing. *Never said a single word?*

How do you know she didn't? the voice returned, and that froze me in the act of putting my toothbrush back in the medicine cabinet. The UFO voice had a point. I had been deep into *All the Way from the Top* by July of '94. Jo could have come in and told me she'd seen Lon Chaney Junior dancing with the queen, doing the Werewolves of London, and I probably would have said "Uh-huh, honey, that's nice" as I went on proofing copy.

"Bullshit," I said to my reflection. "That's just bullshit."

Except it wasn't. When I was really driving on a book I more or less fell out of the world; other than a quick scan of the sports pages, I didn't even read the newspaper. So yes — it *was* possible that Jo had told me she'd run over to the TR after a board meeting in Lewiston or Freeport, it *was* possible that she'd told me she'd run into an old friend — perhaps another student from the photography seminar she'd attended at Bates in 1991 — and it *was* possible she'd told me they'd had dinner together on our deck, eating black trumpet mushrooms she'd picked herself as the sun went down. It was possible she'd told me these things and I hadn't registered a word of what she was saying.

And did I really think I'd get anything I

could trust out of Bonnie Amudson? She'd been Jo's friend, not mine, and Bonnie might feel the statute of limitations hadn't run out on any secrets my wife had told her.

The bottom line was as simple as it was brutal: Jo was four years dead. Best to love her and let all troubling questions lapse. I took a final mouthful of water directly from the tap, swished it around in my mouth, and spat it out.

When I returned to the kitchen to set the coffee-maker for seven A.M., I saw a new message in a new circle of magnets. It read

`blue rose liar ha ha`

I looked at it for a second or two, wondering what had put it there, and why.

Wondering if it was true.

I stretched out a hand and scattered all the letters far and wide. Then I went to bed.

Chapter 13

I caught the measles when I was eight, and I was very ill. "I thought you were going to die," my father told me once, and he was not a man given to exaggeration. He told me about how he and my mother had dunked me in a tub of cold water one night, both of them at least half-convinced the shock of it would stop my heart, but both of them completely convinced that I'd burn up before their eyes if they didn't do *something*. I had begun to speak in a loud, monotonously discursive voice about the bright figures I saw in the room — angels come to bear me away, my terrified mother was sure — and the last time my father took my temperature before the cold plunge, he said that the mercury on the old Johnson & Johnson rectal thermometer had stood at a hundred and six degrees. After that, he said, he didn't dare take it anymore.

I don't remember any bright figures, but I remember a strange period of time that was like being in a funhouse corridor where several different movies were showing at once. The world grew elastic, bulging in places where it had never bulged before, wavering in places where it had always been solid. People — most of them seeming impossibly tall — darted in and out of my room on scissoring, cartoonish legs. Their words all came out booming, with instant echoes. Someone shook a pair of baby-shoes in my face. I seem to remember my brother, Siddy, sticking his hand into his shirt and making repeated arm-fart noises. Continuity broke down. Everything came in segments, weird wieners on a poison string.

In the years between then and the summer I returned to Sara Laughs, I had the usual sicknesses, infections, and insults to the body, but never anything like that feverish interlude when I was eight. I never expected to — believing, I suppose, that such experiences are unique to children, people with malaria, or maybe those suffering catastrophic mental breakdowns. But on the night of July seventh and the morning of July eighth, I lived through a period of time remarkably like that childhood delirium. Dreaming, waking, moving — they were all one. I'll tell you as best I can, but nothing I say can convey the strangeness of that experience. It was as if I had found a secret passage hidden just beyond the wall of the world and went crawling along it.

First there was music. Not Dixieland, because there were no horns, but *like* Dixieland. A primitive, reeling kind of bebop. Three or four acoustic guitars, a harmonica, a stand-up bass (or maybe a pair). Behind all of this was a hard, happy drumming that didn't sound as if it was coming from a real drum; it sounded as if someone with a lot of percussive talent was whopping on a bunch of boxes. Then a woman's voice joined in — a contralto voice, not quite mannish, roughing over the high notes. It was laughing and urgent and ominous all at the same time, and I knew at once that I was hearing Sara Tidwell, who had never cut a record in her life. I was hearing Sara Laughs, and man, she was *rocking*.

"You know we're goin back to MANderley,
We're gonna dance on the SANderley,
I'm gonna sing with the BANderley,
We gonna ball all we CANderley —
Ball me, baby, yeah!"

The basses — yes, there were two — broke out in a barnyard shuffle like the break in Elvis's version of "Baby Let's Play House," and then there was a guitar solo: Son Tidwell playing that chickenscratch thing.

Lights gleamed in the dark, and I thought of a song from the fifties — Claudine Clark singing "Party Lights." And here they were, Japanese lanterns hung from the trees above the path of railroad-tie steps leading from the house to the water. Party lights casting mystic circles of radiance in the dark: red blue and green.

Behind me, Sara was singing the bridge to her Manderley song — mama likes it nasty, mama likes it strong, mama likes to party all night long — but it was fading. Sara and the Red-Top Boys had set up their bandstand in the driveway by the sound, about where George Footman had parked when he came to serve me with Max Devore's subpoena. I was descending toward the lake through circles of radiance, past party lights surrounded by soft-winged moths. One had found its way inside a lamp and it cast a monstrous, batlike shadow against the ribbed paper. The flower-boxes Jo had put beside the steps were full of night-blooming roses. In the light of the Japanese lanterns they looked blue.

Now the band was only a faint murmur; I could hear Sara shouting out the lyric, laughing her way through it as though it were the funniest thing she'd ever heard, all that Manderley-sanderley-canderley stuff, but I could no longer make out the individual words. Much clearer was the lap of the lake against the rocks at the foot of the steps, the hollow clunk of the cannisters under the swimming float, and the cry of a loon drifting out of the darkness. Someone was standing on The Street to my right, at the edge of the lake. I couldn't see his face, but I could see the brown sportcoat and the tee-shirt he was wearing beneath it. The lapels cut off some of the letters of the message, so it looked like this:

ORMA

ER

OUN

I knew what it said anyway — in dreams you almost always know, don't you? NORMAL SPERM COUNT, a Village Cafe yuck-it-up special if ever there was one.

I was in the north bedroom dreaming all this, and here I woke up enough to *know* I was dreaming . . . except it was like waking into another dream, because Bunter's bell was ringing madly and there was someone standing in the hall. Mr. Normal Sperm Count? No, not him. The shadow-shape falling on the door wasn't quite human. It was slumped, the arms indistinct. I sat up into the silver shaking of the bell, clutching a loose puddle of sheet against my naked waist, sure it was the shroud-thing out there — the shroud-thing had come out of its grave to get me.

"Please don't," I said in a dry and trembling voice. "Please don't, please."

The shadow on the door raised its arms. *"It ain't nuthin but a barn-dance sugar!"* Sara Tidwell's laughing, furious voice sang. *"It ain't nuthin but a round-and-round!"*

I lay back down and pulled the sheet over my face in a childish act of denial . . . and there I stood on our little lick of beach, wearing just my undershorts. My feet were ankle-deep in the water. It was warm the way the lake gets by midsummer. My dim shadow was cast two ways, in one direction by the scantling moon which rode low above the water, in another by the Japanese lantern with the moth caught inside it. The man who'd been standing on the path was gone but he had left a plastic owl to mark his place. It stared at me with frozen, gold-ringed eyes.

"Hey Irish!"

I looked out at the swimming float. Jo stood there. She must have just climbed out of the water, because she was still dripping and her hair was plastered against her cheeks. She was wearing the two-piece swimsuit from the photo I'd found, gray with red piping.

"It's been a long time, Irish — what do you say?"

"Say about what?" I called back, although I knew.

"About this!" She put her hands over her breasts and squeezed. Water ran out between her fingers and trickled across her knuckles.

"Come on, Irish," she said from beside and above me, "come on, you bastard, let's go." I felt her strip down the sheet, pulling it easily out of my sleep-numbed fingers. I shut my eyes, but she took my hand and placed it between her legs. As I found that velvety seam and began to stroke it open, she began to rub the back of my neck with her fingers.

"You're not Jo," I said. "Who are you?"

But no one was there to answer. I was in the woods. It was dark, and on the lake the loons were crying. I was walking the path to Jo's studio. It wasn't a dream; I could feel the cool air against my skin and the occasional bite of a rock into my bare sole or heel. A mosquito buzzed around my ear and I waved it away. I was wearing Jockey shorts, and at every step they pulled against a huge and throbbing erection.

"What the hell is this?" I asked as Jo's little barnboard studio loomed in the dark. I looked behind me and saw Sara on her hill, not the woman but the house, a long lodge jutting toward the nightbound lake. "What's happening to me?"

"Everything's all right, Mike," Jo said. She was standing on the float, watching as I swam toward her. She put her hands behind her neck like a calendar model, lifting her breasts more fully into the damp halter. As in the photo, I could see her nipples poking out the cloth. I was swimming in my underpants, and with the same huge erection.

"Everything's all right, Mike," Mattie said in the north bedroom, and I opened my eyes. She was sitting beside me on the bed, smooth and naked in the weak glow of the nightlight. Her hair was down, hanging to her shoulders. Her breasts were tiny, the size of teacups, but the nipples were large and distended. Between her legs, where my hand still lingered, was a powderpuff of blonde hair, smooth as down. Her body was wrapped in shadows like moth-wings, like rose-petals. There was something desperately attractive about her as she sat there — she was like the prize you know you'll never win at the carny shooting gallery or the county fair ringtoss. The one they keep on the top shelf. She reached under the sheet and folded her fingers over the stretched material of my undershorts.

Everything's all right, it ain't nuthin but a round-and-round, said the UFO voice as I climbed the steps to my wife's studio. I stooped, fished for the key from beneath the mat, and took it out.

I climbed the ladder to the float, wet and dripping, preceded by my engorged sex — is there anything, I wonder, so unintentionally comic as a sexually aroused man? Jo stood on the boards in her wet bathing suit. I pulled Mattie into bed with me. I opened the door to Jo's studio. All of these things happened at the same time, weaving in and out of each other like strands of some exotic rope or belt. The thing with Jo felt the most like a dream, the thing in the studio, me crossing the floor and looking down at my old green IBM, the least. Mattie in the north bedroom was somewhere in between.

On the float Jo said, "Do what you want." In the north bedroom Mattie said, "Do what you want." In the studio, no one had to tell me anything. In there I knew *exactly* what I wanted.

On the float I bent my head and put my mouth on one of Jo's breasts and sucked the cloth-covered nipple into my mouth. I tasted damp fabric and dank lake. She reached for me where I stuck out and I slapped her hand away. If she touched me I would come at once. I sucked, drinking back trickles of cotton-water, groping with my own hands, first caressing her ass and then yanking down the bottom half of her suit. I got it off her and she dropped to her knees. I did too, finally getting rid of my wet, clinging underpants and tossing them on top of her bikini panty. We faced each other that way, me naked, her almost.

"Who was the guy at the game?" I panted. "Who was he, Jo?"

"No one in particular, Irish. Just another bag of bones."

She laughed, then leaned back on her haunches and stared at me. Her navel was a tiny black cup. There was something queerly, attractively snakelike in her posture. "Everything down there is death," she said, and pressed her cold palms and white, pruney fingers to my cheeks. She turned my head and then bent it so I was looking into the lake. Under the water I saw decomposing bodies slipping by, pulled by some deep current. Their wet eyes stared. Their fish-nibbled noses gaped. Their tongues lolled between white lips like tendrils of waterweed. Some of the dead trailed pallid balloons of jellyfish guts; some were little more than bone. Yet not even the sight of this floating charnel parade could divert me from what I wanted. I shrugged my head free of her hands, pushed her down on the boards, and finally cooled what was so hard and contentious, sinking it deep. Her moon-silvered eyes stared up at me, through me, and I saw that one pupil was larger than the other. That was how her eyes had looked on the TV monitor when I had identified her in the Derry County Morgue. She was dead. My wife was dead and I was fucking her corpse. Nor could even that realization stop me. "Who was he?" I cried at her, covering her cold flesh as it lay on the wet boards. "Who was he, Jo, for Christ's sake tell me who he was!"

In the north bedroom I pulled Mattie on top of me, relishing the feel of those small breasts against my chest and the length of her entwining legs. Then I rolled her over on the far side of the bed. I felt her hand reaching for me, and slapped it away — if she touched me where she meant to touch me, I would come in an instant. "Spread your legs, hurry," I said, and she did. I closed my eyes, shutting out all other sensory input in favor of this. I pressed forward, then stopped. I made one little adjustment, pushing at my engorged penis with the side of my hand, then rolled my hips and slipped into her like a finger in a silk-lined glove. She looked up at me, wide-eyed, then put a hand on my cheek and turned my head. "Everything out there is death," she said, as if only explaining the obvious. In the window I saw Fifth Avenue between Fiftieth and Sixtieth — all those trendy shops, Bijan and Bally, Tiffany and Bergdorf's and Steuben Glass. And here came Harold Oblowski, northbound and swinging his pigskin briefcase (the one Jo and I had given him for Christmas the year before she died). Beside him, carrying a Barnes and Noble bag by the handles, was the bountiful, beauteous Nola, his secretary. Except her bounty was gone. This was a grinning, yellow-jawed skeleton in a Donna Karan suit and alligator pumps; scrawny, beringed bones instead of fingers gripped the bag-handles. Harold's teeth jutted in his usual agent's grin, now extended to the point of obscenity. His favorite suit, the doublebreasted charcoal-gray from Paul Stuart, flapped on him like a sail in a fresh breeze. All around them, on both sides of the street, walked the living dead — mommy mummies leading baby corpses by the hands or wheeling them in expensive prams, zombie doormen, reanimated skateboarders. Here a tall black man with a last few strips of flesh hanging from his face like cured deer-hide walked his skeletal Alsatian. The cab-drivers were rotting to raga music. The faces looking down from the passing buses were skulls, each wearing its own version of Harold's grin — *Hey, how are ya, how's the wife, how's the kids, writing any good books lately?* The peanut vendors were putrefying. Yet none of it could quench me. I was on fire. I slipped my hands under her buttocks, lifting her, biting at the sheet (the pattern, I saw with no surprise, was blue roses) until I pulled it free of the mattress to keep from biting her on the neck, the shoulder, the breasts, anywhere my teeth could reach. "Tell me who he was!" I shouted at her. "You know, I know you do!" My voice was so muffled by my mouthful of bed-linen that I doubted if anyone but me could have understood it. "Tell me, you bitch!"

On the path between Jo's studio and the

house I stood in the dark with the typewriter in my arms and that dream-spanning erection quivering below its metal bulk — all that ready and nothing willing. Except maybe for the night breeze. Then I became aware I was no longer alone. The shroud-thing was behind me, called like the moths to the party lights. It laughed — a brazen, smoke-broken laugh that could belong to only one woman. I didn't see the hand that reached around my hip to grip me — the typewriter was in the way — but I didn't need to see it to know its color was brown. It squeezed, slowly tightening, the fingers wriggling.

"What do you want to know, sugar?" she asked from behind me. Still laughing. Still teasing. "Do you really want to know at all? Do you want to know or do you want to feel?"

"Oh, you're killing me!" I cried. The typewriter — thirty or so pounds of IBM Selectric — was shaking back and forth in my arms. I could feel my muscles twanging like guitar strings.

"Do you want to know who he was, sugar? That nasty man?"

"Just do me, you bitch!" I screamed. She laughed again — that harsh laughter that was almost like a cough — and squeezed me where the squeezing was best.

"You hold still, now," she said. "You hold

still, pretty boy, 'less you want me to take fright and yank this thing of yours right out by the . . ." I lost the rest as the whole world exploded in an orgasm so deep and strong that I thought it would simply tear me apart. I snapped my head back like a man being hung and ejaculated looking up at the stars. I screamed — I had to — and on the lake, two loons screamed back.

At the same time I was on the float. Jo was gone, but I could faintly hear the sound of the band — Sara and Sonny and the Red-Top Boys tearing through "Black Mountain Rag." I sat up, dazed and spent, fucked hollow. I couldn't see the path leading up to the house, but I could discern its switchback course by the Japanese lanterns. My underpants lay beside me in a little wet heap. I picked them up and started to put them on, only because I didn't want to swim back to shore with them in my hand. I stopped with them stretched between my knees, looking at my fingers. They were slimed with decaying flesh. Puffing out from beneath several of the nails were clumps of torn-out hair. Corpsehair.

"Oh Jesus," I moaned. The strength went out of me. I flopped into wetness. I was in the north-wing bedroom. What I had landed in was hot, and at first I thought it was come. The dim glow of the nightlight showed darker stuff, however. Mattie was gone and the bed was full of blood. Lying in the middle of that soaking pool was something I at first glance took to be a clump of flesh or a piece of organ. I looked more closely and saw it was a stuffed animal, a black-furred object matted red with blood. I lay on my side looking at it, wanting to bolt out of the bed and flee from the room but unable to do it. My muscles were in a dead swoon. Who had I really been having sex with in this bed? And what had I done to her? In God's name, what?

"I don't believe these lies," I heard myself say, and as though it were an incantation, I was slapped back together. That isn't exactly what happened, but it's the only way of saying that seems to come close to whatever did. There were three of me — one on the float, one in the north bedroom, one on the path — and each one felt that hard slap, as if the wind had grown a fist. There was rushing blackness, and in it the steady silver shaking of Bunter's bell. Then it faded, and I faded with it. For a little while I was nowhere at all.

I came back to the casual chatter of birds on summer vacation and to that peculiar red darkness that means the sun is shining through your closed eyelids. My neck was stiff, my head was canted at a weird angle, my legs were folded awkwardly beneath me, and I was hot.

I lifted my head with a wince, knowing even as I opened my eyes that I was no longer in bed, no longer on the swimming float, no longer on the path between the house and the studio. It was floorboards under me, hard and uncompromising.

The light was dazzling. I squinched my eyes closed again and groaned like a man with a hangover. I eased them back open behind my cupped hands, gave them time to adjust, then cautiously uncovered them, sat all the way up, and looked around. I was in the upstairs hall, lying under the broken air conditioner. Mrs. Meserve's note still hung from it. Sitting outside my office door was the green IBM with a piece of paper rolled into it. I looked down at my feet and saw that they were dirty. Pine needles were stuck to my soles, and one toe was scratched. I got up, staggered a little (my right leg had gone to sleep), then braced a hand against the wall and stood steady. I looked down at myself. I was wearing the Jockeys I'd gone to bed in, and I didn't look as if I'd had an accident in them. I pulled out the waistband and peeked inside. My cock looked as it usually did; small and soft, curled up and asleep in its thatch of hair. If Noonan's Folly had been adventuring in the night, there was no sign of it now.

"It sure felt like an adventure," I croaked.

I armed sweat off my forehead. It was stifling up here. "Not the kind I ever read about in *The Hardy Boys*, though."

Then I remembered the blood-soaked sheet in the north bedroom, and the stuffed animal lying on its side in the middle of it. There was no sense of relief attached to the memory, that thank-God-it-was-only-a-dream feeling you get after a particularly nasty nightmare. It felt as real as any of the things I'd experienced in my measles fever-delirium . . . and all those things *had* been real, just distorted by my overheated brain.

I staggered to the stairs and limped down them, holding tight to the bannister in case my tingling leg should buckle. At the foot I looked dazedly around the living room, as if seeing it for the first time, and then limped down the north-wing corridor.

The bedroom door was ajar and for a moment I couldn't bring myself to push it all the way open and go in. I was very badly scared, and my mind kept trying to replay an old episode of *Alfred Hitchcock Presents*, the one about the man who strangles his wife during an alcoholic blackout. He spends the whole half hour looking for her, and finally finds her in the pantry, bloated and open-eyed. Kyra Devore was the only kid of stuffed-animal age I'd met recently, but she had been sleeping peacefully under her cabbage-rose coverlet when I left her mother and headed home. It was stupid to think I had driven all the way back to Wasp Hill Road, probably wearing nothing but my Jockeys, that I had —

What? Raped the woman? Brought the child here? In my sleep?

I got the typewriter, in my sleep, didn't I? It's sitting right upstairs in the goddam hallway.

Big difference between going thirty yards through the woods and five miles down the road to —

I wasn't going to stand out here listening to those quarrelling voices in my head. If I wasn't crazy — and I didn't think I was — listening to those contentious assholes would probably send me there, and by the express. I reached out and pushed the bedroom door open.

For a moment I actually *saw* a spreading octopus-pattern of blood soaking into the sheet, that's how real and focused my terror was. Then I closed my eyes tight, opened them, and looked again. The sheets were rumpled, the bottom one mostly pulled free. I could see the quilted satin hide of the mattress. One pillow lay on the far edge of the bed. The other was scrunched down at the foot. The throw rug — a piece of Jo's work — was askew, and my water-glass lay overturned on the nighttable. The bedroom looked as if it might have been the site of a brawl or an orgy, but not a murder. There was no blood and no little stuffed animal with black fur.

I dropped to my knees and looked under the bed. Nothing there — not even dust-kitties, thanks to Brenda Meserve. I looked at the ground-sheet again, first passing a hand over its rumpled topography, then pulling it back down and resecuring the elasticized corners. Great invention, those sheets; if women gave out the Medal of Freedom instead of a bunch of white politicians who never made a bed or washed a load of clothes in their lives, the guy who thought up fitted sheets would undoubtedly have gotten a piece of that tin by now. In a Rose Garden ceremony.

With the sheet pulled taut, I looked again. No blood, not a single drop. There was no stiffening patch of semen, either. The former I hadn't really expected (or so I was already telling myself), but what about the latter? At the very least, I'd had the world's most creative wet-dream — a triptych in which I had screwed two women and gotten a handjob from a third, all at the same time. I thought I had that morning-after feeling, too, the one you get when the previous night's sex has been of the headbusting variety. But if there had been fireworks, where was the burnt gunpowder?

"In Jo's studio, most likely," I told the

empty, sunny room. "Or on the path between here and there. Just be glad you didn't leave it in Mattie Devore, bucko. An affair with a post-adolescent widow you don't need."

A part of me disagreed; a part of me thought Mattie Devore was exactly what I *did* need. But I hadn't had sex with her last night, any more than I had had sex with my dead wife out on the swimming float or gotten a handjob from Sara Tidwell. Now that I saw I hadn't killed a nice little kid either, my thoughts turned back to the typewriter. Why had I gotten it? Why bother?

Oh man. What a silly question. My wife might have been keeping secrets from me, maybe even having an affair; there might be ghosts in the house; there might be a rich old man half a mile south who wanted to put a sharp stick into me and then break it off; there might be a few toys in my own humble attic, for that matter. But as I stood there in a bright shaft of sunlight, looking at my shadow on the far wall, only one thought seemed to matter: I had gone out to my wife's studio and gotten my old typewriter, and there was only one reason to do something like that.

I went into the bathroom, wanting to get rid of the sweat on my body and the dirt on my feet before doing anything else. I reached for the shower-handle, then stopped. The tub was full of water. Either I had for some reason filled it during my sleepwalk . . . or something else had. I reached for the drain-lever, then stopped again, remembering that moment on the shoulder of Route 68 when my mouth had filled up with the taste of cold water. I realized I was waiting for it to happen again. When it didn't, I opened the bathtub drain to let out the standing water and started the shower.

I could have brought the Selectric downstairs, perhaps even lugged it out onto the deck where there was a little breeze coming over the surface of the lake, but I didn't. I had brought it all the way to the door of my office, and my office was where I'd work . . . if I *could* work. I'd work in there even if the temperature beneath the roofpeak built to a hundred and twenty degrees . . . which, by three in the afternoon, it just might.

The paper rolled into the machine was an old pink-carbon receipt from Click!, the photo shop in Castle Rock where Jo had bought her supplies when we were down here. I'd put it in so that the blank side faced the Courier type-ball. On it I had typed the names of my little harem, as if I had tried in some struggling way to report on my three-faceted dream even while it was going on:

```
    Jo Sara Mattie Jo Sara Mattie
      Mattie Mattie Sara Sara
Jo Johanna Sara Jo MattieSaraJo.
```

Below this, in lower case:

```
normal sperm count sperm norm
         all's rosy
```

I opened the office door, carried the type-writer in, and put it in its old place beneath the poster of Richard Nixon. I pulled the pink slip out of the roller, balled it up, and tossed it into the wastebasket. Then I picked up the Selectric's plug and stuck it in the baseboard socket. My heart was beating hard and fast, the way it had when I was thirteen and climbing the ladder to the high board at the Y-pool. I had climbed that ladder three times when I was twelve and then slunk back down it again; once I turned thirteen, there could be no chickening out — I really had to do it.

I thought I'd seen a fan hiding in the far corner of the closet, behind the box marked GADGETS. I started in that direction, then turned around again with a ragged little laugh. I'd had moments of confidence before, hadn't I? Yes. And then the iron bands had clamped around my chest. It would be stupid to get out the fan and then discover I had no business in this room after all.

"Take it easy," I said, "take it easy." But I couldn't, no more than that narrow-chested boy in the ridiculous purple bathing suit had been able to take it easy when he walked to the end of the diving board, the pool so green below him, the upraised faces of the boys and girls in it so small, so *small*.

I bent to one of the drawers on the right side of the desk and pulled so hard it came all the way out. I got my bare foot out of its landing zone just in time and barked a gust of loud, humorless laughter. There was half a ream of paper in the drawer. The edges had that faintly crispy look paper gets when it's been sitting for a long time. I no more than saw it before remembering I had brought my own supply — stuff a good deal fresher than this. I left it where it was and put the drawer back in its hole. It took several tries to get it on its tracks; my hands were shaking.

At last I sat down in my desk chair, hearing the same old creaks as it took my weight and the same old rumble of the casters as I rolled it forward, snugging my legs into the kneehole. Then I sat facing the keyboard, sweating hard, still remembering the high board at the Y, how springy it had been under my bare feet as I walked its length, remembering the echoing quality of the voices below me, remembering the smell of chlorine and the steady low throb of the air-exchangers: *fwung-fwung-fwung-fwung,* as if the water had its own secret heartbeat. I had stood at the end of the board wondering (and not for the first time!) if you could be paralyzed if you hit the water wrong. Probably not, but you could die of fear. There were documented cases of that in *Ripley's Believe It or Not,* which served me as science between the ages of eight and fourteen.

Go on! Jo's voice cried. My version of her voice was usually calm and collected; this time it was shrill. *Stop dithering and go on!*

I reached for the IBM's rocker-switch, now remembering the day I had dropped my Word Six program into the PowerBook's trash. *Goodbye, old pal,* I had thought.

"Please let this work," I said. "Please."

I lowered my hand and flicked the switch. The machine came on. The Courier ball did a preliminary twirl, like a ballet dancer standing in the wings, waiting to go on. I picked up a piece of paper, saw my sweaty fingers were leaving marks, and didn't care. I rolled it into the machine, centered it, then wrote

Chapter One

and waited for the storm to break.

Chapter 14

The ringing of the phone — or, more accurately, the way I *received* the ringing of the phone — was as familiar as the creaks of my chair or the hum of the old IBM Selectric. It seemed to come from far away at first, then to approach like a whistling train coming down on a crossing.

There was no extension in my office or Jo's; the upstairs phone, an old-fashioned rotary-dial, was on a table in the hall between them — in what Jo used to call "no-man's-land." The temperature out there must have been at least ninety degrees, but the air still felt cool on my skin after the office. I was so oiled with sweat that I looked like a slightly pot-bellied version of the muscle-boys I sometimes saw when I was working out.

"Hello?"

"Mike? Did I wake you? Were you sleeping?" It was Mattie, but a different one from last night. This one wasn't afraid or even tentative; this one sounded so happy she was almost bubbling over. It was almost certainly the Mattie who had attracted Lance Devore.

"Not sleeping," I said. "Writing a little."

"Get out! I thought you were retired."

"I thought so, too," I said, "but maybe I was a little hasty. What's going on? You sound over the moon."

"I just got off the phone with John Storrow —"

Really? How long had I been on the second floor, anyway? I looked at my wrist and saw nothing but a pale circle. It was half-past freckles and skin o'clock, as we used to say when we were kids; my watch was downstairs in the north bedroom, probably lying in a puddle of water from my overturned night-glass.

"— his age, and that he can subpoena the other son!"

"Whoa," I said. "You lost me. Go back and slow down."

She did. Telling the hard news didn't take long (it rarely does): Storrow was coming up tomorrow. He would land at County Airport and stay at the Lookout Rock Hotel in Castle View. The two of them would spend most of Friday discussing the case. "Oh, and he found a lawyer for you," she said. "To go with you to your deposition. I think he's from Lewiston."

It all sounded good, but what mattered a lot more than the bare facts was that Mattie had recovered her will to fight. Until this morning (if it *was* still morning; the light coming in the window above the broken air conditioner suggested that if it was, it wouldn't be much longer) I hadn't realized how gloomy the young woman in the red sundress and tidy white sneakers had been. How far down the road to believing she would lose her child.

"This is great. I'm so glad, Mattie."

"And you did it. If you were here, I'd give you the biggest kiss you ever had."

"He told you you could win, didn't he?"

"Yes."

"And you believe him."

"Yes!" Then her voice dropped a little. "He wasn't exactly thrilled when I told him I'd had you over to dinner last night, though."

"No," I said. "I didn't think he would be."

"I told him we ate in the yard and he said we only had to be inside together for sixty seconds to start the gossip."

"I'd say he's got an insultingly low opinion of Yankee lovin," I said, "but of course he's from New York."

She laughed harder than my little joke warranted, I thought. Out of semi-hysterical relief that she now had a couple of protectors? Because the whole subject of sex was a tender one for her just now? Best not to speculate.

"He didn't paddle me too hard about it, but he made it clear that he would if we did it again. When this is over, though, I'm having you for a *real* meal. We'll have everything you like, just the way you like it."

Everything you like, just the way you like it. And she was, by God and Sonny Jesus, completely unaware that what she was saying might have another meaning — I would have bet on it. I closed my eyes for a moment, smiling. Why not smile? Everything she was saying sounded absolutely great, especially once you cleared the confines of Michael Noonan's dirty mind. It sounded like we might have the expected fairy-tale ending, if we could keep our courage and hold our course. And if I could restrain myself from making a pass at a girl young enough to be my daughter . . . outside of my dreams, that was. If I couldn't, I probably deserved whatever I got. But Kyra wouldn't. She was the hood ornament in all this, doomed to go wherever the car took her. If I got any of the wrong ideas, I'd do well to remember that.

"If the judge sends Devore home empty-handed, I'll take you out to Renoir Nights in Portland and buy you nine courses of French chow," I said. "Storrow, too. I'll even spring for the legal beagle I'm dating on Friday. So who's better than me, huh?"

"No one I know," she said, sounding serious. "I'll pay you back for this, Mike. I'm down now, but I won't always be down. If it takes me the rest of my life, I'll pay you back."

"Mattie, you don't have to —"

"I *do*," she said with quiet vehemence. "I *do*. And I have to do something else today, too."

"What's that?" I loved hearing her sound the way she did this morning — so happy and free, like a prisoner who has just been pardoned and let out of jail — but already I was looking longingly at the door to my office. I couldn't do much more today, I'd end up baked like an apple if I tried, but I wanted another page or two, at least. Do what you want, both women had said in my dreams. Do what you want.

"I have to buy Kyra the big teddybear they have at the Castle Rock Wal-Mart," she said. "I'll tell her it's for being a good girl because I can't tell her it's for walking in the middle of the road when you were coming the other way."

"Just not a black one," I said. The words were out of my mouth before I knew they were even in my head.

"Huh?" Sounding startled and doubtful.

"I said bring me back one," I said, the words once again out and down the wire before I even knew they were there.

"Maybe I will," she said, sounding amused. Then her tone grew serious again. "And if I said anything last night that made you unhappy, even for a minute, I'm sorry. I never for the world —"

"Don't worry," I said. "I'm not unhappy. A little confused, that's all. In fact I'd pretty much forgotten about Jo's mystery date." A lie, but in what seemed to me to be a good cause.

"That's probably for the best. I won't keep you — go on back to work. It's what you want to do, isn't it?"

I was startled. "What makes you say that?"

"I don't know, I just . . ." She stopped. And I suddenly knew two things: What she had been about to say, and that she wouldn't say it. *I dreamed about you last night. I dreamed about us together. We were going to make love and one of us said "Do what you want." Or maybe, I don't know, maybe we both said it.*

Perhaps sometimes ghosts were alive — minds and desires divorced from their bodies, unlocked impulses floating unseen. Ghosts from the id, spooks from low places.

"Mattie? Still there?"

"Sure, you bet. Do you want me to stay in touch? Or will you hear all you need from John Storrow?"

"If you don't stay in touch, I'll be pissed at you. Royally."

She laughed. "I will, then. But not when you're working. Goodbye, Mike. And thanks again. So much."

I told her goodbye, then stood there for a

moment looking at the old-fashioned Bakelite phone handset after she had hung up. She'd call and keep me updated, but not when I was working. How would she know when that was? She just would. As I'd known last night that she was lying when she said Jo and the man with the elbow patches on the sleeves of his sportcoat had walked off toward the parking lot. Mattie had been wearing a pair of white shorts and a halter top when she called me, no dress or skirt required today because it was Wednesday and the library was closed on Wednesday.

You don't know any of that. You're just making it up.

But I wasn't. If I'd been making it up, I probably would have put her in something a little more suggestive — a Merry Widow from Victoria's Secret, perhaps.

That thought called up another. *Do what you want,* they had said. Both of them. *Do what you want.* And that was a line I knew. While on Key Largo I'd read an *Atlantic Monthly* essay on pornography by some feminist. I wasn't sure which one, only that it hadn't been Naomi Wolf or Camille Paglia. This woman had been of the conservative stripe, and she had used that phrase. Sally Tisdale, maybe? Or was my mind just hearing echo-distortions of Sara Tidwell? Whoever it had been, she'd claimed that "do what *I* want" was the basis of erotica which appealed to women and "do what *you* want" was the basis of pornography which appealed to men. Women imagine speaking the former line in sexual situations; men imagine having the latter line spoken *to* them. And, the writer went on, when real-world sex goes bad — sometimes turning violent, sometimes shaming, sometimes just unsuccessful from the female partner's point of view — porn is often the unindicted co-conspirator. The man is apt to round on the woman angrily and cry, "You wanted me to! Quit lying and admit it! You *wanted* me to!"

The writer claimed it was what every man hoped to hear in the bedroom: Do what you want. Bite me, sodomize me, lick between my toes, drink wine out of my navel, give me a hairbrush and raise your ass for me to paddle, it doesn't matter. Do what you want. The door is closed and we are here, but really only *you* are here, I am just a willing extension of your fantasies and only *you* are here. I have no wants of my own, no needs of my own, no taboos. Do what you want to this shadow, this fantasy, this ghost.

I'd thought the essayist at least fifty per cent full of shit; the assumption that a man can find real sexual pleasure only by turning a woman into a kind of jackoff accessory says more about the observer than the participants. This lady had had a lot of jargon and a fair amount of wit, but underneath she was only saying what Somerset Maugham, Jo's old favorite, had had Sadie Thompson say in "Rain," a story written eighty years before: men are pigs, filthy, dirty pigs, all of them. But we are *not* pigs, as a rule, not beasts, or at least not unless we are pushed to the final extremity. And if we are pushed to it, the issue is rarely sex; it's usually territory. I've heard feminists argue that to men sex and territory are interchangeable, and that is very far from the truth.

I padded back to the office, opened the door, and behind me the telephone rang again. And here was another familiar sensation, back for a return visit after four years: that anger at the telephone, the urge to simply rip it out of the wall and fire it across the room. Why did the whole world have to call while I was writing? Why couldn't they just . . . well . . . let me do what I wanted?

I gave a doubtful laugh and returned to the phone, seeing the wet handprint on it from my last call.

"Hello?"

"I said to stay visible while you were with her."

"Good morning to you, too, Lawyer Storrow."

"You must be in another time-zone up

394

there, chum. I've got one-fifteen down here in New York."

"I had dinner with her," I said. "Outside. It's true that I read the little kid a story and helped put her to bed, but —"

"I imagine half the town thinks you're bopping each other's brains out by now, and the other half will think it if I have to show up for her in court." But he didn't sound really angry; I thought he sounded as though he was having a happy-face day.

"Can they make you tell who's paying for your services?" I asked. "At the custody hearing, I mean?"

"Nope."

"At my deposition on Friday?"

"Christ, no. Durgin would lose all credibility as guardian *ad litem* if he went in that direction. Also, they have reasons to steer clear of the sex angle. Their focus is on Mattie as neglectful and perhaps abusive. Proving that Mom isn't a nun quit working around the time *Kramer vs. Kramer* came out in the movie theaters. Nor is that the only problem they have with the issue." He now sounded positively gleeful.

"Tell me."

"Max Devore is eighty-five and divorced. Twice divorced, in point of fact. Before awarding custody to a single man of his age, secondary custody has to be taken into consideration. It is, in fact, the single most important issue, other than the allegations of abuse and neglect levelled at the mother."

"What are those allegations? Do you know?"

"No. Mattie doesn't either, because they're fabrications. She's a sweetie, by the way —"

"Yeah, she is."

"— and I think she's going to make a great witness. I can't wait to meet her in person. Meantime, don't sidetrack me. We're talking about secondary custody, right?"

"Right."

"Devore has a daughter who has been declared mentally incompetent and lives in an institution somewhere in California — Modesto, I think. Not a good bet for custody."

"It wouldn't seem so."

"The son, Roger, is . . ." I heard a faint fluttering of notebook pages. ". . . fifty-four. So he's not exactly a spring chicken, either. Still, there are lots of guys who become daddies at that age nowadays; it's a brave new world. But Roger is a homosexual."

I thought of Bill Dean saying, *Rump-wrangler. Understand there's a lot of that goin around out there in California.*

"I thought you said sex doesn't matter."

"Maybe I should have said *hetero* sex doesn't matter. In certain states — California is one of them — *homo* sex doesn't matter, either . . . or not as much. But this case isn't going to be adjudicated in California. It's going to be adjudicated in Maine, where folks are less enlightened about how well two married men — married to each other, I mean — can raise a little girl."

"Roger Devore is *married?*" Okay. I admit it. I now felt a certain horrified glee myself. I was ashamed of it — Roger Devore was just a guy living his life, and he might not have had much or anything to do with his elderly dad's current enterprise — but I felt it just the same.

"He and a software designer named Morris Ridding tied the knot in 1996," John said. "I found that on the first computer sweep. And if this does wind up in court, I intend to make as much of it as I possibly can. I don't know how much that will be — at this point it's impossible to predict — but if I get a chance to paint a picture of that bright-eyed, cheerful little girl growing up with two elderly gays who probably spend most of their lives in computer chat-rooms speculating about what Captain Kirk and Mr. Spock might have done after the lights were out in officers' country . . . well, if I get that chance, I'll take it."

"It seems a little mean," I said. I heard myself speaking in the tone of a man who wants to be dissuaded, perhaps even laughed at, but that didn't happen.

"Of course it's mean. It feels like swerving up onto the sidewalk to knock over a couple of innocent bystanders. Roger Devore and Morris Ridding don't deal drugs, traffic in little boys, or rob old ladies. But this is custody, and custody does an even better job than divorce of turning human beings into insects. This one isn't as bad as it could be, but it's bad enough because it's so *naked*. Max Devore came up there to his old hometown for one reason and one reason only: to buy a kid. That makes me mad."

I grinned, imagining a lawyer who looked like Elmer Fudd standing outside of a rabbit-hole marked DEVORE with a shotgun.

"My message to Devore is going to be very simple: the price of the kid just went up. Probably to a figure higher than even he can afford."

"*If* it goes to court — you've said that a couple of times now. Do you think there's a chance Devore might just drop it and go away?"

"A pretty good one, yeah. I'd say an excellent one if he wasn't old and used to getting his own way. There's also the question of whether or not he's still sharp enough to know where his best interest lies. I'll try for a meeting with him and his lawyer while I'm up there, but so far I haven't managed to get past his secretary."

"Rogette Whitmore?"

"No, I think she's a step further up the ladder. I haven't talked to her yet, either. But I will."

"Try either Richard Osgood or George Footman," I said. "Either of them may be able to put you in touch with Devore or Devore's chief counsel."

"I'll want to talk to the Whitmore woman in any case. Men like Devore tend to grow more and more dependent on their close advisors as they grow older, and she could be a key to getting him to let this go. She could also be a headache for us. She might urge him to fight, possibly because she really thinks he can win and possibly because she wants to watch the fur fly. Also, she might marry him."

"*Marry* him?"

"Why not? He could have her sign a pre-nup — I could no more introduce that in court than his lawyers could go fishing for who hired Mattie's lawyer — and it would strengthen his chances."

"John, I've seen the woman. She's got to be seventy herself."

"But she's a potential female player in a custody case involving a little girl, and she's a layer between old man Devore and the married gay couple. We just need to keep it in mind."

"Okay." I looked at the office door again,

but not so longingly. There comes a point when you're done for the day whether you want to be or not, and I thought I had reached that point. Perhaps in the evening . . .

"The lawyer I got for you is named Romeo Bissonette." He paused. "Can that be a real name?"

"Is he from Lewiston?"

"Yes, how did you know?"

"Because in Maine, especially around Lewiston, that can be a real name. Am I supposed to go see him?" I didn't want to go see him. It was fifty miles to Lewiston over two-lane roads which would now be crawling with campers and Winnebagos. What I wanted was to go swimming and then take a long nap. A long *dreamless* nap.

"You don't need to. Call him and talk to him a little. He's only a safety net, really — he'll object if the questioning leaves the incident on the morning of July Fourth. About that incident you tell the truth, the whole truth, and nothing but the truth. Got it?"

"Yes."

"Talk to him before, then meet him on Friday at . . . wait . . . it's right here . . ." The notebook pages fluttered again. "Meet him at the Route 120 Diner at nine-fifteen. Coffee. Talk a little, get to know each other, maybe flip for the check. I'll be with Mattie, getting as much as I can. We may want to hire a private dick."

"I love it when you talk dirty."

"Uh-huh. I'm going to see that bills go to your guy Goldacre. He'll send them to your agent, and your agent can —"

"No," I said. "Instruct Goldacre to send them directly here. Harold's a Jewish mother. How much is this going to cost me?"

"Seventy-five thousand dollars, minimum," he said with no hesitation at all. With no apology in his voice, either.

"Don't tell Mattie."

"All right. Are you having any fun yet, Mike?"

"You know, I sort of am," I said thoughtfully.

"For seventy-five grand, you should." We said our goodbyes and John hung up.

As I put my own phone back into its cradle, it occurred to me that I had lived more in the last five days than I had in the last four years.

This time the phone didn't ring and I made it all the way back into the office, but I knew I was definitely done for the day. I sat down at the IBM, hit the RETURN key a couple of times, and was beginning to write myself a next-note at the bottom of the page I'd been working on when the phone interrupted me. What a sour little doodad the telephone is, and what little good news we get from it! Today had been an exception, though, and I thought I could sign off with a grin. I was working, after all — *working*. Part of me still marvelled that I was sitting here at all, breathing easily, my heart beating steadily in my chest, and not even a glimmer of an anxiety attack on my personal event horizon. I wrote:

```
[NEXT: Drake to Raiford. Stops
on the way at vegetable stand
to talk to the guy who runs it,
old source, needs a good & col-
orful    name.    Straw    hat.
DisneyWorld tee- shirt. They
talk about Shackle- ford.]
```

I turned the roller until the IBM spat this page out, stuck it on top of the manuscript, and jotted a final note to myself: "Call Ted Rosencrief about Raiford." Rosencrief was a retired Navy man who lived in Derry. I had employed him as a research assistant on several books, using him on one project to find out how paper was made, what the migratory habits of certain common birds were for another, a little bit about the architecture of pyramid burial rooms for a third. And it's always "a little bit" I want, never "the whole damn thing." As a writer, my motto has always been don't confuse me with the facts. The Arthur Hailey type of fiction is beyond me — I can't read it, let alone write it. I want to know just enough so I can lie colorfully. Rosie knew that, and we had always worked well together.

This time I needed to know a little bit about Florida's Raiford Prison, and what the deathhouse down there is really like. I also needed a little bit on the psychology of serial killers. I thought Rosie would probably be glad to hear from me . . . almost as glad as I was to finally have something to call him about.

I picked up the eight double-spaced pages I had written and fanned through them, still amazed at their existence. Had an old IBM typewriter and a Courier type-ball been the secret all along? That was certainly how it seemed.

What had come out was also amazing. I'd had ideas during my four-year sabbatical; there had been no writer's block in that regard. One had been really great, the sort of thing which certainly would have become a novel if I'd still been able to write novels. Half a dozen to a dozen were of the sort I'd classify "pretty good," meaning they'd do in a pinch . . . or if they happened to unexpectedly grow tall and mysterious overnight, like Jack's beanstalk. Sometimes they do. Most were glimmers, little "what-ifs" that came and went like shooting stars while I was driving or walking or just lying in bed at night and waiting to go to sleep.

The Red-Shirt Man was a what-if. One day I saw a man in a bright red shirt washing the show windows of the JCPenney store in Derry — this was not long before Penney's moved out to the mall. A young man and woman walked under his ladder . . . very bad luck, according to the old superstition. These two didn't know *where* they were walking, though — they were holding hands, drinking deeply of each other's eyes, as completely in love as any two twenty-year-olds in the history of the world. The man was tall, and as I watched, the top of his head came within an ace of clipping the window-washer's feet. If that had happened, the whole works might have gone over.

The entire incident was history in five seconds. Writing *The Red-Shirt Man* took five months. Except in truth, the entire book was done in a what-if second. I imagined a collision instead of a near-miss. Everything else followed from there. The writing was just secretarial.

The idea I was currently working on wasn't one of Mike's Really Great Ideas (Jo's voice carefully made the capitals), but it wasn't a what-if, either. Nor was it much like my old gothic suspense yarns; V. C. Andrews with a prick was nowhere in sight this time. But it felt solid, like the real thing, and this morning it had come out as naturally as a breath.

Andy Drake was a private investigator in Key Largo. He was forty years old, divorced, the father of a three-year-old girl. At the open he was in the Key West home of a woman named Regina Whiting. Mrs. Whiting also had a little girl, hers five years old. Mrs. Whiting was married to an extremely rich developer who did not know what Andy Drake knew: that until 1992, Regina Taylor Whiting had been Tiffany Taylor, a high-priced Miami call-girl.

That much I had written before the phone started ringing. Here is what I knew beyond that point, the secretarial work I'd do over the next several weeks, assuming that my marvellously recovered ability to work held up:

One day when Karen Whiting was three, the phone had rung while she and her mother were sitting in the patio hot tub. Regina thought of asking the yard-guy to answer it, then decided to get it herself — their regular man was out with the flu, and she didn't feel comfortable about asking a stranger for a favor. Cautioning her daughter to sit still, Regina hopped out to answer the phone. When Karen put up a hand to keep from being splashed as her mother left the tub, she dropped the doll she had been bathing. When she bent to pick it up, her hair became caught in one of the hot tub's powerful intakes. (It was reading of a fatal accident like this that had originally kicked the story off in my mind two or three years before.)

The yard-man, some no-name in a khaki shirt sent over by a day-labor outfit, saw what was happening. He raced across the lawn, dove headfirst into the tub, and yanked the child from the bottom, leaving hair and a good chunk of scalp clogging the jet when he did. He'd give her artificial respiration until she began to breathe again. (This would be a wonderful, suspenseful scene, and I couldn't wait to write it.) He would refuse all of the hysterical, relieved mother's offers of recompense, although he'd finally give her an address so that her husband could talk to him. Only both the address and his name, John Sanborn, would turn out to be a fake.

Two years later the ex-hooker with the respectable second life sees the man who saved her child on the front page of the Miami paper. His name is given as John Shackleford and he has been arrested for the rape-murder of a nine-year-old girl. And, the article goes on, he is suspected in over forty other murders, many of the victims children. "Have you caught Baseball Cap?" one of the reporters would yell at the press conference. "Is John Shackleford Baseball Cap?"

"Well," I said, going downstairs, "they sure *think* he is."

I could hear too many boats out on the lake this afternoon to make nude bathing an option. I pulled on my suit, slung a towel over my shoulders, and started down the path — the one which had been lined with glowing paper lanterns in my dream — to wash off the sweat of my nightmares and my unexpected morning's labors.

There are twenty-three railroad-tie steps between Sara and the lake. I had gone down only four or five before the enormity of what had just happened hit me. My mouth began to tremble. The colors of the trees and the sky mixed together as my eyes teared up. A sound began to come out of me — a kind of muffled groaning. The strength ran out of my legs and I sat down hard on a railroad tie. For a moment I thought it was over, mostly just a false alarm, and then I began to cry. I stuffed one end of the towel in my mouth during the worst of it, afraid that if the boaters on the lake heard the sounds coming out of me, they'd think someone up here was being murdered.

I cried in grief for the empty years I had spent without Jo, without friends, and without my work. I cried in gratitude because those workless years seemed to be over. It was too early to tell for sure — one swallow doesn't make a summer and eight pages of hard copy don't make a career re-suscitation — but I thought it really might be so. And I cried out of fear, as well, as we do when some awful experience is finally over or when some terrible accident has been narrowly averted. I cried because I suddenly realized that I had been walking a white line ever since Jo died, walking straight down the middle of the road. By some miracle, I had been carried out of harm's way. I had no idea who had done the carrying, but that was all right — it was a question that could wait for another day.

I cried it all out of me. Then I went on down to the lake and waded in. The cool water felt more than good on my overheated body; it felt like a resurrection.

Chapter 15

"State your name for the record."

"Michael Noonan."

"Your address?"

"Derry is my permanent address, 14 Benton Street, but I also maintain a home in TR-90, on Dark Score Lake. The mailing address is Box 832. The actual house is on Lane Forty-two, off Route 68."

Elmer Durgin, Kyra Devore's guardian *ad litem,* waved a pudgy hand in front of his face, either to shoo away some troublesome insect or to tell me that was enough. I agreed that it was. I felt rather like the little girl in *Our Town* who gave her address as Grover's Corner, New Hampshire, America, the Northern Hemisphere, the World, the Solar System, the Milky Way Galaxy, the Mind of God. Mostly I was nervous. I'd reached the age of forty still a virgin in the area of court proceedings, and although we were in the conference room of Durgin, Peters, and Jarrette on Bridge Street in Castle Rock, this was still a court proceeding.

There was one mentionably odd detail to these festivities. The stenographer wasn't using one of those keyboards-on-a-post that look like adding machines, but a Stenomask, a gadget which fit over the lower half of his face. I had seen them before, but only in old black-and-white crime movies, the ones where Dan Duryea or John Payne is always driving around in a Buick with portholes on the sides, looking grim and smoking a Camel. Glancing over into the corner and seeing a guy who looked like the world's oldest fighter-pilot was weird enough, but hearing everything you said immediately re-peated in a muffled monotone was even weirder.

"Thank you, Mr. Noonan. My wife has read all your books and says you are her fa-vorite author. I just wanted to get that on the record." Durgin chuckled fatly. Why not? He was a fat guy. Most fat people I like — they have expansive natures to go with their expansive waistlines. But there *is* a subgroup which I think of as the Evil Little Fat Folks. You don't want to fuck with the ELFFs if you can help it; they will burn your house and rape your dog if you give them half an excuse and a quarter of an op-portunity. Few of them stand over five-foot-two (Durgin's height, I estimated), and many are under five feet. They smile a lot, but their eyes don't smile. The Evil Little Fat Folks hate the whole world. Mostly they hate folks who can look down the length of their bodies and still see their own feet. This included me, although just barely.

"Please thank your wife for me, Mr.

Durgin. I'm sure she could recommend one for you to start on."

Durgin chuckled. On his right, Durgin's assistant — a pretty young woman who looked approximately seventeen minutes out of law school — chuckled. On my left, Romeo Bissonette chuckled. In the corner, the world's oldest F-111 pilot only went on muttering into his Stenomask.

"I'll wait for the big-screen version," he said. His eyes gave an ugly little gleam, as if he knew a feature film had never been made from one of my books — only a made-for-TV movie of *Being Two* that pulled ratings roughly equal to the National Sofa Refinishing Championships. I hoped that we'd completed this chubby little fuck's idea of the pleasantries.

"I am Kyra Devore's guardian *ad litem*," he said. "Do you know what that means, Mr. Noonan?"

"I believe I do."

"It means," Durgin rolled on, "that I've been appointed by Judge Rancourt to decide — if I can — where Kyra Devore's best interests lie, should a custody judgment become necessary. Judge Rancourt would not, in such an event, be required to base his decision on my conclusions, but in many cases that is what happens."

He looked at me with his hands folded on a blank legal pad. The pretty assistant, on the other hand, was scribbling madly. Perhaps she didn't trust the fighter-pilot. Durgin looked as if he expected a round of applause.

"Was that a question, Mr. Durgin?" I asked and Romeo Bissonette delivered a light, practiced chip to my ankle. I didn't need to look at him to know it wasn't an accident.

Durgin pursed lips so smooth and damp that he looked as if he were wearing a clear gloss on them. On his shining pate, roughly two dozen strands of hair were combed in smooth little arcs. He gave me a patient, measuring look. Behind it was all the intransigent ugliness of an Evil Little Fat Folk. The pleasantries were over, all right. I was sure of it.

"No, Mr. Noonan, that was not a question. I simply thought you might like to know why we've had to ask you to come away from your lovely lake on such a pleasant morning. Perhaps I was wrong. Now, if —"

There was a peremptory knock on the door, followed by your friend and his, George Footman. Today Cleveland Casual had been replaced by a khaki Deputy Sheriff's uniform, complete with Sam Browne belt and sidearm. He helped himself to a good look at the assistant's bustline, displayed in a blue silk blouse, then handed her a folder and a cassette tape recorder. He gave me one brief gander before leaving. *I remember you, buddy,* that glance said. *The smartass writer, the cheap date.*

Romeo Bissonette tipped his head toward me. He used the side of his hand to bridge the gap between his mouth and my ear. "Devore's tape," he said.

I nodded to show I understood, then turned to Durgin again.

"Mr. Noonan, you've met Kyra Devore and her mother, Mary Devore, haven't you?"

How did you get Mattie out of Mary, I wondered . . . and then knew, just as I had known about the white shorts and halter top. Mattie was how Ki had first tried to say *Mary.*

"Mr. Noonan, are we keeping you up?"

"There's no need to be sarcastic, is there?" Bissonette asked. His tone was mild, but Elmer Durgin gave him a look which suggested that, should the ELFFs succeed in their goal of world domination, Bissonette would be aboard the first gulag-bound boxcar.

"I'm sorry," I said before Durgin could reply. "I just got derailed there for a second or two."

"New story idea?" Durgin asked, smiling his glossy smile. He looked like a swamp-toad in a sportcoat. He turned to the old jet

413

pilot, told him to strike that last, then repeated his question about Kyra and Mattie.

Yes, I said, I had met them.

"Once or more than once?"

"More than once."

"How many times have you met them?"

"Twice."

"Have you also spoken to Mary Devore
on the phone?"

Already these questions were moving in a
direction that made me uncomfortable.

"Yes."

"How many times?"

"Three times." The third had come the
day before, when she had asked if I would
join her and John Storrow for a picnic lunch
on the town common after my deposition.
Lunch right there in the middle of town before God and everybody . . . although, with
a New York lawyer to play chaperone, what
harm in that?

"Have you spoken to Kyra Devore on the
telephone?"

What an odd question! Not one anybody
had prepared me for, either. I supposed that
was at least partly why he had asked it.

"Mr. Noonan?"

"Yes, I've spoken to her once."

"Can you tell us the nature of that conversation?"

"Well . . ." I looked doubtfully at
Bissonette, but there was no help there. He

obviously didn't know, either. "Mattie —"

"Pardon me?" Durgin leaned forward as much as he could. His eyes were intent in their pink pockets of flesh. "Mattie?"

"Mattie Devore. *Mary* Devore."

"You call her Mattie?"

"Yes," I said, and had a wild impulse to add: *In bed! In bed I call her that! "Oh Mattie, don't stop, don't stop," I cry!* "It's the name she gave me when she introduced herself. I met her —"

"We may get to that, but right now I'm interested in your telephone conversation with Kyra Devore. When was that?"

"It was yesterday."

"July ninth, 1998."

"Yes."

"Who placed that call?"

"Ma . . . Mary Devore." *Now he'll ask why she called, I thought, and I'll say she wanted to have yet another sex marathon, foreplay to consist of feeding each other chocolate-dipped strawberries while we look at pictures of naked malformed dwarves.*

"How did Kyra Devore happen to speak to you?"

"She asked if she could. I heard her saying to her mother that she had to tell me something."

"What was it she had to tell you?"

"That she had her first bubble bath."

"Did she also say she coughed?"

415

I was quiet, looking at him. In that moment I understood why people hate lawyers, especially when they've been dusted over by one who's good at the job.

"Mr. Noonan, would you like me to repeat the question?"

"No," I said, wondering where he'd gotten his information. Had these bastards tapped Mattie's phone? My phone? Both? Perhaps for the first time I understood on a gut level what it must be like to have half a billion dollars. With that much dough you could tap a lot of telephones. "She said her mother pushed bubbles in her face and she coughed. But she was —"

"Thank you, Mr. Noonan, now let's turn to —"

"Let him finish," Bissonette said. I had an idea he had already taken a bigger part in the proceedings than he had expected to, but he didn't seem to mind. He was a sleepy-looking man with a bloodhound's mournful, trustworthy face. "This isn't a courtroom, and you're not cross-examining him."

"I have the little girl's welfare to think of," Durgin said. He sounded both pompous and humble at the same time, a combination that went together like chocolate sauce on creamed corn. "It's a responsibility I take very seriously. If I seemed to be badgering you, Mr. Noonan, I apologize."

I didn't bother accepting his apology — that would have made us both phonies. "All I was going to say is that Ki was laughing when she said it. She said she and her mother had a bubble-fight. When her mother came back on, she was laughing, too."

Durgin had opened the folder Footman had brought him and was paging rapidly through it while I spoke, as if he weren't hearing a word. "Her mother . . . Mattie, as you call her."

"Yes. Mattie as I call her. How do you know about our private telephone conversation in the first place?"

"That's none of your business, Mr. Noonan." He selected a single sheet of paper, then closed the folder. He held the paper up briefly, like a doctor studying an X-ray, and I could see it was covered with single-spaced typing. "Let's turn to your initial meeting with Mary and Kyra Devore. That was on the Fourth of July, wasn't it?"

"Yes."

Durgin was nodding. "The morning of the Fourth. And you met Kyra Devore first."

"Yes."

"You met her first because her mother wasn't with her at that time, was she?"

"That's a badly phrased question, Mr. Durgin, but I guess the answer is yes."

"I'm flattered to have my grammar corrected by a man who's been on the best-seller lists," Durgin said, smiling. The smile suggested that he'd like to see me sitting next to Romeo Bissonette in that first gulag-bound boxcar. "Tell us about your meeting, first with Kyra Devore and then with Mary Devore. Or Mattie, if you like that better."

I told the story. When I was finished, Durgin centered the tape player in front of him. The nails of his pudgy fingers looked as glossy as his lips.

"Mr. Noonan, you could have run Kyra over, isn't that true?"

"Absolutely not. I was going thirty-five — that's the speed limit there by the store. I saw her in plenty of time to stop."

"Suppose you had been coming the other way, though — heading north instead of south. Would you still have seen her in plenty of time?"

That was a fairer question than some of his others, actually. Someone coming the other way would have had a far shorter time to react. Still . . .

"Yes," I said.

Durgin went up with the eyebrows. "You're sure of that?"

"Yes, Mr. Durgin. I might have had to come down a little harder on the brakes, but —"

"At thirty-five."

"Yes, at thirty-five. I told you, that's the speed limit —"

"— on that particular stretch of Route 68. Yes, you told me that. You did. Is it your experience that most people obey the speed limit on that part of the road?"

"I haven't spent much time on the TR since 1993, so I can't —"

"Come on, Mr. Noonan — this isn't a scene from one of your books. Just answer my questions, or we'll be here all morning."

"I'm doing my best, Mr. Durgin."

He sighed, put-upon. "You've owned your place on Dark Score Lake since the eighties, haven't you? And the speed limit around the Lakeview General Store, the post office, and Dick Brooks's All-Purpose Garage — what's called The North Village — hasn't changed since then, has it?"

"No," I admitted.

"Returning to my original question, then — in your observation, do most people on that stretch of road obey the thirty-five-mile-an-hour limit?"

"I can't say if it's most, because I've never done a traffic survey, but I guess a lot don't."

"Would you like to hear Castle County Sheriff's Deputy Footman testify on where the greatest number of speeding tickets are given out in TR-90, Mr. Noonan?"

"No," I said, quite honestly.

"Did other vehicles pass you while you

were speaking first with Kyra Devore and then with Mary Devore?"

"Yes."

"How many?"

"I don't know exactly. A couple."

"Could it have been three?"

"I guess."

"Five?"

"No, probably not so many."

"But you don't know, exactly, do you?"

"No."

"Because Kyra Devore was upset."

"Actually she had it together pretty well for a —"

"Did she cry in your presence?"

"Well . . . yes."

"Did her mother make her cry?"

"That's unfair."

"As unfair as allowing a three-year-old to go strolling down the middle of a busy highway on a holiday morning, in your opinion, or perhaps not quite as unfair as that?"

"Jeepers, lay off," Mr. Bissonette said mildly. There was distress on his blood-hound's face.

"I withdraw the question," Durgin said.

"Which one?" I asked.

He looked at me tiredly, as if to say he had to put up with assholes like me all the time and he was used to how we behaved. "How many cars went by from the time you

420

picked the child up and carried her to safety to the time when you and the Devores parted company?"

I hated that "carried her to safety" bit, but even as I formulated my answer, the old guy was muttering the question into his Stenomask. And it was in fact what I had done. There was no getting around it.

"I told you, I don't know for sure."

"Well, give me a guesstimate."

Guesstimate. One of my all-time least favorite words. A Paul Harvey word. "There might have been three."

"Including Mary Devore herself? Driving a —" He consulted the paper he'd taken from the folder. "— a 1982 Jeep Scout?"

I thought of Ki saying *Mattie go fast* and understood where Durgin was heading now. And there was nothing I could do about it.

"Yes, it was her and it was a Scout. I don't know what year."

"Was she driving below the posted speed limit, at the posted speed limit, or above the posted speed limit when she passed the place where you were standing with Kyra in your arms?"

She'd been doing at least fifty, but I told Durgin I couldn't say for sure. He urged me to try — *I know you are unfamiliar with the hangman's knot, Mr. Noonan, but I'm sure you can make one if you really work at it* — and I declined as politely as I could.

421

He picked up the paper again. "Mr. Noonan, would it surprise you to know that two witnesses — Richard Brooks, Junior, the owner of Dick's All-Purpose Garage, and Royce Merrill, a retired carpenter — claim that Mrs. Devore was doing well over thirty-five when she passed your location?"

"I don't know," I said. "I was concerned with the little girl."

"Would it surprise you to know that Royce Merrill estimated her speed at *sixty* miles an hour?"

"That's ridiculous. When she hit the brakes she would have skidded sideways and landed upside down in the ditch."

"The skid-marks measured by Deputy Footman indicate a speed of at least fifty miles an hour," Durgin said. It wasn't a question, but he looked at me almost roguishly, as if inviting me to struggle a little more and sink a little deeper into this nasty pit. I said nothing. Durgin folded his pudgy little hands and leaned over them toward me. The roguish look was gone.

"Mr. Noonan, if you hadn't carried Kyra Devore to the side of the road — if you hadn't rescued her — mightn't *her own mother* have run her over?"

Here was the really loaded question, and how should I answer it? Bissonette was certainly not flashing any helpful signals; he seemed to be trying to make meaningful eye-contact with the pretty assistant. I thought of the book Mattie was reading in tandem with "Bartleby" — *Silent Witness*, by Richard North Patterson. Unlike the Grisham brand, Patterson's lawyers almost always seemed to know what they were doing. *Objection, Your Honor, calls for speculation on the part of the witness.*

I shrugged. "Sorry, counsellor, can't say — left my crystal ball home."

Again I saw the ugly flash in Durgin's eyes. "Mr. Noonan, I can assure you that if you don't answer that question here, you are apt to be called back from Malibu or Fire Island or wherever it is you're going to write your next opus to answer it later on."

I shrugged. "I've already told you I was concerned with the child. I can't tell you how fast the mother was going, or how good Royce Merrill's vision is, or if Deputy Footman even measured the right set of skidmarks. There's a whole bunch of rubber on that part of the road, I can tell you. Suppose she *was* going fifty? Even fifty-five, let's say that. She's twenty-one years old, Durgin. At the age of twenty-one, a person's driving skills are at their peak. She probably would have swerved around the child, and easily."

"I think that's quite enough."

"Why? Because you're not getting what you wanted?" Bissonette's shoe clipped my ankle again, but I ignored it. "If you're on

423

Kyra's side, why do you sound as though you're on her grandfather's?"

A baleful little smile touched Durgin's lips. The kind that says *Okay, smart guy, you want to play?* He pulled the tape-recorder a little closer to him. "Since you have mentioned Kyra's grandfather, Mr. Maxwell Devore of Palm Springs, let's talk about him a little, shall we?"

"It's your show."

"Have you ever spoken with Maxwell Devore?"

"Yes."

"In person or on the phone?"

"Phone." I thought about adding that he had somehow gotten hold of my unlisted number, then remembered that Mattie had, too, and decided to keep my mouth shut on that subject.

"When was this?"

"Last Saturday night. The night of the Fourth. He called while I was watching the fireworks."

"And was the subject of your conversation that morning's little adventure?" As he asked, Durgin reached into his pocket and brought out a cassette tape. There was an ostentatious quality to this gesture; in that moment he looked like a parlor magician showing you both sides of a silk handkerchief. And he was bluffing. I couldn't be sure of that . . . and yet I was. Devore had taped our conversation, all right — that underhum really had been too loud, and on some level I'd been aware of that fact even while I was talking to him — and I thought it really was on the cassette Durgin was now slotting into the cassette player . . . but it was a bluff.

"I don't recall," I said.

Durgin's hand froze in the act of snapping the cassette's transparent loading panel shut. He looked at me with frank disbelief . . . and something else. I thought the something else was surprised anger.

"You don't recall? Come now, Mr. Noonan. Surely writers *train* themselves to recall conversations, and this one was only a week ago. Tell me what you talked about."

"I really can't say," I told him in a stolid, colorless voice.

For a moment Durgin looked almost panicky. Then his features smoothed. One polished fingernail slipped back and forth over keys marked REW, FF, PLAY, and REC. "How did Mr. Devore begin the conversation?" he asked.

"He said hello," I said mildly, and there was a short muffled sound from behind the Stenomask. It could have been the old guy clearing his throat; it could have been a suppressed laugh.

Spots of color were blooming in Durgin's

cheeks. "After hello? What then?"

"I don't recall."

"Did he ask you about that morning?"

"I don't recall."

"Didn't you tell him that Mary Devore and her daughter were together, Mr. Noonan? That they were together picking flowers? Isn't that what you told this worried grandfather when he inquired about the incident which was the talk of the township that Fourth of July?"

"Oh boy," Bissonette said. He raised one hand over the table, then touched the palm with the fingers of the other, making a ref's *T*. "Time out."

Durgin looked at him. The flush in his cheeks was more pronounced now, and his lips had pulled back enough to show the tips of small, neatly capped teeth. "What do *you* want?" he almost snarled, as if Bissonette had just dropped by to tell him about the Mormon Way or perhaps the Rosicrucians.

"I want you to stop leading this guy, and I want that whole thing about picking flowers stricken from the record," Bissonette said.

"Why?" Durgin snapped.

"Because you're trying to get stuff on the record that this witness won't say. If you want to break here for awhile so we can make a conference call to Judge Rancourt, get his opinion —"

"I withdraw the question," Durgin said.

He looked at me with a kind of helpless, surly rage. "Mr. Noonan, do you want to help me do my job?"

"I want to help Kyra Devore if I can," I said.

"Very well." He nodded as if no distinction had been made. "Then please tell me what you and Maxwell Devore talked about."

"I can't recall." I caught his eyes and held them. "Perhaps," I said, "you can refresh my recollection."

There was a moment of silence, like that which sometimes strikes a high-stakes poker game just after the last of the bets have been made and just before the players show their hands. Even the old fighter-pilot was quiet, his eyes unblinking above the mask. Then Durgin pushed the cassette player aside with the heel of his hand (the set of his mouth said he felt about it just then as I often felt about the telephone) and went back to the morning of July Fourth. He never asked about my dinner with Mattie and Ki on Tuesday night, and never returned to my telephone conversation with Devore — the one where I had said all those awkward and easily disprovable things.

I went on answering questions until eleven-thirty, but the interview really ended when Durgin pushed the tape-player away with the heel of his hand. I knew it, and I'm pretty sure he did, too.

★ ★ ★

"Mike! Mike, over here!"

Mattie was waving from one of the tables in the picnic area behind the town common's bandstand. She looked vibrant and happy. I waved back and made my way in that direction, weaving between little kids playing tag, skirting a couple of teenagers making out on the grass, and ducking a Frisbee which a leaping German shepherd caught smartly.

There was a tall, skinny redhead with her, but I barely got a chance to notice him. Mattie met me while I was still on the gravel path, put her arms around me, hugged me — it was no prudey little ass-poking-out hug, either — and then kissed me on the mouth hard enough to push my lips against my teeth. There was a hearty smack when she disengaged. She pulled back and looked at me with undisguised delight. "Was it the biggest kiss you've ever had?"

"The biggest in at least four years," I said. "Will you settle for that?" And if she didn't step away from me in the next few seconds, she was going to have physical proof of how much I had enjoyed it.

"I guess I'll have to." She turned to the redheaded guy with a funny kind of defiance. "Was that all right?"

"Probably not," he said, "but at least you're not currently in view of those old boys at the All-Purpose Garage. Mike, I'm John Storrow. Nice to meet you in person."

I liked him at once, maybe because I'd come upon him dressed in his three-piece New York suit and primly setting out paper plates on a picnic table while his curly red hair blew around his head like kelp. His skin was fair and freckled, the kind which would never tan, only burn and then peel in great eczemalike patches. When we shook, his hand seemed to be all knuckles. He had to be at least thirty, but he looked Mattie's age, and I guessed it would be another five years before he was able to get a drink without showing his driver's license.

"Sit down," he said. "We've got a five-course lunch, courtesy of Castle Rock Variety — grinders, which are for some strange reason called 'Italian sandwiches' up here . . . mozzarella sticks . . . garlic fries . . . Twinkies."

"That's only four," I said.

"I forgot the soft-drink course," he said, and pulled three long-neck bottles of S'OK birch beer out of a brown bag. "Let's eat. Mattie runs the library from two to eight on Fridays and Saturdays, and this would be a bad time for her to be missing work."

"How did the readers' circle go last night?" I asked. "Lindy Briggs didn't eat you alive, I see."

She laughed, clasped her hands, and

shook them over her head. "I was a hit! An absolute smashola! I didn't dare tell them I got all my best insights from you —"

"Thank God for small favors," Storrow said. He was freeing his own sandwich from its string and butcher-paper wrapping, doing it carefully and a little dubiously, using just the tips of his fingers.

"— so I said I looked in a couple of books and found some leads there. It was sort of wonderful. I felt like a college kid."

"Good."

"Bissonette?" John Storrow asked. "Where's he? I never met a guy named Romeo before."

"Said he had to go right back to Lewiston. Sorry."

"Actually it's best we stay small, at least to begin with." He bit into his sandwich — they come tucked into long sub rolls — and looked at me, surprised. "This isn't bad."

"Eat more than three and you're hooked for life," Mattie said, and chomped heartily into her own.

"Tell us about the depo," John said, and while they ate, I talked. When I finished, I picked up my own sandwich and played a little catch-up. I'd forgotten how good an Italian can be — sweet, sour, and oily all at the same time. Of course nothing that tastes that good can be healthy; that's a given. I suppose one could formulate a similar postulate about full-body hugs from young girls in legal trouble.

"Very interesting," John said. "Very interesting indeed." He took a mozzarella stick from its grease-stained bag, broke it open, and looked with a kind of fascinated horror at the clotted white gunk inside. "People up here eat this?" he asked.

"People in New York eat fish-bladders," I said. "Raw."

"Touché." He dipped a piece into the plastic container of spaghetti sauce (in this context it is called "cheese-dip" in western Maine), then ate it.

"Well?" I asked.

"Not bad. They ought to be a lot hotter, though."

Yes, he was right about that. Eating cold mozzarella sticks is a little like eating cold snot, an observation I thought I would keep to myself on this beautiful midsummer Friday.

"If Durgin had the tape, why wouldn't he play it?" Mattie asked. "I don't understand."

John stretched his arms out, cracked his knuckles, and looked at her benignly. "We'll probably never know for sure," he said.

He thought Devore was going to drop the suit — it was in every line of his body-language and every inflection of his voice. That was hopeful, but it would be good if Mattie didn't allow herself to become *too* hopeful. John Storrow wasn't as young as he looked, and probably not as guileless, either (or so I fervently hoped), but he *was* young. And neither he nor Mattie knew the story of Scooter Larribee's sled. Or had seen Bill Dean's face when he told it.

"Want to hear some possibilities?"

"Sure," I said.

John put down his sandwich, wiped his fingers, and then began to tick off points. "First, *he* made the call. Taped conversations have a highly dubious value under those circumstances. Second, he didn't exactly come off like Captain Kangaroo, did he?"

"No."

"Third, your fabrication impugns *you,* Mike, but not really very much, and it doesn't impugn Mattie at all. And by the way, that thing about Mattie pushing bubbles in Kyra's face, I love that. If that's the best they can do, they better give it up right now. Last — and this is where the truth probably lies — I think Devore's got Nixon's Disease."

"Nixon's Disease?" Mattie asked.

"The tape Durgin had isn't the only tape. Can't be. And your father-in-law is afraid that if he introduces one tape made by whatever system he's got in Warrington's, we might subpoena all of them. And I'd damn well try."

She looked bewildered. "What could be

on them? And if it's bad, why not just destroy them?"

"Maybe he can't," I said. "Maybe he needs them for other reasons."

"It doesn't really matter," John said. "Durgin was bluffing, and *that's* what matters." He hit the heel of his hand lightly against the picnic table. "I think he's going to drop it. I really do."

"It's too early to start thinking like that," I said at once, but I could tell by Mattie's face — shining more brightly than ever — that the damage was done.

"Fill him in on what else you've been doing," Mattie told John. "Then I've got to get to the library."

"Where do you send Kyra on your workdays?" I asked.

"Mrs. Cullum's. She lives two miles up the Wasp Hill Road. Also in July there's V.B.S. from ten until three. That's Vacation Bible School. Ki loves it, especially the singing and the flannel-board stories about Noah and Moses. The bus drops her off at Arlene's, and I pick her up around quarter of nine." She smiled a little wistfully. "By then she's usually fast asleep on the couch."

John held forth for the next ten minutes or so. He hadn't been on the case long, but had already started a lot of balls rolling. A fellow in California was gathering facts about Roger Devore and Morris Ridding

433

("gathering facts" sounded so much better than "snooping"). John was particularly interested in learning about the quality of Roger Devore's relations with his father, and if Roger was on record concerning his little niece from Maine. John had also mapped out a campaign to learn as much as possible about Max Devore's movements and activities since he'd come back to TR-90. To that end he had the name of a private investigator, one recommended by Romeo Bissonette, my rent-a-lawyer.

As he spoke, paging rapidly through a little notebook he drew from the inside pocket of his suitcoat, I remembered what he'd said about Lady Justice during our telephone conversation: *Slap some handcuffs on that broad's wrists and some tape over her mouth to go along with the blindfold, rape her and roll her in the mud.* That was maybe a bit too strong for what we were doing, but I thought at the very least we were shoving her around a little. I imagined poor Roger Devore up on the stand, having flown three thousand miles in order to be questioned about his sexual preferences. I had to keep reminding myself that his father had put him in that position, not Mattie or me or John Storrow.

"Have you gotten any closer to a meeting with Devore and his chief legal advisor?" I asked.

"Don't know for sure. The line is in the water, the offer is on the table, the puck's on the ice, pick your favorite metaphor, mix em and match em if you desire."

"Got your irons in the fire," Mattie said.

"Your checkers on the board," I added.

We looked at each other and laughed. John regarded us sadly, then sighed, picked up his sandwich, and began to eat again.

"You really have to meet him with his lawyer more or less dancing attendance?" I asked.

"Would you like to win this thing, then discover Devore can do it all again based on unethical behavior by Mary Devore's legal resource?" John returned.

"Don't even joke about it!" Mattie cried.

"I wasn't joking," John said. "It has to be with his lawyer, yes. I don't think it's going to happen, not on this trip. I haven't even got a look at the old *cockuh,* and I have to tell you my curiosity is killing me."

"If that's all it takes to make you happy, show up behind the backstop at the softball field next Tuesday evening," Mattie said. "He'll be there in his fancy wheelchair, laughing and clapping and sucking his damned old oxygen every fifteen minutes or so."

"Not a bad idea," John said. "I have to go back to New York for the weekend — I'm leaving *après* Osgood — but maybe I'll show up on Tuesday. I might even bring my glove." He began clearing up our litter, and once again I thought he looked both prissy and endearing at the same time, like Stan Laurel wearing an apron. Mattie eased him aside and took over.

"No one ate any Twinkies," she said, a little sadly.

"Take them home to your daughter," John said.

"No way. I don't let her eat stuff like this. What kind of mother do you think I am?"

She saw our expressions, replayed what she'd just said, then burst out laughing. We joined her.

Mattie's old Scout was parked in one of the slant spaces behind the war memorial, which in Castle Rock is a World War I soldier with a generous helping of birdshit on his pie-dish helmet. A brand-new Taurus with a Hertz decal above the inspection sticker was parked next to it. John tossed his briefcase — reassuringly thin and not very ostentatious — into the back seat.

"If I can make it back on Tuesday, I'll call you," he told Mattie. "If I'm able to get an appointment with your father-in-law through this man Osgood, I will also call you."

"I'll buy the Italian sandwiches," Mattie said.

He smiled, then grasped her arm in one

hand and mine in the other. He looked like a newly ordained minister getting ready to marry his first couple.

"You two talk on the telephone if you need to," he said, "always remembering that one or both lines may be tapped. Meet in the market if you happen to. Mike, you might feel a need to drop by the local library and check out a book."

"Not until you renew your card, though," Mattie said, giving me a demure glance.

"But no more visits to Mattie's trailer. Is that understood?"

I said yes; she said yes; John Storrow looked unconvinced. It made me wonder if he was seeing something in our faces or bodies that shouldn't be there.

"They are committed to a line of attack which probably isn't going to work," he said. "We can't risk giving them the chance to change course. That means innuendos about the two of you; it also means innuendos about Mike and Kyra."

Mattie's shocked expression made her look twelve again. "Mike and Kyra! What are you talking about?"

"Allegations of child molestation thrown up by people so desperate they'll try anything."

"That's ridiculous," she said. "And if my father-in-law wanted to sling that kind of mud —"

John nodded. "Yes, we'd be obligated to sling it right back. Newspaper coverage from coast to coast would follow, maybe even Court TV, God bless and save us. We want none of that if we can avoid it. It's not good for the grownups, and it's not good for the child. Now or later."

He bent and kissed Mattie's cheek.

"I'm sorry about all this," he said, and he did sound genuinely sorry. "Custody's just this way."

"I think you warned me. It's just that . . . the idea someone might make a thing like that up just because there was no other way for them to win . . ."

"Let me warn you again," he said. His face came as close to grim as its young and good-natured features would probably allow. "What we have is a very rich man with a very shaky case. The combination could be like working with old dynamite."

I turned to Mattie. "Are you still worried about Ki? Still feel she's in danger?"

I saw her think about hedging her response — out of plain old Yankee reserve, quite likely — and then deciding not to. Deciding, perhaps, that hedging was a luxury she couldn't afford.

"Yes. But it's just a feeling, you know."

John was frowning. I supposed the idea that Devore might resort to extralegal means of obtaining what he wanted had occurred to him, as well. "Keep your eye on her as much as you can," he said. "I respect intuition. Is yours based on anything concrete?"

"No," Mattie answered, and her quick glance in my direction asked me to keep my mouth shut. "Not really." She opened the Scout's door and tossed in the little brown bag with the Twinkies in it — she had decided to keep them after all. Then she turned to John and me with an expression that was close to anger. "I'm not sure how to follow that advice, anyway. I work five days a week, and in August, when we do the microfiche update, it'll be six. Right now Ki gets her lunch at Vacation Bible School and her dinner from Arlene Cullum. I see her in the mornings. The rest of the time . . ." I knew what she was going to say before she said it; the expression was an old one. ". . . she's on the TR."

"I could help you find an *au pair*," I said, thinking it would be a hell of a lot cheaper than John Storrow.

"No," they said in such perfect unison that they glanced at each other and laughed. But even while she was laughing, Mattie looked tense and unhappy.

"We're not going to leave a paper trail for Durgin or Devore's custody team to exploit," John said. "Who pays me is one thing. Who pays Mattie's child-care help is another."

"Besides, I've taken enough from you,"

Mattie said. "More than I can sleep easy on. I'm not going to get in any deeper just because I've been having megrims." She climbed into the Scout and closed the door.

I rested my hands on her open window. Now we were on the same level, and the eye-contact was so strong it was disconcerting. "Mattie, I don't have anything else to spend it on. Really."

"When it comes to John's fee, I accept that. Because John's fee is about Ki." She put her hand over mine and squeezed briefly. "This other is about me. All right?"

"Yeah. But you need to tell your babysitter and the people who run this Bible thing that you've got a custody case on your hands, a potentially bitter one, and Kyra's not to go anywhere with anyone, even someone they know, without your say-so."

She smiled. "It's already been done. On John's advice. Stay in touch, Mike." She lifted my hand, gave it a hearty smack, and drove away.

"What do you think?" I asked John as we watched the Scout blow oil on its way to the new Prouty Bridge, which spans Castle Street and spills outbound traffic onto Highway 68.

"I think it's grand she has a well-heeled benefactor and a smart lawyer," John said. He paused, then added: "But I'll tell you something — she somehow doesn't feel lucky to me at all. There's a feeling I get . . . I don't know . . ."

"That there's a cloud around her you can't quite see."

"Maybe. Maybe that's it." He raked his hands through the restless mass of his red hair. "I just know it's something sad."

I knew exactly what he meant . . . except for me there was more. I wanted to be in bed with her, sad or not, right or not. I wanted to feel her hands on me, tugging and pressing, patting and stroking. I wanted to be able to smell her skin and taste her hair. I wanted to have her lips against my ear, her breath tickling the fine hairs within its cup as she told me to do what I wanted, whatever I wanted.

I got back to Sara Laughs shortly before two o'clock and let myself in, thinking about nothing but my study and the IBM with the Courier ball. I was writing again — *writing.* I could still hardly believe it. I'd work (not that it felt much like work after a four-year layoff) until maybe six o'clock, swim, then go down to the Village Cafe for one of Buddy's cholesterol-rich specialties.

The moment I stepped through the door, Bunter's bell began to ring stridently. I stopped in the foyer, my hand frozen on the knob. The house was hot and bright, not a shadow anywhere, but the gooseflesh form-

441

ing on my arms felt like midnight.

"Who's here?" I called.

The bell stopped ringing. There was a moment of silence, and then a woman shrieked. It came from everywhere, pouring out of the sunny, mote-laden air like sweat out of hot skin. It was a scream of outrage, anger, grief . . . but mostly, I think, of horror. And I screamed in response. I couldn't help it. I had been frightened standing in the dark cellar stairwell, listening to the unseen fist thump on the insulation, but this was far worse.

It never stopped, that scream. It faded, as the child's sobs had faded; faded as if the person screaming was being carried rapidly down a long corridor and away from me.

At last it was gone.

I leaned against the bookcase, my palm pressed against my tee-shirt, my heart galloping beneath it. I was gasping for breath, and my muscles had that queer *exploded* feel they get after you've had a bad scare.

A minute passed. My heartbeat gradually slowed, and my breathing slowed with it. I straightened up, took a tottery step, and when my legs held me, took two more. I stood in the kitchen doorway, looking across to the living room. Above the fireplace, Bunter the moose looked glassily back at me. The bell around his neck hung still and chimeless. A hot sunpoint glowed on its side. The only sound was that stupid Felix the Cat clock in the kitchen.

The thought nagging at me, even then, was that the screaming woman had been Jo, that Sara Laughs was being haunted by my wife, and that she was in pain. Dead or not, she was in pain.

"Jo?" I asked quietly. "Jo, are you —"

The sobbing began again — the sound of a terrified child. At the same moment my mouth and nose once more filled with the iron taste of the lake. I put one hand to my throat, gagging and frightened, then leaned over the sink and spat. It was as it had been before — instead of voiding a gush of water, nothing came out but a little spit. The waterlogged feeling was gone as if it had never been there.

I stayed where I was, grasping the counter and bent over the sink, probably looking like a drunk who has finished the party by up-chucking most of the night's bottled cheer. I felt like that, too — stunned and bleary, too overloaded to really understand what was going on.

At last I straightened up again, took the towel folded over the dishwasher's handle, and wiped my face with it. There was tea in the fridge, and I wanted a tall, ice-choked glass of it in the worst way. I reached for the doorhandle and froze. The fruit and vegetable magnets were drawn into a circle again. In the center was this:

help im drown

That's it, I thought. *I'm getting out of here. Right now. Today.*

Yet an hour later I was up in my stifling study with a glass of tea on the desk beside me (the cubes in it long since melted), dressed only in my bathing trunks and lost in the world I was making — the one where a private detective named Andy Drake was trying to prove that John Shackleford was not the serial killer nicknamed Baseball Cap.

This is how we go on: one day at a time, one meal at a time, one pain at a time, one breath at a time. Dentists go on one root-canal at a time; boat-builders go on one hull at a time. If you write books, you go on one page at a time. We turn from all we know and all we fear. We study catalogues, watch football games, choose Sprint over AT&T. We count the birds in the sky and will not turn from the window when we hear the footsteps behind us as something comes up the hall; we say yes, I agree that clouds often look like other things — fish and unicorns and men on horseback — but they are really only clouds. Even when the lightning flashes inside them we say they are only clouds and turn our attention to the next meal, the next pain, the next breath, the next page. This is how we go on.

Chapter 16

The book was big, okay? The book was major.

I was afraid to change *rooms*, let alone pack up the typewriter and my slim just-begun manuscript and take it back to Derry. That would be as dangerous as taking an infant out in a windstorm. So I stayed, always reserving the right to move out if things got too weird (the way smokers reserve the right to quit if their coughs get too heavy), and a week passed. Things happened during that week, but until I met Max Devore on The Street the following Friday — the seventeenth of July, it would have been — the most important thing was that I continued to work on a novel which would, if finished, be called *My Childhood Friend*. Perhaps we always think what was lost was the best . . . or would have been the best. I don't know for sure. What I *do* know is that my real life that week had mostly to do with Andy Drake, John Shackleford, and a shadowy figure standing in the deep background. Raymond Garraty, John Shackleford's childhood friend. A man who sometimes wore a baseball cap.

During that week, the manifestations in the house continued, but at a lower level —

there was nothing like that bloodcurdling scream. Sometimes Bunter's bell rang, and sometimes the fruit and vegetable magnets would re-form themselves into a circle . . . never with words in the middle, though; not that week. One morning I got up and the sugar cannister was overturned, making me think of Mattie's story about the flour. Nothing was written in the spill, but there was a squiggle —

~~~~~~~~~

— as though something had tried to write and failed. If so, I sympathized. I knew what *that* was like.

My depo before the redoubtable Elmer Durgin was on Friday the tenth. On the following Tuesday I took The Street down to Warrington's softball field, hoping for my own peek at Max Devore. It was going on six o'clock when I got within hearing range of the shouts, cheers, and batted balls. A path marked with rustic signs (curlicued *W*'s burned into oak arrows) led past an abandoned boathouse, a couple of sheds, and a gazebo half-buried in blackberry creepers. I eventually came out in deep center field. A litter of potato-chip bags, candy-wrappers, and beer cans suggested that others sometimes watched the games from this vantage-point. I couldn't help thinking about Jo and her mysterious friend, the guy in the old brown sportcoat, the burly guy who had slipped an arm around her waist and led her away from the game, laughing, back toward The Street. Twice over the weekend I'd come close to calling Bonnie Amudson, seeing if maybe I could chase that guy down, put a name on him, and both times I had backed off. Sleeping dogs, I told myself each time. Sleeping dogs, Michael.

I had the area beyond deep center to myself that evening, and it felt like the right distance from home plate, considering the man who usually parked his wheelchair behind the backstop had called me a liar and I had invited him to store my telephone number where the sunshine grows dim.

I needn't have worried in any case. Devore wasn't in attendance, nor was the lovely Rogette.

I did spot Mattie behind the casually maintained chickenwire barrier on the first-base line. John Storrow was beside her, wearing jeans and a polo shirt, his red hair mostly corralled by a Mets cap. They stood watching the game and chatting like old friends for two innings before they saw me — more than enough time for me to feel envious of John's position, and a little jealous as well.

Finally someone lofted a long fly to center, where the edge of the woods served as the only fence. The center fielder backed up, but it was going to be far over his head. It was hit to my depth, off to my right. I moved in that direction without thinking, high-footing through the shrubs that formed a zone between the mown outfield and the trees, hoping I wasn't running through poison ivy. I caught the softball in my out-stretched left hand, and laughed when some of the spectators cheered. The center fielder applauded me by tapping his bare right hand into the pocket of his glove. The batter, meanwhile, circled the bases se-renely, knowing he had hit a ground-rule home run.

I tossed the ball to the fielder and as I re-turned to my original post among the candy-wrappers and beer cans, I looked back in and saw Mattie and John looking at me.

If anything confirms the idea that we're just another species of animal, one with a slightly bigger brain and a *much* bigger idea of our own importance in the scheme of things, it's how much we can convey by ges-ture when we absolutely have to. Mattie clasped her hands to her chest, tilted her head to the left, raised her eyebrows — *My hero.* I held my hands to my shoulders and flipped the palms skyward — *Shucks, ma'am, 't'warn't nothin.* John lowered his head and put his fingers to his brow, as if something there hurt — *You lucky sonofabitch.*

With those comments out of the way, I pointed at the backstop and shrugged a question. Both Mattie and John shrugged back. An inning later a little boy who looked like one giant exploding freckle ran out to where I was, his oversized Michael Jordan jersey churning around his shins like a dress.

"Guy down there gimme fifty cent to say you should call im later on at his hotel over in the Rock," he said, pointing at John. "He say you gimme another fifty cent if there was an answer."

"Tell him I'll call him around nine-thirty," I said. "I don't have any change, though. Can you take a buck?"

"Hey, yeah, swank." He snatched it, turned away, then turned back. He grinned, revealing a set of teeth caught between Act I and Act II. With the softball players in the background, he looked like a Norman Rockwell archetype. "Guy also say tell you that was a bullshit catch."

"Tell him people used to say the same thing about Willie Mays all the time."

"Willie who?"

Ah, youth. Ah, mores. "Just tell him, son. He'll know."

I stayed another inning, but by then the

game was getting drunk, Devore still hadn't shown, and I went back home the way I had come. I met one fisherman standing out on a rock and two young people strolling along The Street toward Warrington's, their hands linked. They said hi and I hi'd them back. I felt lonely and content at the same time. I believe that is a rare kind of happiness.

Some people check their phone answering machines when they get home; that summer I always checked the front of the fridge. Eenie-meenie-chili-beanie, as Bullwinkle Moose used to say, the spirits are about to speak. That night they hadn't, although the fruit and vegetable magnets had re-formed into a sinuous shape like a snake or perhaps the letter *S* taking a nap:

A little later I called John and asked him where Devore had been, and he repeated in words what he had already told me, and much more economically, by gesture. "It's the first game he's missed since he came back," he said. "Mattie tried asking a few people if he was okay, and the consensus seemed to be that he was . . . at least as far as anyone knew."

"What do you mean she *tried* asking a few people?"

450

"I mean that several wouldn't even talk to her. 'Cut her dead,' my parents' generation would have said." *Watch it, buddy,* I thought but didn't say, *that's only half a step from my generation.* "One of her old girlfriends spoke to her finally, but there's a general attitude about Mattie Devore. That man Osgood may be a shitty salesman, but as Devore's Mr. Moneyguy he's doing a wonderful job of separating Mattie from the other folks in the town. *Is* it a town, Mike? I don't quite get that part."

"It's just the TR," I said absently. "There's no real way to explain it. Do you actually believe Devore's bribing *everyone?* That doesn't say much for the old Wordsworthian idea of pastoral innocence and goodness, does it?"

"He's spreading money and using Osgood — maybe Footman, too — to spread stories. And the folks around here seem at least as honest as honest politicians."

"The ones who stay bought?"

"Yeah. Oh, and I saw one of Devore's potential star witnesses in the Case of the Runaway Child. Royce Merrill. He was over by the equipment shed with some of his cronies. Did you happen to notice him?"

I said I had not.

"Guy must be a hundred and thirty," John said. "He's got a cane with a gold head the size of an elephant's asshole."

"That's a *Boston Post* cane. The oldest person in the area gets to keep it."

"And I have no doubt he came by it honestly. If Devore's lawyers put him on the stand, I'll debone him." There was something chilling in John's gleeful confidence.

"I'm sure," I said. "How did Mattie take getting cut dead by her old friends?" I was thinking of her saying that she hated Tuesday nights, hated to think of the softball games going on as they always had at the field where she had met her late husband.

"She did okay," John said. "I think she's given most of them up as a lost cause, anyway." I had my doubts about that — I seem to remember that at twenty-one lost causes are sort of a specialty — but I didn't say anything. "She's hanging in. She's been lonely and scared, I think that in her own mind she might already have begun the process of giving Kyra up, but she's got her confidence back now. Mostly thanks to meeting you. Talk about your fantastically lucky breaks."

Well, maybe. I flashed on Jo's brother Frank once saying to me that he didn't think there was any such thing as luck, only fate and inspired choices. And then I remembered that image of the TR criss-crossed with invisible cables, connections that were unseen but as strong as steel.

"John, I forgot to ask the most important question of all the other day, after I gave my depo. This custody case we're all so concerned about . . . has it even been scheduled?"

"Good question. I've checked three ways to Sunday, and Bissonette has, too. Unless Devore and his people have pulled something really slippery, like filing in another court district, I don't think it has been."

"Could they do that? File in another district?"

"Maybe. But probably not without us finding out."

"So what does it mean?"

"That Devore's on the verge of giving up," John said promptly. "As of now I see no other way of explaining it. I'm going back to New York first thing tomorrow, but I'll stay in touch. If anything comes up here, you do the same."

I said I would and went to bed. No female visitors came to share my dreams. That was sort of a relief.

When I came downstairs to recharge my iced-tea glass late Wednesday morning, Brenda Meserve had erected the laundry whirligig on the back stoop and was hanging out my clothes. This she did as her mother had no doubt taught her, with pants and shirts on the outside and undies on the inside, where any passing nosyparkers couldn't see what you chose to wear closest to your skin.

"You can take these in around four o'clock," Mrs. M. said as she prepared to leave. She looked at me with the bright and cynical eye of a woman who has been "doing for" well-off men her entire life. "Don't you forget and leave em out all night — dewy clothes don't ever feel fresh until they're warshed again."

I told her most humbly that I would remember to take in my clothes. I then asked her — feeling like a spy working an embassy party for information — if the house felt all right to her.

"All right how?" she asked, cocking one wild eyebrow at me.

"Well, I've heard funny noises a couple of times. In the night."

She sniffed. "It's a log house, ennit? Built in relays, so to speak. It settles, one wing against t'other. That's what you hear, most likely."

"No ghosts, huh?" I said, as if disappointed.

"Not that I've ever seen," she said, matter-of-fact as an accountant, "but my ma said there's plenty down here. She said this whole lake is haunted. By the Micmacs that lived here until they was driven out by General Wing, by all the men who went away to the Civil War and died there — over six hundred went from this part of the world, Mr. Noonan, and less than a hundred and fifty came back . . . at least in their bodies. Ma said this side of Dark Score's also haunted by the ghost of that Negro boy who died here, poor tyke. He belonged to one of the Red-Tops, you know."

"No — I know about Sara and the Red-Tops, but not this." I paused. "Did he drown?"

"Nawp, caught in an animal trap. Struggled there for most of a whole day, screaming for help. Finally they found him. They saved the foot, but they shouldn't have. Blood-poisoning set in, and the boy died. Summer of ought-one, that was. It's why they left, I guess — it was too sad to stay. But my ma used to claim the little fella, *he* stayed. She used to say that he's still on the TR."

I wondered what Mrs. M. would say if I told her that the little fella had very likely been here to greet me when I arrived from Derry, and had been back on several occasions since.

"Then there was Kenny Auster's father, Normal," she said. "You know that story, don't you? Oh, that's a terrible story." She looked rather pleased — either at knowing such a terrible story or at having the chance to tell it.

"No," I said. "I know Kenny, though. He's the one with the wolfhound. Blueberry."

"Ayuh. He carpenters a tad and caretakes a tad, just like his father before him. His dad caretook many of these places, you know, and back just after the Second World War was over, Normal Auster drownded Kenny's little brother in his back yard. This was when they lived on Wasp Hill, down where the road splits, one side goin to the old boat-landin and the other to the marina. He didn't drown the tyke in the lake, though. He put him on the ground under the pump and just held him there until the baby was full of water and dead."

I stood there looking at her, the clothes behind us snapping on their whirligig. I thought of my mouth and nose and throat full of that cold mineral taste that could have been well-water as well as lakewater; down here all of it comes from the same deep aquifers. I thought of the message on the refrigerator: *help im drown.*

"He left the baby laying right under the pump. He had a new Chevrolet, and he drove it down here to Lane Forty-two. Took his shotgun, too."

"You aren't going to tell me Kenny Auster's dad committed suicide in my house, are you, Mrs. Meserve?"

She shook her head. "Nawp. He did it on

456

the Brickers' lakeside deck. Sat down on their porch glider and blew his damned baby-murdering head off."

"The Brickers? I don't —"

"You wouldn't. Hasn't been any Brickers on the lake since the sixties. They were from Delaware. Quality folks. You'd think of it as the Warshburn place, I guess, although they're gone, now, too. Place is empty. Every now and then that stark naturalborn fool Osgood brings someone down and shows it off, but he'll never sell it at the price he's asking. Mark my words."

The Washburns I had known — had played bridge with them a time or two. Nice enough people, although probably not what Mrs. M., with her queer backcountry snobbishness, would have called "quality." Their place was maybe an eighth of a mile north of mine along The Street. Past that point, there's nothing much — the drop to the lake gets steep, and the woods are massed tangles of second growth and blackberry bushes. The Street goes on to the tip of Halo Bay at the far north end of Dark Score, but once Lane Forty-two curves back to the highway, the path is for the most part used only by berry-picking expeditions in the summer and hunters in the fall.

Normal, I thought. Hell of a name for a guy who had drowned his infant son under the backyard pump.

"Did he leave a note? Any explanation?"

"Nawp. But you'll hear folks say he haunts the lake, too. Little towns are most likely full of haunts, but I couldn't say aye, no, or maybe myself; I ain't the sensitive type. All I know about your place, Mr. Noonan, is that it smells damp no matter how much I try to get it aired out. I 'magine that's logs. Log buildins don't go well with lakes. The damp gets into the wood."

She had set her purse down between her Reeboks; now she bent and picked it up. It was a countrywoman's purse, black, styleless (except for the gold grommets holding the handles on), and utilitarian. She could have carried a good selection of kitchen appliances in there if she had wanted to.

"I can't stand here natterin all day long, though, much as I might like to. I got one more place to go before I can call it quits. Summer's ha'vest time in this part of the world, you know. Now remember to take those clothes in before dark, Mr. Noonan. Don't let em get all dewy."

"I won't." And I didn't. But when I went out to take them in, dressed in my bathing trunks and coated with sweat from the oven I'd been working in (I had to get the air conditioner fixed, just *had* to), I saw that something had altered Mrs. M.'s arrangements. My jeans and shirts now hung around the pole. The underwear and socks, which had been decorously hidden when Mrs. M. drove up the driveway in her old Ford, were now on the outside. It was as if my unseen guest — *one* of my unseen guests — was saying ha ha ha.

I went to the library the next day, and made renewing my library card my first order of business. Lindy Briggs herself took my four bucks and entered me into the computer, first telling me how sorry she had been to hear about Jo's death. And, as with Bill, I sensed a certain reproach in her tone, as if I were to blame for such improperly delayed condolences. I supposed I was.

"Lindy, do you have a town history?" I asked when we had finished the proprieties concerning my wife.

"We have two," she said, then leaned toward me over the desk, a little woman in a violently patterned sleeveless dress, her hair a gray puffball around her head, her bright eyes swimming behind her bifocals. In a confidential voice she added, "Neither is much good."

"Which one is better?" I asked, matching her tone.

"Probably the one by Edward Osteen. He was a summer resident until the mid-fifties and lived here full-time when he retired. He wrote *Dark Score Days* in 1965 or '66. He had it privately published because he couldn't find a commercial house that would take it. Even the regional publishers passed." She sighed. "The locals bought it, but that's not many books, is it?"

"No, I suppose not," I said.

"He just wasn't much of a writer. Not much of a photographer, either — those little black-and-white snaps of his make my *eyes* hurt. Still, he tells some good stories. The Micmac Drive, General Wing's trick horse, the twister in the eighteen-eighties, the fires in the nineteen-thirties . . ."

"Anything about Sara and the Red-Tops?"

She nodded, smiling. "Finally got around to looking up the history of your own place, did you? I'm glad to hear it. He found an old photo of them, and it's in there. He thought it was taken at the Fryeburg Fair in 1900. Ed used to say he'd give a lot to hear a record made by that bunch."

"So would I, but none were ever made." A haiku by the Greek poet George Seferis suddenly occurred to me: *Are these the voices of our dead friends / or just the gramophone?* "What happened to Mr. Osteen? I don't recall the name."

"Died not a year or two before you and Jo bought your place on the lake," she said. "Cancer."

"You said there were two histories?"

"The other one you probably know — *A History of Castle County and Castle Rock.*

Done for the county centennial, and dry as dust. Eddie Osteen's book isn't very well written, but he wasn't dry. You have to give him that much. You should find them both over there." She pointed to shelves with a sign over them which read OF MAINE IN-TEREST. "They don't circulate." Then she brightened. "Although we will happily take any nickels you should feel moved to feed into our photocopy machine."

Mattie was sitting in the far corner next to a boy in a turned-around baseball cap, showing him how to use the microfilm reader. She looked up at me, smiled, and mouthed the words *Nice catch*. Referring to my lucky grab at Warrington's, presumably. I gave a modest little shrug before turning to the OF MAINE INTEREST shelves. But she was right — lucky or not, it *had* been a nice catch.

"What are you looking for?"

I was so deep into the two histories I'd found that Mattie's voice made me jump. I turned around and smiled, first aware that she was wearing some light and pleasant perfume, second that Lindy Briggs was watching us from the main desk, her welcoming smile put away.

"Background on the area where I live," I said. "Old stories. My housekeeper got me interested." Then, in a lower voice:

"Teacher's watching. Don't look around."

Mattie looked startled — and, I thought, a little worried. As it turned out, she was right to be worried. In a voice that was low-pitched yet still designed to carry at least as far as the desk, she asked if she could reshelve either book for me. I gave her both. As she picked them up she said in what was almost a con's whisper: "That lawyer who represented you last Friday got John a private detective. He says they may have found something interesting about the guardian *ad litem.*"

I walked over to the OF MAINE INTEREST shelves with her, hoping I wasn't getting her in trouble, and asked if she knew what the something interesting might be. She shook her head, gave me a professional little librarian's smile, and I went away.

On the ride back to the house, I tried to think about what I'd read, but there wasn't much. Osteen was a bad writer who had taken bad pictures, and while his stories were colorful, they were also pretty thin on the ground. He mentioned Sara and the Red-Tops, all right, but he referred to them as a "Dixie-Land octet," and even I knew that wasn't right. The Red-Tops might have played some Dixieland, but they had primarily been a blues group (Friday and Saturday nights) and a gospel group (Sunday mornings). Osteen's two-page summary of the Red-Tops' stay on the TR made it clear that he had heard no one else's covers of Sara's tunes.

He confirmed that a child had died of blood-poisoning caused by a traphold wound, a story which sounded like Brenda Meserve's . . . but why wouldn't it? Osteen had likely heard it from Mrs. M.'s father or grandfather. He also said that the boy was Son Tidwell's only child, and that the guitar-player's real name was Reginald. The Tidwells had supposedly drifted north from the whorehouse district of New Orleans — the fabled crib-and-club streets which had been known around the turn of the century as Storyville.

There was no mention of Sara and the Red-Tops in the more formal history of Castle County, and no mention of Kenny Auster's drownded little brother in either book. Not long before Mattie came over to speak to me, I'd had a wild idea: that Son Tidwell and Sara Tidwell were man and wife, and that the little boy (not named by Osteen) had been their son. I found the picture Lindy had mentioned and studied it closely. It showed at least a dozen black people standing in a stiff group in front of what looked like a cattle exhibition. There was an old-fashioned Ferris wheel in the background. It could well have been taken at the Fryeburg Fair, and as old and faded as it was, it had a simple, elemental power that all Osteen's own photos put together could not match. You have seen photographs of western and Depression-era bandidos that have that same look of eerie truth — stern faces above tight ties and collars, eyes not quite lost in the shadows of antique hatbrims.

Sara stood front and center, wearing a black dress and her guitar. She was not outright smiling in this picture, but there seemed to be a smile in her eyes, and I thought they were like the eyes in some paintings, the ones that seem to follow you wherever you move in the room. I studied the photo and thought of her almost spiteful voice in my dream: *What do you want to know, sugar?* I suppose I wanted to know about her and the others — who they had been, what they were to each other when they weren't singing and playing, why they'd left, where they'd gone.

Both of her hands were clearly visible, one posed on the strings of her guitar, the other on the frets, where she had been making a G-chord on an October Fair-day in the year 1900. Her fingers were long, artistic, bare of rings. That didn't necessarily mean that she and Son Tidwell weren't married, of course, and even if they hadn't been, the little boy who'd been caught in the trap could have been born on the wrong side of the blanket.

Except the same ghost of a smile lurked in Son Tidwell's eyes. The resemblance was remarkable. I had an idea that the two of them had been brother and sister, not man and wife.

I thought about these things on my way home, and I thought about cables that were felt rather than seen . . . but mostly I found myself thinking about Lindy Briggs — the way she had smiled at me, the way, a little later on, she had not smiled at her bright young librarian with the high-school certification. That worried me.

Then I got back to the house, and all I worried about was my story and the people in it — bags of bones which were putting on flesh daily.

Michael Noonan, Max Devore, and Rogette Whitmore played out their horrible little comedy scene Friday evening. Two other things which bear narrating happened before that.

The first was a call from John Storrow on Thursday night. I was sitting in front of the TV with a baseball game running soundlessly in front of me (the mute button with which most remote controls come equipped may be the twentieth century's finest invention). I was thinking about Sara Tidwell and Son Tidwell and Son Tidwell's little boy. I was thinking about Storyville, a name any writer just had to love. And in the back of my mind I was thinking about my wife, who had died pregnant.

"Hello?" I said.

"Mike, I have some wonderful news," John said. He sounded near to bursting. "Romeo Bissonette may be a weird name, but there's nothing weird about the detective-guy he found for me. His name is George Kennedy, like the actor. He's good, and he's *fast*. This guy could work in New York."

"If that's the highest compliment you can think of, you need to get out of the city more."

He went on as if he hadn't heard. "Kennedy's real job is with a security firm — the other stuff is strictly in the moonlight. Which is a great loss, believe me. He got most of this on the phone. I can't believe it."

"What specifically can't you believe?"

"Jackpot, baby." Again he spoke in that tone of greedy satisfaction which I found both troubling and reassuring. "Elmer Durgin has done the following things since late May: paid off his car; paid off his camp in Rangely Lakes; caught up on about ninety years of child support —"

"Nobody pays child support for ninety years," I said, but I was just running my mouth to hear it go . . . to let off some of my own building excitement, in truth. " 'T'ain't possible, McGee."

"It is if you have seven kids," John said, and began howling with laughter.

I thought of the pudgy self-satisfied face, the cupid-bow mouth, the nails that looked polished and prissy. "He *don't*," I said.

"He *do*," John said, still laughing. He sounded like a complete lunatic — manic, hold the depressive. "He really do! Ranging in ages from f-fourteen to th-th-*three!* What a b-busy p-p-potent little prick he must have!" More helpless howls. And by now I was howling right along with him — I'd caught it like the mumps. "Kennedy is going to f-f-fax me p-pictures of the whole . . . fam' . . . damily!" We broke up completely, laughing together long-distance. I could picture John Storrow sitting alone in his Park Avenue office, bellowing like a lunatic and scaring the cleaning ladies.

"That doesn't matter, though," he said when he could talk coherently again. "You see what matters, don't you?"

"Yes," I said. "How could he be so stupid?" Meaning Durgin, but also meaning Devore. John understood, I think, that we were talking about both he's at the same time.

"Elmer Durgin's a little lawyer from a little township tucked away in the big woods of western Maine, that's all. How could he

467

know that some guardian angel would come along with the resources to smoke him out? He also bought a boat, by the way. Two weeks ago. It's a twin outboard. A big 'un. It's over, Mike. The home team scores nine runs in the bottom of the ninth and the fucking pennant is *ours*."

"If you say so." But my hand went off on its own expedition, made a loose fist, and knocked on the good solid wood of the coffee-table.

"And hey, the softball game wasn't a total loss." John was still talking between little giggling outbursts like helium balloons.

"No?"

"I'm taken with her."

"Her?"

"Mattie," he said patiently. "Mattie Devore." A pause, then: "Mike? Are you there?"

"Yeah," I said. "Phone slipped. Sorry." The phone hadn't slipped as much as an inch, but it came out sounding natural enough, I thought. And if it hadn't, so what? When it came to Mattie, I would be — in John's mind, at least — below suspicion. Like the country-house staff in an Agatha Christie. He was twenty-eight, maybe thirty. The idea that a man twelve years older might be sexually attracted to Mattie had probably never crossed his mind . . . or maybe just for a second or two there on the common, before he dismissed it as ludicrous. The way Mattie herself had dismissed the idea of Jo and the man in the brown sportcoat.

"I can't do my courtship dance while I'm representing her," he said, "wouldn't be ethical. Wouldn't be safe, either. Later, though . . . you can never tell."

"No," I said, hearing my voice as you sometimes do in moments when you are caught completely flat-footed, hearing it as though it were coming from someone else. Someone on the radio or the record-player, maybe. Are these the voices of our dead friends, or just the gramophone? I thought of his hands, the fingers long and slender and without a ring on any of them. Like Sara's hands in that old photo. "No, you can never tell."

We said goodbye, and I sat watching the muted baseball game. I thought about getting up to get a beer, but it seemed too far to the refrigerator — a safari, in fact. What I felt was a kind of dull hurt, followed by a better emotion: rueful relief, I guess you'd call it. Was he too old for her? No, I didn't think so. Just about right. Prince Charming No. 2, this time in a three-piece suit. Mattie's luck with men might finally be changing, and if so I should be glad. I *would* be glad. And relieved. Because I had a book to write, and never mind the look of white sneakers flashing below a red sundress in the deepening gloom, or the ember of her cigarette dancing in the dark.

Still, I felt really lonely for the first time since I saw Kyra marching up the white line of Route 68 in her bathing suit and flip-flops.

"You funny little man, said Strickland," I told the empty room. It came out before I knew I was going to say anything, and when it did, the channel on the TV changed. It went from baseball to a rerun of *All in the Family* and then to *Ren & Stimpy.* I glanced down at the remote control. It was still on the coffee-table where I'd left it. The TV channel changed again, and this time I was looking at Humphrey Bogart and Ingrid Bergman. There was an airplane in the background, and I didn't need to pick up the remote and turn on the sound to know that Humphrey was telling Ingrid that she was getting on that plane. My wife's all-time favorite movie. She bawled at the end without fail.

"Jo?" I asked. "Are you here?"

Bunter's bell rang once. Very faintly. There had been several presences in the house, I was sure of it . . . but tonight, for the first time, I was positive it was Jo who was with me.

"Who was he, hon?" I asked. "The guy at the softball field, who was he?"

Bunter's bell hung still and quiet. She was in the room, though. I sensed her, something like a held breath.

I remembered the ugly, gibing little message on the refrigerator after my dinner with Mattie and Ki: *blue rose liar ha ha.*

"Who was he?" My voice was unsteady, sounding on the verge of tears. "What were you doing down here with some guy? Were you . . ." But I couldn't bring myself to ask if she had been lying to me, cheating on me. I couldn't ask even though the presence I felt might be, let's face it, only in my own head.

The TV switched away from *Casablanca* and here was everybody's favorite lawyer, Perry Mason, on Nick at Nite. Perry's nemesis, Hamilton Burger, was questioning a distraught-looking woman, and all at once the sound blared on, making me jump.

"I am *not* a liar!" some long-ago TV actress cried. For a moment she looked right out at me, and I was stunned breathless to see Jo's eyes in that black-and-white fifties face. "I *never* lied, Mr. Burger, never!"

"I submit that you did!" Burger responded. He moved in on her, leering like a vampire. "I submit that you —"

The TV suddenly went off. Bunter's bell gave a single brisk shake, and then whatever had been here was gone. But I felt better. *I am* not *a liar . . . I* never *lied, never.*

471

I could believe that if I chose to.

If I chose.

I went to bed, and there were no dreams.

I had taken to starting work early, before the heat could really get a hold on the study. I'd drink some juice, gobble some toast, then sit behind the IBM until almost noon, watching the Courier ball dance and twirl as the pages floated through the machine and came out with writing on them. That old magic, so strange and wonderful. It never really felt like work to me, although I called it that; it felt like some weird kind of mental trampoline I bounced on. Those were springs that took away all the weight of the world for awhile.

At noon I'd break, drive down to Buddy Jellison's greaseatorium for something nasty, then return and work for another hour or so. After that I would swim and take a long dreamless nap in the north bedroom. I had barely poked my head into the master bedroom at the south end of the house, and if Mrs. M. thought this was odd, she kept it to herself.

On Friday the seventeenth, I stopped at the Lakeview General on my way back to the house to gas up my Chevrolet. There are pumps at the All-Purpose Garage, and the go-juice was a penny or two cheaper, but I didn't like the vibe. Today, as I stood in front of the store with the pump on automatic feed, looking off toward the mountains, Bill Dean's Dodge Ram pulled in on the other side of the island. He climbed down and gave me a smile. "How's it going, Mike?"

"Pretty fair."

"Brenda says you're writin up a storm."

"I am," I said, and it was on the tip of my tongue to ask for an update on the broken second-floor air conditioner. The tip of my tongue was where it stayed. I was still too nervous about my rediscovered ability to want to change anything about the environment in which I was doing it. Stupid, maybe, but sometimes things work just because you think they work. It's as good a definition of faith as any.

"Well, I'm glad to hear it. Very glad." I thought he was sincere enough, but he somehow didn't sound like Bill. Not the one who had greeted me back, anyway.

"I've been looking up some old stuff about my side of the lake," I said.

"Sara and the Red-Tops? You always were sort of int'rested in them, I remember."

"Them, yes, but not just them. Lots of history. I was talking to Mrs. M., and she told me about Normal Auster. Kenny's father."

Bill's smile stayed on, and he only paused a moment in the act of unscrewing the cap on his gas tank, but I still had a sense, quite clear, that he had frozen inside. "You wouldn't write about a thing like that, would you, Mike? Because there's a lot of people around here that'd feel it bad and take it wrong. I told Jo the same thing."

"Jo?" I felt an urge to step between the two pumps and over the island so I could grab him by the arm. "What's Jo got to do with this?"

He looked at me cautiously and long. "She didn't tell you?"

"What are you talking about?"

"She thought she might write something about Sara and the Red-Tops for one of the local papers." Bill was picking his words very slowly. I have a clear memory of that, and of how hot the sun was, beating down on my neck, and the sharpness of our shadows on the asphalt. He began to pump his gas, and the sound of the pump's motor was also very sharp. "I think she even mentioned *Yankee* magazine. I c'd be wrong about that, but I don't think I am."

I was speechless. Why would she have kept quiet about the idea to try her hand at a little local history? Because she might have thought she was poaching on my territory? That was ridiculous. She had known me better than that . . . hadn't she?

"When did you have this conversation, Bill? Do you remember?"

"Coss I do," he said. "Same day she come down to take delivery of those plastic owls. Only I raised the subject, because folks had told me she was asking around."

"Prying?"

"I didn't say that," he said stiffly, "you did."

True, but I thought prying was what he meant. "Go on."

"Nothing to go on about. I told her there were sore toes here and there on the TR, same as there are anyplace, and ast her not to tread on any corns if she could help it. She said she understood. Maybe she did, maybe she didn't. All I know is she kep' on asking questions. Listenin to stories from old fools with more time than sense."

"When was this?"

"Fall of '93, winter and spring of '94. Went all around town, she did — even over to Motton and Harlow — with her notebook and little tape-recorder. Anyway, that's all I know."

I realized a stunning thing: Bill was lying. If you'd asked me before that day, I'd have laughed and told you Bill Dean didn't have a lie in him. And he must not have had many, because he did it badly.

I thought of calling him on it, but to what end? I needed to think, and I couldn't do it here — my mind was roaring. Given time, that roar might subside and I'd see it was really nothing, no big deal, but I needed that time. When you start finding out unexpected things about a loved one who's been dead awhile, it rocks you. Take it from me, it does.

Bill's eyes had shifted away from mine, but now they shifted back. He looked both earnest and — I could have sworn it — a little scared.

"She ast about little Kerry Auster, and that's a good example of what I mean about steppin on sore toes. That's not the stuff for a newspaper story or a magazine article. Normal just snapped. No one knows why. It was a terrible tragedy, senseless, and there's still people who could be hurt by it. In little towns things are kind of connected under the surface —"

Yes, like cables you couldn't quite see.

"— and the past dies slower. Sara and those others, that's a little different. They were just . . . just wanderers . . . from away. Jo could have stuck to those folks and it would've been all right. And say — for all I know, she did. Because I never saw a single word she ever wrote. If she did write."

About that he was telling the truth, I felt. But I knew something else, knew it as surely as I'd known Mattie had been wearing white shorts when she called me on her day off. *Sara and those others were just wanderers from away,* Bill had said, but he hesitated in the

476

middle of his thought, substituting wanderers for the word which had come naturally to mind. *Niggers* was the word he hadn't said. *Sara and those others were just niggers from away.*

All at once I found myself thinking of an old story by Ray Bradbury, "Mars Is Heaven." The first space travellers to Mars discover it's Green Town, Illinois, and all their well-loved friends and relatives are there. Only the friends and relatives are really alien monsters, and in the night, while the space travellers think they are sleeping in the beds of their long-dead kinfolk in a place that must be heaven, they are slaughtered to the last man.

"Bill, you're sure she was up here a few times in the off-season?"

"Ayuh. 'T'wasn't just a few times, either. Might have been a dozen times or more. Day-trips, don't you know."

"Did you ever see a fellow with her? Burly guy, black hair?"

He thought about it. I tried not to hold my breath. At last he shook his head. "Few times I saw her, she was alone. But I didn't see her every time she came. Sometimes I only heard she'd been on the TR after she 'us gone again. Saw her in June of '94, headed up toward Halo Bay in that little car a hers. She waved, I waved back. Went down to the house later that evenin to see if she needed anythin, but she'd gone. I didn't see her again. When she died later on that summer, me and 'Vette were so shocked."

Whatever she was looking for, she must never have written any of it down. I would have found the manuscript.

Was that true, though? She had made many trips down here with no apparent attempts at concealment, on one of them she had even been accompanied by a strange man, and I had only found out about these visits by accident.

"This is hard to talk about," Bill said, "but since we've gotten started hard, we might as well go the rest of the way. Livin on the TR is like the way we used to sleep four or even five in a bed when it was January and true cold. If everyone rests easy, you do all right. But if one person gets restless, gets tossing and turning, no one can sleep. Right now you're the restless one. That's how people see it."

He waited to see what I'd say. When almost twenty seconds passed without a word from me (Harold Oblowski would have been proud), he shuffled his feet and went on.

"There are people in town uneasy about the interest you've taken in Mattie Devore, for instance. Now I'm not sayin there's anythin goin on between the two of you — although there's folks who *do* say it — but if you want to stay on the TR you're makin it tough on yourself."

"Why?"

"Comes back to what I said a week and a half ago. She's trouble."

"As I recall, Bill, you said she was *in* trouble. And she is. I'm trying to help her out of it. There's nothing going on between us but that."

"*I* seem to recall telling you that Max Devore is nuts," he said. "If you make him mad, we all pay the price." The pump clicked off and he racked it up. Then he sighed, raised his hands, dropped them. "You think this is easy for me to say?"

"You think it's easy for me to listen to?"

"All right, ayuh, we're in the same skiff. But Mattie Devore isn't the only person on the TR livin hand-to-mouth, you know. There's others got their woes, as well. Can't you understand that?"

Maybe he saw that I understood too much and too well, because his shoulders slumped.

"If you're asking me to stand aside and let Devore take Mattie's baby without a fight, you can forget it," I said. "And I hope that's not it. Because I think I'd have to be quits with a man who'd ask another man to do something like that."

"I wouldn't ask it now anywise," he said, his accent thickening almost to the point of contempt. "It'd be too late, wouldn't it?" And then, unexpectedly, he softened. "Christ, man, I'm worried about *you*. Let the rest of it go hang, all right? Hang high where the crows can pick it." He was lying again, but this time I didn't mind so much, because I thought he was lying to himself. "But you need to have a care. When I said Devore was crazy, that was no figure of speech. Do you think he'll bother with court if court can't get him what he wants? Folks died in those summer fires back in 1933. Good people. One related to me. They burned over half the goddam county and Max Devore set em. That was his going-away present to the TR. It could never be proved, but he did it. Back then he was young and broke, not yet twenty and no law in his pocket. What do you think he'd do now?"

He looked at me searchingly. I said nothing.

Bill nodded as if I *had* spoken. "Think about it. And you remember this, Mike: no man who didn't care for you would ever talk to you straight as I have."

"How straight was that, Bill?" I was faintly aware of some tourist walking from his Volvo to the store and looking at us curiously, and when I replayed the scene in my mind later on, I realized we must have looked like guys on the verge of a fistfight. I remember that I felt like crying out of sadness and bewilderment and an incompletely defined sense of betrayal, but I also remember being furious with this lanky old man — him in his shining-clean cotton undershirt and his mouthful of false teeth. So maybe we *were* close to fighting, and I just didn't know it at the time.

"Straight as I could be," he said, and turned away to go inside and pay for his gas.

"My house is haunted," I said.

He stopped, back to me, shoulders hunched as if to absorb a blow. Then, slowly, he turned back. "Sara Laughs has always been haunted, Mike. You've stirred em up. P'raps you should go back to Derry and let em settle. That might be the best thing." He paused, as if replaying this last to see if he agreed with it, then nodded. He nodded as slowly as he had turned. "Ayuh, that might be best all around."

When I got back to Sara I called Ward Hankins. Then I finally made that call to Bonnie Amudson. Part of me was rooting for her not to be in at the travel agency in Augusta she co-owned, but she was. Halfway through my talk with her, the fax began to print out xeroxed pages from Jo's appointment calendars. On the first one Ward had scrawled, "Hope this helps."

I didn't rehearse what I was going to say

481

to Bonnie; I felt that to do so would be a recipe for disaster. I told her that Jo had been writing something — maybe an article, maybe a series of them — about the township where our summerhouse was located, and that some of the locals had apparently been cheesed off by her curiosity. Some still were. Had she talked to Bonnie? Perhaps showed her an early draft?

"No, huh-uh." Bonnie sounded honestly surprised. "She used to show me her photos, and more herb samples than I honestly cared to see, but she never showed me anything she was writing. In fact, I remember her once saying that she'd decided to leave the writing to you and just —"

" — take a little taste of everything else, right?"

"Yes."

I thought this was a good place to end the conversation, but the guys in the basement seemed to have other ideas. "Was she seeing anyone, Bonnie?"

Silence from the other end. With a hand that seemed at least four miles down my arm, I plucked the fax sheets out of the basket. Ten of them — November of 1993 to August of 1994. Jottings everywhere in Jo's neat hand. Had we even had a fax before she died? I couldn't remember. There was so fucking much I couldn't remember.

"Bonnie? If you know something, please

tell me. Jo's dead, but I'm not. I can forgive her if I have to, but I can't forgive what I don't underst—"

"I'm sorry," she said, and gave a nervous little laugh. "It's just that I didn't understand at first. 'Seeing anyone,' that was just so . . . so foreign to Jo . . . the Jo I knew . . . that I couldn't figure out what you were talking about. I thought maybe you meant a shrink, but you didn't, did you? You meant seeing someone like seeing a guy. A boyfriend."

"That's what I meant." Thumbing through the faxed calendar sheets now, my hand not quite back to its proper distance from my eyes but getting there, getting there. I felt relief at the honest bewilderment in Bonnie's voice, but not as much as I'd expected. Because I'd known. I hadn't even needed the woman in the old *Perry Mason* episode to put in her two cents, not really. It was Jo we were talking about, after all. *Jo.*

"Mike," Bonnie was saying, very softly, as if I might be crazy, "she loved you. She loved *you.*"

"Yes. I suppose she did." The calendar pages showed how busy my wife had been. How productive. S-Ks of Maine . . . the soup kitchens. WomShel, a county-to-county network of shelters for battered women. TeenShel. Friends of Me. Libes.

She had been at two or three meetings a month — two or three a *week* at some points — and I'd barely noticed. I had been too busy with my women in jeopardy. "I loved her too, Bonnie, but she was up to something in the last ten months of her life. She didn't give you any hint of what it might have been when you were riding to meetings of the Soup Kitchens board or the Friends of Maine Libraries?"

Silence from the other end.

"Bonnie?"

I took the phone away from my ear to see if the red LOW BATTERY light was on, and it squawked my name. I put it back.

"Bonnie, what is it?"

"There *were* no long drives those last nine or ten months. We talked on the phone and I remember once we had lunch in Waterville, but there *were* no long drives. She quit."

I thumbed through the fax-sheets again. Meetings noted everywhere in Jo's neat hand, Soup Kitchens of Maine among them.

"I don't understand. She quit the Soup Kitchens board?"

Another moment of silence. Then, speaking carefully: "No, Mike. She quit *all* of them. She finished with Woman Shelters and Teen Shelters at the end of '93 — her term was up then. The other two, Soup Kitchens and Friends of Maine Libraries

. . . she resigned in October or November of 1993."

Meetings noted on all the sheets Ward had sent me. Dozens of them. Meetings in 1993, meetings in 1994. Meetings of boards to which she'd no longer belonged. She had been down here. On all those supposed meeting-days, Jo had been on the TR. I would have bet my life on it.

But why?

Chapter 17

Devore was mad, all right, mad as a hatter, and he couldn't have caught me at a worse, weaker, more terrified moment. And I think that everything from that moment on was almost pre-ordained. From there to the terrible storm they still talk about in this part of the world, it all came down like a rockslide.

I felt fine the rest of Friday afternoon — my talk with Bonnie left a lot of questions unanswered, but it had been a tonic just the same. I made a vegetable stir-fry (atonement for my latest plunge into the Fry-O-Lator at the Village Cafe) and ate it while I watched the evening news. On the other side of the lake the sun was sliding down toward the mountains and flooding the living room with gold. When Tom Brokaw closed up shop, I decided to take a walk north along The Street — I'd go as far as I could and still be assured of getting home by dark, and as I went I'd think about the things Bill Dean and Bonnie Amudson had told me. I'd think about them the way I sometimes walked and thought about plot-snags in whatever I was working on.

I walked down the railroad-tie steps, still feeling perfectly fine (confused, but fine), started off along The Street, then paused to look at the Green Lady. Even with the evening sun shining fully upon her, it was hard to see her for what she actually was — just a birch tree with a half-dead pine standing behind it, one branch of the latter making a pointing arm. It was as if the Green Lady were saying go north, young man, go north. Well, I wasn't exactly young, but I could go north, all right. For awhile, at least.

Yet I stood a moment longer, uneasily studying the face I could see in the bushes, not liking the way the little shake of breeze seemed to make what was nearly a mouth sneer and grin. I think perhaps I started to feel a little bad then, was too preoccupied to notice it. I set off north, wondering what, exactly, Jo might have written . . . for by then I was starting to believe she might have written something, after all. Why else had I found my old typewriter in her studio? I would go through the place, I decided. I would go through it carefully and . . .

help im drown

The voice came from the woods, the water, from myself. A wave of lightheadedness passed through my thoughts, lifting and scattering them like leaves in a breeze. I stopped. All at once I had never felt so bad, so *blighted,* in my life. My chest was tight. My stomach folded in on itself like a cold flower. My eyes filled with chilly water that was nothing like tears, and I knew what was coming. *No,* I tried to say, but the word wouldn't come out.

My mouth filled with the cold taste of lakewater instead, all those dark minerals, and suddenly the trees were shimmering before my eyes as if I were looking up at them through clear liquid, and the pressure on my chest had become dreadfully localized and taken the shapes of hands. They were holding me down.

"Won't it stop doing that?" someone asked — almost cried. There was no one on The Street but me, yet I heard that voice clearly. "Won't it ever stop doing that?"

What came next was no outer voice but alien thoughts in my own head. They beat against the walls of my skull like moths trapped inside a light-fixture . . . or inside a Japanese lantern.

> *help I'm drown*
> > *help I'm drown*
> > > *blue-cap man say git me*
> > > > *blue-cap man say dassn't let me ramble*
> > > *help I'm drown*
> > > > *lost my berries they on the path*
> > > *he holdin me*
> > > > *he face shimmer n look bad*
> > *lemme up lemme up O sweet Jesus*
> > > lemme up
> *oxen free allee allee oxen free PLEASE*
> OXEN FREE *you go on and stop now*
> > *ALLEE OXEN FREE*

she scream my name
 she scream it so LOUD
I bent forward in an utter panic, opened my mouth, and from my gaping, straining mouth there poured a cold flood of . . .

Nothing at all.

The horror of it passed and yet it didn't pass. I still felt terribly sick to my stomach, as if I had eaten something to which my body had taken a violent offense, some kind of ant-powder or maybe a killer mushroom, the kind Jo's fungi guides pictured inside red borders. I staggered forward half a dozen steps, gagging dryly from a throat which still believed it was wet. There was another birch where the bank dropped to the lake, arching its white belly gracefully over the water as if to see its reflection by evening's flattering light. I grabbed it like a drunk grabbing a lamppost.

The pressure in my chest began to ease, but it left an ache as real as rain. I hung against the tree, heart fluttering, and suddenly I became aware that something stank — an evil, polluted smell worse than a clogged septic pool which has simmered all summer under the blazing sun. With it was a sense of some hideous presence giving off that odor, something which should have been dead and wasn't.

Oh stop, allee allee oxen free, I'll do anything only stop, I tried to say, and still nothing came out. Then it was gone. I could smell nothing but the lake and the woods . . . but I could see something: a boy in the lake, a little drowned dark boy lying on his back. His cheeks were puffed out. His mouth hung slackly open. His eyes were as white as the eyes of a statue.

My mouth filled with the unmerciful iron of the lake again. Help me, lemme up, help I'm drown. I leaned out, screaming inside my head, screaming down at the dead face, and I realized *I was looking up at myself,* looking up through the rose-shimmer of sunset water at a white man in blue jeans and a yellow polo shirt holding onto a trembling birch and trying to scream, his liquid face in motion, his eyes momentarily blotted out by the passage of a small perch coursing after a tasty bug, I was both the dark boy and the white man, drowned in the water and drowning in the air, is this right, is this what's happening, tap once for yes twice for no.

I retched nothing but a single runner of spit, and, impossibly, a fish jumped at it. They'll jump at almost anything at sunset; something in the dying light must make them crazy. The fish hit the water again about seven feet from the bank, spanking out a circular silver ripple, and it was gone — the taste in my mouth, the horrible smell, the shimmering drowned face of the Negro child — a Negro, that was how he would have thought of himself — whose name had almost surely been Tidwell.

I looked to my right and saw a gray forehead of rock poking out of the mulch. I thought, *There, right there,* and as if in confirmation, that horrible putrescent smell puffed at me again, seemingly from the ground.

I closed my eyes, still hanging onto the birch for dear life, feeling weak and sick and ill, and that was when Max Devore, that madman, spoke from behind me. "Say there, whoremaster, where's your whore?"

I turned and there he was, with Rogette Whitmore by his side. It was the only time I ever met him, but once was enough. Believe me, once was more than enough.

His wheelchair hardly looked like a wheelchair at all. What it looked like was a motorcycle sidecar crossed with a lunar lander. Half a dozen chrome wheels ran along both sides. Bigger wheels — four of them, I think — ran in a row across the back. None looked to be exactly on the same level, and I realized each was tied into its own suspension-bed. Devore would have a smooth ride over ground a lot rougher than The Street. Above the back wheels was an enclosed engine compartment. Hiding Devore's legs was a fiberglass nacelle, black with red pinstriping, that would not have looked out of place on a racing car. Implanted in the center of it was a gadget that looked like my DSS satellite dish . . . some sort of computerized avoidance system, I guessed. Maybe even an autopilot. The armrests were wide and covered with controls. Holstered on the left side of this machine was a green oxygen tank four feet long. A hose went to a clear plastic accordion tube; the accordion tube led to a mask which rested in Devore's lap. It made me think of the old guy's Stenomask. Coming on the heels of what had just happened, I might have considered this Tom Clancyish vehicle a hallucination, except for the bumper-sticker on the nacelle, below the dish. I BLEED DODGER BLUE, it said.

This evening the woman I had seen outside The Sunset Bar at Warrington's was wearing a white blouse with long sleeves and black pants so tapered they made her legs look like sheathed swords. Her narrow face and hollow cheeks made her resemble Edvard Munch's screamer more than ever. Her white hair hung around her face in a lank cowl. Her lips were painted so brightly red she seemed to be bleeding from the mouth.

She was old and she was ugly, but she was a prize compared to Mattie's father-in-law. Scrawny, blue-lipped, the skin around his eyes and the corners of his mouth a dark exploded purple, he looked like something an archeologist might find in the burial room of a pyramid, surrounded by his stuffed wives and pets, bedizened with his favorite jewels. A few wisps of white hair still clung to his scaly skull; more tufts sprang from enormous ears which seemed to have melted like wax sculptures left out in the sun. He was wearing white cotton pants and a billowy blue shirt. Add a little black beret and he would have looked like a French artist from the nineteenth century at the end of a very long life.

Across his lap was a cane of some black wood. Snugged over the end was a bright red bicycle grip. The fingers grasping it looked powerful, but they were going as black as the cane itself. His circulation was failing, and I couldn't imagine what his feet and his lower legs must look like.

"Whore run off and left you, has she?"

I tried to say something. A croak came out of my mouth, nothing more. I was still holding the birch. I let go of it and tried to straighten up, but my legs were still weak and I had to grab it again.

He nudged a silver toggle switch and the chair came ten feet closer, halving the distance between us. The sound it made was a silky whisper; watching it was like watching an evil magic carpet. Its many wheels rose and fell independent of one another and flashed in the declining sun, which had begun to take on a reddish cast. And as he came closer, I felt the sense of the man. His body was rotting out from under him, but the force around him was undeniable and daunting, like an electrical storm. The woman paced beside him, regarding me with silent amusement. Her eyes were pinkish. I assumed then that they were gray and had picked up a bit of the coming sunset, but I think now she was an albino.

"I always liked a whore," he said. He drew the word out, making it *horrrrrrr.* "Didn't I, Rogette?"

"Yes, sir," she said. "In their place."

"Sometimes their place was on my face!" he cried with a kind of insane perkiness, as if she had contradicted him. "Where is she, young man? Whose face is she sitting on right now? I wonder. That smart lawyer you found? Oh, I know all about him, right down to the Unsatisfactory Conduct he got in the third grade. I make it my business to know things. It's the secret of my success."

With an enormous effort, I straightened up. "What are you doing here?"

"Having a constitutional, same as you. And no law against it, is there? The Street belongs to anyone who wants to use it. You haven't been here long, young whoremaster, but surely you've been here long enough to know that. It's our version of the town common, where good pups and vile dogs may walk side-by-side."

Once more using the hand not bunched around the red bicycle grip, he picked up the oxygen mask, sucked deeply, then dropped it back in his lap. He grinned — an unspeakable grin of complicity that revealed gums the color of iodine.

"She good? That little *horrrrrr* of yours? She must be good to have kept my son prisoner in that nasty little trailer where she lives. And then along comes you even before the worms had finished with my boy's eyes. Does her cunt *suck?*"

"Shut up."

Rogette Whitmore threw back her head and laughed. The sound was like the scream of a rabbit caught in an owl's talons, and my flesh crawled. I had an idea she was as crazy as he was. Thank God they were old. "You struck a nerve there, Max," she said.

"What do you want?" I took a breath . . . and caught a taste of that putrescence again. I gagged. I didn't want to, but I couldn't help it.

Devore straightened in his chair and breathed deeply, as if to mock me. In that moment he looked like Robert Duvall in *Apocalypse Now*, striding along the beach and telling the world how much he loved the smell of napalm in the morning. His grin widened. "Lovely place, just here, isn't it? A cozy spot to stop and think, wouldn't you say?" He looked around. "This is where it happened, all right. Ayuh."

"Where the boy drowned."

I thought Whitmore's smile looked momentarily uneasy at that. Devore didn't. He clutched for his translucent oxygen mask with an old man's overwide grip, fingers that grope rather than reach. I could see little bubbles of mucus clinging to the inside. He sucked deep again, put it down again.

"Thirty or more folks have drowned in this lake, and that's just the ones they know about," he said. "What's one boy, more or less?"

"I don't get it. Were there *two* Tidwell boys who died here? The one that got blood-poisoning and the one —"

"Do you care about your soul, Mr. Noonan? Your immortal soul? God's butterfly caught in a cocoon of flesh that will soon stink like mine?"

I said nothing. The strangeness of what had happened before he arrived was passing. What replaced it was his incredible personal magnetism. I have never in my life felt so much raw force. There was nothing supernatural about it, either, and *raw* is exactly the right word. I might have run. Under other circumstances, I'm sure I would have. It certainly wasn't bravery that kept me where I was; my legs still felt rubbery, and I was afraid I might fall down.

"I'm going to give you one chance to save your soul," Devore said. He raised a bony finger to illustrate the concept of one. "Go away, my fine whoremaster. Right now, in the clothes you stand up in. Don't bother to pack a bag, don't even stop to make sure you turned off the stove-burners. Go. Leave the whore and leave the whorelet."

"Leave them to you."

"Ayuh, to me. I'll do the things that need to be done. Souls are for liberal arts majors, Noonan. I was an engineer."

"Go fuck yourself."

Rogette Whitmore made that screaming-rabbit sound again.

The old man sat in his chair, head lowered, grinning sallowly up at me and looking like something raised from the dead. "Are you sure you want to be the one, Noonan? It doesn't matter to her, you know — you or me, it's all the same to her."

"I don't know what you're talking about." I drew another deep breath, and this time the air tasted all right. I took a step away from the birch, and my legs were all right, too. "And I don't care. You're never getting Kyra. Never in what remains of your scaly life. I'll never see that happen."

"Pal, you'll see plenty," Devore said, grinning and showing me his iodine gums. "Before July's done, you'll likely have seen so much you'll wish you'd ripped the living eyes out of your head in June."

"I'm going home. Let me pass."

"Go home then, how could I stop you?" he asked. "The Street belongs to everyone." He groped the oxygen mask out of his lap again and took another healthy pull. He dropped it into his lap and settled his left hand on the arm of his Buck Rogers wheelchair.

I stepped toward him, and almost before I knew what was happening, he ran the wheelchair at me. He could have hit me and hurt me quite badly — broken one or both of my legs, I don't doubt — but he stopped just short. I leaped back, but only because he allowed me to. I was aware that Whitmore was laughing again.

"What's the matter, Noonan?"

"Get out of my way. I'm warning you."

"Whore made you jumpy, has she?"

I started to my left, meaning to go by him on that side, but in a flash he had turned the chair, shot it forward, and cut me off.

"Get out of the TR, Noonan. I'm giving you good ad—"

I broke to the right, this time on the lake side, and would have slipped by him quite neatly except for the fist, very small and hard, that hammered the left side of my face. The white-haired bitch was wearing a ring, and the stone cut me behind the ear. I felt the sting and the warm flow of blood. I pivoted, stuck out both hands, and pushed her. She fell to the needle-carpeted path with a squawk of surprised outrage. At the next instant something clouted me on the back of the head. A momentary orange glow lit up my sight. I staggered backward in what felt like slow motion, waving my arms, and Devore came into view again. He was slued around in his wheelchair, scaly head thrust forward, the cane he'd hit me with still upraised. If he had been ten years younger, I believe he would have fractured my skull instead of just creating that momentary orange light.

I ran into my old friend the birch tree. I raised my hand to my ear and looked unbelievingly at the blood on the tips of my fingers. My head ached from the blow he had fetched me.

Whitmore was struggling to her feet, brushing pine needles from her slacks and looking at me with a furious smile. Her cheeks had filled in with a thin pink flush. Her too-red lips were pulled back to show small teeth. In the light of the setting sun her eyes looked as if they were burning.

"Get out of my way," I said, but my voice sounded small and weak.

"No," Devore said, and laid the black barrel of his cane on the nacelle that curved over the front of his chair. Now I could see the little boy who had been determined to have the sled no matter how badly he cut his hands getting it. I could see him very clearly. "No, you whore-fucking sissy. I *won't.*"

He shoved the silver toggle switch again and the wheelchair rushed silently at me. If I had stayed where I was, he would have run me through with his cane as surely as any evil duke was ever run through in an Alexandre Dumas story. He probably would have crushed the fragile bones in his right hand and torn his right arm clean out of its socket in the collision, but this man had never cared about such things; he left cost-counting to the little people. If I had hesitated out of shock or incredulity, he would have killed me, I'm sure of it. Instead, I rolled to my left. My sneakers slid on the needle-slippery embankment for a moment. Then they lost contact with the earth and I was falling.

I hit the water awkwardly and much too close to the bank. My left foot struck a sub-merged root and twisted. The pain was huge, something that felt like a thunderclap sounds. I opened my mouth to scream and the lake poured in — that cold metallic dark taste, this time for real. I coughed it out and sneezed it out and floundered away from where I had landed, thinking *The boy, the dead boy's down here, what if he reaches up and grabs me?*

I turned over on my back, still flailing and coughing, very aware of my jeans clinging clammily to my legs and crotch, thinking absurdly about my wallet — I didn't care about the credit cards or driver's license, but I had two good snapshots of Jo in there, and they would be ruined.

Devore had almost run himself over the embankment, I saw, and for a moment I thought he still might go. The front of his chair jutted over the place where I had fallen (I could see the short tracks of my sneakers just to the left of the birch's partially exposed roots), and although the forward wheels were still grounded, the crumbly earth was running out from beneath them in dry little avalanches that rolled down the slope and pit-a-patted into the water, creating interlocking ripple patterns. Whitmore was clinging to the back of the chair, yanking on it, but it was much too heavy for her; if Devore was to be saved, he would have to save himself. Standing waist-deep in the lake with my clothes floating around me, I rooted for him to go over.

The purplish claw of his left hand recaptured the silver toggle switch after several attempts. One finger hooked it backward, and the chair reversed away from the embankment with a final shower of stones and dirt. Whitmore leaped prankishly to one side to keep her feet from being run over.

Devore fiddled some more with his controls, turned the chair to face me where I stood in the water, some seven feet out from the overhanging birch, and then nudged the chair forward until he was on the edge of The Street but safely away from the dropoff. Whitmore had turned away from us entirely; she was bent over with her butt poking in my direction. If I thought about her at all, and I can't remember that I did, I suppose I thought she was getting her breath back.

Devore appeared to be in the best shape of the three of us, not even needing a hit from the oxygen mask sitting in his lap. The late light was full in his face, making him look like a half-rotted jack-o'-lantern which has been soaked with gas and set on fire.

"Enjoying your swim?" he asked, and laughed.

I looked around, hoping to see a strolling couple or perhaps a fisherman looking for a place where he could wet his line one more time before dark . . . and yet at the same time I hoped I'd see no one. I was angry, hurt, and scared. Most of all I was embarrassed. I had been dunked in the lake by a man of eighty-five . . . a man who showed every sign of hanging around and making sport of me.

I began wading to my right — south, back toward my house. The water was about waist-deep, cool and almost refreshing now that I was used to it. My sneakers squelched over rocks and submerged tree-branches. The ankle I'd twisted still hurt, but it was supporting me. Whether it would continue to once I got out of the lake was another question.

Devore twiddled his controls some more. The chair pivoted and came rolling slowly along The Street, keeping pace with me easily.

"I didn't introduce you properly to Rogette, did I?" he said. "She was quite an athlete in college, you know. Softball and field hockey were her specialties, and she's held onto at least some of her skills. Rogette, demonstrate your skills for this young man."

Whitmore passed the slowly moving wheelchair on the left. For a moment she was blocked out by it. When I could see her again, I could also see what she was holding. She hadn't been bent over to get her breath.

Smiling, she strode to the edge of the embankment with her left arm curled against her midriff, cradling the rocks she had picked up from the edge of the path. She selected a chunk roughly the size of a golfball, drew her hand back to her ear, and threw it at me. Hard. It whizzed by my left temple and splashed into the water behind me.

"Hey!" I shouted, more startled than afraid. Even after everything that had preceded it, I couldn't believe this was happening.

"What's wrong with you, Rogette?" Devore asked chidingly. "You never used to throw like a girl. Get him!"

The second rock passed two inches over my head. The third was a potential tooth-smasher. I batted it away with an angry, fearful shout, not noticing until later that it had bruised my palm. At the moment I was only aware of her hateful, smiling face — the face of a woman who has plunked down two dollars in a carny shooting-pitch and means to win the big stuffed teddybear even if she has to blast away all night.

And she threw *fast*. The rocks hailed down around me, some splashing into the ruddy water to my left or right, creating little geysers. I began to backpedal, afraid to turn and swim for it, afraid that she would throw a really big one the minute I did. Still, I had to get out of her range. Devore, meanwhile, was laughing a wheezy old man's laugh, his wretched face crunched in on itself like the face of a malicious apple-doll.

One of her rocks struck me a hard, painful blow on the collarbone and bounced high into the air. I cried out, and she did, too: *"Hai!,"* like a karate fighter who's gotten in a good kick.

So much for orderly retreat. I turned, swam for deeper water, and the bitch brained me. The first two rocks she threw after I began to swim seemed to be range-finders. There was a pause when I had time to think *I'm doing it, I'm getting beyond her area of* . . . and then something hit the back of my head. I felt it and heard it the same way — it went *CLONK!,* like something you'd read in a *Batman* comic.

The surface of the lake went from bright orange to bright red to dark scarlet. Faintly I could hear Devore yelling approval and Whitmore squealing her strange laugh. I took in another mouthful of iron-tasting water and was so dazed I had to remind myself to spit it out, not swallow it. My feet now felt too heavy for swimming, and my goddam sneakers weighed a ton. I put them down to stand up and couldn't find the bottom — I had gotten beyond my depth. I looked in toward the shore. It was spectacular, blazing in the sunset like stage-scenery lit with bright orange and red gels. I was probably twenty feet out from the shore now. Devore and Whitmore were at the edge of The Street, watching. They looked like Dad and Mom in a Grant Wood painting. Devore was using the mask again, but I could see him grinning inside it. Whitmore was grinning, too.

More water sloshed in my mouth. I spit most of it out, but some went down, making me cough and half-retch. I started to sink below the surface and fought my way back up, not swimming but only splashing wildly, expending nine times the energy I needed to stay afloat. Panic made its first appearance, nibbling through my dazed bewilderment with sharp little rat teeth. I realized I could hear a high, sweet buzzing. How many blows had my poor old head taken? One from Whitmore's fist . . . one from Devore's cane . . . one rock . . . or had it been two? Christ, I couldn't remember.

Get hold of yourself, for God's sake — you're not going to let him beat you this way, are you? Drown you like that little boy was drowned?

No, not if I could help it.

I trod water and ran my left hand down the back of my head. Not too far above the nape I encountered a goose-egg that was still rising. When I pressed on it the pain made me feel like throwing up and fainting at the same time. Tears rose in my eyes and rolled down my cheeks. There were only traces of blood on the tips of my fingers when I looked at them, but it was hard to tell about cuts when you were in the water.

"You look like a woodchuck caught out in

the rain, Noonan!" Now his voice seemed to roll to where I was, as if across a great distance.

"Fuck you!" I called. "I'll see you in jail for this!"

He looked at Whitmore. She looked back with an identical expression, and they both laughed. If someone had put an Uzi in my hands at that moment, I would have killed them both with no hesitation and then asked for a second clip so I could machine-gun the bodies.

With no Uzi to hand, I began to dogpaddle south, toward my house. They paced me along The Street, he rolling in his whisper-quiet wheelchair, she walking beside him as solemn as a nun and pausing every now and then to pick up a likely-looking rock.

I hadn't swum enough to be tired, but I was. It was mostly shock, I suppose. Finally I tried to draw a breath at the wrong time, swallowed more water, and panicked completely. I began to swim in toward the shore, wanting to get to where I could stand up. Rogette Whitmore began to fire rocks at me immediately, first using the ones she had lined up between her left arm and her midriff, then those she'd stockpiled in Devore's lap. She was warmed up, she wasn't throwing like a girl anymore, and her aim was deadly. Stones splashed all around me. I batted another away — a big one that likely would have cut open my forehead if it had hit — but her follow-up struck my bicep and tore a long scratch there. Enough. I rolled over and swam back out beyond her range, gasping for breath, trying to keep my head up in spite of the growing ache in the back of my neck.

When I was clear, I trod water and looked in at them. Whitmore had come all the way to the edge of the embankment, wanting to get every foot of distance she could. Hell, every damned inch. Devore was parked behind her in his wheelchair. They were both still grinning, and now their faces were as red as the faces of imps in hell. Red sky at night, sailor's delight. Another twenty minutes and it would be getting dark. Could I keep my head above water for another twenty minutes? I thought so, if I didn't panic again, but not much longer. I thought of drowning in the dark, looking up and seeing Venus just before I went under for the last time, and the panic-rat slashed me with its teeth again. The panic-rat was worse than Rogette and her rocks, much worse.

Maybe not worse than Devore.

I looked both ways along the lakefront, checking The Street wherever it wove out of the trees for a dozen feet or a dozen yards. I didn't care about being embarrassed anymore, but I saw no one. Dear God, where was everybody? Gone to the Mountain View in Fryeburg for pizza, or the Village Cafe for milkshakes?

"What do you want?" I called in to Devore. "Do you want me to tell you I'll butt out of your business? Okay, I'll butt out!"

He laughed.

Well, I hadn't expected it to work. Even if I'd been sincere about it, he wouldn't have believed me.

"We just want to see how long you can swim," Whitmore said, and threw another rock — a long, lazy toss that fell about five feet short of where I was.

They mean to kill me, I thought. *They really do.*

Yes. And what was more, they might well get away with it. A crazy idea, both plausible and implausible at the same time, rose in my mind. I could see Rogette Whitmore tacking a notice to the COMMUNITY DOIN'S board outside the Lakeview General Store.

TO THE MARTIANS OF TR-90, GREETINGS!

Mr. MAXWELL DEVORE, every-one's favorite Martian, will give each resident of the TR ONE HUNDRED DOLLARS if no one will use The Street on FRIDAY EVENING, THE 17th OF JULY, between the hours of SEVEN and NINE P.M. Keep our "SUMMER FRIENDS" away, too! And remember: GOOD MARTIANS are like GOOD MONKEYS: they <u>SEE</u> no evil, <u>HEAR</u> no evil, and <u>SPEAK</u> no evil!

I couldn't really believe it, not even in my current situation . . . and yet I almost could. At the very least I had to grant him the luck of the devil.

Tired. My sneakers heavier than ever. I tried to push one of them off and succeeded only in taking in another mouthful of lakewater. They stood watching me, Devore occasionally picking the mask up from his lap and having a revivifying suck.

I couldn't wait until dark. The sun exits in a hurry here in western Maine — as it does, I guess, in mountain country everywhere — but the twilights are long and lingering. By the time it got dark enough in the west to move without being seen, the moon would have risen in the east.

I found myself imagining my obituary in the *New York Times*, the headline reading POPULAR ROMANTIC SUSPENSE NOVELIST DROWNS IN MAINE. Debra Weinstock would provide them with the author photo from the forthcoming *Helen's Promise*. Harold Oblowski would say all the right things, and he'd also remember to put a modest (but not tiny) death notice in *Publishers Weekly*. He would go half-and-half with Putnam on it, and —

I sank, swallowed more water, and spat it out. I began pummelling the lake again and forced myself to stop. From the shore, I could hear Rogette Whitmore's tinkling laughter. *You bitch*, I thought. *You scrawny bi—*

Mike, Jo said.

Her voice was in my head, but it wasn't the one I make when I'm imagining her side of a mental dialogue or when I just miss her and need to whistle her up for awhile. As if to underline this, something splashed to my right, splashed hard. When I looked in that direction I saw no fish, not even a ripple. What I saw instead was our swimming float, anchored about a hundred yards away in the sunset-colored water.

"I can't swim that far, baby," I croaked.

"Did you say something, Noonan?" Devore called from the shore. He cupped a mocking hand to one of his huge waxlump ears. "Couldn't quite make it out! You sound all out of breath!" More tinkling laughter from Whitmore. He was Johnny Carson; she was Ed McMahon.

You can make it. I'll help you.

511

The float, I realized, might be my only chance — there wasn't another one on this part of the shore, and it was at least ten yards beyond Whitmore's longest rockshot so far. I began to dogpaddle in that direction, my arms now as leaden as my feet. Each time I felt my head on the verge of going under I paused, treading water, telling myself to take it easy, I was in pretty good shape and doing okay, telling myself that if I didn't panic I'd be all right. The old bitch and the even older bastard resumed pacing me, but they saw where I was headed and the laughter stopped. So did the taunts.

For a long time the swimming float seemed to draw no closer. I told myself that was just because the light was fading, the color of the water draining from red to purple to a near-black that was the color of Devore's gums, but I was able to muster less and less conviction for this idea as my breath shortened and my arms grew heavier.

When I was still thirty yards away a cramp struck my left leg. I rolled sideways like a swamped sailboat, trying to reach the bunched muscle. More water poured down my throat. I tried to cough it out, then retched and went under with my stomach still trying to heave and my fingers still looking for the knotted place above the knee.

I'm really drowning, I thought, strangely

calm now that it was happening. *This is how it happens, this is it.*

Then I felt a hand seize me by the nape of the neck. The pain of having my hair yanked brought me back to reality in a flash — it was better than an epinephrine injection. I felt another hand clamp around my left leg; there was a brief but terrific sense of heat. The cramp let go and I broke the surface swimming — *really* swimming this time, not just dogpaddling, and in what seemed like seconds I was clinging to the ladder on the side of the float, breathing in great, snatching gasps, waiting to see if I was going to be all right or if my heart was going to detonate in my chest like a hand grenade. At last my lungs started to overcome my oxygen debt, and everything began to calm down. I gave it another minute, then climbed out of the water and into what was now the ashes of twilight. I stood facing west for a little while, bent over with my hands on my knees, dripping on the boards. Then I turned around, meaning this time to flip them not just a single bird but that fabled double eagle. There was no one to flip it to. The Street was empty. Devore and Rogette Whitmore were gone.

Maybe they were gone. I'd do well to remember there was a lot of Street I couldn't see.

I sat cross-legged on the float until the moon rose, waiting and watching for any movement. Half an hour, I think. Maybe forty-five minutes. I checked my watch, but got no help there; it had shipped some water and stopped at 7:30 P.M. To the other satisfactions Devore owed me I could now add the price of one Timex Indiglo — that's $29.95, asshole, cough it up.

At last I climbed back down the ladder, slipped into the water, and stroked for shore as quietly as I could. I was rested, my head had stopped aching (although the knot above the nape of my neck still throbbed steadily), and I no longer felt off-balance and incredulous. In some ways, that had been the worst of it — trying to cope not just with the apparition of the drowned boy, the flying rocks, and the lake, but with the pervasive sense that none of this could be happening, that rich old software moguls did not try to drown novelists who strayed into their line of sight.

Had tonight's adventure been a case of simple straying into Devore's view, though? A coincidental meeting, no more than that? Wasn't it likely he'd been having me watched ever since the Fourth of July . . . maybe from the other side of the lake, by people with high-powered optical equipment? Paranoid bullshit, I would have said . . . at least I would have said it before the

514

two of them almost sank me in Dark Score Lake like a kid's paper boat in a mud-puddle.

I decided I didn't care who might be watching from the other side of the lake. I didn't care if the two of them were still lurking on one of the tree-shielded parts of The Street, either. I swam until I could feel strands of waterweed tickling my ankles and see the crescent of my beach. Then I stood up, wincing at the air, which now felt cold on my skin. I limped to shore, one hand raised to fend off a hail of rocks, but no rocks came. I stood for a moment on The Street, my jeans and polo shirt dripping, looking first one way, then the other. It seemed I had this little part of the world to myself. Last, I looked back at the water, where weak moonlight beat a track from the thumbnail of beach out to the swimming float.

"Thanks, Jo," I said, then started up the railroad ties to the house. I got about halfway, then had to stop and sit down. I had never been so utterly tired in my whole life.

Chapter 18

I climbed the stairs to the deck instead of going around to the front door, still moving slowly and marvelling at how my legs felt twice their normal weight. When I stepped into the living room I looked around with the wide eyes of someone who has been away for a decade and returns to find everything just as he left it — Bunter the moose on the wall, the *Boston Globe* on the couch, a compilation of *Tough Stuff* crossword puzzles on the end-table, the plate on the counter with the re-mains of my stir-fry still on it. Looking at these things brought the realization home full force — I had gone for a walk, leaving all this normal light clutter behind, and had almost died instead. Had almost been murdered.

I began to shake. I went into the north-wing bathroom, took off my wet clothes, and threw them into the tub — *splat*. Then, still shaking, I turned and stared at myself in the mirror over the washbasin. I looked like someone who has been on the losing side in a barroom brawl. One bicep bore a long, clotting gash. A blackish-purple bruise was unfurling what looked like shadowy wings on my left collarbone. There was a bloody furrow on my neck and behind my ear, where the lovely Rogette had caught me with the stone in her ring.

I took my shaving mirror and used it to check the back of my head. "Can't you get that through your thick skull?" my mother used to shout at me and Sid when we were kids, and now I thanked God that Ma had apparently been right about the thickness factor, at least in my case. The spot where Devore had struck me with his cane looked like the cone of a recently extinct volcano. Whitmore's bull's-eye had left a red wound that would need stitches if I wanted to avoid a scar. Blood, rusty and thin, stained the nape of my neck all around the hairline. God knew how much had flowed out of that unpleasant-looking red mouth and been washed away by the lake.

I poured hydrogen peroxide into my cupped palm, steeled myself, and slapped it onto the gash back there like aftershave. The bite was monstrous, and I had to tighten my lips to keep from crying out. When the pain started to fade a little, I soaked cotton balls with more peroxide and cleaned my other wounds.

I showered, threw on a tee-shirt and a pair of jeans, then went into the hall to phone the County Sheriff. There was no need for directory assistance; the Castle Rock P.D. and County Sheriff's numbers were on the IN CASE OF EMERGENCY card thumbtacked to the bulletin board, along with numbers for the fire department, the ambulance service, and the 900-number where you could get three answers to that day's *Times* crossword puzzle for a buck-fifty.

I dialled the first three numbers fast, then began to slow down. I got as far as 955-960 before stopping altogether. I stood there in the hall with the phone pressed against my ear, visualizing another headline, this one not in the decorous *Times* but the rowdy *New York Post*. NOVELIST TO AGING COMPU-KING: "YOU BIG BULLY!" Along with side-by-side pictures of me, looking roughly my age, and Max Devore, looking roughly a hundred and six. *The Post* would have great fun telling its readers how Devore (along with his companion, an elderly lady who might weigh ninety pounds soaking wet) had lumped up a novelist half his age — a guy who looked, in his photograph, at least, reasonably trim and fit.

The phone got tired of holding only six of the required seven numbers in its rudimentary brain, double-clicked, and dumped me back to an open line. I took the handset away from my ear, stared at it for a moment, and then set it gently back down in its cradle.

I'm not a sissy about the sometimes whimsical, sometimes hateful attention of the press, but I'm wary, as I would be around a bad-tempered fur-bearing mammal. America has turned the people who entertain it into weird high-class whores, and the media jeers at any "celeb" who dares complain about his or her treatment. "Quitcha bitchin!" cry the newspapers and the TV gossip shows (the tone is one of mingled triumph and indignation). "Didja really think we paid ya the big bucks just to sing a song or swing a Louisville Slugger? Wrong, asshole! We pay so we can be amazed when you do it well — whatever 'it' happens to be in your particular case — and also because it's gratifying when you fuck up. The truth is you're supplies. If you cease to be amusing, we can always kill you and eat you."

They can't *really* eat you, of course. They can print pictures of you with your shirt off and say you're running to fat, they can talk about how much you drink or how many pills you take or snicker about the night you pulled some starlet onto your lap at Spago and tried to stick your tongue in her ear, but they can't really eat you. So it wasn't the thought of the *Post* calling me a crybaby or being a part of Jay Leno's opening monologue that made me put the phone down; it was the realization that I had no proof. No one had seen us. And, I realized, finding an alibi for himself and his personal assistant would be the easiest thing in the world for Max Devore.

There was one other thing, too, the

capper: imagining the County Sheriff sending out George Footman, aka daddy, to take my statement on how the mean man had knocked li'l Mikey into the lake. How the three of them would laugh later about that!

I called John Storrow instead, wanting him to tell me I was doing the right thing, the only thing that made any sense. Wanting him to remind me that only desperate men were driven to such desperate lengths (I would ignore, at least for the time being, how the two of them had laughed, as if they were having the time of their lives), and that nothing had changed in regard to Ki Devore — her grandfather's custody case still sucked bogwater.

I got John's recording machine at home and left a message — just call Mike Noonan, no emergency, but feel free to call late. Then I tried his office, mindful of the scripture according to John Grisham: young lawyers work until they drop. I listened to the firm's recording machine, then followed instructions and punched STO on my phone keypad, the first three letters of John's last name.

There was a click and he came on the line — another recorded version, unfortunately. "Hi, this is John Storrow. I've gone up to Philly for the weekend to see my mom and dad. I'll be in the office on Monday; for the rest of the week, I'll be out on business.

From Tuesday to Friday you'll probably have the most luck trying to reach me at . . ."

The number he gave began 207-955, which meant Castle Rock. I imagined it was the hotel where he'd stayed before, the nice one up on the View. "Mike Noonan," I said. "Call me when you can. I left a message on your apartment machine, too."

I went in the kitchen to get a beer, then only stood there in front of the refrigerator, playing with the magnets. Whoremaster, he'd called me. *Say there, whoremaster, where's your whore?* A minute later he had offered to save my soul. Quite funny, really. Like an alcoholic offering to take care of your liquor cabinet. *He spoke of you with what I think was genuine affection,* Mattie had said. *Your great-grandfather and his great-grandfather shit in the same pit.*

I left the fridge with all the beer still safe inside, went back to the phone, and called Mattie.

"Hi," said another obviously recorded voice. I was on a roll. "It's me, but either I'm out or not able to come to the phone right this minute. Leave a message, okay?" A pause, the mike rustling, a distant whisper, and then Kyra, so loud she almost blew my ear off: *"Leave a HAPPY message!"* What followed was laughter from both of them, cut off by the beep.

"Hi, Mattie, it's Mike Noonan," I said. "I just wanted —"

I don't know how I would have finished that thought, and I didn't have to. There was a click and then Mattie herself said, "Hello, Mike." There was such a difference between this dreary, defeated-sounding voice and the cheerful one on the tape that for a moment I was silenced. Then I asked her what was wrong.

"Nothing," she said, then began to cry. "Everything. I lost my job. Lindy fired me."

Firing wasn't what Lindy had called it, of course. She'd called it "belt-tightening," but it was firing, all right, and I knew that if I looked into the funding of the Four Lakes Consolidated Library, I would discover that one of the chief supporters over the years had been Mr. Max Devore. And he'd continue to be one of the chief supporters . . . if, that was, Lindy Briggs played ball.

"We shouldn't have talked where she could see us doing it," I said, knowing I could have stayed away from the library completely and Mattie would be just as gone. "And we probably should have seen this coming."

"John Storrow *did* see it." She was still crying, but making an effort to get it under control. "He said Max Devore would probably want to make sure I was as deep in the corner as he could push me, come the custody hearing. He said Devore would want to make sure I answered 'I'm unemployed, Your Honor' when the judge asked where I worked. I told John Mrs. Briggs would never do anything so low, especially to a girl who'd given such a brilliant talk on Melville's 'Bartleby.' Do you know what he told me?"

"No."

"He said, 'You're very young.' I thought that was a patronizing thing to say, but he was right, wasn't he?"

"Mattie —"

"What am I going to do, Mike? What am I going to do?" The panic-rat had moved on down to Wasp Hill Road, it sounded like.

I thought, quite coldly: *Why not become my mistress? Your title will be "research assistant," a perfectly jake occupation as far as the IRS is concerned. I'll throw in clothes, a couple of charge cards, a house — say goodbye to the rustbucket doublewide on Wasp Hill Road — and a two-week vacation: how does February on Maui sound? Plus Ki's education, of course, and a hefty cash bonus at the end of the year. I'll be considerate, too. Considerate and discreet. Once or twice a week, and never until your little girl is fast asleep. All you have to do is say yes and give me a key. All you have to do is slide over when I slide in. All you have to do is let me do what I want — all through the dark, all through the night, let me touch where I want to touch, let me do what I want to do, never say no, never say stop.*

I closed my eyes.

"Mike? Are you there?"

"Sure," I said. I touched the throbbing gash at the back of my head and winced. "You're going to do just fine, Mattie. You —"

"The trailer's not paid for!" she nearly wailed. "I have two overdue phone bills and they're threatening to cut off the service! There's something wrong with the Jeep's transmission, and the rear axle, as well! I can pay for Ki's last week of Vacation Bible School, I guess — Mrs. Briggs gave me three weeks' pay in lieu of notice — but how will I buy her *shoes?* She outgrows everything so *fast* . . . there's holes in all her shorts and most of her g-g-goddam underwear . . ."

She was starting to weep again.

"I'm going to take care of you until you get back on your feet," I said.

"No, I can't let —"

"You can. And for Kyra's sake, you will. Later on, if you still want to, you can pay me back. We'll keep tabs on every dollar and dime, if you like. But I'm going to take care of you." *And you'll never take off your clothes when I'm with you. That's a promise, and I'm going to keep it.*

"Mike, you don't have to do this."

"Maybe, maybe not. But I *am* going to do it. You just try and stop me." I'd called meaning to tell her what had happened to me — giving her the humorous version — but that now seemed like the worst idea in the world. "This custody thing is going to be over before you know it, and if you can't find anyone brave enough to put you to work down here once it is, I'll find someone up in Derry who'll do it. Besides, tell me the truth — aren't you starting to feel that it might be time for a change of scenery?"

She managed a scrap of a laugh. "I guess you could say that."

"Heard from John today?"

"Actually, yes. He's visiting his parents in Philadelphia but he gave me the number there. I called him."

He'd said he was taken with her. Perhaps she was taken with him, as well. I told myself the thorny little tug I felt across my emotions at the idea was only my imagination. Tried to tell myself that, anyway. "What did he say about you losing your job the way you did?"

"The same things you said. But he didn't make me feel safe. You do. I don't know why." I did. I was an older man, and that is our chief attraction to young women: we make them feel safe. "He's coming up again Tuesday morning. I said I'd have lunch with him."

Smoothly, not a tremor or hesitation in my voice, I said: "Maybe I could join you."

Mattie's own voice warmed at the suggestion; her ready acceptance made me feel paradoxically guilty. "That would be great! Why don't I call him and suggest that you both come over here? I could barbecue again. Maybe I'll keep Ki home from V.B.S. and make it a foursome. She's hoping you'll read her another story. She really enjoyed that."

"That sounds great," I said, and meant it. Adding Kyra made it all seem more natural, less of an intrusion on my part. Also less like a date on theirs. John could not be accused of taking an unethical interest in his client. In the end he'd probably thank me. "I believe Ki might be ready to move on to 'Hansel and Gretel.' How are you, Mattie? All right?"

"Much better than I was before you called."

"Good. Things are going to be all right."

"Promise me."

"I think I just did."

There was a slight pause. "Are *you* all right, Mike? You sound a little . . . I don't know . . . a little strange."

"I'm okay," I said, and I was, for someone who had been pretty sure he was drowning less than an hour ago. "Can I ask you one question before I go? Because this is driving me crazy."

"Of course."

"The night we had dinner, you said Devore told you his great-grandfather and mine knew each other. Pretty well, according to him."

"He said they shit in the same pit. I thought that was elegant."

"Did he say anything else? Think hard."

She did, but came up with nothing. I told her to call me if something about that conversation did occur to her, or if she got lonely or scared, or if she started to feel worried about anything. I didn't like to say too much, but I had already decided I'd have to have a frank talk with John about my latest adventure. It might be prudent to have the private detective from Lewiston — George Kennedy, like the actor — put a man or two on the TR to keep an eye on Mattie and Kyra. Max Devore was mad, just as my caretaker had said. I hadn't understood then, but I did now. Any time I started to doubt, all I had to do was touch the back of my head.

I returned to the fridge and once more forgot to open it. My hands went to the magnets instead and again began moving them around, watching as words formed, broke apart, evolved. It was a peculiar kind of writing . . . but it *was* writing. I could tell by the way I was starting to trance out.

That half-hypnotized state is one you cultivate until you can switch it on and off at will . . . at least you can when things are going well. The intuitive part of the mind unlocks itself when you begin work and rises to a height of about six feet (maybe ten on good days). Once there, it simply hovers, sending black-magic messages and bright pictures. For the balance of the day that part is locked to the rest of the machinery and goes pretty much forgotten . . . except on certain occasions when it comes loose on its own and you trance out unexpectedly, your mind making associations which have nothing to do with rational thought and glaring with unexpected images. That is in some ways the strangest part of the creative process. The muses are ghosts, and sometimes they come uninvited.

My house is haunted.

Sara Laughs has always been haunted . . . you've stirred em up.

stirred, I wrote on the refrigerator. But it didn't look right, so I made a circle of fruit and vegetable magnets around it. That was better, much. I stood there for a moment, hands crossed over my chest as I crossed them at my desk when I was stuck for a word or a phrase, then took off *stirr* and put on *haunt,* making *haunted.*

"It's haunted in the circle," I said, and barely heard the faint chime of Bunter's bell, as if in agreement.

I took the letters off, and as I did found

528

myself thinking how odd it was to have a lawyer named Romeo —

(*romeo* went in the circle)

— and a detective named George Kennedy.

(*george* went up on the fridge)

I wondered if Kennedy could help me with Andy Drake —

(*drake* on the fridge)

— maybe give me some insights. I'd never written about a private detective before and it's the little stuff —

(*rake* off, leave the *d*, add *etails*)

— that makes the difference. I turned a 3 on its back and put an I beneath it, making a pitchfork. The devil's in the details.

From there I went somewhere else. I don't know where, exactly, because I was tranced out, that intuitive part of my mind up so high a search-party couldn't have found it. I stood in front of my fridge and played with the letters, spelling out little pieces of thought without even thinking about them. You mightn't believe such a thing is possible, but every writer knows it is.

What brought me back was light splashing across the windows of the foyer. I looked up and saw the shape of a car pulling to a stop behind my Chevrolet. A cramp of terror seized my belly. That was a moment when I would have given everything I owned for a loaded gun. Because it was Footman. Had to be. Devore had called him when he and Whitmore got back to Warrington's, had told him Noonan refuses to be a good Martian so get over there and fix him.

When the driver's door opened and the dome-light in the visitor's car came on, I breathed a conditional sigh of relief. I didn't know who it was, but it sure wasn't "daddy." This fellow didn't look as if he could take care of a housefly with a rolled-up newspaper . . . although, I supposed, there were plenty of people who had made that same mistake about Jeffrey Dahmer.

Above the fridge was a cluster of aerosol cans, all of them old and probably not ozone-friendly. I didn't know how Mrs. M. had missed them, but I was pleased she had. I took the first one my hand touched — Black Flag, excellent choice — thumbed off the cap, and stuck the can in the left front pocket of my jeans. Then I turned to the drawers on the right of the sink. The top one contained silverware. The second one held what Jo called "kitchenshit" — everything from poultry thermometers to those gadgets you stick in corncobs so you don't burn your fingers off. The third one down held a generous selection of mismatched steak knives. I took one, put it in the right front pocket of my jeans, and went to the door.

★ ★ ★

The man on my stoop jumped a little when I turned on the outside light, then blinked through the door at me like a near-sighted rabbit. He was about five-four, skinny, pale. He wore his hair cropped in the sort of cut known as a wiffle in my boyhood days. His eyes were brown. Guarding them was a pair of horn-rimmed glasses with greasy-looking lenses. His little hands hung at his sides. One held the handle of a flat leather case, the other a small white oblong. I didn't think it was my destiny to be killed by a man with a business card in one hand, so I opened the door.

The guy smiled, the anxious sort of smile people always seem to wear in Woody Allen movies. He was wearing a Woody Allen outfit too, I saw — faded plaid shirt a little too short at the wrists, chinos a little too baggy in the crotch. *Someone must have told him about the resemblance*, I thought. *That's got to be it.*

"Mr. Noonan?"

"Yes?"

He handed me the card. NEXT CENTURY REAL ESTATE, it said in raised gold letters. Below this, in more modest black, was my visitor's name.

"I'm Richard Osgood," he said as if I couldn't read, and held out his hand. The American male's need to respond to that gesture in kind is deeply ingrained, but that night I resisted it. He held his little pink paw out a moment longer, then lowered it and wiped the palm nervously against his chinos. "I have a message for you. From Mr. Devore."

I waited.

"May I come in?"

"No," I said.

He took a step backward, wiped his hand on his pants again, and seemed to gather himself. "I hardly think there's any need to be rude, Mr. Noonan."

I wasn't being rude. If I'd wanted to be rude, I would have treated him to a faceful of roach-repellent. "Max Devore and his minder tried to drown me in the lake this evening. If my manners seem a little off to you, that's probably it."

Osgood's look of shock was real, I think. "You must be working too hard on your latest project, Mr. Noonan. Max Devore is going to be eighty-six on his next birthday — if he makes it, which now seems to be in some doubt. Poor old fella can hardly even walk from his chair to his bed anymore. As for Rogette —"

"I see your point," I said. "In fact I saw it twenty minutes ago, without any help from you. I hardly believe it myself, and I was there. Give me whatever it is you have for me."

"Fine," he said in a prissy little "all right, *be* that way" voice. He unzipped a pouch on the front of his leather bag and brought out a white envelope, business-sized and sealed. I took it, hoping Osgood couldn't sense how hard my heart was thumping. Devore moved pretty damned fast for a man who travelled with an oxygen tank. The question was, what kind of move was this?

"Thanks," I said, beginning to close the door. "I'd tip you the price of a drink, but I left my wallet on the dresser."

"Wait! You're supposed to read it and give me an answer."

I raised my eyebrows. "I don't know where Devore got the notion that he could order me around, but I have no intention of allowing his ideas to influence my behavior. Buzz off."

His lips turned down, creating deep dimples at the corners of his mouth, and all at once he didn't look like Woody Allen at all. He looked like a fifty-year-old real-estate broker who had sold his soul to the devil and now couldn't stand to see anyone yank the boss's forked tail. "Piece of friendly advice, Mr. Noonan — you want to watch it. Max Devore is no man to fool around with."

"Luckily for me, I'm not fooling around."

I closed the door and stood in the foyer, holding the envelope and watching Mr.

Next Century Real Estate. He looked pissed off and confused — no one had given him the bum's rush just lately, I guessed. Maybe it would do him some good. Lend a little perspective to his life. Remind him that, Max Devore or no Max Devore, Richie Osgood would still never stand more than five-feet-seven. Even in cowboy boots.

"Mr. Devore wants an answer!" he called through the closed door.

"I'll phone," I called back, then slowly raised my middle fingers in the double eagle I'd hoped to give Max and Rogette earlier. "In the meantime, perhaps you could convey this."

I almost expected him to take off his glasses and rub his eyes. He walked back to his car instead, tossed his case in, then followed it. I watched until he had backed up to the lane and I was sure he was gone. Then I went into the living room and opened the envelope. Inside was a single sheet of paper, faintly scented with the perfume my mother had worn when I was just a kid. White Shoulders, I think it's called. Across the top — neat, ladylike, printed in slightly raised letters — was

Rogette D. Whitmore

Below it was this message, written in a slightly shaky feminine hand:

Dear Mr. Noonan,

Max wishes me to convey how glad he was to meet you! I must echo that sentiment. You are a very amusing and entertaining fellow! We enjoyed your antics ever so much.

Now to business. M. offers you a very simple deal: if you promise to cease asking questions about him, and if you promise to cease all legal maneuvering — if you promise to let him rest in peace, so to speak — then Mr. Devore promises to cease efforts to gain custody of his granddaughter. If this suits, you need only tell Mr. Osgood "I agree." He will carry the message! Max hopes to return to California by private jet v4ery soon — he has business which can be put off no longer, although he has enjoyed his time here and has found you particularly interesting. He wants me to remind you that custody has its responsibilities, and urges you not to forget he said so.

Rogette

P.S. He reminds me that you didn't answer his question — does her cunt suck? Max is quite curious on that point.

R.

I read this note over a second time, then a third. I started to put it on the table, then read it a fourth time. It was as if I couldn't get the sense of it. I had to restrain an urge to fly to the telephone and call Mattie at once. It's over, Mattie, I'd say. Taking your job and dunking me in the lake were the last two shots of the war. He's giving up.

No. Not until I was absolutely sure.

I called Warrington's instead, where I got my fourth answering machine of the night. Devore and Whitmore hadn't bothered with anything warm and fuzzy, either; a voice as cold as a motel ice-machine simply told me to leave my message at the sound of the beep.

"It's Noonan," I said. Before I could go any further there was a click as someone picked up.

"Did you enjoy your swim?" Rogette Whitmore asked in a smoky, mocking voice.

If I hadn't seen her in the flesh, I might have imagined a Barbara Stanwyck type at her most coldly attractive, coiled on a red velvet couch in a peach-silk dressing gown, telephone in one hand, ivory cigarette holder in the other.

"If I'd caught up with you, Ms. Whitmore, I would have made you understand my feelings perfectly."

"Oooo," she said. "My thighs are a-tingle."

"Please spare me the image of your thighs."

"Sticks and stones, Mr. Noonan," she said. "To what do we owe the pleasure of your call?"

"I sent Mr. Osgood away without a reply."

"Max thought you might. He said, 'Our young whoremaster believes in the value of a personal response. You can tell that just looking at him.'"

"He gets the uglies when he loses, doesn't he?"

"Mr. Devore doesn't *lose*." Her voice dropped at least forty degrees and all the mocking good humor bailed out on the way down. "He may change his goals, but he doesn't *lose*. You were the one who looked like a loser tonight, Mr. Noonan, paddling around and yelling out there in the lake. You were scared, weren't you?"

"Yes. Badly."

"You were right to be. I wonder if you know how lucky you are?"

"May I tell you something?"

"Of course, Mike — may I call you Mike?"

"Why don't you just stick with Mr. Noonan. Now — are you listening?"

"With bated breath."

"Your boss is old, he's nutty, and I suspect he's past the point where he could effectively manage a Yahtzee scorecard, let alone a custody suit. He was whipped a week ago."

"Do you have a point?"

"As a matter of fact I do, so get it right: if either of you ever tries anything remotely like that again, I'll come after that old fuck and jam his snot-smeared oxygen mask so far up his ass he'll be able to aerate his lungs from the bottom. And if I see you on The Street, Ms. Whitmore, I'll use you for a shotput. Do you understand me?"

I stopped, breathing hard, amazed and also rather disgusted with myself. If you had told me I'd had such a speech in me, I would have scoffed.

After a long silence I said: "Ms. Whitmore? Still there?"

"I'm here," she said. I wanted her to be furious, but she actually sounded amused. "Who has the uglies now, Mr. Noonan?"

"I do," I said, "and don't you forget it, you rock-throwing bitch."

"What is your answer to Mr. Devore?"

"We have a deal. I shut up, the lawyers shut up, he gets out of Mattie and Kyra's life. If, on the other hand, he continues to —"

"I know, I know, you'll bore him and stroke him. I wonder how you'll feel about all this a week from now, you arrogant, stupid creature?"

Before I could reply — it was on the tip of my tongue to tell her that even at her best she still threw like a girl — she was gone.

I stood there with the telephone in my hand for a few seconds, then hung it up. Was it a trick? It felt like a trick, but at the same time it didn't. John needed to know about this. He hadn't left his parents' number on his answering machine, but Mattie had it. If I called her back, though, I'd be obligated to tell her what had just happened. It might be a good idea to put off any further calls until tomorrow. To sleep on it.

I stuck my hand in my pocket and damned near impaled it on the steak knife hiding there. I'd forgotten all about it. I took it out, carried it back into the kitchen, and returned it to the drawer. Next I fished out the aerosol can, turned to put it back on top of the fridge with its elderly brothers, then stopped. Inside the circle of fruit and vege-table magnets was this:

d
go
w
19n

Had I done that myself? Had I been so far into the zone, so tranced out, that I had put a mini-crossword on the refrigerator without remembering it? And if so, what did it mean?

Maybe someone else put it up, I thought. *One of my invisible roommates.*

"Go down 19n," I said, reaching out and touching the letters. A compass heading? Or maybe it meant *Go 19 Down.* That suggested crosswords again. Sometimes in a puzzle you get a clue which reads simply *See 19 Across* or *See 19 Down.* If that was the meaning here, what puzzle was I supposed to check?

"I could use a little help here," I said, but there was no answer — not from the astral plane, not from inside my own head. I finally got the can of beer I'd been promising myself and took it back to the sofa. I picked up my *Tough Stuff* crossword book and looked at the puzzle I was currently working. "Liquor Is Quicker," it was called, and it was filled with the stupid puns which only crossword addicts find amusing. Tipsy actor? Marlon Brandy. Tipsy southern novel? Tequila Mockingbird. Drives the

D.A. to drink? Bourbon of proof. And the definition of 19 Down was Oriental nurse, which every cruciverbalist in the universe knows is amah. Nothing in "Liquor Is Quicker" connected to what was going on in my life, at least that I could see.

I thumbed through some of the other puzzles in the book, looking at 19 Downs. Marble worker's tool (chisel). CNN's favorite howler, 2 wds (wolfblitzer). Ethanol and dimethyl ether, e.g. (isomers). I tossed the book aside in disgust. Who said it had to be this particular crossword collection, anyway? There were probably fifty others in the house, four or five in the drawer of the very end-table on which my beer can stood. I leaned back on the sofa and closed my eyes.

I always liked a whore . . . sometimes their place was on my face.

This is where good pups and vile dogs may walk side-by-side.

There's no town drunk here, we all take turns.

This is where it happened. Ayuh.

I fell asleep and woke up three hours later with a stiff neck and a terrible throb in the back of my head. Thunder was rumbling thickly far off in the White Mountains, and the house seemed very hot. When I got up from the couch, the backs of my thighs more or less peeled away from the fabric. I shuffled down to the north wing like an old, old man, looked at my wet clothes, thought about taking them into the laundry room, and then decided if I bent over that far, my head might explode.

"You ghosts take care of it," I muttered. "If you can change the pants and the underwear around on the whirligig, you can put my clothes in the hamper."

I took three Tylenol and went to bed. At some point I woke a second time and heard the phantom child sobbing.

"Stop," I told it. "Stop it, Ki, no one's going to take you anywhere. You're safe." Then I went back to sleep again.

Chapter 19

The telephone was ringing. I climbed toward it from a drowning dream where I couldn't catch my breath, rising into early sunlight, wincing at the pain in the back of my head as I swung my feet out of bed. The phone would quit before I got to it, they almost always do in such situations, and then I'd lie back down and spend a fruitless ten minutes wondering who it had been before getting up for good.

Ringgg . . . ringgg . . . ringgg . . .

Was that ten? A dozen? I'd lost count. Someone was really dedicated. I hoped it wasn't trouble, but in my experience people don't try that hard when the news is good. I touched my fingers gingerly to the back of my head. It hurt plenty, but that deep, sick ache seemed to be gone. And there was no blood on my fingers when I looked at them.

I padded down the hall and picked up the phone. "Hello?"

"Well, you won't have to worry about testifyin at the kid's custody hearin anymore, at least."

"Bill?"

"Ayuh."

"How did you know . . ." I leaned around the corner and peered at the waggy, annoying cat-clock. Twenty minutes past seven and already sweltering. Hotter'n a bugger, as us TR Martians like to say. "How do you know he decided —"

"I don't know nothing about his business one way or t'other." Bill sounded touchy. "He never called to ask my advice, and I never called to give him any."

"What's happened? What's going on?"

"You haven't had the TV on yet?"

"I don't even have the coffee on yet."

No apology from Bill; he was a fellow who believed that people who didn't get up until after six A.M. deserved whatever they got. I was awake now, though. And had a pretty good idea of what was coming.

"Devore killed himself last night, Mike. Got into a tub of warm water and pulled a plastic bag over his head. Mustn't have taken long, with his lungs the way they were."

No, I thought, probably not long. In spite of the humid summer heat that already lay on the house, I shivered.

"Who found him? The woman?"

"Ayuh, sure."

"What time?"

" 'Shortly before midnight,' they said on the Channel 6 news."

Right around the time I had awakened on the couch and taken myself stiffly off to bed, in other words.

"Is she implicated?"

"Did she play Kevorkian, you mean? The news report I saw didn't say nothin about that. The gossip-mill down to the Lakeview General will be turnin brisk by now, but I ain't been down yet for my share of the grain. If she helped him, I don't think she'll ever see trouble for it, do you? He was eighty-five and not well."

"Do you know if he'll be buried on the TR?"

"California. She said there'd be services in Palm Springs on Tuesday."

A sense of surpassing oddness swept over me as I realized the source of Mattie's problems might be lying in a chapel filled with flowers at the same time The Friends of Kyra Devore were digesting their lunches and getting ready to start throwing the Frisbee around. *It's going to be a celebration,* I thought wonderingly. *I don't know how they're going to handle it in The Little Chapel of the Microchips in Palm Springs, but on Wasp Hill Road they're going to be dancing and throwing their arms in the sky and hollering Yes, Lawd.*

I'd never been glad to hear of anyone's death before in my life, but I was glad to hear of Devore's. I was sorry to feel that way, but I did. The old bastard had dumped me in the lake . . . but before the night was over, he was the one who had drowned. Inside a plastic bag he had drowned, sitting in a tub of tepid water.

"Any idea how the TV guys got onto it so fast?" It wasn't *superfast*, not with seven hours between the discovery of the body and the seven o'clock news, but TV news people have a tendency to be lazy.

"Whitmore called em. Had a press conference right there in Warrin'ton's parlor at two o'clock this morning. Took questions settin on that big maroon plush sofa, the one Jo always used to say should be in a saloon oil paintin with a naked woman lyin on it. Remember?"

"Yeah."

"I saw a coupla County deputies walkin around in the background, plus a fella I reckonized from Jaquard's Funeral Home in Motton."

"That's bizarre," I said.

"Ayuh, body still upstairs, most likely, while Whitmore was runnin her gums . . . but she claimed she was just followin the boss's orders. Said he left a tape sayin he'd done it on Friday night so as not to affect the cump'ny stock price and wanted Rogette to call in the press right off and assure folks that the cump'ny was solid, that between his son and the Board of Directors, everythin was goin to be just acey-deucey. Then she told about the services in Palm Springs."

"He commits suicide, then holds a two A.M. press conference by proxy to soothe the stockholders."

"Ayuh. And it sounds just like him."

A silence fell between us on the line. I tried to think and couldn't. All I knew was that I wanted to go upstairs and work, aching head or no aching head. I wanted to rejoin Andy Drake, John Shackleford, and Shackleford's childhood friend, the awful Ray Garraty. There was madness in my story, but it was a madness I understood.

"Bill," I said at last, "are we still friends?"

"Christ, yes," he said promptly. "But if there's people around who seem a little stand-offy to you, you'll know why, won't you?"

Sure I'd know. Many would blame the old man's death on me. It was crazy, given his physical condition, and it would by no means be a majority opinion, but the idea would gain a certain amount of credence, at least in the short run — I knew that as well as I knew the truth about John Shackleford's childhood friend.

Kiddies, once upon a time there was a goose that flew back to the little unincorporated township where it had lived as a downy gosling. It began laying lovely golden eggs, and the townsfolk all gathered around to marvel and receive their share. Now, however, that goose was cooked and someone had to take the heat. I'd get some, but Mattie's kitchen might get a few degrees toastier than mine; she'd had the temerity to fight for her child instead of silently handing Ki over.

"Keep your head down the next few weeks," Bill said. "That'd be my idea. In fact, if you had business that took you right out of the TR until all this settles down, that might be for the best."

"I appreciate the sense of what you're saying, but I can't. I'm writing a book. If I pick up my shit and move, it's apt to die on me. It's happened before, and I don't want it to happen this time."

"Pretty good yarn, is it?"

"Not bad, but that's not the important thing. It's . . . well, let's just say this one's important to me for other reasons."

"Wouldn't it travel as far as Derry?"

"Are you trying to get rid of me, William?"

"I'm tryin to keep an eye out, that's all — caretakin's my job, y'know. And don't say you weren't warned: the hive's gonna buzz. There's two stories goin around about you, Mike. One is that you're shacking with Mattie Devore. The other is that you came back to write a hatchet-job on the TR. Pull out all the old skeletons you can find."

"Finish what Jo started, in other words. Who's been spreading that story, Bill?"

Silence from Bill. We were back on earth-quake ground again, and this time that ground felt shakier than ever.

"The book I'm working on is a novel," I said. "Set in Florida."

"Oh, ayuh?" You wouldn't think three little syllables could have so much relief in them.

"Think you could kind of pass that around?"

"I think I could," he said. "If you tell Brenda Meserve, it'd get around even faster and go even farther."

"Okay, I will. As far as Mattie goes —"

"Mike, you don't have to —"

"I'm not shacking with her. That was never the deal. The deal was like walking down the street, turning the corner, and seeing a big guy beating up a little guy." I paused. "She and her lawyer are planning a barbecue at her place Tuesday noon. I'm planning to join them. Are people from town going to think we're dancing on Devore's grave?"

"Some will. Royce Merrill will. Dickie Brooks will. Old ladies in pants, Yvette calls em."

"Well fuck them," I said. "Every last one."

"I understand how you feel, but tell her not to shove it in folks' faces," he almost pleaded. "Do that much, Mike. It wouldn't kill her to drag her grill around back of her

549

trailer, would it? At least with it there, folks lookin out from the store or the garage wouldn't see nothing but the smoke."

"I'll pass on the message. And if I make the party, I'll put the barbecue around back myself."

"You'd do well to stay away from that girl and her child," Bill said. "You can tell me it's none of my business, but I'm talkin to you like a Dutch uncle, tellin you for your own good."

I had a flash of my dream then. The slick, exquisite tightness as I slipped inside her. The little breasts with their hard nipples. Her voice in the darkness, telling me to do what I wanted. My body responded almost instantly. "I know you are," I said.

"All right." He sounded relieved that I wasn't going to scold him — take him to school, he would have said. "I'll let you go n have your breakfast."

"I appreciate you calling."

"Almost didn't. Yvette talked me into it. She said, 'You always liked Mike and Jo Noonan best of all the ones you did for. Don't you get in bad with him now that he's back home.' "

"Tell her I appreciate it," I said.

I hung up the phone and looked at it thoughtfully. We seemed to be on good terms again . . . but I didn't think we were exactly friends. Certainly not the way we had been. That had changed when I realized Bill was lying to me about some things and holding back about others; it had also changed when I realized what he had almost called Sara and the Red-Tops.

You can't condemn a man for what may only be a figment of your own imagination.

True, and I'd try not to do it . . . but I knew what I knew.

I went into the living room, snapped on the TV, then snapped it off again. My satellite dish got fifty or sixty different channels, and not a one of them local. There was a portable TV in the kitchen, however, and if I dipped its rabbit-ears toward the lake I'd be able to get WMTW, the ABC affiliate in western Maine.

I snatched up Rogette's note, went into the kitchen, and turned on the little Sony tucked under the cabinets with the coffee-maker. *Good Morning America* was on, but they would be breaking for the local news soon. In the meantime I scanned the note, this time concentrating on the mode of expression rather than the message, which had taken all of my attention the night before.

Hopes to return to California by private jet very soon, she had written.

Has business which can be put off no longer, she had written.

If you promise to let him rest in peace, she had written.

It was a goddam suicide note.

"You knew," I said, rubbing my thumb over the raised letters of her name. "You knew when you wrote this, and probably when you were chucking rocks at me. But why?"

Custody has its responsibilities, she had written. *Don't forget he said so.*

But the custody business was over, right? Not even a judge that was bought and paid for could award custody to a dead man.

GMA finally gave way to the local report, where Max Devore's suicide was the leader. The TV picture was snowy, but I could see the maroon sofa Bill had mentioned, and Rogette Whitmore sitting on it with her hands folded composedly in her lap. I thought one of the deputies in the background was George Footman, although the snow was too heavy for me to be completely sure.

Mr. Devore had spoken frequently over the last eight months of ending his life, Whitmore said. He had been very unwell. He had asked her to come out with him the previous evening, and she realized now that he had wanted to look at one final sunset. It had been a glorious one, too, she added. I could have corroborated that; I remembered the sunset very well, having almost drowned by its light.

Rogette was reading Devore's statement

when my phone rang again. It was Mattie, and she was crying in hard gusts.

"The news," she said, "Mike, did you see . . . do you know . . ."

At first that was all she could manage that was coherent. I told her I did know, Bill Dean had called me and then I'd caught some of it on the local news. She tried to reply and couldn't speak. Guilt, relief, horror, even hilarity — I heard all those things in her crying. I asked where Ki was. I could sympathize with how Mattie felt — until turning on the news this morning she'd believed old Max Devore was her bitterest enemy — but I didn't like the idea of a three-year-old girl watching her mom fall apart.

"Out back," she managed. "She's had her breakfast. Now she's having a d-doll p-p-p . . . doll pi-p-pic—"

"Doll picnic. Yes. Good. Let it go, then. All of it. Let it out."

She cried for two minutes at least, maybe longer. I stood with the telephone pressed to my ear, sweating in the July heat, trying to be patient.

I'm going to give you one chance to save your soul, Devore had told me, but this morning he was dead and his soul was wherever it was. He was dead, Mattie was free, I was writing. Life should have felt wonderful, but it didn't.

At last she began to get her control back. "I'm sorry. I haven't cried like that — really, really cried — since Lance died."

"It's understandable and you're allowed."

"Come to lunch," she said. "Come to lunch *please*, Mike. Ki's going to spend the afternoon with a friend she met at Vacation Bible School, and we can talk. I need to talk to someone . . . God, my head is spinning. Please say you'll come."

"I'd love to, but it's a bad idea. Especially with Ki gone."

I gave her an edited version of my conversation with Bill Dean. She listened carefully. I thought there might be an angry outburst when I finished, but I'd forgotten one simple fact: Mattie Stanchfield Devore had lived around here all her life. She knew how things worked.

"I understand that things will heal quicker if I keep my eyes down, my mouth shut, and my knees together," she said, "and I'll do my best to go along, but diplomacy only stretches so far. That old man was trying to take my daughter away, don't they realize that down at the goddam general store?"

"*I* realize it."

"I know. That's why I wanted to talk to you."

"What if we had an early supper on the Castle Rock common? Same place as Friday? Say five-ish?"

554

"I'd have to bring Ki —"

"Fine," I said. "Bring her. Tell her I know 'Hansel and Gretel' by heart and am willing to share. Will you call John in Philly? Give him the details?"

"Yes. I'll wait another hour or so. God, I'm so happy. I know that's wrong, but I'm so happy I could *burst!*"

"That makes two of us." There was a pause on the other end. I heard a long, watery intake of breath. "Mattie? All right?"

"Yes, but how do you tell a three-year-old her grandfather died?"

Tell her the old fuck slipped and fell headfirst into a Glad Bag, I thought, then pressed the back of my hand against my mouth to stifle a spate of lunatic cackles.

"I don't know, but you'll have to do it as soon as she comes in."

"I will? Why?"

"Because she's going to see you. She's going to see your face."

I lasted exactly two hours in the upstairs study, and then the heat drove me out — the thermometer on the stoop read ninety-five degrees at ten o'clock. I guessed it might be five degrees warmer on the second floor.

Hoping I wasn't making a mistake, I unplugged the IBM and carried it downstairs. I was working without a shirt, and as I crossed the living room, the back of the typewriter slipped in the sweat coating my midriff and I almost dropped the outdated sonofabitch on my toes. That made me think of my ankle, the one I'd hurt when I fell into the lake, and I set the typewriter aside to look at it. It was colorful, black and purple and reddish at the edges, but not terribly inflated. I guessed my immersion in the cool water had helped keep the swelling down.

I put the typewriter on the deck table, rummaged out an extension cord, plugged in beneath Bunter's watchful eye, and sat down facing the hazy blue-gray surface of the lake. I waited for one of my old anxiety attacks to hit — the clenched stomach, the throbbing eyes, and, worst of all, that sensation of invisible steel bands clamped around my chest, making it impossible to breathe. Nothing like that happened. The words flowed as easily down here as they had upstairs, and my naked upper body was loving the little breeze that puffed in off the lake every now and again. I forgot about Max Devore, Mattie Devore, Kyra Devore. I forgot about Jo Noonan and Sara Tidwell. I forgot about myself. For two hours I was back in Florida. John Shackleford's execution was nearing. Andy Drake was racing the clock.

It was the telephone that brought me back, and for once I didn't resent interruption. If undisturbed, I might have gone on writing until I simply melted into a sweaty pile of goo on the deck.

It was my brother. We talked about Mom — in Siddy's opinion she was now short an entire roof instead of just a few shingles — and her sister, Francine, who had broken her hip in June. Sid wanted to know how I was doing, and I told him I was doing all right, I'd had some problems getting going on a new book but now seemed to be back on track (in my family, the only permissible time to discuss trouble is when it's over). And how was the Sidster? Kickin, he said, which I assumed meant just fine — Siddy has a twelve-year-old, and consequently his slang is always up-to-date. The new accounting business was starting to take hold, although he'd been scared for awhile (first I knew of it, of course). He could never thank me enough for the bridge loan I'd made him last November. I replied that it was the least I could do, which was the absolute truth, especially when I considered how much more time — both in person and on the phone — he spent with our mother than I did.

"Well, I'll let you go," Siddy told me after a few more pleasantries — he never says goodbye or so long when he's on the phone, it's always *well, I'll let you go,* as if he's been holding you hostage. "You want to keep cool up there, Mike — Weather Channel says it's going to be hotter than hell in New England all weekend."

"There's always the lake if things get too bad. Hey Sid?"

"Hey what?" Like *I'll let you go, Hey what* went back to childhood. It was sort of comforting; it was also sort of spooky.

"Our folks all came from Prout's Neck, right? I mean on Daddy's side." Mom came from another world entirely — one where the men wear Lacoste polo shirts, the women always wear full slips under their dresses, and everyone knows the second verse of "Dixie" by heart. She had met my dad in Portland while competing in a college cheerleading event. Materfamilias came from Memphis quality, darlin, and didn't let you forget it.

"I guess so," he said. "Yeah. But don't go asking me a lot of family-tree questions, Mike — I'm still not sure what the difference is between a nephew and a cousin, and I told Jo the same thing."

"Did you?" Everything inside me had gone very still . . . but I can't say I was surprised. Not by then.

"Uh-huh, you bet."

"What did she want to know?"

"Everything I knew. Which isn't much. I could have told her all about Ma's great-great-grandfather, the one who got killed by the Indians, but Jo didn't seem to care about any of Ma's folks."

"When would this have been?"

"Does it matter?"

"It might."

"Okay, let's see. I think it was around the time Patrick had his appendectomy. Yeah, I'm sure it was. February of '94. It might have been March, but I'm pretty sure it was February."

Six months from the Rite Aid parking lot. Jo moving into the shadow of her own death like a woman stepping beneath the shade of an awning. Not pregnant, though, not yet. Jo making day-trips to the TR. Jo asking questions, some of the sort that made people feel bad, according to Bill Dean . . . but she'd gone on asking just the same. Yeah. Because once she got onto something, Jo was like a terrier with a rag in its jaws. Had she been asking questions of the man in the brown sportcoat? Who *was* the man in the brown sportcoat?

"Pat was in the hospital, sure. Dr. Alpert said he was doing fine, but when the phone rang I jumped for it — I half-expected it to be him, Alpert, saying Pat had had a relapse or something."

"Where in God's name did you get this sense of impending doom, Sid?"

"I dunno, buddy, but it's there. Anyway, it's not Alpert, it's Johanna. She wants to know if we had any ancestors — three, maybe even four generations back — who lived there where you are, or in one of the surrounding towns. I told her I didn't know, but you might. Know, I mean. She said she didn't want to ask you because it was a surprise. Was it a surprise?"

"A big one," I said. "Daddy was a lobsterman —"

"Bite your tongue, he was an *artist* — 'a seacoast primitive.' Ma still calls him that." Siddy wasn't quite laughing.

"Shit, he sold lobster-pot coffee-tables and lawn-puffins to the tourists when he got too rheumatic to go out on the bay and haul traps."

"*I* know that, but Ma's got her marriage edited like a movie for television."

How true. Our own version of Blanche Du Bois. "Dad was a lobsterman in Prout's Neck. He —"

Siddy interrupted, singing the first verse of "Papa Was a Rollin' Stone" in a horrible offkey tenor.

"Come on, this is serious. He had his first boat from his father, right?"

"That's the story," Sid agreed. "Jack Noonan's *Lazy Betty*, original owner Paul Noonan. Also of Prout's. Boat took a hell of a pasting in Hurricane Donna, back in 1960. I think it was Donna."

Two years after I was born. "And Daddy put it up for sale in '63."

"Yep. I don't know whatever became of it, but it was Grampy Paul's to begin with, all right. Do you remember all the lobster stew we ate when we were kids, Mikey?"

"Seacoast meatloaf," I said, hardly thinking about it. Like most kids raised on the coast of Maine, I can't imagine ordering lobster in a restaurant — that's for flat-landers. I was thinking about Grampy Paul, who had been born in the 1890s. Paul Noonan begat Jack Noonan, Jack Noonan begat Mike and Sid Noonan, and that was really all I knew, except the Noonans had all grown up a long way from where I now stood sweating my brains out.

They shit in the same pit.

Devore had gotten it wrong, that was all — when we Noonans weren't wearing polo shirts and being Memphis quality, we were Prout's Neckers. It was unlikely that Devore's great-grandfather and my own would have had anything to do with each other in any case; the old rip had been twice my age, and that meant the generations didn't match up.

But if he had been *totally* wrong, what had Jo been on about?

"Mike?" Sid asked. "Are you there?"

"Yeah."

"Are you okay? You don't sound so great, I have to tell you."

"It's the heat," I said. "Not to mention

your sense of impending doom. Thanks for calling, Siddy."

"Thanks for being there, brother."

"Kickin," I said.

I went out to the kitchen to get a glass of cold water. As I was filling it, I heard the magnets on the fridge begin sliding around. I whirled, spilling some of the water on my bare feet and hardly noticing. I was as excited as a kid who thinks he may glimpse Santa Claus before he shoots back up the chimney.

I was barely in time to see nine plastic letters drawn into the circle from all points of the compass. CARLADEAN, they spelled . . . but only for a second. Some presence, tremendous but unseen, shot past me. Not a hair on my head stirred, but there was still a strong sense of being buffeted, the way you're buffeted by the air of a passing express train if you're standing near the platform yellow-line when the train bolts through. I cried out in surprise and groped my glass of water back onto the counter, spilling it. I no longer felt in need of cold water, because the temperature in the kitchen of Sara Laughs had dropped off the table.

I blew out my breath and saw vapor, as you do on a cold day in January. One puff, maybe two, and it was gone — but it had been there, all right, and for perhaps five seconds the film of sweat on my body turned to what felt like a slime of ice.

CARLADEAN exploded outward in all directions — it was like watching an atom being smashed in a cartoon. Magnetized letters, fruits, and vegetables flew off the front of the refrigerator and scattered across the kitchen. For a moment the fury which fuelled that scattering was something I could almost taste, like gunpowder.

And something gave way before it, going with a sighing, rueful whisper I had heard before: *"Oh Mike. Oh Mike."* It was the voice I'd caught on the Memo-Scriber tape, and although I hadn't been sure then, I was now — it was Jo's voice.

But who was the other one? Why had it scattered the letters?

Carla Dean. Not Bill's wife; that was Yvette. His mother? His grandmother?

I walked slowly through the kitchen, collecting fridge-magnets like prizes in a scavenger hunt and sticking them back on the Kenmore by the handful. Nothing snatched them out of my hands; nothing froze the sweat on the back of my neck; Bunter's bell didn't ring. Still, I wasn't alone, and I knew it.

CARLADEAN: Jo had wanted me to know. Something else hadn't. Something else had shot past me like the Wabash Cannonball, trying to scatter the letters before I could read them.

Jo was here; a boy who wept in the night was here, too.

And what else?

What else was sharing my house with me?

Chapter 20

I didn't see them at first, which wasn't surprising; it seemed that half of Castle Rock was on the town common as that sultry Saturday afternoon edged on toward evening. The air was bright with hazy midsummer light, and in it kids swarmed over the playground equipment, a number of old men in bright red vests — some sort of club, I assumed — played chess, and a group of young people lay on the grass listening to a teenager in a headband playing the guitar and singing one I remembered from an old Ian and Sylvia record, a cheery tune that went

"Ella Speed was havin her lovin fun,
John Martin shot Ella with a
   Colt forty-one . . ."

I saw no joggers, and no dogs chasing Frisbees. It was just too goddam hot.

I was turning to look at the bandshell, where an eight-man combo called The Castle Rockers was setting up (I had an idea "In the Mood" was about as close as they got to rock and roll), when a small person hit me from behind, grabbing me just above the knees and almost dumping me on the grass.

"Gotcha!" the small person cried gleefully.

"Kyra Devore!" Mattie called, sounding both amused and irritated. "You'll knock him down!"

I turned, dropped the grease-spotted McDonald's bag I had been carrying, and lifted the kid up. It felt natural, and it felt wonderful. You don't realize the weight of a healthy child until you hold one, nor do you fully comprehend the life that runs through them like a bright wire. I didn't get choked up ("Don't go all corny on me, Mike," Siddy would sometimes whisper when we were kids at the movies and I got wet-eyed at a sad part), but I thought of Jo, yes. And the child she had been carrying when she fell down in that stupid parking lot, yes to that, too.

Ki was squealing and laughing, her arms outspread and her hair hanging down in two amusing clumps accented by Raggedy Ann and Andy barrettes.

"Don't tackle your own quarterback!" I yelled, grinning, and to my delight she yelled it right back at me: "Don't taggle yer own quartermack! Don't taggle yer own quartermack!"

I set her on her feet, both of us laughing. Ki took a step backward, tripped herself, and sat down on the grass, laughing harder than ever. I had a mean thought, then, brief

566

but oh so clear: if only the old lizard could see how much he was missed. How sad we were at his passing.

Mattie walked over, and tonight she looked as I'd half-imagined her when I first met her — like one of those lovely children of privilege you see at the country club, either goofing with their friends or sitting seriously at dinner with their parents. She was in a white sleeveless dress and low heels, her hair falling loose around her shoulders, a touch of lipstick on her mouth. Her eyes had a brilliance in them that hadn't been there before. When she hugged me I could smell her perfume and feel the press of her firm little breasts.

I kissed her cheek; she kissed me high up on the jaw, making a smack in my ear that I felt all the way down my back. "Say things are going to be better now," she whispered, still holding me.

"Lots better now," I said, and she hugged me again, tight. Then she stepped away. "You better have brought plenty food, big boy, because we plenty hungry womens. Right, Kyra?"

"I taggled my own quartermack," Ki said, then leaned back on her elbows, giggling deliciously at the bright and hazy sky.

"Come on," I said, and grabbed her by the middle. I toted her that way to a nearby picnic table, Ki kicking her legs and waving her arms and laughing. I set her down on the bench; she slid off it and beneath the table, boneless as an eel and still laughing.

"All right, Kyra Elizabeth," Mattie said. "Sit up and show the other side."

"Good girl, good girl," she said, clambering up beside me. "That's the other side to me, Mike."

"I'm sure," I said. Inside the bag there were Big Macs and fries for Mattie and me. For Ki there was a colorful box upon which Ronald McDonald and his unindicted co-conspirators capered.

"Mattie, I got a Happy Meal! Mike got me a Happy Meal! They have toys!"

"Well see what yours is."

Kyra opened the box, poked around, then smiled. It lit up her whole face. She brought out something that I at first thought was a big dustball. For one horrible second I was back in my dream, the one of Jo under the bed with the book over her face. *Give me that,* she had snarled. *It's my dust-catcher.* And something else, too — some other association, perhaps from some other dream. I couldn't get hold of it.

"Mike?" Mattie asked. Curiosity in her voice, and maybe borderline concern.

"It's a doggy!" Ki said. "I won a doggy in my Happy Meal!"

Yes, of course. A dog. A little stuffed dog. And it was gray, not black . . . although why

568

I'd care about the color either way I didn't know.

"That's a pretty good prize," I said, taking it. It was soft, which was good, and it was gray, which was better. Being gray made it all right, somehow. Crazy but true. I handed it back to her and smiled.

"What's his name?" Ki asked, jumping the little dog back and forth across her Happy Meal box. "What doggy's name, Mike?"

And, without thinking, I said, "Strickland."

I thought she'd look puzzled, but she didn't. She looked delighted. "Stricken!" she said, bouncing the dog back and forth in ever-higher leaps over the box. "Stricken! Stricken! My dog Stricken!"

"Who's this guy Strickland?" Mattie asked, smiling a little. She had begun to unwrap her hamburger.

"A character in a book I read once," I said, watching Ki play with the little puffball dog. "No one real."

"My grampa died," she said five minutes later.

We were still at the picnic table but the food was mostly gone. Strickland the stuffed puffball had been set to guard the remaining french fries. I had been scanning the ebb and flow of people, wondering who was here from the TR observing our tryst and simply

569

burning to carry the news back home. I saw no one I knew, but that didn't mean a whole lot, considering how long I'd been away from this part of the world.

Mattie put down her burger and looked at Ki with some anxiety, but I thought the kid was okay — she had been giving news, not expressing grief.

"I know he did," I said.

"Grampa was awful old." Ki pinched a couple of french fries between her pudgy little fingers. They rose to her mouth, then gloop, all gone. "He's with Lord Jesus now. We had all about Lord Jesus in V.B.S."

Yes, Ki, I thought, *right now Grampy's probably teaching Lord Jesus how to use Pixel Easel and asking if there might be a whore handy.*

"Lord Jesus walked on water and also changed the wine into macaroni."

"Yes, something like that," I said. "It's sad when people die, isn't it?"

"It would be sad if Mattie died, and it would be sad if you died, but Grampy was old." She said it as though I hadn't quite grasped this concept the first time. "In heaven he'll get all fixed up."

"That's a good way to look at it, hon," I said.

Mattie did maintenance on Ki's drooping barrettes, working carefully and with a kind of absent love. I thought she glowed in the summer light, her skin in smooth, tanned contrast to the white dress she had probably bought at one of the discount stores, and I understood that I loved her. Maybe that was all right.

"I miss the white nana, though," Ki said, and this time she did look sad. She picked up the stuffed dog, tried to feed him a french fry, then put him down again. Her small, pretty face looked pensive now, and I could see a whisper of her grandfather in it. It was far back but it was there, perceptible, another ghost. "Mom says white nana went back to California with Grampy's early remains."

"*Earthly* remains, Ki-bird," Mattie said. "That means his body."

"Will white nana come back and see me, Mike?"

"I don't know."

"We had a game. It was all rhymes." She looked more pensive than ever.

"Your mom told me about that game," I said.

"She won't be back," Ki said, answering her own question. One very large tear rolled down her right cheek. She picked up "Stricken," stood him on his back legs for a second, then put him back on guard-duty. Mattie slipped an arm around her, but Ki didn't seem to notice. "White nana didn't really like me. She was just pretending to like me. That was her *job*."

Mattie and I exchanged a glance.

"What makes you say that?" I asked.

"Don't know," Ki said. Over by where the kid was playing the guitar, a juggler in whiteface had started up, working with half a dozen colored balls. Kyra brightened a little. "Mommy-bommy, may I go watch that funny white man?"

"Are you done eating?"

"Yeah, I'm full."

"Thank Mike."

"Don't taggle yer own quartermack," she said, then laughed kindly to show she was just pulling my leg. "Thanks, Mike."

"Not a problem," I said, and then, because that sounded a little old-fashioned: "Kickin."

"You can go as far as that tree, but no farther," Mattie said. "And you know why."

"So you can see me. I will."

She grabbed Strickland and started to run off, then stopped and looked over her shoulder at me. "I guess it was the fridgea-fator people," she said, then corrected herself very carefully and seriously. "The *ree-fridge-a-rator* people." My heart took a hard double beat in my chest.

"It was the refrigerator people what, Ki?" I asked.

"That said white nana didn't really like me." Then she ran off toward the juggler, oblivious to the heat.

Mattie watched her go, then turned back to me. "I haven't talked to anybody about Ki's fridgeafator people. Neither has she, until now. Not that there are any real people, but the letters seem to move around by themselves. It's like a Ouija board."

"Do they spell things?"

For a long time she said nothing. Then she nodded. "Not always, but sometimes." Another pause. "*Most* times, actually. Ki calls it mail from the people in the refrigerator." She smiled, but her eyes were a little scared. "Are they special magnetic letters, do you think? Or have we got a poltergeist working the lakefront?"

"I don't know. I'm sorry I brought them, if they're a problem."

"Don't be silly. You gave them to her, and you're a tremendously big deal to her right now. She talks about you all the time. She was much more interested in picking out something pretty to wear for you tonight than she was in her grandfather's death. I was supposed to wear something pretty, too, Kyra insisted. She's not that way about people, usually — she takes them when they're there and leaves them when they're gone. That's not such a bad way for a little girl to grow up, I sometimes think."

"You both dressed pretty," I said. "That much I'm sure of."

"Thanks." She looked fondly at Ki, who

stood by the tree watching the juggler. He had put his rubber balls aside and moved on to Indian clubs. Then she looked back at me. "Are we done eating?"

I nodded, and Mattie began to pick up the trash and stuff it back into the take-out bag. I helped, and when our fingers touched, she gripped my hand and squeezed. "Thank you," she said. "For everything you've done. Thank you so damn much."

I squeezed back, then let go.

"You know," she said, "it's crossed my mind that Kyra's moving the letters around herself. Mentally."

"Telekinesis?"

"I guess that's the technical term. Only Ki can't spell much more than 'dog' and 'cat.' "

"What's showing up on the fridge?"

"Names, mostly. Once it was yours. Once it was your wife's."

"Jo?"

"The whole thing — JOHANNA. And NANA. Rogette, I presume. JARED shows up sometimes, and BRIDGET. Once there was KITO." She spelled it.

"Kito," I said, and thought: *Kyra, Kia, Kito. What is this?* "A boy's name, do you think?"

"I know it is. It's Swahili, and means precious child. I looked it up in my baby-name book." She glanced toward her own precious child as we walked across the grass to the nearest trash barrel.

"Any others that you can remember?"

She thought. "REG has showed up a couple of times. And once there was CARLA. You understand that Ki can't even read these names as a rule, don't you? She has to ask me what they say."

"Has it occurred to you that Kyra might be copying them out of a book or a magazine? That she's learning to write using the magnetic letters on the fridge instead of paper and pencil?"

"I suppose that's possible . . ." She didn't look as if she believed it, though. Not surprising. I didn't believe it myself.

"I mean, you've never actually seen the letters moving around by themselves on the front of the fridge, have you?" I hoped I sounded as unconcerned asking this question as I wanted to.

She laughed a bit nervously. "God, no!"

"Anything else?"

"Sometimes the fridgeafator people leave messages like HI and BYE and GOOD GIRL. There was one yesterday that I wrote down to show you. Kyra asked me to. It's *really* weird."

"What is it?"

"I'd rather show you, but I left it in the glove compartment of the Scout. Remind me when we go."

Yes. I would.

"This is some spooky shit, *señor*," she said. "Like the writing in the flour that time."

I thought about telling her I had my own fridgeafator people, then didn't. She had enough to worry about without that . . . or so I told myself.

We stood side-by-side on the grass, watching Ki watch the juggler. "Did you call John?" I asked.

"You bet."

"His reaction?"

She turned to me, laughing with her eyes. "He actually sang a verse of 'Ding Dong, the Witch Is Dead.' "

"Wrong sex, right sentiment."

She nodded, her eyes going back to Kyra. I thought again how beautiful she looked, her body slim in the white dress, her features clean and perfectly made.

"Was he pissed at me inviting myself to lunch?" I asked.

"Nope, he loved the idea of having a party."

A party. He loved the idea. I began to feel rather small.

"He even suggested we invite your lawyer from last Friday. Mr. Bissonette? Plus the private detective John hired on Mr. Bissonette's recommendation. Is that okay with you?"

"Fine. How about you, Mattie? Doing okay?"

"Doing okay," she agreed, turning to me. "I *did* have several more calls than usual today. I'm suddenly quite popular."

"Uh-oh."

"Most were hangups, but one gentleman took time enough to call me a cunt, and there was a lady with a very strong Yankee accent who said, 'Theah, you bitch, you've killed him. Aaa you satisfied?' She hung up before I could tell her yes, very satisfied, thanks." But Mattie didn't look satisfied; she looked unhappy and guilty, as if she had literally wished him dead.

"I'm sorry."

"It's okay. Really. Kyra and I have been alone for a long time, and I've been scared for most of it. Now I've made a couple of friends. If a few anonymous phone calls are the price I have to pay, I'll pay it."

She was very close, looking up at me, and I couldn't stop myself. I put the blame on summer, her perfume, and four years without a woman. In that order. I slipped my arms around her waist, and remember perfectly the texture of her dress beneath my hands; the slight pucker at the back where the zipper hid in its sleeve. I remember the sensation of the cloth moving against the bare skin beneath. Then I was kissing her, very gently but very thoroughly — anything worth doing is worth doing right — and she was kissing me back in exactly the same spirit, her mouth curious but not afraid. Her lips were warm and smooth and held some faint sweet taste. Peaches, I think.

We stopped at the same time and pulled back a little from each other. Her hands were still on my shoulders. Mine were on the sides of her waist, just above her hips. Her face was composed enough, but her eyes were more brilliant than ever, and there were slants of color in her cheeks, rising along the cheekbones.

"Oh boy," she said. "I really wanted that. Ever since Ki tackled you and you picked her up I've wanted it."

"John wouldn't think much of us kissing in public," I said. My voice wasn't quite even, and my heart was racing. Seven seconds, one kiss, and every system in my body was red-lining. "In fact, John wouldn't think much of us kissing at all. He fancies you, you know."

"I know, but I fancy *you.*" She turned to check on Ki, who was still standing obediently by the tree, watching the juggler. Who might be watching *us?* Someone who had come over from the TR on a hot summer evening to get ice cream at Frank's Tas-T-Freeze and enjoy a little music and society on the common? Someone who traded for fresh vegetables and fresh gossip at the Lakeview General? A regular at the All-Purpose Garage? This was insanity, and it stayed insanity no matter how you cut it. I dropped my hands from her waist.

"Mattie, they could put our picture next to 'indiscreet' in the dictionary."

She took her hands off my shoulders and stepped back a pace, but her brilliant eyes never left mine. "I know that. I'm young but not entirely stupid."

"I didn't mean —"

She held up a hand to stop me. "Ki goes to bed around nine — she can't seem to sleep until it's mostly dark. I stay up later. Come and visit me, if you want to. You can park around back." She smiled a little. It was a sweet smile; it was also incredibly sexy. "Once the moon's down, that's an area of discretion."

"Mattie, you're young enough to be my daughter."

"Maybe, but I'm not. And sometimes people can be too discreet for their own good."

My body knew so emphatically what it wanted. If we had been in her trailer at that moment it would have been no contest. It was almost no contest anyway. Then something recurred to me, something I'd thought about Devore's ancestors and my own: the generations didn't match up. Wasn't the same thing true here? And I don't believe that people automatically have a right to what they want, no matter how badly they want it. Not every thirst should be slaked. Some things are just wrong — I guess that's what I'm trying to say. But I wasn't sure this was one of them, and I wanted her, all right. So much. I kept thinking about how her dress had slid when I put my arms around her waist, the warm feel of her skin just beneath. And no, she wasn't my daughter.

"You said your thanks," I told her in a dry voice. "And that's enough. Really."

"You think this is *gratitude?*" She voiced a low, tense laugh. "You're forty, Mike, not eighty. You're not Harrison Ford, but you're a good-looking man. Talented and interesting, too. And I like you such an awful lot. I want you to be with me. Do you want me to say please? Fine. Please be with me."

Yes, this was about more than gratitude — I suppose I'd known that even when I was using the word. I'd known she was wearing white shorts and a halter top when she called on the phone the day I went back to work. Had she also known what I was wearing? Had she dreamed she was in bed with me, the two of us screwing our brains out while the party lights shone and Sara Tidwell played her version of the white nana rhyming game, all that crazy Manderley-sanderley-canderley stuff? Had Mattie dreamed of telling me to do what she wanted?

And there were the fridgeafator people.

580

They were another kind of sharing, an even spookier kind. I hadn't quite had nerve enough to tell Mattie about mine, but she might know anyway. Down low in her mind. Down below in her mind, where the blue-collar guys moved around in the zone. Her guys and my guys, all part of the same strange labor union. And maybe it wasn't an issue of morality *per se* at all. Something about it — about *us* — just felt dangerous.

And oh so attractive.

"I need time to think," I said.

"This isn't about what you think. What do you *feel* for me?"

"So much it scares me."

Before I could say anything else, my ears caught a familiar series of chord-changes. I turned toward the kid with the guitar. He had been working through a repertoire of early Dylan, but now he swung into something chuggy and up-tempo, something that made you want to grin and pat your hands together.

> *"Do you want to go fishin*
> *here in my fishin hole?*
> *Said do you want to fish some, honey,*
> *here in my fishin hole?*
> *You want to fish in my pond, baby,*
> *you better have a big long pole."*

"Fishin Blues." Written by Sara Tidwell,

originally performed by Sara and the Red-Top Boys, covered by everyone from Ma Rainey to the Lovin' Spoonful. The raunchy ones had been her specialty, double-entendre so thin you could read a newspaper through it . . . although reading hadn't been Sara's main interest, judging by her lyrics.

Before the kid could go on to the next verse, something about how you got to wiggle when you wobble and get that big one way down deep, The Castle Rockers ran off a brass flourish that said "Shut up, everybody, we're comin atcha." The kid quit playing his guitar; the juggler began catching his Indian clubs and dropping them swiftly onto the grass in a line. The Rockers launched themselves into an extremely evil Sousa march, music to commit serial murders by, and Kyra came running back to us.

"The jugster's done. Will you tell me the story, Mike? Hansel and Panzel?"

"It's Hansel and *Gretel,*" I said, "and I'll be happy to. But let's go where it's a little quieter, okay? The band is giving me a headache."

"Music hurt your headie?"

"A little bit."

"We'll go by Mattie's car, then."

"Good thought."

Kyra ran ahead to stake out a bench on

the edge of the common. Mattie gave me a long warm look, then her hand. I took it. Our fingers folded together as if they had been doing it for years. I thought, *I'd like it to be slow, both of us hardly moving at all. At first, anyway. And would I bring my nicest, longest pole? I think you could count on that.* And then, afterward, we'd talk. Maybe until we could see the furniture in the first early light. When you're in bed with someone you love, particularly for the first time, five o'clock seems almost holy.

"You need a vacation from your own thoughts," Mattie said. "I bet most writers do from time to time."

"That's probably true."

"I wish we were home," she said, and I couldn't tell if her fierceness was real or pretend. "I'd kiss you until this whole conversation became irrelevant. And if there were second thoughts, at least you'd be having them in my bed."

I turned my face into the red light of the westering sun. "Here or there, at this hour Ki would still be up."

"True," she said, sounding uncharacteristically glum. "True."

Kyra reached a bench near the sign reading TOWN COMMON PARKING and climbed up on it, holding the little stuffed dog from Mickey D's in one hand. I tried to pull my hand away as we approached her and Mattie held it firm. "It's all right, Mike. At V.B.S. they hold hands with their friends everywhere they go. It's big people who make it into a big deal."

She stopped, looked at me.

"I want you to know something. Maybe it won't matter to you, but it does to me. There wasn't anyone before Lance and no one after. If you come to me, you'll be my second. I'm not going to talk with you about this again, either. Saying please is all right, but I won't beg."

"I don't —"

"There's a pot with tomato plants in it by the trailer steps. I'll leave a key under it. Don't think. Just come."

"Not tonight, Mattie. I can't."

"You can," she replied.

"Hurry *up*, slowpokes!" Kyra cried, bouncing on the bench.

"*He's* the slow one!" Mattie called back, and poked me in the ribs. Then, in a much lower voice: "You are, too." She unwound her hand from mine and ran toward her daughter, her brown legs scissoring below the hem of the white dress.

In my version of "Hansel and Gretel" the witch was named Depravia. Kyra stared at me with huge eyes when I got to the part where Depravia asks Hansel to poke out his finger so she can see how plump he's getting.

"Is it too scary?" I asked.

Ki shook her head emphatically. I glanced at Mattie to make sure. She nodded and waved a hand for me to go on, so I finished the story. Depravia went into the oven and Gretel found her secret stash of winning lottery tickets. The kids bought a Jet Ski and lived happily ever after on the eastern side of Dark Score Lake. By then The Castle Rockers were slaughtering Gershwin and sunset was nigh. I carried Kyra to Scoutie and strapped her in. I remembered the first time I'd helped put the kid into her car-seat, and the inadvertent press of Mattie's breast.

"I hope there isn't a bad dream for you in that story," I said. Until I heard it coming out of my own mouth, I hadn't realized how fundamentally awful that one is.

"I won't have bad dreams," Kyra said matter-of-factly. "The fridgeafator people will keep them away." Then, carefully, reminding herself: *Ree-fridge-a-rator.* She turned to Mattie. "Show him the crosspatch, Mommy-bommy."

"Cross*word.* But thanks, I would've forgotten." She thumbed open the glove compartment and took out a folded sheet of paper. "It was on the fridge this morning. I copied it down because Ki said you'd know what it meant. She said you do crossword puzzles. Well, she said crosspatches, but I got the idea."

Had I told Kyra that I did crosswords? Almost certainly not. Did it surprise me that she knew? Not at all. I took the sheet of paper, unfolded it, and looked at what was printed there:

```
        d
       go
        w
    ninety2
```

"Is it a crosspatch puzzle, Mike?" Kyra asked.

"I guess so — a very simple one. But if it means something, I don't know what it is. May I keep this?"

"Yes," Mattie said.

I walked her around to the driver's side of the Scout, reaching for her hand again as we went. "Just give me a little time. I know that's supposed to be the girl's line, but —"

"Take the time," she said. "Just don't take too much."

I didn't want to take *any*, which was just the problem. The sex would be great, I knew that. But after?

There might *be* an after, though. I knew it and she did, too. With Mattie, "after" was a real possibility. The idea was a little scary, a little wonderful.

I kissed the corner of her mouth. She laughed and grabbed me by the earlobe.

"You can do better," she said, then looked at Ki, who was sitting in her car-seat and gazing at us interestedly. "But I'll let you off this time."

"Kiss Ki!" Kyra called, holding out her arms, so I went around and kissed Ki. Driving home, wearing my dark glasses to cut the glare of the setting sun, it occurred to me that maybe I could be Kyra Devore's father. That seemed almost as attractive to me as going to bed with her mother, which was a measure of how deep I was in. And going deeper, maybe.

Deeper still.

Sara Laughs seemed very empty after having Mattie in my arms — a sleeping head without dreams. I checked the letters on the fridge, saw nothing there but the normal scatter, and got a beer. I went out on the deck to drink it while I watched the last of the sunset. I tried to think about the refrigerator people and crosspatches that had appeared on both refrigerators: "go down nineteen" on Lane Forty-two and "go down ninety-two" on Wasp Hill Road. Different vectors from the land to the lake? Different spots on The Street? Shit, who knew?

I tried to think about John Storrow and how unhappy he was apt to be if he found out there was — to quote Sara Laughs, who got to the line long before John Mellencamp

— another mule kicking in Mattie Devore's stall. But mostly what I thought about was holding her for the first time, kissing her for the first time. No human instinct is more powerful than the sex-drive when it is fully aroused, and its awakening images are emotional tattoos that never leave us. For me, it was feeling the soft bare skin of her waist just beneath her dress. The slippery feel of the fabric . . .

I turned abruptly and hurried through the house to the north wing, almost running and shedding clothes as I went. I turned the shower on to full cold and stood under it for five minutes, shivering. When I got out I felt a little more like an actual human being and a little less like a twitching bundle of nerve endings. And as I toweled dry, something else recurred to me. At some point I had thought of Jo's brother Frank, had thought that if anyone besides myself would be able to feel Jo's presence in Sara Laughs, it would be him. I hadn't gotten around to inviting him down yet, and now wasn't sure I wanted to. I had come to feel oddly possessive, almost jealous, about what was happening here. And yet if Jo had been writing something on the quiet, Frank might know. Of course she hadn't confided in him about the pregnancy, but —

I looked at my watch. Quarter past nine. In the trailer near the intersection of Wasp

Hill Road and Route 68, Kyra was probably already asleep . . . and her mother might already have put her extra key under the pot near the steps. I thought of her in the white dress, the swell of her hips just below my hands and the smell of her perfume, then pushed the images away. I couldn't spend the whole night taking cold showers. Quarter past nine was still early enough to call Frank Arlen.

He picked up on the second ring, sounding both happy to hear from me and as if he'd gotten three or four cans further into the sixpack than I had so far done. We passed the usual pleasantries back and forth — most of my own almost entirely fictional, I was dismayed to find — and he mentioned that a famous neighbor of mine had kicked the bucket, according to the news. Had I met him? Yes, I said, remembering how Max Devore had run his wheelchair at me. Yes, I'd met him. Frank wanted to know what he was like. That was hard to say, I told him. Poor old guy was stuck in a wheelchair and suffering from emphysema.

"Pretty frail, huh?" Frank asked sympathetically.

"Yeah," I said. "Listen, Frank, I called about Jo. I was out in her studio looking around, and I found my typewriter. Since then I've kind of gotten the idea she was writing something. It might have started as a little piece about our house, then widened. The place is named after Sara Tidwell, you know. The blues singer."

A long pause. Then Frank said, "I know." His voice sounded heavy, grave.

"What else do you know, Frank?"

"That she was scared. I think she found out something that scared her. I think that mostly because —"

That was when the light finally broke. I probably should have known from Mattie's description, *would* have known if I hadn't been so upset. "You were down here with her, weren't you? In July of 1994. You went to the softball game, then you went back up The Street to the house."

"How do you know that?" he almost barked.

"Someone saw you. A friend of mine." I was trying not to sound mad and not succeeding. I *was* mad, but it was a relieved anger, the kind you feel when your kid comes dragging into the house with a shamefaced grin just as you're getting ready to call the cops.

"I almost told you a day or two before we buried her. We were in that pub, do you remember?"

Jack's Pub, right after Frank had beaten the funeral director down on the price of Jo's coffin. Sure I remembered. I even remembered the look in his eyes when I'd told him Jo had been pregnant when she died.

He must have felt the silence spinning out, because he came back sounding anxious. "Mike, I hope you didn't get any —"

"What? Wrong ideas? I thought maybe she was having an affair, how's that for a wrong idea? You can call that ignoble if you want, but I had my reasons. There was a lot she wasn't telling me. What did she tell *you?*"

"Next to nothing."

"Did you know she quit all her boards and committees? Quit and never said a word to me?"

"No." I didn't think he was lying. Why would he, at this late date? "Jesus, Mike, if I'd known that —"

"What happened the day you came down here? Tell me."

"I was at the printshop in Sanford. Jo called me from . . . I don't remember, I think a rest area on the turnpike."

"Between Derry and the TR?"

"Yeah. She was on her way to Sara Laughs and wanted me to meet her there. She told me to park in the driveway if I got there first, not to go in the house . . . which I could have; I know where you keep the spare key."

Sure he did, in a Sucrets tin under the deck. I had shown him myself.

"Did she say why she didn't want you to go inside?"

"It'll sound crazy."

"No it won't. Believe me."

"She said the house was dangerous."

For a moment the words just hung there. Then I asked, "Did you get here first?"

"Uh-huh."

"And waited outside?"

"Yes."

"Did you see or sense anything dangerous?"

There was a long pause. At last he said, "There were lots of people out on the lake — speedboaters, water-skiers, you know how it is — but all the engine-noise and the laughter seemed to kind of . . . stop dead when it got near the house. Have you ever noticed that it seems quiet there even when it's not?"

Of course I had; Sara seemed to exist in its own zone of silence. "Did it feel *dangerous*, though?"

"No," he said, almost reluctantly. "Not to me, anyway. But it didn't feel exactly empty, either. I felt . . . fuck, I felt *watched*. I sat on one of those railroad-tie steps and waited for my sis. Finally she came. She parked behind my car and hugged me . . . but she never took her eyes off the house. I asked her what she was up to and she said she couldn't tell me, and that I couldn't tell you we'd been there. She said something like, 'If he finds out on his own, then it's meant to be. I'll have to tell him sooner or later, anyway. But I can't now, because I need his whole attention. I can't get that while he's working.' "

I felt a flush crawl across my skin. "She said that, huh?"

"Yeah. Then she said she had to go in the house and do something. She wanted me to wait outside. She said if she called, I should come on the run. Otherwise I should just stay where I was."

"She wanted someone there in case she got in trouble."

"Yeah, but it had to be someone who wouldn't ask a lot of questions she didn't want to answer. That was me. I guess that was always me."

"And?"

"She went inside. I sat on the hood of my car, smoking cigarettes. I was still smoking then. And you know, I *did* start to feel something then that wasn't right. As if there might be someone in the house who'd been waiting for her, someone who didn't like her. Maybe someone who wanted to hurt her. Probably I just picked that up from Jo — the way her nerves seemed all strung up, the way she kept looking over my shoulder at the house even while she was hugging me — but it seemed like something else. Like a . . . I don't know . . ."

"Like a vibe."

"Yes!" he almost shouted. "A vibration. But not a good vibration, like in the Beach Boys song. A *bad* vibration."

"What happened?"

"I sat and waited. I only smoked two cigarettes so I don't guess it could have been longer than twenty minutes or half an hour, but it seemed longer. I kept noticing how the sounds from the lake seemed to make it most of the way up the hill and then just kind of . . . *quit*. And how there didn't seem to be any birds, except far off in the distance.

"Once she came out. I heard the deck door bang, and then her footsteps on the stairs over on that side. I called to her, asked if she was okay, and she said fine. She said for me to stay where I was. She sounded a little short of breath, as if she was carrying something or had been doing some chore."

"Did she go to her studio or down to the lake?"

"I don't know. She was gone another fifteen minutes or so — time enough for me to smoke another butt — and then she came back out the front door. She checked to make sure it was locked, and then she came up to me. She looked a lot better. Relieved. The way people look when they do some dirty job they've been putting off, finally get it behind them. She suggested we walk down that path she called The Street to the resort that's down there —"

"Warrington's."

"Right, right. She said she'd buy me a beer and a sandwich. Which she did, out at the end of this long floating dock."

The Sunset Bar, where I had first glimpsed Rogette.

"Then you went to have a look at the softball game."

"That was Jo's idea. She had three beers to my one, and she insisted. Said someone was going to hit a longshot homer into the trees, she just knew it."

Now I had a clear picture of the part Mattie had seen and told me about. Whatever Jo had done, it had left her almost giddy with relief. She had ventured into the house, for one thing. Had dared the spirits in order to do her business and survived. She'd had three beers to celebrate and her discretion had slipped . . . not that she had behaved with any great stealth on her previous trips down to the TR. Frank remembered her saying if I found out on my own then it was meant to be — *que sera, sera*. It wasn't the attitude of someone hiding an affair, and I realized now that all her behavior suggested a woman keeping a short-term secret. She would have told me when I finished my stupid book, if she had lived. If.

"You watched the game for awhile, then

went back to the house along The Street."

"Yes," he said.

"Did either of you go in?"

"No. By the time we got there, her buzz had worn off and I trusted her to drive. She was laughing while we were at the softball game, but she wasn't laughing by the time we got back to the house. She looked at it and said, 'I'm done with her. I'll never go through that door again, Frank.'"

My skin first chilled, then prickled.

"I asked her what was wrong, what she'd found out. I knew she was writing something, she'd told me that much —"

"She told everyone but me," I said . . . but without much bitterness. I knew who the man in the brown sportcoat had been, and any bitterness or anger — anger at Jo, anger at myself — paled before the relief of that. I hadn't realized how much that fellow had been on my mind until now.

"She must have had her reasons," Frank said. "You know that, don't you?"

"But she didn't tell you what they were."

"All I know is that it started — whatever it was — with her doing research for an article. It was a lark, Jo playing Nancy Drew. I'm pretty sure that at first not telling you was just to keep it a surprise. She read books but mostly she talked to people — listened to their stories of the old days and teased them into looking for old letters . . .

diaries . . . she was good at that part of it, I think. Damned good. You don't know any of this?"

"No," I said heavily. Jo hadn't been having an affair, but she *could* have had one, if she'd wanted. She could have had an affair with Tom Selleck and been written up in *Inside View* and I would have gone on tapping away at the keys of my PowerBook, blissfully unaware.

"Whatever she found out," Frank said, "I think she just stumbled over it."

"And you never told me. Four years and you never told me any of it."

"That was the last time I was with her," Frank said, and now he didn't sound apologetic or embarrassed at all. "And the last thing she asked of me was that I not tell you we'd been to the lake house. She said she'd tell you everything when she was ready, but then she died. After that I didn't think it mattered. Mike, she was my sister. She was my sister and I promised."

"All right. I understand." And I did — just not enough. What had Jo discovered? That Normal Auster had drowned his infant son under a handpump? That back around the turn of the century an animal trap had been left in a place where a young Negro boy would be apt to come along and step into it? That another boy, perhaps the incestuous child of Son and Sara Tidwell, had been drowned by his mother in the lake, she maybe laughing that smoke-broken, lunatic laugh as she held him down? You gotta wiggle when you wobble, honey, and hold that young 'un way down deep.

"If you need me to apologize, Mike, consider it done."

"I don't. Frank, do you remember anything else she might have said that night? Anything at all?"

"She said she knew how you found the house."

"She said *what?*"

"She said that when it wanted you, it called you."

At first I couldn't reply, because Frank Arlen had completely demolished one of the assumptions I'd made about my married life — one of the biggies, one of those that seem so basic you don't even think about questioning them. Gravity holds you down. Light allows you to see. The compass needle points north. Stuff like that.

This assumption was that Jo was the one who had wanted to buy Sara Laughs back when we saw the first real money from my writing career, because Jo was the "house person" in our marriage, just as I was the "car person." Jo was the one who had picked our apartments when apartments were all we could afford, Jo who hung a picture here and asked me to put up a shelf there. Jo was the one who had fallen in love with the Derry house and had finally worn down my resistance to the idea that it was too big, too busy, and too broken to take on. Jo had been the nest-builder.

She said that when it wanted you, it called you.

And it was probably true. No, I could do better than that, if I was willing to set aside the lazy thinking and selective remembering. It was *certainly* true. I was the one who had first broached the idea of a place in western Maine. I was the one who collected stacks of real-estate brochures and hauled them home. I'd started buying regional magazines like *Down East* and always began at the back, where the real-estate ads were. It was I who had first seen a picture of Sara Laughs in a glossy handout called *Maine Retreats*, and it was I who had made the call first to the agent named in the ad, and then to Marie Hingerman after badgering Marie's name out of the Realtor.

Johanna had also been charmed by Sara Laughs — I think anyone would have been charmed by it, seeing it for the first time in autumn sunshine with the trees blazing all around it and drifts of colored leaves blowing up The Street — but it was I who had actively sought the place out.

Except that was more lazy thinking and selective remembering. Wasn't it? Sara had sought me out.

Then how could I not have known it until now? And how was I led here in the first place, full of unknowing happy ignorance?

The answer to both questions was the same. It was also the answer to the question of how Jo could have discovered something distressing about the house, the lake, maybe the whole TR, and then gotten away with not telling me. I'd been gone, that's all. I'd been zoning, tranced out, writing one of my stupid little books. I'd been hypnotized by the fantasies going on in my head, and a hypnotized man is easy to lead.

"Mike? Are you still there?"

"I'm here, Frank. But I'll be goddamned if I know what could have scared her so."

"She mentioned one other name I remember: Royce Merrill. She said he was the one who remembered the most, because he was so old. And she said, 'I don't want Mike to talk to him. I'm afraid that old man might let the cat out of the bag and tell him more than he should know.' Any idea what she meant?"

"Well . . . it's been suggested that a splinter from the old family tree wound up here, but my mother's people are from Memphis. The Noonans are from Maine, but not from this part." Yet I no longer entirely believed this.

"Mike, you sound almost sick."

600

"I'm okay. Better than I was, actually."

"And you understand why I didn't tell you any of this until now? I mean, if I'd known the ideas you were getting . . . if I'd had any *clue* . . ."

"I think I understand. The ideas didn't belong in my head to begin with, but once that shit starts to creep in . . ."

"When I got back to Sanford that night and it was over, I guess I thought it was just more of Jo's 'Oh fuck, there's a shadow on the moon, nobody go out until tomorrow.' She was always the superstitious one, you know — knocking on wood, tossing a pinch of salt over her shoulder if she spilled some, those four-leaf-clover earrings she used to have . . ."

"Or the way she wouldn't wear a pullover if she put it on backward by mistake," I said. "She claimed doing that would turn around your whole day."

"Well? Doesn't it?" Frank asked, and I could hear a little smile in his voice.

All at once I remembered Jo completely, right down to the small gold flecks in her left eye, and wanted nobody else. Nobody else would do.

"She thought there was something bad about the house," Frank said. "That much I *do* know."

I drew a piece of paper to me and jotted *Kia* on it. "Yes. And by then she may have suspected she was pregnant. She might have been afraid of . . . influences." There were influences here, all right. "You think she got most of this from Royce Merrill?"

"No, that was just a name she mentioned. She probably talked to dozens of people. Do you know a guy named Kloster? Gloster? Something like that?"

"Auster," I said. Below *Kia* my pencil was making a series of fat loops that might have been cursive letter *l*'s or hair ribbons. "Kenny Auster. Was that it?"

"It sounds right. In any case, you know how she was once she really got going on a thing."

Yes. Like a terrier after rats.

"Mike? Should I come up there?"

No. Now I was sure. Not Harold Oblowski, not Frank, either. There was a process going on in Sara, something as delicate and as organic as rising bread in a warm room. Frank might interrupt that process . . . or be hurt by it.

"No, I just wanted to get it cleared up. Besides, I'm writing. It's hard for me to have people around when I'm writing."

"Will you call if I can help?"

"You bet," I said.

I hung up the telephone, thumbed through the book, and found a listing for R. MERRILL on the Deep Bay Road. I called the number, listened to it ring a dozen times, then hung up. No newfangled answering machine for Royce. I wondered idly where he was. Ninety-five seemed a little too old to go dancing at the Country Barn in Harrison, especially on a close night like this one.

I looked at the paper with *Kia* written on it. Below the fat *l*-shapes I wrote *Kyra,* and remembered how, the first time I'd heard Ki say her name, I'd thought it was "Kia" she was saying. Below *Kyra* I wrote *Kito,* hesitated, then wrote *Carla.* I put these names in a box. Beside them I jotted *Johanna, Bridget,* and *Jared.* The fridgeafator people. Folks who wanted me to go down nineteen and go down ninety-two.

"Go down, Moses, you bound for the Promised Land," I told the empty house. I looked around. Just me and Bunter and the waggy clock . . . except it wasn't.

When it wanted you, it called you.

I got up to get another beer. The fruits and vegetables were in a circle again. In the middle, the letters now spelled:

```
lye stille
```

As on some old tombstones — *God grant she lye stille.* I looked at these letters for a long time. Then I remembered the IBM was still out on the deck. I brought it in, plonked it on the dining-room table, and began to work on my current stupid little book. Fifteen minutes and I was lost, only faintly aware of thunder someplace over the lake, only faintly aware of Bunter's bell shivering from time to time. When I went back to the fridge an hour or so later for another beer and saw that the words in the circle now said

ony lye stille

I hardly noticed. At that moment I didn't care if they lay stille or danced the hucklebuck by the light of the silvery moon. John Shackleford had begun to remember his past, and the child whose only friend he, John, had been. Little neglected Ray Garraty.

I wrote until midnight came. By then the thunder had faded away but the heat held on, as oppressive as a blanket. I turned off the IBM and went to bed . . . thinking, so far as I can remember, nothing at all — not even about Mattie, lying in her own bed not so many miles away. The writing had burned off all thoughts of the real world, at least temporarily. I think that, in the end, that's what it's for. Good or bad, it passes the time.

Chapter 21

I was walking north along The Street. Japanese lanterns lined it, but they were all dark because it was daylight — *bright* daylight. The muggy, smutchy look of mid-July was gone; the sky was that deep sapphire shade which is the sole property of October. The lake was deepest indigo beneath it, sparkling with sunpoints. The trees were just past the peak of their autumn colors, burning like torches. A wind out of the south blew the fallen leaves past me and between my legs in rattly, fragrant gusts. The Japanese lanterns nodded as if in approval of the season. Up ahead, faintly, I could hear music. Sara and the Red-Tops. Sara was belting it out, laughing her way through the lyric as she always had . . . only, how could laughter sound so much like a snarl?

"White boy, I'd never kill a child of mine. That you'd even think it!"

I whirled, expecting to see her right behind me, but there was no one there. Well . . .

The Green Lady was there, only she had changed her dress of leaves for autumn and become the Yellow Lady. The bare pine-branch behind her still pointed the way: go north, young man, go north. Not much farther down the path was another birch, the one I'd held onto when that terrible drowning sensation had come over me again.

I waited for it to come again now — for my mouth and throat to fill up with the iron taste of the lake — but it didn't happen. I looked back at the Yellow Lady, then beyond her to Sara Laughs. The house was there, but much reduced: no north wing, no south wing, no second story. No sign of Jo's studio off to the side, either. None of those things had been built yet. The ladybirch had travelled back with me from 1998; so had the one hanging over the lake. Otherwise —

"Where am I?" I asked the Yellow Lady and the nodding Japanese lanterns. Then a better question occurred to me. "*When* am I?" No answer. "It's a dream, isn't it? I'm in bed and dreaming."

Somewhere out in the brilliant, gold-sparkling net of the lake, a loon called. Twice. *Hoot once for yes, twice for no,* I thought. *Not a dream, Michael. I don't know exactly what it is — spiritual time-travel, maybe — but it's not a dream.*

"Is this really happening?" I asked the day, and from somewhere back in the trees, where a track which would eventually come to be known as Lane Forty-two ran toward a dirt road which would eventually come to be known as Route 68, a crow cawed. Just once.

I went to the birch hanging over the lake, slipped an arm around it (doing it lit a trace memory of slipping my hands around Mattie's waist, feeling her dress slide over her skin), and peered into the water, half-wanting to see the drowned boy, half-fearing to see him. There was no boy there, but something lay on the bottom where he had been, among the rocks and roots and waterweed. I squinted and just then the wind died a little, stilling the glints on the water. It was a cane, one with a gold head. A *Boston Post* cane. Wrapped around it in a rising spiral, their ends waving lazily, were what appeared to be a pair of ribbons — white ones with bright red edges. Seeing Royce's cane wrapped that way made me think of high-school graduations, and the baton the class marshal waves as he or she leads the gowned seniors to their seats. Now I understood why the old crock hadn't answered the phone. Royce Merrill's phone-answering days were all done. I knew that; I also knew I had come to a time before Royce had even been born. Sara Tidwell was here, I could hear her singing, and when Royce had been born in 1903, Sara had already been gone for two years, she and her whole Red-Top family.

"Go down, Moses," I told the ribbon-wrapped cane in the water. "You bound for the Promised Land."

607

I walked on toward the sound of the music, invigorated by the cool air and rushing wind. Now I could hear voices as well, lots of them, talking and shouting and laughing. Rising above them and pumping like a piston was the hoarse cry of a side-show barker: "Come on in, folks, *hurr*-ay, *hurr*-ay, *hurr*-ay! It's all on the inside but you've got to *hurr*-ay, next show starts in ten minutes! See Angelina the Snake-Woman, she shimmies, she shakes, she'll bewitch your eye and steal your heart, but don't get too close for her bite is *poy*-son! See Hando the Dog-Faced Boy, terror of the South Seas! See the Human Skeleton! See the Human Gila Monster, relic of a time God forgot! See the Bearded Lady and all the Killer Martians! It's on the inside, yessirree, so *hurr*-ay, *hurr*-ay, *hurr*-ay!"

I could hear the steam-driven calliope of a merry-go-round and the bang of the bell at the top of the post as some lumberjack won a stuffed toy for his sweetie. You could tell from the delighted feminine screams that he'd hit it almost hard enough to pop it off the post. There was the snap of .22s from the shooting gallery, the snoring moo of someone's prize cow . . . and now I began to smell the aromas I have associated with county fairs since I was a boy: sweet fried dough, grilled onions and peppers, cotton candy, manure, hay. I began to walk faster as the strum of guitars and thud of double basses grew louder. My heart kicked into a higher gear. I was going to see them perform, actually see Sara Laughs and the Red-Tops live and onstage. This was no crazy three-part fever-dream, either. This was happening right now, so hurr-ay, hurr-ay, hurr-ay.

The Washburn place (the one that would always be the Bricker place to Mrs. M.) was gone. Beyond where it would eventually be, rising up the steep slope on the eastern side of The Street, was a flight of broad wooden stairs. They reminded me of the ones which lead down from the amusement park to the beach at Old Orchard. Here the Japanese lanterns were lit in spite of the brightness of the day, and the music was louder than ever. Sara was singing "Jimmy Crack Corn."

I climbed the stairs toward the laughter and shouts, the sounds of the Red-Tops and the calliope, the smells of fried food and farm animals. Above the stairhead was a wooden arch with

WELCOME TO FRYEBURG FAIR
WELCOME TO THE 20TH CENTURY

printed on it. As I watched, a little boy in short pants and a woman wearing a shirtwaist and an ankle-length linen skirt walked under the arch and toward me. They shimmered, grew gauzy. For a moment I could see their skeletons and the bone grins which lurked beneath their laughing faces. A moment later and they were gone.

Two farmers — one wearing a straw hat, the other gesturing expansively with a corncob pipe — appeared on the Fair side of the arch in exactly the same fashion. In this way I understood that there was a barrier between The Street and the Fair. Yet I did not think it was a barrier which would affect me. I was an exception.

"Is that right?" I asked. "Can I go in?"

The bell at the top of the Test Your Strength pole banged loud and clear. Bong once for yes, twice for no. I continued on up the stairs.

Now I could see the Ferris wheel turning against the brilliant sky, the wheel that had been in the background of the band photo in Osteen's *Dark Score Days*. The framework was metal, but the brightly painted gondolas were made of wood. Leading up to it like an aisle leading up to an altar was a broad, sawdust-strewn midway. The sawdust was there for a purpose; almost every man I saw was chewing tobacco.

I paused for a few seconds at the top of the stairs, still on the lake side of the arch. I was afraid of what might happen to me if I passed under. Afraid of dying or disappearing, yes, but mostly of never being able to return the way I had come, of being condemned to spend eternity as a visitor to the turn-of-the-century Fryeburg Fair. That was also like a Ray Bradbury story, now that I thought of it.

In the end what drew me into that other world was Sara Tidwell. I had to see her with my own eyes. I had to watch her sing. *Had* to.

I felt a tingling as I stepped beneath the arch, and there was a sighing in my ears, as of a million voices, very far away. Sighing in relief? Dismay? I couldn't tell. All I knew for sure was that being on the other side was different — the difference between looking at a thing through a window and actually being there; the difference between observing and participating.

Colors jumped out like ambushers at the moment of attack. The smells which had been sweet and evocative and nostalgic on the lake side of the arch were now rough and sexy, prose instead of poetry. I could smell dense sausages and frying beef and the vast shadowy aroma of boiling chocolate. Two kids walked past me sharing a paper cone of cotton candy. Both of them were clutching knotted hankies with their little bits of change in them. "Hey kids!" a barker in a dark blue shirt called to them. He was wearing arm-garters and his smile revealed one splendid gold tooth. "Knock over the milk-bottles and win a prize! I en't had a loser all day!"

Up ahead, the Red-Tops swung into "Fishin Blues." I'd thought the kid on the common in Castle Rock was pretty good, but this version made the kid's sound old and slow and clueless. It wasn't cute, like an antique picture of ladies with their skirts held up to their knees, dancing a decorous version of the black bottom with the edges of their bloomers showing. It wasn't something Alan Lomax had collected with his other folk songs, just one more dusty American butterfly in a glass case full of them; this was smut with just enough shine on it to keep the whole struttin bunch of them out of jail. Sara Tidwell was singing about the dirty boogie, and I guessed that every overalled, straw-hatted, plug-chewing, callus-handed, clodhopper-wearing farmer standing in front of the stage was dreaming about doing it with her, getting right down to where the sweat forms in the crease and the heat gets hot and the pink comes glimmering through.

I started walking in that direction, aware of cows mooing and sheep blatting from the exhibition barns — the Fair's version of my childhood Hi-Ho Dairy-O. I walked past the shooting gallery and the ringtoss and the penny-pitch; I walked past a stage where The Handmaidens of Angelina were weaving in a slow, snakelike dance with their hands pressed together as a guy with a turban on his head and shoepolish on his face tooted a flute. The picture painted on stretched canvas suggested that Angelina — on view inside for just one tenth of a dollar, neighbor — would make these two look like old boots. I walked past the entrance to Freak Alley, the corn-roasting pit, the Ghost House, where more stretched canvas depicted spooks coming out of broken windows and crumbling chimneys. *Everything in there is death,* I thought . . . but from inside I could hear children who were very much alive laughing and squealing as they bumped into things in the dark. The older among them were likely stealing kisses. I passed the Test Your Strength pole, where the gradations leading to the brass bell at the top were marked BABY NEEDS HIS BOTTLE, SISSY, TRY AGAIN, BIG BOY, HE-MAN, and, just below the bell itself, in red: HERCULES! Standing at the center of a little crowd a young man with red hair was removing his shirt, revealing a heavily muscled upper torso. A cigar-smoking carny held a hammer out to him. I passed the quilting booth, a tent where people were sitting on benches and playing Bingo, the baseball pitch. I passed them all and hardly noticed. I was in the zone, tranced out. "You'll have to call him back," Jo had sometimes told Harold when he phoned, "Michael is currently in the Land of Big Make-Believe." Only now nothing felt like pretend and the only thing that interested me was the stage at the base of the Ferris wheel. There were eight black folks up there on it, maybe ten. Standing at the front, wearing a guitar and whaling on it as she sang, was Sara Tidwell. She was alive. She was in her prime. She threw back her head and laughed at the October sky.

What brought me out of this daze was a cry from behind me: "Wait up, Mike! Wait up!"

I turned and saw Kyra running toward me, dodging around the strollers and gamesters and midway gawkers with her pudgy knees pumping. She was wearing a little white sailor dress with red piping and a straw hat with a navy-blue ribbon on it. In one hand she clutched Strickland, and when she got to me she threw herself confidently forward, knowing I would catch her and swing her up. I did, and when her hat started to fall off I caught it and jammed it back on her head.

"I taggled my own quartermack," she said, and laughed. "Again."

"That's right," I said. "You're a regular Mean Joe Green." I was wearing overalls (the tail of a wash-faded blue bandanna stuck out of the bib pocket) and manure-stained workboots. I looked at Kyra's white socks and saw they were homemade. I would find no discreet little label reading Made in Mexico or Made in China if I took off her straw hat and looked inside, either. This hat had been most likely Made in Motton, by some farmer's wife with red hands and achy joints.

"Ki, where's Mattie?"

"Home, I guess. She couldn't come."

"How did you get here?"

"Up the stairs. It was a lot of stairs. You should have waited for me. You could have carrot me, like before. I want to hear the music."

"Me too. Do you know who that is, Kyra?"

"Yes," she said, "Kito's mom. Hurry up, slowpoke!"

I walked toward the stage, thinking we'd have to stand at the back of the crowd, but they parted for us as we came forward, me carrying Kyra in my arms — the lovely sweet weight of her, a little Gibson Girl in her sailor dress and ribbon-accented straw hat. Her arm was curled around my neck and they parted for us like the Red Sea had parted for Moses.

They didn't turn to look at us, either. They were clapping and stomping and bellowing along with the music, totally involved. They stepped aside unconsciously, as if some kind of magnetism were at work here — ours positive, theirs negative. The few women in the crowd were blushing but clearly enjoying themselves, one of them laughing so hard tears were streaming down her face. She looked no more than twenty-two or -three. Kyra pointed to her and said matter-of-factly: "You know Mattie's boss at the liberry? That's her nana."

Lindy Briggs's grandmother, and fresh as a daisy, I thought. *Good Christ.*

The Red-Tops were spread across the stage and under swags of red, white, and blue bunting like some time-travelling rock band. I recognized all of them from the picture in Edward Osteen's book. The men wore white shirts, arm-garters, dark vests, dark pants. Son Tidwell, at the far end of the stage, was wearing the derby he'd had on in the photo. Sara, though . . .

"Why is the lady wearing Mattie's dress?" Kyra asked me, and she began to tremble.

"I don't know, honey. I can't say." Nor could I argue — it was the white sleeveless dress Mattie had been wearing on the common, all right.

Onstage, the band was smoking through an instrumental break. Reginald "Son" Tidwell strolled over to Sara, feet ambling, hands a brown blur on the strings and frets of his guitar, and she turned to face him. They put their foreheads together, she laughing and he solemn; they looked into each other's eyes and tried to play each

616

other down, the crowd cheering and clapping, the rest of the Red-Tops laughing as they played. Seeing them together like that, I realized that I had been right: they were brother and sister. The resemblance was too strong to be missed or mistaken. But mostly what I looked at was the way her hips and butt switched in that white dress. Kyra and I might be dressed in turn-of-the-century country clothes, but Sara was thoroughly modern Millie. No bloomers for her, no petticoats, no cotton stockings. No one seemed to notice that she was wearing a dress that stopped above her knees — that she was all but naked by the standards of this time. And under Mattie's dress she'd be wearing garments the like of which these people had never seen: a Lycra bra and hip-hugger nylon panties. If I put my hands on her waist, the dress would slip not against an unwelcoming corset but against soft bare skin. Brown skin, not white. *What do you want, sugar?*

Sara backed away from Son, shaking her ungirdled, unbustled fanny and laughing. He strolled back to his spot and she turned to the crowd as the band played the turn-around. She sang the next verse looking directly at me.

"Before you start in fishin
you better check your line.

Said before you start in fishin, honey,
  you better check on your line.
I'll pull on yours, darlin,
  and you best tug on mine."

The crowd roared happily. In my arms, Kyra was shaking harder than ever. "I'm scared, Mike," she said. "I don't like that lady. She's a scary lady. She stole Mattie's dress. I want to go home."

It was as if Sara heard her, even over the rip and ram of the music. Her head cocked back on her neck, her lips peeled open, and she laughed at the sky. Her teeth were big and yellow. They looked like the teeth of a hungry animal, and I decided I agreed with Kyra: she was a scary lady.

"Okay, hon," I murmured in Ki's ear. "We're out of here."

But before I could move, the sense of the woman — I don't know how else to say it — fell upon me and held me. Now I understood what had shot past me in the kitchen to knock away the CARLADEAN letters; the chill was the same. It was almost like identifying a person by the sound of their walk.

She led the band to the turnaround once more, then into another verse. Not one you'd find in any written version of the song, though:

"I ain't gonna hurt her, honey,

not for all the treasure in the worl'.
Said I wouldn't hurt your baby,
not for diamonds or for pearls.
Only one black-hearted bastard
dare to touch that little girl."

The crowd roared as if it were the funniest thing they'd ever heard, but Kyra began to cry. Sara saw this and stuck out her breasts — much bigger breasts than Mattie's — and shook them at her, laughing her trademark laugh as she did. There was a parodic coldness about this gesture . . . and an emptiness, too. A sadness. Yet I could feel no compassion for her. It was as if the heart had been burned out of her and the sadness which remained was just another ghost, the memory of love haunting the bones of hate.

And how her laughing teeth leered.

Sara raised her arms over her head and this time shook it all the way down, as if reading my thoughts and mocking them. Just like jelly on a plate, as some other old song of the time has it. Her shadow wavered on the canvas backdrop, which was a painting of Fryeburg, and as I looked at it I realized I had found the Shape from my Manderley dreams. It was Sara. Sara was the Shape and always had been.

No, Mike. That's close, but it's not right.

Right or wrong, I'd had enough. I turned,

putting my hand on the back of Ki's head and urging her face down against my chest. Both her arms were around my neck now, clutching with panicky tightness.

I thought I'd have to bull my way back through the crowd — they had let me in easily enough, but they might be a lot less amenable to letting me back out. *Don't fuck with me, boys,* I thought. *You don't want to do that.*

And they didn't. Onstage Son Tidwell had taken the band from E to G, someone began to bang a tambourine, and Sara went from "Fishin Blues" to "Dog My Cats" without a single pause. Out here, in front of the stage and below it, the crowd once more drew back from me and my little girl without looking at us or missing a beat as they clapped their work-swollen hands together. One young man with a port-wine stain swimming across the side of his face opened his mouth — at twenty he was already missing half his teeth — and hollered *"Yee-HAW!"* around a melting glob of tobacco. It was Buddy Jellison from the Village Cafe, I realized . . . Buddy Jellison magically rolled back in age from sixty-eight to twenty. Then I realized the hair was the wrong shade — light brown instead of black (although he was pushing seventy and looking it in every other way, Bud hadn't a single white hair in his head). This was

Buddy's grandfather, maybe even his great-grandfather. I didn't give a shit either way. I only wanted to get out of here.

"Excuse me," I said, brushing by him.

"There's no town drunk here, you meddling son of a bitch," he said, never looking at me and never missing a beat as he clapped. "We all just take turns."

It's a dream after all, I thought. *It's a dream and that proves it.*

But the smell of tobacco on his breath wasn't a dream, the smell of the crowd wasn't a dream, and the weight of the frightened child in my arms wasn't a dream, either. My shirt was hot and wet where her face was pressed. She was crying.

"Hey, Irish!" Sara called from the stage, and her voice was so like Jo's that I could have screamed. She wanted me to turn back — I could feel her will working on the sides of my face like fingers — but I wouldn't do it.

I dodged around three farmers who were passing a ceramic bottle from hand to hand and then I was free of the crowd. The midway lay ahead, wide as Fifth Avenue, and at the end of it was the arch, the steps, The Street, the lake. Home. If I could get to The Street we'd be safe. I was sure of it.

"Almost done, Irish!" Sara shrieked after me. She sounded angry, but not too angry to laugh. "You gonna get what you want, sugar, all the comfort you need, but you want to let me finish my bi'ness. Do you hear me, boy? Just stand clear! Mind me, now!"

I began to hurry back the way I had come, stroking Ki's head, still holding her face against my shirt. Her straw hat fell off and when I grabbed for it, I got nothing but the ribbon, which pulled free of the brim. No matter. We had to get out of here.

On our left was the baseball pitch and some little boy shouting "Willy hit it over the fence, Ma! Willy hit it over the fence!" with monotonous, brain-croggling regularity. We passed the Bingo, where some woman howled that she had won the turkey, by glory, every number was covered with a button and she had won the turkey. Overhead, the sun dove behind a cloud and the day went dull. Our shadows disappeared. The arch at the end of the midway drew closer with maddening slowness.

"Are we home yet?" Ki almost moaned. "I want to go home, Mike, please take me home to my mommy."

"I will," I said. "Everything's going to be all right."

We were passing the Test Your Strength pole, where the young man with the red hair was putting his shirt back on. He looked at me with stolid dislike — the instinctive mistrust of a native for an interloper, perhaps

— and I realized I knew him, too. He'd have a grandson named Dickie who would, toward the end of the century to which this fair had been dedicated, own the All-Purpose Garage on Route 68.

A woman coming out of the quilting booth stopped and pointed at me. At the same moment her upper lip lifted in a dog's snarl. I knew that face, too. From where? Somewhere around town. It didn't matter, and I didn't want to know even if it did.

"We never should have come here," Ki moaned.

"I know how you feel," I said. "But I don't think we had any choice, hon. We —"

They came out of Freak Alley, perhaps twenty yards ahead. I saw them and stopped. There were seven in all, long-striding men dressed in cutters' clothes, but four didn't matter — those four looked faded and white and ghostly. They were sick fellows, maybe dead fellows, and no more dangerous than daguerreotypes. The other three, though, were real. As real as the rest of this place, anyway. The leader was an old man wearing a faded blue Union Army cap. He looked at me with eyes I knew. Eyes I had seen measuring me over the top of an oxygen mask.

"Mike? Why we stoppin?"

"It's all right, Ki. Just keep your head down. This is all a dream. You'll wake up tomorrow morning in your own bed."

" 'Kay."

The jacks spread across the midway hand to hand and boot to boot, blocking our way back to the arch and The Street. Old Blue-Cap was in the middle. The ones on either side of him were much younger, some by maybe as much as half a century. Two of the pale ones, the almost-not-there ones, were standing side-by-side to the old man's right, and I wondered if I could burst through that part of their line. I thought they were no more flesh than the thing which had thumped the insulation of the cellar wall . . . but what if I was wrong?

"Give her over, son," the old man said. His voice was reedy and implacable. He held out his hands. It was Max Devore, he had come back, even in death he was seeking custody. Yet it *wasn't* him. I knew it wasn't. The planes of this man's face were subtly different, the cheeks gaunter, the eyes a brighter blue.

"Where am *I?*" I called to him, accenting the last word heavily, and in front of Angelina's booth, the man in the turban (a Hindu who perhaps hailed from Sandusky, Ohio) put down his flute and simply watched. The snake-girls stopped dancing and watched, too, slipping their arms around each other and drawing together for comfort. "Where am *I*, Devore? If our great-grandfathers shit in the same pit, then where am *I?*"

"Ain't here to answer your questions. Give her over."

"I'll take her, Jared," one of the younger men — one of those who were really *there* — said. He looked at Devore with a kind of fawning eagerness that sickened me, mostly because I knew who he was: Bill Dean's father. A man who had grown up to be one of the most respected elders in Castle County was all but licking Devore's boots.

Don't think too badly of him, Jo whispered. *Don't think too badly of any of them. They were very young.*

"You don't need to do nothing," Devore said. His reedy voice was irritated; Fred Dean looked abashed. "He's going to hand her over on his own. And if he don't, we'll take her together."

I looked at the man on the far left, the third of those that seemed totally real, totally there. Was this me? It didn't look like me. There was something in the face that seemed familiar but —

"Hand her over, Irish," Devore said. "Last chance."

"No."

Devore nodded as if this was exactly what he had expected. "Then we'll take her. This has got to end. Come on, boys."

They started toward me and as they did I

realized who the one on the end — the one in the caulked treewalker boots and flannel loggers' pants — reminded me of: Kenny Auster, whose wolfhound would eat cake 'til it busted. Kenny Auster, whose baby brother had been drowned under the pump by Kenny's father.

I looked behind me. The Red-Tops were still playing, Sara was still laughing, shaking her hips with her hands in the sky, and the crowd was still plugging the east end of the midway. That way was no good, anyway. If I went that way, I'd end up raising a little girl in the early years of the twentieth century, trying to make a living by writing penny dreadfuls and dime novels. That might not be so bad . . . but there was a lonely young woman miles and years from here who would miss her. Who might even miss us both.

I turned back and saw the jackboys were almost on me. Some of them more here than others, more vital, but all of them dead. All of them damned. I looked at the towhead whose descendants would include Kenny Auster and asked him, "What did you do? What in Christ's name did you men do?"

He held out his hands. "Give her over, Irish. That's all *you* have to do. You and the woman can have more. All the more you want. She's young, she'll pop em out like watermelon seeds."

I was hypnotized, and they would have taken us if not for Kyra. "What's happening?" she screamed against my shirt. "Something smells! Something smells *so bad! Oh Mike, make it stop!*"

And I realized I could smell it, too. Spoiled meat and swampgas. Burst tissue and simmering guts. Devore was the most alive of all of them, generating the same crude but powerful magnetism I had felt around his great-grandson, but he was as dead as the rest of them, too: as he neared I could see the tiny bugs which were feeding in his nostrils and the pink corners of his eyes. *Everything down here is death,* I thought. *Didn't my own wife tell me so?*

They reached out their tenebrous hands, first to touch Ki and then to take her. I backed up a step, looked to my right, and saw more ghosts — some coming out of busted windows, some slipping from red-brick chimneys. Holding Kyra in my arms, I ran for the Ghost House.

"Get him!" Jared Devore yelled, startled. "Get him, boys! Get that punk! Goddammit!"

I sprinted up the wooden steps, vaguely aware of something soft rubbing against my cheek — Ki's little stuffed dog, still clutched in one of her hands. I wanted to look back and see how close they were getting, but I didn't dare. If I stumbled —

"Hey!" the woman in the ticket booth cawed. She had clouds of gingery hair, makeup that appeared to have been applied with a garden-trowel, and mercifully resembled no one I knew. She was just a carny, just passing through this benighted place. Lucky her. "Hey, mister, you gotta buy a ticket!"

No time, lady, no time.

"Stop him!" Devore shouted. "He's a goddam punk thief! That ain't his young 'un he's got! Stop him!" But no one did and I rushed into the darkness of the Ghost House with Ki in my arms.

Beyond the entry was a passage so narrow I had to turn sideways to get down it. Phosphorescent eyes glared at us in the gloom. Up ahead was a growing wooden rumble, a loose sound with a clacking chain beneath it. Behind us came the clumsy thunder of caulk-equipped loggers' boots rushing up the stairs outside. The ginger-haired carny was hollering at them now, she was telling them that if they broke anything inside they'd have to give up the goods. "You mind me, you damned rubes!" she shouted. "That place is for kids, not th' likes of you!"

The rumble was directly ahead of us. Something was turning. At first I couldn't make out what it was.

"Put me down, Mike!" Kyra sounded excited. "I want to go through by myself!"

I set her on her feet, then looked nervously back over my shoulder. The bright light at the entryway was blocked out as they tried to cram in.

"You asses!" Devore yelled. "Not all at the same time! Sweet weeping Jesus!" There was a smack and someone cried out. I faced front just in time to see Kyra dart through the rolling barrel, holding her hands out for balance. Incredibly, she was laughing.

I followed, got halfway across, then went down with a thump.

"Ooops!" Kyra called from the far side, then giggled as I tried to get up, fell again, and was tumbled all the way over. The bandanna fell out of my bib pocket. A bag of horehound candy dropped from another pocket. I tried to look back, to see if they had got themselves sorted out and were coming. When I did, the barrel hurled me through another inadvertent somersault. Now I knew how clothes felt in a dryer.

I crawled to the end of the barrel, got up, took Ki's hand, and let her lead us deeper into the Ghost House. We got perhaps ten paces before white bloomed around her like a lily and she screamed. Some animal — something that sounded like a huge cat — hissed heavily. Adrenaline dumped into my bloodstream and I was about to jerk her backward into my arms again when the hiss came once more. I felt hot air on my ankles, and Ki's dress made that bell-shape around her legs again. This time she laughed instead of screaming.

"Go, Ki!" I whispered. "Fast."

We went on, leaving the steam-vent behind. There was a mirrored corridor where we were reflected first as squat dwarves and then as scrawny ectomorphs with long white vampire features. I had to urge Kyra on again; she wanted to make faces at herself. Behind us, I heard cursing lumberjacks trying to negotiate the barrel. I could hear Devore cursing, too, but he no longer seemed so . . . well, so *eminent*.

There was a sliding-pole that landed us on a big canvas pillow. This made a loud farting noise when we hit it, and Ki laughed until fresh tears spilled down her cheeks, rolling around and kicking her feet in glee. I got my hands under her arms and yanked her up.

"Don't taggle yer own quartermack," she said, then laughed again. Her fear seemed to have entirely departed.

We went down another narrow corridor. It smelled of the fragrant pine from which it had been constructed. Behind one of these walls, two "ghosts" were clanking chains as mechanically as men working on a shoe-factory assembly line, talking about where they were going to take their girls tonight and who was going to bring some "red-eye engine," whatever that was. I could no longer hear anyone behind us. Kyra led the way confidently, one of her little hands holding one of my big ones, pulling me along. When we came to a door painted with glowing flames and marked THIS WAY TO HADES, she pushed through it with no hesitation at all. Here red isinglass topped the passage like a tinted skylight, imparting a rosy glow I thought far too pleasant for Hades.

We went on for what felt like a very long time, and I realized I could no longer hear the calliope, the hearty *bong!* of the Test Your Strength bell, or Sara and the Red-Tops. Nor was that exactly surprising. We must have walked a quarter of a mile. How could any county fair Ghost House be so big?

We came to three doors then, one on the left, one on the right, and one set into the end of the corridor. On one a little red tricycle was painted. On the door facing it was my green IBM typewriter. The picture on the door at the end looked older, somehow — faded and dowdy. It showed a child's sled. *That's Scooter Larribee's,* I thought. *That's the one Devore stole.* A rash of gooseflesh broke out on my arms and back.

"Well," Kyra said brightly, "here are our

toys." She lifted Strickland, presumably so he could see the red trike.

"Yeah," I said. "I guess so."

"Thank you for taking me away," she said. "Those were scary men but the spooky-house was fun. Nighty-night. Stricken says nighty-night, too." It still came out sounding exotic — *tiu* — like the Vietnamese word for sublime happiness.

Before I could say another word, she had pushed open the door with the trike on it and stepped through. It snapped shut behind her, and as it did I saw the ribbon from her hat. It was hanging out of the bib pocket of the overalls I was wearing. I looked at it a moment, then tried the knob of the door she had just gone through. It wouldn't turn, and when I slapped my hand against the wood it was like slapping some hard and fabulously dense metal. I stepped back, then cocked my head in the direction from which we'd come. There was nothing. Total silence.

This is the between-time, I thought. *When people talk about "slipping through the cracks," this is what they really mean. This is the place where they really go.*

You better get going yourself, Jo told me. *If you don't want to find yourself trapped here, maybe forever, you better get going yourself.*

I tried the knob of the door with the type-writer painted on it. It turned easily. Behind it was another narrow corridor — more wooden walls and the sweet smell of pine. I didn't want to go in there, something about it made me think of a long coffin, but there was nothing else to do, nowhere else to go. I went, and the door slammed shut behind me.

Christ, I thought. *I'm in the dark, in a closed-in place . . . it's time for one of Michael Noonan's world-famous panic attacks.*

But no bands clamped themselves over my chest, and although my heart-rate was high and my muscles were still jacked on adrenaline, I was under control. Also, I realized, it wasn't entirely dark. I could only see a little, but enough to make out the walls and the plank floor. I wrapped the dark blue ribbon from Ki's hat around my wrist, tucking one end underneath so it wouldn't come loose. Then I began to move forward.

I went on for a long time, the corridor turning this way and that, seemingly at random. I felt like a microbe slipping through an intestine. At last I came to a pair of wooden arched doorways. I stood before them, wondering which was the correct choice, and realized I could hear Bunter's bell faintly through the one to my left. I went that way and as I walked, the bell grew steadily louder. At some point the sound of the bell was joined by the mutter of thunder. The autumn cool had left the air and it was hot again — stifling. I looked down and saw that the biballs and clodhopper shoes were gone. I was wearing thermal underwear and itchy socks.

Twice more I came to choices, and each time I picked the opening through which I could hear Bunter's bell. As I stood before the second pair of doorways, I heard a voice somewhere in the dark say quite clearly: "No, the President's wife wasn't hit. That's his blood on her stockings."

I walked on, then stopped when I realized my feet and ankles no longer itched, that my thighs were no longer sweating into the longjohns. I was wearing the Jockey shorts I usually slept in. I looked up and saw I was in my own living room, threading my way carefully around the furniture as you do in the dark, trying like hell not to stub your stupid toe. I could see a little better; faint milky light was coming in through the windows. I reached the counter which separates the living room from the kitchen and looked over it at the waggy-cat clock. It was five past five.

I went to the sink and turned on the water. When I reached for a glass I saw I was still wearing the ribbon from Ki's straw hat on my wrist. I unwound it and put it on the counter between the coffee-maker and the kitchen TV. Then I drew myself some cold water, drank it down, and made my way cautiously along the north-wing corridor by the pallid yellow glow of the bathroom nightlight. I peed (*you*-rinated, I could hear Ki saying), then went into the bedroom. The sheets were rumpled, but the bed didn't have the orgiastic look of the morning after my dream of Sara, Mattie, and Jo. Why would it? I'd gotten out of it and had myself a little sleepwalk. An extraordinarily vivid dream of the Fryeburg Fair.

Except that was bullshit, and not just because I had the blue silk ribbon from Ki's hat. None of it had the quality of dreams on waking, where what seemed plausible becomes immediately ridiculous and all the colors — both those bright and those ominous — fade at once. I raised my hands to my face, cupped them over my nose, and breathed deeply. Pine. When I looked, I even saw a little smear of sap on one pinky finger.

I sat on the bed, thought about dictating what I'd just experienced into the MemoScriber, then flopped back on the pillows instead. I was too tired. Thunder rumbled. I closed my eyes, began to drift away, and then a scream ripped through the house. It was as sharp as the neck of a broken bottle. I sat up with a yell, clutching at my chest.

It was Jo. I had never heard her scream like that in our life together, but I knew who it was, just the same. "Stop hurting her!" I shouted into the darkness. "Whoever you are, *stop hurting her!*"

She screamed again, as if something with a knife, clamp, or hot poker took a malicious delight in disobeying me. It seemed to come from a distance this time, and her third scream, while just as agonized as the first two, was farther away still. They were diminishing as the little boy's sobbing had diminished.

A fourth scream floated out of the dark, then Sara was silent. Breathless, the house breathed around me. Alive in the heat, aware in the faint sound of dawn thunder.

Chapter 22

I was finally able to get into the zone, but couldn't do anything once I got there. I keep a steno pad handy for notes — character lists, page references, date chronologies — and I doodled in there a little bit, but the sheet of paper in the IBM remained blank. There was no thundering heartbeat, no throbbing eyes or difficulty breathing — no panic attack, in other words — but there was no story, either. Andy Drake, John Shackleford, Ray Garraty, the beautiful Regina Whiting . . . they stood with their backs turned, refusing to speak or move. The manuscript was sitting in its accustomed place on the left side of the typewriter, the pages held down with a pretty chunk of quartz I'd found on the lane, but nothing was happening. Zilch.

I recognized an irony here, perhaps even a moral. For years I had fled the problems of the real world, escaping into various Narnias of my imagination. Now the real world had filled up with bewildering thickets, there were things with teeth in some of them, and the wardrobe was locked against me.

Kyra, I had printed, putting her name inside a scalloped shape that was supposed to be a cabbage rose. Below it I had drawn a piece of bread with a beret tipped rakishly on the top crust. Noonan's conception of French toast. The letters L.B. surrounded with curlicues. A shirt with a rudimentary duck on it. Beside this I had printed *QUACK QUACK*. Below *QUACK QUACK* I had written *Ought to fly away "Bon Voyage."*

At another spot on the sheet I had written *Dean, Auster,* and *Devore.* They were the ones who had seemed the most there, the most dangerous. Because they had descendants? But surely all seven of those jacks must, mustn't they? In those days most families were whoppers. And where had *I* been? I had asked, but Devore hadn't wanted to say.

It didn't feel any more like a dream at nine-thirty on a sullenly hot Sunday morning. Which left exactly what? Visions? Time-travel? And if there was a purpose to such travel, what was it? What was the message, and who was trying to send it? I remembered clearly what I'd said just before passing from the dream in which I had sleepwalked out to Jo's studio and brought back my typewriter: *I don't believe these lies.* Nor would I now. Until I could see at least some of the truth, it might be safer to believe nothing at all.

At the top of the sheet upon which I was doodling, in heavily stroked letters, I printed the word DANGER!, then circled it. From the circle I drew an arrow to Kyra's name. From her name I drew an arrow to *Ought to fly away "Bon Voyage"* and added *MATTIE.*

Below the bread wearing the beret I drew a little telephone. Above it I put a cartoon balloon with R-R-RINGGG! in it. As I finished this, the cordless phone rang. It was sitting on the deck rail. I circled *MATTIE* and picked up the phone.

"Mike?" She sounded excited. Happy. Relieved.

"Yeah," I said. "How are you?"

"Great!" she said, and I circled L.B. on my pad.

"Lindy Briggs called ten minutes ago — I just got off the phone with her. Mike, she's giving me my job back! Isn't that wonderful?"

Sure. And wonderful how it would keep her in town. I crossed out *Ought to fly away "Bon Voyage,"* knowing that Mattie wouldn't go. Not now. And how could I ask her to? I thought again *If only I knew a little more . . .*

"Mike? Are you —"

"It's very wonderful," I said. In my mind's eye I could see her standing in the kitchen, drawing the kinked telephone cord through her fingers, her legs long and coltish below her denim shorts. I could see the shirt she was wearing, a white tee with a yellow duck paddling across the front. "I hope Lindy had the good grace to sound ashamed of

639

herself." I circled the tee-shirt I'd drawn.

"She did. And she was frank enough to kind of . . . well, disarm me. She said the Whitmore woman talked to her early last week. Was very frank and to the point, Lindy said. I was to be let go immediately. If that happened, the money, computer equipment, and software Devore funnelled into the library would keep coming. If it didn't, the flow of goods and money would stop immediately. She said she had to balance the good of the community against what she knew was wrong . . . she said it was one of the toughest decisions she ever had to make . . ."

"Uh-huh." On the pad my hand moved of its own volition like a planchette gliding over a Ouija board, printing the words PLEASE CAN'T I PLEASE. "There's probably some truth in it, but Mattie . . . how much do you suppose *Lindy* makes?"

"I don't know."

"I bet it's more than any three other small-town librarians in the state of Maine combined."

In the background I heard Ki: "Can I talk, Mattie? Can I talk to Mike? Please can't I please?"

"In a minute, hon." Then, to me: "Maybe. All I know is that I have my job back, and I'm willing to let bygones be bygones."

On the page, I drew a book. Then I drew

a series of interlocked circles between it and the duck tee-shirt.

"Ki wants to talk to you," Mattie said, laughing. "She says the two of you went to the Fryeburg Fair last night."

"Whoa, you mean I had a date with a pretty girl and slept through it?"

"Seems that way. Are you ready for her?"

"Ready."

"Okay, here comes the chatterbox."

There was a rustling as the phone changed hands, then Ki was there. "I taggled you at the Fair, Mike! I taggled my own quartermack!"

"Did you?" I asked. "That was quite a dream, wasn't it, Ki?"

There was a long silence at the other end. I could imagine Mattie wondering what had happened to her telephone chatterbox. At last Ki said in a hesitating voice: "You there too." *Tiu.* "We saw the snake-dance ladies . . . the pole with the bell on top . . . we went in the spookyhouse . . . you fell down in the barrel! It wasn't a dream . . . was it?"

I could have convinced her that it was, but all at once that seemed like a bad idea, one that was dangerous in its own way. I said: "You had on a pretty hat and a pretty dress."

"*Yeah!*" Ki sounded enormously relieved. "And *you* had on —"

"Kyra, stop. Listen to me."

641

She stopped at once.

"It's better if you don't talk about that dream too much, I think. To your mom or to anyone except me."

"Except you."

"Yes. And the same with the refrigerator people. Okay?"

"Okay. Mike, there was a lady in Mattie's clothes."

"I know," I said. It was all right for her to talk, I was sure of it, but I asked anyway: "Where's Mattie now?"

"Waterin the flowers. We got lots of flowers, a billion at least. I have to clean up the table. It's a chore. I don't mind, though. I like chores. We had French toast. We always do on Sundays. It's yummy, 'specially with strawberry syrup."

"I know," I said, drawing an arrow to the piece of bread wearing the beret. "French toast is great. Ki, did you tell your mom about the lady in her dress?"

"No. I thought it might scare her." She dropped her voice. "Here she comes!"

"That's all right . . . but we've got a secret, right?"

"Yes."

"Now can I talk to Mattie again?"

"Okay." Her voice moved off a little. "Mommy-bommy, Mike wants to talk to you." Then she came back. "Will you bizzit us today? We could go on another picnic."

"I can't today, Ki. I have to work."

"Mattie never works on Sunday."

"Well, when I'm writing a book, I write every day. I have to, or else I'll forget the story. Maybe we'll have a picnic on Tuesday, though. A barbecue picnic at your house."

"Is it long 'til Tuesday?"

"Not too long. Day after tomorrow."

"Is it long to write a book?"

"Medium-long."

I could hear Mattie telling Ki to give her the phone.

"I will, just one more second. Mike?"

"I'm here, Ki."

"I love you."

I was both touched and terrified. For a moment I was sure my throat was going to lock up the way my chest used to when I tried to write. Then it cleared and I said, "Love you, too, Ki."

"Here's Mattie."

Again there was the rustly sound of the telephone changing hands, then Mattie said: "Did that refresh your recollection of your date with my daughter, sir?"

"Well," I said, "it certainly refreshed hers." There was a link between Mattie and me, but it didn't extend to this — I was sure of it.

She was laughing. I loved the way she sounded this morning and I didn't want to bring her down . . . but I didn't want her mistaking the white line in the middle of the road for the crossmock, either.

"Mattie, you still need to be careful, okay? Just because Lindy Briggs offered you your old job back doesn't mean everyone in town is suddenly your friend."

"I understand that," she said. I thought again about asking if she'd consider taking Ki up to Derry for awhile — they could live in my house, stay for the duration of the summer if that was what it took for things to return to normal down here. Except she wouldn't do it. When it came to accepting my offer of high-priced New York legal talent, she'd had no choice. About this she did. Or thought she did, and how could I change her mind? I had no logic, no connected facts; all I had was a vague dark shape, like something lying beneath nine inches of snowblind ice.

"I want you to be careful of two men in particular," I said. "One is Bill Dean. The other is Kenny Auster. He's the one —"

"— with the big dog who wears the neckerchief. He —"

"That's Booberry!" Ki called from the middle distance. "Booberry licked my facie!"

"Go out and play, hon," Mattie said.

"I'm clearun the table."

"You can finish later. Go on outside now." There was a pause as she watched Ki go out the door, taking Strickland with her. Although the kid had left the trailer, Mattie still spoke in the lowered tone of someone who doesn't want to be overheard. "Are you trying to scare me?"

"No," I said, drawing repeated circles around the word DANGER. "But I want you to be careful. Bill and Kenny may have been on Devore's team, like Footman and Osgood. Don't ask me why I think that might be, because I have no satisfactory answer. It's only a feeling, but since I got back on the TR, my feelings are different."

"What do you mean?"

"Are you wearing a tee-shirt with a duck on it?"

"How do you know that? Did Ki tell you?"

"Did she take the little stuffed dog from her Happy Meal out with her just now?"

A long pause. At last she said "My God" in a voice so low I could hardly hear it. Then again: "How —"

"I don't *know* how. I don't know if you're still in a . . . a bad situation, either, or why you might be, but I feel that you are. That you both are." I could have said more, but I was afraid she'd think I'd gone entirely off the rails.

"He's *dead!*" she burst out. "That old man is *dead!* Why can't he leave us alone?"

"Maybe he has. Maybe I'm wrong about all this. But there's no harm in being careful, is there?"

"No," she said. "Usually that's true."

"Usually?"

"Why don't you come and see me, Mike? Maybe *we* could go to the Fair together."

"Maybe this fall we will. All three of us."

"I'd like that."

"In the meantime, I'm thinking about the key."

"Thinking is half your problem, Mike," she said, and laughed again. Ruefully, I thought. And I saw what she meant. What she didn't seem to understand was that feeling was the other half. It's a sling, and in the end I think it rocks most of us to death.

I worked for a while, then carried the IBM back into the house and left the manuscript on top. I was done with it, at least for the time being. No more looking for the way back through the wardrobe; no more Andy Drake and John Shackleford until this was over. And, as I dressed in long pants and a button-up shirt for the first time in what felt like weeks, it occurred to me that perhaps something — some force — had been trying to sedate me with the story I was telling. With the ability to work again. It made sense; work had always been my drug of choice, even better than booze or the Mellaril I still kept in the bathroom medicine cabinet. Or maybe work was only the delivery system, the hypo with all the dreamy dreams inside it. Maybe the real drug was the zone. Being in the zone. Feeling it, you sometimes hear the basketball players say. I was in the zone and I was really feeling it.

I grabbed the keys to the Chevrolet off the counter and looked at the fridge as I did. The magnets were circled again. In the middle was a message I'd seen before, one that was now instantly understandable, thanks to the extra Magnabet letters:

help her

"I'm doing my best," I said, and went out.

Three miles north on Route 68 — by then you're on the part of it which used to be known as Castle Rock Road — there's a greenhouse with a shop in front of it. Slips 'n Greens, it's called, and Jo used to spend a fair amount of time there, buying gardening supplies or just noodling with the two women who ran the place. One of them was Helen Auster, Kenny's wife.

I pulled in there at around ten o'clock that Sunday morning (it was open, of course; during tourist season almost every Maine shopkeeper turns heathen) and parked next to a Beamer with New York plates. I paused long enough to hear the weather forecast on the radio — continued hot and humid for another forty-eight hours at least — and then got out. A woman wearing a bathing suit, a skort, and a giant yellow sunhat emerged from the shop with a bag of peat moss cradled in her arms. She gave me a little smile. I returned it with eighteen per cent interest. She was from New York, and that meant she wasn't a Martian.

The shop was even hotter and damper than the white morning outside. Lila Proulx, the co-owner, was on the phone. There was a little fan beside the cash register and she was standing directly in front of it, flapping the front of her sleeveless blouse. She saw me and twiddled her fingers in a wave. I twiddled mine back, feeling like someone else. Work or no work, I was still zoning. Still feeling it.

I walked around the shop, picking up a few things almost at random, watching Lila out of the corner of my eye and waiting for her to get off the phone so I could talk to her . . . and all the time my own private hyperdrive was humming softly away. At last she hung up and I came to the counter.

"Michael Noonan, what a sight for sore eyes you are!" she said, and began ringing up my purchases. "I was awfully sorry to hear about Johanna. Got to get that right up front. Jo was a pet."

"Thanks, Lila."

"Welcome. Don't need to say any more

648

about it, but with a thing like that it's best to put it right up front. I've always believed it, always will believe it. Right up front. Going to do a little gardening, are you?" *Gointer do a little ga'adnin, aaa you?*

"If it ever cools off."

"Ayuh! Isn't it wicked?" She flapped the top of her blouse again to show me how wicked it was, then pointed at one of my purchases. "Want this one in a special bag? Always safe, never sorry, that's my motto."

I nodded, then looked at the little blackboard tilted against the counter. FRESH BLUEBERRYS, the chalked message read. THE CROP IS IN!

"I'll have a pint of berries, too," I said. "As long as they're not Friday's. I can do better than Friday."

She nodded vigorously, as if to say she knew damned well I could. "These were on the bush yest'y. That fresh enough for you?"

"Good as gold," I said. "Blueberry's the name of Kenny's dog, isn't it?"

"Ain't he a funny one? God, I love a big dog, if he's behaved." She turned, got a pint of berries from her little fridge, and put them in another bag for me.

"Where's Helen?" I asked. "Day off?"

"Not her," Lila said. "If she's in town, you can't get her out of this place 'less you beat her with a stick. She and Kenny and the kids went down Taxachusetts. Them and her

649

brother's family club together and get a sea-side cottage two weeks every summer. They all went. Old Blueberry, he'll chase seagulls until he drops." She laughed — it was a loud and hearty one. It made me think of Sara Tidwell. Or maybe it was the way Lila looked at me as she did it. There was no laughter in her eyes. They were small and considering, coldly curious.

Would you for Christ's sake quit it? I told myself. *They can't all be in on it together, Mike!*

Couldn't they, though? There *is* such a thing as town consciousness — anyone who doubts it has never been to a New England town meeting. Where there's a conscious-ness, is there not likely to be a subcon-scious? And if Kyra and I were doing the old mind-meld thing, could not other people in TR-90 also be doing it, perhaps without even knowing it? We all shared the same air and land; we shared the lake and the aquifer which lay below everything, buried water tasting of rock and minerals. We shared The Street as well, that place where good pups and vile dogs could walk side-by-side.

As I started out with my purchases in a cloth carry-handle bag, Lila said: "What a shame about Royce Merrill. Did you hear?"

"No," I said.

"Fell down his cellar stairs yest'y evening. What a man his age was doing going down

650

such a steep flight of steps is beyond me, but I suppose once you get to his age, you have your own reasons for doing things."

Is he dead? I started to ask, then rephrased. It wasn't the way the question was expressed on the TR. "Did he pass?"

"Not yet. Motton Rescue took him to Castle County General. He's in a coma." *Comber,* she said it. "They don't think he'll ever wake up, poor fella. There's a piece of history that'll die with him."

"I suppose that's true." *Good riddance,* I thought. "Does he have children?"

"No. There have been Merrills on the TR for two hundred years; one died at Cemetery Ridge. But all the old families are dying out now. You have a nice day, Mike." She smiled. Her eyes remained flat and considering.

I got into my Chevy, put the bag with my purchases in it on the passenger seat, then simply sat for a moment, letting the air conditioner pour cool air on my face and neck. Kenny Auster was in Taxachusetts. That was good. A step in the right direction.

But there was still my caretaker.

"Bill's not here," Yvette said. She stood in the door, blocking it as well as she could (you can only do so much in that regard when you're five-three and weigh roughly a hundred pounds), studying me with the gimlet gaze of a nightclub bouncer denying re-entry to a drunk who's been tossed out on his ear once already.

I was on the porch of the neat-as-ever-you-saw Cape Cod which stands at the top of Peabody Hill and looks all the way across New Hampshire and into Vermont's back yard. Bill's equipment sheds were lined up to the left of the house, all of them painted the same shade of gray, each with its own sign: DEAN CARETAKING, No. 1, No. 2, and No. 3. Parked in front of No. 2 was Bill's Dodge Ram. I looked at it, then back at Yvette. Her lips tightened a little more. Another notch and I figured they'd be gone entirely.

"He went to North Conway with Butch Wiggins," she said. "They went in Butch's truck. To get —"

"No need lying for me, dear heart," Bill said from behind her.

It was still over an hour shy of noon, and on the Lord's Day to boot, but I had never heard a man who sounded more tired. He clumped down the hall, and as he came out of its shadows and into the light — the sun was finally burning through the murk — I saw that Bill now looked his age. Every year of it, and maybe ten more to grow on. He was wearing his usual khaki shirt and pants — Bill Dean would be a Dickies man until the day he died — but his shoulders looked slumped, almost sprained, as if he'd spent a week lugging buckets that were too heavy for him. The falling-away of his face had finally begun, an indefinable something that makes the eyes look too big, the jaw too prominent, the mouth a bit loose. He looked old. There were no children to carry on the family line of work, either; all the old families were dying out, Lila Proulx had said. And maybe that was a good thing.

"Bill —" she began, but he raised one of his big hands to stop her. The callused fingertips shook a little.

"Go in the kitchen a dight," he told her. "I need to talk to my *compadre* here. 'T'won't take long."

Yvette looked at him, and when she looked back at me, she had indeed reached zero lip-surface. There was just a black line where they had been, like a mark dashed off with a pencil. I saw with woeful clarity that she hated me.

"Don't you tire him out," she said to me. "He hasn't been sleepin. It's the heat." She walked back down the hall, all stiff back and high shoulders, disappearing into shadows that were probably cool. It always seems to be cool in the houses of old people, have you noticed?

Bill came out onto the porch and put his big hands into the pockets of his pants without offering to shake with me. "I ain't got nothin to say to you. You and me's quits."

"Why, Bill? Why are we quits?"

653

He looked west, where the hills stepped into the burning summer haze, disappearing in it before they could become mountains, and said nothing.

"I'm trying to help that young woman."

He gave me a look from the corners of his eyes that I could read well enough. "Ayuh. Help y'self right into her pants. I see men come up from New York and New Jersey with their young girls. Summer weekends, ski weekends, it don't matter. Men who go with girls that age always look the same, got their tongues run out even when their mouths are shut. Now you look the same."

I felt both angry and embarrassed, but I resisted the urge to chase him in that direction. That was what he wanted.

"What happened here?" I asked him. "What did your fathers and grandfathers and great-grandfathers do to Sara Tidwell and her family? You didn't just move them on, did you?"

"Didn't have to," Bill said, looking past me at the hills. His eyes were moist almost to the point of tears, but his jaw was set and hard. "They moved on themselves. Never was a nigger who didn't have an itchy foot, my dad used to say."

"Who set the trap that killed Son Tidwell's boy? Was it your father, Bill? Was it Fred?"

His eyes moved; his jaw never did. "I

dunno what you're talking about."

"I hear him crying in my house. Do you know what it's like to hear a dead child crying in your house? *Some bastard trapped him like a weasel and I hear him crying in my fucking house!*"

"You're going to need a new caretaker," Bill said. "I can't do for you no more. Don't want to. What I want is for you to get off my porch."

"What's happening? Help me, for Christ's sake."

"I'll help you with the toe of my shoe if you don't get going on your own."

I looked at him a moment longer, taking in the wet eyes and the set jaw, his divided nature written on his face.

"I lost my wife, you old bastard," I said. "A woman you claimed to love."

Now his jaw moved at last. He looked at me with surprise and injury. "That didn't happen *here*," he said. "That didn't have anything to do with *here*. She might've been off the TR because . . . well, she might've had her reasons to be off the TR . . . but she just had a stroke. Would have happened anywhere. *Anywhere.*"

"I don't believe that. I don't think you do, either. *Something followed her to Derry,* maybe because she was pregnant . . ."

Bill's eyes widened. I gave him a chance to say something, but he didn't take it.

". . . or maybe just because she knew too much."

"She had a stroke." Bill's voice wasn't quite even. "I read the obituary myself. She had a damn *stroke.*"

"What did she find out? Talk to me, Bill. Please."

There was a long pause. Until it was over I allowed myself the luxury of thinking I might actually be getting through to him.

"I've only got one more thing to say to you, Mike — stand back. For the sake of your immortal soul, stand back and let things run their course. They will whether you do or don't. This river has almost come to the sea; it won't be dammed by the likes of you. Stand back. For the love of Christ."

Do you care about your soul, Mr. Noonan? God's butterfly caught in a cocoon of flesh that will soon stink like mine?

Bill turned and walked to his door, the heels of his workboots clodding on the painted boards.

"Stay away from Mattie and Ki," I said. "If you so much as go near that trailer —"

He turned back, and the hazy sunshine glinted on the tracks below his eyes. He took a bandanna from his back pocket and wiped his cheeks. "I ain't stirrin from this house. I wish to God I'd never come back from my vacation in the first place, but I did — mostly on your account, Mike. Those two down on Wasp Hill have nothing to fear from me. No, not from *me*."

He went inside and closed the door. I stood there looking at it, feeling unreal — surely I could not have had such a deadly conversation with Bill Dean, could I? Bill who had reproached me for not letting folks down here share — and perhaps ease — my grief for Jo, Bill who had welcomed me back so warmly?

Then I heard a *clack* sound. He might not have locked his door while he was at home in his entire life, but he had locked it now. The *clack* was very clear in the breathless July air. It told me everything I had to know about my long friendship with Bill Dean. I turned and walked back to my car, my head down. Nor did I turn when I heard a window run up behind me.

"Don't you ever come back here, you town bastard!" Yvette Dean cried across the sweltering dooryard. "You've broken his heart! Don't you ever come back! Don't you ever! Don't you *ever!*"

"Please," Mrs. M. said. "Don't ask me any more questions, Mike. I can't afford to get in Bill Dean's bad books, any more'n my ma could afford to get into Normal Auster's or Fred Dean's."

I shifted the phone to my other ear. "All I want to know is —"

"In this part of the world caretakers pretty well run the whole show. If they say to a summer fella that he should hire this carpenter or that 'lectrician, why, that's who the summer fella hires. Or if a caretaker says this one should be fired because he ain't proving reliable, he is fired. Or *she*. Because what goes once for plumbers and landscapers and 'lectricians has always gone twice for housekeepers. If you want to be recommended — and *stay* recommended — you have to keep on the sunny side of people like Fred and Bill Dean, or Normal and Kenny Auster. Don't you see?" She was almost pleading. "When Bill found out I told you about what Normal Auster did to Kerry, oooo he was so mad at me."

"Kenny Auster's brother — the one Normal drowned under the pump — his name was Kerry?"

"Ayuh. I've known a lot of folks name their kids alike, think it's cute. Why, I went to school with a brother and sister named Roland and Rolanda Therriault, I think Roland's in Manchester now, and Rolanda married that boy from —"

"Brenda, just answer one question. I'll never tell. Please?"

I waited, my breath held, for the click that would come when she put her telephone back in its cradle. Instead, she spoke three words in a soft, almost regretful voice. "What is it?"

"Who was Carla Dean?"

I waited through another long pause, my hand playing with the ribbon that had come off Ki's turn-of-the-century straw hat.

"You dassn't tell anyone I told you anything," she said at last.

"I won't."

"Carla was Bill's twin sister. She died sixty-five years ago, during the time of the fires." The fires Bill claimed had been set by Ki's grandfather — his going-away present to the TR. "I don't know just how it happened. Bill never talks about it. If you tell him I told you, I'll never make another bed in the TR. He'll see to it." Then, in a hopeless voice, she said: "He may know anyway."

Based on my own experiences and surmises, I guessed she might be right about that. But even if she was, she'd have a check from me every month for the rest of her working life. I had no intention of telling her that over the telephone, though — it would scald her Yankee soul. Instead I thanked her, assured her again of my discretion, and hung up.

I sat at the table for a moment, staring blankly at Bunter, then said: "Who's here?"

No answer.

"Come on," I said. "Don't be shy. Let's go nineteen or ninety-two down. Barring that, let's talk."

Still no answer. Not so much as a shiver of the bell around the stuffed moose's neck. I spied the scribble of notes I'd made while talking to Jo's brother and drew them toward me. I had put *Kia, Kyra, Kito,* and *Carla* in a box. Now I scribbled out the bottom line of that box and added the name *Kerry* to the list. *I've known a lot of folks name their kids alike,* Mrs. M. had said. *They think it's cute.*

I didn't think it was cute; I thought it was creepy.

It occurred to me that at least two of these soundalikes had drowned — Kerry Auster under a pump, Kia Noonan in her mother's dying body when she wasn't much bigger than a sunflower seed. And I had seen the ghost of a third drowned child in the lake. Kito? Was that one Kito? Or was Kito the one who had died of blood-poisoning?

They name their kids alike, they think it's cute.

How many soundalike kids had there been to start with? How many were left? I thought the answer to the first question didn't matter, and that I knew the answer to the second one already. *This river has almost come to the sea,* Bill had said.

Carla, Kerry, Kito, Kia . . . all gone. Only Kyra Devore was left.

I got up so fast and hard that I knocked over my chair. The clatter in the silence made me cry out. I was leaving, and right

660

now. No more telephone calls, no more playing Andy Drake, Private Detective, no more depositions or half-assed wooings of the lady fair. I should have followed my instincts and gotten the fuck out of Dodge that first night. Well, I'd go now, just get in the Chevy and haul ass for Der—

Bunter's bell jangled furiously. I turned and saw it bouncing around his neck as if batted to and fro by a hand I couldn't see. The sliding door giving on the deck began to fly open and clap shut like something hooked to a pulley. The book of *Tough Stuff* crossword puzzles on the end-table and the DSS program guide blew open, their pages riffling. There was a series of rattling thuds across the floor, as if something enormous were crawling rapidly toward me, pounding its fists as it came.

A draft — not cold but warm, like the rush of air produced by a subway train on a summer night — buffeted past me. In it I heard a strange voice which seemed to be saying *Bye-BY, bye-BY, bye-BY,* as if wishing me a good trip home. Then, as it dawned on me that the voice was actually saying *Ki-Ki, Ki-Ki, Ki-Ki,* something struck me and knocked me violently forward. It felt like a large soft fist. I buckled over the table, clawing at it to stay up, overturning the lazy susan with the salt and pepper shakers on it, the napkin holder, the little vase Mrs. M. had

661

filled with daisies. The vase rolled off the table and shattered. The kitchen TV blared on, some politician talking about how inflation was on the march again. The CD player started up, drowning out the politician; it was the Rolling Stones doing a cover of Sara Tidwell's "I Regret You, Baby." Upstairs, one smoke alarm went off, then another, then a third. They were joined a moment later by the warble-whoop of the Chevy's car alarm. The whole world was cacophony.

Something hot and pillowy seized my wrist. My hand shot forward like a piston and slammed down on the steno pad. I watched as it pawed clumsily to a blank page, then seized the pencil which lay nearby. I gripped it like a dagger and then something wrote with it, not guiding my hand but *raping* it. The hand moved slowly at first, almost blindly, then picked up speed until it was flying, almost tearing through the sheet:

help her don't go help her don't go help her help don't don't baby please don't go help her help her help her

I had almost reached the bottom of the page when the cold descended again, that outer cold that was like sleet in January, chilling my skin and crackling the snot in my nose and sending two shuddery puffs of white air from my mouth. My hand clenched and the pencil snapped in two. Behind me, Bunter's bell rang out one final furious convulsion before falling silent. Also from behind me came a peculiar double pop, like the sound of champagne corks being drawn. Then it was over. Whatever it had been or however many they had been, it was finished. I was alone again.

I turned off the CD player just as Mick and Keith moved on to a white-boy version of Howling Wolf, then ran upstairs and pushed the reset buttons on the smoke-detectors. I leaned out the window of the big guest bedroom while I was up there, aimed the fob of my keyring down at the Chevrolet, and pushed the button on it. The alarm quit.

With the worst of the noise gone I could hear the TV cackling away in the kitchen. I went down, killed it, then froze with my hand still on the off button, looking at Jo's annoying waggy-cat clock. Its tail had finally stopped switching, and its big plastic eyes lay on the floor. They had popped right out of its head.

★ ★ ★

I went down to the Village Cafe for supper, snagging the last Sunday *Telegram* from the rack (COMPUTER MOGUL DEVORE DIES IN WESTERN MAINE TOWN WHERE HE GREW UP, the headline read) before sitting down at the counter. The accompanying photo was a studio shot of Devore that looked about thirty years old. He was smiling. Most people do that quite naturally. On Devore's face it looked like a learned skill.

I ordered the beans that were left over from Buddy Jellison's Saturday-night bean-hole supper. My father wasn't much for aphorisms — in my family dispensing nuggets of wisdom was Mom's job — but as Daddy warmed up the Saturday-night yelloweyes in the oven on Sunday afternoon, he would invariably say that beans and beef stew were better the second day. I guess it stuck. The only other piece of fatherly wisdom I can remember receiving was that you should always wash your hands after you took a shit in a bus station.

While I was reading the story on Devore, Audrey came over and told me that Royce Merrill had passed without recovering consciousness. The funeral would be Tuesday afternoon at Grace Baptist, she said. Most of the town would be there, many folks just to see Ila Meserve awarded the *Boston Post* cane. Did I think I'd get over? No, I said, probably not. I thought it prudent not to add that I'd likely be attending a victory party at Mattie Devore's while Royce's funeral was going on down the road.

The usual late-Sunday-afternoon flow of customers came and went while I ate, people ordering burgers, people ordering beans, people ordering chicken salad sandwiches, people buying sixpacks. Some were from the TR, some from away. I didn't notice many of them, and no one spoke to me. I have no idea who left the napkin on my newspaper, but when I put down the A section and turned to find the sports, there it was. I picked it up, meaning only to put it aside, and saw what was written on the back in big dark letters: GET OFF THE TR.

I never found out who left it there. I guess it could have been any of them.

Chapter 23

The murk came back and transformed that Sunday night's dusk into a thing of decadent beauty. The sun turned red as it slid down toward the hills and the haze picked up the glow, turning the western sky into a nosebleed. I sat out on the deck and watched it, trying to do a crossword puzzle and not getting very far. When the phone rang, I dropped *Tough Stuff* on top of my manuscript as I went to answer it. I was tired of looking at the title of my book every time I passed.

"Hello?"

"What's going on up there?" John Storrow demanded. He didn't even bother to say hi. He didn't sound angry, though; he sounded totally pumped. "I'm missing the whole goddam soap opera!"

"I invited myself to lunch on Tuesday," I said. "Hope you don't mind."

"No, that's good, the more the merrier." He sounded as if he absolutely meant it. "What a summer, huh? What a summer! Anything happen just lately? Earthquakes? Volcanoes? Mass suicides?"

"No mass suicides, but the old guy died," I said.

"Shit, the whole *world* knows Max Devore kicked it," he said. "Surprise me, Mike!

Stun me! Make me holler boy-howdy!"

"No, the *other* old guy. Royce Merrill."

"I don't know who you — oh, wait. The one with the gold cane who looked like an exhibit from *Jurassic Park*?"

"That's him."

"Bummer. Otherwise . . . ?"

"Otherwise everything's under control," I said, then thought of the popped-out eyes of the cat-clock and almost laughed. What stopped me was a kind of surety that Mr. Good Humor Man was just an act — John had really called to ask what, if anything, was going on between me and Mattie. And what was I going to say? Nothing yet? One kiss, one instant blue-steel hard-on, the fundamental things apply as time goes by?

But John had other things on his mind. "Listen, Michael, I called because I've got something to tell you. I think you'll be both amused and amazed."

"A state we all crave," I said. "Lay it on me."

"Rogette Whitmore called, and . . . you didn't happen to give her my parents' number, did you? I'm back in New York now, but she called me in Philly."

"I didn't *have* your parents' number. You didn't leave it on either of your machines."

"Oh, right." No apology; he seemed too excited to think of such mundanities. I began to feel excited myself, and I didn't even know what the hell was going on. "I gave it to Mattie. Do you think the Whitmore woman called Mattie to get it? Would Mattie give it to her?"

"I'm not sure that if Mattie came upon Rogette flaming in a thoroughfare, she'd piss on her to put her out."

"Vulgar, Michael, *très vulgarino*." But he was laughing. "Maybe Whitmore got it the same way Devore got yours."

"Probably so," I said. "I don't know what'll happen in the months ahead, but right now I'm sure she's still got access to Max Devore's personal control panel. And if anyone knows how to push the buttons on it, it's probably her. Did she call from Palm Springs?"

"Uh-huh. She said she'd just finished a preliminary meeting with Devore's attorneys concerning the old man's will. According to her, Grampa left Mattie Devore eighty million dollars."

I was struck silent. I wasn't amused yet, but I was certainly amazed.

"Gets ya, don't it?" John said gleefully.

"You mean he left it to Kyra," I said at last. "Left it in trust to *Kyra*."

"No, that's just what he did not do. I asked Whitmore three times, but by the third I was starting to understand. There was method in his madness. Not much, but a little. You see, there's a condition. If he left the money to the minor child instead of to the mother, the condition would have no weight. It's funny when you consider that Mattie isn't long past minor status herself."

"Funny," I agreed, and thought of her dress sliding between my hands and her smooth bare waist. I also thought of Bill Dean saying that men who went with girls that age always looked the same, had their tongues run out even if their mouths were shut.

"What string did he put on the money?"

"That Mattie remain on the TR for one year following Devore's death — until July 17, 1999. She can leave on day-trips, but she has to be tucked up in her TR-90 bed every night by nine o'clock, or else the legacy is forfeit. Did you ever hear such a bullshit thing in your life? Outside of some old George Sanders movie, that is?"

"No," I said, and recalled my visit to the Fryeburg Fair with Kyra. *Even in death he's seeking custody,* I had thought, and of course this was the same thing. He wanted them here. Even in death he wanted them on the TR.

"It won't fly?" I asked.

"Of *course* it won't fly. Fucking crackpot might as well have written he'd give her eighty million dollars if she used blue tampons for a year. But she'll get the eighty mil, all right. My heart is set on it. I've already talked to three of our estate guys, and . . . you don't think I should bring one of them up with me on Tuesday, do you? Will Stevenson'll be the point man in the estate phase, if Mattie agrees." He was all but babbling. He hadn't had a thing to drink, I'd've bet the farm on it, but he was sky-high on all the possibilities. We'd gotten to the happily-ever-after part of the fairy tale, as far as he was concerned; Cinderella comes home from the ball through a cash cloudburst.

". . . course Will's a little bit old," John was saying, "about three hundred or so, which means he's not exactly a fun guy at a party, but . . ."

"Leave him home, why don't you?" I said. "There'll be plenty of time to carve up Devore's will later on. And in the immediate future, I don't think Mattie's going to have any problem observing the bullshit condition. She just got her job back, remember?"

"Yeah, the white buffalo drops dead and the whole herd scatters!" John exulted. "Look at em go! And the new multimillionaire goes back to filing books and mailing out overdue notices! Okay, Tuesday we'll just party."

"Good."

"Party 'til we puke."

"Well . . . maybe us older folks will just

670

party until we're mildly nauseated, would that be all right?"

"Sure. I've already called Romeo Bissonette, and he's going to bring George Kennedy, the private detective who got all that hilarious shit on Durgin. Bissonette says Kennedy's a scream when he gets a drink or two in him. I thought I'd bring some steaks from Peter Luger's, did I tell you that?"

"I don't believe you did."

"Best steaks in the world. Michael, do you realize what's happened to that young woman? *Eighty million dollars!*"

"She'll be able to replace Scoutie."

"Huh?"

"Nothing. Will you come in tomorrow night or on Tuesday?"

"Tuesday morning around ten, into Castle County Airport. New England Air. Mike, are you all right? You sound odd."

"I'm all right. I'm where I'm supposed to be. I think."

"What's that supposed to mean?"

I had wandered out onto the deck. In the distance thunder rumbled. It was hotter than hell, not a breath of breeze stirring. The sunset was fading to a baleful afterglow. The sky in the west looked like the white of a bloodshot eye.

"I don't know," I said, "but I have an idea the situation will clarify itself. I'll meet you at the airport."

"Okay," he said, and then, in a hushed, almost reverential voice: "Eighty million motherfucking American dollars."

"It's a whole lotta lettuce," I agreed, and wished him a good night.

I drank black coffee and ate toast in the kitchen the next morning, watching the TV weatherman. Like so many of them these days, he had a slightly mad look, as if all those Doppler radar images had driven him to the brink of something. I think of it as the Millennial Video Game look.

"We've got another thirty-six hours of this soup to work through and then there's going to be a big change," he was saying, and pointed to some dark gray scum lurking in the Midwest. Tiny animated lightning-bolts danced in it like defective sparkplugs. Beyond the scum and the lightning-bolts, America looked clear all the way out to the desert country, and the posted temperatures were fifteen degrees cooler. "We'll see temps in the mid-nineties today and can't look for much relief tonight or tomorrow morning. But tomorrow afternoon these frontal storms will reach western Maine, and I think most of you are going to want to keep updated on weather conditions. Before we get back to cooler air and bright clear skies on Wednesday, we're probably going to see violent thunderstorms, heavy rain, hail in some locations. Tornados are rare in Maine, but some towns in western and central Maine could see them tomorrow. Back to you, Earl."

Earl, the morning news guy, had the innocent beefy look of a recent retiree from the Chippendales and read off the Tele-PrompTer like one. "Wow," he said. "That's quite a forecast, Vince. Tornados a possibility."

"Wow," I said. "Say wow again, Earl. Do it 'til I'm satisfied."

"Holy cow," Earl said just to spite me, and the telephone rang. I went to answer it, giving the waggy clock a look as I went by. The night had been quiet — no sobbing, no screaming, no nocturnal adventures — but the clock was disquieting, just the same. It hung there on the wall eyeless and dead, like a message full of bad news.

"Hello?"

"Mr. Noonan?"

I knew the voice, but for a moment couldn't place it. It was because she had called me Mr. Noonan. To Brenda Meserve I'd been Mike for almost fifteen years.

"Mrs. M.? Brenda? What —"

"I can't work for you anymore," she said, all in a rush. "I'm sorry I can't give you proper notice — I never stopped work for anyone without giving notice, not even that old drunk Mr. Croyden — but I have to.

Please understand."

"Did Bill find out I called you? I swear to God, Brenda, I never said a word —"

"No. I haven't spoken to him, nor he to me. I just can't come back to Sara Laughs. I had a bad dream last night. A terrible dream. I dreamed that . . . something's mad at me. If I come back, I could have an accident. It would look like an accident, at least, but . . . it wouldn't be."

That's silly, Mrs. M., I wanted to say. You're surely past the age where you believe in campfire stories about ghoulies and ghosties and long-leggedy beasties.

But of course I could say no such thing. What was going on in my house was no campfire story. I knew it, and she knew I did.

"Brenda, if I've caused you any trouble, I'm truly sorry."

"Go away, Mr. Noonan . . . Mike. Go back to Derry and stay for awhile. It's the best thing you could do."

I heard the letters sliding on the fridge and turned. This time I actually saw the circle of fruits and vegetables form. It stayed open at the top long enough for four letters to slide inside. Then a little plastic lemon plugged the hole and completed the circle.

yats

the letters said, then swapped themselves around, making

stay

Then both the circle and the letters broke up.

"Mike, *please*." Mrs. M. was crying. "Royce's funeral is tomorrow. Everyone in the TR who matters — the old-timers — will be there."

Yes, of course they would. The old ones, the bags of bones who knew what they knew and kept it to themselves. Except some of them had talked to my wife. Royce himself had talked to her. Now he was dead. So was she.

"It would be best if you were gone. You could take that young woman with you, maybe. Her and her little girl."

But could I? I somehow didn't think so. I thought the three of us were on the TR until this was over . . . and I was starting to have an idea of when that would be. A storm was coming. A summer storm. Maybe even a tornado.

"Brenda, thanks for calling me. And I'm not letting you go. Let's just call it a leave of absence, shall we?"

"Fine . . . whatever you want. Will you at least think about what I said?"

"Yes. In the meantime, I don't think I'd

675

tell anyone you called me, all right?"

"No!" she said, sounding shocked. Then: "But they'll know. Bill and Yvette . . . Dickie Brooks at the garage . . . old Anthony Weyland and Buddy Jellison and all the others . . . they'll know. Goodbye, Mr. Noonan. I'm so sorry. For you and your wife. Your poor wife. I'm so sorry." Then she was gone.

I held the phone in my hand for a long time. Then, like a man in a dream, I put it down, crossed the room, and took the eyeless clock off the wall. I threw it in the trash and went down to the lake for a swim, remembering that W. F. Harvey story "August Heat," the one that ends with the line "The heat is enough to drive a man mad."

I'm not a bad swimmer when people aren't pelting me with rocks, but my first shore-to-float-to-shore lap was tentative and unrhythmic — ugly — because I kept expecting something to reach up from the bottom and grab me. The drowned boy, maybe. The second lap was better, and by the third I was relishing the increased kick of my heart and the silky coolness of the water rushing past me. Halfway through the fourth lap I pulled myself up the float's ladder and collapsed on the boards, feeling better than I had since my encounter with Devore and Rogette Whitmore on Friday night. I was still in the zone, and on top of that I was experiencing a glorious endorphin rush. In that state, even the dismay I'd felt when Mrs. M. told me she was resigning her position ebbed away. She would come back when this was over; of course she would. In the meantime, it was probably best she stay away.

Something's mad at me. I could have an accident.

Yes indeed. She might cut herself. She might fall down a flight of cellar stairs. She might even have a stroke running across a hot parking lot.

I sat up and looked at Sara on her hill, the deck jutting out over the drop, the railroad ties descending. I'd only been out of the water for a few minutes, but already the day's sticky heat was folding over me, stealing my rush. The water was still as a mirror. I could see the house reflected in it, and in the reflection Sara's windows became watchful eyes.

I thought that the focus of all the phenomena — the epicenter — was very likely on The Street between the real Sara and its drowned image. *This is where it happened,* Devore had said. And the old-timers? Most of them probably knew what I knew: that Royce Merrill had been murdered. And wasn't it possible — wasn't it *likely* — that what had killed him might come among them as they sat in their pews or gathered afterward around his grave? That it might steal some of their force — their guilt, their memories, their *TR*-ness — to help it finish the job?

I was very glad that John was going to be at the trailer tomorrow, and Romeo Bissonette, and George Kennedy, who was so amusing when he got a drink or two in him. Glad it was going to be more than just me with Mattie and Ki when the old folks got together to give Royce Merrill his sendoff. I no longer cared very much about what had happened to Sara and the Red-Tops, or even about what was haunting my house. What I wanted was to get through tomorrow, and for Mattie and Ki to get through tomorrow. We'd eat before the rain started and then let the predicted thunderstorms come. I thought that, if we could ride them out, our lives and futures might clarify with the weather.

"Is that right?" I asked. I expected no answer — talking out loud was a habit I had picked up since returning here — but somewhere in the woods east of the house, an owl hooted. Just once, as if to say it was right, get through tomorrow and things will clarify. The hoot almost brought something else to mind, some association that was ultimately too gauzy to grasp. I tried once or twice, but the only thing I could come up with was the title of a wonderful old novel — *I Heard the Owl Call My Name*.

I rolled forward off the float and into the water, grasping my knees against my chest like a kid doing a cannonball. I stayed under as long as I could, until the air in my lungs started to feel like some hot bottled liquid, and then I broke the surface. I trod water about thirty yards out until I had my breath back, then set my sights on the Green Lady and stroked for shore.

I waded out, started up the railroad ties, then stopped and went back to The Street. I stood there for a moment, gathering my courage, then walked to where the birch curved her graceful belly out over the water. I grasped that white curve as I had on Friday evening and looked into the water. I was sure I'd see the child, his dead eyes looking up at me from his bloating brown face, and that my mouth and throat would once more fill with the taste of the lake: *help I'm drown, lemme up, oh sweet Jesus lemme up.* But there was nothing. No dead boy, no ribbon-wrapped *Boston Post* cane, no taste of the lake in my mouth.

I turned and peered at the gray forehead of rock poking out of the mulch. I thought *There, right there,* but it was only a conscious and unspontaneous thought, the mind voicing a memory. The smell of decay and the certainty that something awful had happened right there was gone.

When I got back up to the house and went for a soda, I discovered the front of the refrigerator was bare and clean. Every magnetic letter, every fruit and vegetable, was gone. I never found them. I might have, probably would have, if there had been more time, but on that Monday morning time was almost up.

I dressed, then called Mattie. We talked about the upcoming party, about how excited Ki was, about how nervous Mattie was about going back to work on Friday — she was afraid that the locals would be mean to her, but in an odd, womanly way she was even more afraid that they would be *cold* to her, snub her. We talked about the money, and I quickly ascertained that she didn't believe in the reality of it. "Lance used to say his father was the kind of man who'd show a piece of meat to a starving dog and then eat it himself," she said. "But as long as I have my job back, I won't starve and neither will Ki."

"But if there really *are* big bucks . . . ?"

"Oh, gimme-gimme-gimme," she said, laughing. "What do you think I am, crazy?"

"Nah. By the way, what's going on with Ki's fridgeafator people? Are they writing any new stuff?"

"That is the weirdest thing," she said. "They're gone."

"The fridgeafator people?"

"I don't know about them, but the magnetic letters you gave her sure are. When I asked Ki what she did with them, she started crying and said Allamagoosalum took them. She said he ate them in the middle of the night, while everyone was sleeping, for a snack."

"Allama-*who*-salum?"

"Allamagoosalum," Mattie said, sounding wearily amused. "Another little legacy from her grandfather. It's a corruption of the Micmac word for 'boogeyman' or 'demon' — I looked it up at the library. Kyra had a good many nightmares about demons and wendigos and the allamagoosalum late last winter and this spring."

"What a sweet old grandpa he was," I said sentimentally.

"Right, a real pip. She was miserable over losing the letters; I barely got her calmed down before her ride to V.B.S. came. Ki wants to know if you'll come to Final Exercises on Friday afternoon, by the way. She and her friend Billy Turgeon are going to flannelboard the story of baby Moses."

"I wouldn't miss it," I said . . . but of course I did. We all did.

"Any idea where her letters might have gone, Mike?"

"No."

"Yours are still okay?"

"Mine are fine, but of course mine don't spell anything," I said, looking at the empty door of my own fridgeafator. There was sweat on my forehead. I could feel it creeping down into my eyebrows like oil. "Did you . . . I don't know . . . sense anything?"

"You mean did I maybe hear the evil alphabet-thief as he slid through the window?"

"You know what I mean."

"I suppose so." A pause. "I thought I heard something in the night, okay? About three this morning, actually. I got up and went into the hall. Nothing was there. But . . . you know how hot it's been lately?"

"Yes."

"Well, not in my trailer, not last night. It was cold as ice. I swear I could almost see my breath."

I believed her. After all, I *had* seen mine.

"Were the letters on the front of the fridge then?"

"I don't know. I didn't go up the hall far enough to see into the kitchen. I took one look around and then went back to bed. I almost *ran* back to bed. Sometimes bed feels safer, you know?" She laughed nervously. "It's a kid thing. Covers are boogeyman kryptonite. Only at first, when I got in . . . I don't know . . . I thought someone was in there already. Like someone had been hiding on the floor underneath and then . . . when I went to check the hall . . . they got in. Not a nice someone, either."

Give me my dust-catcher, I thought, and shuddered.

"What?" Mattie asked sharply. "What did you say?"

"I asked who did you think it was? What was the first name that came into your mind?"

"Devore," she said. "*Him.* But there was no one there." A pause. "I wish *you'd* been there."

"I do, too."

"I'm glad. Mike, do you have any ideas at all about this? Because it's very freaky."

"I think maybe . . ." For a moment I was on the verge of telling her what had happened to my own letters. But if I started talking, where would it stop? And how much could she be expected to believe? ". . . maybe Ki took the letters herself. Went walking in her sleep and chucked them under the trailer or something. Do you think that could be?"

"I think I like the idea of Kyra strolling around in her sleep even less than the idea of ghosts with cold breath taking the letters off the fridge," Mattie said.

"Take her to bed with you tonight," I said, and felt her thought come back like an arrow: *I'd rather take you.*

What she said, after a brief pause, was: "Will you come by today?"

"I don't think so," I said. She was noshing on flavored yogurt as we talked, eating it in little nipping bites. "You'll see me tomorrow, though. At the party."

"I hope we get to eat before the thunderstorms. They're supposed to be bad."

"I'm sure we will."

"And are you still thinking? I only ask because I dreamed of you when I finally fell asleep again. I dreamed of you kissing me."

"I'm still thinking," I said. "Thinking hard."

But in fact I don't remember thinking about anything very hard that day. What I remember is drifting further and further into that zone I've explained so badly. Near dusk I went for a long walk in spite of the heat — all the way out to where Lane Forty-two joins the highway. Coming back I stopped on the edge of Tidwell's Meadow, watching the light fade out of the sky and listening to thunder rumble somewhere over New Hampshire. Once more there was that sense of how thin reality was, not just here but everywhere; how it was stretched like skin over the blood and tissue of a body we can never know clearly in this life. I looked at trees and saw arms; I looked at bushes and saw faces. Ghosts, Mattie had said. Ghosts with cold breath.

Time was also thin, it seemed to me. Kyra and I had really been at the Fryeburg Fair — some version of it, anyway; we had really visited the year 1900. And at the foot of the meadow the Red-Tops were almost there now, as they once had been, in their neat little cabins. I could almost hear the sound of their guitars, the murmur of their voices and laughter; I could almost see the gleam of their lanterns and smell their beef and pork frying. *"Say baby, do you remember me?"* one of her songs went, *"Well I ain't your honey like I used to be."*

Something rattled in the underbrush to my left. I turned that way, expecting to see Sara step out of the woods wearing Mattie's dress and Mattie's white sneakers. In this gloom, they would seem almost to float by themselves, until she got close to me . . .

There was no one there, of course, it had undoubtedly been nothing but Chuck the Woodchuck headed home after a hard day at the office, but I no longer wanted to be out here, watching as the light drained out of the day and the mist came up from the ground. I turned for home.

Instead of going into the house when I got back, I made my way along the path to Jo's studio, where I hadn't been since the night I had taken my IBM back in a dream. My way was lit by intermittent flashes of heat lightning.

The studio was hot but not stale. I could smell a peppery aroma that was actually pleasant, and wondered if it might be some of Jo's herbs. There was an air conditioner out here, and it worked — I turned it on and then just stood in front of it a little while. So much cold air on my overheated body was probably unhealthy, but it felt wonderful.

I didn't feel very wonderful otherwise, however. I looked around with a growing sense of something too heavy to be mere sadness; it felt like despair. I think it was caused by the contrast between how little of Jo was left in Sara Laughs and how much of her was still out here. I imagined our marriage as a kind of playhouse — and isn't that what marriage is, in large part? playing house? — where only half the stuff was held down. Held down by little magnets or hidden cables. Something had come along and picked up our playhouse by one corner — easiest thing in the world, and I supposed I should be grateful that the something hadn't decided to draw back its foot and kick the poor thing all the way over. It just picked up that one corner, you see. My stuff stayed put, but all of Jo's had slid . . .

Out of the house and down here.

"Jo?" I asked, and sat down in her chair. There was no answer. No thumps on the wall. No crows or owls calling from the woods. I put my hand on her desk, where the typewriter had been, and slipped my hand across it, picking up a film of dust.

"I miss you, honey," I said, and began to cry.

When the tears were over — again — I wiped my face with the tail of my tee-shirt like a little kid, then just looked around. There was the picture of Sara Tidwell on her desk and a photo I didn't remember on the wall — this latter was old, sepia-tinted, and woodsy. Its focal point was a man-high birchwood cross in a little clearing on a slope above the lake. That clearing was gone from the geography now, most likely, long since filled in by trees.

I looked at her jars of herbs and mushroom sections, her filing cabinets, her sections of afghan. The green rag rug on the floor. The pot of pencils on the desk, pencils she had touched and used. I held one of them poised over a blank sheet of paper for a moment or two, but nothing happened. I had a sense of life in this room, and a sense of being watched . . . but not a sense of being *helped*.

"I know some of it but not enough," I said. "Of all the things I don't know, maybe the one that matters most is who wrote 'help her' on the fridge. Was it you, Jo?"

No answer.

I sat awhile longer — hoping against hope, I suppose — then got up, turned off the air conditioning, turned off the lights, and went back to the house, walking in soft bright stutters of unfocused lightning. I sat on the deck for a little while, watching the night. At some point I realized I'd taken the length of blue silk ribbon out of my pocket and was winding it nervously back and forth between my fingers, making half-assed cat's cradles. Had it really come from the year 1900? The idea seemed perfectly crazy and perfectly sane at the same time. The night hung hot and hushed. I imagined old folks all over the TR — perhaps in Motton and Harlow, too — laying out their funeral clothes for tomorrow. In the doublewide trailer on Wasp Hill Road, Ki was sitting on the floor, watching a videotape of *The Jungle Book* — Baloo and Mowgli were singing "The Bare Necessities." Mattie was on the couch with her feet up, reading the new Mary Higgins Clark and singing along. Both were wearing shorty pajamas, Ki's pink, Mattie's white.

After a little while I lost my sense of them; it faded the way radio signals sometimes do late at night. I went into the north bedroom, undressed, and crawled onto the top sheet of my unmade bed. I fell asleep almost at once.

I woke in the middle of the night with someone running a hot finger up and down the middle of my back. I rolled over and when the lightning flashed, I saw there was a woman in bed with me. It was Sara Tidwell. She was grinning. There were no pupils in her eyes. "Oh sugar, I'm almost back," she whispered in the dark. I had a sense of her reaching out for me again, but when the next flash of lightning came, that side of the bed was empty.

Chapter 24

Inspiration isn't always a matter of ghosts moving magnets around on refrigerator doors, and on Tuesday morning I had a flash that was a beaut. It came while I was shaving and thinking about nothing more than remembering the beer for the party. And like the best inspirations, it came out of nowhere at all.

I hurried into the living room, not quite running, wiping the shaving cream off my face with a towel as I went. I glanced briefly at the *Tough Stuff* crossword collection lying on top of my manuscript. That had been where I'd gone first in an effort to decipher "go down nineteen" and "go down ninety-two." Not an unreasonable starting-point, but what did *Tough Stuff* have to do with TR-90? I had purchased the book at Mr. Paperback in Derry, and of the thirty or so puzzles I'd completed, I'd done all but half a dozen in Derry. TR ghosts could hardly be expected to show an interest in my Derry crossword collection. The telephone book, on the other hand —

I snatched it off the dining-room table. Although it covered the whole southern part of Castle County — Motton, Harlow, and Kashwakamak as well as the TR — it was pretty thin. The first thing I did was check the white pages to see if there *were* at least ninety-two. There were. The *Y*'s and *Z*'s finished up on page ninety-seven.

This was the answer. Had to be.

"I got it, didn't I?" I asked Bunter. "This is it."

Nothing. Not even a tinkle from the bell.

"Fuck you — what does a stuffed moosehead know about a telephone book?"

Go down nineteen. I turned to page nineteen of the telephone book, where the letter *F* was prominently showcased. I began to slip my finger down the first column and as it went, my excitement faded. The nineteenth name on page nineteen was Harold Failles. It meant nothing to me. There were also Feltons and Fenners, a Filkersham and several Finneys, half a dozen Flahertys and more Fosses than you could shake a stick at. The last name on page nineteen was Framingham. It also meant nothing to me, but —

Framingham, Kenneth P.

I stared at that for a moment. A realization began to dawn. It had nothing to do with the refrigerator messages.

You're not seeing what you think you're seeing, I thought. *This is like when you buy a blue Buick —*

"You see blue Buicks everywhere," I said. "Practically got to kick em out of your way.

Yeah, that's it." But my hands were shaking as I turned to page ninety-two.

Here were the *T*'s of southern Castle County, along with a few *U*'s like Alton Ubeck and Catherine Udell just to round things out. I didn't bother checking the ninety-second entry on the page; the phone book wasn't the key to the magnetic cross-patches after all. It did, however, suggest something enormous. I closed the book, just held it in my hands for a moment (happy folks with blueberry rakes on the front cover), then opened it at random, this time to the *M*'s. And once you knew what you were looking for, it jumped right out at you.

All those *K*'s.

Oh, there were Stevens and Johns and Marthas; there was Meserve, G., and Messier, V., and Jayhouse, T. And yet, again and again, I saw the initial *K* where people had exercised their right not to list their first name in the book. There were at least twenty *K*-initials on page fifty alone, and another dozen *C*-initials. As for the actual names themselves . . .

There were twelve Kenneths on this random page in the M-section, including three Kenneth Moores and two Kenneth Munters. There were four Catherines and two Katherines. There were a Casey, a Kiana, and a Kiefer.

"Holy Christ, it's like fallout," I whispered.

I thumbed through the book, not able to believe what I was seeing and seeing it anyway. Kenneths, Katherines, and Keiths were everywhere. I also saw Kimberly, Kim, and Kym. There were Cammie, Kia (yes, and we had thought ourselves so original), Kiah, Kendra, Kaela, Keil, and Kyle. Kirby and Kirk. There was a woman named Kissy Bowden, and a man named Kito Rennie — Kito, the same name as one of Kyra's fridgeafator people. And everywhere, outnumbering such usually common initials as *S* and *T* and *E*, were those *K*'s. My eyes danced with them.

I turned to look at the clock — didn't want to stand John Storrow up at the airport, Christ no — and there was no clock there. Of course not. Old Krazy Kat had popped his peepers during a psychic event. I gave a loud, braying laugh that scared me a little — it wasn't particularly sane.

"Get hold of yourself, Mike," I said. "Take a deep breath, son."

I took the breath. Held it. Let it out. Checked the digital readout on the microwave. Quarter past eight. Plenty of time for John. I turned back to the telephone book and began to riffle rapidly through it. I'd had a second inspiration — not a megawatt blast like the first one, but a lot more accurate, it turned out.

Western Maine is a relatively isolated area — it's a little like the hill country of the border South — but there has always been at least some inflow of folks from away ("flatlanders" is the term the locals use when they are feeling contemptuous), and in the last quarter of the century it has become a popular area for active seniors who want to fish and ski their way through retirement. The phone book goes a long way toward separating the newbies from the long-time residents. Babickis, Parettis, O'Quindlans, Donahues, Smolnacks, Dvoraks, Blindermeyers — all from away. All flatlanders. Jalberts, Meserves, Pillsburys, Spruces, Therriaults, Perraults, Stanchfields, Starbirds, Dubays — all from Castle County. You see what I'm saying, don't you? When you see a whole column of Bowies on page twelve, you know that those folks have been around long enough to relax and really spread those Bowie genes.

There were a few *K*-initials and *K*-names among the Parettis and the Smolnacks, but only a few. The heavy concentrations were all attached to families that had been here long enough to absorb the atmosphere. To breathe the fallout. Except it wasn't radiation, exactly, it —

I suddenly imagined a black headstone taller than the tallest tree on the lake, a monolith which cast its shadow over half of Castle County. This picture was so clear and so terrible that I covered my eyes, dropping the phone book on the table. I backed away from it, shuddering. Hiding my eyes actually seemed to enhance the image further: a grave-marker so enormous it blotted out the sun; TR-90 lay at its foot like a funeral bouquet. Sara Tidwell's son had drowned in Dark Score Lake . . . or *been* drowned in it. But she had marked his passing. Memorialized it. I wondered if anyone else in town had ever noticed what I just had. I didn't suppose it was all that likely; when you open a telephone book you're looking for a specific name in most cases, not reading whole pages line by line. I wondered if *Jo* had noticed — if she'd known that almost every longtime family in this part of the world had, in one way or another, named at least one child after Sara Tidwell's dead son.

Jo wasn't stupid. I thought she probably had.

I returned to the bathroom, relathered, started again from scratch. When I finished, I went back to the phone and picked it up. I poked in three numbers, then stopped, looking out at the lake. Mattie and Ki were up and in the kitchen, both of them wearing aprons, both of them in a fine froth of excitement. There was going to be a party!

They would wear pretty new summer clothes, and there would be music from Mattie's boombox CD player! Ki was helping Mattie make biscuits for strewberry snortcake, and while the biscuits were baking they would make salads. If I called Mattie up and said *Pack a couple of bags, you and Ki are going to spend a week at Disney World*, Mattie would assume I was joking, then tell me to hurry up and finish getting dressed so I'd be at the airport when John's plane landed. If I pressed, she'd remind me that Lindy had offered her her old job back, but the offer would close in a hurry if Mattie didn't show up promptly at two P.M. on Friday. If I continued to press, she would just say no.

Because I wasn't the only one in the zone, was I? I wasn't the only one who was really feeling it.

I returned the phone to its recharging cradle, then went back into the north bedroom. By the time I'd finished dressing, my fresh shirt was already feeling wilted under the arms; it was as hot that morning as it had been for the last week, maybe even hotter. But I'd be in plenty of time to meet the plane. I had never felt less like partying, but I'd be there. Mikey on the spot, that was me. Mikey on the goddam spot.

John hadn't given me his flight number,

but at Castle County Airport, such niceties are hardly necessary. This bustling hub of transport consists of three hangars and a terminal which used to be a Flying A gas station — when the light's strong on the little building's rusty north side, you can still see the shape of that winged *A*. There's one runway. Security is provided by Lassie, Breck Pellerin's ancient collie, who spends her days crashed out on the linoleum floor, cocking an ear at the ceiling whenever a plane lands or takes off.

I popped my head into Pellerin's office and asked him if the ten from Boston was on time. He said it 'twas, although he hoped the paa'ty I was meetin planned to either fly back out before mid-afternoon or stay the night. Bad weather was comin in, good gorry, yes. What Breck Pellerin referred to as *'lectrical* weather. I knew exactly what he meant, because in my nervous system that electricity already seemed to have arrived.

I went out to the runway side of the terminal and sat on a bench advertising Cormier's Market (FLY INTO OUR DELI FOR THE BEST MEATS IN MAINE). The sun was a silver button stuck on the eastern slope of a hot white sky. Headache weather, my mother would have called it, but the weather was due to change. I would hold onto the hope of that change as best I could.

At ten past ten I heard a wasp-whine from

the south. At quarter past, some sort of twin-engine plane dropped out of the murk, flopped onto the runway, and taxied toward the terminal. There were only four passengers, and John Storrow was the first one off. I grinned when I saw him. I had to grin. He was wearing a black tee-shirt with WE ARE THE CHAMPIONS printed across the front and a pair of khaki shorts which displayed a perfect set of city shins: white and bony. He was trying to manage both a Styrofoam cooler and a briefcase. I grabbed the cooler maybe four seconds before he dropped it, and tucked it under my arm.

"Mike!" he cried, lifting one hand palm out.

"John!" I returned in much the same spirit (*evoe* is the word that comes immediately to the crossword aficionado's mind), and slapped him five. His homely-handsome face split in a grin, and I felt a little stab of guilt. Mattie had expressed no preference for John — quite the opposite, in fact — and he really hadn't solved any of her problems; Devore had done that by topping himself before John had so much as a chance to get started on her behalf. Yet still I felt that nasty little poke.

"Come on," he said. "Let's get out of this heat. You have air conditioning in your car, I presume?"

"Absolutely."

698

"What about a cassette player? You got one of those? If you do, I'll play you something that'll make you chortle."

"I don't think I've ever heard that word actually used in conversation, John."

The grin shone out again, and I noticed what a lot of freckles he had. Sheriff Andy's boy Opie grows up to serve at the bar. "I'm a lawyer. I use words in conversation that haven't even been invented yet. You have a tape-player?"

"Of course I do." I hefted the cooler. "Steaks?"

"You bet. Peter Luger's. They're —"

"— the best in the world. You told me."

As we went into the terminal, someone said, "Michael?"

It was Romeo Bissonette, the lawyer who had chaperoned me through my deposition. In one hand he had a box wrapped in blue paper and tied with a white ribbon. Beside him, just rising from one of the lumpy chairs, was a tall guy with a fringe of gray hair. He was wearing a brown suit, a blue shirt, and a string tie with a golf-club on the clasp. He looked more like a farmer on auction day than the sort of guy who'd be a scream when you got a drink or two into him, but I had no doubt this was the private detective. He stepped over the comatose collie and shook hands with me. "George Kennedy, Mr. Noonan. I'm pleased to meet you. My wife has read every single book you ever wrote."

"Well thank her for me."

"I will. I have one in the car — a hardcover . . ." He looked shy, as so many people do when they get right to the point of asking. "I wonder if you'd sign it for her at some point."

"I'd be delighted to," I said. "Right away's best, then I won't forget." I turned to Romeo. "Good to see you, Romeo."

"Make it Rommie," he said. "Good to see you, too." He held out the box. "George and I clubbed together on this. We thought you deserved something nice for helping a damsel in distress."

Kennedy now *did* look like a man who might be fun after a few drinks. The kind who might just take a notion to hop onto the nearest table, turn a tablecloth into a kilt, and dance. I looked at John, who gave the kind of shrug that means hey, don't ask *me*.

I pulled off the satin bow, slipped my finger under the Scotch tape holding the paper, then looked up. I caught Rommie Bissonette in the act of elbowing Kennedy. Now they were both grinning.

"There's nothing in here that's going to jump out at me and go booga-booga, is there, guys?" I asked.

"Absolutely not," Rommie said, but his grin widened.

Well, I can be as good a sport as the next guy. I guess. I unwrapped the package, opened the plain white box inside, revealed a square pad of cotton, lifted it out. I had been smiling all through this, but now I felt the smile curl up and die on my mouth. Something went twisting up my spine as well, and I think I came very close to dropping the box.

It was the oxygen mask Devore had had on his lap when he met me on The Street, the one he'd snorted from occasionally as he and Rogette paced me, trying to keep me out deep enough to drown. Rommie Bissonette and George Kennedy had brought it to me like the scalp of a dead enemy and I was supposed to think it was *funny* —

"Mike?" Rommie asked anxiously. "Mike, are you okay? It was just a joke —"

I blinked and saw it wasn't an oxygen mask at all — how in God's name could I have been so stupid? For one thing, it was bigger than Devore's mask; for another, it was made of opaque rather than clear plastic. It was —

I gave a tentative chuckle. Rommie Bissonette looked tremendously relieved. So did Kennedy. John only looked puzzled.

"Funny," I said. "Like a rubber crutch." I pulled out the little mike from inside the mask and let it dangle. It swung back and forth on its wire, reminding me of the waggy clock's tail.

"What the hell is it?" John asked.

"Park Avenue lawyer," Rommie said to George, broadening his accent so it came out *Paa-aak Avenew lawyah*. "Ain't nevah seen one of these, have ya, chummy? Nossir, coss not." Then he reverted to normalspeak, which was sort of a relief. I've lived in Maine my whole life, and for me the amusement value of burlesque Yankee accents has worn pretty thin. "It's a Stenomask. The stenog keeping the record at Mike's depo was wearing one. Mike kept looking at him —"

"It freaked me out," I said. "Old guy sitting in the corner and mumbling into the Mask of Zorro."

"Gerry Bliss freaks a lot of people out," Kennedy said. He spoke in a low rumble. "He's the last one around here who wears em. He's got ten or eleven left in his mudroom. I know, because I bought that one from him."

"I hope he stuck it to you," I said.

"I thought it would make a nice memento," Rommie said, "but for a second there I thought I'd given you the box with the severed hand in it — I hate it when I mix up my gift-boxes like that. What's the deal?"

"It's been a long hot July," I said. "Put it down to that." I hung the Stenomask's strap over one finger, dangling it that way.

"Mattie said to be there by eleven," John told us. "We're going to drink beer and throw the Frisbee around."

"I can do both of those things quite well," George Kennedy said.

Outside in the tiny parking lot George went to a dusty Altima, rummaged in the back, and came out with a battered copy of *The Red-Shirt Man*. "Frieda made me bring this one. She has the newer ones, but this is her favorite. Sorry about how it looks — she's read it about six times."

"It's my favorite, too," I said, which was true. "And I like to see a book with mileage." That was also true. I opened the book, looked approvingly at a smear of long-dried chocolate on the flyleaf, and then wrote: *For Frieda Kennedy, whose husband was there to lend a hand. Thanks for sharing him, and thanks for reading, Mike Noonan.*

That was a long inscription for me — usually I just stick to *Best wishes* or *Good luck,* but I wanted to make up for the curdled expression they had seen on my face when I opened their innocent little gag present. While I was scribbling, George asked me if I was working on a new novel.

"No," I said. "Batteries currently on recharge." I handed the book back.

"Frieda won't like that."

"No. But there's always *Red-Shirt*."

"We'll follow you," Rommie said, and a

rumble came from deep in the west. It was no louder than the thunder which had rumbled on and off for the last week, but this wasn't dry thunder. We all knew it, and we all looked in that direction.

"Think we'll get a chance to eat before it storms?" George asked me.

"Yeah. Just about barely."

I drove to the gate of the parking lot and glanced right to check for traffic. When I did, I saw John looking at me thoughtfully.

"What?"

"Mattie said you *were* writing, that's all. Book go tits-up on you or something?"

My Childhood Friend was just as lively as ever, in fact . . . but it would never be finished. I knew that this morning as well as I knew there was rain on the way. The boys in the basement had for some reason decided to take it back. Asking why might not be such a good idea — the answers might be unpleasant.

"Something. I'm not sure just what." I pulled out onto the highway, checked behind me, and saw Rommie and George following in George's little Altima. America has become a country full of big men in little cars. "What do you want me to listen to? If it's home karaoke, I pass. The last thing on earth I want to hear is you singing 'Bubba Shot the Jukebox Last Night.'"

"Oh, it's better than that," he said. "Miles better."

He opened his briefcase, rooted through it, and came out with a plastic cassette box. The tape inside was marked 7-20-98 — yesterday. "I love this," he said. He leaned forward, turned on the radio, then popped the cassette into the player.

I was hoping I'd already had my quota of nasty surprises for the morning, but I was wrong.

"Sorry, I just had to get rid of another call," John said from my Chevy's speakers in his smoothest, most lawyerly voice. I'd have bet a million dollars that his bony shins hadn't been showing when this tape was made.

There was a laugh, both smoky and grating. My stomach seized up at the sound of it. I remembered seeing her for the first time standing outside The Sunset Bar, wearing black shorts over a black tank-style swimsuit. Standing there and looking like a refugee from crash-diet hell.

"You mean you had to turn on your tape-recorder," she said, and now I remembered how the water had seemed to change color when she nailed me that really good one in the back of the head. From bright orange to dark scarlet it had gone. And then I'd started drinking the lake. "That's okay. Tape anything you want."

John reached out suddenly and ejected the cassette. "You don't need to hear this," he said. "It's not substantive. I thought you'd get a kick out of her blather, but . . . man, you look terrible. Do you want me to drive? You're white as a fucking sheet."

"I can drive," I said. "Go on, play it. Afterward I'll tell you about a little adventure I had Friday night . . . but you're going to keep it to yourself. They don't have to know" — I jerked my thumb over my shoulder at the Altima — "and Mattie doesn't have to know. Especially Mattie."

He reached for the tape, then hesitated. "You're sure?"

"Yeah. It was just hearing her again out of the blue like that. The quality of her voice. Christ, the reproduction is good."

"Nothing but the best for Avery, McLain, and Bernstein. We have very strict protocols about what we can tape, by the way. If you were wondering."

"I wasn't. I imagine none of it's admissible in litigation anyway, is it?"

"In certain rare cases a judge might let a tape in, but that's not why we do it. A tape like this saved a man's life four years ago, right around the time I joined the firm. That guy is now in the Witness Protection Program."

"Play it."

He leaned forward and pushed the button.

John: "How is the desert, Ms. Whitmore?"

Whitmore: "Hot."

John: "Arrangements progressing nicely? I know how difficult times like this can —"

Whitmore: "You know very little, counsellor, take it from me. Can we cut the crap?"

John: "Consider it cut."

Whitmore: "Have you conveyed the conditions of Mr. Devore's will to his daughter-in-law?"

John: "Yes ma'am."

Whitmore: "Her response?"

John: "I have none to give you now. I may have after Mr. Devore's will has been probated. But surely you know that such codicils are rarely if ever accepted by the courts."

Whitmore: "Well, if that little lady moves out of town, we'll see, won't we?"

John: "I suppose we will."

Whitmore: "When is the victory party?"

John: "Excuse me?"

Whitmore: "Oh please. I have sixty different appointments today, plus a boss to bury tomorrow. You're going up there to celebrate with her and her daughter, aren't you? Did you know she's invited the writer? Her fuck-buddy?"

John turned to me gleefully. "Do you hear

how pissed she sounds? She's trying to hide it, but she can't. It's eating her up inside!"

I barely heard him. I was in the zone with what she was saying

(*the writer her fuck-buddy*)

and what was *under* what she was saying. Some quality beneath the words. *We just want to see how long you can swim,* she had called out to me.

John: "I hardly think what I or Mattie's friends do is any of your business, Ms. Whitmore. May I respectfully suggest that you party with your friends and let Mattie Devore party with h—"

Whitmore: "Give him a message."

Me. She was talking about me. Then I realized it was even more personal than that — she was talking *to* me. Her body might be on the other side of the country, but her voice and spiteful spirit were right here in the car with us.

And Max Devore's will. Not the meaningless shit his lawyers had put down on paper but his *will*. The old bastard was as dead as Damocles, but yes, he was definitely still seeking custody.

John: "Give who a message, Ms. Whitmore?"

Whitmore: "Tell him he never answered

Mr. Devore's question."
John: "What question is that?"

Does her cunt suck?

Whitmore: "Ask him. He'll know."
John: "If you mean Mike Noonan, you can ask him yourself. You'll see him in Castle County Probate Court this fall."
Whitmore: "I hardly think so. Mr. Devore's will was made and witnessed out here."
John: "Nevertheless, it will be probated in Maine, where he died. My heart is set on it. And when you leave Castle County the next time, Rogette, you will do so with your education in matters of the law considerably broadened."

For the first time she sounded angry, her voice rising to a reedy caw.

Whitmore: "If you think —"
John: "I don't think. I know. Goodbye, Ms. Whitmore."
Whitmore: "You might do well to stay away from —"

There was a click, the hum of an open line, then a robot voice saying "Nine-forty A.M. . . . Eastern Daylight . . . July . . . twentieth." John punched EJECT, collected his tape, and stored it back in his briefcase.

"I hung up on her." He sounded like a man telling you about his first skydive. "I actually did. She was mad, wasn't she? Wouldn't you say she was seriously pissed?"

"Yeah." It was what he wanted to hear but not what I really believed. Pissed, yes. *Seriously* pissed? Maybe not. Because Mattie's location and state of mind hadn't been her concern; Rogette had called to talk to me. To tell me she was thinking of me. To bring back memories of how it felt to tread water with the back of your head gushing blood. To freak me out. And she had succeeded.

"What was the question you didn't answer?" John asked me.

"I don't know what she meant by that," I said, "but I *can* tell you why hearing her turned me a little white in the gills. If you can be discreet, and if you want to hear."

"We've got eighteen miles to cover; lay it on me."

I told him about Friday night. I didn't clutter my version with visions or psychic phenomena; there was just Michael Noonan out for a sunset walk along The Street. I'd been standing by a birch tree which hung over the lake, watching the sun drop toward the mountains, when they came up behind me. From the point where Devore charged me with his wheelchair to the point where I finally got back onto solid ground, I stuck pretty much to the truth.

When I finished, John was at first utterly silent. It was a measure of how thrown for a loop he was; under normal circumstances he was every bit the chatterbox Ki was.

"Well?" I asked. "Comments? Questions?"

"Lift your hair so I can see behind your ear."

I did as he asked, revealing a big Band-Aid and a large area of swelling. John leaned forward to study it like a little kid observing his best friend's battle-scar during recess. "Holy shit," he said at last.

It was my turn to say nothing.

"Those two old fucks tried to drown you."

I said nothing.

"They tried to drown you for helping Mattie."

Now I *really* said nothing.

"And you never reported it?"

"I started to," I said, "then realized I'd make myself look like a whiny little asshole. And a liar, most likely."

"How much do you think Osgood might know?"

"About them trying to drown me? Nothing. He's just a messenger boy."

A little more of that unusual quiet from John. After a few seconds of it he reached out and touched the lump on the back of my head.

"Ow!"

"Sorry." A pause. "Jesus. Then he went

back to Warrington's and pulled the pin. Jesus. Michael, I never would have played that tape if I'd known —"

"It's all right. But don't even think of telling Mattie. I'm wearing my hair over my ear like that for a reason."

"Will you *ever* tell her, do you think?"

"I might. Some day when he's been dead long enough so we can laugh about me swimming with my clothes on."

"That might be awhile," he said.

"Yeah. It might."

We drove in silence for a bit. I could sense John groping for a way to bring the day back to jubilation, and loved him for it. He leaned forward, turned on the radio, and found something loud and nasty by Guns 'n Roses — welcome to the jungle, baby, we got fun and games.

"Party 'til we puke," he said. "Right?"

I grinned. It wasn't easy with the sound of the old woman's voice still clinging to me like light slime, but I managed. "If you insist," I said.

"I do," he said. "Most certainly."

"John, you're a good guy for a lawyer."

"And you're a good one for a writer."

This time the grin on my face felt more natural and stayed on longer. We passed the marker reading TR-90, and as we did, the sun burned through the haze and flooded the day with light. It seemed like an omen of better times ahead, until I looked into the west. There, black in the bright, I could see the thunderheads building up over the White Mountains.

Chapter 25

For men, I think, love is a thing formed of equal parts lust and astonishment. The astonishment part women understand. The lust part they only think they understand. Very few — perhaps one in twenty — have any concept of what it really is or how deep it runs. That's probably just as well for their sleep and peace of mind. And I'm not talking about the lust of satyrs and rapists and molesters; I'm talking about the lust of shoe-clerks and high-school principals.

Not to mention writers and lawyers.

We turned into Mattie's dooryard at ten to eleven, and as I parked my Chevy beside her rusted-out Jeep, the trailer door opened and Mattie came out on the top step. I sucked in my breath, and beside me I could hear John sucking in his.

She was very likely the most beautiful young woman I have ever seen in my life as she stood there in her rose-colored shorts and matching middy top. The shorts were not short enough to be cheap (my mother's word) but plenty short enough to be provocative. Her top tied in floppy string bows across the shoulders and showed just enough tan to dream on. Her hair hung to her shoulders. She was smiling and waving.

I thought, *She's made it — take her into the country-club dining room now, dressed just as she is, and she shuts everyone else down.*

"Oh Lordy," John said. There was a kind of dismayed longing in his voice. "All that and a bag of chips."

"Yeah," I said. "Put your eyes back in your head, big boy."

He made cupping motions with his hands as if doing just that. George, meanwhile, had pulled his Altima in next to us.

"Come on," I said, opening my door. "Time to party."

"I can't touch her, Mike," John said. "I'll melt."

"Come on, you goof."

Mattie came down the steps and past the pot with the tomato plant in it. Ki was behind her, dressed in an outfit similar to her mother's, only in a shade of dark green. She had the shys again, I saw; she kept one steadying hand on Mattie's leg and one thumb in her mouth.

"The guys are here! The guys are here!" Mattie cried, laughing, and threw herself into my arms. She hugged me tight and kissed the corner of my mouth. I hugged her back and kissed her cheek. Then she moved on to John, read his shirt, patted her hands together in applause, and then hugged him. He hugged back pretty well for a guy who was afraid he might melt, I thought, picking her up off her feet and swinging her around in a circle while she hung onto his neck and laughed.

"Rich lady, rich lady, rich lady!" John chanted, then set her down on the cork soles of her white shoes.

"Free lady, free lady, free lady!" she chanted back. "The hell with rich!" Before he could reply, she kissed him firmly on the mouth. His arms rose to slip around her, but she stepped back before they could catch hold. She turned to Rommie and George, who were standing side-by-side and looking like fellows who might want to explain all about the Mormon Church.

I took a step forward, meaning to do the introductions, but John was taking care of that, and one of his arms managed to accomplish its mission after all — it circled her waist as he led her forward toward the men.

Meanwhile a little hand slipped into mine. I looked down and saw Ki looking up at me. Her face was grave and pale and every bit as beautiful as her mother's. Her blonde hair, freshly washed and shining, was held back with a velvet scrunchy.

"Guess the fridgeafator people don't like me now," she said. The laughter and insouciance were gone, at least for the moment. She looked on the verge of tears. "My letters all went bye-bye."

I picked her up and set her in the crook of my arm as I had on the day I'd met her walking down the middle of Route 68 in her bathing suit. I kissed her forehead and then the tip of her nose. Her skin was perfect silk. "I know they did," I said. "I'll buy you some more."

"Promise?" Doubtful dark blue eyes fixed on mine.

"Promise. And I'll teach you special words like zygote and bibulous. I know lots of special words."

"How many?"

"A hundred and eighty."

Thunder rumbled in the west. It didn't seem louder, but it was more focused, somehow. Ki's eyes went in that direction, then came back to mine. "I'm scared, Mike."

"Scared? Of what?"

"Of I don't know. The lady in Mattie's dress. The men we saw." Then she looked over my shoulder. "Here comes Mommy." I have heard actresses deliver the line *Not in front of the children* in that exact same tone of voice. Kyra wiggled in the circle of my arms. "Land me."

I landed her. Mattie, John, Rommie, and George came over to join us. Ki ran to Mattie, who picked her up and then eyed us like a general surveying her troops.

"Got the beer?" she asked me.

"Yessum. A case of Bud and a dozen mixed sodas, as well. Plus lemonade."

"Great. Mr. Kennedy —"

"George, ma'am."

"George, then. And if you call me ma'am again, I'll punch you in the nose. I'm Mattie. Would you drive down to the Lakeview General" — she pointed to the store on Route 68, about half a mile from us — "and get some ice?"

"You bet."

"Mr. Bissonette —"

"Rommie."

"There's a little garden at the north end of the trailer, Rommie. Can you find a couple of good-looking lettuces?"

"I think I can handle that."

"John, let's get the meat into the fridge. As for you, Michael . . ." She pointed to the barbecue. "The briquets are the self-lighting kind — just drop a match and stand back. Do your duty."

"Aye, good lady," I said, and dropped to my knees in front of her. That finally got a giggle out of Ki.

Laughing, Mattie took my hand and pulled me back onto my feet. "Come on, Sir Galahad," she said. "It's going to rain. I want to be safe inside and too stuffed to jump when it does."

In the city, parties begin with greetings at

the door, gathered-in coats, and those peculiar little air-kisses (when, exactly, did *that* social oddity begin?). In the country, they begin with chores. You fetch, you carry, you hunt for stuff like barbecue tongs and oven mitts. The hostess drafts a couple of men to move the picnic table, then decides it was actually better where it was and asks them to put it back. And at some point you discover that you're having fun.

I piled briquets until they looked approximately like the pyramid on the bag, then touched a match to them. They blazed up satisfyingly and I stood back, wiping my forearm across my forehead. Cool and clear might be coming, but it surely wasn't in hailing distance yet. The sun had burned through and the day had gone from dull to dazzling, yet in the west black-satin thunderheads continued to stack up. It was as if night had burst a blood-vessel in the sky over there.

"Mike?"

I looked around at Kyra. "What, honey?"

"Will you take care of me?"

"Yes," I said with no hesitation at all.

For a moment something about my response — perhaps only the quickness of it — seemed to trouble her. Then she smiled. "Okay," she said. "Look, here comes the ice-man!"

George was back from the store. He

parked and got out. I walked over with Kyra, she holding my hand and swinging it possessively back and forth. Rommie came with us, juggling three heads of lettuce — I didn't think he was much of a threat to the guy who had fascinated Ki on the common Saturday night.

George opened the Altima's back door and brought out two bags of ice. "The store was closed," he said. "Sign said WILL RE-OPEN AT 5 P.M. That seemed a little too long to wait, so I took the ice and put the money through the mail-slot."

They'd closed for Royce Merrill's funeral, of course. Had given up almost a full day's custom at the height of the tourist season to see the old fellow into the ground. It was sort of touching. I thought it was also sort of creepy.

"Can I carry some ice?" Kyra asked.

"I guess, but don't frizzicate yourself," George said, and carefully put a five-pound bag of ice into Ki's outstretched arms.

"Frizzicate," Kyra said, giggling. She began walking toward the trailer, where Mattie was just coming out. John was behind her and regarding her with the eyes of a gutshot beagle. "Mommy, look! I'm frizzicating!"

I took the other bag. "I know the icebox is outside, but don't they keep a padlock on it?"

"I am friends with most padlocks," George said.

"Oh. I see."

"Mike! Catch!" John tossed a red Frisbee. It floated toward me, but high. I jumped for it, snagged it, and suddenly Devore was back in my head: *What's wrong with you, Rogette? You never used to throw like a girl. Get him!*

I looked down and saw Ki looking up. "Don't think about sad stuff," she said.

I smiled at her, then flipped her the Frisbee. "Okay, no sad stuff. Go on, sweetheart. Toss it to your mom. Let's see if you can."

She smiled back, turned, and made a quick, accurate flip to her mother — the toss was so hard that Mattie almost flubbed it. Whatever else Kyra Devore might have been, she was a Frisbee champion in the making.

Mattie tossed the Frisbee to George, who turned, the tail of his absurd brown suitcoat flaring, and caught it deftly behind his back. Mattie laughed and applauded, the hem of her top flirting with her navel.

"Showoff!" John called from the steps.

"Jealousy is such an ugly emotion," George said to Rommie Bissonette, and flipped him the Frisbee. Rommie floated it back to John, but it went wide and bonked off the side of the trailer. As John hurried

721

down the steps to get it, Mattie turned to me. "My boombox is on the coffee-table in the living room, along with a stack of CDs. Most of them are pretty old, but at least it's music. Will you bring them out?"

"Sure."

I went inside, where it was hot in spite of three strategically placed fans working overtime. I looked at the grim, mass-produced furniture, and at Mattie's rather noble effort to impart some character: the van Gogh print that should not have looked at home in a trailer kitchenette but did, Edward Hopper's *Nighthawks* over the sofa, the tie-dyed curtains that would have made Jo laugh. There was a bravery here that made me sad for her and furious at Max Devore all over again. Dead or not, I wanted to kick his ass.

I went into the living room and saw the new Mary Higgins Clark on the sofa end-table with a bookmark sticking out of it. Lying beside it in a heap were a couple of little-girl hair ribbons — something about them looked familiar to me, although I couldn't remember ever having seen Ki wearing them. I stood there a moment longer, frowning, then grabbed the boombox and CDs and went back outside. "Hey, guys," I said. "Let's rock."

I was okay until she danced. I don't know

if it matters to you, but it does to me. I was okay until she danced. After that I was lost.

We took the Frisbee around to the rear of the house, partly so we wouldn't piss off any funeral-bound townies with our rowdiness and good cheer, mostly because Mattie's back yard was a good place to play — level ground and low grass. After a couple of missed catches, Mattie kicked off her party-shoes, dashed barefoot into the house, and came back in her sneakers. After that she was a lot better.

We threw the Frisbee, yelled insults at each other, drank beer, laughed a lot. Ki wasn't much on the catching part, but she had a phenomenal arm for a kid of three and played with gusto. Rommie had set the boombox up on the trailer's back step, and it spun out a haze of late-eighties and early-nineties music: U2, Tears for Fears, the Eurythmics, Crowded House, A Flock of Seagulls, Ah-Hah, the Bangles, Melissa Etheridge, Huey Lewis and the News. It seemed to me that I knew every song, every riff.

We sweated and sprinted in the noon light. We watched Mattie's long, tanned legs flash and listened to the bright runs of Kyra's laughter. At one point Rommie Bissonette went head over heels, all the change spilling out of his pockets, and John laughed until he had to sit down. Tears rolled from his eyes. Ki ran over and plopped on his defenseless lap. John stopped laughing in a hurry. "Ooof!" he cried, looking at me with shining, wounded eyes as his bruised balls no doubt tried to climb back inside his body.

"Kyra *Devore!*" Mattie cried, looking at John apprehensively.

"I taggled my own quartermack," Ki said proudly.

John smiled feebly at her and staggered to his feet. "Yes," he said. "You did. And the ref calls fifteen yards for squashing."

"Are you okay, man?" George asked. He looked concerned, but his voice was grinning.

"I'm fine," John said, and spun him the Frisbee. It wobbled feebly across the yard. "Go on, throw. Let's see whatcha got."

The thunder rumbled louder, but the black clouds were all still west of us; the sky overhead remained a harmless humid blue. Birds still sang and crickets hummed in the grass. There was a heat-shimmer over the barbecue, and it would soon be time to slap on John's New York steaks. The Frisbee still flew, red against the green of the grass and trees, the blue of the sky. I was still in lust, but everything was still all right — men are in lust all over the world and damned near all of the time, and the icecaps don't melt. But she danced, and everything changed.

It was an old Don Henley song, one driven by a really nasty guitar riff.

"Oh God, I love this one," Mattie cried. The Frisbee came to her. She caught it, dropped it, stepped on it as if it were a hot red spot falling on a nightclub stage, and began to shake. She put her hands first behind her neck and then on her hips and then behind her back. She danced standing with the toes of her sneakers on the Frisbee. She danced without moving. She danced as they say in that song — like a wave on the ocean.

*"The government bugged the men's room
in the local disco lounge,
And all she wants to do is dance, dance . . .
To keep the boys from selling
all the weapons they can scrounge,
And all she wants to do, all she wants to do
is dance."*

Women are sexy when they dance — incredibly sexy — but that wasn't what I reacted to, or how I reacted. The lust I was coping with, but this was more than lust, and not copeable. It was something that sucked the wind out of me and left me feeling utterly at her mercy. In that moment she was the most beautiful thing I had ever seen, not a pretty woman in shorts and a middy top dancing in place on a Frisbee, but Venus revealed. She was everything I had missed during the last four years, when I'd been so badly off I didn't know I was missing anything. She robbed me of any last defenses I might have had. The age difference didn't matter. If I looked to people like my tongue was hanging out even when my mouth was shut, then so be it. If I lost my dignity, my pride, my sense of self, then so be it. Four years on my own had taught me there are worse things to lose.

How long did she stand there, dancing? I don't know. Probably not long, not even a minute, and then she realized we were looking at her, rapt — because to some degree they all saw what I saw and felt what I felt. For that minute or however long it was, I don't think any of us used much oxygen.

She stepped off the Frisbee, laughing and blushing at the same time, confused but not really uncomfortable. "I'm sorry," she said. "I just . . . I love that song."

"All she wants to do is dance," Rommie said.

"Yes, sometimes that's all she wants," Mattie said, and blushed harder than ever. "Excuse me, I have to use the facility." She tossed me the Frisbee and then dashed for the trailer.

I took a deep breath, trying to steady myself back to reality, and saw John doing the same thing. George Kennedy was wearing a mildly stunned expression, as if someone had fed him a light sedative and it was finally taking effect.

Thunder rumbled. This time it *did* sound closer.

I skimmed the Frisbee to Rommie. "What do you think?"

"I think I'm in love," he said, and then seemed to give himself a small mental shake — it was a thing you could see in his eyes. "I also think it's time we got going on those steaks if we're going to eat outside. Want to help me?"

"Sure."

"I will, too," John said.

We walked back to the trailer, leaving George and Kyra to play toss. Kyra was asking George if he had ever caught any crinimals. In the kitchen, Mattie was standing beside the open fridge and stacking steaks on a platter. "Thank God you guys came in. I was on the point of giving up and gobbling one of these just the way it is. They're the most beautiful things I ever saw."

"You're the most beautiful thing *I* ever saw," John said. He was being totally sincere, but the smile she gave him was distracted and a little bemused. I made a mental note to myself: never compliment a woman on her beauty when she has a couple of raw steaks in her hands. It just doesn't turn the windmill somehow.

"How are you at barbecuing meat?" she asked me. "Tell the truth, because these are way too good to mess up."

"I can hold my own."

"Okay, you're hired. John, you're assisting. Rommie, help me do salads."

"My pleasure."

George and Ki had come around to the front of the trailer and were now sitting in lawn-chairs like a couple of old cronies at their London club. George was telling Ki how he had shot it out with Rolfe Nedeau and the Real Bad Gang on Lisbon Street in 1993.

"George, what's happening to your *nose?*" John asked. "It's getting so long."

"Do you mind?" George asked. "I'm having a conversation here."

"Mr. Kennedy has caught lots of crooked crinimals," Kyra said. "He caught the Real Bad Gang and put them in Supermax."

"Yes," I said. "Mr. Kennedy also won an Academy Award for acting in a movie called *Cool Hand Luke.*"

"That's absolutely correct," George said. He raised his right hand and crossed the two fingers. "Me and Paul Newman. Just like that."

"We have his pusgetti sauce," Ki said gravely, and that got John laughing again. It didn't hit me the same way, but laughter is catching; just watching John was enough to break me up after a few seconds. We were howling like a couple of fools as we slapped the steaks on the grill. It's a wonder we didn't burn our hands off.

"Why are they laughing?" Ki asked George.

"Because they're foolish men with little tiny brains," George said. "Now listen, Ki — I got them all except for the Human Headcase. He jumped into his car and I jumped into mine. The details of that chase are nothing for a little girl to hear —"

George regaled her with them anyway while John and I stood grinning at each other across Mattie's barbecue. "This is great, isn't it?" John said, and I nodded.

Mattie came out with corn wrapped in aluminum foil, followed by Rommie, who had a large salad bowl clasped in his arms and negotiated the steps carefully, trying to peer over the top of the bowl as he made his way down them.

We sat at the picnic table, George and Rommie on one side, John and I flanking Mattie on the other. Ki sat at the head, perched on a stack of old magazines in a lawn-chair. Mattie tied a dishtowel around her neck, an indignity Ki submitted to only because (a) she was wearing new clothes, and (b) a dishtowel wasn't a baby-bib, at least technically speaking.

We ate hugely — salad, steak (and John

was right, it really was the best I'd ever had), roasted corn on the cob, "strewberry snortcake" for dessert. By the time we'd gotten around to the snortcake, the thunderheads were noticeably closer and there was a hot, jerky breeze blowing around the yard.

"Mattie, if I never eat a meal as good as this one again, I won't be surprised," Rommie said. "Thanks ever so much for having me."

"Thank *you*," she said. There were tears standing in her eyes. She took my hand on one side and John's on the other. She squeezed both. "Thank you all. If you knew what things were like for Ki and me before this last week . . ." She shook her head, gave John and me a final squeeze, and let go. "But that's over."

"Look at the baby," George said, amused.

Ki had slumped back in her lawn-chair and was looking at us with glazing eyes. Most of her hair had come out of the scrunchy and lay in clumps against her cheeks. There was a dab of whipped cream on her nose and a single yellow kernel of corn sitting in the middle of her chin.

"I threw the Frisbee six fousan times," Kyra said. She spoke in a distant, declamatory tone. "I tired."

Mattie started to get up. I put my hand on her arm. "Let me?"

She nodded, smiling. "If you want."

I picked Kyra up and carried her around to the steps. Thunder rumbled again, a long, low roll that sounded like the snarl of a huge dog. I looked up at the encroaching clouds, and as I did, movement caught my eye. It was an old blue car heading west on Wasp Hill Road toward the lake. The only reason I noticed it was that it was wearing one of those stupid bumper-stickers from the Village Cafe: HORN BROKEN — WATCH FOR FINGER.

I carried Ki up the steps and through the door, turning her so I wouldn't bump her head. "Take care of me," she said in her sleep. There was a sadness in her voice that chilled me. It was as if she knew she was asking the impossible. "Take care of me, I'm little, Mama says I'm a little guy."

"I'll take care of you," I said, and kissed that silky place between her eyes again. "Don't worry, Ki, go to sleep."

I carried her to her room and put her on her bed. By then she was totally conked out. I wiped the cream off her nose and picked the corn-kernel off her chin. I glanced at my watch and saw it was ten 'til two. They would be gathering at Grace Baptist by now. Bill Dean was wearing a gray tie. Buddy Jellison had a hat on. He was standing behind the church with some other men who were smoking before going inside.

I turned. Mattie was in the doorway.

731

"Mike," she said. "Come here, please."

I went to her. There was no cloth between her waist and my hands this time. Her skin was warm, and as silky as her daughter's. She looked up at me, her lips parted. Her hips pressed forward, and when she felt what was hard down there, she pressed harder against it.

"Mike," she said again.

I closed my eyes. I felt like someone who has just come to the doorway of a brightly lit room full of people laughing and talking. And dancing. Because sometimes that *is* all we want to do.

I want to come in, I thought. *That's what I want to do, all I want to do. Let me do what I want. Let me —*

I realized I was saying it aloud, whispering it rapidly into her ear as I held her with my hands going up and down her back, my fingertips ridging her spine, touching her shoulderblades, then coming around in front to cup her small breasts.

"Yes," she said. "What we both want. Yes. That's fine."

Slowly, she reached up with her thumbs and wiped the wet places from under my eyes. I drew back from her. "The key —"

She smiled a little. "You know where it is."

"I'll come tonight."

"Good."

"I've been . . ." I had to clear my throat. I looked at Kyra, who was deeply asleep. "I've been lonely. I don't think I knew it, but I have been."

"Me too. And I knew it for both of us. Kiss, please."

I kissed her. I think our tongues touched, but I'm not sure. What I remember most clearly is the *liveness* of her. She was like a dreidel lightly spinning in my arms.

"Hey!" John called from outside, and we sprang apart. "You guys want to give us a little help? It's gonna rain!"

"Thanks for finally making up your mind," she said to me in a low voice. She turned and hurried back up the doublewide's narrow corridor. The next time she spoke to me, I don't think she knew who she was talking to, or where she was. The next time she spoke to me, she was dying.

"Don't wake the baby," I heard her tell John, and his response: "Oh, sorry, sorry."

I stood where I was a moment longer, getting my breath, then slipped into the bathroom and splashed cold water on my face. I remember seeing a blue plastic whale in the bathtub as I turned to take a towel off the rack. I remember thinking that it probably blew bubbles out of its spout-hole, and I even remember having a momentary glimmer of an idea — a children's story about a spouting whale. Would you call him Willie? Nah, too obvious. Wilhelm, now — *that* had a fine round ring to it, simultaneously grand and amusing. Wilhelm the Spouting Whale.

I remember the bang of thunder from overhead. I remember how happy I was, with the decision finally made and the night to look forward to. I remember the murmur of men's voices and the murmur of Mattie's response as she told them where to put the stuff. Then I heard all of them going back out again.

I looked down at myself and saw a certain lump was subsiding. I remember thinking there was nothing so absurd-looking as a sexually excited man and knew I'd had this same thought before, perhaps in a dream. I left the bathroom, checked on Kyra again — rolled over on her side, fast asleep — and then went down the hall. I had just reached the living room when gunfire erupted outside. I never confused the sound with thunder. There was a moment when my mind fumbled toward the idea of backfires — some kid's hotrod — and then I knew. Part of me had been expecting something to happen . . . but it had been expecting ghosts rather than gunfire. A fatal lapse.

It was the rapid *pah! pah! pah!* of an auto-fire weapon — a Glock nine-millimeter, as it turned out. Mattie screamed — a high, drilling scream that froze my blood. I heard John cry out in pain and George Kennedy bellow, "Down, down! For the love of Christ, *get her down!*"

Something hit the trailer like a hard spatter of hail — a rattle of punching sounds running from west to east. Something split the air in front of my eyes — I heard it. There was an almost-musical *sproing* sound, like a snapping guitar string. On the kitchen table, the salad bowl one of them had just brought in shattered.

I ran for the door and nearly dived down the cement-block steps. I saw the barbecue overturned, with the glowing coals already setting patches of the scant front-yard grass on fire. I saw Rommie Bissonette sitting with his legs outstretched, looking stupidly down at his ankle, which was soaked with blood. Mattie was on her hands and knees by the barbecue with her hair hanging in her face — it was as if she meant to sweep up the hot coals before they could cause some real trouble. John staggered toward me, holding out a hand. The arm above it was soaked with blood.

And I saw the car I'd seen before — the nondescript sedan with the joke sticker on it. It had gone up the road — the men inside making that first pass to check us out — then turned around and come back. The shooter was still leaning out the front passenger window. I could see the stubby smoking weapon in his hands. It had a wire stock. His features were a blue blank broken only by huge gaping eyesockets — a ski-mask.

Overhead, thunder gave a long, awakening roar.

George Kennedy was walking toward the car, not hurrying, kicking hot spilled coals out of his way as he went, not bothering about the dark-red stain that was spreading on the right thigh of his pants, reaching behind himself, not hurrying even when the shooter pulled back in and shouted "Go go go!" at the driver, who was also wearing a blue mask, George not hurrying, no, not hurrying a bit, and even before I saw the pistol in his hand, I knew why he had never taken off his absurd Pa Kettle suit jacket, why he had even played Frisbee in it.

The blue car (it turned out to be a 1987 Ford registered to Mrs. Sonia Belliveau of Auburn and reported stolen the day before) had pulled over onto the shoulder and had never really stopped rolling. Now it accelerated, spewing dry brown dust out from under its rear tires, fishtailing, knocking Mattie's RFD box off its post and sending it flying into the road.

George still didn't hurry. He brought his hands together, holding his gun with his right and steadying with his left. He squeezed off five deliberate shots. The first two went into the trunk — I saw the holes appear. The third blew in the back window of the departing Ford, and I heard someone shout in pain. The fourth went I don't know where. The fifth blew the left rear tire. The Ford veered to that side. The driver almost brought it back, then lost it completely. The car ploughed into the ditch thirty yards below Mattie's trailer and rolled over on its side. There was a *whumpf!* and the rear end was engulfed in flames. One of George's shots must have hit the gas-tank. The shooter began struggling to get out through the passenger window.

"Ki . . . get Ki . . . away . . ." A hoarse, whispering voice.

Mattie was crawling toward me. One side of her head — the right side — still looked all right, but the left side was a ruin. One dazed blue eye peered out from between clumps of bloody hair. Skull-fragments littered her tanned shoulder like bits of broken crockery. How I would love to tell you I don't remember any of this, how I would love to have someone else tell you that Michael Noonan died before he saw that, but I cannot. *Alas* is the word for it in the cross-word puzzles, a four-letter word meaning to express great sorrow.

"Ki . . . Mike, get Ki . . ."

I knelt and put my arms around her. She

struggled against me. She was young and strong, and even with the gray matter of her brain bulging through the broken wall of her skull she struggled against me, crying for her daughter, wanting to reach her and protect her and get her to safety.

"Mattie, it's all right," I said. Down at the Grace Baptist Church, at the far end of the zone I was in, they were singing "Blessed Assurance" . . . but most of their eyes were as blank as the eye now peering at me through the tangle of bloody hair. "Mattie, stop, rest, it's all right."

"Ki . . . get Ki . . . don't let them . . ."

"They won't hurt her, Mattie, I promise."

She slid against me, slippery as a fish, and screamed her daughter's name, holding out her bloody hands toward the trailer. The rose-colored shorts and top had gone bright red. Blood spattered the grass as she thrashed and pulled. From down the hill there was a guttural explosion as the Ford's gas-tank exploded. Black smoke rose toward a black sky. Thunder roared long and loud, as if the sky were saying *You want noise? Yeah? I'll give you noise.*

"Say Mattie's all right, Mike!" John cried in a wavering voice. "Oh for God's sake say she's —"

He dropped to his knees beside me, his eyes rolling up until nothing showed but the whites. He reached for me, grabbed my shoulder, then tore damned near half my shirt off as he lost his battle to stay conscious and fell on his side next to Mattie. A curd of white goo bubbled from one corner of his mouth. Twelve feet away, near the overturned barbecue, Rommie was trying to get on his feet, his teeth clenched in pain. George was standing in the middle of Wasp Hill Road, reloading his gun from a pouch he'd apparently had in his coat pocket and watching as the shooter worked to get clear of the overturned car before it was engulfed. The entire right leg of George's pants was red now. *He may live but he'll never wear that suit again, I thought.*

I held Mattie. I put my face down to hers, put my mouth to the ear that was still there and said: "Kyra's okay. She's sleeping. She's fine, I promise."

Mattie seemed to understand. She stopped straining against me and collapsed to the grass, trembling all over. "Ki . . . Ki . . ." This was the last of her talking on earth. One of her hands reached out blindly, groped at a tuft of grass, and yanked it out.

"Over here," I heard George saying. "Get over here, motherfuck, don't you even *think* about turning your back on me."

"How bad is she?" Rommie asked, hobbling over. His face was as white as paper. And before I could reply: "Oh Jesus. Holy Mary Mother of God, pray for us sinners now and at the hour of our death. Blessed be the fruit of thy womb Jesus. Oh Mary born without sin, pray for us who have recourse to Thee. Oh no, oh Mike, no." He began again, this time lapsing into Lewiston street-French, what the old folks call La Parle.

"Quit it," I said, and he did. It was as if he had only been waiting to be told. "Go inside and check on Kyra. Can you?"

"Yes." He started toward the trailer, holding his leg and lurching along. With each lurch he gave a high yip of pain, but somehow he kept going. I could smell burning tufts of grass. I could smell electric rain on a rising wind. And under my hands I could feel the light spin of the dreidel slowing down as she went.

I turned her over, held her in my arms, and rocked her back and forth. At Grace Baptist the minister was now reading Psalm 139 for Royce: If I say, Surely the darkness shall cover me, even the night shall be light. The minister was reading and the Martians were listening. I rocked her back and forth in my arms under the black thunderheads. I was supposed to come to her that night, use the key under the pot and come to her. She had danced with the toes of her white sneakers on the red Frisbee, had danced like a wave on the ocean, and now she was dying in my arms while the grass burned in little clumps and the man who had fancied her as much as I had lay unconscious beside her, his right arm painted red from the short sleeve of his WE ARE THE CHAMPIONS tee-shirt all the way down to his bony, freckled wrist.

"Mattie," I said. "Mattie, Mattie, Mattie." I rocked her and smoothed my hand across her forehead, which on the right side was miraculously unsplattered by the blood that had drenched her. Her hair fell over the ruined left side of her face. "Mattie," I said. "Mattie, Mattie, oh Mattie."

Lightning flashed — the first stroke I had seen. It lit the western sky in a bright blue arc. Mattie trembled strongly in my arms — all the way from neck to toes she trembled. Her lips pressed together. Her brow furrowed, as if in concentration. Her hand came up and seemed to grab for the back of my neck, as a person falling from a cliff may grasp blindly at anything to hold on just a little longer. Then it fell away and lay limply on the grass, palm up. She trembled once more — the whole delicate weight of her trembled in my arms — and then she was still.

Chapter 26

After that I was mostly in the zone. I came out a few times — when that scratched-out scrap of genealogy fell from inside one of my old steno books, for instance — but those interludes were brief. In a way it was like my dream of Mattie, Jo, and Sara; in a way it was like the terrible fever I'd had as a child, when I'd almost died of the measles; mostly it was like nothing but itself. It was just the zone. I was feeling it. I wish to God I hadn't been.

George came over, herding the man in the blue mask ahead of him. George was limping now, and badly. I could smell hot oil and gasoline and burning tires. "Is she dead?" George asked. "Mattie?"

"Yes."

"John?"

"Don't know," I said, and then John twitched and groaned. He was alive, but there was a lot of blood.

"Mike, listen," George began, but before he could say more, a terrible liquid screaming began from the burning car in the ditch. It was the driver. He was cooking in there. The shooter started to turn that way, and George raised his gun. "Move and I'll kill you."

"You can't let him die like that," the

742

shooter said from behind his mask. "You couldn't let a dog die like that."

"He's dead already," George said. "You couldn't get within ten feet of that car unless you were in an asbestos suit." He reeled on his feet. His face was as white as the spot of whipped cream I'd wiped off the end of Ki's nose. The shooter made as if to go for him and George brought the gun up higher. "The next time you move, don't stop," George said, "because I won't. Guaranteed. Now take that mask off."

"No."

"I'm done fucking with you, Jesse. Say hello to God." George pulled back the hammer of his revolver.

The shooter said, "Jesus Christ," and yanked off his mask. It was George Footman. Not much surprise there. From behind him, the driver gave one more shriek from within the Ford fireball and then was silent. Smoke rose in black billows. More thunder roared.

"Mike, go inside and find something to tie him with," George Kennedy said. "I can hold him another minute — two, if I have to — but I'm bleeding like a stuck pig. Look for strapping tape. That shit would hold Houdini."

Footman stood where he was, looking from Kennedy to me and back to Kennedy again. Then he peered down at Highway 68, which was eerily deserted. Or perhaps it wasn't so eerie, at that — the coming storms had been well forecast. The tourists and summer folk would be under cover. As for the locals . . .

The locals were . . . sort of listening. That was at least close. The minister was speaking about Royce Merrill, a life which had been long and fruitful, a man who had served his country in peace and in war, but the old-timers weren't listening to him. They were listening to us, the way they had once gathered around the pickle barrel at the Lakeview General and listened to prize-fights on the radio.

Bill Dean was holding Yvette's wrist so tightly his fingernails were white. He was hurting her . . . but she wasn't complaining. She *wanted* him to hold onto her. Why?

"Mike!" George's voice was perceptibly weaker. "Please, man, help me. This guy is dangerous."

"Let me go," Footman said. "You'd better, don't you think?"

"In your wettest dreams, motherfuck," George said.

I got up, went past the pot with the key underneath, went up the cement-block steps. Lightning exploded across the sky, followed by a bellow of thunder.

Inside, Rommie was sitting in a chair at the kitchen table. His face was even whiter than George's. "Kid's okay," he said, forcing the words. "But she looks like waking up . . . I can't walk anymore. My ankle's totally fucked."

I moved for the telephone.

"Don't bother," Rommie said. His voice was harsh and trembling. "Tried it. Dead. Storm must already have hit some of the other towns. Killed some of the equipment. Christ, I never had anything hurt like this in my life."

I went to the drawers in the kitchen and began yanking them open one by one, looking for strapping tape, looking for clothesline, looking for any damned thing. If Kennedy passed out from blood-loss while I was in here, the other George would take his gun, kill him, and then kill John as he lay unconscious on the smoldering grass. With them taken care of, he'd come in here and shoot Rommie and me. He'd finish with Kyra.

"No he won't," I said. "He'll leave her alive."

And that might be even worse.

Silverware in the first drawer. Sandwich bags, garbage bags, and neatly banded stacks of grocery-store coupons in the second. Oven mitts and potholders in the third —

"Mike, where's my Mattie?"

I turned, as guilty as a man who has been

caught mixing illegal drugs. Kyra stood at the living-room end of the hall with her hair falling around her sleep-flushed cheeks and her scrunchy hung over one wrist like a bracelet. Her eyes were wide and panicky. It wasn't the shots that had awakened her, probably not even her mother's scream. I had wakened her. My thoughts had wakened her.

In the instant I realized it I tried to shield them somehow, but I was too late. She had read me about Devore well enough to tell me not to think about sad stuff, and now she read what had happened to her mother before I could keep her out of my mind.

Her mouth dropped open. Her eyes widened. She shrieked as if her hand had been caught in a vise and ran for the door.

"No, Kyra, no!" I sprinted across the kitchen, almost tripping over Rommie (he looked at me with the dim incomprehension of someone who is no longer completely conscious), and grabbed her just in time. As I did, I saw Buddy Jellison leaving Grace Baptist by a side door. Two of the men he had been smoking with went with him. Now I understood why Bill was holding so tightly to Yvette, and loved him for it — loved both of them. Something wanted him to go with Buddy and the others . . . but Bill wasn't going.

Kyra struggled in my arms, making big

convulsive thrusts at the door, gasping in breath and then screaming it out again. *"Let me go, want to see Mommy, let me go, want to see Mommy, let me go —"*

I called her name with the only voice I knew she would really hear, the one I could use only with her. She relaxed in my arms little by little, and turned to me. Her eyes were huge and confused and shining with tears. She looked at me a moment longer and then seemed to understand that she mustn't go out. I put her down. She just stood there a moment, then backed up until her bottom was against the dishwasher. She slid down its smooth white front to the floor. Then she began to wail — the most awful sounds of grief I have ever heard. She understood completely, you see. I had to show her enough to keep her inside, I had to . . . and because we were in the zone together, I could.

Buddy and his friends were in a pickup truck headed this way. BAMM CONSTRUCTION, it said on the side.

"Mike!" George cried. He sounded panicky. "You got to hurry!"

"Hold on!" I called back. "Hold on, George!"

Mattie and the others had started stacking picnic things beside the sink, but I'm almost positive that the stretch of Formica counter above the drawers had been clean and bare when I hurried after Kyra. Not now. The yellow sugar cannister had been overturned. Written in the spilled sugar was this:

go now

"No shit," I muttered, and checked the remaining drawers. No tape, no rope. Not even a lousy set of handcuffs, and in most well-equipped kitchens you can count on finding three or four. Then I had an idea and looked in the cabinet under the sink. When I went back out, our George was swaying on his feet and Footman was looking at him with a kind of predatory concentration.

"Did you get some tape?" George Kennedy asked.

"No, something better," I said. "Tell me, Footman, who actually paid you? Devore or Whitmore? Or don't you know?"

"Fuck you," he said.

I had my right hand behind my back. Now I pointed down the hill with my left one and endeavored to look surprised. "What the hell's Osgood doing? Tell him to go away!"

Footman looked in that direction — it was instinctive — and I hit him in the back of the head with the Craftsman hammer I'd found in the toolbox under Mattie's sink.

748

The sound was horrible, the spray of blood erupting from the flying hair was horrible, but worst of all was the feeling of the skull giving way — a spongy collapse that came right up the handle and into my fingers. He went down like a sandbag, and I dropped the hammer, gagging.

"Okay," George said. "A little ugly, but probably the best thing you could have done under . . . under the . . ."

He didn't go down like Footman — it was slower and more controlled, almost graceful — but he was just as out. I picked up the revolver, looked at it, then threw it into the woods across the road. A gun was nothing for me to have right now; it could only get me into more trouble.

A couple of other men had also left the church; a carful of ladies in black dresses and veils, as well. I had to hurry on even faster. I unbuckled George's pants and pulled them down. The bullet which had taken him in the leg had torn into his thigh, but the wound looked as if it was clotting. John's upper arm was a different story — it was still pumping out blood in frightening quantities. I yanked his belt free and cinched it around his arm as tightly as I could. Then I slapped him across the face. His eyes opened and stared at me with a bleary lack of recognition.

"Open your mouth, John!" He only stared

at me. I leaned down until our noses were almost touching and screamed, *"OPEN YOUR MOUTH! DO IT NOW!"* He opened it like a kid when the nurse tells him just say aahh. I stuck the end of the belt between his teeth. "Close!" He closed. "Now hold it," I said. "Even if you pass out, hold it."

I didn't have time to see if he was paying attention. I got to my feet and looked up as the whole world went glare-blue. For a second it was like being inside a neon sign. There was a black suspended river up there, roiling and coiling like a basket of snakes. I had never seen such a baleful sky.

I dashed up the cement-block steps and into the trailer again. Rommie had slumped forward onto the table with his face in his folded arms. He would have looked like a kindergartner taking a timeout if not for the broken salad bowl and the bits of lettuce in his hair. Kyra still sat with her back to the dishwasher, weeping hysterically.

I picked her up and realized that she had wet herself. "We have to go now, Ki."

"I want Mattie! I want Mommy! *I want my Mattie, make her stop being hurt! Make her stop being dead!"*

I hurried across the trailer. On the way to the door I passed the end-table with the Mary Higgins Clark novel on it. I noticed the tangle of hair ribbons again — ribbons perhaps tried on before the party and then discarded in favor of the scrunchy. They were white with bright red edges. Pretty. I picked them up without stopping, stuffed them into a pants pocket, then switched Ki to my other arm.

"I want Mattie! I want Mommy! *Make her come back!*" She swatted at me, trying to make me stop, then began to buck and kick in my arms again. She drummed her fists on the side of my head. "Put me down! Land me! Land me!"

"No, Kyra."

"Put me down! Land me! Land me! put me down!"

I was losing her. Then, as we came out onto the top step, she abruptly stopped struggling. "Give me Stricken! I want Stricken!"

At first I had no idea what she was talking about, but when I looked where she was pointing I understood. Lying on the walk not far from the pot with the key underneath it was the stuffed toy from Ki's Happy Meal. Strickland had put in a fair amount of outside playtime from the look of him — the light-gray fur was now dark-gray with dust — but if the toy would calm her, I wanted her to have it. This was no time to worry about dirt and germs.

"I'll give you Strickland if you promise to close your eyes and not open them until I tell you. Will you promise?"

"I promise," she said. She was trembling in my arms, and great globular tears — the kind you expect to see in fairy-tale books, never in real life — rose in her eyes and went spilling down her cheeks. I could smell burning grass and charred beefsteak. For one terrible moment I thought I was going to vomit, and then I got it under control.

Ki closed her eyes. Two more tears fell from them and onto my arm. They were hot. She held out one hand, groping. I went down the steps, got the dog, then hesitated. First the ribbons, now the dog. The ribbons were probably okay, but it seemed wrong to give her the dog and let her bring it along. It seemed wrong but . . .

It's gray, Irish, the UFO voice whispered. *You don't need to worry about it because it's gray. The stuffed toy in your dream was black.*

I didn't know exactly what the voice was talking about and had no time to care. I put the stuffed dog in Kyra's open hand. She held it up to her face and kissed the dusty fur, her eyes still closed.

"Maybe Stricken can make Mommy better, Mike. Stricken a magic dog."

"Just keep your eyes closed. Don't open them until I say."

She put her face against my neck. I carried her across the yard and to my car that way. I put her on the passenger side of the front seat. She lay down with her arms over her head and the dirty stuffed dog clutched in one pudgy hand. I told her to stay just like that, lying down on the seat. She made no outward sign that she heard me, but I knew that she did.

We had to hurry because the old-timers were coming. The old-timers wanted this business over, wanted this river to run into the sea. And there was only one place we could go, only one place where we might be safe, and that was Sara Laughs. But there was something I had to do first.

I kept a blanket in the trunk, old but clean. I took it out, walked across the yard, and shook it down over Mattie Devore. The hump it made as it settled around her was pitifully slight. I looked around and saw John staring at me. His eyes were glassy with shock, but I thought maybe he was coming back. The belt was still clamped in his teeth; he looked like a junkie preparing to shoot up.

"Iss ant eee," he said — *This can't be.* I knew exactly how he felt.

"There'll be help here in just a few minutes. Hang in there. I have to go."

"Go air?"

I didn't answer. There wasn't time. I stopped and took George Kennedy's pulse. Slow but strong. Beside him, Footman was deep in unconsciousness, but muttering thickly. Nowhere near dead. It takes a lot to kill a daddy. The jerky wind blew the smoke from the overturned car in my direction, and now I could smell cooking flesh as well as barbecued steak. My stomach clenched again.

I ran to the Chevy, dropped behind the wheel, and backed out of the driveway. I took one more look — at the blanket-covered body, at the three knocked-over men, at the trailer with the line of black bulletholes wavering down its side and its door standing open. John was up on his good elbow, the end of the belt still clamped in his teeth, looking at me with uncomprehending eyes. Lightning flashed so brilliantly I tried to shield my eyes from it, although by the time my hand was up, the flash had gone and the day was as dark as late dusk.

"Stay down, Ki," I said. "Just like you are."

"I can't hear you," she said in a voice so hoarse and choked with tears that I could barely make out the words. "Ki's takin a nap wif Stricken."

"Okay," I said. "Good."

I drove past the burning Ford and down to the foot of the hill, where I stopped at the rusty bullet-pocked stop-sign. I looked right and saw the pickup truck parked on the shoulder. BAMM CONSTRUCTION on the side. Three men crowded together in the cab, watching me. The one by the passenger window was Buddy Jellison; I could tell him by his hat. Very slowly and deliberately, I raised my right hand and gave them the finger. None of them responded and their stony faces didn't change, but the pickup began to roll slowly toward me.

I turned left onto 68, heading for Sara Laughs under a black sky.

Two miles from where Lane Forty-two branches off the highway and winds west to the lake, there stood an old abandoned barn upon which one could still make out faded letters reading DONCASTER DAIRY. As we approached it, the whole eastern side of the sky lit up in a purple-white blister. I cried out, and the Chevy's horn honked — by itself, I'm almost positive. A thorn of lightning grew from the bottom of that light-blister and struck the barn. For a moment it was still completely there, glowing like something radioactive, and then it spewed itself in all directions. I have never seen anything even remotely like it outside of a movie theater. The thunderclap which followed was like a bombshell. Kyra screamed and slid onto the floor on the passenger side of the car with her hands clapped to her ears. She still clutched the little stuffed dog in one of them.

A minute later I topped Sugar Ridge. Lane Forty-two splits left from the highway at the bottom of the ridge's north slope. From the top I could see a wide swath of TR-90 — woods and fields and barns and farms, even a darkling gleam from the lake. The sky was as black as coal dust, flashing almost constantly with internal lightnings. The air had a clear ochre glow. Every breath I took tasted like the shavings in a tinderbox. The topography beyond the ridge stood out with a surreal clarity I cannot forget. That sense of mystery swarmed my heart and mind, that sense of the world as thin skin over unknowable bones and gulfs.

I glanced into the rearview mirror and saw that the pickup truck had been joined by two other cars, one with a V-plate that means the vehicle is registered to a combat veteran of the armed services. When I slowed down, they slowed down. When I sped up, they sped up. I doubted they would follow us any farther once I turned onto Lane Forty-two, however.

"Ki? Are you okay?"

"Sleepun," she said from the footwell.

"Okay," I said, and started down the hill.

I could just see the red bicycle reflectors marking my turn onto Forty-two when it began to hail — great big chunks of white ice that fell out of the sky, drummed on the roof like heavy fingers, and bounced off the hood. They began to heap in the gutter where my windshield wipers hid.

"What's happening?" Kyra cried.

"It's just hail," I said. "It can't hurt us." This was barely out of my mouth when a hailstone the size of a small lemon struck my side of the windshield and then bounced high into the air again, leaving a white mark from which a number of short cracks radiated. Were John and George Kennedy lying helpless out in this? I turned my mind in that direction, but could sense nothing.

When I made the left onto Lane Forty-two, it was hailing almost too hard to see. The wheelruts were heaped with ice. The white faded out under the trees, though. I headed for that cover, flipping on my headlights as I went. They cut bright cones through the pelting hail.

As we went into the trees, that purple-white blister glowed again, and my rearview mirror went too bright to look at. There was a rending, crackling crash. Kyra screamed again. I looked around and saw a huge old spruce toppling slowly across the lane, its ragged stump on fire. It carried the electrical lines with it.

Blocked in, I thought. *This end, probably the other end, too. We're here. For better or for worse, we're here.*

The trees grew over Lane Forty-two in a canopy except for where the road passed beside Tidwell's Meadow. The sound of the hail in the woods was an immense splintery rattle. Trees *were* splintering, of course; it was the most damaging hail ever to fall in that part of the world, and although it spent itself in fifteen minutes, that was long enough to ruin a season's worth of crops.

Lightning flashed above us. I looked up and saw a large orange fireball being chased by a smaller one. They ran through the trees to our left, setting fire to some of the high branches. We came briefly into the clear at Tidwell's Meadow, and as we did the hail changed to torrential rain. I could not have continued driving if we hadn't run back into the woods almost immediately, and as it was the canopy provided just enough cover so I could creep along, hunched over the wheel and peering into the silver curtain falling through the fan of my headlights. Thunder boomed constantly, and now the wind began to rise, rushing through the trees like a contentious voice. Ahead of me, a leaf-heavy branch dropped into the road. I ran over it and listened to it thunk and scrape and roll against the Chevy's under-carriage.

Please, nothing bigger, I thought . . . or maybe I was praying. *Please let me get to the house. Please let us get to the house.*

By the time I reached the driveway the wind was howling a hurricane. The writhing trees and pelting rain made the entire world seem on the verge of wavering into insubstantial gruel. The driveway's slope had turned into a river, but I nosed the Chevy down it with no hesitation — we couldn't stay out here; if a big tree fell on the car, we'd be crushed like bugs in a Dixie cup.

I knew better than to use the brakes — the car would have heeled sideways and perhaps have been swept right down the slope toward the lake, rolling over and over as it went. Instead I dropped the transmission into low range, toed two notches into the emergency brake, and let the engine pull us down with the rain sheeting against the windshield and turning the log bulk of the house into a phantom. Incredibly, some of the lights were still on, shining like bathysphere portholes in nine feet of water. The generator was working, then . . . at least for the time being.

Lightning threw a lance across the lake, green-blue fire illuminating a black well of water with its surface lashed into surging whitecaps. One of the hundred-year-old pines which had stood to the left of the railroad-tie steps now lay with half its length in the water. Somewhere behind us another tree went over with a vast crash. Kyra covered her ears.

"It's all right, honey," I said. "We're here, we made it."

I turned off the engine and killed the lights. Without them I could see little; almost all the day had gone out of the day. I tried to open my door and at first couldn't. I pushed harder and it not only opened, it was ripped right out of my hand. I got out and in a brilliant stroke of lightning saw Kyra crawling across the seat toward me, her face white with panic, her eyes huge and brimming with terror. My door swung back and hit me in the ass hard enough to hurt. I ignored it, gathered Ki into my arms, and turned with her. Cold rain drenched us both in an instant. Except it really wasn't like rain at all; it was like stepping under a waterfall.

"My doggy!" Ki shrieked. Shriek or not, I could hardly hear her. I could see her face, though, and her empty hands. "Stricken! I drop Stricken!"

I looked around and yes, there he was, floating down the macadam of the driveway and past the stoop. A little farther on, the rushing water spilled off the paving and down the slope; if Strickland went with the flow, he'd probably end up in the woods somewhere. Or all the way down to the lake.

"Stricken!" Ki sobbed. "My *DOGGY!*"

Suddenly nothing mattered to either of us but that stupid stuffed toy. I chased down the driveway after it with Ki in my arms, oblivious of the rain and wind and brilliant flashes of lightning. And yet it was going to beat me to the slope — the water in which it was caught was running too fast for me to catch up.

What snagged it at the edge of the paving was a trio of sunflowers waving wildly in the wind. They looked like God-transported worshippers at a revival meeting: *Yes, Jeesus! Thankya Lawd!* They also looked familiar. It was of course impossible that they should be the same three sunflowers which had been growing up through the boards of the stoop in my dream (and in the photograph Bill Dean had taken before I came back), and yet it was them; beyond doubt it *was* them. Three sunflowers like the three weird sisters in *Macbeth*, three sunflowers with faces like searchlights. I had come back to Sara Laughs; I was in the zone; I had returned to my dream and this time it had possessed me.

"Stricken!" Ki bending and thrashing in my arms, both of us too slippery for safety. "Please, Mike, *please!*"

Thunder exploded overhead like a basket of nitro. We both screamed. I dropped to one knee and snatched up the little stuffed dog. Kyra clutched it, covered it with frantic kisses. I lurched to my feet as another thunderclap sounded, this one seeming to run through the air like some crazy liquid bullwhip. I looked at the sunflowers, and they seemed to look back at me — *Hello, Irish, it's been a long time, what do you say?* Then, re-settling Ki in my arms as well as I could, I turned and slogged for the house. It wasn't easy; the water in the driveway was now ankle-deep and full of melting hailstones. A branch flew past us and landed pretty much where I'd knelt to pick up Strickland. There was a crash and a series of thuds as a bigger branch struck the roof and went rolling down it.

I ran onto the back stoop, half-expecting the Shape to come rushing out to greet us, raising its baggy not-arms in gruesome good fellowship, but there was no Shape. There was only the storm, and that was enough.

Ki was clutching the dog tightly, and I saw with no surprise at all that its wetting, combined with the dirt from all those hours of outside play, had turned Strickland black. It was what I had seen in my dream after all.

Too late now. There was nowhere else to go, no other shelter from the storm. I opened the door and brought Kyra Devore inside Sara Laughs.

The central portion of Sara — the heart of the house — had stood for almost a hundred years and had seen its share of storms. The one that fell on the lakes region that July afternoon might have been the worst of them, but I knew as soon as we were inside, both of us gasping like people who have narrowly escaped drowning, that it would almost certainly withstand this one as well.

The log walls were so thick it was almost like stepping into some sort of vault. The storm's crash and bash became a noisy drone punctuated by thunderclaps and the occasional loud thud of a branch falling on the roof. Somewhere — in the basement, I guess — a door had come loose and was clapping back and forth. It sounded like a starter's pistol. The kitchen window had been broken by the topple of a small tree. Its needly tip poked in over the stove, making shadows on the counter and the stove-burners as it swayed. I thought of breaking it off and decided not to. At least it was plugging the hole.

I carried Ki into the living room and we looked out at the lake, black water prinked up in surreal points under a black sky. Lightning flashed almost constantly, revealing a ring of woods that danced and swayed in a frenzy all around the lake. As solid as the house was, it was groaning deeply within itself as the wind pummelled it and tried to push it down the hill.

There was a soft, steady chiming. Kyra lifted her head from my shoulder and looked around.

"You have a moose," she said.

"Yes, that's Bunter."

"Does he bite?"

"No, honey, he can't bite. He's like a . . . like a doll, I suppose."

"Why is his bell ringing?"

"He's glad we're here. He's glad we made it."

I saw her want to be happy, and then I saw her realizing that Mattie wasn't here to be happy with. I saw the idea that Mattie would never be here to be happy with glimmer in her mind . . . and felt her push it away. Over our heads something huge crashed down on the roof, the lights flickered, and Ki began to weep again.

"No, honey," I said, and began to walk with her. "No, honey, no, Ki, don't. Don't, honey, don't."

"I want my mommy! *I want my Mattie!*"

I walked her the way I think you're supposed to walk babies who have colic. She understood too much for a three-year-old, and her suffering was consequently more terrible than any three-year-old should have to bear. So I held her in my arms and walked her, her shorts damp with urine and rainwater under my hands, her arms fever-hot around my neck, her cheeks slathered with snot and tears, her hair a soaked clump from our brief dash through the downpour, her breath acetone, her toy a strangulated black clump that sent dirty water trickling over her knuckles. I walked her. Back and forth we went through Sara's living room, back and forth through dim light thrown by the overhead and one lamp. Generator light is never quite steady, never quite still — it seems to breathe and sigh. Back and forth through the ceaseless low chiming of Bunter's bell, like music from that world we sometimes touch but never really see. Back and forth beneath the sound of the storm. I think I sang to her and I know I touched her with my mind and we went deeper and deeper into that zone together. Above us the clouds ran and the rain pelted, dousing the fires the lightning had started in the woods. The house groaned and the air eddied with gusts coming in through the broken kitchen window, but through it all there was a feeling of rueful safety. A feeling of coming home.

At last her tears began to taper off. She lay with her cheek and the weight of her heavy head on my shoulder, and when we passed the lakeside windows I could see her eyes looking out into the silver-dark storm, wide and unblinking. Carrying her was a tall man with thinning hair. I realized I could see the dining-room table right through us. *Our reflections are ghosts already,* I thought.

"Ki? Can you eat something?"

"Not hung'y."

"Can you drink a glass of milk?"

"No, cocoa. I cold."

"Yes, of course you are. And I have cocoa."

I tried to put her down and she held on

with panicky tightness, scrambling against me with her plump little thighs. I hoisted her back up again, this time settling her against my hip, and she subsided.

"Who's here?" she asked. She had begun to shiver. "Who's here 'sides us?"

"I don't know."

"There's a boy," she said. "I saw him there." She pointed Strickland toward the sliding glass door which gave on the deck (all the chairs out there had been over-turned and thrown into the corners; one of the set was missing, apparently blown right over the rail). "He was black like on that funny show me and Mattie watch. There are other black people, too. A lady in a big hat. A man in blue pants. The rest are hard to see. But they watch. They watch us. Don't you see them?"

"They can't hurt us."

"Are you sure? Are you, are you?"

I didn't answer.

I found a box of Swiss Miss hiding behind the flour cannister, tore open one of the packets, and dumped it into a cup. Thunder exploded overhead. Ki jumped in my arms and let out a long, miserable wail. I hugged her, kissed her cheek.

"Don't put me down, Mike, I scared."

"I won't put you down. You're my good girl."

"I scared of the boy and the blue-pants

man and the lady. I think it's the lady who wore Mattie's dress. Are they ghosties?"

"Yes."

"Are they bad, like the men who chased us at the fair? Are they?"

"I don't really know, Ki, and that's the truth."

"But we'll find out."

"Huh?"

"That's what you thought. 'But we'll find out.' "

"Yes," I said. "I guess that's what I was thinking. Something like that."

I took her down to the master bedroom while the water heated in the kettle, thinking there had to be *something* left of Jo's I could pop her into, but all of the drawers in Jo's bureau were empty. So was her side of the closet. I stood Ki on the big double bed where I had not so much as taken a nap since coming back, took off her clothes, carried her into the bathroom, and wrapped her in a bathtowel. She hugged it around herself, shaking and blue-lipped. I used another one to dry her hair as best I could. During all of this, she never let go of the stuffed dog, which was now beginning to bleed stuffing from its seams.

I opened the medicine cabinet, pawed through it, and found what I was looking for on the top shelf: the Benadryl Jo had kept around for her ragweed allergy. I thought of checking the expiration date on the bottom of the box, then almost laughed out loud. What difference did *that* make? I stood Ki on the closed toilet seat and let her hold on around my neck while I stripped the child-proof backing from four of the little pink-and-white caplets. Then I rinsed out the tooth-glass and filled it with cold water. While I was doing this I saw movement in the bathroom mirror, which reflected the doorway and the master bedroom beyond. I told myself that I was only seeing the shadows of windblown trees. I offered the caplets to Ki. She reached for them, then hesitated.

"Go on," I said. "It's medicine."

"What kind?" she asked. Her small hand was still poised over the little cluster of caplets.

"Sadness medicine," I said. "Can you swallow pills, Ki?"

"Sure. I taught myself when I was two."

She hesitated a moment longer — looking at me and looking *into* me, I think, ascertaining that I was telling her something I really believed. What she saw or felt must have satisfied her, because she took the caplets and put them in her mouth, one after another. She swallowed them with little birdie-sips from the glass, then said: "I still feel sad, Mike."

"It takes awhile for them to work."

I rummaged in my shirt drawer and found an old Harley-Davidson tee that had shrunk. It was still miles too big for her, but when I tied a knot in one side it made a kind of sarong that kept slipping off one of her shoulders. It was almost cute.

I carry a comb in my back pocket. I took it out and combed her hair back from her forehead and her temples. She was starting to look put together again, but there was still something missing. Something that was connected in my mind with Royce Merrill. That was crazy, though . . . wasn't it?

"Mike? What cane? What cane are you thinking about it?"

Then it came to me. "A candy cane," I said. "The kind with stripes." From my pocket I took the two white ribbons. Their red edges looked almost raw in the uncertain light. "Like these." I tied her hair back in two little ponytails. Now she had her ribbons; she had her black dog; the sunflowers had relocated a few feet north, but they were there. Everything was more or less the way it was supposed to be.

Thunder blasted, somewhere close a tree fell, and the lights went out. After five seconds of dark-gray shadows, they came on again. I carried Ki back to the kitchen, and when we passed the cellar door, something laughed behind it. I heard it; Ki did, too. I could see it in her eyes.

"Take care of me," she said. "Take care of me cause I'm just a little guy. You promised."

"I will."

"I love you, Mike."

"I love you, too, Ki."

The kettle was huffing. I filled the cup to the halfway mark with hot water, then topped it up with milk, cooling it off and making it richer. I took Kyra over to the couch. As we passed the dining-room table I glanced at the IBM typewriter and at the manuscript with the crossword-puzzle book lying on top of it. Those things looked vaguely foolish and somehow sad, like gadgets that never worked very well and now do not work at all.

Lightning lit up the entire sky, scouring the room with purple light. In that glare the laboring trees looked like screaming fingers, and as the light raced across the sliding glass door to the deck I saw a woman standing behind us, by the woodstove. She was indeed wearing a straw hat, with a brim the size of a cartwheel.

"What do you mean, the river is almost in the sea?" Ki asked.

I sat down and handed her the cup. "Drink that up."

"Why did the men hurt my mommy? Didn't they want her to have a good time?"

"I guess not," I said. I began to cry. I held her on my lap, wiping away the tears with the backs of my hands.

"You should have taken some sad-pills, too," Ki said. She held out her cocoa. Her hair ribbons, which I had tied in big sloppy bows, bobbed. "Here. Drink some."

I drank some. From the north end of the house came another grinding, crackling crash. The low rumble of the generator stuttered and the house went gray again. Shadows raced across Ki's small face.

"Hold on," I told her. "Try not to be scared. Maybe the lights will come back." A moment later they did, although now I could hear a hoarse, uneven note in the gennie's roar and the flicker of the lights was much more noticeable.

"Tell me a story," she said. "Tell me about Cinderbell."

"Cinderella."

"Yeah, her."

"All right, but storyguys get paid." I pursed my lips and made sipping sounds.

She held the cup out. The cocoa was sweet and good. The sensation of being watched was heavy and not sweet at all, but let them watch. Let them watch while they could.

"There was this pretty girl named Cinderella —"

"Once upon a time! That's how it starts!

That's how they all start!"

"That's right, I forgot. Once upon a time there was this pretty girl named Cinderella, who had two mean stepsisters. Their names were . . . do you remember?"

"Tammy Faye and Vanna."

"Yeah, the Queens of Hairspray. And they made Cinderella do all the really unpleasant chores, like sweeping out the fireplace and cleaning up the dogpoop in the back yard. Now it just so happened that the noted rock band Oasis was going to play a gig at the palace, and although all the girls had been invited . . ."

I got as far as the part about the fairy god-mother catching the mice and turning them into a Mercedes limousine before the Bena-dryl took effect. It really was a medicine for sadness; when I looked down, Ki was fast asleep in the crook of my arm with her cocoa cup listing radically to port. I plucked it from her fingers and put it on the coffee-table, then brushed her drying hair off her forehead.

"Ki?"

Nothing. She'd gone to the land of Noddy-Blinky. It probably helped that her afternoon nap had ended almost before it got started.

I picked her up and carried her down to the north bedroom, her feet bouncing limply in the air and the hem of the Harley shirt flipping around her knees. I put her on the bed and pulled the duvet up to her chin. Thunder boomed like artillery fire, but she didn't even stir. Exhaustion, grief, Benadryl . . . they had taken her deep, taken her beyond ghosts and sorrow, and that was good.

I bent over and kissed her cheek, which had finally begun to cool. "I'll take care of you," I said. "I promised, and I will."

As if hearing me, Ki turned on her side, put the hand holding Strickland under her jaw, and made a soft sighing sound. Her lashes were dark soot against her cheeks, in startling contrast to her light hair. Looking at her I felt myself swept by love, shaken by it the way one is shaken by a sickness.

Take care of me, I'm just a little guy.

"I will, Ki-bird," I said.

I went into the bathroom and began filling the tub, as I had once filled it in my sleep. She would sleep through it all if I could get enough warm water before the generator quit entirely. I wished I had a bath-toy to give her in case she did wake up, something like Wilhelm the Spouting Whale, but she'd have her dog, and she probably wouldn't wake up, anyway. No freezing baptism under a handpump for Kyra. I was not cruel, and I was not crazy.

I had only disposable razors in the medicine cabinet, no good for the other job ahead of me. Not efficient enough. But one of the kitchen steak knives would do. If I filled the washbasin with water that was really hot, I wouldn't even feel it. A letter *T* on each arm, the top bar drawn across the wrists —

For a moment I came out of the zone. A voice — my own speaking as some combination of Jo and Mattie — screamed: *What are you thinking about? Oh Mike, what in God's name are you thinking about?*

Then the thunder boomed, the lights flickered, and the rain began to pour down again, driven by the wind. I went back into that place where everything was clear, my course indisputable. Let it all end — the sorrow, the hurt, the fear. I didn't want to think anymore about how Mattie had danced with her toes on the Frisbee as if it were a spotlight. I didn't want to be there when Kyra woke up, didn't want to see the misery fill her eyes. I didn't want to get through the night ahead, the day that was coming beyond it, or the day that was coming after that. They were all cars on the same old mystery train. Life was a sickness. I was going to give her a nice warm bath and cure her of it. I raised my arms. In the medicine cabinet mirror a murky figure — a Shape — raised its own in a kind of jocular greeting. It was me. It had been me all along, and that was all right. That was just fine.

★ ★ ★

I dropped to one knee and checked the
water. It was coming in nice and warm.
Good. Even if the generator quit now, it
would be fine. The tub was an old one, a
deep one. As I walked down to the kitchen
to get the knife, I thought about climbing in
with her after I had finished cutting my
wrists in the hotter water of the basin. No, I
decided. It might be misinterpreted by the
people who would come here later on,
people with nasty minds and nastier assumptions. The ones who'd come when the
storm was over and the trees across the road
cleared away. No, after her bath I would dry
her and put her back in bed with Strickland
in her hand. I'd sit across the room from
her, in the rocking chair by the bedroom
windows. I would spread some towels in my
lap to keep as much of the blood off my
pants as I could, and eventually I would go
to sleep, too.

Bunter's bell was still ringing. Much
louder now. It was getting on my nerves,
and if it kept on that way it might even wake
the baby. I decided to pull it down and silence it for good. I crossed the room, and as
I did a strong gust of air blew past me. It
wasn't a draft from the broken kitchen
window; this was that warm subway-air
again. It blew the *Tough Stuff* crossword
book onto the floor, but the paperweight on

775

the manuscript kept the loose pages from following. As I looked in that direction, Bunter's bell fell silent.

A voice sighed across the dim room. Words I couldn't make out. And what did they matter? What did one more manifestation — one more blast of hot air from the Great Beyond — matter?

Thunder rolled and the sigh came again. This time, as the generator died and the lights went out, plunging the room into gray shadow, I got one word in the clear:

Nineteen.

I turned on my heels, making a nearly complete circle. I finished up looking across the shadowy room at the manuscript of *My Childhood Friend.* Suddenly the light broke. Understanding arrived.

Not the crossword book. Not the phone book, either.

My book. My manuscript.

I crossed to it, vaguely aware that the water had stopped running into the tub in the north-wing bathroom. When the generator died, the pump had quit. That was all right, it would be plenty deep enough already. And warm. I would give Kyra her bath, but first there was something I had to do. I had to go down nineteen, and after that I just might have to go down ninety-two. And I could. I had completed just over a hundred and twenty pages of manuscript, so I could. I grabbed the battery-powered lantern from the top of the cabinet where I still kept several hundred actual vinyl records, clicked it on, and set it on the table. It cast a white circle of radiance on the manuscript — in the gloom of that afternoon it was as bright as a spotlight.

On page nineteen of *My Childhood Friend*, Tiffi Taylor — the call-girl who had re-invented herself as Regina Whiting — was sitting in her studio with Andy Drake, reliving the day that John Sanborn (the alias under which John Shackleford had been getting by) saved her three-year-old daughter, Karen. This is the passage I read as the thunder boomed and the rain slashed against the sliding door giving on the deck:

```
FRIEND, by Noonan/Pg. 19

over that way, I was sure of
     it," she said, "but
when I couldn't see her any-
     where, I went to
look in the hot tub." She lit a
     cigarette. "What I
saw made me feel like scream-
     ing, Andy — Karen was
underwater. All that was out
     was her hand . . . the
```

nails were turning purple.
      After that . . . I guess I
dived in, but I don't remember;
      I was zoned out.
Everything from then on is like
      a dream where stuff
runs together in your mind. The
      yard-guy — Sanborn —
shoved me aside and dived. His
      foot hit me in the
throat and I couldn't swallow
      for a week. He yanked
up on Karen's arm. I thought
      he'd pull it off her
damn shoulder, but he got her.
      He got her."
   In the gloom, Drake saw she
      was weeping. "God.
Oh God, I thought she was dead.
      I was sure she was."

I knew at once, but laid my steno pad along the left margin of the manuscript so I could see it better. Reading down, as you'd read a vertical crossword-puzzle answer, the first letter of each line spelled the message which had been there almost since I began the book:

owls undEr stud O

Then, allowing for the indent next-to-last

line from the bottom:

owls undEr studIO

Bill Dean, my caretaker, is sitting behind the wheel of his truck. He has accomplished his two purposes in coming here — welcoming me back to the TR and warning me off Mattie Devore. Now he's ready to go. He smiles at me, displaying those big false teeth, those Roebuckers. "If you get a chance, you ought to look for the owls," he tells me. I ask him what Jo would have wanted with a couple of plastic owls and he replies that they keep the crows from shitting up the woodwork. I accept that, I have other things to think about, but still . . . "It was like she'd come down to do that errand special," he says. It never crosses my mind — not then, at least — that in Indian folklore, owls have another purpose: they are said to keep evil spirits away. If Jo knew that plastic owls would scare the crows off, she would have known that. It was just the sort of information she picked up and tucked away. My inquisitive wife. My brilliant scatterbrain.

Thunder rolled. Lightning ate at the clouds like spills of bright acid. I stood by the dining-room table with the manuscript in my unsteady hands.

"Christ, Jo," I whispered. "What did you find out?"

And why didn't you tell me?

779

But I thought I knew the answer to that. She hadn't told me because I was somehow like Max Devore; his great-grandfather and my own had shit in the same pit. It didn't make any sense, but there it was. And she hadn't told her own brother, either. I took a weird kind of comfort from that.

I began to leaf through the manuscript, my skin crawling.

Andy Drake rarely frowned in Michael Noonan's *My Childhood Friend*. He scowled instead, because there's an owl in every scowl. Before coming to Florida, John Shackleford had been living in Studio City, California. Drake's first meeting with Regina Whiting occurred in her studio. Ray Garraty's last-known address was the Studio Apartments in Key Largo. Regina Whiting's best friend was Steffie Underwood. Steffi's husband was Towle Underwood — there was a good one, two for the price of one.

Owls under studio.

It was everywhere, on every page, just like the *K*-names in the telephone book. A kind of monument, this one built — I was sure of it — not by Sara Tidwell but by Johanna Arlen Noonan. My wife passing messages behind the guard's back, praying with all her considerable heart that I would see and understand.

On page ninety-two Shackleford was talking to Drake in the prison visitors' room

— sitting with his wrists between his knees, looking down at the chain running between his ankles, refusing to make eye-contact with Drake.

FRIEND, by Noonan/Pg. 92

only thing I got to say. Any-
     thing else, fuck,
what good would it do? Life's a
     game, and I
lost. You want me to tell you
     that I yanked
some little kid out of the
     water, pulled her
up, got her motor going again?
     I did, but
not because I'm a hero or a
     saint . . ."

There was more but no need to read it. The message, *owls under studio,* ran down the margin just as it had on page nineteen. As it probably did on any number of other pages as well. I remembered how deliriously happy I had been to discover that the block had been dissolved and I could write again. It had been dissolved all right, but not because I'd finally beaten it or found a way around it. *Jo* had dissolved it. *Jo* had beaten it, and my continued career as a writer of second-rate thrillers had been the least of her concerns when she did it. As I stood there in the flicker-flash of lightning, feeling my unseen guests swirl around me in the unsteady air, I remembered Mrs. Moran, my first-grade teacher. When your efforts to replicate the smooth curves of the Palmer Method alphabet on the blackboard began to flag and waver, she would put her large competent hand over yours and help you.

So had Jo helped me.

I riffled through the manuscript and saw the key words everywhere, sometimes placed so you could actually read them stacked on different lines, one above the other. How hard she had tried to tell me this . . . and I had no intention of doing anything else until I found out why.

I dropped the manuscript back on the table, but before I could re-anchor it, a furious gust of freezing air blew past me, lifting the pages and scattering them everywhere in a cyclone. If that force could have ripped them to shreds, I'm sure that it would have.

No! it cried as I grabbed the lantern's handle. *No, finish the job!*

Wind blew around my face in chill gusts — it was as if someone I couldn't quite see was standing right in front of me and breathing in my face, retreating as I moved forward, huffing and puffing like the big bad wolf outside the houses of the three little pigs.

I hung the lantern over my arm, held my hands out in front of me, and clapped them together sharply. The cold puffs in my face ceased. There was now only the random swirling air coming in through the partially plugged kitchen window. "She's sleeping," I said to what I knew was still there, silently watching. "There's time."

I went out the back door and the wind took me at once, making me stagger sideways, almost knocking me over. And in the wavering trees I saw green faces, the faces of the dead. Devore's was there, and Royce's, and Son Tidwell's. Most of all I saw Sara's.

Everywhere Sara.

No! Go back! You don't need no truck with no owls, sugar! Go back! Finish the job! Do what you came for!

"I don't *know* what I came for," I said. "And until I find out, I'm not doing *any-thing.*"

The wind screamed as if in offense, and a huge branch split off the pine standing to the right of the house. It fell on top of my Chevrolet in a spray of water, denting the roof before rolling off on my side.

Clapping my hands out here would be every bit as useful as King Canute commanding the tide to turn. This was her world, not mine . . . and only the edge of it, at that. Every step closer to The Street and the lake would bring me closer to that

783

world's heart, where time was thin and spirits ruled. Oh dear God, what had happened to cause this?

The path to Jo's studio had turned into a creek. I got a dozen steps down it before a rock turned under my foot and I fell heavily on my side. Lightning zigged across the sky, there was the crack of another breaking branch, and then something was falling toward me. I put my hands up to shield my face and rolled to the right, off the path. The branch splashed to the ground just behind me, and I tumbled halfway down a slope that was slick with soaked needles. At last I was able to pull myself to my feet. The branch on the path was even bigger than the one which had landed on the roof of the car. If it had struck me, it likely would have bashed in my skull.

Go back! A hissing, spiteful wind through the trees.

Finish it! The slobbering, guttural voice of the lake slamming into the rocks and the bank below The Street.

Mind your business! That was the very house itself, groaning on its foundations. *Mind your business and let me mind mine!*

But Kyra *was* my business. Kyra was my daughter.

I picked up the lantern. The housing was cracked but the bulb glowed bright and steady — that was one for the home team.

Bent over against the howling wind, hand raised to ward off more falling branches, I slipped and stumbled my way down the hill to my dead wife's studio.

Chapter 27

At first the door wouldn't open. The knob turned under my hand so I knew it wasn't locked, but the rain seemed to have swelled the wood . . . or had something been shoved up against it? I drew back, crouched a little, and hit the door with my shoulder. This time there was some slight give.

It was her. Sara. Standing on the other side of the door and trying to hold it shut against me. How could she do that? How, in God's name? She was a fucking ghost!

I thought of the BAMM CONSTRUCTION pickup . . . and as if thought were conjuration I could almost see it out there at the end of Lane Forty-two, parked by the highway. The old ladies' sedan was behind it, and three or four other cars were now behind them. All of them with their windshield wipers flopping back and forth, their headlights cutting feeble cones through the downpour. They were lined up on the shoulder like cars at a yard sale. There was no yard sale here, only the old-timers sitting silently in their cars. Old-timers who were in the zone just like I was. Old-timers sending in the vibe.

She was drawing on them. *Stealing* from them. She'd done the same with Devore —

and me too, of course. Many of the manifestations I'd experienced since coming back had likely been created from my own psychic energy. It was amusing when you thought of it.

Or maybe "terrifying" was the word I was actually looking for.

"Jo, help me," I said in the pouring rain. Lightning flashed, turning the torrents a bright brief silver. "If you ever loved me, help me now."

I drew back and hit the door again. This time there was no resistance at all and I went hurtling in, catching my shin on the jamb and falling to my knees. I held onto the lantern, though.

There was a moment of silence. In it I felt forces and presences gathering themselves. In that moment nothing seemed to move, although behind me, in the woods Jo had loved to ramble — with me or without me — the rain continued to fall and the wind continued to howl, a merciless gardener pruning its way through the trees that were dead and almost dead, doing the work of ten gentler years in one turbulent hour. Then the door slammed shut and it began. I saw everything in the glow of the flashlight, which I had turned on without even realizing it, but at first I didn't know exactly what I was seeing, other than the destruction by poltergeist of my wife's beloved crafts and treasures.

The framed afghan square tore itself off the wall and flew from one side of the studio to the other, the black oak frame breaking apart. The heads popped off the dolls poking out of the baby collages like champagne corks at a party. The hanging light-globe shattered, showering me with fragments of glass. A wind began to blow — a cold one — and was quickly joined and whirled into a cyclone by one which was warmer, almost hot. They rolled past me as if in imitation of the larger storm outside.

The Sara Laughs head on the bookcase, the one which appeared to be constructed of toothpicks and lollipop sticks, exploded in a cloud of wood-splinters. The kayak paddle leaning against the wall rose into the air, rowed furiously at nothing, then launched itself at me like a spear. I threw myself flat on the green rag rug to avoid it, and felt bits of broken glass from the shattered light-globe cut into the palm of my hand as I came down. I felt something else, as well — a ridge of something beneath the rug. The paddle hit the far wall hard enough to split into two pieces.

Now the banjo my wife had never been able to master rose in the air, revolved twice, and played a bright rattle of notes that were out of tune but nonetheless unmistakable — wish I was in the land of cotton, old times there are not forgotten. The phrase ended with a vicious BLUNK! that broke all five strings. The banjo whirled itself a third time, its bright steel fittings reflecting fishscale runs of light on the study walls, and then beat itself to death against the floor, the drum shattering and the tuning pegs snapping off like teeth.

The sound of moving air began to — how do I express this? — to *focus* somehow, until it wasn't the sound of air but the sound of voices — panting, unearthly voices full of fury. They would have screamed if they'd had vocal cords to scream with. Dusty air swirled up in the beam of my flashlight, making helix shapes that danced together, then reeled apart again. For just a moment I heard Sara's snarling, smoke-broken voice: *"Git out, bitch! You git on out! This ain't none of yours —"* And then a curious insubstantial thud, as if air had collided with air. This was followed by a rushing wind-tunnel shriek that I recognized: I'd heard it in the middle of the night. Jo was screaming. Sara was hurting her, Sara was punishing her for presuming to interfere, and Jo was screaming.

"No!" I shouted, getting to my feet. "Leave her alone! Leave her be!" I advanced into the room, swinging the lantern in front of my face as if I could beat her away with it. Stoppered bottles stormed past me — some contained dried flowers, some carefully sectioned mushrooms, some woods-herbs. They shattered against the far wall with a brittle xylophone sound. None of them struck me; it was as if an unseen hand guided them away.

Then Jo's rolltop desk rose into the air. It must have weighed at least four hundred pounds with its drawers loaded as they were, but it floated like a feather, nodding first one way and then dipping the other in the opposing currents of air.

Jo screamed again, this time in anger rather than pain, and I staggered backward against the closed door with a feeling that I had been scooped hollow. Sara wasn't the only one who could steal the energy of the living, it appeared. White semeny stuff — ectoplasm, I guess — spilled from the desk's pigeonholes in a dozen little streams, and the desk suddenly launched itself across the room. It flew almost too fast to follow with the eye. Anyone standing in front of it would have been smashed flat. There was a head-splitting shriek of protest and agony — Sara this time, I knew it was — and then the desk struck the wall, breaking through it and letting in the rain and the wind. The rolltop snapped loose of its slot and hung like a jointed tongue. All the drawers shot out. Spools of thread, skeins of yarn, little flora/fauna identification books and woods guides, thimbles, notebooks, knitting needles, dried-up Magic Markers — Jo's early remains, Ki might have called them. They flew everywhere like bones and bits of hair cruelly scattered from a disinterred coffin.

"Stop it," I croaked. "Stop it, both of you. That's enough."

But there was no need to tell them. Except for the furious beat of the storm, I was alone in the ruins of my wife's studio. The battle was over. At least for the time being.

I knelt and doubled up the green rag rug, carefully folding into it as much of the shattered glass from the light as I could. Beneath it was a trapdoor giving on a triangular storage area created by the slope of the land as it dropped toward the lake. The ridge I'd felt was one of the trap's hinges. I had known about this area and had meant to check it for the owls. Then things began to happen and I'd forgotten.

There was a recessed ring in the trapdoor. I grabbed it, ready for more resistance, but it swung up easily. The smell that wafted up froze me in my tracks. Not damp decay, at least not at first, but Red — Jo's favorite perfume. It hung around me for a moment and then it was gone. What replaced it was the smell of rain, roots, and wet earth. Not pleasant, but I had smelled far worse down by the lake near that damned birch tree.

I shone my light down three steep steps. I

could see a squat shape that turned out to be an old toilet — I could vaguely remember Bill and Kenny Auster putting it under here back in 1990 or '91. There were steel boxes — filing cabinet drawers, actually — wrapped in plastic and stacked up on pallets. Old records and papers. An eight-track tape player wrapped in a plastic bag. An old VCR next to it, in another one. And over in the corner —

I sat down, hung my legs over, and felt something touch the ankle I had turned in the lake. I shone my light between my knees and for one moment saw a young black kid. Not the one drowned in the lake, though — this one was older and quite a lot bigger. Twelve, maybe fourteen. The drowned boy had been no more than eight.

This one bared his teeth at me and hissed like a cat. There were no pupils in his eyes; like those of the boy in the lake, his eyes were entirely white, like the eyes of a statue. And he was shaking his head. *Don't come down here, white man. Let the dead rest in peace.*

"But you're not at peace," I said, and shone the light full on him. I had a momentary glimpse of a truly hideous thing. I could see through him, but I could also see *into* him: the rotting remains of his tongue in his mouth, his eyes in their sockets, his brain simmering like a spoiled egg in its case of skull. Then he was gone, and there was nothing but one of those swirling dust-helixes.

I went down, holding the lantern raised. Below it, nests of shadows rocked and seemed to reach upward.

The storage area (it was really no more than a glorified crawlspace) had been floored with wooden pallets, just to keep stuff off the ground. Now water ran beneath these in a steady river, and enough of the earth had eroded to make even crawling unsteady work. The smell of perfume was entirely gone. What had replaced it was a nasty riverbottom smell and — unlikely given the conditions, I know, but it was there — the faint, sullen smell of ash and fire.

I saw what I'd come for almost at once. Jo's mail-order owls, the ones she had taken delivery of herself in November of 1993, were in the northeast corner, where there were only about two feet between the sloped pallet flooring and the underside of the studio. *Gorry, but they looked real,* Bill had said, and Gorry if he wasn't right: in the bright glow of the lantern they looked like birds first swaddled, then suffocated in clear plastic. Their eyes were bright wedding rings circling wide black pupils. Their plastic feathers were painted the dark green of pine needles, their bellies a shade of dirty orange-white. I crawled toward them over the squelching, shifting pallets, the glow of the lantern bobbing back and forth between them, trying not to wonder if that boy was behind me, creeping in pursuit. When I got to the owls, I raised my head without thinking and thudded it against the insulation which ran beneath the studio floor. *Thump once for yes, twice for no, asshole,* I thought.

I hooked my fingers into the plastic which wrapped the owls and pulled them toward me. I wanted to be out of here. The sensation of water running just beneath me was strange and unpleasant. So was the smell of fire, which seemed stronger now in spite of the damp. Suppose the studio was burning? Suppose Sara had somehow set it alight? I'd roast down here even while the storm's muddy runoff was soaking my legs and belly.

One of the owls stood on a plastic base, I saw — the better to set him on your deck or stoop to scare the crows, my dear — but the base the other should have been attached to was missing. I backed toward the trapdoor, holding the lantern in one hand and dragging the plastic sack of owls in the other, wincing each time thunder cannonaded over my head. I'd only gotten a little way when the damp tape holding the plastic gave way. The owl missing its base tilted slowly toward me, its black-gold eyes staring raptly into my own.

A swirl of air. A faint, comforting whiff of Red perfume. I pulled the owl out by the hornlike tufts growing from its forehead and turned it upside down. Where it had once been attached to its plastic base there were now only two pegs with a hollow space between them. Inside the hole was a small tin box that I recognized even before I reached into the owl's belly and chivvied it out. I shone the lantern on its front, knowing what I'd see: JO'S NOTIONS, written in old-fashioned gilt script. She had found the box in an antiques barn somewhere.

I looked at it, my heart beating hard. Thunder boomed overhead. The trapdoor stood open, but I had forgotten about going up. I had forgotten about everything but the tin box I held in my hand, a box roughly the size of a cigar box but not quite as deep. I spread my hand over the cover and pulled it off.

There was a strew of folded papers lying on top of a pair of steno books, the wire-bound ones I keep around for notes and character lists. These had been rubber-banded together. On top of everything else was a shiny black square. Until I picked it up and held it close to the side of the lantern, I didn't realize it was a photo negative.

Ghostly, reversed and faintly orange, I

saw Jo in her gray two-piece bathing suit. She was standing on the swimming float with her hands behind her head.

"Jo," I said, and then couldn't say anything else. My throat had closed up with tears. I held the negative for a moment, not wanting to lose contact with it, then put it back in the box with the papers and steno books. This stuff was why she had come to Sara in July of 1994; to gather it up and hide it as well as she could. She had taken the owls off the deck (Frank had heard the door out there bang) and had carried them out here. I could almost see her prying the base off one owl and stuffing the tin box up its plastic wazoo, wrapping both of them in plastic, then dragging them down here, all while her brother sat smoking Marlboros and feeling the vibrations. The bad vibrations. I doubted if I would ever know all the reasons why she'd done it, or what her frame of mind had been . . . but she had almost certainly believed I'd find my own way down here eventually. Why else had she left the negative?

The loose papers were mostly photocopied press clippings from the *Castle Rock Call* and from the *Weekly News*, the paper which had apparently preceded the *Call*. The dates were marked on each in my wife's neat, firm hand. The oldest clipping was from 1865, and was headed **ANOTHER HOME SAFE**. The returnee was one Jared

Devore, age thirty-two. Suddenly I understood one of the things that had puzzled me: the generations which didn't seem to match up. A Sara Tidwell song came to mind as I crouched there on the pallets with my lantern shining down on that old-timey type. It was the ditty that went *The old folks do it and the young folks, too / And the old folks show the young folks just what to do* . . .

By the time Sara and the Red-Tops showed up in Castle County and settled on what became known as Tidwell's Meadow, Jared Devore would have been sixty-seven or -eight. Old but still hale. A veteran of the Civil War. The sort of older man younger men might look up to. And Sara's song was right — the old folks show the young folks just what to do.

What exactly had they done?

The clippings about Sara and the Red-Tops didn't tell. I only skimmed them, anyway, but the overall tone shook me, just the same. I'd describe it as unfailing genial contempt. The Red-Tops were "our Southern blackbirds" and "our rhythmic darkies." They were "full of dusky good-nature." Sara herself was "a marvellous figure of a Negro woman with broad nose, full lips, and noble brow" who "fascinated men-folk and women-folk alike with her animal high spirits, flashing smile, and raucous laugh."

They were, God keep us and save us, re-

797

views. Good ones, if you didn't mind being called full of dusky good-nature.

I shuffled through them quickly, looking for anything about the circumstances under which "our Southern blackbirds" had left. I found nothing. What I found instead was a clipping from the *Call* marked July 19th (*go down nineteen*, I thought), 1933. The headline read **VETERAN GUIDE, CARETAKER, CANNOT SAVE DAUGHTER.** According to the story, Fred Dean had been fighting the wildfires in the eastern part of the TR with two hundred other men when the wind had suddenly changed, menacing the north end of the lake, which had previously been considered safe. At that time a great many local people had kept fishing and hunting camps up there (this much I knew myself). The community had had a general store and an actual name, Halo Bay. Fred's wife, Hilda, was there with the Dean twins, William and Carla, age three, while her husband was off eating smoke. A good many other wives and kids were in Halo Bay, as well.

The fires had come fast when the wind changed, the paper said — "like marching explosions." They jumped the only firebreak the men had left in that direction and headed for the far end of the lake. At Halo Bay there were no men to take charge, and apparently no women able or willing to do so. They panicked instead, racing to load

798

their cars with children and camp possessions, clogging the one road out with their
vehicles. Eventually one of the old cars or
trucks broke down and as the fires roared
closer, running through woods that hadn't
seen rain since late April, the women who'd
waited found their way out blocked.

The volunteer firefighters came to the
rescue in time, but when Fred Dean got to
his wife, one of a party of women trying to
push a balky stalled Ford coupe out of the
road, he made a terrible discovery. Billy lay
on the floor in the back of the car, fast
asleep, but Carla was missing. Hilda had
gotten them both in, all right — they had
been on the back seat, holding hands just as
they always did. But at some point, after her
brother had crawled onto the floor and
dozed off and while Hilda was stuffing a few
last items into the trunk, Carla must have
remembered a toy or a doll and returned to
the cottage to get it. While she was doing
that, her mother had gotten into their old
DeSoto and driven away without rechecking
the babies. Carla Dean was either still in the
cottage at Halo Bay or making her way up
the road on foot. Either way the fires would
run her down.

The road was too narrow to get a vehicle
turned around and too blocked to get one of
those pointed in the right direction through
the crush. So Fred Dean, hero that he was,

set off on the run toward the smoke-blackened horizon, where bright ribbons of orange had already begun to shine through. The wind-driven fire had crowned and raced to meet him like a lover.

I knelt on the pallets, reading this by the glow of my lantern, and all at once the smell of fire and burning intensified. I coughed . . . and then the cough was choked off by the iron taste of water in my mouth and throat. Once again, this time kneeling in the storage area beneath my wife's studio, I felt as if I were drowning. Once again I leaned forward and retched up nothing but a little spit.

I turned and saw the lake. The loons were screaming on its hazy surface, making their way toward me in a line, beating their wings against the water as they came. The blue of the sky had been blotted out. The air smelled of charcoal and gunpowder. Ash had begun to sift down from the sky. The eastern verge of Dark Score was in flames, and I could hear occasional muffled reports as hollow trees exploded. They sounded like depth charges.

I looked down, wanting to break free of this vision, knowing that in another moment or two it wouldn't be anything so distant as a vision but as real as the trip Kyra and I had made to the Fryeburg Fair. Instead of a plastic owl with gold-ringed eyes, I was looking at a child with bright blue ones. She was sitting on a picnic table, holding out her chubby arms and crying. I saw her as clearly as I saw my own face in the mirror each morning when I shaved. I saw she was about *Kyra's age but much plumper, and her hair is black instead of blonde. Her hair is the shade her brother's will remain until it finally begins to go gray in the impossibly distant summer of 1998, a year she will never see unless someone gets her out of this hell. She wears a white dress and red knee-stockings and she holds her arms out to me, calling* Daddy, Daddy.

I start toward her and then there is a blast of organized heat that tears me apart for a moment — I am the ghost here, I realize, and Fred Dean has just run right through me. Daddy, *she cries, but to him, not me.* Daddy! *and she hugs him, unmindful of the soot smearing her white silk dress and her chubby face as he kisses her and more soot begins to fall and the loons beat their way in toward shore, seeming to weep in shrill lamentation.*

Daddy the fire is coming! *she cries as he scoops her into his arms.*

I know, be brave, *he says.* We're gonna be all right, sugarplum, but you have to be brave.

The fire isn't just coming; it has come. The entire east end of Halo Bay is in flames and now they're moving this way, eating one by one the little cabins where the men like to lay up drunk in hunting season and ice-fishing season. Behind Al LeRoux's, the washing Marguerite hung out that morning is in flames, pants and dresses and underwear burning on lines which are themselves strings of fire. Leaves and bark shower down; a burning ember touches Carla's neck and she shrieks with pain. Fred slaps it away as he carries her down the slope of land to the water.

Don't do it! *I scream. I know all this is beyond my power to change, but I scream at him anyway, try to change it anyway.* Fight it! For Christ's sake, fight it!

Daddy, who is that man? *Carla asks, and points at me as the green-shingled roof of the Dean place catches fire.*

Fred glances toward where she is pointing, and in his face I see a spasm of guilt. He knows what he's doing, that's the terrible thing — way down deep he knows exactly what he is doing here at Halo Bay where The Street ends. He knows and he's afraid that someone will witness his work. But he sees nothing.

Or does he? There is a momentary doubtful widening of the eyes as if he does *spy something — a dancing helix of air, perhaps. Or does he feel me? Is that it? Does he feel a momentary cold draft in all this heat? One that feels like protesting hands, hands that would restrain if they only had substance? Then he looks away; then he is wading into the water beside the Deans' stub of a dock.*

Fred! *I scream.* For God's sake, man, look at her! Do you think your wife put her in a white silk dress by accident? Is that anyone's idea of a play-dress?

Daddy, why are we going in the water? *she asks.*

To get away from the fire, sugarplum.

Daddy, I can't swim!

You won't have to, *he replies, and what a chill I feel at that! Because it's no lie — she won't have to swim, not now, not ever. And at least Fred's way will be more merciful than Normal Auster's when Normal's turn comes — more merciful than the squalling handpump, the gallons of freezing water.*

Her white dress floats around her like a lily. Her red stockings shimmer in the water. She hugs his neck tightly and now they are among the fleeing loons; the loons spank the water with their powerful wings, churning up curds of foam and staring at the man and the girl with their distraught red eyes. The air is heavy with smoke and the sky is gone. I stagger after them, wading — I can feel the cold of the water, although I don't splash and leave no wake. The eastern and northern edges of the lake are both on fire now — there is a burning crescent around us as Fred Dean wades deeper with his daughter, carrying her as if to some baptismal rite. And still he tells himself he is trying to save her, only to save her, just as all her life Hilda will tell herself that the child just wandered back to the cottage to look for a toy, that she was not left behind on purpose, left in her white dress and red stockings to be found by her father, who once did some-thing unspeakable. This is the past, this is the Land of Ago, and here the sins of the fathers are visited on the children, even unto the sev-enth generation, which is not yet.

He takes her deeper and she begins to scream. Her screams mingle with the screams of the loons until he stops the sound with a kiss upon her terrified mouth. "Love you, Daddy loves his sugarplum," *he says, and then lowers her. It is to be a full-immersion baptism, then, except there is no shorebank choir singing "Shall We Gather at the River" and no one shouting* Hal-lelujah! *and he is not letting her come back up. She struggles furiously in the white bloom of her sacrificial dress, and after a moment he cannot bear to watch her; he looks across the lake in-stead, to the west where the fire hasn't yet touched (and never will), to the west where skies are still blue. Ash sifts around him like black rain and the tears pour out of his eyes and as she struggles furiously beneath his hands, trying to free herself from his drowning grip, he tells himself* It was an accident, just a terrible ac-cident, I took her out in the lake because it was the only place I *could* take her, the only place left, and she panicked, she started to struggle, she was all wet and all slippery and I lost my good hold on her and then I lost *any* hold on her and then —

I forget I'm a ghost. I scream "Kia! Hold on, Ki!" and dive. I reach her, I see her terrified face, her bulging blue eyes, her rosebud of a mouth which is trailing a silver line of bubbles toward the surface where Fred stands in water up to his neck, holding her down while he tells himself over and over that he was trying to save her, it was the only way, he was trying to save her, it was the only way. I reach for her, again and again I reach for her, my child, my daughter, my Kia (they are all Kia, the boys as well as the girls, all my daughter), and each time my arms go through her. Worse — oh, far worse — is that now she is reaching for me, her dappled arms floating out, begging for rescue. Her groping hands melt through mine. We cannot touch, because now I am the ghost. I am the ghost and as her struggles weaken I realize that I can't I can't oh I

couldn't breathe — I was drowning.

I doubled over, opened my mouth, and this time a great spew of lakewater came out, soaking the plastic owl which lay on the pallet by my knees. I hugged the JO'S NOTIONS box to my chest, not wanting the contents to get wet, and the movement triggered another retch. This time cold water poured from my nose as well as my mouth. I dragged in a deep breath, then coughed it out.

"This has got to end," I said, but of course this *was* the end, one way or the other. Because Kyra was last.

I climbed up the steps to the studio and sat on the littered floor to get my breath.

Outside, the thunder boomed and the rain fell, but I thought the storm had passed its peak of fury. Or maybe I only hoped.

I rested with my legs hanging down through the trap — there were no more ghosts here to touch my ankles, I don't know how I knew that but I did — and stripped off the rubber bands holding the steno notebooks together. I opened the first one, paged through it, and saw it was almost filled with Jo's handwriting and a number of folded typed sheets (Courier type, of course), single-spaced: the fruit of all those clandestine trips down to the TR during 1993 and 1994. Fragmentary notes, for the most part, and transcriptions of tapes which might still be down below me in the storage space somewhere. Tucked away with the VCR or the eight-track player, perhaps. But I didn't need them. When the time came — if the time came — I was sure I'd find most of the story here. What had happened, who had done it, how it was covered up. Right now I didn't care. Right now I only wanted to make sure that Kyra was safe and stayed safe. There was only one way to do that.

Lye stille.

I attempted to slip the rubber bands around the steno books again, and the one I hadn't looked at slipped out of my wet hand and fell to the floor. A torn slip of green paper fell out. I picked it up and saw this:

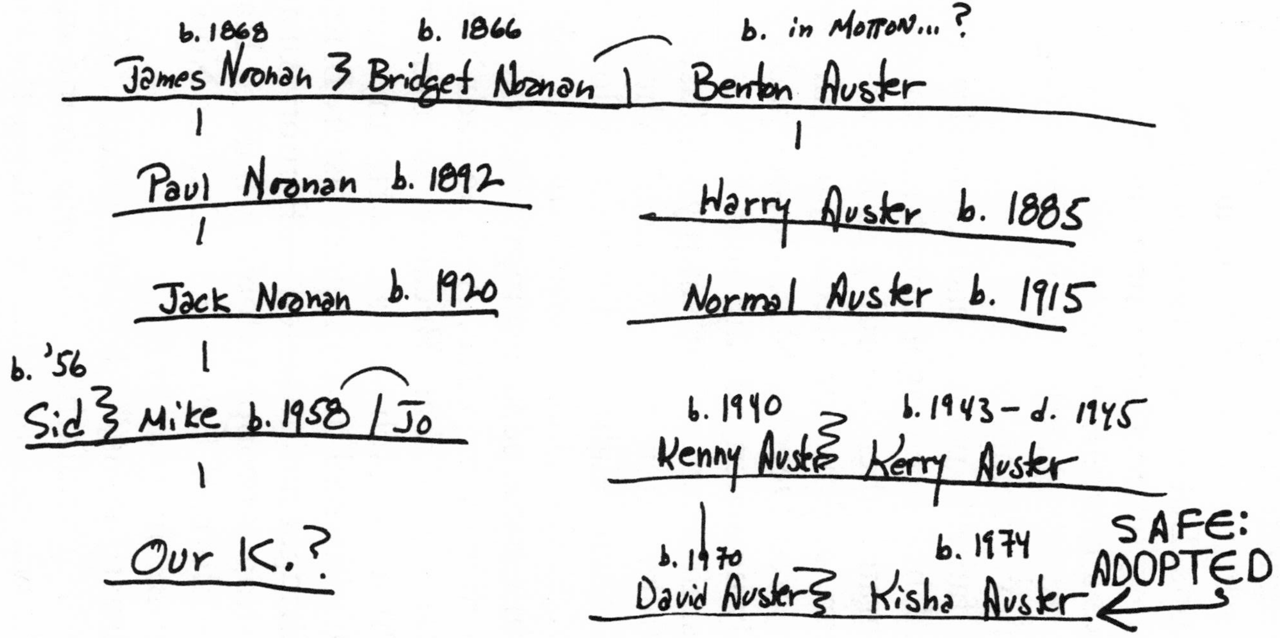
b. 1868
James Noonan
b. 1866
Bridget Noonan
b. in MOTTON... ?
Benton Auster
Paul Noonan b. 1892
Harry Auster b. 1885
Jack Noonan b. 1920
Normal Auster b. 1915
b. '56
Sid
Mike b. 1958 / Jo
b. 1940
Kenny Auster
b. 1943 – d. 1945
Kerry Auster
Our K.?
b. 1970
David Auster
b. 1974
Kisha Auster
SAFE:
ADOPTED

For a moment I came out of that strange and heightened awareness I'd been living in; the world fell back into its accustomed dimensions. But the colors were all too strong, somehow, objects too emphatically *present*. I felt like a battlefield soldier suddenly illuminated by a ghastly white flare, one that shows everything.

My father's people had come from The Neck, I had been right about that much; my great-grandfather according to this was James Noonan, and he had never shit in the same pit as Jared Devore. Max Devore had either been lying when he said that to Mattie . . . or misinformed . . . or simply confused, the way folks often get confused when they reach their eighties. Even a fellow like Devore, who had stayed mostly sharp, wouldn't have been exempt from the occasional nick in his edge. And he hadn't been that far off at that. Because, according to this little scratch of a chart, my great-grandfather had had an older sister, Bridget. And Bridget had married — Benton Auster.

My finger dropped down a line, to Harry Auster. Born of Benton and Bridget Noonan Auster in the year 1885.

"Christ Jesus," I whispered. "Kenny Auster's grandfather was my granduncle. And he was one of them. Whatever they did, Harry Auster was one of them. That's the connection."

I thought of Kyra with sudden sharp terror. She had been up at the house by herself for nearly an hour. How could I have been so stupid? Anyone could have come in while I was under the studio. Sara could have used anyone to —

I realized that wasn't true. The murderers and the child victims had all been linked by blood, and now that blood had thinned, that river had almost reached the sea. There was Bill Dean, but he was staying well away from Sara Laughs. There was Kenny Auster, but Kenny had taken himself and his family off to Taxachusetts. And Ki's closest blood relations — mother, father, grandfather — were all dead.

Only I was left. Only I was blood. Only I could do it. Unless —

I bolted back up to the house as fast as I could, slipping and sliding my way along the soaked path, desperate to make sure she was all right. I didn't think Sara could hurt Kyra herself, no matter how much of that old-timer vibe she had to draw on . . . but what if I was wrong?

What if I was wrong?

Chapter 28

Ki lay fast asleep just as I had left her, on her side with the filthy little stuffed dog clutched under her jaw. It had put a smudge on her neck but I hadn't the heart to take it away from her. Beyond her and to the left, through the open bathroom door, I could hear the steady *plink-plonk-plink* of water falling from the faucet and into the tub. Cool air blew around me in a silky twist, caressing my cheeks, sending a not unpleasurable shiver up my back. In the living room Bunter's bell gave a dim little shake.

Water's still warm, sugar, Sara whispered. *Be her friend, be her daddy. Go on, now. Do what I want. Do what we both want.*

And I *did* want to, which had to be why Jo at first tried to keep me away from the TR and from Sara Laughs. Why she'd made a secret of her possible pregnancy, as well. It was as if I had discovered a vampire inside me, a creature with no interest in what it thought of as talk-show conscience and op-ed page morality. A part that wanted only to take Ki into the bathroom and dunk her into that tub of warm water and hold her under, watching the red-edged white ribbons shimmer the way Carla Dean's white dress and red stockings had shimmered while the woods burned all around her and her father. A part of me would be more than glad to pay the last installment on that old bill.

"Dear God," I muttered, and wiped my face with a shaking hand. "She knows so many tricks. And she's so fucking *strong.*"

The bathroom door tried to swing shut against me before I could go through, but I pushed it open against hardly any resistance. The medicine-cabinet door banged back, and the glass shattered against the wall. The stuff inside flew out at me, but it wasn't a very dangerous attack; this time most of the missiles consisted of toothpaste tubes, toothbrushes, plastic bottles, and a few old Vick's inhalers. Faint, very faint, I could hear her shouting in frustration as I yanked the plug at the bottom of the tub and let the water start gurgling out. There had been enough drowning on the TR for one century, by God. And yet, for a moment I felt an incredibly strong urge to put the plug back in while the water was still deep enough to do the job. Instead I tore it off its chain and threw it down the hall. The medicine-cabinet door clapped shut again and the rest of the glass fell out.

"How many have you had?" I asked her. "How many besides Carla Dean and Kerry Auster and our Kia? Two? Three? Five? How many do you need before you can rest?"

All of them! the answer shot back. It wasn't just Sara's voice, either; it was my own, as well. She'd gotten into me, had snuck in by way of the basement like a burglar . . . and already I was thinking that even if the tub was empty and the water-pump temporarily dead, there was always the lake.

All of them! the voice cried again. *All of them, sugar!*

Of course — only all of them would do. Until then there would be no rest for Sara Laughs.

"I'll help you to rest," I said. "That I promise."

The last of the water swirled away . . . but there was always the lake, always the lake if I changed my mind. I left the bathroom and looked in on Ki again. She hadn't moved, the sensation that Sara was in here with me had gone, Bunter's bell was quiet . . . and yet I felt uneasy, unwilling to leave her alone. I had to, though, if I was to finish my work, and I would do well not to linger. County and State cops would be along eventually, storm or no storm, downed trees or no downed trees.

Yes, but . . .

I stepped into the hall and looked uneasily around. Thunder boomed, but it was losing some of its urgency. So was the wind. What wasn't fading was the sense of something watching me, something that was not-Sara. I stood where I was a moment or two longer, trying to tell myself it was just the sizzle of my overcooked nerves, then walked down the hall to the entry.

I opened the door to the stoop . . . then looked around again sharply, as if expecting to see someone or something lurking behind the far end of the bookcase. A Shape, perhaps. Something that still wanted its dust-catcher. But I was the only Shape left, at least in this part of the world, and the only movement I saw was ripple-shadows thrown by the rain rolling down the windows.

It was still coming down hard enough to redrench me as I crossed my stoop to the driveway, but I paid no attention. I had just been with a little girl when she drowned, had damned near drowned myself not so long ago, and the rain wasn't going to stop me from doing what I had to do. I picked up the fallen branch which had dented the roof of my car, tossed it aside, and opened the Chevy's rear door.

The things I'd bought at Slips 'n Greens were still sitting on the back seat, still tucked into the cloth carry-handle bag Lila Proulx had given me. The trowel and the pruning knife were visible, but the third item was in a plastic sack. *Want this one in a special bag?* Lila had asked me. *Always safe, never sorry.* And later, as I was leaving, she had spoken of Kenny's dog Blueberry chasing seagulls and had given out with a big, hearty laugh. Her eyes hadn't laughed, though. Maybe that's how you tell the Martians from the Earthlings — the Martians can never laugh with their eyes.

I saw Rommie and George's present lying on the front seat: the Stenomask I'd at first mistaken for Devore's oxygen mask. The boys in the basement spoke up then — murmured, at least — and I leaned over the seat to grab the mask by its elastic strap without the slightest idea of why I was doing so. I dropped it into the carry-bag, slammed the car door, then started down the railroad-tie steps to the lake. On the way I paused to duck under the deck, where we had always kept a few tools. There was no pick, but I grabbed a spade that looked up to a piece of gravedigging. Then, for what I thought would be the last time, I followed the course of my dream down to The Street. I didn't need Jo to show me the spot; the Green Lady had been pointing to it all along. Even had she not been, and even if Sara Tidwell did not still stink to the heavens, I think I would have known. I think I would have been led there by my own haunted heart.

There was a man standing between me and the place where the gray forehead of rock guarded the path, and as I paused on the last railroad tie, he hailed me in a rasping voice that I knew all too well.

"Say there, whoremaster, where's your whore?"

He stood on The Street in the pouring rain, but his cutters' outfit — green flannel pants, checked wool shirt — and his faded blue Union Army cap were dry, because the rain was falling through him rather than on him. He looked solid but he was no more real than Sara herself. I reminded myself of this as I stepped down onto the path to face him, but my heart continued to speed up, thudding in my chest like a padded hammer.

He was dressed in Jared Devore's clothes, but this wasn't Jared Devore. This was Jared's great-grandson Max, who had begun his career with an act of sled-theft and ended it in suicide . . . but not before arranging for the murder of his daughter-in-law, who'd had the temerity to refuse him what he had so dearly wanted.

I started toward him and he moved to the center of the path to block me. I could feel the cold baking off him. I am saying exactly what I mean, expressing what I remember as clearly as I can: I could feel the cold baking off him. And yes, it was Max Devore all right, but got up like a logger at a costume party and looking the way he must have around the time his son Lance was born. Old but hale. The sort of man younger men might well look up to. And now, as if the thought had called them, I could see the rest shimmer into faint being behind him, standing in a line across the path. These were the ones who had been with Jared at the Fryeburg Fair, and now I knew who some of them were. Fred Dean, of course, only nineteen years old in '01, the drowning of his daughter still over thirty years away. And the one who had reminded me of myself was Harry Auster, the firstborn of my great-grandfather's sister. He would have been sixteen, barely old enough to raise a fuzz but old enough to work in the woods with Jared. Old enough to shit in the same pit as Jared. To mistake Jared's poison for wisdom. One of the others twisted his head and squinted at the same time — I'd seen that tic before. Where? Then it came to me: in the Lakeview General. This young man was the late Royce Merrill's father. The others I didn't know. Nor did I care to.

"You ain't a-passing by us," Devore said. He held up both hands. "Don't even think about trying. Am I right, boys?"

They murmured growling agreement — the sort you could hear coming from any present-day gang of headbangers or taggers, I imagine — but their voices were distant; actually more sad than menacing. There was some substance to the man in Jared Devore's clothes, perhaps because in life he had been a man of enormous vitality, perhaps because he was so recently dead, but the others were little more than projected images.

I started forward, moving into that baking cold, moving into the smell of him — the same invalid odors which had surrounded him when I'd met him here before.

"Where do you think you're going?" he cried.

"For a constitutional," I said. "And no law against it. The Street's the place where good pups and vile dogs can walk side-by-side. You said so yourself."

"You don't understand," Max-Jared said. "You never will. You're not of that world. That was our world."

I stopped, looking at him curiously. Time was short, I wanted to be done with this . . . but I had to know, and I thought Devore was ready to tell me.

"*Make* me understand," I said. "Convince me that any world was your world." I looked at him, then at the flickering, translucent figures behind him, gauze flesh heaped on shining bones. "Tell me what you did."

"It was all different then," Devore said. "When *you* come down here, Noonan, you might walk all three miles north to Halo Bay and see only a dozen people on The Street. After Labor Day you might not see anyone at all. This side of the lake you have to walk through the bushes that are growing up wild

817

and around the fallen trees — there'll be even more of em after this storm — and even a deadfall or two because nowadays the townfolk don't club together to keep it neat the way they used to. But in our time — ! The woods were bigger then, Noonan, distances were farther to go, and neighboring meant something. Life itself, often enough. Back then this really *was* a street. Can you see?"

I could. If I looked through the phantom shapes of Fred Dean and Harry Auster and the others, I could. They weren't just ghosts; they were shimmerglass windows on another age. I saw

a summer afternoon in the year of . . . 1898? Perhaps 1902? 1907? Doesn't matter. This is a period when all time seems the same, as if time had stopped. This is a time the old-timers remember as a kind of golden age. It is the Land of Ago, the Kingdom of When-I-Was-a-Boy. The sun washes everything with the fine gold light of endless late July; the lake is as blue as a dream, netted with a billion sparks of reflected light. And The Street! It is as smoothly grassed as a lawn and as broad as a boulevard. It is a boulevard, I see, a place where the community fully realizes itself. It is the main conduit of communication, the chief cable in a township criss-crossed with them. I'd felt the existence of these cables all along — even when Jo was alive I felt them under the surface, and here is their point of origin. Folks promenade on The Street, all up and down the east side of Dark Score Lake they promenade in little groups, laughing and conversing under a cloud-stacked summer sky, and this is where the cables all begin. I look and realize how wrong I have been to think of them as Martians, as cruel and calculating aliens. East of their sunny promenade looms the darkness of the woods, glades and hollows where any miserable thing may await, from a foot lopped off in a logging accident to a birth gone wrong and a young mother dead before the doctor can arrive from Castle Rock in his buggy. These are people with no electricity, no phones, no County Rescue Unit, no one to rely upon but each other and a God some of them have already begun to mistrust. They live in the woods and the shadows of the woods, but on fine summer afternoons they come to the edge of the lake. They come to The Street and look in each other's faces and laugh together and then they are truly on the TR — in what I have come to think of as the zone. They are not Martians; they are little lives dwelling on the edge of the dark, that's all.

I see summer people from Warrington's, the men dressed in white flannels, two women in long tennis dresses still carrying their rackets. A fellow riding a tricycle with an enormous front wheel weaves shakily among them. The party of summer folk has stopped to talk with a group of young men from town; the fellows from away

want to know if they can play in the townies'
baseball game at Warrington's on Tuesday
night. Ben Merrill, Royce's father-to-be, says
Ayuh, but we won't go easy on ya just cause
you're from N'Yawk. *The young men laugh;*
so do the tennis girls.

A little farther on, two boys are playing catch
with the sort of raw homemade baseball that is
known as a horsey. Beyond them is a conven-
tion of young mothers, talking earnestly of their
babies, all safely prammed and gathered in their
own group. Men in overalls discuss weather and
crops, politics and crops, taxes and crops. A
teacher from the Consolidated High sits on the
gray stone forehead I know so well, patiently tu-
toring a sullen boy who wants to be somewhere
else and doing anything else. I think the boy will
grow up to be Buddy Jellison's father. Horn
broken — watch for finger, *I think.*

All along The Street folks are fishing, and
they are catching plenty; the lake fairly teems
with bass and trout and pickerel. An artist —
another summer fellow, judging from his smock
and nancy beret — has set up his easel and is
painting the mountains while two ladies watch
respectfully. A giggle of girls passes, whispering
about boys and clothes and school. There is
beauty here, and peace. Devore's right to say
this is a world I never knew. It's

"Beautiful," I said, pulling myself back
with an effort. "Yes, I see that. But what's
your point?"

"My point?" Devore looked almost comically surprised. "She thought she could walk there like everyone else, that's the fucking *point!* She thought she could walk there like a white gal! Her and her big teeth and her big tits and her snotty looks. She thought she was something special, but we taught her different. She tried to walk me down and when she couldn't do that she put her filthy hands on me and tumped me over. But that was all right; we taught her her manners. Didn't we, boys?"

They growled agreement, but I thought some of them — young Harry Auster, for one — looked sick.

"We taught her her place," Devore said. "We taught her she wasn't nothing but a *nigger. This is the word he uses over and over again when they are in the woods that summer, the summer of 1901, the summer that Sara and the Red-Tops become the musical act to see in this part of the world. She and her brother and their whole nigger family have been invited to Warrington's to play for the summer people; they have been fed on champagne and ersters . . . or so says Jared Devore to his little school of devoted followers as they eat their own plain lunches of bread and meat and salted cucumbers out of lard-buckets given to them by their mothers (none of the young men are married, although Oren Peebles is engaged).*

Yet it isn't her growing renown that upsets

Jared Devore. It isn't the fact that she has been to Warrington's; it don't cross his eyes none that she and that brother of hers have actually sat down and eaten with white folks, taken bread from the same bowl as them with their blacknigger fingers. The folks at Warrington's are flatlanders, after all, and Devore tells the silent, attentive young men that he's heard that in places like New York and Chicago white women sometimes even fuck *blackniggers.*

Naw! *Harry Auster says, looking around nervously, as if he expected a few white women to come tripping through the woods way out here on Bowie Ridge.* No white woman'd fuck a nigger! Shoot a pickle!

Devore only gives him a look, the kind that says When you're my age. *Besides, he doesn't care what goes on in New York and Chicago; he saw all the flatland he wanted to during the Civil War . . . and, he will tell you, he never fought that war to free the damned slaves. They can keep slaves down there in the land of cotton until the end of the eternity, as far as Jared Lancelot Devore is concerned. No, he fought in the war to teach those cracker sons of bitches south of Mason and Dixon that you don't pull out of the game just because you don't like some of the rules. He went down to scratch the scab off the end of old Johnny Reb's nose. Tried to leave the United States of America, they had!* The Lord!

No, he doesn't care about slaves and he

doesn't care about the land of cotton and he doesn't care about blackniggers who sing dirty songs and then get treated to champagne and ersters (Jared always says oysters *in just that sarcastic way) in payment for their smut. He doesn't care about anything so long as they keep in their place and let him keep in his.*

But she won't do it. The uppity bitch will not do it. She has been warned to stay off The Street, but she will not listen. She goes anyway, walking along in her white dress just as if there was a white person inside it, sometimes with her son, who has a blacknigger African name and no daddy — his daddy probably just spent the one night with his mommy in a haystack somewhere down Alabama and now she walks around with the get of that just as bold as a brass monkey. She walks The Street as if she has a right to be there, even though not a soul will talk to her —

"But that's not true, is it?" I asked Devore. "That's what really stuck in old great-granddaddy's craw, wasn't it? They *did* talk to her. She had a way about her — that laugh, maybe. Men talked to her about crops and the women showed off their babies. In fact they gave her their babies to hold and when she laughed down at them, they laughed back up at her. The girls asked her advice about boys. The boys . . . they just looked. But *how* they looked, huh? They filled up their eyes, and I expect most of

823

them thought about her when they went out to the privy and filled up their palms."

Devore glowered. He was aging in front of me, the lines drawing themselves deeper and deeper into his face; he was becoming the man who had knocked me into the lake because he couldn't bear to be crossed. And as he grew older he began to fade.

"That was what Jared hated most of all, wasn't it? That they didn't turn aside, didn't turn away. She walked on The Street and no one treated her like a nigger. They treated her like a neighbor."

I was in the zone, deeper in than I'd ever been, down where the town's unconscious seemed to run like a buried river. I could drink from that river while I was in the zone, could fill my mouth and throat and belly with its cold minerally taste.

All that summer Devore had talked to them. They were more than his crew, they were his boys: Fred and Harry and Ben and Oren and George Armbruster and Draper Finney, who would break his neck and drown the next summer trying to dive into Eades Quarry while he was drunk. Only it was the sort of accident that's kind of on purpose. Draper Finney drank a lot between July of 1901 and August of 1902, because it was the only way he could sleep. The only way he could get the hand out of his mind, that hand sticking straight out of the water, clenching and unclenching until you wanted to scream *Won't it stop, won't it ever stop doing that.*

All summer long Jared Devore filled their ears with nigger bitch and uppity bitch. All summer long he told them about their responsibility as men, their duty to keep the community pure, and how they must see what others didn't and do what others wouldn't.

It was a Sunday afternoon in August, a time when traffic along The Street dropped steeply. Later on, by five or so, things would begin to pick up again, and from six to sunset the broad path along the lake would be thronged. But three in the afternoon was low tide. The Methodists were back in session over in Harlow for their afternoon Song Service; at Warrington's the assembled company of vacationing flatlanders was sitting down to a heavy mid-afternoon Sabbath meal of roast chicken or ham; all over the township families were addressing their own Sunday dinners. Those who had already finished were snoozing through the heat of the day — in a hammock, wherever possible. Sara liked this quiet time. Loved it, really. She had spent a great deal of her life on carny midways and in smoky gin-joints, shouting out her songs in order to be heard above the voices of redfaced, unruly drunks, and while part of her loved the excitement

825

and unpredictability of that life, part of her loved the serenity of this one, too. The peace of these walks. She wasn't getting any younger, after all; she had a kid who had now left purt near all his babyhood behind him. On that particular Sunday she must have thought The Street almost *too* quiet. She walked a mile south from the meadow without seeing a soul — even Kito was gone by then, having stopped off to pick berries. It was as if the whole township were

deserted. She knows there's an Eastern Star supper in Kashwakamak, of course, has even contributed a mushroom pie to it because she has made friends of some of the Eastern Star ladies. They'll all be down there getting ready. What she doesn't know is that today is also Dedication Day for the new Grace Baptist Church, the first real church ever to be built on the TR. A slug of locals have gone, heathen as well as Baptist. Faintly, from the other side of the lake, she can hear the Methodists singing. The sound is sweet and faint and beautiful; distance and echo has tuned every sour voice.

She isn't aware of the men — most of them very young men, the kind who under ordinary circumstances dare only look at her from the corners of their eyes — until the oldest one among them speaks. "Wellnow, a black whore in a white dress and a red belt! Damn if that ain't just a little too much color for lakeside. What's wrong with you, whore? Can't you take a hint?"

She turns toward him, afraid but not showing it. She has lived thirty-six years on this earth, has known what a man has and where he wants to put it since she was eleven, and she understands that when men are together like this and full of redeye (she can smell it), they give up thinking for themselves and turn into a pack of dogs. If you show fear they will fall on you like dogs and likely tear you apart like dogs.

Also, they have been laying for her. There can be no other explanation for them turning up like this.

"*What hint is that, sugar?*" *she asks, standing her ground. Where is everyone? Where can they all be? God damn! Across the lake, the Methodists have moved on to "Trust and Obey," a droner if there ever was one.*

"*That you ain't got no business walking where the white folks walk," Harry Auster says. His adolescent voice breaks into a kind of mouse-squeak on the last word and she laughs. She knows how unwise that is, but she can't help it — she's never been able to help her laughter, any more than she's ever been able to help the way men like this look at her breasts and bottom. Blame it on God.*

"*Why, I walk where I do," she says. "I was told this was common ground, ain't nobody got a right to keep me out. Ain't nobody has. You seen em doin it?*"

"*You see us now," George Armbruster says, trying to sound tough.*

827

Sara looks at him with a species of kindly contempt that makes George shrivel up inside. His cheeks glow hot red. "Son," she says, "you only come out now because the decent folks is all somewheres else. Why do you want to let this old fella tell you what to do? Act decent and let a lady walk."

I see it all. As Devore fades and fades, at last becoming nothing but eyes under a blue cap in the rainy afternoon (through him I can see the shattered remains of my swimming float washing against the embankment), I see it all. I see her as she

starts forward, walking straight at Devore. If she stands here jawing with them, something bad is going to happen. She feels it, and she never questions her feelings. And if she walks at any of the others, ole massa'll bore in on her from the side, pulling the rest after. Ole massa in the little ole blue cap is the wheeldog, the one she must face down. She can do it, too. He's strong, strong enough to make these boys one creature, his creature, at least for the time being, but he doesn't have her force, her determination, her energy. In a way she welcomes this confrontation. Reg has warned her to be careful, not to move too fast or try to make real friends until the rednecks (only Reggie calls them "the bull gators") show themselves — how many and how crazy — but she goes her own course, trusts her own deep instincts. And here they are, only seven of em, and really just the one bull gator.

I'm stronger than you, ole massa, she thinks, walking toward him. *She fixes her eyes on his and will not let them drop; his are the ones that drop, his the mouth that quivers uncertainly at one corner, his the tongue that comes out as quick as a lizard's tongue to wet the lips, and all that's good . . . but even better is when he falls back a step. When he does that the rest of them cluster in two groups of three, and there it is, her way through. Faint and sweet are the Methodists, faithy music carrying across the lake's still surface. A droner of a hymn, yes, but sweet across the miles.*

> *When we walk with the Lord*
> *in the light of His word,*
> *what a glory He sheds on our way . . .*

I'm stronger than you, sugar, *she sends,* I'm meaner than you, you may be the bull gator but I'm the queen bee and if you don't want me stingin on you, you best clear me the rest of my path.

"You bitch," he says, but his voice is weak; he is already thinking this isn't the day, there's something about her he didn't quite see until he saw her right up close, some blacknigger hougan he didn't feel until now, better wait for another day, better —

Then he trips over a root or a rock (perhaps it's the very rock behind which she will finally come to rest) and falls down. His cap falls off, showing the big old bald spot on top of his head. His pants split all the way up the seam. And Sara makes a crucial mistake. Perhaps she underestimates Jared Devore's own very considerable personal force, or perhaps she just cannot help herself — the sound of his britches ripping is like a loud fart. In any case she laughs — that raucous, smoke-broken laugh which is her trademark. And her laugh becomes her doom.

Devore doesn't think. He simply gives her the leather from where he lies, big feet in pegged loggers' boots shooting out like pistons. He hits her where she is thinnest and most vulnerable, in the ankles. She hollers in shocked pain as the left one breaks; she goes down in a tumble, losing her furled parasol out of one hand. She draws in breath to scream again and Jared says from where he is lying, "Don't let her! Dassn't let her holler!"

Ben Merrill falls on top of her full-length, all one hundred and ninety pounds of him. The breath she has drawn to scream with whooshes out in a gusty, almost silent sigh instead. Ben, who has never even danced with a woman, let alone lain on top of one like this, is instantly excited by the feel of her struggling beneath him. He wriggles against her, laughing, and when she rakes her nails down his cheek he barely feels it. The way it seems to him, he's all cock and a yard long. When she tries to roll over and get out from under that way, he rolls with her, lets her be on top, and he is totally surprised when she drives her forehead down on his. He sees stars, but he is eighteen years old, as strong as he will ever be, and he loses neither consciousness nor his erection.

Oren Peebles tears away the back of her dress, laughing. "Pig-pile!" he cries in a breathy little whisper, and drops on top of her. Now he is dry-humping her topside and Ben is dry-humping just as enthusiastically from underneath, dry-humping like a billygoat even with the blood pouring down the sides of his head from the split in the center of his brow, and she knows that if she can't scream she is lost. If she can scream and if Kito hears, he'll run and get help, run and get Reg —

But before she can try again, ole massa is squatting beside her and showing her a long-bladed knife. "Make a sound and I'll cut your nose off," he says, and that's when she gives up. They have brought her down after all, partly because she laughed at the wrong time, mostly out of pure buggardly bad luck. Now they will not be stopped, and best that Kito should stay away — please God keep him back where he was, it was a good patch of berries, one that should keep him occupied an hour or more. He loves berry-picking, and it won't take these men an hour. Harry Auster yanks her hair back, tears her dress off one shoulder, and begins to sucker on her neck.

Ole massa the only one not at her. Old massa standing back, looking both ways along The

Street, his eyes slitted and wary; old massa look like a mangy timberwolf done eaten a whole generation of chickenhouse chickens while managing to avoid every trap and snare. "Hey Irish, quit on her a minute," he tells Harry, then widens his wise gaze to the others. "Get her in the puckies, you damn fools. Get her in there deep."

They don't. They can't. They are too eager to have her. They arm-yank her behind the forehead of gray rock and call it good. She doesn't pray easily but she prays now. She prays for them to let her live. She prays for Kito to stay clear, to keep filling his bucket slow by eating every third handful. She prays that if he does take a notion to catch up with her, he will see what's happening and run the other way as fast as he can, run silent and get Reg.

"Stick this in your mouth," George Armbruster pants. "And don't you bite me, you bitch."

They take her top and bottom, back and front, two and three at a time. They take her where anybody coming along can't help but see them, and ole massa stands off a little, looking first at the panting young men grouped around her, kneeling with their trousers down and their thighs scratched from the bushes they are kneeling in, then he peers up and down the path with his wild and wary eyes. Incredibly, one of them — it is Fred Dean — says "Sorry, ma'am" after he's shot his load feels like *halfway up to east bejeezus. It's as if he acci-dentally kicked her in the shin while crossing his legs.*

And it doesn't end. There's come down her throat, come running down the crack of her ass, the young one has bitten the blood right out of her left breast, and it doesn't end. They are young, and by the time the last one has finished, the first one, oh God, the first one is ready again. Across the river the Methodists are now singing "Blessed Assurance, Jesus Is Mine" and as ole massa approaches her she thinks, It's almost over, woman, he the last, hold on hold steady and it be over. *He looks at the skinny redhead and the one who keeps squinching his eye up and tossing his head and tells them to watch the path, he's going to take his turn now that she's broke in.*

He unbuckles his belt, he unbuttons his flies, he pushes down his underwear — dirty black at the knees and dirty yellow at the crotch — and as he drops a knee on either side of her she sees that ole massa's little massa is just as floppy as a snake with its neck broke and before she can stop it, that raucous laugh bursts all unexpected from her again — even lying here covered with the hot jelly spend of her rapists, she can't help but see the funny side.

"Shut up!" Devore growls at her, and smashes the heel of one hard hand across her face, breaking her cheekbone and her nose. "Shut up that howling!"

"Reckon it might get stiffer if it was one of your boys layin here with his rosy red ass stuck up in the air, sugar?" she asks, and then, for the last time, Sara laughs.

Devore draws his hand back to hit her again, his naked loins lying against her naked loins, his penis a flaccid worm between them. But before he can bring the hand down a child's voice cries, "Ma! What they doin to you, Ma? Git off my mama, you bastards!"

She sits up in spite of Devore's weight, her laughter dying, her wide eyes searching Kito out and finding him, a slim young boy of eight standing on The Street, dressed in overalls and a straw hat and brand-new canvas shoes, carrying a tin bucket in one hand. His lips are blue with juice. His eyes are wide with confusion and fright.

"Run, Kito!" *she screams.* "Run away h—"

Red fire explodes in her head; she swoons back into the bushes, hearing ole massa from a great distance: "Get him. Dassn't let him ramble, now."

Then she's going down a long dark slope, she's lost in a Ghost House corridor that leads only deeper and deeper into its own convoluted bowels; from that deep falling place she hears him, she hears, her darling one, he is

screaming. I heard him screaming as I knelt by the gray rock with my carry-bag beside me and no idea how I'd gotten to where I was — I certainly had no memory of walking here. I was crying in shock and horror and pity. Was she crazy? Well, no wonder. No fucking wonder. The rain was steady but no longer apocalyptic. I stared at my fishy-white hands on the gray rock for a few seconds, then looked around. Devore and the others were gone.

The ripe and gassy stench of decay filled my nose — it was like a physical assault. I fumbled in the carry-bag, found the Stenomask Rommie and George had given me as a joke, and slipped it over my mouth and nose with fingers that felt numb and distant. I breathed shallowly and tentatively. Better. Not a lot, but enough to keep from fleeing, which was undoubtedly what she wanted.

"No!" she cried from somewhere behind me as I grabbed the spade and dug in. I tore a great mouth in the ground with the first swipe, and each subsequent one deepened and widened it. The earth was soft and yielding, woven through with mats of thin roots which parted easily under the blade.

"No! Don't you dare!"

I wouldn't look around, wouldn't give her a chance to push me away. She was stronger down here, perhaps because it had happened here. Was that possible? I didn't know and didn't care. All I cared about was getting this done. Where the roots were thicker, I hacked through them with the pruning knife.

"Leave me be!"

Now I *did* look around, risked one quick glance because of the unnatural crackling sounds which had accompanied her voice — which now seemed to *make* her voice. The Green Lady was gone. The birch had somehow become Sara Tidwell: it was Sara's face growing out of the criss-crossing branches and shiny leaves. That rain-slicked face swayed, dissolved, came together, melted away, came together again. For a moment all the mystery I had sensed down here was revealed. Her damp shifting eyes were utterly human. They stared at me with hate and supplication.

"I ain't done!" she cried in a cracked, breaking voice. "He was the worst, don't you understand? He was the worst and it's his blood in her and I won't rest until I *have it out!*"

There was a gruesome ripping sound. She had inhabited the birch, made it into a physical body of some sort and intended to tear it free of the earth. She would come and get me with it if she could; kill me with it if she could. Strangle me in limber branches. Stuff me with leaves until I looked like a Christmas decoration.

"No matter how much of a monster he was, Kyra had nothing to do with what he did," I said. "And you won't have her."

"Yes I *will!*" the Green Lady screamed. The ripping, rending sounds were louder now. They were joined by a hissing, shaky crackle. I didn't look around again. I didn't *dare* look around. I dug faster instead. "Yes I *will* have her!" she cried, and now the voice was closer. She was coming for me but I refused to see; when it comes to walking trees and bushes, I'll stick to *Macbeth*, thanks. "I *will* have her! He took mine and *I mean to take his!*"

"Go away," a new voice said.

The spade loosened in my hands, almost fell. I turned and saw Jo standing below me and to my right. She was looking at Sara, who had materialized into a lunatic's hallucination — a monstrous greenish-black thing that slipped with every step it tried to walk along The Street. She had left the birch behind yet assumed its vitality somehow — the actual tree huddled behind her, black and shrivelled and dead. The creature born of it looked like the Bride of Frankenstein as sculpted by Picasso. In it, Sara's face came and went, came and went.

The Shape, I thought coldly. *It was always real . . . and if it was always me, it was always her, too.*

Jo was dressed in the white shirt and yellow slacks she'd had on the day she died. I couldn't see the lake through her as I had been able to see it through Devore and Devore's young friends; she had materialized herself completely. I felt a curious *draining* sensation at the back of my skull and thought I knew how.

"Git out, bitch!" the Sara-thing snarled. It raised its arms toward Jo as it had raised them to me in my worst nightmares.

"Not at all." Jo's voice remained calm. She turned toward me. "Hurry, Mike. You have to be quick. It's not really her anymore. She's let one of the Outsiders in, and they're very dangerous."

"Jo, I love you."

"I love you t—"

Sara shrieked and then began to spin. Leaves and branches blurred together and lost coherence; it was like watching something liquefy in a blender. The entity which had only looked a little like a woman to begin with now dropped its masquerade entirely. Something elemental and grotesquely inhuman began to form out of the maelstrom. It leaped at my wife. When it struck her, the color and solidity left Jo as if slapped away by a huge hand. She became a phantom struggling with the thing which raved and shrieked and clawed at her.

"Hurry, Mike!" she screamed. *"Hurry!"*

I bent to the job.

The spade struck something that wasn't dirt, wasn't stone, wasn't wood. I scraped along it, revealing a filthy mold-crusted swatch of canvas. Now I dug like a madman, wanting to clear as much of the buried object as I could, wanting to fatten my chances of success as much as I could. Behind me, the Shape screamed in fury and my wife screamed in pain. Sara had given up part of her discorporate self in order to gain her revenge, had let in something Jo called an Outsider. I had no idea what that might be and never *wanted* to know. Sara was its conduit, I knew that much. And if I could take care of her in time —

I reached into the dripping hole, slapping wet earth from the ancient canvas. Faint stencilled letters appeared when I did: J. M. MCCURDIE SAWMILL. McCurdie's had burned in the fires of '33, I knew. I'd seen a picture of it in flames somewhere. As I seized the canvas, the tips of my fingers punching through and letting out a fresh billow of green and gassy stench, I could hear grunting. I could hear

Devore. He's lying on top of her and grunting like a pig. Sara is semiconscious, muttering unintelligibly through bruised lips which are shiny with blood. Devore is looking back over his shoulder at Draper Finney and Fred Dean. They have raced after the boy and brought him back, but he won't stop yelling, he's yelling to beat the band, yelling to wake the dead, and if they can hear the Methodists singing "How I

Love to Tell the Story" over here, *then* they may be able to hear the yowling nigger over there. Devore says "Put him in the water, shut him up." The minute he says it, as though the words are magic words, his cock begins to stiffen.

"What do you mean?" Ben Merrill asks.

"You know goddam well," Jared says. He pants the words out, jerking his hips as he speaks. His narrow ass gleams in the afternoon light. "He seen us! You want to cut his throat, get his blood all over you? Fine by me. Here. Take my knife, be my guest!"

"N-No, Jared!" Ben cries in horror, actually seeming to cringe at the sight of the knife.

He is finally ready. It takes him a little longer, that's all, he ain't a kid like these other ones. But now — ! Never mind her smart mouth, never mind her insolent way of laughing, never mind the whole township. Let them all show up and watch if they like. He slips it to her, what she's wanted all along, what all her kind want. He slips it in and sinks it deep. He continues giving orders even as he rapes her. Up and down his ass goes, tick-tock, just like a cat's tail. "Somebody take care of him! Or do you want to spend forty years rotting in Shawshank because of a nigger boy's tattle?"

Ben seizes one of Kito Tidwell's arms, Oren Peebles the other, but by the time they have dragged him as far as the embankment they have lost their heart. Raping an uppity nigger woman with the gall to laugh at Jared when he fell down and split his britches is one thing. Drowning a scared kid like a kitten in a mudpuddle . . . that's another one altogether.

They loosen their grip, staring into each other's haunted eyes, and Kito pulls free.

"Run, honey!" Sara cries. "Run away and get —" Jared clamps his hands around her throat and begins choking.

The boy trips over his own berry bucket and thumps gracelessly to the ground. Harry and Draper recapture him easily. "What you going to do?" Draper asks in a kind of desperate whine, and Harry replies

"What I have to." That's what he replied, and now I was going to do what I had to — in spite of the stench, in spite of Sara, in spite of my dead wife's shrieks. I hauled the roll of canvas out of the ground. The ropes which had tied it shut at either end held, but the roll itself split down the middle with a hideous burping sound.

"Hurry!" Jo cried. "I can't hold it much longer!"

It snarled; it bayed like a dog. There was a loud wooden crunch, like a door being slammed hard enough to splinter, and Jo wailed. I grabbed for the carry-bag with Slips 'n Greens printed on the front and tore it open as

Harry — the others call him Irish because of

his carrot-colored hair — grabs the struggling kid in a clumsy kind of bearhug and jumps into the lake with him. The kid struggles harder than ever; his straw hat comes off and floats on the water. "Get that!" Harry pants. Fred Dean kneels and fishes out the dripping hat. Fred's eyes are dazed, he's got the look of a fighter about one round from hitting the canvas. Behind them Sara Tidwell has begun to rattle deep in her chest and throat — like the sight of the boy's clenching hand, these sounds will haunt Draper Finney until his final dive into Eades Quarry. Jared sinks his fingers deeper, pumping and choking at the same time, the sweat pouring off him. No amount of washing will take the smell of that sweat out of these clothes, and when he begins to think of it as "murder-sweat," he burns the clothes to get shed of it.

Harry Auster wants to be shed of it all — to be shed of it and never see these men again, most of all Jared Devore, who he now thinks must be Lord Satan himself. Harry cannot go home and face his father unless this nightmare is over, buried. And his mother! How can he ever face his beloved mother, Bridget Auster with her round sweet Irish face and graying hair and comforting shelf of bosom, Bridget who has always had a kind word or a soothing hand for him, Bridget Auster who has been Saved, Washed in the Blood of the Lamb, Bridget Auster who is even now serving pies at the picnic they're having at the new church, Bridget

Auster who is mamma; how can he ever look at her again — or she him — if he has to stand in court on a charge of raping and beating a woman, even a black woman?

So he yanks the clinging boy away — Kito scratches him once, just a nick on the side of the neck, and that night Harry will tell his mamma it was a bush-pricker that caught him unawares and he will let her put a kiss on it — and then he plunges the child into the lake. Kito looks up at him, his face shimmering, and Harry sees a little fish flick by. A perch, he thinks. For an instant he wonders what the boy must see, looking up through the silver shield of the surface at the face of the fellow who's holding him down, the fellow who's drowning him, and then Harry pushes that away. Just a nigger, *he reminds himself desperately.* That's all he is, just a nigger. No kin of yours.

Kito's arm comes out of the water — his dripping dark-brown arm. Harry pulls back, not wanting to be clawed, but the hand doesn't reach for him, only sticks straight up. The fingers curl into a fist. Open. Curl into a fist. Open. Curl into a fist. The boy's thrashing begins to ease, the kicking feet begin to slow down, the eyes looking up into Harry's eyes are taking on a curiously dreamy look, and still that brown arm sticks straight up, still the hand opens and closes, opens and closes. Draper Finney stands on the shore crying, sure that now someone will come along, now someone will see the terrible thing they have done — the terrible thing they are in fact still doing. Be sure your sin will find you out, *it says in the Good Book.* Be sure. *He opens his mouth to tell Harry to quit, maybe it's still not too late to take it back, let him up, let him live, but no sound comes out. Behind him Sara is choking her last. In front of him her drowning son's hand opens and closes, opens and closes, the reflection of it shimmering on the water, and Draper thinks* Won't it stop doing that, won't it ever stop doing that? *And as if it were a prayer that something is now answering, the boy's locked elbow begins to bend and his arm begins to sag; the fingers begin to close again into a fist and then stop. For a moment the hand wavers and then*

I slammed the heel of my hand into the center of my forehead to clear these phantoms away. Behind me there was a frenzied snap and crackle of wet bushes as Jo and whatever she was holding back continued to struggle. I put my hands inside the split in the canvas like a doctor spreading a wound. I yanked. There was a low ripping sound as the roll tore the rest of the way up and down.

Inside was what remained of them — two yellowed skulls, forehead to forehead as if in intimate conversation, a woman's faded red leather belt, a molder of clothes . . . and a heap of bones. Two ribcages, one large and one small. Two sets of legs, one long and one short. The early remains of Sara and Kito Tidwell, buried here by the lake for almost a hundred years.

The larger of the two skulls turned. It glared at me with its empty eyesockets. Its teeth chattered as if it would bite me, and the bones below it began a tenebrous, jittery stirring. Some broke apart immediately; all were soft and pitted. The red belt stirred restlessly and the rusty buckle rose like the head of a snake.

"Mike!" Jo screamed. *"Quick, quick!"*

I pulled the sack out of the carry-bag and grabbed the plastic bottle which had been inside. Lye stille, the Magnabet letters had said; another little word-trick. Another message passed behind the unsuspecting guard's back. Sara Tidwell was a fearsome creature, but she had underestimated Jo . . . and she had underestimated the telepathy of long association, as well. I had gone to Slips 'n Greens, I had bought a bottle of lye, and now I opened it and poured it, smoking, over the bones of Sara and her son.

There was a hissing sound like the one you hear when you open a beer or a bottled soft drink. The belt-buckle melted. The bones turned white and crumpled like things made out of sugar — I had a nightmare image of Mexican children eating candy corpses off long sticks on the Day of the Dead. The eyesockets of Sara's skull widened as the lye filled the dark hollow where her mind, her prodigious talent, and her laughing soul had once resided. It was an expression that looked at first like surprise and then like sorrow.

The jaw fell off; the nubs of the teeth sizzled away.

The top of the skull caved in.

Spread fingerbones jittered, then melted.

"Ohhhhhh . . ."

It whispered through the soaking trees like a rising wind . . . only the wind had died as the wet air caught its breath before the next onslaught. It was a sound of unspeakable grief and longing and surrender. I sensed no hate in it; her hate was gone, burned away in the corrosive I had bought in Helen Auster's shop. The sound of Sara's going was replaced by the plaintive, almost human cry of a bird, and it awakened me from the place where I had been, brought me finally and completely out of the zone. I got shakily to my feet, turned around, and looked at The Street.

Jo was still there, a dim form through which I could now see the lake and the dark clouds of the next thundersquall coming over the mountains. Something flickered beyond her — that bird venturing out of its safe covert for a peek at the re-arranged environment, perhaps — but I barely registered that. It was Jo I wanted to see, Jo who had come God knew how far and suffered God knew how much to help me. She looked exhausted, hurt, in some fundamental way diminished. But the other thing — the Outsider — was gone. Jo, standing in a ring of birch leaves so dead they looked charred, turned to me and smiled.

"Jo! We did it!"

Her mouth moved. I heard the sound, but the words were too distant to make out. She was standing right there, but she might have been calling across a wide canyon. Still, I understood her. I read the words off her lips if you prefer the rational, right out of her mind if you prefer the romantical. I prefer the latter. Marriage is a zone, too, you know. Marriage is a zone.

— *So* that's *all right, isn't it?*

I glanced down into the gaping roll of canvas and saw nothing but stubs and splinters sticking out of a noxious, uneasy paste. I got a whiff, and even through the Stenomask it made me cough and back away. Not corruption; lye. When I looked back around at Jo, she was barely there.

"Jo! Wait!"

— *Can't help. Can't stay.*

Words from another star system, barely glimpsed on a fading mouth. Now she was little more than eyes floating in the dark afternoon, eyes which seemed made of the lake behind them.

— Hurry . . .

She was gone. I slipped and stumbled to the place where she'd been, my feet crunching over dead birch leaves, and grabbed at nothing. What a fool I must have looked, soaked to the skin, wearing a Stenomask askew over the lower half of my face, trying to embrace the wet gray air.

I got the faintest whiff of Red perfume . . . and then only damp earth, lakewater, and the vile stink of lye running under everything. At least the smell of putrefaction was gone; that had been no more real than . . .

Than what? Than *what?* Either it was all real or none of it was real. If none of it was real, I was out of my mind and ready for the Blue Wing at Juniper Hill. I looked over toward the gray rock and saw the bag of bones I had pulled out of the wet ground like a festering tooth. Lazy tendrils of smoke were still rising from its ripped length. *That* much was real. So was the Green Lady, who was now a soot-colored Black Lady — as dead as the dead branch behind her, the one that seemed to point like an arm.

Can't help . . . can't stay . . . hurry.

Couldn't help with what? What more help did I need? It was done, wasn't it? Sara was gone: spirit follows bone, good night sweet ladies, God grant she lye stille.

And still a kind of stinking terror, not so different from the smell of putrescence

848

which had come out of the ground, seemed to sweat out of the air; Kyra's name began to beat in my head, *Ki-Ki, Ki-Ki, Ki-Ki,* like the call of some exotic tropical bird. I started up the railroad-tie steps to the house, and although I was exhausted, by the time I was halfway up I had begun to run.

I climbed the stairs to the deck and went in that way. The house looked the same — save for the broken tree poking in through the kitchen window, Sara Laughs had stood up to the storm very well — but something was wrong. There was something I could almost smell . . . and perhaps I *did* smell it, bitter and low. Lunacy may have its own wild-vetch aroma. It's not the kind of thing I would ever care to research.

In the front hall I stopped, looking down at a heap of paperback books, Elmore Leonards and Ed McBains, lying on the floor. As if they had been raked off the shelf by a passing hand. A flailing hand, maybe. I could also see my tracks there, both coming and going. They had already begun to dry. They should have been the only ones; I had been carrying Ki when we came in. They should have been, but they weren't. The others were smaller, but not so small that I mistook them for a child's.

I ran down the hall to the north bedroom crying her name, and I might as well have been crying *Mattie* or *Jo* or *Sara.* Coming out of my mouth, Kyra's name sounded like the name of a corpse. The duvet had been thrown back onto the floor. Except for the black stuffed dog, lying where it had in my dream, the bed was empty. And Ki was gone.

Chapter 29

I reached for Ki with the part of my mind that had for the last few weeks known what she was wearing, what room of the trailer she was in, and what she was doing there. There was nothing, of course — that link was also dissolved.

I called for Jo — I think I did — but Jo was gone, too. I was on my own. God help me. God help us both. I could feel panic trying to descend and fought it off. I had to keep my mind clear. If I couldn't think, any chance Ki might still have would be lost. I walked rapidly back down the hall to the foyer, trying not to hear the sick voice in the back of my head, the one saying that Ki was lost already, dead already. I knew no such thing, couldn't know it now that the connection between us was broken.

I looked down at the heap of books, then up at the door. The new tracks had come in this way and gone out this way, too. Lightning stroked the sky and thunder cracked. The wind was rising again. I went to the door, reached for the knob, then paused. Something was caught in the crack between the door and the jamb, something as fine and floaty as a strand of spider's silk.

A single white hair.

I looked at it with a sick lack of surprise. I should have known, of course, and if not for the strain I'd been under and the successive shocks of this terrible day, I *would* have known. It was all on the tape John had played for me that morning . . . a time that already seemed part of another man's life.

For one thing, there was the time-check marking the point where John had hung up on her. *Nine-forty A.M., Eastern Daylight,* the robot voice had said, which meant that Rogette had been calling at six-forty in the morning . . . if, that was, she'd really been calling from Palm Springs. That was at least possible; had the oddity occurred to me while we were driving from the airport to Mattie's trailer, I would have told myself that there were no doubt insomniacs all over California who finished their East Coast business before the sun had hauled itself fully over the horizon, and good for them. But there was something else that couldn't be explained away so easily.

At one point John had ejected the tape. He did it because, he said, I'd gone as white as a sheet instead of looking amused. I had told him to go on and play the rest; it had just surprised me to hear her again. *The quality of her voice. Christ, the reproduction is good.* Except it was really the boys in the basement who had reacted to John's tape; my subconscious co-conspirators. And it hadn't been her *voice* that had scared them badly enough to turn my face white. The underhum had done that. The characteristic underhum you always got on TR calls, both those you made and those you received.

Rogette Whitmore had never left TR-90 at all. If my failing to realize that this morning cost Ki Devore her life this afternoon, I wouldn't be able to live with myself. I told God that over and over as I went plunging down the railroad-tie steps again, running into the face of a revitalized storm.

It's a blue-eyed wonder I didn't go flying right off the embankment. Half my swimming float had grounded there, and perhaps I could have impaled myself on its splintered boards and died like a vampire writhing on a stake. What a pleasant thought *that* was.

Running isn't good for people near panic; it's like scratching poison ivy. By the time I had thrown my arm around one of the pines at the foot of the steps to check my progress, I was on the edge of losing all coherent thought. Ki's name was beating in my head again, so loudly there wasn't room for much else.

Then a stroke of lightning leaped out of the sky to my right and knocked the last three feet of trunk out from beneath a huge old spruce which had probably been here when Sara and Kito were still alive. If I'd been looking directly at it I would have been blinded; even with my head turned three-quarters away, the stroke left a huge blue swatch like the aftermath of a gigantic camera flash floating in front of my eyes. There was a grinding, juddering sound as two hundred feet of blue spruce toppled into the lake, sending up a long curtain of spray, which seemed to hang between the gray sky and gray water. The stump was on fire in the rain, burning like a witch's hat.

It had the effect of a slap, clearing my head and giving me one final chance to use my brain. I took a breath and forced myself to do just that. Why had I come down here in the first place? Why did I think Rogette had brought Kyra toward the lake, where I had just been, instead of carrying her away from me, up the driveway to Lane Forty-two?

Don't be stupid. She came down here because The Street's the way back to Warrington's, and Warrington's is where she's been, all by herself, ever since she sent the boss's body back to California in his private jet.

She had sneaked into the house while I was under Jo's studio, finding the tin box in the belly of the owl and studying that scrap of genealogy. She would have taken Ki then if I'd given her the chance, but I didn't. I came hurrying back, afraid something was wrong, afraid someone might be trying to

854

get hold of the kid —

Had Rogette awakened her? Had Ki seen her and tried to warn me before drifting off again? Was that what had brought me in such a hurry? Maybe. I'd still been in the zone then, we'd still been linked then. Rogette had certainly been in the house when I came back. She might even have been in the north-bedroom closet and peering at me through the crack. Part of me had known it, too. Part of me had felt her, felt something that was not-Sara.

Then I'd left again. Grabbed the carry-bag from Slips 'n Greens and come down here. Turned right, turned north. Toward the birch, the rock, the bag of bones. I'd done what I had to do, and while I was doing it, Rogette carried Kyra down the railroad-tie steps behind me and turned left on The Street. Turned south toward Warrington's. With a sinking feeling deep in my belly, I realized I had probably heard Ki . . . might even have seen her. That bird peeking timidly out from cover during the lull had been no bird. Ki was awake by then, Ki had seen me — perhaps had seen Jo, as well — and tried to call out. She had managed just that one little peep before Rogette had covered her mouth.

How long ago had that been? It seemed like forever, but I had an idea it hadn't been long at all — less than five minutes, maybe.

But it doesn't take long to drown a child. The image of Kito's bare arm sticking straight out of the water tried to come back — the hand at the end of it opening and closing, opening and closing, as if it were trying to breathe for the lungs that couldn't — and I pushed it away. I also suppressed the urge to simply sprint in the direction of Warrington's. Panic would take me for sure if I did that.

In all the years since her death I had never longed for Jo with the bitter intensity I felt then. But she was gone; there wasn't even a whisper of her. With no one to depend on but myself, I started south along the tree-littered Street, skirting the blowdowns where I could, crawling under them if they blocked my way entirely, taking the noisy branch-breaking course over the top only as a last resort. As I went I issued what I imagine are all the standard prayers in such a situation, but none of them seemed to get past the image of Rogette Whitmore's face rising in my mind. Her screaming, merciless face.

I remember thinking *This is the outdoor version of the Ghost House.* Certainly the woods seemed haunted to me as I struggled along: trees only loosened in the first grand blow were falling by the score in this follow-up cap of wind and rain. The noise was

856

like great crunching footfalls, and I didn't need to worry about the noise my own feet were making. When I passed the Batchelders' camp, a circular prefab construction sitting on an outcrop of rock like a hat on a footstool, I saw that the entire roof had been bashed flat by a hemlock.

Half a mile south of Sara I saw one of Ki's white hair ribbons lying in the path. I picked it up, thinking how much that red edging looked like blood. Then I stuffed it into my pocket and went on.

Five minutes later I came to an old moss-caked pine that had fallen across the path; it was still connected to its stump by a stretched and bent network of splinters, and squalled like a line of rusty hinges as the surging water lifted and dropped what had been its upper twenty or thirty feet, now floating in the lake. There was space to crawl under, and when I dropped to my knees I saw other knee-tracks, just beginning to fill with water. I saw something else: the second hair ribbon. I tucked it into my pocket with the first.

I was halfway under the pine when I heard another tree go over, this one much closer. The sound was followed by a scream — not pain or fear but surprised anger. Then, even over the hiss of the rain and the wind, I could hear Rogette's voice: *"Come back! Don't go out there, it's dangerous!"*

I squirmed the rest of the way under the tree, barely feeling the stump of a branch which tore a groove in my lower back, got to my feet, and sprinted along the path. If the fallen trees I came to were small, I hurdled them without slowing down. If they were bigger, I scrabbled over with no thought to where they might claw or dig in. Thunder whacked. There was a brilliant stroke of lightning, and in its glare I saw gray barnboard through the trees. On the day I'd first seen Rogette I'd only been able to catch glimpses of Warrington's lodge, but now the forest had been torn open like an old garment — this area would be years recovering. The lodge's rear half had been pretty well demolished by a pair of huge trees that seemed to have fallen together. They had crossed like a knife and fork on a diner's plate and lay on the ruins in a shaggy *X*.

Ki's voice, rising over the storm only because it was shrill with terror: *"Go away! I don't want you, white nana! Go away!"* It was horrible to hear the terror in her voice, but wonderful to hear her voice at all.

About forty feet from where Rogette's shout had frozen me in place, one more tree lay across the path. Rogette herself stood on the far side of it, holding a hand out to Ki. The hand was dripping blood, but I hardly noticed. It was Kyra I noticed.

The dock running between The Street

and The Sunset Bar was a long one — seventy feet at least, perhaps a hundred. Long enough so that on a pretty summer evening you could stroll it hand-in-hand with your date or your lover and make a memory. The storm hadn't torn it away — not yet — but the wind had twisted it like a ribbon. I remember newsreel footage at some childhood Saturday matinee, film of a suspension bridge dancing in a hurricane, and that was what the dock between Warrington's and The Sunset Bar looked like. It jounced up and down in the surging water, groaning in all its slatted joints like a wooden accordion. There had been a rail — presumably to guide those who'd made a heavy night of it safely back to shore — but it was gone now. Kyra was halfway out along this swaying, dipping length of wood. I could see at least three rectangles of blackness between the shore and where she stood, places where boards had snapped off. From beneath the dock came the disturbed *clung-clung-clung* of the empty steel drums that were holding it up. Several of these drums had come unanchored and were floating away. Ki had her arms stretched out for balance like a tightrope walker in the circus. The black Harley-Davidson tee-shirt flapped around her knees and sunburned shoulders.

"Come back!" Rogette cried. Her lank hair flew around her head; the shiny black rain-

coat she was wearing rippled. She was holding both hands out now, one bloody and one not. I had an idea Ki might have bitten her.

"No, white nana!" Ki shook her head in wild negation and I wanted to tell her don't do that, Ki-bird, don't shake your head like that, very bad idea. She tottered, one arm pointed up at the sky and one down at the water so she looked for a moment like an airplane in a steep bank. If the dock had picked that moment to take a hard buck beneath her, Ki would have spilled off the side. She regained some precarious balance instead, although I thought I saw her bare feet slide a little on the slick boards. *"Go away, white nana, I don't want you! Go . . . go take a nap, you look tired!"*

Ki didn't see me; all her attention was fixed on the white nana. The white nana didn't see me, either. I dropped to my belly and squirmed under the tree, pulling myself along with my clawed hands. Thunder rolled across the lake like a big mahogany ball, the sound echoing off the mountains. When I got to my knees again, I saw that Rogette was advancing slowly toward the shore end of the dock. For every step she took forward, Kyra took a shaky, dangerous step backward. Rogette was holding her good hand out, though for a moment I thought this one had begun to bleed as well.

The stuff running through her bunchy fingers was too dark for blood, however, and when she began to talk, speaking in a hideous coaxing voice that made my skin crawl, I realized it was melting chocolate.

"Let's play the game, Ki-bird," Rogette cooed. "Do you want to start?" She took a step. Ki took a compensatory step backward, tottered, caught her balance. My heart stopped, then resumed racing. I closed the distance between myself and the woman as rapidly as I could, but I didn't run; I didn't want her to know a thing until she woke up. *If* she woke up. I didn't care if she did or not. Hell, if I could fracture the back of George Footman's skull with a hammer, I could certainly put a hurt on this horror. As I walked, I laced my hands together into one large fist.

"No? Don't want to start? Too shy?" Rogette spoke in a sugary *Romper Room* voice that made me want to grind my teeth together. "All right, *I'll* start. Happy! What rhymes with happy, Ki-bird? Pappy . . . and nappy . . . you were taking a nappy, weren't you, when I came and woke you up. And lappy . . . would you want to come and sit on my lappy, Ki-bird? We'll feed each other chocolate, just like we used to . . . I'll tell you a new knock-knock joke . . ."

Another step. She had come to the edge of the dock. If she'd thought of it, she could simply have thrown rocks at Kyra as she had at me, thrown until she connected with one and knocked Ki into the lake. But I don't think she got even close to such a notion. Once crazy goes past a certain point, you're on a turnpike with no exit ramps. Rogette had other plans for Kyra.

"Come on, Ki-Ki, play the game with white nana." She held out the chocolate again, gooey Hershey's Kisses dripping through crumpled foil. Kyra's eyes shifted, and at last she saw me. I shook my head, trying to tell her to be quiet, but it was no good — an expression of joyous relief crossed her face. She cried out my name, and I saw Rogette's shoulders go up in surprise.

I ran the last dozen feet, raising my joined hands like a club, but I slipped a little on the wet ground at the crucial moment and Rogette made a kind of ducking cringe. Instead of striking her at the back of the neck as I'd meant to, my joined hands only glanced off her shoulder. She staggered, went to one knee, and was up again almost at once. Her eyes were like little blue arc-lamps, spitting rage instead of electricity. *"You!"* she said, hissing the word over the top of her tongue, turning it into the sound of some ancient curse: *Heeyuuuu!* Behind us Kyra screamed my name, stagger-dancing on the wet wood and waving her arms in an effort to keep from falling in the lake. Water slopped onto the deck and ran over her small bare feet.

"Hold on, Ki!" I called back. Rogette saw my attention shift and took her chance — she spun and ran out onto the dock. I sprang after her, grabbed her by the hair, and it came off in my hand. All of it. I stood there at the edge of the surging lake with her mat of white hair dangling from my fist like a scalp.

Rogette looked over her shoulder, snarling, an ancient bald gnome in the rain, and I thought *It's him, it's Devore, he never died at all, somehow he and the woman swapped identities, she was the one who committed suicide, it was her body that went back to California on the jet —*

Even as she turned the other way again and began to run toward Ki, I knew better. It was Rogette, all right, but she'd come by that hideous resemblance honestly. Whatever was wrong with her had done more than make her hair fall out; it had aged her as well. Seventy, I'd thought, but that had to be at least ten years beyond the actual mark.

I've known a lot of folks name their kids alike, Mrs. M. had told me. *They think it's cute.* Max Devore must have thought so, too, because he had named a son Roger and his daughter Rogette. Perhaps she'd come by the Whitmore part honestly — she might

have been married in her younger years —
but once the wig was gone, her antecedents
were beyond argument. The woman tot-
tering along the wet dock to finish the job
was Kyra's aunt.

Ki began to back up rapidly, making no
effort to be careful and pick her footing.
She was going into the drink; there was no
way she could stay up. But before she could
fall, a wave slapped the dock between them
at a place where some of the barrels had
come loose and the slatted walkway was already partly submerged. Foamy water flew
up and began to twist into one of those
helix shapes I had seen before. Rogette
stopped ankle-deep in the water sloshing
over the dock, and I stopped about twelve
feet behind her.

The shape solidified, and even before I
could make out the face I recognized the
baggy shorts with their fading swirls of color
and the smock top. Only Kmart sells smock
tops of such perfect shapelessness; I think it
may be a federal law.

It was Mattie. A grave gray Mattie,
looking at Rogette with grave gray eyes.
Rogette raised her hands, tottered, tried to
turn. At that moment a wave surged under
the dock, making it rise and then drop like
an amusement-park ride. Rogette went over
the side. Beyond her, beyond the water-

shape in the rain, I could see Ki sprawling on the porch of The Sunset Bar. That last heave had flipped her to temporary safety like a human tiddlywink.

Mattie was looking at me, her lips moving, her eyes on mine. I had been able to tell what Jo was saying, but this time I had no idea. I tried with all my might, but I couldn't make it out.

"Mommy! Mommy!"

The figure didn't so much turn as revolve; it didn't actually seem to be there below the hem of the long shorts. It moved up the dock to the bar, where Ki was now standing with her arms held out.

Something grabbed at my foot.

I looked down and saw a drowning apparition in the surging water. Dark eyes stared up at me from beneath the bald skull. Rogette was coughing water from between lips that were as purple as plums. Her free hand waved weakly up at me. The fingers opened . . . and closed. Opened . . . and closed. I dropped to one knee and took it. It clamped over mine like a steel claw and she yanked, trying to pull me in with her. The purple lips peeled back from yellow toothpegs like those in Sara's skull. And yes — I thought that this time Rogette was the one laughing.

I rocked on my haunches and yanked her up. I didn't think about it; it was pure instinct. I had her by at least a hundred pounds, and three quarters of her came out of the lake like a gigantic, freakish trout. She screamed, darted her head forward, and buried her teeth in my wrist. The pain was immediate and enormous. I jerked my arm up even higher and then brought it down, not thinking about hurting her, wanting only to rid myself of that weasel's mouth. Another wave hit the half-submerged dock as I did. Its rising, splintered edge impaled Rogette's descending face. One eye popped; a dripping yellow splinter ran up her nose like a dagger; the scant skin of her forehead split, snapping away from the bone like two suddenly released windowshades. Then the lake pulled her away. I saw the torn topography of her face a moment longer, up-turned into the torrential rain, wet and as pale as the light from a fluorescent bar. Then she rolled over, her black vinyl raincoat swirling around her like a shroud.

What I saw when I looked back toward The Sunset Bar was another glimpse under the skin of this world, but one far different from the face of Sara in the Green Lady or the snarling, half-glimpsed shape of the Outsider. Kyra stood on the wide wooden porch in front of the bar amid a litter of overturned wicker furniture. In front of her was a waterspout in which I could still see — very faintly — the fading shape of a woman. She was on her knees, holding her arms out.

They tried to embrace. Ki's arms went through Mattie and came out dripping. "Mommy, I can't get you!"

The woman in the water was speaking — I could see her lips moving. Ki looked at her, rapt. Then, for just a moment Mattie turned to me. Our eyes met, and hers were made of the lake. They were Dark Score, which was here long before I came and will remain long after I am gone. I put my hands to my mouth, kissed my palms, and held them out to her. Shimmery hands went up, as if to catch those kisses.

"Mommy don't go!" Kyra screamed, and flung her arms around the figure. She was immediately drenched and backed away with her eyes squinched shut, coughing. There was no longer a woman with her; there was only water running across the boards and dripping through the cracks to rejoin the lake, which comes up from deep springs far below, from the fissures in the rock which underlies the TR and all this part of our world.

Moving carefully, doing my own balancing act, I made my way out along the wavering dock to The Sunset Bar. When I got there I took Kyra in my arms. She hugged me tight, shivering fiercely against me. I could hear the small dicecup rattle of her teeth and smell the lake in her hair.

"Mattie came," she said.

"I know. I saw her."

"Mattie made the white nana go away."

"I saw that, too. Be very still now, Ki. We're going back to solid ground, but you can't move around a lot. If you do, we'll end up swimming."

She was good as gold. When we were on The Street again and I tried to put her down, she clung to my neck fiercely. That was okay with me. I thought of taking her into Warrington's, but didn't. There would be towels in there, probably dry clothes as well, but I had an idea there might also be a bathtub full of warm water waiting in there. Besides, the rain was slackening again and this time the sky looked lighter in the west.

"What did Mattie tell you, hon?" I asked as we walked north along The Street. Ki would let me put her down so we could crawl under the downed trees we came to, but raised her arms to be picked up again on the far side of each.

"To be a good girl and not be sad. But I am sad. I'm *very* sad." She began to cry, and I stroked her wet hair.

By the time we got to the railroad-tie steps she had cried herself out . . . and over the mountains in the west, I could see one small but very brilliant wedge of blue.

"All the woods fell down," Ki said, looking around. Her eyes were very wide.

"Well . . . not all, but a lot of them, I guess."

Halfway up the steps I paused, puffing and seriously winded. I didn't ask Ki if I could put her down, though. I didn't *want* to put her down. I just wanted to catch my breath.

"Mike?"

"What, doll?"

"Mattie told me something else."

"What?"

"Can I whisper?"

"If you want to, sure."

Ki leaned close, put her lips to my ear, and whispered.

I listened. When she was done I nodded, kissed her cheek, shifted her to the other hip, and carried her the rest of the way up to the house.

'T'wasn't the stawm of the century, chummy, and don't you go thinkin that it was. Nossir.

So said the old-timers who sat in front of the big Army medics' tent that served as the Lakeview General that late summer and fall. A huge elm had toppled across Route 68 and bashed the store in like a Saltines box. Adding injury to insult, the elm had carried a bunch of spitting live lines with it. They ignited propane from a ruptured tank, and the whole thing went kaboom. The tent was a pretty good warm-weather substitute, though, and folks on the TR took to saying they was goin down to the MASH for bread and beer — this because you could still see a faded red cross on both sides of the tent's roof.

The old-timers sat along one canvas wall in folding chairs, waving to other old-timers when they went pooting by in their rusty old-timer cars (all certified old-timers own either Fords or Chevys, so I'm well on my way in that regard), swapping their undershirts for flannels as the days began to cool toward cider season and spud-digging, watching the township start to rebuild itself around them. And as they watched they talked about the ice storm of the past winter, the one that knocked out lights and splintered a million trees between Kittery and Fort Kent; they talked about the cyclones that touched down in August of 1985; they talked about the sleet hurricane of 1927. Now *there* was some stawms, they said. *There* was some stawms, by Gorry.

I'm sure they've got a point, and I don't argue with them — you rarely win an argument with a genuine Yankee old-timer, never if it's about the weather — but for me the storm of July 21, 1998, will always be *the* storm. And I know a little girl who feels the same. She may live until 2100, given all the benefits of modern medicine, but I think that for Kyra Elizabeth Devore that will always be *the* storm. The one where her dead mother came to her dressed in the lake.

The first vehicle to come down my driveway didn't arrive until almost six o'clock. It turned out to be not a Castle County police car but a yellow bucket-loader with flashing yellow lights on top of the cab and a guy in a Central Maine Power Company slicker working the controls. The guy in the other seat was a cop, though — was in fact Norris Ridgewick, the County Sheriff himself. And he came to my door with his gun drawn.

The change in the weather the TV guy had promised had already arrived, clouds and storm-cells driven east by a chilly wind running just under gale force. Trees had continued to fall in the dripping woods for at least an hour after the rain stopped. Around five o'clock I made us toasted-cheese sandwiches and tomato soup . . . comfort food, Jo would have called it. Kyra ate listlessly, but she did eat, and she drank a lot of milk. I had wrapped her in another of my tee-shirts and she tied her own hair back. I offered her the white ribbons, but she shook her head decisively and opted for a rubber band instead. "I don't like those ribbons anymore," she said. I decided I didn't, either, and threw them away. Ki

871

watched me do it and offered no objection. Then I crossed the living room to the woodstove.

"What are you doing?" She finished her second glass of milk, wriggled off her chair, and came over to me.

"Making a fire. Maybe all those hot days thinned my blood. That's what my mom would have said, anyway."

She watched silently as I pulled sheet after sheet from the pile of paper I'd taken off the table and stacked on top of the woodstove, balled each one up, and slipped it in through the door. When I felt I'd loaded enough, I began to lay bits of kindling on top.

"What's written on those papers?" Ki asked.

"Nothing important."

"Is it a story?"

"Not really. It was more like . . . oh, I don't know. A crossword puzzle. Or a letter."

"Pretty long letter," she said, and then laid her head against my leg as if she were tired.

"Yeah," I said. "Love letters usually are, but keeping them around is a bad idea."

"Why?"

"Because they . . ." *Can come back to haunt you* was what rose to mind, but I wouldn't say it. "Because they can embarrass you in later life."

"Oh."

"Besides," I said. "These papers are like your ribbons, in a way."

"You don't like them anymore."

"Right."

She saw the box then — the tin box with JO'S NOTIONS written on the front. It was on the counter between the living room and the sink, not far from where old Krazy Kat had hung on the wall. I didn't remember bringing the box up from the studio with me, but I suppose I might not have; I was pretty freaked. I also think it could have come up . . . kind of by itself. I *do* believe such things now; I have reason to.

Kyra's eyes lit up in a way they hadn't since she had wakened from her short nap to find out her mother was dead. She stood on tiptoe to take hold of the box, then ran her small fingers across the gilt letters. I thought about how important it was for a kid to own a tin box. You had to have one for your secret stuff — the best toy, the prettiest bit of lace, the first piece of jewelry. Or a picture of your mother, perhaps.

"This is so . . . *pretty*," she said in a soft, awed voice.

"You can have it if you don't mind it saying JO'S NOTIONS instead of KI'S NOTIONS. There are some papers in it I want to read, but I could put them somewhere else."

She looked at me to make sure I wasn't

kidding, saw I wasn't.

"I'd love it," she said in the same soft, awed voice.

I took the box from her, scooped out the steno books, notes, and clippings, then handed it back to Ki. She practiced taking the lid off and then putting it back on.

"Guess what I'll put in here," she said.

"Secret treasures?"

"Yes!" she said, and actually smiled for a moment. "Who was Jo, Mike? Do I know her? I do, don't I? She was one of the fridge-afator people."

"She —" A thought occurred. I shuffled through the yellowed clippings. Nothing. I thought I'd lost it somewhere along the way, then saw a corner of what I was looking for peeking from the middle of one of the steno notebooks. I slid it out and handed it to Ki.

"What is it?"

"A backwards photo. Hold it up to the light."

She did, and looked for a long time, rapt. Faint as a dream I could see my wife in her hand, my wife standing on the swimming float in her two-piece suit.

"That's Jo," I said.

"She's pretty. I'm glad to have her box for my things."

"I am too, Ki." I kissed the top of her head.

When Sheriff Ridgewick hammered on the door, I thought it wise to answer with my hands up. He looked wired. What seemed to ease the situation was a simple, uncalculated question.

"Where's Alan Pangborn these days, Sheriff?"

"Over New Hampshire," Ridgewick said, lowering his pistol a little (a minute or two later he holstered it without even seeming to be aware he had done so). "He and Polly are doing real well. Except for her arthritis. That's nasty, I guess, but she still has her good days. A person can go along quite awhile if they get a good day every once and again, that's what I think. Mr. Noonan, I have a lot of questions for you. You know that, don't you?"

"Yes."

"First off and most important, do you have the child? Kyra Devore?"

"Yes."

"Where is she?"

"I'll be happy to show you."

We walked down the north-wing corridor and stood just outside the bedroom doorway, looking in. The duvet was pulled up to her chin and she was sleeping deeply. The stuffed dog was curled in one hand — we could just see its muddy tail poking out of her fist at one end and its nose poking out at the other. We stood there for a long time, neither of us saying anything, watching her sleep in the light of a summer evening. In the woods the trees had stopped falling, but the wind still blew. Around the eaves of Sara Laughs it made a sound like ancient music.

Epilogue

It snowed for Christmas — a polite six inches of powder that made the carollers working the streets of Sanford look like they belonged in *It's a Wonderful Life.* By the time I came back from checking Kyra for the third time, it was quarter past one on the morning of the twenty-sixth, and the snow had stopped. A late moon, plump but pale, was peeking through the unravelling fluff of clouds.

I was Christmasing with Frank again, and we were the last two up. The kids, Ki included, were dead to the world, sleeping off the annual bacchanal of food and presents. Frank was on his third Scotch — it had been a three-Scotch story if there ever was one, I guess — but I'd barely drunk the top off my first one. I think I might have gotten into the bottle quite heavily if not for Ki. On the days when I have her I usually don't drink so much as a glass of beer. And to have her three days in a row . . . but shit, *kemo sabe,* if you can't spend Christmas with your kid, what the hell is Christmas for?

"Are you all right?" Frank asked when I sat down again and took another little token sip from my glass.

I grinned at that. Not is *she* all right but

are *you* all right. Well, nobody ever said Frank was stupid.

"You should've seen me when the Department of Human Services let me have her for a weekend in October. I must have checked on her a dozen times before I went to bed . . . and then I *kept* checking. Getting up and peeking in on her, listening to her breathe. I didn't sleep a wink Friday night, caught maybe three hours on Saturday. So this is a big improvement. But if you ever blab any of what I've told you, Frank — if they ever hear about me filling up that bathtub before the storm knocked the gennie out — I can kiss my chances of adopting her goodbye. I'll probably have to fill out a form in triplicate before they even let me attend her high-school graduation."

I hadn't meant to tell Frank the bathtub part, but once I started talking, almost everything spilled out. I suppose it had to spill to someone if I was ever to get on with my life. I'd assumed that John Storrow would be the one on the other side of the confessional when the time came, but John didn't want to talk about any of those events except as they bore on our ongoing legal business, which nowadays is all about Kyra Elizabeth Devore.

"I'll keep my mouth shut, don't worry. How goes the adoption battle?"

"Slow. I've come to loathe the State of

878

Maine court system, and DHS as well. You take the people who work in those bureaucracies one by one and they're mostly fine, but when you put them together . . ."

"Bad, huh?"

"I sometimes feel like a character in *Bleak House*. That's the one where Dickens says that in court nobody wins but the lawyers. John tells me to be patient and count my blessings, that we're making amazing progress considering that I'm that most untrustworthy of creatures, an unmarried white male of middle age, but Ki's been in two foster-home situations since Mattie died, and —"

"Doesn't she have kin in one of those neighboring towns?"

"Mattie's aunt. She didn't want anything to do with Ki when Mattie was alive and has even less interest now. Especially since —"

"— since Ki's not going to be rich."

"Yeah."

"The Whitmore woman was lying about Devore's will."

"Absolutely. He left everything to a foundation that's supposed to foster global computer literacy. With due respect to the number-crunchers of the world, I can't imagine a colder charity."

"How is John?"

"Pretty well mended, but he's never going to get the use of his right arm back entirely.

He damned near died of blood-loss."

Frank had led me away from the entwined subjects of Ki and custody quite well for a man deep into his third Scotch, and I was willing enough to go. I could hardly bear to think of her long days and longer nights in those homes where the Department of Human Services stores away children like knickknacks nobody wants. Ki didn't live in those places but only existed in them, pale and listless, like a well-fed rabbit kept in a cage. Each time she saw my car turning in or pulling up she came alive, waving her arms and dancing like Snoopy on his doghouse. Our weekend in October had been wonderful (despite my obsessive need to check her every half hour or so after she was asleep), and the Christmas holiday had been even better. Her emphatic desire to be with me was helping in court more than anything else . . . yet the wheels still turned slowly.

Maybe in the spring, Mike, John told me. He was a new John these days, pale and serious. The slightly arrogant eager beaver who had wanted nothing more than to go head to head with Mr. Maxwell "Big Bucks" Devore was no longer in evidence. John had learned something about mortality on the twenty-first of July, and something about the world's idiot cruelty, as well. The man who had taught himself to shake with his left hand instead of his right was no longer interested in partying 'til he puked. He was seeing a girl in Philly, the daughter of one of his mother's friends. I had no idea if it was serious or not, Ki's "Unca John" is close-mouthed about that part of his life, but when a young man is of his own accord seeing the daughter of one of his mother's friends, it usually is.

Maybe in the spring: it was his mantra that late fall and early winter. *What am I doing wrong?* I asked him once — this was just after Thanksgiving and another setback.

Nothing, he replied. *Single-parent adoptions are always slow, and when the putative adopter is a man, it's worse.* At that point in the conversation John made an ugly little gesture, poking the index finger of his left hand in and out of his loosely cupped right fist.

That's blatant sex discrimination, John.

Yeah, but usually it's justified. Blame it on every twisted asshole who ever decided he had a right to take off some little kid's pants, if you want; blame it on the bureaucracy, if you want; hell, blame it on cosmic rays if you want. It's a slow process, but you're going to win in the end. You've got a clean record, you've got Kyra saying "I want to be with Mike" to every judge and DHS worker she sees, you've got enough money to keep after them no matter how much they squirm and no matter how many forms they throw at you . . . and most of all, buddy, you've got me.

I had something else, too — what Ki had whispered in my ear as I paused to catch my breath on the steps. I'd never told John about that, and it was one of the few things I didn't tell Frank, either.

Mattie says I'm your little guy now, she had whispered. *Mattie says you'll take care of me.*

I was trying to — as much as the fucking slowpokes at Human Services would let me — but the waiting was hard.

Frank picked up the Scotch and tilted it in my direction. I shook my head. Ki had her heart set on snowman-making, and I wanted to be able to face the glare of early sun on fresh snow without a headache.

"Frank, how much of this do you actually believe?"

He poured for himself, then just sat for a time, looking down at the table and thinking. When he raised his head again there was a smile on his face. It was so much like Jo's that it broke my heart. And when he spoke, he juiced his ordinarily faint Boston brogue.

"Sure and I'm a half-drunk Irishman who just finished listenin to the granddaddy of all ghost stories on Christmas night," he said. "I believe all of it, you silly git."

I laughed and so did he. We did it mostly through the nose, as men are apt to do when up late, maybe in their cups a little, and don't want to wake the house.

"Come on — how much really?"

"All of it," he repeated, dropping the brogue. "Because Jo believed it. And because of her." He nodded his head in the direction of the stairs so I'd know which her he meant. "She's like no other little girl I've ever seen. She's sweet enough, but there's something in her eyes. At first I thought it was losing her mother the way she did, but that's not it. There's more, isn't there?"

"Yes," I said.

"It's in you, too. It's touched you both."

I thought of the baying thing which Jo had managed to hold back while I poured the lye into that rotted roll of canvas. An Outsider, she had called it. I hadn't gotten a clear look at it, and probably that was good. Probably that was very good.

"Mike?" Frank looked concerned. "You're shivering."

"I'm okay," I said. "Really."

"What's it like in the house now?" he asked. I was still living in Sara Laughs. I procrastinated until early November, then put the Derry house up for sale.

"Quiet."

"Totally quiet?"

I nodded, but that wasn't completely true. On a couple of occasions I had awakened with a sensation Mattie had once mentioned — that there was someone in bed with me. But not a dangerous presence. On a couple of occasions I have smelled (or thought I have) Red perfume. And sometimes, even when the air is perfectly still, Bunter's bell will shiver out a few notes. It's as if something lonely wants to say hello.

Frank glanced at the clock, then back at me, almost apologetically. "I've got a few more questions — okay?"

"If you can't stay up until the wee hours on Boxing Day morning," I said, "I guess you never can. Fire away."

"What did you tell the police?"

"I didn't have to tell them much of anything. Footman talked enough to suit them — too much to suit Norris Ridgewick. Footman said that he and Osgood — it was Osgood driving the car, Devore's pet broker — did the drive-by because Devore had made threats about what would happen to them if they didn't. The State cops also found a copy of a wire-transfer among Devore's effects at Warrington's. Two million dollars to an account in the Grand Caymans. The name scribbled on the copy is Randolph Footman. Randolph is George's middle name. Mr. Footman is now residing in Shawshank State Prison."

"What about Rogette?"

"Well, Whitmore was her mother's maiden name, but I think it's safe to say that Rogette's heart belonged to Daddy. She had leukemia, was diagnosed in 1996. In people her age — she was only fifty-seven when she died, by the way — it's fatal in two cases out of every three, but she was doing the chemo. Hence the wig."

"Why did she try to kill Kyra? I don't understand that. If you broke Sara Tidwell's hold on this earthly plane of ours when you dissolved her bones, the curse should have . . . why are you looking at me that way?"

"You'd understand if you'd ever met Devore," I said. "This is the man who lit the whole fucking TR on fire as a way of saying goodbye when he headed west to sunny California. I thought of him the second I pulled the wig off, thought they'd swapped identities somehow. Then I thought *Oh no, it's her all right, it's Rogette, she's just lost her hair somehow.*"

"And you were right. The chemo."

"I was also wrong. I know more about ghosts than I did, Frank. Maybe the most important thing is that what you see first, what you think first . . . that's what's usually true. It was him that day. Devore. He came back at the end. I'm sure of it. At the end it wasn't about Sara, not for him. At the end it wasn't even about Kyra. At the end it was about Scooter Larribee's sled."

Silence between us. For a few moments it was so deep that I could actually hear the house breathing. You can hear that, you

885

know. If you really listen. That's something else I know now.

"Christ," he said at last.

"I don't think Devore came east from California to kill her," I said. "That wasn't the original plan."

"Then what was? Get to know his granddaughter? Mend his fences?"

"God, no. You still don't understand what he was."

"Tell me, then."

"A human monster. He came back to *buy* her, but Mattie wouldn't sell. Then, when Sara got hold of him, he began to plan Ki's death. I suspect that Sara never found a more willing tool."

"How many did she kill in all?" Frank asked.

"I don't know for sure. I don't think I want to. Based on Jo's notes and clippings, I'd say that there were perhaps four other . . . directed murders, shall we call them? . . . in the years between 1901 and 1998. All children, all *K*-names, all closely related to the men who killed her."

"My God."

"I don't think God had much to do with it . . . but she made them pay, all right."

"You're sorry for her, aren't you?"

"Yes. I would have torn her apart before I let her put so much as a finger on Ki, but of course I am. She was raped and murdered.

886

Her child was drowned while she herself lay dying. My God, aren't *you* sorry for her?"

"I suppose I am. Mike, do you know who the other boy was? The crying boy? Was he the one who died of blood-poisoning?"

"Most of Jo's notes concerned that part of it — it's where she got started. Royce Merrill knew the story well. The crying boy was Reg Tidwell, Junior. You have to understand that by September of 1901, when the Red-Tops played their last show in Castle County, almost everyone on the TR knew that Sara and her boy had been murdered, and almost everyone had a good idea of who'd done it.

"Reg Tidwell spent a lot of that August hounding the County Sheriff, Nehemiah Bannerman. At first it was to find them alive — Tidwell wanted a search mounted — and then it was to find their bodies, and then it was to find their killers . . . because once he accepted that they were dead, he never doubted that they'd been murdered.

"Bannerman was sympathetic at first. *Everyone* seemed sympathetic at first. The Red-Top crowd had been treated wonderfully during their time on the TR — that was what infuriated Jared the most — and I think you can forgive Son Tidwell for making a crucial mistake."

"What mistake was that?"

Why, he got the idea that Mars was heaven, I

thought. *The TR must have seemed like heaven to them, right up until Sara and Kito went for a stroll, the boy carrying his berry-bucket, and never came back. It must have seemed that they'd finally found a place where they could be black people and still be allowed to breathe.*

"Thinking they'd be treated like regular folks when things went wrong, just because they'd been treated that way when things were right. Instead, the TR clubbed together against them. No one who had an idea of what Jared and his protégés had done *condoned* it, exactly, but when the chips were down . . ."

"You protect your own, you wash your dirty laundry with the door closed," Frank murmured, and finished his drink.

"Yeah. By the time the Red-Tops played the Castle County Fair, their little community down by the lake had begun to break up — this is all according to Jo's notes, you understand; there's not a whisper of it in any of the town histories.

"By Labor Day the active harassment had started — so Royce told Jo. It got a little uglier every day — a little scarier — but Son Tidwell flat didn't want to go, not until he found out what had happened to his sister and nephew. He apparently kept the blood family there in the meadow even after the others had taken off for friendlier locations.

"Then someone laid the trap. There was a clearing in the woods about a mile east of what's now called Tidwell's Meadow; it had a big birch cross in the middle of it. Jo had a picture of it in her studio. That was where the black community had their services after the doors of the local churches were closed to them. The boy — Junior — used to go up there a lot to pray or just to sit and meditate. There were plenty of folks in the township who knew his routine. Someone put a leghold trap on the little path through the woods that the boy used. Covered it with leaves and needles."

"Jesus," Frank said. He sounded ill.

"Probably it wasn't Jared Devore or his logger-boys who set it, either — they didn't want any more to do with Sara and Son's people after the murders, they kept right clear of them. It might not even have been a friend of those boys. By then they didn't *have* that many friends. But that didn't change the fact that those folks down by the lake were getting out of their place, scratching at things better left alone, refusing to take no for an answer. So someone set the trap. I don't think there was any intent to actually kill the boy, but to maim him? Maybe see him with his foot off, condemned to a lifetime crutch? I think they may have gotten that far in their imagining.

"In any case it worked. The boy stepped

in the trap . . . and for quite awhile they didn't find him. The pain must have been excruciating. Then the blood-poisoning. He died. Son gave up. He had other kids to think about, not to mention the people who'd stuck with him. They packed up their clothes and their guitars and left. Jo traced some of them to North Carolina, where many of the descendants still live. And during the fires of 1933, the ones young Max Devore set, the cabins burned flat."

"I don't understand why the bodies of Sara and her son weren't found," Frank said. "I understand that what you smelled — the putrescence — wasn't there in any physical sense. But surely at the time . . . if this path you call The Street was so popular . . ."

"Devore and the others *didn't* bury them where I found them, not to begin with. They would have started by dragging the bodies deeper into the woods — maybe up to where the north wing of Sara Laughs stands now. They covered them with brush and came back that night. Must have been that night; to leave them any longer would have drawn every carnivore in the woods. They took them someplace else and buried them in that roll of canvas. Jo didn't know where, but my guess is Bowie Ridge, where they'd spent most of the summer cutting. Hell, Bowie Ridge is still pretty isolated.

They put the bodies somewhere; we might as well say there."

"Then how . . . why . . ."

"Draper Finney wasn't the only one haunted by what they did, Frank — they all were. Literally *haunted*. With the possible exception of Jared Devore, I suppose. He lived another ten years and apparently never missed a meal. But the boys had bad dreams, they drank too much, they fought too much, they argued . . . bristled if anyone so much as mentioned the Red-Tops . . ."

"Might as well have gone around wearing signs reading KICK US, WE'RE GUILTY," Frank commented.

"Yes. It probably didn't help that most of the TR was giving them the silent treatment. Then Finney died in the quarry — committed suicide in the quarry, I think — and Jared's logger-boys got an idea. Came down with it like a cold. Only it was more like a compulsion. Their idea was that if they dug up the bodies and reburied them where it happened, things'd go back to normal for them."

"Did Jared go along with the idea?"

"According to Jo's notes, by then they never went near him. They reburied the bag of bones — without Jared Devore's help — where I eventually dug it up. In the late fall or early winter of 1902, I think."

"She *wanted* to be back, didn't she? Sara.

891

Back where she could really work on them."

"And on the whole township. Yes. Jo thought so, too. Enough so she didn't want to go back to Sara Laughs once she found some of this stuff out. Especially when she guessed she was pregnant. When we started trying to have a baby and I suggested the name Kia, how that must have scared her! And I never saw."

"Sara thought she could use you to kill Kyra if Devore played out before he could get the job done — he was old and in bad health, after all. Jo gambled that you'd save her instead. That's what you think, isn't it?"

"Yes."

"And she was right."

"I couldn't have done it alone. From the night I dreamed about Sara singing, Jo was with me every step of the way. Sara couldn't make her quit."

"No, she wasn't a quitter," Frank agreed, and wiped at one eye. "What do you know about your twice-great-aunt? The one that married Auster?"

"Bridget Noonan Auster," I said. "Bridey, to her friends. I asked my mother and she swears up and down she knows nothing, that Jo never asked her about Bridey, but I think she might be lying. The young woman was definitely the black sheep of the family — I can tell just by the sound of Mom's voice when the name comes up. I have no idea how she met Benton Auster. Let's say he was down in the Prout's Neck part of the world visiting friends and started flirting with her at a clambake. That's as likely as anything else. This was in 1884. She was eighteen, he was twenty-three. They got married, one of those hurry-up jobs. Harry, the one who actually drowned Kito Tidwell, came along six months later."

"So he was barely seventeen when it happened," Frank said. "Great God."

"And by then his mother had gotten religion. His terror over what she'd think if she ever found out was part of the reason he did what he did. Any other questions, Frank? Because I'm really starting to fade."

For several moments he said nothing — I had begun to think he was done when he said, "Two others. Do you mind?"

"I guess it's too late to back out now. What are they?"

"The Shape you spoke of. The Outsider. That troubles me."

I said nothing. It troubled me, too.

"Do you think there's a chance it might come back?"

"It always does," I said. "At the risk of sounding pompous, the Outsider eventually comes back for all of us, doesn't it? Because we're all bags of bones. And the Outsider . . . Frank, the Outsider wants what's in the bag."

He mulled this over, then swallowed the rest of his Scotch at a gulp.

"You had one other question?"

"Yes," he said. "Have you started writing again?"

I went upstairs a few minutes later, checked Ki, brushed my teeth, checked Ki again, then climbed into bed. From where I lay I was able to look out the window at the pale moon shining on the snow.

Have you started writing again?

No. Other than a rather lengthy essay on how I spent my summer vacation which I may show to Kyra in some later year, there's been nothing. I know that Harold is nervous, and sooner or later I suppose I'll have to call him and tell him what he already guesses: the machine which ran so sweet for so long has stopped. It isn't broken — this memoir came out with nary a gasp or missed heartbeat — but the machine has stopped, just the same. There's gas in the tank, the sparkplugs spark and the battery bats, but the wordygurdy stands there quiet in the middle of my head. I've put a tarp over it. It's served me well, you see, and I don't like to think of it getting dusty.

Some of it has to do with the way Mattie died. It occurred to me at some point this fall that I had written similar deaths in at least two of my books, and popular fiction is heaped with other examples of the same thing. Have you set up a moral dilemma you don't know how to solve? Is the protagonist sexually attracted to a woman who is much too young for him, shall we say? Need a quick fix? Easiest thing in the world. "When the story starts going sour, bring on the man with the gun." Raymond Chandler said that, or something like it — close enough for government work, *kemo sabe*.

Murder is the worst kind of pornography, murder is let me do what I want taken to its final extreme. I believe that even make-believe murders should be taken seriously; maybe that's another idea I got last summer. Perhaps I got it while Mattie was struggling in my arms, gushing blood from her smashed head and dying blind, still crying out for her daughter as she left this earth. To think I might have written such a hellishly convenient death in a book, *ever*, sickens me.

Or maybe I just wish there'd been a little more time.

I remember telling Ki it's best not to leave love letters around; what I thought but didn't say was that they can come back to haunt you. I am haunted anyway . . . but I will not willingly haunt myself, and when I closed my book of dreams I did so of my own free will. I think I could have poured lye over those dreams as well, but from that I stayed my hand.

I've seen things I never expected to see and felt things I never expected to feel — not the least of them what I felt and still feel for the child sleeping down the hall from me. She's my little guy now, I'm her big guy, and that's the important thing. Nothing else seems to matter half so much.

Thomas Hardy, who supposedly said that the most brilliantly drawn character in a novel is but a bag of bones, stopped writing novels himself after finishing *Jude the Obscure* and while he was at the height of his narrative genius. He went on writing poetry for another twenty years, and when someone asked him why he'd quit fiction he said he couldn't understand why he had trucked with it so long in the first place. In retrospect it seemed silly to him, he said. Pointless. I know exactly what he meant. In the time between now and whenever the Outsider remembers me and decides to come back, there must be other things to do, things that mean more than those shadows. I think I could go back to clanking chains behind the Ghost House wall, but I have no interest in doing so. I've lost my taste for spooks. I like to imagine Mattie would think of Bartleby in Melville's story.

I've put down my scrivener's pen. These days I prefer not to.

Center Lovell, Maine:
May 25th, 1997–February 6th, 1998

About the Author

Stephen King was born in 1947 and has lived most of his life in the state of Maine, attending the University of Maine at Orono, where he met his wife, the novelist Tabitha King. He began writing stories when he was nine years old, encouraged by an aunt who paid him a quarter each time he finished one. Mr. King was teaching high school English when his first novel, *Carrie*, was accepted for publication. He has since written and published more than thirty novels, including *The Shining*, *The Stand*, *It*, *Desperation*, and *The Green Mile*. His stories and novellas have been collected in four volumes, with a fifth to be published in 1999. Numerous films have been based on his stories, including three — *Carrie*, *Stand by Me*, and *Shawshank Redemption* — that received Academy Award nominations. His most recent volume in the Dark Tower series, begun while he was in college, is *Wizard and Glass*, published in 1997. Among many honors for his work over the years, he received in 1996 the O. Henry First Prize Award for his short story, "The Man in the Black Suit," and in 1997 the Poets & Writers' Writers for Writers Award for his support of writers, writing, and reading. Since 1991 he has played rhythm guitar and sung vocals for The Rock Bottom Remainders, a band of writers that performs now and then around the country to promote literacy. Year after year he roots (so far in vain) for the Red Sox to win the World Series.

Awaking from a state of inebriation, he knew that Ham had beheld his nakedness and "told his two brethren." But "Shem and Japheth took a garment, and laid it upon both their shoulders, and went backward, and covered the nakedness of their father ; and their faces were backward, and they saw not their father's nakedness." [1] It is quite natural to suppose, that, humiliated and chagrined at his sinful conduct, and angered at the behavior of his son and grandson, Ham and Canaan, Noah expressed his disapprobation of Canaan. It was *his* desire, on the impulse of the moment, that Canaan should suffer a humiliation somewhat commensurate with his offence ; and, on the other hand, it was appropriate that he should commend the conduct of his other sons, who sought to hide their father's shame. And all this was done without any inspiration. He simply expressed himself as a fallible man.

Bishop Hopkins, however, is pleased to call this a "prophecy." In order to prophesy, in the scriptural meaning of the word, a man must have the divine unction, and must be moved by the Holy Ghost ; and, in addition to this, it should be said, that a true prophecy always comes to pass, — is sure of fulfilment. Noah was not inspired when he pronounced his curse against Canaan, for the sufficient reason that it was not fulfilled. He was not speaking in the spirit of prophecy when he blessed Shem and Japheth, for the good reason that their descendants have often been in bondage. Now, if these words of Noah were prophetic, were inspired of God, we would naturally expect to find *all of Canaan's descendants in bondage,* and all of Shem's out of bondage, — free! If this prophecy — granting this point to the learned bishop for argument's sake — has not been fulfilled, then we conclude one of two things ; namely, these are not the words of God, or they have not been fulfilled. But they were not the words of prophecy, and consequently never had any divine authority. It was Canaan upon whom Noah pronounced the curse : and Canaan was the son of Ham ; and Ham, it is said, is the progenitor of the Negro race. The Canaanites were not bondmen, but freemen, — powerful tribes when the Hebrews invaded their country ; and from the Canaanites descended the bold and intelligent Carthaginians, as is admitted by the majority of writers on this subject. From Ham proceeded the Egyptians, Libyans, the Phu-

---

[1]   Gen. ix. 23.

that this passage establishes clearly and unmistakably the unity of mankind, in that God created them of one blood ; second, he hath determined "the bounds of their habitation," — hath located them geographically. The language quoted is very explicit. "He hath determined the bounds of their habitation," that is, " all the nations of men.[1]   We have, then, the fact, that there are different "nations of men," and that they are all "of one blood," and, therefore, have a common parent. This declaration was made by the Apostle Paul, an inspired writer, a teacher of great erudition, and a scholar in both the Hebrew and the Greek languages.

It should not be forgotten either, that in Paul's masterly discussion of the doctrine of sin, — the fall of man, — he always refers to Adam as the "one man" by whom sin came into the world.[2]   His Epistle to the Romans abounds in passages which prove very plainly the unity of mankind. The Acts of the Apostles, as well as the Gospels, prove the unity we seek to establish.

But there are a few who would admit the unity of mankind, and still insist that the Negro does not belong to the human family. It is so preposterous, that one has a keen sense of humiliation in the assured consciousness that he goes rather low to meet the enemies of God's poor ; but it can certainly do no harm to meet them with the everlasting truth.

In the Gospel of Luke we read this remarkable historical statement : "And as they led him away, they laid hold upon one Simon, a Cyrenian, coming out of the country, and on him they laid the cross, that he might bear it after Jesus." [3]   By referring to the map, the reader will observe that Cyrene is in Libya, on the north coast of Africa. All the commentators we have been able to consult, on the passage quoted below, agree that this man Simon was a Negro, — a black man. John Melville produced a very remarkable sermon from this passage.[4]   And many of the most celebrated pictures of "The Crucifixion," in Europe, represent this Cyrenian as black, and give him a very prominent place in the most tragic scene ever witnessed on this earth. In the Acts

---

[1]   Deut. xxxii. 8, 9 : "When the Most High divided to the nations their inheritance, when he separated the sons of Adam, he set the bounds of the people according to the number of the children of Israel.   For the Lord's portion is his people ; Jacob is the lot of his inheritance."

[2]   Rom. v. 12, 14-21.

[3]   Luke xxiii. 26 ; Acts vi. 9, also second chapter, tenth verse.   Matthew records the same fact in the twenty-seventh chapter, thirty-second verse : "And as they came out, they found a man of Cyrene, Simon by name : him they compelled to bear his cross."

[4]   See Melville's Sermons.

of the Apostles we have a very full and interesting account of the conversion and immersion of the Ethiopian eunuch, "a man of Ethiopia, an eunuch of great authority under Candace, Queen of the Ethiopians, who had the charge of all her treasure, and had come to Jerusalem for to worship." [1] Here, again, we find that all the commentators agree as to the nationality of the eunuch: he was a Negro; and, by implication, the passage quoted leads us to the belief that the Ethiopians were a numerous and wealthy people. Candace was the queen that made war against Augustus Cæsar twenty years before Christ, and, though not victorious, secured an honorable peace.[2] She reigned in Upper Egypt, — up the Nile, — and lived at Meroe, that ancient city, the very cradle of Egyptian civilization.[3]

"In the time of our Saviour (and indeed from that time forward), by Ethiopia was meant, in a general sense, the countries south of Egypt, then but imperfectly known; of one of which that Candace was queen whose eunuch was baptized by Philip. Mr. Bruce, on his return from Abyssinia, found in latitude 16° 38' a place called Chendi, where the reigning sovereign was then a queen; and where a tradition existed that a woman, by name Hendaque (which comes as near as possible to the Greek name Χανδακη), once governed all that country. Near this place are extensive ruins, consisting of broken pedestals and obelisks, which Bruce conjectures to be those of Meroe, the capital of the African Ethiopia, which is described by Herodotus as a great city in his time, namely, four hundred years before Christ; and where, separated from the rest of the world by almost impassable deserts, and enriched by the commercial expeditions of their travelling brethren, the Cushites continued to cultivate, so late as the first century of the Christian era, some portions of those arts and sciences to which the settlers in the cities had always more or less devoted themselves."[4]

But a few writers have asserted, and striven to prove, that the Egyptians and Ethiopians are quite a different people from the Negro. Jeremiah seems to have understood that these people about whom we have been writing were Negroes, — we mean black. "Can the Ethiopian," asks the prophet, "change his skin, or the leopard his spots?" The prophet was as thoroughly aware that the Ethiopian was black, as that the leopard had spots; and Luther's German has for the word "Ethiopia," "Negro-land," —

---

[1] Acts viii. 27.
[2] Pliny says the Ethiopian government subsisted for several generations in the hands of queens whose name was *Candace*.
[3] See Liddell and Scott's Greek Lexicon.
[4] Jones's Biblical Cyclopædia, p. 311.

the country of the blacks.[1] The word "Ethiop" in the Greek literally means "sunburn."

That these Ethiopians were black, we have, in addition to the valuable testimony of Jeremiah, the scholarly evidence of Herodotus, Homer, Josephus, Eusebius, Strabo, and others.

It will be necessary for us to use the term "Cush" farther along in this discussion: so we call attention at this time to the fact, that the Cushites, so frequently referred to in the Scriptures, are the same as the Ethiopians.

Driven from unscriptural and untenable ground on the unity of the races of mankind, the enemies of the Negro, falling back in confusion, intrench themselves in the curse of Canaan. "And Noah awoke from his wine, and knew what his younger son had done unto him. And he said, Cursed be Canaan; a servant of servants shall he be unto his brethren." [2] This passage was the leading theme of the defenders of slavery in the pulpit for many years. Bishop Hopkins says, —

"The heartless irreverence which Ham, the father of Canaan, displayed toward his eminent parent, whose piety had just saved him from the Deluge, presented the immediate *occasion* for this remarkable prophecy; but the actual *fulfilment* was reserved for his posterity after they had lost the knowledge of God, and become utterly polluted by the abominations of heathen idolatry. The Almighty, foreseeing this total degradation of the race, ordained them to servitude or slavery under the descendants of Shem and Japheth, doubtless because *he judged it to be their fittest condition.* And all history proves how accurately the prediction has been accomplished, even to the present day."[3]

Now, the first thing to be done by those who adopt this view is, to prove, beyond a reasonable doubt, that Noah was inspired to pronounce this prophecy. Noah *had* been, as a rule, a righteous man. For more than a hundred years he had lifted up his voice against the growing wickedness of the world. His fidelity to the cause of God was unquestioned; and for his faith and correct living, he and his entire household were saved from the Deluge. But after his miraculous deliverance from the destruction that overcame the old world, his entire character is changed. There is not a single passage to show us that he continued his avocation as a preacher. He became a husbandman; he kept a vineyard; and, more than all, he drank of the wine and got drunk!

---

[1] The term Ethiope was anciently given to all those whose color was darkened by the sun. — *Smyth's Unity of the Human Races*, chap. i. p. 34.
[2] Gen. ix. 24, 25. See also the twenty-sixth and twenty-seventh verses.
[3] Bible Views of Slavery, p. 7.

tim, and the Cushim or Ethiopians, who, colonizing the African side of the Red Sea, subsequently extended themselves indefinitely to the west and south of that great continent. Egypt was called Chemia, or the country of Ham ; and it has been thought that the Egyptian's deity, Hammon or Ammon, was a deification of Ham.[1] The Carthaginians were successful in numerous wars against the sturdy Romans. So in this, as in many other instances, the prophecy of Noah failed.

Following the chapter containing the prophecy of Noah, the historian records the genealogy of the descendants of Ham and Canaan. We will quote the entire account that we may be assisted to the truth.

> "And the sons of Ham; Cush, and Mizraim, and Phut, and Canaan; and the sons of Cush; Seba, and Havilah, and Sabtah, and Raamah, and Sabtechah: and the sons of Raamah; Sheba and Dedan. And Cush begat Nimrod: he began to be a mighty one in the earth. He was a mighty hunter before the Lord: wherefore it is said, Even as Nimrod the mighty hunter before the Lord. And the beginning of his kingdom was Babel, and Erech, and Accad, and Calneh, in the land of Shinar. Out of that land went forth Asshur, and builded Nineveh, and the city Rehoboth, and Calah, and Resen between Nineveh and Calah: the same is a great city. And Mizraim begat Ludim, and Anamim, and Lehabim, and Naphtuhim, and Pathrusim, and Casluhim (out of whom came Philistim), and Caphtorim. And Canaan begat Sidon his first-born, and Heth, and the Jebusite, and the Amorite, and the Girgasite, and the Hivite, and the Arkite, and the Sinite, and the Arvadite, and the Zemarite, and the Hamathite: and afterward were the families of the Canaanites spread abroad. And the border of the Canaanites was from Sidon, as thou comest to Gerar, unto Gaza; as thou goest, unto Sodom, and Gomorrah, and Admah, and Zeboim, even unto Lasha. These are the sons of Ham, after their families, after their tongues, in their countries, and in their nations."[2]

Here is a very minute account of the family of Ham, who it is said was to share the fate of his son Canaan, and a clear account of the children of Canaan. "Nimrod," says the record, "began to be a mighty one in the earth. He was a mighty hunter before the Lord. . . . And the beginning of his kingdom," etc. We find that Cush was the oldest son of Ham, and the father of Nimrod the "mighty one in the earth," whose "kingdom" was so extensive. He founded the Babylonian empire, and was the father of the founder of the city of Nineveh, one of the grandest cities of the ancient world. These wonderful achieve-

---

[1] Plutarch, De Iside et Osiride. See also Dr. Morton, and Ethnological Journal, 4th No p. 172.

[2] Gen. x. 6-20.

ments were of the children of Cush, the ancestor of the Negroes. It is fair to suppose that this line of Ham's posterity was not lacking in powers necessary to found cities and kingdoms, and maintain government.

Thus far we have been enabled to see, according to the Bible record, that the posterity of Canaan did not go into bondage; that it was a powerful people, both in point of numbers and wealth; and, from the number and character of the cities it built, we infer that it was an intellectual posterity. We conclude that thus far there is no evidence, from a biblical standpoint, that Noah's prophecy was fulfilled. But, notwithstanding the absence of scriptural proof as to the bondage of the children of Canaan, the venerable Dr. Mede says, "There never has been a son of Ham who has shaken a sceptre over the head of Japheth. Shem has subdued Japheth, and Japheth has subdued Shem; but Ham has never subdued either." The doctor is either falsifying the facts of history, or is ignorant of history. The Hebrews were in bondage in Egypt for centuries. Egypt was peopled by Misraim, the second son of Ham. Who were the Shemites? They were Hebrews! The Shemites were in slavery to the Hamites. Melchizedek, whose name was expressive of his character, — *king of righteousness* (or a righteous king), was a worthy priest of the most high God; and Abimelech, whose name imports *parental king*, pleaded the integrity of his heart and the righteousness of his nation before God, and his plea was admitted. Yet both these personages appear to have been Canaanites." [1]   Melchizedek and Abimelech were Canaanites, and the most sacred and honorable characters in Old-Testament history. It was Abraham, a Shemite, who, meeting Melchizedek, a Canaanite, gave him a tenth of all his spoils. It was Nimrod, a Cushite, who "went to Asher, and built Nineveh," after subduing the Shemites. So it seems very plain that Noah's prophecy did not come true in every respect, and that it was not the word of God. "And God blessed Noah and his sons." [2]   God pronounces his blessing upon this entire family, and enjoins upon them to "be fruitful and multiply, and replenish the earth." Afterwards Noah seeks to abrogate the blessing of God by his "cursed be Canaan." But this was only the bitter expression of a drunken and humiliated parent lacking divine authority. No doubt he and his other

---

Dr. Bush.   [2] Gen. ix. 1.

two sons conformed their conduct to the spirit of the curse pronounced, and treated the Hamites accordingly. The scholarly Dr. William Jones [1] says that Ham was the youngest son of Noah ; that he had four sons, Cush, Misraim, Phut, and Canaan ; and that they peopled Africa and part of Asia. [2] The Hamites were the offspring of Noah, and one of the three great families that have peopled the earth. [3]

---

[1] Jones's Biblical Cyclopædia, p. 393.   Ps. lxxviii. 51.

[2] Ps. cv. 23.

[3] If Noah's utterance were to be regarded as a prophecy, it applied only to the Canaanites, the descendants of Canaan, Noah's grandson. Nothing is said in reference to any person but Canaan in the supposed prophecy.

CHAPTER II.

THE NEGRO IN THE LIGHT OF PHILOLOGY, ETHNOLOGY, AND EGYPTOLOGY.

Cushim and Ethiopia. — Ethiopians, White and Black. — Negro Characteristics. — The Dark Continent. — The Antiquity of the Negro. — Indisputable Evidence. — The Military and Social Condition of Negroes. — Cause of Color. — The Term Ethiopian.

THERE seems to be a great deal of ignorance and confusion in the use of the word "Negro;"[1] and about as much trouble attends the proper classification of the inhabitants of Africa. In the preceding chapter we endeavored to prove, not that Ham and Canaan were the progenitors of the Negro races, — for that is admitted by the most consistent enemies of the blacks, — but that the human race is *one*, and that Noah's curse was not a divine prophecy.

The term "Negro" seems to be applied chiefly to the dark and woolly-haired people who inhabit Western Africa. But the Negro is to be found also in Eastern Africa.[2] Zonaras says, "Chus is the person from whom the Cuseans are derived. They are the same people as the Ethiopians." This view is corroborated by Josephus,[3] Apuleius, and Eusebius. The Hebrew term "Cush" is translated Ethiopia by the Septuagint, Vulgate, and by almost all other versions, ancient and modern, as well as by the English version. "It is not, therefore, to be doubted that

---

[1] Edward W. Blyden, LL.D., of Liberia, says, "Supposing that this term was originally used as a phrase of contempt, is it not with us to elevate it? How often has it not happened that names originally given in reproach have been afterwards adopted as a title of honor by those against whom it was used? — Methodists, Quakers, etc. But as a proof that no unfavorable signification attached to the word when first employed, I may mention, that, long before the slave-trade began, travellers found the blacks on the coast of Africa preferring to be called Negroes" (see Purchas' Pilgrimage . . .). And in all the pre-slavetrade literature the word was spelled with a capital *N*. It was the slavery of the blacks which afterwards degraded the term. To say that the name was invented to degrade the race, some of whose members were reduced to slavery, is to be guilty of what in grammar is called a *hysteron proteron*. The disgrace became attached to the name in consequence of slavery; and what we propose to do is, now that slavery is abolished, to restore it to its original place and legitimate use, and therefore to restore the capital *N*."

[2] Prichard, vol. ii. p. 44.   [3] Josephus, Antiq., lib. 1, chap. 6.

the term '*Cushim*' has by the interpretation of all ages been translated by 'Ethiopians,' because they were also known by their black color, and their transmigrations, which were easy and frequent."[1] But while it is a fact, supported by both sacred and profane history, that the terms "Cush" and "Ethiopian" were used interchangeably, there seems to be no lack of proof that the same terms were applied frequently to a people who were not Negroes. It should be remembered, moreover, that there were nations who were black, and yet were not Negroes. And the only distinction amongst all these people, who are branches of the Hamitic family, is the texture of the hair. "But it is *equally* certain, as we have seen, that the term 'Cushite' is applied in Scripture to other branches of the same family; as, for instance, to the Midianites, from whom Moses selected his wife, and who could not have been Negroes. The term 'Cushite,' therefore, is used in Scripture as denoting nations who were not black, or in any respect Negroes, and also countries south of Egypt, whose inhabitants were Negroes; and yet both races are declared to be the descendants of Cush, the son of Ham. Even in Ezekiel's day the interior African nations were not of one race; for he represents Cush, Phut, Lud, and Chub, as either themselves constituting, or as being amalgamated with, 'a mingled people' (Ezek. xxx. 5); 'that is to say,' says Faber, 'it was a nation of Negroes who are represented as very numerous, — *all* the mingled people.'"[2]

The term "Ethiopia" was anciently given to all those whose color was darkened by the sun. Herodotus, therefore, distinguishes the Eastern Ethiopians who had straight hair, from the Western Ethiopians who had curly or woolly hair.[3] "They are a twofold people, lying extended in a long tract from the rising to the setting sun."[4]

The conclusion is patent. The words "Ethiopia" and "Cush" were used always to describe a black people, or the country where such a people lived. The term "Negro," from the Latin "*niger*" and the French "*noir*," means black; and consequently is a modern term, with all the original meaning of Cush and Ethiopia, with a single exception. We called attention above to the fact that all Ethiopians were not of the pure Negro type, but were

---

[1] Poole. [2] Smyth's Unity Human Races, chap. 11, p. 41.
[3] Herodotus, vii., 69, 70. Ancient Univ. Hist., vol. xviii. pp. 254, 255. [4] Strabo, vol. i. p. 60.

nevertheless a branch of the original Hamitic family from whence sprang all the dark races. The term "Negro" is now used to designate the people, who, in addition to their dark complexion, have curly or woolly hair. It is in this connection that we shall use the term in this work.[1]

Africa, the home of the indigenous dark races, in a geographic and ethnographic sense, is the most wonderful country in the world. It is thoroughly tropical. It has an area in English square miles of 11,556,600, with a population of 192,520,000 souls. It lies between the latitudes of 38° north and 35° south; and is, strictly speaking, an enormous peninsula, attached to Asia by the Isthmus of Suez. The most northern point is the cape, situated a little to the west of Cabo Blanco, and opposite Sicily, which lies in latitude 37° 20′ 40″ north, longitude 9° 41′ east. Its southernmost point is Cabo d'Agulhas, in 34° 49′ 15″ south; the distance between these two points being 4,330 geographical, or about 5,000 English miles. The westernmost point is Cabo Verde, in longitude 17° 33′ west; its easternmost, Cape Jerdaffun, in longitude 51° 21′ east, latitude 10° 25′ north, the distance between the two points being about the same as its length. The western coasts are washed by the Atlantic, the northern by the Mediterranean, and the eastern by the Indian Ocean. The shape of this "dark continent" is likened to a triangle or to an oval. It is rich in oils, ivory, gold, and precious timber. It has beautiful lakes and mighty rivers, that are the insoluble problems of the present times.

Of the antiquity of the Negro there can be no doubt. He is known as thoroughly to history as any of the other families of men. He appears at the first dawn of history, and has continued down to the present time. The scholarly Gliddon says, that "the hieroglyphical designation of 'KeSH,' exclusively applied to *African* races as distinct from the Egyptian, has been found by Lepsius as far back as the monuments of the sixth dynasty, 3000 B.C. But the great influx of Negro and Mulatto races into Egypt as captives dated from the twelfth dynasty; when, about the twenty-second century, B.C., Pharaoh SESOUR-TASEN extended his conquests up the Nile far into Nigritia. After the eighteenth dynasty the monuments come down to the

---

[1] It is not wise, to say the least, for intelligent Negroes in America to seek to drop the word "Negro." It is a good, strong, and healthy word, and ought to live. It should be covered with glory: let Negroes do it.

third century, A.D., without one single instance in the Pharaonic or Ptolemaic periods that Negro labor was ever directed to any agricultural or utilitarian objects."[1]   The Negro was found in great numbers with the Sukim, Thut, Lubin, and other African nations, who formed the strength of the army of the king of Egypt, Shishak, when he came against Rehoboam in the year 971 B.C. ; and in his tomb, opened in 1849, there were found among his depicted army the exact representation of the genuine Negro race, both in color, hair, and physiognomy.   Negroes are also represented in Egyptian paintings as connected with the military campaigns of the eighteenth dynasty.   They formed a part of the army of Ibrahim Pacha, and were prized as gallant soldiers at Moncha and in South Arabia.[2]   And Herodotus assures us that Negroes were found in the armies of Sesostris and Xerxes ; and, at the present time, they are no inconsiderable part of the standing army of Egypt.[3]   Herodotus states that eighteen of the Egyptian kings were Ethiopians.[4]

It is quite remarkable to hear a writer like John P. Jeffries, who evidently is not very friendly in his criticisms of the Negro, make such a positive declaration as the following : —

"Every rational mind must, therefore, readily conclude that the African race has been in existence, as a distinct people, over four thousand two hundred years ; and how long before that period is a matter of conjecture only, there being no reliable data upon which to predicate any reliable opinion."[5]

It is difficult to find a writer on ethnology, ethnography, or Egyptology, who doubts the antiquity of the Negroes as a distinct people.   Dr. John C. Nott of Mobile, Ala., a Southern man in the widest meaning, in his "Types of Mankind," while he tries to make his book acceptable to Southern slaveholders, strongly maintains the antiquity of the Negro.

"Ethnological science, then, possesses not only the authoritative testimonies of Lepsius and Birch in proof of the existence of Negro races during the twenty-fourth century, B.C., but, the same fact being conceded by all living Egyptologists, we may hence infer that these Nigritian types were contemporary with the earliest Egyptians."[6]

In 1829 there was a remarkable Theban tomb opened by Mr. Wilkinson, and in 1840 it was carefully examined by Harris and

---

[1] Journal of Ethnology, No. 7, p. 310.   •
[2] Pickering's Races of Men, pp. 185–89.
[3] Burckhardt's Travels, p. 341.
[4] Euterpe, lib. 6.
[5] Jeffries's Nat. Hist. of Human Race, p. 315.
[6] Types of Mankind, p. 259.

Gliddon.   There is a most wonderful collection of Negro scenes in it.   Of one of these scenes even Dr. Nott says, —

" A Negress, apparently a princess, arrives at Thebes, drawn in a plaustrum by a pair of humped oxen, the driver and groom being red-colored Egyptians, and, one might almost infer, eunuchs. Following her are multitudes of Negroes and Nubians, bringing tribute from the upper country, as well as black slaves of both sexes and all ages, among which are some *red* children, whose *fathers* were Egyptians. The cause of her advent seems to have been to make offerings in this tomb of a ' royal son of KeS*h* — Amunoph,' who may have been her husband." [1]

It is rather strange that the feelings of Dr. Nott toward the Negro were so far mollified as to allow him to make a statement that destroys his heretofore specious reasoning about the political and social status of the Negro.   He admits the antiquity of the Negro ; but makes a special effort to place him in a servile state at all times, and to present him as a vanquished vassal before Ramses III. and other Egyptian kings.   He sees no change in the Negro's condition, except that in slavery he is better fed and clothed than in his native home.   But, nevertheless, the Negress of whom he makes mention, and the entire picture in the Theban tomb, put down the learned doctor's argument.   Here is a Negro princess with Egyptian driver and groom, with a large army of attendants, going on a long journey to the tomb of her royal husband !

There is little room here to question the political and social conditions of the Negroes. [2]   They either had enjoyed a long and peaceful rule, or by their valor in offensive warfare had won honorable place by conquest.   And the fact that black slaves are mentioned does not in any sense invalidate the historical trustworthiness of the pictures found in this Theban tomb ; for Wilkinson says, in reference to the condition of society at this period, —

" It is evident that both white and black slaves were employed as servants ; they attended on the guests when invited to the house of their mas-

---

[1] Types of Mankind, p. 262.

[2] Even in Africa it is found that Negroes possess great culture. Speaking of Sego, the capital of Bambara, Mr. Park says : " The view of this extensive city, the numerous canoes upon the river, the crowded population, and the cultivated state of the surrounding country, formed altogether a prospect of civilization and magnificence which I little expected to find in the bosom of Africa." See Park's Travels, chap. ii.

Mr. Park also adds, that the population of this city, Sego, is about thirty thousand.   It had mosques, and even ferries were busy conveying men and horses over the Niger.

ter; and, from their being in the families of priests as well as of the military chiefs, we may infer that they were purchased with money, and that the right of possessing slaves was not confined to those who had taken them in war. The traffic in slaves was tolerated by the Egyptians; and it is reasonable to suppose that many persons were engaged . . . in bringing them to Egypt for public sale, independent of those who were sent as part of the tribute, and who were probably, at first, the property of the monarch; nor did any difficulty occur to the Ishmaelites in the purchase of Joseph from his brethren, nor in his subsequent sale to Potiphar on arriving in Egypt."

So we find that slavery was not, at this time, confined to any particular race of people. This Negro princess was as liable to purchase white as black slaves; and doubtless some were taken in successful wars with other nations, while others were purchased as servants.

But we have further evidence to offer in favor of the antiquity of the Negro. In Japan, and in many other parts of the East, there are to be found stupendous and magnificent temples, that are hoary with age. It is almost impossible to determine the antiquity of some of them, in which the idols are exact representations of woolly-haired Negroes, although the inhabitants of those countries to-day have straight hair. Among the Japanese, black is considered a color of good omen. In the temples of Siam we find the idols fashioned like unto Negroes.[1] Osiris, one of the principal deities of the Egyptians, is frequently represented as black.[2] Bubastis, also, the Diana of Greece, and a member of the great Egyptian Triad, is now on exhibition in the British Museum, sculptured in black basalt sitting figure.[3] Among the Hindus, Kali, the consort of Siva, one of their great Triad; Crishna, the eighth incarnation of Vishnu; and Vishnu also himself, the second of the Trimerti or Hindu Triad, are represented of a black color.[4] Dr. Morton says, —

"The Sphinx may have been the shrine of the Negro population of Egypt, who, as a people, were unquestionably under our average size. Three million Buddhists in Asia represent their chief deity, Buddha, with Negro features and hair. There are two other images of Buddha, one at Ceylon and the other at Calanee, of which Lieut. Mahoney says, 'Both these statues agree in having crisped hair and long, pendent ear-rings.'"[5]

---

[1] See Ambassades Mémorables de la Companie des Indes orientales des Provinces Unies vers les Empereurs du Japan, Amst., 1680; and Kaempfer.

[2] Wilkinson's Egypt, vol. iii. p. 340.

[3] Coleman's Mythology of the Hindus, p. 91. Dr. William Jones, vol. iii., p. 377.

[4] Asiatic Researches, vol. vi. pp. 436–448.

[5] Heber's Narrative, vol. i. p. 254.

And the learned and indefatigable Hamilton Smith says, —

"In the plains of India are Nagpoor, and a ruined city without name at the gates of Benares (perhaps the real Kasi of tradition), once adorned with statues of a woolly-haired race." [1]

Now, these substantial and indisputable traces of the march of the Negro races through Japan and Asia lead us to conclude that the Negro race antedates all profane history. And while the great body of the Negro races have been located geographically in Africa, they have been, in no small sense, a cosmopolitan people. Their wanderings may be traced from the rising to the setting sun.

"The remains of architecture and sculpture in India seem to prove an early connection between that country and Africa. . . . The Pyramids of Egypt, the colossal statues described by Pausanias and others, the Sphinx, and the Hermes Canis, which last bears a strong resemblance to the Varaha Avatar, indicate the style of the same indefatigable workmen who formed the vast excavations of Canarah, the various temples and images of Buddha, and the idols which are continually dug up at Gaya or in its vicinity. These and other indubitable facts may induce no ill-grounded opinion, that Ethiopia and Hindustan were peopled or colonized by the same extraordinary race; in confirmation of which it may be added, that the mountaineers of Bengal and Benhar can hardly be distinguished in some of their features, particularly in their lips and noses, from the modern Abyssinians." [2]

There is little room for speculation here to the candid searcher after truth. The evidence accumulates as we pursue our investigations. Monuments and temples, sepulchred stones and pyramids, rise up to declare the antiquity of the Negro races. Hamilton Smith, after careful and critical investigation, reaches the conclusion, that the Negro type of man was the most ancient, and the indigenous race of Asia, as far north as the lower range of the Himalaya Mountains, and presents at length many curious facts which cannot, he believes, be otherwise explained.

"In this view, the first migrations of the Negro stock, coasting westward by catamarans, or in wretched canoes, and skirting South-western Asia, may synchronize with the earliest appearance of the Negro tribes of Eastern Africa, and just precede the more mixed races, which, like the Ethiopians of Asia, passed the Red Sea at the Straits of Bab-el-Mandeb, ascended the Nile, or crossed that river to the west." [3]

Taking the whole southern portion of Asia westward to Arabia, this conjecture — which likewise was a conclusion drawn,

---

[1] Nat. Hist. of the Human Species, pp. 209, 214, 217.
[2] Asiatic Researches, vol. i. p. 427.   Also Sir William Jones, vol. iii. 3d disc.
[3] Nat. Hist. Human Species, p. 126.

after patient research, by the late Sir T. Stanford Raffles —
accounts, more satisfactorily than any other, for the Oriental
habits, ideas, traditions, and words which can be traced among
several of the present African tribes and in the South-Sea Islands.
Traces of this black race are still found along the Himalaya
range from the Indus to Indo-China, and the Malay peninsula,
and in a mixed form all through the southern states to Ceylon.[1]

But it is unnecessary to multiply evidence in proof of the
antiquity of the Negro. His presence in this world was coetaneous with the other families of mankind: here he has toiled with
a varied fortune; and here under God — *his* God — he will, in the
process of time, work out all the sublime problems connected
with his future as a man and a brother.

There are various opinions rife as to the cause of color and
texture of hair in the Negro. The generally accepted theory
years ago was, that the curse of Cain rested upon this race; while
others saw in the dark skin of the Negro the curse of Noah pronounced against Canaan. These two explanations were comforting to that class who claimed that they had a right to buy and sell
the Negro; and of whom the Saviour said, "For they bind heavy
burdens and grievous to be borne, and lay them on men's shoulders; but they themselves will not move them with one of their
fingers."[2] But science has, of later years, attempted a solution of
this problem. Peter Barrère, in his treatise on the subject, takes
the ground that the bile in the human system has much to do
with the color of the skin.[3] This theory, however, has drawn the
fire of a number of European scholars, who have combated it with
more zeal than skill. It is said that the spinal and brain matter
are of a dark, ashy color; and by careful examination it is proven
that the blood of Ethiopians is black. These facts would seem to
clothe this theory with at least a shadow of plausibility. But the
opinion of Aristotle, Strabo, Alexander, and Blumenbach is, that
the climate, temperature, and mode of life, have more to do with
giving color than any thing else. This is certainly true among
animals and plants. There are many instances on record where
dogs and wolves, etc., have turned white in winter, and then assumed a different color in the spring. If you start at the north
and move south, you will find, at first, that the flowers are very

---

[1] Prichard, pp. 188-219.   [2] Matt. xxiii. 4.
[3] Discours sur la cause physicale de la couleur des nègres.

white and delicate; but, as you move toward the tropics, they begin to take on deeper and richer hues until they run into almost endless varieties. Guyot argues on the other side of the question to account for the intellectual diversity of the races of mankind.

"While all the types of animals and of plants go on decreasing in perfection, from the equatorial to the polar regions, in proportion to the temperatures, man presents to our view his purest, his most perfect type, at the very centre of the temperate continents, — at the centre of Asia, Europe, in the regions of Iran, of Armenia, and of the Caucasus; and, departing from this geographical centre in the three grand directions of the lands, the types gradually lose the beauty of their forms, in proportion to their distance, even to the extreme points of the southern continents, where we find the most deformed and degenerate races, and the lowest in the scale of humanity." [1]

The learned professor seeks to carry out his famous geographical argument, and, with great skill and labor, weaves his theory of the influence of climate upon the brain and character of man. But while no scholar would presume to combat the theory that plants take on the most gorgeous hues as one nears the equator, and that the races of mankind take on a darker color in their march toward the equator, certainly no student of Oriental history will assent to the unsupported doctrine, that the intensity of the climate of tropical countries affects the intellectual status of races. If any one be so prejudiced as to doubt this, let him turn to "Asiatic Researches," and learn that the dark races have made some of the most invaluable contributions to science, literature, civil-engineering, art, and architecture that the world has yet known. Here we find the cradle of civilization, ancient and remote.

Even changes and differences in color are to be noted in almost every community.

"As we go westward we observe the light color predominating over the dark; and then, again, when we come within the influence of damp from the sea-air, we find the shade deepened into the general blackness of the coast population."

The artisan and farm-laborer may become exceedingly dark from exposure, and the sailor is frequently so affected by the weather that it is next to impossible to tell his nationality.

"It is well known that the Biscayan women are a shining white, the inhabitants of Granada on the contrary dark, to such an extent, that, in this

---

[1] Earth and Man. Lecture x. pp. 254, 255.

region, the pictures of the blessed Virgin and other saints are painted of the same color." [1]

The same writer calls attention to the fact, that the people on the Cordilleras, who live under the mountains towards the west, and are, therefore, exposed to the Pacific Ocean, are quite, or nearly, as fair in complexion as the Europeans ; whereas, on the contrary, the inhabitants of the opposite side, exposed to the burning sun and scorching winds, are copper-colored. Of this theory of climateric influence we shall say more farther on.

It is held by some eminent physicians in Europe and America, that the color of the skin depends upon substances external to the *cutis vera.* Outside of the *cutis* are certain layers of a substance various in consistence, and scarcely perceptible : here is the home and seat of color ; and these may be regarded as secretions from the vessels of the *cutis.* The dark color of the Negro principally depends on the substance interposed between the true skin and the scarf-skin. This substance presents different appearances : and it is described sometimes as a sort of organized network or reticular tissue ; at others, as a mere mucous or slimy layer ; and it is odd that these somewhat incompatible ideas are both conveyed by the term *reticulum mucosum* given to the intermediate portion of the skin by its orignal discoverer, Malpighi. There is, no doubt, something plausible in all the theories advanced as to the color and hair of the Negro ; but it is verily all speculation. One theory is about as valuable as another.

Nine hundred years before Christ the poet Homer, speaking of the death of Memnon, killed at the siege of Troy, says, " He was received by his Ethiopians." This is the first use of the word Ethiopia in the Greek ; and it is derived from the roots αιθω, "to burn," and ωψ, "face." It is safe to assume, that, when God dispersed the sons of Noah, he fixed the " bounds of their habitation," and, that, from the earth and sky the various races have secured their civilization. He sent the different nations into separate parts of the earth. He gave to each its racial peculiarities, and adaptibility for the climate into which it went. He gave color, language, and civilization ; and, when by wisdom we fail to interpret his inscrutable ways, it is pleasant to know that " he worketh all things after the counsel of his own mind."

---

[1] Blumenbach, p. 107.

CHAPTER III.

PRIMITIVE NEGRO CIVILIZATION.

The Ancient and High Degree of Negro Civilization. — Egypt, Greece, and Rome borrow from the Negro the Civilization that made them Great. — Cause of the Decline and Fall of Negro Civilization. — Confounding the Terms "Negro" and "African."

IT is fair to presume that God gave all the races of mankind civilization to start with. We infer this from the known character of the Creator. Before Romulus founded Rome, before Homer sang, when Greece was in its infancy, and the world quite young, "hoary Meroe" was the chief city of the Negroes along the Nile. Its private and public buildings, its markets and public squares, its colossal walls and stupendous gates, its gorgeous chariots and alert footmen, its inventive genius and ripe scholarship, made it the cradle of civilization, and the mother of art. It was the queenly city of Ethiopia, — for it was founded by colonies of Negroes. Through its open gates long and ceaseless caravans, laden with gold, silver, ivory, frankincense, and palm-oil, poured the riches of Africa into the capacious lap of the city. The learning of this people, embalmed in the immortal hieroglyphic, flowed adown the Nile, and, like spray, spread over the delta of that time-honored stream, on by the beautiful and venerable city of Thebes, — the city of a hundred gates, another monument to Negro genius and civilization, and more ancient than the cities of the Delta, — until Greece and Rome stood transfixed before the ancient glory of Ethiopia! Homeric mythology borrowed its very essence from Negro hieroglyphics; Egypt borrowed her light from the venerable Negroes up the Nile. Greece went to school to the Egyptians, and Rome turned to Greece for law and the science of warfare. England dug down into Rome twenty centuries to learn to build and plant, to establish a government, and maintain it. Thus the flow of civilization has been from the East — the place of light — to the West; from the Oriental to the Occidental. (God fixed the mountains east and west in Europe.)

"Tradition universally represents the earliest men descending, it is true, from the high table-lands of this continent; but it is in the low and fertile plains lying at their feet, with which we are already acquainted, that they unite themselves for the first time in natural bodies, in tribes, with fixed habitations, devoting themselves to husbandry, building cities, cultivating the arts, — in a word, forming well-regulated societies. The traditions of the Chinese place the first progenitors of that people on the high table-land, whence the great rivers flow: they make them advance, station by station, as far as the shores of the ocean. The people of the Brahmins come down from the regions of the Hindo-Khu, and from Cashmere, into the plains of the Indus and the Ganges; Assyria and Bactriana receive their inhabitants from the table-lands of Armenia and Persia.

"These alluvial plains, watered by their twin rivers, were better formed than all other countries of the globe to render the first steps of man, an infant still, easy in the career of civilized life. A rich soil, on which overflowing rivers spread every year a fruitful loam, as in Egypt, and one where the plough is almost useless, so movable and so easily tilled is it, a warm climate, finally, secure to the inhabitants of these fortunate regions plentiful harvests in return for light labor. Nevertheless, the conflict with the river itself and with the desert, — which, on the banks of the Euphrates, as on those of the Nile and the Indus, is ever threatening to invade the cultivated lands, — the necessity of irrigation, the inconstancy of the seasons, keep forethought alive, and give birth to the useful arts and to the sciences of observation. The abundance of resources, the absence of every obstacle, of all separation between the different parts of these vast plains, allow the aggregation of a great number of men upon one and the same space, and facilitate the formation of those mighty primitive states which amaze us by the grandeur of their proportions.

"Each of them finds upon its own soil all that is necessary for a brilliant exhibition of its resources. We see those nations come rapidly forward, and reach in the remotest antiquity a degree of culture of which the temples. and the monuments of Egypt and of India, and the recently discovered palaces. of Nineveh, are living and glorious witnesses.

"Great nations, then, are separately formed in each of these areas, circumscribed by nature within natural limits. Each has its religion, its social principles, its civilization severally. But nature, as we have seen, has separated them; little intercourse is established between them; the social principle on which they are founded is exhausted by the very formation of the social state they enjoy, and is never renewed. A common life is wanting to them: they do not reciprocally share with each other their riches. With them movement is stopped: every thing becomes stable and tends to remain stationary.

"Meantime, in spite of the peculiar seal impressed on each of these Oriental nations by the natural conditions in the midst of which they live, they have, nevertheless, some grand characteristics common to all, some family traits that betray the nature of the continent and the period of human progress to which they belong, making them known on the one side as Asiatic, and on the other side as primitive." [1]

---

[1] Earth and Man, pp. 300–302.

Is it asked what caused the decline of all this glory of the primitive Negro? why this people lost their position in the world's history? Idolatry! Sin![1]

Centuries have flown apace, tribes have perished, cities have risen and fallen, and even empires, whose boast was their duration, have crumbled, while Thebes and Meroe stood. And it is a remarkable fact, that the people who built those cities are less mortal than their handiwork. Notwithstanding their degradation, their woes and wrongs, the perils of the forest and dangers of the desert, this remarkable people have not been blotted out. They still live, and are multiplying in the earth. Certainly they have been preserved for some wise purpose, in the future to be unfolded.

But, again, what was the cause of the Negro's fall from his high state of civilization? It was forgetfulness of God, idolatry! "Righteousness exalteth a nation; but sin is a reproach to any people."

The Negro tribes of Africa are as widely separated by mental, moral, physical, and social qualities as the Irish, Huns, Copts, and Druids are. Their location on the Dark Continent, their surroundings, and the amount of light that has come to them from the outside world, are the thermometer of their civilization. It is as manifestly improper to call all Africans Negroes as to call Americans Indians.

"The Negro nations of Africa differ widely as to their manner of life and their characters, both of mind and body, in different parts of that continent, according as they have existed under different moral and physical conditions. Foreign culture, though not of a high degree, has been introduced among the population of some regions; while from others it has been shut out by almost impenetrable barriers, beyond which the aboriginal people remain secluded amid their mountains and forests, in a state of instinctive existence, — a state from which, history informs us, that human races have hardly emerged, until moved by some impulse from without. Neither Phœnician nor Roman culture seems to have penetrated into Africa beyond the Atlantic region and the desert. The activity and enthusiasm of the propagators of Islám have reached farther. In the fertile low countries beyond the Sahara, watered by rivers which descend northward from the central highlands, Africa has contained for centuries several Negro empires, originally founded by Mohammedans. The Negroes of this part of Africa are people of a very different description from

---

[1] It is a remarkable fact, that the absence of salt in the food of the Eastern nations, especially the dark nations or races, has been very deleterious. An African child will eat salt by the handful; and, once tasting it, will cry for it. The ocean is the womb of nature; and the Creator has wisely designed salt as the savor of life, the preservative element in human food.

the black pagan nations farther towards the South. They have adopted many of the arts of civilized society, and have subjected themselves to governments and political institutions. They practise agriculture, and have learned the necessary, and even some of the ornamental, arts of life, and dwell in towns of considerable extent; many of which are said to contain ten thousand, and even thirty thousand inhabitants, — a circumstance which implies a considerable advancement in industry and the resources of subsistence. All these improvements were introduced into the interior of Africa three or four centuries ago; and we have historical testimony, that in the region where trade and agriculture now prevail the population consisted, previous to the introduction of Islám, of savages as wild and fierce as the natives farther towards the south, whither the missionaries of that religion have never penetrated. It hence appears that human society has not been in all parts of Africa stationary and unprogressive from age to age. The first impulse to civilization was late in reaching the interior of that continent, owing to local circumstances which are easily understood; but, when it had once taken place, an improvement has resulted which is, perhaps, proportional to the early progress of human culture in other more favored regions of the world." [1]

But in our examination of African tribes we shall not confine ourselves to that class of people known as Negroes, but call attention to other tribes as well. And while, in this country, all persons with a visible admixture of Negro blood in them are considered Negroes, it is technically incorrect. For the real Negro was not the sole subject sold into slavery: very many of the noblest types of mankind in Africa have, through the uncertainties of war, found their way to the horrors of the middle passage, and finally to the rice and cotton fields of the Carolinas and Virginias. So, in speaking of the race in this country, in subsequent chapters, I shall refer to them as *colored people* or *Negroes.*

---

[1] Physical History of Mankind, vol. ii. pp. 45, 46.

CHAPTER IV.

NEGRO KINGDOMS OF AFRICA.

BENIN: Its Location. — Its Discovery by the Portuguese. — Introduction of the Catholic Religion. — The King as a Missionary. — His Fidelity to the Church purchased by a White Wife. — Decline of Religion. — Introduction of Slavery. — Suppression of the Trade by the English Government. — Restoration and Peace.
DAHOMEY: Its Location. — Origin of the Kingdom. — Meaning of the Name. — War. — Capture of the English Governor, and his Death. — The Military Establishment. — Women as Soldiers. — Wars and their Objects. — Human Sacrifices. — The King a Despot. — His Powers. — His Wives. — Polygamy. — Kingly Succession. — Coronation. — Civil and Criminal Law. — Revenue System. — Its Future.
YORUBA: Its Location. — Slavery and its Abolition. — Growth of the People of Abeokuta. — Missionaries and Teachers from Sierra Leone. — Prosperity and Peace attend the People. — Capacity of the People for Civilization. — Bishop Crowther. — His Influence.

BENIN.

THE vast territory stretching from the Volta River on the west to the Niger in the Gulf of Benin on the east, the Atlantic Ocean on the south, and the Kong Mountains on the north, embraces the three powerful Negro kingdoms of Benin, Dahomey, and Yoruba. From this country, more than from any other part of Africa, were the people sold into American slavery. Two or three hundred years ago there were several very powerful Negro empires in Western Africa. They had social and political government, and were certainly a very orderly people. But in 1485 Alfonso de Aviro, a Portuguese, discovered Benin, the most easterly province; and as an almost immediate result the slave-trade was begun. It is rather strange, too, in the face of the fact, that, when De Aviro returned to the court of Portugal, an ambassador from the Negro king of Benin accompanied him for the purpose of requesting the presence of Christian missionaries among this people. Portugal became interested, and despatched Fernando Po to the Gulf of Benin; who, after discovering the island that bears his name, ascended the Benin River to Gaton, where he located a Portuguese colony. The Romish Church lifted her standard here. The brothers of the Society of Jesus, if they did not convert the king, certainly had him in a humor to bring all of his regal powers to bear upon his subjects to turn them into 'the Catholic Church. He actually took the contract to turn his subjects over to this Church! But this shrewd savage did not agree to undertake this herculean task for nothing. He wanted a white wife. He told the missionaries that he would deliver his subjects to Christianity for a white wife, and they agreed to furnish her. Some priests were sent to the Island of St. Thomas to hunt the wife. This island had, even at that early day, a considerable white population. A strong appeal was made to the sisters there to consider this matter as a duty to the holy Church. It was set forth as a missionary enterprise. After some contemplation, one of the sisters agreed to accept the hand of the Negro king. It was a noble act, and one for which she should have been canonized, but we believe never was.

The Portuguese continued to come. Gaton grew. The missionary worked with a will. Attention was given to agriculture and commerce. But the climate was wretched. Sickness and death swept the Portuguese as the fiery breath of tropical lightning. They lost their influence over the people. They established the slave-trade, but the Church and slave-pen would not agree. The inhuman treatment they bestowed upon the people gave rise to the gravest suspicions as to the sincerity of the missionaries. History gives us the sum total of a religious effort that was not of God. There isn't a trace of Roman Catholicism in that country, and the last state of that people 'is worse than the former.

The slave-trade turned the heads of the natives. Their cruel and hardened hearts assented to the crime of man-stealing. They turned aside from agricultural pursuits. They left their fish-nets on the seashore, their cattle uncared for, their villages neglected, and went forth to battle against their weaker neighbors. They sold their prisoners of war to slave-dealers on the coast, who gave them rum and tobacco as an exceeding great reward. When war failed to give from its bloody and remorseless jaws the victims for whom a ready market awaited, they turned to duplicity, treachery, and cruelty. "And men's worst enemies were those of their own household." The person suspicioned of witchcraft was speedily found guilty, and adjudged to slavery. The guilty and the innocent often shared the same fate. The thief, the adulterer, and the aged were seized by the rapacity that pervaded the people, and were hurled into the hell of slavery.

Now, as a result of this condition of affairs, the population was depleted, the people grew indolent and vicious, and finally the empire was rent with political feuds. Two provinces was the result. One still bore the name of Benin, the other was called Waree. The capital of the former contains about 38,000 inhabitants, and the chief town and island of Waree only contain about 16,000 of a population.

Finally England was moved to a suppression of the slave-trade at this point. The ocean is very calm along this coast, which enabled her fleets to run down slave-vessels and make prizes of them. This had a salutary influence upon the natives. Peace and quietness came as angels. A spirit of thrift possessed the people. They turned to the cultivation of the fields and to commercial pursuits. On the river Bonny, and along other streams, large and flourishing palm-oil marts sprang up ; and a score or more of vessels are needed to export the single article of palm-oil. The morals of the people are not what they ought to be ; but they have, on the whole, made wonderful improvement during the last fifty years.

DAHOMEY.

This nation is flanked by Ashantee on the west, and Yoruba on the east; running from the seacoast on the south to the Kong mountains on the north. It is one hundred and eighty miles in width, by two hundred in breadth. Whydah is the principal town on the seacoast. The story runs, that, about two hundred and seventy-five years ago, Tacudons, chief of the Foys, carried a siege against the city of Abomey. He made a solemn vow to the gods, that, if they aided him in pushing the city to capitulate, he would build a palace in honor of the victory. He succeeded. He laid the foundations of his palace, and then upon them ripped open the bowels of Da. He called the building *Da-Omi*, which meant Da's belly. He took the title of King of Dahomey, which has remained until the present time. The neighboring tribes, proud and ambitious, overran the country, and swept Whydah and adjacent places with the torch and spear. Many whites fell into their hands as prisoners ; all of whom were treated with great consideration, save the English governor of the above-named town. They put him to death, because, as they charged, he had incited and excited the people of Dahomey to resist their king.

This is a remarkable people. They are as cruel as they are

cunning. The entire population is converted into an army : even women are soldiers. Whole regiments of women are to be found in the army of the king of Dahomey, and they are the best foot-regiments in the kingdom. They are drilled at stated periods, are officered, and well disciplined. The army is so large, and is so constantly employed in predatory raids upon neighboring tribes, that the consuming element is greater than the producing. The object of these raids was threefold : to get slaves for human sacrifices, to pour the blood of the victims on the graves of their ancestors yearly, and to secure human skulls to pave the court of the king and to ornament the walls about the palace ! After a successful war, the captives are brought to the capital of the kingdom. A large platform is erected in the great market space, encircled by a parapet about three feet high. The platform blazes with rich clothes, elaborate umbrellas, and all the evidences of kingly wealth and splendor, as well as the spoils taken in battle. The king occupies a seat in the centre of the platform, attended by his imperturbable wives. The captives, rum, tobacco, and cowries are now ready to be thrown to the surging mob below. They have fought gallantly, and now clamor for their reward. "Feed us, king !" they cry, "feed us, king ! for we are hungry !" and as the poor captives are tossed to the mob they are despatched without ceremony !

But let us turn from this bloody and barbarous scene. The king is the most absolute despot in the world. He is heir-at-law to all his subjects. He is regarded as a demigod. It is unlawful to indicate that the king eats, sleeps, or drinks. No one is allowed to approach him, except his nobles, who at a court levee disrobe themselves of all their elegant garments, and, prostrate upon the ground, they crawl into his royal presence. The whole people are the cringing lickspittles of the nobles in turn. Every private in the army is ambitious to please the king by valor. The king is literally monarch of all he surveys. He is proprietor of the land, and has at his disposal every thing animate or inanimate in his kingdom. He has about three thousand wives.[1] Every man who would marry must buy his spouse from the king ; and, while the system of polygamy obtains everywhere throughout the kingdom, the subject must have care not to secure so many wives that it

---

[1] The king of Dahomey is limited to 3,333 wives ! It is hardly fair to suppose that his majesty feels cramped under the ungenerous act that limits the number of his wives.

would appear that he is attempting to rival the king. The robust women are consigned to the military service. But the real condition of woman in this kingdom is slavery of the vilest type. She owns nothing. She is always in the market, and lives in a state of constant dread of being sold. When the king dies, a large number of his wives are sacrificed upon his grave. This fact inspires them to take good care of him! In case of death, the king's brother, then his nephew, and so on, take the throne. An inauguration generally lasts six days, during which time hundreds of human lives are sacrificed in honor of the new monarch.

The code of Dahomey is very severe. Witchcraft is punished with death; and in this regard stalwart old Massachusetts borrowed from the barbarian. Adultery, is punished by slavery or sudden death. Thieves are also sold into slavery. Treason and cowardice and murder are punished by death. The civil code is as complicated as the criminal is severe. Over every village, is a Caboceer, equivalent to our mayor. He can convene a court by prostrating himself and kissing the ground. The court convenes, tries and condemns the criminal. If it be a death sentence, he is delivered to a man called the Milgan, or equivalent to our sheriff, who is the ranking officer in the state. If the criminal is sentenced to slavery, he is delivered to the Mayo, who is second in rank to the Milgan, or about like our turnkey or jailer. All sentences must be referred to the king for his approval; and all executions take place at the capital, where notice is given of the same by a public crier in the market-places.

The revenue system of this kingdom is oppressive. The majority of slaves taken in war are the property of the king. A tax is levied on each person or slave exported from the kingdom. In relation to domestic commerce, a tax is levied on every article of food and clothing. A custom-service is organized, and the tax-collectors are shrewd and exacting.

The religion of the people is idolatry and fetich, or superstition. They have large houses where they worship snakes; and so great is their reverence for the reptile, that, if any one kills one that has escaped, he is punished with death. But, above their wild and superstitious notions, there is an ever-present consciousness of a Supreme Being. They seldom mention the name of God, and then with fear and trembling.

"The worship of God in the absurd symbol of the lower animals I do not wish to defend: but it is all that these poor savages can do; and is not that less impious than to speak of the Deity with blasphemous familiarity, as our illiterate preachers often do ? " [1]

But this people are not in a hopeless condition of degradation.

"The Wesleyan Missionary Society of England have had a mission-station at Badagry for some years, and not without some important and encouraging tokens of success. . . . The king, it is thought, is more favorable to Christian missions now than he formerly was." [2]

And we say Amen !

YORUBA.

This kingdom extends from the seacoast to the river Niger, by which it is separated from the kingdom of Nufi. It contains more territory than either Benin or Dahomey. Its principal sea-port is Lagos. For many years it was a great slave-mart, and only gave up the traffic under the deadly presence of English guns. Its facilities for the trade were great. Portuguese and Spanish slave-traders took up their abode here, and, teaching the natives the use of fire-arms, made a stubborn stand for their lucrative enterprise; but in 1852 the slave-trade was stopped, and the slavers driven from the seacoast. The place came under the English flag; and, as a result, social order and business enterprise have been restored and quickened. The slave-trade wrought great havoc among this people. It is now about fifty-five years since a few weak and fainting tribes, decimated by the slave-trade, fled to Ogun, a stream seventy-five miles from the coast, where they took refuge in a cavern. In the course of time they were joined by other tribes that fled before the scourge of slave-hunt-ers. Their common danger gave them a commonality of interests. They were, at first, reduced to very great want. They lived for a long time on berries, herbs, roots, and such articles of food as nature furnished without money and without price; but, leagued together to defend their common rights, they grew bold, and began to spread out around their hiding-place, and engage in agriculture. Homes and villages began to rise, and the desert to blossom as the rose. They finally chose a leader, — a wise and judicious man by the name of Shodeke; and one hundred and thirty towns were united under one government. In 1853, less than a generation, a feeble people had grown to be nearly one

---

[1] Savage Africa, p. 51.   [2] Western Africa, p. 207.

hundred thousand (100,000) ; and Abeokuta, named for their cave, contains at present nearly three hundred thousand souls.

In 1839 some colored men from Sierra Leone, desirous of engaging in trade, purchased a small vessel, and called at Lagos and Badagry. They had been slaves in this country, and had been taken to Sierra Leone, where they had received a Christian education. Their visit, therefore, was attended with no ordinary interest. They recognized many of their friends and kindred, and were agreeably surprised at the wonderful change that had taken place in so short a time. They returned to Sierra Leone, only to inspire their neighbors with a zeal for commercial and missionary enterprise. Within three years, five hundred of the best colored people of Sierra Leone set out for Lagos and Badagry on the seacoast, and then moved overland to Abeokuta, where they intended to make their home. In this company of noble men were merchants, mechanics, physicians, school-teachers, and clergymen. Their people had fought for deliverance from physical bondage: these brave missionaries had come to deliver them from intellectual and spiritual bondage. The people of Abeokuta gave the missionaries a hearty welcome. The colony received new blood and energy. School-buildings and churches rose on every hand. Commerce was revived, and even agriculture received more skilful attention. Peace and and plenty began to abound. Every thing wore a sunny smile, and many tribes were bound together by the golden cords of civilization, and sang their *Te Deum* together. Far-away England caught their songs of peace, and sent them agricultural implements, machinery, and Christian ministers and teachers. So, that, nowhere on the continent of Africa is there to be found so many renewed households, so many reclaimed tribes, such substantial results of a vigorous, Christian civilization.

The forces that quickened the inhabitants of Abeokuta were not all objective, exoteric: there were subjective and inherent forces at work in the hearts of the people. They were capable of civilization, — longed for it; and the first blaze of light from without aroused their slumbering forces, and showed them the broad and ascending road that led to the heights of freedom and usefulness. That they sought this road with surprising alacrity, we have the most abundant evidence. Nor did all the leaders come from abroad. Adgai, in the Yoruba language, but Crowther, in English, was a native of this country. In 1822 he was sold into slavery at the port of Badagry. The vessel that was to bear him away to the "land of chains and stocks" was captured by a British man-of-war, and taken to Sierra Leone. Here he came under the influence of Christian teachers. He proved to be one of the best pupils in his school. He received a classical education, fitted for the ministry, and then hastened back to his native country to carry the gospel of peace. It is rather remarkable, but he found his mother and several sisters still "in the gall of bitterness and in the bonds of iniquity." The son and brother became their spiritual teacher, and, ere long, had the great satisfaction of seeing them "clothed, in their right mind, and sitting at the feet of Jesus." His influence has been almost boundless. A man of magnificent physical proportions, — tall, a straight body mounted by a ponderous head, shapely, with a kind eye, benevolent face, a rich cadence in his voice, — the "black Bishop" Crowther is a princely looking man, who would attract the attention of cultivated people anywhere. He is a man of eminent piety, broad scholarship, and good works. He has translated the Bible into the Yoruba language, founded schools, and directed the energies of his people with a matchless zeal. His beautiful and beneficent life is an argument in favor of the possibilities of Negro manhood so long injured by the dehumanizing influences of slavery. Others have caught the inspiration that has made Bishop Crowther's life "as terrible as an army with banners" to the enemies of Christ and humanity, and are working to dissipate the darkness of that land of night.

CHAPTER V.

THE ASHANTEE EMPIRE.

Its Location and Extent. — Its Famous Kings. — The Origin of the Ashantees Obscure. — The War with Denkera. — The Ashantees against the Field conquer two Kingdoms and annex them. — Death of Osai Tutu. — The Envy of the King of Dahomey. — Invasion of the Ashantee Country by the King of Dahomey. — His Defeat shared by his Allies. — Akwasi pursues the Army of Dahomey into its own Country. — Gets a Mortal Wound and suffers a Humiliating Defeat. — The King of Dahomey sends the Royal Kudjoh his Congratulations. — Kwamina deposed for attempting to introduce Mohammedanism into the Kingdom. — The Ashantees conquer the Mohammedans. — Numerous Wars. — Invasion of the Fanti Country. — Death of Sir Charles McCarthy. — Treaty. — Peace.

THE kingdom of Ashantee lies between the Kong Mountains and the vast country of the Fantis. The country occupied by the Ashantees was, at the first, very small; but by a series of brilliant conquests they finally secured a territory of three hundred square miles. One of their most renowned kings, Osai Tutu, during the last century, added to Ashantee by conquest the kingdoms of Sarem, Buntuku, Warsaw, Denkera, and Axim. Very little is known as to the origin of the Ashantees. They were discovered in the early part of the eighteenth century in the great valley between the Kong Mountains and the river Niger, from whence they were driven by the Moors and Mohammedan Negroes. They exchanged the bow for fire-arms, and soon became a warlike people. Osai Tutu led in a desperate engagement against the king of Denkera, in which the latter was slain, his army was put to rout, and large quantities of booty fell into the hands of the victorious Ashantees. The king of Axim unwittingly united his forces to those of the discomforted Denkera, and, drawing the Ashantees into battle again, sustained heavy losses, and was put to flight. He was compelled to accept the most exacting conditions of peace, to pay the king of the Ashantees four thousand ounces of gold to defray the expenses of the war, and have his territory made tributary to the conqueror. In a subsequent battle Osai Tutu was surprised and killed. His courtiers and wives were made prisoners, with much goods. This enraged the Ashantees, and they reeked vengeance on the heads of the inhabitants of Kromanti, who laid the disastrous ambuscade. They failed, however, to recover the body of their slain king; but many of his attendants were retaken, and numerous enemies, whom they sacrificed to the manes of their dead king at Kumasi.

After the death of the noble Osai Tutu, dissensions arose among his followers. The tribes and kingdoms he had bound to his victorious chariot-wheels began to assert their independence. His life-work began to crumble. Disorder ran riot; and, after a few ambitious leaders were convinced that the throne of Ashantee demanded brains and courage, they cheerfully made way for the coronation of Osai Opoko, brother to the late king. He was equal to the existing state of affairs. He proved himself a statesman, a soldier, and a wise ruler. He organized his army, and took the field in person against the revolting tribes. He reconquered all the lost provinces. He defeated his most valorous foe, the king of Gaman, after driving him into the Kong Mountains. When his jealous underlings sought his overthrow by conspiracy, he conquered them by an appeal to arms. His rule was attended by the most lasting and beneficent results. He died in 1742, and was succeeded by his brother, Osai Akwasi.

The fame and military prowess of the kings of the Ashantees were borne on every passing breeze, and told by every fleeing fugitive. The whole country was astounded by the marvellous achievements of this people, and not a little envy was felt among adjoining nations. The king of Dahomey especially felt like humiliating this people in battle. This spirit finally manifested itself in feuds, charges, complaints, and, laterally, by actual hostilities. The king of Dahomey felt that he had but one rival, the king of Ashantee. He felt quite sure of victory on account of the size, spirit, and discipline of his army. It was idle at this time, and was ordered to the Ashantee border. The first engagement took place near the Volta. The king of Dahomey had succeeded in securing an alliance with the armies of Kawaku and Bourony, but the valor and skill of the Ashantees were too much for the invading armies. If King Akwasi had simply maintained his defensive position, his victory would have been lasting; but, overjoyed at his success, he unwittingly pursued the enemy beyond the Volta, and carried war into the kingdom of Dahomey. Troops fight with great desperation in their own country. The Ashantee

army was struck on its exposed flanks, its splendid companies of
Caboceers went down before the intrepid Amazons. Back to the
Volta, the boundary-line between the two empires, fled the routed
Ashantees. Akwasi received a mortal wound, from which he died
in 1752, when his nephew, Osai Kudjoh, succeeded to the throne.

Three brothers had held the sceptre over this empire, but
now it passed to another generation. The new king was worthy
of his illustrious family. After the days of mourning for his
royal uncle were ended, before he ascended the throne, several
provinces revolted. He at once took the field, subdued his recalcitrant subjects, and made them pay a heavy tribute. He won
other provinces by conquest, and awed the neighboring tribes
until an unobstructed way was open to his invincible army across
the country to Cape Palmas. His fame grew with each military
manœuvre, and each passing year witnessed new triumphs.
Fawning followed envy in the heart of the king of Dahomey;
and a large embassy was despatched to the powerful Kudjoh, con-
gratulating him upon his military achievements, and seeking a
friendly alliance between the two governments. Peace was now
restored; and the armies of Ashantee very largely melted into
agricultural communities, and great prosperity came. But King
Kudjoh was growing old in the service of his people; and, as he
could no longer give his personal attention to public affairs, dissensions arose in some of the remote provinces. With impaired
vision and feeble health he, nevertheless, put an army into the
field to punish the insubordinate tribes; but before operations
began he died. His grandson, Osai Kwamina, was designated as
legal successor to the throne in 1781. He took a solemn vow
that he would not enter the palace until he secured the heads of
Akombroh and Afosee, whom he knew had excited and incited
the people to rebellion against his grandfather. His vengeance
was swift and complete. The heads of the rebel leaders were
long kept at Kumasi as highly prized relics of the reign of King
Kwamina. His reign was brief, however. He was deposed for
attempting to introduce the Mohammedan religion into the kingdom. Osai Apoko was crowned as his successor in 1797. The
Gaman and Kongo armies attached themselves to the declining
fortunes of the deposed king, and gave battle for his lost crown.
It was a lost cause. The new king could wield his sword as well
as wear a crown. He died of a painful sickness, and was succeeded by his son, Osai Tutu Kwamina, in 1800.

The new king was quite youthful, — only seventeen; but he inherited splendid qualities from a race of excellent rulers. He re-organized his armies, and early won a reputation for courage, sagacity, and excellent ability, extraordinary in one so young. He inherited a bitter feeling against the Mohammedans, and made up his mind to chastise two of their chiefs, Ghofan and Ghobago, and make the territory of Banna tributary to Ashantee. He invaded their country, and burned their capital. In an engagement fought at Kaha, the entire Moslem army was defeated and captured. The king of Ghofan was wounded and made prisoner, and died in the camp of the Ashantee army. Two more provinces were bound to the throne of Kwamina; and we submit that this is an historical anomaly, in that a pagan people subdued an army that emblazoned its banner with the faith of *the one God!*

The Ashantee empire had reached the zenith of its glory. Its flag waved in triumph from the Volta to Bossumpea, and the Kong Mountains had echoed the exploits of the veterans that formed the strength of its army. The repose that even this uncivilized people longed for was denied them by a most unfortunate incident.

Asim was a province tributary to the Ashantee empire. Two of the chiefs of Asim became insubordinate, gave offence to the king, and then fled into the country of the Fantis, one of the most numerous and powerful tribes on the Gold Coast. The Fantis promised the fugitives armed protection. There was no extradition treaty in those days. The king despatched friendly messengers, who were instructed to set forth the faults of the offending subjects, and to request their return. The request was contemptuously denied, and the messengers subjected to a painful death. The king of Ashantee invaded the country of the enemy, and defeated the united forces of Fanti and Asim. He again made them an offer of peace, and was led to believe it would be accepted. But the routed army was gathering strength for another battle, although Chibbu and Apontee had indicated to the king that the conditions of peace were agreeable. The king sent an embassy to learn when a forma' submission would take place; and they, also, were put to death. King Osai Tutu Kwamina took "*the great oath*," and vowed that he would never return from the seat of war or enter his capital without the heads of the rebellious chiefs.

The Ashantee army shared the desperate feelings of their leader; and a war was begun, which for cruelty and carnage has

no equal in the annals of the world's history.   Pastoral communities, hamlets, villages, and towns were swept by the red waves of
remorseless warfare.   There was no mercy in battle: there were
no prisoners taken by day, save to be spared for a painful death at
nightfall.   Their groans, mingling with the shouts of the victors,
made the darkness doubly hideous; and the blood of the vanquished army, but a short distance removed, ran cold at the
thoughts of the probable fate that waited them on the morrow.
Old men and old women, young men and young women, the
rollicking children whose light hearts knew no touch of sorrow,
as well as the innocent babes clinging to the agitated bosoms of
their mothers, — unable to distinguish between friend or foe, —
felt the cruel stroke of war.   All were driven to an inhospitable
grave in the place where the fateful hand of war made them its
victims, or perished in the sullen waters of the Volta.   For nearly
a hundred miles "the smoke of their torment" mounted the skies.
Nothing was left in the rear of the Ashantee army, not even
cattle or buildings.   Pursued by a fleet-footed and impartial disaster, the fainting Fantis and their terrified allies turned their
faces toward the seacoast.   And why?   Perhaps this fleeing army
had a sort of superstitious belief that the sea might help them.
Then, again, they knew that there were many English on the Gold
Coast; that they had forts and troops.   They trusted, also, that
the young king of the Ashantees would not follow his enemy
under the British flag and guns.   They were mistaken.   The two
revolting chiefs took refuge in the fort at Anamabo.   On came
the intrepid king, thundering at the very gates of the English
fort.   The village was swept with the hot breath of battle.   Thousands perished before this invincible army.   The English soldiers
poured hot shot and musketry into the columns of the advancing
army; but on they marched to victory with an impurturbable air,
worthy of "*the old guard*" under Ney at Waterloo.   Preparations
were completed for blowing up the walls of the fort; and it
would have been but a few hours until the king of Ashantee
would have taken the governor's chair, had not the English capitu-
lated.   During the negotiations one of the offending chiefs made
good his escape to a little village called Cape Coast; but the other
was delivered up, and, having been taken back to Kumasi, was
tortured to death.   Twelve thousand persons fell in the engagement at Anamabo, and thousands of lives were lost in other
engagements.   This took place in 1807.

In 1811 the king of Ashantee sent an army to Elmina to protect his subjects against predatory bands of Fantis. Three or four battles were fought, and were invariably won by the Ashantee troops.

Barbarians have about as long memories as civilized races. They are a kind-hearted people, but very dangerous and ugly when they are led to feel that they have been injured. "*The great oath*" means a great deal; and the king was not happy in the thought that one of the insolent chiefs had found refuge in the town of Cape Coast, which was in the Fanti country. So in 1817 he invaded this country, and called at Cape Coast, and reduced the place to the condition of a siege. The English authorities saw the Fantis dying under their eyes, and paid the fine imposed by the King of Ashantee, rather than bury the dead inhabitants of the beleaguered town. The Ashantees retired.

England began to notice the Ashantees. They had proven themselves to be a most heroic, intelligent, and aggressive people. The Fantis lay stretched between them and the seacoast. The frequent invasion of this country, for corrective purposes as the Ashantees believed, very seriously interrupted the trade of the coast; and England began to feel it. The English had been defeated once in an attempt to assist the Fantis, and now thought it wise to turn attention to a pacific policy, looking toward the establishment of amicable relations between the Ashantees and themselves. There had never been any unpleasant relations between the two governments, except in the instance named. The Ashantees rather felt very kindly toward England, and for prudential and commercial reasons desired to treat the authorities at the coast with great consideration. They knew that the English gave them a market for their gold, and an opportunity to purchase manufactured articles that they needed. But the Fantis, right under the English flag, receiving a rent for the ground on which the English had their fort and government buildings, grew so intolerably abusive towards their neighbors, the Ashantees, that the British saw nothing before them but interminable war. It was their desire to avoid it if possible. Accordingly, they sent an embassy to the king of the Ashantees, consisting of Gov. James, of the fort at Akra, a Mr. Bowdich, nephew to the governor-in-chief at Cape Coast, a Mr. Hutchinson, and the surgeon of the English settlement, Dr. Teddlie. Mr. Bowdich headed the embassy to the royal court, where they were kindly received. A treaty was made. The rent that the Fantis had been receiving for ground occupied by the English — four ounces of gold per month — was to be paid to the king of Ashantee, as his by right of conquest. Diplomatic relations were to be established between the two governments, and Mr. Hutchinson was to remain at Kumasi as the British resident minister. He was charged with the carrying out of so much of the treaty as related to his government. The treaty was at once forwarded to the home government, and Mr. Dupuis was appointed consul of his Majesty's government to the court of Ashantee. A policy was outlined that meant the opening up of commerce with the distant provinces of the Ashantee empire along the Kong Mountains. In those days it took a long time to sail from England to the Gold Coast in Western Africa; and before Consul Dupuis reached the coast, the king of Ashantee was engaged in a war with the king of Gaman. The Ashantee army was routed. The news of the disaster was hailed by the Fantis on the coast with the most boisterous and public demonstrations. This gave the king of Ashantee offence. The British authorities were quite passive about the conduct of the Fantis, although by solemn treaty they had become responsible for their deportment. The Fantis grew very insulting and offensive towards the Ashantees. The king of the latter called the attention of the authorities at the Cape to the conduct of the Fantis, but no official action was taken. In the mean while Mr. Dupuis was not allowed to proceed on his mission to the capital of the Ashantees. Affairs began to assume a very threatening attitude; and only after the most earnest request was he permitted to proceed to the palace of the king of Ashantee. He received a hearty welcome at the court, and was entertained with the most lavish kindness. After long and painstaking consideration, a treaty was decided upon that was mutually agreeable; but the self-conceited and swaggering insolence of the British authorities on the coast put it into the waste-basket. The commander of the British squadron put himself in harmony with the local authorities, and refused to give Consul Dupuis transportation to England for the commissioners of the Ashantee government, whom he had brought to the coast with the intention of taking to London with him.

A war-cloud was gathering. Dupuis saw it. He sent word to the king of Ashantee to remember his oath, and refrain from hostilities until he could communicate with the British government. The treaty stipulated for the recognition, by the British authorities, of the authority of the Ashantee king over the Fantis. Only those immediately around the fort were subject to English law, and then not to an extent to exempt them from tax imposed by the Ashantee authorities.

In the midst of these complications, Parliament, by a special act, abolished the charter of the African Company. This put all its forts, arsenals, and stations under the direct control of the crown. Sir Charles McCarthy was made governor-general of the British possessions on the Gold Coast, and took up his headquarters at Cape Coast in March, 1822. Two months had passed now since Dupuis had sailed for England; and not a syllable had reached the king's messenger, who, all this time, had waited to hear from England. The country was in an unsettled state. Gov. McCarthy was not equal to the situation. He fell an easy prey to the fawning and lying Fantis. They received him as the champion of their declining fortunes, and did every thing in their power to give him an unfriendly opinion of the Ashantees. The king of the Ashantees began to lose faith in the British. His faithful messenger returned from the coast bearing no friendly tidings. The king withdrew his troops from the seacoast, and began to put his army upon a good war-footing. When all was in readiness a Negro sergeant in the British service was seized, and put to a torturous death. This was a signal for the grand opening. Of course the British were bound to demand redress. Sir Charles McCarthy was informed by some Fantis scouts that the king of Ashantee, at the head of his army, was marching for Cape Coast. Sir Charles rallied his forces, and went forth to give him battle. His object was to fight the king at a distance from the cape, and thus prevent him from devastating the entire country as in former wars. Sir Charles McCarthy was a brave man, and worthy of old England; but in this instance his courage was foolhardy. He crossed the Prah River to meet a wily and desperate foe. His troops were the worthless natives, hastily gathered, and were intoxicated with the hope of deliverance from Ashantee rule. He should have waited for the trained troops of Major Chisholm. This was his fatal mistake. His pickets felt the enemy early in the morning of the 21st of January, 1824. A lively skirmish followed. In a short time the clamorous warhorns of the advancing Ashantees were heard, and a general engagement came on. The first fighting began along a shallow stream. The Ashantees came up with the courage and measured tread of a well-disciplined army. They made a well-directed charge to gain the opposite bank of the stream, but were repulsed by an admirable bayonet charge from Sir Charles's troops. The Ashantees then crossed the stream above and below the British army, and fell with such desperation upon its exposed and naked flanks, that it was bent into the shape of a letter A, and hurled back toward Cape Coast in dismay. Wounded and exhausted, toward evening Sir Charles fled from his exposed position to the troops of his allies under the command of the king of Denkera. He concentrated his artillery upon the heaviest columns of the enemy ; but still they came undaunted, bearing down upon the centre like an avalanche. Sir Charles made an attempt to retreat with his staff, but met instant death at the hands of the Ashantees. His head was removed from the body and sent to Kumasi. His heart was eaten by the chiefs of the army that they might imbibe his courage, while his flesh was dried and issued in small rations among the line-officers for the same purpose. His bones were kept at the capital of the Ashantee kingdom as national fetiches.[1]

Major Chisholm and Capt. Laing, learning of the disaster that had well-nigh swallowed up Sir Charles's army, retreated to Cape Coast. There were about thirty thousand troops remaining, but they were so terrified at the disaster of the day that they could not be induced to make a stand against the gallant Ashantees. The king of Ashantee, instead of following the routed army to the gates of Cape Coast, where he could have dealt it a death-blow, offered the English conditions of peace. Capt. Ricketts met the Ashantee messengers at Elmina, and heard from them the friendly messages of the king. The Ashantees only wanted the British to surrender Kudjoh Chibbu of the province of Denkera ; but this fugitive from the Ashantee king, while negotiations were pending, resolved to rally the allied armies and make a bold stroke. He crossed the Prah at the head of a con-

---

[1] The following telegram shocks the civilized world. It serves notice on the Christians of the civilized world, that, in a large missionary sense, they have come far short of their duty to the "nations beyond," who sit in darkness and the shadow of death.

"MASSACRE OF MAIDENS. LONDON, Nov. 10, 1881. — Advices from Cape Coast Castle report that the king of Ashantee killed two hundred young girls for the purpose of using their blood for mixing mortar for repair of one of the state buildings. The report of the massacre was received from a refugee chosen for one of the victims. Such wholesale massacres are known to be a custom with the king." — *Cinn. Commercial.*

siderable force, and fell upon the Ashantee army in its camp. The English were charmed by this bold stroke, and sent a reserve force; but the whole army was again defeated by the Ashantees, and came back to Cape Coast in complete confusion.

The Ashantee army were at the gates of the town. Col. Southerland arrived with re-enforcements, but was beaten into the fort by the unyielding courage of the attacking force. A new king, Osai Ockote, arrived with fresh troops, and won the confidence of the army by marching right under the British guns, and hissing defiance into the face of the foe. The conflict that fol lowed was severe, and destructive to both life and property. All the native and British forces were compelled to retire to the fort; while the Ashantee troops, inspired by the dashing bearing of their new king, closed in around them like tongues of steel. The invading army was not daunted by the belching cannon that cut away battalion after battalion. On they pressed for revenge and victory. The screams of fainting women and terrified children, the groans of the dying, and the bitter imprecations of desperate combatants, — a mingling medley, — swelled the great diapason of noisy battle. The eyes of the beleaguered were turned toward the setting sun, whose enormous disk was leaning against the far-away mountains, and casting his red and vermilion over the dusky faces of dead Ashantees and Fantis; and, imparting a momentary beauty to the features of the dead white men who fell so far away from home and friends, he sank to rest. There was a sad, far-off look in the eye of the impatient sailor who kept his lonely watch on the vessel that lay at rest on the sea. Night was wished for, prayed for, yearned for. It came at last, and threw its broad sable pinions over the dead, the dying, and the living. Hostilities were to be renewed in the morning; but the small-pox broke out among the soldiers, and the king of Ashantee retired.

Sir Neill Campbell was appointed governor-general at Cape Coast. One of his first acts was to call for all the chiefs of the Fantis, and give them to understand that hostilities between themselves and the king of Ashantee must stop. He then required Osai Ockoto to deposit four thousand ounces of gold ($72,000), as a bond to keep the peace. In case he provoked hostilities, the seventy-two thousand dollars were to be used to purchase ammunition with which'to chastise him. In 1831 the king was obliged to send two of his royal family, Kwanta Missah, his own son, and Ansah, the son of the late king, to be held as hostages. These boys were sent to England, where they were educated, but are now residents of Ashantee.

Warsaw and Denkera, interior provinces, were lost to the Ashantee empire; but, nevertheless, it still remains one of the most powerful Negro empires of Western Africa.

The king of Ashantee has a fair government. His power is well-nigh absolute. He has a House of Lords, who have a check-power. Coomassi is the famous city of gold, situated in the centre of the empire. The communication through to the seacoast is unobstructed; and it is rather remarkable that the Ashantees are the only nation in Africa, who, living in the interior, have direct communication with the Caucasian. They have felt the somewhat elevating influence of Mohammedanism, and are not unconscious of the benefits derived by the literature and contact of the outside world. They are a remarkable people: brave, generous, industrious, and mentally capable. The day is not distant when the Ashantee kingdom will be won to the Saviour, and its inhabitants brought under the beneficent influences of Christian civilization.

CHAPTER VI.

THE NEGRO TYPE.

Climate the Cause. — His Geographical Theatre. — He is susceptible to Christianity and Civilization.

IF the reader will turn to a map of Africa, the Mountains of the Moon[1] will be found to run right through the centre of that continent. They divide Africa into two almost equal parts. In a dialectic sense, also, Africa is divided. The Mountains of the Moon, running east and west, seem to be nature's dividing line between two distinct peoples. North of these wonderful mountains the languages are numerous and quite distinct, and lacking affinity. For centuries these tribes have lived in the same latitude, under the same climatic influences, and yet, without a written standard, have preserved the idiomatic coloring of their tribal language without corruption. Thus they have eluded the fate that has overtaken all other races who without a written language, living together by the laws of affinity, sooner or later have found one medium of speech as inevitable as necessary.

But coming south of the Mountains of the Moon, until we reach the Cape of Good Hope, there is to be found one great family. Nor is the difference between the northern and southern tribes only linguistic. The physiological difference between these people is great. They range in color from the dead black up to pure white, and from the dwarfs on the banks of the Casemanche to the tall and giant-like Vei tribe of Cape Mount.

"The Fans which inhabit the mountain terraces are altogether of a different complexion from the seacoast tribes. Their hair is longer: that of the women hangs down in long braids to their shoulders, while the men have tolerably long two-pointed beards. It would be impossible to find such long hair among the coast tribes, even in a single instance.

"In the low, swampy land at the mouth of the Congo, one meets with typical Negroes; and there again, as one reaches a higher soil, one finds a different class of people.

"The Angolese resemble the Fula. They are scarcely ever black. Their

---

[1] See Keith Johnson's Map of Africa, 1863.

hands and feet are exquisitely small; and in every way they form a contrast with the slaves of the Portuguese, who, brought for the most part from the Congo, are brutal and debased.

" I have divided Africa into three grand types, — the Ethiopian, the intermediate, and the Negro. In the same manner the Negro may be divided into three sub-classes : —

" The bronze-colored class : gracefully formed, with effeminate features, small hands and feet, long fingers, intelligent minds, courteous and polished manners. Such are the Mpongwe of the Gaboon, the Angolese, the Fanti of the Gold Coast, and most probably the Haoussa of the Niger, a tribe with which I am not acquainted.

" The black-skinned class : athletic shapes, rude manners, less intelligence, but always with some good faculties, thicker lips, broader noses, but seldom prognathous to any great degree. Such are the Wollof, the Kru-men, the Benga of Corisco, and the Cabinda of Lower Guinea, who hire themselves out as sailors in the Congo and in Angola precisely as do the Kru-men of North Guinea.

" Lastly, the typical Negroes : an exceptional race even among the Negroes, whose disgusting type it is not necessary to re-describe. They are found chiefly along the coast between the Casemanche and Sierra Leone, between Lagos and the Cameroons, in the Congo swamps, and in certain swampy plains and mountain-hollows of the interior." [1]

That climate has much to do with physical and mental character, we will not have to prove to any great extent. It is a fact as well established as any principle in pathology. Dr. Joseph Brown says, —

" It is observed that the natives of marshy districts who permanently reside in them lose their whole bodily and mental constitution, contaminated by the poison they inhale. Their aspect is sallow and prematurely senile, so that children are often wrinkled, their muscles flaccid, their hair lank, and frequently pale, the abdomen tumid, the stature stunted, and the intellectual and moral character low and degraded. They rarely attain what in more wholesome regions would be considered old age. In the marshy districts of certain countries, — for example, Egypt, Georgia, and Virginia, — the extreme term of life is stated to be forty in the latter place. . . . In portions of Brittany which adjoin the Loire, the extreme duration of life is fifty, at which age the inhabitant wears the aspect of eighty in a healthier district. It is remarked that the inferior animals, and even vegetables, partake of the general deprivation : they are stunted and short-lived."

In his " Ashango Land," Paul B. du Chaillu devotes a large part of his fifteenth chapter to the Obongos, or Dwarfs. Nearly all African explorers and travellers have been much amazed at the diversity of color and stature among the tribes they met. This

---

[1] Savage Africa, pp. 403, 404.

diversity in physical and mental character owes its existence to the diversity and perversity of African climate.

The Negro, who is but a fraction of the countless indigenous races of Africa, has been carried down to his low estate by the invincible forces of nature. Along the ancient volcanic tracts are to be found the Libyan race, with a tawny complexion, features quite Caucasian, and long black hair. On the sandstones are to be found an intermediate type, darker somewhat than their progenitors, lips thick, and nostrils wide at the base. Then comes the Negro down in the alluvia, with dark skin, woolly hair, and prognathous development.

"The Negro forms an exceptional race in Africa. He inhabits that immense tract of marshy land which lies between the mountains and the sea, from Senegal to Benguela, and the low lands of the eastern side in the same manner. He is found in the parts about Lake Tchad, in Sennaar, along the marshy banks of rivers, and in several isolated spots besides."[1]

The true Negro inhabits Northern Africa. When his country, of which we know absolutely nothing, has been crowded, the nomadic portion of the population has poured itself over the mountain terraces, and, descending into the swamps, has become degraded in body and mind.

Technically speaking, we do not believe the Negro is a distinct species.

"It is certain that the woolly hair, the prognathous development, and the deep black skin of the typical Negro, are not peculiar to the African continent."[2]

The Negro is found in the low, marshy, and malarious districts. We think the Negro is produced in a descending scale. The African who moves from the mountain regions down into the miasmatic districts may be observed to lose his stature, his complexion, his hair, and his intellectual vigor : he finally becomes the Negro. Pathologically considered, he is weak, sickly, and short-lived. His legs are slender and almost calf-less : the head is developed in the direction of the passions, while the whole form is destitute of symmetry.

"It will be understood that the typical Negroes, with whom the slavers are supplied, represent the dangerous, the destitute, and diseased classes of African society. They may be compared to those which in England fill our

---

[1] Savage Africa, p. 400.　　　　[2] Savage Africa, p. 412.

jails, our workhouses, and our hospitals.   So far from being equal to us, the polished inhabitants of Europe, as some ignorant people suppose, they are immeasurably below the Africans themselves.

" The typical Negro is the true savage of Africa; and I must paint the deformed anatomy of his mind, as I have already done that of his body.

" The typical Negroes dwell in petty tribes, where all are equal except the women, who are slaves; where property is common, and where, consequently, there is no property at all; where one may recognize the Utopia of philosophers, and observe the saddest and basest spectacles which humanity can afford.

" The typical Negro, unrestrained by moral laws, spends his days in sloth, his nights in debauchery.   He smokes hashish till he stupefies his senses or falls into convulsions; he drinks palm-wine till he brings on a loathsome disease; he abuses children, stabs the poor brute of a woman whose hands keep him from starvation, and makes a trade of his own offspring.   He swallows up his youth in premature vice; he lingers through a manhood of disease, and his tardy death is hastened by those who no longer care to find him food. . . . If you wish to know what they have been, and to what we may restore them, look at the portraits which have been preserved of the ancient Egyptians: and in those delicate and voluptuous forms; in those round, soft features; in those long, almond-shaped, half-closed, languishing eyes; in those full pouting lips, large smiling mouths, and complexions of a warm and copper-colored tint, — you will recognize the true African type, the women-men of the Old World, of which the Negroes are the base, the depraved caricatures." [1]

But the Negro is not beyond the influences of civilization and Christianization.   Hundreds of thousands have perished in the cruel swamps of Africa; hundreds of thousands have been devoured by wild beasts of the forests; hundreds of thousands have perished before the steady and murderous columns of stronger tribes; hundreds of thousands have perished from fever, smallpox, and cutaneous diseases; hundreds of thousands have been sold into slavery; hundreds of thousands have perished in the "middle-passage;" hundreds of thousands have been landed in this New World in the West: and yet hundreds of thousands are still swarming in the low and marshy lands of Western Africa. Poor as this material is, out of it we have made, here in the United States, six million citizens; and out of this cast-away material of Africa, God has raised up many children.

To the candid student of ethnography, it must be conclusive that the Negro is but the most degraded and disfigured type of the primeval African.   And still, with all his interminable woes and wrongs, the Negro on the west coast of Africa, in Liberia

---

[1] Savage Africa, p. 430.

and Sierra Leone, as well as in the southern part of the United States, shows that centuries of savagehood and slavery have not drained him of all the elements of his manhood. History furnishes us with abundant and specific evidence of his capacity to civilize and Christianize. We shall speak of this at length in a subsequent chapter.

CHAPTER VII.

AFRICAN IDIOSYNCRASIES.

PATRIARCHAL GOVERNMENT. — CONSTRUCTION OF VILLAGES. — NEGRO ARCHITECTURE. — ELECTION OF KINGS. — CORONATION CEREMONY. — SUCCESSION. — AFRICAN QUEENS. — LAW, CIVIL AND CRIMINAL. — PRIESTS. — THEIR FUNCTIONS. — MARRIAGE. — WARFARE. — AGRICULTURE. — MECHANIC ARTS. — BLACKSMITHS.

ALL the tribes on the continent of Africa are under, to a greater or less degree, the patriarchal form of government. It is usual for writers on Africa to speak of "kingdoms" and "empires;" but these kingdoms are called so more by compliment than with any desire to convey the real meaning that we get when the empire of Germany or kingdom of Spain is spoken of. The patriarchal government is the most ancient in Africa. It is true that great kingdoms have risen in Africa; but they were the result of devastating wars rather than the creation of political genius or governmental wisdom.

" Pangola is the child or vassal of Mpende. Sandia and Mpende are the only independent chiefs from Kebrabasa to Zumbo, and belong to the tribe Manganja. The country north of the mountains, here in sight from the Zambesi, is called Senga, and its inhabitants Asenga or Basenga; but all appear to be of the same family as the rest of the Manganja and Maravi. Formerly all the Manganja were united under the government of their great chief, Undi, whose empire extended from Lake Shirwa to the River Loangwa; but after Undi's death it fell to pieces, and a large portion of it on the Zambesi was absorbed by their powerful Southern neighbors, the Bamjai. This has been the inevitable fate of every African empire from time immemorial. A chief of more than ordinary ability arises, and, subduing all his less powerful neighbors, founds a kingdom, which he governs more or less wisely till he dies. His successor, not having the talents of the conqueror, cannot retain the dominion, and some of the abler under-chiefs set up for themselves; and, in a few years, the remembrance only of the empire remains. This, which may be considered as the normal state of African society, gives rise to frequent and desolating wars, and the people long in vain for a power able to make all dwell in peace. In this light a European colony would be considered by the natives as an inestimable boon to inter-tropical Africa. Thousands of industrious natives would gladly settle around it, and engage in that peaceful pursuit of agriculture and trade of which they are so fond; and, undistracted by wars or rumors of wars, might listen to the purifying and ennobling truths of the gospel of Jesus Christ. The Manganja on the Zambesi, like their countrymen on the Shire, are fond of agriculture; and, in addition to the usual varieties of food, cultivate tobacco and cotton in quantities more than equal to their wants. To the question, 'Would they work for Europeans?' an affirmative answer may be given; if the Europeans belong to the class which can pay a reasonable price for labor, and not to that of adventurers who want employment for themselves. All were particularly well clothed from Sandia's to Pangola's; and it was noticed that all the cloth was of native manufacture, the product of their own looms. In Senga a great deal of iron is obtained from the ore, and manufactured very cleverly." [1]

The above is a fair description of the internecine wars that have been carried on between the tribes in Africa, back "to a time whereof the memory of man runneth not to the contrary." In a preceding chapter we gave quite an extended account of four Negro empires. We call attention here to the villages of these people, and shall allow writers who have paid much attention to this subject to give their impressions. Speaking of a village of the Aviia tribe called Mandji, Du Chaillu says, —

"It was the dirtiest village I had yet seen in Africa, and the inhabitants appeared to me of a degraded class of Negroes. The shape and arrangement of the village were quite different from any thing I had seen before. The place was in the form of a quadrangle, with an open space in the middle not more than ten yards square; and the huts, arranged in a continuous row on two sides, were not more than eight feet high from the ground to the roof. The doors were only four feet high, and of about the same width, with sticks placed across on the inside, one above the other, to bar the entrance. The place for the fire was in the middle of the principal room, on each side of which was a little dark chamber; and on the floor was an *orala*, or stage, to smoke meat upon. In the middle of the yard was a hole dug in the ground for the reception of offal, from which a disgusting smell arose, the wretched inhabitants being too lazy or obtuse to guard against this by covering it with earth.

"The houses were built of a framework of poles, covered with the bark of trees, and roofed with leaves. In the middle of the village stood the public shed, or palaver-house, — a kind of town-hall found in almost all West-African villages. A large fire was burning in it, on the ground; and at one end of the shed stood a huge wooden idol, painted red and white, and rudely fashioned in the shape of a woman. The shed was the largest building in the village, for it was ten feet high, and measured fifteen feet by ten. It is the habit of the lazy negroes of these interior villages — at least, the men — to spend almost the whole day lying down under the palaver-shed, feeding their morbid imaginations with tales of witchcraft, and smoking their *condoquais*."

---

[1] Livingstone's Expedition to the Zambesi, pp. 216, 217.

But all the villages of these poor children of the desert are not so untidy as the one described above. There is a wide difference in the sanitary laws governing these villages.

"The Ishogo villages are large. Indeed, what most strikes the traveller in coming from the seacoast to this inland country, is the large size, neatness, and beauty of the villages. They generally have about one hundred and fifty or one hundred and sixty huts, arranged in streets, which are very broad and kept remarkably clean. Each house has a door of wood which is painted in fanciful designs with red, white, and black. One pattern struck me as simple and effective; it was a number of black spots margined with white, painted in regular rows on a red ground. But my readers must not run away with the idea that the doors are like those of the houses of civilized people; they are seldom more than two feet and a half high. The door of my house was just twenty-seven inches high. It is fortunate that I am a short man, otherwise it would have been hard exercise to go in and out of my lodgings. The planks of which the doors are made are cut with great labor by native axes out of trunks of trees, one trunk seldom yielding more than one good plank. My hut, an average-sized dwelling, was twenty feet long and eight feet broad. It was divided into three rooms or compartments, the middle one, into which the door opened, being a little larger than the other two. . . . Mokenga is a beautiful village, containing about one hundred and sixty houses; they were the largest dwellings I had yet seen on the journey. The village was surrounded by a dense grove of plantain-trees, many of which had to be supported by poles, on account of the weight of the enormous bunches of plantains they bore. Little groves of lime-trees were scattered everywhere, and the limes, like so much golden fruit, looked beautiful amidst the dark foliage that surrounded them. Tall, towering palm-trees were scattered here and there. Above and behind the village was the dark green forest. The street was the broadest I ever saw in Africa; one part of it was about one hundred yards broad, and not a blade of grass could be seen in it. The *Sycobii* were building their nests everywhere, and made a deafening noise, for there were thousands and thousands of these little sociable birds." [1]

The construction of houses in villages in Africa is almost uniform, as far as our studies have led us. [2] Or, rather, we ought to modify this statement by saying there are but two plans of construction. One is where the houses are erected on the rectilinear, the other is where they are built on the circular plan. In the more warlike tribes the latter plan prevails. The hillsides and elevated places near the timber are sought as desirable locations for villages. The plan of architecture is simple. The diameter is first considered, and generally varies from ten to fifteen feet. A circle is drawn in the ground, and then long flexible sticks are driven into the earth. The builder, standing inside of the circle,

---

[1] Ashango Land, pp. 288, 289, 291, 292.   [2] Western Africa, p. 257 *sq.*

binds the sticks together at the top; where they are secured together by the use of the "monkey-rope," a thick vine that stretches itself in great profusion from tree to tree in that country. Now, the reader can imagine a large umbrella with the handle broken off even with the ribs when closed up, and without any cloth, — nothing but the ribs left. Now open it, and place it on the ground before you, and you have a fair idea of the hut up to the present time. A reed thatching is laid over the frame, and secured firmly by parallel lashings about fifteen inches apart. The door is made last by cutting a hole in the side of the hut facing toward the centre of the contemplated circle of huts.[1] The door is about eighteen inches in height, and just wide enough to admit the body of the owner. The sharp points, after the cutting, are guarded by plaited twigs. The door is made of quite a number of stout sticks driven into the ground at equal distances apart, through which, in and out, are woven pliant sticks. When this is accomplished, the maker cuts off the irregular ends to make it fit the door, and removes it to its place. Screens are often used inside to keep out the wind: they are made so as to be placed in whatever position the wind is blowing. Some of these houses are built with great care, and those with domed roofs are elaborately decorated inside with beads of various sizes and colors.

The furniture consists of a few mats, several baskets, a milk-pail, a number of earthen pots, a bundle of assagais, and a few other weapons of war. Next, to guard against the perils of the rainy season, a ditch about two feet in width and of equal depth is made about the new dwelling. Now multiply this hut by five hundred, preserving the circle, and you have the village. The *palaver-house*, or place for public debates, is situated in the centre of the circle of huts. Among the northern and southern tribes, a fence is built around their villages, when they are called "kraals." The space immediately outside of the fence is cleared, so as to put an enemy at a disadvantage in an attack upon the village. Among the agricultural tribes, as, for example, the Kaffirs, they drive their cattle into the kraal, and for the young build pens.

The other method of building villages is to have one long street, with a row of houses on each side, rectangular in shape.

---

[1] Through the Dark Continent, vol. i. p. 489.

They are about twenty-five or thirty feet in length, and about twelve to fifteen feet in width. Six or eight posts are used to join the material of the sides to. The roofs are flat. Three rooms are allowed to each house. The two end rooms are larger than the centre one, where the door opens out into the street. Sometimes these rooms are plastered, but it is seldom ; and then it is in the case of the well-to-do class.[1]

We said, at the beginning of this chapter, that the government in Africa was largely patriarchal ; and yet we have called attention to four great kingdoms. There is no contradiction here, although there may seem to be ; for even kings are chosen by ballot, and a sort of a house of lords has a veto power over royal edicts.

"Among the tribes which I visited in my explorations I found but one form of government, which may be called the patriarchal. There is not sufficient national unity in any of the tribes to give occasion for such a despotism as prevails in Dahomey, and in other of the African nationalities. I found the tribes of equatorial Africa greatly dispersed, and, in general, no bond of union between parts of the same tribe. A tribe is divided up into numerous *clans*, and these again into numberless little villages, each of which last possesses an independent chief. The villages are scattered; are often moved for death or witchcraft, as I have already explained in the narrative ; and not infrequently are engaged in war with each other.

"The chieftainship is, to a certain extent, hereditary, the right of succession vesting in the brother of the reigning chief or king. The people, however, and particularly the elders of the village, have a veto power, and can, for sufficient cause, deprive the lineal heir of his succession, and put in over him some one thought of more worth. In such cases the question is put to the vote of the village ; and, where parties are equally divided as to strength, there ensue sometimes long and serious palavers before all can unite in a choice. The chief is mostly a man of great influence prior to his accession, and generally an old man when he gains power.

"His authority, though greater than one would think, judging from the little personal deference paid to him, is final only in matters of every-day use. In cases of importance, such as war, or any important removal, the elders of the village meet together and deliberate in the presence of the whole population, which last finally decide the question.

"The elders, who possess other authority, and are always in the counsels of the chief, are the oldest members of important families in the village. Respect is paid to them on account of their years, but more from a certain regard for 'family,' which the African has very strongly wherever I have known him. These families form the aristocracy."[2]

Here are democracy and aristocracy blended somewhat. The king's power seems to be in deciding everyday affairs, while

---

[1] *Uncivilized Races of Men*, vol. i. chap. vii.   [2] *Equatorial Africa*, pp. 377, 378.

the weighty matters which affect the whole tribe are decided by the elders and the people. Mr. Reade says of such government, —

"Among these equatorial tribes the government is patriarchal, which is almost equivalent to saying that there is no government at all. The tribes are divided into clans. Each clan inhabits a separate village, or group of villages; and at the head of each is a patriarch, the parody of a king. They are distinguished from the others by the grass-woven cap which they wear on their heads, and by the staff which they carry in their hands. They are always rich and aged: therefore they are venerated; but, though they can exert influence, they cannot wield power; they can advise, but they cannot command. In some instances, as in that of Quenqueza, King of the Rembo, the title and empty honors of royalty are bestowed upon the most influential patriarch in a district. This is a vestige of higher civilization and of ancient empire which disappears as one descends among the lower tribes." [1]

"The African form of government is patriarchal, and, according to the temperament of the chief, despotic, or guided by the counsel of the elders of the tribe. Reverence for loyalty sometimes leads the mass of the people to submit to great cruelty, and even murder, at the hands of a despot or madman; but, on the whole, the rule is mild; and the same remark applies in a degree to their religion." [2]

When a new king is elected, he has first to repair to the pontiff's house, who — apropos of priests — is more important than the king himself. The king prostrates himself, and, with loud cries, entreats the favor of this high priest. At first the old man inside, with a gruff voice, orders him away, says he cannot be annoyed; but the king enumerates the presents he has brought him, and finally the door opens, and the priest appears, clad in white, a looking-glass on his breast, and long white feathers in his head. The king is sprinkled, covered with dust, walked over, and then, finally, the priest lies upon him. He has to swear that he will obey, etc.; and then he is allowed to go to the coronation. Then follow days and nights of feasting, and, among some tribes, human sacrifices.

The right of succession is generally kept on the male side of the family. The crown passes from brother to brother, from uncle to nephew, from cousin to cousin. Where there are no brothers, the son takes the sceptre. In all our studies on Africa, we have found only two women reigning. A woman by the name of Shinga ascended the throne of the Congo empire in 1640. She rebelled against the ceremonies sought to be intro-

---

[1] *Savage Africa*, p. 216.　　[2] *Expedition to Zambesi*, pp. 626, 627.

duced by Portuguese Catholic priests, who incited her nephew to treason. Defeated in several pitched battles, she fled into the Jaga country, where she was crowned with much success. In 1646 she won her throne again, and concluded an honorable peace with the Portuguese. The other queen was the blood-thirsty Tembandumba of the Jagas. She was of Arab blood, and a cannibal by practice. She fought many battles, achieved great victories, flirted with beautiful young savages, and finally was poisoned.

The African is not altogether without law.

"Justice appears, upon the whole, to be pretty fairly administered among the Makololo. A headman took some beads and a blanket from one of his men who had been with us; the matter was brought before the chief; and he immediately ordered the goods to be restored, and decreed, moreover, that no headman should take the property of the men who had returned. In theory all the goods brought back belonged to the chief; the men laid them at his feet, and made a formal offer of them all: he looked at the articles, and told the men to keep them. This is almost invariably the case. Tuba Mokoro, however, fearing lest Sekeletu might take a fancy to some of his best goods, exhibited only a few of his old and least valuable acquisitions. Masakasa had little to show: he had committed some breach of native law in one of the villages on the way, and paid a heavy fine rather than have the matter brought to the doctor's ears. Each carrier is entitled to a portion of the goods in his bundle, though purchased by the chief's ivory; and they never hesitate to claim their rights: but no wages can be demanded from the chief if he fails to respond to the first application." [1]

We have found considerable civil and criminal law among the different tribes. We gave an account of the civil and criminal code of Dahomey in the chapter on that empire. In the Congo country all civil suits are brought before a judge. He sits on a mat under a large tree, and patiently hears the arguments *pro* and *con.* His decisions are final. There is no higher court, and hence no appeal. The criminal cases are brought before the *Chitomé,* or priest. He keeps a sacred fire burning in his house that is never suffered to go out. He is supported by the lavish and delicate gifts of the people, and is held to be sacred. No one is allowed to approach his house except on the most urgent business. He never dies, so say the people. When he is seriously sick his legal successor steals quietly into his house, and beats his brains out, or strangles him to death. It is his duty to hear all criminal cases, and to this end he makes a periodical circuit

---

[1] Livingstone's Expedition to the Zambesi, pp. 307, 308.

among the tribe. Murder, treason, adultery, killing the escaped snakes from the fetich-house, — and often stealing, — are punished by death, or by being sold into slavery. A girl who loses her standing, disgraces her family by an immoral act, is banished from the tribe. And in case of seduction the man is tied up and flogged. In case of adultery a large sum of money must be paid. If the guilty one is unable to pay the fine, then death or slavery is the penalty.

"Adultery is regarded by the Africans as a kind of theft. It is a vice, therefore, and so common that one might write a Decameron of native tales like those of Boccaccio. And what in Boccaccio is more poignant and more vicious than this song of the Benga, which I have often heard them sing, young men and women together, when no old men were present ? —

> 'The old men young girls married.
> The young girls made the old men fools;
> For they love to kiss the young men in the dark,
> Or beneath the green leaves of the plantain-tree.
> The old men then threatened the young men,
> And said, "You make us look like fools;
> But we will stab you with our knives till your blood runs forth!"
> "Oh, stab us, stab us!" cried the young men gladly,
> "*For then your wives will fasten up our wounds.*"'"[1]

The laws of marriage among many tribes are very wholesome and elevating. When the age of puberty arrives, it is the custom in many tribes for the elderly women, who style themselves *Negemba*, to go into the forest, and prepare for the initiation of the *igonji*, or novice. They clear a large space, build a fire, which is kept burning for three days. They take the young woman into the fetich-house, — a new one for this ceremony, — where they go through some ordeal, that, thus far, has never been understood by men. When a young man wants a wife, there are two things necessary; viz., he must secure her consent, and then buy her. The apparent necessary element in African courtship is not a thing to be deprecated by the contracting parties. On the other hand, it is the *sine qua non* of matrimony. It is proof positive when a suitor gives cattle for his sweetheart, first, that he is wealthy; and, second, that he greatly values the lady he fain would make his bride. He first seeks the favor of the girl's parents. If she have none, then her next of kin, as in Israel in the days of Boaz. For it is a law among many tribes, that a young girl

---

[1] Savage Africa, p. 219.

shall never be without a guardian.   When the relatives are favorably impressed with the suitor, they are at great pains to sound his praise in the presence of the girl; who, after a while, consents to see him.   The news is conveyed to him by a friend or relative of the girl.   The suitor takes a bath, rubs his body with palm-oil, dons his best armor, and with beating heart and proud stride hastens to the presence of the fastidious charmer.   She does not speak.   He sits down, rises, turns around, runs, and goes through many exercises to show her that he is sound and healthy.   The girl retires, and the anxious suitor receives the warm congratulations of the spectators on his noble bearing.   The fair lady conveys her assent to the waiting lover, and the village rings with shouts of gladness.   Next come the preliminary matters before the wedding.   Marriage among most African tribes is a coetaneous contract.   The bride is delivered when the price is paid by the bridegroom.   No goods, no wife.   Then follow the wedding and feasting, firing of guns, blowing of horns, music, and dancing.[1]

Polygamy is almost universal in Africa, and poor woman is the greater sufferer from the accursed system.   It is not enough that she is drained of her beauty and strength by the savage passions of man: she is the merest abject slave everywhere. The young women are beautiful, but it is only for a brief season: it soon passes like the fragile rose into the ashes of premature old age.   In Dahomey she is a soldier; in Kaffir-land she tends the herds, and builds houses; and in Congo without her industry man would starve.   Everywhere man's cruel hand is against her. Everywhere she is the slave of his unholy passions.[2]

It is a mistaken notion that has obtained for many years, that the Negro in Africa is physically the most loathsome of all mankind.   True, the Negro has been deformed by degradation and abuse; but this is not his normal condition.   We have seen native Africans who were jet black, woolly-haired, and yet possessing fine teeth, beautiful features, tall, graceful, and athletic.

"In reference to the status of the Africans among the nations of the earth, we have seen nothing to justify the notion that they are of a different 'breed' or 'species' from the most civilized.   The African is a man with every

---

[1] See Savage Africa, p. 207.   Livingstone's Life-Work, pp. 47, 48.   Uncivilized Races of Men, vol. i. pp. 71–86; also Du Chaillu and Denham and Clappterton.

[2] Savage Africa, pp. 424, 425.

attribute of human kind. Centuries of barbarism have had the same deterio-
rating effects on Africans as Prichard describes them to have had on certain
of the Irish who were driven, some generations back, to the hills in Ulster and
Connaught; and these depressing influences have had such moral and physical
effects on some tribes, that ages probably will be.required to undo what ages
have done. This degradation, however, would hardly be given as a reason for
holding any race in bondage, unless the advocate had sunk morally to the
same low state. Apart from the frightful loss of life in the process by which,
it is pretended, the Negroes are better provided for than in a state of liberty
in their own country, it is this very system that perpetuates, if not causes, the
unhappy condition with which the comparative comfort of some of them in
slavery is contrasted.

" Ethnologists reckon the African as by no means the lowest of the human
family. He is nearly as strong physically as the European; and, as a race, is
wonderfully persistent among the nations of the earth. Neither the diseases
nor the ardent spirits which proved so fatal to North-American Indians, South-
Sea Islanders, and Australians, seem capable of annihilating the Negroes.
Even when subjected to that system so destructive to human life, by which
they are torn from their native soil, they spring up irrepressibly, and darken
half the new continent. They are gifted by nature with physical strength
capable of withstanding the sorest privations, and a lightheartedness which,
as a sort of compensation, enables them to make the best of the worst situations. It is like that power which the human frame possesses of withstanding
heat, and to an extent which we should never have known, had not an adventurous surgeon gone into an oven, and burnt his fingers with his own watch.
The Africans have wonderfully borne up under unnatural conditions that would
have proved fatal to most races.

" It is remarkable that the power of resistance under calamity, or, as some
would say, adaptation for a life of servitude, is peculiar only to certain tribes
on the continent of Africa. Climate cannot be made to account for the fact
that many would pine in a state of slavery, or voluntarily perish. No Kroo-
man can be converted into a slave, and yet he is an inhabitant of the low,
unhealthy west coast; nor can any of the Zulu or Kaffir tribes be reduced to
bondage, though all these live on comparatively elevated regions. We have
heard it stated by men familiar with some of the Kaffirs, that a blow, given
even in play by a European, must be returned. A love of liberty is observable
in all who have the Zulu blood, as the Makololo, the Watuta, and probably the
Masai. But blood does not explain the fact. A beautiful Barotse woman at
Naliele, on refusing to marry a man whom she did not like, was in a pet given
by the headman to some Mambari slave-traders from Benguela. Seeing her
fate, she seized one of their spears, and, stabbing herself, fell down dead." [1]

Dr. David Livingstone is certainly entitled to our utmost confidence in all matters that he writes about. Mr. Archibald Forbes
says he has seen Africans dead upon the field of battle that would
measure nine feet; and it was only a few months ago that we

---

[1] Livingstone's Expedition to the Zambesi, pp. 625, 626.

had the privilege of seeing a Zulu who was eight feet and eleven inches in height. As to the beauty of the Negro, nearly all African travellers agree.

"But if the women of Africa are brutal, the men of Africa are feminine. Their faces are smooth; their breasts are frequently as full as those of European women; their voices are never gruff or deep; their fingers are long; and they can be very proud of their rosy nails. While the women are nearly always ill-shaped after their girlhood, the men have gracefully moulded limbs, and always after a feminine type, — the arms rounded, the legs elegantly formed, without too much muscular development, and the feet delicate and small.

"When I first went ashore on Africa, viz., at Bathurst, I thought all the men who passed me, covered in their long robes, were women, till I saw one of the latter sex, and was thereby disenchanted.

"While no African's face ever yet reminded me of a man whom I had known in England, I saw again and again faces which reminded me of women; and on one occasion, in Angola, being about to chastise a *carregadore*, he sank on his knees as I raised my stick, clasped his hands, and looked up imploringly toward me, — was so like a young lady I had once felt an affection for, that, in spite of myself, I flung the stick away, fearing to commit a sacrilege.

"Ladies on reading this will open their eyes, and suppose that either I have very bad taste, or that I am writing fiction. But I can assure them that among the Angolas, and the Mpongwe, and the Mandingoes, and the Fula, I have seen men whose form and features would disgrace no petticoats, — not even satin ones at a drawing-room.

"While the women are stupid, sulky, and phlegmatic, the men are vivacious, timid, inquisitive, and garrulous beyond belief. They make excellent domestic servants, are cleanly, and even tedious in the nicety with which they arrange dishes on a table or clothes on a bed. They have also their friendships after the manner of woman, embracing one another, sleeping on the same mat, telling one another their secrets, betraying them, and getting terribly jealous of one another (from pecuniary motives) when they happen to serve the same master.

"They have none of that austerity, that reserve, that pertinacity, that perseverance, that strong-headed stubborn determination, or that ferocious courage, which are the common attributes of our sex. They have, on the other hand, that delicate tact, that intuition, that nervous imagination, that quick perception of character, which have become the proverbial characteristics of cultivated women. They know how to render themselves impenetrable; and if they desire to be perfidious, they wear a mask which few eyes can see through, while at the same time a certain sameness of purpose models their character in similar moulds. Their nature is an enigma; but solve it, and you have solved the race. They are inordinately vain : they buy looking-glasses; they will pass hours at their toilet, in which their wives must act as *femmes de chambre;* they will spend all their money on ornaments and dress, in which they can display a charming taste. They are fond of music, of dancing, and are not insensible to the beauties of nature. They are indolent, and have little ambition except to be admired and well spoken of. They are so sensitive that a harsh word will rankle in their hearts, and make them unhappy for a length of time ; and they will strip themselves to pay the *griots* for their flattery, and to escape their satire. Though naturally timid, and loath to shed blood, they witness without horror the most revolting spectacles which their religion sanctions ; and, though awed by us their superiors, a real injury will transform their natures, and they will take a speedy and merciless revenge.

"According to popular belief, the Africans are treacherous and hostile. The fact is, that all Africans are supposed to be Negroes, and that which is criminal is ever associated with that which is hideous. But, with the exception of some Mohammedan tribes toward the north, one may travel all over Africa without risking one's life. They may detain you ; they may rob you, if you are rich ; they may insult you, and refuse to let you enter their country, if you are poor : but your life is always safe till you sacrifice it by some imprudence.

"In ancient times the blacks were known to be so gentle to strangers that many believed that the gods sprang from them. Homer sings of the Ocean, father of the gods ; and says that, when Jupiter wishes to take a holiday, he visits the sea, and goes to the banquets of the blacks, — a people humble, courteous, and devout." [1]

We have quoted thus extensively from Mr. Reade because he has given a fair account of the peoples he met. He is a good writer, but sometimes gets real funny !

It is a fact that all uncivilized races are warlike. The tribes of Africa are a vast standing army. Fighting seems to be their employment. We went into this matter of armies so thoroughly in the fourth chapter that we shall not have much to say here. The bow and arrow, the spear and assagai were the primitive weapons of African warriors ; but they have learned the use of fire-arms within the last quarter of a century. The shield and assagai are not, however, done away with. The young Prince Napoleon, whose dreadful death the reader may recall, was slain by an assagai. These armies are officered, disciplined, and drilled to great perfection, as the French and English troops have abundant reason to know.

"The Zulu tribes are remarkable for being the only people in that part of Africa who have practised war in an European sense of the word. The other tribes are very good at bush-fighting, and are exceedingly crafty at taking an enemy unawares, and coming on him before he is prepared for them. Guerilla warfare is, in fact, their only mode of waging battle ; and, as is necessarily the case in such warfare, more depends on the exertion of individual combatants than on the scientific combinations of masses. But the Zulu tribe have, since the time of Tchaka, the great inventor of military tactics, carried on war in a manner approaching the notions of civilization.

---

[1] Savage Africa, pp. 426, 427.

" Their men are organized into regiments, each subdivided into companies, and each commanded by its own chief, or colonel ; while the king, as commanding general, leads his forces to war, disposes them in battle-array, and personally directs their movements. They give an enemy notice that they are about to march against him, and boldly meet him in the open field. There is a military etiquette about them which some of our own people have been slow to understand. They once sent a message to the English commander that they would 'come and breakfast with him.' He thought it was only a joke, and was very much surprised when the Kaffirs, true to their promise, came pouring like a torrent over the hills, leaving him barely time to get his men under arms before the dark enemies arrived." [1]

And there are some legends told about African wars that would put the "Arabian Nights" to the blush.[2]

In Africa, as in districts of Germany and Holland, woman is burdened with agricultural duties. The soil of Africa is very rich,[3] and consequently Nature furnishes her untutored children with much spontaneous vegetation. It is a rather remarkable fact, that the average African warrior thinks it a degradation for him to engage in agriculture. He will fell trees, and help move a village, but *will not* go into the field to work. The women — generally the married ones — do the gardening. They carry the seed on their heads in a large basket, a hoe on their shoulder, and a baby slung on the back. They scatter the seed over the ground, and then break up the earth to the depth of three or four inches.

" Four or five gardens are often to be seen round a kraal, each situated so as to suit some particular plant. Various kinds of crops are cultivated by the Kaffirs, the principal being maize, millet, pumpkins, and a kind of spurious sugar-cane in great use throughout Southern Africa, and popularly known by the name of 'sweet-reed.' The two former constitute, however, the necessaries of life, the latter belonging rather to the class of luxuries. The maize, or, as it is popularly called when the pods are severed from the stem, 'mealies,' is the very staff of life to a Kaffir; as it is from the mealies that is made the thick porridge on which the Kaffir chiefly lives. If a European hires a Kaffir, whether as guide, servant, or hunter, he is obliged to supply him with a stipulated quantity of food, of which the maize forms the chief ingredient. Indeed, so long as the native of Southern Africa can get plenty of porridge and sour milk, he is perfectly satisfied with his lot. When ripe, the ears of maize are removed from the stem, the leafy envelope is stripped off, and they are hung in pairs over sticks until they are dry enough to be taken to the storehouse." [4]

---

[1] Uncivilized Races of Men, vol. i. p. 94.
[2] Through the Dark Continent, vol. i. p. 344 *sq.*; also vol. ii. pp. 87, 88.
[3] Livingstone's Zambesi, pp. 613–617.
[4] Uncivilized Races of Men, vol. i. p. 146.

The cattle are cared for by the men, and women are not allowed to engage in the hunt for wild animals. The cattle among the mountain and sandstone tribes are of a fine stock; but those of the tribes in the alluvia, like their owners, are small and sickly.

The African pays more attention to his weapons of offensive warfare than he does to his wives; but in many instances he is quite skilful in the handicrafts.

"The Ishogo people are noted throughout the neighboring tribes for the superior quality and fineness of the *bongos*, or pieces of grass-cloth, which they manufacture. They are industrious and skilful weavers. In walking down the main street of Mokenga, a number of *ouandjas*, or houses without walls, are seen, each containing four or five looms, with the weavers seated before them weaving the cloth. In the middle of the floor of the *ouandjay* a wood-fire is seen burning; and the weavers, as you pass by, are sure to be seen smoking their pipes, and chatting to one another whilst going on with their work. The weavers are all men, and it is men also who stitch the *bongos* together to make *denguis* or robes of them; the stitches are not very close together, nor is the thread very fine, but the work is very neat and regular, and the needles are of their own manufacture. The *bongos* are very often striped, and sometimes made even in check patterns; this is done by their dyeing some of the threads of the warp, or of both warp and woof, with various simple colors; the dyes are all made of decoctions of different kinds of wood, except for black, when a kind of iron-ore is used. The *bongos* are employed as money in this part of Africa. Although called grass-cloth by me, the material is not made of grass, but of the delicate and firm cuticle of palm leaflets, stripped off in a dexterous manner with the fingers."[1]

Nearly all his mechanical genius seems to be exhausted in the perfection of his implements of war; and Dr. Livingstone is of the opinion, that when a certain perfection in the arts is reached, the natives pause. This, we think, is owing to their far remove from other nations. Livingstone says, —

"The races of this continent seem to have advanced to a certain point and no farther; their progress in the arts of working iron and copper, in pottery, basket-making, spinning, weaving, making nets, fish-hooks, spears, axes, knives, needles, and other things, whether originally invented by this people or communicated by another instructor, appears to have remained in the same rude state for a great number of centuries. This apparent stagnation of mind in certain nations we cannot understand; but, since we have in the latter ages of the world made what we consider great progress in the arts, we have unconsciously got into the way of speaking of some other races in much the same tone as that used by the Celestials in the Flowery Land. These same Chinese

---

[1] Ashango Land, pp. 290, 291.

anticipated us in several most important discoveries by as many centuries as we may have preceded others. In the knowledge of the properties of the magnet, the composition of gunpowder, the invention of printing, the manufacture of porcelain, of silk, and in the progress of literature, they were before us. But then the power of making further discoveries was arrested, and a stagnation of the intellect prevented their advancing in the path of improvement or invention."

Mr. Wood says, —

"The natives of Southern Africa are wonderful proficients in forging iron; and, indeed, a decided capability for the blacksmith's art seems to be inherent in the natives of Africa, from north to south, and from east to west. None of the tribes can do very much with the iron, but the little which they require is worked in perfection. As in the case with all uncivilized beings, the whole treasures of the art are lavished on their weapons; and so, if we wish to see what an African savage can do with iron, we must look at his spears, knives, and arrows — the latter, indeed, being but spears in miniature."

The blacksmith, then, is a person of some consequence in his village. He gives shape and point to the weapons by which game is to be secured and battles won. All seek his favor.

"Among the Kaffirs, a blacksmith is a man of considerable importance, and is much respected by the tribe. He will not profane the mystery of his craft by allowing uninitiated eyes to inspect his various processes, and therefore carries on his operations at some distance from the kraal. His first care is to prepare the bellows. The form which he uses prevails over a very large portion of Africa, and is seen, with some few modifications, even among the many islands of Polynesia. It consists of two leathern sacks, at the upper end of which is a handle. To the lower end of each sack is attached the hollow horns of some animal, that of the cow or eland being most commonly used; and when the bags are alternately inflated and compressed, the air passes out through the two horns.

"Of course the heat of the fire would destroy the horns if they were allowed to come in contact with it; and they are therefore inserted, not into the fire, but into an earthenware tube which communicates with the fire. The use of valves is unknown; but as the two horns do not open into the fire, but into the tube, the fire is not drawn into the bellows as would otherwise be the case. This arrangement, however, causes considerable waste of air, so that the bellows-blower is obliged to work much harder than would be the case if he were provided with an instrument that could conduct the blast directly to its destination. The ancient Egyptians used a bellows of precisely similar construction, except that they did not work them entirely by hand. They stood with one foot on each sack, and blew the fire by alternately pressing on them with the feet, and raising them by means of a cord fastened to their upper ends.

"When the blacksmith is about to set to work, he digs a hole in the ground, in which the fire is placed; and then sinks the earthenware tube in a sloping direction, so that the lower end opens at the bottom of the hole, while the upper end projects above the level of the ground. The two horns are next inserted into the upper end of the earthenware tube; and the bellows are then fastened in their places, so that the sacks are conveniently disposed for the hands of the operator, who sits between them. A charcoal-fire is then laid in the hole, and is soon brought to a powerful heat by means of the bellows. A larger stone serves the purpose of an anvil, and a smaller stone does duty for a hammer. Sometimes the hammer is made of a conical piece of iron, but in most cases a stone is considered sufficient. The rough work of hammering the iron into shape is generally done by the chief blacksmith's assistants, of whom he has several, all of whom will pound away at the iron in regular succession. The shaping and finishing the article is reserved by the smith for himself. The other tools are few and simple, and consist of punches and rude pinchers made of two rods of iron.

"With these instruments the Kaffir smith can cast brass into various ornaments. Sometimes he pours it into a cylindrical mould, so as to make a bar from which bracelets and similar ornaments can be hammered, and sometimes he makes studs and knobs by forming their shape in clay moulds." [1]

Verily, the day will come when these warlike tribes shall beat their spears into pruning-hooks, and their assagais into plough-shares, and shall learn war no more! The skill and cunning of their artificers shall be consecrated to the higher and nobler ends of civilization, and the noise of battle shall die amid the music of a varied industry!

---

[1] Uncivilized Races of Men, vol. i. pp. 97, 98.

CHAPTER VIII.

LANGUAGES, LITERATURE, AND RELIGION.

STRUCTURE OF AFRICAN LANGUAGES. — THE MPONGWE, MANDINGO, AND GREBO. — POETRY : EPIC, IDYLLIC, AND MISCELLANEOUS. — RELIGIONS AND SUPERSTITIONS.

PHILOLOGICALLY the inhabitants of Africa are divided into two distinct families. The dividing line that Nature drew across the continent is about two degrees north of the equator. Thus far science has not pushed her investigations into Northern Africa ; and, therefore, little is known of the dialects of that section. But from what travellers have learned of portions of different tribes that have crossed the line, and made their way as far as the Cape of Good Hope, we infer, that, while there are many dialects in that region, they all belong to one common family. During the Saracen movement, in the second century of the Christian era, the Arab turned his face toward Central Africa. Everywhere traces of his language and religion are to be found. He transformed whole tribes of savages. He built cities, and planted fields ; he tended flocks, and became trader. He poured new blood into crumbling principalities, and taught the fingers of the untutored savage to war. His religion, in many places, put out the ineffectual fires of the fetich-house, and lifted the grovelling thoughts of idolaters heavenward. His language, like the new juice of the vine, made its way to the very roots of Negro dialects, and gave them method and tone. In the song and narrative, in the prayer and precept, of the heathen, the Arabic comes careering across each sentence, giving cadence and beauty to all.

On the heels of the Mohammedan followed the Portuguese, the tried and true servants of Rome, bearing the double swords and keys. Not so extensive as the Arab, the influence of the Portuguese, nevertheless, has been quite considerable.

All along the coast of Northern Guinea, a distance of nearly fifteen hundred miles, — from Cape Mesurado to the mouth of the Niger, — the Kree, Grebo, and Basa form one general family, and speak the Mandu language. On the Ivory Coast another language is spoken between Frisco and Dick's Cove. It is designated as the Avĕkwŏm language, and in its verbal and inflective character is not closely related to the Mandu. The dialects of Popo, Dahomey, Ashantee, and Akra are resolvable into a family or language called the *Fantyipin.* All these dialects, to a greater or less extent, have incorporated many foreign words, — Dutch, French, Spanish, English, Portuguese, and even many words from Madagascar. The language of the Gold and Ivory Coasts we find much fuller than those on the Grain Coast. Wherever commerce or mechanical enterprise imparts a quickening touch, we find the vocabulary of the African amplified. Susceptible, apt, and cunning, the coast tribes, on account of their intercourse with the outside world, have been greatly changed. We are sorry that the change has not always been for the better. Uncivilized sailors, and brainless and heartless speculators, have sown the rankest seeds of an effete Caucasian civilization in the hearts of the unsuspecting Africans. These poor people have learned to cheat, lie, steal; are capable of remarkable diplomacy and treachery; have learned well the art of flattery and extreme cruelty. Mr. Wilson says, —

" The Sooahelee, or Swahere language, spoken by the aboriginal inhabitants of Zanzibar, is very nearly allied to the Mpongwe, which is spoken on the western coast in very nearly the same parallel of latitude. *One-fifth of the words of these two dialects are either the same, or so nearly so that they may easily be traced to the same root.*"

The Italics are our own. The above was written just a quarter of a century ago.

" The language of Uyanzi seemed to us to be a mixture of almost all Central African dialects. Our great stock of native words, in all dialects, proved of immense use to me; and in three days I discovered, after classifying and comparing the words heard from the Wy-anzi with other African words, that I· was tolerably proficient, at least for all practical purposes, in the Kiyanzi dialect." [1]

Mr. Stanley wrote the above in Africa in March, 1877. It was but a repetition of the experiences of Drs. Livingstone and Kirk, that, while the dialects west and south-west of the Mountains of the Moon are numerous, and apparently distinct, they are

---

[1] Stanley's Through the Dark Continent, vol. ii. pp. 320, 321; see, also, pp. 3, 78, 123, 245, 414.

referable to one common parent.   The Swahere language has held
its place from the beginning.   Closely allied to the Mpongwe, it
is certainly one of great strength and beauty.

"This great family of languages — if the Mpongwe dialect may be taken
as a specimen — is remarkable, for its beauty, elegance, and perfectly philosophical arrangements, as well as for its almost indefinite expansibility.   In these
respects it not only differs essentially and radically from all the dialects north
of the Mountains of the Moon, but they are such as may well challenge a
comparison with any known language in the world." [1]

The dialects of Northern Africa are rough, irregular in structure, and unpleasant to the ear.   The Mpongwe we are inclined
to regard as the best of all the dialects we have examined.   It is
spoken, with but slight variations, among the Mpongwe, Ayomba,
Oroungou, Rembo, Camma, Ogobay, Anenga, and Ngaloi tribes.
A careful examination of several other dialects leads us to suspect
that they, too, sustain a distant relationship to the Mpongwe.

Next to this remarkable language comes the Bakalai, with
its numerous dialectic offspring, scattered amongst the following tribes: the Balengue, Mebenga, Bapoukow, Kombe, Mbiki,
Mbousha, Mbondemo, Mbisho, Shekiani, Apingi, Evili, with other
tribes of the interior.

The two families of languages we have just mentioned — the
Mpongwe and the Bakalai — are distinguished for their system and
grammatical structure.   It is surprising that these unwritten languages should hold their place among roving, barbarous tribes
through so many years.   In the Mpongwe language and its
dialects, the liquid and semi-vowel *r* is rolled with a fulness and
richness harmonious to the ear.   The Bakalai and its branches
have no *r;* and it is no less true that all tribes that exclude this
letter from their dialects are warlike, nomadic, and much inferior
to the tribes that use it freely.

The Mpongwe language is spoken on each side of the
Gabun, at Cape Lopez, and at Cape St. Catharin in Southern
Guinea; the Mandingo, between Senegal and the Gambia; and
the Grebo language, in and about Cape Palmas.   It is about
twelve hundred miles from Gabun to Cape Palmas, about two
thousand miles from Gabun to Senegambia, and about six hundred miles from Cape Palmas to Gambia.   It is fair to presume
that these tribes are sufficiently distant from each other to be

---

[1] Western Africa, p. 455.

called strangers. An examination of their languages may not
fail to interest.

It has been remarked somewhere, that a people's homes are
the surest indications of the degree of civilization they have
attained. It is certainly true, that deportment has much to do
with the polish of language. The disposition, temperament, and
morals of a people who have no written language go far toward
giving their language its leading characteristics. The Grebo
people are a well-made, quick, and commanding-looking people.
In their intercourse with one another, however, they are unpol-
ished, of sudden temper, and revengeful disposition.[1] Their
language is consequently *monosyllabic.* A great proportion of
Grebo words are of the character indicated. A few verbs will
illustrate. *Kba*, carry; *la*, kill; *ya*, bring; *mu*, go; *wa*, walk;
ni, do; and so on. This is true of objects, or nouns. *Ge*, farm;
bro, earth; *wĕnh*, sun; *tu*, tree; *gi*, leopard; *na*, fire; *yi*, eye; *bo*,
leg; *lu*, head; *nu*, rain; *kai*, house. The Grebo people seem to
have no idea of syllabication. They do not punctuate; but,
speaking with the rapidity with which they move, run their words
together until a whole sentence might be taken for one word. If
any thing has angered a Grebo he will say, "*E ya mu kra wudi;*"
being interpreted, "It has raised a great bone in my throat." But
he says it so quickly that he pronounces it in this manner,
yamukroure. There are phrases in this language that are beyond
the ability of a foreigner to pronounce. It has no contractions,
and often changes the first and second person of the personal pro-
noun, and the first and second person plural, by lowering or pitch-
ing the voice. The orthography remains the same, though the
significations of those words are radically different.

The Mpongwe language is largely polysyllabic. It is burdened
with personal pronouns, and its adjectives have numerous changes
in addition to their degrees of comparison. We find no inflec-
tions to suggest case or gender. The adjective *mpolo*, which
means "large," carries seven or eight forms. While it is impossible to tell whether a noun is masculine, feminine, or neuter, they
use one adjective for all four declensions, changing its form to
suit each.

The following form of declensions will serve to impart a
clearer idea of the arbitrary changes in the use of the adjective:

---

[1] Western Africa, p. 456.

First Declension. { Singular, *nyare mpolu*, a large cow.
{ Plural, *inyare impolu*, large cows.

Second Declension. { Singular, *egara evolu*, a large chest.
{ Plural, *gara volu*, large chests.

Third Declension. { Singular, *idâmbe ivolu*, a large sheep.
{ Plural, *idâmbe ampolu*, large sheep.

Fourth Declension. { Singular, *omamba ompolu*, a large snake.
{ Plural, *imamba impolu*, large snakes. [1]

We presume it would be a difficult task for a Mpongwe to explain the arbitrary law by which such changes are made. And yet he is as uniform and strict in his obedience to this law as if it were written out in an Mpongwe grammar, and taught in every village.

His verb has four moods; viz., indicative, imperative, conditional, and subjunctive. The auxiliary particle gives the indicative mood its grammatical being. The imperative is formed from the present of the indicative by changing its initial consonant into its reciprocal consonant as follows: —

> *tonda*, to love.
> *ronda*, love thou.
> *denda*, to do.
> *lenda*, do thou.

The conditional mood has a form of its own; but the conjunctive particles are used as auxiliaries at the same time, and different conjunctive particles are used with different tenses. The subjunctive, having but one form, in a sentence where there are two verbs is used as the second verb.[2] So by the use of the auxiliary particles the verb can form the infinitive and potential mood. The Mpongwe verb carries four tenses, — present, past or historical, perfect past, and future. Upon the principle of alliteration the perfect past tense, representing an action as completed, is formed from the present tense by prefixing *a*, and by changing *a*-final into *i:* for example, *tŏnda*, "to love;" *atŏndi*, "did love." The past or historical tense is derived from the imperative by prefixing *a*, and by changing *a*-final into *i.* Thus *rŏnda*, "love;" *arŏndi*, "have loved." The future tense is constructed by the aid of the auxiliary particle *be*, as follows: *mi be tŏnda*, "I am going to love."

We have not been able to find a Mandingo grammar, except Mr. MacBrair's, which is, as far as we know, the only one in

---

[1] Western Africa, p. 470.   [2] Equatorial Africa, p. 531.

existence. We have had but little opportunity to study the structure of that language. But what scanty material we have at hand leads us to the conclusion that it is quite loosely put together. The saving element in its verb is the minuteness with which it defines the time of an action. The causative form is made by the use of a suffix. It does not use the verb "to go" or "come" in order to express a future tense. Numerous particles are used in the substantive verb sense. The Mandingo language is rather smooth. The letters *v* and *z* are not in it. About one-fifth of the verbs and nouns commence with vowels, and the noun always terminates in the letter *o*.

Here is a wide and interesting field for philologists: it should be cultivated.

The African's nature is as sunny as the climate he lives in. He is not brutal, as many advocates of slavery have asserted. It is the unanimous testimony of all explorers of, and travellers through, the Dark Continent, that the element of gentleness predominates among the more considerable tribes; that they have a keen sense of the beautiful, and are susceptible of whatever culture is brought within their reach. The Negro nature is not sluggish, but joyous and vivacious. In his songs he celebrates victories, and laughs at death with the complacency of the Greek Stoics.

> "Rich man and poor fellow, all men must die:
> Bodies are only shadows. Why should I be sad?"[1]

He can be deeply wrought upon by acts of kindness; and bears a friendship to those who show him favor, worthy of a better state of society. When Henry M. Stanley (God bless him! noble, brave soul!) was about emerging from the Dark Continent, he made a halt at Kabinda before he ended his miraculous journey at Zanzibar on the Pacific Ocean. He had been accompanied in his perilous journey by stout-hearted, brave, and faithful natives. Their mission almost completed, they began to sink into that listlessness which is often the precursor of death. They had been true to their master, and were now ready to die as bravely as they had lived. Read Mr. Stanley's account without emotion if you can:—

> "'Do you wish to see Zanzibar, boys?' I asked.
> "'Ah, it is far. Nay, speak not, master. We shall never see it,' they replied.

---

[1] Savage Africa, p. 212.

" 'But you will die if you go on in this way. Wake up — shake your-selves — show yourselves to be men.'

" 'Can a man contend with God? Who fears death? Let us die undis-turbed, and be at rest forever,' they answered.

" Brave, faithful, loyal souls! They were, poor fellows, surrendering them-selves to the benumbing influences of a listlessness and fatal indifference to life! Four of them died in consequence of this strange malady at Loanda, three more on board her Majesty's ship Industry, and one woman breathed her last the day after we arrived at Zanzibar. But in their sad death they had one consolation, in the words which they kept constantly repeating to them-selves —

" ' We have brought our master to the great sea, and he has seen his white brothers. La il Allah, il Allah! There is no God but God!' they said — and died.

" It is not without an overwhelming sense of grief, a choking in the throat, and swimming eyes, that I write of those days; for my memory is still busy with the worth and virtues of the dead. In a thousand fields of incident, adventure, and bitter trials, they had proved their stanch heroism and their fortitude; they had lived and endured nobly. I remember the enthusiasm with which they responded to my appeals; I remember their bold bearing during the darkest days; I remember the Spartan pluck, the indomitable courage, with which they suffered in the days of our adversity. Their voices again loyally answer me, and again I hear them address each other upon the necessity of standing by the 'master.' Their boat-song, which contained sentiments similar to the following : —

> ' The pale-faced stranger, lonely here,
> In cities afar, where his name is dear,
> Your Arab truth and strength shall show;
> He trusts in us, row, Arabs, row ' —

despite all the sounds which now surround me, still charms my listening ear. [1] . . .

" They were sweet and sad moments, those of parting. What a long, long, and true friendship was here sundered! Through what strange vicissitudes of life had they not followed me! What wild and varied scenes had we not seen together! What a noble fidelity these untutored souls had exhibited! The chiefs were those who had followed me to Ujiji in 1871; they had been wit-nesses of the joy of Livingstone at the sight of me; they were the men to whom I intrusted the safe-guard of Livingstone on his last and fatal journey, who had mourned by his corpse at Muilala, and borne the illustrious dead to the Indian Ocean.

" And in a flood of sudden recollection, all the stormy period here ended rushed in upon my mind; the whole panorama of danger and tempest through which these gallant fellows had so stanchly stood by me — these gallant fel-lows now parting from me. Rapidly, as in some apocalyptic vision, every scene of strife with Man and Nature, through which these poor men and women had borne me company, and solaced me by the simple sympathy of

---

[1] Through the Dark Continent, vol. ii. pp. 470, 471.

common suffering, came hurrying across my memory; for each face before me was associated with some adventure or some peril, reminded me of some triumph or of some loss. What a wild, weird retrospect it was, — that mind's flash over the troubled past! so like a troublous dream!

"And for years and years to come, in many homes in Zanzibar, there will be told the great story of our journey, and the actors in it will be heroes among their kith and kin. For me too they are heroes, these poor, ignorant children of Africa, for, from the first deadly struggle in savage Ituru to the last staggering rush into Embomma, they had rallied to my voice like veterans, and in the hour of need they had never failed me. And thus, aided by their willing hands and by their loyal hearts, the expedition had been successful, and the three great problems of the Dark Continent's geography had been fairly settled." [1]

How many times we have read this marvellous narrative of Stanley's march through the Dark Continent, we do not know; but we do know that every time we have read it with tears and emotion, have blessed the noble Stanley, and thanked God for the grand character of his black followers! There is no romance equal to these two volumes. The trip was one awful tragedy from beginning to end, and the immortal deeds of his untutored guards are worthy of the famous *Light Brigade.*

On the fourth day of August, 1877, Henry M. Stanley arrived at the village of Nsanda on his way to the ocean. He had in his command one hundred and fifteen souls. Foot-sore, travel-soiled, and hungry, his people sank down exhausted. He tried to buy food from the natives; but they, with an indifference that was painful, told them to wait until market-day. A foraging party scoured the district for food, but found none. Starvation was imminent. The feeble travellers lay upon the ground in the camp, with death pictured on their dusky features. Stanley called his boat-captains to his tent, and explained the situation. He knew that he was within a few days march of Embomma, and that here were located one Englishman, one Frenchman, one Spaniard, and one Portuguese. He told the captains that he had addressed a letter to these persons for aid; and that resolute, swift, and courageous volunteers were needed to go for the relief, — without which the whole camp would be transformed into a common graveyard. We will now quote from Mr. Stanley again in proof of the noble nature of the Negro : —

"The response was not long coming; for Uledi sprang up and said, 'O master, don't talk more! I am ready now. See, I will only buckle on my belt,

---

[1] *Through the Dark Continent,* vol. ii. pp. 482, 483.

and I shall start at once, and nothing will stop me.   I will follow on the track like a leopard.'

" 'And I am one,' said Kachéché.   ' Leave us alone, master.   If there are white men at Embomma, we will find them out.   We will walk and walk, and when we cannot walk we will crawl.'

" ' Leave off talking, men,' said Muini Pembé, 'and allow others to speak, won't you?   Hear me, my master.   I am your servant.   I will outwalk the two.   I will carry the letter, and plant it before the eyes of the white men.'

" ' I will go too, sir,' said Robert.

" 'Good!   It is just as I should wish it; but, Robert, you cannot follow these three men.   You will break down, my boy.'

" 'Oh, we will carry him if he breaks down,' said Uledi.   'Won't we, Kachéché ? "

" '*Inshallah !* ' responded Kachéché decisively.   'We must have Robert along with us, otherwise the white men won't understand us.' "

What wonderful devotion !   What sublime self-forgetfulness! The world has wept over such stories as Bianca and Héloise, and has built monuments that will stand, —

> " *While Fame her record keeps,*
> *Or Honor paints the hallowed spot*
> *Where Valor proudly sleeps,*" —

and yet these black heroes are unremembered.   "I will follow the track like a leopard," gives but a faint idea of the strong will of Uledi ; and Kachéché's brave words are endowed with all the attributes of that heroic *abandon* with which a devoted general hurls the last fragment of wasting strength against a stubborn enemy.   And besides, there is something so tender in these words that they seem to melt the heart.   "We will walk and walk, and when we cannot walk we will crawl !"   We have never read but one story that approaches this narrative of Mr. Stanley, and that was the tender devotion of Ruth to her mother-in-law.   We read it in the Hebrew to Dr. O. S. Stearns of Newton, Mass. ; and confess that, though it has been many years since, the blessed impression still remains, and our confidence in humanity is strengthened thereby.

Here are a few white men in the wilds of Africa, surrounded by the uncivilized children of the desert.   They have money and valuable instruments, a large variety of gewgaws that possessed the power of charming the fancy of the average savage ; and therefore the whites would have been a tempting prey to the blacks.   But not a hair of their head was harmed.   The white men had geographical fame to encourage them in the struggle, —

friends and loved ones far away beyond the beautiful blue sea. These poor savages had nothing to steady their purposes save a paltry sum of money as day-wages, — no home, no friends ; and yet they were as loyal as if a throne were awaiting them. No, no ! nothing waited on their heroic devotion to a magnificent cause but a lonely death when they had brought the "master" to the sea. When their stomachs, pinched by hunger; when their limbs, stiff from travel ; when their eyes, dim with the mists of death ; when every vital force was slain by an heroic ambition to serve the great Stanley ; when the fires of endeavor were burnt to feeble embers, — then, and only then, would these faithful Negroes fail in the fulfilment of their mission, so full of peril, and yet so grateful to them, because it was in the line of *duty*.

Cicero urged virtue as necessary to effective oratory. The great majority of Negroes in Africa are both orators and logicians. A people who have such noble qualities as this race seems to possess has, as a logical necessity, the poetic element in a large degree.

In speaking of Negro poetry, we shall do so under three different heads ; viz., the *Epic, Idyllic, Religious*, or miscellaneous.

The epic poetry of Africa, so far as known, is certainly worthy of careful study. The child must babble before it can talk, and all barbarians have a sense of the sublime in speech. Mr. Taine, in his "History of English Literature," speaking of early Saxon poetry, says, —

"One poem nearly whole, and two or three fragments, are all that remain of this lay-poetry of England. The rest of the pagan current, German and barbarian, was arrested or overwhelmed, first by the influx of the Christian religion, then by the conquest of the Norman-French. But what remains more than suffices to show the strange and powerful poetic genius of the race, and to exhibit beforehand the flower in the bud.

"If there has ever been anywhere a deep and serious poetic sentiment, it is here. They do not speak : they sing, or rather they shout. Each little verse is an acclamation, which breaks forth like a growl ; their strong breasts heave with a groan of anger or enthusiasm, and a vehement or indistinct phrase or expression rises suddenly, almost in spite of them, to their lips. There is no art, no natural talent, for describing, singly and in order, the different parts of an object or an event. The fifty rays of light which every phenomenon emits in succession to a regular and well-directed intellect, come to them at once in a glowing and confused mass, disabling them by their force and convergence. Listen to their genuine war-chants, unchecked and violent, as became their terrible voices ! To this day, at this distance of time, separated as they are by manners, speech, ten centuries, we seem to hear them still." [1]

---

[1] History of English Literature, vol. i. pp. 48, 49.

This glowing description of the poetry of the primitive and hardy Saxon gives the reader an excellent idea of the vigorous, earnest, and gorgeous effusions of the African. Panda was king of the Kaffirs. He was considered quite a great warrior. It took a great many *isi-bongas* to describe his virtues. His chief *isi-bongas* was "O-Elephant." This was chosen to describe his strength and greatness. Mr. Wood gives an account of the song in honor of Panda : —

> " 1. Thou brother of the Tchaks, *considerate forder,*
> 2. A *swallow which fled in the sky;*
> 3. A swallow with a whiskered breast ;
> 4. Whose cattle was ever in so huddled a crowd,
> 5. They stumble for room when they ran.
> 6. Thou false adorer of the valor of another,
> 7. That valor thou tookest at the battle of Makonko.
> 8. Of the stock of N'dabazita, *ramrod of brass,*
> 9. *Survivor alone of all other rods;*
> 10. Others they broke and left this in the soot,
> 11. Thinking to burn at some rainy cold day.
> 12. *Thigh of the bullock of Inkakavini,*
> 13. Always delicious if only 'tis roasted,
> 14. It will always be tasteless if boiled.
> 15. The woman from Mankeba is delighted ;
> 16. She has seen the leopards of Jama,
> 17. Fighting together between the Makonko.
> 18. He passed between the Jutuma and Ihliza,
> 19. The Celestial who thundered between the Makonko.
> 20. I praise thee, O king ! son of Jokwane, the son of Undaba,
> 21. The merciless opponent of every conspiracy.
> 22. Thou art an *elephant,* an *elephant,* an *elephant.*
> 23. All glory to thee, thou *monarch who art black.*"

" The first *isi-bonga,* in line 1, alludes to the ingenuity with which Panda succeeded in crossing the river so as to escape out of the district where Dingan exercised authority. In the second line, 'swallow which fled in the sky' is another allusion to the secrecy with which he managed his flight, which left no more track than the passage of a swallow through the air. Lines 4 and 5 allude to the wealth, i.e., the abundance of cattle, possessed by Panda. Line 6 asserts that Panda was too humble-minded, and thought more of the power of Dingan than it deserved; while line 7 offers as proof of this assertion, that, when they came to fight, Panda conquered Dingan. Lines 8 to 11 all relate to the custom of seasoning sticks by hanging them over the fireplaces in Kaffir huts. Line 14 alludes to the fact that meat is very seldom roasted by the Kaffirs, but is almost invariably boiled, or rather stewed, in closed vessels. In line 15 the ' woman from Mankebe' is Panda's favorite wife. In line 19, 'The Celestial' alludes to the name of the great Zulu tribe over which Panda reigned ; the word 'Zulu' meaning celestial, and having much the same import as the same word when employed by the Chinese to denote their origin. Line 21 refers to the attempts of Panda's rivals to dethrone him, and the ingenious manner in which he contrived to defeat their plans by forming judicious alliances."

There is a daring insolence, morbid vanity, and huge description in this song of Panda, that make one feel like admitting that the sable bard did his work of flattery quite cleverly. It should not be forgotten by the reader, that, in the translation of these songs, much is lost of their original beauty and perspicuity. The following song was composed to celebrate the war triumphs of Dinga, and is, withal, exciting, and possessed of good movement. It is, in some instances, much like the one quoted above :—

> " Thou needy offspring of Umpikazi,
> Eyer of the cattle of men ;
> Bird of Maube, fleet as a bullet,
> Sleek, erect, of beautiful parts ;
> Thy cattle like the comb of the bees ;
> O head too large, too huddled to move ;
> Devourer of Moselekatze, son of Machobana ;
> Devourer of 'Swazi, son of Sobuza ;
> Breaker of the gates of Machobana ;
> Devourer of Gundave of Machobana ;
> A monster in size, of mighty power ;
> Devourer of Ungwati of ancient race ;
> Devourer of the kingly Uomape ;
> Like heaven above, raining and shining."

The poet has seen fit to refer to the early life of his hero, to call attention to his boundless riches, and, finally, to celebrate his war achievements. It is highly descriptive, and in the Kaffir language is quite beautiful.

Tchaka sings a song himself, the ambitious sentiments of which would have been worthy of Alexander the Great or Napoleon Bonaparte. He had carried victory on his spear throughout all Kaffir-land. Everywhere the tribes had bowed their submissive necks to his yoke ; everywhere he was hailed as king. But out of employment he was not happy. He sighed for more tribes to conquer, and thus delivered himself : —

> " Thou hast finished, finished the nations !
> Where will you go out to battle now ?
> Hey ! where will you go out to battle now ?
> Thou hast conquered kings !
> Where are you going to battle now ?

Thou hast finished, finished the nations !
Where are you going to battle now ?
Hurrah, hurrah, hurrah !
Where are you going to battle now ? ''

There is really something modern in this deep lament of the noble savage !

The following war song of the Wollof, though it lacks the sonorous and metrical elements of real poetry, contains true military aggressiveness, mixed with the theology of the fatalist.

A WAR SONG.

"I go in front. I fear not death. I am not afraid. If I die, I will take my blood to bathe my head.

"The man who fears nothing marches always in front, and is never hit by the murderous ball. The coward hides himself behind a bush, and is killed.

"Go to the battle. It is not lead that kills. It is Fate which strikes us, and which makes us die."

Mr. Reade says of the musicians he met up the Senegal, —

"There are three classes of these public minstrels, — 1, those who play such vulgar instruments as the flute and drum; 2, those who play on the ballafond, which is the marimba of Angola and South America, and on the harp; 3, those who sing the legends and battle-songs of their country, or who improvise satires or panegyrics. This last class are dreaded, though despised. They are richly rewarded in their lifetime, but after death they are not even given a decent burial. If they were buried in the ground, it would become barren ; if in the river, the water would be poisoned, and the fish would die : so they are buried in hollow trees.

The idyllic poetry of Africa is very beautiful in its gorgeous native dress. It requires some knowledge of their mythology in order to thoroughly understand all their figures of speech. The following song is descriptive of the white man, and is the production of a Bushman.

"*In the blue palace of the deep sea*
Dwells a strange creature :
His skin as white as salt ;
His hair long and tangled as the sea-weed.
He is more great than the princes of the earth ;
He is clothed with the skins of fishes, —
Fishes more beautiful than birds.
His house is built of brass rods ;
His garden is a forest of tobacco.
On his soil white beads are scattered
Like sand-grains on the seashore."

The following idyl, extemporized by one of Stanley's black soldiers, on the occasion of reaching Lake Nyanza, possesses more energy of movement, perspicuity of style, and warm, glowing imagery, than any song of its character we have yet met with from the lips of unlettered Negroes. It is certainly a noble song of triumph. It swells as it rises in its mission of praise. It breathes the same victorious air of the song of Miriam : "*Sing ye to the Lord, for he hath triumphed gloriously ; the horse and the rider hath he thrown into the sea.*" And in the last verse the child-nature of the singer riots like " The May Queen " of Tennyson.

THE SONG OF TRIUMPH.

"Sing, O friends, sing; the journey is ended :
Sing aloud, O friends ; sing to the great Nyanza.
Sing all, sing loud, O friends, sing to the great sea ;
Give your last look to the lands behind, and then turn to the sea.

Long time ago you left your lands,
Your wives and children, your brothers and your friends ;
Tell me, have you seen a sea like this
Since you left the great salt sea ?

CHORUS.

Then sing, O friends ! sing; the journey is ended :
Sing aloud, O friend ! sing to this great sea.

This sea is fresh, is good and sweet ;
Your sea is salt, and bad, unfit to drink.
This sea is like wine to drink for thirsty men ;
The salt sea — bah ! it makes men sick.

Lift up your heads, O men, and gaze around ;
Try if you can see its end.
See, it stretches moons away,
This great, sweet, fresh-water sea.

We come from Usukuma land,
The land of pastures, cattle, sheep and goats,
The land of braves, warriors, and strong men,
And, lo ! this is the far-known Usukuma sea.

Ye friends, ye scorned at us in other days.
Ah, ha ! Wangwana. What say ye now ?
Ye have seen the land, its pastures and its herds,
Ye now see the far-known Usukuma sea.
Kaduma's land is just below ;
He is rich in cattle, sheep, and goats.
The Msungu is rich in cloth and beads ;
His hand is open, and his heart is free.

To-morrow the Msungu must make us strong
With meat and beer, wine and grain.
We shall dance and play the livelong day,
And eat and drink, and sing and play."

The religious and miscellaneous poetry is not of the highest
order. One of the most remarkable men of the Kaffir tribe was
Sicana, a powerful chief and a Christian. He was a poet, and
composed hymns, which he repeated to his people till they could
retain them upon their memories. The following is a specimen
of his poetical abilities, and which the people are still accustomed
to sing to a low monotonous air : —

" Ulin guba inkulu siambata tina
Ulodali bom' unadali pezula,
Umdala undala idala izula,
Yebinza inquinquis zixeliela.
UTIKA umkula gozizuline,
Yebinza inquinquis nozilimele.
Umze uakonana subiziele,
Umkokeli ua sikokeli tina,
Uenza infama zenza go bomi ;
Imali inkula subiziele,
Wena wena q'aba inyaniza,
Wena wena kaka linyaniza,
Wena wena klati linyaniza ;
Invena inh'inani subiziele,
Ugaze laku ziman' heba wena,
Usanhla zaku ziman' heba wena,
Umkokili ua, sikokeli tina :
Ulodali bom' uadali pezula,
Umdala uadala idala izula."

TRANSLATION.

" Mantle of comfort ! God of love !
The Ancient One on high !
Who guides the firmament above,
The heavens, and starry sky ;

Creator, Ruler, Mighty One ;
The only Good, All-wise, —
To him, the great eternal God,
Our fervent prayers arise.

Giver of life, we call on him,
On his high throne above,
Our Rock of refuge still to be,
Of safety and of love ;

Our trusty shield, our sure defence,
Our leader, still to be:
We call upon our pitying God,
Who makes the blind to see.

We supplicate the Holy Lamb
Whose blood for us was shed,
Whose feet were pierced for guilty man,
Whose hands for us have bled;

Even our God who gave us life,
From heaven, his throne above,
The great Creator of the world,
Father, and God of love."

When any person is sick, the priests and devout people consult their favorite spirits. At Goumbi, in Equatorial Africa, this ceremony is quite frequent. Once upon a time the king fell sick. Quengueza was the name of the afflicted monarch. Ilogo was a favorite spirit who inhabited the moon. The time to invoke the favor of this spirit is during the full moon. The moon, in the language of Equatorial Africa, is Ogouayli. Well, the people gathered in front of the king's house, and began the ceremony, which consisted chiefly in singing the following song: —

" Ilogo, we ask thee !
Tell who has bewitched the king !

Ilogo, we ask thee,
What shall we do to cure the king ?

The forests are thine, Ilogo !
The rivers are thine, Ilogo !

The moon is thine !
O moon ! O moon ! O moon !
Thou art the house of Ilogo !
Shall the king die ? O Ilogo !
O Ilogo ! O moon ! O moon !" [1]

In African caravans or processions, there is a man chosen to go in front and sing, brandishing a stick somewhat after the manner of our band-masters. The song is rather an indifferent howl, with little or no relevancy. It is a position much sought after, and affords abundant opportunity for the display of the voice.

---

[1] Equatorial Africa, pp. 448, 449.

Such a person feels the dignity of the position. The following is a sample : —

> *" Shove him on !*
> *But is he a good man ?*
> *No, I think he's a stingy fellow :*
> *Shove him on !*
> *Let him drop in the road, then.*
> *No, he has a big stick :*
> *Shove him on !*
> *Oh, matta-bicho ! matta-bicho !*
> *Who will give me matta-bicho ? "*

Of this song Mr. Reade says, —

" *Matta-bicho* is a bunda compound meaning *kill-worm;* the natives supposing that their entrails are tormented by a small worm, which it is necessary to kill with raw spirits. From the frequency of their demand, it would seem to be the worm that ever gnaws, and that their thirst is the fire which is never quenched."

The Griot, as we have already mentioned, sings for money. He is a most accomplished parasite and flatterer. He makes a study of the art. Here is one of his songs gotten up for the occasion.

I.

" The man who had not feared to pass the seas through a love of study and of science heard of the poor Griot. He had him summoned. He made him sing songs which made the echoes of the Bornou mountains, covered with palm-trees, ring louder and louder as the sounds flew over the summits of the trees.

II.

" The songs touched the heart of the great white man, and the dew of his magnificence fell upon the Griot's head. Oh ! how can he sing the wonderful deeds of the Toubab? His voice and his breath would not be strong enough to sing that theme. He must be silent, and let the lion of the forest sing his battles and his victories.

III.

" Fatimata heard the songs of the Griot. She heard, too, the deeds which the Toubab had accomplished. She sighed, and covered her head with her robe. Then she turned to her young lover, and she said, ' Go to the wars; let the flying ball kill thee: for Fatimata loves thee no longer. The white man fills her thoughts.' "

The most beautiful nursery song ever sung by any mother, in any language, may be heard in the Balengi county, in Central Africa. There is wonderful tenderness in it, — tenderness that would melt the coldest heart. It reveals a bright spot in the heart-life of this people.[1]

" Why dost thou weep, my child?
The sky is bright; the sun is shining: why dost thou weep?
Go to thy father: he loves thee; go, tell him why thou weepest.
What! thou weepest still! Thy father loves thee; I caress thee: yet still
    thou art sad.
Tell me then, my child, why dost thou weep?"

It is not so very remarkable, when we give the matter thought, that the African mother should be so affectionate and devoted in her relations to her children. The diabolical system of polygamy has but this one feeble apology to offer in Africa. The wives of one man may quarrel, but the children always find loving maternal arms ready to shelter their heads against the wrath of an indifferent and cruel father. The mother settles all the disputes of the children, and cares for them with a zeal and tenderness that would be real beautiful in many American mothers; and, in return, the children are very noble in their relations to their mothers. "Curse me, but do not speak ill of my mother," is a saying in vogue throughout nearly all Africa. The old are venerated, and when they become sick they are abandoned to die alone.

It is not our purpose to describe the religions and superstitions of Africa.[2] To do this would occupy a book. The world knows that this poor people are idolatrous, — *" bow down to wood and stone."* They do not worship the true God, nor conform their lives unto the teachings of the Saviour. They worship snakes, the sun, moon, and stars, trees, and water-courses. But the bloody human sacrifice which they make is the most revolting feature of their spiritual degradation. Dr. Prichard has gone into this subject more thoroughly than our time or space will allow.

"Nowhere can the ancient African religion be studied better than in the kingdom of Congo. Christianity in Abyssinia, and Mohammedanism in Northern Guinea, have become so mingled with pagan rites as to render it extremely difficult to distinguish between them.

---

[1] On the intellectual faculties of the Negro, see Prichard, third ed., 1837, vol. ii. p. 346, sect. iii. Peschel's Races of Men, p. 462, *sq.*, especially Blumenbach's Life and Works, p. 305, *sq* Western Africa, p. 379, — all of chap. xi.

[2] See Prichard, fourth ed., 1841, vol. i. p. 197, sect. v. Moffat's Southern Africa; Uncivilized Races of Men, vol. i. pp. 183-219.

"The inhabitants of Congo, whom I take as a true type of the tribes of Southern Guinea generally, and of Southern Central Africa, believe in a supreme Creator, and in a host of lesser divinities. These last they represent by images; each has its temple, its priests, and its days of sacrifice, as among the Greeks and Romans."[1]

The false religions of Africa are but the lonely and feeble reaching out of the human soul after the true God.

---

[1] Savage Africa, p. 287, *sq.*

CHAPTER IX.

SIERRA LEONE.

Its Discovery and Situation. — Natural Beauty. — Founding of a Negro Colony. — The Sierra Leone Company. — Fever and Insubordination. — It becomes an English Province. — Character of its Inhabitants. — Christian Missions, etc.

SIERRA LEONE was discovered and named by Piedro de Cintra. It is a peninsula, about thirty miles in length by about twenty-five in breadth, and is situated 8° and 30' north latitude, and is about 13½° west longitude. Its topography is rather queer. On the south and west its mountains bathe their feet in the Atlantic Ocean, and on the east and north its boundaries are washed by the river and bay of Sierra Leone. A range of mountains, co-extensive with the peninsula, — forming its backbone, — rises between the bay of Sierra Leone and the Atlantic Ocean, from two to three thousand feet in altitude. Its outlines are as severe as Egyptian architecture, and the landscape view from east or west is charming beyond the power of description. Freetown is the capital, with about twenty thousand inhabitants, situated on the south side of Sierra Leone River, and hugged in by an amphitheatre of beautiful hills and majestic mountains.

"On the side of the hill [says Mr. Reed] which rises behind the town is a charming scene, which I will attempt to describe. You have seen a rural hamlet, where each cottage is half concealed by its own garden. Now convert your linden into graceful palm, your apples into oranges, your gooseberry-bushes into bananas, your thrush which sings in its wicker cage into a gray parrot whistling on a rail; . . . sprinkle this with strange and powerful perfumes; place in the west a sun flaming among golden clouds in a prussian-blue sea, dotted with white sails; imagine those mysterious and unknown sounds, those breathings of the earth-soul, with which the warm night of Africa rises into life, — and then you will realize one of those moments of poetry which reward poor travellers for long days and nights of naked solitude." [1]

In 1772 Lord Mansfield delivered his celebrated opinion on the case of the Negro man Sommersett, whose master, having

---

[1] Savage Africa, p. 25.

abandoned him in a sick condition, afterwards sought to reclaim him. The decision was to the effect that no man, white or black, could set foot on British soil and remain a slave. The case was brought at the instance of Mr. Granville Sharp. The decision created universal comment. Many Negroes in New England, who had found shelter under the British flag on account of the proclamation of Sir Henry Clinton, went to England. Free Negroes from other parts — Jamaica, St. Thomas, and San Domingo — hastened to breathe the free air of the British metropolis. Many came to want, and wandered about the streets of London, strangers in a strange land. Granville Sharp, a man of great humanity, was deeply affected by the sad condition of these people. He consulted with Dr. Smeathman, who had spent considerable time in Africa; and they conceived the plan of transporting them to the west coast of Africa, to form a colony.[1] The matter was agitated in London by the friends of the blacks, and finally the government began to be interested. A district of about twenty square miles was purchased by the government of Naimbanna, king of Sierra Leone, on which to locate the proposed colony. About four hundred Negroes and sixty white persons, the greater portion of the latter being "women of the town," [2] were embarked on "The Nautilus," Capt. Thompson, and landed at Sierra Leone on the 9th of May, 1787. The climate was severe, the sanitary condition of the place vile, and the habits of the people immoral. The African fever, with its black death-stroke, reaped a harvest; while the irregularities and indolence of the majority of the colonists, added to the deeds of plunder perpetrated by predatory bands of savages, reduced the number of the colonists to about sixty-four souls in 1791.

The dreadful news of the fate of the colony was borne to the philanthropists in England. But their faith in colonization stood as unblanched before the revelation as the Iron Duke at Waterloo. An association was formed under the name of "St. George's Bay," but afterwards took the name of the "Sierra Leone Company," with a capital stock of one million two hundred and fifty thousand dollars, with such humanitarians as Granville Sharp, Thornton, Wilberforce, and Clarkson among its directors. The object of the company was to push forward the work of colonization. One

---

[1] Précis sur l'Établissement des Colonies de Sierra Léona et de Boulama, etc. Par C. B. Wadström, pp. 3–28.

[2] Wadström Essay on Colonization, p. 220.

hundred Europeans landed at Sierra Leone in the month of February, 1792, and were followed in March by eleven hundred and thirty-one Negroes. A large number of them had served in the British army during the Revolutionary War in America, and, accepting the offer of the British Government, took land in this colony as a reward for services performed in the army. Another fever did its hateful work; and fifty or sixty Europeans, and many blacks, fell under its parching and consuming touch.[1] Jealous feuds rent the survivors, and idleness palsied every nerve of industry in the colony. In 1794 a French squadron besieged the place, and the people sustained a loss of about two hundred and fifty thousand dollars. Once more an effort was made to revive the place, and get its drowsy energies aroused in the discharge of necessary duties. Some little good began to show itself; but it was only the tender bud of promise, and was soon trampled under the remorseless heel of five hundred and fifty insurrectionary maroons from Jamaica and Nova Scotia.

The indifferent character of the colonists, and the hurtful touch of the climate, had almost discouraged the friends of the movement in England. It was now the year 1800. This vineyard planted by good men yielded "nothing but leaves." No industry had been developed, no substantial improvement had been made, and the future was veiled in harassing doubts and fears. The money of the company had almost all been expended. The company barely had the signs of organic life in it, but the light of a beautiful Christian faith had not gone out across the sea in stalwart old England. The founders of the colony believed that good management would make the enterprise succeed: so they looked about for a master hand to guide the affair. On the 8th of August, 1807, the colony was surrendered into the hands of the Crown, and was made an English colony. During the same year in which this transfer was made, Parliament declared the slave-trade piracy; and a naval squadron was stationed along the coast for the purpose of suppressing it. At the first, many colored people of good circumstances, feeling that they would be safe under the English flag, moved from the United States to Sierra Leone. But the chief source of supply of population was the captured slaves, who were always unloaded at this place.

---

[1] This led to the sending of 119 whites, along with a governor, as counsellors, physicians, soldiers, clerks, overseers, artificers, settlers, and servants. Of this company 57 died within the year, 22 returned, and 40 remained. See Wadström, pp. 121, *sq.*

When the English Government took charge of Sierra Leone, the
population was 2,000, the majority of whom were from the West
Indies or Nova Scotia. In 1811 it was nearly 5,000; in 1820 it
was 12,000; it 1833 it was 30,000; in 1835 it was 35,000; in 1844
it was 40,000; in 1869 it was 55,374, with but 129 white men.
On the 31st of March, 1827, the slaves that had been captured
and liberated by the English squadron numbered 11,878; of which
there were 4,701 males above, and 1,875 under, fourteen years of
age. There were 2,717 females above, and 1,517 under, the age
of fourteen, besides 1,068 persons who, settled in Freetown, working in the timber-trade.

With the dreadful scourge of slavery driven from the sea, the
sanitary condition of the place greatly improved; and with a
vigorous policy of order and education enforced, Sierra Leone
began to bloom and blossom as a rose. When the slaver disappeared, the merchant-vessel came on her peaceful mission of
commerce.

The annual trade-returns presented to Parliament show that
the declared value of British and Irish produce and manufactures
exported to the West Coast of Africa, arranged in periods of five
years each, has been as follows:—

EXPORTS FROM GREAT BRITAIN.

1846–50 .	. . £2,773,408;	or a yearly average of £554,681
1851–55 .	. . 4,314,752; " " "	862,950
1856–60 .	. . 5,582,941; " " "	1,116,588
1861–63 .	. . 4,216,045; " " "	1,405,348

IMPORTS.

The same trade-returns show that the imports of African
produce from the West Coast into Great Britain have been as
follows. The "official value" is given before 1856, after that date
the "computed real value" is given.

Official value, 1851–55	. . . £4,154,725;	average, £830,945
Computed real value, 1856–60 .	. 9,376,251;	" 1,875,250
. " " " 1861–63 .	. 5,284,611;	" 1,761,537

The value of African produce has decreased during the last
few years in consequence of the discovery of the petroleum or
rock-oil in America. In 1864 between four and five thousand
bales of cotton were shipped to England.

It is to be borne in mind, that under the system which existed
when Sierra Leone, the Gambia, and Gold Coast settlements were

maintained for the promotion of the slave-trade, the lawful commerce was only £20,000 annually, and that now the amount of tonnage employed in carrying legal merchandise is greater than was ever engaged in carrying slaves.[1] W. Winwood Reade visited Sierra Leone during the Rebellion in America; but, being somewhat prejudiced against the Negro, we do not expect any thing remarkably friendly. But we quote from him the view he took of the people he met there: —

"The inhabitants of the colony may be divided into four classes: —

"First, The street-venders, who cry cassada-cakes, palm-oil, pepper, pieces of beef, under such names as *agedee, aballa, akalaray*, and which are therefore as unintelligible as the street-cries of London. This is the costermonger type.

"Second, The small market-people, who live in frame houses, sell nails, fish-hooks, tape, thread, ribbons, etc., and who work at handicrafts in a small way.

"Third, The shopkeepers, who inhabit frame houses on stone foundations, and within which one may see a sprinkling of mahogany, a small library of religious books, and an almost English atmosphere of comfort.

"Lastly, The liberated Africans of the highest grade, who occupy two-story stone houses enclosed all around by spacious piazzas, the rooms furnished with gaudy richness; and the whole their own property, being built from the proceeds of their . . . thrift."

When England abolished the slave-trade on the West Coast of Africa, Christianity arose with healing in her wings. Until slavery was abolished in this colony, missionary enterprises were abortive; but when the curse was put under the iron heel of British prohibition, the Lord did greatly bless the efforts of the missionary. The Episcopal Church — "the Church of England" — was the first on the ground in 1808; but it was some years before any great results were obtained. In 1832 this Church had 638 communicants, 294 candidates for baptism, 684 sabbath-school pupils, and 1,388 children in day-schools. This Church carried its missionary work beyond its borders to the tribes that were "sitting in darkness;" and in 1850 had built 54 seminaries and schools, had 6,600 pupils, 2,183 communicants, and 7,500 attendants on public worship. It is pleasant to record that out of 61 teachers, 56 *were native Africans!* In 1865 there were sixteen missionary societies along the West Coast of Africa. Seven were American, six English, two German, and one West-Indian. These societies maintained 104 European or American

---

[1] See Livingstone's Zambesi, pp. 633, 634.

missionaries, had 110 mission-stations, 13,000 scholars, 236 schools, 19,000 registered communicants; representing a Christian population of 60,000 souls.

The Wesleyan Methodists began their work in 1811; and in 1831 they had two missionaries, 294 members in their churches, and 160 pupils in school. They extended their missions westward to the Gambia, and eastward toward Cape Coast Castle, Badagry, Abbeokuta, and Kumasi; and in this connection, in 1850, had 44 houses of worship, 13 out-stations, 42 day-schools, 97 teachers, 4,500 pupils in day and sabbath schools, 6,000 communicants, 560 on probation, and 14,600 in attendance on public worship. In 1850 the population of Sierra Leone was 45,000; of which 36,000 were Christians, against 1,734 Mohammedans.

Sierra Leone represents the most extensive composite population in the world for its size. About one hundred different tribes are represented, with as many different languages or dialects. Bishop Vidal, under direction of the British Parliament, gave special attention to this matter, and found not less than one hundred and fifty-one distinct languages, besides several dialects, spoken in Sierra Leone. They were arranged under twenty-six groups, and yet fifty-four are unclassified that are as distinct as German and French. "God makes the wrath of man to praise him, and the remainder thereof he will restrain." Through these numerous languages, poor benighted Africa will yet hear the gospel.

Some years ago Dr. Ferguson, who was once governor of the Sierra Leone colony, and himself a colored man, wrote an extended account of the situation there, which was widely circulated in England and America at the time. It is so manifestly just and temperate in tone, so graphic and minute in description, that we reproduce it *in extenso :* —

"1. Those most recently arrived are to be found occupying mud houses and small patches of ground in the neighborhood of one or other of the villages (the villages are about twenty in number, placed in different parts of the colony, grouped in three classes or districts; namely, mountain, river, and sea districts). The majority remain in their locations as agriculturists; but several go to reside in the neighborhood of Freetown, looking out for work as laborers, farm-servants, servants to carry wood and water, grooms, house-servants, etc.; others cultivate vegetables, rear poultry and pigs, and supply eggs, for the Sierra Leone market. Great numbers are found offering for sale in the public market and elsewhere a vast quantity of cooked edible substances — rice, corn, and cassava cakes; heterogeneous compounds of rice and corn-flower, yams, cassava, palm-oil, pepper, pieces of beef, mucilaginous vegetables, etc., etc., under names quite unintelligible to a stranger, such as *aagedee, aballa, akalaray, cabona,* etc., etc., cries which are shouted along the streets of Freetown from morn till night. These, the lowest grade of liberated Africans, are a harmless and well-disposed people; there is no poverty among them, nor begging; their habits are frugal and industrious; their anxiety to possess money is remarkable: but their energies are allowed to run riot and be wasted from the want of knowledge requisite to direct them in proper channels.

"2. Persons of grade higher than those last described are to be found occupying frame houses: they drive a petty trade in the market, where they expose for sale nails, fish-hooks, door-hinges, tape, thread, ribbons, needles, pins, etc. Many of this grade also look out for the arrival of canoes from the country laden with oranges, *kolas,* sheep, bullocks, fowls, rice, etc., purchase the whole cargo at once at the water-side, and derive considerable profit from selling such articles by retail in the market and over the town. Many of this grade are also occupied in curing and drying fish. an article which always sells well in the market, and is in great request by people at a distance from the water-side, and in the interior of the country. A vast number of this grade are tailors, straw-hat makers, shoemakers, cobblers, blacksmiths, carpenters, masons, etc. Respectable men of this grade meet with ready mercantile credits amounting from twenty pounds to sixty pounds ; and the class is very numerous.

"3. Persons of grade higher than that last mentioned are found occupying frame houses reared on a stone foundation of from six to ten feet in height. These houses are very comfortable; they are painted outside and in; have piazzas in front and rear, and many of them all round ; a considerable sprinkling of mahogany furniture of European workmanship is to be found in them ; several books are to be seen lying about, chiefly of a religious character ; and a general air of domestic comfort pervades the whole, which, perhaps more than any thing else, bears evidence of the advanced state of intelligence at which they have arrived. This grade is nearly altogether occupied in shopkeeping, hawking, and other mercantile pursuits. At sales of prize goods, public auctions, and every other place affording a probability of cheap bargains, they are to be seen in great numbers, where they club together in numbers of from three to six, seven, or more, to purchase large lots or unbroken bales. And the scrupulous honesty with which the subdivision of the goods is afterwards made cannot be evidenced more thoroughly than this: that, common as such transactions are, they have never yet been known to become the subject of controversy or litigation. The principal streets of Freetown, as well as the approaches to the town, are lined on each side by an almost continuous range of booths and stalls, among which almost every article of merchandise is offered for sale, and very commonly at a cheaper rate than similar articles are sold in the shops of the merchants.

" Two rates of profit are recognized in the mercantile transactions of the European merchants; namely, a wholesale and retail profit, the former varying from thirty to fifty per cent, the latter from fifty to one hundred per cent. The working of the retail trade in the hands of Europeans requires a considerable outlay in the shape of shop-rent, shopkeepers' and clerks' wages, etc. The liberated Africans were not slow in observing nor in seizing on the advantages which their peculiar position held out for the successful prosecution of the retail trade.

"Clubbing together, as before observed, and holding ready money in their hands, the merchants are naturally anxious to execute for them considerable orders on such unexceptionable terms of payment; while, on the other hand, the liberated Africans, seeing clearly their advantage, insist most pertinaciously on the lowest possible percentage of wholesale profit.

"Having thus become possessed of the goods at the lowest possible ready-money rate, their subsequent transactions are not clogged with the expense of shop-rents, shopkeepers' and clerks' wages and subsistence, etc., etc., expenses unavoidable to Europeans. They are therefore enabled at once to undersell the European retail merchants, and to secure a handsome profit to themselves; a consummation the more easily attained, aided as it is by the extreme simplicity and abstemiousness of their mode of living, which contrast so favorably for them with the expensive and almost necessary luxuries of European life. Many of this grade possess large canoes, with which they trade in the upper part of the river, along shore, and in the neighboring rivers; bringing down rice, palm-oil, cam-wood, ivory, hides, etc., etc., in exchange for British manufactures. They are all in easy circumstances, readily obtaining mercantile credits from sixty pounds to two hundred pounds. Persons of this and the grade next to be mentioned evince great anxiety to become possessed of houses and lots in old Freetown. These lots are desirable because of their proximity to the market-place and the great thoroughfares, and also for the superior advantages which they afford for the establishment of their darling object, — 'a retail store.' Property of this description has of late years become much enhanced in value, and its value is still increasing, solely from the annually increasing numbers and prosperity of this and the next grade. The town-lots originally granted to the Nova-Scotian settlers and the Maroons are, year after year, being offered for sale by public auction; and in every case liberated Africans are the purchasers. A striking instance of their desire to possess property of this description, and of its increasing value, came under my immediate notice a few months ago.

"The gentlemen of the Church Missionary Society having been for some time looking about in quest of a lot on which to erect a new chapel, a lot suitable for the purpose was at length offered for sale by public auction; and at a meeting of the society's local committee, it was resolved, in order to secure the purchase of the property in question, to offer as high as sixty pounds. The clergyman delegated for this purpose, at my recommendation, resolved, on his own responsibility, to offer, if necessary, as high as seventy pounds; but, to the surprise and mortification of us all, the lot was knocked down at upward of ninety pounds, and a liberated African was the purchaser. He stated very kindly that if he had known the society were desirous of purchasing the lot he would not have opposed them; he nevertheless manifested no desire of transferring to them the purchase, and even refused an advance of ten pounds on his bargain.

"4. Persons of the highest grade of liberated Africans occupy comfortable two-story stone houses, enclosed all round with spacious piazzas. These houses are their own property, and are built from the proceeds of their own industry. In several of them are to be seen mahogany chairs, tables, sofas, and four-post bedsteads, pier-glasses, floor-cloths, and other articles indicative of domestic comfort and accumulating wealth.

" Persons of this grade, like those last described, are almost wholly engaged in mercantile pursuits. Their transactions, however, are of greater magnitude and value, and their business is carried on with an external appearance of respectability commensurate with their superior pecuniary means : thus, instead of exposing their wares for sale in booths or stalls by the way-side, they are to be found in neatly fitted-up shops on the ground-floors of their stone dwelling-houses.

" Many individual members of this grade have realized very considerable sums of money, — sums which, to a person not cognizant of the fact, would appear to be incredible. From the studied manner in which individuals conceal their pecuniary circumstances from the world, it is difficult to obtain a correct knowledge of the wealth of the class generally. The devices to which they have recourse in conducting a bargain are often exceedingly ingenious ; and to be reputed rich might materially interfere with their success on such occasions. There is nothing more common than to hear a plea of poverty set up and most pertinaciously urged, in extenuation of the terms of a purchase, by persons whose outward condition, comfortable well-furnished houses, and large mercantile credits, indicate any thing but poverty.

" There are circumstances, however, the knowledge of which they cannot conceal, and which go far to exhibit pretty clearly the actual state of matters : such as, *First*, the facility with which they raise large sums of cash prompt' at public auctions. *Second*, the winding up of the estates of deceased persons. (Peter Newland, a liberated African, died a short time before I left the colony : and his estate realized, in houses, merchandise, and cash, upward of fifteen hundred pounds.) *Third*, the extent of their mercantile credits. I am well acquainted with an individual of this grade who is much courted and caressed by every European merchant in the colony, who has transactions in trade with all of them, and whose name, shortly before my departure from the colony, stood on the debtor side of the books of one of the principal merchants to the amount of nineteen hundred pounds, to which sum it had been reduced from three thousand pounds during the preceding two months. A highly respectable female has now, and has had for several years, the government contract for the supplying of fresh beef to the troops and the naval squadron ; and I have not heard that on a single occasion there has been cause of complaint for negligence or non-fulfilment of the terms of the contract. *Fourth*, many of them at the present moment have their children being educated in England at their own expense. There is at Sierra Leone a very fine regiment of colonial militia, more than eight-tenths of which are liberated Africans. The amount of property which they have acquired is ample guaranty for their loyalty, should that ever be called in question. They turn out with great alacrity and cheerfulness on all occasions for periodical drill. But perhaps the most interesting point of view in which the liberated Africans are to be seen, and that which will render their moral condition most intelligible to those at a distance, is where they sit at the Quarter Sessions as petty, grand, and special jurors. They constitute a considerable part of the jury at every session ; and I have repeatedly heard the highest legal authority in the colony express his satisfaction with their decisions."

But this account was written at the early sunrise of civilization in Sierra Leone. Now civilization is at its noonday tide, and the hopes of the most sanguine friends of the liberated Negro have been more than realized. How grateful this renewed spot on the edge of the Dark Continent would be to the weary and battle-dimmed vision of Wilberforce, Sharp, and other friends of the colony! And if they still lived, beholding the wonderful results, would they not gladly say, "Lord, now lettest thou thy servant depart in peace, according to thy word : for mine eyes have seen thy salvation which thou hast prepared before the face of all people ; a light to lighten the Gentiles, and the glory of thy people Israel " ?

CHAPTER X.

THE REPUBLIC OF LIBERIA.

LIBERIA. — ITS LOCATION. — EXTENT. — RIVERS AND MOUNTAINS. — HISTORY OF THE FIRST COLONY. — THE NOBLE MEN WHO LAID THE FOUNDATION OF THE LIBERIAN REPUBLIC — NATIVE TRIBES. — TRANSLATION OF THE NEW TESTAMENT INTO THE VEI LANGUAGE. — THE BEGINNING AND TRIUMPH OF CHRISTIAN MISSIONS TO LIBERIA. — HISTORY OF THE DIFFERENT DENOMINATIONS ON THE FIELD. — A MISSIONARY REPUBLIC OF NEGROES. — TESTIMONY OF OFFICERS OF THE ROYAL NAVY AS TO THE EFFICIENCY OF THE REPUBLIC IN SUPPRESSING THE SLAVE-TRADE. — THE WORK OF THE FUTURE.

THAT section of country on the West Coast of Africa known as Liberia, extending from Cape Palmas to Cape Mount, is about three hundred miles coastwise. Along this line there are six colonies of Colored people, the majority of the original settlers being from the United States. The settlements are Cape Palmas, Cape Mesurado, Cape Mount, River Junk, Basa, and Sinon. The distance between them varies from thirty-five to one hundred miles, and the only means of communication is the coast-vessels. Cape Palmas, though we include it under the general title of Liberia, was founded by a company of intelligent Colored people from Maryland. This movement was started by the indefatigable J. H. B. Latrobe and Mr. Harper of the Maryland Colonization Society. This society purchased at Cape Palmas a territory of about twenty square miles, in which there was at that time — more than a half-century ago — a population of about four thousand souls. Within two years from the time of the first purchase, this enterprising society held deeds from friendly proprietors for eight hundred square miles, embracing the dominions of nine kings, who bound themselves to the colonists in friendly alliance. This territory spread over both banks of the Cavally River, and from the ocean to the town of Netea, which is thirty miles from the mouth of the river. In the immediate vicinity of Cape Palmas, — say within an area of twenty miles, — there was a native population of twenty-five thousand. Were we to go toward the interior from the Cape about forty-five or fifty miles, we should find a population of at least seventy thousand natives, the majority of whom we are sure are anxious to enjoy the blessings of education, trade, civilization, and Christianity. The country about Cape Palmas is very beautiful and fertile. The cape extends out into the sea nearly a mile, the highest place being about one hundred and twenty-five feet. Looking from the beach, the ground rises gradually until its distant heights are crowned with heavy, luxuriant foliage and dense forest timber. And to plant this colony the Maryland Legislature appropriated the sum of two hundred thousand dollars! And the colony has done worthily, has grown rapidly, and at present enjoys all the blessings of a Christian community. Not many years ago it declared its independence.

But Liberia, in the proper use of the term, is applied to all the settlements along the West Coast of Africa that were founded by Colored people from the United States. It is the most beautiful spot on the entire coast. The view is charming in approaching this country. Rev. Charles Rockwell says, —

"One is struck with the dark green hue which the rank and luxuriant growth of forest and of field everywhere presents. In this respect it strongly resembles in appearance the dark forests of evergreens which line a portion of the coast of Eastern Virginia. . . . At different points there are capes or promontories rising from thirty or forty to one or two hundred feet above the level of the sea; while at other places the land, though somewhat uneven, has not, near the sea, any considerable hills. In some places near the mouths of the rivers are thickly wooded marshes; but on entering the interior of the country the ground gradually rises, the streams become rapid, and at the distance of twenty miles or more from the sea, hills, and beyond them mountains, are often met with."

The physical, social, and political bondage of the Colored people in America before the war was most discouraging. They were mobbed in the North, and sold in the South. It was not enough that they were isolated and neglected in the Northern States: they were proscribed by the organic law of legislatures, and afflicted by the most burning personal indignities. They had a few friends; but even their benevolent acts were often hampered by law, and strangled by caste-prejudice. Following the plans of Granville Sharp and William Wilberforce, Liberia was founded as a refuge to all Colored men who would avail themselves of its blessings.

Colonization societies sprang into being in many States, and large sums of money were contributed to carry out the objects of these organizations. Quite a controversy arose inside of anti-slavery societies, and much feeling was evinced; but the men who believed colonization to be the solution of the slavery question went forward without wavering or doubting. In March, 1820, the first emigrants sailed for Africa, being eighty-six in number; and in January, 1822, founded the town of Monrovia, named for President Monroe. Rev. Samuel J. Mills, while in college in 1806, was moved by the Holy Spirit to turn his face toward Africa as a missionary. His zeal for missionary labor touched the hearts of Judson, Newell, Nott, Hall, and Rice, who went to mission-fields in the East as early as 1812.[1] The American Colonization Society secured the services of the Rev. Samuel J. Mills and Rev. Ebenezer Burgess to locate the colony at Monrovia. Mr. Mills found an early, watery grave; but the report of Mr. Burgess gave the society great hope, and the work was carried forward.

The first ten years witnessed the struggles of a noble band of Colored people, who were seeking a new home on the edge of a continent given over to the idolatry of the heathen. The funds of the society were not as large as the nature and scope of the work demanded. Emigrants went slowly, not averaging more than 170 per annum, — only 1,232 in ten years: but the average from the first of January, 1848, to the last of December, 1852, was 540 yearly; and, in the single year of 1853, 782 emigrants arrived at Monrovia. In 1855 the population of Monrovia and Cape Palmas had reached about 8,000.

Going south from Monrovia for about one hundred miles, and inland about twenty, the country was inhabited by the Bassa tribe and its branches; numbering about 130,000 souls, and speaking a common language. "They were peaceful, domestic, and industrious; and, after fully supplying their own wants, furnish a large surplus of rice, oil, cattle, and other articles of common use, for exportation." [2] This tribe, like the Veis, of whom we shall make mention subsequently, have reduced their language to a written system. The New Testament has been translated into their language by a missionary, and they have had the gospel these many years in their own tongue.

The "Greybo language," spoken in and about Cape Palmas, has been reduced to a written form; and twenty thousand copies

---

[1] Ethiope, p. 197.   [2] Foreign Travel and Life at Sea, vol. ii. p. 359.

of eleven different works have been printed and distributed. There are about seventy-five thousand natives within fifty miles of Cape Palmas ; and, as a rule, they desire to avail themselves of the blessings of civilization. The Veis occupy about fifty miles of seacoast; extending from Gallinas River, one hundred miles north of Monrovia, and extending south to Grand Mount. Their territory runs back from the seacoast about thirty miles, and they are about sixteen thousand strong.

This was a grand place to found a Negro state, — a *missionary republic*, as Dr. Christy terms it. When the republic rose, the better, wealthier class of free Colored people from the United States embarked for Liberia. Clergymen, physicians, merchants, mechanics, and school-teachers turned their faces toward the new republic, with an earnest desire to do something for themselves and race ; and history justifies the hopes and prayers of all sincere friends of Liberia. Unfortunately, at the first, many white men were more anxious to get the Negro out of the country than to have him do well when out ; and, in many instances, some unworthy Colored people got transportation to Liberia, of whom Americans were rid, but of whom Liberians could not boast. But the law of the survival of the fittest carried the rubbish to the bottom. The republic grew and expanded in every direction. From year to year new blood and fresh energy were poured into the social and business life of the people ; and England, America, and other powers acknowledged the republic by sending resident ministers there.

The servants of Christ saw, at the earliest moment of the conception to build a black government in Africa, that the banner of the cross must wave over the new colony, if good were to be expected. The Methodist Church, with characteristic zeal and aggressiveness, sent with the first colonists several members of their denomination and two "local preachers ;" and in March, 1833, the Rev. Melville B. Cox, an ordained minister of this church, landed at Monrovia. The mission experienced many severe trials ; but the good people who had it in charge held on with great tenacity until the darkness began to give away before the light of the gospel. Nor did the Board of the Methodist Missionary Society in America lose faith. They appropriated for this mission, in 1851, $22,000 ; in 1852, $26,000 ; in 1853, $32,957 ; and in 1854, $32,957. In the report of the board of managers for 1851, the following encouraging statement occurs : —

" All eyes are now turned toward this new republic on the western coast of Africa as the star of hope to the colored people, both bond and free, in the United States. The republic is establishing and extending itself; and its Christian population is in direct contact with the natives, both Pagans and Mohammedans. Thus the republic has, indirectly, a powerful missionary influence, and its moral and religious condition is a matter of grave concern to the Church. Hence the Protestant Christian missions in Liberia are essential to the stability and prosperity of the republic; and the stability and prosperity of the republic are necessary to the protection and action of the missions. It will thus appear that the Christian education of the people is the legitimate work of the missions."

At this time (1851) they had an annual Conference, with three districts, with as many presiding elders, whose duty it was to visit all the churches and schools in their circuit. The Conference had 21 members, all of whom were colored men. The churches contained 1,301 members, of whom 115 were on probation, and 116 were natives. There were 20 week-day schools, with 839 pupils, 50 of whom were natives. Then there were seven schools among the natives, with 127 faithful attendants.

Bishop Scott, of the General Conference of the Methodist Episcopal Church, was, by order of his Conference, sent on an official visit to Liberia. He spent more than two months among the missions, and returned in 1853 much gratified with the results garnered in that distant field.

" The government of the republic of Liberia, which is formed on the model of our own, and is wholly in the hands of colored men, seems to be exceedingly well administered. I never saw so orderly a people. I saw but one intoxicated colonist while in the country, and I heard not one profane word. The sabbath is kept with singular strictness, and the churches crowded with attentive and orderly worshippers." [1]

The above is certainly re-assuring, and had its due influence among Christian people at the time it appeared. At an anniversary meeting of the Methodist Church, held in Cincinnati, O., in the same year, 1853, Bishop Ames gave utterance to sentiments in regard to the character of the government of Liberia that quite shocked some pro-slavery people who held "*hired pews*" in the Methodist Church. His utterances were as brave as they were complimentary.

---

[1] Bishop Scott's Letter in the Colonization Herald, October, 1853.

" Nations reared under religious and political restraint are not capable of self-government, while those who enjoy only partially these advantages have set an example of such capability. We have in illustration of this a well-authenticated historical fact: we refer to the colored people of this country, who, though they have grown up under the most unfavorable circumstances, were enabled to succeed in establishing a sound republican government in Africa. They have given the most clear and indubitable evidence of their capability of self-government, and in this respect have shown a higher grade of manhood than the polished Frenchman himself." [1]

The Presbyterian Board of Missions sent Rev. J. B. Pinny into the field in 1833. In 1837, missions were established among the natives, and were blessed with very good results. In 1850 there were, under the management of this denomination, three congregations, with 116 members, two ordained ministers, and a flourishing sabbath-school. A high-school was brought into existence in 1852, with a white gentleman, the Rev. D. A. Wilson, as its principal. It was afterward raised into a college, and was always crowded.

The American Protestant-Episcopal Church raised its missionary standard in Liberia in 1836. The Rev. John Payne was at the head of this enterprise, assisted by six other clergymen, until 1850, when he was consecrated missionary bishop for Africa. He was a white gentleman of marked piety, rare scholarship, and large executive ability. The station at Monrovia was under the care of the Rev. Alexander Crummell, an educated and eloquent preacher of the Negro race. There was an excellent training-school for religious and secular teachers ; there are several boarding-schools for natives, with an average attendance of a hundred ; and up to 1850 more than a thousand persons had been brought into fellowship with this church.

The Foreign Missionary Board of the Southern Baptist Convention in 1845 turned its attention to this fruitful field. In 1855, ten years after they began work, they had 19 religious and secular teachers, 11 day-schools, 400 pupils, and 484 members in their churches. There were 13 mission-stations, and all the teachers were colored men.

We have said, a few pages back in this chapter, that the Methodist Church was first on the field when the colony of Liberia was founded. We should have said *one* of the first ; because we find, in "Gammell's History of the American Baptist

---

[1] In Methodist Missionary Advocate, 1853.

Missions," that the Baptists were in this colony as missionaries in 1822; that under the direction of the Revs. Lot Carey and Collin Teage, two intelligent Colored Baptists, a church was founded. Mr. Carey was a man of most exemplary character. He had received an education in Virginia, where he had resided as a freeman for some years, having purchased his freedom by his personal efforts, and where also he was ordained in 1821.

"In September, 1826, he was unanimously elected vice-agent of the colony; and on the return of Mr. Ashmun to the United States, in 1828, he was appointed to discharge the duties of governor in the interim, — a task which he performed during the brief remnant of his life with wisdom, and with credit to himself. His death took place in a manner that was fearfully sudden and extraordinary. The natives of the country had committed depredations upon the property of the colony, and were threatening general hostilities. Mr. Carey, in his capacity as acting governor, immediately called out the military forces of the colony, and commenced vigorous measures for repelling the assault and protecting the settlements. He was at the magazine, engaged in superintending the making of cartridges, when, by the oversetting of a lamp, a large mass of powder became ignited, and produced an explosion which resulted in the death of Mr. Carey, and seven others who were engaged with him. In this sudden and awful manner perished an extraordinary man, — one who in a higher sphere might have developed many of the noblest energies of character, and who, even in the humble capacity of a missionary among his own benighted brethren, deserves a prominent place in the list of those who have shed lustre upon the African race.

"At the period of Mr. Carey's death, the church of which he was the pastor contained a hundred members, and was in a highly flourishing condition. It was committed to the charge of Collin Teage, who now returned from Sierra Leone, and of Mr. Waring, one of its members, who had lately been ordained a minister. The influences which had commenced with the indefatigable founder of the mission continued to be felt long after he had ceased to live. The church at Monrovia was increased to two hundred members; and the power of the gospel was manifested in other settlements of the Colonization Society, and even among the rude natives of the coast, of whom nearly a hundred were converted to Christianity, and united with the several churches of the colony." [1]

We regret that statistics on Liberia are not as full as desirable; but we have found enough to convince us that the cause of religion, education, and republican government are in safe hands, and on a sure foundation. There are now more than three thousand members within their churches. The sabbath-schools have about eighteen hundred children, seven hundred of whom are

---

[1] Gammell's History of the American Baptist Missions, pp. 248, 249.

natives ;[1] and in the day-schools are gathered about two thousand bright and promising pupils.

Many noble soldiers of the cross have fallen on this field, where a desperate battle has been waged between darkness and light, heathenism and religion, the wooden gods of men and the only true God who made heaven and earth. Many have been mortally touched by the poisonous breath of African fever, and, like the sainted Gilbert Haven, have staggered back to home and friends to die. Few of the white teachers have been able to remain on the field. During the first thirty years of missionary effort in the field, the mortality among the white missionaries was terrible. Up to 1850 the Episcopal Church had employed twenty white teachers, but only three of them were left. The rest died, or were driven home by the climate. Of nineteen missionaries sent out by the Presbyterian Church up to 1850, nine died, seven returned home, and but three remained. The Methodist Church sent out thirteen white teachers : six died, six returned home, and but one remained. Among the colored missionaries the mortality was reduced to a minimum. Out of thirty-one in the employ of the Methodist Church, only seven died natural deaths, and fourteen remained in the service. On this subject of mortality, Bishop Payne says, —

" It is now very generally admitted, that Africa must be evangelized chiefly by her own children. It should be our object to prepare them, so far as we may, for their great work. And since colonists afford the most advanced material for raising up the needed instruments, it becomes us, in wise co-operation with Providence, to direct our efforts in the most judicious manner to them. To do this, the most important points should be occupied, to become in due time radiating centres of Christian influence to colonists and natives."[2]

In thirty-three years Liberia gained wonderfully in population, and, at the breaking-out of the Rebellion in the United States, had about a hundred thousand souls, besides the three hundred thousand natives in the vast territory over which her government is recognized. Business of every kind has grown up. The laws are wholesome ; the law-makers intelligent and upright ; the army and navy are creditable, and the republic is in every sense a grand success. Mr. Wilson says, —

---

[1] Edward W. Blyden, LL.D., president of Liberia College, a West Indian, is a scholar of marvellous erudition, a writer of rare abilities, a subtle reasoner, a preacher of charming graces, and one of the foremost Negroes of the world. He is himself the best argument in favor of the Negro's capacity for Christian civilization. He ranks amongst the world's greatest linguists.

[2] Report of Bishop Payne, June 6, 1853.

"Trade is the chosen employment of the great mass of the Liberians, and some of them have been decidedly successful in this vocation. It consists in the exchange of articles of American or European manufacture for the natural products of the country; of which palm-oil, cam-wood, and ivory are the principal articles. Cam-wood is a rich dye-wood, and is brought to Monrovia on the shoulders of the natives from a great distance. It is worth in the European and American markets from sixty to eighty dollars per ton. The ivory of this region does not form an important item of commerce. Palm-oil is the main article of export, and is procured along the seacoast between Monrovia and Cape Palmas. The Liberian merchants own a number of small vessels, built by themselves, and varying in size from ten or fifteen to forty or fifty tons. These are navigated by the Liberian sailors, and are constantly engaged in bringing palm-oil to Monrovia, from whence it is again shipped in foreign vessels for Liverpool or New York. I made inquiry, during a short sojourn at this place in 1852 on my way to this country, about the amount of property owned by the wealthier merchants of Monrovia, and learned that there were four or five who were worth from fifteen thousand to twenty thousand dollars, a large number who owned property to the amount of ten thousand dollars, and perhaps twelve or fifteen who were worth as much as five thousand dollars. The property of some of these may have increased materially since that time.

"The settlers along the banks of the St. Paul have given more attention to the cultivation of the soil. They raise sweet-potatoes, cassava, and plantains, for their own use, and also supply the Monrovia market with the same. Ground-nuts and arrow-root are also cultivated, but to a very limited extent. A few individuals have cultivated the sugar-cane with success, and have manufactured a considerable quantity of excellent sugar and molasses. Some attention has been given to the cultivation of the coffee-tree. It grows luxuriantly, and bears most abundantly. The flavor of the coffee is as fine as any in the world; and, if the Liberians would give the attention to it they ought, it would probably be as highly esteemed as any other in the world. It is easily cultivated, and requires little or no outlay of capital; and we are surprised that it has not already become an article of export. The want of disposition to cultivate the soil is, perhaps, the most discouraging feature in the prospects of Liberia. Mercantile pursuits are followed with zeal and energy, but comparatively few are willing to till the ground for the means of subsistence."

Liberia had its first constitution in 1825. It was drawn at the instance of the Colonization Society in the United States. It set forth the objects of the colony, defined citizenship, and declared the objects of the government. It remained in force until 1836. In 1839 a "Legislative Council" was created, and the constitution amended to meet the growing wants of the government. In 1847 Liberia declared herself an independent republic. The first article of the constitution of 1847 reads as follows: —

"ARTICLE I., SECTION I. All men are born equally free and independent, and among their natural, inherent and inalienable rights are the rights of enjoying and defending *life* and LIBERTY."

This section meant a great deal to a people who had abandoned their homes in the United States, where a chief justice of the Supreme Court had declared that "a Negro has no rights which a white man is bound to respect," — a country where the Federal Congress had armed every United-States marshal in all the Northern States with the inhuman and arbitrary power to apprehend, load with chains, and hurl back into the hell of slavery, every poor fugitive who sought to find a home in a professedly free section of " the *land of the free and the home of the brave.*" These brave black pilgrims, who had to leave " the freest land in the world " in order to get their freedom, did not intend that the solemn and formal declaration of principles contained in their constitution should be reduced to a *reductio ad absurdum*, as those in the American Constitution were by the infamous *Fugitive-slave Law.* And in section 4 of their constitution they prohibit " the sum of all villanies " — *slavery!* The article reads : —

" There shall be no slavery within this republic. Nor shall any citizen of this republic, or any person resident therein, deal in slaves, either within or without this republic."

They had no measure of *compromise* by which slavery could be carried on beyond certain limits " for highly commercial and business interests of a portion of their fellow-citizens." Liberians might have grown rich by merely suffering the slave-trade to be carried on among the natives. The constitution fixed a scale of revenue, and levied a tariff on all imported articles. A customs-service was introduced, and many reforms enforced which greatly angered a few avaricious white men whose profession as *men-stealers* was abolished by the constitution. Moreover, there were others who for years had been trading and doing business along the coast, without paying any duties on the articles they exported. The new government.incurred their hostility.

In April, 1850, the republic of Liberia entered into a treaty with England, and in article nine of said treaty bound herself to the suppression of the slave-trade in the following explicit language : —

" Slavery and the slave-trade being perpetually abolished in the republic of Liberia, the republic engages that a law shall be passed declaring it to be piracy for any *Liberian citizen* or vessel to be engaged or concerned in the slave-trade."

Notwithstanding the above treaty, the enemies of the republic circulated the report in England and America that the Liberian government was secretly engaged in the slave-trade. The friends of colonization in both countries were greatly alarmed by the rumor, and sought information in official quarters, — of men on the ground. The following testimony will show that the charge was malicious : —

" Capt. Arabian, R.N., in one of his despatches says, 'Nothing had been done more to suppress the slave-trade in this quarter than the constant intercourse of the natives with these industrious colonists;' and again, 'Their character is exceedingly correct and moral, their minds strongly impressed with religious feeling, and their domestic habits remarkably neat and comfortable.' 'Wherever the influence of Liberia extends, the slave-trade has been abandoned by the natives.'

" Lieut. Stott, R.N., in a letter to Dr. Hodgkin, dated July, 1840, says, it (Liberia) promises to be the only successful institution on the coast of Africa, keeping in mind its objects ; viz., 'that of raising the African slave into a free man, the extinction of the slave-trade, and the religious and moral improvement of Africa;' and adds, 'The surrounding Africans are aware of the nature of the colony, taking refuge when persecuted by the few neighboring slave-traders. The remnant of a tribe has lately fled to and settled in the colony on land granted them. Between my two visits, a lapse of only a few days, four or five slaves sought refuge from their master, who was about to sell, or had sold, them to the only slave-factory on the coast. The native chiefs in the neighborhood have that respect for the colonists that they have made treaties for the abolition of the slave-trade.'

" Capt. Irving, R.N., in a letter to Dr. Hodgkin, Aug. 3, 1840, observes, 'You ask me if they aid in the slave-trade ? I assure you, no ! and I am sure the colonists would feel themselves much hurt should they know such a question could possibly arise in England. In my opinion it is the best and safest plan for the extinction of the slave-trade, and the civilization of Africa; for it is a well-known fact, that wherever their flag flies it is an eye-sore to the slave-dealers.'

" Capt. Herbert, R.N.: 'With regard to the present state of slave-taking in the colony of Liberia, I have never known one instance of a slave being owned or disposed of by a colonist. On the contrary, I have known them to render great facility to our cruisers in taking vessels engaged in that nefarious traffic.'

" Capt. Dunlop, who had abundant opportunities for becoming acquainted with Liberia during the years 1848–50, says, 'I am perfectly satisfied no such thing as domestic slavery exists in any shape amongst the citizens of the republic.'

" Commodore Sir Charles Hotham, commander-in-chief of her British Majesty's squadron on the western coast of Africa, in a letter to the Secretary of the Admiralty, dated April 7, 1847, and published in the Parliamentary Returns, says, 'On perusing the correspondence of my predecessors, I found a great difference of opinion existing as to the views and objects of the settlers;

some even accusing the governor of lending himself to the slave-trade. After discussing the whole subject with officers and others best qualified to judge on the matter, I not only satisfied my own mind that there is no reasonable cause for such a suspicion, but further, that this establishment merits all the support we can give it; for it is only through their means that we can hope to improve the African race.' Subsequently, in 1849, the same officer gave his testimony before the House of Lords, in the following language : 'There is no necessity for the squadron watching the coast between Sierra Leone and Cape Palmas, as the Liberian territory intervenes, and there the slave-trade has been extinguished.'"[1]

The government was firmly and wisely administered, and its friends everywhere found occasion for great pleasure in its marked success. While the government had more than a quarter of a million of natives under its care, the greatest caution was exercised in dealing with them legally. The system was not so complicated as our Indian system, but the duties of the officers in dealing with the uncivilized tribes were as delicate as those of an Indian agent in the United States.

"The history of a single case will illustrate the manner in which Liberia exerts her influence in preventing the native tribes from warring upon each other. The territory of Little Cape Mount, Grand Cape Mount, and Gallinas was purchased, three or four years since, and added to the Republic. The chiefs, by the term of sale, transferred the rights of sovereignty and of soil to Liberia, and bound themselves to obey her laws. The government of Great Britain had granted to Messrs. Hyde, Hodge, & Co., of London, a contract for the supply of laborers from the coast of Africa to the planters of her West India colonies. This grant was made under the rule for the substitution of *apprentices*, to supply the lack of labor produced by the emancipation of the slaves. The agents of Messrs. Hyde, Hodge, & Co. visited Grand Cape Mount, and made an offer of ten dollars per head to the chiefs for each person they could supply as *emigrants* for this object. The offer excited the cupidity of some of the chiefs ; and to procure the emigrants and secure the bounty one of them, named Boombo, of Little Cape Mount, resorted to war upon several of the surrounding tribes. He laid waste the country, burned the towns and villages, captured and murdered many of the inhabitants, carried off hundreds of others, and robbed several factories in that region belonging to merchants in Liberia. On the 26th of February, 1853, President Roberts issued his proclamation enjoining a strict observance of the law regulating passports, and forbidding the sailing of any vessel with emigrants without first visiting the port of Monrovia, where each passenger should be examined as to his wishes. On the 1st of March the president, with two hundred men, sailed for Little Cape Mount, arrested Boombo and fifty of his followers, summoned a council of the other chiefs at Monrovia for his trial on the 14th, and returned home with his prisoners. At the time appointed, the trial was held, Boombo was found

---

[1] Colonization Herald, December, 1852.

guilty of '*high misdemeanor,*' and sentenced 'to make restitution, restoration, and reparation of goods stolen, people captured, and damages committed; to pay a fine of five hundred dollars, and be imprisoned for two years.' When the sentence was pronounced, the convict shed tears, regarding the ingredient of imprisonment in his sentence to be almost intolerable. These rigorous measures, adopted to maintain the authority of the government and majesty of the laws, have had a salutary influence upon the chiefs. No outbreaks have since occurred, and but little apprehension of danger for the future is entertained." [1]

The republic did a vast amount of good bfeore the Great Rebellion in the United States, but since emancipation its population has been fed by the natives who have been educated and converted to Christianity. Professor David Christy, the great colonizationist, said in a lecture delivered in 1855, —

"If, then, a colony of colored men, beginning with less than a hundred, and gradually increasing to nine thousand, has in thirty years established an independent republic amidst a savage people, destroyed the slave-trade on six hundred miles of the African coast, put down the heathen temples in one of its largest counties, afforded security to all the missions within its limits, and now casts its shield over three hundred thousand native inhabitants, what may not be done in the next thirty years by colonization and missions combined, were sufficient means supplied to call forth all their energies?"

The circumstances that led to the founding of the Negro republic in the wilds of Africa perished in the fires of civil war. The Negro is free everywhere; but the republic of Liberia stands, and should stand until its light shall have penetrated the gloom of Africa, and until the heathen shall gather to the brightness of its shining. May it stand through the ages as a Christian republic, as a faithful light-house along the dark and trackless sea of African paganism!

---

[1] Ethiope, pp. 207, 208.

CHAPTER XI.

RÉSUMÉ.

THE UNITY OF THE HUMAN FAMILY RE-AFFIRMED — GOD GAVE ALL RACES OF MEN CIVILIZATION — THE ANTIQUITY OF THE NEGRO BEYOND DISPUTE — IDOLATRY THE CAUSE OF THE DEGRADATION OF THE AFRICAN RACES. — HE HAS ALWAYS HAD A PLACE IN HISTORY, THOUGH INCIDENTAL. — NEGRO TYPE CAUSED BY DEGRADATION. — NEGRO EMPIRES AN EVIDENCE OF CRUDE ABILITY FOR SELF-GOVERNMENT. — INFLUENCE OF THE TWO CHRISTIAN GOVERNMENTS ON THE WEST COAST UPON THE HEATHEN — ORATION ON EARLY CHRISTIANITY IN AFRICA. — THE DUTY OF CHRISTI-ANITY TO EVANGELIZE AFRICA.

THE preceding ten chapters are introductory in their nature. We felt that they were necessary to a history of the Colored race in the United States. We desired to explain and explode two erroneous ideas, — the curse of Canaan, and the theory that the Negro is a distinct species, — that were educated into our white countrymen during the long and starless night of the bondage of the Negro. It must appear patent to every honest student of God's word, that the slavery interpretation of the curse of Canaan is without warrant of Scripture, and at war with the broad and catholic teachings of the New Testament. It is a sad commentary on American civilization to find even a few men like Helper, " Ariel," and the author of " The Adamic Race " still croaking about the inferiority of the Negro ; but it is highly gratifying to know that they no longer find an audience or readers, not even in the South. A man never hates his neighbors until he has injured them. Then, in justification of his unjustifiable conduct, he uses slander for argument.

During the late war thousands of mouths filled with vituperative wrath against the colored race were silenced as in the presence of the heroic deeds of " the despised race," and since the war the obloquy of the Negro's enemies has been turned into the most fulsome praise.

We stand in line and are in harmony with history and historians — modern and ancient, sacred and profane — on the subject of the unity of the human family. There are, however, a few who differ; but their wild, incoherent, and unscholarly theories deserve the mercy of our silence.

It is our firm conviction, and it is not wholly unsupported by history, that the Creator gave all the nations arts and sciences. Where nations have turned aside to idolatry they have lost their civilization. The Canaanites, Jebusites, Hivites, etc., the idolatrous [1] nations inhabiting the land of Canaan, were the descendants of Canaan; and the only charge the Lord brought against them when he commanded Joshua to exterminate them was, that they were his enemies [2] in all that that term implies. The sacred record tells us that they were a warlike, powerful people,[3] living in walled cities, given to agriculture, and possessing quite a respectable civilization ; but they were idolaters — God's enemies.

It is worthy of emphasis, that the antiquity of the Negro race is beyond dispute. This is a fact established by the most immutable historical data, and recorded on the monumental brass and marble of the Oriental nations of the most remote period of time. The importance and worth of the Negro have given him a place in all the histories of Egypt, Greece, and Rome. His position, it is true, in all history up to the present day, has been accidental, incidental, and collateral; but it is sufficient to show how he has been regarded in the past by other nations. His brightest days were when history was an infant; and, since he early turned from God, he has found the cold face of hate and the hurtful hand of the Caucasian against him. The Negro type is the result of degradation. It is nothing more than the lowest strata of the African race. Pouring over the venerable mountain terraces, an abundant stream from an abundant and unknown source, into the malarial districts, the genuine African has gradually degenerated into the typical Negro. His blood infected with the poison of his low habitation, his body shrivelled by disease, his intellect veiled in pagan superstitions, the noblest yearnings of his soul strangled at birth by the savage passions of a nature abandoned to sensuality; — the poor Negro of Africa deserves more our pity than our contempt.

It is true that the weaker tribes, or many of the Negroid type, were the chief source of supply for the slave-market in this country for many years ; but slavery in the United States — a severe ordeal through which to pass to citizenship and civilization

---

[1] Deut. xii. 2, 3, also 30th verse.   [2] Deut. vi. 19.   [3] Deut. vii. 7.

— had the effect of calling into life many a slumbering and dying attribute in the Negro nature. The cruel institution drove him from an extreme idolatry to an extreme religious exercise of his faith in worship. And now that he is an American citizen, — the condition and circumstances which rendered his piety appropriate abolished, — he is likely to move over to an extreme rationalism.

The Negro empires to which we have called attention are an argument against the theory that he is without government; and his career as a soldier [1] would not disgrace the uniform of an American soldier. Brave, swift in execution, terrible in the onslaught, tireless in energy, obedient to superiors, and clannish to a fault, — the abilities of these black soldiers are worthy of a good cause.

On the edge of the Dark Continent, Sierra Leone and Liberia have sprung up as light-houses on a dark and stormy ocean of lost humanity. Hundreds of thousands of degraded Negroes have been snatched from the vile swamps, and Christianity has been received and appreciated by them. These two Negro settlements have solved two problems; viz., the Negro's ability to administer a government, and the capacity of the native for the reception of education and Christian civilization. San Domingo and Jamaica have their lessons too, but it is not our purpose to write the history of the Colored people of the world. The task may be undertaken some time in the future, however.

It must be apparent to the interested friends of languishing Africa, that there are yet two more problems presented for our solution; and they are certainly difficult of solution. First, we must solve the problem of African geography; second, we must redeem by the power of the gospel, with all its attending blessings, the savage tribes of Africans who have never heard the beautiful song of the angels: *"Glory to God in the highest, and on earth peace, good-will toward men."* That this work will be done we do not doubt. We have great faith in the outcome of the missionary work going on now in Africa; and we are especially encouraged by the wide and kindly interest awakened on behalf of Africa by the noble life-work of Dr. David Livingstone, and the thrilling narrative of Mr. Henry M. Stanley.

It is rather remarkable now, in the light of recent events, that we should have chosen a topic at the close of both our academic

---

[1] News comes to us from Egypt that Arabi Pacha's best artillerists are Negro soldiers.

and theological course that we can see now was in line with this work so near our heart. The first oration was on "The Footsteps of the Nation," the second was "Early Christianity in Africa." Dr. Livingstone had just fallen a martyr to the cause of geography, and the orators and preachers of enlightened Christendom were busy with the virtues and worth of the dead. It was on the tenth day of June, 1874, that we delivered the last-named oration ; and we can, even at this distance, recall the magnificent audience that greeted it, and the feeling with which we delivered it. We were the first Colored man who had ever taken a diploma from that venerable and world-famed institution (Newton Seminary, Newton Centre, Mass.), and therefore there was much interest taken in our graduation. We were ordained on the following evening at Watertown, Mass. ; and the original poem written for the occasion by our pastor, the Rev. Granville S. Abbott, D.D., contained the following significant verses : —

> "Ethiopia's hands long stretching,
>   Mightily have plead with God ;
> Plead not vainly : time is fetching
>   Answers, as her faith's reward.
>   God is faithful,
>   Yea, and Amen is his word.
>
> Countless prayers, so long ascending,
>   Have their answer here and now ;
> Threads of purpose, wisely meeting
>   In an ordination vow.
>   Afric brother,
>   To thy mission humbly bow."

The only, and we trust sufficient, apology we have to offer to the reader for mentioning matters personal to the author is, that we are deeply touched in reading the oration, after many years, in the original manuscript, preserved by accident. It is fitting that it should be produced here as bearing upon the subject in hand.

EARLY CHRISTIANITY IN AFRICA.

ORATION BY GEORGE W. WILLIAMS,

ON THE OCCASION OF HIS GRADUATION FROM NEWTON THEOLOGICAL SEMINARY, NEWTON CENTRE, MASS., JUNE 10, 1874.

Africa was one of the first countries to receive Christianity. Simon, a Cyrenian, from Africa, bore the cross of Jesus for him to Calvary. There was more in that singular incident than we are apt to recognize, for the time soon came when Africa did indeed take up the Saviour's cross.

The African, in his gushing love, welcomed the new religion to his country and to his heart. He was willing to share its persecutions, and endure shame for the cross of Christ.

Africa became the arena in which theological gladiators met in dubious strife. It was the scene of some of the severest doctrinal controversies of the early Church. Here men and women, devoted to an idea, stood immovable, indomitable as the pyramids, against the severest persecution. Her sons swelled the noble army of martyrs and confessors. The eloquence of their shed blood has been heard through the centuries, and pleads the cause of the benighted to-day.

It was Africa that gave the Christian Church Athanasius and Origen, Cyprian, Tertullian, and Augustine, her greatest writers and teachers. Athanasius, the missionary of monachism to the West, was the indefatigable enemy of Arianism, the bold leader of the catholic party at Alexandria, at the early age of thirty (30) elevated to its bishopric, one of the most important sees in the East. Ever conscientious and bold, the whole Christian Church felt his influence, while emperors and kings feared his power. His life was stormy, because he loved the truth and taught it in all boldness. He hated his own life for the truth's sake. He counted all things but loss, that he might gain Christ. He was often in perils by false brethren, was driven out into the solitary places of the earth, — into the monasteries of the Thebaid; and yet he endured as ·seeing Him who is invisible, looking for the reward of the promise, knowing that He who promised is faithful.

Origen was an Alexandrian by birth and culture, an able preacher, a forcible writer, and a theologian of great learning. His influence while living was great, and was felt long after his death.

In North Africa, Cyprian, the great writer of Church polity, a pastor and teacher of rare gifts, was the first bishop to lay down his life for the truth's sake.

The shadows of fifteen centuries rest upon his name; but it is as fadeless to-day as when a weeping multitude followed him to his martyrdom, and exclaimed, "Let us die with our holy bishop."

The weary centuries intervene, and yet the student of Church polity is fascinated and instructed by the brilliant teachings of Cyprian. His bitterest enemies — those who have most acrimoniously assailed him — have at length recognized in him the qualities of a great writer and teacher; and his puissant name, sending its influence along the ages, attracts the admiration of the ecclesiastical scholars of every generation.

Tertullian, the leader of the Montanists, fiery, impulsive, the strong preacher, the vigorous writer, the bold controversialist, organized a sect which survived him, though finally disorganized through the influence of Augustine, the master theologian of the early Church, indeed of the Church universal.

Other fathers built theological systems that flourished for a season; but the system that Augustine established survived him, has survived the intervening centuries, and lives to-day.

Africa furnished the first dissenters from an established church, — the Donatists. They were the Separatists and Puritans of the early Church.

Their struggle was long, severe, but useless. They were condemned, not convinced; discomfited, not subdued; and the patient, suffering, indomitable spirit they evinced shows what power there is in a little truth held in faith.

Christianity had reached its zenith in Africa. It was her proudest hour. Paganism had been met and conquered. The Church had passed through a baptism of blood, and was now wholly consecrated to the cause of its Great Head. Here Christianity flowered; here it brought forth rich fruit in the lives of its tenacious adherents. Here the acorn had become the sturdy oak, under which the soldiers of the cross pitched their tents. The African Church had triumphed gloriously.

But, in the moment of signal victory, the Saracens poured into North Africa, and Mohammedanism was established upon the ruins of Christianity.

The religion of Christ was swept from its moorings, the saint was transformed into the child of the desert, and quiet settlements became bloody fields where brother shed brother's blood.

Glorious and sublime as was the triumph of Christianity in North Africa, we must not forget that only a narrow belt of that vast country, on the Mediterranean, was reached by Christianity. Its western and southern portions are yet almost wholly unknown. Her vast deserts, her mighty rivers, and her dusky children are yet beyond the reach of civilization; and her forests have been the grave of many who would explore her interior. To-day England stands by the new-made grave of the indomitable Livingstone, — her courageous son, who, as a missionary and geographer spent his best days and laid down his life in the midst of Africa.

For nearly three centuries Africa has been robbed of her sable sons. For nearly three centuries they have toiled in bondage, unrequited, in this youthful republic of the West. They have grown from a small company to be an exceedingly great people, — five millions in number. No longer chattels, they are human beings; no longer bondmen, they are freemen, with almost every civil disability removed.

Their weary feet now press up the mount of science. Their darkened intellect now sweeps, unfettered, through the realms of learning and culture. With his Saxon brother, the African slakes his insatiable thirstings for knowledge at the same fountain. In the Bible, he reads not only the one unalterable text, "Servants, obey your masters," but also, "Ye are all brethren." "God hath made of one blood all nations of men for to dwell on all the face of the earth." "He is no respecter of persons."

The Negro in this country has begun to enjoy the blessings of a free citizenship. Under the sunny sky of a Christian civilization he hears the clarion voices of progress about him, urging him onward and upward. From across the ocean, out of the jungles of Africa, come the voices of the benighted and perishing. Every breeze is freighted with a Macedonian call, "Ye men of the African race, come over and help us!"

> "Shall we, whose souls are lighted
> By wisdom from on high, —
> Shall we, to men benighted
> The lamp of life deny?"

God often permits evil on the ground of man's free agency, but he does not commit evil.

The Negro of this country can turn to his Saxon brothers and say, as Joseph said to his brethren who wickedly sold him, "As for you, ye meant it unto evil, but God meant it unto good; that we, after learning your arts and sciences, might return to Egypt and deliver the rest of our brethren who are yet in the house of bondage."

That day will come! Her chains will be severed by the sword of civilization and liberty. Science will penetrate her densest forests, and climb her loftiest mountains, and discover her richest treasures. The Sun of righteousness, and the star of peace, shall break upon her sin-clouded vision, and smile upon her renewed households. The anthem of the Redeemer's advent shall float through her forests, and be echoed by her mountains. Those dusky children of the desert, who now wander and plunder, will settle to quiet occupations of industry. Gathering themselves into villages, plying the labors of handicraft and agriculture, they will become a well-disciplined society, instead of being a roving, barbarous horde.

The sabbath bells will summon from scattered cottages smiling populations, linked together by friendship, and happy in all the sweetness of domestic charities. Thus the glory of her latter day shall be greater than at the beginning, *and Ethiopia shall stretch forth her hands unto God.*

It is our earnest desire and prayer, that the friends of missions in all places where God in his providence may send this history will give the subject of the civilization and Christianization of Africa prayerful consideration. The best schools the world can afford should be founded on the West Coast of Africa. The native should be educated at home, and mission-stations should be planted under the very shadow of the idol-houses of the heathen. The best talent and abundant means have been sent to Siam, China, and Japan. Why not send the best talent and needful means to Liberia, Sierra Leone, and Cape Palmas, that native missionaries may be trained for the outposts of the Lord? There is not a more promising mission-field in the world than Africa, and yet our friends in America take so little interest in this work! The Lord is going to save that Dark Continent, and it behooves his servants here to honor themselves in doing something to hasten the completion of this inevitable work! Africa is to be redeemed by the African, and the white Christians of this country can aid the work by munificent contributions. Will you do it, brethren? God help you!

Part II.

SLAVERY IN THE COLONIES.[1]

CHAPTER XII.

THE COLONY OF VIRGINIA.

1619–1775.

INTRODUCTION OF THE FIRST SLAVES. — "THE TREASURER" AND THE DUTCH MAN-OF-WAR. — THE CORRECT DATE. — THE NUMBER OF SLAVES. — WERE THERE TWENTY, OR FOURTEEN? — LITIGATION ABOUT THE POSSESSION OF THE SLAVES. — CHARACTER OF THE SLAVES IMPORTED, AND THE CHARACTER OF THE COLONISTS. — RACE PREJUDICES. — LEGAL ESTABLISHMENT OF SLAVERY. — WHO ARE SLAVES FOR LIFE. — DUTIES ON IMPORTED SLAVES. — POLITICAL AND MILITARY PROHIBITIONS AGAINST NEGROES. — PERSONAL RIGHTS. — CRIMINAL LAWS AGAINST SLAVES. — EMANCIPATION. — HOW BROUGHT ABOUT. — FREE NEGROES. — THEIR RIGHTS. — MORAL AND RELIGIOUS TRAINING. — POPULATION. — SLAVERY FIRMLY ESTABLISHED.

VIRGINIA was the mother of slavery as well as "the mother of Presidents." Unfortunate for her, unfortunate for the other colonies, and thrice unfortunate for the poor Colored people, who from 1619 to 1863 yielded their liberty, their toil, — unrequited, — their bodies and intellects to an institution that ground them to powder. No event in the history of North America has carried with it to its last analysis such terrible forces. It touched the brightest features of social life, and they faded under the contact of its poisonous breath. It affected legislation, local and national; it made and destroyed statesmen; it prostrated and bullied honest public sentiment; it strangled the voice of the press, and awed the pulpit into silent acquiescence; it organized the judiciary of States, and wrote decisions for judges; it gave States their political being, and afterwards dragged them

---

[1] A Flemish favorite of Charles V. having obtained of his king a patent, containing an exclusive right of importing four thousand Negroes into America, sold it for twenty-five thousand ducats to some Genoese merchants, who first brought into a regular form the commerce for slaves between Africa and America. — HOLMES's *American Annals*, vol. i. p. 35.

by the fore-hair through the stormy sea of civil war; laid the parricidal fingers of Treason against the fair throat of Liberty, — and through all time to come no event will be more sincerely deplored than the introduction of slavery into the colony of Virginia during the last days of the month of August in the year 1619!

The majority of writers on American history, as well as most histories on Virginia, from Beverley to Howison, have made a mistake in fixing the date of the introduction of the first slaves. Mr. Beverley, whose history of Virginia was printed in London in 1772, is responsible for the error, in that nearly all subsequent writers — excepting the laborious and scholarly Bancroft and the erudite Campbell — have repeated his mistake. Mr. Beverley, speaking of the burgesses having "met the Governor and Council at James Town in May 1620," adds in a subsequent paragraph, "In August following a Dutch Man of War landed twenty Negroes for sale; which were the first of that kind that were carried into the country."[1] By "August following," we infer that Beverley would have his readers understand that this was in 1620. But Burk, Smith, Campbell, and Neill gave 1619 as the date.[2] But we are persuaded to believe that the first slaves were landed at a still earlier date. In Capt. John Smith's history, printed in London in 1629, is a mere incidental reference to the introduction of slaves into Virginia. He mentions, under date of June 25, that the "governor and councell caused Burgesses to be chosen in all places,"[3] which is one month later than the occurrence of this event as fixed by Beverley. Smith speaks of a vessel named "George" as having been "sent to Newfoundland" for fish, and, having started in May, returned after a voyage of "seven weeks." In the next sentence he says, "About the last of August came in a dutch man of warre that sold vs twenty Negars."[4] Might not he have meant "about the end of last August" came the Dutch man-of-war, etc.? All historians, except two, agree that these slaves were landed in August, but disagree as to the year. Capt. Argall, of whom so much complaint was made by the Virginia Company to Lord Delaware,[5] fitted out the ship "Treasurer" at the expense of the Earl of Warwick, who sent him "an olde commission of hostility from the Duke of Savoy against the Span-

[1] R. Beverley's History of Virginia, pp. 35, 36.   [2] See Campbell, p. 144; Burk, vol. i. p. 326.   [3] Smith, vol. ii. pp. 38, 39.   [4] Smith's History of Virginia, vol. ii. p. 39.   [5] Virginia Company of London, p. 117, *sq.*

yards," for a "filibustering" cruise to the West Indies.[1] And, "after several acts of hostility committed, and some purchase gotten, she returns to Virginia at the end of ten months or there-abouts."[2] It was in the early autumn of 1618,[3] that Capt. Edward (a son of William) Brewster was sent into banishment by Capt. Argall; and this, we think, was one of the last, if not *the* last official act of that arbitrary governor. It was certainly before this that the ship "Treasurer," manned "with the ablest men in the colony," sailed for "the Spanish dominions in the Western hemisphere." Under date of June 15, 1618, John Rolfe, speaking of the death of the Indian Powhatan, which took place in April, says, "Some private differences happened betwixt Capt. Bruster and Capt. Argall," etc.[4] Capt. John Smith's information, as secured from Master Rolfe, would lead to the conclusion that the difficulty which took place between Capt. Edward Brewster and Capt. Argall occurred in the spring instead of the autumn, as Neill says. If it be true that "The Treasurer" sailed in the early spring of 1618, Rolfe's statement as to the time of the strife between Brewster and Argall would harmonize with the facts in reference to the length of time the vessel was absent as recorded in Burk's history. But if Neill is correct as to the time of the quarrel, — for we maintain that it was about this time that Argall left the colony, — then his statement would tally with Burk's account of the time the vessel was on the cruise. If, therefore, she sailed in October, 1618, being absent ten months, she was due at Jamestown in August, 1619.

But, nevertheless, we are strangely moved to believe that 1618 was the memorable year of the landing of the first slaves in Virginia. And we have one strong and reliable authority on our side. Stith, in his history of Virginia, fixes the date in 1618.[5] On the same page there is an account of the trial and sentence of Capt. Brewster. The ship "Treasurer" had evidently left England in the winter of 1618. When she reached the Virginia colony, she was furnished with a new crew and abundant supplies for her cruise. Neill says she returned with booty and "a certain number of negroes." Campbell agrees that it was some time before the landing of the Dutch man-of-war that "The Treasurer" returned to Virginia. He says, "She returned to Virginia after

---

[1] Campbell, p. 144.   [2] Burk, vol. i. p. 319.   [3] Neill, p. 120.   [4] Smith, vol. ii. p. 37.
[5] There were two vessels, The Treasurer and the Dutch man-of-war; but the latter, no doubt, put the first slaves ashore.

some ten months with her booty, which consisted of captured negroes, who were not left in Virginia, because Capt. Argall had gone back to England, but were put on the Earl of Warwick's plantation in the Somer Islands." [1]

During the last two and one-half centuries the readers of the history of Virginia have been mislead as to these two vessels, the Dutch man-of-war and "The Treasurer." The Dutch man-of-war did land the first slaves; but the ship "Treasurer" was the first to bring them to this country, in 1618.

When in 1619 the Dutch man-of-war brought the first slaves to Virginia, Capt. Miles Kendall was deputy-governor. The man-of-war claimed to sail under commission of the Prince of Orange. Capt. Kendall gave orders that the vessel should not land in any of his harbors: but the vessel was without provisions; and the Negroes, *fourteen* in number, were tendered for supplies. Capt. Kendall accepted the slaves, and, in return, furnished the man-of-war with the coveted provisions. In the mean while Capt. Butler came and assumed charge of the affairs of the Virginia Company, and dispossessed Kendall of his slaves, alleging that they were the property of the Earl of Warwick. He insisted that they were taken from the ship "Treasurer," [2] "with which the said Holland man-of-war had consorted." Chagrined, and wronged by Gov. Butler, Capt. Kendall hastened back to England to lay his case before the London Company, and to seek equity. The Earl of Warwick appeared in court, and claimed the Negroes as his property, as having belonged to his ship, "The Treasurer." Every thing that would embarrass Kendall was introduced by the earl. At length, as a final resort, charges were formally preferred against him, and the matter referred to Butler for decision. Capt. Kendall did not fail to appreciate the gravity of his case, when charges were preferred against him in London, and the trial ordered before the man of whom he asked restitution! The case remained in *statu quo* until July, 1622, when the court made a disposition of the case. Nine of the slaves were to be delivered to Capt. Kendall, "and the rest to be consigned to the company's use." This decision was reached by the court after the Earl of Warwick had submitted the case to the discretion and judicial impartiality of the judges. The court gave instructions to Capt. Bernard, who was then the governor, to see that its order was

---

[1] Campbell, p. 144.   [2] Burk, Appendix, p. 316, Declaration of Virginia Company, 7th May, 1623.

enforced. But while the order of the court was *in transitu*, Bernard died. The earl, learning of the event, immediately wrote a letter, representing that the slaves should *not* be delivered to Kendall; and an advantage being taken — purely technical — of the omission of the name of the captain of the Holland man-of-war, Capt. Kendall never secured his nine slaves.

It should be noted, that while Rolfe, in Capt. Smith's history, fixes the number of slaves in the Dutch vessel at *twenty*, — as also does Beverley, — it is rather strange that the Council of Virginia, in 1623, should state that the commanding officer of the Dutch man-of-war told Capt. Kendall that "he had fourteen Negroes on board!"[1] Moreover, it is charged that the slaves taken by "The Treasurer" were divided up among the sailors; and that they, having been cheated out of their dues, asked judicial interference.[2] Now, these slaves from "The Treasurer" "were placed on the Earl of Warwick's lands in Bermudas, and there kept and detained to his Lordship's use." There are several things apparent; viz., that there is a mistake between the statement of the Virginia Council in their declaration of May 7, 1623, about the number of slaves landed by the man-of-war, and the statements of Beverley and Smith. And if Stith is to be relied upon as to the slaves of "The Treasurer" having been taken to the "Earl of Warwick's lands in Bermudas, and there kept," his lordship's claim to the slaves Capt. Kendall got from the Dutch man-of-war was not founded in truth or equity!

Whether the number was fourteen or twenty, it is a fact, beyond historical doubt, that the Colony of Virginia purchased the first Negroes, and thus opened up the nefarious traffic in human flesh. It is due to the Virginia Colony to say, that these slaves were forced upon them; that they were taken in exchange for food given to relieve the hunger of famishing sailors; that white servitude[3] was common, and many whites were convicts[4] from England; and the extraordinary demand for laborers may have deadened the moral sensibilities of the colonists as to the enormity of the great crime to which they were parties. Women were sold for wives,[5] and sometimes were kidnapped[6] in England and sent into the colony. There was nothing in the moral atmosphere of the colony inimical to the spirit of bondage that was

---

[1] See Burk, vol. i. p. 326. [2] Stith, Book III. pp. 153, 154.
[3] Beverley, 235, *sq.* [4] Campbell, 147.
[5] Beverley, p. 248. [6] Court and Times of James First, ii. p. 108; also, Neill p. 121.

manifest so early in the history of this people. England had always held her sceptre over slaves of some character : villeins in the feudal era, stolen Africans under Elizabeth and under the house of the Tudors ; Caucasian children — whose German blood could be traced beyond the battle of Hastings — in her mines, factories, and mills ; and vanquished Brahmans in her Eastern possessions. How, then, could we expect less of these " knights " and "adventurers" who " degraded the human race by an exclusive respect for the privileged classes " ? [1]

The institution of slavery once founded, it is rather remarkable that its growth was so slow. According to the census of Feb. 16, 1624, there were but twenty-two in the entire colony.[2] There were eleven at Flourdieu Hundred, three in James City, one on James Island, one on the plantation opposite James City, four at Warisquoyak, and two at Elizabeth City. In 1648 the population of Virginia was about fifteen thousand, with a slave population of three hundred.[3] The cause of the slow increase of slaves was not due to any colonial prohibition. The men who were engaged in tearing unoffending Africans from their native home were some time learning that this colony was at this time a ready market for their helpless victims. Whatever feeling or scruple, if such ever existed, the colonists had in reference to the subject of dealing in the slave-trade, was destroyed at conception by the golden hopes of large gains. The latitude, the products of the soil, the demand for labor, the custom of the indenture of white servants, were abundant reasons why the Negro should be doomed to bondage for life.

The subjects of slavery were the poor unfortunates that the strong push to the outer edge of organized African society, where, through neglect or abuse, they are consigned to the mercy of avarice and malice. We have already stated that the weaker tribes of Africa are pushed into the alluvial flats of that continent; where they have perished in large numbers, or have become the prey of the more powerful tribes, who consort with slave-hunters. Disease, tribal wars in Africa, and the merciless greed of slave-hunters, peopled the colony of Virginia with a class that was expected to till the soil. African criminals, by an immemorial usage, were sold into slavery as the highest penalty, save death ; and often this was preferred to bondage. Many such criminals

---

[1] Bancroft, vol. i. p. 468.   [2] Neill, p. 121.   [3] Hist. Tracts, vol. ii. Tract viii.

found their way into the colony. To be bondmen among neighboring tribes at home was dreaded beyond expression; but to wear chains in a foreign land, to submit to the dehumanizing treatment of cruel taskmasters, was an ordeal that fanned into life the last dying ember of manhood and resentment.

The character of the slaves imported, and the pitiable condition of the white servants, produced rather an anomalous result. "Male servants, and slaves of both sex" were bound together by the fellowship of toil. But the distinction "made between them in their clothes and food" [1] drew a line, not between their social condition, — for it was the same, — but between their nationality. First, then, was social estrangement, next legal difference, and last of all political disagreement and strife. In order to oppress the weak, and justify the unchristian distinction between God's creatures, the persons who would bolster themselves into respectability must have the aid of law. Luther could march fearlessly to the Diet of Worms if every tile on the houses were a devil; but Macbeth was conquered by the remembrance of the wrong he had done the virtuous Duncan and the unoffending Banquo, long before he was slain by Macduff. A guilty conscience always needs a multitude of subterfuges to guard against dreaded contingencies. So when the society in the Virginia Colony had made up its mind that the Negroes in their midst were 'mere heathen,[2] they stood ready to punish any member who had the temerity to cross the line drawn between the races. It was not a mitigating circumstance that the white servants of the colony who came into natural contact with the Negroes were "disorderly persons," or convicts sent to Virginia by an order of the king of England. It was fixed by public sentiment and law that there should be no relation between the races. The first prohibition was made "September 17th, 1630." Hugh Davis, a white servant, was publicly flogged "before an assembly of Negroes and others," for defiling himself with a Negro. It was also required that he should confess as much on the following sabbath.[3]

In the winter of 1639, on the 6th of January, during the incumbency of Sir Francis Wyatt, the General Assembly passed the first prohibition against Negroes. "All persons," doubtless including fraternizing Indians, "except Negroes," were required to secure arms and ammunition, or be subject to a fine, to be

---

[1] Beverley, p. 236. [2] Campbell, p. 145. [3] Hening, vol. i. p. 146; also p. 552.

imposed by "the Governor and Council." [1]   The records are too scanty, and it is impossible to judge, at this remote day, what was the real cause of this law. We have already called attention to the fact that the slaves were but a mere fraction of the *summa summarum* of the population.   It could not be that the brave Virginians were afraid of an insurrection! Was it another reminder that the "Negroes were heathen," and, therefore, not entitled to the privileges of Christian freemen? It was not the act of that government, which in its conscious rectitude "can put ten thousand to flight," but was rather the inexcusable feebleness of a diseased conscience, that staggers off for refuge "when no man pursueth."

Mr. Bancroft thinks that the "special tax upon female slaves" [2] was intended to discourage the traffic. It does not so seem to us. It seems that the Virginia Assembly was endeavoring to establish friendly relations with the Dutch and other nations in order to secure "trade." Tobacco was the chief commodity of the colonists. They intended by the act [3] of March, 1659, to guarantee the most perfect liberty "to trade with" them. They required, however, that foreigners should "give bond and pay the impost of tenn shillings per hogshead laid upon all tobacco exported to any fforreigne dominions." The same act recites, that whenever any slaves were sold for tobacco, the amount of imposts would only be "two shillings per hogshead," which was only the nominal sum paid by the colonists themselves. This act was passed several years before the one became a law that is cited by Mr. Bancroft. It seems that much trouble had been experienced in determining who were taxable in the colony. It is very clear that the LIV. Act of March, 1662, which Mr. Bancroft thinks was intended to discourage the importation of slaves by taxing female slaves, seeks only to determine who shall be taxable. It is a general law, declaring "that *all* male persons, of what age soever imported into this country shall be brought into lysts and be liable to the payment of all taxes, and all negroes, male and female being imported shall be accompted tythable, and all Indian servants male or female however procured being adjudged sixteen years of age shall be likewise tythable from which none shall be exempted." [4] Beverley says that "the male servants, and slaves of both sexes," were employed together. It seems that white women were so

---

[1] Hening, vol. i. p 226.   [2] Bancroft, vol. i. p. 178.   [3] Hening, vol. i. p. 540.   [4] Ibid., vol. ii. p. 84.

scarce as to be greatly respected. But female Negroes and Indians were taxable; although Indian children, unlike those of Negroes, were not held as slaves.[1] Under the LIV. Act there is but one class exempted from tax, — white females, and, we might add, persons under sixteen years of age.[2] So what Mr. Bancroft mistakes as repressive legislation against the slave-trade is only an exemption of white women, and intended to encourage their coming into the colony.

The legal distinction between slaves and servants was, "slaves for life, and servants for a time."[3] Slavery existed from 1619 until 1662, without any sanction in law. On the 14th of December, 1662, the foundations of the slave institution were laid in the old law maxim, "*Partus sequitur ventrum*," — that the issue of slave mothers should follow their condition.[4] Two things were accomplished by this act; viz., slavery received the direct sanction of statutory law, and it was also made hereditary. On the 6th of March, 1655, — seven years before the time mentioned above, — an act was passed declaring that all Indian children brought into the colony by friendly Indians should not be treated as slaves,[5] but be instructed in the trades.[6] By implication, then, slavery existed legally at this time; but the act of 1662 was the first direct law on the subject. In 1670 a question arose as to whether Indians taken in war were to be servants for a term of years, or for life. The act passed on the subject is rather remarkable for the language in which it is couched; showing, as it does, that it was made to relieve the Indian, and fix the term of the Negro's bondage beyond a reasonable doubt. "*It is resolved* and enacted that all servants not being christians imported into this colony by shipping shall be slaves for their lives; but what shall come by land shall serve, if boyes or girles, until thirty yeares of age, if men or women twelve yeares and no longer."[7] This remarkable act was dictated by fear and policy. No doubt the Indian was as thoroughly despised as the Negro; but the Indian was on his native soil, and, therefore, was a more dangerous[8] subject. Instructed by the past, and fearful of the future, the sagacious colonists declared by this act, that those who "shall come by land" should not be assigned to servitude for life. While this act was passed to define the legal status of the Indian, at the same time,

---

[1] Hening, vol. i. p. 396.   [2] Burk, vol. ii. Appendix, p. xxiii.   [3] Beverley, p. 235.
[4] Hening, vol. ii. p. 170; see, also, vol. iii. p. 140.   [5] Beverley, p. 195.
[6] Hening, vol. i. p. 396.   [7] Ibid., vol. ii. p. 283.   [8] Campbell, p. 160; also Bacon's Rebellion.

and with equal force, it determines the fate of the Negro who is so unfortunate as to find his way into the colony. *"All servants not being christians imported into this colony by shipping shall be slaves for their lives."* Thus, in 1670, Virginia, not abhorring the insti-tution, solemnly declared that "all servants not christians" — heathen Negroes — coming into her "colony by shipping" — there was no other way for them to come! — should *"be slaves for their lives!"*

In 1682 the colony was in a flourishing condition. Opulence generally makes men tyrannical, and great success in business makes them unmerciful. Although Indians, in special acts, had not been classed as slaves, but only accounted "servants for a term of years," the growing wealth and increasing number of the colonists seemed to justify them in throwing off the mask. The act of the 3d of October, 1670, defining who should be slaves, was repealed at the November session of the General Assembly of 1682. Indians were now made slaves,[1] and placed upon the same legal footing with the Negroes. The sacred rite of baptism[2] did not alter the condition of children — Indian or Negro — when born in slavery. And slavery, as a cruel and inhuman institution, flourished and magnified with each returning year.

Encouraged by friendly legislation, the Dutch plied the slave-trade with a zeal equalled only by the enormous gains they reaped from the planters. It was not enough that faith had been broken with friendly Indians, and their children doomed by statute to the hell of perpetual slavery; it was not sufficient that the Indian and Negro were compelled to serve, unrequited, for their lifetime. On the 4th of October, 1705, "an act declaring the Negro, Mulatto, and Indian slaves, within this dominion, to be real estate,"[3] was passed without a dissenting voice. Before this time they had been denominated by the courts as chattels : now they were to pass in law as real estate. There were, however, several provisos to this act. Merchants coming into the colony with slaves, not sold, were not to be affected by the act until the slaves had actually passed in a *bonâ-fide* sale. Until such time their slaves were contemplated by the law as chattels. In case a master died without lawful heirs, his slaves did not escheat, but were regarded as other personal estate or property. Slave prop-

---

[1] Hening, vol. ii. pp. 490, 491.   [2] Ibid., vol. ii. p. 260; see, also, vol. iii. p. 460.
[3] Ibid., vol. iii. p. 333.

erty was liable to be taken in execution for the payment of debts, and was recoverable by a personal action.[1]

The only apology for enslaving the Negroes we can find in all the records of this colony is, that they "were heathen." Every statute, from the first to the last, during the period the colony was under the control of England, carefully mentions that all persons — Indians and Negroes — who "are not christians" are to be slaves. And their conversion to Christianity afterwards did not release them from their servitude.[2]

The act making Indian, Mulatto, and Negro slaves real property, passed in October, 1705, under the reign of Queen Anne, and by her approved, was "explained" and "amended" in February, 1727, during the reign of King George II. Whether the act received its being out of a desire to prevent fraud, like the "Statutes of Frauds," is beyond finding out. But it was an act that showed that slavery had grown to be so common an institution as not to excite human sympathy. And the attempt to "explain" and "amend" its cruel provisions was but a faint precursor of the evils that followed. Innumerable lawsuits grew out of the act, and the courts and barristers held to conflicting interpretations and constructions. Whether complaints were made to his Majesty, the king, the records do not relate; or whether he was moved by feelings of humanity is quite as difficult to understand. But on the 31st of October, 1751, he issued a proclamation repealing the act declaring slaves real estate.[3] The proclamation abrogated nine other acts, and quite threw the colony into confusion.[4] It is to be hoped that the king was animated by the noblest impulses in repealing one of the most dehumanizing laws that ever disgraced the government of any civilized people. The General Assembly, on the 15th of April, 1752, made an appeal to the king, "humbly" protesting against the proclamation. The law-makers in the colony were inclined to doubt the king's prerogative in this matter. They called the attention of his Majesty to the fact that he had given the "Governor" "full power and authority with the advice and consent of the council" to make needful laws; but they failed

---

[1] Hening, vol. iii. pp. 334, 335. [2] Ibid., vol. iii. p. 448; see, also, vol. v. p. 548.

[3] Hildreth, in his History of the United States, says that the law making "Negroes, Mulattoes, and Indians" real estate "continued to be the law so long as Virginia remained a British colony." This is a mistake, as the reader can see. The law was repealed nearly a quarter of a century before Virginia ceased to be a British colony.

[4] Hening, vol. v. p. 432, *sq.*

to realize fully that his Majesty, in accordance with the proviso contained in the grant of authority made to the governor and council of the colony, was using his veto. They recited the causes which induced them to enact the law, recounted the benefits accruing to his Majesty's subjects from the conversion of human beings into real property,[1] and closed with a touching appeal for the retention of the act complained of, so that slaves *"might not at the same time be real estate in some respects, personal in others, and bothe in others!"* History does not record that the brusque old king was at all moved by this earnest appeal and convincing argument of the Virginia Assembly.

In 1699 the government buildings at James City were destroyed. The General Assembly, in an attempt to devise means to build a new Capitol, passed an act on the 11th of April of the aforesaid year, fixing a "duty on servants and slaves imported "[2] into the colony. Fifteen shillings was the impost tax levied upon every servant imported, "not born in England or Wales, and twenty shillings for every Negro or other slave" thus imported. The revenue arising from this tax on servants and slaves was to go to the building of a new Capitol. Every slave-vessel was inspected by a customs-officer. The commanding officer of the vessel was required to furnish the names and number of the servants and slaves imported, the place of their birth, and pay the duty imposed upon each before they were permitted to be landed. This act was to be in force for the space of "three years from the publication thereof, and no longer."[3] But, in the summer of 1701, it was continued until the 25th day of December, 1703. The act was passed as a temporary measure to secure revenue with which to build the Capitol.[4] Evidently it was not intended to remain a part of the code of the colony. In 1732 it was revived by an act, the preamble of which leads us to infer that the home government was not friendly to its passage. In short, the act is preceded by a prayer for permission to pass it. Whatever may have been the feeling in England in reference to levying imposts upon servants and slaves, it is certain the colonists were in hearty accord with the spirit and letter of the act. It must be clear to every honest student of history, that there never was, up to this time, an attempt made to cure the growing evils of

---

[1] Beverley, p. 98.
[3] Hening, vol. iii. p. 195.
[2] Hening, vol. iii, pp. 193, 194.
[4] Burk, vol. ii. Appendix, p. xxii.

slavery. When a tax was imposed upon slaves imported, the object in view was the replenishing of the coffers of the colonial government. In 1734 another act was passed taxing imported slaves, because it had "been found very easy to the subjects of this colony, and no ways burthensome to the traders in slaves." The additional reason for continuing the law was, "that a competent revenue" might be raised "for preventing or lessening a poll-tax." [1] And in 1738, this law being "found, by experience, to be an easy expedient for raising a revenue towards the lessening a pooll-tax, always grievous to the people of this colony, and is in no way burthensom to the traders in slaves," it was re-enacted. In every instance, through all these years, the imposition of a tax on slaves imported into the colony had but one end in view, — the raising of revenue. In 1699 the end sought through the taxing of imported slaves was the building of the Capitol ; in 1734 it was to lighten the burden of taxes on the subjects in the colony ; but, in 1740, the object was to get funds to raise and transport troops in his Majesty's service. [2] The original duty remained ; and an additional levy of five per centum was required on each slave imported, over and above the twenty shillings required by previous acts.

In 1742 the tax was continued, because it was "necessary" "to discharge the public debts." [3] And again, in 1745, it was still believed to be necessary "for supporting the public expense." [4] The act, in a legal sense, expired by limitation, but in spirit remained in full force until revived by the acts of 1752-53. [5] In the spring of 1755 the General Assembly increased the tax on imported slaves above the amount previously fixed by law. [6] The duty at this time was ten per centum on each slave sold into the colony. The same law was reiterated in 1757, [7] and, when it had expired by limitation, was revived in 1759, to be in force for "the term of seven years from thence next following." [8]

Encouraged by the large revenue derived from the tax imposed on servants and slaves imported into the colony from foreign parts, the General Assembly stood for the revival of the impost-tax. The act of 1699 required the tax at the hands of "the importer," and from as many persons as engaged in the slave-trade who were subjects of Great Britain, and residents of the colony; but the tax at length became a burden to them. In

---

[1] Hening, vol. iv. p. 394. [2] Ibid., vol. v. pp. 92, 93. [3] Ibid., vol. v. pp. 160, 161.
[4] Ibid., vol. v. pp. 318, 319. [5] Ibid., vol. vi. pp. 217, 218. [6] Ibid., vol. vii. p. 466.
[7] Ibid., vol. vii. p. 81. [8] Ibid., vol. vii. p. 281.

order to evade the law and escape the tax, they frequently went into Maryland and the Carolinas, and bought slaves, ostensibly for their own private use, but really to sell in the local market. To prevent this, an act was passed imposing a tax of twenty per centum on all such sales ;[1] but there was a great outcry made against this act. Twenty per centum of the gross amount on each slave, paid by the person making the purchase, was a burden that planters bore with ill grace. The question of the reduction of the tax to ten per centum was vehemently agitated. The argument offered in favor of the reduction was three-fold ; viz., "very burthensom to the fair purchaser," inimical "to the settlement and improvement of the lands" in the colony, and a great hinderance to "the importation of slaves, and thereby lessens the fund arising upon the duties upon slaves."[2] The reduction was made in May, 1760; and, under additional pressure, the additional duty on imported slaves to be "paid by the buyer" was taken off altogether.[3] But in 1766 the duty on imported slaves was revived ;[4] and in 1772 an act was passed reviving the "additional duty" on "imported slaves, and was continued in force until the colonies threw off the British yoke in 1775."[5]

In all this epoch, from 1619 down to 1775, there is not a scrap of history to prove that the colony of Virginia ever sought to prohibit in any manner the importation of slaves. That she encouraged the traffic, we have abundant testimony; and that she enriched herself by it, no one can doubt.

During the period of which we have just made mention above, the slaves in this colony had no political or military rights. As early as 1639,[6] the Assembly *excused* them from owning or carrying arms; and in 1705 they were barred by a special act from holding or exercising "any office, ecclesiastical, civil, or military, or any place of publick trust or power,"[7] in the colony. If found with a "gun, sword, club, staff, or other weopon,"[8] they were turned over to the constable, who was required to administer "twenty lashes on his or her bare back." There was but one exception made. Where Negro and Indian slaves lived on the border of the colony, frequently harassed by predatory bands of hostile Indians, they could bear arms by first getting written

---

[1] Hening, vol. vii. p. 338.   [2] Ibid., vol. vii. p. 363.   [3] Ibid., vol. vii. p. 383.
[4] Ibid., vol. viii. pp. 190, 191, 237, 336, 337.   [5] Ibid., vol. viii. pp. 530, 532.
[6] Ibid., vol. i. p. 226.   [7] Ibid., vol. iii. p. 251.
[8] Ibid., vol. iii. p. 459; also vol. iv. p. 131, vol. vi. p. 109, and vol. ii. p. 481.

license from their master;[1] but even then they were kept under surveillance by the whites.

Personal rights, we cannot see that the slaves had any. They were not allowed to leave the plantation on which they were held as chattel or real estate, without a written certificate or pass from their master, which was only granted under the most urgent circumstances.[2] If they dared lift a hand against any white man, or "Christian" (?) as they loved to call themselves, they were punished by thirty lashes ; and if a slave dared to resist his master while he was correcting him, he could be killed ; and the master would be guiltless in the eyes of the law.[3] If a slave remained on another plantation more than four hours, his master was liable to a fine of two hundred pounds of tobacco.[4] And if any white person had any commercial dealings with a slave, he was liable to imprisonment for one month without bail, and compelled to give security in the sum of ten pounds.[5] If a slave had earned and owned a horse and buggy, it was lawful to seize them ;[6] and the church-warden was charged with the sale of the articles. Even with the full permission of his master, if a slave were found going about the colony trading any articles for his or master's profit, his master was liable to a fine of ten pounds ; which fine went to the church-warden, for the benefit of the poor of the parish in which the slave did the trading.[7]

In all the matters of law, civil and criminal, the slave had no rights. Under an act of 1705, Catholics, Indian and Negro slaves, were denied the right to appear as "witnesses in any cases whatsoever," "not being christians;"[8] but this was modified somewhat in 1732, when Negroes, Indians, and Mulattoes were admitted as witnesses in the trial of slaves.[9] In criminal causes the slave could be arrested, cast into prison, tried, and condemned, with but one witness against him, and sentenced without a jury. The solemnity and dignity of "trial by jury," of which Englishmen love to boast, was not allowed the criminal slave.[10] And, when a slave was executed, a value was fixed upon him ; and the General Assembly was required to make an appropriation covering the value of the slave to indemnify the master.[11] More than five slaves meeting together, "to rebel or make insur-

[1] Hening., vol. vi. p. 110.   [2] Ibid., vol. ii. p. 481.   [3] Ibid., vol. ii. p. 270.
[4] Ibid., vol. ii. p. 493.   [5] Ibid., vol. iii. p. 451.   [6] Ibid., vol. iii. pp. 459, 460.
[7] Ibid., vol. viii. p. 360.   [8] Ibid., vol. iii. p. 298.   [9] Ibid., vol. iv. p. 327.
[10] Ibid., vol. iii. p. 103.   [11] Ibid., vol. iii. p. 270, and vol. iv. p. 128.

rection " was considered " felony ; " and they were liable to " suffer death, and be utterly excluded the benefit of clergy ; " [1] but, where one slave was guilty of manslaughter in killing another slave, he was allowed the benefit of clergy.[2]   In case of burglary by a slave, he was not allowed the benefit of the clergy, except " said breaking, in the case of a freeman, would be burglary." [3] And the only humane feature in the entire code of the colony was an act passed in 1772, providing that no slave should be condemned to suffer " unless four of the judges " before whom he is tried " concur." [4]

The free Negroes of the colony of Virginia were but little removed by law from their unfortunate brothers in bondage. Their freedom was the act of individuals, with but one single exception.   In 1710 a few recalcitrant slaves resolved to offer armed resistance to their masters, whose treatment had driven them to the verge of desperation.   A slave of Robert Ruffin, of Surry County, entered into the plot, but afterwards revealed it to the masters of the rebellious slaves.   As a reward for his services, the General Assembly, on the 9th of October, 1710, gave him his manumission papers, with the added privilege to remain in the colony.[5]   For the laws of the colony required " that no negro, mulatto, or indian slaves " should be set free " except for some meritorious services."   The governor and council were to decide upon the merits of the services, and then grant a license to the master to set his slave at liberty.[6]   If any master presumed to emancipate a slave without a license granted according to the act of 1723, his slave thus emancipated could be taken up by the church-warden for the parish in which the master of the slave resided, and sold " by public outcry."   The money accruing from such sale was to be used for the benefit of the parish.[7]   But if a slave were emancipated according to law, the General Assembly paid the master so much for him, as in the case of slaves executed by the authorities.   But it was seldom that emancipated persons were permitted to remain in the colony.   By the act of 1699 they were required to leave the colony within six months after they had secured their liberty, on pain of having to pay a fine of " ten pounds sterling to the church-wardens of the parish ; " which money was to be used in transporting the liberated slave out of

[1] Hening, vol. iv. p. 126, and vol. vi. p. 104, *sq.*   [2] Ibid., vol. viii. p. 139.
[3] Ibid., vol. viii. p. 522.   [4] Ibid., vol. viii. p. 523.   [5] Ibid., vol. iii. pp. 536, 537.
[6] Ibid., vol. iv. p. 132.   [7] Ibid., vol. vi. p. 112.

the country.[1] If slave women came in possession of their freedom, the law sought them out, and required of them to pay taxes ;[2]
a burden from which their white sisters, and even Indian women,
were exempt.

If free Colored persons in the colony ever had the right of
franchise, there is certainly no record of it. We infer, however,
from the act of 1723, that previous to that time they had exercised
the voting privilege. For that act declares "that no free negro
shall hereafter have any vote at the election."[3] Perhaps they had
had a vote previous to this time ; but it is mere conjecture, unsupported by historical proof. Being denied the right of suffrage did
not shield them from taxation. All free Negroes, male and female,
were compelled to pay taxes.[4] They contributed to the support
of the colonial government, and yet they had no voice in the
government. They contributed to the building of schoolhouses,
but were denied the blessings of education.

Free Negroes were enlisted in the militia service, but were
not permitted to bear arms. They had to attend the trainings,
but were assigned the most servile duties.[5] They built fortifications, pitched and struck tents, cooked, drove teams, and in some
instances were employed as musicians. Where free Negroes
were acting as housekeepers, they were allowed to have fire-
arms in their possession ;[6] and if they lived on frontier plantations, as we have made mention already, they were permitted to
use arms under the direction of their employers.

In a moral and religious sense, the slaves of the colony of
Virginia received little or no attention from the Christian Church.
All intercourse was cut off between the races. Intermarrying of
whites and blacks was prohibited by severe laws.[7] And the most
common civilities and amenities of life were frowned down when
intended for a Negro. The plantation was as religious as the
Church, and the Church was as secular as the plantation. The
"white christians" hated the Negro, and the Church bestowed
upon him a most bountiful amount of neglect.[8] Instead of receiving religious instruction from the clergy, slaves were given to
them in part pay for their ministrations to the whites, — for their
"use and encouragement."[9] It was as late as 1756 before any

---

[1] Hening, vol. iii. pp. 87, 88.   [2] Ibid., vol. ii. p. 267.   [3] Ibid., vol. iv. pp. 133, 134.
[4] Ibid., vol. iv. p. 133.   [5] Ibid., vol. vii. p. 95 ; and vol. vi. p. 533.
[6] Ibid., vol. iv. p. 131.   [7] Ibid., vol. iii. p. 87.   [8] Campbell, p. 529.
[9] Burk, vol. ii. Appendix, p. xiii.

white minister had the piety and courage to demand instruction for the slaves.[1]   The prohibition against instruction for these poor degraded vassals is not so much a marvel after all.   For in 1670, when the white population was forty thousand, servants six thousand, and slaves two thousand, Sir William Berkeley, when inquired of by the home government as to the condition of education in the colony, replied : —

"The same course that is taken in England out of towns, — every man according to his ability instructing his children.   We have forty-eight parishes, and our ministers are well paid, and by my consent should be better *if they would pray oftener and preach less.*   But of all other commodities, so of this, *the worst are sent us,* and we had few that we could boast of, since the persecution of Cromwell's tyranny drove divers worthy men hither.   But I thank God, *there are no free schools nor printing,* and I hope we shall not have these hundred years : for *learning* has brought disobedience and heresy and sects into the world ; and *printing* has divulged them, and libels against the best government.   God keep us from both ! "[2]

Thus was the entire colony in ignorance and superstition, and it was the policy of the home government to keep out the light.   The sentiments of Berkeley were applauded in official circles in England, and most rigorously carried out by his successor who, in 1682, with the concurrence of the council, put John Buckner under bonds for introducing the art of printing into the colony.[3]   This prohibition continued until 1733.   If the whites of the colony were left in ignorance, what must have been the mental and moral condition of the slaves ?   The ignorance of the whites made them the pliant tools of the London Company, and the Negroes in turn were compelled to submit to a condition "of rather rigorous servitude."[4]   This treatment had its reflexive influence on the planters.   Men fear most the ghosts of their sins, and for cruel deeds rather expect and dread "the reward in the life that now is."   So no wonder Dinwiddie wrote the father of Charles James Fox in 1758 : "We dare not venture to part with any of our white men any distance, as we must have a watchful eye over our negro slaves."

In 1648, as we mentioned some pages back, there were about three hundred slaves in the colony.   Slow coming at first, but at length they began to increase rapidly, so that in fifty years they

---

[1] Foot's Sketches, First Series, p. 291.   [2] Hening, vol. ii. p. 517.
[3] Hening, vol. ii. p. 518.   [4] Campbell, p. 383.

had increased one hundred per cent. In 1671 they were two thousand strong, and all, up to that date, direct from Africa. In 1715 there were twenty-three thousand slaves against seventy-two thousand whites.[1] By the year 1758 the slave population had increased to the alarming number of over one hundred thousand, which was a little less than the numerical strength of the whites.

During this period of a century and a half, slavery took deep root in the colony of Virginia, and attained unwieldy and alarming proportions. It had sent its dark death-roots into the fibre and organism of the political, judicial, social, and religious life of the people. It was crystallized now into a domestic institution. It existed in contemplation of legislative enactment, and had high judicial recognition through the solemn forms of law. The Church had proclaimed it a " sacred institution," and the clergy had covered it with the sanction of their ecclesiastical office. There it stood, an organized system, — the dark problem of the uncertain future : more terrible to the colonists in its awful, spectral silence during the years of the Revolution than the victorious guns of the French and Continental armies, which startled the English lion from his hurtful hold at the throat of white men's liberties — black men had no country, no liberty — in this new world in the West. But, like the dead body of the Roman murderer's victim, slavery was a curse that pursued the colonists evermore.

---

[1] Chalmers's American Colonies, vol. ii. p. 7.

CHAPTER XIII.

THE COLONY OF NEW YORK.

1628–1775.

SETTLEMENT OF NEW YORK BY THE DUTCH IN 1609. — NEGROES INTRODUCED INTO THE COLONY, 1628. — THE TRADE IN NEGROES INCREASED. — TOBACCO EXCHANGED FOR SLAVES AND MERCHANDISE. — GOVERNMENT OF THE COLONY. — NEW NETHERLAND FALLS INTO THE HANDS OF THE ENGLISH, AUG. 27, 1664. — VARIOUS CHANGES. — NEW LAWS ADOPTED. — LEGISLATION. — FIRST REPRESENTATIVES ELECTED IN 1683. — IN 1702 QUEEN ANNE INSTRUCTS THE ROYAL GOVERNOR IN REGARD TO THE IMPORTATION OF SLAVES. — SLAVERY RESTRICTIONS. — EXPEDITION TO EFFECT THE CONQUEST OF CANADA UNSUCCESSFUL. — NEGRO RIOT. — SUPPRESSED BY THE EFFICIENT AID OF TROOPS. — FEARS OF THE COLONISTS. — NEGRO PLOT OF 1741. — THE ROBBERY OF HOGG'S HOUSE. — DISCOVERY OF A PORTION OF THE GOODS. — THE ARREST OF HUGHSON, HIS WIFE, AND IRISH PEGGY. — CRIMINATION AND RECRIMINATION. — THE BREAKING-OUT OF NUMEROUS FIRES. — THE ARREST OF SPANISH NEGROES. — THE TRIAL OF HUGHSON. — TESTIMONY OF MARY BURTON. — HUGHSON HANGED. — THE ARREST OF MANY OTHERS IMPLICATED IN THE PLOT. — THE HANGING OF CÆSAR AND PRINCE. — QUACK AND CUFFEE BURNED AT THE STAKE. — THE LIEUTENANT-GOVERNOR'S PROCLAMATION. — MANY WHITE PERSONS ACCUSED OF BEING CONSPIRATORS. — DESCRIPTION OF HUGHSON'S MANNER OF SWEARING THOSE HAVING KNOWLEDGE OF THE PLOT. — CONVICTION AND HANGING OF THE CATHOLIC PRIEST URY. — THE SUDDEN AND UNEXPECTED TERMINATION OF THE TRIAL. — NEW LAWS MORE STRINGENT TOWARD SLAVES ADOPTED.

FROM the settlement of New York by the Dutch in 1609, down to its conquest by the English in 1664, there is no reliable record of slavery in that colony. That the institution was coeval with the Holland government, there can be no historical doubt. During the half-century that the Holland flag waved over the New Netherlands, slavery grew to such proportions as to be regarded as a necessary evil. As early as 1628 the irascible slaves from Angola,[1] Africa, were the fruitful source of widespread public alarm. A newly settled country demanded a hardy and energetic laboring class. Money was scarce, the colonists poor, and servants few. The numerous physical obstructions across the path of material civilization suggested cheap but efficient labor. White servants were few, and the cost of securing them from abroad was a great hinderance to their increase. The Dutch had possessions on the coast of Guinea and in Brazil, and

---

[1] Brodhead's History of New York, vol. i. p. 184.

hence they found it cheap and convenient to import slaves to perform the labor of the colony.[1]

The early slaves went into the pastoral communities, worked on the public highways, and served as valets in private families. Their increase was stealthy, their conduct insubordinate, and their presence a distressing nightmare to the apprehensive and conscientious.

The West India Company had offered many inducements to its patroons.[2] And its pledge to furnish the colonists with "as many blacks as they conveniently could," was scrupulously performed.[3] In addition to the slaves furnished by the vessels plying between Brazil and the coast of Guinea, many Spanish and Portuguese prizes were brought into the Netherlands, where the slaves were made the chattel property of the company. An urgent and extraordinary demand for labor, rather than the cruel desire to traffic in human beings, led the Dutch to encourage the bringing of Negro slaves. Scattered widely among the whites, treated often with the humanity that characterized the treatment bestowed upon the white servants, there was little said about slaves in this period. The majority of them were employed upon the farms, and led quiet and sober lives. The largest farm owned by the company was "*cultivated by the blacks;*"[4] and this fact was recorded as early as the 19th of April, 1638, by "Sir William Kieft, Director-General of New Netherland." And, although the references to slaves and slavery in the records of Amsterdam are incidental, yet it is plainly to be seen that the institution was purely patriarchal during nearly all the period the Hollanders held the Netherlands.

Manumission of slaves was not an infrequent event.[5] Sometimes it was done as a reward for meritorious services, and sometimes it was prompted by the holy impulses of humanity and justice. The most cruel thing done, however, in this period, was to hold as slaves in the service of the company the children of Negroes who were lawfully manumitted. "All their children already born, or yet to be born, remained obligated to serve the company as slaves." In cases of emergency the liberated fathers of these bond children were required to serve "by water or by land" in the defence of the Holland government.[6] It is gratify-

---

[1] O'Callaghan's History of New Netherlands, pp. 384, 385. [2] Brodhead, vol. i. p. 194.
[3] Ibid., vol. i. pp. 196, 197. [4] Dunlap's History of New York, vol. i. p. 58.
[5] O'Callaghan, p. 385. [6] Van Tienhoven.

ing, however, to find the recorded indignation of some of the best citizens of the New Netherlands against the enslaving of the children of free Negroes. It was severely denounced, as contrary to justice and in "violation of the law of nature." "How any one born of a free Christian mother" could, notwithstanding, be a slave, and be obliged to remain such, passed their comprehension.[1] It was impossible for them to explain it." And, although "they were treated just like Christians," the moral sense of the people could not excuse such a flagrant crime against humanity.[2]

Director-General Sir William Kieft's unnecessary war, "without the knowledge, and much less the order, of the XIX., and against the will of the Commonality there," had thrown the Province into great confusion. Property was depreciating, and a feeling of insecurity seized upon the people. Instead of being a source of revenue, New Netherlands, as shown by the books of the Amsterdam Chamber, had cost the company, from 1626 to 1644, inclusive, "over five hundred and fifty thousand guilders, deducting the returns received from there." It was to be expected that the slaves would share the general feeling of uneasiness and expectancy. Something had to be done to stay the panic so imminent among both classes of the colonists, bond and free. The Bureau of Accounts made certain propositions to the company calculated to act as a tonic upon the languishing hopes of the people. After reciting many methods by which the Province was to be rejuvenated, it was suggested "that it would be wise to permit the patroons, colonists, and other farmers to import as many Negroes from the Brazils as they could purchase for cash, to assist them on their farms ; as (it was maintained) these slaves could do more work for their masters, and were less expensive, than the hired laborers engaged in Holland, and conveyed to New Netherlands, "*by means of much money and large promises.*"[3]

Nor was the substitution of slave labor for white a temporary expedient. Again in 1661 a loud call for more slaves was heard.[4] In the October treaty of the same year, the Dutch yielded to the seductive offer of the English, "to deliver two or three thousand hogsheads of tobacco annually . . . in return for negroes and merchandise." At the first the Negro slave was regarded as a cheap laborer, — a blessing to the Province ; but after a while the

---

[1] Hildreth, vol. i. p. 441 ; also Hol. Doc., III. p. 351   [2] Annals of Albany, vol. ii. pp. 55–60.
[3] O'Callaghan, p. 353.   N. Y. Col. Docs., vol. ii. pp. 368, 369.   [4] Brodhead, vol. i. p. 697.

cupidity of the English induced the Hollanders to regard the Negro as a coveted, marketable chattel.

"In its scheme of political administration, the West-India Company ex-hibited too often a mercantile and selfish spirit; and in encouraging commerce in Negro slaves, it established an institution which subsisted many generations after its authority had ceased." [1]

The Dutch colony was governed by the Dutch and Roman law. The government was tripartite, — executive, legislative, and judicial, — all vested in, and exercised by, the governor and coun-cil. There seemed to be but little or no necessity for legislation on the slavery question. The Negro seemed to be a felt need in the Province, and was regarded with some consideration by the kind-hearted Hollanders. Benevolent and social, they desired to see all around them happy. The enfranchised African might and did obtain a freehold; while the Negro who remained under an institution of patriarchal simplicity, scarcely knowing he was in bondage, danced merrily at the best, in "kermis," at Christmas and Pinckster.[2] There were, doubtless, a few cases where the slaves received harsh treatment from their masters; but, as a rule, the jolly Dutch fed and clothed their slaves as well as their white servants. There were no severe rules to strip the Negroes of their personal rights, — such as social amusements or public feasts when their labors had been completed. During this entire period, they went and came among their class without let or hinderance. They were married, and given in marriage;[3] they sowed, and, in many instances, gathered an equitable share of the fruits of their labors. If there were no schools for them, there were no laws against an honest attempt to acquire knowledge at seasonable times. The Hollanders built their government upon the hearth-stone, believing it to be the earthly rock of ages to a nation that would build wisely for the future. And while it is true that they regarded commerce as the life-blood of the material existence of a people, they nevertheless found their inspiration for multifarious duties in the genial sunshine of the family circle. A nation thus constituted could not habilitate slavery with all the hideous features it wore in Virginia and Massachusetts. The slaves could not escape the good influences of the mild government of the New Netherlands, nor could the Hollanders withhold the bright-ness and goodness of their hearts from their domestic slaves.

---

[1] Brodhead, vol. i. p. 746. [2] Ibid., vol. i. p. 748. [3] Valentine's Manual for 1861, pp. 640–664.

On the 27th of August, 1664, New Netherlands fell into the hands of the English; and the city received a new name, — New York, after the famous Duke of York. When the English colors were run up over Fort Amsterdam, it received a new name, "Fort James." In the twenty-four articles in which the Hollanders surrendered their Province, there is no direct mention of slaves or slavery. The only clause that might be construed into a reference to the slaves is as follows: "IV. If any inhabitant have a mind to remove himself, he shall have a year and six weeks from this day to remove himself, wife, children, *servants*, goods, and to dispose of his lands here." There was nothing in the articles of capitulation hostile to slavery in the colony.

During the reign of Elizabeth, the English government gave its royal sanction to the slave-traffic. "In 1562 Sir John Hawkins, Sir Lionel Duchet, Sir Thomas Lodge, and Sir William Winter" — all "honorable men" — became the authors of the greatest curse that ever afflicted the earth. Hawkins, assisted by the aforenamed gentlemen, secured a ship-load of Africans from Sierra Leone, and sold them at Hispaniola. Many were murdered on the voyage, and cast into the sea. The story of this atrocity coming to the ears of the queen, she was horrified. She summoned Hawkins into her presence, in order to rebuke him for his crime against humanity. He defended his conduct with great skill and eloquence. He persuaded her Royal Highness that it was an act of humanity to remove the African from a bad to a better country, from the influences of idolatry to the influences of Christianity. Elizabeth afterwards encouraged the slave-trade.

So when New Netherlands became an English colony, slavery received substantial official encouragement, and the slave became the subject of colonial legislation.

The first laws under the English Government were issued under the patent to the Duke of York, on the 1st of March, 1665, and were known as "the Duke's Laws." It is rather remarkable that they were fashioned after the famous "Massachusetts Fundamentals," adopted in 1641. These laws have the following caption: "*Laws collected out of the several laws now in force in his majesty's American colonies and plantations.*" The first mention of slavery is contained in a section under the caption of "Bond Slavery."

"No Christian shall be kept in Bondslavery, villenage, or Captivity, Except Such who shall be Judged thereunto by Authority, or such as willing have sold or shall sell themselves, In which Case a Record of Such servitude shall be entered in the Court of Sessions held for that Jurisdiction where Such Masters shall Inhabit, provided that nothing in the Law Contained shall be to the prejudice of Master or Dame who have or shall by any Indenture or Covenant take Apprentices for Terme of Years, or other Servants for Term of years or Life." [1]

By turning to the first chapter on Massachusetts, the reader will observe that the above is the Massachusetts law of 1641 with but a very slight alteration. We find no reference to slavery directly, and the word slave does not occur in this code at all. Article 7, under the head of "Capital Laws," reads as follows: "If any person forcibly stealeth or carrieth away any mankind he shall be put to death."

On the 27th of January, 1683, Col. Thomas Dongan was sent to New York as its governor, and charged with carrying out a long list of instructions laid down by his Royal Highness the Duke of York. Gov. Dongan arrived in New York during the latter part of August; and on the 13th of September, 1683, the council sitting at Fort James promulgated an order calling upon the people to elect representatives. On the 17th October, 1683, the General Assembly met for the first time at Fort James, in the city of New York. It is a great misfortune that the journals of both houses are lost. The titles of the Acts passed have been preserved, and so far we are enabled to fairly judge of the character of the legislation of the new assembly. On the 1st November, 1683, the Assembly passed *"An Act for naturalizing all those of foreign nations* at present inhabiting within this province and professing Christianity, and for encouragement for others to come and settle within the same." [2] This law was re-enacted in 1715, and provided, that "nothing contained in this Act is to be construed to discharge or set at liberty any servant, bondman or slave, but only to have relation to such persons as are free at the making hereof." [3]

So the mild system of domestic slavery introduced by the Dutch now received the sanction of positive British law. Most of the slaves in the Province of New York, from the time they were first introduced, down to 1664, had been the property of the West-India Company. As such they had small plots of land to

---

[1] New York Hist. Coll., vol. i. pp. 322, 323.   [2] Journals of Legislative Council, vol. i. p xii.
[3] Bradford's Laws, p. 125.

work for their own benefit, and were not without hope of emancipation some day. But under the English government the condition of the slave was clearly defined by law and one of great hardships. On the 24th of October, 1684, an Act was passed in which slavery was for the first time regarded as a legitimate institution in the Province of New York under the English government.[1]

The slave-trade grew. New York began to feel the necessity of a larger number of slaves. In 1702 her "most gracious majesty," Queen Anne, among many instructions to the royal governor, directed that the people "take especial care, that God Almighty be devoutly and duly served," and that the "Royal African Company of England" "take especial care that the said Province may have a constant and sufficient supply of merchantable Negroes, at moderate rates."[2] It was a marvellous zeal that led the good queen to build up the Church of England alongside of the institution of human slavery. It was an impartial zeal that sought their mutual growth, — the one intended by our divine Lord to give mankind absolute liberty, the other intended by man to rob mankind of the great boon of freedom! But with the sanction of statutory legislation, and the silent acquiescence of the Church, the foundations of the institution of slavery were firmly laid in the approving conscience of a selfish public. Dazzled by prospective riches, and unscrupulous in the methods of accumulations, the people of the Province of New York clamored for more exacting laws by which to govern the slaves.[3] Notwithstanding Lord Cornbury had received the following instructions from the crown, "you shall endeavor to get a law passed for the restraining of any inhuman severity . . . to find out the best means to facilitate and encourage the conversion of Negroes and Indians to the Christian religion," the Colonial Assembly (the same year, 1702) passed severe laws against the slaves. It was "*An Act for regulating slaves,*" but was quite lengthy and specific. It was deemed "*not lawful to trade with negro slaves,*" and the violation of this law was followed by fine and imprisonment. "*Not above three slaves may meet together:*" if they did they were liable to be whipped by a justice of the peace, or sent to jail. "*A common whipper to be appointed,*"

---

[1] Journals, etc., N.Y., vol. i. p. xiii.   [2] Dunlap's Hist. of N.Y., vol. i. p. 260.
[3] Booth's Hist. of N.Y., vol. i. p. 270-272.

showed that the justices had more physical exercise than they cared for. "*A slave not to strike a freeman*," indicated that the slaves in New York as in Virginia were accounted as heathen. "*Penalty for concealing slaves*," and the punishment of Negroes for stealing, etc., were rather severe, but only indicated the temper of the people at that time.[1]

The recommendations to have Negro and Indian slaves baptized gave rise to considerable discussion and no little alarm. As was shown in the chapter on Virginia, the proposition to baptize slaves did not meet with a hearty indorsement from the master-class. The doctrine had obtained in most of the colonies, that a man was a freeman by virtue of his membership in a Christian church, and hence eligible to office. To escape the logic of this position, the dealer in human flesh sought to bar the door of the Church against the slave. But in 1706 "*An Act to encourage the baptizing of Negro, Indian, and mulatto slaves*," was passed in the hope of quieting the public mind on this question.

"WHereas divers of her Majesty's good Subjects, Inhabitants of this Colony, now are, and have been willing that such Negroe, Indian, and Mulatto Slaves, who belong to them, and desire the same, should be baptized, but are deterred and hindered therefrom by reason of a groundless Opinion that hath spread itself in this Colony, that by the baptizing of such Negro, Indian, or Mulatto Slave, they would become Free, and ought to be set at liberty. In order therefore to put an end to all such Doubts and scruples as have, or hereafter at any time may arise about the same —

"*Be it enacted, &c.*, that the baptizing of a Negro, Indian, or Mulatto Slave shall not be any cause or reason for the setting them or any of them at liberty.

"*And be it, &c.*, that all and every Negro, Indian, Mulatto and Mestee bastard child and children, who is, are, and shall be born of any Negro, Indian, or Mestee, shall follow the state and condition of the mother and be esteemed, reputed, taken and adjudged a slave and slaves to all intents and purposes whatsoever.

"*Provided always, and be it*, &c., That no slave whatsoever in this colony shall at any time be admitted as a witness for or against any freeman in any case, matter or cause, civil or criminal, whatsoever."[2]

---

[1] On the 22d of March, 1680, the following proclamation was issued: "Whereas, several inhabitants within this city have and doe dayly harbour, entertain and countenance Indian and neger slaves in their houses, and to them sell and deliver wine, rum, and other strong liquors, for which they receive money or goods which by the said Indian and negro slaves is pilfered, purloyned, and stolen from their several masters, by which the publick peace is broken, the damage of the master is produced, etc., therefore they are prohibited, etc.; and if neger or indian slave make application for these forbidden articles, immediate information is to be given to his master or to the mayor or oldest alderman." — DUNLAP, vol. ii. Appendix, p. cxxviii.

[2] Bradford Laws, p. 81.

So when the door of the Christian Church was opened to the Negro, he was to appear at the sacred altar with his chains on. Though emancipated from the bondage of Satan, he nevertheless remained the abject slave of the Christian colonists. Claiming spiritual kinship with Christ, the Negro could be sold at the pleasure of his master, and his family hearthstone trodden down by the slave-dealer. The humane feature of the system of slavery under the simple Dutch government, of allowing slaves to acquire an interest in the soil, was now at an end. The tendency to manumit faithful slaves called forth no approbation. The colonists grew cold and hard-fisted. They saw not God's image in the slave, — only so many dollars. There were no strong men in the pulpits of the colony who dared brave the avaricious spirit of the times. Not satisfied with colonial legislation, the municipal government of the city of New York passed, in 1710,[1] an ordinance forbidding Negroes, Indians, and Mulatto slaves from appearing "in the streets after nightfall without a lantern with a lighted candle in it."[2] The year before, a slave-market was erected at the foot of Wall Street, where slaves of every description were for sale. Negroes, Indians, and Mulattoes; men, women, and children; the old, the middle-aged, and the young, — all, as sheep in shambles, were daily declared the property of the highest cash-bidder. And what of the few who secured their freedom? Why, the law of 1712 declared that no Negro, Indian, or Mulatto that shall hereafter be set free "shall hold any land or real estate, but the same shall escheat."[3] There was, therefore, but little for the Negro in either state, — bondage or freedom. There was little in this world to allure him, to encourage him, to help him. The institution under which he suffered was one huge sepulchre, and he was buried alive.

The poor grovelling worm turns under the foot of the pedestrian. The Negro winched under his galling yoke of British colonial oppression.

A misguided zeal and an inordinate desire of conquest had

---

[1] The ordinance referred to was re-enacted on the 22d of April, 1731, and reads as follows: "No Negro, Mulatto, or Indian slave, above the age of fourteen, shall presume to appear in any of the streets, or in any other place of this city on the south side of Fresh Water, in the night time, above an hour after sunset, without a lanthorn and candle in it (unless in company with his owner or some white belonging to the family). Penalty, the watch-house that night; next day, prison, until the owner pays 4*s*, and before discharge, the slave to be whipped not exceeding forty lashes." — DUNLAP, vol. ii. Appendix, p. clxiii.

[2] Booth, vol. i. p. 271.   [3] Hurd's Bondage and Freedom, vol. i. p. 281.

led the Legislature to appropriate ten thousand pounds sterling toward an expedition to effect the conquest of Canada. Acadia had just fallen into the hands of Gov. Francis Nicholson without firing a gun, and the news had carried the New Yorkers off their feet. "On to Canada!" was the shibboleth of the adventurous colonists; and the expedition started. Eight transports, with eight hundred and sixty men, perished amid the treacherous rocks and angry waters of the St. Lawrence. The troops that had gone overland returned in chagrin. The city was wrapped in gloom : the Legislature refused to do any thing further; and here the dreams of conquest vanished. The city of New York was thrown on the defensive. The forts were repaired, and every thing put in readiness for an emergency. Like a sick man the colonists started at every rumor. On account of bad faith the Iroquois were disposed to mischief.

In the feeble condition of the colonial government, the Negro grew restless. At the first, as previously shown, the slaves were very few, but now, in 1712, were quite numerous. The Negro, the Quaker, and the Papist were a trinity of evils that the colonists most dreaded. The Negro had been badly treated; and an attempt on his part to cast off the yoke was not improbable, in the mind of the master-class. The fears of the colonists were at length realized. A Negro riot broke out. A house was burned, and a number of white persons killed; and, had it not been for the prompt and efficient aid of the troops, the city of New York would have been reduced to ashes.

Now, what was the condition of the slaves in the Christian colony of New York? They had no family relations : for a long time they lived together by common consent. They had no property, no schools, and, neglected in life, were abandoned to burial in a common ditch after death. They dared not lift their hand to strike a Christian or a Jew. Their testimony was excluded by the courts, and the power of their masters over their bodies extended sometimes to life and limb. This condition of affairs yielded its bitter fruit at length.

"Here we see the effects of that blind and wicked policy which induced England to pamper her merchants and increase her revenues, by positive instructions to the governours of her colonies, strictly enjoining them (for the good of the African company, and for the emoluments expected from the assiento contract), to fix upon America a vast negro population, torn from their homes and brought hither by force. New York was at this time filled with negroes; every householder who could afford to keep servants, was surrounded by blacks, some pampered in indolence, all carefully kept in ignorance, and considered, erroneously, as creatures whom the white could not do without, yet lived in dread of. They were feared, from their numbers, and from a consciousness, however stifled, that they were injured and might seek revenge or a better condition." [1]

The Negro plot of 1741 furnishes the most interesting and thrilling chapter in the history of the colony of New York. Unfortunately for the truth of history, there was but one historian [2] of the affair, and he an interested judge; and what he has written should be taken *cum grano salis.* His book was intended to defend the action of the court that destroyed so many innocent lives, but no man can read it without being thoroughly convinced that the decision of the court was both illogical and cruel. There is nothing in this country to equal it, except it be the burning of the witches at Salem. But in stalwart old England the Popish Plot in 1679, started by Titus Oates, is the only occurrence in human history that is so faithfully reproduced by the Negro plot. Certainly history repeats itself. Sixty-two years of history stretch between the events. One tragedy is enacted in the metropolis of the Old World, the other in the metropolis of the New World. One was instigated by a perjurer and a heretic, the other by an indentured servant, in all probability from a convict ship. The one was suggested by the hatred of the Catholics, and the other by hatred of the Negro. And in both cases the evidence that convicted and condemned innocent men and women was wrung from the lying lips of doubtful characters by an overwrought zeal on the part of the legal authorities.

Titus Oates, who claimed to have discovered the *"Popish Plot,"* was a man of the most execrable character. He was the son of an Anabaptist, took orders in the Church, and had been settled in a small living by the Duke of Norfolk. Indicted for perjury, he effected an escape in a marvellous manner. While a chaplain in the English navy he was convicted of practices not fit to be mentioned, and was dismissed from the service. He next sought communion with the Church of Rome, and made his way into the Jesuit College of St. Omers. After a brief residence among the students, he was deputed to perform a confidential mission to Spain, and, upon his return to St. Omers, was dismissed to the world on account of his habits, which were very

---

[1] Dunlap, vol. i. p. 323.   [2] Judge Daniel Horsemanden.

distasteful to Catholics. He boasted that he had only joined them to get their secrets. Such a man as this started the cry of the Popish Plot, and threw all England into a state of consternation. A chemist by the name of Tongue, on the 12th of August, 1678, had warned the king against a plot that was directed at his life, etc. But the king did not attach any importance to the statement until Tongue referred to Titus Oates as his authority. The latter proved himself a most arrant liar while on the stand : but the people were in a credulous state of mind, and Oates became the hero of the hour ; [1] and under his wicked influence many souls were hurried into eternity. Read Hume's account of the Popish Plot, and then follow the bloody narrative of the Negro plot of New York, and see how the one resembles the other.

" Some mysterious design was still suspected in every enterprise and profession : arbitrary power and Popery were apprehended as the scope of all projects : each breath or rumor made the people start with anxiety : their enemies, they thought, were in their very bosom, and had gotten possession of their sovereign's confidence. While in this timorous, jealous disposition, the cry of a *plot* all on a sudden struck their ears : they were wakened from their slumber, and like men affrightened and in the dark, took every figure for a spectre. The terror of each man became the source of terror to another. And a universal panic being diffused, reason and argument, and common-sense and common humanity, lost all influence over them. From this disposition of men's minds we are to account for the progress of the *Popish Plot*, and the credit given to it ; an event which would otherwise appear prodigious and altogether inexplicable." [2]

On the 28th of February, 1741, the house of one Robert Hogg, Esq., of New-York City, a merchant, was robbed of some fine linen, medals, silver coin, etc. Mr. Hogg's house was situated on the corner of Broad and Mill Streets, the latter sometimes being called Jew's Alley. The case was given to the officers of the law to look up.

The population of New-York City was about ten thousand, about two thousand of whom were slaves. On the 18th of March the chapel in the fort took fire from some coals carelessly left by an artificer in a gutter he had been soldering. The roof was of shingles ; and a brisk wind from the south-east started a fire, that was not observed until it had made great headway. In those times the entire populace usually turned out to assist in extinguishing fires ; but this fire being in the fort, the fear of an

---

[1] Hume, vol. vi. pp. 171–212.   [2] Ibid., vol. vi. p. 171.

explosion of the magazine somewhat checked their usual celerity on such occasions. The result was, that all the government buildings in the fort were destroyed. A militia officer by the name of Van Horne, carried away by the belief that the fire was purposely set by the Negroes, caused the beating of the drums and the posting of the "night watch." And for his vigilance he was nicknamed "Major Drum." The "Major's" apprehensions, however, were contagious. The fact that the governor reported the true cause of the fire to the Legislature had but little influence in dispossessing the people of their fears of a Negro plot. The next week the chimney of Capt. Warren's house near the fort took fire, but was saved with but slight damage. A few days after this the storehouse of a Mr. Van Zandt was found to be on fire, and it was said at the time to have been occasioned by the carelessness of a smoker. In about three days after, two fire-alarms were sounded. One was found to be a fire in some hay in a cow-stable near a Mr. Quick's house. It was soon extinguished. The other alarm was on account of a fire in the kitchen loft of the dwelling of a Mr. Thompson. On the next day coals were discovered under the stables of a Mr. John Murray on Broadway. On the next morning an alarm called the people to the residence of Sergeant Burns, near the fort ; and in a few hours the dwelling of a Mr. Hilton, near Fly Market, was found to be on fire. But the flames in both places were readily extinguished. It was thought that the fire was purposely set at Mr. Hilton's, as a bundle of tow was found near the premises. A short time before these strange fires broke out, a Spanish vessel, partly manned by Spanish Catholic Negroes, had been brought into the port of New York as a prize. All the crew that were Negroes were hurried into the Admiralty Court ; where they were promptly condemned to slavery, and an order issued for their sale. The Negroes pleaded their freedom in another country, but had no counsel to defend them. A Capt. Sarly purchased one of these Negroes. Now, Capt. Sarly's house adjoined that of Mr. Hilton's ; and so, when the latter's house was discovered to be on fire, a cry was raised, "The Spanish Negroes ! The Spanish ! Take up the Spanish Negroes !" Some persons took it upon themselves to question Capt. Sarly's Negro about the fires, and it is said that he behaved in an insolent manner ; whereupon he was sent to jail. A magistrate gave orders to the constables to arrest and incarcerate the rest of the Spanish Negroes. The magistrates held a meeting the same day, in the afternoon; and, while they were deliberating about the matter, another fire broke out in Col. Phillipes's storehouse. Some of the white people cried "Negro! Negro!" and "Cuff Phillipes!" Poor Cuff, startled at the cry, ran to his master's house, from whence he was dragged to jail by an excited mob. Judge Horsemanden says, —

"Many people had such terrible apprehensions on this occasion that several Negroes (many of whom had assisted to put out the fire) who were met in the streets, were hurried away to jail; and when they were there they were continued some time in confinement before the magistrates could spare time to examine into their several cases."[1]

Let the reader return now to the robbery committed in Mr. Hogg's house on the 28th of February. The officers thought they had traced the stolen goods to a public house on the North River, kept by a person named John Hughson. This house had been a place of resort for Negroes; and it was searched for the articles, but nothing was found. Hughson had in his service an indentured servant, — a girl of sixteen years, — named Mary Burton. She intimated to a neighbor that the goods were concealed in Hughson's house, but that it would be at the expense of her life to make this fact known. This information was made known to the sheriff, and he at once apprehended the girl and produced her before Alderman Banker. This benevolent officer promised the girl her freedom on the ground that she should tell all she knew about the missing property. For prudential reasons the Alderman ordered Mary Burton to be taken to the City Hall, corner Wall and Nassua Streets. On the 4th of March the justices met at the City Hall. In the mean while John Hughson and his wife had been arrested for receiving stolen goods. They were now examined in the presence of Mary Burton. Hughson admitted that some goods had been brought to his house, produced them, and turned them over to the court. It appears from the testimony of the Burton girl that another party, dwelling in the house of the Hughson's, had taken part in receiving the stolen articles. She was a girl of bad character, called Margaret Sorubiero, *alias* Solinburgh, *alias* Kerry, but commonly called Peggy Carey. This woman had lived in the home of the Hughsons for about ten months, but at one time during this period had remained a short while at the house of John Rommes, near the new Bat-

---

[1] Horsemanden's Negro Plot, p. 29.

tery, but had returned to Hughson's again. The testimony of Mary Burton went to show that a Negro by the name of Cæsar Varick, but called Quin, on the night in which the burglary was committed, entered Peggy's room through the window. The next morning Mary Burton saw "speckled linen" in Peggy's room, and that the man Varick gave the deponent two pieces of silver. She further testified that Varick drank two mugs of punch, and bought of Hughson a pair of stockings, giving him a lump of silver; and that Hughson and his wife received and hid away the linen.[1] Mr. John Varick (it was spelled Vaarck then), a baker, the owner of Cæsar, occupied a house near the new Battery, the kitchen of which adjoined the yard of John Romme's house. He found some of Robert Hogg's property under his kitchen floor, and delivered it to the mayor. Upon this revelation Romme fled to New Jersey, but was subsequently captured at Brunswick. He had followed shoemaking and tavern-keeping, and was, withal, a very suspicious character.

Up to this time nothing had been said about a Negro plot. It was simply a case of burglary. Hughson had admitted receiving certain articles, and restored them; Mr. Varick had found others, and delivered them to the mayor.

The reader will remember that the burglary took place on the 28th of February; that the justices arraigned the Hughsons, Mary Burton, and Peggy Carey on the 4th of March; that the first fire broke out on the 18th, the second on the 25th, of March, the third on the 1st of April, and the fourth and fifth on the 4th of April; that on the 5th of April coals were found disposed so as to burn a haystack, and that the day following two houses were discovered to be on fire.

On the 11th of April the Common Council met. The following gentlemen were present: John Cruger, Esq., mayor; the recorder, Daniel Horsemanden; aldermen, Gerardus Stuyvesant, William Romaine, Simon Johnson, John Moore, Christopher Banker, John Pintard, John Marshall; assistants, Henry Bogert, Isaac Stoutenburgh, Philip Minthorne, George Brinckerhoff, Robert Benson, and Samuel Lawrence. Recorder Horsemanden sug-

---

[1] As far back as 1684 the following was passed against the entertainment of slaves: "No person to countenance or entertain any negro or Indian slave, or sell or deliver to them any strong liquor, without liberty from his master, or receive from them any money or goods; but, upon any offer made by a slave, to reveal the same to the owner, or to the mayor, under penalty of £5." — DUNLAP, vol. ii. Appendix, p. cxxxiii.

gested to the council that the governor be requested to offer rewards for the apprehension of the incendiaries and all persons implicated, and that the city pay the cost, etc. It was accordingly resolved that the lieutenant-governor be requested to offer a reward of one hundred pounds current money of the Province to any white person, and pardon, if concerned; and twenty pounds, freedom, and, if concerned, pardon to any slave (the master to be paid twenty-five pounds); and to any free Negro, Mulatto, or Indian, forty-five pounds and pardon, if concerned. The mayor and the recorder (Horsemanden), called upon Lieut.-Gov. Clark, and laid the above resolve before him.

The city was now in a state of great excitement. The air was peopled with the wildest rumors.

On Monday the 13th of April each alderman, assistant, and constable searched his ward. The militia was called out, and sentries posted at the cross-streets. While the troops were patrolling the streets, the aldermen were examining Negroes in reference to the origin of the fires. Nothing was found. The Negroes denied all knowledge of the fires or a plot.

On the 21st of April, 1741, the Supreme Court convened.[1] Judges Frederick Phillipse and Daniel Horsemanden called the *grand jury*. The members were as follows: Robert Watts, merchant, foreman; Jeremiah Latouche, Joseph Read, Anthony Rutgers, John M'Evers, John Cruger, jun., John Merrit, Adoniah Schuyler, Isaac DePeyster, Abraham Ketteltas, David Provoost, Rene Hett, Henry Beeckman, jun., David van Horne, George Spencer, Thomas Duncan, and Winant Van Zandt, —all set down as merchants, —a respectable, intelligent, and influential grand jury! Judge Phillipse informed the jury that the people "have been put into many frights and terrors," in regard to the fires; that it was their duty to use "all lawful means" to discover the guilty parties, for there was "much room to suspect" that the fires were not accidental. He told them that there were many persons in jail upon whom suspicion rested; that arson was felony at common law, even though the fire is extinguished, or goes out itself; that arson was a deep crime, and, if the perpetrators were not apprehended and punished, "who can say he is safe, or where will it end?" The learned judge then went on to deliver a moral lecture against the wickedness of selling "penny drams" to Negroes,

---

[1] Horsemanden's Negro Plot, p. 33.

without the consent of their masters.   In conclusion, he charged
the grand jury to present "all conspiracies, combinations and
other offences."

It should be kept in mind that Mary Burton was only a witness
in the burglary case already mentioned.   Up to that time there
had been no fires.   The fires, and wholesale arrests of innocent
Negroes, followed the robbery.   But the grand jury called Mary
Burton to testify in reference to the fires.   She refused to be
sworn.   She was questioned concerning the fires, but gave no
answer.   Then the proclamation of the mayor, offering protection, pardon, freedom, and one hundred pounds, was read.   It had
the desired effect.   The girl opened her mouth, and spake all the
words that the jury desired.   At first she agreed to tell all she
knew about the stolen goods, but would say nothing about the
fires.   This declaration led the jury to infer that she could, but
would not say any thing about the fires.   After a moral lecture
upon her duty in the matter in the light of eternal reward, and a
reiteration of the proffered reward that then awaited her wise
decision, her memory brightened, and she immediately began to
tell *all* she knew.   She said that a Negro named Prince, belonging to a Mr. Auboyman, and Prince (Varick) brought the goods,
stolen from Mr. Hogg's house, to the house of her master, and
that Hughson, his wife, and Peggy (Carey) received them;
further, that Cæsar, Prince, and Cuffee (Phillipse) had frequently
met at Hughson's tavern, and discoursed about burning the fort;
that they had said they would go down to the Fly (the east end of
the city), and burn the entire place; and that Hughson and his
wife had assented to these insurrectionary remarks, and promised
to assist them.   She added, by way of fulness and emphasis, that
when a handful of wretched slaves, seconded by a miserable and
ignorant white tavern-keeper, should have lain the city in ashes,
and murdered eight or nine thousand persons, — then Cæsar
should be governor, Hughson king, and Cuffee supplied with
abundant riches!   The loquacious Mary remembered that this
intrepid trio had said, that when they burned the city it would be
in the night, so they could murder the people as they came out of
their homes.   It should not be forgotten that *all* the fires broke
out in the daytime!

It is rather remarkable and should be observed, that this wonderful witness stated that her master, John Hughson, had threatened to poison her if she told anybody that the stolen goods were

in his house; that all the Negroes swore they would burn her if she told; and that, when they talked of burning the town during their meetings, there were no white persons present save her master, mistress, and Peggy Carey.

The credulous Horsemanden tells us that "the evidence of a conspiracy," not only to burn the city, but also "to destroy and murder the people," was most "astonishing to the grand jury!" But that any white person should confederate with slaves in such a wicked and cruel purpose was astounding beyond measure! And the grand jury was possessed of the same childlike faith in the ingenious narrative of the wily Mary. In their report to the judges, they set forth in strong terms their faith in the statements of the deponent, and required the presence of Peggy Carey. The extent of the delusion of the judges, jury, and people may be seen in the fact, that, immediately upon the report of the jury, the judges summoned the entire bar of the city of New York to meet them. The following gentlemen responded to the call: Messrs. Murray, Alexander, Smith, Chambers, Nichols, Lodge, and Jameson. All the lawyers were present except the attorney-general. By the act of 1712, "for preventing, suppressing and punishing the conspiracy and insurrection of negroes and other slaves," [1] a justice of the peace could try the refractory slaves at once. But here was a deep, dark, and bloody plot to burn the city and murder its inhabitants, in which *white* persons were implicated. This fact led the learned judges to conclude it wise and prudent to refer this whole matter to the Supreme Court. And the generous offer of the *entire* bar of New-York City to assist, in turns, in every trial, should remain evermore an indestructible monument to their unselfish devotion to their city, the existence of which was threatened by less than a score of ignorant, penniless Negro slaves!

By the testimony of Mary Burton, Peggy Carey stood convicted as one of the conspirators. She had already languished in jail for more than a month. The judges thought it advisable to examine her in her cell. They tried to cajole her into criminating others; but she stoutly denied all knowledge of the fires, and said "that if she should accuse anybody of any such thing, she must accuse innocent persons, and wrong her own soul."

On the 24th of April, Cæsar Varick, Prince Auboyman, John

---

[1] Bradford's Laws, pp. 141-144.

Hughson, his wife, and Peggy Carey were arraigned for felony, and pleaded not guilty. Cæsar and Prince were first put on trial. As they did not challenge the jury, the following gentlemen were sworn : Messrs. Roger French, John Groesbeck, John Richard, Abraham Kipp, George Witts, John Thurman, Patrick Jackson, Benjamin Moore, William Hammersley, John Lashiere, Joshua Sleydall, and John Shurmer. "Guilty!" as charged in the indictment. They had committed the robbery, so said the jury.

On the 3d of May one Arthur Price, a common thief, was committed to jail for theft. He occupied a cell next to the notorious Peggy Carey. In order to bring himself into favor with the judges, he claimed to have had a conversation with Peggy through the hole in the door. Price says she told him that "she was afraid of those fellows" (the Negroes); that if they said any thing in any way involving her she would hang every one of them; that she did not care to go on the stand again unless she was called; that when asked if she intended to set the town on fire she said no; but she knew about the plot; that Hughson and his wife "were sworn with the rest;" that she was not afraid of "Prince, Cuff, Cæsar, and Fork's Negro — not Cæsar, but another," because they "were all true-hearted fellows." This remarkable conversation was flavored throughout with the vilest species of profanity. Notwithstanding this interview was between a common Irish prostitute and a wretched sneak-thief, it had great weight with the solemn and upright judges.

In the midst of this trial, seven barns were burnt in the town of Hackinsack. Two Negroes were suspected of the crime, but there was not the slightest evidence that they were guilty. But one of them said that he had discharged a gun at the party who set his master's barn on fire, but did not kill any one. The other one was found loading a gun with two bullets. This was enough to convict. They were burnt alive at a stake. This only added fuel to the flame of public excitement in New York.

On the 6th of May (Wednesday) two more arrests were made, — Hughson's daughter Sarah, suspected of being a confederate, and Mr. Sleydall's Negro Jack, — on suspicion of having put fire to Mr. Murray's haystack. On the same day the judges arraigned the white persons implicated in the case, — John Hughson, his wife, and Peggy Carey. The jury promptly found them guilty of "receiving stolen goods." "Peggy Carey," says Recorder Horsemanden, "seeming to think it high time to do something to recommend herself to mercy, made a voluntary confession." This vile, foul-mouthed prostitute takes the stand, and gives a new turn to the entire affair. She removes the scene of the conspiracy to another tavern near the new Battery, where John Romme had made a habit of entertaining, *contrary to law*, Negro slaves. Peggy had seen many meetings at this place, particularly in December, 1740. At that time she mentioned the following Negroes as being present : Cuff, Brash, Curacoa, Cæsar, Patrick, Jack, Cato ; but *her* especial Cæsar Varick was not implicated ! Romme administered an oath to all these Negroes, and then made a proposition to them ; viz., that they should destroy the fort, burn the town, and bring the spoils to him. He engaged to divide with them, and take them to a new country, where he would give them their freedom. Mrs. Romme was present during this conversation ; and, after the Negroes had departed, she and the deponent (Peggy) were sworn by Romme to eternal secrecy. Mrs. Romme denied swearing to the conspiracy, but acknowledged that her husband had received stolen goods, that he sold drams to Negroes who kept game-fowls there ; but that never more than three Negroes came at a time. She absconded in great fright. It has been mentioned that Peggy Carey had lived at the tavern of John Romme for a short time, and that articles belonging to Mr. Hogg had been found under the kitchen floor of the house next to Romme's.

The judges evidently reasoned that all Negroes would steal, or that stealing was incident upon or implied by the condition of the slave. Then Romme kept a "tippling-house," and defied the law by selling "drams" to Negroes. Now, a man who keeps a "tippling-house" was liable to encourage a conspiracy.

A full list of the names of the persons implicated by Peggy was handed to the proper officers, and those wicked persons apprehended. They were brought before the redoubtable Peggy for identification. She accused them of being sworn conspirators. They all denied the charge. Then they were turned over to Mary Burton ; and she, evidently displeased at Peggy's attempt to rival her in the favor of the powerful judges, testified that she knew them not. But it was vain. Peggy had the ear of the court, and the terror-stricken company was locked up in the jail. Alarmed at their helpless situation, the ignorant Negroes began "to accuse one another, as it would seem, by way of injuring an enemy and guarding themselves."

Cæsar and Prince, having been tried and convicted of felony, were sentenced to be hanged.   The record says, —

"Monday, 11th of May. Cæsar and Prince were executed this day at the gallows, according to sentence : they died very stubbornly, without confessing *any thing about the conspiracy :* and denied that *they knew any thing about it to the last.* The body of Cæsar was accordingly hung in chains." [1]

On the 13th of May, 1741, a solemn fast was observed ; "because many houses and dwellings had been fired about our ears, without any discovery of the cause or occasion of them, which had put us into the utmost consternation." Excitement ran high. Instead of getting any light on the affair, the plot thickened.

On the 6th of May, Hughson, his wife, and Peggy Carey had been tried and found guilty, as has already been stated.   Sarah Hughson, daughter of the Hughsons, was in jail.   Mary Burton was the heroine of the hour.   Her word was law, Whoever she named was produced in court.   The sneak-thief, Arthur Price, was employed by the judges to perform a mission that was at once congenial to his tastes and in harmony with his criminal education.   He was sent among the incarcerated Negroes to administer punch, in the desperate hope of getting more "confessions !"   Next, he was sent to Sarah Hughson to persuade her to accuse her father and mother of complicity in the conspiracy. He related a conversation he had with Sarah, but she denied it to his teeth with great indignation.   This vile and criminal method of securing testimony of a conspiracy never brought the blush to the cheek of a single officer of the law.   "None of these things moved" them.   They were themselves so completely lost in the general din and excitement, were so thoroughly convinced that a plot existed, and that it was their duty to prove it in some manner or other, — that they believed every thing that went to establish the guilt of any one.

Even a feeble-minded boy was arrested, and taken before the grand jury.   He swore that he knew nothing of the plot to burn the town, but the kind magistrates told him that if he would tell the truth he should not be hanged.   Ignorant as these helpless slaves were, they now understood "telling the truth" to mean to criminate some one in the plot, and thus gratify the inordinate hunger of the judges and jury for testimony relating to a

---

[1] Horsemanden's Negro Plot, p. 60.

"conspiracy." This Negro imbecile began his task of telling "what he knew," which was to be rewarded by allowing him to leave without being hung! He deposed that Quack desired him to burn the fort; that Cuffee said he would fire one house, Cura-coa Dick another, and so on *ad infinitum.* He was asked by one of the learned gentlemen, "what the Negroes intended by all this mischief?" He answered, "To kill all the gentlemen and take their wives; that one of the fellows already hanged, was to be an officer in the Long Bridge Company, and the other, in the Fly Company." [1]

On the 25th of May a large number of Negroes were arrested. The boy referred to above (whose name was Sawney, or Sandy) was called to the stand again on the 26th, when he grew very talkative. He said that "at a meeting of Negroes he was called in and frightened into undertaking to burn the slip Market;" that he witnessed some of the Negroes in their attempts to burn certain houses; that at the house of one Comfort, he, with others, was sworn to secrecy and fidelity to each other; said he was never at either tavern, Hughson's nor Romme's; and ended his revelations by accusing a woman of setting fire to a house, and of murdering her child. As usual, after such confessions, more arrests followed. Quack and Cuffee were tried and convicted of felony, "for wickedly and maliciously conspiring with others to burn the town and murder the inhabitants." This was an occasion to draw forth the eloquence of the attorney-general; and in fervid utterance he pictured the Negroes as "monsters, devils, etc." A Mr. Rosevelt, the master of Quack, swore that his slave was home when the fire took place in the fort; and Mr. Phillipse, Cuffee's master, testified as much for his servant. But this testimony was not what the magistrates wanted: so they put a soldier on the stand who swore that Quack *did* come to the fort the day of the fire; that his wife lived there, and when he insisted on going in he (the sentry) knocked him down, but the officer of the guard passed him in. Lawyer Smith, "whose eloquence had disfranchised the Jews," was called upon to sum up. He thought too much favor had been shown the Negroes, in that they had been accorded a trial as if they were freemen; that the wicked Negroes might have been proceeded against in a most summary manner; that the Negro witnesses had been treated with too much consid-

---

[1] The city of New York was divided into parts at that time, and comprised two militia districts.

eration ; that " the law requires no oath to be administered to
them ; and, indeed, it would be a profanation of it to administer
it to a heathen in a legal form ; " that " the monstrous ingratitude
of this black tribe is what exceedingly aggravates their guilt ; "
that their condition as slaves was one of happiness and peace ;
that " they live without care ; are commonly better fed and
clothed than the poor of most Christian countries ; they are
indeed slaves," continued the eloquent and logical attorney, " but
under the protection of the law : none can hurt them with impunity ; but notwithstanding all the kindness and tenderness with
which they have been treated among us, yet this is the second
attempt of this same kind that this brutish and bloody species of
mankind have made within one age ! " Of course the jury knew
their duty, and merely went through the form of going out and
coming in immediately with a verdict of " guilty." The judge
sentenced them to be chained to a stake and burnt to death, —
" and the Lord have mercy upon your poor wretched souls." His
Honor told them that " they should be thankful that their feet
were caught in the net ; that the mischief had fallen upon their
own pates." He advised them to consider the tenderness and
humanity with which they had been treated ; that they were the
most abject wretches, the very outcasts of the nations of the
earth ; and, therefore, they should look to their souls, for as to
their bodies, they would be burnt.

These poor fellows were accordingly chained to the stake the
next Sunday ; but, before the fuel was lighted, Deputy Sheriff
More and Mr. Rosevelt again questioned Quack and Cuffee, and
reduced their confessions to paper, for they had stoutly protested
their innocence while in court. In hope of being saved they
confessed, in substance, that Hughson contrived to burn the town,
and kill the people ; that a company of Negroes voted Quack the
proper person to burn the fort, because his wife lived there ; that
he did set the chapel on fire with a lighted stick ; that Mary
Burton had told the truth, and that she could implicate many
more if she would, etc. All this general lying was done with the
understanding that the confessors were to be reprieved until the
governor could be heard from. But a large crowd had gathered
to witness the burning of these poor Negroes, and they compelled
the sheriff to proceed with the ceremonies. The convicted slaves
were burned.

On the 1st of June the boy Sawney was again put upon the

witness-stand. His testimony led to the arrest of more Negroes. He charged them with having been sworn to the plot, and with having sharp penknives with which to kill white men. One Fortune testified that he never knew of houses where conspirators met, nor did he know Hughson, but accuses Sawney, and Quack who had been burnt. The next witness was a Negro girl named Sarah. She was frightened out of her senses. She foamed at the mouth, uttered the bitterest imprecations, and denied all knowledge of a conspiracy. But the benevolent gentlemen who conducted the trial told her that others had said certain things in proof of the existence of a conspiracy, that the only way to save her life was to acknowledge that there had been a conspiracy to burn the town and kill the inhabitants. She then assented to all that was told her, and thereby implicated quite a number of Negroes ; but, when her testimony was read to her, she again denied all. She was without doubt a fit subject for an insane-asylum rather than for the witness-stand, in a cause that involved so many human lives.

It will be remembered that John Hughson, his wife, and daughter had been in the jail for a long time. He now desired to be called to the witness-stand. He begged to be sworn, that in the most solemn manner he might deny all knowledge of the conspiracy, and exculpate his wife and child. But the modest recorder reminded him of the fact that he stood convicted as a felon already, that he and his family were doomed to be hanged, and that, therefore, it would be well for him to "confess all." He was sent back to jail unheard. Already condemned to be hung, the upright magistrates had Hughson tried again for "conspiracy" on the 4th of June! The indictments were three in number: *First*, that Hughson, his wife, his daughter, and Peggy Carey, with three Negroes, Cæsar, Prince, and Cuffee, conspired in March last to set fire to the house in the fort. *Second*, That Quack (already burnt) did set fire to and burn the house, and that the prisoners, Hughson, his wife, daughter Sarah, and Peggy, encouraged him so to do. *Third*, That Cuffee (already burnt) did set fire to Phillipse's house, and burnt it ; and they, the prisoners, procured and encouraged him so to do. Hughson, his family, and Peggy pleaded not guilty to all the above indictments. The attorney-general delivered a spirited address to the jury, which was more forcible than elegant. He denounced the unlucky Hughson as "infamous, inhuman, an arch-rebel against God, his

king, and his country, — a devil incarnate," etc. He was ably
assisted by eminent counsel for the king, — Joseph Murray, James
Alexander, William Smith, and John Chambers. Mary Burton was
called again. She swore that Negroes used to go to Hughson's
at night, eat and drink, and sometimes buy provisions; that
Hughson did swear the Negroes to secrecy in the plot; that she
herself had seen seven or eight guns and swords, a bag of shot,
and a barrel of gunpowder at Hughson's house; that the prisoner
told her he would kill her if she ever revealed any thing she knew
or saw; wanted her to swear like the rest, offered her silk gowns,
and gold rings, — but none of those tempting things moved the
virtuous Mary. Five other witnesses testified that they heard
Quack and Cuffee say to Hughson while in jail, "This is what you
have brought us to." The Hughsons had no counsel, and but three
witnesses. One of them testified that he had lived in Hughson's
tavern about three months during the past winter, and had never
seen Negroes furnished entertainment there. The two others said
that they had never seen any evil in the man nor in his house, etc.

"William Smith, Esq." now took the floor to sum up. He
told the jury that it was "black and hellish" to burn the town,
and then kill them all; that John Hughson, by his complicity in
this crime, had made himself blacker than the Negroes; that the
credit of the witnesses was good, and that there was nothing left
for them to do but to find the prisoners guilty, as charged in the
indictment. The judge charged the jury, that the evidence
against the prisoners "is ample, full, clear, and satisfactory.
They were found guilty in twenty minutes, and on the 8th of
June were brought into court to receive sentence. The judge
told them that they were guilty of a terrible crime; that they had
not only made Negroes their equals, but superiors, by waiting
upon, keeping company with, entertaining them with meat, drink,
and lodging; that the most amazing part of their conduct was
their part in a plot to burn the town, and murder the inhabitants,
— to have consulted with, aided, and abetted the "black seed of
Cain," was an unheard of crime, — that although "with uncommon
assurance they deny the fact, and call on God, as a witness of
their innocence, He, out of his goodness and mercy, has confounded them, and proved their guilt, to the satisfaction of the
court and jury." After a further display of forensic eloquence,
the judge sentenced them "to be hanged by the neck 'till dead,"
on Friday, the 12th of June, 1741.

The Negro girl Sarah, referred to above, who was before the jury on the 1st of June in such a terrified state of body and mind, was re-called on the 5th of June. She implicated twenty Negroes, whom she declared were present at the house of Comfort, whetting their knives, and avowing that "they would kill white people." On the 6th of June, Robin, Cæsar, Cook, Cuffee, and Jack, another Cuffee, and Jamaica were arrested, and put upon trial on the 8th of June. It is a sad fact to record, even at this distance, that these poor blacks, without counsel, friends, or money, were tried and convicted upon the evidence of a poor ignorant, hysterical girl, and the "dying confession" of Quack and Cuffee, who "confessed" with the understanding that they should be free! Tried and found guilty on the 8th, without clergy or time to pray, they were burned at the stake the next day! Only Jack found favor with the court, and that favor was purchased by perjury. He was respited until it "was found how well he would deserve further favor." It was next to impossible to understand him, so two white gentlemen were secured to act as interpreters. Jack testified to having seen Negroes at Hughson's tavern; that "when they were eating, he said they began to talk about setting the houses on fire:" he was so good as to give the names of about fourteen Negroes whom he heard say that they would set their masters' houses on fire, and then rush upon the whites and kill them; that at one of these meetings there were five or six Spanish Negroes present, whose conversation he could not understand; that they waited a month and a half for the Spaniards and French to come, but when they came not, set fire to the fort. As usual, more victims of these confessors swelled the number already in the jail; which was, at this time, full to suffocation.

On the 19th of June the lieutenant-governor issued a proclamation of freedom to all who would "confess and discover" before the 1st of July. Several Indians were in the prison, charged with conspiracy. The confessions and discoveries were numerous. Every Negro charged with being an accomplice of the unfortunate wretches that had already perished at the stake began to accuse some one else of complicity in the plot. They all knew of many Negroes who were going to cut the white people's throats with penknives; and when the town was in flames they were to "meet at the end of Broadway, next to the fields!" And it must be recorded, to the everlasting disgrace of the judiciary

of New York, that scores of ignorant, helpless, and innocent
Negroes — and a few white people too — were convicted upon
the confessions of the terror-stricken witnesses! There is not a
court to-day in all enlightened Christendom that would accept as
evidence — not even circumstantial — the incoherent utterances
of these Negro "confessors." And yet an intelligent (?) New-
York court thought the evidence "clear (?), and satisfactory!"

But the end was not yet reached. A new turn was to be
given to the notorious Mary Burton. The reader will remember
that she said that there never were any white persons present
when the burning of the town was the topic of conversation,
except her master and mistress and Peggy Carey. But on the
25th of June the budding Mary accused Rev. John Ury, a reputed
Catholic priest, and a schoolmaster in the town, and one Campbell, also a school-teacher, of having visited Hughson's tavern
with the conspirators.

On the 26th of June, nine more Negroes were brought before
the court and arraigned. Seven pleaded guilty in the hope of a
reprieve: two were tried and convicted upon the testimony of
Mary Burton. Eight more were arraigned, and pleaded guilty;
followed by seven more, some of whom pleaded guilty, and some
not guilty. Thus, in one day, the court was enabled to dispose of
twenty-four persons.

On the 27th of June, one Adam confessed that he knew of
the plot, but said he was enticed into it by Hughson, three years
before; that Hughson told him that he knew a man who could
forgive him all his sins. So between John Hughson's warm rum,
and John Ury's ability to forgive sin, the virtuous Adam found
all his scruples overcome; and he took the oath. A Dr. Hamilton
who lodged at Holt's, and the latter also, are brought into court as
accused of being connected with the plot. It was charged that
Holt directed his Negro Joe to set fire to the play-house at the
time he should indicate. At the beginning of the trial only four
white persons were mentioned; but now they began to multiply,
and barrels of powder to increase at a wonderful rate. The confessions up to this time had been mere repetitions. The arrests
were numerous, and the jail crowded beyond its capacity. The
poor Negroes implicated were glad of an opportunity to "confess" against some one else, and thereby save their own lives.
Recorder Horsemanden says, "Now many negroes began to
squeak, in order to lay hold of the benefit of the proclamation."

He deserves the thanks of humanity for his frankness! For before the proclamation there were not more than seventy Negroes in jail; but, within eight days after it was issued, thirty more frightened slaves were added to the number. And Judge Horsemanden says, " 'Twas difficult to find room for them, nor could we see any likelihood of stopping the impeachments." The Negroes turned to accusing white persons, and seven or eight were arrested. The sanitary condition of the prison now became a subject of grave concern. The judges and lawyers consulted together, and agreed to pardon some of the prisoners to make room in the jail. They also thought it prudent to lump the confessions, and thereby facilitate their work; but the confessions went on, and the jail filled up again.

The Spanish Negroes taken by an English privateer, and adjudged to slavery by the admiralty court, were now taken up, tried, convicted, and sentenced to be hung. Five others received sentence the same day.

The bloody work went on. The poor Negroes in the jail, in a state of morbid desperation, turned upon each other the blistering tongue of accusation. They knew that they were accusing each other innocently, — as many confessed afterwards, — but this was the last straw that these sinking people could see to catch at, and this they did involuntarily. "Victims were required; and those who brought them to the altar of Moloch, purchased their own safety, or, at least, their lives."

On the 2d of July, one Will was produced before Chief-Justice James DeLancy. He plead guilty, and was sentenced to be burnt to death on the 4th of July. On the 6th of July, eleven plead guilty. One Dundee implicates Dr. Hamilton with Hughson in giving Negroes rum and swearing them to the plot. A white man by the name of William Nuill deposed that a Negro — belonging to Edward Kelly, a butcher — named London swore by God that if he should be arrested and cast into the jail, he would hang or burn all the Negroes in New York, guilty or not guilty. On this same day five Negroes were hanged. One of them was "hung in chains" upon the same gibbet with Hughson. And the Christian historian says "the town was amused" on account of a report that Hughson had turned black and the Negro white! The vulgar and sickening description of the condition of the bodies, in which Mr. Horsemanden took evident relish, we withhold from the reader. It was rumored that a Negro doctor had administered poison to the convicts, and hence the change in the bodies after death.

In addition to the burning of the Negro Will, on the 4th of July, was the sensation created by his accusing two white soldiers, Kane and Kelly, with complicity in the conspiracy. Kane was examined the next day : said that he had never been to the house of John Romme; acknowledged that he had received a stolen silver spoon, given to his wife, and sold it to one Van Dype, a silversmith ; that he never knew John Ury, etc. Knowing Mary Burton was brought forward, — as she always was when the trials began to lag, — and accused Kane. He earnestly denied the accusation at first, but finally confessed that he was at Hughson's in reference to the plot on two several occasions, but was induced to go there "by Corker, Coffin, and Fagan." After his tongue got limbered up, and his memory refreshed, he criminated Ury. He implicated Hughson's father and three brothers, Hughson's mother-in-law, an old fortune-teller, as being parties to the plot as sworn "to burn, and kill ;" that Ury christened some of the Negroes, and even had the temerity to attempt to proselyte him, Kane; that Ury asked him if he could read Latin, could he read English ; to both questions he answered no ; that the man Coffin read to him, and descanted upon the benefits of being a Roman Catholic; that they could forgive sins, and save him from hell ; and that if he had not gone away from their company they might have seduced him to be a Catholic ; that one Conolly, on Governor's Island, admitted that he was "bred up a priest;" that one Holt, a dancing-master, also knew of the plot; and then described the mystic ceremony of swearing the plotters. He said, "There was a black ring made on the floor, about a foot and a half in diameter; and Hughson bid every one put off the left shoe and put their toes within the ring ; and Mrs. Hughson held a bowl of punch over their heads, as the Negroes stood around the circle, and Hughson pronounced the oath above mentioned, (something like a freemason's oath and penalties,) and every negro severally repeated the oath after him, and then Hughson's wife fed them with a draught out of the bowl."

This was "new matter," so to speak, and doubtless broke the monotony of the daily recitals to which their honors had been listening all summer. Kane was about to deprive Mary Burton of her honors ; and, as he could not write, he made his mark. A peddler named Coffin was arrested and examined. He denied all knowledge of the plot, never saw Hughson, never was at his place, saw him for the first time when he was executed; had never seen Kane but once, and then at Eleanor Waller's, where they drank beer together. But the court committed him. Kane and Mary Burton accused Edward Murphy. Kane charged David Johnson, a hatter, as one of the conspirators; while Mary Burton accuses Andrew Ryase, "little Holt," the dancing-master, John Earl, and seventeen soldiers, — all of whom were cast into prison.

On the 16th of July nine Negroes were arraigned: four plead guilty, two were sentenced to be burnt, and the others to be hanged. On the next day seven Negroes plead guilty. One John Schultz came forward, and made a deposition that perhaps had some little influence on the court and the community at large. He swore that a Negro man slave, named Cambridge, belonging to Christopher Codwise, Esq., did on the 9th of June, 1741, confess to the deponent, in the presence of Codwise and Richard Baker, that the confession he had made before Messrs. Lodge and Nichols was entirely false; viz., that he had confessed himself guilty of participating in the conspiracy; had accused a Negro named Cajoe through fear; that he had heard some Negroes talking together in the jail, and saying that if they did not confess they would be hanged; that what he said about Horsefield Cæsar was a lie; that he had never known in what section of the town Hughson lived, nor did he remember ever hearing his name, until it had become the town talk that Hughson was concerned in a plot to burn the town and murder the inhabitants.

This did not in the least abate the zeal of Mary Burton and William Kane. They went on in their work of accusing white people and Negroes, receiving the approving smiles of the magistrates. Mary Burton says that John Earl, who lived in Broadway, used to come to Hughson's with ten soldiers at a time; that these white men were to command the Negro companies; that John Ury used to be present; and that a man near the Mayor's Market, who kept a shop where she (Mary Burton) got rum from, a doctor, by nationality a Scotchman, who lived by the Slip, and another dancing-master, named Corry, used to meet with the conspirators at Hughson's tavern.

On the 14th of July, John Ury was examined, and denied ever having been at Hughson's, or knowing any thing about the conspiracy; said he never saw any of the Hughsons, nor did he know Peggy Carey. But William Kane, the soldier, insisted that Ury did visit the house of Hughson. Ury was again committed. On the next day eight persons were tried and convicted upon the evidence of Kane and Mary Burton. The jail was filling up again, and the benevolent magistrates pardoned fourteen Negroes. Then they turned their judicial minds to the case of William Kane *vs.* John Ury. First, he was charged with having counselled, procured, and incited a Negro slave, Quack, to burn the king's house in the fort : to which he pleaded not guilty. Second, that being a priest, made by the authority of the pretended See of Rome, he had come into the Province and city of New York after the time limited by law against Jesuits and Popish priests, passed in the eleventh year of William III., and had remained for the space of seven months ; that he had announced himself to be an ecclesiastical person, made and ordained by the authority of the See of Rome ; and that he had appeared so to be by celebrating masses and granting absolution, etc. To these charges Ury pleaded not guilty, and requested a copy of the indictments, but was only allowed a copy of the second ; and pen, ink, and paper grudgingly granted him. His private journal was seized, and a portion of its contents used as evidence against him. The following was furnished to the grand jury : —

"Arrived at Philadelphia the 17th of February, 1738. At Ludinum, 5th March. — To Philadelphia, 29th April. — Began school at Burlington, 18th June. Omilta Jacobus Atherthwaite, 27th July. — Came to school at Burlington, 23d January, 1740. — Saw ———, 7th May. — At five went to Burlington, to Piercy, the madman. — Went to Philadelphia, 19th May. — Went to Burlington, 18th June. — At six in the evening to Penefack, to Joseph Ashton. — Began school at Dublin under Charles Hastie, at eight pounds a year, 31st July, ———, 15th October, ———, 27th ditto. — Came to John Croker (at the Fighting Cocks), New York, 2d November. — I boarded gratis with him, 7th November, — Natura Johannis Pool, 26th December. — I began to teach with John Campbell, 6th April, 1741. — Baptized Timothy Ryan, born 18th April, 1740, son of John Ryan and Mary Ryan, 18th May. — Pater Confessor Butler, two Anni, no sacramentum non confessio." [1]

On the 21st of July, Sarah Hughson, who had been respited, was put on the witness-stand again. There were some legal errors in the indictments against Ury, and his trial was postponed until the next term ; but he was arraigned on a new indictment. The energies of the jury and judges received new life. Here was a

---

man who was a Catholic, — or had been a Catholic, — and the spirit
of religious intolerance asserted itself. Sarah Hughson remem
bered having seen Ury at her father's house on several occasions ;
had seen him make a ring with chalk on the floor, make all the
Negroes stand around it, while he himself would stand in the
middle, with a cross, and swear the Negroes. This was also "new
matter :" nothing of this kind was mentioned in the first confession. But this was not all. She had seen Ury preach to the
Negroes, forgive their sins, and baptize some of them ! She said
that Ury wanted her to confess to him, and that Peggy confessed
to him in French.

On the 24th of July, Elias Desbroses, confectioner, being
called, swore that Ury had come to his shop with one Webb, a
carpenter, and inquired for sugar-bits, or wafers, and asked him
"whether a minister had not his wafers of him ? or, whether that
paste, which the deponent showed him, was not made of the same
ingredients as the Luthern minister's ?" or words to that effect :
the deponent told Ury that if he desired such things a joiner
would make him a mould ; and that when he asked him whether
he had a congregation, Ury "waived giving him an answer."

On the 27th of July, Mr. Webb, the carpenter, was called to
the witness-stand and testified as follows : That he had met Ury
at John Croker's (at the Fighting Cocks), where he became acquainted with him ; that he had heard him read Latin and English so admirably that he employed him to teach his child ; that
finding out that he was a school-teacher, he invited him to board
at his house without charge ; that he understood from him that
he was a non-juring minister, had written a book that had drawn
the fire of the Church, was charged with treason, and driven out
of England, sustaining the loss of "a living" worth fifty pounds a
year ; that on religious matters the deponent could not always
comprehend him ; that the accused said Negroes were only fit for
slaves, and to put them above that condition was to invite them
to cut your throats. The observing Horsemanden was so much
pleased with the above declaration, that he gives Ury credit in a
footnote for understanding the dispositions of Negroes ![1] Farther
on Mr. Webb says, that, after one Campbell removed to Hughson's, Ury went thither, and so did the deponent on three different
times, and heard him read prayers after the manner of the Church

---

[1] Horsemanden's Negro Plot, p. 284.

of England; but in the prayer for the king he only mentioned "our sovereign lord the King," and not "King George." He said that Ury pleaded against drunkenness, debauchery, and Deists; that he admonished every one to keep his own minister; that when the third sermon was delivered one Mr. Hildreth was present, when Ury found fault with certain doctrines, insisted that good works as well as faith were necessary to salvation; that he announced that on a certain evening he would preach from the text, "Upon this rock I will build my church, and the gates of hell shall not prevail against it; and whosoever sins ye remit, they are remitted, and whosoever sins ye retain, they are retained."

The judges, delighted with this flavor added to the usually dry proceedings, thought they had better call Sarah Hughson; that if she were grateful for her freedom she would furnish the testimony their honors desired. Sarah was accordingly called. She is recommended for mercy. She is, of course, to say what is put in her mouth, to give testimony such as the court desires. So the fate of the poor schoolmaster was placed in the keeping of the fateful Sarah.

On the 28th of July another grand jury was sworn, and, like the old one, was composed of merchants. The following persons composed it: Joseph Robinson, James Livingston, Hermanus Rutgers, jun., Charles LeRoux, Abraham Boelen, Peter Rutgers, Jacobus Roosevelt, John Auboyneau, Stephen Van Courtlandt, jun., Abraham Lynsen, Gerardus Duyckinck, John Provost, Henry Lane, jun., Henry Cuyler, John Roosevelt, Abraham DePeyster, Edward Hicks, Joseph Ryall, Peter Schuyler, and Peter Jay.[1]

Sarah Hughson had been pardoned. John Ury was brought into court, when he challenged some of the jury. William Hammersley, Gerardus Beekman, John Shurmur, Sidney Breese, Daniel Shatford, Thomas Behenna, Peter Fresneau, Thomas Willett, John Breese, John Hastier, James Tucker, and Brandt Schuyler were sworn to try him. Barring formalities, he was arraigned upon the old indictment; viz., felony, in inciting and exciting the Negro slave Quack to set fire to the governor's house. The king's counsel were the attorney-general, Richard Bradley, and Messrs. Murray, Alexander, Smith, and Chambers. Poor Ury had no counsel, no sympathizers. The attorney-general, in an opening speech to the jury, said that certain evidence was to be produced

---

[1] Horsemanden's Negro Plot, p. 286.

showing that the prisoner at the bar was guilty as charged in the indictment ; that he had a letter that he desired to read to them, which had been sent to Lieut.-Gov. Clark, written by Gen. Oglethorpe ("the visionary Lycurgus of Georgia"), bearing date of the 16th of May. The following is a choice passage from the letter referred to : —

"Some intelligence I had of a villanous design of a very extraordinary nature, and if true very important, viz., that the Spaniards had employed emissaries to burn all the magazines and considerable towns in the English North America, and thereby to prevent the subsisting of the great expedition and fleet in the West Indies ; and for this purpose many priests were employed, who pretended to be physicians, dancing-masters, and other such kinds of occupations, and under that pretence to get admittance and confidence in families." [1]

The burden of his effort was the wickedness of Popery and the Roman-Catholic Church. The first witness called was the irrepressible Mary Burton. She began by rehearsing the old story of setting fire to the houses : but this time she varied it somewhat ; it was not the fort that was to be burnt first, but Croker's, near a coffee-house, by the long bridge. She remembered the ring drawn with chalk, saw things in it that looked like rats (the good Horsemanden throws a flood of light upon this otherwise dark passage by telling his reader that it was the Negroes' black toes !) ; that she peeped in once and saw a black thing like a child, and Ury with a book in his hand, and at this moment she let a silver spoon drop, and Ury chased her, and would have caught her, had she not fallen into a bucket of water, and thus marvellously escaped ! But the rule was to send this curious Mary to bed when any thing of an unusual nature was going on. Ury asked her some questions.

"*Prisoner.* — You say you have seen me several times at Hughson's, what clothes did I usually wear?

"*Mary Burton.* — I cannot tell what clothes you wore particularly.

"*Prisoner.* — That is strange, and know me so well ? "

She then says several kinds, but particularly, or chiefly, a riding-coat, and often a brown coat, trimmed with black.

"*Prisoner.* — I never wore such a coat. What time of the day did I used to come to Hughson's?

"*M. Burton.* — You used chiefly to come in the night-time, and when I have been going to bed I have seen you undressing in Peggy's room, as if you

---

[1] Colonial Hist. of N. Y., vol. vi. p. 199.

were to lie there; but I cannot say that you did, for you were always gone before I was up in the morning.

"*Prisoner.* — What room was I in when I called Mary, and you came up, as you said?

"*M. Burton.* — In the great room, up stairs.

"*Prisoner.* — What answer did the Negroes make, when I offered to forgive them their sins, as you said?

"*M. Burton.* — I don't remember." [1]

William Kane, the soldier, took the stand. He was very bold to answer all of Ury's questions. He saw him baptize a child, could forgive sins, and wanted to convert him! Sarah Hughson was next called, but Ury objected to her because she had been convicted. The judge informed him that she had been pardoned, and was, therefore, competent as a witness. Judge Horsemanden was careful to produce newspaper scraps to prove that the court of France had endeavored to create and excite revolts and insurrections in the English colonies, and ended by telling a pathetic story about an Irish schoolmaster in Ulster County who drank the health of the king of Spain! [2] This had great weight with the jury, no doubt. Poor Ury, convicted upon the evidence of three notorious liars, without counsel, was left to defend himself. He addressed the jury in an earnest and intelligent manner. He showed where the evidence clashed; that the charges were not in harmony with his previous character, the silence of Quack and others already executed. He showed that Mr. Campbell took possession of the house that Hughson had occupied, on the 1st of May; that at that time Hughson and his wife were in jail, and Sarah in the house; that Sarah abused Campbell, and that he reproved her for the foul language she used; and that this furnished her with an additional motive to accuse him; that he never knew Hughson or any of the family. Mr. John Croker testified that Ury never kept company with Negroes, nor did he receive them at Croker's house up to the 1st of May, for all the plotting was done before that date; that he was a quiet, pious preacher, and an excellent schoolmaster; that he taught Webb's child, and always declared himself a non-juring clergyman of the Church of England. But the fatal revelation of this friend of Ury's was, that Webb made him a desk; and the jury thought they saw in it an altar for a Catholic priest! That was enough. The attorney-general told the jury that the prisoner was a Romish priest, and

---

[1] Horsemanden's Negro Plot, pp. 292, 293.   [2] Ibid., pp. 298, 299, note.

then proceeded to prove the exceeding sinfulness of that Church. Acknowledging the paucity of the evidence intended to prove him a priest, the learned gentleman hastened to dilate upon all the dark deeds of Rome, and thereby poisoned the minds of the jury against the unfortunate Ury. He was found guilty, and on the 29th of August, 1741, was hanged, professing his innocence, and submitting cheerfully to a cruel and unjust death as a servant of the Lord.[1]

The trials of the Negroes had continued, but were somewhat overshadowed by that of the reputed Catholic priest. On the 18th of July seven Negroes were hanged, including a Negro doctor named Harry. On the 23d of July a number of white persons were fined for keeping disorderly houses, — entertaining Negroes; while nine Negroes were, the same day, released from jail on account of a lack of evidence! On the 15th of August a Spanish Negro was hanged. On the 31st of August, Corry (the dancing-master), Ryan, Kelly, and Coffin — all white persons — were dismissed because no one prosecuted; while the reader must have observed that the evidence against them was quite as strong as that offered against any of the persons executed, by the lying trio Burton, Kane, and Sarah. But Mr. Smith the historian gives the correct reason why these trials came to such a sudden end.

" The whole summer was spent in the prosecutions; every new trial led to further accusations: a coincidence of slight circumstances, was magnified by the general terror into violent presumptions; tales collected without doors, mingling with the proofs given at the bar, poisoned the minds of the jurors; and the sanguinary spirit of the day suffered no check till Mary, the capital informer, bewildered by frequent examinations and suggestions, lost her first impressions, and began to touch characters, which malice itself did not dare to suspect." [2]

The 24th of September was solemnly set apart for public thanksgiving for the escape of the citizens from destruction!

As we have already said, this " Negro plot " has but one parallel in the history of civilization. It had its origin in a diseased public conscience, inflamed by religious bigotry, accelerated by hired liars, and consummated in the blind and bloody action of a court and jury who imagined themselves sitting over a powder-magazine. That a robbery took place, there was abun· dant evidence in the finding of some of the articles, and the

---

[1] Horsemanden's Negro Plot, pp. 221, 222.   [2] Smith's Hist. of N. Y., vol. 11. pp; 59, 60.

admissions of Hughson and others; but there was not a syllable of competent evidence to show that there was an organized plot. And the time came, after the city had gotten back to its accustomed quietness, that the most sincere believers in the "Negro plot" were converted to the opinion that the zeal of the magistrates had not been "according to knowledge." For they could not have failed to remember that the Negroes were considered heathen, and, therefore, not sworn by the court; that they were not allowed counsel; that the evidence was indirect, contradictory, and malicious, while the trials were hasty and unfair. From the 11th of May to the 29th of August, one hundred and fifty-four Negroes were cast into prison; fourteen of whom were burnt, eighteen hanged, seventy-one transported, and the remainder pardoned. During the same space of time twenty-four whites were committed to prison; four of whom were executed, and the remainder discharged. The number arrested was one hundred and seventy-eight, thirty-six executed, and seventy-one transported! What a terrible tragedy committed in the name of law and Christian government! Mary Burton, the Judas Iscariot of the period, received her hundred pounds as the price of the blood she had caused to be shed; and the curtain fell upon one of the most tragic events in all the history of New York or of the civilized world.[1]

The legislature turned its attention to additional legislation upon the slavery question. Severe laws were passed against the Negroes. Their personal rights were curtailed until their condition was but little removed from that of the brute creation. We have gone over the voluminous records of the Province of New York, and have not found a single act calculated to ameliorate the condition of the slave.[2] He was hated, mistrusted, and feared. Nothing was done, of a friendly character, for the slave in the

---

[1] "On the 6th of March, 1742, the following order was passed by the Common Council: 'Ordered, that the indentures of Mary Burton be delivered up to her, and that she be discharged from the remainder of her servitude, and three pounds paid her, to provide necessary clothing.' The Common Council had purchased her indentures from her master, and had kept her and them, until this time." — DUNLAP, vol. ii. Appendix, p. clxvii.

[2] On the 17th of November, 1767, a bill was brought into the House of Assembly "to prevent the unnatural and unwarrantable custom of enslaving mankind, and the importation of slaves into this province." It was changed into an act "for laying an impost on Negroes imported." This could not pass the governor and council; and it was afterward known that Benning I. Wentworth, the governor of New Hampshire, had received instructions not to pass any law "imposing duties on negroes imported into that province." Hutchinson of Massachusetts had similar instructions. The governor and his Majesty's council knew this at the time.

Province of New York, until threatening dangers from without taught the colonists the importance of husbanding all their resources. The war between the British colonies in North America and the mother country gave the Negro an opportunity to level, by desperate valor, a mountain of prejudice, and wipe out with his blood the dark stain of 1741. History says he did it.

CHAPTER XIV.

THE COLONY OF MASSACHUSETTS.

1633–1775.

THE EARLIEST MENTIONS OF NEGROES IN MASSACHUSETTS. — PEQUOD INDIANS EXCHANGED FOR NEGROES. — VOYAGE OF THE SLAVE-SHIP "DESIRE" IN 1638. — FUNDAMENTAL LAWS ADOPTED. — HEREDITARY SLAVERY. — KIDNAPPING NEGROES. — GROWTH OF SLAVERY IN THE SEVENTEENTH CENTURY. — TAXATION OF SLAVES. — INTRODUCTION OF INDIAN SLAVES PROHIBITED. — THE POSITION OF THE CHURCH RESPECTING THE BAPTISM OF SLAVES. — SLAVE MARRIAGE. — CONDITION OF FREE NEGROES. — PHILLIS WHEATLEY THE AFRICAN POETESS. — HER LIFE. — SLAVERY RECOGNIZED IN ENGLAND IN ORDER TO BE MAINTAINED IN THE COLONIES. — THE EMANCIPATION OF SLAVES. — LEGISLATION FAVORING THE IMPORTATION OF WHITE SERVANTS, BUT PROHIBITING THE CLANDESTINE BRINGING-IN OF NEGROES. — JUDGE SEWALL'S ATTACK ON SLAVERY. — JUDGE SAFFIN'S REPLY TO JUDGE SEWALL.

HAD the men who gave the colony of Massachusetts its political being and Revolutionary fame known that the Negro — so early introduced into the colony as a slave — would have been in the future Republic for years the insoluble problem, and at last the subject of so great and grave economic and political concern, they would have committed to the jealous keeping of the chroniclers of their times the records for which the historian of the Negro seeks so vainly in this period. Stolen as he was from his tropical home; consigned to a servitude at war with man's intellectual and spiritual, as well as with his physical, nature; the very lowest of God's creation, in the estimation of the Roundheads of New England; a stranger in a strange land, — the poor Negro of Massachusetts found no place in the sympathy or history of the Puritan, — Christians whose deeds and memory have been embalmed in song and story, and given to an immortality equalled only by the indestructibility of the English language. The records of the most remote period of colonial history have preserved a silence on the question of Negro slavery as ominous as it is conspicuous. What data there are concerning the introduction of slavery are fragmentary, uncertain, and unsatisfactory, to say the least. There is but one work bearing the luminous stamp of historical trustworthiness, and which turns a flood

of light on the dark records of the darker crime of human slavery
in Massachusetts. And we are sure it is as complete as the ripe
scholarship, patient research, and fair and fearless spirit of its
author, could make it.[1]

The earliest mention of the presence of Negroes in Massachusetts is in connection with an account of some Indians who were
frightened at a Colored man who had lost his way in the tangled
path of the forest. The Indians, it seems, were "worse scared
than hurt, who seeing a blackamore in the top of a tree looking
out for his way which he had lost, surmised he was *Abamacho*, or
the devil; deeming all devils that are blacker than themselves:
and being near to the plantation, they posted to the English, and
entreated their aid to conjure this devil to his own place, who
finding him to be a poor wandering blackamore, conducted him to
his master." [2] This was in 1633. It is circumstantial evidence
of a twofold nature; i.e., it proves that there were Negroes in the
colony at a date much earlier than can be fixed by reliable data,
and that the Negroes were slaves. It is a fair presumption that
this "wandering blackamore" who was conducted "to his *master*" was not the only Negro slave in the colony. Slaves generally
come in large numbers, and consequently there must have been
quite a number at this time.

Negro slavery in Massachusetts was the safety-valve to the
pent-up vengeance of the Pequod Indians. Slavery would have
been established in Massachusetts, even if there had been no
Indians to punish by war, captivity, and duplicity. Encouraged
by the British authorities, avarice and gain would have quieted
the consciences of Puritan slave-holders. But the Pequod war
was the early and urgent occasion for the founding of slavery
under the foster care of a *free church and free government!* As
the Pequod Indians would "not endure the yoke," would not
remain "as servants," [3] they were sent to Bermudas [4] and exchanged for Negroes,[5] with the hope that the latter would "endure

---

[1] George H. Moore, LL.D., for many years librarian of the New-York Historical Society,
but at present the efficient superintendent of the Lenox Library, in his "Notes on the History of
Slavery in Massachusetts," has summoned nearly all the orators and historians of Massachusetts
to the bar of history. He leaves them open to one of three charges; viz., evading the truth, ignorance of it, or falsifying the record. And in addition to this work, which is authority, his
"Additional Notes" glow with an energy and perspicuity of style which lead me to conclude that
Dr. Moore works admirably under the spur; and that his refined sarcasm, unanswerable logic, and
critical accuracy give him undisputed place amongst the ablest writers of our times.

[2] Wood's New-England Prospect, 1634, p. 77. [3] Slavery in Mass., p. 7.

[4] Ibid., pp. 4, 5, and 6. [5] Elliott's New-England Hist., pp. 167–205.

the yoke" more patiently.   The first importation of slaves from Barbados, secured in exchange for Indians, was made in 1637, the first year of the Pequod war, and was doubtless kept up for many years.

But in the following year we have the most positive evidence that New England had actually engaged in the slave-trade.

"Mr. Pierce, in the Salem ship, the Desire, returned from the West Indies after seven months.   He had been at Providence, and brought some cotton, and tobacco, and negroes, &c., from thence, and salt from Tertugos. . . . Dry fish and strong liquors are the only commodities for those parts.   He met there two men-of-war, sent forth by the lords, &c., of Providence with letters of mart, who had taken divers prizes from the spaniard and many negroes." [1]

"The Desire" was built at Marblehead in 1636; [2] was of one hundred and twenty tons, and perhaps one of the first built in the colony.   There is no positive proof that "The Mayflower," after landing the holy Pilgrim Fathers, was fitted out for a slave-cruise!   But there is no evidence to destroy the belief that "The Desire" was built for the slave-trade.   Within a few years from the time of the building of "The Desire," there were quite a number of Negro slaves in Massachusetts.   "John Josselyn, Gen't" in his "Two Voyages to New England," made in "1638, 1663," and printed for the first time in 1674,[3] gives an account of an attempt to breed slaves in Massachusetts.

"The Second of *October*, (1639) about 9 of the clock in the morning, Mr. *Maverick's* Negro woman came to my chamber window, and in her own Countrey language and tune sang very loud and shril, going out to her, she used a great deal of respect towards me, and willingly would have expressed her grief in *English;* but I apprehended it by her countenance and deportment, whereupon I repaired to my host, to learn of him the cause, and resolved to entreat him in her behalf, for that I understood before, that she had been a Queen in her own Countrey, and observed a very humble and dutiful garb used towards her by another Negro who was her maid.   Mr. *Maverick* was desirous to have a breed of Negroes, and therefore seeing she would not yield by persuasions

---

[1] Winthrop's Journal, Feb. 26, 1638, vol. i. p. 254; see, also, Felt, vol. ii. p. 230.

[2] Dr. Moore backs his statement as to the time The Desire was built by quoting from Winthrop, vol. i. p. 193.   But there is a mistake somewhere as to the correct date.   Winthrop says she was built in 1636; but I find in Mr. Drake's "Founders of New England," pp. 31, 32, this entry: "More (June) XXth, 1635.   In the Desire de Lond. Pearce, and bond for New Eng. p'r cert. frō ij Justices of Peace and ministers of All Saints lionian in Northampton."   If she sailed in 1635, she must have been built earlier.

[3] Dr. George H. Moore says Josselyn's Voyages were printed in 1664.   This is an error. They were not published until ten years later, in 1674.   In 1833 the Massachusetts Historical Society printed the work in the third volume and third series of their collection.

to company with a Negro young man he had in his house; he commanded him will'd she nill'd she to go to bed to her, which was no sooner done but she kickt him out again, this she took in high disdain beyond her slavery, and this was the cause of her grief." [1]

It would appear, at first blush, that slavery was an individual speculation in the colony; but the voyage of the ship "Desire" was evidently made with a view of securing Negro slaves for sale. Josselyn says, in 1627, that the English colony on the Island of Barbados had "in a short time increased to twenty thousand, besides Negroes." [2] And in 1637 he says that the New Englanders "sent the male children of Pequets to the Bermudus." [3] It is quite likely that many individuals of large means and estates had a few Negro slaves quite early, — perhaps earlier than we have any record; but as a public enterprise in which the colony was interested, slavery began as early as 1638. "It will be observed," says Dr. Moore, "that this first entrance into the slave-trade was not a private, individual speculation. It was the enterprise of the authorities of the colony. And on the 13th of March, 1639, it was ordered by the General Court "that 3*l* 8*s* should be paid Lieftenant Davenport for the present, for charge disbursed for the slaves, which, when they have earned it, hee is to repay it back againe." The marginal note is " Lieft. Davenport to keep ye slaves." (Mass. Rec. i. 253.[4]) So there can be. no doubt as to the permanent establishment of the institution of slavery as early as 1639, while before that date the institution existed in a patriarchal condition. But there isn't the least fragment of history to sustain the haphazard statement of Emory Washburn, that slavery existed in Massachusetts "from the time Maverick was found dwelling on Noddle's Island in 1630." [5] We are sure this assertion lacks the authority of historical data. It is one thing for a historian to think certain events happened at a particular time, but it is quite another thing to be able to cite reliable authority in proof of the assertion.[6] But no doubt Mr. Washburn relies upon Mr. Palfrey, who refers his reader to Mr.

---

[1] Josselyn, p. 28.   [2] Ibid., p. 250.   [3] Ibid., p. 258.   [4] Slavery in Mass., p 9.
[5] Mass. Hist. Coll., vol. iv. 4th Series, p. 333, *sq.*
[6] Mr. Bancroft (Centenary Edition, vol. i. p. 137) says, " The earliest importation of Negro slaves into New England was made in 1637, from Providence Isle, in the Salem ship Desire." But Winthrop (vol. i. p. 254, under date of the 26th of February, 1638) says, " The Desire returned from the West Indies after seven months." He also states (ibid., p. 193) that The Desire was "built at Marblehead in 1636." But this may or may not be true according to the old method of keeping time.

Josselyn. Palfrey says, "Before Winthrop's arrival, there were two negro slaves in Massachusetts, held by Mr. Maverick, on Noddle's Island." [1] Josselyn gives the only account we have of the slaves on Noddle's Island. The incident that gave rise to this scrap of history occurred on the 2d of October, 1639. Winthrop was chosen governor in the year 1637.[2] It was in this year, on the 26th of February, that the slave-ship "Desire" landed a cargo of Negroes in the colony. Now, if Mr. Palfrey relies upon Josselyn for the historical trustworthiness of his statement that there were two Negroes in Massachusetts before Winthrop arrived, he has made a mistake. There is no proof for the assertion. That there were three Negroes on Noddle's Island, we have the authority of Josselyn, but nothing more. And if the Negro queen who kicked Josselyn's man out of bed had been as long in the island as Palfrey and Washburn indicate, she would have been able to explain her grief to Josselyn in English. We have no doubt but what Mr. Maverick got his slaves from the ship "Desire" in 1638, the same year Winthrop was inaugurated governor.

In Massachusetts, as in the other colonies, slavery made its way into individual families first; thence into communities, where it was clothed with the garment of usage and custom;[3] and, finally, men longing to enjoy the fruit of unrequited labor gave it the sanction of statutory law. There was not so great a demand for slaves in Massachusetts as in the Southern States; and yet they had their uses in a domestic way, and were, consequently, sought after. As early as 1641 Massachusetts adopted a body of fundamental laws. The magistrates,[4] armed with authority from the crown of Great Britain, had long exercised a power which wellnigh trenched upon the personal rights of the people. The latter desired a revision of the laws, and such modifications of the power and discretion of the magistrates as would be in sympathy with the spirit of personal liberty that pervaded the minds of the colonists. But while the people sought to wrest an arbitrary power from the unwilling hands of their judges, they found no pity in their hearts for the poor Negroes in their midst, who, having served as slaves because of their numerical weakness and the passive silence of justice, were now to become the legal

[1] Palfrey's Hist. of N. E., vol. ii. p. 30, note. [2] Josselyn, p. 257.
[3] Elliott's New-England Hist., vol. ii. pp. 57, 58. [4] Hildreth, vol. i. p. 270, *sq.*

and statutory vassals — for their life-time — of a liberty-loving and liberty-seeking people! In the famous "Body of Liberties" is to be found the first statute establishing slavery in the United States. It is as follows : —

"It is ordered by this court, and the authority thereof; that there shall never be any bond slavery, villainage or captivity amongst us, unless it be lawful captives taken in just wars, as willingly sell themselves or are sold to us, and such shall have the liberties and christian usage which the law of God established in Israel concerning such persons doth morally require; provided this exempts none from servitude, who shall be judged thereto by authority." [1]

We have omitted the old spelling, but none of the words, as they appeared in the original manuscript. There isn't the shadow of a doubt but what this law has been preserved inviolate. [2]

There has been considerable discussion about the real bearing of this statute. Many zealous historians, in discussing it, have betrayed more zeal for the good name of the Commonwealth than for the truth of history. Able lawyers — and some of them still survive — have maintained, with a greater show of learning than of facts, that this statute abolished slavery in Massachusetts. But, on the other hand, there are countless lawyers who pronounce it a plain and unmistakable law, "creating and establishing slavery." An examination of the statute will help the reader to a clear understanding of it. To begin with, this law received its being from the existent *fact* of slavery in the colony. From the practice of a few holding Negroes as slaves, it became general and prodigious. Its presence in society called for lawful regulations concerning it. While it is solemnly declared "that there shall never be any bond slavery, villianage, or captivity" in the colony, there were three provisos; viz., "lawful captives taken in just wares," those who would "sell themselves or are sold to us," and such as "shall be judged thereto by authority." Under the foregoing conditions slavery was plainly established in Massachusetts. The "just wares" were the wars against the Pequod Indians. That these were made prisoners and slaves, we have the universal testimony of all writers on the history of Massachusetts. Just what class of people would "sell themselves" into slavery we are at a loss to know! We can, however, understand the meaning of the words, "or are sold to us." This was an open door for the traffic in human beings; for it made it lawful for to sell slaves to

---

[1] Ancient Charters and Laws of Mass., pp. 52, 23.   [2] Slavery in Mass., p. 13, note.

the colonists, and lawful for the latter to purchase them. Those who were "judged thereto by authority" were those in slavery already and such as should come into the colony by shipping.

This statute is wide enough to drive a load of hay through. It is not the work of a novice, but the labored and skilful product of great law learning.

"The law must be interpreted in the light of contemporaneous facts of history. At the time it was made (1641), what had its authors to provide for?

"1. Indian slaves — their captives taken in war.

"2. Negro slaves — their own importations of 'strangers,' obtained by purchase or exchange.

"3. Criminals — condemned to slavery as a punishment for offences.

"In this light, and only in this light, is their legislation intelligible and consistent. It is very true that the code of which this law is a part 'exhibits throughout the hand of the practised lawyer, familiar with the principles and securities of English Liberty;' but who had ever heard, at that time, of the 'common-law rights' of Indians and Negroes, or anybody else but Englishmen?

"Thus stood the statute through the whole colonial period, and it was never expressly repealed. Based on the Mosaic code, it is an absolute recognition of slavery as a legitimate status, and of the right of one man to sell himself as well as that of another man to buy him. It sanctions the slave-trade, and the perpetual bondage of Indians and Negroes, their children and their children's children, and entitles Massachusetts to precedence over any and all the other colonies in similar legislation. It anticipates by many years any thing of the sort to be found in the statutes of Virginia, or Maryland, or South Carolina, and nothing like it is to be found in the contemporary codes of her sister colonies in New England." [1]

The subject had been carefully weighed; and, lacking authority for legalizing a crime against man, the Mosaic code was cited, and in accordance with its *humane* provisions, slaves were to be treated. But it was *authority* for slavery that the cunning lawyer who drew the statute was seeking, and not precedents to determine the kind of treatment to be bestowed upon the slave. Under it "human slavery existed for nearly a century and a half without serious challenge;" [2] and here, as well as in Virginia, it received the sanction of the Church and courts. It grew with its growth, and strengthened with its strength; until, as an organic institution, it had many defenders and few apologists. [3]

"This article gives express sanction to the slave-trade, and the practice of holding Negroes and Indians in perpetual bondage, anticipating by many

---

[1] Slavery in Mass., pp. 18, 19.   [2] Ibid., p. 12.   [3] Elliott's New-England Hist., vol. i. p. 383.

years any thing of the sort to be found in the statutes of Virginia or Mary-land." [1]

And it is rather strange, in the light of this plain statute establishing and legalizing the purchase of slaves, that Mr. Washburn's statement, unsustained, should receive the public indorsement of so learned a body as the Massachusetts Historical Society!

"But, after all [says Mr. Washburn], the laws on this subject, as well as the practice of the government, were inconsistent and anomalous, indicating clearly, that whether Colony or Province, so far as it felt free to follow its own inclinations, uncontrolled by the action of the mother country, Massachusetts was hostile to slavery as an institution!" [2]

No doubt Massachusetts was "inconsistent" in seeking liberty for her white citizens while forging legal chains for the Negro. And how far the colony "felt free to follow its own inclinations" Chief-Justice Parsons declares from the bench. Says that eminent jurist, —

"Slavery was introduced into this country [Massachusetts] soon after its first settlement, and was tolerated until the ratification of the present Constitution — of 1780." [3]

So here we find an eminent authority declaring that slavery followed hard upon the heels of the Pilgrim Fathers, "and was tolerated" until 1780. Massachusetts "felt free" to tear from the iron grasp of the imperious magistrates the liberties of the people, but doubtless felt not "free" enough to blot out "the crime and folly of an evil time." And yet for years lawyers and clergymen, orators and statesmen, historians and critics, have stubbornly maintained, that, while slavery did creep into the colony, and did exist, it was "not probably by force of any law, for none such is found or known to exist." (?) [4]

Slavery having been firmly established in Massachusetts, the next step was to make it hereditary. This was done under the sanction of the highest and most solemn forms of the courts of law. It is not our purpose to give this subject the attention it merits, in this place; but in a subsequent chapter it will receive due attention. We will, however, say in passing, that it was the opinion of many lawyers in the last century, some of whom served upon the bench in Massachusetts, that children followed the

---

[1] Hildreth, vol. i. p. 278.   [2] Mass. Hist. Coll., vol. iv. 4th Series, p. 334.
[3] Quoted by Dr. Moore, p. 20.   [4] Commonwealth *vs.* Aves, 18 Pickering, p. 208.

condition of their mothers.   Chief-Justice Parsons held that "the issue of the female slave, according to the maxim of the civil law, was the property of her master."   And, subsequently, Chief-Justice Parker rendered the following opinion : —

"The practice was . . . to consider such issue as slaves, and the property of the master of the parents, liable to be sold and transferred like other chattels, and as assets in the hands of executors and administrators. . . . We think there is no doubt that, at any period of our history, the issue of a slave husband and a free wife would have been declared free.   His children, if the issue of a marriage with a slave, would, immediately on their birth, become the property of his master, or of the master of the female slave." [1]

This decision is strengthened by the statement of Kendall in reference to the wide-spread desire of Negro slaves to secure free Indian wives, in order to insure the freedom of their children. He says, —

"While slavery was supposed to be maintainable by law in Massachusetts, there was a particular temptation to Negroes for taking Indian wives, the children of Indian women being acknowledged to be free." [2]

We refer the reader, with perfect confidence, to our friend Dr. George H. Moore, who, in his treatment of this particular feature of slavery in Massachusetts, has, with great research, put down a number of zealous friends of the colony who have denied, with great emphasis, that any child was ever born into slavery there. Neither the opinion of Chief-Justice Dana, nor the naked and barren assertions of historians Palfrey, Sumner, and Washburn, — great though the men were, — can dispose of the *historical reality of hereditary slavery in Massachusetts*, down to the adoption of the Constitution of 1780.

The General Court of Massachusetts issued an order in 1645 [3] for the return of certain kidnapped or stolen Negroes to their native country.   It has been variously commented upon by historians and orators.   The story runs, that a number of ships, plying between New-England seaport towns and Madeira and the Canaries, made it their custom to call on the coast of Guinea "to trade for negroes."   Thus secured, they were disposed of in the

---

[1] Andover *vs.* Canton, Mass. Reports, 551, 552, quoted by Dr. Moore.

[2] Kendall's Travels, vol. ii. p. 179.

[3] The following note, if it refers to the kidnapped Negroes, gives an earlier date, — "29th May, 1644.   Mr. Blackleach his petition about the Mores was consented to, to be committed to the eld^rs, to enforme us of the mind of God herein, & then further to consider it." — *Mass. Records*, vol. ii. p. 67.

slave-markets of Barbadoes and the West Indies. The New-England slave-market did not demand a large supply. Situated on a cold, bleak, and almost sterile coast, Massachusetts lacked the conditions to make slave-trading as lucrative as the Southern States ; but, nevertheless, she disposed of quite a number, as the reader will observe when we examine the first census. A ship from the town of Boston consorted with "some Londoners" with the object of gaining slaves. Mr. Bancroft [1] says that "upon the Lord's day, invited the natives aboard one of their ships," and then made prisoners of such as came ; which is not mentioned by Hildreth.[2] The latter writer says, that "on pretence of some quarrel with the natives," landed a small cannon called a "murderer," attacked the village on Sunday ; and having burned the village, and killed many, made a few prisoners. Several of these prisoners fell to the Boston ship. On account of a disagreement between the captain and under officers of the ship, as well as the owners, the story of the above affair was detailed before a Boston court. Richard Saltonstall was one of the magistrates before whom the case was tried. He was moved by the recital of the cruel wrong done the Africans, and therefore presented a petition to the court, charging the captain and mate with the threefold crime of "murder," "man-stealing," and "sabbath-breaking."[3]

---

[1] Bancroft, Centennial edition, vol. i. p. 137.   [2] Hildreth, vol. i. p. 282.

[3] The petition is rather a remarkable paper, and is printed below. It is evident that the judge was in earnest. And yet the court, while admitting the petition, tried the case on only one ground, man-stealing.

To the honored general court.

The oath I took this yeare att my enterance upon the place of assistante was to this effect: That I would truly endeavour the advancement of the gospell and the good of the people of this plantation (to the best of my skill) dispencing justice equally and impartially (according to the laws of God and this land) in all cases wherein I act by virtue of my place. I conceive myself called by virtue of my place to act (according to this oath) in the case concerning the negers taken by captain Smith and Mr. Keser; wherein it is apparent that Mr. Keser gave chace to certaine negers; and upon the same day tooke divers of them; and at another time killed others; and burned one of their townes. Omitting several misdemeanours, which accompained these acts above mentioned, I conceive the acts themselves to bee directly contrary to these following laws (all of which are capitall by the word of God; and two of them by the lawes of this jurisdiction).

The act (or acts) of murder (whether by force or fraude) are expressly contrary both to the law of God, and the law of this country.

The act of stealing negers, or taking them by force (Whether it be considered as theft or robbery) is (as I conceive) expressly contrary, both to the law of God, and the law of this country.

The act of chaceing the negers (as aforesayde) upon the sabbath day (being a servile worke and such as cannot be considered under any other heade) is expressly capitall by the law of God.

These acts and outrages being committed where there was noe civill government, which might call them to accompt, and the persons, by whom they were committed beeing of our jurisdiction, I conceive this court to bee the ministers of God in this case, and therefore my humble request is that the severall offenders

It seems that by the Fundamental Laws, adopted by the people in 1641, the first two offences were punishable by death, and all of them "capitall, by the law of God." The court doubted its jurisdiction over crimes committed on the distant coast of Guinea. But article ninety-one of "The Body of Liberties" determined who were lawful slaves, — those who sold themselves or were sold, "lawful captives taken in just wares," and those "judged thereto by authority." Had the unfortunate Negroes been purchased, there was no law in Massachusetts to free them from their owners; but having been kidnapped, unlawfully obtained, the court felt that it was its plain duty to bear witness against the "sin of man-stealing." For, in the laws adopted in 1641, among the "Capital Laws," at the latter part of article ninety-four is the following: "If any man stealeth a man, or mankind, he shall surely be put to death.".[1] There is a marginal reference to Exod. xxi. 16. Dr. Moore does not refer to this in his elaborate discussion of statute on "bond slavery." And Winthrop says that the magistrates decided that the Negroes, "having been procured not honestly by purchase, but by the unlawful act of kidnaping," should be returned to their native country. That there was a criminal code in the colony, there can be no doubt; but we have searched for it in vain. Hildreth[2] says it was printed in 1649, but that there is now no copy extant.

The court issued an order about the return of the kidnapped Negroes, which we will give in full, on account of its historical value, and because of the difference of opinion concerning it.

"The general court conceiving themselves bound by the first opportunity to bear witness against the heinous, and crying sin of man-stealing, as also to prescribe such timely redress for what is past, and such a law for the future, as may sufficiently deter all others belonging to us to have to do in such vile and odious courses, justly abhorred of all good and just men, do order that the negro interpreter with others unlawfully taken, be by the first opportunity at the charge of the country for the present, sent to his native country (Guinea) and a letter with him of the indignation of the court thereabouts, and justice thereof, desiring our honored governor would please put this order in execution."[3]

may be imprisoned by the order of this court, and brought into their deserved censure in convenient time; and this I humbly crave that soe the sinn they have committed may be upon their own heads, and not upon ourselves (as otherwise it will.)   Yrs in all christean observance,

RICHARD SALTONSTALL.

The house of deputs thinke meete that this petition shall be granted, and desire our magistrats concurrance herein.   EDWARD RAWSON.

—COFFIN'S *Newbury*, pp. 335, 336.

[1] Laws Camb., 1675, p. 15.   [2] Hildreth, vol. i. p. 368.   [3] Coffin, p. 335.

This "protest against man-stealing" has adorned and flavored many an oration on the "position of Massachusetts" on the slavery question. It has been brought out "to point a moral and adorn a tale" by the proud friends of the Commonwealth; but the law quoted above against "man-stealing," the language of the "protest," the statute on "bond servitude," and the practices of the colonists for many years afterwards, prove that many have gloried, but not according to the truth.[1] When it came to the question of damages, the court said : "For the negars (they being none of his, *but stolen*) we thinke meete to allow. nothing." [2]

So the decision of the court was based upon law, — the prohibition against "man-stealing." And it should not be forgotten that many of the laws of the colony were modelled after the Mosaic code. It is referred to, apologetically, in the statute of 1641 ; and no careful student can fail to read between the lines the desire there expressed to refer to the Old Testament as authority for slavery. Now, slaves were purchased by Abraham, and the New-England "doctors of the law" were unwilling to have slaves stolen when they could be bought[3] so easily. Dr. Moore says, in reference to the decision, —

"In all the proceedings of the General Court on this occasion, there is not a trace of anti-slavery opinion or sentiment, still less of anti-slavery legislation; though both have been repeatedly claimed for the honor of the colony." [4]

And Dr. Moore is not alone in his opinion ; for Mr. Hildreth says this case "in which Saltonstall was concerned has been magnified by too precipitate an admiration into a protest on the part of Massachusetts against the African slave-trade. So far, however, from any such protest being made, at the very birth of the foreign commerce of New England the African slave-trade became a regular business." [5] There is now, therefore, no room to doubt but what the decision was rendered on a technical point of law, and not inspired by an anti-slavery sentiment.

As an institution, slavery had at first a stunted growth in Massachusetts, and did not increase its victims to any great extent until near the close of the seventeenth century. But when it did begin a perceptible growth, it made rapid and prodigious strides. In 1676 there were about two hundred slaves in

---

[1] Drake (p. 288) says, "This act, however, was afterwards repealed or disregarded."
[2] Mass. Records, vol. ii. p. 129.   [3] Moore, Appendix, 251, *sq.*
[4] Slavery in Mass., p. 30.   [5] Hildreth, vol. i. p. 282.

the colony, and they were chiefly from Guinea and Madagascar.[1] In 1680 Gov. Bradstreet, in compliance with a request made by the home government, said that the slave-trade was not carried on to any great extent. They were introduced in small lots, and brought from ten to forty pounds apiece. He thought the entire number in the colony would not reach more than one hundred and twenty-five. Few were born in the colony, and none had been baptized up to that time.[2] The year 1700 witnessed an unprecedented growth in the slave-trade. From the 24th of January, 1698, to the 25th of December, 1707,[3] two hundred Negroes were imported into the colony, — quite as many as in the previous sixty years. In 1708 Gov. Dudley's report to the board of trade fixed the number of Negroes at five hundred and fifty, and suggested that they were not so desirable as white servants, who could be used in the army, and in time of peace turn their attention to planting. The prohibition against the Negro politically and in a military sense, in that section of the country, made him almost valueless to the colonial government struggling for deliverance from the cruel laws of the mother country. The white servant could join the "minute-men," plough with his gun on his back, go to the church, and, having received the blessing of the parish minister, could hasten to battle with the proud and almost boastful feelings of a Christian freeman ! But the Negro, bond and free, was excluded from all these sacred privileges. Wronged, robbed of his freedom, — the heritage of all human kind, — he was suspicioned and contemned for desiring that great boon. On the 17th of February, 1720, Gov. Shute placed the number of slaves — including a few Indians — in Massachusetts at two thousand. During the same year thirty-seven males and sixteen females were imported into the colony.[4] We are unable to discover whether these were counted in the enumeration furnished by Gov. Shute or not. We are inclined to think they were included. In 1735 there were two thousand six hundred[5] bond and free in the colony; and within the next seventeen years the Negro population of Boston alone reached 1,541.[6]

---

[1] Slavery in Mass., p. 49. See, also, Drake's Boston, p. 441, note.
[2] Mass. Hist. Coll., vol. viii. 3d Series, p. 337.   [3] Slavery in Mass., p. 50.
[4] Coll. Amer. Stat. Asso., vol. i. p. 586.   [5] Douglass's British Settlements, vol. i. p. 531.
[6] Drake, p. 714. I cannot understand how Dr. Moore gets 1,514 slaves in Boston in 1742, except from Douglass. His "1742" should read 1752, and his "1,514" slaves should read 1,541 slaves.

In 1754 the colonial government found it necessary to establish a system of taxation. Gov. Shirley was required to inform the House of Representatives as to the different kinds of taxable property. And from a clause in his message, Nov. 19, 1754, on the one hundred and nineteenth page of the Journal, we infer two things ; viz., that slaves were chattels or real estate, and, therefore, taxable. The governor says, "There is one part of the Estate, viz., the Negro slaves, which I am at a loss how to come at the knowledge of, without your assistance." In accordance with the request for assistance on this matter, the Legislature instructed the assessors of each town and district within the colony to secure a correct list of all Negro slaves, male and female, from sixteen years old and upwards, to be deposited in the office of the secretary of state.[1] The result of this enumeration was rather surprising; as it fixed the Negro population at 4,489, — quite an increase over the last enumeration. Again, in 1764–65, another census of the Negroes was taken ; and they were found to be 5,779.

Here, as in Virginia, an impost tax was imposed upon all Negro slaves imported into the colony. We will quote section 3 of the Act of October, 1705, requiring duty upon imported Negroes ; because many are disposed to discredit some historical statements about slavery in Massachusetts.

"SECT. 3. And be it further enacted by the authority aforesaid, that from and after the first day of May, in the year one thousand seven hundred and six, every master of ship or vessel, merchant or other person, importing or bringing into this province any negroe or negroes, male or female, of what age soever, shall enter their number, names and sex in the impost office; and the master shall insert the same in the manifest of his lading, and shall pay to the commissioner and receiver of the impost, four pounds per head for every such negro, male or female ; and as well the master, as the ship or vessel wherein they are brought, shall be security for payment of the said duty; and both or either of them shall stand charged in the law therefor to the commissioner, who may deny to grant a clearing for such ship or vessel, until payment be made, or may recover the same of the master, at the commissioner's election,

---

[1] "There is a curious illustration of 'the way of putting it' in Massachusetts, in Mr. Felt's account of this 'census of slaves,' in the Collections of the American Statistical Association, vol. i. p. 208. He says that the General Court passed this order 'for the purpose of having an accurate account of slaves in our Commonwealth, *as a subject in which the people were becoming much interested, relative to the cause of liberty!*' There is not a particle of authority for this suggestion — such a motive for their action never existed anywhere but in the imagination of the writer himself !" — *Slavery in Mass.*, p. 51, note.

by action of debt, bill, plaint or information in any of her majesty's courts of record within this province." [1]

A fine of eight pounds was imposed upon any person refusing or neglecting to make a proper entry of each slave imported, in the "Impost Office." If a Negro died within six weeks after his arrival, a drawback was allowed. If any slave was sold again into another Province or plantation within a year after his arrival, a drawback was allowed to the person who paid the impost duty. A subsequent and more stringent law shows that there was no desire to abate the traffic. In August, 1712, a law was passed "prohibiting the importation or bringing into the province any Indian servants or slaves;" [2] but it was only intended as a check upon the introduction of the Tuscaroras and other "revengeful" Indians from South Carolina.[3] Desperate Indians and insubordinate Negroes were the occasion of grave fears on the part of the colonists.[4] Many Indians had been cruelly dealt with in war; in peace, enslaved and wronged beyond their power of endurance. Their stoical nature led them to the performance of desperate deeds. There is kinship in suffering. There is an unspoken language in sorrow that binds hearts in the indissoluble fellowship of resolve. Whatever natural and national differences existed between the Indian and the Negro — one from the bleak coasts of New England, the other from the tropical coast of Guinea — were lost in the commonality of degradation and interest. The more heroic spirits of both races began to grow restive under the yoke. The colonists were not slow to observe this, and hence this law was to act as a restraint upon and against "their rebellion and hostilities." And the reader should understand that it was not an anti-slavery measure. It was not "hostile to slavery" as a system: it was but the precaution of a guilty and ever-gnawing public conscience.

Slavery grew. There was no legal obstacle in its way. It had the sanction of the law, as we have already shown, and what was better still, the sympathy of public sentiment. The traffic in slaves appears to have been more an object in Boston than at

---

[1] Ancient Charters and Laws of Mass., p. 748.
[2] Ibid.
[3] Slavery in Mass., p. 61.
[4] Hildreth, vol. ii. pp. 269, 270.

any period before or since. For a time dealers had no hesitation in advertising them for sale in their own names. At length a very few who advertised would refer purchasers to "inquire of the printer, and know further." [1] This was in 1727, fifteen years after the afore-mentioned Act became a law, and which many apologists would interpret as a specific and direct prohibition against slavery; but there is no reason for such a perversion of so plain an Act.

Slavery in Massachusetts, as elsewhere, in self-defence had to claim as one of its necessary and fundamental principles, that the slave was either *naturally* inferior to the other races, or that, by some fundamentally inherent law in the institution itself, the master was justified in placing the lowest possible estimate upon his slave property. "Property" implied absolute control over the thing possessed. It carried in its broad meaning the awful fact, not alone of ownership, but of the supremacy of the will of the owner. Mr. Addison says, —

"What color of excuse can there be for the contempt with which we treat this part of our species, that we should not put them upon the common foot of humanity, that we should only *set an insignificant fine upon the man who murders them;* nay, that we should, as much as in us lies, cut them off from the prospect of happiness in another world, as well as in this, and deny them that which we look upon as the proper means for obtaining it?" [2]

None whatever! And yet the Puritans put the Negro slaves in their colony on a level with "horses and hogs." Let the intelligent American of to-day read the following remarkable note from Judge Sewall's diary, and then confess that facts are stranger than fiction.

"1716. I essayed June 22, to prevent Indians and Negroes being rated with Horses and Hogs; but could not prevail. Col. Thaxter bro't it back, and gave as a reason of yr Nonagreement, They were just going to make a new valuation." [3]

It had been sent to the deputies, and was by them rejected, and then returned to the judge by Col. Thaxter. The House was "just going to make a New Valuation" of the property in the

---

[1] Drake's Boston, p. 574. [2] Spectator, No. 215, Nov. 6, 1711.
[3] Slavery in Mass., p. 64.

colony, and hence did not care to exclude slaves from the list of chattels,[1] in which they had always been placed.

"In 1718, all Indian, Negro, and Mulatto servants for life were estimated as other Personal Estate — viz.: Each male servant *for life* above fourteen years of age, at fifteen pounds value; each female servant for life, above fourteen years of age, at ten pounds value. The assessor might make abatement for cause of age or infirmity. Indian, Negro, and Mulatto Male servants *for a term of years* were to be numbered and rated as other Polls, and not as Personal Estate. In 1726, the assessors were required to estimate Indian, Negro, and Mulatto servants proportionably as other Personal Estate, according to their sound judgment and discretion. In 1727, the rule of 1718 was restored, but during one year only, for in 1728 the law was the same as that of 1726; and so it probably remained, including all such servants, as well for term of years as for life, in the ratable estates. We have seen the supply-bills for 1736, 1738, 1739, and 1740, in which this feature is the same.

"And thus they continued to be rated with horses, oxen, cows, goats, sheep, and swine, until after the commencement of the War of the Revolution."[2]

On the 22d of April, 1728, the following notice appeared in a Boston newspaper : —

"Two very likely Negro girls. Enquire two doors from the Brick Meeting-house in Middle-street. At which place is to be sold women's stays, children's good callamanco stiffened-boddy'd coats, and childrens' stays of all sorts, and women's hoop-coats; all at very reasonable rates."[3]

So the "likely Negro girls" were mixed up in the sale of "women's stays" and "hoop-coats"! It was bad enough to "rate Negroes with Horses and Hogs," but to sell them with second-hand clothing was an incident in which is to be seen the low depth to which slavery had carried the Negro by its cruel weight. A human being could be sold like a cast-off garment, and pass without a bill of sale.[4] The announcement that a "likely Negro

---

[1] "In the inventory of the estate of Samuel Morgaridge, who died in 1754, I find,

'Item, three negroes . . . . £133, 6s., 8d.

Item, flax . . . . £12, 2s., 8.'

"In the inventory of Henry Rolfe's estate, taken in April, 1711, I find the following, namely,

'Fifteen sheep, old and young . . . . £3, 15s.

An old gun 2

An old Negroe man 10   0

£13   7s.'"

— Coffin, p. 188.

[2] Slavery in Mass., pp. 64, 65.   [3] Drake, 583, note.

[4] Here is a sample of the sales of those days: "In 1716, Rice Edwards, of Newbury, ship-wright, sells to Edmund Greenleaf 'my whole personal estate with all my goods and chattels as also *one negro man*, one cow, three pigs with timber, plank, and boards." — Coffin, p. 337.

woman about nineteen years and a child about six months of age *to be sold together or apart* " [1] did not shock the Christian sensibilities of the people of Massachusetts. A babe six months old could be torn from the withered and famishing bosom of the young mother, and sold with other articles of merchandise. How bitter and how cruel was such a separation, mothers [2] only can know; and how completely lost a community and government are that regard with complacency a hardship so diabolical, the Christians of America must be able to judge.

The Church has done many cruel things in the name of Christianity. In the dark ages it filled the minds of its disciples with fear, and their bodies with the pains of penance. It burned Michael Servetus, and it strangled the scientific opinions of Galileo. And in stalwart old Massachusetts it thought it was doing God's service in denying the Negro slave the right of Christian baptism."

"The famous French *Code Noir* of 1685 obliged every planter to have his Negroes baptized, and properly instructed in the doctrines and duties of Christianity. Nor was this the only important and humane provision of that celebrated statute, to which we may seek in vain for any parallel in British Colonial legislation." [3]

On the 25th of October, 1727, Matthias Plant [4] wrote, in answer to certain questions put to him by "the secretary of the Society for the Propagation of the Gospel," as follows:—

"6. Negro slaves, one of them is desirous of baptism, but *denied by her master*, a woman of wonderful sense, and prudent in matters, of equal knowledge in Religion with most of her sex, far exceeding any of her own nation that ever yet I heard of." [5]

It was nothing to her master that she was "desirous of baptism," "of wonderful sense," "prudent in matters," and "of equal knowledge in religion with most of her sex!" She was a Negro slave, and as such was denied the blessings of the Christian Church.

---

1 New-England Weekly Journal, No. 267, May 1, 1732.

2 A child one year and a half old — a nursing child sold from the bosom of its mother! — and *for life!* — COFFIN, p. 337.

3 Slavery in Mass., p. 96. Note.

4 Eight years after this, on the 22d of June, 1735, Mr. Plant records in his diary: "I wrote Mr. Salmon of Barbadoes to send me a Negro." (Coffin, p. 338.) It doesn't appear that the reverend gentleman was opposed to slavery!

5 Note quoted by Dr. Moore, p. 58.

"The system of personal servitude was fast disappearing from Western Europe, where the idea had obtained that it was inconsistent with Christian duty for Christians to hold Christians as slaves. But this charity did not extend to heathen and infidels. The same system of morality which held the possessions of unbelievers as lawful spoils of war, delivered over their persons also to the condition of servitude. Hence, in America, the slavery of the Indians, and presently of Negroes, whom experience proved to be much more capable of enduring the hardships of that condition."[1]

And those who were so fortunate as to secure baptism were not freed thereby.[2] In Massachusetts no Negro ever had the courage to seek his freedom through this door, and, therefore, there was no necessity for legislation there to define the question; but in the Southern colonies the law declared that baptism did not secure the liberty of the subject. As early as 1631 a law was passed admitting no man to the rights of "freemen" who was not a member of some church within the limits of the jurisdiction of the colony.[3] The blessings of a "freeman" were reserved for church-members only. Negroes were not admitted to the church, and, therefore, were denied the rights of a freeman.[4] Even the mother country had no bowels of compassion for the Negro. In 1677 the English courts held that a Negro slave was *property*.

"That, being usually bought and sold among merchants as merchandise, and *also being infidels*, there might be a property in them sufficient to maintain trover."[5]

So as "infidels" the Negro slaves of Massachusetts were deprived of rights and duties belonging to a member of the Church and State.

"Zealous for religion as the colonists were, very little effort was made to convert the Negroes, owing partly, at least, to a prevalent opinion that neither Christian brotherhood nor the law of England would justify the holding Chris-

---

[1] Hildreth, vol. i. p. 44.

[2] "For they tell the Negroes, that they must believe in Christ, and receive the Christian faith, and that they must receive the sacrament, and be baptized, and so they do; but still they keep them slaves for all this." — MACY'S *Hist. of Nantucket*, pp. 280, 281.

[3] Ancient Charters and Laws of Mass., p. 117.

[4] Mr. Palfrey relies upon a single reference in Winthrop for the historical trustworthiness of his statement that a Negro slave could be a member of the church. He thinks, however, that this "presents a curious question," and wisely reasons as follows: "As a church-member, he was eligible to the political franchise; and, if he should be actually invested with it, he would have a part in making laws to govern his master, — laws with which his master, if a non-communicant, would have had no concern except to obey them. But it is improbable that the Court would have made a slave — while a slave — a member of the Company, though he were a communicant. — PALFREY, vol. ii. p. 30. Note.

[5] Butts *vs.* Penny, 2 Lev., p. 201; 3 Kib., p. 785.

tians as slaves. Nor could repeated colonial enactments to the contrary entirely root out this idea, for it was not supposed that a colonial statute could set aside the law of England." [1]

But the deeper reason the colonists had for excluding slaves from baptism, and hence citizenship, was twofold ; viz., to keep in harmony with the Mosaic code in reference to "strangers" and " Gentiles," and to keep the door of the Church shut in the face of the slave ; because to open it to him was to emancipate him in course of time. Religious and secular knowledge were not favorable to slavery. The colonists turned to the narrow, national spirit of the Old Testament, rather than to the broad and catholic spirit of the New Testament, for authority to withhold the mercies of the Christian religion from the Negro slaves in their midst.

The rigorous system of domestic slavery established in the colony of Massachusetts bore its bitter fruit in due season. It was impossible to exclude the slaves from the privileges of the Church and State without inflicting a moral injury upon the holy marriage relation. In the contemplation of the law the slave was a chattel, an article of merchandise. The custom of separating parent and child, husband and wife, was very clear proof that the marriage relation was either positively ignored by the institution of slavery, or grossly violated under the slightest pretext. All well-organized society or government rests upon this sacred relation. But slavery, with lecherous grasp and avaricious greed, trailed the immaculate robes of marriage in the moral filth of the traffic in human beings. True, there never was any prohibition against the marriage of one slave to another slave, — for they *tried* to breed slaves in Massachusetts ! — but there never was any law encouraging the lawful union of slaves until after the Revolutionary War, in 1786. We rather infer from the following in the Act of October, 1705, that the marriage relation among slaves had been left entirely to the caprices of the master.

" And no master shall unreasonably deny marriage to his Negro with one of the same nation; any law, usage or custom to the contrary notwithstanding." [2]

We have not been able to discover "any law " positively prohibiting marriage among slaves ; but there was a custom denying

---

[1] Hildreth, vol. ii. p. 426.   [2] Ancient Charters and Laws of Mass., p. 748.

marriage to the Negro, that at length received the weight of positive law. Mr. Palfrey says, —

"From the reverence entertained by the fathers of New England for the
nuptial tie, it is safe to infer that slave husbands and wives were never separated." [1]

We have searched faithfully to find the slightest justification
for this inference of Mr. Palfrey, but have not found it. There
is not a line in any newspaper of the colony, until 1710, that indicates the concern of the people in the lawful union of slaves.
And there was no legislation upon the subject until 1786, when
an "Act for the orderly Solemnization of Marriage" passed. That
Negro slaves were united in marriage, there is abundant evidence,
but not many in this period. It was almost a useless ceremony
when "the customs and usages" of slavery separated them at the
convenience of the owner. The master's power over his slaves
was almost absolute. If he wanted to sell the children and keep
the parents, his decision was not subject to any court of law. It
was final. If he wanted to sell the wife of his slave man into the
rice-fields of the Carolinas or into the West India Islands, the
tears of the husband only exasperated the master. "The fathers
of New England" had *no* reverence for the "nuptial tie" among
their slaves, and, therefore, tore slave families asunder without
the least compunction of conscience. "Negro children were considered an incumbrance in a family, and, when weaned, were
given away like puppies," says the famous Dr. Belknap. But
after the Act of 1705, "their banns were published like those of
white persons;" and public sentiment began to undergo a change
on the subject. The following Negro marriage was prepared by
the Rev. Samuel Phillips of Andover. His ministry did not commence until 1710; and, therefore, this marriage was prepared
subsequent to that date. He realized the need of something, and
acted accordingly.

"You, Bob, do now, in ye Presence of God and these Witnesses, Take
Sally to be your wife;

"Promising, that so far as shall be consistent with ye Relation which you
now Sustain as a servant, you will Perform ye Part of an Husband towards
her: And in particular, as you shall have ye Opportunity & Ability, you will
take proper Care of her in Sickness and Health, in Prosperity & Adversity;

"And that you will be True & Faithful to her, and will Cleave to her

---

[1] Palfrey, vol. ii. p. 30. Note.

only, so long as God, in his Providence, shall continue your and her abode in Such Place (or Places) as that you can conveniently come together. — Do You thus Promise?

"You, Sally, do now, in ye Presence of God, and these Witnesses, Take Bob to be your Husband;

"Promising, that so far as your present Relation as a Servant shall admit, you will Perform the Part of a Wife towards him: and in particular,

"You Promise that you will Love him; And that as you shall have the Opportunity & Ability, you will take a proper Care of him in Sickness and Health; in Prosperity and Adversity:

"And you will cleave to him only, so long as God, in his Providence, shall continue his & your Abode in such Place (or Places) as that you can come together. — Do you thus Promise? I then, agreeable to your Request, and with ye Consent of your Masters & Mistresses, do Declare that you have License given you to be conversant and familiar together as Husband and Wife, so long as God shall continue your Places of Abode as aforesaid; And so long as you Shall behave yourselves as it becometh servants to doe:

"For you must both of you bear in mind that you remain still, as really and truly as ever, your Master's Property, and therefore it will be justly expected, both by God and Man, that you behave and conduct yourselves as Obedient and faithful Servants towards your respective Masters & Mistresses for the Time being:

"And finally, I exhort and Charge you to beware lest you give place to the Devil, so as to take occasion from the license now given you, to be lifted up with Pride, and thereby fall under the Displeasure, not of Man only, but of God also; for it is written, that God resisteth the Proud but giveth Grace to the humble.

"I shall now conclude with Prayer for you, that you may become good Christians, and that you may be enabled to conduct as such; and in particular, that you may have Grace to behave suitably towards each Other, as also dutifully towards your Masters & Mistresses, Not with Eye Service as Men pleasers, ye Servants of Christ doing ye Will of God from ye heart, &c.

["ENDORSED] NEGRO MARRIAGE."

Where a likely Negro woman was courted by the slave of another owner, and wanted to marry, she was sold, as a matter of humanity, "with her wearing apparel" to the owner of the man. "A Bill of Sale of a Negro Woman Servant in Boston in 1724, recites that 'Whereas Scipio, of Boston aforesaid, Free Negro Man and Laborer, proposes Marriage to Margaret, the Negro Woman Servant of the said Dorcas Marshall [a Widow Lady of Boston]: Now to the Intent that the said Intended Marriage may take Effect, and that the said Scipio may Enjoy the said Margaret without any Interruption,' etc., she is duly sold, with her apparel, for Fifty Pounds."[2] Within the next twenty years the Governor

---

[1] Hist. Mag., vol. v., 2d Series, by Dr. G. H. Moore.   [2] Slavery in Mass., p. 57, note.

and his Council found public opinion so modified on the question of marriage among the blacks, that they granted a Negro a divorce on account of his wife's adultery with a white man. But in Quincy's Reports, page 30, note, quoted by Dr. Moore, in 1758 the following rather loose decision is recorded : that the child of a female slave never married according to any of the forms prescribed by the laws of this land, by another slave, who "had kept her company with her master's consent," was not a bastard.

The Act of 1705 forbade any "christian" from marrying a Negro, and imposed a fine of fifty pounds upon any clergyman who should join a Negro and "christian" in marriage. It stood as the law of the Commonwealth until 1843, when it was repealed by an "Act relating to Marriage between Individuals of Certain Races."

As to the political rights of the Negro, it should be borne in mind, that, as he was excluded from the right of Christian baptism, hence from the Church ; and as only church-members enjoyed the rights of freemen, it is clear that the Negro was not admitted to the exercise of the duties of a freeman.[1] Admitting that there were instances where Negroes received the rite of baptism, it was so well understood as not entitling them to freedom or political rights, that it was never questioned during this entire period. Free Negroes were but little better off than the slaves. While they might be regarded as owning their own labor, political rights and ecclesiastical privileges were withheld from them.

"They became the objects of a suspicious legislation, which deprived them of most of the rights of freemen, and reduced them to a social position very similar, in many respects, to that which inveterate prejudice in many parts of Europe has fixed upon the Jews."

Though nominally free, they did not come under the head of "Christians." Neither freedom, nor baptism in the Church, could free them from the race-malice of the whites, that followed them like the fleet-footed "Furies." There were special regulations for free Negroes. The Act of 1703, forbidding slaves from being out at night after the hour of nine o'clock, extended to free Negroes.[2] In 1707 an Act was passed "regulating of free negroes."[3] It recites that "free negroes and mulattos, able of body, and fit for

---

[1] I use the term freeman, because the colony being under the English crown, there were no citizens. All were British subjects.

[2] Ancient Charters and Laws of Mass., p. 746.   [3] Ibid., p. 386.

labor, who are not charged with trainings, watches, and other services," [1] shall perform service equivalent to militia training. They were under the charge of the officer in command of the military company belonging to the district where they resided. They did fatigue-duty. And the only time, that, by law, the Negro was admitted to the trainings, was between 1652 and 1656. But there is no evidence that the Negroes took advantage of the law. Public sentiment is more potent than law. In May, 1656, the law of 1652, admitting Negroes to the trainings, was repealed.

"For the better ordering and settling of severall cases in the military companyes within this jurisdiction, which, upon experience, are found either wanting or inconvenient, it is ordered and declared by this Court and the authoritie thereof, that henceforth no negroes or Indians, although servants to the English, shal be armed or permitted to trayne, and yᵗ no other person shall be exempted from trayning but such as some law doth priveledge." [2]

And Gov. Bradstreet, in his report to the "Committee for Trade," made in May, 1680, says, —

"We account all generally from Sixteen to Sixty that are healthfull and strong bodys, both House-holders and Servants fit to beare Armes, *except Negroes* and *slaves*, whom wee arme not." [3]

The law of 1707 — which is the merest copy of the Virginia law on the same subject — requires free Negroes to answer fire-alarms with the company belonging to their respective precincts. They were not allowed to entertain slave friends at their houses, without the permission of the owner of the slaves. To all prohibitions there was affixed severe fines in large sums of money. In case of a failure to pay these fines, the delinquent was sent to the House of Correction; where, under severe discipline, he was constrained to work out his fine at the rate of one shilling per day! If a Negro "presume to smite or strike any person of the English, or other christian nation," he was publicly flogged by the justice before whom tried, at the discretion of that officer.

During this period the social condition of the Negroes, bond

---

[1] Mr. Palfrey is disposed to hang a very weighty matter on a very slender thread of authority. He says, "In the list of men capable of bearing arms, at Plymouth, in 1643, occurs the name of 'Abraham Pearse, the Black-moore,' from which we infer . . . that Negroes were not dispensed from military service in that colony" (History of New England, vol. ii. p. 30, note). This single case is borne down by the laws and usages of the colonists on this subject. Negroes as a class were absolutely excluded from the military service, from the commencement of the colony down to the war with Great Britain.

[2] Slavery in Mass., Appendix, p. 243.   [3] Mass. Hist. Soc. Coll., vol. viii. 3d Series, p. 336.

and free, was very deplorable. The early records of the town of Boston preserve the fact that one Thomas Deane, in the year 1661, was prohibited from employing a Negro in the manufacture of hoops, under a penalty of twenty shillings; for what reason is not stated."[1] No churches or schools, no books or teachers, they were left to the gloom and vain imaginations of their own fettered intellects. John Eliot "had long lamented it with a Bleeding and Burning Passion, that the English used their Negroes but as their Horses or their Oxen, and that so little care was taken about their immortal souls; he looked upon it as a Prodigy, that any wearing the *Name* of *Christians* should so much have the *Heart* of *Devils* in them, as to prevent and hinder the Instruction of the poor *Blackamores*, and confine the souls of their miserable Slaves to a *Destroying Ignorance*, merely for fear of thereby losing the Benefit of their Vassalage; but now he made a motion to the *English* within two or three Miles of him, that at such a time and place they would send their *Negroes* once a week unto him: For he would then *Catechise* them, and *Enlighten* them, to the utmost of his power in things of their Everlasting Peace; however, he did not live to make much progress in this undertaking."[2] The few faint voices of encouragement, that once in a great while reached them from the pulpit[3] and forum, were as strange music, mellowed and sweetened by the distance. The free and slave Negroes were separated by law, were not allowed to communicate together to any great extent. They were not allowed in numbers greater than three, and then, if not in the service of some white person, were liable to be arrested, and sent to the House of Correction.

" The slave was the property of his master as much as his ox or his horse; *he had no civil rights* but that of protection from cruelty; he could acquire no property nor dispose of any[4] without the consent of his master. . . . We think he had not the capacity to communicate a civil relation to his children, which he did not enjoy himself, except as the property of his master."[5]

With but small means the free Negroes of the colony were unable to secure many comforts in their homes. They were hated and dreaded more than their brethren in bondage. They could

---

[1] Lyman's Report, 1822.   [2] Mather's Magnalia, Book III., p. 207.   Compare also p. 209.
[3] Elliott's New-England Hist., vol. ii. p. 165.
[4] Mr. Palfrey comes again with his single and exceptional case, asking us to infer a rule therefrom. See History of New England, note, p. 30.
[5] Chief-Justice Parker, in Andover *vs.* Canton, 13 Mass. p. 550.

judge, by contrast, of the abasing influences of slavery. They were only nominally free ; because they were taxed [1] without representation, — had no voice in the colonial government.

But, notwithstanding the obscure and neglected condition of the free Negroes, some of them by their industry, frugality, and aptitude won a place in the confidence and esteem of the more humane of the white population. Owning their own time, many of the free Negroes applied themselves to the acquisition of knowledge. Phillis Wheatley, though nominally a slave for some years, stood at the head of the intellectual Negroes of this period. She was brought from Africa to the Boston slave-market, where, in 1761, she was purchased by a benevolent white lady by the name of Mrs. John Wheatley. She was naked, save a piece of dirty carpet about her loins, was delicate of constitution, and much fatigued from a rough sea-voyage. Touched by her modest demeanor and intelligent countenance, Mrs. Wheatley chose her from a large company of slaves. It was her intention to teach her the duties of an ordinary domestic ; but clean clothing and wholesome diet effected such a radical change in the child for the better, that Mrs. Wheatley changed her plans, and began to give her private instruction. Eager for learning, apt in acquiring, though only eight years old, she greatly surprised and pleased her mistress. Placed under the instruction of Mrs. Wheatley's daughter, Phillis learned the English language sufficiently well as to be able to read the most difficult portions of the Bible with ease and accuracy. This she accomplished in less than a year and a half. She readily mastered the art of writing ; and within four years from the time she landed in the slave-market in Boston, she was able to carry on an extensive correspondence on a variety of topics.

Her ripening intellectual faculties attracted the attention of the refined and educated people of Boston, many of whom sought her society at the home of the Wheatleys. It should be remembered, that this period did not witness general culture among the masses of white people, and certainly no facilities for the education of Negroes. And yet some cultivated white persons gave Phillis encouragement, loaned her books, and called her out on matters of a literary character. Having acquired the principles of an English education, she turned her attention to the study of

---

[1] Slavery in Mass., p. 62.

the Latin language, [1] and was able to do well in it.   Encouraged by her success, she translated one of Ovid's tales.   The translation was considered so admirable that it was published in Boston by some of her friends.   On reaching England it was republished, and called forth the praise of many of the reviews.

Her manners were modest and refined.   Her nature was sensitive and affectionate.   She early gave signs of a deep spiritual experience,[2] which gave tone and character to all her efforts in composition and poetry.   There was a charming vein of gratitude in all her private conversations and public utterances, which her owners did not fail to recognize and appreciate.   Her only distinct recollection of her native home was, that every morning early *her mother poured out water before the rising sun.*   Her growing intelligence and keen appreciation of the blessings of civilization overreached mere animal grief at the separation from her mother.   And as she knew more of the word of God, she became more deeply interested in the condition of her race.

At the age of twenty her master emancipated her.   Naturally delicate, the severe climate of New England, and her constant application to study, began to show on her health.   Her friend and mother, for such she proved herself to be, Mrs. Wheatley, solicitous about her health, called in eminent medical counsel, who prescribed a sea-voyage.   A son of Mrs. Wheatley was about to visit England on mercantile business, and therefore took Phillis with him.   For the previous six years she had cultivated her taste for poetry; and, at this time, her reputation was quite well established.   She had corresponded with persons in England in social circles, and was not a stranger to the English.   She was heartily welcomed by the leaders of the society of the British metropolis, and treated with great consideration.   Under all the trying circumstances of high social life, among the nobility and rarest literary genius of London, this redeemed child of the desert, coupled to a beautiful modesty the extraordinary powers of an incomparable conversationalist.   She carried London by storm.   Thoughtful people praised her; titled people dined her; and the press extolled the name of Phillis Wheatley, the African poetess.

---

[1] Mott's Sketches, p. 17.

[2] At the early age of sixteen, in the year 1770, Phillis was baptized into the membership of the society worshipping in the "Old South Meeting-House."   The gifted, eloquent, and noble Dr. Sewall was the pastor.   This was an exception to the rule, that slaves were not baptized into the Church.

Prevailed upon by admiring friends, in 1773 [1] she gave her poems to the world. They were published in London in a small octavo volume of about one hundred and twenty pages, comprising thirty-nine pieces. It was dedicated to the Countess of Huntingdon, with a picture of the poetess, and a letter of recommendation signed by the governor and lieutenant-governor, with many other "respectable citizens of Boston."

TO THE PUBLIC.

As it has been repeatedly suggested to the publisher, by persons who have seen the manuscript, that numbers would be ready to suspect they were not really the writings of PHILLIS, he has procured the following attestation, from the most respectable characters in *Boston*, that none might have the least ground for disputing their *Original*.

We, whose Names are under-written, do assure the World, that the Poems specified in the following page were (as we verily believe) written by PHILLIS, a young Negro Girl, who was, but a few Years since, brought, an uncultivated Barbarian, from *Africa*, and has ever since been, and now is, under the disadvantage of serving as a Slave in a family in this town. She has been examined by some of the best judges, and is thought qualified to write them.

His Excellency, THOMAS HUTCHINSON, *Governor.*
The Hon. ANDREW OLIVER, *Lieutenant Governor.*

Hon. Thomas Hubbard,	*Rev.* Charles Chauncy,
Hon. John Erving,	*Rev.* Mather Byles,
Hon. James Pitts,	*Rev.* Ed. Pemberton,
Hon. Harrison Gray,	*Rev.* Andrew Elliot,
Hon. James Bowdoin,	*Rev.* Samuel Cooper,
John Hancock, *Esq.*	*Rev.* Samuel Mather,
Joseph Green, *Esq.*	*Rev.* John Moorhead,
Richard Cary, *Esq.*	*Mr.* John Wheatley, her master.

The volume has passed through several English and American editions, and is to be found in all first-class libraries in the country. Mrs. Wheatley sickened, and grieved daily after Phillis. A picture of her little ward, sent from England, adorned her bedroom; and she pointed it out to visiting friends with all the sincere pride of a mother. On one occasion she exclaimed to a friend, "See! Look at my Phillis! Does she not seem as though she would speak to me?" Getting no better, she sent a loving

---

[1] All writers I have seen on this subject — and I think I have seen all — leave the impression that Miss Wheatley's poems were first published in London. This is not true. The first published poems from her pen were issued in Boston in 1770. But it was a mere pamphlet edition, and has long since perished.

request to Phillis to come to her at as early a moment as possible. With a deep sense of gratitude to Mrs. Wheatley for countless blessings bestowed upon her, Phillis hastened to return to Boston. She found her friend and benefactor just living, and shortly had the mournful satisfaction of closing her sightless eyes. The husband and daughter followed the wife and mother quickly to the grave. Young Mr. Wheatley married, and settled in England. Phillis was alone in the world.

"She soon after received an offer of marriage from a respectable colored man, of Boston. The name of this individual was *John* Peters.[1] He kept a grocery in Court Street, and was a man of handsome person. He wore a wig, carried a cane, and quite acted out ' *the gentleman.*' In an evil hour, he was accepted; and, though he was a man of talents and information, — writing with fluency and propriety, and, at one period, reading law, — he proved utterly unworthy of the distinguished woman who honored him by her alliance."

Her married life was brief. She was the mother of one child, that died early. Ignorant of the duties of domestic life, courted and flattered by the cultivated, Peters's jealousy was at length turned into harsh treatment. Tenderly raised, and of a delicate constitution, Phillis soon went into decline, and died Dec. 5, 1784, in the thirty-first[2] year of her life, greatly beloved and sincerely mourned by all whose good fortune it had been to know of her high mental endowments and blameless Christian life.

Her influence upon the rapidly growing anti-slavery sentiment of Massachusetts was considerable. The friends of humanity took pleasure in pointing to her marvellous achievements, as an evidence of what the Negro could do under favorable circumstances. From a state of nudity in a slave-market, a stranger to the English language, this young African girl had won her way over the rough path of learning; had conquered the spirit of caste in the best society of conservative old Boston; had brought two continents to her feet in admiration and amazement at the rare poetical accomplishments of a child of Africa![3]

She addressed a poem to Gen. Washington that pleased the old warrior very much. We have never seen it, though we have searched diligently. Mr. Sparks says of it, —

---

[1] All the historians but Sparks omit the given name of Peters. It was John.

[2] The date usually given for her death is 1780, while her age is fixed at twenty-six. The best authority gives the dates above, and I think they are correct.

[3] " Her correspondence was sought, and it extended to persons of distinction even in England; among whom may be named the Countess of Huntingdon, Whitefield, and the Earl of Dartmouth." — SPARKS's *Washington*, vol. iii. p. 298, note.

" I have not been able to find, among Washington's papers, the letter and poem addressed to him. They have doubtless been lost. From the circumstance of her invoking the muse in his praise, and from the tenor of some of her printed pieces, particularly one addressed to King George seven years before, in which she compliments him on the repeal of the Stamp Act, it may be inferred, that she was a Whig in politics after the American way of thinking; and it might be curious to see in what manner she would eulogize liberty and the rights of man, while herself, nominally at least, in bondage." [1]

Gen. Washington, in a letter to Joseph Reed, bearing date of the 10th of February, 1776, from Cambridge, refers to the letter and poem as follows : —

" I recollect nothing else worth giving you the trouble of, unless you can be amused by reading a letter and poem addressed to me by Miss Phillis Wheatley. In searching over a parcel of papers the other day, in order to destroy such as were useless, I brought it to light again. At first, with a view of doing justice to her poetical genius, I had a great mind to publish the poem; but not knowing whether it might not be considered rather as a mark of my own vanity, than as a compliment to her, I laid it aside,[2] till I came across it again in the manner just mentioned." [3]

This gives the world an " inside " view of the brave old general's opinion of the poem and poetess ; but the " outside " view, as expressed to Phillis, is worthy of reproduction at this point.

CAMBRIDGE, 28 February, 1776.

MISS PHILLIS, — Your favor of the 26th of October did not reach my hands, till the middle of December. Time enough, you will say, to have given an answer ere this. Granted. But a variety of important occurrences, continually interposing to distract the mind and withdraw the attention, I hope will apologize for the delay, and plead my excuse for the seeming but not real neglect. I thank you most sincerely for your polite notice of me, in the elegant lines you enclosed; and however undeserving I may be of such encomium and panegyric, the style and manner exhibit a striking proof of your poetical talents; in honor of which, and as a tribute justly due to you, I would have published the poem, had I not been apprehensive, that, while I only meant to give the world this new instance of your genius, I might have incurred the imputation of vanity. This, and nothing else, determined me not to give it place in the public prints.

If you should ever come to Cambridge, or near head-quarters, I shall be happy to see a person so favored by the Muses, and to whom nature has been so liberal and beneficent in her dispensations.

I am, with great respect, your obedient, humble servant,

GEORGE WASHINGTON.[4]

---

[1] Sparks's Washington, vol. iii. p. 299, note.

[2] This destroys the last hope I have nursed for nearly six years that the poem might yet come to light. Somehow I had overlooked this note.

[3] Sparks's Washington, vol iii. p. 288.   [4] Ibid., vol. iii. pp. 297, 298.

This letter is a handsome compliment to the poetess, and does honor to both the head and heart of the general. His modesty, so characteristic, has deprived history of its dues. But it is consoling to know that the sentiments of the poem found a response in the patriotic heart of the *first soldier of the Revolution, and the Father of his Country !*

While Phillis Wheatley stands out as one of the most distinguished characters of this period, and who, as a Colored person, had no equal, yet she was not the only individual of her race of intellect and character. A Negro boy from Africa was purchased by a Mr. Slocum, who resided near New Bedford, Mass. After he acquired the language, he turned his thoughts to freedom, and in a few years, by working beyond the hours he devoted to his master, was enabled to buy himself from his master. He married an Indian woman named Ruth Moses, and settled at Cutterhunker, in the Elizabeth Islands, near New Bedford. In a few years, through industry and frugality, John Cuffe — the name he took as a freeman — was enabled to purchase a good farm of one hundred (100) acres. Every year recorded new achievements, until John Cuffe had a wide reputation for wealth, honesty, and intelligence. He applied himself to books, and secured, as the ripe fruit of his studious habits, a fair business education. Both himself and wife were Christian believers ; and to lives of industry and increasing secular knowledge, they added that higher knowledge which makes alive to "everlasting life." Ten children were born unto them, — four boys and six girls. One of the boys, Paul Cuffe, became one of the most distinguished men of color Massachusetts has produced. The reader will be introduced to him in the proper place in the history. John Cuffe died in 1745, leaving behind, in addition to considerable property, a good name, which is of great price.[1]

Richard Dalton, Esq., of Boston, owned a Negro boy whom he taught to read any Greek writer without hesitancy. Mr. Dalton was afflicted with weak eyes ; and his fondness for the classics would not allow him to forego the pleasure of them, and hence his Negro boy Cæsar was instructed in the Greek.[2] "The Boston Chronicle" of Sept. 21, 1769, contains the following advertisement : "To be sold, a Likely Little negroe boy, who *can speak the French language,* and very fit for a Valet."

---

[1] Armistead's A Tribute to the Negro, pp. 460, 461.   [2] Douglass, vol. ii. p. 345, note.

With increasing evidence of the Negro's capacity for mental improvement, and fitness for the duties and blessings of a freeman, and the growing insolence and rigorous policy of the mother country, came a wonderful change in the colony. The Negroes were emboldened to ask for and claim rights as British subjects, and the more humane element among the whites saw in a relaxation of the severe treatment of the blacks security and immunity in war. But anti-slavery sentiment in Massachusetts was not born of a genuine desire to put down a wicked and cruel traffic in human beings. Two things operated in favor of humane treatment of the slaves, — an impending war, and the decision of Lord Mansfield in the Sommersett case. The English government was yearly increasing the burdens of the colonists. The country was young, its resources little known. The people were largely engaged in agricultural pursuits. There were no tariff laws encouraging or protecting the labor or skill of the people. Civil war seemed inevitable. Thoughtful men began to consider the question as to which party the Negroes of the colony would contribute their strength. It was no idle question to determine whether the Negroes were Tories or Whigs. As early as 1750 the questions as to the legality of holding Negroes in slavery in British colonies began to be discussed in England and New England. "What, precisely, the English law might be on the subject of slavery, still remained a subject of doubt." [1] Lord Holt held that slavery was a condition unknown to English law, — that the being in England was evidence of freedom. This embarrassed New-England planters in taking their slaves to England. The planters banded for their common cause, and secured the written opinion of Yorke and Talbot, attorney and solicitor general of England. They held that slaves *could* be held in England as well as in America; that baptism did not confer freedom: and the opinion stood as sound law for nearly a half-century. [2] The men in England who lived on the money wrung from the slave-trade, the members of the Royal African Company, came to the rescue of the institution of slavery. In order to maintain it by law in the American colonies, it had to be recognized in England. The people of Massachusetts took a lively interest in the question. In 1761, at a meeting "in the old court-house," James Otis, [3] in a

---

[1] Hildreth, vol. ii. p. 426. [2] Pearce *vs.* Lisle, Ambler, 76.

[3] It may sound strangely in the ears of some friends and admirers of the gifted John Adams to hear now, after the lapse of many years, what he had to say of the position Otis took. His

speech against the "writs of assistance," struck a popular chord on the questions of "The Rights of the Colonies," afterwards published (1764) by order of the Legislature. He took the broad ground, "that the colonists, black and white, born here, are free-born British subjects and entitled to all the essential rights of such."[1] In 1766 Nathaniel Appleton and James Swan distinguished themselves in their defence of the doctrines of "liberty for all." It became the general topic of discussion in private and public, and country lyceums and college societies took it up as a subject of forensic disputation.[2] In the month of May, 1766, the representatives of the people were instructed to advocate the total abolition of slavery. And on the 16th of March, 1767, a resolution was offered to see whether the instructions should be adhered to, and was unanimously carried in the affirmative. But it should be remembered that British troops were in the colony, in the streets of Boston. The mutterings of the distant thunder of revolution could be heard. Public sentiment was greatly tempered toward the Negroes. On the 31st of May, 1609, the House of Representatives of Massachusetts resolved against the presence of troops, and besought the governor to remove them. His Excellency disclaimed any power under the circumstances to interfere. The House denounced a standing army in time of peace, without the consent of the General Court, as "without precedent, and unconstitutional."[3] In 1769 one of the courts of Massachusetts gave a decision friendly to a slave, who was the plaintiff. This stimulated the Negroes to an exertion for freedom. The entire colony was in a feverish state of excitement. An anonymous Tory writer reproached Bostonians for desiring freedom when they themselves enslaved others.

---

mild views on slavery were as deserving of scrutiny as those of the elder Quincy. Mr. Adams says: "Nor were the poor negroes forgotten. Not a Quaker in Philadelphia, or Mr. Jefferson, of Virginia, ever asserted the rights of negroes in stronger terms. Young as I was, and ignorant as I was, I shuddered at the doctrine he taught; and I have all my lifetime shuddered, and still shudder, at the consequences that may be drawn from such premises. Shall we say, that the rights of masters and servants clash, and can be decided only by force? I adore the idea of gradual abolitions! But who shall decide how fast or how slowly these abolitions shall be made?"

[1] Hildreth, vol. ii. pp. 564, 565.

[2] Coffin says, "In October of 1773, an action was brought against Richard Greenleaf, of Newburyport, by Cæsar [Hendrick], a colored man, whom he claimed as his slave, for holding him in bondage. He laid the damages at fifty pounds. The council for the plaintiff, in whose favor the jury brought in their verdict and awarded him eighteen pounds' damages and costs, was John Lowell, Esq., afterward Judge Lowell. This case excited much interest, as it was the first, if not the only one of the kind, that ever occurred in the county."

[3] Hildreth, vol. ii. pp. 550, 551.

" ' What ! ' cries our good people here, ' Negro slaves in Boston ! It cannot be.' It is nevertheless true. For though the Bostonians have grounded their rebellion on the 'immutable laws of nature,' yet, notwithstanding their resolves about freedom in their Town-meetings, they actually have in town 2,000 Negro slaves." [1]

These trying and exasperating circumstances were but the friendly precursors of a spirit of universal liberty.

In England the decision of Lord Mansfield in the Sommersett case had encouraged the conscientious few who championed the cause of the slave. Charles Stewart, Esq., of Boston, Mass., had taken to London with him his Negro slave, James Sommersett. The Negro was seized with a sickness in the British metropolis, and was thereupon abandoned by his master. He afterwards regained his health, and secured employment. His master, learning of his whereabouts, had him arrested, and placed in confinement on board the vessel "Ann and Mary," Capt. John Knowls, commander, then lying in the Thames, but soon to sail for Jamaica, where Sommersett was to be sold.

"On the 3rd of Dec., 1771, affidavits were made by Thomas Walklin, Elizabeth Cade, and John Marlow, that James Sommersett, a Negro, was confined in irons on board a ship called the *Ann* and *Mary*, John Knowls commander, lying in the Thames, and bound for Jamaica. Lord Mansfield, upon the prayer of the above subscribers, allowed a writ of *habeas corpus*, requiring the return of the body of Sommersett before his lordship with an explanation of the cause of his detention. On the 9th of Dec., Capt. Knowls produced the body of Sommersett in Court. Lord Mansfield, after a preliminary examination, referred the matter to the Court of King's Bench, and, therefore, took sureties, and bound Sommersett over 'till ' the 2nd day of the next Hillary term.' At the time appointed the defendant, with counsel, the reputed master of the Negro man Sommersett, and Capt. John Knowls, appeared before the court. Capt. Knowls recited the reasons that led him to detain Sommersett ; whereupon the counsel for the latter asked for time in which to prepare an argument against the return. Lord Mansfield gave them until the 7th of February. At the time appointed Mr. Sergeant Davy and Mr. Sergeant Glynn argued against the return, and had further argument ' postponed 'till Easter term,' when Mr. Mansfield, Mr. Alleyne, and Mr. Hargrave argued on the same side. ' The only question before us is whether the cause on the return is sufficient. If it is, the Negro must be remanded ; if it is not, he must be discharged. The return states that the slave departed and· refused to serve, whereupon he was kept to be sold abroad. So high an act of dominion must be recognized by the law of the country where it is used. The power of a master over his slave has been exceedingly different in different countries.

---

[1] Drake, p. 729, note.   [2] I use the English spelling, — Sommersett.

The state of slavery is of such a nature that it is incapable of being introduced on any reasons, moral or political, but only by positive law, which preserves its force long after the reasons, occasions, and time itself from whence it was created is erased from memory. It is so odious that nothing can be suffered to support it but positive law. Whatever inconveniences, therefore, may follow from the decision, I cannot say this case is allowed or approved by the law of England, and therefore the black must be discharged.'"

The influence of this decision was wide-spread, and hurtful to slavery in the British colonies in North America. It poured new life into the expiring hopes of the Negroes, and furnished a rule of law for the advocates of "freedom for all." It raised a question of law in all the colonies as to whether the colonial governments could pass an Act legalizing that which was "contrary to English law." [1]

Notwithstanding the general and generous impulse for liberty, the indissoluble ties of avarice, and the greed for the unearned gains of the slave-trade, made public men conserve to conserve the interests of those directly interested in the inhuman traffic.

"In an age when the interests of trade guided legislation, this branch of commerce possessed paramount attractions. Not a statesman exposed its enormities; and, if Richard Baxter echoed the opinions of Puritan Massachusetts, if Southern drew tears by the tragic tale of Oronooko, if Steele awakened a throb of indignation by the story of Inkle and Yarico, if Savage and Shenstone pointed their feeble couplets with the wrongs of 'Afric's sable children,' if the Irish metaphysician Hutcheson, struggling for a higher system of morals, —justly stigmatized the traffic; yet no public opinion lifted its voice against it. English ships, fitted out in English cities, under the special favor of the royal family, of the ministry, and of parliament, stole from Africa, in the years from 1700 to 1750, probably a million and a half of souls, of whom one-eighth were buried in the Atlantic, victims of the passage; and yet in England no general indignation rebuked the enormity; for the public opinion of the age was obedient to materialism." [2]

Humane masters who desired to emancipate their slaves were embarrassed by a statute unfriendly to manumission. The Act of 1703 [3] deterred many persons from emancipating their slaves on account of its unjust and hard requirements. And under it quite a deal of litigation arose. It required every master who desired to liberate his slave, before doing so, to furnish a bond to the treasurer of the town or place in which he resided, in a sum not

---

[1] Hildreth, vol. ii. p. 567.   [2] Bancroft, 12th ed. vol. iii. p. 412.
[3] Ancient Charters and Laws of Mass., pp. 745, 746.

less than fifty pounds.[1] This was to indemnify the town or place in case the Negro slave thus emancipated should, through lameness or sickness, become a charge. In case a master failed to furnish such security, his emancipated slaves were still contemplated by the law as in bondage, "notwithstanding any manumission or instrument of freedom to them made or given." Judge Sewall, in a letter to John Adams, cites a case in point.

"A man, by will, gives his Negro his liberty, and leaves him a legacy. The executor consents that the Negro shall be free, but refuseth to give bond to the selectmen to indemnify the town against any charge for his support in case he should become poor (without which, by the province law, he is not manumitted), or to pay him the legacy.

"*Query.* Can he recover the legacy, and how?

"I have just observed that in your last you desire me to say something towards discouraging you from removing to Providence; and you say, any thing will do. ` At present, I only say, you will do well enough where you are. I will explain myself, and add something further, in some future letter. I have not time to enlarge now, for which I believe you will not be inconsolably grieved. So, to put you out of pain, your hearty friend,

JONATHAN SEWALL."[2]

Mr. Adams replied as follows: —

"Now. *En mesure le manner.* The testator intended plainly that his negro should have his liberty and a legacy; therefore the law will presume that he intended his executor should do all that without which he could have neither. That this indemnification was not in the testator's mind, cannot be proved from the will any more than it could be proved, in the first case above, that the testator did not know a fee-simple would pass a will without the word heirs; nor than, in the second case, that the devise of a trust, that might continue forever, would convey a fee-simple without the like words. I take it, therefore, that the executor of this will is, by implication, obliged to give bonds to the town treasurer, and, in his refusal, is a wrongdoer; and I cannot think he ought to be allowed to take advantage of his own wrong, so much as to allege this want of an indemnification to evade an action of the case brought for the legacy by the negro himself.

"But why may not the negro bring a special action of the case against the executor, setting forth the will, the devise of freedom and a legacy, and then

---

[1] The following is from Felt's Salem, vol. ii. pp. 415, 416, and illustrates the manner in which the law was complied with: "1713. Ann, relict of Governor Bradstreet, frees Hannah, a negro servant. 171;, Dec. 21. William and Samuel Upton, of this town, liberate Thomas, who has faithfully served their father, John Upton, of Reading. They give security to the treasurer, that they will meet all charges, which may accrue against the said black man. 1721, May 27. Elizur Keyser does the same for his servant, Cato, after four years more, and then the latter was to receive two suits of clothes. . . . 1758, June 5. The heirs of John Turner, having freed two servants, Titus and Rebeckah, give bonds to the selectmen, that they shall be no public charge."

[2] John Adams's Works, vol. i. p. 51.

the necessity of indemnification by the province law, and then a refusal to indemnify, and, of consequence, to set free and to pay the legacy?

"Perhaps the negro is free at common law by the devise. Now, the province law seems to have been made only to oblige the master to maintain his manumitted slave, and not to declare a manumission in the master's lifetime, or at his death, void. Should a master give his negro his freedom, under his hand and seal, without giving bond to the town, and should afterwards repent and endeavor to recall the negro into servitude, would not that instrument be a sufficient discharge against the master?"[1]

It is pleaded in extenuation of this Act, that it was passed to put a stop to the very prevalent habit of emancipating old and decrepit Negroes after there was no more service in them. If this be true, it reveals a practice more cruel than slavery itself.

In 1702 the representatives of the town of Boston were "desired to promote the encouraging the bringing of White servants and to put a period to Negroes being slaves."[2] This was not an anti-slavery measure, as some have wrongly supposed.[3] It was not a resolution or an Act: it was simply a request; and one that the "Representatives" did not grant for nearly a century afterwards.

"In 1718, a committee of both Houses prepared a bill entitled 'An Act for the Encouraging the Importation of White Male Servants, and the preventing the Clandestine bringing in of Negroes and Molattoes.'"

It was read in Council a first time on the 16th of June, and "sent down recommended" to the House; where it was also read a first time on the same day. The next day it was read a second time, and, "on the question for a third reading, decided in the negative."[4] In 1706 an argument or "Computation that the Importation of Negroes is not so profitable as that of White Servants," was published in Boston.[5] It throws a flood of light upon the Act mentioned above, and shows that the motives that inspired the people who wanted a period put to the holding of Negroes as slaves were grossly material and selfish. It was the first published article on the subject, and is worthy of reproduc-

---

[1] Adams's Works, vol. i. p. 55.   [2] Drake, p. 525.

[3] The late Senator Sumner, in a speech delivered on the 28th of June, 1854, refers to this as "the earliest testimony from any official body against negro slavery." Even the weight of the senator's assertion cannot resist the facts of history. The "resolve" instructing the "representatives" was never carried; but, on the contrary, the next Act was the law of 1703 restricting manumission!

[4] Journal H. of R., 15, 16. General Court Records, x. 282.   [5] Slavery in Mass., p. 106.

tion in full. It is reprinted from "The Boston News-Letter," No. 112, June 10, 1706, in the New-York Historical Society.

"By last Year's Bill of Mortality for the Town of *Boston*, in *Number* 100 *News-Letter*, we are furnished with a List of 44 Negroes dead last year, which being computed one with another at 30*l.* per Head, amounts to the Sum of One Thousand three hundred and Twenty Pounds, of which we would make this Remark: That the Importing of Negroes into this or the Neighboring Provinces is not so beneficial either to the Crown or Country, as White Servants would be.

" For Negroes do not carry Arms to defend the Country as Whites do.

"Negroes are generally Eye-Servants, great Thieves, much addicted to Stealing, Lying and Purloining.

" They do not People our Country as Whites would do whereby we should be strengthened against an Enemy.

"By Encouraging the Importing of White Men Servants, allowing somewhat to the Importer, most Husbandmen in the Country might be furnished with Servants for 8, 9, or 10*l.* a Head, who are not able to launch out 40 or 50*l.* for a Negro the now common Price.

"A Man then might buy a White Man Servant we suppose for 10*l.* to serve 4 years, and Boys for the same price to Serve 6, 8, or 10 years; If a White Servant die, the Loss exceeds not 10*l.* but if a Negro dies, 'tis a very great loss to the Husbandman; Three years Interest of the price of the Negro, will near upon if not altogether purchase a White Man Servant.

" If necessity call for it, that the Husbandman must fit out a Man against the Enemy; if he has a Negro he cannot send him, but if he has a White Servant, 'twill answer the end, and perhaps save his son at home.

"Were Merchants and Masters Encouraged as already said to bring in Men Servants, there needed not be such Complaint against Superiors Impressing our Children to the War, there would then be Men enough to be had without Impressing.

"The bringing in of such Servants would much enrich this Province, because Husbandmen would not only be able far better to manure what Lands are already under Improvement, but would also improve a great deal more that now lyes waste under Woods, and enable this Province to set about raising of Naval Stores, which would be greatly advantageous to the Crown of England, and this Province.

" For the raising of Hemp here, so as to make Sail-cloth and Cordage to furnish but our own shipping, would hinder the Importing it, and save a considerable sum in a year to make Returns for which we now do, and in time might be capacitated to furnish England not only with Sail-cloth and Cordage, but likewise with Pitch, Tar, Hemp, and other Stores which they are now obliged to purchase in Foreign Nations.

" Suppose the Government here should allow Forty Shillings per head for five years, to such as should Import every of these years 100 White Men Servants, and each to serve 4 years, the cost would be but 200*l.* a year, and a 1000*l.* for the 5 years. The first 100 Servants, being free the 4th year they serve the 5th for Wages, and the 6th there is 100 that goes out into the Woods, and settles a 100 Families to Strengthen and Baracado us from the Indians, and also a 100 Families more every year successively.

" And here you see that in one year the Town of Boston has lost 1320*l.* by 44 Negroes, which is also a loss to the Country in general, and for a less loss (if it may improperly be so called) for a 1000*l.* the Country may have 500 Men in 5 years time for the 44 Negroes dead in one year.

" A certain person within these 6 years had two Negroes dead computed both at 60*l.* which would have procured him six white Servants at 10*l.* per head to have Served 24 years, at 4 years apiece, without running such a great risque, and the Whites would have strengthened the Country, that Negroes do not.

" 'Twould do well that none of those Servants be liable to be Impressed during their Service of Agreement at their first Landing.

" That such Servants being Sold or Transported out of this Province during the time of their Service, the Person that buys them be liable to pay 3*l.* into the Treasury."

Comment would be superfluous. It is only necessary for the reader to note that there is not a humane sentiment in the entire article.

But universal liberty was not without her votaries. All had not bowed the knee to Baal. The earliest friend of the Indian and the Negro was the scholarly, pious, and benevolent Samuel Sewall, at one time one of the judges of the Superior Court of Massachusetts, and afterwards the chief justice. He hated slavery with a righteous hatred, and early raised his voice and used his pen against it. He contributed the first article against slavery printed in the colony. It appeared as a tract, on the 24th of June, 1700, and was " Printed by Bartholomew Green and John Allen." It is withal the most remarkable document of its kind we ever saw. It is reproduced here to show the reader what a learned Christian judge thought of slavery one hundred and eighty-two years ago.

" THE SELLING OF JOSEPH A MEMORIAL.

" By the Hon'ble JUDGE SEWALL in New England.

" FORASMUCH *as* LIBERTY *is in real value next unto Life; None ought to part with it themselves, or deprive others of it, but upon most mature consideration.*

" The Numerousness of Slaves at this Day in the Province, and the Uneasiness of them under their Slavery, hath put many upon thinking whether the Foundation of it be firmly and well laid; so as to sustain the Vast Weight that is built upon it. It is most certain that all Men, as they are the Sons of *Adam,* are Co-heirs, and have equal Right unto Liberty, and all other outward

Comforts of Life. GOD *hath given the Earth [with all its commodities] unto the Sons of Adam, Psal.,* 115, 16. *And hath made of one Blood all Nations of Men, for to dwell on all the face of the Earth, and hath determined the Times before appointed, and the bounds of their Habitation : That they should seek the Lord. Forasmuch then as we are the Offspring of* GOD, &c. *Acts,* 17, 26, 27, 29. Now, although the Title given by the last ADAM doth infinitely better Men's Estates, respecting GOD and themselves ; and grants them a most beneficial and inviolable Lease under the Broad Seal of Heaven, who were before only Tenants at Will ; yet through the Indulgence of GOD to our First Parents after the Fall, the outward Estate of all and every of their Children, remains the same as to one another. So that Originally, and Naturally, there is no such thing as Slavery. *Joseph* was rightfully no more a slave to his Brethren, than they were to him ; and they had no more Authority to *Sell* him, than they had to *Slay* him. And if *they* had nothing to do to sell him ; the *Ishmaelites* bargaining with them, and paying down Twenty pieces of Silver, could not make a Title. Neither could *Potiphar* have any better Interest in him than the *Ishmaelites* had. *Gen.* 37, 20, 27, 28. For he that shall in this case plead *Alteration of Property,* seems to have forfeited a great part of his own claim to Humanity. There is no proportion between Twenty Pieces of Silver and LIBERTY. The Commodity itself is the Claimer. If *Arabian* Gold be imported in any quantities, most are afraid to meddle with it, though they might have it at easy rates ; lest it should have been wrongfully taken from the Owners, it should kindle a fire to the Consumption of their whole Estate. 'Tis pity there should be more Caution used in buying a Horse, or a little lifeless dust, than there is in purchasing Men and Women : Whereas they are the Offspring of GOD, and their Liberty is,

> . . . *Auro pretiofior Omni.*

" And seeing GOD hath said, *He that Stealeth a Man, and Selleth him, or if he be found in his Hand, he shall surely be put to Death.* Exod. 21, 16. This Law being of Everlasting Equity, wherein Man-Stealing is ranked among the most atrocious of Capital Crimes : What louder Cry can there be made of that Celebrated Warning

> *Caveat Emptor!*

" And all things considered, it would conduce more to the Welfare of the Province, to have White Servants for a Term of Years, than to have Slaves for Life. Few can endure to hear of a Negro's being made free ; and indeed they can seldom use their Freedom well ; yet their continual aspiring after their forbidden Liberty, renders them Unwilling Servants. And there is such a disparity in their Conditions, Colour, and Hair, that they can never embody with us, & grow up in orderly Families, to the Peopling of the Land ; but still remain in our Body Politick as a kind of extravasat Blood. As many Negro Men as there are among us, so many empty Places are there in our Train Bands, and the places taken up of Men that might make Husbands for our Daughters. And the Sons and Daughters of *New England* would become more like *Jacob* and *Rachel,* if this Slavery were thrust quite out of Doors. Moreover it is too well known what Temptations Masters are under, to connive at the Fornication of their Slaves;.lest they should be obliged to find them Wives, or pay their Fines.   It seems to be practically pleaded that they might be lawless ; 'tis thought much of, that the Law should have satisfaction for their Thefts, and other Immoralities ; by which means, *Holiness to the Lord* is more rarely engraven upon this sort of Servitude.   It is likewise most lamentable to think, how in taking Negroes out of *Africa,* and selling of them here, That which GOD has joined together, Men do boldly rend asunder ; Men from their Country, Husbands from their Wives, Parents from their Children.   How horrible is the Uncleanness, Mortality, if not Murder, that the Ships are guilty of that bring great Crowds of these miserable Men and Women.   Methinks when we are bemoaning the barbarous Usage of our Friends and Kinsfolk in *Africa,* it might not be unreasonable to enquire whether we are not culpable in forcing the *Africans* to become Slaves amongst ourselves.   And it may be a question whether all the Benefit received by *Negro* Slaves will balance the Accompt of Cash laid out upon them ; and for the Redemption of our own enslaved Friends out of *Africa.*   Besides all the Persons and Estates that have perished there.

" Obj. 1.   *These Blackamores are of the Posterity of Cham, and therefore are under the Curse of Slavery.*   Gen. 9, 25, 26, 27.

" *Ans.*   Of all Offices, one would not beg this ; viz. Uncall'd for, to be an Executioner of the Vindictive Wrath of God ; the extent and duration of which is to us uncertain.   If this ever was a Commission ; How do we know but that it is long since out of Date ?   Many have found it to their Cost, that a Prophetical Denunciation of Judgment against a Person or People, would not warrant them to inflict that evil.   If it would, *Hazael* might justify himself in all he did against his master, and the *Israelites* from 2 *Kings* 8, 10, 12.

" But it is possible that by cursory reading, this Text may have been mistaken.   For *Canaan* is the Person Cursed three times over, without the mentioning of *Cham.*   Good Expositors suppose the Curse entailed on him, and that this Prophesie was accomplished in the Extirpation of the *Canaanites,* and in the Servitude of the *Gibeonites.   Vide Pareum.*   Whereas the Blackmores are not descended of *Canaan,* but of Cush. Psal. 68, 31.   *Princes shall come out of Egypt* [Mizraim].   *Ethiopia* [Cush] *shall soon stretch out her hands unto God.*   Under which Names, all *Africa* may be comprehended ; and their Promised Conversion ought to be prayed for.   *Jer.* 13, 23.   *Can the Ethiopian change his Skin ?*   This shows that Black Men are the Posterity of *Cush.*   Who time out of mind have been distinguished by their Colour.   And for want of the true, *Ovid* assigns a fabulous cause of it.

> *Sanguine tum credunt in corpora summa vocato*
> *Æthiopum populos nigrum traxisse colorem.*   Metamorph. lib. 2.

" Obj. 2.   *The* Nigers *are brought out of a Pagan Country, into places where the Gospel is preached.*

" *Ans.*   Evil must not be done, that good may come of it.   The extraordinary and comprehensive Benefit accruing to the Church of God, and to *Joseph* personally, did not rectify his Brethren's Sale of him.

" Obj. 3.   *The Africans have Wars one with another : Our Ships bring lawful Captives taken in those wars.*

"*Answ.* For aught is known, their Wars are much such as were between *Jacob's* Sons and their Brother *Joseph.* If they be between Town and Town; Provincial or National: Every War is upon one side Unjust. An Unlawful War can't make lawful Captives. And by receiving, we are in danger to promote, and partake in their Barbarous Cruelties. I am sure, if some Gentlemen should go down to the *Brewsters* to take the Air, and Fish: And a stronger Party from *Hull* should surprise them, and sell them for Slaves to a Ship outward bound; they would think themselves unjustly dealt with; both by Sellers and Buyers. And yet 'tis to be feared, we have no other Kind of Title to our *Nigers. Therefore all things whatsoever ye would that men should do to you, do you even so to them: for this is the Law and the Prophets.* Matt. 7, 12.

"Obj. 4. Abraham *had Servants bought with his money and born in his House.*

"*Ans.* Until the Circumstances of *Abraham's* purchase be recorded, no Argument can be drawn from it. In the mean time, Charity obliges us to conclude, that He knew it was lawful and good.

"It is Observable that the *Israelites* were strictly forbidden the buying or selling one another for Slaves. *Levit.* 25. 39. 46. *Jer.* 34, 8-22. And GOD gaged His Blessing in lieu of any loss they might conceit they suffered thereby, *Deut.* 15. 18. And since the partition Wall is broken down, inordinate Self-love should likewise be demolished. GOD expects that Christians should be of a more Ingenuous and benign frame of Spirit. Christians should carry it to all the World, as the *Israelites* were to carry it one towards another. And for Men obstinately to persist in holding their Neighbours and Brethren under the Rigor of perpetual Bondage, seems to be no proper way of gaining Assurance that God has given them Spiritual Freedom. Our Blessed Saviour has altered the Measures of the ancient Love Song, and set it to a most Excellent New Tune, which all ought to be ambitious of Learning. *Matt.* 5. 43. 44. *John* 13. 34. These *Ethiopians*, as black as they are, seeing they are the Sons and Daughters of the First *Adam*, the Brethren and Sisters of the Last ADAM, and the Offspring of GOD; They ought to be treated with a Respect agreeable.

"*Servitus perfecta voluntaria, inter Christianum & Christianum, ex parte servi patientis saepe est licita, quia est necessaria; sed ex parte domini agentis, & procurando & exercendo, vix potest esse licita; quia non convenit regulæ illi generali: Quaecunque volueritis ut faciant vobis homines, ita & vos facite eis. Matt.* 7, 12.

"*Perfecta servitus paenae, non potest jure locum habere, nisi ex delicto gravi quod ultimum supplicium aliquo modo meretur: quia Libertas ex naturali æstimatione proxime accedit ad vitam ipsam, & eidem a multis præferri solet.*

"Ames. Cas. Confc. Lib. 5. Cap. 23. Thes. 2. 3."

Judge Sewall's attack on slavery created no little stir in Boston; and the next year, 1701, Judge John Saffin, an associate of Judge Sewall, answered it in quite a lengthy paper.[1] Having furnished

---

[1] It was thought to be lost for some years, until Dr. George H. Moore secured a copy from George Brinley, Esq., of Hartford, Conn., and reproduced it in his Notes.

Judge Sewall's paper, it is proper that Judge Saffin's reply should likewise have a place here.

"JUDGE SAFFIN'S REPLY TO JUDGE SEWALL, 1701.

"A Brief and Candid Answer to a late Printed Sheet, *Entituled,* The Selling of Joseph.

"THAT Honourable and Learned Gentleman, the Author of a Sheet, Entituled, *The Selling of Joseph, A* Memorial, seems from thence to draw this conclusion, that because the Sons of *Jacob* did very ill in selling their Brother *Joseph* to the *Ishmaelites*, who were Heathens, therefore it is utterly unlawful to Buy and Sell Negroes, though among Christians; which Conclusion I presume is not well drawn from the Premises, nor is the case parallel; for it was unlawful for the *Israelites* to Sell their Brethren upon any account, or pretence whatsoever during life. But it was not unlawful for the Seed of *Abraham* to have Bond men, and Bond women either born in their House, or bought with their Money, as it is written of *Abraham, Gen.* 14. 14. &* ,21. 10. &* *Exod.* 21. 16. &* *Levit.* 25. 44. 45. 46 *v.* After the giving of the law: And in *Josh.* 9. 23. That famous Example of the *Gibeonites* is a sufficient proof where there no other.

"To speak a little to the Gentlemans first Assertion: *That none ought to part with their Liberty themselves, or deprive others of it but upon mature consideration;* a prudent exception, in which he grants, that upon some consideration a man may be deprived of his Liberty. And then presently in his next Position or Assertion he denies it, *viz.: It is most certain, that all men as they are the Sons of* Adam *are Coheirs, and have equal right to Liberty, and all other Comforts of Life,* which he would prove out of *Psal.* 115. 16. *The Earth hath he given to the Children of Men.* True, but what is all this to the purpose, to prove that all men have equal right to Liberty, and all outward comforts of this life; which Position seems to invert the Order that God hath set in the World, who hath Ordained different degrees and orders of men, some to be High and Honourable, some to be Low and Despicable; some to be Monarchs, Kings, Princes and Governours, Masters and Commanders, others to be Subjects, and to be Commanded; Servants of sundry sorts and degrees, bound to obey; yea, some to be born Slaves, and so to remain during their lives, as hath been proved. Otherwise there would be a meer parity among men, contrary to that of the Apostle, I. *Cor.* 12 *from the* 13 *to the* 26 *verse,* where he sets forth (by way of comparison) the different sorts and offices of the Members of the Body, indigitating that they are all of use, but not equal, and of Like dignity. So God hath set different Orders and Degrees of Men in the World, both in Church and Common weal. Now, if this Position of parity should be true, it would then follow that the ordinary Course of Divine Providence of God in the World should be wrong, and unjust, (which we must not dare to think, much less to affirm) and all the sacred Rules, Precepts and Commands of the Almighty which he hath given the Sons of Men to observe and keep in their respective Places, Orders and Degrees, would be to no purpose; which unaccountably derogate from the Divine Wisdom of the most High, who hath made nothing in vain, but hath Holy Ends in all his Dispensations to the Children of men.

"In the next place, this worthy Gentleman makes a large Discourse concerning the Utility and Conveniency to keep the one, and inconveniency of the other; respecting white and black Servants, which conduceth most to the welfare and benefit of this Province: which he concludes to be white men, who are in many respects to be preferred before Blacks; who doubts that? doth it therefore follow, that it is altogether unlawful for Christians to buy and keep Negro Servants (for this is the thesis) but that those that have them ought in Conscience to set them free, and so lose all the money they cost (for we must not live in any known sin) this seems to be his opinion; but it is a Question whether it ever was the Gentleman's practice? But if he could perswade the General Assembly to make an Act, That all that have Negroes, and do set them free, shall be Reimbursed out of the Publick Treasury, and that there shall be no more Negroes brought into the country; 'tis probable there would be more of his opinion; yet he would find it a hard task to bring the Country to consent thereto; for then the Negroes must be all sent out of the Country, or else the remedy would be worse than the disease; and it is to be feared that those Negroes that are free, if there be not some strict course taken with them by Authority, they will be a plague to this Country.

"*Again*, If it should be unlawful to deprive them that are lawful Captives, or Bondmen of their Liberty for Life being Heathens; it seems to be more unlawful to deprive our Brethren, of our own or other Christian Nations of the Liberty, (though but for a time) by binding them to Serve some Seven, Ten, Fifteen, and some Twenty Years, which oft times proves for their whole Life, as many have been; which in effect is the same in Nature, though different in the time, yet this was allow'd among the *Jews* by the Law of God; and is the constant practice of our own and other Christian Nations in the World: the which our Author by his Dogmatical Assertions doth condem as Irreligious; which is Diametrically contrary to the Rules and Precepts which God hath given the diversity of men to observe in their respective Stations, Callings, and Conditions of Life, as hath been observed.

"And to illustrate his Assertion our Author brings in by way of Comparison the Law of God against man Stealing, on pain of Death: Intimating thereby, that Buying and Selling of Negro's is a breach of that Law, and so deserves Death: A severe Sentence: But herein he begs the Question with a *Caveat Emptor.* For, in that very Chapter there is a Dispensation to the People of *Israel*, to have Bond men, Women and Children, even of their own Nation in some case; and Rules given therein to be observed concerning them; Verse the 4*th.* And in the before cited place, *Levit* 25. 44, 45, 46. Though the *Israelites* were forbidden (ordinarily) to make Bond men and Women of their own Nation, but of Strangers they might: the words run thus, verse 44. *Both thy Bond men, and thy Bond maids which thou shalt have shall be of the Heathen, that are round about you : of them shall you Buy Bond men and Bond maids, &c.* See also, I *Cor.* 12. 13. Whether we be Bond or Free, which shows that in the times of the New Testament, there were Bond men also, &c.

"*In fine*, The sum of this long Haurange, is no other, than to compare the Buying and Selling of Negro's unto the Stealing of Men, and the Selling of

Joseph by his Brethren, which bears no proportion therewith, nor is there any congruiety therein, as appears by the foregoing Texts.

"Our Author doth further proceed to answer some Objections of his own framing, which he supposes some might raise.

"Object. I. *That these Blackamores are of the Posterity of* Cham, *and therefore under the Curse of Slavery.* Gen. 9. 25, 26, 27. The which the Gentleman seems to deny, saying, *they ware the Seed of Canaan that were Cursed, &c.*

"*Answ.* Whether they were so or not, we shall not dispute: this may suffice, that not only the seed of *Cham* or *Canaan,* but any lawful Captives of other Heathen Nations may be made Bond men as hath been proved.

"Obj. 2. *That the Negroes are brought out of Pagan Countreys into places where the Gospel is preached.* To which he Replies, *that we must not doe Evil that Good may come of it.*

"*Ans.* To which we answer, That it is no Evil thing to bring them out of their own Heathenish Country, where they may have the knowledge of the True God, be Converted and Eternally saved.

"Obj. 3. *The* Affricans *have Wars one with another;* our Ships bring lawful Captives taken in those Wars.

"To which our Author answers Conjecturally, and Doubtfully, *for aught we know,* that which may or may not be; which is insignificant, and proves nothing. He also compares the Negroes Wars, one Nation with another, with the Wars between *Joseph* and his Brethren. But where doth he read of any such War? We read indeed of a Domestick Quarrel they had with him, they envyed and hated *Joseph;* but by what is Recorded, he was meerly passive and meek as a Lamb. This Gentleman farther adds, *That there is not any War but is unjust on one side, &c.* Be it so, what doth that signify: We read of lawful Captives taken in the Wars, and lawful to be Bought and Sold without contracting the guilt of the *Agressors;* for which we have the example of *Abraham* before quoted; but if we must stay while both parties Warring are in the right, there would be no lawful Captives at all to be Bought; which seems to be rediculous to imagine, and contrary to the tenour of Scripture, and all Humane Histories on that subject.

"Obj. 4. *Abraham had Servants bought with his Money, and born in his House.* Gen. 14. 14. To which our worthy Author answers, *until the Circumstances of Abraham's purchase be recorded, no Argument can be drawn from it.*

"*Ans.* To which we Reply, this is also Dogmatical, and proves nothing. He farther adds, *In the mean time Charity Obliges us to conclude, that he knew it was lawful and good.* Here the gentleman yields the case; for if we are in Charity bound to believe *Abrahams* practice, in buying and keeping *Slaves* in his house to be lawful and good: then it follows, that our Imitation of him in this his Moral Action, is as warrantable as that of his Faith; *who is the Father of all them that believe.* Rom. 4. 16.

"In the close all, Our Author Quotes two more places of Scripture, *viz.,* Levit. 25. 46, and *Jer.* 34, from the 8. to the 22. *v.* To prove that the people of Israel were strictly forbidden the Buying and Selling one another for *Slaves:* who questions that? and what is that to the case in hand? What a strange piece of Logick is this? 'Tis unlawful for Christians to Buy and Sell one another for slaves. *Ergo*, It is unlawful to Buy and Sell Negroes that are lawful Captiv'd Heathens.

"And after a Serious Exhortation to us all to Love one another according to the Command of Christ. *Math.* 5, 43, 44. This worthy Gentleman con· cludes with this Assertion, *That these Ethiopeans as Black as they are, seeing they are the Sons and Daughters of the first* Adam; *the Brethren and Sisters of the Second* Adam, *and the Offspring of God; we ought to treat them with a respect agreeable.*

"*Ans.* We grant it for a certain and undeniable verity, That all Mankind are the Sons and Daughters of *Adam*, and the Creatures of God: But it doth not therefore follow that we are bound to love and respect all men alike; this under favour we must take leave to deny; we ought in charity, if we see our Neighbour in want, to relieve them in a regular way, but we are not bound to give them so much of our Estates, as to make them equal with ourselves, be-cause they are our Brethren, the Sons of *Adam*, no, not our own natural Kins-men: We are Exhorted *to do good unto all, but especially to them who are of the Household of Faith, Gal.* 6. 10. And we are to love, honour and respect all men according to the gift of God that is in them: I may love my Servant well, but my Son better; Charity begins at home, it would be a violation of common prudence, and a breach of good manners, to treat a Prince like a Peasant. And this worthy Gentleman would deem himself much neglected, if we should show him no more Defference than to an ordinary Porter: And therefore these florid expressions, the Sons and Daughters of the First *Adam*, the Brethren and Sisters of the Second *Adam*, and the Offspring of God, seem to be misapplied to import and insinuate, that we ought to tender Pagan Negroes with all love, kindness, and equal respect as to the best of men.

"By all which it doth evidently appear both by Scripture and Reason, the practice of the People of God in all Ages, both before and after the giving of the Law, and in the times of the Gospel, that there were Bond men, Women and Children commonly kept by holy and good men, and improved in Service; and therefore by the Command of God, *Lev.* 25, 44, and their venerable Example, we may keep Bond men, and use them in our Service still; yet with all candour, moderation and Christian prudence, according to their state and condition consonant to the Word of God."

Judge Sewall had dealt slavery a severe blow, and opened up an agitation on the subject that was felt during the entire Revolu· tionary struggle. He became the great apostle of liberty, the father of the anti-slavery movement in the colony. He was the bold and stern John the Baptist of that period, "the voice of one crying in the wilderness" of bondage, to prepare the way for freedom.

The Quakers, or Friends as they were called, were perhaps the earliest friends of the slaves, but, like Joseph of Arimathæa, were "secretly" so, for fear of the "Puritans." But they early recorded their disapprobation of slavery as follows:—

26th day of yᵉ 9th mo. 1716.

" An epistle from the last Quarterly Meeting was read in this, and yᵉ matter referred to this meeting, viz., whether it is agreeable to truth for friends to purchase slaves and keep them term of liffe, was considered, and yᵉ sense and judgment of this meeting is, that it is not agreeable to truth for friends to purchase slaves and hold them term of liffe.

" Nathaniel Starbuck, junʳ is to draw out this meeting's judgment concerning friends not buying slaves and keeping them term of liffe, and send it to the next Quarterly Meeting, and to sign it in yᵉ meeting's behalf." [1]

Considering the prejudice and persecution that pursued this good people, their testimony against slavery is very remarkable. In 1729–30 Elihu Coleman of Nantucket, a minister of the society of Friends, wrote a book against slavery, published in 1733, entitled, "*A Testimony against that Anti-Christian Practice of* MAKING SLAVES OF MEN.[2] It was well written, and the truth fearlessly told for the conservative, self-seeking period he lived in. He says, —

" I am not unthoughtful of the ferment or stir that such discourse as this may make among some, who (like Demetrius of old) may say, by this craft we have our wealth, which caused the people to cry out with one voice, great is Diana of the Ephesians, whom all Asia and the world worship."

He examined and refuted the arguments put forth in defence of slavery, charged slaveholders with idleness, and contended that slavery was the mother of vice, at war with the laws of nature and of God. Others caught the spirit of reform, and the agitation movement gained recruits and strength every year. Felt says, " 1765. Pamphlets and newspapers discuss the subjects of slavery with increasing zeal." The colonists were aroused. Men were taking one side or the other of a question of great magnitude. In 1767 an anonymous tract of twenty octavo pages against slavery made its appearance in Boston. It was written by Nathaniel Appleton, a co-worker with Otis, and an advanced thinker on the subject of emancipation. It was in the form of a letter addressed to a friend, and was entitled, " Considerations on Slavery." The Rev. Samuel Webster Salisbury published on the 2d of March, 1769, " An Earnest Address to my Country on Slavery." He opened his article with an argument showing the inconsistency of a Christian people holding slaves, pictured the evil results of slavery, and then asked, —

---

[1] History of Nantucket, p. 281.   [2] Coffin, p. 338; also History of Nantucket, pp. 279, 280.

" What then is to be done? Done! for God's sake break every yoke and let these oppressed ones *go free without delay* — let them taste the sweets of that *liberty*, which we so highly prize, and are so earnestly supplicating God and man to grant us : nay, which we claim as the natural right of every man. Let me beseech my countrymen to put on bowels of compassion for these their *brethren* (for so I must call them,) yea, let me beseech you for your own sake and for God's sake, *to break every yoke* and let the oppressed go free." [1]

Begun among the members of the bar and the pulpit, the common folk at length felt a lively interest in the subject of emancipation. An occasional burst of homely, vigorous eloquence from the pulpit on the duties of the hour inflamed the conscience of the pew with a noble zeal for a righteous cause. The afflatus of liberty sat upon the people as cloven tongues. Every village, town, and city had its orators whose only theme was emancipation. " The pulpit and the press were not silent, and sermons and essays in behalf of the enslaved Africans were continually making their appearance." The public conscience was being rapidly educated, and from the hills of Berkshire to the waters of Massachusetts Bay the fires of liberty were burning.

---

[1] Coffin, p. 338.

CHAPTER XV.

THE COLONY OF MASSACHUSETTS, — CONTINUED.

1633–1775.

THE ERA OF PROHIBITORY LEGISLATION AGAINST SLAVERY. — BOSTON INSTRUCTS HER REPRESENTA-
TIVES TO VOTE AGAINST THE SLAVE-TRADE. — PROCLAMATION ISSUED BY GOV. DUMMER AGAINST
THE NEGROES, APRIL 13, 1723. — PERSECUTION OF THE NEGROES. — "SUING FOR LIBERTY." —
LETTER OF SAMUEL ADAMS TO JOHN PICKERING, JUN., ON BEHALF OF NEGRO MEMORIALISTS. —
A BILL FOR THE SUPPRESSION OF THE SLAVE-TRADE PASSES. — IS VETOED BY GOV. GAGE, AND
FAILS TO BECOME A LAW.

THE time to urge legislation on the slavery question had
come. Cultivated at the first as a private enterprise, then
fostered as a patriarchal institution, slavery had grown to
such gigantic proportions as to be regarded as an unwieldy evil,
and subversive of the political stability of the colony. Men
winked at the "day of its small things," and it grew. Little
legislation was required to regulate it, and it began to take root in
the social and political life of the people. The necessities for
legislation in favor of slavery increased. Every year witnessed
the enactment of laws more severe, until they appeared as scars
upon the body of the laws of the colony. To erase these scars
was the duty of the hour.

It was now 1755. More than a half-century of agitation and
discussion had prepared the people for definite action. Manumission and petition were the first methods against slavery. On
the 10th of March, 1755, the town of Salem instructed their representative, Timothy Pickering, to petition the General Court
against the importation of slaves.[1] The town of Worcester, in
June, 1765, instructed their representative to "use his influence
to obtain a law to put an end to that unchristian and impolitic
practice of making slaves of the human species, and that he give
his vote for none to serve in His Majesty's Council, who will use
their influence against such a law." [2] The people of Boston, in

---

[1] Felt, vol. ii. p, 416.　　　　[2] Newspaper Literature, vol. i. p. 31.

the month of May, 1766, instructed their representatives as
follows : —

"And for the total abolishing of slavery among us, that you move for a law
to prohibit the importation and the purchasing of slaves for the future." [1]

And in the following year, 1767, on the 16th of March, the
question was put as to whether the town should adhere to its
previous instructions in favor of the suppression of the slave-
trade, and passed in the affirmative.   Nearly all the towns, especially those along the coast, those accessible by mails and newspapers, had recorded their vote, in some shape or other, against
slavery.   The pressure for legislation on the subject was great.
The country members of the Legislature were almost a unit in
favor of the passage of a bill prohibiting the further importation
of slaves.   The opposition came from the larger towns, but the
opposers were awed by the determined bearing of the enemies of
the slave-trade.   The scholarship, wealth, and piety of the colony
were steadily ranging to the side of humanity.

On the 13th of March, 1767, a bill was introduced in the
House of Representatives "to prevent the *unwarrantable and
unlawful* Practice or Custom of inslaving Mankind in this Province, and the importation of slaves into the same." [2]   It was read
the first time, when a dilatory motion was offered that the bill lie
over to the next session, which was decided in the negative.   An
amendment was offered to the bill, limiting it "to a certain time,"
which was carried ; and the bill made a special order for a second
reading on the following day.   It was accordingly read on the
14th, when a motion was made to defer it for a third reading to
the next "May session."   The friends of the bill voted down this
dilatory motion, and had the bill made the special order of the
following Monday, — it now being Saturday.   On Sunday there
must have been considerable lobbying done, as can be seen by
the vote taken on Monday.   After it was read, and the debate
was concluded, it was "*Ordered that the Matter subside*, and that
Capt. Sheaffe, Col. Richmond, and Col. Bourne, be a Committee to bring in a Bill for laying a Duty of Impost on slaves importing into this Province." [3]   This was a compromise, that, as
will be seen subsequently, impaired the chances of positive and
wholesome legislation against slavery.   The original bill dealt a

---

[1] Lyman's Report, quoted by Dr. Moore.   [2] House Journal, p. 387.   [3] Ibid.

double blow: it struck at the slave-trade in the Province, and levelled the institution already in existence. But some secret influences were set in operation, that are forever hidden from the searching eye of history; and the friends of liberty were bullied or cheated. There was no need of a bill imposing an impost tax on slaves imported, for such a law had been in existence for more than a half-century. If the tax were not heavy enough, it could have been increased by an amendment of a dozen lines. On the 17th the substitute was brought in by the special committee appointed by the Speaker the previous day. The rules requiring bills to be read on three several days were suspended, the bill ordered to a first and second reading, and then made the special order for eleven o'clock on the next day, Wednesday, the 18th. The motion to lie on the table until the "next May" was defeated. An amendment was then offered to limit the life of the bill to one year, which was carried, and the bill recommitted. On the afternoon of the same day it was read a third time, and placed on its passage with the amendment. It passed, was ordered engrossed, and was "sent up by Col. Bowers, Col. Gerrish, Col. Leonard, Capt. Thayer, and Col. Richmond." On the 19th of March it was read a first time in the council. On the 20th it was read a second time, and passed to be engrossed "as taken into a new draft." When it reached the House for concurrence, in the afternoon of the same day, it was "Read and unanimously non-concurred, and the House adhere to their own vote, sent up for concurrence." [1]

Massachusetts has gloried much and long in this Act to prohibit "the Custom of enslaving mankind;" but her silver-tongued orators and profound statesmen have never possessed the courage to tell the plain truth about its complete failure. From the first it was harassed by dilatory motions and amendments directed to its life; and the substitute, imposing an impost tax on imported slaves for one year, showed plainly that the friends of the original bill had been driven from their high ground. It was like applying for the position of a major-general, and then accepting the place of a corporal. It was as though they had asked for a fish, and accepted a serpent instead. It seriously lamed the cause of emancipation. It filled the slaves with gloom, and their friends with apprehension. On the other hand, those who profited by

---

[1] House Journals; see, also, Gen. Court Records, May, 1763, to May, 1767, p. 485.

barter in flesh and blood laughed secretly to themselves at the abortive attempt of the anti-slavery friends to call a halt on the trade. They took courage. For ten weary years the voices lifted for the freedom of the slave were few, faint, and far between. The bill itself has been lost. What its subject-matter was, is left to uncertain and unsatisfactory conjecture. All we know is from the title just quoted. But it was, nevertheless, the only direct measure offered in the Provincial Legislature against slavery during the entire colonial period, and came nearest to passage of any. But "a miss is as good as a mile!"

It was now the spring season of 1771. Ten years had flown, and no one in all the Province of Massachusetts had had the courage to attempt legislation friendly to the slave. The scenes of the preceding year were fresh in the minds of the inhabitants of Boston. The blood of the martyrs to liberty was crying from the ground. The "red coats" of the British exasperated the people. The mailed hand, the remorseless steel finger, of English military power was at the throat of the rights of the people. The colony was gasping for independent political life. A terrible struggle for liberty was imminent. The colonists were about to contend for all that men hold dear, — their wives, their children, their homes, and their country. But while they were panting for an untrammelled existence, to plant a free nation on the shores of North America, they were robbing Africa every year of her sable children, and condemning them to a bondage more cruel than political subjugation. This glaring inconsistency imparted to reflecting persons a new impulse toward anti-slavery legislation.

In the spring of 1771 the subject of suppressing the slave-trade was again introduced into the Legislature. On the 12th of April a bill " *To prevent the Importation of slaves from Africa* " was introduced, and read the first time, and, upon the question "When shall the bill be read again?" was ordered to a second reading on the day following at ten o'clock. Accordingly, on the 13th, the bill was read a second time, and postponed till the following Tuesday morning. On the 16th it was recommitted. On the 19th of the same month a "Bill to prevent the Importation of Negro slaves into this Province" was read a first time, and ordered to a second reading "to-morrow at eleven o'clock." On the following day it was read a second time, and made the special order for three o'clock on the following Monday. On the 22d, Monday, it was read a third time, and placed upon its passage and engrossed. On the 24th it passed the House. When it reached the Council James Otis proposed an amendment, and a motion prevailed that the bill lie upon the table. But it was taken from the table, and the amendment of Otis was concurred in by the House. It passed the Council in the latter part of April, but failed to receive the signature of the governor, on the ground that he was "not authorized by Parliament." [1] The same reason for refusing his signature was set up by Gen. Gage. Thus the bill failed. Gov. Hutchinson gave his reasons to Lord Hillsborough, secretary of state for the colonies. The governor thought himself restrained by "instructions" to colonial governors "from assenting to any laws of a new and unusual nature." In addition to the foregoing, his Excellency doubted the lawfulness of the legislation to which the "scruple upon the minds of the people in many parts of the province" would lead them; and that he had suggested the propriety of transmitting the bill to England to learn "his Majesty's pleasure" thereabouts. Upon these reasons Dr. Moore comments as follows : —

"These are interesting and important suggestions. It is apparent that at this time there was no special instruction to the royal governor of Massachusetts, forbidding his approval of acts against the slave-trade. Hutchinson evidently doubted the genuineness of the 'chief motive' which was alleged to be the inspiration of the bill, the 'meerly moral' scruple against slavery; but his reasonings furnish a striking illustration of the changes which were going on in public opinion, and the gradual softening of the harsher features of slavery under their influence. The non-importation agreement throughout the Colonies, by which America was trying to thwart the commercial selfishness of her rapacious Mother, had rendered the provincial viceroys peculiarly sensitive to the slightest manifestation of a disposition to approach the sacred precincts of those prerogatives by which King and Parliament assumed to bind their distant dependencies: and the 'spirit of non-importation' which Massachusetts had imperfectly learned from New York was equally offensive to them, whether it interfered with their cherished 'trade with Africa,' or their favorite monopolies elsewhere."

Discouraged by the failure of the House and General Court to pass measures hostile to the slave-trade, the people in the outlying towns began to instruct their representatives, in unmistakable language, to urge the enactment of repressive legislation on this subject. At a town meeting in Salem on the 18th of May, 1773,[2] the representatives were instructed to prevent, by appro-

---

[1] Slavery in Mass., pp. 131, 132.   [2] Felt, vol. ii. pp. 416, 417.

priate legislation, the further importation of slaves into the colony, as "repugnant to the natural rights of mankind, and highly preju-dicial to the Province." On the very next day, May 19, 1773, at a similar meeting in the town of Leicester, the people gave among other instructions to Thomas Denny, their representative, the fol-lowing on the question of slavery: —

"And, as we have the highest regard for (so as even to revere the name of) liberty, we cannot behold but with the greatest abhorrence any of our fellow-creatures in a state of slavery.

"Therefore we strictly enjoin you to use your utmost influence that a stop may be put to the slave-trade by the inhabitants of this Province; which, we apprehend, may be effected by one of these two ways: either by laying a heavy duty on every negro imported or brought from Africa or elsewhere into this Province; or by making a law, that every negro brought or imported as afore-said should be a free man or woman as soon as they come within the jurisdic-tion of it; and that every negro child that shall be born in said government after the enacting such law should be free at the same age that the children of white people are; and, from the time of their birth till they are capable of earning their living, to be maintained by the town in which they are born, or at the expense of the Province, as shall appear most reasonable.

"Thus, by enacting such a law, in process of time will the blacks become free; or, if the Honorable House of Representatives shall think of a more eligible method, we shall be heartily glad of it. But whether you can justly take away or free a negro from his master, who fairly purchased him, and (although illegally; for such is the purchase of any person against their consent unless it be for a capital offence) which the custom of this country has justified him in, we shall not determine; but hope that unerring Wisdom will direct you in this and all your other important undertakings." [1]

Medford instructed the representative to "use his utmost influence to have a final period put to that most cruel, inhuman and unchristian practice, the slave-trade." At a town meeting the people of Sandwich voted, on the 18th of May, 1773, "that our representative is instructed to endeavor to have an Act passed by the Court, to prevent the importation of *slaves* into this country, and that all children that shall be born of such Africans as are now slaves among us, shall, after such Act, be free at 21 yrs. of age." [2]

This completes the list of towns that gave instructions to their representatives, as far as the record goes. But there doubtless were others; as the towns were close together, and as the "spirit of liberty was rife in the land."

---

[1] Hist. of Leicester, pp. 442, 443. [2] Freeman's Hist. of Cape Cod, vol. ii. pp. 114, 115.

The Negroes did not endure the yoke without complaint. Having waited long and patiently for the dawn of freedom in the colony in vain, a spirit of unrest seized them. They grew sullen and desperate. The local government started, like a sick man, at every imaginary sound, and charged all disorders to the Negroes. If a fire broke out, the "Negroes did it,"—in fact, the Negroes, who were not one-sixth of the population, were continually committing depredations against the whites! On the 13th of April, 1723, Lieut.-Gov. Dummer issued a proclamation against the Negroes, which contained the following preamble:—

"Whereas, within some short time past, many fires have broke out within the town of Boston, and divers buildings have thereby been consumed: which fires have been designedly and industriously kindled by some villanous and desperate negroes, or other dissolute people, as appears by the confession of some of them (who have been examined by the authority), and many concurring circumstances; and it being vehemently suspected that they have entered into a combination to burn and destroy the town, I have therefore thought fit, with the advice of his Majesty's council, to issue forth this proclamation," etc.

On Sunday, the 18th of April, 1723, the Rev. Joseph Sewall preached a sermon suggested "by the late fires yᵗ have broke out in Boston, supposed to be purposely set by yᵉ negroes." The town was greatly exercised. Everybody regarded the Negroes with distrust. Special measures were demanded to insure the safety of the town. The selectmen of Boston passed "nineteen articles" for the regulation of the Negroes. The watch of the town was increased, and the military called out at the sound of every fire-alarm "to keep the slaves from breaking out"! In August, 1730, a Negro was charged with burning a house in Malden; which threw the entire community into a panic. In 1755 two Negro slaves were put to death for poisoning their master, John Codman of Charlestown. One was hanged, and the other burned to death. In 1766 all slaves who showed any disposition to be free were "transported and exchanged for small negroes." [1] In 1768 Capt. John Willson, of the Fifty-ninth Regiment, was accused of exciting the slaves against their masters; assuring them that the soldiers had come to procure their freedom, and that, "with their assistance, they should be able to drive the Liberty Boys to the Devil." The following letter from Mrs. John Adams to her husband, dated at the Boston Garrison,

---

[1] Boston Gazette, Aug. 17, 1761.

22d September, 1774, gives a fair idea of the condition of the public pulse, and her pronounced views against slavery.

"There has been in town a conspiracy of the negroes. At present it is kept pretty private, and was discovered by one who endeavored to dissuade them from it. He being threatened with his life, applied to Justice Quincy for protection. They conducted in this way, got an Irishman to draw up a petition to the Governor [Gage], telling him they would fight for him provided he would arm them, and engáge to liberate them if he conquered. And it is said that he attended so much to it, as to consult Percy upon it, and one Lieutenant Small has been very busy and active. There is but little said, and what steps they will take in consequence of it I know not. I wish most sincerely there was not a slave in the province ; it always appeared a most iniquitous scheme to me to fight ourselves for what we are daily robbing and plundering from those who have as good a right to freedom as we have. You know my mind upon this subject."[1]

The Negroes of Massachusetts were not mere passive observers of the benevolent conduct of their white friends. They were actively interested in the agitation going on in their behalf. Here, as in no other colony, the Negroes showed themselves equal to the emergencies that arose, and capable of appreciating the opportunities to strike for their own rights. The Negroes in the colony at length struck a blow for their liberty. And it was not the wild, indiscriminate blow of Turner, nor the military measure of Gabriel ; not the remorseless logic of bludgeon and torch, — but the sober, sensible efforts of *men* and *women* who believed their condition abnormal, and slavery prejudicial to the largest growth of the human intellect. The eloquence of Otis, the impassioned appeals of Sewall, and the zeal of Eliot had rallied the languishing energies of the Negroes, and charged their hearts with the divine passion for liberty. They had learned to spell out the letters of freedom, and the meaning of the word had quite ravished their fainting souls. They had heard that the royal charter declared all the colonists British subjects ; they had devoured the arguments of their white friends, and were now prepared to act on their own behalf. The slaves of Greece and Rome, it is true, petitioned the authorities for a relaxation of the severe laws that crushed their manhood ; but they were captives from other nations, noted for government and a knowledge of the science of warfare. But it was left to the Negroes of Massachu-

---

[1] Letters of Mrs. Adams, p. 20.

setts to force their way into courts created only for white men, and win their cause!

On Wednesday, Nov. 5, 1766, John Adams makes the following record in his diary: —

"5. Wednesday. Attended Court; heard the trial of an action of trespass, brought by a mulatto woman, for damages, for restraining her of her liberty. This is called suing for liberty; the first action that ever I knew of the sort, though I have heard there have been many."[1]

So as early as 1766 Mr. Adams records a case of "suing for liberty;" and though it was the first he had known of, nevertheless, he had "heard there have been many." *How* many of these cases were in Massachusetts it cannot be said with certainty, but there were "many." The case to which Mr. Adams makes reference was no doubt that of Jenny Slew *vs.* John Whipple, jun., cited by Dr. Moore. It being the earliest case mentioned anywhere in the records of the colony, great interest attaches to it.

"JENNY SLEW of Ipswich in the County of Essex, spinster, Pltff., agst. JOHN WHIPPLE, Jun., of said Ipswich Gentleman, Deft., in a Plea of Trespass for that the said John on the 29th day of January, A.D. 1762, at Ipswich aforesaid with force and arms took her the said Jenny, held and kept her in servitude as a slave in his service, and has restrained her of her liberty from that time to the fifth of March last without any lawful right & authority so to do and did her other injuries against the peace & to the damage of said Jenny Slew as she saith the sum of twenty-five pounds. This action was first brought at last March Court at Ipswich when & where the parties appeared & the case was continued by order of Court to the then next term when and where the Pltff appeared & the said John Whipple Jun, came by Edmund Trowbridge, Esq. his attorney & defended when he said that there is no such person in nature as Jenny Slew of Ipswich aforesaid, Spinster, & this the said John was ready to verify wherefore the writ should be abated & he prayed judgment accordingly which plea was overruled by the Court and afterwards the said John by the said Edmund made a motion to the Court & praying that another person might endorse the writ & be subject to cost if any should finally be for the Court but the Court rejected the motion and then Deft. saving his plea in abatement aforesaid said that he is not guilty as the plaintiff contends, & thereof put himself on the Country, & then the cause was continued to this term, and now the Pltff. reserving to herself the liberty of joining issue on the Deft's plea aforesaid in the appeal says that the defendant's plea aforesaid is an insufficient answer to the Plaintiff's declaration aforesaid and by law she is not held to reply thereto & she is ready to verify wherefore for want of a sufficient answer to the Plaintiff's declaration aforesaid she prays judg-

ment for her damages & costs & the defendant consenting to the waiving of
the demurrer on the appeal said his plea aforesaid is good & because the
Pltff refuses to reply thereto He prays judgment for his cost. It is considered
by the Court that the defendant's plea in chief aforesaid is good & that the
said John Whipple recover of the said Jenny Slew costs tax at   the
Pltff appealed to the next Superior Court of Judicature to be holden for this
County & entered into recognizance with sureties as the law directs for prosecuting her appeal to effect." *Records of the Inferior Court of C. C. P., Vol.—,*
(Sept. 1760 *to July* 1766), *page* 502.

"JENNY SLEW of Ipswich, in the County of Essex, Spinster, Appellant,
versus JOHN WHIPPLE, Jr. of said Ipswich, Gentleman Appellee from the
judgment of an Inferior Court of Common Pleas held at Newburyport within
and for the County of Essex on the last Tuesday of September 1765 when and
where the appellant was plaint., and the appellee was defendant in a plea of
trespass, for that the said John upon the 29th day of January, A.D. 1762, at
Ipswich aforesaid with force and arms took her the said Jenny held & kept her
in servitude as a slave in his service & has restrained her of her liberty from
that time to the fifth of March 1765 without any lawful right or authority so
to do & did other injuries against the Peace & to the damage of the said
Jenny Slew, as she saith, the sum of twenty-five pounds, at which Inferior
Court, judgment was rendered upon the demurrer then that the said John
Whipple recover against the said Jenny Slew costs. This appeal was brought
forward at the Superior Court of Judicature &c., holden at Salem, within & for
the County of Essex on the first Tuesday of last November, from whence it
was continued to the last term of this Court for this County by consent & so
from thence unto this Court, and now both parties appeared & the demurrer
aforesaid being waived by consent & issue joined upon the plea tendered at
said Inferior Court & on file. The case after full hearing was committed to
a jury sworn according to law to try the same who returned their verdict therein upon oath, that is to say, they find for appellant reversion of the former
judgment four pounds money damage & costs. It's therefore considered by
the Court, that the former judgment be reversed & that the said Slew recover
against the said Whipple the sum of four pounds lawful money of this Province damage & costs taxed 9*l.* 9*s.* 6*d.*

"Exon. issued 4 Dec. 1766." *Records of the Superior Court of Judica-*
ture (vol. 1766–7), *page* 175.

The next of the "freedom cases," in chronological order, was
the case of Newport *vs.* Billing, and was doubtless the one in
which John Adams was engaged in the latter part of September,
1768.[1] It was begun in the Inferior Court, where the decision
was against the slave, Amos Newport. The plaintiff took an
appeal to the highest court in the colony; and that court gave as
its solemn opinion, "that the said Amos [Newport] was not a
freeman, as he alleged, but the proper slave of the said Joseph

---

[1] Adams's Works, vol. ii. p. 213.

[Billing]." [1] It should not be lost sight of, that not only the Fundamental laws of 1641, but the highest court in Massachusetts, held, as late as 1768, that there was property in man !

The case of James *vs.* Lechmere is the one "which has been for more than half a century the grand *cheval de bataille* of the champions of the historic fame of Massachusetts." [2]   Richard Lechmere resided in Cambridge, and held to servitude for life a Negro named "James."   On the 2d of May, 1769, this slave began an action in the Inferior Court of Common Pleas.   The action was "in trespass for assault and battery, and imprisoning and holding the plaintiff in servitude from April 11, 1758, to the date of the writ."   The judgment of the Inferior Court was adverse to the slave ; but on the 31st of October, 1769, the Superior Court of Suffolk had the case settled by compromise.   A long line of worthies in Massachusetts have pointed with pride to this decision as the legal destruction of slavery in that State.   But it "*is shown by the records and files of Court to have been brought up from the Inferior Court by sham demurrer, and, after one or two continuances, settled by the parties.*" [3]   The truth of history demands that the facts be given to the world.   It will not be pleasant for the people of Massachusetts to have this delusion torn from their affectionate embrace.   It was but a mere historical chimera, that ought not to have survived a single day ; and, strangely enough, it has existed until the present time among many intelligent people.   This case has been cited for the last hundred years as having settled the question of bond servitude in Massachusetts, when the fact is, there was no decision in this instance !   And the claim that Richard Lechmere's slave James was adjudged free "upon the same grounds, substantially, as those upon which Lord Mansfield discharged Sommersett," is absurd and baseless. [4]   For on the 27th of April, 1785 (thirteen years after the famous decision), Lord Mansfield himself said, in reference to the Sommersett case, "that his decision went no farther than that the master cannot by force compel the slave to go out of the kingdom."   Thirty-five years of suffering and degradation remained for the Africans after the decision of Lord Mansfield.   His lordship's decision was ren-

---

[1] Records, 1768, fol., p. 284.

[2] This is the case referred to by the late Charles Sumner in his famous speech in answer to Senator Butler of South Carolina; see also Slavery in Mass., p. 115, 116; Washburn's Judicial Hist. of Mass., p. 202; Mass. Hist. Soc. Proc., 1863–64, p. 322.

[3] Records, 1769, fol. p. 196.   Gray in Quincy's Reports, p. 30, note, quoted by Dr. Moore.

[4] Slavery in Mass., pp. 115, 116, note.

dered on the 22d of June, 1772; and in 1807, thirty-five years afterwards, the British government abolished the slave-trade. And then,
after twenty-seven years more of reflection, slavery was abolished
in English possessions. *So, sixty-two years after Lord Mansfield's decision, England emancipated her slaves!* It took only two
generations for the people to get rid of slavery under the British
flag. How true, then, that "facts are stranger than fiction"!

In 1770 John Swain of Nantucket brought suit against Elisha
Folger, captain of the vessel "Friendship," for allowing a Mr.
Roth to receive on board his ship a Negro boy named "Boston,"
and for the recovery of the slave. This was a jury-trial in the
Court of Common Pleas. The jury brought in a verdict in favor
of the slave, and he was "manumitted by the magistrates." John
Swain took an appeal from the decision of the Nantucket Court
to the Supreme Court of Boston, but never prosecuted it.[1] In
1770, in Hanover, Plymouth County, a Negro asked his master to
grant him his freedom as *his right*. The master refused; and the
Negro, with assistance of counsel, succeeded in obtaining his
liberty.[2]

"In October of 1773, an action was brought against Richard Greenleaf, of
Newburyport, by Cæsar [Hendrick,] a colored man, whom he claimed as his
slave, for holding him in bondage. He laid the damages at fifty pounds. The
counsel for the plaintiff, in whose favor the jury brought in their verdict and
awarded him eighteen pounds damages and costs, was John Lowell, esquire,
afterward judge Lowell. This case excited much interest, as it was the first,
if not the only one of the kind, that ever occurred in the county."[3]

This case is mentioned in full by Mr. Dane in his "Abridgment and Digest of American Law," vol. ii. p. 426.

In the Inferior Court of Common Pleas, in the county of
Essex, July term in 1774, a Negro slave of one Caleb Dodge of
Beverly brought an action against his master for restraining his
liberty. The jury gave a verdict in favor of the Negro, on the
ground that there was "no law of the Province to hold a man to
serve for life."[4] This is the only decision we have been able to
find based upon such a reason. The jury may have reached this
conclusion from a knowledge of the provisions of the charter of
the colony; or they may have found a verdict in accordance with

---

[1] Lyman's Report, 1822.   [2] Slavery in Mass., p. 118.   [3] Hist. of Newbury, p. 339.
[4] The Watchman's Alarm, p. 28, note; also Slavery in Mass., p. 119.

the charge of the court.   The following significant language in the
charter of the colony could not have escaped the court : —

"That all and every of the subjects of us, our heirs and successors, which
go to and inhabit within our said province and territory, and every of their
children which shall happen to be born there, or on the seas in going thither,
or returning from thence, shall have and enjoy all liberties and immunities of
free and natural subjects within the dominions of us, our heirs and successors,
to all intents, constructions, and purposes whatsoever, as if they and every of
them were born within our realm of England."

The Rev. Dr. Belknap, speaking of these cases which John
Adams speaks of as "suing for liberty," gives an idea of the line
of argument used by the Negroes : —

"On the part of the blacks it was pleaded, that the royal charter expressly
declared all persons born or residing in the province, to be as free as the King's
subjects in Great Britain; that by the laws of England, no man could be deprived of his liberty but by the judgment of his peers; that the laws of the
province respecting an evil existing, and attempting to mitigate or regulate it,
did not authorize it; and, on some occasions, the plea was, that though the
slavery of the parents be admitted, yet no disability of that kind could descend
to children." [1]

The argument pursued by the masters was, —

"The pleas on the part of the masters were, that the negroes were purchased in open market, and bills of sale were produced in evidence; that the
laws of the province recognized slavery as existing in it, by declaring that no
person should manumit his slave without giving bond for his maintenance." [2]

It is well that posterity should know the motives that inspired
judges and juries to grant these Negroes their prayer for liberty.

"In 1773, etc., some slaves did recover against their masters; but these
cases are no evidence that there could not be slaves in the Province, for sometimes masters permitted their slaves to recover, to get clear of maintaining them
as *paupers* when old and infirm; the effect, as then generally understood, of a
judgment against the master on this point of slavery; hence, a very feeble
defence was often made by the masters, especially when sued by the old or
infirm slaves, as the masters could not even manumit their slaves, without in-
demnifying their towns against their maintenance, as town paupers."

And Chief-Justice Parsons, in the case of Winchendon *vs.*
Hatfield, in error, says, —

"Several negroes, born in this country of imported slaves demanded their
freedom of their masters by suit at law, and obtained it by a judgment of court.

---

[1] Mass. Hist. Soc. Coll., vol. iv. 1st Series, pp. 202, 203.   [2] Hildreth, vol. ii. p. 564.

The defence of the master was feebly made, for such was the temper of the times, that a restless discontented slave was worth little ; and when his freedom was obtained in a course of legal proceedings, the master was not holden for his future support, if he became poor."

Thus did the slaves of Massachusetts fill their mouths with arguments, and go before the courts. The majority of them, aged and infirm, were allowed to gain their cause in order that their masters might be relieved from supporting their old age. The more intelligent, and, consequently, the more determined ones, were allowed to have their freedom from prudential reasons, more keenly felt than frankly expressed by their masters. In some instances, however, noble, high-minded Christians, on the bench and on juries, were led to their conclusions by broad ideas of justice and humanity. But the spirit of the age was cold and materialistic. With but a very few exceptions, the most selfish and constrained motives conspired to loose the chains of the bondmen in the colony.

The slaves were not slow to see that the colonists were in a frame of mind to be persuaded on the question of emancipation. Their feelings were at white heat in anticipation of the Revolutionary struggle, and the slaves thought it time to strike out a few sparks of sympathy.

On the 25th of June, 1773, a petition was presented to the House of Representatives, and read before that body during the afternoon session. It was the petition "of Felix Holbrook, and others, Negroes, praying that they may be liberated from a state of Bondage, and made Freemen of this Community ; and that this Court would give and grant to them some part of the unimproved Lands belonging to the Province, for a settlement, or relieve them in such other Way as shall seem good and wise upon the Whole." After its reading, a motion prevailed to refer it to a select committee for consideration, with leave to report at any time. It was therefore "ordered, that Mr. Hancock, Mr. Greenleaf, Mr. Adams, Capt. Dix, Mr. Pain, Capt. Heath, and Mr. Pickering consider this Petition, and report what may be proper to be done." [1] It was a remarkably strong committee. There were the patriotic Hancock, the scholarly Greenleaf, the philosophic Pickering, and the eloquent Samuel Adams. It was natural that the Negro petitioners should have expected something. Three days after the committee

---

[1] House Journal, p. 85, quoted by Dr. Moore.

was appointed, on the 28th of June, they recommended "that the further Consideration of the Petition be referred till next session." The report was adopted, and the petition laid over until the "*next session.*" [1]

But the slaves did not lose heart. They found encouragement among a few noble spirits, and so were ready to urge the Legislature to a consideration of their petition at the next session, in the winter of 1774. The following letter shows that they were anxious and earnest.

"SAMUEL ADAMS TO JOHN PICKERING, JR.

" BOSTON, Jany. 8, 1774.

" *Sir,* —

As the General Assembly will undoubtedly meet on the 26th of this month, the Negroes whose petition lies on file, and is referred for consideration, are very solicitous for the Event of it, and having been informed that you intended to consider it at your leisure Hours in the Recess of the Court, they earnestly wish you would compleat a Plan for their Relief. And in the meantime, if it be not too much Trouble, they ask it as a favor that you would by a Letter enable me to communicate to them the general outlines of your Design. I am, with sincere regard," etc.[2]

It is rather remarkable, that on the afternoon of the first day of the session, — Jan. 26, 1774, — the " Petition of a number of Negro Men, which was entered on the Journal of the 25th of June last, and referred for Consideration to this session," was " read again, together, with a Memorial of the same Petitioners, and *Ordered*, that Mr. Speaker, Mr. Pickering, Mr. Hancock, Mr. Adams, Mr. Phillips, Mr. Pain, and Mr. Greenleaf consider the same and report." [3] The public feeling on the matter was aroused. It was considered as important as, if not more important than, any measure before the Legislature.

The committee were out until March, considering what was best to do about the petition. On the 2d of March, 1774, they reported to the House "a Bill to prevent the Importation of Negroes and others as slaves into this Province," when it was read a first time. On the 3d of March it was read a second time in the morning session; in the afternoon session, read a third time, and passed to be engrossed. It was then sent up to the Council to be concurred in, by Col. Gerrish, Col. Thayer, Col.

<small>[1] House Journal, p. 94.   [2] Slavery in Mass., p. 136.   [3] House Journal, p. 104.</small>

Bowers, Mr. Pickering. and Col. Bacon.[1] On the next day the bill "passed in Council with Amendments,"[2] and was returned to the House. On the 5th of March the House agreed to concur in Council amendments, and on the 7th of March passed the bill as amended. On the day following it was placed upon its passage in the Council, and carried. It was then sent down to the governor to receive his signature, in order to become the law of the Province. That official's approval was withheld; and the reason given was, "the secretary said (on returning the approved bills) that his Excellency had not had time to consider the other Bills that had been laid before him."[3]

It is quite fortunate that the bill was preserved ;[4] for it is now, in the certain light of a better civilization, a document of great historic value.

"ANNO REGNI REGIS GEORGII TERTII &C. DECIMO QUARTO.

" AN ACT to prevent the importation of Negroes or other Persons as Slaves into this Province; and the purchasing them within the same; *and for making provision for relief of the children of such as are already subjected to slavery Negroes Mulattoes & Indians born within this Province.*

"WHEREAS the Importation of Persons as Slaves into this Province has been found detrimental to the interest of his Majesty's subjects therein; And it being apprehended that the abolition thereof will be beneficial to the Province —

"*Be it therefore Enacted* by the Governor Council and House of Representatives that whoever shall after the Tenth Day of April next import or bring into this Province by Land or Water any Negro or other Person or Persons whether Male or Female as a Slave or Slaves shall for each and every such Person so imported or brought into this Province forfeit and pay the sum of one hundred Pounds to be recovered by presentment or indictment of a Grand Jury and when so recovered to be to his Majesty for the use of this Government: or by action of debt in any of his Majesty's Courts of Record and in case of such recovery the one moiety thereof to be to his majesty for the use of this Government the other moiety to the Person or Persons who shall sue for the same.

"*And be it further Enacted* that from and after the Tenth Day of April next any Person or Persons that shall purchase any Negro or other Person or Persons as a Slave or Slaves imported or brought into this Province as aforesaid shall forfeit and pay for every Negro or other Person so purchased Fifty Pounds to be recovered and disposed of in the same way and manner as before directed.

---

[1] House Journal, p. 224.   [2] Ibid., p. 226.
[3] House Journal, Gen. Court Records, xxx. pp. 248, 264 ; also, Slavery in Mass., p. 137.
[4] Mass. Archives, Domestic Relations, 1643–1774, vol. ix. p. 457.

"*And be it further Enacted* that every Person, concerned in importing or bringing into this Province, or purchasing any such Negro or other Person or Persons as aforesaid within the same; who shall be unable, or refuse, to pay the Penalties or forfeitures ordered by this Act; shall for every such offence suffer Twelve months' imprisonment without Bail or mainprise.

"*Provided* allways that nothing in this act contained shall extend to subject to the Penalties aforesaid the Masters, Mariners, Owners or Freighters of any such Vessel or Vessels, as before the said Tenth Day of April next shall have sailed from any Port or Ports in this Province, for any Port or Ports not within this Government, for importing or bringing into this Province any Negro or other Person or Persons as Slaves who in the prosecution of the same voyage may be imported or brought into the same. *Provided* he shall not offer them or any of them for sale.

"*Provided* also that this act shall not be construed to extend to any such Person or Persons, occasionally hereafter coming to reside within this Province, or passing thro' the same, who may bring such Negro or other Person or Persons as necessary servants into this Province provided that the stay or residence of such Person or Persons shall not exceed Twelve months or that such Person or Persons within said time send such Negro or other Person or Persons out of this Province there to be and remain, and also that during said Residence such Negro or other Person or Persons shall not be sold or alienated within the same.

"ᴠ *And be it further Enacted and declared that nothing in this act contained shall extend or be construed to extend for retaining or holding in perpetual servitude any Negro or other Person or Persons now inslaved within this Province but that every such Negro or other Person or Persons shall be intituled to all the Benefits such Negro or other Person or Persons might by Law have been intituled to, in case this act had not been made.*

"In the House of Representatives March 2, 1774. Read a first & second Time. March 3, 1774. Read a third Time & passed to be engrossed. Sent up for concurrence. T. CUSHING, *Spkr.*

"In Council March 3, 1774. Read a first time. 4. Read a second Time and passed in Concurrence to be Engrossed with the Amendment at ᴠ dele the whole Clause. Sent down for concurrence.

THOS. FLUCKER, *Secry.*

"In the House of Representatives March 4, 1774. Read and concurred.

T. CUSHING, *Spkr.*"

Like all other measures for the suppression of the slave-trade, this bill failed to become a law. If Massachusetts desired to free herself from this twofold cross of woe, — even if her great jurists could trace the law that justified the abolition of the curse, in the pages of the royal charter, — were not the British governors of the Province but conserving the corporation interests of the home government and the members of the Royal African Company? By the Treaty of Utrecht, England had agreed to furnish the Spanish West Indies with Negroes for the space of thirty years. She had aided all her colonies to establish slavery, and had sent her navies to guard the vessels that robbed Africa of five hundred thousand souls annually.[1] This was the cruel work of England. For all her sacrifices in the war, the millions of treasure she had spent, the blood of her children so prodigally shed, with the glories of Blenheim, of Ramillies, of Oudenarde and Malplaquet, England found her consolation and reward in seizing and enjoying, as the lion's share of results of the grand alliance against the Bourbons, the exclusive right for thirty years of selling African slaves to the Spanish West Indies and the coast of America![2] Why *should* Gov. Hutchinson sign a bill that was intended to choke the channel of a commerce in human souls that was so near the heart of the British throne?

Gov. Hutchinson was gone, and Gen. Gage was now governor. He convened the General Court at Salem, in June, 1774. On the 10th of June the same bill that Gov. Hutchinson had refused to sign was introduced, with a few immaterial changes, and pushed to a third reading, and engrossed the same day. It was called up on the 16th of June, and passed. It was sent up to the Council, where it was read a third time, and concurred in. But the next day the General Court was dissolved! And over the grave of this, the last attempt at legislation to suppress the slave-trade in Massachusetts, was written: *"Not to have been consented* to by the governor"!

These repeated efforts at anti-slavery legislation were strategic and politic. The gentlemen who hurried those bills through the House and Council, almost regardless of rules, knew that the royal governors would never affix their signatures to them. But the colonists, having put themselves on record, could appeal to the considerate judgment of the impatient Negroes; while the refusal of the royal governors to give the bills the force of law did much to drive the Negroes to the standard of the colonists. In the long night of darkness that was drawing its sable curtains about the colonial government, the loyalty of the Negroes was the lonely but certain star that threw its peerless light upon the pathway of the child of England so soon to be forced to lift its parricidal hand against its rapacious and cruel mother.

---

[1] Ethiope, p. 12.   [2] Bolingbroke, pp. 346-348.

CHAPTER XVI.

THE COLONY OF MARYLAND.

1634–1775.

MARYLAND UNDER THE LAWS OF VIRGINIA UNTIL 1630.—FIRST LEGISLATION ON THE SLAVERY QUESTION IN 1637-38.—SLAVERY ESTABLISHED BY STATUTE IN 1663.—THE DISCUSSION OF SLAVERY. —AN ACT PASSED ENCOURAGING THE IMPORTATION OF NEGROES AND WHITE SLAVES IN 1671.—AN ACT LAYING AN IMPOST ON NEGROES AND WHITE SERVANTS IMPORTED INTO THE COLONY.—DUTIES IMPOSED ON RUM AND WINE.—TREATMENT OF SLAVES AND PAPISTS.—CONVICTS IMPORTED INTO THE COLONY.—AN ATTEMPT TO JUSTIFY THE CONVICT-TRADE.—SPIRITED REPLIES. —THE LAWS OF 1723, 1729, 1752.—RIGHTS OF SLAVES.—NEGRO POPULATION IN 1728.—INCREASE OF SLAVERY IN 1756.—NO EFFORTS MADE TO PREVENT THE EVILS OF SLAVERY.—THE REVOLUTION NEARING.—NEW LIFE FOR THE NEGROES.

U P to the 20th of June, 1630, the territory that at present constitutes the State of Maryland was included within the limits of the colony of Virginia. During that period the laws of Virginia obtained throughout the entire territory.

In 1637 [1] the first assembly of the colony of Maryland agreed upon a number of bills, but they never became laws. The list is left, but nothing more. The nearest and earliest attempt at legislation on the slavery question to be found is a bill that was introduced *"for punishment of ill servants."* During the earlier years of the existence of slavery in Virginia, the term "servant" was applied to Negroes as well as to white persons. The legal distinction between slaves and servants was, "servants for a term of years," — white persons ; and "servants for life," — Negroes. In the first place, there can be no doubt but what Negro slaves were a part of the population of this colony from its organization; [2] and, in the second place, the above-mentioned bill of 1637 for the *"punishment of ill servants"* was intended, doubtless, to apply

---

[1] Dr. Abiel Holmes, in his American Annals, vol. ii. p. 5, says, "Maryland now contained about thirty-six thousand persons, of white men from sixteen years of age and upwards, and negroes male, and female from sixteen to sixty." I infer from this statement that slavery was in existence in Maryland in 1634; and I cannot find any thing in history to lead me to doubt but that slavery was born with the colony.

[2] Cabinet Cyclopædia, vol. i. p. 61.

to Negro servants, or slaves. So few were they in number, that they were seldom referred to as "slaves." They were "servants;" and that appellation dropped out only when the growth of slavery as an institution, and the necessity of specific legal distinction, made the Negro the only person that was suited to the condition of absolute property.

In 1638 there was a list of bills that reached a second reading, but never passed. There was one bill *"for the liberties of the people,"* that declared "all Christian inhabitants (slaves only excepted) to have and enjoy all such rights, liberties, immunities, privileges and free customs, within this province, as any natural born subject of England hath or ought to have or enjoy in the realm of England, by force or virtue of the common law or statute law of England, saving in such cases as the same are or may be altered or changed by the laws and ordinances of this province." [1] There is but one mention made of "slaves" in the above Act, but in none of the other Acts of 1638. There are certain features of the Act worthy of special consideration. The reader should keep the facts before him, that by the laws of England no Christian could be held in slavery; that in the Provincial governments the laws were made to conform with those of the home government; that, in specifying the rights of the colonists, the Provincial assemblies limited the immunities and privileges conferred by the Magna Charta upon British subjects, to Christians; that Negroes were considered heathen, and, therefore, denied the blessings of the Church and State; that even where Negro slaves were baptized, it was held by the courts in the colonies, and was the law-opinion of the solicitor-general of Great Britain, that they were not *ipso facto* free; [2] and that, where Negroes were free, they had no rights in the Church or State. So, while this law of 1638 did not say that Negroes *should* be slaves, in designating those who were to enjoy the rights of freemen, it excludes the Negro, and thereby fixes his condition as a slave by implication. If he were not named as a freeman, it was the intention of the law-makers that

---

[1] See Bacon's Laws; also Holmes's Annals, vol. i. p. 250.

[2] The following appeared in the Plantation Laws, printed in London in 1705: "Where any negro or slave, being in servitude or bondage, is or shall become Christian, and receive the sacrament of baptism, the same shall not nor ought not to be deemed, adjudged or construed to be a manumission or freeing of any such negro or slave, or his or her issue, from their servitude or bondage, but that notwithstanding they shall at all times hereafter be and remain in servitude and bondage as they were before baptism, any opinion, matter or thing to the contrary notwithstanding."

he should remain a bondman, — the exception to an established rule of law.[1]

In subsequent Acts reference was made to "servants," "fugitives," "runaways," etc. ; but the first statute in this colony establishing slavery was passed in 1663. It was "*An Act concerning negroes and other slaves.*" It enacts section one : —

"All negroes or other slaves within the province, and all negroes and other slaves to be hereafter imported into the province, shall serve *durante vita ;* and all children born of any negro or other slave, shall be slaves as their fathers were for the term of their lives."

Section two : —

"And forasmuch as divers freeborn *English* women, forgetful of their free condition, and to the disgrace of our nation, do intermarry with negro slaves, by which also divers suits may arise, touching the issue of such women, and a great damage doth befall the master of such negroes, for preservation whereof for deterring such free-born women from such shameful matches, *be it enacted*, &c.: That whatsoever free-born woman shall intermarry with any slave, from and after the last day of the present assembly, shall serve the master of such slave during the life of her husband; and that all the issue of such free-born women, so married, shall be slaves as their fathers were."

Section three : —

"And be it further enacted, that all the issues of *English*, or other free-born women, that have already married negroes, shall serve the master of their parents, till they be thirty years of age and no longer."[2]

Section one is the most positive and sweeping statute we have ever seen on slavery. It fixes the term of servitude for the longest time man can claim, — the period of his earthly existence, — and dooms the children to a service from which they were to find discharge only in death. Section two was called into being on account of the intermarriage of white women with slaves. Many of these women had been indentured as servants to pay their passage to this country, some had been sent as convicts, while still others had been apprenticed for a term of years. Some of them, however, were very worthy persons. No little confusion attended the fixing of the legal status of the issue of such marriages ; and it was to deter Englishwomen from such alliances, and to determine the status of the children before the courts, that this section was passed. Section three was clearly an *ex post*

---

[1] McSherry's Hist. of Maryland, p. 86.   [2] Freedom and Bondage, vol. i. p. 249.

facto law : but the public sentiment of the colony was reflected in it ; and it stood, and was re-enacted in 1676.

Like Virginia, the colony of Maryland found the soil rich, and the cultivation of tobacco a profitable enterprise. The country was new, and the physical obstructions in the way of civilization numerous and formidable. Of course all could not pursue the one path that led to agriculture. Mechanic and trade folk were in great demand. Laborers were scarce, and the few that could be obtained commanded high wages. The Negro slave's labor could be made as cheap as his master's conscience and heart were small. Cheaper labor became the cry on every hand, and the Negro was the desire of nearly all white men in the colony.[1] In 1671 the Legislature passed "*An Act encouraging the importation of negroes and slaves into*" the colony, which was followed by another and similar Act in 1692. Two motives inspired the colony to build up the slave-trade ; viz., to have more laborers, and to get something for nothing. And, as soon as Maryland was known to be a good market for slaves, the traffic increased with wonderful rapidity. Slaves soon became the bone and sinew of the working-force of the colony. They were used to till the fields, to fell the forests, to assist mechanics, and to handle light crafts along the water-courses. They were to be found in all homes of opulence and refinement ; and, unfortunately, their presence in such large numbers did much to lower honorable labor in the estimation of the whites, and to enervate women in the best white society. While the colonists persuaded themselves that slavery was an institution indispensable to the colony, its evil effects soon became apparent. It were impossible to engage the colony in the slave-trade, and escape the bad results of such an inhuman enterprise. It made men cruel and avaricious.

It was the motion of individuals to have legislative encouragement tendered the venders of human flesh and blood ; but the time came when the government of the colony saw that an impost tax upon the slaves imported into the colony would not impair the trade, while it would aid the government very materially. In 1696 "*An Act laying an imposition on negroes, slaves and white persons imported*" into the colony was passed. It is plain from the reading of the caption of the above bill, that it was intended to reach three classes of persons ; viz., Negro servants, Negro

[1] McMahon's Hist. of Maryland, vol. i. p. 274.

slaves, and white servants. The word "imported" means such persons as could not pay their passage, and were therefore indentured to the master of the vessel. When they arrived, their time was hired out, if they were free, for a term of years, at so much per year;[1] but if they were slaves the buyer had to pay all claims against this species of property before he could acquire a fee simple in the slave. Some historians have too frequently misinterpreted the motive and aim of the colonial Legislatures in imposing an impost tax upon Negroes and other servants imported into their midst. The fact that the law applied to white persons does not aid in an interpretation that would credit the makers of the act with feelings of humanity. A people who could buy and sell wives did not hesitate to see in the indentured white servants property that ought to be taxed. Why not? These white servants represented so many dollars invested, or so many years of labor in prospect! So all persons imported into the colony of Maryland, "Negroes, slaves, and white persons," were taxed as any other marketable article. A swift and remorseless civilization against the stolid forces of nature made men indiscriminate and cruel in their impulses to obtain. Public sentiment had been formulated into law: the law contemplated "servants and slaves" as chattel property; and the political economists of the Province saw in this species of property rich gains for the government. It was condition, circumstances, that made the servant or slave; but at length it was nationality, color.

When, on the threshold of the eighteenth century, "white indentured" servants were rapidly ceasing to exist under color or sanction of law, religious bigotry and ecclesiastical intolerance joined hands with the supporters of Negro slavery in a crusade[2]

---

[1] The following form was used for a long time in Maryland for binding out a servant.

This Indenture *made the   day of   in the   yeere of our Soveraigne Lord King* Charles, *&c betweene   of the one party,* and   on the *other party,* Witnesseth, *that the said   doth hereby covenant promise, and grant, to and with the said   his Executors and Assignes, to serve him from the day of the date hereof, vntill his first and next arrivall in Maryland; and after for and during the tearme of   yeeres, in such service and imployment, as the said   or his assignes shall there imploy him, according to the custome of the Countrey in the like kind. In consideration whereof, the said   doth promise and grant, to and with the said   to pay for his passing, and to find him with Meat, Drinke, Apparell and Lodging, with other necessaries during the said terme; and at the end of the said terme, to give him one whole yeeres provision of Corne, and fifty acres of Land, according to the order of the countrey. In witnesse whereof, the said   hath hereunto put his hand and seale, the day and yeere above written.*

Sealed and delivered in the presence of

— *Relation of the state of Maryland, pp.* 62, 63.

[2] Modern Traveller, vol. i. pp. 122, 123.

against the Irish Catholics. In 1704 the Legislature passed "*An Act imposing three pence per gallon on rum and wine, brandy and spirits, and twenty shillings per poll for negroes, for raising a supply to defray the public charge of this province, and twenty shillings, per poll, on Irish servants, to prevent the importing too great a number of Irish papist into this province.*" Although this Act was intended to remain on the statute-books only three years, its life was prolonged by a supplemental Act, and it disgraced the colony for twenty-one years. As in New York, so here, the government regarded the slave and Papist with feelings of hatred and fear. The former was only suited to a condition of perpetual bondage, the latter to be ostracized and driven out from before the face of the exclusive Protestants of that period. Both were cruelly treated; one on account of his face, the other on account of his faith.

"Unfortunately for the professors of the Catholic religion, by the force of circumstances which it is not necessary to detail, their religious persuasions became identified, in the public mind, with opposition to the principles of the revolution. Their political disfranchisement was the consequence. Charles Calvert, the deposed proprietary, shared the common fate of his Catholic brethren. Sustained and protected by the crown in the enjoyment of his mere private rights, the general jealousy of Catholic power denied him the government of the province."[1]

A knowledge of the antecedents of the master-class will aid the reader to a more accurate conception of the character of the institution of slavery in the colony of Maryland.

It is not very pleasing for the student of history at this time to remember that the British colonies in North America received into their early life the worst poison of European society, — the criminal element. From the first the practice of transporting convicts into the colonies obtained. And, during the reign of George I., statutes were passed "authorizing transportation as a commutation punishment for clergyable felonies." These con- victs were transported by private shippers, and then sold into the colony; and thus it became a gainful enterprise. From 1700 until 1760 this nefarious and pestiferous traffic greatly increased. At length it became, as already indicated, the subject of a special impost tax. Three or four hundred convicts were imported into the colony annually, and the people began to complain.[2] In "The

---

[1] McMahon's Maryland, vol. i. p. 278.   [2] 1st Pitkin's United States, p. 133.

Maryland Gazette" of the 30th of July, 1767, a writer attempted to show that the convict element was not to be despised, but was rather a desirable addition to the Province.   He says, —

"I suppose that for these last thirty years, communibus annis, there have been at least 600 convicts per year imported into this province: and these have probably gone into 400 families."

After answering some objections to their importation because of the contagious diseases likely to be communicated by them, he furt' er remarks, —

"This makes at least 400 to one, that they do no injury to the country in way complained of: and the people's continuing to buy and receive them so constantly, shows plainly the general sense of the country about the matter; notwithstanding a few gentlemen seem so angry that convicts are imported here at all, and would, if they could, by spreading this terror, prevent the people's buying them. I confess I am one, says he, who think a young country cannot be settled, cultivated, and improved, without people of some sort: and that it is much better for the country to receive convicts than slaves. The wicked and bad amongst them, that come into this province, mostly run away to the northward, mix with their people, and pass for honest men: whilst those more innocent, and who came for very small offences, serve their times out here, behave well, and become useful people."

This attempt to justify the *convict trade* elicited two able and spirited replies over the signatures of "Philanthropos" and "C. D." appearing in "Green's Gazette" of 20th of August, 1767, in which the writer of the first article is handled "with the gloves off."

"His remarks [says Philanthropos] remind me of the observation of a great philosopher, who alleges that there is a certain race of men of so selfish a cast, that they would even set a neighbour's house on fire, for the convenience of roasting an egg at the blaze. That these are not the reveries of fanciful speculatists, the author now under consideration is in a great measure a proof; for who, but a man swayed with the most sordid selfishness, would endeavor to disarm the people of all caution against such imminent danger, lest their just apprehensions should interfere with his little schemes of profit? And who but such a man would appear publicly as an advocate for the importation of felons, the scourings of jails, and the abandoned outcasts of the British nation, as a mode in any sort eligible for peopling a young country?"

In another part of his reply he remarks, —

"In confining the indignation because of their importation to a few, and representing that the general sense of the people is in favor of this vile importation, he is guilty of the most shameful misrepresentation and the grossest calumny upon the whole province. What opinion must our mother country, and our sister colonies, entertain of our virtue, when they see it confidently asserted in the Maryland Gazette, that we are fond of peopling our country with the most abandoned profligates in the universe? Is this the way to purge ourselves from that false and bitter reproach, so commonly thrown upon us, *that we are the descendants of convicts?* As far as it has lain in my way to be acquainted with the general sentiments of the people upon this subject, I solemnly declare, that the most discerning and judicious amongst them esteem it the greatest grievance imposed upon us by our mother country."

The writer felt that a young country could not be settled "without people of some sort," and that it was better to secure "convicts than slaves." Upon what grounds precisely this defender of buying convict labor based his conclusion that he would rather have "convicts than slaves" is not known. It could not have been that he believed the convicts of England more industrious or skilful than Negro slaves? Or, had he theoretical objections to slavery as a permanent institution? Perhaps the writer had himself graduated from the criminal class! But there were gentlemen who differed with him, and couched their objections to the convict system of importation in very vigorous English. On the 20th of August, 1767, two articles appeared in "Greene's Gazette." Says one of these writers, —

"For who, but a man swayed with the most sordid selfishness, would endeavor to disarm the people of all caution against such imminent danger, lest their just apprehensions should interfere with his little schemes of profit? And who but such a man would appear publicly as an advocate for the importation of felons, the scourings of jails, and the abandoned outcasts of the British nation, as a mode in any sort eligible for peopling a young country?"

There can be no doubt but that many of the convicts thus imported, having served out their time, in a brief season became slave-drivers and slave-owners. With hearts reduced to flinty hardness in the fires of unrestrained passions, the convict element, as it became absorbed in the great free white population of the Province,[1] created a most positive sentiment in favor of a cruel code for the government of the Negro slave. There were two motives that inspired the ex-convict to cruelty to the Negro: to

[1] McMahone says of this convict element: "The pride of this age revolts at the idea of going back to such as these, for the roots of a genealogical tree; and they, whose delight it would be, to trace their blood through many generations of stupid, sluggish, imbecile ancestors, with no claim to merit but the name they carry down, will even submit to be called '*novi homines,*' if a convict stand in the line of ancestry."

divert attention from himself, and to persuade himself, in his doubting mind, that the Negro was inferior to him by *nature.* It was, no doubt, a great undertaking; but the findings of such a court must have been comforting to an anxious conscience! The result can be judged. Maryland made a slave-code, which, for cruelty and general inhumanity, has no equal in the South.[1] The Maryland laws of 1715 contained, in chapter forty-four, an act with one hundred and thirty-five sections relating to Negro slaves. A most rigorous pass-system was established. By section six, no Negro or other servant was allowed to leave the county without a pass under the seal of the county in which their master resided; for which pass the slave or other servant was compelled to pay ten pounds of tobacco, or one shilling in money. If such persons were apprehended, a justice of the peace could impose such fines and inflict such punishment as were fixed by the law applying to runaways. By the Act of 1723, chapter fifteen, under the caption of *"An Act to prevent the tumultuous meeting and other irregularities of negroes and other slaves,"* the severity of the laws was increased tenfold. According to section four, a Negro or other slave who had the temerity to strike a white person, was to have his ears *"cropt on order of a Justice."* Section six denies slaves the right of possession of property: they could not own cattle. Section seven gave authority to any white man to kill a Negro who resisted an attempt to arrest him; and by a supplemental Act of 1751, chapter fourteen, the owner of a slave thus killed was to be paid out of the public treasury. In 1729 an Act was passed providing, that upon the conviction of certain crimes, Negroes and other slaves shall be not only hanged, but the body should be quartered, and exposed to public view. When slaves grew old and infirm in the service of their masters, and the latter were inspired by a desire to compliment the faithfulness of their servants by emancipation, the law came in and forbade manumission by the "last will or testament," or the making free in any way of Negro slaves. It was a temporary Act, passed in 1752, void of every element of humanity; and yet it stood as the law of the colony for twenty long years.

In 1748 the Negro population of Maryland was thirty-six thousand, and still rapidly increasing.

---

[1] With perhaps the single exception of South Carolina, of which the reader will learn more farther on.

"By a 'very accurate census,' taken this year, this was found to be the number of white inhabitants in Maryland : —

	FREE.	SERVANTS.	CONVICTS.	TOTAL.
Men . . .	24,058	3,576	1,507	29,141
Women . .	23,521	1,824	386	25,731
Boys . . .	26,637	1,048	67	27,752
Girls . . .	24,141	422	21	24,584
	98,357	6,870	1,981	107,208

"By the same account the total number of mulattoes in Maryland amounted to 3,592; and the total number of Negroes, to 42,764. Pres. Stiles' MS. It was reckoned (say the authors of Univ. Hist.), that above 2,000 Negro slaves were annually imported into Maryland."[1]

In 1756 the blacks had increased to 46,225, and in 1761 to 49,675. There was nothing in the laws to prohibit the instruction of Negroes, and yet no one dared to brave public sentiment on that point. The churches gave no attention or care to the slaves. During the first half or three-quarters of a century there was an indiscriminate mingling and marrying among the Negroes and white servants ; and, although this was forbidden by rigid statutes, it went on to a considerable extent. The half-breed, or Mulatto, population increased ;[2] and so did the number of free Negroes. The contact of these two elements — of slaves and convicts — was neither prudent nor healthy. The Negroes suffered from the touch of the moral contagion of this effete matter driven out of European society. Courted as rather agreeable companions by the convicts at first, the Negro slaves were at length treated worse by the ex-convicts than by the most intelligent and opulent slave-dealers in all the Province. And with no rights in the courts, incompetent to hold an office of any kind, the free Negroes were in almost as disagreeable a situation as the slaves.

From the founding of the colony of Maryland in 1632 down to the Revolutionary War, there is no record left us that any effort was ever made to cure the most glaring evils of slavery. For the Negro this was one long, starless night of oppression and out-

---

[1] American Annals.

[2] Dr. Holmes says, " The total number of mulattoes in Maryland amounted to 3,592," in 1755.

rage. No siren's voice whispered to him of a distant future, propitious and gracious to hearts almost insensible to a throb of joy, to minds unconscious of the feeblest rays of light. Being *absolute* property, it was the right of the master to say how much food, or what quantity of clothing, his slave should have. There were no rules by which a slave could claim the privilege of ceasing from labor at the close of the day. No, the master had the same right to work his slaves after nightfall as to drive his horse morning, noon, and night. Poor clothes, rough and scanty diet, wretched quarters, overworked, neglected in body and mind, the Negroes of Maryland had a sore lot.

The Revolution was nearing. Public attention was largely occupied with the Stamp Act and preparations for hostilities. The Negro was left to toil on; and, while at this time there was no legislation sought for slavery, there was nothing done that could be considered hostile to the institution. The Negroes hailed the mutterings of the distant thunders of revolution as the precursor of a new era to them. It did furnish an opportunity for them in Maryland to prove themselves patriots and brave soldiers. And how far their influence went to mollify public sentiment concerning them, will be considered in its appropriate place. Suffice it now to say, that cruel and hurtful, unjust and immoral, as the institution of slavery was, it had not robbed the Negro of a lofty conception of the fundamental principles that inspired white men to resist the arrogance of England; nor did it impair his enthusiasm in the cause that gave birth to a new republic amid the shock of embattled arms.

CHAPTER XVII.

THE COLONY OF DELAWARE.

1636–1775.

THE TERRITORY OF DELAWARE SETTLED IN PART BY SWEDES AND DANES, ANTERIOR TO THE YEAR 1638. — THR DUKE OF YORK TRANSFERS THE TERRITORY OF DELAWARE TO WILLIAM PENN. — PENN GRANTS THE COLONY THE PRIVILEGE OF SEPARATE GOVERNMENT. — SLAVERY INTRODUCED ON THE DELAWARE AS EARLY AS 1636. — COMPLAINT AGAINST PETER ALRICKS FOR USING OXEN AND NEGROES BELONGING TO THE COMPANY. — THE FIRST LEGISLATION ON THE SLAVERY QUESTION IN THE COLONY. — AN ENACTMENT OF A LAW FOR THE BETTER REGULATION OF SERVANTS. — AN ACT RESTRAINING MANUMISSION.

ANTERIOR to the year 1638, the territory now occupied by the State of Delaware was settled in part by Swedes and Danes. It has been recorded of them that they early declared that it was "not lawful to buy and keep slaves." [1] But the Dutch claimed the territory. When New Netherlands was ceded to the Duke of York, Delaware was occupied by his representatives. On the 24th of August, 1682, the Duke transferred that territory to William Penn. [2] But in 1703 Penn surrendered the old form of government, and gave the Delaware counties the privilege of a separate administration under the *Charter of Privileges.* Delaware inaugurated a legislature, but remained under the Council and Governor of Pennsylvania. But slavery made its appearance on the Delaware as early as 1636. [3]

"At this early period there appears to have been slavery on the Delaware. As one Coinclisse was 'condemned, on the 3d of February, to serve the company with the blacks on South River for wounding a soldier at Fort Amsterdam. He was also to pay a fine to the fiscal, and damages to the wounded soldier.' On the 22d, a witness testifying in the case of Governor Van Twiller, (the governor of New Neitherlands before Kieft,) who was charged with neglect and mismanagement of the company's affairs, said that

---

[1] Dr. Stevens, in his History of Georgia, vol. i. p. 288, says, "In the Swedish and German colony, which Gustavus Adolphus planted in Delaware, and which in many points resembled the plans of the Trustees, negro servitude was disallowed." But he gives no authority, I regret.

[2] See Laws of Delaware, vol. i. Appendix, pp. 1–4.   [3] Albany Records, vol. ii. p. 10.

'he had in his custody for Van Twiller, at Fort Hope and Nassau, twenty-four to thirty goats, and that *three negroes bought by the director* in 1636, were since employed in his private service.' Thus it will be seen that slavery was introduced on the Delaware as early as 1636, though probably not in this State, as the Dutch at that time had no settlement here."¹

And on the 15th of September, 1657, complaint was made that Peter Alricks had "used the company's oxen and negroes;" thus showing that there were quite a number of Negroes in the colony at the time mentioned. In September, 1661, there was a meeting between Calvert, D'Hinoyossa, Peter Alricks, and two Indian chiefs, to negotiate terms of peace. At this meeting the Marylanders agreed to furnish the Dutch annually three thousand hogsheads of tobacco, provided the Dutch would "supply them with negroes and other commodities."² Negroes were numerous, and an intercolonial traffic in slaves was established.

The first legislation on the slavery question in the colony of Delaware was had in 1721. "*An Act for the trial of Negroes*" provided that two justices and six freeholders should have full power to try "negro and mulatto slaves" for heinous offences. In case slaves were executed, the Assembly paid the owner two-thirds the value of such slave. It forbade convocations of slaves, and made it a misdemeanor to carry arms. During the same year an Act was passed punishing adultery and fornication. In case of children of a white woman by a slave, the county court bound them out until they were thirty-one years of age. In 1739 the Legislature passed an Act for the better regulation of servants and slaves, consisting of sixteen articles. It provided that no indentured servant should be sold into another government without the approval of at least one justice. Such servant could not be assigned over except before a justice. If a person manumitted a slave, good security was required: if he failed to do this, the manumission was of no avail. If free Negroes did not care for their children, they were liable to be bound out. In 1767 the Legislature passed another Act restraining manumission. It recites : —

"SECTION 2. *And be it enacted by the honorable John Penn, esq. with his Majesty's royal approbation, Lieutenant Governor and Commander in Chief of the counties of New-Castle, Kent and Sussex, upon Delaware, and province of Pennsylvania, under the honorable Thomas Penn and Richard Penn, esquires,*

---

¹ Vincent's History of Delaware, p. 159.   ² Ibid., p. 381.

true and absolute proprietaries of the said counties and province, by and with the advice and consent of the Representatives of the freemen of the said counties, in General Assembly met, and by the authority of the same, That if any master or mistress shall, by will or otherwise, discharge or set free any Mulatto or Negro slave or slaves; he or she, or his or her executors or administrators, at the next respective County Court of Quarter Sessions, shall enter into a recognizance with sufficient sureties, to be taken in the name of the Treasurer of the said county for the time being, in the sum of Sixty Pounds for each slave so set free, to indemnify the county from any charge they or any of them may be unto the same, in case of such Negro or Mulattoe's being sick, or otherwise rendered incapable to support him or herself; and that until such recognizance be given, no such Negro or Mulatto shall be deemed free." [1]

The remainder of the slave code in this colony was like unto those of the other colonies, and therefore need not be described. Negroes had no rights, ecclesiastical or political. They had no property, nor could they communicate a relation of any character. They had no religious or secular training, and none of the blessings of home life. Goaded to the performance of the most severe tasks, their only audible reply was an occasional growl. It sent a feeling of terror through their inhuman masters, and occasioned them many ugly dreams.

---

[1] Laws of Delaware, vol. i. p. 436.

CHAPTER XVIII.

THE COLONY OF CONNECTICUT.

1646–1775.

The Founding of Connecticut, 1631-36. — No Reliable Data given for the Introduction of Slaves. — Negroes were first introduced by Ship during the Early Years of the Colony. — "Committee for Trade and Foreign Plantations." — Interrogating the Governor as to the Number of Negroes in the Colony in 1680. — The Legislature (1690) passes a Law pertaining to the Purchase and Treatment of Slaves and Free Persons. — An Act passed by the General Court in 1711, requiring Persons manumitting Slaves to maintain them. — Regulating the Social Conduct of Slaves in 1723. — The Punishment of Negro, Indian, and Mulatto Slaves, for the Use of Profane Language, in 1630. — Lawfulness of Indian and Negro Slavery recognized by Code, Sept. 5, 1646. — Limited Rights of Free Negroes in the Colony. — Negro Population in 1762. — Act against Importation of Slaves, 1774.

ALTHOUGH the colony of Connecticut was founded between the years 1631 and 1636, there are to be found no reliable data by which to fix the time of the introduction of slavery there.[1] Like the serpent's entrance into the Garden of Eden, slavery entered into this colony stealthily; and its power for evil was discovered only when it had become a formidable social and political element. Vessels from the West Coast of Africa, from the West Indies, and from Barbadoes, landed Negroes for sale in Connecticut during the early years of its settlement. And for many years slavery existed here, without sanction of law, it is true, but perforce of custom. Negroes were bought as laborers and domestics, and it was a long time before their number called for special legislation. But, like a cancer, slavery grew until there was not a single colony in North America that could boast of its ability to check the dreadful curse. When the first slaves were introduced into this colony, can never be known; but, that there were Negro slaves from the beginning, we have the strongest

---

[1] In the Capital Laws of Connecticut, passed on the 1st of December, 1642, the tenth law reads as follows: "10. If any man stealeth a man or mankind, he shall be put to death. Ex. 21 16." But this was the law in Massachusetts, and yet slavery existed there for one hundred and forty-three (143) years.

historical presumption. For nearly two decades there was no reference made to slavery in the records of the colony.

In 1680 "the Committee for Trade and Foreign Plantations" addressed to the governors of the North-American plantations or colonies a series of questions. Among the twenty-seven questions put to Gov. Leete of Connecticut, were two referring to Negroes. The questions were as follows: —

"17. What number of English, Scotch, Irish or Forreigners have (for these seaven yeares last past, or any other space of time) come yearly to plant and inhabit within your Corporation. And also, what Blacks and Slaves have been brought in within the said time, and att what rates?

"18. What number of Whites, Blacks or Mulattos have been born and christened, for these seaven yeares last past, or any other space of time, for as many yeares as you are able to state on account of?"[1]

To these the governor replied as follows: —

"17. *Answ.* For English, Scotts and Irish, there are so few come in that we cannot give a certain accot. Som yeares come none; sometimes, a famaly or two, in a year. And for Blacks, there comes sometimes 3 or 4 in a year from Barbadoes; and they are sold usually at the rate of 22li. a piece, sometimes more and sometimes less, according as men can agree with the master of vessells, or merchants that bring them hither.

"18. *Answ.* We can give no accot. of the perfect number of either born; but fewe blacks; and but two blacks christened, as we know of."[2]

It is evident that the number of slaves was not great at this time, and that they were few and far between. The sullen and ofttimes revengeful spirit of the Indians had its effect upon the few Negro slaves in the colony. Sometimes they were badly treated by their masters, and occasionally they would run away. The country was new, the settlements scattered; and slavery as an institution, at this time and in this colony, in its infancy. The spirit of insubordination among the slave population seemed to call aloud for legislative restriction. In October, 1690, the Legislature passed the following bill: —

"Whereas many persons of this Colony doe for their necessary use purchase negroe seruants, and often times the sayd seruants run away to the great wronge, damage and disapoyntment of their masters and owners, for prevention of which for [221] the future, as much as ‖ may be, it is ordered by this Court that Whateuer negroe or negroes shall hereafter, at any time, be fownd wandring out of the towne bownds or place to which they doe belong, without

---

[1] Conn. Col. Recs., 1678–89, p. 293.   [2] Ibid., p. 298.

a ticket or pass from the authority, or their masters or owners, shall be stopt and secured by any of the inhabitants, or such as shall meet with them, and brought before the next authority to be examined and returned to their owners, who shall sattisfy for the charge if any be; and all ferrymen within this Colony are hereby required not to suffer any negroe without such certificate, to pass ouer their ferry by assisting them therein, upon the penalty of twenty shillings, to be payd as a fine to the county treasury, and to be leuyed upon theire estates for non-payment in way of distresse by warrant from any one Assistant or Comʳ. This order to be obserued as to vagrant and susspected persons fownd wandring from town to town, haueing no passes; such to be seized for examination and farther disspose by the authority; and if any negroes are free and for themselues, trauelling without such ticket or certificate, they to bear the charge themselues of their takeing up." [1]

The general air of complaint that pervades the above bill leaus to the conclusion that it was required by an alarming state of affairs. The pass-system was a copy from the laws of the older colonies where slavery had long existed. By implication free Negroes had to secure from the proper authorities a certificate of freedom; and the bill required them to carry it, or pay the cost of arrest.

One of the most palpable evidences of the humanity of the Connecticut government was the following act passed in May, 1702 : —

"Whereas it is observed that some persons in this Colonie having purchased Negro or Malatta Servants or Slaves, after they have spent the principall part of their time and strength in their masters service, doe sett them at liberty, and the said slaves not being able to provide necessaries for themselves may become a charge and burthen to the towns where they have served: for prevention whereof,

"It is ordered and enacted by this Court and the authority thereof: That every person in this Colonie that now is or hereafter shall be owner of a negro or mulatta servant or slave, and after some time of his or her being taken into imployment in his or her service, shall sett such servant or slave at liberty to provide for him or herselfe, if afterwards such servant or slave shall come to want, every such servant shall be relieved at the onely cost and charge of the person in whose service he or she was last reteined or taken, and by whome sett at liberty, or at the onely cost and charge of his or her heirs, executors or administrators, any law, usage or custome to the contrary notwithstanding." [2]

Massachusetts had acted and did act very cowardly about this matter. But Connecticut showed great wisdom and humanity in making a just and equitable provision for such poor and decrepit slaves as might find themselves turned out to charity after a long

---

[1] Conn. Col. Recs., 1689–1706, p. 40.   [2] Ibid., 1689–1706, pp. 375, 376.

life of unrequited toil. Slavery was in itself "the sum of all villanies," — the blackest curse that ever scourged the earth. To buy and sell human beings ; to tear from the famishing breast of the mother her speechless child ; to separate the husband from the wife of his heart ; to wring riches .from the unpaid toil of human beings ; to tear down the family altar, and let lecherous beasts, who claim the name of "Christian," run over defenceless womanhood as swine over God's altar ! — is there any thing worse, do you ask ? Yes ! To work a human being from youth to old age, to appropriate the labor of that being exclusively, to rob it of the blessings of this life, to poison every domestic charity, to fetter the intellect by the power of fatal ignorance, to withhold the privileges of the gospel of love ; and then, when the hollow cough comes under an inclement sky, when the shadows slant, when the hand trembles, when the gait is shuffling, when the ear is deaf, the eye dim, when desire faileth, — then to turn that human being out to die is by far the profoundest crime man can be guilty of in his dealings with mankind ! And slavery had so hardened men's hearts, that the above act was found to be necessary to teach the alphabet of human kindness. No wonder human forbearance was strained to its greatest tension when masters, thus liberating their slaves, assumed the lofty air of humanitarians who had actually done a noble act in manumitting a slave !

In 1708 the General Court was called upon to legislate against the commercial communion that had gone on between the slaves and free persons in an unrestricted manner for a long time. Slaves would often steal articles of household furniture, wares, clothing, etc., and sell them to white persons. And, in order to destroy the ready market this wide-spread kleptomania found, an Act was passed making it a misdemeanor for a free person to purchase any article from slaves. It is rather an interesting law, and is quoted in full.

"Whereas divers rude and evil minded persons for the sake of filthie lucre do frequently receive from Indians, malattoes and negro servants, money and goods stolen or obteined by other indirect and unlawful means, thereby incouraging such servants to steal from their masters and others : for redress whereof,

[35] *Be it enacted by the Governour, Council and Representatives, in General Court assembled, and by the authoritie of the same,* That every free person whomsoever, which shall presume either openly or privately to buy or receive of or from any Indian, molato or negro servant or slave, any goods, money, merchandize, wares, or provisions, without order from the master or

mistress of such servant or slave, every person so offending and being thereof convicted, shall be sentenced to restore all such money, goods, wares, merchandizes, or provisions, unto the partie injured, in specie, (if not altered,) and also forfeit to the partie double the value thereof over and above, or treble the value where the same are disposed of or made away. And if the person so offending be unable, or shall not make restitution as awarded, then to be openly whipt with so many stripes (not exceeding twentie,) as the court or justices that have cognizance of such offence shall order, or make satisfaction by service. And the Indian, negro, or molatto servant or slave, of or from whom such goods, money, wares, merchandizes or provisions shall be received or bought, if it appear to be stolen, or that shall steal any money, goods, or chattells, and be thereof convicted, although the buyer or receiver be not found, shall be punished by whipping not exceeding thirtie stripes, and the money, goods or chattels shall be restored to the partie injured, if it be found. And every assistant and justice of peace in the countie where such offence is committed, is hereby authorized to hear and determine all offences against this law, provided the damage exceed not the sum of fortie shillings." [1]

On the same day another act was passed, charging that as Mulatto and Negro slaves had become numerous in parts of the colony, destined to become insubordinate, abusive of white people, etc., and is as follows : —

"And whereas negro and molatto servants or slaves are become numerous in some parts of this Colonie, and are very apt to be turbulent, and often quarrelling with white people to the great disturbance of the peace :

"*It is therefore ordered and enacted by the Governour, Council and Representatives, in General Court assembled, and by the authoritie of the same,* That if any negro or malatto servant or slave disturb the peace, or shall offer to strike any white person, and be thereof convicted, such negro or malatto servant or slave shall be punished by whipping, at the discretion of the court, assistant, or justice of the peace that shall have cognizance thereof, not exceeding thirtie stripes for one offence." [2]

In 1711 the General Court of Connecticut Colony signally distinguished itself by the passage of an act in harmony with that of 1702. It was found that indentured servants as well as slaves had been made the victims of the cruel policy of turning slaves and servants out into the world without means of support after they had become helpless, or had served out their time. This class of human beings had been cast aside, like a squeezed lemon, to be trodden under the foot of men. The humane and thoughtful men of the colony demanded a remedy at law, and it came in the following admirable bill : —

---

[1] Conn. Col. Recs., 1706–16, p. 52. [2] Ibid., pp. 52, 53.

" An Act relating to Slaves, and such in particular as shall happen to become Servants for Time.

" *It is ordered and enacted by the Governour, Council and Representatives, in General Court assembled, and by the authority of the same,* That all slaves set at liberty by their owners, and all negro, malatto,͈or Spanish Indians, who are servants to masters for time, in case they come to want, after they shall be so set at liberty, or the time of their said service be expired, shall be relieved by such owners or masters respectively, their heirs, executors, or administrators ; and upon their, or either of their refusal so to do, the said slaves and servants shall be relieved by the selectmen of the towns to which they belong, and the said selectmen shall recover of the said owners or masters, their heirs, executors, or administrators, all the charge and cost they were at for such relief, in the usual manner as in the case of any other debts." [1]

In 1723 an Act was passed regulating the social conduct, and restricting the personal rights, of slaves. The slaves were quite numerous at this time, and hence the colonists deemed it proper to secure repressive legislation. It is strange how anticipatory the colonies were during the zenith of the slavery institution ! They were always expecting something of the slaves. No doubt they thought that it would be but the normal action of goaded humanity if the slaves should rise and cut their masters' throats. The colonists lived in mortal dread of their slaves, and the character of the legislation was but the thermometer of their fear. This Act was a slight indication of the unrest of the people of this colony on the slavery question : —

" [376] AN ACT TO PREVENT THE DISORDER OF NEGRO AND INDIAN SERVANTS AND SLAVES IN THE NIGHT SEASON.

" *Be it enacted by the Governour, Council and Representatives, in General Court assembled, and by the authority of the same,* That from and after the publication of this act, if any negro or Indian servant or slave shall be found abroad from home in the night season, after nine of the clock, without special order from his or their master or mistress, it shall be lawful for any person or persons to apprehend and secure such negro or Indian servant or slave so offending, and him or them bring before the next assistant or justice of peace ; which assistant or justice of peace shall have full power to pass sentence upon such negro or Indian servant or slave so offending, and order him or them to be publickly whipt on his or their naked body, not exceeding ten stripes, and pay cost of court, except his or their master or mistress shall redeem them by paying a fine not exceeding twenty shillings.

" *And it is hereby enacted by the authority aforesaid,* That if any such negro or Indian servant or slave as abovesaid shall have entertainment in any house after nine of the clock as aforesaid, except to do any business they may be sent

---

[1] Conn. Col. Recs., 1706–16, p. 233.

upon, the head of the family that entertaineth or tolerates them in his or their house, or any the dependencies thereof, and being convicted thereof before any one assistant or justice of the peace, who shall have power to hear and determine the same, shall forfeit the sum of twenty shillings, one-half to the complainer and the other half to the treasury of the town where the offence is committed; any law or usage to the contrary notwithstanding. And that it shall be the duty of the several grand-jurors and constables and tything-men, to make diligent enquiry into and present of all breaches of this act." [1]

The laws regulating slavery in the colony of Connecticut, up to this time, had stood, and been faithfully enforced. There had been a few infractions of the law, but the guilty had been punished. And in addition to statutory regulation of slaves, the refractory ones were often summoned to the bar of public opinion and dealt with summarily. Individual owners of slaves felt themselves at liberty to use the utmost discretion in dealing with this species of their property. So on every hand the slave found himself scrutinized, suspicioned, feared, hated, and hounded by the entire community of whites who were by law a perpetual *posse comitatus.* The result of too great vigilance and severe censorship was positive and alarming. It made the slave desperate. It intoxicated him with a malice that would brook no restraint. It is said that the use of vigorous adjectives and strong English is a relief to one in moments of trial. But even this was denied the oppressed slaves in Connecticut; for in May, 1730, a bill was passed punishing them for using strong language.

"AN ACT FOR THE PUNISHMENT OF NEGROES, INDIAN AND MOLATTO SLAVES, FOR SPEAKING DEFAMATORY WORDS.

" *Be it enacted by the Governour, Council and Representatives, in General Court assembled, and by the authority of the same,* That if any Negro, Indian or Molatto slave shall utter, publish and speak such words of any person that would by law be actionable if the same were uttered, published or spoken by any free person of any other, such Negro, Indian or Molatto slave, being thereof convicted before any one assistant or justice of the peace, (who are hereby impowred to hear and determine the same,) shall be punished by whipping, at the discretion of the assistant or justice before whom the tryal is, (respect being had to the circumstances of the case,) not exceeding forty stripes. And the said slave, so convict, shall be sold to defray all charges arising thereby, unless the same be by his or their master or mistress paid and answered, &c." [2]

The above act is the most remarkable document in this period of its kind. And yet there are two noticeable features in it: viz.,

---

[1] Conn. Col. Recs., 1717-25, pp. 390, 391.   [2] Ibid., 1726-35, p. 290.

the slave is to be proceeded against the same as if he were a free person ; and he was to be entitled to offer evidence, enter his plea, and otherwise defend himself against the charge. This was more than was allowed in any of the other colonies.

On the 9th of September, 1730, Gov. J. Talcott, in a letter to the "Board of Trade," said that there were "about 700 Indian and Negro slaves" in the colony. The most of these were Negro slaves. For on the 8th of July, 1715, a proclamation was issued by the governor against the importation of Indians;[1] and on the 13th of October, 1715, a bill was passed "*prohibiting the Importation or bringing into*" the colony any Indian slaves. It was an exact copy of the Act of May, 1712, passed in the colony of Massachusetts.

The colony of Connecticut never established slavery by direct statute; but in adopting a code which was ordered by the General Court of Hartford to be "copied by the secretary into the book of public records," it gave the institution legal sanction. This code was signed on the 5th of September, 1646. It recognized the lawfulness of Indian and Negro slavery. This was done under the confederacy of the "United Colonies of New England."[2] For some reason the part of the code recognizing slavery is omitted from the revised laws of 1715. In this colony, as in Massachusetts, only members of the church, "and living within the jurisdiction," could be admitted to the rights of freemen. In 1715 an Act was passed requiring persons who desired to become "freemen of this corporation," to secure a certificate from the selectmen that they were "persons of quiet and peaceable behavior and civil conversation, of the age of twenty-one years, and freeholders." This provision excluded all free Negroes. It was impossible for one to secure such a certificate. Public sentiment alone would have frowned upon such an innovation upon the customs and manners of the Puritans. On the 17th of May, 1660, the following Act was passed: "It is ordered by this court, that neither Indian nor negar serv[ts] shall be required to traine, watch or ward in the Collo:"[3]

To determine the status of the Negro here, this Act was necessary. He might be free, own his own labor; but if the law excluded him from the periodical musters and trainings, from the

---

[1] Conn. Col. Recs., 1706-16, pp. 515, 516. [2] Hazard, State Papers, vol. ii. pp. 1-6.
[3] Conn. Col. Recs., vol. i. p. 349.

church and civil duties, his freedom was a mere *misnomer*. It is difficult to define the rights of a free Negro in this colony. He was restricted in his relations with the slaves, and in his intercourse with white people was regarded with suspicion. If he had, in point of law, the right to purchase property, the general prejudice that confronted him on every hand made his warmest friends judiciously conservative. There were no provisions made for his intellectual or spiritual growth. He was regarded by both the religious and civil government, under which he lived, as a heathen. Even his accidental conversion could not change his condition, nor mollify the feelings of the white Christians (?) about him. Like the wild animal, he was possessed with the barest privilege of getting something to eat. Beyond this he had nothing. Everywhere he turned, he felt the withering glance of a suspicious people. Prejudice and proscriptive legislation cast their dark shadows on his daily path ; and the conscious superiority of the whites consigned him to the severest drudgery for his daily bread. The recollection of the past was distressing, the trials and burdens of the present were almost unbearable, while the future was one shapeless horror to him.

Perhaps the lowly and submissive acquiescence of the Negroes, bond and free, had a salutary effect upon the public mind. There is something awfully grand in an heroic endurance of undeserved pain. The white Christians married, and were given in marriage ; they sowed and gathered rich harvests ; they bought and built happy homes ; beautiful children were born unto them ; they built magnificent churches, and worshipped the true God : the present was joyous, and the future peopled with sublime anticipation. The contrast of these two peoples in their wide-apart conditions must have made men reflective. And added to this came the loud thunders of the Revolution. Connecticut had her orators, and they touched the public heart with the glowing coals of patriotic resolve. They felt the insecurity of their own liberties, and were now willing to pronounce in favor of the liberty of the Negroes. The inconsistency of asking for freedom, praying for freedom, fighting for freedom, and dying for freedom, when they themselves held thousands of human beings in bondage the most cruel the world ever knew, helped the cause of the slave. In 1762 the Negro population of this colony was four thousand five hundred and ninety.[1]

---

[1] Pres. Stiles's MSS.

Public sentiment was aroused on the slavery question ; and in October, 1774, the following prohibition was directed at slavery : —

"*Act against importation of slaves* — " No Indian, negro, or mulatto slave shall at any time hereafter be brought or imported into this State, by sea or land, from any place or places whatsoever, to be disposed of, left or sold, within this State." [1]

The above bill was brief, but pointed ; and showed that Connecticut was the only one of the New-England colonies that had the honesty and courage to legislate against slavery. And the patriotism and incomparable valor of the Negro soldiers of Connecticut, who proudly followed the Continental flag through the fires of the Revolutionary War, proved that they were worthy of the humane sentiment that demanded the Act of 1774.

---

[1] Freedom and Bondage, vol. i. pp. 272, 273.

CHAPTER XIX.

THE COLONY OF RHODE ISLAND.

1647–1775.

COLONIAL GOVERNMENT IN RHODE ISLAND, MAY, 1647. — AN ACT PASSED TO ABOLISH SLAVERY IN 1652, BUT WAS NEVER ENFORCED. — AN ACT SPECIFYING WHAT TIMES INDIAN AND NEGRO SLAVES SHOULD NOT APPEAR IN THE STREETS. — AN IMPOST-TAX ON SLAVES (1708). — PENALTIES IMPOSED ON DISOBEDIENT SLAVES. — ANTI-SLAVERY SENTIMENT IN THE COLONIES RECEIVES LITTLE ENCOURAGEMENT. — CIRCULAR LETTER FROM THE BOARD OF TRADE TO THE GOVERNOR OF THE ENGLISH COLONIES RELATIVE TO NEGRO SLAVES. — GOVERNOR CRANSTON'S REPLY. — LIST OF MILITIA-MEN, INCLUDING WHITE AND BLACK SERVANTS. — ANOTHER LETTER FROM THE BOARD OF TRADE. — AN ACT PREVENTING CLANDESTINE IMPORTATIONS AND EXPORTATIONS OF PAS-SENGERS, NEGROES, OR INDIAN SLAVES. — MASTERS OF VESSELS REQUIRED TO REPORT THE NAMES AND NUMBER OF PASSENGERS TO THE GOVERNOR. — VIOLATION OF THE IMPOST-TAX LAW ON SLAVES PUNISHED BY SEVERE PENALTIES. — APPROPRIATION BY THE GENERAL ASSEMBLY, JULY 5, 1715, FROM THE FUND DERIVED FROM THE IMPOST-TAX, FOR THE PAVING OF THE STREETS OF NEWPORT. — AN ACT PASSED DISPOSING OF THE MONEY RAISED BY IMPOST-TAX. — IMPOST-LAW REPEALED, MAY, 1732. — AN ACT RELATING TO FREEING MULATTO AND NEGRO SLAVES PASSED 1728. — AN ACT PASSED PREVENTING MASTERS OF VESSELS FROM CARRYING SLAVES OUT OF THE COLONY, JUNE 17, 1757. — EVE OF THE REVOLUTION. — AN ACT PROHIBITING IMPORTATION OF NEGROES INTO THE COLONY IN 1774. — THE POPULATION OF RHODE ISLAND IN 1730 AND 1774.

INDIVIDUAL Negroes were held in bondage in Rhode Island from the time of the formation of the colonial government there, in May, 1647, down to the close of the eighteenth century. Like her sister colonies, she early took the poison of the slave-traffic into her commercial life, and found it a most difficult political task to rid herself of it. The institution of slavery was never established by statute in this colony; but it was so firmly rooted five years after the establishment of the government, that it required the positive and explicit prohibition of law to destroy it. On the 19th of May, 1652, the General Court passed the following Act against slavery. It is the earliest positive prohibition against slavery in the records of modern nations.

"Whereas, there is a common course practiced amongst English men to buy negers, to that end they may have them for service or slaves forever; for the preventinge of such practices among us, let it be ordered, that no blacke mankind or white being forced by covenant bond, or otherwise, to serve any man or his assignes longer than ten yeares, or until they come to bee twentie-four yeares of age, if they bee taken in under fourteen, from the time of their cominge within the liberties of this Collonie. And at the end or terme of ten yeares to sett them free, as the manner is with the English servants. And that man that will not let them goe free, or shall sell them away elsewhere, to that end that they may bee enslaved to others for a long time, hee or they shall forfeit to the Collonie forty pounds." [1]

The above law was admirable, but there was lacking the public sentiment to give it practical force in the colony. It was never repealed, and yet slavery flourished under it for a century and a half. Mr. Bancroft says, "The law was not enforced, but the principle lived among the people." [2] No doubt the principle lived among the people; but, practically, they did but little towards emancipating their slaves until the Revolutionary War cloud broke over their homes. There is more in the statement Mr. Bancroft makes than the casual reader is likely to discern.

The men who founded Rhode Island, or Providence Plantation as it was called early, were of the highest type of Christian gentlemen. They held advanced ideas on civil government and religious liberty. They realized, to the full, the enormity of the sinfulness of slavery; but while they hesitated to strike down what many men pronounced a necessary social evil, it grew to be an institution that governed more than it could be governed. The institution was established. Slaves were upon the farms, in the towns, and in the families, of those who could afford to buy them. The population of the colony was small; and to manumit the slaves in whom much money was invested, or to suddenly cut off the supply from without, was more than the colonists felt able to perform. The spirit was willing, but the flesh was weak.

For a half-century there was nothing done by the General Court to check or suppress the slave-trade, though the Act of 1652 remained the law of the colony. The trade was not extensive. No vessels from Africa touched at Newport or Providence. The source of supply was Barbadoes; and, occasionally, some came by land from other colonies. Little was said for or against slavery during this period. It was a question difficult to handle. The sentiment against it was almost unanimous. It was an evil; but how to get rid of it, was the most important thing to be considered. During this period of perplexity, there was an ominous silence on slavery. The conservatism of the colonists produced

---

[1] R. I. Col. Recs., vol. i. p. 243.   [2] Bancroft, vol. i. 5th ed. p. 175.

the opposite in the Negro population. They began to think and talk about their "rights." The Act of 1652 had begun to bear fruit. At the expiration of ten years' service, slaves began to demand their freedom-papers. This set the entire Negro class in a state of expectancy. Their eagerness for liberty was interpreted by the more timid among the whites as the signal for disorder. A demand was made for legislation that would curtail the personal liberties of the Negroes in the evenings. It is well to produce the Act of Jan. 4, 1703, that the reader may see the similarity of the laws passed in the New-England colonies against Negroes : —

"An Act to restrict negroes and Indians for walking in unseasonable times in the night, and at other times not allowable.

"Voted, Be it enacted by this Assembly and the authority thereof, and it is hereby enacted, If any negroes or Indians, either freemen, servants, or slaves, do walk in the streets of the town of Newport, or any other town in this Collony, after nine of the clock of the night, without a certificate from their masters, or some English person of said family with them, or some lawfull excuse for the same, that it shall be lawfull for any person to take them up and deliver them to a Constable, to be secured, or see them secured, till the next morning, and then to be brought before some Justice of the Peace in said town, to be dealt withall, according to the recited Act, which said Justice shall cause said person or persons so offending, to be whipped at the publick whipping post in said town, not exceeding fifteen stripes upon their naked backs, except their incorrigible behavior require more. And all free negroes and free Indians to be under the same penalty, without a lawful excuse for their so being found walking in the streets after such unseasonable time of night.

"And be it further enacted, All and every house keeper, within said town or towns or Collony, that shall entertain men's servants, either negroes or Indians, without leave of their masters or to whom they do belong, after said set time of the night before mentioned, and being convicted of the same before any one Justice of the Peace, he or they shall pay for each his defect five shillings in money, to be for the use of the poor in the town where the person lives; and if refused to be paid down, to be taken by distraint by a warrant to any one Constable, in said town; any Act to the contrary notwithstanding." [1]

It is rather remarkable that this Act should prohibit free Negroes and free Indians from walking the streets after nine o'clock. In this particular this bill had no equal in any of the other colonies. This act seemed to be aimed with remarkable precision at the Negroes as a class, both bond and free. The influence of free Negroes upon the slaves had not been in harmony with the condition of the latter; and the above Act was

---

[1] R. I. Col. Recs., vol. iii. pp. 492, 493.

intended as a reminder, in part, to free Negroes and Indians. It went to show that there was but little meaning in the word "free," when placed before a Negro's name. No such restriction could have been placed upon the personal rights of a white colonist; for, under the democratical government of the colony, a subject was greater than the government. No law could stand that was inimical to his rights as a freeman. But the free Negro had no remedy at law. He was literally between two conditions, bondage and freedom.

Attention has been called to the fact, that the Act of 1652 was never enforced. In April, 1708, an Act, laying an impost-tax upon slaves imported into the colony, was passed which really gave legal sanction to the slave-trade.[1] The following is the Act referred to : —

"And it is further enacted by the authority aforesaid, that whereas, by an act of Assembly, in February last past, concerning the importing negroes, one article of said act, expressing that three pounds money shall be paid into the treasury for each negro imported into this colony; but upon exporting such negro in time limited in said act, said three pounds were to be drawn out of the treasury again by the importer:

"It is hereby enacted, that said sum for the future, shall not be drawn out, but there continued for the use in said act expressed; any act to the contrary, notwithstanding."[2]

The Act referred to as having passed "in February last past," cannot be found.[3] But, from the one quoted above, it is to be inferred that two objects were aimed at, viz. : First, under the codes of Massachusetts and Virginia, a drawback was allowed to an importer of a Negro who exported him within a stated time : the Rhode-Island Act of "February" had allowed importers this privilege. Second, notwithstanding the loud-sounding Act of 1652, this colony was not only willing to levy an impost-tax upon all slaves imported; but, in her greed for "blood money," even denied the importer the mean privilege, in exporting his slave, of drawing his rebate ! The consistency of Rhode Island must have been a jewel that the other colonies did not covet.

The last section of the Act of 1703 was directed against "house

---

[1] There is no law making the manufacturing of whiskey legal in the United States; and yet the United-States government makes laws to regulate the business, and collects a revenue from it. It exists by and with the consent of the government, and, in a sense, is legal.

[2] R. I. Col. Recs., vol. iv. p. 34.

[3] I have searched diligently for the Act of February, among the Rhode-Island Collections and Records, but have not found it. It was evidently more comprehensive than the above Act.

keepers," who were to be fined for entertaining Negro or Indian slaves after nine o'clock.   In 1708 another Act was passed, supplemental to the one of 1703, and added stripes as a penalty for non-payment of fines.   Many white persons in the larger towns had grown rather friendly towards the slaves; and, even where they did not speak out in public against the enslavement of human beings, their hearts led them to the performance of many little deeds of kindness.   They discovered many noble attributes in the Negro character, and were not backward in expressing their admiration.   When summoned before a justice, and fined for entertaining Negroes after nine o'clock, they paid the penalty with a willingness and alacrity that alarmed the slave-holding caste.   This was regarded as treason.   Some could not pay the fine, and, hence, went free.   The new Act intended to remedy this.   It was as follows: —

" An Act to prevent the entertainment of Negroes, &c.

"Whereas, there is a law in this colony to suppress any persons from entertaining of negro slaves or Indian servants that are not their own, in their houses, or unlawfully letting them have strong drink, whereby they were damnified, such persons were to pay a fine of five shillings, and so by that means go unpunished, there being no provision made [of] what corporeal punishment they should have, if they have not wherewith to pay:

"Therefore, it is now enacted, that any such delinquent that shall so offend, if he or she shall not have or procure the sum of ten shillings for each defect, to be paid down before the authority before whom he or she hath been legally convicted, he or she shall be by order of said authority, publicly whipped upon their naked back, not exceeding ten stripes; any act to the contrary, notwithstanding." [1]

It is certain that what little anti-slavery sentiment there was in the British colonies in North America during the first century of their existence received no encouragement from Parliament. From the beginning, the plantations in this new world in the West were regarded as the hotbeds in which slavery would thrive, and bring forth abundant fruit, to the great gain of the English government.   All the appointments made by the crown were expected to be in harmony with the plans to be carried out in the colonies.   From the settlement of Jamestown down to the breaking out of the war, and the signing of the Declaration of Independence, not a single one of the royal governors ever suffered his sense of duty to the crowned heads to be warped by local

---

[1] R. I. Col. Recs., vol. iv. p. 50.

views on "the right of slavery." The Board of Trade was untiring in its attention to the colonies. And no subject occupied greater space in the correspondence of that colossal institution than slavery. The following circular letter, addressed to the governors of the colonies, is worthy of reproduction here, rather than in the Appendix. It is a magnificent window, that lets the light in upon a dark subject. It gives a very fair idea of the profound concern that the home government had in foreign and domestic slavery.

"CIRCULAR LETTER FROM THE BOARD OF TRADE TO THE GOVERNORS OF THE ENGLISH COLONIES, RELATIVE TO NEGRO SLAVES.

"APRIL 17, 1708.

"SIR: Some time since, the Queen was pleased to refer to us a petition relating to the trade of Africa, upon which we have heard what the Royal African Company, and the separate traders had to offer; and having otherwise informed ourselves, in the best manner we could, of the present state of that trade, we laid the same before Her Majesty. The consideration of that trade came afterwards into the house of commons, and a copy of our report was laid before the house; but the session being then too far spent to enter upon a matter of so great weight, and other business intervening, no progress was made therein. However, it being absolutely necessary that a trade so beneficial to the kingdom should be carried on to the greatest advantage, there is no doubt but the consideration thereof will come early before the Parliament at their next meeting; and as the well supplying of the plantations and colonies with sufficient number of negroes at reasonable prices, is in our opinion the chief point to be considered in regard to that trade, and as hitherto we have not been able to know how they have been supplied by the company, or by separate traders, otherwise than according to the respective accounts given by them, which for the most part are founded upon calculations made from their exports on one side and the other, and do differ so very much, that no certain judgment can be made upon those accounts.

"Wherefore, that we may be able at the next meeting of the Parliament to lay before both houses when required, an exact and authentic state of that trade, particularly in regard to the several plantations and colonies; we do hereby desire and strictly require you, that upon the receipt hereof, you do inform yourself from the proper officers or otherwise, in the best manner you can, what number of negroes have been yearly imported directly from Africa into Jamaica, since the 24th of June, 1698, to the 25th of December, 1707, and at what rate per head they have been sold each year, one with another, distinguishing the numbers that have been imported on account of the Royal African Company, and those which have been imported by separate traders; as likewise the rates at which such negroes have been sold by the company and by separate traders. We must recommend it to your care to be as exact and diligent therein as possibly you can, and with the first opportunity to transmit to us such accounts as aforesaid, that they may arrive here in due time, as also duplicates by the first conveyance.

"And that we may be the better able to make a true judgment of the present settlement of that trade, we must further recommend it to you to confer with some of the principal planters and inhabitants within your government touching that matter, and to let us know how the negro trade was carried on, and the island of Jamaica supplied with negroes till the year 1698, when that trade was laid open by act of Parliament; how it has been carried on, and negroes supplied since that time, or in what manner they think the said trade may best be managed for the benefit of the plantations.

"We further desire you will inform us what number of ships, if any, are employed from Jamaica to the coast of Africa in the negro trade, and how many separate traders are concerned therein.

"Lastly, whatever accounts you shall from time to time send us touching these matters of the negro trade, we desire that the same may be distinct, and not intermixed with other matters; and that for the time to come, you do transmit to us the like half yearly accounts of negroes, by whom imported and at what rates sold; the first of such subsequent accounts, to begin from Christmas, 1707, to which time those now demanded, are to be given. So we bid you heartily farewell,

"Your very loving friends,

"STAMFORD,
HERBERT,
PH. MEADOWS,
I. PULTENEY,
R. MONCKTON.

"P. S. We expect the best account you can give us, with that expedition which the shortness of the time requires.

"Memorandum. This letter, mutatis mutandis, was writ to the Governors of Barbadoes, the Leeward Islands, Bermuda, New York, New Jersey, Maryland, the President of the Council of Virginia, the Governor of New Hampshire and the Massachusetts Bay, the Deputy Governor of Pennsylvania, the Lords proprietors of Carolina, the Governors and Companies of Connecticut and Rhode Island."[1]

The good Queen of England was interested in the traffic in human beings; and although the House of Commons was too busy to give attention to "a matter of so great weight," the "Board of Trade" felt that it was "absolutely necessary that a trade so beneficial to the kingdom should be carried on to the greatest advantage." England never gave out a more cruel document than the above circular letter. To read it now, under the glaring light of the nineteenth century, will almost cause the English-speaking people of the world to doubt even "the truth of history." Slavery did not exist at sufferance. It was a crime

---

[1] R. I. Col. Recs., vol. iv. pp. 53, 54.

against the weak, ignorant, and degraded children of Africa, systematically perpetrated by an organized Christian government, backed by an army that grasped the farthest bounds of civilization, and a navy that overshadowed the oceans.

The reply of the governor of Rhode Island was not as encouraging as their lordships could have wished.

GOVERNOR CRANSTON'S REPLY.

"May it please your Lordships: In obedience to your Lordships' commands of the 15th of April last, to the trade of Africa.

"We, having inspected into the books of Her Majesty's custom, and informed ourselves from the proper officers thereof, by strict inquiry, can lay before your Lordships no other account of that trade than the following, viz.:

"1. That from the 24th of June, 1698, to the 25th of December, 1707, we have not had any negroes imported into this colony from the coast of Africa, neither on the account of the Royal African Company, or by any of the separate traders.

"2. That on the 30th day of May, 1696, arrived at this port from the coast of Africa, the brigantine Seaflower, Thomas Windsor, master, having on board her forty-seven negroes, fourteen of which he disposed of in this colony, for betwixt £30 and £35 per head; the rest he transported by land for Boston, where his owners lived.

"3. That on the 10th of August, the 19th and 28th of October, in the year 1700, sailed from this port three vessels, directly for the coast of Africa; the two former were sloops, the one commanded by Nicho's Hillgroue, the other by Jacob Bill; the last a ship, commanded by Edwin Carter, who was part owner of the said three vessels, in company with Thomas Bruster, and John Bates, merchants, of Barbadoes, and separate traders from thence to the coast of Africa; the said three vessels arriving safe to Barbadoes from the coast of Africa, where they made the disposition of their negroes.

"4. That we have never had any vessels from the coast of Africa to this colony, nor any trade there, the brigantine above mentioned, excepted.

"5. That the whole and only supply of negroes to this colony, is from the island of Barbadoes; from whence is imported one year with another, betwixt twenty and thirty; and if those arrive well and sound, the general price is from £30 to £40 per head.

"According to your Lordships' desire, we have advised with the chiefest of our planters, and find but small encouragement for that trade to this colony; since by the best computation we can make, there would not be disposed in this colony above twenty or thirty at the most, annually; the reasons of which are chiefly to be attributed to the general dislike our planters have for them, by reason of their turbulent and unruly tempers.

"And that most of our planters that are able and willing to purchase any of them, are supplied by the offspring of those they have already, which increase daily; and that the inclination of our people in general, is to employ white servants before Negroes.

"Thus we have given our Lordships a true and faithful account of what hath occurred, relating to the trade of Africa from this colony; and if, for the future, our trade should be extended to those parts, we shall not fail transmitting accounts thereof according to your Lordships' orders, and that at all times be ready to show ourselves,

"Your Lordships' obedient servant,

"SAMUEL CRANSTON, *Governor.*

"NEWPORT, ON RHODE ISLAND, December 5, 1708." [1]

So in nine years there had been no Negro slaves imported into the colony; that in 1696 fourteen had been sold to the colonists for between thirty pounds and thirty-five pounds apiece; that this was the only time a vessel direct from the coast of Africa had touched in this colony; that the supply of Negro slaves came from Barbadoes, and that the colonists who would purchase slaves were supplied by the offspring of those already in the plantation; and that the colonists preferred white servants to black slaves. The best that can be said of Gov. Cranston's letter is, it was very respectful in tone. The following table was one of the enclosures of the letter. It is given in full on account of its general interest: —

"A list of the number of freemen and militia, with the servants, white and black, in the respective towns; as also the number of inhabitants in Her Majesty's colony of Rhode Island, &c., December the 5th, 1708.

TOWNS.	FREEMEN.	MILITIA.	WHITE SERVANTS.	BLACK SERVANTS.	TOTAL NUMBER OF INHABITANTS.
Newport . . .	190	358	20	220	2,203
Providence. . .	241	283	6	7	1,446
Portsmouth . .	98	104	8	40	628
Warwick . . .	80	95	4	10	480
Westerly . . .	95	100	5	20	570
New Shoreham .	38	47	—	6	208
Kingstown. . .	200	282	—	85	1,200
Jamestown. . .	33	28	9	32	206
Greenwich . . .	40	65	3	6	240
Total . . .	1,015	1,362	56	426	7,181

[1] R. I. Coll. Recs., vol. iv. pp. 54, 55.

"It is to be understood that all men within this colony, from the age of sixteen to the age of sixty years, are of the militia, so that all freemen above and under said ages, are inclusive in the abovesaid number of the militia.

"As to the increase or decrease of the inhabitants within five years last past, we are not capable to give an exact account, by reason there was no list ever taken before this (the militia excepted), which hath increased since the 14th of February, 1704–5 (at which time a list was returned to your Lordships), the number of 287.

"SAMUEL CRANSTON, *Governor.*

"NEWPORT, ON RHODE ISLAND, December the 5th, 1708." [1]

The Board of Trade replied to Gov. Cranston, under date of "Whitehall, January 16th, 1709–10.," saying they should be glad to hear from him "in regard to Negroes," etc.[2]

The letter of inquiry from the Board of Trade imparted to slave-dealers an air of importance and respectability. The institution was not near so bad as it had been thought to be ; the royal family were interested in its growth ; it was a gainful enterprise ; and, more than all, as a matter touching the conscience, the Bible and universal practice had sanctified the institution. To attempt to repeal the Act of 1652 would have been an occasion unwisely furnished for anti-slavery men to use to a good purpose. The bill was a dead letter, and its enemies concluded to let it remain on the statute-book of the colony.

The experiment of levying an impost-tax upon Negro slaves imported into the colony had proved an enriching success. After 1709 the slave-trade became rather brisk. As the population increased, public improvements became necessary, — there were new public buildings in demand, roads to be repaired, bridges to be built, and the poor and afflicted to be provided for. To do all this, taxes had to be levied upon the freeholders. A happy thought struck the leaders of the government. If men *would* import slaves, and the freemen of the colony *would* buy them, they should pay a tax as a penalty for their sin.[3] And the people easily accommodated their views to the state of the public treasury.

Attention has been called already to the impost Act of 1708. On the 27th of February, 1712, the General Assembly passed "*An Act for preventing clandestine importations and exportations*

---

[1] R. I. Col. Recs., vol. iv. p. 59.   [2] J. Carter Brown's Manuscripts, vol. viii. Nos. 506, 512.
[3] It was a specious sort of reasoning. I learn that the bank over on the corner is to be robbed to-night at twelve o'clock. Shall I go and rob it at ten o'clock ; because, if I do not do so, another person will, two hours later ?

of passengers, or negroes, or Indian slaves into or out of this colony," etc. The Act is quite lengthy. It required masters of vessels to report to the governor the names and number of all passengers landed into the colony, and not to carry away any person without a pass or permission from the governor, upon pain of a fine of fifty pounds current money of New England. Persons desiring to leave the colony had to give public notice for ten days in the most public place in the colony; and it specifies the duties of naval officers, and closes with the following in reference to Negro slaves, calling attention to the impost Act of 1708:—

"It was then and there enacted, that for all negroes imported into this colony, there shall be £3 current money, of New England, paid into the general treasury of this colony for each negro, by the owner or importer of said negro; reference being had unto the said act will more fully appear.

"But were laid under no obligation by the said act, to give an account to the Governor what negroes they did import, whereby the good intentions of said act were wholly frustrated and brought to no effect; and by the clandestinely hiding and conveying said negroes out of the town into the country, where they lie concealed:

"For the prevention of which for the future, it is hereby enacted by the authority aforesaid, that from and after the publication of this act, all masters of vessels that shall come into the harbor of Newport, or into any port of this government, that hath imported any negroes or Indian slaves, shall, before he puts on shore in any port of this government, or in the town of Newport, any negroes or Indian slaves, or suffers any negroes or Indian slaves to be put on shore by any person whatsoever, from on board his said vessel, deliver unto the naval officer in the town of Newport, a fair manifest under his hand, which shall specify the full number of negroes and Indian slaves he hath imported in his said vessel, of what sex, with their names, the names of their owners, or of those they are consigned to; to the truth of which manifest so given in, the said master shall give his corporal oath, or solemn engagement unto the said naval officer, who is hereby empowered to administer the same unto him; which said manifest being duly sworn unto, the said naval officer shall make a fair entry thereof in a book, which shall be prepared for that use, whereunto the said master shall set his hand. . . .

"And when the said master hath delivered his said manifest and sworn to it, as abovesaid, and before he hath landed on shore, or suffer to be landed, any negroes or Indian slaves as aforesaid, he, the said master, shall pay to the naval officer the sum of £3 current money, of New England, for each negro; and the sum of forty shillings of the like money for each Indian that shall be by him imported into this colony, or that shall be brought into this colony in the vessel whereof he is master.

"But if he hath not ready money to pay down, as aforesaid, he shall then give unto the said naval officer a bill, as the law directs, to pay unto him the full sum above mentioned, for each and every negro and Indian imported as above said, which bill shall run payable in ten days from the entering the manifest as above said; and if at the end of the ten days, the said master shall refuse to pay the full contents of his bill, that then the said naval officer shall deliver the said bill unto the Governor, or in his absence, to the next officer of the peace, as aforesaid who shall immediately proceed with the said master in the manner above said, by committing of him to Her Majesty's jail, where he shall remain without bail or mainprize, until he hath paid unto the naval officer, for the use of this colony, double the sum specified in his said bill, and all charges that shall accrue thereby; which money shall be paid out by the said naval officer, as the General Assembly of this colony shall order the same.

"And it is further enacted, that the naval officer who now is, and who ever shall be for the future put into said office, shall at his entering into the said office, take his engagement to the faithful performance of the above said acts. And for his encouragement, shall have such fees as are hereafter mentioned at the end of this act.

"And for the more effectual putting in execution those acts, and that none may plead ignorance :

"It is enacted by the authority aforesaid, that all masters of vessels trading to this government, shall give bond, with sufficient surety in the naval office, for the sum of £50, current money of New England."[1]

We have omitted a large portion of the bill, because of its length; but have quoted sufficient to give an excellent idea of the marvellous caution taken by the good Christians of Rhode Island to get every cent due them on account of the slave-trade, which their prohibition did not prohibit. It was a carefully drawn bill for those days.

The diligence of the public officers in the seaport town of Newport was richly rewarded. The slave-trade now had the sanction and regulation of colonial law. The demand for Negro laborers was not affected in the least, while traders did not turn aside on account of three pounds per head tax upon every slave sold into Rhode Island. On the 5th of July, 1715, the General Assembly appropriated a portion of the fund derived from the impost-tax on imported Negroes to repairing the streets ; and then strengthened and amplified the original law on impost-duties, etc. The following is the Act : —

"This Assembly, taking into consideration that Newport is the metropolitan town in this colony, and that all the courts of judicature within this colony are held there; and also, that it is the chief market town in the government; and that it hath very miry streets, especially that leading from the ferry, or landing place, up to the colony house, so that the members of the courts are very much discommoded therewith, and is a great hindrance to the transporting of pro-

---

[1] R. I. Col. Recs., vol. iv. pp. 133-135.

visions, &c., in and out of the said towns, to the great loss of the inhabitants thereof ; —

" Therefore, be it enacted by this present Assembly, and by the authority thereof it is enacted, that the sum of £289 17s. 3d., now lying in the naval officer's hand, (being duties paid to this colony for importing of slaves), shall be, and is hereby granted to the town of Newport, towards paving the streets of Newport, from the ferry place, up to the colony house, in said Newport; to be improved by their directors, such as they shall, at their quarter meetings appoint for the same.

" And whereas, there was an act of Assembly, made at Newport, in the year 1701–2, for the better preventing of fraud, and cozen, in paying the duties for importing of negro and Indian slaves into this colony, and the same being found in some clauses deficient, for the effecting of the full intent and purpose thereof ; —

" Therefore, it is hereby enacted by the authority aforesaid, that every master of ship, or vessel, merchant or other person or persons, importing or bringing into this colony any negro slave or slaves of what age soever, shall enter their number, names, and sex in the naval office; and the master shall insert the same in the manifest of his lading, and shall pay to the naval officer in Newport, £3 per head, for the use of this colony, for every negro, male or female, so imported, or brought in. And every such master, merchant, or other person, refusing or neglecting to pay the said duty within ten days after they are brought ashore in said colony, then the said naval officer, on knowledge thereof, shall enter an action and sue [for] the recovery of the same, against him or them, in an action of debt, in any of His Majesty's courts of record, within this colony.

" And if any master of ship or vessel, merchant or others, shall refuse or neglect to make entry, as aforesaid, of all negroes imported in such ship or vessel, or be convicted of not entering the full number, such master, merchant, or other person, shall forfeit and pay the sum of £6, for every one that he shall refuse or neglect to make entry, of one moiety thereof to His Majesty, for and towards the support of the government of this colony; and the other moiety to him or them that shall inform or sue for the same; to be recovered by the naval officer in manner as above said.

" And also, all persons that shall bring any negro or negroes into this colony, from any of His Majesty's provinces adjoining, shall in like manner enter the number, names and sex, of all such negroes, in the above said office, under the penalty of the like forfeiture, as above said; and to be recovered in like manner by the naval officer, and shall pay into the said office within the time above limited, the like sum of £3 per head; and for default of payment, the same to be recovered by the naval officer in like manner as aforesaid.

" Provided always, that if any gentleman, who is not a resident in this colony, and shall pass through any part thereof, with a waiting man or men with him, and doth not reside in this colony six months, then such waiting men shall be free from the above said duty; the said gentleman giving his solemn engagement, that they are not for sale; any act or acts, clause or clauses of acts, to the contrary hereof, in any ways, notwithstanding.

" Provided, that none of the clauses in the aforesaid act, shall extend to any masters or vessels, who import negroes into this colony, directly from the coast of Africa.

" And it is further enacted by the authority aforesaid, that the money raised by the impost of negroes, as aforesaid, shall be disposed of as followeth, viz. :

" The one moiety of the said impost money to be for the use of the town of Newport, to be disposed of by the said town towards paving the streets of said town, and for no other use whatsoever, for and during the full time of seven years from the publication of this act; and that £60 of said impost money be for, and towards the erecting of a substantial bridge over Potowomut river, at or near the house of Ezekiel Hunt, in East Greenwich, and to no other use whatsoever.

" And that Major Thomas Frye and Capt. John Eldredge be the persons appointed to order and oversee the building of said bridge, and to render an account thereof, to the Assembly; and the said Major Frye and Capt. Eldredge to be paid for their trouble and pains, out of the remaining part of said impost money; and the remainder of said impost money to be disposed of as the Assembly shall from time to time see fit." [1]

And in October, 1717, the following order passed the assembly : —

" It is ordered by this Assembly, that the naval officer pay out of the impost money on slaves, £100, to the overseer that oversees the paving of the streets of Newport, to be improved for paying the charges of paving said streets." [2]

The fund accruing from the impost-duty on slaves was regarded with great favor everywhere, especially in Newport. It had cleaned her streets and lightened the burdens of taxation which rested so grievously upon the freeholders. There was no voice lifted against the iniquitous traffic, and the conscience of the colony was at rest. In June, 1729, the following Act was passed : —

" An Act disposing of the money raised in this colony on importing negro slaves into this colony.

" Forasmuch as there is an act of Assembly made in this colony the 27th day of February, A.D. 1711, laying a duty of £3 per head on all slaves imported into this colony, as is in said act is expressed; and several things of a public nature requiring a fund to be set apart for carrying them on ; —

" Be it therefore enacted by the General Assembly, and by the authority of the same it is enacted and declared, that henceforward all monies that shall be raised in this colony by the aforesaid account, on any slaves imported into this colony, shall be employed, the one moiety thereof for the use of the town of Newport, towards paving and amending the streets thereof; and the other moiety, for, and towards the support, repairing and mending the great bridges

---

[1] R. I. Col. Recs., vol. iv. pp. 191–193.   [2] R. I. Col. Recs., vol. iv. p. 225.

on the main, in the country roads, and for no other use whatsoever; any thing in the aforesaid act to the contrary, in anywise notwithstanding." [1]

It is wonderful how potential the influence of money is upon mankind. The sentiments of the good people had been scattered to the winds; and they had found a panacea for the violated convictions of the wrong of slavery in the reduction of their taxes, new bridges, and cleansed streets. Conscience had been bribed into acquiescence, and the iniquity thrived. There were those who still endeavored to escape the vigilance of the naval officers, and save the three pounds on each slave. But the diligence and liberality of the authorities were not to be outdone by the skulking stinginess of Negro-smugglers. On the 18th of June, 1723, the General Assembly passed the following order: —

"Voted, that Mr. Daniel Updike, the attorney general, be, and he hereby is ordered, appointed and empowered to gather in the money due to this colony, for the importation of negroes, and to prosecute, sue and implead such person or persons as shall refuse to pay the same; and that he be allowed five shillings per head, for every slave that shall be hereafter imported into this colony, out of the impost money; and that he be also allowed ten per cent. more for all such money as he shall recover of the outstanding debts; and in all respects to have the like power as was given to the naval officer by the former act." [2]

The above illustrates the spirit of the times. There was a mania for this impost-tax upon stolen Negroes, and the law was to be enforced against all who sought to evade its requirements. But the Assembly had a delicate sense of equity, as well as an inexorable opinion of the precise demands of the law in its letter and spirit. On the 19th of June, 1716, the following was passed: —

"It is ordered by this Assembly, that the duty of two sucking slaves imported into this colony by Col. James Vaughan, of Barbadoes, be remitted to the said James Vaughan." [3]

It was not below the dignity of the Legislature of the colony of Rhode Island to pass a bill of relief for Col. Vaughan, and refund to him the six pounds he had paid to land his two sucking Negro baby slaves! In June, 1731, the naval officer, James Cranston, called the attention of the Assembly to the case of one Mr. Royall, — who had imported forty-five Negroes into the colony, and

---

[1] R. I. Col. Recs., vol. iv. pp. 423, 424.   [2] Ibid., p. 330.   [3] Ibid., vol. iv. p. 209.

after a short time sold sixteen of them into the Province of Massachusetts Bay, where there was also an impost-tax, — and asked directions. The Assembly replied as follows : —

"Upon consideration whereof, it is voted and ordered, that the duty to this colony of the said sixteen negroes transported into the Massachusetts Bay, as aforesaid, be taken off and remitted ; but that he collect the duty of the other twenty-nine." [1]

But the zeal of the colony in seeking the enforcement of the impost-law created a strong influence against it from without ; and by order of the king the entire law was repealed in May, 1732. [2]

The cruel practice of manumitting aged and helpless slaves became so general in this plantation, that the General Assembly passed a law regulating it, in February, 1728. It was borrowed very largely from a similar law in Massachusetts, and reads as follows : —

"An Act relating to freeing mulatto and negro slaves.

"Forasmuch, as great charge, trouble and inconveniences have arisen to the inhabitants of divers towns in this colony, by the manumitting and setting free mulatto and negro slaves ; for remedying whereof, for the future, —

"Be it enacted by the General Assembly of this colony, and by the authority of the same it is enacted, that no mulatto or negro slave, shall be hereafter manumitted, discharged or set free, or at liberty, until sufficient security be given to the town treasurer of the town or place where such person dwells, in a valuable sum of not less than £100, to secure and indemnify the town or place from all charge for, or about such mulatto or negro, to be manumitted and set at liberty, in case he or she by sickness, lameness or otherwise, be rendered incapable to support him or herself.

"And no mulatto or negro hereafter manumitted, shall be deemed or accounted free, for whom security shall not be given as aforesaid, but shall be the proper charge of their respective masters or mistresses, in case they should stand in need of relief and support ; notwithstanding any manumission or instrument of freedom to them made and given ; and shall be liable at all times to be put forth to service by the justices of the peace, or wardens of the town." [3]

It is very remarkable that there were no lawyers to challenge the legality of such laws as the above, which found their way into the statute books of all the New-England colonies. There could be no conditional emancipation. If a slave were set at liberty, why he was free, and, if he afterwards became a pauper, was entitled to the same care as a white freeman. But it is not diffi-

---

[1] R. I. Col. Recs., vol. iv. p. 454.   [2] Ibid., vol. iv. p. 471.   [3] Ibid., vol. iv. pp. 415, 416.

cult to see that the status of a free Negro was difficult of definition. When the Negro slave grew old and infirm, his master no
longer cared for him, and the public was protected against him by
law. Death was his most beneficent friend.

In October, 1743, a widow lady named Comfort Taylor, of
Bristol County, Massachusetts Bay, sued and obtained judgment
against a Negro named Cuff Borden for two hundred pounds, and
cost of suit "for a grievous trespass." Cuff was a slave. An
ordinary execution would have gone against his person : he would
have been imprisoned, and nothing more. In view of this condition of affairs, Mrs. Taylor petitioned the General Assembly of
Rhode Island, praying that authority be granted the sheriff to sell
Cuff, as other property, to satisfy the judgment. The Assembly
granted her prayer as follows : —

"Upon consideration whereof, it is voted and resolved, that the sheriff of
the said county of Newport, when he shall receive the execution against the
said negro Cuff, be, and he is hereby fully empowered to sell said negro Cuff
as other personal estate ; and after the fine of £20 be paid into the general
treasury, and all other charges deducted out of the price of said negro, the
remainder to be appropriated in said satisfying said execution." [1]

This case goes to show that in Rhode Island Negro slaves
were rated, at law, as chattel property, and could be taken in
execution to satisfy debts as other personal property.

A great many slaves availed themselves of frequent opportunities of going away in privateers and other vessels. With but
little before them in this life, they were even willing to risk being
sold into slavery at some other place, that they might experience
a change. They made excellent seamen, and were greatly desired
by masters of vessels. This went on for a long time. The loss
to the colony was great ; and the General Assembly passed the
subjoined bill as a check to the stampede that had become quite
general : —

"An Act to prevent the commanders of privateers, or masters
of any other vessels, from carrying slaves out of this colony.

"Whereas, it frequently happens that the commanders of privateers, and
masters of other vessels, do carry off slaves that are the property of inhabitants of this colony, and that without the privity or consent of their masters
or mistresses ; and whereas, there is no law of this colony for remedying so
great an evil, —

---

[1] R. I. Col. Recs., vol. v. pp. 72, 73.

"Be it therefore enacted by this General Assembly, and by the authority of the same, it is enacted, that from and after the publication of this act, if any commander of a private man of war, or master of a merchant ship or other vessel, shall knowingly carry away from, or out of this colony, a slave or slaves, the property of any inhabitant thereof, the commander of such privateer, or the master of the said merchant ship or vessel, shall pay, as a fine, the sum of £500, to be recovered by the general treasurer of this colony for the time being, by bill, plaint, or information in any court of record within this colony.

"And be it further enacted by the authority aforesaid, that the owner or owners of any slave or slaves that may be carried away, as aforesaid, shall have a right of action against the commander of the said privateer, or master of the said merchant ship or vessel, or against the owner or owners of the same, in which the said slave or slaves is, or are carried away; and by the said action or suit, recover of him or them, double damages.

"And whereas, disputes may arrise respecting the knowledge that the owner or owners, commanders or masters of the said private men of war, merchant ships or vessels may have of any slave or slaves being on board a privateer, or merchant ship or vessel, —

"Be it therefore further enacted, and by the authority aforesaid, it is enacted, that when any owner or owners of any slave or slaves in this colony, shall suspect that a slave or slaves, to him, her or them belonging, is, or are, on board any private man of war, or merchant ship or vessel, the owner or owners of such slave or slaves may make application, either to the owner or owners, or to the commander or master of the said ship or vessel, before its sailing, and inform him or them thereof; which being done in the presence of one or more substantial witness or witnesses, the said information or application shall amount to, and be construed, deemed and taken to be a full proof of his or their knowledge thereof; provided, the said slave or slaves shall go in any such ship or vessel.

"And be it further enacted by the authority aforesaid, that if the owner or owners of any slave or slaves in this colony, or any other person or persons, legally authorized by the owner or owners of a slave or slaves, shall attempt to go on board any privateer, or a merchant ship or vessel, to search for his, her or their slave or slaves, and the commander or master of such ship or vessel, or other officer or officers on board the same, in the absence of the commander or master, shall refuse to permit such owner or owners of a slave or slaves, or other person or persons, authorized, as aforesaid, to go on board and search for the slave or slaves by him, her or them missed, or found absent, such refusal shall be deemed, construed, and taken to be full proof that the owner or owners, commander or master of the said privateer or other ship or vessel, hath, or have a real knowledge that such slave or slaves is, or are on board.

"And this act shall be forthwith published, and therefrom have, and take force and effect, in and throughout this colony.

"Accordingly the said act was published by the beat of drum, on the 17th day of June, 1757, a few minutes before noon, by

"THO. WARD, Secretary." [1]

---

[1] R. I. Col. Recs., vol. vi. pp. 64, 65.

The education of the Negro slave in this colony was thought to be inimical to the best interests of the master class. Ignorance was the *sine qua non* of slavery. The civil government and ecclesiastical establishment ground him, body and spirit, as between "the upper and nether millstones." But the Negro was a good listener, and was not unconscious of what was going on around him. He was neither blind nor deaf.

The fires of the Revolutionary struggle began to melt the frozen feelings of the colonists towards the slaves. When they began to feel the British lion clutching at the throat of their own liberties, the bondage of the Negro stared them in the face. They knew the Negro's power of endurance, his personal courage, his admirable promptitude in the performance of difficult tasks, and his desperate spirit when pressed too sharply. The thought of such an ally for the English army, such an element in their rear, was louder in their souls than the roar of the enemy's guns. The act of June, 1774, shows how deeply the people felt on the subject.

"AN ACT PROHIBITING THE IMPORTATION OF NEGROES INTO THIS COLONY.

Whereas, the inhabitants of America are generally engaged in the preservation of their own rights and liberties, among which, that of personal freedom must be considered as the greatest; as those who are desirous of enjoying all the advantages of liberty themselves, should be willing to extend personal liberty to others; —

"Therefore, be it enacted by this General Assembly, and by the authority thereof it is enacted, that for the future, no negro or mulatto slave shall be brought into this colony; and in case any slave shall hereafter be brought in, he or she shall be, and are hereby, rendered immediately free, so far as respects personal freedom, and the enjoyment of private property, in the same manner as the native Indians.

"Provided, nevertheless, that this law shall not extend to servants of persons travelling through this colony, who are not inhabitants thereof, and who carry them out with them, when they leave the same.

"Provided, also, that nothing in this act shall extend, or be deemed to extend, to any negro or mulatto slave, belonging to any inhabitant of either of the British colonies, islands or plantations, who shall come into this colony, with an intention to settle or reside, for a number of years, therein; but such negro or mulatto, so brought into this colony, by such person inclining to settle or reside therein, shall be, and remain, in the same situation, and subject in like manner to their master or mistress, as they were in the colony or plantation from whence they removed.

"Provided, nevertheless, that if any person, so coming into this colony, to settle or reside, as aforesaid, shall afterwards remove out of the same, such person shall be obliged to carry all such negro or mulatto slaves, as also all such as shall be born from them, out of the colony with them.

"Provided, also, that nothing in this act shall extend, or be deemed to extend, to any negro or mulatto slave brought from the coast of Africa, into the West Indies, on board any vessel belonging to this colony, and which negro or mulatto slave could not be disposed of in the West Indies, but shall be brought into this colony.

"Provided, that the owner of such negro or mulatto slave give bond to the general treasurer of the said colony, within ten days after such arrival in the sum of £100, lawful money, for each and every such negro or mulatto slave so brought in, that such negro or mulatto slave shall be exported out of the colony, within one year from the date of such bond; if such negro or mulatto be alive, and in a condition to be removed.

"Provided, also, that nothing in this act shall extend, or be deemed to extend, to any negro or mulatto slave that may be on board any vessel belonging to this colony, now at sea, in her present voyage."[1]

In 1730 the population of Rhode Island was, whites, 15,302; Indians, 985; Negroes, 1,648; total, 17,935. In 1749 there were 28,439 whites, and 3,077 Negroes. Indians were not given this year. In 1756 the whites numbered 35,939, the Negroes 4,697. In 1774 Rhode Island contained 9,439 families, Newport had 9,209 inhabitants. The whites in the entire colony numbered 54,435, the Negroes, 3,761, and the Indians, 1,482.[2] It will be observed that the Negro population fell off between the years 1749 and 1774. It is accounted for by the fact mentioned before, — that many ran away on ships that came into the Province.

The Negroes received better treatment at this time than at any other period during the existence of the colony. There was a general relaxation of the severe laws that had been so rigidly enforced. They took great interest in public meetings, devoured with avidity every scrap of news regarding the movements of the Tory forces, listened with rapt attention to the patriotic conversations of their masters, and when the storm-cloud of war broke were as eager to fight for the independence of North America as their masters.

---

[1] R. I. Col. Recs., vol. vii. pp. 251, 252.
[2] American Annals, vol. ii. pp. 107, 155, 156, 184, and 265.

CHAPTER XX.

THE COLONY OF NEW JERSEY.

1664–1775.

New Jersey passes into the Hands of the English. — Political Powers conveyed to Berkeley and Carteret. — Legislation on the Subject of Slavery during the Eighteenth Century. — The Colony divided into East and West Jersey. — Separate Governments. — An Act concerning Slavery by the Legislature of East Jersey. — General Apprehension respecting the rising of Negro and Indian Slaves. — East and West Jersey surrender their Rights of Government to the Queen. — An Act for regulating the Conduct of Slaves. — Impost-Tax of Ten Pounds levied upon each Negro imported into the Colony. — The General Court passes a Law regulating the Trial of Slaves. — Negroes ruled out of the Militia Establishment upon Condition. — Population of the Jerseys in 1738 and 1745.

THE colony of New Jersey passed into the control of the English in 1664; and the first grant of political powers, upon which the government was erected, was conveyed by the Duke of York to Berkeley and Carteret during the same year.. In the "Proprietary Articles of Concession," the words *servants, slaves, and Christian servants* occur. It was the intention of the colonists to draw a distinction between "*servants for a term of years*," and "*servants for life*," between white servants and black slaves, between Christians and pagans.

When slavery was introduced into Jersey is not known.[1] There is no doubt but that it made its appearance there almost as early as in New Netherlands. The Dutch, the Quakers, and the English held slaves. But the system was milder here than in any of the other colonies. The Negroes were scattered among the families of the whites, and were treated with great humanity. Legislation on the subject of slavery did not begin until the middle of the eighteenth century, and it was not severe. Before this time, say three-quarters of a century, a few Acts had been passed calculated to protect the slave element from the sin of intoxication. In 1675 an Act passed, imposing fines and punish-

---

[1] It is unfortunate that there is no good history of New Jersey. The records of the Historical Society of that State are not conveniently printed, nor valuable in colonial data.

ments upon any white person who should transport, harbor, or entertain "apprentices, servants, or slaves." It was perfectly natural that the Negroes should be of a nomadic disposition. They had no homes, no wives, no children, — nothing to attach them to a locality. Those who resided near the seacoast watched, with unflagging interest, the coming and going of the mysterious white-winged vessels. They hung upon the storied lips of every fugitive, and dreamed of lands afar where they might find that liberty for which their souls thirsted as the hart for the water-brook. Far from their native country, without the blessings of the Church, or the warmth of substantial friendship, they fell into a listless condition, a somnolence that led them to stagger against some of the regulations of the Province. Their wandering was not inspired by any subjective, inherent, generic evil : it was but the tossing of a weary, distressed mind under the dreadful influences of a hateful dream. And what little there is in the early records of the colony of New Jersey is at once a compliment to the humanity of the master, and the docility of the slave.

In 1676 the colony was divided into East and West Jersey, with separate governments. The laws of East Jersey, promulgated in 1682, contained laws prohibiting the entertaining of fugitive servants, or trading with Negroes. The law respecting fugitive servants was intended to destroy the hopes of runaways in the entertainment they so frequently obtained at the hands of benevolent Quakers and other enemies of "indenture" and slavery. The law-makers acted upon the presumption, that as the Negro had no property, did not own himself, he could not sell any article of his own. All slaves who attempted to dispose of any article were regarded with suspicion. The law made it a misdemeanor for a free person to purchase any thing from a slave, and hence cut off a source of revenue to the more industrious slaves, who by their frugality often prepared something for sale.

In 1694 *"an Act concerning slaves"* was passed by the Legislature of East Jersey. It provided, among other things, for the trial of *"negroes and other slaves, for felonies punishable with death, by a jury of twelve persons before three justices of the peace ; for theft, before two justices ; the punishment by whipping."* Here was the grandest evidence of the high character of the white population in East Jersey. In every other colony in North America the Negro was denied the right of "trial by jury," so sacred to Englishmen. In Virginia, Maryland, Massachusetts, Connecticut, — in all the colonies, — the Negro went into court convicted, went out convicted, and was executed, upon the frailest evidence imaginable. But here in Jersey the only example of justice was shown toward the Negro in North America. "Trial by jury" implied the right to be sworn, and give competent testimony. A Negro slave, when on trial for his life, was accorded the privilege of being tried by twelve honest white colonists before *three* justices of the peace. This was in striking contrast with the conduct of the colony of New York, where Negroes were arrested upon the incoherent accusations of dissolute whites and terrified blacks. It gave the Negroes a new and an anomalous position in the New World. It banished the cruel theory of Virginia, New York, and Connecticut, that the Negro was a pagan, and therefore should not be sworn in courts of justice, and threw open a wide door for his entrance into a more hopeful state than he had, up to that time, dared to anticipate. It allowed him to infer that his life was a little more than that of the brute that perisheth; that he could not be dragged by malice through the forms of a trial, without jury, witness, counsel, or friend, to an ignominious death, that was to be regretted only by his master, and his regrets to be solaced by the Legislature paying "the price;" that the law regarded him as a man, whose life was too dear to be committed to the disposition of irascible men, whose prejudices could be mollified only in extreme cruelty or cold-blooded murder. It had much to do toward elevating the character of the Negro in New Jersey. It first fired his heart with the noble impulse of gratitude, and then led him to *hope*. And how much that little word means! It causes the soul to spread its white pinions to every favoring breeze, and hasten on to a propitious future. And then the fact that Negroes had rights acknowledged by the statutes, and respectfully accorded them by the courts, had its due influence upon the white colonists. The men, or class of men, who have rights not challenged, command the respect of others. The fact clothes them with dignity as with a garment. And then, by the inevitable logic of the position of the courts of East Jersey, the colonists were led to the conclusion that the Negroes among them had other rights. And, as it has been said already, they received better treatment here than in any other colony in the country.

In West Jersey happily the word "slave" was omitted from the laws. Only servants and runaway servants were mentioned, and the selling of rum to Negroes and Indians was strictly forbidden.

The fear of insurrection among Indians and Negroes was general throughout all of the colonies. One a savage, and the other untutored, they knew but two manifestations, — gratitude and revenge. It was deemed a wise precaution to keep these unfortunate people as far removed from the exciting influences of rum as possible. Chapter twenty-three of a law passed in West Jersey in 1676, providing for publicity in judicial proceedings, concludes as follows : —

"That all and every person and persons inhabiting the said province, shall, as far as in us lies, be free from oppression and slavery." [1]

In 1702 the proprietors of East and West Jersey surrendered their rights of government to the queen. The Province was immediately placed with New York, and the government committed to the hands of Lord Cornbury.[2] In 1704 *"An Act for regulating negroe, Indian and mulatto slaves within the province of New Jersey,"* was introduced, but was tabled and disallowed. The Negroes had just cause for the fears they entertained as to legislation directed at the few rights they had enjoyed under the Jersey government. Their fellow-servants over in New York had suffered under severe laws, and at that time had no privilege in which they could rejoice. In 1713 the following law was passed : —

"*An act for regulating slaves.* (1 Nev. L., c. 10.) Sect. 1. Against trading with slaves. 2. For arrest of slaves being without pass. 3. Negro belonging to another province, not having license, to be whipped and committed to jail. 4. Punishment of slaves for crimes to be by three or more' justices of the peace, with five of the principal freeholders, without a grand jury; seven agreeing, shall give judgment. 5. Method in such causes more particularly described. Provides that 'the evidence of Indian, negro, or mulatto slaves shall be admitted and allowed on trials of such slaves, on all causes criminal.' 6. Owner may demand a jury. 7, 8. Compensation to owners for death of slave. 9. A slave for attempting to ravish any white woman, or presuming 'to assault or strike any free man or woman professing Christianity,' any two

---

[1] *Freedom and Bondage*, vol. i. p. 283.

[2] The following were the instructions his lordship received, concerning the treatment of Negro slaves : "You shall endeavour to get a law past for the restraining of any inhuman severity, which by ill masters or overseers may be used towards their Christian servants and their slaves, and that provision be made therein that the wilfull killing of Indians and negroes may be punished with death, and that a fit penalty be emposed for the maiming of them." — *Freedom and Bondage*, vol. i. p. 280, note.

justices have discretionary powers to inflict corporal punishment, not extending to life or limb. 10. Slaves, for stealing, to be whipped. 11. Penalties on justices, &c., neglecting duty. 12. Punishment for concealing, harboring, or entertaining slaves of others. 13. Provides that no Negro, Indian, or mulatto that shall thereafter be made free, shall hold any real estate in his own right, in fee simple or fee tail. 14. 'And whereas it is found by experience that free Negroes are an idle, slothful people, and prove very often a charge to the place where they are,' enacts that owners manumitting, shall give security, &c." [1]

Nearly all the humane features of the Jersey laws were supplanted by severe prohibitions, requirements, and penalties. The trial by jury was construed to mean that one Negro's testimony was good against another Negro in a trial for a felony, allowing the owner of the slave to demand a jury. Humane masters were denied the right to emancipate their slaves, and the latter were prohibited from owning real property in fee simple or fee tail. Having stripped the Negro of the few rights he possessed, the General Court, during the same year, went on to reduce him to absolute property, and levied an impost-tax of ten pounds upon every Negro imported into the colony, to remain in force for seven years.

In 1754 an Act provided, that in the borough of Elizabeth any white servant or servants, slave or slaves, which shall "be brought before the Mayor, &c., by their masters or other inhabitant of the Borough, for any misdemeanor rude or disorderly behavior, may be committed to the workhouse to hard labor and receive correction not exceeding thirty lashes." [2] This Act was purely local in character, and indiscriminate in its application to every class of servants. It was nothing more than a police regulation, and as such was a wholesome law.

In 1768 the General Court passed *An Act to regulate the trial of slaves for murder and other crimes and to repeal so much of an act, &c.* Sections one and two provided for the trial of slaves by the ordinary higher criminal courts. Section three provided that the expenses incurred in the execution of slaves should be levied upon all the owners of able-bodied slaves in the county, by order of the justices presiding at the trial. Section four repealed sections four, five, six, and seven of the Act of 1713. This was significant. It portended a better feeling toward the Negroes, and illumined the dark horizon of slavery with the distant light of

---

[1] Freedom and Bondage, vol. i. p. 284.   [2] Hurd, vol. i. p. 285.

hope. A strong feeling in favor of better treatment for Negro slaves made itself manifest at this time. When the Quaker found the prejudice against himself subsiding, he turned, like a good Samaritan, to pour the wine of human sympathy into the lacerated feelings of the Negro. Private instruction was given to them in many parts of Jersey. The gospel was expounded to them in its beauty and simplicity, and produced its good fruit in better lives.

The next year, 1769, a mercenary spirit inspired and secured the passage of another Act levying a tax upon imported slaves, and requiring persons manumitting slaves to give better securities. It reads, —

" Whereas duties on the importation of negroes in several of the neighboring colonies hath, on experience, been found beneficial in the introduction of sober industrious foreigners, to settle under his Majesty's allegiance, and the promoting a spirit of industry among the inhabitants in general, in order therefore to promote the same good designs in this government and that such as purchase slaves may contribute some equitable proportion of the public burdens." [1]

How an impost-tax upon imported slaves would be "beneficial in the introduction of sober industrious foreigners," is not easily perceived ; and how it would promote "a spirit of industry among the inhabitants in general," is a problem most difficult of solution. But these were the lofty reasons that inspired the General Court to seek to fill the coffers of the Province with money drawn from the slave-lottery, where human beings were raffled off to the highest bidders in the colony. The cautious language in which the Act was couched indicated the sensitive state of the public conscience on slavery at that time. They were afraid to tell the truth. They did not dare to say to the people : We propose to repair the streets of your towns, the public roads, and lighten the burden of taxation, by saying to men-stealers, we will allow you to sell your cargoes of slaves into this colony provided you share the spoils of your superlative crime ! No, they had to tell the people that the introduction of Negro slaves, upon whom there was a tax, would entice sober and industrious white people to come among them, and would quicken the entire Province with a spirit of thrift never before witnessed !

In 1760 the Negro was ruled out of the militia establishment upon a condition. The law provided against the enlistment of any "*young man under the age of twenty-one years, or any slaves who are so for terms of life, or apprentices,*" without leave of their masters.   This was the mildest prohibition against the entrance of the slave into the militia service in any of the colonies. There is nothing said about the employment of the free Negroes in this service; and it is fair to suppose, in view of the mild character of the laws, that they were not excluded.   In settlements where the German and Quaker elements predominated, the Negro found that his "lines had fallen unto him in pleasant places, and that he had a goodly heritage."   In the coast towns, and in the great centres of population, the white people were of a poorer class.   Many were adventurers, cruel and unscrupulous in their methods.   The speed with which the people sought to obtain a competency wore the finer edges of their feeling to the coarse grain of selfishness; and they not only drew themselves up into the miserable rags of their own selfish aggrandizements as far as all competitors were concerned, but regarded slavery with imperturbable complacency.

In 1738 the population of the Jerseys was, whites, 43,388; blacks, 3,981.   In 1745 the whites numbered 56,797, and the blacks, 4,606.[1]

---

[1] American Annals, vol. ii. pp. 127, 143.

CHAPTER XXI.

THE COLONY OF SOUTH CAROLINA.

1665–1775.

THE CAROLINAS RECEIVE TWO DIFFERENT CHARTERS FROM THE CROWN OF GREAT BRITAIN. — ERA
OF SLAVERY LEGISLATION. — LAW ESTABLISHING SLAVERY. — THE SLAVE POPULATION OF THIS
PROVINCE REGARDED AS CHATTEL PROPERTY. — TRIAL OF SLAVES. — INCREASE OF SLAVE POPU-
LATION. — THE INCREASE IN THE RICE-TRADE. — SEVERE LAWS REGULATING THE PRIVATE AND
PUBLIC CONDUCT OF SLAVES. — PUNISHMENT OF SLAVES FOR RUNNING AWAY. — THE LIFE OF
SLAVES REGARDED AS OF LITTLE CONSEQUENCE BY THE VIOLENT MASTER CLASS. — AN ACT
EMPOWERING TWO JUSTICES OF THE PEACE TO INVESTIGATE TREATMENT OF SLAVES. — AN ACT
PROHIBITING THE OVERWORKING OF SLAVES. — SLAVE-MARKET AT CHARLESTON. — INSURRECTION.
— A LAW AUTHORIZING THE CARRYING OF FIRE-ARMS AMONG THE WHITES — THE ENLISTMENT
OF SLAVES TO SERVE IN TIME OF ALARM. — NEGROES ADMITTED TO THE MILITIA SERVICE. —
COMPENSATION TO MASTERS FOR THE LOSS OF SLAVES KILLED BY THE ENEMY OR WHO DESERT.
— FEW SLAVES MANUMITTED. — FROM 1754–1776 LITTLE LEGISLATION ON THE SUBJECT OF
SLAVERY. — THREATENING WAR BETWEEN ENGLAND AND HER PROVINCIAL DEPENDENCIES. — THE
EFFECT UPON PUBLIC SENTIMENT.

THE Carolinas received two different charters from the crown
of Great Britain. The first was witnessed by the king at
Westminster, March 24, 1663; the second, June 30, 1665.
The last charter was surrendered to the king by seven of the eight
proprietors on the 25th July, 1729. The government became
regal; and the Province was immediately divided into North and
South Carolina by an order of the British Council, and the boundaries between the two governments fixed.

There were Negro slaves in the Carolinas from the earliest
days of their existence. The era of slavery legislation began about
the year 1690. The first Act for the "*Better Ordering of Slaves*"
was "read three times and passed, and ratified in open Parliament,
the seventh day of February, Anno Domini, 1690." It bore the
signatures of Seth Sothell, G. Muschamp, John Beresford, and
John Harris. It contained fifteen articles of the severest character. On the 7th of June, 1712, the first positive law establishing
slavery passed, and was signed.[1] The entire Act embraced thirty-

---

[1] An eminent lawyer, chief justice of the Supreme Court of the State of ——, and a
warm personal friend of mine, recently said to me, during an afternoon stroll, that he never knew
that slavery was ever established by statute in any of the British colonies in North America.

five sections. Section one is quoted in full because of the interest that centres in it in connection with the problem of slavery legislation in the colonies.

" 1. *Be it therefore enacted*, by his Excellency, William, Lord Craven, Palatine, and the rest of the true and absolute Lords and Proprietors of this Province, by and with the advice and consent of the rest of the members of the General Assembly, now met at Charlestown, for the South-west part of this Province, and by the authority of the same, That all negroes, mulatoes, mustizoes or Indians, which at any time heretofore have been sold, or now are held or taken to be, or hereafter shall be bought and sold for slaves, are hereby declared slaves; and they, and their children, are hereby made and declared slaves, to all intents and purposes; excepting all such negroes, mulatoes, mustizoes or Indians, which heretofore have been, or hereafter shall be, for some particular merit, made and declared free, either by the Governor and council of this Province, pursuant to any Act or law of this Province, or by their respective owners or masters; and also, excepting all such negroes, mulatoes, mustizoes or Indians, as can prove they ought not to be sold for slaves. And in case any negro, mulatoe, mustizoe or Indian, doth lay claim to his or her freedom, upon all or any of the said accounts, the same shall be finally heard and determined by the Governor and council of this Province." [1]

The above section was re-enacted into another law, containing forty-three sections, passed on the 23d of February, 1722. Virginia declared that children should follow the condition of their mothers, but never passed a law in any respect like unto this most remarkable Act. South Carolina has the unenviable reputation of being the only colony in North America where by positive statute the Negro was doomed to perpetual bondage.[2] On the 10th of May, 1740, an act regulating slaves, containing fifty sections, recites : —

" WHEREAS, in his Majesty's plantations in America, slavery has been introduced and allowed, and the people commonly called negroes, Indians, mulattoes and mustizoes, have been deemed absolute slaves, and the subjects of property in the hands of particular persons, the extent of whose power over such slaves ought to be settled and limited by positive laws, so that the slave may be kept in due subjection and obedience, and the owners and other persons having the care and government of slaves may be restrained from exercising too great rigour and cruelty over them, and that the public peace and order of this Province may be preserved: We pray your most sacred Majesty that it may be enacted." [3]

---

[1] Statutes of S. C., vol. vii. p. 352.

[2] Virginia made slavery statutory as did other colonies, but we have no statute so explicit as the above. But slavery was slavery in all the colonies, cruel and hurtful.

[3] Statutes of S. C., vol. vii. p. 397.

The first section of this Act was made more elaborate than any other law previously passed. It bore all the marks of ripe scholarship and profound law learning. The first section is produced here : —

" 1. *And be it enacted,* by the honorable William Bull, Esquire, Lieutenant Governor and Commander-in-chief, by and with the advice and consent of his Majesty's honorable Council, and the Commons House of Assembly of this Province, and by the authority of the same, That all negroes and Indians, (free Indians in amity with this government, and negroes, mulattoes and mustizoes, who are now free, excepted,) mulattoes or mustizoes who now are, or shall hereafter be, in this Province, and all their issue and offspring, born or to be born, shall be, and they are hereby declared to be, and remain forever hereafter, absolute slaves, and shall follow the condition of the mother, and shall be deemed, held, taken, reputed and adjudged in law, to be chattels personal, in the hands of their owners and possessors, and their executors, administrators and assigns, to all intents, constructions and purposes whatsoever; *provided always,* that if any negro, Indian, mulatto or mustizo, shall claim his or her freedom, it shall and may be lawful for such negro, Indian, mulatto or mustizo, or any person or persons whatsoever, on his or her behalf, to apply to the justices of his Majesty's court of common pleas, by petition or motion, either during the sitting of the said court, or before any of the justices of the same court, at any time in the vacation ; and the said court, or any of the justices thereof, shall, and they are hereby fully impowered to, admit any person so applying to be guardian for any negro, Indian, mulatto or mustizo, claiming his, her or their freedom ; and such guardians shall be enabled, entitled and capable in law, to bring an action of trespass in the nature of ravishment of ward, against any person who shall claim property in, or who shall be in possession of, any such negro, Indian, mulatto or mustizo ; and the defendant shall and may plead the general issue on such action brought, and the special matter may and .shall be given in evidence, and upon a general or special verdict found, judgment shall be given according to the very right of the cause, without having any regard to any defect in the proceedings, either in form or substance ; and if judgment shall be given for the plaintiff, a special entry shall be made, declaring that the ward of the plaintiff is free, and the jury shall assess damages which the plaintiff's ward hath sustained, and the court shall give judgment, and award execution, against the defendant for such damage, with full costs of suit ; but in case judgment shall be given for the defendant, the said court is hereby fully impowered to inflict such corporal punishment, not extending to life or limb, on the ward of the plaintiff, as they, in their discretion, shall think fit ; *provided always,* that in any action or suit to be brought in pursuance of the direction of this Act, the burthen of the proof shall lay on the plaintiff, and it shall be always presumed that every negro, Indian, mulatto and mustizo, is a slave, unless the contrary can be made appear, the Indians in amity with this government excepted, in which case the burthen of the proof shall lye on the defendant ; *provided also,* that nothing in this Act shall be construed to hinder or restrain any other court of law or equity in this Province, from determining the property of slaves, or their right of freedom, which now have cognizance or jurisdiction of the same, when the same shall happen to come in judgment before such courts, or any of them, always taking this Act for their direction therein." [1]

The entire slave population of this Province was regarded as *chattel property, absolutely.* They could be seized in execution as in the case of other property, but not, however, if there were other chattels available.   In case of "burglary, robbery, burning of houses, killing or stealing of any meat or other cattle, or other petty injuries, as maiming one of the other, stealing of fowls, provisions, or such like trespass or injuries," a justice of the peace was to be informed.   He issued a warrant for the arrest of the offender or offenders, and summoned all competent witnesses. After examination, if found guilty, the offender or offenders were committed to jail.   The justice then notified the justice next to him to be associated with him in the trial.   He had the authority to fix the day and hour of the trial, to summon witness, and "three discreet and sufficient freeholders."   The justices then swore the "freeholders," and, after they had tried the case, had the authority to pronounce the sentence of death, "or such other punishment" as they felt meet to fix.   "The solemnity of a jury" was never accorded to slaves.   "Three freeholders" could dispose of human life in such cases, and no one could hinder. [2]   The confession of the accused slave, and the testimony of another slave, were "held for good and convincing evidence in all petty larcenies or trespasses not exceeding forty shillings."   In the case of a Negro on trial for his life, "the oath of Christian evidence" was required, or the "positive evidence of two Negroes or slaves," in order to convict.

The increase of slaves was almost phenomenal.   The rice-trade had grown to enormous proportions.   The physical obstruction gave away rapidly before the incessant and stupendous efforts of Negro laborers.   The colonists held out most flattering inducements to Englishmen to emigrate into the Province.   The home government applauded the zeal and executive abilities of the local authorities.   Attention was called to the necessity of legislation for the government of the vast Negro population in the colony.   The code of South Carolina was without an example among the civilized governments of modern times.   It was unlawful for any free

---

[1] Statutes of S. C., vol. vii. pp. 397, 398.   [2] Ibid., vol. vii. pp. 343, 344.

person to inhabit or trade with Negroes.[1] Slaves could not leave the plantation on which they were owned, except in livery, or armed with a pass, signed by their master, containing the name of the possessor. For a violation of this regulation they were whipped on the naked back. No man was allowed to conduct a "plantation, cow-pen or stock," that shall be six miles distant from his usual place of abode, and wherein six Negroes were employed, without one or more white persons were residing on the place.[2] Negro slaves found on another plantation than the one to which they belonged, "on the Lord's Day, fast days, or holy-days," even though they could produce passes, were seized and whipped. If a slave were found "keeping any horse, horses, or neat cattle," any white man, by warrant, could seize the animals, and sell them through the church-wardens ; and the money arising from such sale was devoted to the poor of the parish in which said presumptuous slaves resided. If more than seven slaves were found travelling on the highway, except accompanied by a white man, it was lawful for any white man to apprehend each and every one of such slaves, and administer twenty lashes upon their bare back. No slave was allowed to hire out his time. Some owners of slaves were poor, and, their slaves being trusty and industrious, permitted them to go out and get whatever work they could, with the understanding that the master was to have the wages. An Act was passed in 1735, forbidding such transactions, and fining the persons who hired slaves who had no written certificate from their masters setting forth the terms upon which the work was to be done. No slave could hire a house or plantation. No amount of industry could make him an exception to the general rule. If he toiled faithfully for years, amassed a fortune for his master, earned quite a competence for himself during the odd moments he caught from a busy life, and then, with acknowledged character and business tact, he sought to hire a plantation or buy a house, the law came in, and pronounced it a misdemeanor, for which both purchaser and seller had to pay in fines, stripes, and imprisonment. A slave could not keep in his own name, or that of his master, any kind of a house of entertainment. He was even prohibited by law from selling corn or rice in the Province. The penalty was a fine of forty shillings,

---

[1] This Act, passed on the 16th of March, 1696, was made "perpetual" on the 12th of December, 1712. It remained throughout the entire period. See Statutes of S. C., vol. ii. p. 598.

[2] Statutes of S. C., vol. vii. p. 363.

and the forfeiture of the articles for sale. They could not keep a boat or canoe.

The cruelties of the code are without a parallel, as applied to the correction of Negro slaves.

"If any negro or Indian slave [says the act of Feb. 7, 1690] shall offer any violence, by stricking or the like, to any white person, he shall for the first offence be severely whipped by the constable, by order of any justice of peace; and for the second offence, by like order, shall be severely whipped, his or her nose slit, and face burnt in some place; and for the third offence, to be left to two justices and three sufficient freeholders, to inflict death, or any other punishment, according to their discretion."

As the penalties for the smallest breach of the slave-code grew more severe, the slaves grew more restless and agitated. Sometimes under great fear they would run away for a short time, in the hope that their irate masters would relent. But this, instead of helping, hindered and injured the cause of the slaves. Angered at the conduct of their slaves, the master element, having their representatives on the floor of the Assembly, secured the passage of the following brutal law:—

"That every slave of above sixteen years of age, that shall run away from his master, mistress or overseer, and shall so continue for the space of twenty days at one time, shall, by his master, mistress, overseer or head of the family's procurement, for the first offence, be publicly and severely whipped, not exceeding forty lashes; and in case the master, mistress, overseer, or head of the family, shall neglect to inflict such punishment of whipping, upon any negro or slave that shall so run away, for the space of ten days, upon complaint made thereof, within one month, by any person whatsoever, to any justice of the peace, the said justice of the peace shall, by his warrant directed to the constable, order the said negro or slave to be publicly and severely whipped, the charges of such whipping, not exceeding twenty shillings, to be borne by the person neglecting to have such runaway negro whipped, as before directed by this Act. And in case such negro or slave shall run away a second time, and shall so continue for the space of twenty days, he or she, so offending, shall be branded with the letter R, on the right cheek. And in case the master, mistress, overseer, or head of the family, shall neglect to inflict the punishment upon such slave running away the second time, the person so neglecting shall forfeit the sum of ten pounds, and upon any complaint made by any person, within one month, to any justice of the peace, of the neglect of so punishing any slave for running away the second time, such justice shall order the constable to inflict the same punishment upon such slave, or cause the same to be done, the charges thereof, not exceeding thirty shillings, to be borne by the person neglecting to have the punishment inflicted. And in case such negro or slave shall run away the third time, and shall so continue for the space of thirty days, he or she, so offending, for the third offence, shall be severely whipped, not exceeding forty lashes, and shall have one of his ears cut off; and in case the master, mistress, overseer or head of the family, shall neglect to inflict the punishment upon such slave running away the third time, the person so neglecting shall forfeit the sum of twenty pounds, and upon any complaint made by any person, within two months, to any justice of the peace, of the neglect of the so punishing any slave for running away the third time, the said justice shall order the constable to inflict the same punishment upon such slave, or cause the same to be done, the charges thereof, not exceeding forty shillings, to be borne by the person neglecting to have the punishment inflicted. And in case such male negro or slave shall run away the fourth time, and shall so continue for the space of thirty days, he, so offending, for the fourth offence, by order or procurement of the master, mistress, overseer or head of the family, shall be gelt; and in case the negro or slave that shall be gelt, shall die, by reason of his gelding, and without any neglect of the person that shall order the same, the owner of the negro or slave so dying, shall be paid for him, out of the public treasury. And if a female slave shall run away the fourth time, then she shall, by order of her master, mistress or overseer, be severely whipped, and be branded on the left cheek with the letter R, and her left ear cut off. And if the owner, if in this Province, or in case of his absence, if his agent, factor or attorney, that hath the charge of the negro or slave, by this Act required to be gelt, whipped, branded and the ear cut off, for the fourth time of running away, shall neglect to have the same done and executed, accordingly as the same is ordered by this Act, for the space of twenty days after such slave is in his or their custody, that then such owner shall lose his property to the said slave, to him or them that will sue for the same, by information, at any time within six months, in the court of common pleas in this Province. And every person who shall so recover a slave by information, for the reasons aforesaid, shall, within twenty days after such recovery, inflict such punishment upon such slave as his former owner or head of a family ought to have done, and for neglect of which he lost his property to the said slave, or for neglect thereof shall forfeit fifty pounds; and in case any negro slave so recovered by information, and gelt, shall die, in such case, the slave so dying shall not be paid for out of the public treasury. And in case any negro or slave shall run away the fifth time, and shall so continue by the space of thirty days at one time, such slave shall be tried before two justices of the peace and three freeholders, as before directed by this Act in case of murder, and being by them declared guilty of the offence, it shall be lawful for them to order the cord of one of the slave's legs to be cut off above the heel, or else to pronounce sentence of death upon the slave, at the discretion of the said justices; and any judgment given after the first offence, shall be sufficient conviction to bring the offenders within the penalty for the second offence; and after the second, within the penalty of the third; and so for the inflicting the rest of the punishments." [1]

If any slave attempted to run away from his or her master, and go out of the Province, he or she could be tried before two

---

[1] Statutes of S. C., vol. vii. pp. 359, 360.

justices and three freeholders, and sentenced to suffer a most cruel death.   If it could be proved that any Negro, free or slave, had endeavored to persuade or entice any other Negro to run off out of the Province, upon conviction he was punished with forty lashes, and branded on the forehead with a red hot iron, "that the mark thereof may remain."   If a white man met a slave, and demanded of him to show his ticket, and the slave refused, the law empowered the white man "to beat, maim, or assault; and if such Negro or slave" could not "be taken, to kill him," if he would not "shew his ticket."

The cruel and barbarous code of the slave-power in South Carolina produced, in course of time, a re-action in the opposite direction.   The large latitude that the law gave to white people in their dealings with the hapless slaves made them careless and extravagant in the use of their authority.   It educated them into a brood of tyrants.   They did not care any more for the life of a Negro slave than for the crawling worm in their path.   Many white men who owned no slaves poured forth their wrathful invectives and cruel blows upon the heads of innocent Negroes with the slightest pretext.   They pushed, jostled, crowded, and kicked the Negro on every occasion.   The young whites early took their lessons in abusing God's poor and helpless children; while an overseer was prized more for his brutal powers — to curse, beat, and torture — than for any ability he chanced to possess for business management.   The press and pulpit had contemplated this state of affairs until they, too, were the willing abettors in the most cruel system of bondage that history has recorded.   But no man wants his horse driven to death, if it is a beast.   No one cares to have every man that passes kick his dog, even if it is not the best dog in the community.   It is *his* dog, and that makes all the difference in the world.   The men who did the most cruel things to the slaves they found in their daily path were, as a rule, without slaves or any other kind of property.   They used their authority unsparingly.   Common-sense taught the planters that better treatment of the slaves meant better work, and increased profits for themselves.   A small value was finally placed upon a slave's life, — fifty pounds.   Fifty pounds paid into the public treasury by a man who, "of wantonness, or only of bloody-mindedness, or cruel intention," had killed "a negro or other slave of his own," was enough to appease the public mind, and atone for a cold-blooded murder !   If he killed another man's slave, the law demanded that he pay fifty pounds current money into the public treasury, and the full price of the slave to the owner, but was "not to be liable to any other punishment or forfeiture for the same." [1] The law just referred to, passed in 1712, was re-enacted in 1722. One change was made in it : i.e., if a white servant, having no property, killed a slave, three justices could bind him over to the master whose slave he killed to serve him for five years. This law had a wholesome effect upon irresponsible white men, who often presumed upon their nationality, having neither brains, money, nor social standing, to punish slaves.

In 1740, May 10, the following Act became a law ; showing that there had been a wonderful change in public sentiment respecting the treatment of slaves : —

"XXXVII. And *whereas*, cruelty is not only highly unbecoming those who profess themselves christians, but is odious in the eyes of all men who have any sense of virtue or humanity; therefore, to restrain and prevent barbarity being exercised towards slaves, *Be it enacted* by the authority aforesaid, That if any person or persons whosoever, shall wilfully murder his own slave, or the slave of any other person. every such person shall, upon conviction thereof, forfeit and pay the sum of seven hundred pounds. current money, and shall be rendered, and is hereby declared altogether and forever incapable of holding, exercising, enjoying or receiving the profits of any office, place or employment, civil or military, within this Province: And in case any such person shall not be able to pay the penalty and forfeitures hereby inflicted and imposed, every such person shall be sent to any of the frontier garrisons of this Province, or committed to the work house in Charlestown, there to remain for the space of seven years, and to serve or to be kept at hard labor. And in case the slave murdered shall be the property of any other person than the offender, the pay usually allowed by the public to the soldiers of such garrison, or the profits of the labor of the offender, if committed to the work house in Charlestown, shall be paid to the owner of the slave murdered. And if any person shall, on a sudden heat of passion, or by undue correction, kill his own slave, or the slave of any other person, he shall forfeit the sum of three hundred and fifty pounds, current money. And in case any person or persons shall wilfully cut out the tongue, put out the eye, castrate, or cruelly scald, burn, or deprive any slave of any limb or member, or shall inflict any other cruel punishment, other than by whipping or beating with a horse-whip, cow-skin, switch or small stick, or by putting irons on, or confining or imprisoning such slave, every such person shall, for every such offence, forfeit the sum of one hundred pounds, current money." [2]

It may be said truthfully that the slaves in the colony of South Carolina were accorded treatment as good as that bestowed upon

---

[1] Statutes of S. C., vol. vii p. 363.   [2] Ibid., vol. vii. pp. 410, 411.

horses, in 1750. But their social condition was most deplorable. The law positively forbid the instruction of slaves, and the penalty was "one hundred pounds current money." For a few years Saturday afternoon had been allowed them as a day of recreation, but as early as 1690 it was forbidden by statute. In the same year an Act was passed declaring that slaves should "have convenient clothes, once every year; and that no slave" should "be free by becoming a christian,[1] but as to payments of debts" were "deemed and taken as all other goods and chattels." Their houses were searched every fortnight "for runaway slaves" and "stolen goods." Druggists were not allowed to employ a Negro to handle medicines, upon pain of forfeiting twenty pounds current money for every such offence. Negroes were not allowed to practise medicine, nor administer drugs of any kind, except by the direction of some white person. Any gathering of Negroes could be broken up at the discretion of a justice living in the district where the meeting was in session.

Poor clothing and insufficient food bred wide-spread discontent among the slaves, and attracted public attention.[2] Many masters endeavored to get on as cheaply as possible in providing for their slaves. In 1722 the Legislature passed an Act empowering two justices of the peace to inquire as to the treatment of slaves on the several plantations; and if any master neglected his slaves in food and raiment, he was liable to a fine of not more than fifty shillings. In May, 1740, an Act was passed requiring masters to see to it that their slaves were not overworked. The time set for them to work, was "from the 25th day of March to the 25th day of September," not "more than fifteen hours in four-and-twenty;" and "from the 25th day of September to the 25th day of March," not "more than fourteen hours in four-and-twenty."

---

[1] The following is the Act of the 7th of June, 1690. "XXXIV. Since charity, and the christian religion, which we profess, obliges us to wish well to the souls of all men, and that religion may not be made a pretence to alter any man's property and right, and that no person may neglect to baptize their negroes or slaves, or suffer them to be baptized, for fear that thereby they should be manumitted and set free, Be it therefore enacted by the authority aforesaid, that it shall be, and is hereby declared, lawful for any negro or Indian slave, or any other slave or slaves whatsoever, to receive and profess the christian faith, and be thereinto baptized; but that notwithstanding such slave or slaves shall receive and profess the christian religion, and be baptized, he or they shall not thereby be manumitted or set free, or his or their owner. master or mistress lose his or their civil right, property and authority over such slave or slaves, but that the slave or slaves, with respect to his servitude, shall remain and continue in the same state and condition that he or they was in before the making of this act." — *Statutes of S. C.,* vol. vii. pp. 364, 365.

[2] In 1740 an Act was passed requiring masters to provide "sufficient clothing" for their slaves.

The history of the impost-tax on slaves imported into the Province of South Carolina is the history of organized greed, ambition, and extortion. Many were the gold sovereigns that were turned into the official coffers at Charleston! With a magnificent harbor, and a genial climate, no city in the South could rival it as a slave-market. With an abundant supply from without, and a steady demand from within, the officials at Charleston felt assured that high impost-duties could not interfere with the slave-trade; while the city would be a great gainer by the traffic, both mediately and immediately.

Sudden and destructive insurrections were the safety-valves to the institution of slavery. A race long and cruelly enslaved may endure the yoke patiently for a season: but like the sudden gathering of the summer clouds, the pelting rain, the vivid, blinding lightning, the deep, hoarse thundering, it will assert itself some day; and then it is indeed a day of judgment to the task-masters! The Negroes in South Carolina endured a most cruel treatment for a long time; and, when "the day of their wrath" came, they scarcely knew it themselves, much less the whites. Florida was in the possession of the Spaniards. Its governor had sent out spies into Georgia and South Carolina, who held out very flattering inducements to the Negroes to desert their masters and go to Florida. Moreover, there was a Negro regiment in the Spanish service, whose officers were from their own race. Many slaves had made good their escape, and joined this regiment. It was allowed the same uniform and pay as the Spanish soldiers had. The colony of South Carolina was fearing an enemy from without, while behold their worst enemy was at their doors! In 1740 some Negroes assembled themselves together at a town called Stone, and made an attack upon two young men, who were guarding a warehouse, and killed them. They seized the arms and ammunition, effected an organization by electing one of their number captain; and, with boisterous drums and flying banners, they marched off "like a disciplined company." They entered the house of one Mr. Godfrey, slew him, his wife, and child, and then fired his dwelling. They next took up their march towards Jacksonburgh, and plundered and burnt the houses of Sacheveral, Nash, Spry, and others. They killed all the white people they found, and recruited their ranks from the Negroes they met. Gov, Bull was "returning to Charleston from the southward, met them, and, observing them armed, quickly rode out of their way." [1] In a march of twelve miles, they had wrought a work of great destruction. News reached Wiltown, and the militia were called out. The Negro insurrectionists were intoxicated with their triumph, and drunk from rum they had taken from the houses they had plundered. They halted in an open field to sing and dance; and, during their hilarity, Capt. Bee, at the head of the troops of the district, fell upon them, and, having killed several, captured all who did not make their escape in the woods.

The Province was thrown into intense excitement. The Legislature called attention to the insurrection,[2] and declared legal some very questionable and summary acts. In 1743 the people had not recovered from the fright they received from the insurrection. On the 7th of May, 1743, an Act was passed requiring every white male inhabitant, who resorted "to any church or any other public place of divine worship, within" the Province to "carry with him a gun or a pair of horse pistols, in good order and fit for service, with at least six charges of gun-powder and ball," upon pain of paying "twenty shillings."

As there was a law against teaching slaves to read and write, there were no educated preachers. If a Negro desired to preach to his fellow-slaves, he had to secure written permission from his master. While Negroes were sometimes baptized into the communion of the Church, — usually the Episcopal Church, — they were allowed only in the gallery, or organ-loft, of white congregations, in small numbers. No clergyman ventured to break unto this benighted people the bread of life. They were abandoned to the superstitions and religious fanaticisms incident to their condition.

In 1704 an Act was passed *"for raising and enlisting such slaves as shall be thought serviceable to this Province in time of Alarms."* It required, within thirty days after the publication of the Act, that the commanders of military organizations throughout the Province should appoint "five freeholders," "sober and discreet men," who were to make a complete list of all the able-bodied slaves in their respective districts. Three of them were competent to decide upon the qualifications of a slave. After the completion of the list, the freeholders mentioned above notified the owners to appear before them upon a certain day, and show

---

[1] Hist. S. C. and Georgia, vol. ii. p. 73.　　　[2] Statutes of S. C., vol. vii. p. 416.

cause why their slaves should not be chosen for the service of the colony. The slaves were then enlisted, and their masters charged with the duty of arming them "with a serviceable lance, hatchet or gun, with sufficient amunition and hatchets, according to the conveniency of the said owners, to appear under the colours of the respective captains, in their several divisions, throughout" the Province, for the performance of such "public service" as required. If an owner refused to equip or permit his slave to respond to alarms, he was fined five pounds for each neglect, which was to be paid to the captain of the company to which the slave belonged. If a slave were killed by the enemy "in the line of duty," the owner of such slave was paid out of the public treasury such sum of money as three freeholders, under oath, should award. The Negroes did admirably ; and four years later, on the 24th of April, 1708, the Legislature re-enacted the bill making them militia-men. The last Act contained ten sections, and bears evidence of the pleasure the whites took in the employment of Negroes as their defenders. If a Negro were taken prisoner by the enemy, and effected his escape back into the Province, he was emancipated. And if a Negro captured and killed an enemy, he was emancipated, but if wounded himself, was set free at the public expense. If he deserted to the enemy, his master was paid for his loss.

Few slaves were manumitted. The law required that masters who emancipated their slaves should make provisions for transporting them out of the Province. If they were found in the Province twelve months after they were set free, the manumission was considered void, except approved by the Legislature.

From 1754 till 1776 there was little legislation on the subject of slavery. The pressure from without made men conservative about slavery, and radical on the question of the rights and liberties of the colonies. The threatening war between England and her provincial dependencies made men humane and patriotic ; and during these years of anxiety and excitement, the weary slaves breathed a better atmosphere, and enjoyed the rare sensation of confidence and benevolence.

CHAPTER XXII.

THE COLONY OF NORTH CAROLINA.

1669–1775.

The Geographical Situation of North Carolina Favorable to the Slave-Trade. — The Locke
Constitution adopted. — William Sayle commissioned Governor. — Legislative Career
of the Colony. — The Introduction of the Established Church of England into the
Colony. — The Rights of Negroes controlled absolutely by their Masters. — An Act
respecting Conspiracies. — The Wrath of Ill-natured Whites visited upon their Slaves.
— An Act against the Emancipation of Slaves. — Limited Rights of Free Negroes.

THE geographical situation of North Carolina was favorable
to the slave-trade.

Through the genius of Shaftesbury, and the subtle cunning of John Locke, Carolina received, and for a time adopted,
the most remarkable constitution ever submitted to any people
in any age of the world. The whole affair was an insult to
humanity, and in its fundamental elements bore the palpable
evidences of the cruel conclusions of an exclusive philosophy.
"No elective franchise could be conferred upon a freehold of less
than fifty acres," while all executive power was vested in the
proprietors themselves. Seven courts were controlled by forty-
two counsellors, twenty-eight of whom held their places through
the gracious favor of the proprietary and "the nobility." Trial
by jury was concluded by the opinions of the majority.

"The instinct of aristocracy dreads the moral power of a proprietary
yeomanry; the perpetual degradation of the cultivators of the soil was enacted.
The leet-men, or tenants, holding ten acres of land at a fixed rent, were not
only destitute of political franchises, but were adscripts to the soil; 'under the
jurisdiction of their lord, without appeal;' and it was added, 'all the children
of leet-men shall be leet-men, and so to all generations.'" [1]

The men who formed the rank and file of the yeomanry of the
colony of North Carolina were ill prepared for a government

---

[1] Bancroft, vol. ii. 5th ed. p. 148.

launçhed upon the immense scale of the Locke Constitution. The
hopes and fears, the feuds and debates, the vexatious and insoluble problems, of the political science of government which had
clouded the sky of the most astute and ambitous statesmen of
Europe, were dumped into this remarkable instrument. The
distance between the people and the nobility was sought to be
made illimitable, and the right to govern was based upon permanent property conditions. Hereditary wealth was to go arm in
arm with political power.

The constitution was signed on the 21st of July, 1669, and
William Sayle was commissioned as governor. The legislative
career of the Province began in the fall of the same year; and
history must record that it was one of the most remarkable and
startling North America ever witnessed. The portions of the constitution which refer to the institution of slavery are as follows: —

"97th. But since the natives of that place, who will be concerned in our
plantation, are utterly strangers to Christianity, whose idolatry, ignorance or
mistake, gives us no right to expel or use them ill; and those who remove from
other parts to plant there, will unavoidably be of different opinions, concerning
matters of religion, the liberty whereof they will expect to have allowed them,
and it will not be reasonable for us on this account to keep them out; that civil
peace may be obtained amidst diversity of opinions, and our agreement and
compact with all men, may be duly and faithfully observed; the violation
whereof, upon what pretence soever, cannot be without great offence to
Almighty God, and great scandal to the true religion which we profess; and
also that Jews, Heathens and other dissenters from the purity of the Christian
religion, may not be scared and kept at a distance from it, but by having an
opportunity of acquainting themselves with the truth and reasonableness of its
doctrines, and the peaceableness and inoffensiveness of its professors, may by
good usage and persuasion, and all those convincing methods of gentleness
and meekness, suitable to the rules and design of the gospel, be won over to
embrace, and unfeignedly receive the truth; therefore any seven or more persons agreeing in any religion, shall constitute a church or profession, to which
they shall give some name, to distinguish it from others. . . .

"101st. No person above seventeen years of age, shall have any benefit
or protection of the law, or be capable of any place of profit or honor, who is
not a member of some church or profession, having his name recorded in some
one, and but one religious record, at once. . . .

"107th. Since charity obliges us to wish well to the souls of all men, and
religion ought to alter nothing in any man's civil estate or right, it shall be
lawful for slaves as well as others, to enter themselves and be of what church
or profession any of them shall think best, and thereof be as fully members
as any freemen. But yet no slave shall hereby be exempted from that civil
dominion his master hath over him, but be in all things in the same state and
condition he was in before. . . .

"110th. Every freeman of Carolina, shall have absolute power and authority over his negro slaves, of what opinion or religion soever."[1]

Though the Locke Constitution was adopted by the proprietaries, March 1, 1669, it may be doubted whether it ever had the force of law, as it was never ratified by the local Legislature. Article one hundred and ten, granting absolute power and authority to a master over his Negro slave, is without a parallel in the legislation of the colonies. And while the slave might enter the Christian Church, and his humanity thereby be recognized, it was strangely inconsistent to place his life at the disposal of brutal masters, who "neither feared God nor regarded man."

The Negro slaves in North Carolina occupied the paradoxical position of being eligible to membership in the Christian Church, and the absolute property of their white brothers. In the second draught of the constitution, signed in March, 1670, against the eloquent protest of John Locke, the section on religion was amended so as, while tolerating every religious creed, to declare "the Church of England" the only true Orthodox Church, and the national religion of the Province. This, in the face of the fact that the great majority of all the Christians who flocked to the New World were dissenters, separatists, and nonconformists, can only be explained in the light of the burning zeal of the Church of England to out-Herod Herod, — to carry the Negroes into the communion of the State church for political purposes. It was the most sordid motive that impelled the churchmen to open the church to the slave. His membership did not change his condition, nor secure him immunity from the barbarous treatment the institution of slavery bestowed upon its helpless victims.

In the eyes of the law the Negro, being *absolute property*, had no rights, except those temporarily delegated by the master ; and he acted in the relation of an agent. Negro slaves were not allowed "to raise horses, cattle or hogs ;" and if any stock were found in their possession six months after the passage of the Act of 1741, they were to be seized by the sheriff of the county, and sold by the church-wardens of the parish. The profits arising from such sales went, one half to the parish, the other half to the informer.[2] A slave was not suffered to go off of the plantation where he was appointed to live, without a pass signed by his

---

[1] Statutes of S. C., vol. i. pp. 53–55.　　　[2] Public Acts of N. C., vol. i. p. 64.

master or the overseer. There was an exception made in the case of Negroes wearing liveries. Negro slaves were not allowed the use of fire-arms or other weapons, except they were armed with a certificate from their master granting the coveted permission. If they hunted with arms, not having a certificate, any Christian could apprehend them, seize the weapons, deliver the slave to the first justice of the peace; who was authorized to administer, without ceremony, twenty lashes upon his or her bare back, and send him or her home. The master had to pay the cost of arrest and punishment. The one exception to this law was, that one Negro on each plantation or in each district could carry a gun to shoot game for his master and protect stock, etc.; but his certificate was to be in his possession all the time. If a Negro went from the plantation on which he resided, to another plantation or place, he was required by statute to travel in the most generally frequented road. If caught in another road, not much travelled, except in the company of a white man, it was lawful for the man who owned the land through which he was passing to seize him, and administer not more than forty lashes. If Negroes visited each other in the night season, — the only time they could visit, — the ones who were found on another plantation than their master's were punished with lashes on their naked back, not exceeding forty; while the Negroes who had furnished the entertainment received twenty lashes for their hospitality. In case any slave, who had not been properly fed and clothed by his master, was convicted of stealing cattle, hogs, or corn from another man, an action of trespass could be maintained against the master in the general or county court, and damages recovered.[1]

Here, as in the other colonies, the greatest enemy of the colonists was an accusing conscience. The people started at every breath of rumor, and always imagined their slaves conspiring to cut their throats. There was nothing in the observed character of the slaves to justify the wide-spread consternation that filled the public mind. Nor was there any occasion to warrant the passage of the Act of 1741, respecting conspiracies among slaves. It is a remarkable document, and is produced here.

"XLVII. *And be it further enacted by the authority aforesaid,* That if any number of negroes or other slaves, that is to say, three, or more, shall, at any

---

[1] This is an instance of humanity in the North-Carolina code worthy of special note. It stands as the only instance of justice toward the over-worked and under-fed slaves of the colony.

time hereafter, consult, advise or conspire to rebel, or make insurrection, or shall plot or conspire the murder of any person or persons whatsoever, every such consulting, plotting or conspiring, shall be adjudged and deemed felony; and the slave or slaves convicted thereof, in manner herein after directed, shall suffer death.

"XLVIII. *And be it further enacted by the authority aforesaid,* That every slave committing such offence, or any other crime or misdemeanor, shall forthwith be committed. by any justice of the peace, to the common jail of the county within which the said offence shall be committed, there to be safely kept; and that the sheriff of such county, upon such commitment, shall forthwith certify the same to any Justice in the commission for the said court for the time being, resident in the county, who is thereupon required and directed to issue a summons for two or more Justices of the said court, and four freeholders, such as shall have slaves in the said county; which said three Justices and four freeholders, owners of slaves, are hereby impowered and required upon oath, to try all manner of crimes and offences, that shall be committed by any slave or slaves, at the court house of the county, and to take for evidence, the confession of the offender, the oath of one or more credible witnesses, or such testimony of negroes, mulattoes or Indians, bond or free, with pregnant circumstances, as to them shall seem convincing, without the solemnity of a jury; and the offender being then found guilty, to pass such judgment upon such offender, according to their discretion, as the nature of the crime or offence shall require; and on such judgment, to award execution.

"XLIX. *Provided always, and be it enacted,* That it shall and may be lawful for each and every Justice, being in the commission of the peace for the county where any slave or slaves shall be tried, by virtue of this act, (who is owner of slaves) to sit upon such trial, and act as a member of such court, though he or they be not summoned thereto: anything herein before contained to the contrary, in any wise, notwithstanding.

"L. And to the end such negro, mulatto or Indian, bond or free, not being christians, as shall hereafter be produced as an evidence on the trial of any slave or slaves, for capital or other crimes, may be under the greater obligation to declare the truth; *Be, it further enacted,* There where any such negro, mulatto or Indian, bond or free, shall, upon due proof made, or pregnant circumstances, appearing before any county court within this government, be found to have given a false testimony, every such offender shall, without further trial, be ordered, by the said court, to have one ear nailed to the pillory, and there stand for the space of one hour, and the said ear to be cut off, and thereafter the other ear nailed in like manner. and cut off, at the expiration of one other hour; and moreover, to order every such offender thirty-nine lashes, well laid on, on his or her bare back, at the common whipping post.

"LI. *And be it further enacted by the authority aforesaid,* That at every such trial of slaves committing capital or other offences, the first person in commission sitting on such trial, shall, before the examination of every negro, mulatto or Indian, not being a christian, charge such to declare the truth.

"LII. *Provided always, and it is hereby intended,* That the master, owner or overseer of any slave, to be arraigned and tried by virtue of this act, may appear at the trial, and make what just defence he can for such slave or slaves;

so that such defence do not relate to any formality in the proceeding on the trial." [1]

The manner of conducting the trials of Negroes charged with felony or misdemeanor was rather peculiar. Upon one or more white persons' testimony, or the evidence of Negroes and Indians, bond or free, the unfortunate defendant, "without the solemnity of a jury," before three justices and four freeholders, could be hurried through a trial, convicted, sentenced to die a dreadful death, and then be executed without the officiating presence of a minister of the gospel.

The unprecedented discretion allowed to masters in the government led to the most tragic results. Men were not only reckless of the lives of their own slaves, but violent toward those belonging to others. If a Negro showed the least independence in conversation with a white man, he could be murdered in cold blood; and it was only a case of a contumacious slave getting his dues. But men became so prodigal in the exercise of this authority that the public became alarmed, and the Legislature called a halt on the master-class. At first the Legislature paid for the slaves who were destroyed by the consuming wrath of ill-natured whites, but finally allowed an action to lie against the persons who killed a slave. This had a tendency to reduce the number of murdered slaves; but the fateful clause in the Locke Constitution had educated a voracious appetite for blood, and the extremest cruel treatment continued without abatement.

The free Negro population was very small in this colony. The following act on manumission differs so widely from the law on this point in the other colonies, that it is given as an illustration of the severe character of the legislation of North Carolina against the emancipation of Negroes.

"LVI. *And be it further enacted by the authority aforesaid,* That no Negro or mulatto slaves shall be set free, upon any pretence whatsoever, except for meritorious services, to be adjudged and allowed of by the county court, and Licence thereupon first had and obtained: and that where any slave shall be set free by his or her master or owner, otherwise than is herein before directed, it shall and may be lawful for the church-wardens of the parish wherein such negro, mulatto or Indian, shall be found, at the expiration of six months, next after his or her being set free, and they are hereby authorized and required, to take up and sell the said negro, mulatto or Indian, as a slave, at the next court to

[1] Public Acts of N. C., p. 65.

be held for the said county, at public vendue : and the monies arising by such sale, shall be applied to the use of the parish, by the vestry thereof : and if any negro, mulatto or Indian slave, set free otherwise than is herein directed, shall depart this province, within six months next after his or her freedom, and shall afterwards return into this government, it shall and may be lawful for the church-wardens of the parish where such negro or mulatto shall be found, at the expiration of one month, next after his or her return into this government to take up such negro or mulatto, and sell him or them, as slaves, at the next court to be held for the county, at public vendue ; and the monies arising thereby, to be applied, by the vestry, to the use of the parish, as aforesaid." [1]

The free Negroes were badly treated. They were not allowed any communion with the slaves. A free Negro man was not allowed to marry a white woman, nor even a Negro slave woman without the consent of her master. If he formed an alliance with a white woman, her offspring were bound out, or sold by the church-wardens, until they obtained their majority.[2] If the white woman were an indentured servant, she was constrained to serve an additional year. If she were a free woman, she was sold for two years by the church-wardens. Free Negroes were greatly despised and shunned by both slaves and white people.

As a conspicuous proof of the glaring hypocrisy of the "nobility," who, in the constitution, threw open the door of the Church to the Negro, it should be said, that, during the period from the founding of the Province down to the colonial war, no attempt was ever made, through the ecclesiastical establishment, to dissipate the dark clouds of ignorance that enveloped the Negro's mind. They were left in a state of ignorance and crime. The gravest social evils were winked at by masters, whose lecherous examples were the occasion for the most grievous offending of the slaves. The Mulattoes and other free Negroes were taxed. They had no place in the militia, nor could they claim the meanest rights of the humblest "leetman."

---

[1] Public Acts of N. C., p. 66.   [2] The Act of 1741 says, "until 31 years of age."

CHAPTER XXIII.

THE·COLONY OF NEW HAMPSHIRE.

1679–1775.

ANTERIOR to the year 1679, the provincial government of Massachusetts exercised authority over the territory that now comprises the State of New Hampshire. It is not at all improbable, then, that slavery existed in this colony from the beginning of its organic existence. As early as 1683 it was set upon by the authorities as a wicked and hateful institution. On the 14th of March, 1684, the governor of New Hampshire assumed the responsibility of releasing a Negro slave from bondage. The record of the fact is thus preserved : —

" The governor tould Mr. Jaffery's negro hee might goe from his master, hee would clere him under hande and sele, so the fello no more attends his master's consernes." [1]

It may be inferred from the above, that the royal governor of the Province felt the pressure of public sentiment on the question of anti-slavery. While this colony copied its criminal code from Massachusetts, its people seemed to be rather select, and, on the question of human rights, far in advance of the people of Massachusetts. The twelfth article was: "If any man stealeth mankind he shall be put to death or otherwise grievously punished." The entire code — the first one — was rejected in England as "fanatical and absurd." [2] It was the desire of this new and

---

[1] Belknap's Hist. of N. H., vol. i. p. 333.   [2] Hildreth, vol. i. p. 501.

feeble colony to throw every obstacle in the way of any legal recognition of slavery. The governors of all the colonies received instruction in regard to the question of slavery, but the governor of New Hampshire had received an order from the crown to have the tax on imported slaves removed. The royal instructions, dated June 30, 1761, were as follows : —

"You are not to give your assent to, or pass any law imposing duties on negroes imported into New Hampshire." [1]

New Hampshire never passed any law establishing slavery, but in 1714 enacted several laws regulating the conduct of servants. One was *An Act to prevent disorders in the night :* —

"Whereas great disorders, insolencies and burglaries are ofttimes raised and committed in the night time by Indian, negro and mulatto servants and slaves, to the disquiet and hurt of her Majesty's good subjects, for the prevention whereof *Be it,* &c. — that no Indian, negro or mulatto servant or slave may presume to be absent from the families where they respectively belong, or be found abroad in the night time after nine o'clock; unless it be upon errand for their respective masters." [2]

The instructions against the importation of slaves were in harmony with the feelings of the great majority of the people. They felt that slavery would be a hinderance rather than a help to them, and in the selection of servants chose white ones. If the custom of holding men in bondage had become a part of the institutions of Massachusetts, — so like a cancer that it could not be removed without endangering the political and commercial life of the colony, — the good people of New Hampshire, acting in the light of experience, resolved, upon the threshold of their provincial life, to oppose the introduction of slaves into their midst. The first result was, that they learned quite early that they could get on without slaves ; and, second, the traders in human flesh discovered that there was no demand for slaves in New Hampshire. Even nature fought against the crime ; and Negroes were found to be poorly suited to the climate, and, of course, were an expensive luxury in that colony.

But, nevertheless, there were slaves in New Hampshire. The majority of them had gone in during the time the colony was a part of the territory of Massachusetts. They had been purchased by men who regarded them as indispensable to them. They had

---

[1] Gordon's Hist. of Am. Rev., vol. v, Letter 2.   [2] Freedom and Bondage, vol. i. p. 266.

lived long in many families; children had been born unto them, and in many instances they were warmly attached to their owners. But all masters were not alike. Some treated their servants and slaves cruelly. The neglect in some cases was worse than stripes or over-work. Some were poorly clad and scantily fed; and, thus exposed to the inclemency of the severe climate, many were precipitated into premature graves. Even white and Indian servants shared this harsh treatment. The Indians endured greater hardships than the Negroes. They were more lofty in their tone, more sensitive in their feelings, more revengeful in their disposition. They were both hated and feared, and the public sentiment against them was very pronounced. A law, passed in 1714, forbid their importation into the colony under a heavy penalty.

In 1718 it was found necessary to pass a law to check the severe treatment inflicted upon servants and slaves. *An Act for restraining inhuman severities* recited, —

"For the prevention and restraining of inhuman severities which by evil masters or overseers, may be used towards their Christian servants, that from and after the publication hereof, if any man smite out the eye or tooth of his man servant or maid servant, or otherwise maim or disfigure them much, unless it be by mere casualty, he shall let him or her go free from his service, and shall allow such further recompense as the court of quarter sessions shall adjudge him. 2. That if any person or persons whatever in this province shall wilfully kill his Indian or negroe servant or servants he shall be punished with death." [1]

There were slaves in New Hampshire down to the breaking-out of the war in the colonies, but they were only slaves in name. Few in number, widely scattered, they felt themselves closely identified with the interests of the colonists.

---

[1] *Freedom and Bondage*, vol. i. p. 267.

CHAPTER XXIV.

THE COLONY OF PENNSYLVANIA.

1681–1775.

ORGANIZATION OF THE GOVERNMENT OF PENNSYLVANIA. — THE SWEDES AND DUTCH PLANT SETTLE-
MENTS ON THE WESTERN BANK OF THE DELAWARE RIVER. — THE GOVERNOR OF NEW YORK
SEEKS TO EXERCISE JURISDICTION OVER THE TERRITORY OF PENNSYLVANIA — THE FIRST LAWS
AGREED UPON IN ENGLAND. — PROVISIONS OF THE LAW. — MEMORIAL AGAINST SLAVERY DRAUGHTED
AND ADOPTED BY THE GERMANTOWN FRIENDS. — WILLIAM PENN PRESENTS A BILL FOR THE
BETTER REGULATION OF SERVANTS. — AN ACT PREVENTING THE IMPORTATION OF NEGROES AND
INDIANS. — RIGHTS OF NEGROES. — A DUTY LAID UPON NEGROES AND MULATTO SLAVES. — THE
QUAKER THE FRIEND OF THE NEGRO — ENGLAND BEGINS TO THREATEN HER DEPENDENCIES IN
NORTH AMERICA. — THE PEOPLE OF PENNSYLVANIA REFLECT UPON THE PROBABLE OUTRAGES
THEIR NEGROES MIGHT COMMIT.

L ONG before there was an organized government in Pennsylvania, the Swedes and Dutch had planted settlements on
the western bank of the Delaware River.   But the English
crown claimed the soil; and the governor of New York, under
patent from the Duke of York, sought to exercise jurisdiction
over the territory.   On the 11th of July, 1681, "Conditions and
Concessions were agreed upon by William Penn, Proprietary,"
and the persons who were "adventurers and purchasers in the
same province."   Provision was made for the punishment of
persons who should injure Indians, and that the planter injured
by them should "not be his own judge upon the Indian."   All controversies arising between the whites and the Indians were to be
settled by a council of twelve persons, — six white men and six
Indians.

The first laws for the government of the colony were agreed
upon in England, and in 1682 went into effect.   Provision was
made for the registering of all servants, their full names, amount
of wages paid, and the time when they received their remuneration.   It was strictly required that servants should not be kept
beyond the time of their indenture, should be kindly treated, and
the customary outfit furnished at the time of their freedom.

The baneful custom of enslaving Negroes had spread through

every settlement in North America, and was even "tolerated in Pennsylvania under the specious pretence of the religious instruction of the slave." [1] In 1688 Francis Daniel Pastorius draughted a memorial against slavery, which was adopted by the Germantown Friends, and by them sent up to the Monthly Meeting, and thence to the Yearly Meeting at Philadelphia. [2] The original document was found by Nathan Kite of Philadelphia in 1844. [3] It was a remarkable document, and the first protest against slavery issued by any religious body in America. Speaking of the slaves, Pastorius asks, "Have not these negroes as much right to fight for their freedom as you have to keep them slaves?" He believed the time would come, —

> "When, from the gallery to the farthest seat,
> Slave and slave-owner shall no longer meet,
> But all sit equal at the Master's feet."

He regarded the "buying, selling, and holding men in slavery, as inconsistent with the christian religion." When his memorial came before the Yearly Meeting for action, it confessed itself "unprepared to act," and voted it "not proper then to give a positive judgment in the case." In 1696 the Yearly Meeting pronounced against the further importation of slaves, and adopted measures looking toward their moral improvement. George Keith, catching the holy inspiration of humanity, with a considerable following, denounced the institution of slavery "as contrary to the religion of Christ, the rights of man, and sound reason and policy." [4]

While these efforts were, to a certain extent, abortive, yet, nevertheless, the Society of the Friends made regulations for the better treatment of the enslaved Negroes. The sentiment thus created went far toward deterring the better class of citizens from purchasing slaves. To his broad and lofty sentiments of humanity, the pious William Penn sought to add the force of positive law. The published views of George Fox, given at Barbadoes in 1671, in his "Gospel Family Order, being a short discourse concerning the ordering of Families, both of Whites, Blacks, and Indians," had a salutary effect upon the mind of Penn. In 1700

---

[1] Gordon's History of Penn., p. 114.   [2] Whittier's Penn. Pilgrim, p. viii.
[3] The memorial referred to was printed *in extenso* in The Friend, vol. xviii. No 16.
[4] Minutes of Yearly Meeting, Watson's MS. Coll.   Bettle's notices of N. S. Minutes, Penn. Hist. Soc.

he proposed to the Council " *the necessitie of a law* [*among others*] *about y[e] marriages of negroes.*" The bill was referred to a joint committee of both houses, and they brought in a bill "*for regulating Negroes in their Morals and Marriages* &c." It reached a second reading, and was lost.[1] Penn regarded the teaching of Negroes the sanctity of the marriage relation as of the greatest importance to the colony, and the surest means of promoting pure morals. Upon what grounds it was rejected is not known. He presented, at the same session of the Assembly, another bill, which provided "*for the better regulation of servants in this province and territories.*" He desired the government of slaves to be prescribed and regulated by law, rather than by the capricious whims of masters. No servant was to be sold out of the Province without giving his consent, nor could he be assigned over except before a justice of the peace. It provided for a regular allowance to servants at the expiration of their time, and required them to serve five days extra for every day's absence from their master without the latter's assent. A penalty was fixed for concealing runaway slaves, and a reward offered for apprehending them. No free person was allowed to deal with servants, and justices and sheriffs were to be punished for neglecting their duties in the premises.

In case a Negro was guilty of murder, he was tried by two justices, appointed by the governor, before six freeholders. The manner of procedure was prescribed, and the nature of the sentence and acquittal. Negroes were not allowed to carry a gun or other weapons. Not more than four were allowed together, upon pain of a severe flogging. An Act for raising revenue was passed, and a duty upon imported slaves was levied, in 1710. In 1711–12, an Act was passed "*to prevent the importation of negroes and Indians*" into the Province. A general petition for the emancipation of slaves by law was presented to the Legislature during this same year; but the wise law-makers replied, that "it was neither just nor convenient to set them at liberty." The bill passed on the 7th of June, 1712, but was disapproved by Great Britain, and was accordingly repealed by an Act of Queen Anne, Feb. 20, 1713. In 1714 and 1717, Acts were passed to check the importation of slaves. But the English government, instead of being touched by the philanthropic endeavors of the people of

---

[1] Colonial Rec., vol. i. pp. 598, 606. See also *Votes* of Assembly, vol. i. pp. 120–122.

Pennsylvania, was seeking, for purposes of commercial trade and gain, to darken the continent with the victims of its avarice.

Negroes had no political rights in the Province. Free Negroes were prohibited from entertaining Negro or Indian slaves, or trading with them. Masters were required, when manumitting slaves, to furnish security, as in the other colonies. Marriages between the races were forbidden. Negroes were not allowed to be abroad after nine o'clock at night.

In 1773 the Assembly passed "*An Act making perpetual the Act entitled, An Act for laying a duty on negroes and mulatto slaves,*" etc., and added ten pounds to the duty. The colonists did much to check the vile and inhuman traffic; but, having once obtained a hold, it did eat like a canker. It threw its dark shadow over personal and collective interests, and poisoned the springs of human kindness in many hearts. It was not alone hurtful to the slave: it transformed and blackened character everywhere, and fascinated those who were anxious for riches beyond the power of moral discernment. Here, however, as in New Jersey, the Negro found the Quaker his practical friend; and his upper and better life received the pruning advice, refining and elevating influence, of a godly people. . But intelligence in the slave was an occasion of offending, and prepared him to realize his deplorable situation. So to enlighten him was to excite in him a deep desire for liberty, and, not unlikely, a feeling of revenge toward his enslavers. So there was really danger in the method the guileless Friends adopted to ameliorate the condition of the slaves.

When England began to breathe out threatenings against her contumacious dependencies in North America, the people of Pennsylvania began to reflect upon the probable outrages their Negroes would, in all probability, commit. They inferred that the Negroes would be their enemy because they were their slaves. This was the equitable findings of a guilty conscience. They did not dare expect less than the revengeful hate of the beings they had laid the yoke of bondage upon; and verily they found themselves with "fears within, and fightings without."

CHAPTER XXV.

THE COLONY OF GEORGIA.

1732–1775.

GEORGIA ONCE INCLUDED IN THE TERRITORY OF CAROLINA. — THE THIRTEENTH COLONY PLANTED IN NORTH AMERICA BY THE ENGLISH GOVERNMENT. — SLAVES RULED OUT ALTOGETHER BY THE TRUSTEES. — THE OPINION OF GEN. OGLETHORPE CONCERNING SLAVERY. — LONG AND BITTER DISCUSSION IN REGARD TO THE ADMISSION OF SLAVERY INTO THE COLONY. — SLAVERY INTRODUCED. — HISTORY OF SLAVERY IN GEORGIA.

GEORGIA was once included in the territory of Carolina, and extended from the Savannah to the St. John's River.

A corporate body, under the title of "The Trustees for establishing the Colony of Georgia," was created by charter, bearing date of June 9, 1732. The life of their trust was for the space of twenty-one years. The rules by which the trustees sought to manage the infant were rather novel; but as a discussion of them would be irrelevant, mention can be made only of that part which related to slavery. Georgia was the last colony — the thirteenth — planted in North America by the English government. Special interest centred in it for several reasons, that will be explained farther on.

The trustees ruled out slavery altogether. Gen. John Oglethorpe, a brilliant young English officer of gentle blood, the first governor of the colony, was identified with "the Royal African Company, which alone had the right of planting forts and trading on the coast of Africa." He said that "slavery is against the gospel, as well as the fundamental law of England. We refused, as trustees, to make a law permitting such a horrid crime." Another of the trustees, in a sermon preached on Sunday, Feb. 17, 1734, at St. George's Church, Hanover Square, London, declared, "Slavery, the misfortune, if not the dishonor, of other plantations, is absolutely proscribed. Let avarice defend it as it will, there is an honest reluctance in humanity against buying and selling, and regarding those of our own species as our wealth and possessions." Beautiful sentiments! Eloquent testimony against the crime of the ages! At first blush the student of history is apt to praise the sublime motives of the "trustees," in placing a restriction against the slave-trade. But the declaration of principles quoted above is not borne out by the facts of history. On this point Dr. Stevens, the historian of Georgia, observes, "Yet in the official publications of that body [the trustees], its inhibition is based only on political and prudential, and not on humane and liberal grounds; and even Oglethorpe owned a plantation and negroes near Parachucla in South Carolina, about forty miles above Savannah."[1] To this reliable opinion is added : —

"The introduction of slaves was prohibited to the colony of Georgia for some years, not from motives of humanity, but for the reason it was encouraged elsewhere, to wit: the interest of the mother country. It was a favorite idea with the 'mother country,' to make *Georgia* a protecting barrier for the Carolinas, against the Spanish settlements south of her, and the principal Indian tribes to the west; to do this, a strong settlement of white men was sought to be built up, whose arms and interests would defend her northern plantations. The introduction of slaves was held to be unfavorable to this scheme, and hence its prohibition. During the time of the prohibition, Oglethorpe himself was a slave-holder in Carolina."[2]

The reasons that led the trustees to prohibit slavery in the colony are put thus tersely : —

"1st. Its expense; which the poor emigrant would be entirely unable to sustain, either in the first cost of a negro, or his subsequent keeping. 2d. Because it would induce idleness, and render labour degrading. 3d. Because the settlers, being freeholders of only fifty-acre lots, requiring but one or two extra hands for their cultivation, the German servants would be a third more profitable than the blacks. Upon the last original design I have mentioned, in planting this colony, they also based an argument against their admission, viz., that the cultivation of silk and wine, demanding skill and nicety, rather than strength and endurance of fatigue, the whites were better calculated for such labour than the negroes. These were the prominent arguments, drawn from the various considerations of internal and external policy, which influenced the Trustees in making this prohibition. Many of them, however, had but a temporary bearing; none stood the test of experience."[3]

It is clear, then, that the founders of the colony of Georgia were not moved by the noblest impulses to prohibit slavery within

---

[1] Stephens's Journal, vol. iii. p. 281.   [2] Freedom and Bondage, vol. i. p. 310, note.
[3] Stevens's Hist. of Georgia, vol. i. p. 289.

their jurisdiction. In the chapter on South Carolina, attention was called to the influence of the Spanish troops in Florida on the recalcitrant Negroes in the Carolinas, the Negro regiment with subalterns from their own class, and the work of Spanish emissaries among the slaves. The home government thought it wise to build up Georgia out of white men, who could develop its resources, and bear arms in defence of British possessions along an extensive border exposed to a pestiferous foe. But the Board of Trade soon found this an impracticable scheme, and the colonists themselves began to clamor "for the use of negroes." [1] The first petition for the introduction and use of Negro slaves was offered to the trustees in 1735. This prayer was promptly and positively denied, and for fifteen years they refused to grant all requests for the use of Negroes. They adhered to their prohibition in letter and spirit. Whenever and wherever Negroes were found in the colony, they were sold back into Carolina. In the month of December, 1738, a petition, addressed to the trustees, including nearly all the names of the foremost colonists, set forth the distressing condition into which affairs had drifted under the enforcement of the prohibition, and declared that "the use of negroes, with proper limitations, which, if granted, would both occasion great numbers of white people to come here, and also to render us capable to subsist ourselves, by raising provisions upon our lands, until we could make some produce fit for export, in some measure to balance our importations." But instead of securing a favorable hearing, the petition drew the fire of the friends of the prohibition against the use of Negroes. On the 3d of January, 1739, a petition to the trustees combating the arguments of the above-mentioned petition, and urging them to remain firm, was issued at Darien. This was followed by another one, issued from Ebenezer on the 13th of March, in favor of the position occupied by the trustees. A great many Scotch and German people had settled in the colony; and, familiar with the arts of husbandry, they became the ardent supporters of the trustees. James Habersham, the "*dear fellow-traveller,*" of Whitefield, exclaimed, —

"I once thought, it was unlawful to keep negro slaves, but I am now induced to think God may have a higher end in permitting them to be brought to this Christian country, than merely to support their masters. Many of the

---

[1] Bancroft, vol. iii. 12th ed. p. 427.

poor slaves in America have already been made freemen of the heavenly Jerusalem, and possibly a time may come when many thousands may embrace the gospel, and thereby be brought into the glorious liberty of the children of God. These, and other considerations, appear to plead strongly for a limited use of negroes; for, while we can buy provisions in Carolina cheaper than we can here, no one will be induced to plant much."

But the trustees stood firm against the subtle cunning of the politicians, and the eloquent pleadings of avarice.

On the 7th October, 1741, a large meeting was held at Savannah, and a petition drawn, in which the land-holders and settlers presented their grievances to the English authorities in London. On the 26th of March, 1742, Mr. Thomas Stephens, armed with the memorial, as the agent of the memorialists, sailed for London. While the document ostensibly set forth their wish for a definition of "the tenure of the lands," really the burden of the prayer was for "*Negroes.*" He presented the memorial to the king, and his Majesty referred it to a committee of the "Lords of Council for Plantation Affairs." This committee transferred a copy of the memorial to the trustees, with a request for their answer. About this time Stephens presented a petition to Parliament, in which he charged the trustees with direliction of duty, improper use of the public funds, abuse of their authority, and numerous other sins against the public welfare. It created a genuine sensation. The House resolved to go into a "committee of the whole," to consider the petitions and the answer of the trustees. The answer of the trustees was drawn by the able pen of the Earl of Egmont, and by them warmly approved on the 3d of May, and three days later was read to the House of Commons. A motion prevailed "that the petitions do lie upon the table," for the perusal of the members, for the space of one week. At the expiration of the time fixed, Stephens appeared, and all the petitions of the people of Georgia to the trustees in reference to "the tenure of lands," and for "the use of negroes," were laid before the honorable body. In the committee of the whole the affairs of the colony were thoroughly investigated; and, after a few days session, Mr. Carew reported a set of resolutions, being the sense of the committee after due deliberation upon the matters before them : —

"That the province of Georgia, in America, by reason of its situation, may be an useful barrier to the British provinces on the continent of America against the French and Spaniards, and Indian nations in their interests; that the ports and harbours within the said province may be a good security to the trade and navigation of this kingdom; that the said province, by reason of the fertility of the soil, the healthfulness of the climate, and the convenience of the rivers, is a proper place for establishing a settlement, and may contribute greatly to the increasing trade of this kingdom; that it is very necessary and advantageous to this nation that the colony of Georgia should be preserved and supported; that it will be an advantage to the colony of Georgia to permit the importation of rum into the said colony from any of the British colonies; that the petition of Thomas Stephens contains false, scandalous and malicious charges, tending to asperse the characters of the Trustees for Establishing the Colony of Georgia, in America."

When the resolution making the importation of rum lawful reached a vote, it was amended by adding, "As also the use of negroes, who may be employed there with advantage to the colony, under proper regulations and restrictions." It was lost by a majority of nine votes. A resolution prevailed calling Thomas Stephens to the bar of the House, "to be reprimanded on his knees by Mr. Speaker," for his offence against the trustees.

On the next day Stephens, upon his bended knees at the bar of the House of Commons, before the assembled statesmen of Great Britain, was publicly reprimanded by the speaker, and discharged after paying his fees. Thus ended the attempt of the people of the colony of Georgia to secure permission, over the heads of the trustees, to introduce slaves into their service.

The dark tide of slavery influence was dashing against the borders of the colony. The people were discouraged. Business was stagnated. Internal dissatisfaction and factional strife wore hard upon the spirit of a people trying to build up and develop a new country. Then the predatory incursions of the Spaniards, and the threatening attitude of the Indians, unnerved the entire Province. In this state of affairs white servants grew insolent and insubordinate. Those whose term of service expired refused to work. In this dilemma many persons boldly put the rule of the trustees under foot, and hired Negroes from the Carolinas. At length the trustees became aware of the clandestine importation of Negroes into the colony, and thereupon gave the magistrates a severe reproval. On the 2d of October, 1747, they received the following reply : —

" We are afraid, sir, from what you have wrote in relation to negroes, that the Honourable Trustees have been misinformed as to our conduct relating thereto; for we can with great assurance assert, that this Board has always acted an uniform part in discouraging the use of negroes in this colony, well knowing it to be disagreeable to the Trustees, as well as contrary to an act existing for the prohibition of them, and always gave it in charge to those whom we had put in possession of lands, not to attempt the introduction or use of negroes. But notwithstanding our great caution, some people from Carolina, soon after settling lands on the Little Ogeechee, found means of bringing and employing a few negroes on the said lands, some time before it was discovered to us; upon which they thought it high time to withdraw them, for fear of being seized, and soon after withdrew themselves and families out of the colony, which appears to us at present to be the resolution of divers others." [1]

It was charged that the law-officers knew of the presence of Negroes in Georgia; that their standing and constant toast was, " *the one thing needful* " (Negroes); and that they themselves had surreptitiously aided in the procurement of Negroes for the colony. The supporters of the colonists grew less powerful as the struggle went forward. The most active grew taciturn and conservative. The advocates of Negro labor became bolder, and more acrimonious in debate; and at length the champions of exclusive white labor shrank into silence, appalled at the desperation of their opponents. The Rev. Martin Bolzius, one of the most active supporters of the trustees, wrote those gentlemen on May 3, 1748: —

"Things being now in such a melancholy state, I must humbly beseech your honors, not to regard any more our or our friend's petitions against negroes."

The Rev. George Whitefield and James Habersham used their utmost influence upon the trustees to obtain a modification of the prohibition against "the use of negroes." On the 6th of December, 1748, Rev. Whitefield, speaking of a plantation and Negroes he had purchased, wrote the trustees: —

"Upwards of five thousand pounds have been expended in that undertaking, and yet very little proficiency made in the cultivation of my tract of land, and that entirely owing to the necessity I lay under of making use of white hands. Had a negro been allowed, I should now have had a sufficiency to support a great many orphans, without expending above half the sum which has been laid out. An unwillingness to let so good a design drop, and having a rational conviction that it must necessarily, if some other method was not fixed upon to prevent it — these two considerations, honoured gentlemen, prevailed on me about two years ago, through the bounty of my good friends, to purchase a plantation in South Carolina, where negroes are allowed. Blessed

---

[1] Stevens's Hist. of Georgia, vol. i. p. 307.

be God, this plantation has succeeded; and though at present I have only eight working hands, yet in all probability there will be more raised in one year, and with a quarter the expense, than has been produced at Bethesda for several years last past. This confirms me in the opinion I have entertained for a long time, that *Georgia never can or will be a flourishing province without negroes are allowed.*" [1]

The sentiment in favor of the importation of Negro slaves had become well-nigh unanimous. The trustees began to waver. On the 10th of January, 1749, another petition was presented to the trustees. It was carefully drawn, and set forth the restrictions under which slaves should be introduced. On the 16th of May following, it was read to the trustees; and they resolved to have it "presented to His Majesty in council." They also asked that the prohibition against the introduction of Negroes, passed in " 1735, be repealed." The Earl of Shaftesbury, at the head of a special committee, draughted a bill repealing the prohibition. On the 26th of October, 1749, a large and influential committee of twenty-seven drew up and signed a petition urging the immediate introduction of slavery, with certain limitations. The paper was duly attested, and returned to the trustees. The opposition to the introduction of slavery into the colony of Georgia had been conquered; and, after a long and bitter struggle, slavery was firmly and legally established in this the last Province of the English in the Western world. The colonists were jubilant.

The charter under which the trustees acted expired by limitation in 1752, and a new form of government was established under the Board of Trade. The royal commission appointed a governor and council. One of the first ordinances enacted by them was one whereby " all offences committed by slaves were to be tried by a single justice, without a jury, who was to award execution, and, in capital cases, to set a value on the slave, to be paid out of the public treasury." At the first session of the Assembly in 1755, a law was passed *"for the regulation and government of slaves."* In 1765 an Act was passed establishing a pass system, and the rest of the legislation in respect to slaves was a copy of the laws of South Carolina.

The history of slavery in Georgia during this period is unparalleled and incomparably interesting. It illustrates the power of the institution, and shows that there was no Province sufficiently

---

[1] Whitefield's Works, vol. ii. pp. 90, 105, 208.

independent of its influence so as to expel it from its jurisdiction. Like the Angel of Death that passed through Egypt, there was no colony that it did not smite with its dark and destroying pinions. The dearest, the sublimest, interests of humanity were prostrated by its defiling touch. It shut out the sunlight of human kindness; it paled the fires of hope; it arrested the development of the branches of men's better natures, and peopled their lower being with base and consuming desires; it placed the " *Golden Rule* " under the unholy heel of time-servers and self-seekers; it made the Church as secular as the 'Change, and the latter as pious as the former : it was a gigantic system, at war with the civilization of the Roundheads and Puritans, and an intolerable burden to a people who desired to build a new nation in this New World in the West.

Part III.

THE NEGRO DURING THE REVOLUTION.

CHAPTER XXVI.

MILITARY EMPLOYMENT OF NEGROES.

1775–1780.

"Many black soldiers were in the service during all stages of the war." — SPARKS.

THE COLONIAL STATES IN 1715. — RATIFICATION OF THE NON-IMPORTATION ACT BY THE SOUTHERN COLONIES. — GEORGE WASHINGTON PRESENTS RESOLUTIONS AGAINST SLAVERY, IN A MEETING AT FAIRFAX COURT-HOUSE, VA. — LETTER WRITTEN BY BENJAMIN FRANKLIN TO DEAN WOODWARD, PERTAINING TO SLAVERY. — LETTER TO THE FREEMEN OF VIRGINIA FROM A COMMITTEE, CONCERNING THE SLAVES BROUGHT FROM JAMAICA. — SEVERE TREATMENT OF SLAVES IN THE COLONIES MODIFIED. — ADVERTISEMENT IN "THE BOSTON GAZETTE" OF THE RUNAWAY SLAVE CRISPUS ATTUCKS. — THE BOSTON MASSACRE. — ITS RESULTS. — CRISPUS ATTUCKS SHOWS HIS LOYALTY. — HIS SPIRITED LETTER TO THE TORY GOVERNOR OF THE PROVINCE. — SLAVES ADMITTED INTO THE ARMY. — THE CONDITION OF THE CONTINENTAL ARMY. — SPIRITED DEBATE IN THE CONTINENTAL CONGRESS, OVER THE DRAUGHT OF A LETTER TO GEN. WASHINGTON. — INSTRUCTIONS TO DISCHARGE ALL SLAVES AND FREE NEGROES IN HIS ARMY. — MINUTES OF THE MEETING HELD AT CAMBRIDGE. — LORD DUNMORE'S PROCLAMATION. — PREJUDICE IN THE SOUTHERN COLONIES. — NEGROES IN VIRGINIA FLOCK TO THE BRITISH ARMY. — CAUTION TO THE NEGROES PRINTED IN A WILLIAMSBURG PAPER. — THE VIRGINIA CONVENTION ANSWERS THE PROCLAMATION OF LORD DUNMORE. — GEN. GREENE, IN A LETTER TO GEN. WASHINGTON, CALLS ATTENTION TO THE RAISING OF A NEGRO REGIMENT ON STATEN ISLAND. — LETTER FROM A HESSIAN OFFICER. — CONNECTICUT LEGISLATURE ON THE SUBJECT OF EMPLOYMENT OF NEGROES AS SOLDIERS. — GEN. VARNUM'S LETTER TO GEN. WASHINGTON, SUGGESTING THE EMPLOYMENT OF NEGROES, SENT TO GOV. COOKE. — THE GOVERNOR REFERS VARNUM'S LETTER TO THE GENERAL ASSEMBLY. — MINORITY PROTEST AGAINST ENLISTING SLAVES TO SERVE IN THE ARMY. — MASSACHUSETTS TRIES TO SECURE LEGAL ENLISTMENTS OF NEGRO TROOPS. — LETTER OF THOMAS KENCH TO THE COUNCIL AND HOUSE OF REPRESENTATIVES, BOSTON, MASS. — NEGROES SERVE IN WHITE ORGANIZATIONS UNTIL THE CLOSE OF THE AMERICAN REVOLUTION. — NEGRO SOLDIERS SERVE IN VIRGINIA. — MARYLAND EMPLOY NEGROES. — NEW YORK PASSES AN ACT PROVIDING FOR THE RAISING OF TWO COLORED REGIMENTS. — WAR IN THE MIDDLE AND SOUTHERN COLONIES. — HAMILTON'S LETTER TO JOHN JAY. — COL. LAURENS'S EFFORTS TO RAISE NEGRO TROOPS IN SOUTH CAROLINA. — PROCLAMATION OF SIR HENRY CLINTON INDUCING NEGROES TO DESERT THE REBEL ARMY. — LORD CORNWALLIS ISSUES A PROCLAMATION OFFERING PROTECTION TO ALL NEGROES SEEKING HIS COMMAND. — COL. LAURENS IS CALLED TO FRANCE ON IMPORTANT BUSINESS. — HIS PLAN FOR SECURING BLACK LEVIES FOR THE SOUTH UPON HIS RETURN. — HIS LETTERS TO GEN. WASHINGTON IN REGARD TO HIS FRUITLESS PLANS. — CAPT. DAVID HUMPHREYS RECRUITS A COMPANY OF COLORED INFANTRY IN CONNECTICUT. — RETURN OF NEGROES IN THE ARMY IN 1778.

THE policy of arming the Negroes early claimed the anxious consideration of the leaders of the colonial army during the American Revolution. England had been crowding her American plantations with slaves at a fearful rate; and, when hostilities actually began, it was difficult to tell whether the American army or the ministerial army would be able to secure the Negroes as allies. In 1715 the royal governors of the colonies gave the Board of Trade the number of the Negroes in their respective colonies. The slave population was as follows : —

	NEGROES.		NEGROES.
New Hampshire	150	Maryland	9,500
Massachusetts	2,000	Virginia	23,000
Rhode Island	500	North Carolina	3,700
Connecticut	1,500	South Carolina	10,500
New York	4,000		
New Jersey	1,500	Total	58,850
Pennsylvania and Delaware	2,500		

Sixty years afterwards, when the Revolution had begun, the slave population of the thirteen colonies was as follows : —

	NEGROES.		NEGROES.
Massachusetts	3,500	Maryland	80,000
Rhode Island	4,373	Virginia	165,000
Connecticut	5,000	North Carolina	75,000
New Hampshire	629	South Carolina	110,000
New York	15,000	Georgia	16,000
New Jersey	7,600		
Pennsylvania	10,000	Total	501,102
Delaware	9,000		

Such a host of beings was not to be despised in a great military struggle. Regarded as a neutral element that could be used simply to feed an army, to perform fatigue duty, and build fortifications, the Negro population was the object of fawning favors of the white colonists. In the NON-IMPORTATION COVENANT, passed by the Continental Congress at Philadelphia, on the 24th of October, 1774, the second resolve indicated the feeling of the representatives of the people on the question of the slave-trade : —

" 2. We will neither import nor purchase, any slave imported after the first day of December next; after which time, we will wholly discontinue the slave-trade, and will neither be concerned in it ourselves, nor will we hire our vessels, nor sell our commodities or manufactures to those who are concerned in it." [1]

---

[1] Journal of the Continental Congress.

It, with the entire covenant, received the signatures of all the delegates from the twelve colonies.[1] The delegates from the Southern colonies were greatly distressed concerning the probable attitude of the slave element. They knew that if that ignorant mass of humanity were inflamed by some act of strategy of the enemy, they might sweep their homes and families from the face of the earth. The cruelties of the slave-code, the harsh treatment of Negro slaves, the lack of confidence in the whites everywhere manifested among the blacks, — as so many horrid dreams, harassed the minds of slaveholders by day and by night. They did not even possess the courage to ask the slaves to remain silent and passive during the struggle between England and themselves. The sentiment that adorned the speeches of orators, and graced the writings of the colonists, during this period, was "the equality of the rights of all men." And yet the slaves who bore their chains under their eyes, who were denied the commonest rights of humanity, who were rated as chattels and real property, were living witnesses to the insincerity and inconsistency of this declaration. But it is a remarkable fact, that all the Southern colonies, in addition to the action of their delegates, ratified the Non-Importation Covenant. The Maryland Convention on the 8th of December, 1774; South Carolina Provincial Congress on the 11th January, 1775; Virginia Convention on the 22d March, 1775; North Carolina Provincial Congress on the 23d of August, 1775; Delaware Assembly on the 25th of March, 1775 (refused by Gov. John Penn); and Georgia, — passed the following resolves thereabouts : —

"1. *Resolved*, That this Congress will adopt, and carry into execution, all and singular the measures and recommendations of the late Continental Congress.

"4. *Resolved*, That we will neither import or [nor] purchase any slave imported from Africa or elsewhere after this date."

Meetings were numerous and spirited throughout the colonies, in which, by resolutions, the people expressed their sentiments in reference to the mother country. On the 18th of July, 1774, at a meeting held in Fairfax Court-House, Virginia, a series of twenty-

---

[1] The Hon. Peter Force, in an article to The National Intelligencer, Jan. 16 and 18, 1855, says: "Southern colonies, jointly with all the others, and separately each for itself, did agree to prohibit the importation of slaves, voluntarily and in. good faith." Georgia was not represented in this Congress, and, therefore, could not sign.

four resolutions was presented by George Washington, chairman of the committee on resolutions, three of which were directed against slavery.

"17. *Resolved*, That it is the opinion of this meeting, that, during our present difficulties and distress, no slaves ought to be imported into any of the British colonies on this continent; and we take this opportunity of declaring our most earnest wishes to see an entire stop for ever put to such a wicked, cruel, and unnatural trade. . . .

"21. *Resolved*, That it is the opinion of this meeting, that this and the other associating colonies should break off all trade, intercourse, and dealings with that colony, province, or town, which shall decline, or refuse to agree to, the plan which shall be adopted by the General Congress. . . .

"24. *Resolved*, That George Washington and Charles Broadwater, lately elected our representatives to serve in the General Assembly, be appointed to attend the Convention at Williamsburg on the first day of August next, and present these resolves, as the sense of the people of this county upon the measures proper to be taken in the present alarming and dangerous situation of America."

Mr. Sparks comments upon the resolutions as follows : —

"The draught, from which the resolves are printed, I find among Washington's papers, in the handwriting of George Mason, by whom they were probably drawn up; yet, as they were adopted by the Committee of which Washington was chairman, and reported by him as moderator of the meeting, they may be presumed to express his opinions, formed on a perfect knowledge of the subject, and after cool deliberation. This may indeed be inferred from his letter to Mr. Bryan Fairfax, in which he intimates a doubt only as to the article favoring the idea of a further petition to the king. He was opposed to such a step, believing enough had been done in this way already; but he yielded the point in tenderness to the more wavering resolution of his associates.

"These resolves are framed with much care and ability, and exhibit the question then at issue, and the state of public feeling, in a manner so clear and forcible as to give them a special claim to a place in the present work, in addition to the circumstance of their being the matured views of Washington at the outset of the great Revolutionary struggle in which he was to act so conspicuous a part. . . .

"Such were the opinions of Washington, and his associates in Virginia, at the beginning of the Revolutionary contest. The seventeenth resolve merits attention, from the pointed manner in which it condemns the slave-trade." [1]

Dr. Benjamin Franklin, in a letter to Dean Woodward, dated April 10, 1773, says, —

"I have since had the satisfaction to learn that a disposition to abolish slavery prevails in North America; that many of the Pennsylvanians have set

---

[1] Sparks's Washington, vol. ii. pp. 488-495.

their slaves at liberty; and that even the Virginia Assembly have petitioned the king for permission to make a law for preventing the importation of more into that Colony. This request, however, will probably not be granted. as their former laws of that kind have always been repealed, and as the interest of a few merchants here has more weight with Government than that of thousands at a distance." [1]

Virginia gave early and positive proof that she was in earnest on the question of non-importation. One John Brown, a merchant of Norfolk, broke the rules of the colony by purchasing imported slaves, and was severely rebuked in the following article :—

" 'TO THE FREEMEN OF VIRGINIA:

" 'COMMITTEE CHAMBER, NORFOLK, March 6, 1775.

" ' Trusting to your sure resentment against the enemies of your country, we, the committee, elected by ballot for the Borough of Norfolk, hold up for your just indignation Mr. John Brown, merchant of this place.

" ' On Thursday, the 2d of March, this committee were informed of the arrival of the brig Fanny, Capt. Watson, with a number of slaves for Mr. Brown; and, upon inquiry, it appeared they were shipped from Jamaica as his property, and on his account; that he had taken great pains to conceal their arrival from the knowledge of the committee; and that the shipper of the slaves, Mr. Brown's correspondent, and the captain of the vessel, were all fully apprised of the Continental prohibition against that article.

" ' From the whole of this transaction, therefore, we, the committee for Norfolk Borough, do give it as our unanimous opinion, that the said John Brown has wilfully and perversely violated the Continental Association to which he had with his own hand subscribed obedience; and that, agreeable to the eleventh article, we are bound forthwith to publish the truth of the case, to the end that all such foes to the rights of British America may be publicly known and universally contemned as the enemies of American liberty, and that every person may henceforth break off all dealings with him.' "

And the first delegation from Virginia to Congress in August, 1774, had instructions as follows, drawn by Thomas Jefferson :—

" For the most trifling reasons, and sometimes for no conceivable reason at all, his Majesty has rejected laws of the most salutary tendency. *The abolition of domestic slavery is the great object of desire in those Colonies, where it was, unhappily, introduced in their infant state. But, previous to the enfranchisement of the slaves we have, it is necessary to exclude all further importations from Africa.* Yet our repeated attempts to effect this by prohibitions, and by imposing duties which might amount to a prohibition, have been hitherto defeated by his Majesty's negative; thus preferring the immediate advantages

---

[1] Sparks's Franklin, vol. viii. p. 42.

of a few British corsairs to the lasting interests of the American States, and to the rights of human nature, deeply wounded by this infamous practice." [1]

It is scarcely necessary to mention the fact, that there were several very cogent passages in the first draught of the Declaration of Independence that were finally omitted. The one most pertinent to this history is here given : —

"He has waged cruel war against human nature itself, violating its most sacred rights of life and liberty in the persons of a distant people who never offended him; captivating and carrying them into slavery in another hemisphere, or to incur miserable death in their transportation thither. This piratical warfare, the opprobrium of *Infidel* powers, is the warfare of the *Christian* king of Great Britain. Determined to keep open a market where *men* should be bought and sold, he has prostituted his negative for suppressing every legislative attempt to prohibit or to restrain this execrable commerce. And, that this assemblage of horrors might want no fact of distinguished die, he is now exciting those very people to rise in arms among us, and to purchase that liberty of which he has deprived them, by murdering the people on whom he also obtruded them; thus paying off former crimes committed against the *liberties* of one people with crimes which he urges them to commit against the *lives* of another." [2]

The solicitude concerning the slavery question was not so great in the Northern colonies. The slaves were not so numerous as in the Carolinas and other Southern colonies. The severe treatment of slaves had been greatly modified, the spirit of masters toward them more gentle and conciliatory, and the public sentiment concerning them more humane. Public discussion of the Negro question, however, was cautiously avoided. The failure of attempted legislation friendly to the slaves had discouraged their friends, while the critical situation of public affairs made the supporters of slavery less aggressive. On the 25th of October, 1774, an effort was made in the Provincial Congress of Massachusetts to re-open the discussion, but it failed. The record of the attempt is as follows : —

"Mr. Wheeler brought into Congress a letter directed to Doct. Appleton, purporting the propriety, that while we are attempting to free ourselves from our present embarrassments, and preserve ourselves from slavery, that we also take into consideration the state and circumstances of the negro slaves in this province. The same was read, and it was moved that a committee be appointed to take the same into consideration. After some debate thereon, the question was put, whether the matter now subside, and it passed in the affirmative." [3]

---

[1] Jefferson's Works, vol. i. p. 135.   [2] Ibid., pp. 23, 24.
[3] Journals of the Provincial Congress of Mass., p. 29.

Thus ended the attempt to call the attention of the people's representatives to the inconsistency of their doctrine and practice on the question of the equality of human rights.   Further agitation of the question, followed by the defeat of just measures in the interest of the slaves, was deemed by many as dangerous to the colony.   The discussions were watched by the Negroes with a lively interest; and failure led them to regard the colonists as their enemies, and greatly embittered them.   Then it was difficult to determine just what would be wisest to do for the enslaved in this colony.   The situation was critical: a bold, clear-headed, loyal-hearted man was needed.

On Tuesday, Oct. 2, 1750, "The Boston Gazette, or Weekly Journal," contained the following advertisement: —

"RAN-away from his master *Wiiliam Brown* of *Framingham*, on the 30th of *Sept.* last, a Molatto Fellow, about 27 Years of Age, named *Crispas*, 6 Feet 2 Inches high, short curl'd Hair, his Knees nearer together than common; had on a light colour'd Bear-skin Coat, plain brown Fustain Jacket, or brown all-Wool one, new Buckskin Breeches, blue Yarn Stockings, and a checked woolen Shirt.

"Whoever shall take up said Run-away, and convey him to his abovesaid Master, shall have *ten Pounds*, old Tenor Reward, and all necessary Charges paid.   And all Masters of Vessels and others, are hereby cautioned against concealing or carrying off said Servant on Penalty of the Law.   *Boston, October* 2, 1750."

During the month of November, — the 13th and 20th, — a similar advertisement appeared in the same paper; showing that the "Molatto Fellow" had not returned to his master.

Twenty years later "Crispas's" name once more appeared in the journals of Boston.   This time he was not advertised as a runaway slave, nor was there reward offered for his apprehension.   His soul and body were beyond the cruel touch of master; the press had paused to announce his apotheosis, and to write the name of the Negro patriot, soldier, and martyr to the ripening cause of the American Revolution, in fadeless letters of gold, — CRISPUS ATTUCKS!

On March 5, 1770, occurred the Boston Massacre; and, while it was not the real commencement of the Revolutionary struggle, it was the bloody drama that opened the most eventful and thrilling chapter in American history.   The colonists had endured, with obsequious humility, the oppressive acts of Britain, the swaggering insolence of the ministerial troops, and the sneers of her hired minions. The aggressive and daring men had found themselves hampered by the conservative views of a large class of colonists, who feared lest some one should take a step not exactly according to the law. But while the "wise and prudent" were deliberating upon a legal method of action, there were those, who, "made of sterner stuff," reasoned right to the conclusion, that they had rights as colonists that ought to be respected. That there was cause for just indignation on the part of the people towards the British soldiers, there is no doubt. But there is reason to question the time and manner of the assault made by the citizens. Doubtless they had "a zeal, but not according to knowledge." There is no record to controvert the fact of the leadership of Crispus Attucks. A manly-looking fellow, six feet two inches in height, he was a commanding figure among the irate colonists. His enthusiasm for the threatened interests of the Province, his loyalty to the teachings of Otis, and his willingness to sacrifice for the cause of equal rights, endowed him with a courage, which, if tempered with better judgment, would have made him a military hero in his day. But consumed by the sacred fires of patriotism, that lighted his path to glory, his career of usefulness ended at the beginning. John Adams, as the counsel for the soldiers, thought that the patriots Crispus Attucks led were a "rabble of saucy boys, negroes, mulattoes, &c.," who could not restrain their emotion. Attucks led the charge with the shout, "The way to get rid of these soldiers is to attack the main-guard ; strike at the root : this is the nest." A shower of missiles was answered by the discharge of the guns of Capt. Preston's company. The exposed and commanding person of the intrepid Attucks went down before the murderous fire. Samuel Gray and Jonas Caldwell were also killed, while Patrick Carr and Samuel Maverick were mortally wounded.

The scene that followed beggared description. The people ran from their homes and places of business into the streets, white with rage. The bells rang out the alarm of danger. The bodies of Attucks and Caldwell were carried into Faneuil Hall, where their strange faces were viewed by the largest gathering of people ever before witnessed. Maverick was buried from his mother's house in Union Street, and Gray from his brother's residence in Royal Exchange Lane. But Attucks and Caldwell, strangers in the city, without relatives, were buried from Faneuil Hall, so justly called " *the Cradle of Liberty.*" The four hearses formed a junction in King Street; and from thence the procession moved in columns six deep, with a long line of coaches containing the first citizens of Boston. The obsequies were witnessed by a very large and respectful concourse of people. The bodies were deposited in one grave, over which a stone was placed bearing this inscription : —

> "Long as in Freedom's cause the wise contend,
> Dear to your country shall your fame extend;
> While to the world the lettered stone shall tell
> Where Caldwell, Attucks, Gray and Maverick fell."

Who was Crispus Attucks? A Negro whose soul, galling under the destroying influence of slavery, went forth a freeman, went forth not only to fight for *his* liberty, but to give his life as an offering upon the altar of *American liberty*. He was not a madcap, as some would have the world believe. He was not ignorant of the issues between the American colonies and the English government, between the freemen of the colony and the dictatorial governors. Where he was during the twenty years from 1750 to 1770, is not known; but doubtless in Boston, where he had heard the fiery eloquence of Otis, the convincing arguments of Sewall, and the tender pleadings of Belknap. He had learned to spell out the fundamental principles that should govern well-regulated communities and states; and, having come to the rapturous consciousness of his freedom in fee simple, the brightest crown God places upon mortal man, he felt himself neighbor and friend. His patriotism was not a mere spasm produced by sudden and exciting circumstances. It was an education; and knowledge comes from experience; and the experience of this black hero was not of a single day. Some time before the memorable 5th of March, Crispus addressed the following spirited letter to the Tory governor of the Province : —

"To THOMAS HUTCHINSON: *Sir,* — You will hear from us with astonishment. You ought to hear from us with horror. You are chargeable before God and man, with our blood. The soldiers were but passive instruments, mere machines; neither moral nor voluntary agents in our destruction, more than the leaden pellets with which we were wounded. You was a free agent. You acted, coolly, deliberately, with all that premeditated malice, not against us in particular, but against the people in general, which, in the sight of the law, is an ingredient in the composition of murder. You will hear further from us hereafter.   CRISPUS ATTUCKS." [1]

---

[1] Adams's Works, vol. ii. p. 322.

This was the declaration of war. It was fulfilled. The world has heard from him; and, more, the English-speaking world will never forget the noble daring and excusable rashness of Attucks in the holy cause of liberty! Eighteen centuries before he was saluted by death and kissed by immortality, another Negro bore the cross of Christ to Calvary for him. And when the colonists were staggering wearily under their cross of woe, a Negro came to the front, and bore that cross to the victory of glorious martyrdom!

And the people did not agree with John Adams that Attucks led "a motley rabble," but a band of patriots. Their evidence of the belief they entertained was to be found in the annual commemoration of the "5th of March," when orators, in measured sentences and impassioned eloquence, praised the hero-dead. In March, 1775, Dr. Joseph Warren, who a few months later, as Gen. Warren, made Bunker Hill the shrine of New-England patriotism, was the orator. On the question of human liberty, he said, —

" That personal freedom is the natural right of every man, and that property, or an exclusive right to dispose of what he has honestly acquired by his own labor, necessarily arises therefrom, are truths which common sense has placed beyond the reach of contradiction. And no man, or body of men, can, without being guilty of flagrant injustice, claim a right to dispose of the persons or acquisitions of any other man, or body of men, unless it can be proved that such a right has arisen from some compact between the parties, in which it has been explicitly and freely granted."

These noble sentiments were sealed by his blood at Bunker Hill, on the 17th of June, 1775, and are the amulet that will protect his fame from the corroding touch of centuries of time

The free Negroes of the Northern colonies responded to the call "*to arms,*" that rang from the placid waters of Massachusetts Bay to the verdant hills of Berkshire, and from Lake Champlain to the upper waters of the Hudson. Every Northern colony had its Negro troops, not as separate organizations, — save the black regiment of Rhode Island, — but scattered throughout all of the white organizations of the army. At the first none but free Negroes were received into the army; but before peace came Negroes were not only admitted, they were purchased, and sent into the war, with an offer of freedom and fifty dollars bounty at the close of their service. On the 29th of May, 1775, the "*Committee of Safety*" for the Province of Massachusetts passed the following resolve against the enlistment of Negro slaves as soldiers : —

"Resolved, That it is the opinion of this committee, as the contest now between Great Britain and the colonies respects the liberties and privileges of the latter, which the colonies are determined to maintain, that the admission of any persons, as soldiers, into the army now raising, but only such as are free-men, will be inconsistent with the principles that are to be supported, and reflect dishonor on this colony, and that no slaves be admitted into this army upon any consideration whatever." [1]

On Tuesday, the 6th of June, 1775, "A resolve of the com-mittee of safety, relative to the [admission] of slaves into the army was read, and ordered to lie on the table for further con-sideration." [2]   But this was but another evidence of the cold, conservative spirit of Massachusetts on the question of other people's rights.

The Continental army was in bad shape.   Its arms and cloth-ing, its discipline and efficiency, were at such a low state as to create the gravest apprehensions and deepest solicitude.   Gen. George Washington took command of the army in and around Boston, on the 3d of July, 1775, and threw his energies into the work of organization.   On the 10th of July he issued instructions to the recruiting-officers of Massachusetts Bay, in which he for-bade the enlistment of any "negro," or "any Person who is not an American born, unless such Person has a Wife and Family and is a settled resident in this Country." [3]   But, nevertheless, it is a curious fact, as Mr. Bancroft says, "the roll of the army at Cam-bridge had from its first formation borne the names of men of color."   "Free negroes stood in the ranks by the side of white men.   In the beginning of the war they had entered the pro-vincial army ; the first general order which was issued by Ward, had required a return, among other things, of the 'complexion'

---

[1] Journals of the Provincial Congress of Mass., p. 553.   [2] Ibid., p. 302.

[3] The following is a copy of Gen. Gates's order to recruiting-officers : —

"You are not to enlist any deserter from the Ministerial Army, or any stroller, negro, or vagabond, or person suspected of being an enemy to the liberty of America, nor any under eighteen years of age.

"As the cause is the best that can engage men of courage and principle to take up arms, so it is expected that none but such will be accepted by the recruiting officer.   The pay, provision, &c., being so ample, it is not doubted but that the officers sent upon this service will, without delay, complete their respective corps, and march the men forthwith to camp.

"You are not to enlist any person who is not an American born, unless such person has a wife and family, and is a settled resident in this country.   The persons you enlist must be provided with good and complete arms."

— MOORE'S *Diary of the American Revolution*, vol. i. p. 110.

of the soldiers; and black men like others were retained in the service after the troops were adopted by the continent." There is no room to doubt. Negroes were in the army from first to last, but were there in contravention of law and positive prohibition.[1]

On the 29th of September, 1775, a spirited debate occurred in the Continental Congress, over the draught of a letter to Gen. Washington, reported by Lynch, Lee, and Adams. Mr. Rutledge of South Carolina moved that the commander-in-chief be instructed to discharge all slaves and free Negroes in his army. The Southern delegates supported him earnestly, but his motion was defeated. Public attention was called to the question, and at length the officers of the army debated it. The following minute of a meeting held at Cambridge preserves and reveals the sentiment of the general officers of the army on the subject : —

"At a council of war, held at head-quarters, October 8th, 1775, present: His Excellency, General Washington; Major-Generals Ward, Lee, and Putnam; Brigadier-Generals Thomas, Spencer, Heath, Sullivan, Greene, and Gates — the question was proposed:

"'Whether it will be advisable to enlist any negroes in the new army? or whether there be a distinction between such as are slaves and those who are free?'

"It was agreed unanimously to reject all slaves; and, by a great majority, to reject negroes altogether."

Ten days later, Oct. 18, 1775, a committee of conference met at Cambridge, consisting of Dr. Franklin, Benjamin Harrison, and Thomas Lynch, who conferred with Gen. Washington, the deputy-governors of Connecticut and Rhode Island, and the Committee of the Council of Massachusetts Bay. The object of the conference was the renovation and improvement of the army. On the 23d of October, the employment of Negroes as soldiers came before the conference for action, as follows : —

"Ought not negroes to be excluded from the new enlistment, especially such as are slaves? all were thought improper by the council of officers."

"*Agreed* that they be rejected altogether."

---

[1] The Provincial Congress of South Carolina, Nov. 20, 1775, passed the following resolve : —

"On motion, *Resolved*, That the colonels of the several regiments of militia throughout the Colony have leave to enroll such a number of able male slaves, to be employed as pioneers and laborers, as public exigencies may require; and that a daily pay of seven shillings and sixpence be allowed for the service of each such slave while actually employed."

— *American Archives*, 4th Series, vol. lv. p. 6.

In his General Orders, issued from headquarters on the 12th of November, 1775, Washington said, —

"Neither negroes, boys unable to bear arms, nor old men unfit to endure the fatigues of the campaign, are to be enlisted." [1]

But the general repaired this mistake the following month. Lord Dunmore had issued a proclamation declaring "all indented servants, negroes, or others (appertaining to rebels) free." Fearing lest many Negroes should join the ministerial army, in General Orders, 30th December, Washington wrote : —

"As the General is informed that numbers of free negroes are desirous of enlisting, he gives leave to the recruiting officers to entertain them, and promises to lay the matter before the Congress, who, he doubts not, will approve of it."

Lord Dunmore's proclamation is here given : —

"*By his Excellency the Right Honorable* JOHN, *Earl of* DUNMORE, *his Majesty's Lieutenant and Governor-General of the Colony and Dominion of Virginia, and Vice-Admiral of the same,* —

"A PROCLAMATION.

"As I have ever entertained hopes that an accommodation might have taken place between *Great Britain* and this Colony, without being compelled by my duty to this most disagreeable but now absolutely necessary step, rendered so by a body of armed men, unlawfully assembled, firing on his Majesty's tenders; and the formation of an army, and that army now on their march to attack his Majesty's troops, and destroy the well-disposed subject of this Colony: To defeat such treasonable purposes, and that all such traitors and their abettors may be brought to justice, and that the peace and good order of this Colony may be again restored, which the ordinary course of the civil law is unable to effect, I have thought fit to issue this my Proclamation; hereby declaring, that, until the aforesaid good purposes can be obtained, I do, in virtue of the power and authority to me given by his Majesty, determine to execute martial law, and cause the same to be executed, throughout this Colony. And, to the end that peace and good order may the sooner be restored, I do require every person capable of bearing arms to resort to his Majesty's standard, or be looked upon as traitors to his Majesty's Crown and Government, and thereby become liable to the penalty the law inflicts upon such offences, — such as forfeiture of life, confiscation of lands, &c., &c. And I do hereby further declare all indented servants, negroes, or others, (appertaining to Rebels,) free, that are able and willing to bear arms, they joining his Majesty's troops, as soon as may be, for the more speedily reducing this Colony to a proper sense of their duty to his Majesty's crown and dignity. I do further

---

[1] Sparks's Washington, vol. iii. p. 155, note.

order and require all his Majesty's liege subjects to retain their quit-rents, or any other taxes due, or that may become due, in their own custody, till such time as peace may be again restored to this at present most unhappy country, or demanded of them, for their former salutary purposes, by officers properly authorized to receive the same.

"Given under my hand, on board the Ship *William*, off *Norfolk*, the seventh day of November, in the sixteenth year of his Majesty's reign.

"DUNMORE.

"God save the King!" [1]

On account of this, on the 31st of December, Gen. Washington wrote the President of Congress as follows :—

"It has been represented to me, that the free negroes, who have served in this army, are very much dissatisfied at being discarded. As it is to be apprehended, that they may seek employ in the ministerial army, I have presumed to depart from the resolution respecting them, and have given license for their being enlisted. If this is disapproved of by Congress, I will put a stop to it." [2]

This letter was referred to a committee consisting of Messrs. Wythe, Adams, and Wilson. On the 16th of January, 1776, they made the following report :—

"That the free negroes who have served faithfully in the army at Cambridge may be re-enlist — therein, but no others." [3]

This action on the part of Congress had reference to the army around Boston, but it called forth loud and bitter criticism from the officers of the army at the South. In a letter to John Adams, dated Oct. 24, 1775, Gen. Thomas indicated that there was some feeling even before the action of Congress was secured. He says, —

"I am sorry to hear that any prejudices should take place in any Southern colony, with respect to the troops raised in this. I am certain the insinuations you mention are injurious, if we consider with what precipitation we were obliged to collect an army. In the regiments at Roxbury, the privates are equal to any that I served with in the last war; very few old men, and in the ranks very few boys. Our fifers are many of them boys. We have some negroes; but I look on them, in general, equally serviceable with other men for fatigue; and, in action, many of them have proved themselves brave.

"I would avoid all reflection, or any thing that may tend to give umbrage; but there is in this army from the southward a number called riflemen, who are

---

[1] Force's American Archives, 4th Series, vol. iii. p. 1,385.

[2] Sparks's Washington, vol. iii. p. 218.   [3] Journals of Congress, vol. ii. p. 26.

as indifferent men as I ever served with. These privates are mutinous, and often deserting to the enemy; unwilling for duty of any kind; exceedingly vicious; and, I think, the army here would be as well without as with them. But to do justice to their officers, they are, some of them, likely men."

The Dunmore proclamation was working great mischief in the Southern colonies. The Southern colonists were largely engaged in planting, and, as they were Tories, did not rush to arms with the celerity that characterized the Northern colonists. At an early moment in the struggle, the famous Rev. Dr. Hopkins of Rhode Island wrote the following pertinent extract : —

" God is so ordering it in his providence, that it seems absolutely necessary something should speedily be done with respect to the slaves among us, in order to our safety, and to prevent their turning against us in our present struggle, in order to get their liberty. Our oppressors have planned to gain the blacks, and induce them to take up arms against us, by promising them liberty on this condition; and this plan they are prosecuting to the utmost of their power, by which means they have persuaded numbers to join them. And should we attempt to restrain them by force and severity, keeping a strict guard over them, and punishing them severely who shall be detected in attempting to join our opposers, this will only be making bad worse, and serve to render our inconsistence, oppression, and cruelty more criminal, perspicuous, and shocking, and bring down the righteous vengeance of Heaven on our heads. The only way pointed out to prevent this threatening evil is to set the blacks at liberty ourselves by some public acts and laws, and then give them proper encouragement to labor, or take arms in the defence of the American cause, as they shall choose. This would at once be doing them some degree of justice, and defeating our enemies in the scheme that they are prosecuting." [1]

On Sunday, the 24th of September, 1775, John Adams recorded the following conversation, that goes to show that Lord Dunmore's policy was well matured : —

" In the evening, Mr. Bullock and Mr. Houston, two gentlemen from Georgia, came into our room, and smoked and chatted the whole evening. Houston and Adams disputed the whole time in good humor. They are both dabs at disputation, I think. Houston, a lawyer by trade, is one of course, and Adams is not a whit less addicted to it than the lawyers. The question was, whether all America was not in a state of war, and whether we ought to confine ourselves to act upon the defensive only? He was for acting offensively, next spring or this fall, if the petition was rejected or neglected. If it was not answered, and favorably answered, he would be for acting against Britain and Britons, as, in open war, against French and Frenchmen; fit privateers, and take their ships anywhere. These gentlemen give a melancholy account of

---

[1] Hopkins's Works, vol. ii. p. 584.

the State of Georgia and South Carolina. They say that if one thousand regular troops should land in Georgia, and their commander be provided with arms and clothes enough, and proclaim freedom to all the negroes who would join his camp, twenty thousand negroes would join it from the two Provinces in a fortnight. The negroes have a wonderful art of communicating intelligence among themselves; it will run several hundreds of miles in a week or fortnight. They say, their only security is this; that all the king's friends, and tools of government, have large plantations, and property in negroes; so that the slaves of the Tories would be lost, as well as those of the Whigs." [1]

The Negroes in Virginia sought the standards of the ministerial army, and the greatest consternation prevailed among the planters. On the 27th of November, 1775, Edmund Pendleton wrote to Richard Lee that the slaves were daily flocking to the British army.

" The Governour, hearing of this, marched out with three hundred and fifty soldiers, Tories and slaves, to Kemp's Landing; and after setting up his standard, and issuing his proclamation, declaring all persons Rebels who took up arms for the country, and inviting all slaves, servants, and apprentices to come to him and receive arms, he proceeded to intercept Hutchings and his party, upon whom he came by surprise, but received, it seems, so warm a fire, that the ragamuffins gave way. They were, however, rallied on discovering that two companies of our militia gave way; and left Hutchings and Dr. Reid with a volunteer company, who maintained their ground bravely till they were overcome by numbers, and took shelter in a swamp. The slaves were sent in pursuit of them; and one of Col. Hutchings's own, with another, found him. On their approach, he discharged his pistol at his slave, but missed him; and was taken by them, after receiving a wound in his face with a sword. The number taken or killed, on either side, is not ascertained. It is said the Governour went to Dr. Reid's shop, and, after taking the medicines and dressings neces-sary for his wounded men, broke all the others to pieces. Letters mention that slaves flock to him in abundance; but I hope it is magnified." [2]

But the dark stream of Negroes that had set in toward the English troops, where they were promised the privilege of bearing arms and their freedom, could not easily be stayed. The proclamation of Dunmore received the criticism of the press, and the Negroes were appealed to and urged to stand by their "true friends." A Williamsburg paper, printed on the 23d of November, 1775, contained the following well-written plea :—

---

[1] Works of John Adams, vol. ii. p. 428.
[2] Force's American Archives, 4th Series, vol. iv. p. 202.

"CAUTION TO THE NEGROES.

"The second class of people for whose sake a few remarks upon this proclamation seem necessary is the Negroes. They have been flattered with their freedom, if they be able to bear arms, and will speedily join Lord Dunmore's troops. To none, then, is freedom promised, but to such as are able to do Lord Dunmore service. The aged, the infirm, the women and children, are still to remain the property of their masters, — of masters who will be provoked to severity, should part of their slaves desert them. Lord Dunmore's declaration, therefore, is a cruel declaration to the Negroes. He does not pretend to make it out of any tenderness to them, but solely upon his own account; and, should it meet with success, it leaves by far the greater number at the mercy of an enraged and injured people. But should there be any amongst the Negroes weak enough to believe that Lord Dunmore intends to do them a kindness, and wicked enough to provoke the fury of the Americans against their defenceless fathers and mothers, their wives, their women and children, let them only consider the difficulty of effecting their escape, and what they must expect to suffer if they fall into the hands of the Americans. Let them further consider what must be their fate should the English prove conquerors. If we can judge of the future from the past, it will not be much mended. Long have the Americans, moved by compassion and actuated by sound policy, endeavored to stop the progress of slavery. Our Assemblies have repeatedly passed acts, laying heavy duties upon imported Negroes; by which they meant altogether to prevent the horrid traffick. But their humane intentions have been as often frustrated by the cruelty and covetousness of a set of English merchants, who prevailed upon the King to repeal our kind and merciful acts, little, indeed, to the credit of his humanity. Can it, then, be supposed that the Negroes will be better used by the English, who have always encouraged and upheld this slavery, than by their present masters, who pity their condition; who wish, in general, to make it as easy and comfortable as possible; *and who would, were it in their power, or were they permitted, not only prevent any more Negroes from losing their freedom, but restore it to such as have already unhappily lost it?* No: the ends of Lord Dunmore and his party being answered, they will either give up the offending Negroes to the rigor of the laws they have broken, or sell them in the West Indies, where every year they sell many thousands of their miserable brethren, to perish either by the inclemency of weather or the cruelty of barbarous masters. Be not then, ye Negroes, tempted by this proclamation to ruin yourselves. I have given you a faithful view of what you are to expect; and declare before God, in doing it, I have considered your welfare, as well as that of the country. Whether you will profit by my advice, I cannot tell; but this I know, that, whether we suffer or not, if *you* desert us, *you* most certainly will." [1]

But the Negroes had been demoralized, and it required an extraordinary effort to quiet them. On the 13th of December, the Virginia Convention put forth an answer to the proclamation

---

[1] Force's American Archives, 4th Series, vol. iii. p. 1,387.

of Lord Dunmore. On the 14th of December a proclamation was issued "offering pardon to such slaves as shall return to their duty within ten days after the publication thereof." The following was their declaration : —

"By the Representatives of the People of the Colony and Dominion of Virginia, assembled in General Convention,

"A DECLARATION.

"Whereas Lord Dunmore, by his Proclamation dated on board the ship 'William,' off Norfolk, the seventh day of November, 1775, hath offered freedom to such able-bodied slaves as are willing to join him, and take up arms against the good people of this Colony, giving thereby encouragement to a general insurrection, which may induce a necessity of inflicting the severest punishments upon those unhappy people, already deluded by his base and insidious arts ; and whereas, by an act of the General Assembly now in force in this Colony, it is enacted, that all negro or other slaves, conspiring to rebel or make insurrection, shall suffer death, and be excluded all benefit of clergy ; — we think it proper to declare, that all slaves who have been or shall be seduced, by his Lordship's Proclamation, or other arts, to desert their masters' service, and take up arms against the inhabitants of this Colony, shall be liable to such punishment as shall hereafter be directed by the General Convention. And to the end that all such who have taken this unlawful and wicked step may return in safety to their duty, and escape the punishment due to their crimes, we hereby promise pardon to them, they surrendering themselves to Colonel William Woodford or any other commander of our troops, and not appearing in arms after the publication hereof. And we do further earnestly recommend it to all humane and benevolent persons in this Colony to explain and make known this our offer of mercy to those unfortunate people." [1]

Gen. Washington was not long in observing the effects of the Dunmore proclamation. He began to fully realize the condition of affairs at the South, and on Dec. 15 wrote Joseph Reed as follows : —

"If the Virginians are wise, that arch-traitor to the rights of humanity, Lord Dunmore, should be instantly crushed, if it takes the force of the whole army to do it ; otherwise, like a snow-ball in rolling, his army will get size, some through fear, some through promises, and some through inclination, joining his standard : but that which renders the measure indispensably necessary is the negroes ; for, if he gets formidable, numbers of them will be tempted to join who will be afraid to do it without." [2]

---

[1] Force's American Archives, 4th Series, vol. iv. pp. 84, 85.

[2] Life and Correspondence of Joseph Reed, vol. i. p. 135.

The slaves themselves were not incapable of perceiving the cunning of Lord Dunmore.   England had forced slavery upon the colonists against their protest, had given instructions to the royal governors concerning the increase of the traffic, and therefore could not be more their friends than the colonists.   The number that went over to the enemy grew smaller all the while, and finally the British were totally discouraged in this regard.   Lord Dunmore was unwilling to acknowledge the real cause of his failure to secure black recruits, and so he charged it to the fever.

"LORD DUNMORE TO THE SECRETARY OF STATE.

[No. 1.]   "Ship 'Dunmore,' in Elizabeth River, Virginia,
                                            30th March, 1776.

.   .   .   .

"Your Lordship will observe by my letter, No. 34, that I have been endeavouring to raise two regiments here — one of white people, the other of black. The former goes on very slowly, but the latter very well, and would have been in great forwardness, had not a fever crept in amongst them, which carried off a great many very fine fellows."

[No. 3.]   "Ship 'Dunmore,' in Gwin's Island Harbour, Virginia,
                                            June 26, 1776.

"I am extremely sorry to inform your Lordship, that that fever, of which I informed you in my letter No. 1, has proved a very malignant one, and has carried off an incredible number of our people, especially the blacks. Had it not been for this horrid disorder, I am satisfied I should have had two thousand blacks; with whom I should have had no doubt of penetrating into the heart of this Colony." [1]

While the colonists felt, as Dr. Hopkins had written, that something ought to be done toward securing the services of the Negroes, yet their representatives were not disposed to legislate the Negro into the army.   He was there, and still a conservative policy was pursued respecting him.   Some bold officers took it upon themselves to receive Negroes as soldiers.   Gen. Greene, in a letter to Gen. Washington, called attention to the raising of a Negro regiment on Staten Island.

                                            "Camp on Long Island,
                                            July 21, 1776, two o'clock.

"Sir; Colonel Hand reports seven large ships are coming up from the Hook to the Narrows.

"A negro belonging to one Strickler, at Gravesend, was taken prisoner (as

---

[1] Force's American Archives, 5th Series, vol. ii. pp. 160, 162.

he says) last Sunday at Coney Island. Yesterday he made his escape, and was taken prisoner by the rifle-guard. He reports eight hundred negroes collected on Staten Island, this day to be formed into a regiment.

"I am your Excellency's most obedient, humble servant,

"N. GREENE.

"*To his Excellency* GEN. WASHINGTON, *Headquarters, New York.*"[1]

To the evidence already produced as to the indiscriminate employment of Negroes as soldiers in the American army, the observations of a foreign officer are added. Under date of the 23d of October, 1777, a Hessian officer wrote:[2] —

"From here to Springfield, there are few habitations which have not a negro family dwelling in a small house near by. The negroes are here as fruitful as other cattle. The young ones are well foddered, especially while they are still calves. Slavery is, moreover, very gainful. The negro is to be considered just as the bond-servant of a peasant. The negress does all the coarse work of the house, and the little black young ones wait on the little white young ones. *The negro can take the field, instead of his master; and therefore no regiment is to be seen in which there are not negroes in abundance: and among them there are able-bodied, strong, and brave fellows.* Here, too, there are many families of free negroes, who live in good houses, have property, and live just like the rest of the inhabitants."[3]

In the month of May, 1777, the Legislature of Connecticut sought to secure some action on the subject of the employment of Negroes as soldiers."

"In May, 1777, the General Assembly of Connecticut appointed a Committee 'to take into consideration the state and condition of the negro and mulatto slaves in this State, and what may be done for their emancipation.' This Committee, in a report presented at the same session (signed by the chairman, the Hon. Matthew Griswold of Lyme), recommended —

"'That the effective negro and mulatto slaves be allowed to enlist with the Continental battalions now raising in this State, under the following regulations and restrictions: viz., that all such negro and mulatto slaves as can procure, either by bounty, hire, or in any other way, such a sum to be paid to their masters as such negro or mulatto shall be judged to be reasonably worth by the selectmen of the town where such negro or mulatto belongs, shall be allowed to enlist into either of said battalions, and shall thereupon be, de facto, *free and emancipated;* and that the master of such negro or mulatto shall be exempted from the support and maintenance of such negro or mulatto, in case

---

[1] Force's American Archives, 5th Series, vol. i. p. 486.

[2] During a few months of study in New-York City, I came across the above in the library of the N. Y. Hist. Soc.

[3] Schloezer's Briefwechsel, vol. iv. p. 365.

such negro or mulatto shall hereafter become unable to support and maintain himself.

" ' And that, in case any such negro or mulatto slave shall be disposed to enlist into either of said battalions during the [war], he shall be allowed so to do: and such negro or mulatto shall be appraised by the selectmen of the town to which he belongs; and his master shall be allowed to receive the bounty to which such slave may be entitled, and also one-half of the annual wages of such slave during the time he shall continue in said service; provided, however, that said master shall not be allowed to receive such part of said wages after he shall have received so much as amounts, together with the bounty, to the sum at which he was appraised.' "

In the lower house the report was put over to the next session, but when it reached the upper house it was rejected.

"You will see by the Report of Committee, May, 1777, that General Varnum's plan for the enlistment of slaves had been anticipated in Connecticut; with this difference, that Rhode Island *adopted* it, while Connecticut did *not*.

"The two States reached nearly the same *results* by different methods. The unanimous declaration of the officers at Cambridge, in the winter of 1775, *against* the enlistment of slaves, — confirmed by the Committee of Congress, — had some weight, I think, with the Connecticut Assembly, so far as the formal enactment of a law *authorizing* such enlistments was in question. At the same time, Washington's license to *continue* the enlistment of negroes was regarded as a rule of action, both by the selectmen in making up, and by the State Government in accepting, the quota of the towns. The process of draughting, in Connecticut, was briefly this: The able-bodied men, in each town, were divided into 'classes ;' and each class was required to furnish one or more men, as the town's quota required, to answer a draught. Now, the Assembly, at the same session at which the proposition for enlisting slaves was rejected (May, 1777), passed an act providing that any *two* men belonging to this State, ' who should procure an able-bodied soldier or recruit to enlist into either of the Continental battalions to be raised from this State,' should themselves be exempted from draught during the continuance of such enlistment. Of recruits or draughted men thus furnished, neither the selectmen nor commanding officers questioned the *color* or the civil *status :* white and black, bond and free, if 'able-bodied,' went on the roll together, accepted as the representatives of their ' class,' or as substitutes for their employers. At the next session (October, 1777), an act was passed which gave more direct encouragement to the enlistment of slaves. By this existing law, the master who emancipated a slave was not released from the liability to provide for his support. This law was now so amended, as to authorize the selectmen of any town, on the application of the master, — after 'inquiry into the age, abilities, circumstances, and character' of the servant or slave, and being satisfied ' that it was likely to be consistent with his real advantage, and that it was probable that he would be able to support himself,' — to grant liberty for his emancipation, and to discharge the master ' from any charge or cost which may be occasioned by maintaining or supporting the servant or slave made free as aforesaid.' This enactment enabled the selectmen to offer an additional inducement to enlistment, for making up the quota of the town. The slave (or servant for term of years) might receive his freedom: the master might secure exemption from draught, and a discharge from future liabilities, to which he must otherwise have been subjected. In point of fact, some hundreds of blacks — slaves and freemen — were enlisted, from time to time, in the regiments of the State troops and of the Connecticut line. *How* many, it is impossible to tell; for, from first to last, the company or regimental rolls indicate *no distinctions* of color. The *name* is the only guide: and, in turning over the rolls of the Connecticut line, the frequent recurrence of names which were exclusively appropriated to negroes and slaves, shows how considerable was their proportion of the material of the Connecticut army; while such surnames as 'Liberty,' 'Freeman,' 'Freedom,' &c., by scores, indicate with what anticipations, and under what inducements, they entered the service.

"As to the efficiency of the service they rendered, I can say nothing from the records, except what is to be gleaned from scattered files, such as one of the petitions I send you. So far as my acquaintance extends, almost every family has its traditions of the good and faithful service of a black servant or slave, who was killed in battle, or served through the war, and came home to tell stories of hard fighting, and draw his pension. In my own native town, — not a large one, — I remember five such pensioners, three of whom, I believe, had been slaves, and, in fact, *were* slaves to the day of their death; for (and this explains the uniform action of the General Assembly on petitions for emancipation) neither the towns nor the State were inclined to exonerate the master, at a time when slavery was becoming unprofitable, from the obligation to provide for the old age of his slave." [1]

Gen. Varnum, a brave and intelligent officer from Rhode Island, early urged the employment of Negro soldiers. He communicated his views to Gen. Washington, and he referred the correspondence to the governor of Rhode Island.

GEN. WASHINGTON TO GOV. COOKE.

"HEADQUARTERS, 2d January, 1778.

"SIR: — Enclosed you will receive a copy of a letter from General Varnum to me, upon the means which might be adopted for completing the Rhode Island troops to their full proportion in the Continental army. I have nothing to say in addition to what I wrote the 29th of the last month on this important subject, but to desire that you will give the officers employed in this business all the assistance in your power.

"I am with great respect, sir,
"Your most obedient servant,
"G. WASHINGTON.

"TO GOVERNOR COOKE." [2]

---

[1] An Historical Research (Livermore), pp. 114-116.   [2] R. I. Col. Recs., vol. viii. p. 640.

The letter of Gen. Varnum to Gen. Washington, in reference to the employment of Negroes as soldiers, is as follows : —

GEN. VARNUM TO GEN. WASHINGTON.

"CAMP, January 2d, 1778.

" SIR : — The two battalions from the State of Rhode Island being small, and there being a necessity of the state's furnishing an additional number to make up their proportion in the Continental army; the field officers have represented to me the propriety of making one temporary battalion from the two, so that one entire corps of officers may repair to Rhode Island, in order to receive and prepare the recruits for the field. It is imagined that a battalion of negroes can be easily raised there. Should that measure be adopted, or recruits obtained upon any other principle, the service will be advanced. The field officers who go upon this command, are Colonel Greene, Lieutenant Colonel Olney, and Major Ward; seven captains, twelve lieutenants, six ensigns, one paymaster, one surgeon and mates, one adjutant and one chaplain.

" I am Your Excellency's most obedient servant,

"J. M. VARNUM.

" TO HIS EXCELLENCY GENERAL WASHINGTON." [1]

Gov. Cooke wrote Gen. Washington as follows : —

"STATE OF RHODE ISLAND, &c.
" PROVIDENCE, January 19th, 1778.

" SIR : — Since we had the honor of addressing Your Excellency by Mr. Thompson, we received your favor of the 2d of January current, enclosing a proposition of Gen. Varnum's for raising a battalion of negroes.

" We in our letter of the 15th current, of which we send a duplicate, have fully represented our present circumstances, and the many difficulties we labor under, in respect to our filling up the Continental battalions. In addition thereto, will observe, that we have now in the state's service within the government, two battalions of infantry, and a regiment of artillery who are enlisted to serve until the 16th day of March next; and the General Assembly have ordered two battalions of infantry, and a regiment of artillery, to be raised, to serve until the 16th of March, 1779. So that we have raised and kept in the field, more than the proportion of men assigned us by Congress.

" The General Assembly of this state are to convene themselves on the second Monday of February next, when your letters will be laid before them, and their determination respecting the same, will be immediately transmitted to Your Excellency.

" I have the honor to be, &c.,

" NICHOLAS COOKE.

"TO GEN. WASHINGTON." [2]

---

[1] R. I. Col. Recs., vol. viii. p. 641.   [2] Ibid., vol. viii. p. 524.

The governor laid the above letters before the General Assembly, at their February session; and the following act was passed : —

" Whereas, for the preservation of the rights and liberties of the United States, it is necessary that the whole powers of government should be exerted in recruiting the Continental battalions; and whereas, His Excellency Gen. Washington hath enclosed to this state a proposal made to him by Brigadier General Varnum, to enlist into the two battalions, raising by this state, such slaves as should be willing to enter into the service; and whereas, history affords us frequent precedents of the wisest, the freest, and bravest nations having liberated their slaves, and enlisted them as soldiers to fight in defence of their country; and also whereas, the enemy, with a great force, have taken possession of the capital, and of a greater part of this state; and this state is obliged to raise a very considerable number of troops for its own immediate defence, whereby it is in a manner rendered impossible for this state to furnish recruits for the said two battalions, without adopting the said measure so recommended.

" It is voted and resolved, that every able-bodied negro, mulatto, or Indian man slave, in this state, may enlist into either of the said two battalions, to serve during the continuance of the present war with Great Britain.

" That every slave, so enlisting, shall be entitled to, and receive, all the bounties, wages, and encouragements, allowed by the Continental Congress, to any soldier enlisting into their service.

" It is further voted and resolved, that every slave, so enlisting, shall, upon his passing muster before Col. Christopher Greene, be immediately discharged from the service of his master or mistress, and be absolutely FREE, as though he had never been encumbered with any kind of servitude or slavery.

" And in case such slave shall, by sickness or otherwise, be rendered unable to maintain himself, he shall not be chargeable to his master or mistress; but shall be supported at the expense of the state.

" And whereas, slaves have been, by the laws, deemed the property of their owners, and therefore compensation ought to be made to the owners for the loss of their service, —

" It is further voted and resolved, that there be allowed, and paid by this state, to the owner, for every such slave so enlisting, a sum according to his worth; at a price not exceeding £120 for the most valuable slave; and in proportion for a slave of less value.

" Provided, the owner of said slave shall deliver up to the officer, who shall enlist him, the clothes of the said slave; or otherwise he shall not be entitled to said sum.

" And for settling and ascertaining the value of such slaves, —

" It is further voted and resolved, that a committee of five be appointed, to wit:

" One from each county; any three of whom, to be a quorum, to examine the slaves who shall be so enlisted, after they shall have passed muster, and to set a price upon each slave according to his value, as aforesaid.

" It is further voted and resolved, that upon any ablebodied negro, mulatto, or Indian slave, enlisting as aforesaid, the officer who shall so enlist him, after he shall have passed muster, as aforesaid, shall deliver a certificate thereof, to the master or mistress of said negro, mulatto, or Indian slave; which shall discharge him from the service of his said master or mistress, as aforesaid.

"It is further voted and resolved, that the committee who shall estimate the value of any slave, as aforesaid, shall give a certificate of the sum at which he may be valued, to the owner of said slave; and the general treasurer of this state is hereby empowered and directed to give unto the said owner of the said slave, his promissory note, as treasurer, as aforesaid, for the sum of money at which he shall be valued, as aforesaid, payable on demand, with interest at the rate of six per cent. per annum; and that said notes, which shall be so given, shall be paid with the money which is due to this state, and is expected from Congress; the money which has been borrowed out of the general treasury, by this Assembly, being first re-placed." [1]

This measure met with some opposition, but it was too weak to effect any thing. The best thing the minority could do was to enter a written protest.

"PROTEST AGAINST ENLISTING SLAVES TO SERVE IN THE ARMY.

"We, the subscribers, beg leave to dissent from the vote of the lower house, ordering a regiment of negroes to be raised for the Continental service, for the following reasons, viz.:

"1st. Because, in our opinion, there is not a sufficient number of negroes in the state, who would have an inclination to enlist, and would pass muster, to constitute a regiment; and raising several companies of blacks, would not answer the purposes intended; and therefore the attempt to constitute said regiment would prove abortive, and be a fruitless expense to the state.

"2d. The raising such a regiment, upon the footing proposed, would suggest an idea and produce an opinion in the world, that the state had purchased a band of slaves to be employed in the defence of the rights and liberties of our country, which is wholly inconsistent with those principles of liberty and constitutional government, for which we are so ardently contending; and would be looked upon by the neighboring states in a contemptible point of view, and not equal to their troops; and they would therefore be unwilling that we should have credit for them, as for an equal number of white troops; and would also give occasion to our enemies to suspect that we are not able to procure our own people to oppose them in the field; and to retort upon us the same kind of ridicule we so liberally bestowed upon them, on account of Dunmore's regiment of blacks; or possibly might suggest to them the idea of employing black regiments against us.

"3d. The expense of purchasing and enlisting said regiment, in the manner proposed, will vastly exceed the expenses of raising an equal number of white men; and at the same time will not have the like good effect.

"4th. Great difficulties and uneasiness will arise in purchasing the negroes

---

[1] R. I. Col. Recs., vol. viii. pp. 358-360.

from their masters; and many of the masters will not be satisfied with any prices allowed.

"JOHN NORTHUP,	GEORGE PIERCE,
"JAMES BABCOK, JR.,	SYLVESTER GARDNER,
"OTHNIEL GORTON,	SAMUEL BABCOCK." [1]

Upon the passage of the Act, Gov. Cooke hastened to notify Gen. Washington of the success of the project.

"PROVIDENCE, February 23d, 1778.

"SIR:— I have been favored with Your Excellency's letter of the [3d instant,][2] enclosing a proposal made to you by General Varnum, for recruiting the two Continental battalions raised by this state.

"I laid the letter before the General Assembly at their session, on the second Monday in this month; who, considering the pressing necessity of filling up the Continental army, and the peculiarly difficult circumstances of this state, which rendered it in a manner impossible to recruit our battalions in any other way, adopted the measure.

"Liberty is given to every effective slave to enter the service during the war; and upon his passing muster, he is absolutely made free, and entitled to all the wages, bounties and encouragements given by Congress to any soldier enlisting into their service. The masters are allowed at the rate of £120, for the most valuable slave; and in proportion to those of less value.

"The number of slaves in this state is not great; but it is generally thought that three hundred, and upwards, will be enlisted.

"I am, with great respect, sir,

"Your Excellency's most obedient, humble servant,

"NICHOLAS COOKE.

"TO GEN. WASHINGTON." [3]

Where masters had slaves in the army, they were paid an annual interest on the appraised value of the slaves, out of the public treasury, until the end of the military service of such slaves.[4] If owners presented certificates from the committee appointed to appraise enlisted Negroes, they were paid in part or in full in "Continental loan-office certificates." [5] The reader will remember, that it has been already shown that Negroes, both bond and free, were excluded from the militia of Massachusetts; and, furthermore, that both the Committee of Safety and the Provincial Congress had opposed the enlistment of Negroes. The first move in the colony to secure legal enlist-

---

[1] R. I. Col. Recs., vol. viii. p. 361.
[2] This is evidently a mistake, as Washington's letter was dated Jan. 2, as the reader will see.
[3] R. I. Col. Recs., vol. viii. p. 526.   [4] Ibid., p. 376.   [5] Ibid., p. 465.

ments and separate organizations of Colored troops was a communication to the General Assembly of Massachusetts, 3d of April, 1778.

"*To the Honorable Council, and House of Representatives, Boston, or at Roxbury.*

"HONORED GENTLEMEN, — At the opening of this campaign, our forces should be all ready, well equipped with arms and ammunition, with clothing sufficient to stand them through the campaign, their wages to be paid monthly, so as not to give the soldiery so much reason of complaint as it is the general cry from the soldiery amongst whom I am connected.

"We have accounts of large re-enforcements a-coming over this spring against us; and we are not so strong this spring, I think, as we were last. Great numbers have deserted; numbers have died, besides what is sick, and incapable of duty, or bearing arms in the field.

"I think it is highly necessary that some new augmentation should be added to the army this summer, — all the re-enforcements that can possibly be obtained. For now is the time to exert ourselves or never; for, if the enemy can get no further hold this campaign than they now possess, we [have] no need to fear much from them hereafter.

"A re-enforcement can quick be raised of two or three hundred men. Will your honors grant the liberty, and give me the command of the party? And what I refer to is negroes. We have divers of them in our service, mixed with white men. But I think it would be more proper to raise a body by themselves, than to have them intermixed with the white men; and their ambition would entirely be to outdo the white men in every measure that the fortune of war calls a soldier to endure. And I could rely with dependence upon them in the field of battle, or to any post that I was sent to defend with them; and they would think themselves happy could they gain their freedom by bearing a part of subduing the enemy that is invading our land, and clear a peaceful inheritance for their masters, and posterity yet to come, that they are now slaves to.

"The method that I would point out to your Honors in raising a detachment of negroes; — that a company should consist of a hundred, including commissioned officers; and that the commissioned officers should be white, and consist of one captain, one captain-lieutenant, two second lieutenants; the orderly sergeant white; and that there should be three sergeants black, four corporals black, two drums and two fifes black, and eighty-four rank and file. These should engage to serve till the end of the war, and then be free men. And I doubt not, that no gentleman that is a friend to his country will disapprove of this plan, or be against his negroes enlisting into the service to maintain the cause of freedom, and suppress the worse than savage enemies of our land.

"I beg your Honors to grant me the liberty of raising one company, if no more. It will be far better than to fill up our battalions with runaways and deserters from Gen. Burgoyne's army, who, after receiving clothing and the bounty, in general make it their business to desert from us. In the lieu thereof, if they are [of] a mind to serve in America, let them supply the families of those gentlemen where those negroes belong that should engage.

"I rest, relying on your Honor's wisdom in this matter, as it will be a quick way of having a re-enforcement to join the grand army, or to act in any other place that occasion shall require; and I will give my faith and assurance that I will act upon honor and fidelity, should I take the command of such a party as I have been describing.

"So I rest till your Honors shall call me; and am your very humble and obedient servant,

"THOMAS KENCH,

"In Col. Craft's Regiment of Artillery, now on Castle Island.

"CASTLE ISLAND, April 3, 1778."

A few days later he addressed another letter to the same body.

" *To the Honorable Council in Boston.*

"The letter I wrote before I heard of the disturbance with Col. Seares, Mr. Spear, and a number of other gentlemen, concerning the freedom of negroes, in Congress Street. It is a pity that riots should be committed on the occasion, as it is justifiable that negroes should have their freedom, and none amongst us be held as slaves, as freedom and liberty is the grand controversy that we are contending for; and I trust, under the smiles of Divine Providence, we shall obtain it, if all our minds can be united; and putting the negroes into the service will prevent much uneasiness, and give more satisfaction to those that are offended at the thoughts of their servants being free.

"I will not enlarge, for fear I should give offence; but subscribe myself

"Your faithful servant,

"THOMAS KENCH.

"CASTLE ISLAND, April 7, 1778." [1]

On the 11th of April the first letter was referred to a joint committee, with instructions "to consider the same, and report." On the 17th of April, "a resolution of the General Assembly of Rhode Island for enlisting Negroes in the public service " was referred to the same committee. In the Militia Act of 1775, the exceptions were, "Negroes, Indians, and mulattoes." By the act of May, 1776, providing for the re-enforcement of the American army, it was declared that, " Indians, negroes, and mulattoes, shall not be held to take up arms or procure any person to do it in their room." By another act, passed Nov. 14, 1776, looking toward the improvement of the army, "Negroes, Indians, and mulattoes " were excluded. During the year 1776 an order was issued for taking the census of all males above sixteen, but excepted "Negroes, Indians, and mulattoes." But after some reverses to the American army, Massachusetts passed a resolve on Jan. 6,

---

[1] MSS. Archives of Mass., vol. cxcix. pp. 80, 84.

1777, "for raising every seventh man to complete our quota," "without any exceptions, save the people called Quakers." This was the nearest Massachusetts ever got toward recognizing Negroes as soldiers. And on the 5th of March, 1778, Benjamin Goddard, for the selectmen, Committee of Safety, and militia officers of the town of Grafton, protested against the enlistment of the Negroes in his town.

It is not remarkable, in view of such a history, that Massachusetts should have hesitated to follow the advice of Thomas Kench. On the 28th of April, 1778, a law was draughted following closely the Rhode-Island Act. But no separate organization was ordered; and, hence, the Negroes served in white organizations till the close of the American Revolution.

There is nothing in the records of Virginia to show that there was ever any legal employment of Negroes as soldiers; but, from the following, it is evident that free Negroes *did* serve, and that there was no prohibition against them, providing they showed their certificates of freedom: —

"And whereas several negro slaves have deserted from their masters, and under pretence of being free men have enlisted as soldiers: For prevention whereof, *Be it enacted*, that it shall not be lawful for any recruiting officer within this commonwealth to enlist any negro or mulatto into the service of this or either of the United States, until such negro or mulatto shall produce a certificate from some justice of the peace for the county wherein he resides that he is a free man." [1]

Maryland employed Negroes as soldiers, and sent them into regiments with white soldiers. John Cadwalder of Annapolis, wrote Gen. Washington on the 5th of June, 1781, in reference to Negro soldiers, as follows: —

"We have resolved to raise, immediately, seven hundred and fifty negroes, to be incorporated with the other troops; and a bill is now almost completed." [2]

The legislature of New York, on the 20th of March, 1781, passed the following Act, providing for the raising of two regiments of blacks: —

"SECT. 6. — And be it further enacted by the authority aforesaid, that any person who shall deliver one or more of his or her able-bodied male slaves to any warrant officer, as aforesaid, to serve in either of the said regiments or

---

[1] Hening, vol. ix. 280.
[2] Sparks's Correspondence of the American Revolution, vol. iii. p. 331.

independent corps, and produce a certificate thereof, signed by any person authorized to muster and receive the men to be raised by virtue of this act, and produce such certificate to the Surveyor-General, shall, for every male slave so entered and mustered as aforesaid, be entitled to the location and grant of one right, in manner as in and by this act is directed; and shall be, and hereby is, discharged from any future maintenance of such slave, any law to the contrary notwithstanding: And such slave so entered as aforesaid, who shall serve for the term of three years or until regularly discharged, shall, immediately after such service or discharge, be, and is hereby declared to be, a free man of this State." [1]

The theatre of the war was now transferred from the Eastern to the Middle and Southern colonies. Massachusetts alone had furnished, and placed in the field, 67,907 men; while all the colonies south of Pennsylvania, put together, had furnished but 50,493, — or 8,414 *less* than the single colony of Massachusetts.[2] It was a difficult task to get the whites to enlist at the South. Up to 1779, nearly all the Negro soldiers had been confined to the New-England colonies. The enemy soon found out that the Southern colonies were poorly protected, and thither he moved. The Hon. Henry Laurens of South Carolina, an intelligent and observing patriot, wrote Gen. Washington on the 16th of March, 1779, concerning the situation at the South : —

"Our affairs [he wrote] in the Southern department are more favorable than we had considered them a few days ago; nevertheless, the country is greatly distressed, and will be more so unless further reinforcements are sent to its relief. Had we arms for three thousand such black men as I could select in Carolina, I should have no doubt of success in driving the British out of Georgia, and subduing East Florida, before the end of July." [3]

Gen. Washington sent the following conservative reply : —

"The policy of our arming slaves is in my opinion a moot point, unless the enemy set the example. For, should we begin to form battalions of them, I have not the smallest doubt, if the war is to be prosecuted, of their following us in it, and justifying the measure upon our own ground. The contest then must be, who can arm fastest. And where are our arms? Besides, I am not clear that a discrimination will not render slavery more irksome to those who remain in it. Most of the good and evil things in this life are judged of by comparison; and I fear a comparison in this case will be productive of much discontent in those, who are held in servitude. But, as this is a subject that has never employed much of my thoughts, these are no more than the first crude ideas that have struck me upon the occasion." [4]

---

[1] Laws of the State of New York, chap. xxxii. (March 20, 1781, 4th Session).
[2] The American Loyalist, p. 30, second edition.
[3] Sparks's Washington, vol. vi. p. 204, note.   [4] Ibid., vol. vi. p. 204.

The gifted and accomplished Alexander Hamilton, a member of Washington's military family, was deeply interested in the plan suggested by the Hon. Henry Laurens, whose son was on Washington's staff.   Col. John Laurens was the bearer of the following remarkable letter from Hamilton to John Jay, President of Congress.

" HEADQUARTERS, March 14, 1779.

"To JOHN JAY.

"DEAR SIR, — Col. Laurens, who will have the honor of delivering you this letter, is on his way to South Carolina, on a project which I think, in the present situation of affairs there, is a very good one, and deserves every kind of support and encouragement.   This is, to raise two, three, or four battalions of negroes, with the assistance of the government of that State, by contributions from the owners, in proportion to the number they possess.   If you should think proper to enter upon the subject with him, he will give you a detail of his plan.   He wishes to have it recommended by Congress to the State ; and, as an inducement, that they should engage to take those battalions into Continental pay.

"It appears to me, that an expedient of this kind, in the present state of Southern affairs, is the most rational that can be adopted, and promises very important advantages.   Indeed, I hardly see how a sufficient force can be collected in that quarter without it ; and the enemy's operations there are growing infinitely more serious and formidable.   I have not the least doubt that the negroes will make very excellent soldiers with proper management ; and I will venture to pronounce, that they cannot be put into better hands than those of Mr. Laurens.   He has all the zeal, intelligence, enterprise, and every other qualification, necessary to succeed in such an undertaking.   It is a maxim with some great military judges, that, with sensible officers, soldiers can hardly be too stupid ; and, on this principle, it is thought that the Russians would make the best troops in the world, if they were under other officers than their own. The King of Prussia is among the number who maintain this doctrine ; and has a very emphatic saying on the occasion, which I do not exactly recollect. I mention this because I hear it frequently objected to the scheme of embodying negroes, that they are too stupid to make soldiers.   This is so far from appearing to me a valid objection, that I think their want of cultivation (for their natural faculties are probably as good as ours), joined to that habit of subordination which they acquire from a life of servitude, will make them sooner become soldiers than our white inhabitants.   Let officers be men of sense and sentiment ; and the nearer the soldiers approach to machines, perhaps the better.

"I foresee that this project will have to combat much opposition from prejudice and self-interest.   The contempt we have been taught to entertain for the blacks makes us fancy many things that are founded neither in reason nor experience ; and an unwillingness to part with property of so valuable a kind will furnish a thousand arguments to show the impracticability or pernicious tendency of a scheme which requires such a sacrifice.   But it should be considered, that, if we do not make use of them in this way, the enemy probably will; and that the best way to counteract the temptations they will hold out will be to offer them ourselves. An essential part of the plan is to give them their freedom with their muskets. This will secure their fidelity, animate their courage, and, I believe, will have a good influence upon those who remain, by opening a door to their emancipation. This circumstance, I confess, has no small weight in inducing me to wish the success of the project; for the dictates of humanity, and true policy, equally interest me in favor of this unfortunate class of men.

"With the truest respect and esteem,

"I am, Sir, your most obedient servant,

"ALEX. HAMILTON." [1]

The condition of the Southern States became a matter of Congressional solicitude. The letter of Col. Hamilton was referred to a special committee on the 29th of March, 1779. It was represented that South Carolina especially was in great danger. The white population was small; and, while there were some in the militia service, it was thought necessary to keep as large a number of whites at home as possible. The fear of insurrection, the desertion [2] of Negroes to the enemy, and the exposed condition of her border, intensified the anxiety of the people. The only remedy seemed to lie in the employment of the more fiery spirits among the Negroes as the defenders of the rights and interests of the colonists. Congress rather hesitated to act, — it was thought that that body lacked the authority to order the enlistment of Negroes in the States, — and therefore recommended to "the states of South Carolina and Georgia, if they shall think the same expedient, to take measures immediately for raising three thousand able-bodied negroes." After some consideration the following plan was recommended by the special committee, and adopted : —

"IN CONGRESS, March 29, 1779.

"The Committee, consisting of Mr. Burke, Mr. Laurens, Mr. Armstrong, Mr. Wilson, and Mr. Dyer, appointed to take into consideration the circumstances of the Southern States, and the ways and means for their safety and defence, report, —

. . . .

"That the State of South Carolina, as represented by the delegates of the said State and by Mr. Huger, who has come hither, at the request of the Governor of the said State, on purpose to explain the particular circumstances thereof, is unable to make any effectual efforts with militia, by reason of the great proportion of citizens necessary to remain at home to prevent insurrections among the negroes, and to prevent the desertion of them to the enemy.

---

[1] Life of John Jay, by William Jay, vol. ii. pp. 31, 32.

[2] Ramsay, the historian of South Carolina says, "It has been computed by good judges, that, between 1775 and 1783, the State of South Carolina lost twenty-five thousand negroes."

" That the state of the country, and the great numbers of those people among them, expose the inhabitants to great danger from the endeavors of the enemy to excite them either to revolt or desert.

" That it is suggested by the delegates of the said State and by Mr. Huger, that a force might be raised in the said State from among the negroes, which would not only be formidable to the enemy from their numbers, and the discipline of which they would very readily admit, but would also lessen the danger from revolts and desertions, by detaching the most vigorous and enterprising from among the negroes.

" That, as this measure may involve inconveniences peculiarly affecting the States of South Carolina and Georgia, the Committee are of the opinion that the same should be submitted to the governing powers of the said States; and if the said powers shall judge it expedient to raise such a force, that the United States ought to defray the expense thereof: whereupon,

" Resolved, That it be recommended to the States of South Carolina and Georgia, if they shall think the same expedient, to take measures immediately for raising three thousand able-bodied negroes.

" That the said negroes be formed into separate corps, as battalions, according to the arrangements adopted for the main army, to be commanded by white commissioned and non-commissioned officers.

" That the commissioned officers be appointed by the said States.

" That the non-commissioned officers may, if the said States respectively shall think proper, be taken from among the non-commissioned officers and soldiers of the Continental battalions of the said States respectively.

" That the Governors of the said States, together with the commanding officer of the Southern army, be empowered to incorporate the several Continental battalions of their States with each other respectively, agreeably to the arrangement of the army, as established by the resolutions of May 27, 1778; and to appoint such of the supernumerary officers to command the said negroes as shall choose to go into that service.

" Resolved, That Congress will make provision for paying the proprietors of such negroes as shall be enlisted for the service of the United States during the war a full compensation for the property, at a rate not exceeding one thousand dollars for each active, able-bodied negro man of standard size, not exceeding thirty-five years of age, who shall be so enlisted and pass muster.

" That no pay or bounty be allowed to the said negroes; but that they be clothed and subsisted at the expense of the United States. [1]

" That every negro who shall well and faithfully serve as a soldier to the end of the present war, and shall then return his arms, be emancipated, and receive the sum of fifty dollars." [1]

Congress supplemented the foregoing measure by commissioning young Col. Laurens to carry forward the important work suggested.   The gallant young officer was indeed worthy of the following resolutions : —

---

[1] Secret Journals of Congress, vol. i pp. 107-110.

" Whereas John Laurens, Esq., who has heretofore acted as aide-de-camp to the Commander-in-chief, is desirous of repairing to South Carolina, with a design to assist in defence of the Southern States ; —

" *Resolved,* That a commission of lieutenant-colonel be granted to the said John Laurens, Esq." [1]

He repaired to South Carolina, and threw all his energies into his noble mission. That the people did not co-operate with him, is evidenced in the following extract from a letter he subsequently wrote to Col. Hamilton : —

" Ternant will relate to you how many violent struggles I have had between duty and inclination, — how much my heart was with you, while I appeared to be most actively employed here. But it appears to me, that I should be inexcusable in the light of a citizen, if I did not continue my utmost efforts for carrying the plan of the black levies into execution, while there remain the smallest hopes of success." [2]

The enemy was not slow in discovering the division of sentiment among the colonists as to the policy of employing Negroes as soldiers. And the suspicions of Gen. Washington, indicated to Henry Laurens, in a letter already quoted, were not groundless. On the 30th of June, 1779, Sir Henry Clinton issued a proclamation to the Negroes. It first appeared in " The Royal Gazette " of New York, on the 3d of July, 1779.

" By his Excellency Sir HENRY CLINTON, K.B. General and Commander-in-chief of all his Majesty's Forces within the Colonies laying on the Atlantic Ocean, from Nova Scotia to West-Florida, inclusive, &c., &c., &.

" PROCLAMATION.

" Whereas the enemy have adopted a practice of enrolling NEGROES among their Troops, I do hereby give notice That all NEGROES taken in arms, or upon any military Duty, shall be purchased for [*the public service at*] a stated Price ; the money to be paid to the Captors.

" But I do most strictly forbid any Person to sell or claim Right over any NEGROE, the property of a Rebel, who may take Refuge with any part of this Army : And I do promise to every NEGROE who shall desert the Rebel Standard, full security to follow within these Lines, any Occupation which he shall think proper.

" Given under my Hand, at Head-Quarters, PHILLIPSBURGH, the 30th day of June, 1779.

" H. CLINTON.
" By his Excellency's command,

" JOHN SMITH, *Secretary.*"

---

[1] Journals of Congress, vol. v. p. 123.   [2] Works of Hamilton, vol. i. pp. 114, 115.

The proclamation had effect. Many Negroes, weary of the hesitancy of the colonists respecting acceptance of their services, joined the ministerial army. On the 14th of February, 1780, Col. Laurens wrote Gen. Washington, from Charleston, S.C., as follows : —

" Private accounts say that General Prevost is left to command at Savannah ; that his troops consist of the Hessians and Loyalists that were there before, re-enforced by a corps of blacks and a detachment of savages. It is generally reported that Sir Henry Clinton commands the present expedition." [1]

Lord Cornwallis also issued a proclamation, offering protection to all Negroes who should seek his command. But the treatment he gave them, as narrated by Mr. Jefferson in a letter to Dr. Gordon, a few years after the war, was extremely cruel, to say the least.

" Lord Cornwallis destroyed all my growing crops of corn and tobacco; he burned all my barns, containing the same articles of the last year, having first taken what corn he wanted; he used, as was to be expected, all my stock of cattle, sheep, and hogs, for the sustenance of his army, and carried off all the horses capable of service; of those too young for service he cut the throats; and he burned all the fences on the plantation, so as to leave it an absolute waste. *He carried off also about thirty slaves. Had this been to give them freedom, he would have done right;* but it was to consign them to inevitable death from the small-pox and putrid fever, then raging in his camp. This I knew afterwards to be the fate of twenty-seven of them. I never had news of the remaining three, but presume they shared the same fate. When I say that Lord Cornwallis did all this, I do not mean that he carried about the torch in his own hands, but that it was all done under his eye; the situation of the house, in which he was, commanding a view of every part of the plantation, so that he must have seen every fire. I relate these things on my own knowledge, in a great degree, as I was on the ground soon after he left it. He treated the rest of the neighborhood somewhat in the same style, but not with that spirit of total extermination with which he seemed to rage over my possessions. Wherever he went, the dwelling-houses were plundered of every thing which could be carried off. Lord Cornwallis's character in England would forbid the belief that he shared in the plunder; but that his table was served with the plate thus pillaged from private houses, can be proved by many hundred eye-witnesses. From an estimate I made at that time, on the best information I could collect, I suppose *the State of Virginia lost, under Lord Cornwallis's hand, that year, about thirty thousand slaves; and that, of these, twenty-seven thousand died of the small-pox and camp-fever; and the rest were partly sent to the West Indies, and exchanged for rum, sugar, coffee, and fruit; and partly sent to New York, from whence they went, at the peace, either to Nova Scotia*

---

[1] Sparks's Correspondence of the American Revolution, vol. ii. p. 402.

or to England. From this last place, I believe, they have been lately sent to Africa. History will never relate the horrors committed by the British Army in the Southern States of America." [1]

Col. Laurens was called from the South, and despatched to France on an important mission in 1780. But the effort to raise Negro troops in the South was not abandoned.

On the 13th of March, 1780, Gen. Lincoln, in a letter to Gov. Rutledge of South Carolina, dated at Charleston, urged the importance of raising a Negro regiment at once. He wrote, —

"Give me leave to add once more, that I think the measure of raising a black corps a necessary one; that I have great reason to believe, if permission is given for it, that many men would soon be obtained. I have repeatedly urged this matter, not only because Congress have recommended it, and because it thereby becomes my duty to attempt to have it executed, but because my own mind suggests the utility and importance of the measure, as the safety of the town makes it necessary."

James Madison saw in the emancipation and arming of the Negroes the only solution of the vexatious Southern problem. On the 20th of November, 1780, he wrote Joseph Jones as follows : —

"Yours of the 18th came yesterday. I am glad to find the Legislature persist in their resolution to recruit their line of the army for the war; though, without deciding on the expediency of the mode under their consideration, would it not be as well to liberate and make soldiers at once of the blacks themselves, as to make them instruments for enlisting white soldiers? It would certainly be more consonant with the principles of liberty, which ought never to be lost sight of in a contest for liberty: and, with white officers and a majority of white soldiers, no imaginable danger could be feared from themselves, as there certainly could be none from the effect of the example on those who should remain in bondage; experience having shown that a freedman immediately loses all attachment and sympathy with his former fellow-slaves." [2]

The struggle went on between Tory and Whig, between traitor and patriot, between selfishness and the spirit of noble consecration to the righteous cause of the Americans. Gen. Greene wrote from North Carolina on the 28th of February, 1781, to Gen. Washington as follows : —

"The enemy have ordered two regiments of negroes to be immediately embodied, and are drafting a great proportion of the young men of that State [South Carolina], to serve during the war." [3]

---

[1] Jefferson's Works, vol. ii. p. 426.   [2] Madison Papers, p. 68.
[3] Sparks's Correspondence of the American Revolution, vol. iii. p. 246.

Upon his return to America, Col. Laurens again espoused his favorite and cherished plan of securing black levies for the South. But surrounded and hindered by the enemies of the country he so dearly loved, and for the honor and preservation of which he gladly gave his young life, his plans were unsuccessful. In two letters to Gen. Washington, a few months before he fell fighting for his country, he gave an account of the trials that beset his path, which he felt led to honorable duty. The first bore date of May 19, 1782.

"The plan which brought me to this country was urged with all the zeal which the subject inspired, both in our Privy Council and Assembly; but the single voice of reason was drowned by the howlings of a triple-headed monster, in which prejudice, avarice, and pusillanimity were united. It was some degree of consolation to me, however, to perceive that truth and philosophy had gained some ground; the suffrages in favor of the measure being twice as numerous as on a former occasion. Some hopes have been lately given me from Georgia; but I fear, when the question is put, we shall be outvoted there with as much disparity as we have been in this country.

. . . .

"I earnestly desire to be where any active plans are likely to be executed, and to be near your Excellency on all occasions in which my services can be acceptable. The pursuit of an object which, I confess, is a favorite one with me, because I always regarded the interests of this country and those of the Union as intimately connected with it, has detached me more than once from your family; but those sentiments of veneration and attachment with which your Excellency has inspired me, keep me always near you, with the sincerest and most zealous wishes for a continuance of your happiness and glory." [1]

The second was dated June 12, 1782, and breathes a despondent air : —

"The approaching session of the Georgia Legislature, and the encouragement given me by Governor Howley, who has a decisive influence in the counsels of that country, induce me to remain in this quarter for the purpose of taking new measures on the subject of our black levies. The arrival of Colonel Baylor, whose seniority entitles him to the command of the light troops, affords me ample leisure for pursuing the business in person; and I shall do it with all the tenacity of a man making a last effort on so interesting an occasion." [2]

Washington's reply showed that he, too, had lost faith in the patriotism of the citizens of the South to a great degree. He wrote his faithful friend : —

"I must confess that I am not at all astonished at the failure of your plan. That spirit of freedom, which, at the commencement of this contest, would

---

[1] Sparks's Correspondence of the American Revolution, vol. iii. p. 506.   [2] Ibid., p. 515.

have gladly sacrificed every thing to the attainment of its object, has long since subsided, and every selfish passion has taken its place. It is not the public but private interest which influences the generality of mankind; nor can the Americans any longer boast an exception. Under these circumstances, it would rather have been surprising if you had succeeded; nor will you, I fear, have better success in Georgia." [1]

Although the effort of the Legislature of Connecticut to authorize the enlistment of Negroes in 1777 had failed, many Negroes, as has been shown, served in regiments from that State; and a Negro company was organized. When white officers refused to serve in it, the gallant David Humphreys volunteered his services, and became the captain.

"In November, 1782, he was, by resolution of Congress, commissioned as a Lieutenant-Colonel, with order that his commission should bear date from the 23d of June, 1780, when he received his appointment as aide-de-camp to the Commander-in-chief. He had, when in active service, given the sanction of his name and influence in the establishment of a company of colored infantry, attached to Meigs', afterwards Butler's, regiment, in the Connecticut line. He continued to be the nominal captain of that company until the establishment of peace." [2]

The following was the roster of his company : —

"*Captain,*
DAVID HUMPHREYS.

Privates,

Jack Arabus,	Brister Baker,	John Ball,
John Cleveland,	Cæsar Bagdon,	John McLean,
Phineas Strong,	Gamaliel Terry,	Jesse Vose,
Ned Fields,	Lent Munson,	Daniel Bradley,
Isaac Higgins,	Heman Rogers,	Sharp Camp,
Lewis Martin,	Job Cæsar,	Jo Otis,
Cæsar Chapman,	John Rogers,	James Dinah,
Peter Mix,	Ned Freedom,	Solomon Sowtice,
Philo Freeman,	Ezekiel Tupham,	Peter Freeman,
Hector Williams,	Tom Freeman,	Cato Wilbrow,
Juba Freeman,	Congo Zado,	Cuff Freeman,
Cato Robinson,	Peter Gibbs,	Juba Dyer,
Prince George,	Prince Johnson,	Andrew Jack,
Prince Crosbee,	Alex. Judd,	Peter Morando,
Shubael Johnson,	Pomp Liberty,	Peter Lion,
Tim Cæsar,	Cuff Liberty,	Sampson Cuff,
Jack Little,	Pomp Cyrus,	Dick Freedom,
Bill Sowers,	Harry Williams,	Pomp McCuff." [3]
Dick Violet,	Sharp Rogers,	

---

[1] Sparks's Washington, vol. viii. pp. 322, 323.
[2] Biographical Sketch in " The National Portrait Gallery of Distinguished Americans."
[3] Colored Patriots of the Revolution, p. 134.

But notwithstanding the persistent and bitter opposition to the employment of slaves, from the earliest hours of the Revolutionary War till its close, Negroes, bond and free, were in all branches of the service. It is to be regretted that the exact number cannot be known. Adjutant-Gen. Scammell made the following official return of Negro soldiers in the main army, under Washington's immediate command, two months after the battle of Monmouth; but the Rhode-Island regiment, the Connecticut, New York, and New-Hampshire troops are not mentioned. Incomplete as it is, it is nevertheless official, and therefore correct as far as it goes.

RETURN OF NEGROES IN THE ARMY, 24TH AUG., 1778.

BRIGADES.	PRESENT.	SICK ABSENT.	ON COMMAND.	TOTAL.
North Carolina . .	42	10	6	58
Woodford . . .	36	3	1	40
Muhlenburg . . .	64	26	8	98
Smallwood . . .	20	3	1	24
2d Maryland . . .	43	15	2	60
Wayne	2	—	—	2
2d Pennsylvania .	[33]	[1]	[1]	[35]
Clinton	33	2	4	39
Parsons	117	12	19	148
Huntington . . .	56	2	4	62
Nixon	26	—	1	27
Patterson	64	13	12	89
Late Learned . .	34	4	8	46
Poor	16	7	4	27
Total	586	98	71	755

ALEX. SCAMMELL, *Adj.-Gen.*[1]

It is gratifying to record the fact, that the Negro was enrolled as a soldier in the war of the American Revolution. What he did will be recorded in the following chapter.

---

[1] This return was discovered by the indefatigable Dr. George H. Moore. It is the only document of the kind in existence.

CHAPTER XXVII.

NEGROES AS SOLDIERS.

1775–1783.

THE NEGRO AS A SOLDIER. — BATTLE OF BUNKER HILL. — GALLANTRY OF NEGRO SOLDIERS. — PETER
SALEM, THE INTREPID BLACK SOLDIER. — BUNKER-HILL MONUMENT. — THE NEGRO SALEM POOR
DISTINGUISHES HIMSELF BY DEEDS OF DESPERATE VALOR. — CAPTURE OF GEN. LEE. — CAPTURE
OF GEN. PRESCOTT. — BATTLE OF RHODE ISLAND. — COL. GREENE COMMANDS A NEGRO REGI-
MENT. — MURDER OF COL. GREENE IN 1781. — THE VALOR OF THE NEGRO SOLDIERS.

A S soldiers the Negroes went far beyond the most liberal
expectations of their stanchest friends. Associated with
white men, many of whom were superior gentlemen, and
nearly all of whom were brave and enthusiastic, the Negro soldiers
of the American army became worthy of the cause they fought to
sustain. Col. Alexander Hamilton had said, "*their natural faculties are as good as ours;*" and the assertion was supported by
their splendid behavior on all the battle-fields of the Revolution.
Endowed by nature with a poetic element, faithful to trusts, abiding in friendships, bound by the golden threads of attachment to
places and persons, enthusiastic in personal endeavor, sentimental
and chivalric, they made hardy and intrepid soldiers. The daring,
boisterous enthusiasm with which they sprang to arms disarmed
racial prejudice of its sting, and made friends of foes.

Their cheerfulness in camp, their celerity in the performance
of fatigue-duty, their patient endurance of heat and cold, hunger
and thirst, and their bold efficiency in battle, made them welcome
companions everywhere they went. The officers who frowned at
their presence in the army at first, early learned, from experience,
that they were the equals of any troops in the army for severe
service in camp, and excellent fighting in the field.

The battle of Bunker Hill was one of the earliest and most
important of the Revolution. Negro soldiers were in the action
of the 17th of June, 1775, and nobly did their duty. Speaking of
this engagement, Bancroft says, —

"Nor should history forget to record that, as in the army at Cambridge, so also in this gallant band, the free negroes of the colony had their representatives." [1]

Two Negro soldiers especially distinguished themselves, and rendered the cause of the colonists great service. Major Pitcairn was a gallant officer of the British marines. He led the charge against the redoubt, crying exultingly, "The day is ours!" His sudden appearance and his commanding air at first startled the men immediately before him. They neither answered nor fired, probably not being exactly certain what was next to be done. At this critical moment, a Negro soldier stepped forward, and, aiming his musket directly at the major's bosom, blew him through.[2] Who was this intrepid black soldier, who at a critical moment stepped to the front, and with certain aim brought down the incarnate enemy of the colonists? What was his name, and whence came he to battle? His name was Peter Salem, a private in Col. Nixon's regiment of the Continental Army.

"He was born in Framingham [Massachusetts], and was held as a slave, probably until he joined the army; whereby, if not before, he became free. . . . Peter served faithfully as a soldier, during the war." [3]

Perhaps Salem was then a slave: probably he thought of the chains and stripes from whence he had come, of the liberty to be purchased in the ordeals of war, and felt it his duty to show himself worthy of his position as an American soldier. He proved that his shots were as effective as those of a white soldier, and that he was not wanting in any of the elements that go to make up the valiant soldier. Significant indeed that a Negro was the first to open the hostilities between Great Britain and the colonies, — the first to pour out his blood as a precious libation on the altar of a people's rights; and that here, at Bunker Hill, when the crimson and fiery tide of battle seemed to be running hard against the small band of colonists, a Negro soldier's steady musket brought down the haughty form of the arch-rebel, and turned victory to the weak! England had loaded the African with chains, and doomed him to perpetual bondage in the North-American colonies; and when she came to forge political chains, in the flames of fratricidal war, for an English-speaking people, the Negro, whom she had grievously wronged, was first to meet her soldiers, and welcome them to a hospitable grave.

---

[1] Bancroft, vol. vii., 6th ed., p. 421.   [2] An Historical Research, p. 93.   [3] History of Leicester, p. 267.

Bunker-hill Monument has a charm for loyal Americans ; and the Negro, too, may gaze upon its enduring magnificence. It commemorates the deeds, not of any particular soldier, but all who stood true to the principles of equal rights and free government on that memorable " 17th of June."

"No name adorns the shaft; but ages hence, though our alphabets may become as obscure as those which cover the monuments of Nineveh and Babylon, its uninscribed surface (on which monarchs might be proud to engrave their titles) will perpetuate the memory of the 17th of June. It is the monument of the day, of the event, of the battle of Bunker Hill; of all the brave men who shared its perils, — alike of Prescott and Putnam and Warren, the chiefs of the day, and the colored man, Salem, who is reported to have shot the gallant Pitcairn, as he mounted the parapet. Cold as the clods on which it rests, still as the silent heavens to which it soars, it is yet vocal, eloquent, in their undivided praise." [1]

The other Negro soldier who won for himself rare fame and distinguished consideration in the action at Bunker Hill was Salem Poor. Delighted with his noble bearing, his superior officers could not refrain from calling the attention of the civil authorities to the facts that came under their personal observation. The petition that set forth his worth as a brave soldier is still preserved in the manuscript archives of Massachusetts : —

" *To the Honorable General Court of the Massachusetts Bay.*

"The subscribers beg leave to report to your Honorable House (which we do in justice to the character of so brave a man), that, under our own observation, we declare that a negro man called Salem Poor, of Col. Frye's regiment, Capt. Ames' company, in the late battle at Charlestown, behaved like an experienced officer, as well as an excellent soldier. To set forth particulars of his conduct would be tedious. We would only beg leave to say, in the person of this said negro centres a brave and gallant soldier. The reward due to so great and distinguished a character, we submit to the Congress.

"Jona. Brewer, Col.	Eliphalet Bodwell, Sgt.
Thomas Nixon, Lt.-Col.	Josiah Foster, Lieut.
Wm. Prescott, Colo.	Ebenr. Varnum, 2d Lieut.
Ephm. Corey, Lieut.	Wm. Hudson Ballard, Cpt.
Joseph Baker, Lieut.	William Smith, Cap.
Joshua Row, Lieut.	John Morton, Sergt. [?]
Jonas Richardson, Capt.	Lieut. Richard Welsh.

"Cambridge, Dec. 5, 1775.

" In Council, Dec. 21, 1775. — Read, and sent down.

"Perez Morton, *Dep'y Sec'y.*" [2]

---

[1] Orations and Speeches of Everett, vol. iii. p. 529.
[2] MS. Archives of Massachusetts, vol. clxxx. p. 241.

How many other Negro soldiers behaved with cool and determined valor at Bunker Hill, it is not possible to know. But many were there : they did their duty as faithful men, and their achievements are the heritage of the free of all colors under our one flag. Col. Trumbull, an artist as well as a soldier, who was stationed at Roxbury, witnessed the engagement from that elevation. Inspired by the scene, when it was yet fresh in his mind, he painted the historic picture of the battle in 1786. He represents several Negroes in good view, while conspicuous in the foreground is the redoubtable Peter Salem. Some subsequent artists — mere copyists — have sought to consign this black hero to oblivion, but 'tis vain. Although the monument at Bunker Hill "does not bear his name, the pencil of the artist has portrayed the scene, the pen of the impartial historian has recorded his achievement, and the voice of the eloquent orator has resounded his valor."

Major Samuel Lawrence "at one time commanded a company whose rank and file were all Negroes, of whose courage, military discipline, and fidelity he always spoke with respect. On one occasion, being out reconnoitring with this company, he got so far in advance of his command, that he was surrounded, and on the point of being made prisoner by the enemy. The men, soon discovering his peril, rushed to his rescue, and fought with the most determined bravery till that rescue was effectually secured. He never forgot this circumstance, and ever after took especial pains to show kindness and hospitality to any individual of the colored race who came near his dwelling." [1]

Gen. Lee, of the American army, was captured by Col. Harcourt of the British army. It was regarded as a very distressing event ; and preparations were made to capture a British officer of the same rank, so an exchange could be effected. Col. Barton of the Rhode-Island militia, a brave and cautious officer, was charged with the capture of Major-Gen. Prescott, commanding the royal army at Newport. On the night of the 9th of July, 1777, Col. Barton, with forty men, in two boats with muffled oars, evaded the enemy's boats, and, being taken for the sentries at Prescott's headquarters, effected that officer's capture — a Negro taking him. The exploit was bold and successful.

" They landed about five miles from Newport, and three-quarters of a mile from the house, which they approached cautiously, avoiding the main guard,

---

[1] Memoir of Samuel Lawrence, by Rev. S. K. Lothrop, D.D., pp. 8, 9.

which was at some distance. *The Colonel went foremost, with a stout, active negro close behind him, and another at a small distance; the rest followed so as to be near, but not seen.*

"A single sentinel at the door saw and hailed the Colonel; he answered by exclaiming against, and inquiring for, rebel prisoners, but kept slowly advancing. The sentinel again challenged him, and required the countersign. He said he had not the countersign, but amused the sentry by talking about rebel prisoners, and still advancing till he came within reach of the bayonet, which, he presenting, the Colonel suddenly struck aside and seized him. He was immediately secured, and ordered to be silent, on pain of instant death. *Meanwhile, the rest of the men surrounding the house, the negro, with his head, at the second stroke forced a passage into it, and then into the landlord's apartment. The landlord at first refused to give the necessary intelligence; but, on the prospect of present death he pointed to the General's chamber, which being instantly opened by the negro's head, the Colonel calling the General by name, told him he was a prisoner.*" [1]

Another account was published by a surgeon of the army, and is given here : —

"*Albany*, Aug. 3, 1777. — The pleasing information is received here that Lieut.-Col. Barton, of the Rhode-Island militia, planned a bold exploit for the purpose of surprising and taking Major-Gen. Prescott, the commanding officer of the royal army at Newport. Taking with him, in the night, about forty men, in two boats, with oars muffled, he had the address to elude the vigilance of the ships-of-war and guard-boats : and, having arrived undiscovered at the quarters of Gen. Prescott, they were taken for the sentinels; and the general was not alarmed till his captors were at the door of his lodging-chamber, which was fast closed. *A negro man, named Prince, instantly thrust his beetle head through the panel door, and seized his victim while in bed.* . . . This event is extremely honorable to the enterprising spirit of Col. Barton, and is considered as ample retaliation for the capture of Gen. Lee by Col. Harcourt. The event occasions great joy and exultation, as it puts in our possession an officer of equal rank with Gen. Lee, by which means an exchange may be obtained. Congress resolved that an elegant sword should be presented to Col. Barton for his brave exploit." [2]

Col. Barton evidently entertained great respect for the valor and trustworthiness of the Negro soldier whom he made the chief actor in a most hazardous undertaking. It was the post of honor ; and the Negro soldier Prince discharged the duty assigned him in a manner that was entirely satisfactory to his superior officer, and crowned as one of the most daring and brilliant *coups d'état* of the American Revolution.

---

[1] Frank Moore's Diary of the American Revolution, vol. i. p. 468.
[2] Thatcher's Military Journal, p. 87.

The battle of Rhode Island, fought on the 29th of August, 1778, was one of the severest of the Revolution. Newport was laid under siege by the British. Their ships-of-war moved up the bay on the morning of the action, and opened a galling fire upon the exposed right flank of the American army ; while the Hessian columns, stretching across a chain of the "highland," attempted to turn Gen. Greene's flank, and storm the advanced redoubt. The heavy cannonading that had continued since nine in the morning was now accompanied by heavy skirmishing ; and the action began to be general all along the lines. The American army was disposed in three lines of battle ; the first extended in front of their earthworks on Butt's Hill, the second in rear of the hill, and the third as reserve a half-mile in the rear of the advance line. At ten o'clock the battle was at white heat. The British vessels kept up a fire that greatly annoyed the Americans, but imparted courage to the Hessians and British infantry. At length the foot columns massed, and swept down the slopes of Anthony's Hill with the impetuosity of a whirlwind. But the American columns received them with the intrepidity and coolness of veterans. The loss of the enemy was fearful.

"Sixty were found dead in one spot. At another, thirty Hessians were buried in one grave. Major-Gen. Greene commanded on the right. Of the four brigades under his immediate command, Varnum's, Glover's, Cornell's and Greene's, all suffered severely, but Gen. Varnum's perhaps the most. A third time the enemy, with desperate courage and increased strength, attempted to assail the redoubt, and would have carried it but for the timely aid of two continental battalions despatched by Sullivan to support his almost exhausted troops. It was in repelling these furious onsets, that the newly raised black regiment, under Col. Greene, distinguished itself by deeds of desperate valor. Posted behind a thicket in the valley, they three times drove back the Hessians who charged repeatedly down the hill to dislodge them; and so determined were the enemy in these successive charges, that the day after the battle the Hessian colonel, upon whom this duty had devolved, applied to exchange his command and go to New York, because he dared not lead his regiment again to battle, lest his men should shoot him for having caused them so much loss." [1]

A few years later the Marquis de Chastellux, writing of this regiment, said, —

"The 5th [of January, 1781] I did not set out till eleven, although I had thirty miles' journey to Lebanon. At the passage to the ferry, I met with a detachment of the Rhode-Island regiment, the same corps we had with us

---

[1] Arnold's History of Rhode Island, vol. ii. pp. 427, 428.

all the last summer, but they have since been recruited and clothed. The greatest part of them are negroes or mulattoes; but they are strong, robust men, and those I have seen had a very good appearance." [1]

On the 14th of May, 1781, the gallant Col. Greene was surprised and murdered at Point's Bridge, New York; but it was not effected until his brave black soldiers had been cut to pieces in defending their leader. It was one of the most touching and beautiful incidents of the war, and illustrates the self-sacrificing devotion of Negro soldiers to the cause of American liberty.

At a meeting of the Congregational and Presbyterian Anti-Slavery Society, at Francestown, N.H., the Rev. Dr. Harris, himself a Revolutionary soldier, spoke thus complimentarily of the Rhode-Island Negro regiment: —

"Yes, a regiment of *negroes*, fighting for *our* liberty and independence, — not a white man among them but the officers, — stationed in this same dangerous and responsible position. Had they been unfaithful, or given away before the enemy, all would have been lost. *Three times in succession* were they attacked, with most desperate valor and fury, by well disciplined and veteran troops, and *three times* did they successfully repel the assault, and thus preserve our army from capture. They fought through the war. They were brave, hardy troops. They helped to gain our liberty and independence."

From the opening to the closing scene of the Revolutionary War; from the death of Pitcairn to the surrender of Cornwallis; on many fields of strife and triumph, of splendid valor and republican glory; from the hazy dawn of unequal and uncertain conflict, to the bright morn of profound peace; through and out of the fires of a great war that gave birth to a new, a grand republic, — the Negro soldier fought his way to undimmed glory, and made for himself a magnificent record in the annals of American history. Those annals have long since been committed to the jealous care of the loyal citizens of the Republic black men fought so heroically to snatch from the iron clutches of Britain.

---

[1] Chastellux' Travels, vol. i. p. 454; London, 1789.

CHAPTER XXVIII.

LEGAL STATUS OF THE NEGRO DURING THE REVOLUTION.

1775–1783.

THE NEGRO WAS CHATTEL OR REAL PROPERTY. — HIS LEGAL STATUS DURING HIS NEW RELATION AS A SOLDIER. — RESOLUTION INTRODUCED IN THE MASSACHUSETTS HOUSE OF REPRESENTATIVES TO PREVENT THE SELLING OF TWO NEGROES CAPTURED UPON THE HIGH SEAS. — THE CONTINENT-AL CONGRESS APPOINTS A COMMITTEE TO CONSIDER WHAT SHOULD BE DONE WITH NEGROES TAKEN BY VESSELS OF WAR IN THE SERVICE OF THE UNITED COLONIES. — CONFEDERATION OF THE NEW STATES. — SPIRITED DEBATE IN CONGRESS RESPECTING THE DISPOSAL OF RECAPTURES. — THE SPANISH SHIP "VICTORIA" CAPTURES AN ENGLISH VESSEL HAVING ON BOARD THIRTY-FOUR NEGROES TAKEN FROM SOUTH CAROLINA. — THE NEGROES RECAPTURED BY VESSELS BELONGING TO THE STATE OF MASSACHUSETTS. — THEY ARE DELIVERED TO THOMAS KNOX, AND CONVEYED TO CASTLE ISLAND. — COL. PAUL REVERE HAS CHARGE OF THE SLAVES ON CASTLE ISLAND. — MASSACHUSETTS PASSES A LAW PROVIDING FOR THE SECURITY, SUPPORT, AND EXCHANGE OF PRISONERS BROUGHT INTO THE STATE. — GEN. HANCOCK RECEIVES A LETTER FROM THE GOV-ERNOR OF SOUTH CAROLINA RESPECTING THE DETENTION OF NEGROES. — IN THE PROVINCIAL ARTICLES BETWEEN THE UNITED STATES OF AMERICA AND HIS BRITANNIC MAJESTY, NEGROES WERE RATED AS PROPERTY. — AND ALSO IN THE DEFINITE TREATY OF PEACE BETWEEN THE UNITED STATES OF AMERICA AND HIS BRITANNIC MAJESTY. — AND ALSO IN THE TREATY OF PEACE OF 1814, BETWEEN HIS BRITANNIC MAJESTY AND THE UNITED STATES, NEGROES WERE DESIGNATED AS PROPERTY. — GEN. WASHINGTON'S LETTER TO BRIG.-GEN. RUFUS PUTNAM IN REGARD TO A NEGRO IN HIS REGIMENT CLAIMED BY MR. HOBBY. — ENLISTMENT IN THE ARMY DID NOT ALWAYS WORK A PRACTICAL EMANCIPATION.

WHEN the Revolutionary War began, the legal status of the Negro slave was clearly defined in the courts of all the colonies. He was either chattel or real property. The question naturally arose as to his legal status during his new rela-tion as a soldier. Could he be taken as property, or as a prisoner of war? Was he booty, or was he entitled to the usage of civil-ized warfare, — a freeman, and therefore to be treated as such?

The Continental Congress, Nov. 25, *1775,* passed a resolution recommending the several colonial legislatures to establish courts that should give jurisdiction to courts, already in existence, to dispose of "cases of capture." In fact, and probably in law, Congress exercised power in cases of appeal. Moreover, Congress had prescribed a rule for the distribution of prizes. But, curiously enough, Massachusetts, in 1776, passed an Act declaring, that, in case captures were made by the forces of the colony, the local authorities should have complete jurisdiction in their distribution; but, when prizes or captives were taken upon colonial territory by the forces of the United Colonies, the distributions should be made in accordance with the laws of Congress. This was but a single illustration of the divided sovereignty of a crude government. That there was need of a uniform law upon this question, there could be no doubt, especially in a war of the magnitude of the one that was then being waged.

On the 13th of September, 1776, a resolution was introduced into the Massachusetts House of Representatives, "to prevent the sale of two negro men lately brought into this state, as prisoners taken on the high seas, and advertised to be sold at Salem, the 17th inst., by public auction." [1] The resolve in full is here given: —

"IN THE HOUSE OF REPRESENTATIVES, SEPT. 13, 1776:

"WHEREAS this House is credibly informed that two negro men lately brought into this State as prisoners taken on the High Seas are advertised to be sold at Salem, the 17th instant, by public auction,

"*Resolved*, That the selling and enslaving the human species is a direct violation of the natural rights alike vested in all men by their Creator, and utterly inconsistent with the avowed principles on which this and the other United States have carried their struggle for liberty even to the last appeal, and therefore, that all persons connected with the said negroes be and they hereby are forbidden to sell them or in any manner to treat them otherways than is already ordered for the treatment of prisoners of war taken in the same vessell or others in the like employ and if any sale of the said negroes shall be made, it is hereby declared null and void.

"Sent up for concurrence.

"SAML. FREEMAN, *Speaker*, P. T.

"IN COUNCIL, Sept. 14, 1776. Read and concurred as taken into a new draught. Sent down for concurrence.

"JOHN AVERY, *Dpy. Secy.*

"IN THE HOUSE OF REPRESENTATIVES, Sept. 14, 1776. Read and non-concurred, and the House adhere to their own vote. Sent up for concurrence.

"J. WARREN, *Speaker.*

"IN COUNCIL, Sept. 16, 1776. Read and concurred as now taken into a new draft. Sent down for concurrence.

"JOHN AVERY, *Dpy. Secy.*

---

[1] Felt says, in History of Salem, vol. ii. p. 278: "Sept. 17 [1776]. At this date two slaves, taken on board of a prize, were to have been sold here; but the General Court forbid the sale, and ordered such prisoners to be treated like all others."

"In the House of Representatives, Sept. 16, 1779. Read and concurred.

"J. Warren, *Speaker.*

"Consented to.

"Jer. Powell,	Jabez Fisher,
W. Sever,	B. White,
B. Greenleaf,	Moses Gill,
Caleb Cushing,	Dan'l Hopkins,
B. Chadbourn,	Benj. Austin,
John Whetcomb,	Wm. Phillips,
Eldad Taylor,	D. Sewall,
S. Holten,	Dan'l Hopkins."

On the Journal of the House, p. 106, appears the following record : —

"David Sewall, Esq., brought down the resolve which passed the House yesterday, forbidding the sale of two negroes, with the following vote of Council thereon, viz.: *In Council*, Sept. 14, 1776. Read and concurred, as taken into a new draught. Sent down for concurrence. Read and non-concurred, and the House adhere to their own vote. Sent up for concurrence."

The resolve, as it originally appeared, was dragged through a tedious debate, non-concurred in by the House, recommitted, remodelled, and sent back, when it finally passed.

"LXXXIII. Resolve forbidding the sale of two Negroes brought in as Prisoners; Passed September 14, [16th,] 1776.

"Whereas this Court is credibly informed that two Negro Men lately taken on the High Seas, on board the sloop *Hannibal*, and brought into this State as Prisoners, are advertized to be sold at *Salem*, the 17th instant, by public Auction:

"*Resolved*, That all Persons concerned with the said Negroes be, and they are hereby forbidden to sell them, or in any manner to treat them otherwise than is already ordered for the Treatment of Prisoners taken in like manner; and if any Sale of the said Negroes shall be made it is hereby declared null and void; and that whenever it shall appear that any Negroes are taken on the High Seas and brought as Prisoners into this State, they shall not be allowed to be Sold, nor treated any otherwise than as Prisoners are ordered to be treated who are taken in like Manner." [1]

It looked like a new resolve. The pronounced and advanced sentiment in favor of the equal rights of all created beings had been taken out; and it appeared now as a war measure, warranted upon military policy. This is the only chaplet that the most

---

[1] Resolves, p. 14. Quoted by Dr. Moore from the original documents.

devout friends of Massachusetts can weave out of her acts on the Negro problem during the colonial period, to place upon her brow. It attracted wide-spread and deserved attention.

During the following month, on the 14th of October, 1776, the Continental Congress appointed a special committee, Messrs. Lee, Wilson, and Hall, "to consider what is to be done with Negroes taken by vessels of war, in the service of the United States." Here was a profound legal problem presented for solution. According to ·ancient custom and law, slaves came as the bloody logic of war. War between nations was of necessity international; but while this truth had stood through many cen- turies, the conversion of the Northern nations of Europe into organized society greatly modified the old doctrine of slavery. Coming under the enlightening influences of modern international law, war captives could not be reduced to slavery.[1] This doctrine was thoroughly understood, doubtless, in the North-American colonies as in Europe. But the almost universal doctrine of property in the Negro, and his status in the courts of the colo- nies, gave the royal army great advantage in the appropriation of Negro captives, under the plea that they were "property," and hence legitimate "spoils of war;" while, on the part of the colo- nists, to declare that captured Negroes were entitled to the treatment of "prisoners of war," was to reverse a principle of law as old as their government. It was, in fact, an abandonment of the claim of property in the Negro. It was a recognition of his rights as a soldier, a bestowal of the highest favors known in the treatment of captives of war.[2] But there was another diffi- culty in the way. Slavery had been recognized in the venerable memorials of the most remote nations. This condition was coeval with the history of all nations, but nowhere regarded as a relation of a local character. It grew up in social compacts, in organized communities of men, and in great and powerful states. It was recognized in private international law; and the relation of master and slave was guarded in their local *habitat*, and respected wherever found.[3] And this relation, this property in man, did

---

[1] Mr. Motley, "Rise of Dutch Republic," vol. i. p. 151, says that in the sixteenth century, in wars between European states, the captor had a property in his prisoner, which was assignable.

[2] Law of Freedom and Bondage, vol. i. p. 158.

[3] Mr. Hurd says, "In ascribing slavery to the law of nations it is a very common error to use that term not in the sense of universal jurisprudence — the Roman *jus gentium* — but in the modern sense of public international law, and to give the custom of enslaving prisoners of war, in

not cease because the slave sought another nation, for it was recognized in all the commercial transactions of nations. Now, upon this principle, the colonists were likely to claim their right to property in slaves captured.

The confederation of the new States was effected on the 1st of March, 1781. Art. IX. gave the "United States in Congress assembled" the exclusive authority of making laws to govern the disposal of all captures made by land or water; to decide which were legal; how prizes taken by the land or naval force of the government should be appropriated, and the right to establish courts of competent jurisdiction in such case, etc. The first legislation under this article was an Act establishing a court of appeals on the 4th of June, 1781. It was discussed on the 25th of June, and again, on the 17th of July, took up a great deal of time; but was recommitted. The committee were instructed to prepare an ordinance regulating the proceedings of the admiralty cases, in the several States, in instances of capture; to codify all resolutions and laws upon the subject; and to request the States to enact such provisions as would be in harmony with the reserved rights of the Congress in such cases as were specified in the Ninth Article. Accordingly, on the 21st of September, 1781, the committee reported to Congress the results of their labor, in a bill on the subject of captures. Upon the question of agreeing to the following section, the yeas and nays were demanded by Mr. Mathews of South Carolina:—

"On the recapture by a citizen of any negro, mulatto, Indian, or other person from whom labor or service is lawfully claimed by *another citizen,* specific restitution shall be adjudged to the claimant, whether the original capture shall have been made on land or water, a reasonable salvage being paid by the claimant to the recaptor, not exceeding one-fourth part of the value of such labor or service, to be estimated according to the laws of the State *of which the claimant shall be a citizen:* but if the service of such negro, mulatto, Indian or other person, captured below high-water mark, shall not be legally claimed *by a citizen of these United States,* he shall be set at liberty."

The delegates from North Carolina, Delaware, New Jersey, and Connecticut, refrained from voting; South Carolina voted in the negative: but it was carried by twenty-eight yeas, against two nays. After a spirited debate, continuing through several days,

illustration: as if the legal condition of other slaves who had never been taken in war were not equally *jure gentium* according to the Roman jurisprudence." See Mr. Webster's speech, 7th March, 1850; Works, vol. v. p. 329.

and having received several amendments, it finally passed on Dec. 4, 1781, as follows : —

" On the recapture by a citizen of any negro, mulatto, Indian, or other person, from whom labor or service is lawfully claimed by *a State or a citizen of a State,* specific restitution shall be adjudged to the claimant, whether the original capture shall have been made on land or water, *and without regard to the time of possession by the enemy,* a reasonable salvage being paid by the claimant to the recaptor, not exceeding 1-4th of the value of such labor or service, to be estimated according to the laws of the State *under which the claim shall be made.*

" But if the service of such negro, mulatto, Indian, or other person, captured below high water mark, shall not be legally claimed *within a year and a day from the sentence of the Court,* he shall be set at liberty."

It should be carefully observed that the above law refers only to *recaptures.* It would be interesting to know the views the committee entertained in reference to slaves captured by the ministerial army. Nothing was said about this interesting feature of the case. Why Congress did not claim proper treatment of the slaves captured by the enemy while in the service of the United Colonies, is not known. Doubtless its leaders saw where the logic of such a position would lead them. The word "another" was left out of the original measure, and was made to read, in the one that passed, "*a State or citizen ;*" as if it were feared that, by implication, a Negro would be recognized as a *citizen.*

By the proclamation of Sir Henry Clinton, already mentioned in the preceding chapter, Negroes were threatened with sale for "the public service;" and Mr. Jefferson in his letter to Mr. Gordon (see preceding chapter), says the enemy sold the Negroes captured in Virginia into the West Indies. After the capture of Stony Point by Gen. Wayne, concerning two Negroes who fell into his hands, he wrote to Lieut.-Col. Meigs, from New Windsor on the 25th of July, 1779, as follows : —

" The wish of the officers to free the three Negroes after a few Years Service meets my most hearty approbation but as the Chance of War or other Incidents may prevent the officer [owner] from Compling with the Intention of the Officers it will be proper for the purchaser or purchasers to sign a Condition in the Orderly Book.

" . . . I wou'd cheerfully join them in their Immediate Manumission — if a few days makes no material difference I could wish the sale put off until a Consultation may be had, & the opinion of the Officers taken on this Business." [1]

---

[1] Dawson's Stony Point, pp. 111, 118.

In June, 1779, a Spanish ship called "Victoria" sailed from Charleston, S.C., for Cadiz. During the first part of her voyage she was run down by a British privateer; but, instead of being captured, she seized her assailant, and found on board thirty-four Negroes, whom the English vessel had taken from plantations in South Carolina. The Spaniards got the Negroes on board their ship, disabled the English vessel, and then dismissed her. Within a few days she was taken by two British letters-of-marque, and headed for New York. During her passage thither she was re-captured by the "Hazard" and "Tyrannicide," armed vessels in the service of Massachusetts, and taken into the port of Boston. By direction of the Board of War she was ordered into the charge of Capt. Johnson, and was unloaded on the 21st of June. The Board of War reported to the Legislature that there were thirty-four Negroes "taken on the high seas and brought into the state." On the 23d of June [1779] the Legislature ordered "that Gen. Lovell, Capt. Adams, and Mr. Cranch, be a committee to consider what is proper to be done with a number of negroes brought into port in the prize ship called the [1] Lady Gage." [2] On the 24th of June, "the committee appointed to take into consideration the state and circumstances of a number of negroes lately brought into the port of Boston, reported a resolve directing the Board of War to inform our delegates in Congress of the state of facts relative to them, to put them into the barracks on Castle Island, and cause them to be supplied and employed." [3] The resolve passed without opposition.

"CLXXX. *Resolve on the Representation of the Board of War respecting a number of negroes captured and brought into this State.* Passed June 24, 1779.

"On the representation made to this Court by the Board of War, respecting a number of negroes brought into the Port of Boston, on board the Prize Ship Victoria:

"*Resolved,* that the Board of War be and they are hereby directed forthwith to write to our Delegates in Congress, informing them of the State of Facts relating to said Negroes, requesting them to give information thereof to the Delegates from the State of *South Carolina*, that so proper measures may be taken for the return of said Negroes, agreeable to their desire.

"And it is further *Resolved*, that the Board of War be and they hereby are directed to put the said Negroes, in the mean time, into the barracks on Castle Island in the Harbor of Boston, and cause them to be supplied with such

---

[1] Dr. Moore thinks this the wrong name. The resolve proves it.
[2] House Journal, p. 60.   [3] Ibid., pp. 63, 64.

Provision and Clothing as shall be necessary for their comfortable support, putting them under the care and direction of some Prudent person or Persons, whose business it shall be to see that the able-bodied men may be usefully employed during their stay in carrying on the Fortifications on said Island, or elsewhere within the said Harbor; and that the Women be employed according to their ability in Cooking, Washing, etc. And that the said Board of War keep an exact Account of their Expenditures in supporting said Negroes." [1]

The Negroes were delivered to Thomas Knox on the 28th of June, and were conveyed "to Castle Island pr. Order of Court." The Board of War voted the "34 Negroes delivered" rations. Lieut.-Col. Paul Revere was instructed to "issue to the Negroes at Castle Island — 1 lb. of Beef, 1 lb. of Rice pr. day." The following letter is not without interest : —

"WAR OFFICE, 28 June, 1779.

"LT.-COL. REVERE,

"Agreeable to a Resolve of Court we send to Castle Island and place under your care the following Negroes, viz.:

[19] Men,
[10] Women,
[5] Children,

lately brought into this Port in the Spanish retaken Ship Victoria. The Men are to be employed on the Fortifications there or elsewhere in the Harbor, in the most useful manner, and the Women and Children, according to their ability, in Cooking, Washing, etc. They are to be allowed for their subsistence One lb. of Beef, and one lb. of Rice per day each, which Commissary Salisbury will furnish upon your order, and this to continue until our further orders.

"By Order of the Board."

In accordance with the order of the Legislature, made on the 24th of June, the president of the Board of War, Samuel P. Savage, wrote a letter to the Massachusetts delegates in Congress, dated "War Office June 29th 1779," calling attention to the re-captured Negroes. The letter closed with the following : —

"Every necessary for the speedy discharge of these people, we have no doubt you will take, that as much expense as possible may be saved to those who call themselves their owners."

The writer was at pains to enumerate, in his letter, such slaves as he was enabled to locate.

"5 Men 4 Women 4 Boys 1 Girl belonging to Mr. Wm. Vryne.
"9 Men 1 Woman belonging to Mr. Anthony Pawley.

---

[1] Resolves, p. 51.

"1 Man belonging to Mr. Thomas Todd.

"2 Men 3 Women belonging to Mr. Henry Lewis.

"2 Men 2 Women belonging to Mr. William Pawley.

"One of the negroes is an elderly sensible man, calls himself James, and says he is free, which we have no reason to doubt the truth of. He also says that he with the rest of the Negroes were taken from a place called George-town."[1]

Pending the action of the *lawful* owners of these captives, the council instructed the commandant of Castle Island, Col. Paul Revere, to place out to service, in different towns, some of the Negroes, with the understanding that they should be delivered up to the authorities on their order. Some were delivered to gentlemen who desired them as servants. But in the fall of 1779 quite a number were still on the island, as may be seen by the following touching letter : —

"BOSTON, Octr. 12, 1779.   A Return of ye Negroes at Castle Island, Viz. :

"NEGRO MEN.

"1. ANTHONY.	6. BOBB.	11. JUNE.
2. PARTRICK.	7. ANTHONEY.	12. RHODICK.
3. PADDE.	8. ADAM.	13. JACK.
4. ISAAC.	9. JACK.	14. FULLER.
5. QUASH.	10. GYE.	15. LEWIS.

" *The above men are stout fellows.*

"NEGRO BOYS.

"No. 1. SMART.

2. RICHARD.

" *Boys very small.*

"NEGRO WOOMEN.	NEGRO GIRLS.
"No. 1. KITTEY.	No. 1. LYSETT.
2. LUCY.	2. SALLY.
3. MILLEY.	3. MERCY.
4. LANDER.	
" *Pretty large.*	*Rather stout.*

" *Gentlemen,*

" *The Scituation of these Negroes is pitiable with respect to Cloathing.*

" *I am, Gent.*

" *Your very hum. Servt.*

" *John Hancock.*"[2]

"OCT. 12, 1779."

---

[1] Mass. Archives, vol. cli., pp. 292-294.

[2] The indefatigable Dr. George H. Moore copied the letter from the original manuscript. The portions in Italics are in the handwriting of Hancock. I have been placed under many obligations to my friend Dr. Moore.

In the mean time some of the reputed owners of the Negroes at Castle Island had come from Charleston, S.C., to secure their property. When they arrived in Boston they secured the services of John Codman, Isaac Smith, and William Smith, who on the 15th of November, 1779, petitioned the Council for the "restitution" of slaves taken by a British privateer, and retaken by two armed vessels of Massachusetts. A committee was appointed to consider the petitions, and report what action should be taken in the matter. Two days later another petition was presented to the Council by one John Winthrop, "praying that certain negroes, who were brought into this state by the Hazard and Tyrannicide, may be delivered to him." It was referred to the committee appointed on the 15th of November. On the 18th of November, "Jabez Fisher, Esq., brought down a report of the Committee of both Houses on the petition of Isaac Smith, being by way of resolve, directing the Board of War to deliver so many of the negroes therein mentioned, as are now alive. Passed in Council, and sent down for concurrence." The order of ·the House is, "Read and concurred, as taken into a new draught. Sent up for concurrence."

It is printed among the resolves of November, 1779.

"XXXI. Resolve relinquishing this state's claim to a number of Negroes, passed November 18, 1779.

"Whereas a number of negroes were re-captured and brought into this State by the armed vessels Hazard and Tyrannicide, and have since been supported at the expense of this State, and as the original owners of said Negroes now apply for them:

"Therefore *Resolved*, That this Court hereby relinquish and give up any claim they may have upon the said owners for re-capturing said negroes: Provided they pay to the Board of War of this State the expence that has arisen for the support and clothing of the Negroes aforesaid." [1]

On the 12th of April, 1780, Massachusetts passed an Act providing more effectually "for the security, support, and exchange of prisoners of war brought into the State." It declares that

"All Prisoners of War, whether captured by the Army or Navy of the United States, or armed Ships or Vessels of any of the United States, or by the Subjects, Troops, Ships, or Vessels of War of this State, and brought into the same, or cast on shore by shipwreck on the coast thereof . . . . all such prisoners, so brought in or cast on shore (including Indians, Negroes, and

---

[1] Resolves, p. 131.

Molatoes) be treated in all respects as prisoners of war to the United States, any law or resolve of this Court to the contrary notwithstanding." [1]

The above Act was passed in compliance with a resolution of Congress, Jan. 13, 1780; and it repealed an Act of 1777, that made no provisions for the capture of Negroes.

On the 23d of January, 1784, Gov. Hancock sent a message to the Legislature, transmitting correspondence received during the adjournment of the Legislature from Oct. 28, 1783, to Jan. 21, 1784. Calling the attention of the Legislature to this correspondence, he referred to a letter from "His Excellency the Governor of South Carolina, respecting the detention of some Negroes here, belonging to the subjects of that state. I have communicated it to the Judges of the Supreme Judicial Court — their observations upon it are with the Papers. I have made no reply to the letter, judging it best to have your decision upon it." [2] The same papers on the same day were read in the Senate, and a joint committee of both houses was appointed. The committee reported to both branches of the Legislature on the 23d of March, 1784, and the report was adopted. A request was made of the governor to furnish copies of the opinions of the judges, etc.

"CLXXI. Order requesting the Governor to write to Governor *Guerard* of *South Carolina*, inclosing the letter of the Judges of the Supreme Judicial Court, March, 23d, 1784.

"*Ordered*, that his Excellency the Governor be requested to write to His Excellency *Benjamin Guerard*, Governor of *South Carolina*, inclosing for the information of Governor Guerard, the letter of the Judges of the Supreme Judicial Court of this Commonwealth, with the copy in the said letter referred to, upon the subject of Governor *Guerard's* letter, dated the sixth October, 1783."

The papers referred to seem to have been lost, but extracts are here produced : —

"GOVERNOR GUERARD TO GOVERNOR HANCOCK, 6th October, 1783.

EXTRACT. "That such adoption is favoring rather of the Tyranny of Great Britain which occasioned her the loss of these States — that no act of British Tyranny could exceed the encouraging the negroes from the State owning them to desert their owners to be emancipated — that it seems arbitrary and domination — assuming for the Judicial Department of any one State, to prevent a restoration voted by the Legislature and ordained by Congress.

---

[1] Laws, 1780, chap. v. pp. 283, 284.   [2] Journal, vol. iv. pp. 308, 309.

That the liberation of our negroes disclosed a specimen of Puritanism I should not have expected from gentlemen of my Profession."

MEMORANDUM. "He had demanded fugitives, carried off by the British, captured by the North, and not given up by the interference of the Judiciary.' 'Governor Hancock referred the subject to the Judges."

"JUDGES CUSHING AND SARGENT TO GOVERNOR HANCOCK, Boston, Dec. 20, 1783.

EXTRACT. "How this determination is an attack upon the spirit, freedom, dignity, independence, and sovereignty of South Carolina, we are unable to conceive. That this has any connection with, or relation to Puritanism, we believe is above yr Excellency's comprehension as it is above ours. We should be sincerely sorry to do any thing inconsistent with the Union of the States, which is and must continue to be the basis of our Liberties and Independence; on the contrary we wish it may be strengthened, confirmed, and endure for ever." [1]

By the Treaty of Peace in 1783, Negroes were put in the same category with horses and other articles of property.[2]

"Negroes [says Mr. Hamilton], by the laws of the States, in which slavery is allowed, are personal property. They, therefore, on the principle of those laws, like horses, cattle and other movables, were liable to become booty — and belonged to the enemy, [captor] as soon as they came into his hands. Belonging to him, he was free either to apply them to his own use, or set them at liberty. If he did the latter, the grant was irrevocable, restitution was impossible. Nothing in the laws of nations or in those of Great Britain, will authorize the resumption of liberty, once granted to a human being." [3]

On the 6th of May, 1783, Gen. Washington wrote Sir Guy Carleton : —

"In the course of our conversation on this point, I was surprised to hear you mention, that an embarkation had already taken place, in which a large number of negroes had been carried away. Whether this conduct is consonant to, or how far it may be deemed an infraction of the treaty, is not for me to decide. I cannot, however, conceal from you, that my private opinion is, that the measure is totally different from the letter and spirit of the treaty. But waiving the discussion of the point, and leaving its decision to our respective sovereigns, I find it my duty to signify my readiness, in conjunction with your Excellency, to enter into any agreement, or take any measures, which may be deemed expedient, to prevent the future carrying away of any negroes, or other property of the American inhabitants." [4]

---

[1] From Mr. Bancroft's MSS., America, 1783, vol. ii. Quoted by Dr. Moore.
[2] Sparks's Washington, vol. viii. p. 428, note.   [3] Works of Hamilton, vol. vii. p. 191.
[4] Sparks's Washington, vol. viii. pp. 431, 432.

In his reply, dated New York, May 12, 1783, Sir Guy Carleton says, —

"I enclose a copy of an order, which I have given out to prevent the carrying away any negroes or other property of the American inhabitants." [1]

It is clear, that notwithstanding the Act of the Massachusetts Legislature, and in the face of the law of Congress on the question of recaptures, Gen. Washington, the Congress of the United Colonies, and subsequently of the United States, regarded Negroes as *property* from the beginning to the end of the war. The following treaties furnish abundant proof that Negroes were regarded as property during the war, by the American government : —

"PROVISIONAL ARTICLES BETWEEN THE UNITED STATES OF AMERICA AND HIS BRITANNIC MAJESTY.

"Agreed upon by and between Richard Oswald, Esquire the Commissioner of His Britannic Majesty, for treating of Peace with the Commissioners of the United States of America, in behalf of his said Majesty, on one part, and John Adams, Benjamin Franklin, John Jay and Henry Laurens, four of the Commissioners of the said States, etc., etc., etc.

"Article VII. * * * All prisoners on both sides shall be set at liberty, and His Britannic Majesty shall with all convenient speed, and without causing any destruction, or carrying away any '*negroes or other* property' of the American inhabitants, withdraw all his armies, garrisons and fleets from the said United States, and from every port, place and harbour within the same. * * *

"Done at Paris, Nov. 30, 1782.

"RICHARD OSWALD, [L.S.]
"JOHN ADAMS,   [L.S.]
"B. FRANKLIN,   [L.S.]
"JOHN JAY,   [L.S.]
"HENRY LAURENS,   [L.S.]" [2]

"DEFINITE TREATY OF PEACE, BETWEEN THE UNITED STATES OF AMERICA AND HIS BRITANNIC MAJESTY.

"Article VII. * * * And His Britannic Majesty shall, with all convenient speed, and without causing any destruction, or carrying away any '*negroes or other property*' of the American inhabitants, withdraw all his armies, etc., etc., etc. * * *

"Done at Paris, Sept. 3, 1783.

"D. HARTLEY. [L.S.]
"JOHN ADAMS, [L.S.]
"B. FRANKLIN, [L.S.]
"JOHN JAY,   [L.S.]" [3]

---

[1] Sparks's Washington, vol. viii., Appendix, p. 544.
[2] U. S. Statutes at large, vol. viii. pp. 54, 57.   [3] Ibid., pp. 80, 83.

"TREATY OF PEACE AND AMITY, BETWEEN HIS BRITANNIC MAJESTY AND THE UNITED STATES OF AMERICA,

"[Ratified and confirmed by and with the advice and consent of the Senate, Feb. 11, 1815.]

"Article I. * * * Shall be restored without delay, and without causing any destruction, or carrying away any of the artillery or other public property originally captured in the said forts or places, and which shall remain therein upon the exchange of the ratifications of this treaty, or any '*slaves or other private property.*' * * * *

"Done, in triplicate, at Ghent, Dec. 24, 1814.

"GAMBIER,	[L.S.]
"HENRY GOULBURN,	[L.S.]
"WILLIAM ADAMS,	[L.S.]
"JOHN QUINCY ADAMS,	[L.S.]
"J. A. BAYARD,	[L.S.]
"H. CLAY,	[L.S.]
"JONA. RUSSELL,	[L.S.]
"ALBERT GALLATIN.	[L.S.]" [1]

It was not a difficult matter to retake Negroes captured by the enemy, and then treat them as prisoners of war. But no officer in the American army, no member of Congress, had the moral courage to proclaim that property ceased in a man the moment he donned the uniform of a Revolutionary soldier, and that all Negro soldiers captured by the enemy should be treated as prisoners of war. So, all through the war with Britain, the Negro soldier was liable to be claimed as property; and every bayonet in the army was at the command of the master to secure his property, even though it had been temporarily converted into an heroic soldier who had defended the country against its foes. The unprecedented spectacle was to be witnessed, of a master hunting his slaves under the flag of the nation. And at the close of hostilities many Negro soldiers were called upon to go back into the service of their masters; while few secured their freedom as a reward for their valor. The following letter of Gen. Washington, addressed to Brig.-Gen. Rufus Putnam, afterwards printed at Marietta, O., from his papers, indicates the regard the Father of his Country had for the rights of the master, though those rights were pushed into the camp of the army where many brave Negroes were found; and it also illustrates the legal strength of such a claim : —

---

[1] U. S. Statutes at large, vol. viii. p. 218.

"HEAD QUARTERS, Feb. 2, 1783.

"SIR, — Mr. Hobby having claimed as his property a negro man now serving in the Massachusetts Regiment, you will please to order a court of inquiry, consisting of five as respectable officers as can be found in your brigade, to examine the validity of the claim, the manner in which the person in question came into service, and the propriety of his being discharged or retained in service. Having inquired into the matter, with all the attending circumstances, they will report to you their opinion thereon; which you will report to me as soon as conveniently may be.

"I am, Sir, with great respect,
"Your most obedient servant,

"G. WASHINGTON.

"P.S. — All concerned should be notified to attend.
"Brig.-Gen. PUTNAM."

Enlistment in the army did not work a practical emancipation of the slave, as some have thought. Negroes were rated as chattel property by both armies and both governments during the entire war. This is the cold fact of history, and it is not pleasing to contemplate. The Negro occupied the anomalous position of an American slave and an American soldier. He was a soldier in the hour of danger, but a chattel in time of peace.

CHAPTER XXIX.

THE NEGRO INTELLECT. — BANNEKER THE ASTRONOMER.[1] —
FULLER THE MATHEMATICIAN. — DERHAM THE PHYSICIAN.

STATUTORY PROHIBITION AGAINST THE EDUCATION OF NEGROES. — BENJAMIN BANNEKER, THE NEGRO
ASTRONOMER AND PHILOSOPHER. — HIS ANTECEDENTS. — YOUNG BANNEKER AS A FARMER AND
INVENTOR. — THE MILLS OF ELLICOTT & CO. — BANNEKER CULTIVATES HIS MECHANICAL GENIUS
AND MATHEMATICAL TASTES. — BANNEKER'S FIRST CALCULATION OF AN ECLIPSE SUBMITTED FOR
INSPECTION IN 1789. — HIS LETTER TO MR. ELLICOTT. — THE TESTIMONY OF A PERSONAL ACQUAINT-
ANCE OF BANNEKER AS TO HIS UPRIGHT CHARACTER. — HIS HOME BECOMES A PLACE OF INTER-
EST TO VISITORS. — RECORD OF HIS BUSINESS TRANSACTIONS. — MRS. MASON'S VISIT TO HIM. —
SHE ADDRESSES HIM IN VERSE. — BANNEKER REPLIES BY LETTER TO HER. — PREPARES HIS FIRST
ALMANAC FOR PUBLICATION IN 1792. — TITLE OF HIS ALMANAC. — BANNEKER'S LETTER TO THOMAS
JEFFERSON. — THOMAS JEFFERSON'S REPLY. — BANNEKER INVITED TO ACCOMPANY THE COMMIS-
SIONERS TO RUN THE LINES OF THE DISTRICT OF COLUMBIA. — BANNEKER'S HABITS OF STUDYING
THE HEAVENLY BODIES. — MINUTE DESCRIPTION GIVEN TO HIS SISTERS IN REFERENCE TO THE
DISPOSITION OF HIS PERSONAL PROPERTY AFTER DEATH. — HIS DEATH. — REGARDED AS THE
MOST DISTINGUISHED NEGRO OF HIS TIME. — FULLER THE MATHEMATICIAN, OR "THE VIRGINIA
CALCULATOR." — FULLER OF AFRICAN BIRTH, BUT STOLEN AND SOLD AS A SLAVE INTO VIRGINIA.
— VISITED BY MEN OF LEARNING. — HE WAS PRONOUNCED TO BE A PRODIGY IN THE MANIPULA-
TION OF FIGURES. — HIS DEATH. — DERHAM THE PHYSICIAN. — SCIENCE OF MEDICINE REGARDED
AS THE MOST INTRICATE PURSUIT OF MAN. — EARLY LIFE OF JAMES DERHAM. — HIS KNOWL-
EDGE OF MEDICINES, HOW ACQUIRED. — HE BECOMES A PROMINENT PHYSICIAN IN NEW ORLEANS.
— DR. RUSH GIVES AN ACCOUNT OF AN INTERVIEW WITH HIM. — WHAT THE NEGRO RACE PRO-
DUCED BY THEIR GENIUS IN AMERICA.

FROM the moment slavery gained a foothold in North America
until the direful hour that witnessed its dissolution amid the
shock of embattled arms, learning was the forbidden fruit
that no Negro dared taste. Positive and explicit statutes everywhere, as fiery swords, drove him away hungry from the tree
of intellectual life; and all persons were forbidden to pluck the
fruit for him, upon pain of severe penalties. Every yearning for
intellectual food was answered by whips and thumb-screws.

But, notwithstanding the state of almost instinctive ignorance
in which slavery held the Negro, there were those who occasionally

---

[1] William Wells Brown, William C. Nell, and all the Colored men whose efforts I have seen,
have made a number of very serious mistakes respecting Banneker's parentage, age, accomplishments, etc. *He was of mixed blood.* His mother's name was not Molly Morton, but one of his
sisters bore that name.

I have used the Memoirs of Banneker, prepared by J. H. B. Latrobe and J. Saurin Norris,
and other valuable material from the Maryland Historical Society.

astounded the world with the brightness of their intellectual genius. There were some Negroes whose minds ran the gauntlet of public proscription on one side and repressive laws on the other, and safely gained eminence in *astronomy, mathematics,* and *medicine.*

BANNEKER THE ASTRONOMER.

BENJAMIN BANNEKER, the Negro *astronomer* and *philosopher,* was born in Maryland, on the 9th of November, 1731. His maternal grandmother was a white woman, a native of England, named *Molly Welsh.* She came to Maryland in a shipload of white emigrants, who, according to the custom of those days, were sold to pay their passage. She served her master faithfully for seven years, when, being free, she purchased a small farm, at a nominal price. Soon after she bought two Negro slaves from a ship that had come into the Chesapeake Bay, and began life anew. Both of these Negroes proved to be men of more than ordinary fidelity, industry, and intelligence. One of them, it was said, was the son of an African king. She gave him his freedom, and then married him. His name was Banneker.[1] Four children were the fruit of this union; but the chief interest centres in only one, —a girl, named Mary. Following the example of her mother, she also married a native of Africa: but both tradition and history preserve an unbroken silence respecting his life, with the single exception that, embracing the Christian religion, he was baptized "Robert Banneker;" and the record of his death is thus preserved, in the family Bible: *"Robert Banneker departed this life, July ʸᵉ 10th 1759."* Thus it is evident that he took his wife's surname. Benjamin Banneker was the only child of Robert and Mary Banneker.

Young Benjamin was a great favorite with his grandmother, who taught him to read. She had a sincere love of the Sacred Scriptures, which she did not neglect to inculcate into the youthful heart of her grandson. In the neighborhood, — at that time an almost desolate spot, — a school was conducted where the master admitted several Colored children, with the whites, to the benefits of his instructions. It was a "pay school," and thither young Banneker was sent at a very tender age. His application to his studies was equalled by none. When the other pupils were

---

[1] In the most remote records the name was written *Banneky.*

playing, he found great pleasure in his books. How long he remained in school, is not known.

His father purchased a farm of one Richard Gist, and here he spent the remnant of his days.

When young Banneker had obtained his majority, he gave attention to the various interests of farm-life. He was industrious, intelligent in his labors, scrupulously neat in the management of his grounds, cultivated a valuable garden, was gentle in his treatment of stock, — horses, cows, etc., — and was indeed comfortably situated. During those seasons of leisure which come to agriculturists, he stored his mind with useful knowledge. Starting with the Bible, he read history, biography, travels, romance, and such works on general literature as he was able to borrow. His mind seemed to turn with especial satisfaction to mathematics, and he acquainted himself with the most difficult problems.

He had a taste also for mechanics. He conceived the idea of making a timepiece, a clock, and about the year 1770 constructed one. With his imperfect tools, and with no other model than a borrowed watch, it had cost him long and patient labor to perfect it, to make the variation necessary to cause it to strike the hours, and produce a concert of correct action between the hour, the minute, and the second machinery. He confessed that its regularity in pointing out the progress of time had amply rewarded all his pains in its construction.[1]

In 1773 Ellicott & Co. built flour-mills in a valley near the banks of the Patapsco River. Banneker watched the mills go up ; and, when the machinery was set in motion, looked on with interest, as he had a splendid opportunity of observing new principles of mechanism. He made many visits to the mills, and became acquainted with their proprietors ; and, till the day of his death, he found in the Ellicotts kind and helpful friends.

After a short time the Ellicotts erected a store, where, a little later, a post-office, was opened. To this point the farmers and gentlemen, for miles around, used to congregate. Banneker often called at the post-office, where, after overcoming his natural modesty and diffidence, he was frequently called out in conversations covering a variety of topics. His conversational powers, his inexhaustible fund of information, and his broad learning (for

---

[1] J. Saurin Norris's sketch.

those times and considering his circumstances), made him the connoisseur of that section. At times he related, in modest terms, the difficulties he was constrained to encounter in order to acquire the knowledge of books he had, and the unsatisfied longings he still had for further knowledge. His fame as a mathematician was already established, and with the increasing facilities of communication his accomplishments and achievements were occupying the thought of many intelligent people.

"By this time he had become very expert in the solution of difficult mathematical problems, which were then, more than in this century, the amusement of persons of leisure; and they were frequently sent to him from scholars residing in different parts of our country who wished to test his capacity. He is reported to have been successful in every case, and, sometimes, he returned with his answers, questions of his own composition conveyed in rhyme."

The following question was propounded to Mr. George Ellicott, and was solved by Benjamin Hallowell of Alexandria.

> "A Cooper and Vintner sat down for a talk,
> Both being so groggy, that neither could walk,
> Says Cooper to Vintner, 'I'm the first of my trade,
> There's no kind of vessel, but what I have made,
> And of any shape, Sir, — just what you will, —
> And of any size, Sir, — from a ton to a gill!'
> 'Then,' says the Vintner, 'you're the man for me, —
> Make me a vessel, if we can agree.
> The top and the bottom diameter define,
> To bear that proportion as fifteen to nine;
> Thirty-five inches are just what I crave,
> No more and no less, in the depth, will I have;
> Just thirty-nine gallons this vessel must hold, —
> Then I will reward you with silver or gold, —
> Give me your promise, my honest old friend?'
> 'I'll make it to-morrow, that you may depend!'
> So the next day the Cooper his work to discharge,
> Soon made the new vessel, but made it too large; —
> He took out some staves, which made it too small,
> And then cursed the vessel, the Vintner and all.
> He beat on his breast, 'By the Powers!' — he swore,
> He never would work at his trade any more!
> Now my worthy friend, find out, if you can,
> The vessel's dimensions and comfort the man!
> "BENJAMIN BANNEKER."

The greater diameter of Banneker's tub must be 24.746 inches; the less diameter, 14.8476 inches.

He was described by a gentleman who had often met him at Ellicott's Mills as "of black complexion, medium stature, of uncommonly soft and gentlemanly manners and of pleasing colloquial powers."

Fortunately Mr. George Ellicott was a gentleman of exquisite literary taste and critical judgment. He discovered in Banneker the elements of a cultivated gentleman and profound scholar. He threw open his library to this remarkable Negro, loaded him with books and astronomical instruments, and gave him the emphatic assurance of sympathy and encouragement. He occasionally made Banneker a visit, when he would urge upon him the importance of making astronomical calculations for almanacs. Finally, in the spring of 1789, Banneker submitted to Mr. Ellicott his first projection of an eclipse. It was found to contain a slight error; and, having kindly pointed it out, Mr. Ellicott received the following reply from Banneker : —

LETTER OF BENJAMIN BANNEKER TO GEORGE ELLICOTT.

"SIR, — I received your letter at the hand of Bell but found nothing strange to me In the Letter Concerning the number of Eclipses, tho according to authors the Edge of the penumber only touches the Suns Limb in that Eclips, that I left out of the Number — which happens April 14th day, at 37 minutes past 7 o'clock in the morning, and is the first we shall have; but since you wrote to me, I drew in the Equations of the Node which will cause a small Solar Defet, but as I did not intend to publish, I was not so very peticular as I should have been, but was more intent upon the true method of projecting a Solar Eclips — It is an easy matter for us when a Diagram is laid down before us, to draw one in resemblance of it, but it is a hard matter for young Tyroes in Astronomy, when only the Elements for the projection is laid down before him to draw his diagram with any degree of Certainty.

"Says the Learned LEADBETTER, the projection, I shall here describe, is that mentioned by Mr. Flamsted. When the sun is in Cancer, Leo, Virgo, Libra, Scorpio or, Sagitary, the Axes of the Globe must lie to the right hand of the Axes of the Ecliptic, but when the sun is in Capricorn, Aquarius, Pisces, Aries, Taurus, or Gemini, then to the left.

"Says the wise author FERGUSON, when the sun is in Capercorn, Aquarius, Pisces, Aries, Taurus, and Gemeni, the Northern half of the Earths Axes lies to the right hand of the Axes of the Ecliptic and to the left hand, whilst the Sun is on the other six signs.

"Now Mr. Ellicott, two such learned gentlemen as the above mentioned, one in direct opposition to the other, stagnates young beginners, but I hope the stagnation will not be of long duration, for this I observe that Leadbetter counts the time on the path of Vertex 1. 2. 3 &c. from the right to the left hand or from the consequent to the antecedent, — But Ferguson on the path of Vertex counts the time 1. 2. 3 &c. from the left to the right hand, according to the order of numbers, so that that is regular, shall compensate for irregularity. Now sir if I can overcome this difficulty I doubt not being able to calculate a Common Almanac. — Sir no more

"But remain your faithful friend,

"B. BANNEKER.

"MR. GEORGE ELLICOTT, *Oct.* 13*th*, 1789."

His mother, an active, intelligent, slight-built Mulatto, with long black hair, had exercised a tender but positive influence over him. His character, so far as is known, was without blemish, with the single exception of an occasional use of ardent spirits. He found himself conforming too frequently to the universal habit of the times, social drinking. Liquors and wines were upon the tables and sideboards of the best families, and wherever Banneker went it confronted him. He felt his weakness in this regard, and resolved to abstain from the use of strong drink. Some time after returning from a visit to Washington, in company with the commissioners who laid out the District of Columbia, he related to his friends that during the entire absence from home he had abstained from the use of liquors; adding, "I feared to trust myself even with wine, lest it should steal away the little sense I have." On a leaf of one of his almanacs, appears the following in his own handwriting : —

"Evil communications corrupt good manners, I hope to live to hear, that good communication corrects 'bad manners.'"

He had a just appreciation of his own strength. He hated vice of every kind ; and, while he did not connect himself to any church, he was deeply attached to the *Society of Friends*. He was frequently seen in their meeting-house. He usually occupied the rear bench, where he would sit with uncovered head, leaning upon his staff, wrapt in profound meditation. The following letter addressed to Mr. J. Saurin Norris shows that his character was upright : —

"In the year 1800, I commenced my engagements in the store of Ellicott's Mills, where my first acquaintance with Benjamin Banneker began. He often came to the store to purchase articles for his own use ; and, after hearing him converse, I was always anxious to wait upon him. After making his purchases, he usually went to the part of the store where George Ellicott was in the habit of sitting, to converse with him about the affairs of our Government and other matters. He was very precise in conversation and exhibited deep reflection. His deportment whenever I saw him, appeared to be perfectly upright and correct, and he seemed to be acquainted with every thing of importance that was passing in the country.

"I recollect to have seen his Almanacs in my father's house, and believe they were the only ones used in the neighborhood at the time. He was a large man inclined to be fleshy, and was far advanced in years, when I first saw him, I remember being once at his house, but do not recollect any thing about the comforts of his establishment, nor of the old clock, about which you enquired. He was fond of, and well qualified, to work out abstruse questions in arithmetic. I remember, he brought to the store, one which he had composed himself, and presented to George Ellicott for solution. I had a copy which I have since lost; but the character and deportment of the man being so wholly different from any thing I had ever seen from one of his color, his question made so deep an impression on my mind I have ever since retained a perfect recollection of it, except two lines, which do not alter the sense. I remember that George Ellicott, was engaged in making out the answer, and cannot now say that he succeeded, but have no doubt he did. I have thus, briefly given you my recollections of Benjamin Banneker. I was young when he died, and doubtless many incidents respecting him, have, from the time which has since elapsed, passed from my recollection:

"CHARLES W. DORSEY, *of Elkridge.*"

After the death of his mother, Banneker dwelt alone until the day of his death, having never married. His manners were gentle and engaging, his benevolence proverbial. His home became a place of great interest to visitors, whom he always received cordially, and treated hospitably all who called.

"We found the venerable star-gazer," says the author of the Memoir of Susanna Mason, "under a wide spreading pear tree, leaden with delicious fruit; he came forward to meet us, and bade us welcome to his lowly dwelling. It was built of logs, one story in height, and was surrounded by an orchard. In one corner of the room, was suspended a clock of his own construction, *which* was a true hearald of departing hours. He was careful in the little affairs of life as well as in the great matters. He kept record of all his business transactions, literary and domestic. The following extracts from his Account Book exhibit his love for detail.

"'Sold on the 2nd of April, 1795, to Buttler, Edwards & Kiddy, the right of an Almanac, for the year 1796, for the sum of 80 dollars, equal to £30.

"'On the 30th of April, 1795, lent John Ford five dollars. £1 17s. 6d.

"'12th of December, 1797, bought a pound of candles at 1s. 8d.

"'Sold to John Collins 2 qts. of dried peaches 6d. "1 qt. mead 4d.

"'On the 26th of March, came Joshua Sanks with 3 or 4 bushels of turnips to feed the cows.

"'13th of April, 1803, planted beans and sowed cabbage seed.'

"He took down from a shelf a little book, wherein he registered the names of those, by whose visits he felt particularly honored, and recorded my mother's name upon the list; he then, diffidently, but very respectfully, requested her acceptance of one of his Almanacs in manuscript."

Within a few days after this visit Mrs. Mason addressed him in a poetical letter, which found its way into the papers of the section, and was generally read. The subjoined portions are sufficient to exhibit the character of the effusion. The admonitory lines at the end doubtless refer to his early addiction to strong drink.

"*An Address to* BENJAMIN BANNEKER, *an African Astronomer, who presented the Author with a Manuscript Almanac in* 1796."

> "Transmitted on the wings of Fame,
> Thine *eclat* sounding with thy name,
> Well pleased, I heard, ere 'twas my lot
> To see thee in thy humble cot.
> That genius smiled upon thy birth,
> And application called it forth;
> That times and tides thou could'st presage,
> And traverse the Celestial stage,
> Where shining globes their circles run,
> In swift rotation round the sun;
> Could'st tell how planets in their way,
> From order ne'er were known to stray.
> Sun, moon and stars, when they will rise,
> When sink below the upper skies;
> When an eclipse shall veil their light,
> And, hide their splendor from our sight.
>
> .   .   .   .
>
> Some men whom private walks pursue,
> Whom fame ne'er ushered into view,
> May run their race, and few observe
> To right or left, if they should swerve,
> Their blemishes would not appear,
> Beyond their lives a single year. —
> But thou, a man exalted high,
> Conspicuous in the world's keen eye,
> On record now, thy name's enrolled,
> And future ages will be told, —
> There lived a man named BANNEKER,
> An African Astronomer! —
> Thou need'st to have a special care,
> Thy conduct with thy talent square,
> That no contaminating vice,
> Obscure thy lustre in our eyes."

During the following year Banneker sent the following letter to his good friend Mrs. Mason: —

"*August 26th,* 1797.

"DEAR FEMALE FRIEND: —

"I have thought of you every day since I saw you last, and of my promise in respect of composing some verses for your amusement, but I am very much indisposed, and have been ever since that time. I have a constant pain in my head, a palpitation in my flesh, and I may say I am attended with a complication of disorders, at this present writing, so that I cannot with any pleasure or delight, gratify your curiosity in that particular, at this present time, yet I say my will is good to oblige you, if I had it in my power, because you gave me good advice, and edifying language, in that piece of poetry which you was pleased to present unto me, and I can but love and thank you for the same; and if ever it should be in my power to be serviceable to you, in any measure, your reasonable requests, shall be armed with the obedience of,

"Your sincere friend and well-wisher,

"BENJAMIN BANNEKER.

"MRS. SUSANNA MASON.

"N.B. The above is mean writing, done with trembling hands. B. B."

With the use of Mayer's Tables, Ferguson's Astronomy, and Leadbeater's Lunar Tables, Banneker had made wonderful progress in his astronomical investigations. He prepared his first almanac for publication in 1792. Mr. James McHenry became deeply interested in him, and, convinced of his talent in this direction, wrote a letter to the firm of Goddard & Angell, publishers of almanacs, in Baltimore. They became the sole publishers of Banneker's almanacs till the time of his death. In an editorial note in the first almanac, they say, —

"They feel gratified in the opportunity of presenting to the public, through their press, what must be considered as an extraordinary effort of genius; a complete and accurate Ephemeris for the year 1792, calculated by a sable descendant of Africa," etc.

And they further say, —

"That they flatter themselves that a philanthropic public, in this enlightened era, will be induced to give their patronage and support to this work, not only on account of its intrinsic merits, (it having met the approbation of several of the most distinguished astronomers of America, particularly the celebrated Mr. Rittenhouse,) but from similar motives to those which induced the editors to give this calculation the preference, — the ardent desire of drawing modest merit from obscurity, and controverting the long-established illiberal prejudice against the blacks."

The title of his almanac is given below as a matter of historic interest.

"Benjamin Banneker's Pennsylvania, Delaware, Virginia, and Maryland Almanac and Ephemeris, for the year of our Lord 1792, being Bissextile or leap year, and the sixteenth year of American Independence, which commenced July 4, 1776: containing the motions of the Sun and Moon, the true places and aspects of the Planets, the rising and setting of the Sun, and the rising, setting, and southing, place and age of the Moon, &c. The Lunations, Conjunctions, Eclipses, Judgment of the Weather, Festivals, and remarkable days."

He had evidently read Mr. Jefferson's Notes on Virginia; and touched by the humane sentiment there exhibited, as well as saddened by the doubt expressed respecting the intellect of the Negro, Banneker sent him a copy of his first almanac, accompanied by a letter which pleaded the cause of his race, and in itself, was a refutation of the charge that the Negro had no intellectual outcome.

"MARYLAND, BALTIMORE COUNTY, August 19, 1791.

"SIR,

"I am fully sensible of the greatness of the freedom I take with you on the present occasion; a liberty which seemed scarcely allowable, when I reflected on that distinguished and dignified station in which you stand, and the almost general prejudice which is so prevalent in the world against those of my complexion.

"It is a truth too well attested, to need a proof here, that we are a race of beings, who have long laboured under the abuse and censure of the world; that we have long been looked upon with an eye of contempt; and considered rather as brutish than human, and scarcely capable of mental endowments.

"I hope I may safely admit, in consequence of the report which has reached me, that you are a man far less inflexible in sentiments of this nature, than many others; that you are measurably friendly, and well disposed towards us; and that you are willing to lend your aid and assistance for our relief from those many distresses, and numerous calamities, to which we are reduced.

"If this is founded in truth, I apprehend you will embrace every opportunity to eradicate that train of absurd and false ideas and opinions, which so generally prevail with respect to us: and that your sentiments are concurrent with mine, which are, that one universal Father hath given being to us all; that He hath not only made us all of one flesh, but that He hath also, without partiality, afforded us all the same sensations, and endowed us all with the same faculties; and that however variable we may be in society or religion, however diversified in situation or in colour, we are all of the same family, and stand in the same relation to Him.

"If these are sentiments of which you are fully persuaded, you cannot but acknowledge, that it is the indispensable duty of those, who maintain for themselves the rights of human nature, and who profess the obligations of Christianity, to extend their powers and influence to the relief of every part of the human race, from whatever burden or oppression they may unjustly labour under; and this, I apprehend, a full conviction of the truth and obligation of these principles should lead all to.

"I have long been convinced, that if your love for yourselves, and for those inestimable laws which preserved to you the rights of human nature, was founded on sincerity you could not but be solicitous, that every individual, of whatever rank or distinction, might with you equally enjoy the blessings thereof; neither could you rest satisfied short of the most active effusion of your exertions, in order to their promotion from any state of degradation, to which the unjustifiable cruelty and barbarism of men may have reduced them.

"I freely and cheerfully acknowledge, that I am of the African race, and in that colour which is natural to them, of the deepest dye; and it is under a sense of the most profound gratitude to the Supreme Ruler of the Universe, that I now confess to you, that I am not under that state of tyrannical thraldom, and inhuman captivity, to which too many of my brethren are doomed, but that I have abundantly tasted of the fruition of those blessings, which proceed from that free and unequalled liberty with which you are favoured; and which I hope you will willingly allow you have mercifully received, from the immediate hand of that Being from whom proceedeth every good and perfect gift.

"Suffer me to recall to your mind that time, in which the arms of the British crown were exerted, with every powerful effort, in order to reduce you to a state of servitude: look back, I entreat you, on the variety of dangers to which you were exposed; reflect on that period in which every human aid appeared unavailable, and in which even hope and fortitude wore the aspect of inability to the conflict, and you cannot but be led to a serious and grateful sense of your miraculous and providential preservation; you cannot but acknowledge, that the present freedom and tranquillity which you enjoy, you have mercifully received, and that it is the peculiar blessing of heaven.

"This, Sir, was a time when you clearly saw into the injustice of a state of Slavery, and in which you had just apprehensions of the horrors of its condition. It was then that your abhorrence thereof was so excited, that you publicly held forth this true and invaluable doctrine, which is worthy to be recorded and remembered in all succeeding ages: 'We hold these truths to be self-evident, that all men are created equal; that they are endowed by their Creator with certain inalienable rights, and that among these are, life, liberty, and the pursuit of happiness.'

"Here, was a time in which your tender feelings for yourselves had engaged you thus to declare; you were then impressed with proper ideas of the great violation of liberty, and the free possession of those blessings, to which you were entitled by nature; but, sir, how pitiable is it to reflect, that although you were so fully convinced of the benevolence of the Father of Mankind, and of his equal and impartial distribution of these rights and privileges which he hath conferred upon them, that you should at the same time counteract his mercies, in detaining by fraud and violence, so numerous a part of my brethren under groaning captivity and cruel oppression, that you should at the same time be found guilty of that most criminal act, which you professedly detested in others, with respect to yourselves.

"Your knowledge of the situation of my brethren is too extensive to need a recital here; neither shall I presume to prescribe methods by which they may be relieved, otherwise than by recommending to you and all others, to wean yourselves from those narrow prejudices which you have imbibed with respect to them, and as Job proposed to his friends, 'put your soul in their soul's stead;' thus shall your hearts be enlarged with kindness and benevolence towards them; and thus shall you need neither the direction of myself or others, in what manner to proceed herein.

"And now, sir, although my sympathy and affection for my brethren hath caused my enlargement thus far, I ardently hope, that your candour and generosity will plead with you in my behalf, when I state that it was not originally my design; but having taken up my pen in order to present a copy of an almanac which I have calculated for the succeeding year, I was unexpectedly led thereto.

"This calculation is the production of my arduous study, in my advanced stage of life; for having long had unbounded desires to become acquainted with the secrets of nature, I have had to gratify my curiosity herein through my own assiduous application to astronomical study, in which I need not recount to you the many difficulties and disadvantages which I have had to encounter.

"And although I had almost declined to make my calculation for the ensuing year, in consequence of the time which I had allotted for it being taken up at the federal territory, by the request of Mr. Andrew Ellicott, yet I industriously applied myself thereto, and hope I have accomplished it with correctness and accuracy. I have taken the liberty to direct a copy to you, which I humbly request you will favourably receive; and although you may have the opportunity of perusing it after its publication, yet I desire to send it to you in manuscript previous thereto, that thereby you might not only have an earlier inspection, but that you might also view it in my own handwriting.

"And now, sir, I shall conclude, and subscribe myself, with the most profound respect,

"Your most obedient humble servant,

"BENJAMIN BANNEKER."

Mr. Jefferson, who was Secretary of State under President Washington, sent the great Negro the following courteous reply:—

"PHILADELPHIA, Aug. 30, 1791.

"SIR,—I thank you sincerely for your letter of the 19th instant, and for the almanac it contained. Nobody wishes more than I do to see such proofs as you exhibit, that Nature has given to our black brethren talents equal to those of the other colors of men, and that the appearance of a want of them is owing only to the degraded condition of their existence, both in Africa and America. I can add, with truth, that no one wishes more ardently to see a good system commenced for raising the condition, both of their body and mind, to what it ought to be, as fast as the imbecility of their present existence, and other circumstances which cannot be neglected, will admit. I have taken the liberty of sending your almanac to Monsieur de Condorcet, Secretary of the Academy of Sciences, at Paris, and members of the Philanthropic Society, because I considered it a document to which your whole color had a right, for their justification against the doubts which have been entertained of them.

"I am, with great esteem, sir,

"Your most obedient servant,

"THO. JEFFERSON.

"MR. BENJAMIN BANNEKER, near Ellicott's }
Lower Mills, Baltimore county." [1]   }

---

[1] Jefferson's Works, vol. iii. p. 291.

The only time Banneker was ever absent from his home any distance was when "the Commissioners to run the lines of the District of Columbia" — then known as the "Federal Territory" — invited him to accompany them upon their mission. Mr. Norris says : —

"Banneker's deportment throughout the whole of this engagement, secured their respect, and there is good authority for believing, that his endowments led the commissioners to overlook the color of his skin, to converse with him freely, and enjoy the clearness and originality of his remarks on various subjects. It is a fact, that they honored him with an invitation to a daily seat at their table; but this, with his usual modesty, he declined. They then ordered a side table laid for him, in the same apartment with themselves. On his return, he called to give an account of his engagements, at the house of one of his friends. He arrived on horseback, dressed in his usual costume ;— a full suit of drab cloth, surmounted by a broad brimmed beaver hat. He seemed to have been re-animated by the presence of the eminent men with whom he had mingled in the District, and gave a full account of their proceedings."

His habits of study were rather peculiar. At nightfall, wrapped in a great cloak, he would lie prostrate upon the ground, where he spent the night in contemplation of the heavenly bodies. At sunrise he would retire to his dwelling, where he spent a portion of the day in repose. But as he seemed to require less sleep than most people, he employed the hours of the afternoons in the cultivation of his garden, trimming of fruit-trees, or in observing the habits and flight of his bees. When his service and attention were not required out-doors, he busied himself with his books, papers, and mathematical instruments, at a large oval table in his house. The situation of Banneker's dwelling was one which would be admired by every lover of nature, and furnished a fine field for the observation of celestial phenomena. It was about half a mile from the Patapsco River, and commanded a prospect of the near and distant hills upon its banks, which have been so justly celebrated for their picturesque beauty. A never-failing spring issued from beneath a large golden-willow tree in the midst of his orchard.[1] The whole situation was charming, inspiring, and no doubt helped him in the solution of difficult problems.

There is no reliable data to enlighten us as to the day of his death ; but it is the opinion of those who lived near him, and their

---

[1] See Norris, paper on Banneker.

descendants, that he died in the fall of 1804. It was a bright, beautiful day, and feeling unwell he walked out on the hills to enjoy the sunlight and air. During his walk he came across a neighbor, to whom he complained of being sick. They both returned to his house, where, after lying down upon his couch, he became speechless, and died peacefully. During a previous sickness he had charged his sisters, Minta Black and Molly Morten, that, so soon as he was dead, all the books, instruments, etc., which Mr. Ellicott had loaned him, should be taken back to the benevolent lender; and, as a token of his gratitude, all his manuscripts containing all his almanacs, his observations and writings on various subjects, his letter to Thomas Jefferson, and that gentleman's reply, etc., were given to Mr. Ellicott.[1] On the day of his death, faithful to the instructions of their brother, Banneker's sisters had all the articles moved to Mr. Ellicott's house; and their arrival was the first sad news of the astronomer's death. To the promptness of these girls in carrying out his orders is the gratitude of the friends of science due for the preservation of the results of Banneker's labors. During the performance of the last sad rites at the grave, two days after his death, his house was discovered to be on fire. It burnt so rapidly that it was impossible to save any thing: so his clock and other personal property perished in the flames. He had given to one of his sisters a feather-bed, upon which he had slept for many years; and she, fortunately and thoughtfully, removed it when he died, and prized it as the only memorial of her distinguished brother. Some years after, she had occasion to open the bed, when she discovered a purse of money — another illustration of his careful habits and frugality.

Benjamin Banneker was known favorably on two continents, and at the time of his death was the most intelligent and distinguished Negro in the United States.

FULLER THE MATHEMATICIAN.

One of the standing arguments against the Negro was, that he lacked the faculty of solving mathematical problems. This charge

---

[1] All of Banneker's literary remains were published by J. H. B. Latrobe in the Maryland Historical Society, and in the Maryland Colonization Journal in 1845. The Memoir of Banneker was somewhat marred by a too precipitous and zealous attempt to preach the doctrine of colonization.

was made without a disposition to allow him an opportunity to submit himself to a proper test. It was equivalent to putting out a man's eyes, and then asserting boldly that he cannot see; of manacling his ankles, and charging him with the inability to run. But notwithstanding all the prohibitions against instructing the Negro, and his far remove from intellectual stimulants, the subject to whom attention is now called had within his own untutored intellect the elements of a great mathematician.

Thomas Fuller, familiarly known as the Virginia Calculator, was a native of Africa. At the age of fourteen he was stolen, and sold into slavery in Virginia, where he found himself the property of a planter residing about four miles from Alexandria. He did not understand the art of reading or writing, but by a marvellous faculty was able to perform the most difficult calculations. Dr. Benjamin Rush of Philadelphia, Penn., in a letter addressed to a gentleman residing in Manchester, Eng., says that hearing of the phenomenal mathematical powers of "Negro Tom," he, in company with other gentlemen passing through Virginia, sent for him. One of the gentlemen asked him how many seconds a man of seventy years, some odd months, weeks, and days, had lived. He gave the exact number in a minute and a half. The gentleman took a pen, and after some figuring told Tom he must be mistaken, as the number was too great. "'Top, massa!" exclaimed Tom, "you hab left out de leap-years!" And sure enough, on including the leap-years in the calculation, the number given by Tom was correct.

"He was visited by William Hartshorn and Samuel Coates," says Mr. Needles, "of this city (Philadelphia), and gave correct answers to all their questions: such as, How many seconds there are in a year and a half? In two minutes he answered 47,304,000. How many seconds in seventy years, seventeen days, twelve hours? In one minute and a half, 2,110,500,800.[1]

That he was a prodigy, no one will question.[2] He was the wonder of the age. The following appeared in several newspapers at the time of his death: —

"DIED — Negro Tom, the famous African calculator, aged 80 years. He was the property of Mrs. Elizabeth Cox, of Alexandria. Tom was a very black man. He was brought to this country at the age of fourteen, and was sold as a slave with many of his unfortunate countrymen. This man was a

---

[1] Needles's Hist. Memoir of the Penn. Society for Promoting the Abolition of Slavery, p. 32.
[2] J. P. Brissot de Warville's Travels in the U. S., vol. i. p. 243.

prodigy. Though he could neither read nor write, he had perfectly acquired the use of enumeration. He could give the number of months, days, weeks, hours, minutes, and seconds, for any period of time that a person chose to mention, allowing in his calculations for all the leap years that happened in the time. He would give the number of poles, yards, feet, inches, and barley-corns in a given distance — say, the diameter of the earth's orbit — and in every calculation he would produce the true answer in less time than ninety-nine out of a hundred men would take with their pens. And what was, perhaps, more extraordinary, though interrupted in the progress of his calculations, and engaged in discourse upon any other subject, his operations were not thereby in the least deranged; he would go on where he left off, and could give any and all of the stages through which the calculation had passed.

"Thus died Negro Tom, this untaught arithmetician, this untutored scholar. Had his opportunities of improvement been equal to those of thousands of his fellow-men, neither the Royal Society of London, the Academy of Science at Paris, nor even a Newton himself need have been ashamed to acknowledge him a brother in science."[1]

DERHAM THE PHYSICIAN.

Through all time the science of medicine has been regarded as ranking among the most intricate and delicate pursuits man could follow. Our Saviour was called "the Great Physician," and St. Luke "the beloved physician." No profession brings a man so near to humanity, and no other class of men have a higher social standing than those who are consecrated to the "art of healing." Such a position demands of a man not only profound research in the field of medicine, but the rarest intellectual and social gifts and accomplishments. For a Negro to gain such a position in the nineteenth century would require merit of unusual order. But in the eighteenth century, when slavery had cast its long, dark shadows over the entire life of the nation, for a Negro, born and reared a slave, to obtain fame in medicine second to none on the continent, was an achievement that justly challenged the admiration of the civilized world.

Dr. James Derham was born a slave in Philadelphia in 1762. His master was a physician. James was taught to read and write, and early rendered valuable assistance to his master in compounding medicines. Endowed with more than average intelligence, he took a great liking to the science of medicine, and absorbed all the information that came within his observation. On the death of his master he was sold to the surgeon of the Sixteenth British Regi-

---

[1] Columbian Centinal of Boston, Dec. 29, 1790.

ment, at that time stationed in Philadelphia. At the close of the war he was sold to Dr. Robert Dove of New Orleans, a humane and intelligent man, who employed him as his assistant in a large business. He grew in a knowledge of his profession every day, was prompt and faithful in the discharge of the trusts reposed in him, and thereby gained the confidence of his master. Dr. Dove was so much pleased with him, that he offered him his freedom upon very easy terms, requiring only two or three years' service. At the end of the time designated, Dr. Derham entered into the practice of medicine upon his own account. He acquired the English, French, and Spanish languages so as to speak them fluently, and built up a practice in a short time worth three thousand dollars a year.[1] He married, and attached himself to the Episcopal Church, in 1788, and at twenty-six years of age was regarded as one of the most eminent physicians in New Orleans.

Dr. Rush of Philadelphia, in "The American Museum" for January, 1789, gave an interesting account of this distinguished "Negro physician." Says Dr. Rush, —

"I have conversed with him upon most of the acute and epidemic diseases of the country where he lives. I expected to have suggested some new medicines to him, but he suggested many more to me. He is very modest and engaging in his manners. He speaks French fluently, and has some knowledge of the Spanish."[2]

Phillis Wheatley has been mentioned already. So, in the midst of darkness and oppression, the Negro race in America, without the use of the Christian church, schoolhouse, or printing-press, produced a *poetess*, an *astronomer*, a *mathematician*, and a *physician*, who, had they been white, would have received monuments and grateful memorials at the hands of their countrymen. But even their color cannot rob them of the immortality their genius earned.

---

[1] Brissot de Warville's New Travels in the U. S., ed. 1794, vol. i. p. 242.

[2] For an account of Fuller and Derham, see De la Littérature des Nègres, ou Recherches sur leurs Facultés intellectuelles, leurs Qualités morales et leur Littérature; suivies de Notices sur la Vie et les Ouvrages des Nègres qui se sont distingués dans les Sciences, les Lettres et les Arts. Par H. GRÉGOIRE, ancien Évêque de Blois, membre du Sénat conservateur, de l'Institut national, de la Société royale des Sciences de Göttingue, etc. Paris : MDCCCVIII.

CHAPTER XXX.

SLAVERY DURING THE REVOLUTION.

1775–1783.

PROGRESS OF THE SLAVE-TRADE. — A GREAT WAR FOR THE EMANCIPATION OF THE COLONIES FROM POLITICAL BONDAGE. — CONDITION OF THE SOUTHERN STATES DURING THE WAR. — THE VIRGINIA DECLARATION OF RIGHTS. — IMMEDIATE LEGISLATION AGAINST SLAVERY DEMANDED. — ADVERTISEMENT FROM "THE INDEPENDENT CHRONICLE." — PETITION OF MASSACHUSETTS SLAVES. — AN ACT PREVENTING THE PRACTICE OF HOLDING PERSONS IN SLAVERY — ADVERTISEMENTS FROM " THE CONTINENTAL JOURNAL." — A LAW PASSED IN VIRGINIA LIMITING THE RIGHTS OF SLAVES. — LAW EMANCIPATING ALL SLAVES WHO SERVED IN THE ARMY. — NEW YORK PROMISES HER NEGRO SOLDIERS FREEDOM. — A CONSCIENTIOUS MINORITY IN FAVOR OF THE ABOLITION OF THE SLAVE-TRADE. — SLAVERY FLOURISHES DURING THE ENTIRE REVOLUTIONARY PERIOD.

THE thunder of the guns of the Revolution did not drown the voice of the auctioneer. The slave-trade went on. A great war for the emancipation of the colonies from the political bondage into which the British Parliament fain would precipitate them did not depreciate the market value of human flesh. Those whose hearts were not enlisted in the war skulked in the rear, and gloated over the blood-stained shekels they wrung from the domestic slave-trade. While the precarious condition of the Southern States during the war made legislation in support of the institution of slavery impolitic, there were, nevertheless, many severe laws in force during this entire period. In the New England and Middle States there was heard an occasional voice for the oppressed ; but it was generally strangled at the earliest moment of its being by that hell-born child, avarice. On the 21st of September, 1776, William Gordon of Roxbury, Mass., wrote,—

"The Virginians begin their Declaration of Rights with saying, 'that *all* men are born equally free and independent, and have certain inherent natural rights, of which they cannot, by any compact, deprive themselves or their posterity; among which are the enjoyment of life and *liberty*.' The Congress declare that they 'hold these truths to be self-evident, that all men are created *equal*, that they are endowed by their Creator with certain *inalienable rights*, that among these are life, *liberty* and pursuit of happiness.' The Continent has rung with affirmations of the like import. If these, Gentlemen, are our genuine sentiments, and we are not provoking the Deity, by acting hypocritically to serve a turn, let us apply earnestly and heartily to the extirpation of slavery from among ourselves. Let the State allow of nothing beyond servitude for a stipulated number of years, and that only for seven or eight, when persons are of age, or till they are of age : and let the descendants of the Africans born among us, be viewed as free-born; and be wholly at their own disposal when one-and-twenty, the latter part of which age will compensate for the expense of infancy, education, and so on."

No one gave heed. Two months later, Nov. 14, there appeared in "The Independent Chronicle" of Boston a plan for gradual emancipation; and on the 28th of the same month, in the same paper there appeared a communication demanding specific and immediate legislation against slavery. But all seemed vain : there were few moral giants among the friends of "liberty for all;" and the comparative silence of the press and pulpit gave the advocates of human slavery an easy victory.

Boston, the home of Warren, and the city that witnessed the first holy offering to liberty, busied herself through all the perilous years of the war in buying and selling human beings. The following are but a few of the many advertisements that appeared in the papers of the city of Boston during the war :[1] —

From "The Independent Chronicle," Oct. 3, 1776 : —

"*To be* SOLD A stout, hearty, likely NEGRO GIRL, fit for either Town or Country. Inquire of Mr. *Andrew Gillespie, Dorchester, Octo.* 1., 1776."

From the same, Oct. 10 : —

"A hearty NEGRO MAN, with a small sum of Money to be given away."

From the same, Nov. 28 : —

"To SELL — A Hearty likely NEGRO WENCH about 12 or 13 Years of Age, has had the Small Pox, can wash, iron, card, and spin, etc., for no other Fault but for want of Employ."

From the same, Feb. 27, 1777 : —

"WANTED a NEGRO GIRL between 12 and 20 Years of Age, for which a good Price will be given, if she can be recommended."

From "The Continental Journal," April 3, 1777 : —

"*To be* SOLD, a likely Negro Man, twenty-two years old, has had the small-pox, can do any sort of business; sold for want of employment."

---

[1] See Slavery in Mass., p. 178.

" *To be* SOLD, a large, commodious Dwelling House, Barn, and Out-houses, with any quantity of land from 1 to 50 acres, as the Purchaser shall choose within 5 miles of Boston. Also a smart well-tempered NEGRO BOY of 14 years old, not to go out of this State and *sold for 15 years only, if he continues to behave well.*"

From "The Independent Chronicle," May 8, 1777 : —

" *To be* SOLD, for want of employ, a likely strong NEGRO GIRL, about 18 years old, understands all sorts of household business, and can be well recommended."

The strange and trying vicissitudes through which the colonies had passed exposed their hypocrisy, revealed the weakness of their government, and forced them to another attempt at the extirpation of slavery. The valorous conduct of the Negro soldiers in the army had greatly encouraged their friends and emboldened their brethren, who still suffered from the curse of slavery. The latter were not silent when an opportunity presented to claim the rights they felt their due. On the 18th of March, 1777, the following petition was addressed, by the slaves in Boston, to the Legislature : —

"PETITION OF MASSACHUSETTS SLAVES.

" The petition of a great number of negroes, who are detained in a state of slavery in the very bowels of a free and Christian country, humbly showing, —

" That your petitioners apprehend that they have, in common with all other men, a natural and inalienable right to that freedom, which the great Parent of the universe hath bestowed equally on all mankind, and which they have never forfeited by any compact or agreement whatever. But they were unjustly dragged by the cruel hand of power from their dearest friends, and some of them even torn from the embraces of their tender parents, — from a populous, pleasant and plentiful country, and in violation of the laws of nature and of nations, and in defiance of all the tender feelings of humanity, brought hither to be sold like beasts of burthen, and, like them, condemned to slavery for life — among a people possessing the mild religion of Jesus — a people not insensible of the sweets of national freedom, nor without a spirit to resent the unjust endeavors of others to reduce them to a state of bondage and subjection.

" Your Honors need not to be informed that a life of slavery like that of your petitioners, deprived of every social privilege, of every thing requisite to render life even tolerable, is far worse than non-existence.

" In imitation of the laudable example of the good people of these States, your petitioners have long and patiently waited the event of petition after petition, by them presented to the legislative body of this State, and cannot but with grief reflect that their success has been but too similar.

"They cannot but express their astonishment that it has never been considered, that every principle from which America has acted, in the course of her unhappy difficulties with Great Britain, bears stronger than a thousand arguments in favor of your humble petitioners. They therefore humbly beseech Your Honors to give their petition its due weight and consideration, and cause an act of the legislature to be passed, whereby they may be restored to the enjoyment of that freedom, which is the natural right of all men, and their children (who were born in this land of liberty) may not be held as slaves after they arrive at the age of twenty-one years. So may the inhabitants of this State (no longer chargeable with the inconsistency of acting themselves the part which they condemn and oppose in others) be prospered in their glorious struggles for liberty, and have those blessings secured to them by Heaven, of which benevolent minds cannot wish to deprive their fellow-men.

"And your petitioners, as in duty bound, shall ever pray : —

> LANCASTER HILL,
> PETER BESS,
> BRISTER SLENFEN,
> PRINCE HALL,
> JACK PIERPONT, [his X mark.]
> NERO FUNELO, [his X mark.]
> NEWPORT SUMNER, [his X mark.]"

The following entry, bearing the same date, was made : —

"A petition of Lancaster Hill, and a number of other Negroes, praying the Court to take into consideration their state of bondage, and pass an act whereby they may be restored to the enjoyment of that freedom which is the natural right of all men. Read and committed to Judge Sargent, Mr. Dalton, Mr. Appleton, Col. Brooks, and Mr. Story."

There is no record of the action of the committee, if any were ever had ; but at the afternoon session of the Legislature, Monday, June 9, 1777, a bill was introduced to prevent "the Practice of holding persons in Slavery." It was "read a first time, and ordered to be read again on Friday next, at 10 o'clock A.M." Accordingly, on the 13th of June, the bill was "read a second time, and after Debate thereon, it was moved and seconded, That the same lie upon the Table, and that Application be made to Congress on the subject thereof ; and the Question being put, it passed in the affirmative, and Mr. Speaker, Mr. Wendell, and Col. Orne, were appointed a Committee to prepare a letter to Congress accordingly, and report." The last action, as far as indicated by the journal, was had on Saturday, June 14, when "the Committee appointed to prepare a Letter to Congress, on the subject of the Bill for preventing the Practice of holding Persons in

Slavery, reported." It was "Read and ordered to lie." [1] And so it did "lie," for that was the end of the matter.

Judge Sargent, who was chairman of the committee appointed on the 18th of March, 1777, was doubtless the author of the following bill : —

"STATE OF MASSACHUSETTS BAY. IN THE YEAR OF OUR LORD, 1777.

"AN ACT for preventing the practice of holding persons in Slavery.

"WHEREAS, the practice of holding Africans and the children born of them, or any other persons, in Slavery, is unjustifiable in a civil government, at a time when they are asserting their natural freedom ; wherefore, for preventing such a practice for the future, and establishing to every person residing within the State the invaluable blessing of liberty.

"*Be it Enacted*, by the Council and House of Representatives, in General Court assembled, and by the authority of the same, — That all persons, whether black or of other complexion, above 21 years of age, now held in Slavery, shall, from and after the   day of   next, be free from any subjection to any master or mistress, who have claimed their servitude by right of purchase, heirship, free gift, or otherwise, and they are hereby entitled to all the freedom, rights, privileges and immunities that do, or ought of right to belong to any of the subjects of this State, any usage or custom to the contrary notwithstanding.

"*And be it Enacted*, by the authority aforesaid, that all written deeds, bargains, sales or conveyances, or contracts without writing, whatsoever, for conveying or transferring any property in any person, or to the service and labor of any person whatsoever, of more than twenty-one years of age, to a third person, except by order of some court of record for some crime, that has been, or hereafter shall be made, or by their own voluntary contract for a term not exceeding seven years, shall be and hereby are declared null and void.

"And WHEREAS, divers persons now have in their service negroes, mulattoes or others who have been deemed their slaves or property, and who are now incapable of earning their living by reason of age or infirmities, and may be desirous of continuing in the service of their masters or mistresses, — *be it therefore Enacted*, by the authority aforesaid, that whatever negro or mulatto, who shall be desirous of continuing in the service of his master or mistress, and shall voluntarily declare the same before two justices of the County in which said master or mistress resides, shall have a right to continue in the service, and to a maintenance from their master or mistress, and if they are incapable of earning their living, shall be supported by the said master or mistress, or their heirs, during the lives of said servants, any thing in this act to the contrary notwithstanding.

"*Provided*, nevertheless, that nothing in this act shall be understood to prevent any master of a vessel or other person from bringing into this State any persons, not Africans, from any other part of the world, except the United States of America, and selling their service for a term of time not exceeding five years, if twenty-one years of age, or, if under twenty-one, not exceeding the time

---

[1] House Journal, pp. 19, 25.

when he or she so brought into the State shall be twenty-six years of age, to pay for and in consideration of the transportation and other charges said master of vessel or other person may have been at, agreeable to contracts made with the persons so transported, or their parents or guardians in their behalf, before they are brought from their own country." [1]

On the back of the bill the following indorsement was written by some officer of the Legislature : " Ordered to lie till the second Wednesday of the next Session of the General Court." This might have ended the struggle for the extinction of slavery in Massachusetts, had not the people at this time made an earnest demand for a State constitution. As the character of the constitution was discussed, the question of slavery divided public sentiment. If it were left out of the constitution, then the claims of the master would forever lack the force of law ; if it were inserted as part of the constitution, it would evidence the insincerity of the people in their talk about the equality of the rights of man, etc. The Legislature — Convention of 1777–78 — prepared, debated, and finally approved and submitted to the people, a draught of a constitution for the State, on the 28th of February, 1778. The framers of the constitution seemed to lack the courage necessary to declare in favor of the freedom of the faithful blacks who had rendered such efficient aid to the cause of the colonists. The prevailing sentiment of the people demanded an article in the constitution denying Negroes the right of citizens. It may be fortunate for the fame of the Commonwealth that the record of the debates on the article denying Negroes the right of suffrage has not been preserved. The article is here given : —

" V. Every male inhabitant of any town in this State, being *free*, and twenty-one years of age, *excepting Negroes, Indians and Mulattoes*, shall be intitled to vote for a Representative or Representatives, as the case may be," etc.

By this article three classes of inhabitants were excluded from the rights, blessings, and duties of citizenship ; and the institution of slavery was recognized as existing by sanction of law. But the constitution was rejected by the people, by an overwhelming majority ; not, however, on account of the fifth article, but because the instrument was obnoxious to them on general principles.

The defeat of the constitution did not temper public sentiment on the question of Negro slavery, for the very next year the

---

[1] Mass. Archives : Revolutionary Resolves, vol. vii. p. 133.

domestic trade seemed to receive a fresh impetus. The following advertisements furnish abundant proof of the undiminished vigor of the enterprise.

From "The Continental Journal," Nov. 25, 1779: —

" *To be* SOLD A likely NEGRO GIRL, 16 years of Age, for no fault, but want of employ."

From the same, Dec. 16, 1779: —

" *To be* SOLD, A Strong likely NEGRO GIRL," etc.

From "The Independent Chronicle," March 9, 1780: —

" *To be* SOLD, for want of employment, an exceeding likely NEGRO GIRL, aged sixteen."

From the same, March 30 and April 6, 1780: —

" *To be* SOLD, very Cheap, for no other Reason than for want of Employ, an exceeding Active NEGRO BOY, aged fifteen. Also, a likely NEGRO GIRL, aged seventeen."

From "The Continental Journal," Aug. 17, 1780: —

" *To be* SOLD, a likely NEGRO BOY."

From the same, Aug. 24 and Sept. 7: —

" *To be* SOLD or LETT, for a term of years, a strong, hearty, likely NEGRO GIRL."

From the same, Oct. 19 and 26, and Nov. 2: —

" *To be* SOLD, a likely NEGRO BOY, about eighteen years of Age, fit for to serve a Gentleman, to tend horses or to work in the Country."

From the same, Oct. 26, 1780: —

" *To be* SOLD, a likely NEGRO BOY, about 13 years old, well calculated to wait on a Gentleman. Inquire of the Printer."
" *To be* SOLD, a likely young COW and CALF. Inquire of the Printer."

"Independent Chronicle," Dec. 14, 21, 28, 1780: —

"A NEGRO CHILD, *soon expected, of a good breed*, may be owned by any Person inclining to take it, and Money with it."

"Continental Journal," Dec. 21, 1780, and Jan. 4, 1781: —

" *To be* SOLD, a hearty, strong NEGRO WENCH, about 29 years of age, fit for town or country."

From " The Continental Journal," March 1, 1781 : —

" *To be* SOLD, an extraordinary likely NEGRO WENCH, 17 years old, she can be warranted to be strong, healthy and good-natured, *has no notion of Freedom*, has been always used to a Farmer's Kitchen and dairy, and is not known to have any failing, but being with Child, which is the only cause of her being sold."

It is evident, from the wording of the last advertisement quoted, that the Negroes were sniffing the air of freedom that occasionally blew from the victorious battle-fields, where many of their race had distinguished themselves by the most intrepid valor. They began to get " *notions of freedom*," and this depreciated their market value.

Dr. William Gordon, the steadfast, earnest, and intelligent friend of the Negro, was deposed as chaplain of both branches of the Legislature on account of his vehement protest against the adoption of the fifth article of the constitution by that body. But his zeal was not thereby abated. He continued to address able articles to the public, and wrought a good work upon the public conscience.

In Virginia, notwithstanding Negroes were among the State's most gallant defenders, a law was passed in October, 1776, "declaring tenants of lands or slaves in taille to hold the same in fee simple." Under the circumstances, after the war had begun, and after the declaration by the State of national independence, it was a most remarkable law.

" That any person who now hath, or hereafter may have, any estate in fee taille, general or special, in any lands or slaves in possession, or in the use or trust of any lands or slaves in possession, or who now is or hereafter may be entitled to any such estate taille in reversion or remainder, after the determination of any estate for life or lives, or of any lesser estate, whether such estate taille hath been or shall be created by deeds, will, act of assembly, or by any other ways or means, shall from henceforth, or from the commencement of such estate taille, stand *ipso facto* seized, possessed, or entitled of, in, or to such lands or slaves, or use in lands or slaves, so held or to be held as aforesaid, in possession, reversion, or remainder, in full and absolute fee simple, in like manner as if such deed, will, act of assembly, or other instrument, had conveyed the same to him in fee simple; any words, limitations, or conditions, in the said deed, will, act of assembly, or other instrument, to the contrary notwithstanding." [1]

---

[1] Hening, vol. ix. p. 226.

But the valor of the Negro soldier had great influence upon the public mind, and inspired the people in many of the States to demand public recognition of deserving Negroes. It has been noted already, that in South Carolina, if a Negro, having been captured by the enemy, made good his escape back into the State, he was emancipated; and, if wounded in the line of duty, was rewarded with his freedom. Rhode Island purchased her Negroes for the army, and presented them with fifty dollars bounty and a certificate of freedom at the close of the war. Even Virginia, the mother of slavery, remembered, at the close of the war, the brave Negroes who had fought in her regiments. In October, 1783, the following Act was passed emancipating all slaves who had served in the army with the permission of their masters. It is to be regretted, however, that *all* slaves who had served in the army were not rewarded with their freedom.

"I. WHEREAS it hath been represented to the present general assembly, that during the course of the war, many persons in this state had caused their slaves to enlist in certain regiments or corps raised within the same, having tendered such slaves to the officers appointed to recruit forces within the state, as substitutes for free persons, whose lot or duty it was to serve in such regiments or corps, at the same time representing to such recruiting officers that the slaves so enlisted by their direction and concurrence were freemen; and it appearing further to this assembly, that on the expiration of the term of enlistment of such slaves that the former owners have attempted again to force them to return to a state of servitude, contrary to the principles of justice, and to their own solemn promise.

"II. And whereas it appears just and reasonable that all persons enlisted as aforesaid, who have faithfully served agreeable to the terms of their enlistment, and have thereby of course contributed towards the establishment of American liberty and independence, should enjoy the blessings of freedom as a reward for their toils and labours; *Be it therefore enacted*, That each and every slave who by the appointment and direction of his owner, hath enlisted in any regiment or corps raised within this state, either on continental or state establishment, and hath been received as a substitute for any free person whose duty or lot it was to serve in such regiment or corps, and hath served faithfully during the term of such enlistment, or hath been discharged from such service by some officer duly authorized to grant such discharge, shall from and after the passing of this act, be fully and compleatly emancipated, and shall be held and deemed free in as full and ample a manner as if each and every of them were specially named in this act; and the attorney-general for the commonwealth, is hereby required to commence an action, *in forma pauperis*, in behalf of any of the persons above described who shall after the passing of this act be detained in servitude by any person whatsoever; and if upon such prosecution it shall appear that the pauper is entitled to his freedom in consequence

of this act, a jury shall be empannelled to assess the damages for his detention." [1]

New York enlisted her Negro soldiers under a statutory
promise of freedom.   They were required to serve three years, or
until regularly discharged.   Several other States emancipated a
few slaves who had served faithfully in the army ; and the recital
of the noble deeds of black soldiers was listened to with great
interest, had an excellent effect upon many white men after
the war, and went far towards mollifying public sentiment on the
slavery question.

If Massachusetts were ever moved by the valor of her black
soldiers to take any action recognizing their services, the record
has not been found up to the present time.   After commemorat-
ing the 5th of March for a long time, as a day on which to inflame
the public zeal for the cause of freedom, her Legislature refused to
mark the grave of the first martyr of the Revolution, Crispus
Attucks !

Slavery flourished during the entire Revolutionary period.   It
enjoyed the silent acquiescence of the pulpit, the support of the
public journals, the sanction of the courts, and the indorsement
of the military establishment.   In a free land (?), under the flag
of the government Negroes fought, bled, sacrificed, and died to
establish, slavery held undisputed sway.   The colonial government, built by the cruel and voracious avarice of Britain, crumbled
under the master-stroke of men who desired political and religious
liberty more than jewelled crowns ; but the slave institution stood
unharmed by the shock of embattled arms.   The colonists asked
freedom for themselves and children, but forged chains for
Negroes and their children.   And while a few individual Negro
slaves were made a present of themselves at the close of the war,
on account of their gallant service, hundreds of thousands of
their brethren were still retained in bondage.

---

[1] Hening, vol. xi. pp. 308, 309.

CHAPTER XXXI.

SLAVERY AS A POLITICAL AND LEGAL PROBLEM.

1775–1800.

BRITISH COLONIES IN NORTH AMERICA DECLARE THEIR INDEPENDENCE. — A NEW GOVERNMENT
ESTABLISHED. — SLAVERY THE BANE OF AMERICAN CIVILIZATION. — THE TORY PARTY ACCEPT
THE DOCTRINE OF PROPERTY IN MAN. — THE DOCTRINE OF THE LOCKE CONSTITUTION IN THE
SOUTH. — THE WHIG PARTY THE DOMINANT POLITICAL ORGANIZATION IN THE NORTHERN
STATES. — SLAVERY RECOGNIZED UNDER THE NEW GOVERNMENT. — ANTI-SLAVERY AGITATION IN
THE STATES. — ATTEMPTED LEGISLATION AGAINST SLAVERY. — ARTICLES OF CONFEDERATION. —
THEIR ADOPTION IN 1778. — DISCUSSION CONCERNING THE DISPOSAL OF THE WESTERN TERRITORY.
— MR. JEFFERSON'S RECOMMENDATION. — AMENDMENT BY MR. SPAIGHT. — CONGRESS IN NEW
YORK IN 1787. — DISCUSSION RESPECTING THE GOVERNMENT OF THE WESTERN TERRITORY. — CON-
VENTION AT PHILADELPHIA TO FRAME THE FEDERAL CONSTITUTION. — PROCEEDINGS OF THE CON-
VENTION. — THE SOUTHERN STATES STILL ADVOCATE SLAVERY. — SPEECHES ON THE SLAVERY
QUESTION BY LEADING STATESMEN. — CONSTITUTION ADOPTED BY THE CONVENTION IN 1787. —
FIRST SESSION OF CONGRESS UNDER THE FEDERAL CONSTITUTION HELD IN NEW YORK IN 1789.
— THE INTRODUCTION OF A TARIFF-BILL. — AN ATTEMPT TO AMEND IT BY INSERTING A CLAUSE
LEVYING A TAX ON SLAVES BROUGHT BY WATER. — EXTINCTION OF SLAVERY IN MASSACHUSETTS.
— A CHANGE IN THE PUBLIC OPINION OF THE MIDDLE AND EASTERN STATES ON THE SUBJECT
OF SLAVERY. — DR. BENJAMIN FRANKLIN'S ADDRESS TO THE PUBLIC FOR PROMOTING THE ABOLI-
TION OF SLAVERY. — MEMORIAL TO THE UNITED-STATES CONGRESS. — CONGRESS IN 1790. —
BITTER DISCUSSION ON THE RESTRICTION OF THE SLAVE-TRADE. — SLAVE POPULATION. —
VERMONT AND KENTUCKY ADMITTED INTO THE UNION. — A LAW PROVIDING FOR THE RETURN
OF FUGITIVES FROM " LABOR AND SERVICE." — CONVENTION OF FRIENDS HELD IN PHILADELPHIA.
— AN ACT AGAINST THE FOREIGN SLAVE-TRADE. — MISSISSIPPI TERRITORY. — CONSTITUTION OF
GEORGIA REVISED. — NEW YORK PASSES A BILL FOR THE GRADUAL EXTINCTION OF SLAVERY. —
CONSTITUTION OF KENTUCKY REVISED. — SLAVERY AS AN INSTITUTION FIRMLY ESTABLISHED.

THE charge that the mother-country forced slavery upon the
British colonies in North America held good until the
colonies threw off the yoke, declared their independence,
and built a new government, on the 4th of July, 1776. After the
promulgation of the gospel of human liberty, the United States
of America could no longer point to England as the "first man
Adam" of the accursed sin of slavery. Henceforth the American
government, under the new dispensation of peace and the equality
of all men, was responsible for the continuance of slavery, both
as a political and legal problem.

Slavery did not escheat to the English government upon the
expiration of its authority in North America. It became the

dreadful inheritance of the new government, and the eyesore of American civilization. Instead of expelling it from the political institutions of the country, it gradually became a factor of great power. Instead of ruling it out of the courts, it was clothed with the ample garments of judicial respectability.

The first article of the immortal Declaration of Independence was a mighty shield of beautifully wrought truths, that the authors intended should protect every human being on the American Continent.

> "*We hold these truths to be self-evident:—that all men are created equal, that they are endowed by their Creator with certain inalienable rights; that among these are life, liberty, and the pursuit of happiness. That to secure these rights, governments are instituted among men, deriving their just powers from the consent of the governed; that whenever any form of government becomes destructive of these ends, it is the right of the people to alter or to abolish it, and to institute a new government, laying its foundation on such principles, and organizing its powers in such form, as to them shall seem most likely to effect their safety and happiness.*"

It was to be expected, that, after such a declaration of principles, the United States would have abolished slavery and the slave-trade forever. While the magic words of the Declaration of Independence were not the empty "palaver" of a few ambitious leaders, yet the practices of the local and the national government belied the grand sentiments of that instrument. From the earliest moment of the birth of the United-States government, slavery began to receive political support and encouragement. Though it was the cruel and depraved offspring of the British government, it nevertheless was adopted by the *free government* of America. Political policy seemed to dictate the methods of a political recognition of the institution. And the fact that the slave-trade was prohibited by Congress at an early day, and by many of the colonies also, did not affect the institution in a local sense.

The Tory party accepted the doctrine of property in man, without hesitation or reservation. Their political fealty to the Crown, their party exclusiveness, and their earnest desire to co-operate with the Royal African Company in the establishment of the slave institution in America, made them, as per necessity, the political guardians of slavery. The institution once planted, property in man having been acquired, it was found to be a difficult task to uproot it. Moreover, the loss of the colonies to the

British Crown did not imply death to the Tory party. It doubtless suffered organically; but its individual members did not
forfeit their political convictions, nor suffer their interest in the
slave-trade to abate. The new States were ambitious to acquire
political power. The white population of the South was small
when compared with that of the North; but the slave population,
added to the former, swelled it to alarming proportions.

The local governments of the South had been organized upon
the fundamental principles of the Locke Constitution. . The
government was lodged with the few, and their rights were built
upon landed estates and political titles and favors. Slaves in the
Carolinas and Virginias answered to the vassals and villeins of
England. This aristocratic element in Tory politics was in
harmony, even in a republic, with the later wish of the South to
build a great political "government upon Slavery as its chief
corner-stone." Added to this was the desire to abrogate the law
of indenture of white servants, and thus to the odium of slavery
to loan the powerful influence of caste, — ranging the Caucasian
against the Ethiopian, the intelligent against the ignorant, the
strong against the weak.

New England had better ideas of popular government for and
of the people, but her practical position on slavery was no better
than any State in the South. The Whig party was the dominant
political organization throughout the Northern States; but the
universality of slavery made dealers in human flesh members of
all parties.

The men who wrote the Declaration of Independence deprecated slavery, as they were pronounced Whigs; but nevertheless
many of them owned slaves. They wished the evil exterminated,
but confessed themselves ignorant of a plan by which to carry
their desire into effect. The good desires of many of the people,
born out of the early days of the struggle for independent existence, perished in their very infancy; and, as has been shown, all
the States, and the Congress of the United States, recognized
slavery as existing under the new political government.

But public sentiment changes in a country where the intellect
is unfettered. First, on the eve of the Revolutionary War, Congress and nearly all the States pronounced against slavery; a few
years later they all recognized the sacredness of slave property;
and still later all sections of the United States seemed to have
been agitated by anti-slavery sentiments. In 1780 the Legislature

of Pennsylvania prohibited the further introduction of slaves, and gave freedom to the children of all slaves born in the State. Delaware resolved "that no person hereafter imported from Africa ought to be held in slavery under any pretense whatever." In 1784 Connecticut and Rhode Island modified their slave-code, and forbade further importations of slaves. In 1778 Virginia passed a law prohibiting the importation of slaves, and in 1782 repealed the law that confined the power of emancipating to the Legislature, only on account of meritorious conduct. Private emancipations became very numerous, and the sentiment in its favor pronounced. But the restriction was re-enacted in about ten years. The eloquence of Patrick Henry and the logic of Thomas Jefferson went far to enlighten public sentiment; but the political influence of the institution grew so rapidly that in 1785, but two years after the war, Washington wrote LaFayette, "petitions for the abolition of slavery, presented to the Virginia Legislature, could scarcely obtain a hearing." Maryland, New York, and New Jersey prohibited the slave-trade; but the institution held its place among the people until 1830. North Carolina attempted to prohibit in 1777, but failed; but in 1786 declared the slave-trade "*of evil consequences and highly impolitic.*" South Carolina and Georgia refused to act, and the slave-trade continued along their shores.

After the adoption of the Articles of Confederation in 1778, the Continental Congress found itself charged with the responsibility of deciding the conflicting claims of the various States to the vast territory stretching westward from the Ohio River. The war over, the payment of the public debt thus incurred demanded the consideration of the people and of their representatives. Massachusetts, Connecticut, New York, Virginia, North Carolina, and Georgia laid claim to boundless tracts of lands outside of their State boundaries. But New Hampshire, Rhode Island, New Jersey, Maryland, Delaware, and South Carolina, making no such claims, and lacking the resources to pay their share of the war debt, suggested that the other States should cede all the territory outside of their State lines, to the United States Government, to be used towards liquidating the entire debt. The proposition was accepted by the States named; but not, however, without some modification. Virginia reserved a large territory beyond the Ohio with which to pay the bounties of her soldiers, while Connecticut retained a portion of the Reserve since so famous in the history of Ohio. The duty of framing an ordinance for the government of the Western territory was referred to a select committee by Congress, consisting of Mr. Jefferson of Virginia (chairman), Mr. Chase of Maryland, and Mr. Howell of Rhode Island. The plan reported by the committee contemplated the whole region included within our boundaries west of the old thirteen States, and as far south as our thirty-first degree north latitude. The plan proposed the ultimate division of this territory into seventeen States; eight of which were to be located below the parallel of the Falls of the Ohio (now Louisville), and nine above it. But the most interesting rule reported by Mr. Jefferson was the following, on the 19th of April, 1784 : —

"That after the year 1800, of the Christian era, there shall be neither slavery nor involuntary servitude in any of the said *states*, otherwise than in punishment of crimes, whereof the party shall have been convicted to be personally guilty."

Mr. Spaight of North Carolina moved to amend the report by striking out the above clause, which was seconded by Mr. Reed of South Carolina. The question, upon a demand for the yeas and nays, was put: "Shall the words moved to be stricken out stand?" The question was lost, and the words were stricken out. The ordinance was further amended, and finally adopted on the 23d of April.

The last Continental Congress was held in the city of New York in 1787. The question of the government of the Western territory came up. A committee was appointed on this subject, with Nathan Dane of Massachusetts as chairman. On the 11th of July the committee reported "An Ordinance for the government of the Territory of the United States, *Northwest of the Ohio.*" It embodied many of the features of Mr. Jefferson's bill, concluding with six unalterable articles of perpetual compact, the last being the following: "There shall be neither slavery nor involuntary servitude in the said territory, otherwise than in punishment of crimes, whereof the parties shall be duly convicted." When upon its passage, a stipulation was added for the delivery of fugitives from "labor or service;"[1] and in this shape the entire ordinance passed on the 13th of July, 1787.

Thus it is clear that under the Confederation slavery existed,

---

[1] St. Clair Papers, vol. i. p. 120.

a part of the political government, as a legal fact. There was no effort made by Congress to abolish it. Mr. Jefferson simply sought to arrest its progress, and confine it to the original thirteen States.

On the 25th of May, 1787, the convention to frame the Federal Constitution met at Philadelphia, although the day appointed was the 14th. George Washington was chosen president, a committee chosen to report rules of proceeding, and a secretary appointed. The sessions were held with closed doors, and all the proceedings were secret. It contained the most eminent men in the United States, — generals of the army, statesmen, lawyers, and men of broad scholarship. The question of congressional apportionment was early before them, and there was great diversity of opinion. But, as there was no census, therefore there could be no just apportionment until an enumeration of the people was taken. Until that was accomplished, the number of delegates was fixed at sixty-five. Massachusetts was the only State in the Union where slavery did not exist. The Northern States desired representation according to the free inhabitants only ; while all of the Southern States, where the great mass of slaves was, wanted representation according to the entire population, bond and free. Some of the Northern delegates urged their view with great force and eloquence. Mr. Patterson of New Jersey said he regarded slaves as mere property. They were not represented in the States : why should they be in the general government ? They were not allowed to vote : why should they be represented ? He regarded it as an encouragement to the slave-trade. Mr. Wilson of Pennsylvania said, "Are they admitted as citizens ? then, why not on an equality with citizens ? Are they admitted as property ? then, why is not other property admitted into the computation ?" It was evident that neither extreme view could carry : so the proposition carried to reckon three-fifths of the slaves in estimating taxes, and to make taxation the basis of representation. New Jersey and Delaware voted Nay ; Massachusetts and South Carolina were divided ; and New York was not represented, her delegates having failed to arrive.

It was apparent during the early stages of the debates, that a constitution had to be made that would be acceptable to the Southern delegates. A clause was inserted relieving the Southern States from duties on exports, and upon the importation of slaves ; and that no navigation act should be passed except by a two-thirds vote. By denying Congress the authority of giving preference to American over foreign shipping, it was designed to secure cheap transportation for Southern exports ; but, as the shipping was largely owned in the Eastern States, their delegates were zealous in their efforts to prevent any restriction of the power of Congress to enact navigation laws. It has been already shown that all the States, with the exception of North Carolina, South Carolina, and Georgia, had prohibited the importation of slaves. The prohibition of duties on the importation of slaves was demanded by the delegates from South Carolina and Georgia. They assured the Convention that without such a provision they could never give their assent to the constitution. This declaration dragooned some Northern delegates into a support of the restriction, but provoked some very plain remarks concerning slavery. Mr. Pinckney said, that, "If the Southern States were let alone, they would probably of themselves stop importations. He would himself, as a citizen of South Carolina, vote for it."

Mr. Sherman remarked that "the abolition of slavery seemed to be going on in the United States, and that the good sense of the several states would probably by degrees complete it ;" and Mr. Ellsworth thought that "slavery, in time, will not be a speck in our country." Mr. Madison said "he thought it *wrong* to admit in the Constitution the idea of property in men."

Slavery, notwithstanding the high-sounding words just quoted, was recognized in and by three separate clauses of the Constitution. The word "slave" was excluded, but the language does not admit of any doubt.

"ART. I. SECT. 2. . . . Representatives and direct taxes shall be apportioned among the several States which may be included within this Union, according to their respective numbers ; which shall be determined by adding to the whole number of free persons, including those bound to service for a term of years, and excluding Indians not taxed, *three-fifths of all other persons.*[1] . . .

"ART. I. SECT. 9. The migration or importation of such *persons* as any of the States now existing shall think proper to admit, shall not be prohibited by the Congress prior to the year one thousand eight hundred and eight ; but a tax or duty may be imposed on such importation, not exceeding ten dollars for each person. . . .

"ART. IV. SECT. 2. . . . No *person* held to service or labor in one State, under the laws thereof, escaping into another, shall, in consequence of any law or regulation therein, be discharged from such service or labor, but shall be

---

[1] The clause " three-fifths of all other persons " refers to Negro slaves. The Italics are our own. The Negro is referred to as a *person* all through the Constitution.

delivered up on claim of the party to whom such service or labor may be due."

The debate on the above was exciting and interesting, as the subject of slavery was examined in all its bearings. Finally the Constitution was submitted to Gouverneur Morris of Pennsylvania, to receive the finishing touches of his facile pen. On the 8th of August, 1787, during the debate, he delivered the following speech : —

"He never would concur in upholding domestic slavery. It was a nefarious institution. It was the curse of Heaven on the States where it prevailed. Compare the free regions of the Middle States, where a rich and noble cultivation marks the prosperity and happiness of the people, with the misery and poverty which overspread the barren wastes of Virginia, Maryland, and the other States having slaves. Travel through the whole continent, and you behold the prospect continually varying with the appearance and disappearance of slavery. The moment you leave the Eastern States, and enter New York, the effects of the institution become visible. Passing through the Jerseys, and entering Pennsylvania, every criterion of superior improvement witnesses the change. Proceed southwardly, and every step you take through the great regions of slaves presents a desert, increasing with the increasing proportion of these wretched beings. Upon what principle is it that the slaves shall be computed in the representation? Are they men? Then make them citizens, and let them vote. Are they property? Why, then, is no other property included? The houses in this city (Philadelphia) are worth more than all the wretched slaves who cover the rice-swamps of South Carolina. The admission of slaves into the representation, when fairly explained, comes to this, — that the inhabitant of Georgia and South Carolina, who goes to the coast of Africa, and, in defiance of the most sacred laws of humanity, tears away his fellow-creatures from their dearest connections, and damns them to the most cruel bondage, shall have more votes in a government instituted for the protection of the rights of mankind than the citizen of Pennsylvania or New Jersey, who views with a laudable horror so nefarious a practice. He would add, that domestic slavery is the most prominent feature in the aristocratic countenance of the proposed Constitution. The vassalage of the poor has ever been the favorite offspring of aristocracy. And what is the proposed compensation to the Northern States for a sacrifice of every principle of right, of every impulse of humanity? They are to bind themselves to march their militia for the defence of the Southern States, for their defence against those very slaves of whom they complain. They must supply vessels and seamen in case of foreign attack. The Legislature will have indefinite power to tax them by excises and duties on imports, both of which will fall heavier on them than on the Southern inhabitants; for the bohea tea used by a Northern freeman will pay more tax than the whole consumption of the miserable slave, which consists of nothing more than his physical subsistence and the rag that covers his nakedness. On the other side, the Southern States are not to be restrained from importing fresh supplies of wretched Africans, at once to increase the danger of attack and the difficulty of defence : nay, they are to be encouraged to it by an assurance of having their votes in the National Government increased in proportion; and are, at the same time, to have their exports and their slaves exempt from all contributions for the public service. Let it not be said that direct taxation is to be proportioned to representation. It is idle to suppose that the General Government can stretch its hand directly into the pockets of the people scattered over so vast a country. They can only do it through the medium of exports, imports, and excises. For what, then, are all the sacrifices to be made? He would sooner submit himself to a tax for paying for all the negroes in the United States than saddle posterity with such a Constitution." [1]

Mr. Rufus King of Massachusetts in the same debate said, —

"The admission of slaves was a most grating circumstance to his mind, and he believed would be so to a great part of the people of America. He had not made a strenuous opposition to it heretofore, because he had hoped that this concession would have produced a readiness, which had not been manifested, to strengthen the General Government, and to mark a full confidence in it. The report under consideration had, by the tenor of it, put an end to all those hopes. In two great points, the hands of the Legislature were absolutely tied. The importation of slaves could not be prohibited. Exports could not be taxed. Is this reasonable? What are the great objects of the general system? First, defence against foreign invasion; secondly, against internal sedition. Shall all the States, then, be bound to defend each? and shall each be at liberty to introduce a weakness which will render defence more difficult? Shall one part of the United States be bound to defend another part, and that other part be at liberty, not only to increase its own danger, but to withhold the compensation for the burden? If slaves are to be imported, shall not the exports produced by their labor supply a revenue, the better to enable the General Government to defend their masters? There was so much inequality and unreasonableness in all this, that the people of the Northern States could never be reconciled to it. No candid man could undertake to justify it to them. He had hoped that some accommodation would have taken place on this subject; that, at least, a time would have been limited for the importation of slaves. He never could agree to let them be imported without limitation, and then be represented in the National Legislature. Indeed, he could so little persuade himself of the rectitude of such a practice, that he was not sure he could assent to it under any circumstances. At all events, either slaves should not be represented, or exports should be taxable."

Mr. Roger Sherman of Connecticut, —

"Regarded the slave-trade as iniquitous : but, the point of representation having been settled after much difficulty and deliberation, he did not think himself bound to make opposition; especially as the present article, as amended, did not preclude any arrangement whatever on that point, in another place of the report." [2]

---

[1] Madison Papers, Elliot, vol. v. pp 392, 393.   [2] Ibid., vol. v. pp. 391, 392.

Mr. Luther Martin of Maryland, in the debate, Tuesday, Aug. 21, —

"Proposed to vary Art. 7, Sect. 4, so as to allow a prohibition or tax on the importation of slaves. In the first place, as five slaves are to be counted as three free men in the apportionment of representatives, such a clause would leave an encouragement to this traffic. In the second place, slaves weakened one part of the Union, which the other parts were bound to protect: the privilege of importing them was therefore unreasonable. And, in the third place, it was inconsistent with the principles of the Revolution, and dishonorable to the American character, to have such a feature in the Constitution.

"Mr. RUTLEDGE did not see how the importation of slaves could be encouraged by this section. He was not apprehensive of insurrections, and would readily exempt the other States from the obligation to protect the Southern against them. Religion and humanity had nothing to do with this question: interest alone is the governing principle with nations. The true question at present is, whether the Southern States shall or shall not be parties to the Union. If the Northern States consult their interest, they will not oppose the increase of slaves, which will increase the commodities of which they will become the carriers.

"Mr. ELLSWORTH was for leaving the clause as it stands. Let every State import what it pleases. The morality or wisdom of slavery are considerations belonging to the States themselves. What enriches a part enriches the whole, and the States are the best judges of their particular interest. The old Confederation had not meddled with this point; and he did not see any greater necessity for bringing it within the policy of the new one.

"Mr. PINCKNEY. South Carolina can never receive the plan if it prohibits the slave-trade. In every proposed extension of the powers of Congress, that State has expressly and watchfully excepted that of meddling with the importation of Negroes. *If the States be all left at liberty on 'this subject, South Carolina may perhaps, by degrees, do of herself what is wished, as Virginia and Maryland have already done.*

" Adjourned.

" WEDNESDAY, Aug. 22.

"*In Convention.* — Art. 7, Sect. 4, was resumed.

"Mr. SHERMAN was for leaving the clause as it stands. He disapproved of the slave-trade; yet, as the States were now possessed of the right to import slaves, as the public good did not require it to be taken from them, and as it was expedient to have as few objections as possible to the proposed scheme of government, he thought it best to leave the matter as we find it. . . . He urged on the Convention the necessity of despatching its business.

"Col. MASON. This infernal traffic originated in the avarice of British merchants. The British Government constantly checked the attempts of Virginia to put a stop to it. The present question concerns, not the importing States alone, but the whole Union. The evil of having slaves was experienced during the late war. Had slaves been treated as they might have been by the enemy, they would have proved dangerous instruments in their hands. But their folly dealt by the slaves as it did by the Tories. He mentioned the dangerous insurrections of the slaves in Greece and Sicily, and the instructions given by Cromwell to the commissioners sent to Virginia, — to arm the servants and slaves, in case other means of obtaining its submission should fail. Maryland and Virginia, he said, had already prohibited the importation of slaves expressly. North Carolina had done the same in substance. All this would be in vain, if South Carolina and Georgia be at liberty to import. The Western people are already calling out for slaves for their new lands; and will fill that country with slaves, if they can be got through South Carolina and Georgia. Slavery discourages arts and manufactures. The poor despise labor when performed by slaves. They prevent the emigration of whites, who really enrich and strengthen a country. *They produce the most pernicious effect on manners. Every master of slaves is born a petty tyrant. They bring the judgment of heaven on a country. As nations cannot be rewarded or punished in the next world, they must be in this. By an inevitable chain of causes and effects, Providence punishes national sins by national calamities.* He lamented that some of our Eastern brethren had, from a lust of gain, embarked in this nefarious traffic. As to the States being in possession of the right to import, this was the case with many other rights, now to be properly given up. He held it essential, in every point of view, that the General Government should have power to prevent the increase of slavery.

"Mr. ELLSWORTH, as he had never owned a slave, could not judge of the effects of slavery on character. He said, however, that, if it was to be considered in a moral light, we ought to go further, and free those already in the country. As slaves also multiply so fast in Virginia and Maryland, that it is cheaper to raise than import them, whilst in the sickly rice-swamps foreign supplies are necessary, if we go no further than is urged, we shall be unjust towards South Carolina and Georgia. Let us not intermeddle. As population increases, poor laborers will be so plenty as to render slaves useless. *Slavery, in time, will not be a speck in our country.* Provision is already made in Connecticut for abolishing it; and the abolition has already taken place in Massachusetts. As to the danger of insurrections from foreign influence, that will become a motive to kind treatment of the slaves.

"Gen. PINCKNEY declared it to be his firm opinion, that if himself and all his colleagues were to sign the Constitution, and use their personal influence, it would be of no avail towards obtaining the assent of their constituents. South Carolina and Georgia cannot do without slaves. As to Virginia, she will gain by stopping the importations. Her slaves will rise in value, and she has more than she wants. It would be unequal to require South Carolina and Georgia to confederate on such unequal terms. He said, the royal assent, before the Revolution, had never been refused to South Carolina as to Virginia. He contended, that the importation of slaves would be for the interest of the whole Union. The more slaves, the more produce to employ the carrying-trade; the more consumption also; and, the more of this, the more revenue for the common treasury. He admitted it to be reasonable, that slaves should be dutied like other imports; but should consider a rejection of the clause as an exclusion of South Carolina from the Union.

"Mr. BALDWIN had conceived national objects alone to be before the Convention; not such as, like the present, were of a local nature. Georgia was decided on this point. That State has always hitherto supposed a General Government to be the pursuit of the Central States, who wished to have a vortex for every thing; that her distance would preclude her from equal advantage; and that she could not prudently purchase it by yielding national powers. From this it might be understood in what light she would view an attempt to abridge one of her favorite prerogatives. *If left to herself, she may probably put a stop to the evil.* As one ground for this conjecture, he took notice of the sect of ———, which, he said, was a respectable class of people, who carried their ethics beyond the mere *equality of men,*—extending their humanity to the claims of the whole animal creation.

" Mr. WILSON observed, that, *if South Carolina and Georgia were themselves disposed to get rid of the importation of slaves in a short time, as had been suggested, they would never refuse to unite because the importation might be prohibited.* As the section now stands, all articles imported are to be taxed. Slaves alone are exempt. This is, in fact, a bounty on that article.

" Mr. GERRY thought we had nothing to do with the conduct of the States as to slaves, but ought to be careful not to give any sanction to it.

" Mr. DICKINSON considered it as inadmissible, on every principle of honor and safety, that the importation of slaves should be authorized to the States by the Constitution. The true question was, whether the national happiness would be promoted or impeded by the importation; and this question ought to be left to the National Government, not to the States particularly interested. If England and France permit slavery, slaves are, at the same time, excluded from both those kingdoms. Greece and Rome were made unhappy by their slaves. He could not believe that the Southern States would refuse to confederate on the account apprehended; especially as the power was not likely to be immediately exercised by the General Government.

" Mr. WILLIAMSON stated the law of North Carolina on the subject; to wit, that it did not directly prohibit the importation of slaves. It imposed a duty of £5 on each slave imported from Africa, £10 on each from elsewhere, and £50 on each from a State licensing manumission. He thought the Southern States could not be members of the Union, if the clause should be rejected; and it was wrong to force any thing down not absolutely necessary, and which any State must disagree to.

" Mr. KING thought the subject should be considered in a political light only. If two States will not agree to the Constitution, as stated on one side, he could affirm with equal belief, on the other, that great and equal opposition would be experienced from the other States. He remarked on the exemption of slaves from duty, whilst every other import was subjected to it, as an inequality that could not fail to strike the commercial sagacity of the Northern and Middle States.

" Mr. LANGDON was strenuous for giving the power to the General Government. He could not, with a good conscience, leave it with the States, who could then go on with the traffic, without being restrained by the opinions here given, *that they will themselves cease to import slaves.*

" Gen. PINCKNEY thought himself bound to declare candidly, that he did not think South Carolina would stop her importations of slaves in any short time; but only stop them occasionally, as she now does. He moved to commit the clause, that slaves might be made liable to an equal tax with other imports; which he thought right, and which would remove one difficulty that had been started.

"Mr. RUTLEDGE. If the Convention thinks that North Carolina, South Carolina, and Georgia will ever agree to the plan, unless their right to import slaves be untouched, the expectation is vain. The people of those States will never be such fools as to give up so important an interest. He was strenuous against striking out the section, and seconded the motion of Gen. Pinckney for a commitment.

"Mr. GOUVERNEUR MORRIS wished the whole subject to be committed, including the clauses relating to taxes on exports and to a navigation act. These things may form a bargain among the Northern and Southern States.

"Mr. BUTLER declared, that he never would agree to the power of taxing exports.

"Mr. SHERMAN said it was better to let the Southern States import slaves than to. part with them, if they made that a *sine quâ non*. He was opposed to a tax on slaves imported, as making the matter worse, because it implied they were *property*. He acknowledged, that, if the power of prohibiting the importation should be given to the General Government, it would be exercised. He thought it would be its duty to exercise the power.

"Mr. READ was for the commitment, provided the clause concerning taxes on exports should also be committed.

"Mr. SHERMAN observed, that that clause had been agreed to, and therefore could not be committed.

"Mr. RANDOLPH was for committing, in order that some middle ground might, if possible, be found. He could never agree to the clause as it stands. He would sooner risk the Constitution. He dwelt on the dilemma to which the Convention was exposed. By agreeing to the clause, it would revolt the Quakers, the Methodists, and many others in the States having no slaves. On the other hand, two States might be lost to the Union. Let us then, he said, try the chance of a commitment." [1]

Three days later (Saturday, Aug. 25) the debate on the subject was resumed, and the report of the committee of eleven was taken up. It was in the following words : —

"Strike out so much of the fourth section as was referred to the Committee, and insert 'The migration or importation of such persons as the several States, now existing, think proper to admit, shall not be prohibited by the Legislature prior to the year 1800; but a tax or duty may be imposed on such migration or importation, at a rate not exceeding the average of the duties laid on imports.'

.   .   .   .

"Gen. PINCKNEY moved to strike out the words 'the year eighteen hundred' as the year limiting the importation of slaves, and to insert the words 'the year eighteen hundred and eight.'

"Mr. GORHAM seconded the motion.

"Mr. MADISON. Twenty years will produce all the mischief that can be apprehended from the liberty to import slaves. So long a term will be more

---

[1] Madison Papers, Elliot, vol. v. pp. 457-461.

dishonorable to the American character than to say nothing about it in the Constitution.

"On the motion, which passed in the affirmative, —

"New Hampshire, Massachusetts, Connecticut, Maryland, North Carolina, South Carolina, Georgia, ay, — 7; New Jersey, Pennsylvania, Delaware, Virginia, no, — 4.

"Mr. GOUVERNEUR MORRIS was for making the clause read at once, —

"'The importation of slaves into North Carolina, South Carolina, and Georgia, shall not be prohibited,' &c. This, he said, would be most fair, and would avoid the ambiguity by which, under the power with regard to naturalization, the liberty reserved to the States might be defeated. He wished it to be known, also, that this part of the Constitution was a compliance with those States. If the change of language, however, should be objected to by the members from those States, he should not urge it.

"Col. MASON was not against using the term 'slaves,' but against naming North Carolina, South Carolina, and Georgia, lest it should give offence to the people of those States.

"Mr. SHERMAN liked a description better than the terms proposed, which had been declined by the old Congress, and were not pleasing to some people.

"Mr. CLYMER concurred with Mr. Sherman.

"Mr. WILLIAMSON said, that, both in opinion and practice, he was against slavery; but thought it more in favor of humanity, from a view of all circumstances, to let in South Carolina and Georgia on those terms, than to exclude them from the Union.

"Mr. GOUVERNEUR MORRIS withdrew his motion.

"Mr. DICKINSON wished the clause to be confined to the States which had not themselves prohibited the importation of slaves; and, for that purpose, moved to amend the clause so as to read, —

"'The importation of slaves into such of the States as shall permit the same shall not be prohibited by the Legislature of the United States until the year 1808;' —

"which was disagreed to, *nem. con.*

"The first part of the Report was then agreed to, amended as follows: —

"'The migration or importation of such persons as the several States now existing shall think proper to admit shall not be prohibited by the Legislature prior to the year 1808.'

"New Hampshire, Massachusetts, Connecticut, Maryland, North Carolina, South Carolina, Georgia, ay, - - 7; New Jersey, Pennsylvania, Delaware, Virginia, no, — 4." [1]

The above specimens of the speeches on the slavery question, during the debate, are sufficient to furnish a fair idea of the personal opinion of the great thinkers of that time on slavery. It is clear that it was the wish of the great majority of the Northern delegates to abolish the institution, in a domestic as well as in

---

[1] Madison Papers, Elliot, vol. v. pp. 477, 478.

a foreign sense; but they were not strong enough to resist the temptation to compromise their profoundest convictions on a question as broad and far-reaching as the Union that they were met to launch anew. Thus by an understanding, or, as Gouverneur Morris called it, "a bargain," between the commercial representatives of the Northern States and the delegates of South Carolina and Georgia, and in spite of the opposition of Maryland and Virginia, the unrestricted power of Congress to enact navigation-laws was conceded to the Northern merchants; and to the Carolina rice-planters, as an equivalent, twenty years' continuance of the African slave-trade. This was the third great "compromise" of the Constitution. The other two were the concession to the smaller States of an equal representation in the Senate; and, to the slaveholders, the counting three-fifths of the slaves in determining the ratio of representation. If this third compromise differed from the other two by involving not merely a political but a moral sacrifice, there was this partial compensation about it, that it was not permanent like the others, but expired, by limitation, at the end of twenty years.[1]

The Constitution was adopted by the Convention, and signed, on the 17th of September, 1787. It was then forwarded to Congress, then in session in New-York City, with the recommendation that that body submit it to the State conventions for ratification; which was accordingly done. Delaware adopted it on the 7th of December, 1787; Pennsylvania, Dec. 12; New Jersey, Dec. 18; Georgia, Jan. 2, 1788; Connecticut, Jan. 9; Massachusetts, Feb. 7; Maryland, April 28; South Carolina, May 23; New Hampshire, June 21 (and, being the ninth ratifying, gave effect to the Constitution); Virginia ratified June 27; New York, July 26. North Carolina gave a conditional ratification on the 7th of August, but Congress did not receive it until January, 1790; nor that of Rhode Island, until June of the same year.

At the conclusion of the deliberations of the convention that framed the Constitution, it was voted that its journal be intrusted to the custody of George Washington. He finally deposited it in the State Department, and it was printed in 1818 by order of Congress.

The first session of Congress, under the new Constitution, was

---

[1] Examine Hildreth and the Secret Debates on the subject of the "compromises."

held in the city of New York, in 1789. A quorum was obtained on the 6th of April; and the first measure brought up for consideration was a tariff-bill which Mr. Parker of Virginia sought to amend by inserting a clause levying an impost-tax of ten dollars upon every slave brought by water. "He was sorry the Constitution prevented Congress from prohibiting the importation altogether. It was contrary to revolution principles, and ought not to be permitted." Thus the question of slavery made its appearance early at the first session of the first Congress under the present Constitution. At that time Georgia was the only State in the Union that seemed to retain a pecuniary interest in the importation of slaves. Even South Carolina had passed an Act prohibiting for one year the importation of slaves. In this, as on several occasions before, she was actuated on account of the low prices of produce, — too low to be remunerative. But, notwithstanding this, Mr. Smith, the member from the Charleston district, grew quite captious over the proposition of the gentleman from Virginia. He

"Hoped that such an important and serious proposition would not be hastily adopted. It was rather a late moment for the first introduction of a subject so big with serious consequences. No one topic had been yet introduced so important to South Carolina and the welfare of the Union."

Mr. Sherman got the floor, and said he

"Approved the object of the motion, but did not think it a fit subject to be embraced in this bill. He could not reconcile himself to the insertion of human beings, as a subject of impost, among goods, wares, and merchandise. He hoped the motion would be withdrawn for the present, and taken up afterwards as an independent subject."

Mr. Jackson of Georgia

"Was not surprised, however others might be so, at the quarter whence this motion came. Virginia, as an old settled State, had her complement of slaves, and the natural increase being sufficient for her purpose, she was careless of recruiting her numbers by importation. But gentlemen ought to let their neighbors get supplied before they imposed such a burden. He knew this business was viewed in an odious light at the Eastward, because the people there were capable of doing their own work, and had no occasion for slaves. But gentlemen ought to have some feeling for others. Surely they do not mean to tax us for every comfort and enjoyment of life, and, at the same time, to take from us the means of procuring them! He was sure, from the unsuitableness of the motion to the business now before the house, and the want of time to consider it, the gentleman's candor would induce him to withdraw it.

Should it ever be brought forward again, he hoped it would comprehend the white slaves as well as the black, imported from all the jails of Europe; wretches convicted of the most flagrant crimes, who were brought in and sold without any duty whatever. They ought to be taxed equally with Africans, and he had no doubt of the equal constitutionality and propriety of such a course."

Mr. Parker of Virginia obtained the floor again, and proceeded to reply to the remarks offered upon his amendment by Sherman, Jackson, and Smith. He declared, —

"That, having introduced the motion on mature reflection, he did not like to withdraw it. The gentleman from Connecticut had said that human beings ought not to be enumerated with goods, wares, and merchandise. Yet he believed they were looked upon by African traders in that light. He hoped Congress would do all in their power to restore to human nature its inherent privileges; to wipe off, if possible, the stigma under which America labored; to do away the inconsistence in our principles justly charged upon us; and to show, by our actions, the pure beneficence of the doctrine held out to the world in our Declaration of Independence."

Mr. Ames of Massachusetts

"Detested slavery from his soul; but he had some doubts whether imposing a duty on their importation would not have an appearance of countenancing the practice."

Mr. Madison made an eloquent speech in support of Mr. Parker's amendment. He said, —

"The confounding men with merchandise might be easily avoided by altering the title of the bill; it was, in fact, the very object of the motion to prevent men, so far as the power of Congress extended, from being confounded with merchandise. The clause in the Constitution allowing a tax to be imposed, though the traffic could not be prohibited for twenty years, was inserted, he believed, for the very purpose of enabling Congress to give some testimony of the sense of America with respect to the African trade. By expressing a national disapprobation of that trade, it is to be hoped we may destroy it, and so save ourselves from reproaches, and our posterity from the imbecility ever attendant on a country filled with slaves. This was as much the interest of South Carolina and Georgia as of any other States. Every addition they received to their number of slaves tended to weakness, and rendered them less capable of self-defence. In case of hostilities with foreign nations, their slave population would be a means, not of repelling invasions, but of inviting attack. It was the duty of the general government to protect every part of the Union against danger, as well internal as external. Every thing, therefore, which tended to increase this danger, though it might be a local affair, yet, if it involved national expense or safety, became of concern to every part of the

Union, and a proper subject for the consideration of those charged with the general administration of the government."

Mr. Bland approved the position taken by Mr. Madison, while Mr. Burke of South Carolina charged the gentlemen with having wasted the time of Congress upon a useless proposition. . He contended, that, while slaves were not mentioned in the Constitution, they would come under the general five per cent *ad valorem* duty on all unenumerated articles, which would be equivalent to the proposition of the gentleman from Virginia. Mr. Madison replied by saying, that no collector of customs would presume to apply the terms "goods," "wares," and "merchandise" to persons. Mr. Sherman followed him in the same strain, and denied that persons were anywhere recognized as property in the Constitution. Finally, at the suggestion of Mr. Madison, Mr. Parker consented to withdraw his motion with the understanding that a separate bill should be brought in. A committee was appointed to discharge that duty, but the noble resolve found a quiet grave in the committee-room.

The failure of this first attempt, under the new Constitution, to restrict slavery, did not lame the cause to any great extent. It was rather accelerated. The manner and spirit of the debate on the subject quickened public thought, animated the friends of the Negro, and provoked many people to good works. Slavery had ceased to exist in Massachusetts. Several suits, entered by slaves against their masters for restraining their liberty, had been won. The case of Elizabeth Freeman, better known as "Mum Bet," was regarded as the first-fruits of the Massachusetts Declaration of Rights in the new Constitution of 1780. The Duke de la Rochefoucault Laincort gives the following interesting account of the extinction of slavery in Massachusetts : —

"In 1781, some negroes, prompted by private suggestion, maintained that they were not slaves: they found advocates, among whom was Mr. Sedgwick, now a member of the Senate of the United States; and the cause was carried before the Supreme Court. Their counsel pleaded, 1°. That no antecedent law had established slavery, and that the laws which seemed to suppose it were the offspring of error in the legislators, who had no authority to enact them : — 2°, That such laws, even if they had existed, were annulled by the new Constitution. They gained the cause under both aspects : and the solution of this first question that was brought forward set the negroes entirely at liberty, and at the same time precluded their pretended owners from all claim to indemnification, since they were proved to have possessed and held them in slavery without any right.   As there were only a few slaves in Massachusetts, the decision passed without opposition, and banished all further idea of slavery." [1]

Mr. Nell gives an account of the legal death of slavery in Massachusetts, but unfortunately does not cite any authority. John Quincy Adams, in reply to a question put by John C. Spencer, stated that "a note had been given for the price of a slave in 1787.   This note was sued, and the Court ruled that the maker had received no consideration, as a man could not be sold. From that time forward, slavery died in the Old Bay State." There were several suits instituted by slaves against their reputed masters in 1781–82; but there are strong evidences that slavery died a much slower death in Massachusetts than many are willing to admit.   James Sullivan wrote to Dr. Belknap in 1795 : —

"In 1781, at the Court in Worcester County, an indictment was found against a white man named Jennison for assaulting, beating, and imprisoning Quock Walker, a black.   He was tried at the Supreme Judicial Court in 1783. His defence was, that the black was his slave, and that the beating, etc., was the necessary restraint and correction of the master.   This was answered by citing the aforesaid clause in the declaration of rights.   The judges and jury were of opinion that he had no right to imprison or beat the negro.   He was found guilty and fined 40 shillings.   This decision put an end to the idea of slavery in Massachusetts." [2]

There are two things in the above that throw considerable uncertainty about the subject as to the precise date of the end of slavery in the Commonwealth.   First, the' suit referred to was tried in 1783, three years after the adoption of the new Constitution.   Second, the good doctor does not say that the decision sealed the fate of slavery, but only that it "was a mortal wound to slavery in Massachusetts."

From 1785–1790, there was a wonderful change in the public opinion of the Middle and Eastern States on the subject of slavery.   Most of them had passed laws providing for gradual emancipation.   The Friends of New York, New Jersey, and Pennsylvania began to organize a crusade against domestic slavery. In the fall of 1789, while the Congressional debates were still fresh in the minds of the people, the venerable Dr. Benjamin Franklin, as president of the "Pennsylvania Society for Promoting the Abolition of Slavery," etc., issued the following letter : —

---

[1] Travels, etc., vol. ii. p. 166.   [2] M. H. S. Coll., 5th Series, III., p. 403.

"AN ADDRESS TO THE PUBLIC.

"*From the Pennsylvania Society for Promoting the Abolition of Slavery, and the Relief of Free Negroes unlawfully held in Bondage.*

"It is with peculiar satisfaction we assure the friends of humanity, that, in prosecuting the design of our association, our endeavors have proved successful, far beyond our most sanguine expectations.

"Encouraged by this success, and by the daily progress of that luminous and benign spirit of liberty which is diffusing itself throughout the world, and humbly hoping for the continuance of the divine blessing on our labors, we have ventured to make an important addition to our original plan; and do therefore earnestly solicit the support and assistance of all who can feel the tender emotions of sympathy and compassion, or relish the exalted pleasure of beneficence.

"Slavery is such an atrocious debasement of human nature, that its very extirpation, if not performed with solicitous care, may sometimes open a source of serious evils.

"The unhappy man, who has long been treated as a brute animal, too frequently sinks beneath the common standard of the human species. The galling chains that bind his body do also fetter his intellectual faculties, and impair the social affections of his heart. Accustomed to move like a mere machine, by the will of a master, reflection is suspended; he has not the power of choice; and reason and conscience have but little influence over his conduct, because he is chiefly governed by the passion of fear. He is poor and friendless; perhaps worn out by extreme labor, age, and disease.

"Under such circumstances, freedom may often prove a misfortune to himself, and prejudicial to society.

"Attention to emancipated black people, it is therefore to be hoped, will become a branch of our national police; but, as far as we contribute to promote this emancipation, so far that attention is evidently a serious duty incumbent on us, and which we mean to discharge to the best of our judgment and abilities.

"To instruct, to advise, to qualify those who have been restored to freedom, for the exercise and enjoyment of civil liberty; to promote in them habits of industry; to furnish them with employments suited to their age, sex, talents, and other circumstances; and to procure their children an education calculated for their future situation in life, — these are the great outlines of the annexed plan, which we have adopted, and which we conceive will essentially promote the public good, and the happiness of these our hitherto too much neglected fellow-creatures.

"A plan so extensive cannot be carried into execution without considerable pecuniary resources, beyond the present ordinary funds of the Society. We hope much from the generosity of enlightened and benevolent freemen, and will gratefully receive any donations or subscriptions for this purpose which may be made to our Treasurer, James Starr, or to James Pemberton, Chairman of our Committee of Correspondence.

"Signed by order of the Society,

"B. FRANKLIN, *President.*

"PHILADELPHIA, 9th of November, 1789."

And as his last public act, Franklin gave his signature to the subjoined memorial to the United-States Congress: —

"The memorial respectfully showeth, —

"That, from a regard for the happiness of mankind, an association was formed several years since in this State, by a number of her citizens, of various religious denominations, for promoting the abolition of slavery, and for the relief of those unlawfully held in bondage. A just and acute conception of the true principles of liberty, as it spread through the land, produced accessions to their numbers, many friends to their cause, and a legislative co-operation with their views, which, by the blessing of Divine Providence, have been successfully directed to the relieving from bondage a large number of their fellow-creatures of the African race. They have also the satisfaction to observe, that, in consequence of that spirit of philanthropy and genuine liberty which is generally diffusing its beneficial influence, similar institutions are forming at home and abroad.

" That mankind are all formed by the same Almighty Being, alike objects of his care, and equally designed for the enjoyment of happiness, the Christian religion teaches us to believe, and the political creed of Americans fully coincides with the position. Your memorialists, particularly engaged in attending to the distresses arising from slavery, believe it their indispensable duty to present this subject to your notice. They have observed, with real satisfaction, that many important and salutary powers are vested in you for 'promoting the welfare and securing the blessings of liberty to the people of the United States'; and as they conceive that these blessings ought rightfully to be administered, without distinction of color, to all descriptions of people, so they indulge themselves in the pleasing expectation, that nothing which can be done for the relief of the unhappy objects of their care, will be either omitted or delayed.

"From a persuasion that equal liberty was originally the portion, and is still the birth-right, of all men; and influenced by the strong ties of humanity, and the principles of their institution, your memorialists conceive themselves bound to use all justifiable endeavors to loosen the bands of slavery, and promote a general enjoyment of the blessings of freedom. Under these impressions, they earnestly entreat your serious attention to the subject of slavery; that you will be pleased to countenance the restoration of liberty to those unhappy men, who alone, in this land of freedom, are degraded into perpetual bondage, and who, amidst the general joy of surrounding freemen, are groaning in servile subjection; that you will devise means for removing this inconsistency from the character of the American people; that you will promote mercy and justice towards this distressed race; and that you will step to the very verge of the power vested in you for discouraging every species of traffic in the persons of our fellow-men.

"BENJ. FRANKLIN, *President.*

"PHILADELPHIA, February 3, 1790."

The session of Congress held in 1790 was stormy. The slavery question came back to haunt the members. On the 12th of February, the memorial from the Pennsylvania society was read. It provoked fresh discussion, and greatly angered many of the Southern members. As soon as its reading was completed, the " Quaker Memorial," that had been read the day previous, was called up; and Mr. Hartley moved its commitment. A long and spirited debate ensued. It was charged that the memorial was "a mischievous attempt, an improper interference, at the best, an act of imprudence;" and that it "would sound an alarm and blow the trumpet of sedition through the Southern States." Mr. Scott of Pennsylvania replied by saying, "I cannot entertain a doubt that the memorial is strictly agreeable to the Constitution. It respects a part of the duty particularly assigned to us by that instrument." Mr. Sherman was in favor of the commitment of the memorial, and gave his reasons *in extenso.* Mr. Smith of South Carolina said, "Notwithstanding all the calmness with which some gentlemen have viewed the subject, they will find that the mere discussion of it will create alarm.. We have been told that, if so, we should have avoided discussion by saying nothing. But it was not for that purpose we were sent here. We look upon this measure as an attack upon property; it is, therefore, our duty to oppose it by every means in our power. When we entered into a political connection with the other States, this property was there. It had been acquired under a former government conformably to the laws and constitution, and every attempt to deprive us of it must be in the nature of an *ex post facto* law, and, as such, forbidden by our political compact." Following the unwise and undignified example set by the gentlemen who had preceded him on that side of the question, he slurred the Quakers. "His constituents wanted no lessons in religion and morality, and least of all from such teachers."

Madison, Gerry, Boudinot, and Page favored commitment. Upon the question to commit, the yeas and nays being demanded, the reference was made by a vote of forty-three to eleven. Of the latter, six were from Georgia and South Carolina, two from Virginia, two from Maryland, and one from New York. A special committee was announced, to whom the memorial was referred, consisting of one member from each of the following States: New Hampshire, Massachusetts, Connecticut, New York, New Jersey, Pennsylvania, and Virginia. At the end of a month, the committee made the following report to Congress:—

"1st. That the general government was expressly restrained, until the year 1808, from prohibiting the importation of any persons whom any of the existing states might till that time think proper to admit. 2d. That, by a fair construction of the constitution, congress was equally restrained from interfering to emancipate slaves within the states, such slaves having been born there, or having been imported within the period mentioned. 3d. That congress had no power to interfere in the internal regulation of particular states relative to the instruction of slaves in the principles of morality and religion, to their comfortable clothing, accommodation, and subsistence, to the regulation of marriages or the violation of marital rights, to the separation of children and parents, to a comfortable provision in cases of age or infirmity, or to the seizure, transportation, and sale of free negroes; but entertained the fullest confidence in the wisdom and humanity of the state legislature that, from time to time, they would revise their laws, and promote these and all other measures tending to the happiness of the slaves. The fourth asserted that congress had authority to levy a tax of ten dollars, should they see fit to exact it, upon every person imported under the special permission of any of the states. The fifth declared the authority of congress to interdict or to regulate the African slave-trade, so far as it might be carried on by citizens of the United States for the supply of foreign countries, and also to provide for the humane treatment of slaves while on their passage to any ports of the United States into which they might be admitted. The sixth asserted the right of congress to prohibit foreigners from fitting out vessels in the United States to be employed in the supply of foreign countries with slaves from Africa. The seventh expressed an intention on the part of congress to exercise their authority to its full extent to promote the humane objects aimed at in the Quaker's memorial."

Mr. Tucker took the floor against the report of the committee, and, after a bitter speech upon the unconstitutionality of meddling with the slavery question in any manner, moved a substitute for the whole, in which he pronounced the recommendations of the committee "as unconstitutional, and tending to injure some of the States of the Union." Mr. Jackson seconded the motion in a rather intemperate speech, which was replied to by Mr. Vining. The substitute of Mr. Tucker was declared out of order. Mr. Benson moved to recommit in hopes of getting rid of the subject, but the motion was overwhelmingly voted down. The report was taken up article by article. The three first resolutions (those relating to the authority of Congress over slavery in the States) were adopted; while the second and third were merged into one, stripped of its objectionable features. But on the fourth the debate was carried to a high pitch. This one related to the ten-dollar tax. Mr. Tucker moved to amend by striking out the fourth resolution. Considerable discussion followed; and, upon the question being put, it was carried by one vote. The fifth resolution, affirming the power of Congress to regulate the slave-trade, drew the fire of Jackson, Smith, and Tucker. Mr. Madison offered to modify it somewhat. It was argued by the opponents of this resolution, that Congress, under the plea of regulating the trade, might prohibit it entirely. Mr. Vining of Delaware, somewhat out of patience with the demands of the Southern members, told those gentlemen very plainly that they ought to be satisfied with the changes already made to gratify them; that they should show some respect to the committee; that all the States from Virginia to New Hampshire had passed laws prohibiting the slave-trade; and then delivered an eloquent defence of the Quakers. The resolution, as modified by Mr. Madison, carried.

The sixth resolution, relating to the foreign slave-trade carried on from ports of the United States, received considerable attention. Mr. Scott made an elaborate speech upon it, in which he claimed, that, if it were a question as to the power of Congress to regulate the foreign slave-trade, he had no doubts as to the authority of that body. "I desire," said that gentleman, "that the world should know, I desire that those people in the gallery, about whom so much has been said, should know, that there is at least one member on this floor who believes that Congress have ample powers to do all they have asked respecting the African slave-trade. Nor do I doubt that Congress will, whenever necessity or policy dictates the measure, exercise those powers." Mr. Jackson attempted to reply. He started out with a labored argument showing the divine origin of slavery, quoting Scriptures; showed that the Greeks and Romans had held slaves, etc. He was followed and supported by Smith of South Carolina. Boudinot obtained the floor, and, after defending the Quakers and praising Franklin, declared that there was nothing unreasonable in the memorial; that it simply requested them "to go to the utmost verge of the Constitution," and not beyond it. Further debate was had, when the sixth resolution was adopted.

The seventh resolution, pledging Congress to exert their full powers for the restriction of the slave-trade — and, as some understood it, to discountenance slavery — was struck out. The committee then arose and reported the resolutions to the house. The next day, the 23d March, 1790, after some preliminary business was disposed of, a motion was made to take up the report of the committee. Ames, Madison, and others thought the matter, having occupied so much of the time of the house, should be left where it was; or rather, as Mr. Madison expressed it, simply entered on the Journals as a matter of public record. After some little discussion, this motion prevailed by a vote of twenty-nine to twenty-five. The entry was accordingly made as follows: —

"That the migration or importation of such persons as any of the states now existing shall think proper to admit, can not be prohibited by congress prior to the year 1808.

"That congress have no right to interfere in the emancipation of slaves, or in the treatment of them, in any of the states, it remaining with the several states alone to provide any regulations therein which humanity and true policy require.

"That congress have authority to restrain the citizens of the United States from carrying on the African slave-trade for the purpose of supplying foreigners with slaves, and of providing by proper regulations for the humane treatment, during their passage, of slaves imported by the said citizens into the said states admitting such importation.

"That congress have also authority to prohibit foreigners from fitting out vessels in any port of the United States for transporting persons from Africa to any foreign port."

The census of 1790 gave the slave population of the States as follows: —

SLAVE POPULATION. — CENSUS OF 1790.

Connecticut	2,759
Delaware	8,887
Georgia	29,264
Kentucky	11,830
Maryland	103,036
New Hampshire	158
New Jersey	11,423
New York	21,324
North Carolina	100,572
Pennsylvania	3,737
Rhode Island	952
South Carolina	107,094
Vermont	17
Virginia	293,427
Territory south of Ohio	3,417

Aggregate, 697,897.

Vermont was admitted into the Union on the 18th of February, 1791; and the first article of the Bill of Rights declared that "no male person born in this country, or brought from over sea, ought to be bound by law to serve any person as a servant, slave, or apprentice after he arrives at the age of twenty-one years, nor female, in like manner, after she arrives at the age of twenty-one years, unless they are bound by their own consent after they arrive at such age, or are bound by law for the payment of debts, damages, fines, costs, or the like." This provision was contained in the first Constitution of that State, and, therefore, it was the first one to abolish and prohibit slavery in North America.

On the 4th of February, 1791, Kentucky was admitted into the Union by Act of Congress, though it had no Constitution. But the next year a Constitution was framed. By it the Legislature was denied the right to emancipate slaves without the consent of the owner, nor without paying the full price of the slaves before emancipating them; nor could any laws be passed prohibiting emigrants from other states from bringing with them persons deemed slaves by the laws of any other states in the Union, so long as such persons should be continued as slaves in Kentucky. The Legislature had power to prohibit the bringing into the state slaves for the purpose of sale. Masters were required to treat their slaves with humanity, to properly feed and clothe them, and to abstain from inflicting any punishment extending to life and limb. Laws could be passed granting owners the right to emancipate their slaves, but requiring security that the slaves thus emancipated should not become a charge upon the county.

During the session of Congress in 1791, the Pennsylvania Society for the Abolition of Slavery presented another memorial, calling upon Congress to exercise the powers they had been declared to possess by the report of the committee which had been spread upon the Journals of the house. Thus emboldened, other anti-slavery societies, of Rhode Island, Connecticut, New York, Virginia, and a few local societies of Maryland, presented memorials praying for the suppression of slavery in the United States. They were referred to a select committee; and, as they made no report, New Hampshire and Massachusetts, the next year, called the attention of Congress to the subject. On the 24th of November, 1792, a Mr. Warner Mifflin, an anti-slavery Quaker from Delaware, addressed a memorial to Congress on the general subject of slavery, which was read and laid upon the table without debate. On the 26th of November, Mr. Stute of North Carolina offered some sharp remarks upon the presumption of the Quaker, and moved that the petition be returned to the petitioner, and that the clerk be instructed to erase the entry from the Journal. This provoked a heated discussion; but at length the petition was returned to the author, and the motion to erase the record from the Journal was withdrawn by the mover.

In 1793 a law was passed providing for the return of fugitives from justice and from service. "In case of the escape out of any state or territory of any person held to service or labor under the laws thereof, the person to whom such labor was due, his agent, or attorney, might seize the fugitive and carry him before any United States judge, or before any magistrate of the city, town, or county in which the arrest was made ; and such judge or magistrate, on proof to his satisfaction, either oral or by affidavit before any other magistrate, that the person seized was really a fugitive, and did owe labor as alleged, was to grant a certificate to. that effect to the claimant, this certificate to serve as sufficient warrant for the removal of the fugitive to the state whence he had fled. Any person obstructing in any way such seizure or removal, or harboring or concealing any fugitive after notice, was liable to a penalty of $500, to be recovered by the claimant."

In 1794 an anti-slavery convention was held in Philadelphia, in which nearly all of the abolition societies of the country were represented. A memorial, carefully avoiding constitutional objections, was drawn and addressed to Congress to do whatever they could toward the suppression of the slave-trade. This memorial, with several other petitions, was referred to a special committee. In due time they reported a bill, which passed without much opposition. It was the first act of the government toward repressing the slave-trade, and was as mild as a summer's day. On Wednesday, the 7th of January, 1795, another meeting was held in Philadelphia, the second, to consider anti-slavery measures. The Act of Congress was read.

"*An Act to prohibit the carrying on the Slave-trade from the United States to any foreign place or country.*

"SECTION I. BE *it enacted by the Senate and House of Representatives of the United States of America, in Congress assembled,* That no citizen or citizens of the United States, or foreigner, or any other person coming into, or residing within the same, shall, for himself or any other person whatsoever, either as master, factor or owner, build, fit, equip, load or otherwise prepare any ship or vessel, within any port or place of the said United States, nor shall cause any ship or vessel to sail from any port or place within the same, for the purpose of carrying on any trade or traffic in slaves, to any foreign country; or for the purpose of procuring, from any foreign kingdom, place or country, the inhabitants of such kingdom, place or country, to be transported to any foreign country, port or place whatever, to be sold or disposed of, as slaves: And if.

any ship or vessel shall be so fitted out, as aforesaid, for the said purposes, or shall be caused to sail, so as aforesaid, every such ship or vessel, her tackle, furniture, apparel and other appurtenances, shall be forfeited to the United States; and shall be liable to be seized, prosecuted and condemned, in any of the circuit courts or district court for the district, where the said ship or vessel may be found and seized.

"SECTION II. *And be it further enacted,* That all and every person, so building, fitting out, equipping, loading, or otherwise preparing, or sending away, any ship or vessel, knowing, or intending, that the same shall be employed in such trade or business, contrary to the true intent and meaning of this act, or any ways aiding or abetting therein, shall severally forfeit and pay the sum of two thousand dollars, one moiety thereof, to the use of the United States, and the other moiety thereof, to the use of him or her, who shall sue for and prosecute the same.

"SECTION III. *And be it further enacted,* That the owner, master or factor of each and every foreign ship or vessel, clearing out for any of the coasts or kingdoms of Africa, or suspected to be intended for the slave-trade, and the suspicion being declared to the officer of the customs, by any citizen, on oath or affirmation, and such information being to the satisfaction of the said officer, shall first give bond with sufficient sureties, to the Treasurer of the United States, that none of the natives of Africa, or any other foreign country or place, shall be taken on board the said ship or vessel, to be transported, or sold as slaves, in any other foreign port or place whatever, within nine months thereafter.

"SECTION IV. *And be it further enacted,* That if any citizen or citizens of the United States shall, contrary to the true intent and meaning of this act, take on board, receive or transport any such persons, as above described, in this act, for the purpose of selling them as slaves, as aforesaid, he or they shall forfeit and pay, for each and every person, so received on board, transported, or sold as aforesaid, the sum of two hundred dollars, to be recovered in any court of the United States proper to try the same; the one moiety thereof, to the use of the United States, and the other moiety to the use of such person or persons, who shall sue for and prosecute the same.

"FREDERICK AUGUSTUS MUHLENBERG,
Speaker of the House of Representatives.

"JOHN ADAMS,
Vice-President of the United States, and
President of the Senate.

"Approved — March the twenty-second, 1794.
G⁰: WASHINGTON, *President of the United States.*"

In 1797 Congress again found themselves confronted by the dark problem of slavery, that would not down at their bidding. The Yearly Meeting of the Quakers of Philadelphia sent a memorial to Congress, complaining that about one hundred and thirty-four Negroes, and others whom they knew not of, having been lawfully emancipated, were afterwards reduced to bondage by an *ex post facto* law passed by North Carolina, in 1777, for that cruel purpose. After considerable debate, the memorial went to a committee, who subsequently reported that the matter complained of was purely of judicial cognizance, and that Congress had no authority in the premises.

During the same session a bill was introduced creating all that portion of the late British Province of West Florida, within the jurisdiction of the United States, into a government to be called the Mississippi Territory. It was to be conducted in all respects like the territory north-west of the Ohio, with the single exception that slavery should not be prohibited. During the discussion of this section of the bill, Mr. Thatcher of Massachusetts moved to amend by striking out the exception as to slavery, so as to make it conform to the ideas expressed by Mr. Jefferson a few years before in reference to the Western Territory. But, after a warm debate, Mr. Thatcher's motion was lost, having received only twelve votes. An amendment of Mr. Harper of South Carolina, offered a few days later, prohibiting the introduction of slaves into the new Mississippi Territory, from without the limits of the United States, carried without opposition.

Georgia revised her Constitution in 1798, and prohibited the importation of slaves "from Africa or any foreign place." Her slave-code was greatly moderated. Any person maliciously killing or dismembering a slave was to suffer the same punishment as if the act had been committed upon a free white person, except in case of insurrection, or "unless such death should happen by accident, in giving such slave moderate correction." But, like Kentucky, the Georgia constitution forbade the emancipation of slaves without the consent of the individual owner; and encouraged emigrants to bring slaves into the State.

In 1799, after three failures, the Legislature of New York passed a bill for the gradual extinction of slavery. It provided that all persons in slavery at the time of the passage of the bill should remain in bondage for life, but all their children, born after the fourth day of July next following, were to be free, but were required to remain under the direction of the owner of their parents, males until twenty-eight, and females until twenty-five. Exportation of slaves was disallowed; and if the attempt were made, and the parties apprehended, the slaves were to be free *instanter*. Persons moving into the State were not allowed to bring slaves, except they had owned them for a year previous to coming into the State.

In 1799 Kentucky revised her Constitution to meet the wants of a growing State. An attempt was made to secure a provision providing for gradual emancipation. It was supported by Henry Clay, who, as a young lawyer and promising orator, began on that occasion a brilliant political career that lasted for a half-century. But not even his magic eloquence could secure the passage of the humane amendment, and in regard to the question of slavery the Constitution received no change.

As the shadows gathered about the expiring days of the eighteenth century, it was clear to be seen that slavery, as an institution, had rooted itself into the political and legal life of the American Republic. An estate prolific of evil, fraught with danger to the new government, abhorred and rejected at first, was at length adopted with great political sagacity and deliberateness, and then guarded by the solemn forms of constitutional law and legislative enactments.

being driven from their strongholds from the very center, for control into the field.

In 1787 Kentucky sought a chance to establish for itself the rank of sovereign statehood. An attempt was made to remove friction by making the admission conditional. Representations by Virginia representatives, voting, laws and prohibitions, etc. ... men on that occasion a brilliant political precept that insisted in a half-century. But not even this magic eloquence could secure the passage of the famous amendment, and in regard to the question of slavery the Constitution received no change.

As we have gathered about the eighteenth days of the eighteenth century, it was clear to be seen that slavery as an institution had rooted itself into the political and legal life of the American Republic. An earnest profile of evil, fraught with difficulty to the new generation, inherited and reserved it that it was to be adjusted with great bitterness and strife; and then punished by the sterner forms of constitutional law and legislative enactment.

APPENDIX.

Part I

PRELIMINARY CONSIDERATIONS.

CHAPTER I.

THE UNITY OF MANKIND.

In Acts xvii. 26 the apostle says, "And God hath made of one blood all nations of men to dwell on the face of the earth, and hath determined the times before appointed, and the bounds of their habitation." In Mark xvi. 15, 16, is recorded that remarkable command of our Saviour, "Go ye into all the world, and preach the gospel to every creature. He that believeth and is baptized shall be saved; but he that believeth not shall be damned." (See also Matt. xxviii. 18, 20.) Now there is a very close connection between the statement here made by the apostle, and the command here given by our Lord Jesus Christ; for it was in obedience to this command that the apostle was at that time at Athens. There, amid the proud and conceited philosophers of Greece, in the centre of their resplendent capital, surrounded on every hand by their noblest works of art and their proudest monuments of learning, the apostle proclaims the equality of all men, their common origin, guilt, and danger, and their universal obligations to receive and embrace the gospel. The Athenians, like other ancient nations, and like them, too, in opposition to their own mythology, regarded themselves as a peculiar and distinct race, created upon the very soil which they inhabited, and pre-eminently elevated above the barbarians of the earth, — as they regarded the other races of men. Paul, however, as an inspired and infallible teacher, authoritatively declares that "God who made the world and all things therein," "hath made of one blood," and caused to descend from one original pair the whole species of men, who are now by His providential direction so propagated as to inhabit "all the face of the earth," having marked out in his eternal and unerring counsel the determinate periods for their inhabiting, and the boundaries of the regions they should inhabit.

The apostle in this passage refers very evidently to the record of the early colonization and settling of the earth contained in the books of Moses. Some Greek copies preserve only the word ενος, leaving out αιματος, a reading which the vulgar Latin follows. The Arabic version, to explain both, has *ex homine*, or as De Dieu renders it, *ex Adamo uno*, there being but the difference of one letter in the Eastern languages between *dam* and *adam*, the one denoting blood, and the other man. But if we take this passage as our more ordinary copies read it, εξενος αιματος, it is still equally plain that the meaning is not that all mankind were made of the same uniform matter, as the author of the work styled Pre-Adamites weakly imagined, for on that ground, not only mankind, but the whole world might be said to be *ex henos haimatos*, i.e., of the same

443

blood, since all things in the world were at first formed out of the same matter. The word *αιμα* therefore must be here rendered in the same sense as that in which it occurs in the best Greek authors — *the stock out of which men come.* Thus Homer says, —

"Ει ετεον γ' εμος εστι και αιματος ημετεροιο."

In like manner those who are near relations, are called by Sophocles οι προς αιματος. And hence the term *consanguinity,* employed to denote nearness of relation. Virgil uses *sanguis* in the same sense.

" *Trojano a sanguine duci.*"

So that the apostle's meaning is, that however men now are dispersed in their habitations, and however much they differ in language and customs from each other, yet they were all originally of the same stock, and derived their succession from the first man whom God created, that is, from Adam, from which name the Hebrew word for blood — i.e. *dam* — is a derivative.

Neither can it be conceived on what account Adam in the Scripture is called "the first man," and said to be "made a living soul," and "of the earth earthy," unless it is to denote that he was absolutely the first of his kind, and was, therefore, designed to be the standard and measure of all the races of men. And thus when our Saviour would trace up all things to the beginning, he illustrates his doctrine by quoting those words which were pronounced after Eve was formed. "But from the beginning of the creation, God made them male and female; for this cause shall a man leave father and mother and cleave unto his wife." Now nothing can be more plain and incontrovertible than that those of whom these words were spoken, were the first male and female which were made in "the beginning of the creation." It is equally evident that these words were spoken of Adam and Eve : for "Adam said, This is now bone of my bone, and flesh of my flesh; therefore shall a man leave his father and his mother, and shall cleave unto his wife." If the Scriptures then of the New Testament be true, it is most plain and evident that all mankind are descended from Adam.[1]

THE CURSE OF CANAAN.

It is not necessary — nay, it is not admissible — to take the words of Noah, as to Shem and Japheth, as *prophetic.* We shall presently see that, as prophetic, they have failed. Let us not, in expounding Scripture, introduce the *supernatural* when the *natural* is adequate. Noah had now known the peculiarities of his sons long enough, and well enough, to be able to make some probable conjecture as to their future course, and their success or failure in life. It is what parents do now-a-days. They say of one son, He will succeed, — he is so dutiful, so economical, so industrious. They say of another, This one will make a good lawyer — he is so sharp in an argument. Of another, they say, We will educate him for the ministry, for he has suitable qualifications. While of another they may be constrained to predict that he will not succeed, because he is indolent, and selfish, and sensual. Does it require special inspiration for a father, having ordinary common sense, to discover the peculiar talents and dispositions of his children, and to predict the probable future of each of them? Sometimes they hit it : sometimes they miss it. Shall it not be conceded to Noah that he could make as probable a conjecture, as to his sons, as your father made as to you, or as you think yourselves competent to make for either of your sons? Noah made a

---

[1] The Unity of the Human Races, pp. 14-17.

good hit. What he said as to the future of his sons, and of their posterity, has turned out, in some respects, as he said it would, but *not exactly,* — not so exactly as to authorize our calling his words an inspired prophecy, as we shall presently show.

But, if we set out to establish or to justify slavery upon these words of Noah, on the assumption GOD *spake* by Noah as to the curse and blessings here recorded, we have a right to expect to find the facts of history to correspond. If the facts of history do not correspond with these words of Noah, then God did not speak them by Noah as his own. Let us face this matter. It is said, by those who interpret the curse of Canaan as divine authority for slavery, that God *has hereby ordained that the descendants of Ham shall be slaves.* The descendants of Shem are not, of course, doomed to that curse. Now, upon the supposition that these are the words of God, and not the denunciations of an irritated father just awaking from his drunkenness, we ought not to find any of *Canaan's descendants out of a condition of slavery, nor any of the descendants of Shem in it.* If we do, then either these are not God's words, or God's words have not come true.

But it is a fact that not all of Ham's entire descendants, nor even of Canaan's descendants (on whom *alone,* and not *at all on Ham,* nor on his three other sons, Noah's 'curse fell), are now, *nor ever have been,* as a whole, in a state of bondage. The Canaanites were not slaves, but free and powerful tribes, when the Hebrews entered their territory. The Carthaginians, it is generally admitted, were descended from Canaan. They certainly were free and powerful when, in frequent wars, they contended, often with success, against the formidable Romans. If the curse of Noah was intended for all the descendants of Ham, it signally failed in the case of the first military hero mentioned in the Bible, who was the founder of a world-renowned city and empire. I refer to Nimrod, who was a son of Cush, the oldest son of Ham. Of this Nimrod the record is, "He began to be a mighty one in the earth: he was a mighty hunter before the Lord: and the beginning of his kingdom was Babel, and Erech, and Accad, and Calneh, in the land of Shinar. Out of that land went forth Asshur and builded Nineveh, and the city Rehoboth, and Calah, and Resen, between Nineveh and Calah; the same is a great city." This is Bible authority, informing us that the grandson of Ham (Nimrod, the son of Cush) was a mighty man — *the great man* of the world, in his day — the founder of the Babylonian empire, and the ancestor of the founder of the city of Nineveh, one of the grandest cities of the ancient world. We are not led to conclude, from these wonderful achievements by the posterity of Cush (who was the progenitor of the Negroes), that this line of Ham's descendants was so *weak in intellect* as to be unable to set up and maintain a government.[1]

CHAPTER III.

NEGRO CIVILIZATION.

DR. WISEMAN has also shown that both Aristotle and Herodotus describe the Egyptians — to whom Homer, Lycurgus, Solon, Pythagoras, and Plato resorted for wisdom — as having the black skin, the crooked legs, the distorted feet and the woolly hair of the Negro, from which we do not wish, or feel it necessary to infer that the Egyptians were Negroes, but *first* that the ideas of degradation and *not-human,* associated with the dark-colored African races of people *now,* were not attached to them

---

[1] Curse of Canaan, pp. 5-7. By Rev. C. H. Edgar.

at an early period of their history; and *secondly*, that while depicted as Negroes, the Egyptians were regarded by these profound ancients — the one a naturalist and the other a historian — as one of the branches of the human family, and as identified with a nation of whose descent from Ham there is no question.[1] Egyptian antiquity, not claiming priority of social existence for itself, often pointed to the regions of Habesh, or high African Ethiopia, and sometimes to the North, for the seat of the gods and demigods, because both were the intermediate stations of the progenitor tribes.[2]

There is, therefore, every reason to believe that the primitive Egyptians were conformed much more to the African than to the European form and physiognomy, and therefore that there was a time when learning, commerce, arts, manufactures, etc., were all associated with a form and character of the human race now regarded as the evidence only of degradation and barbarous ignorance.

But why question this fact when we can refer to the ancient and once glorious kingdoms of Meroe, Nubia, and Ethiopia, and to the prowess and skill of other ancient and interior African Nations? And among the existing nations of interior Africa, there is seen a manifold diversity as regards the blackest races. The characteristics of the most truly Negro race are not found in *all*, nor to the same degree in *many*.

Clapperton and other travellers among the Negro tribes of interior Africa, attest the superiority of the pure Negroes above the mixed races around them, in all moral characteristics, and describe also large and populous kingdoms with numerous towns, well-cultivated fields, and various manufactures, such as weaving, dyeing, tanning, working in iron and other metals, and in pottery.[3]

From the facts we have adduced it seems to follow, that one of the earliest races of men of whose existence, civilization and physiognomy, we have any remaining proofs, were dark or black colored. "We must," says Prichard, "for the present look upon the black races as the aborigines of Kelænonesia, or Oceanica, — that is as the immemorial and primitive inhabitants. There is no reason to doubt that they were spread over the Austral island long before the same or the contiguous regions were approached by the Malayo-Polynesians. We cannot say definitely how far back this will carry us, but as the distant colonizations of the Polynesians probably happened before the island of Java received arts and civilization from Hindustan, it must be supposed to have preceded by some ages the Javan era of Batara Guru, and therefore to have happened before the Christian era."

The Negro race is known to have existed 3,345 years, says Dr. Morton, 268 years later than the earliest notice of the white race, of which we have distinct mention B.C. 2200. This makes the existence of a Negro race certain about 842 years after the flood, according to the Hebrew chronology; or 1650 years after the flood, according to the Septuagint chronology, which may very possibly have been the original Hebrew chronology. There is thus ample time given for the multiplication and diffusion of man over the earth, and for the formation — either by natural or supernatural causes, in combination with the anomalous and altogether extraordinary condition of the earth — of all the various races of men.

It is also apparent from the architecture, and other historical evidences of their character, that dark or black races, with more or less of the Negro physiognomy, were in the earliest period of their known history cultivated and intelligent, having kingdoms, arts, and manufactures. And Mr. Pickering assures us that there is no fact to show that Negro slavery is not of modern origin. The degradation of this race of men therefore, must be regarded as the result of external causes, and not of natural, inherent and original incapacity.[4]

---

[1] See Dr. Wiseman's Lectures on the connection between Science and Revealed Religion, Am ed., pp. 95, 98.

[2] See Nat. Hist. Human Species, p. 373.   [3] See British Encyclopædia, vol. ii. pp. 237, 238.

[4] Tiedeman, on the Brain of the Negro, in the Phil. Trans., 1838, p. 497.

CHAPTER VI.

NEGRO TYPE.

It has often been said that, independently of the woolly hair and the complexion of the Negroes, there are sufficient differences between them and the rest of mankind to mark them as a very peculiar tribe. This is true, and yet the principal differences are perhaps not so constant as many persons imagine. In our West Indian colonies very many Negroes, especially females, are seen, whose figures strike Europeans as remarkably beautiful. This would not be the case if they deviated much from the idea prevalent in Europe, or from the European standard of beauty. Yet the slaves in the colonies, particularly in those of England, were brought from the west coast of intertropical Africa, where the peculiarities of figure, which in our eyes constitute deformity in the Negro, are chiefly prevalent. The black people imported into the French and to some of the Portuguese colonies, from the eastern coast of the African continent, and from Congo, are much better made. The most degraded and savage nations are the ugliest. Among the most improved and the partially civilized, as the Ashantees, and other interior States, the figure and the features of the native people approach much more to the European. The ugliest Negro tribes are confined to the equatorial countries; and on both sides of the equator, as we advance towards the temperate zones, the persons of the inhabitants are most handsome and well formed.

In a later period of this work I shall cite authors who have proved that many races belonging to this department of mankind are noted for the beauty of their features, and their fine stature and proportions. Adanson has made this observation of the Negroes on the Senegal. He thus describes the men. "Leur taille est pour l'ordinaire au-dessus de la mediocre, bien prise et sans défaut. Ils sont forts, robustes, et d'un tempérament propre à la fatigue. Ils ont les yeux noirs et bien fendus, peu de barbe, les traits du visage assez agréables." They are complete Negroes, for it is added that their complexion is of a fine black, that their hair is black, frizzled, cottony, and of extreme fineness. The women are said to be of nearly equal stature with the men, and equally well made. "Leur visage est d'une douceur extrême. Elles ont les yeux noirs, bien fendus, la bouche et les lèvres petites, et les traits du visage bien proportionnés. Il s'en trouve plusieurs d'une beauté parfaite." Mr. Rankin, a highly intelligent traveller, who reports accurately and without prejudice the results of his personal observation, has recently given a similar testimony in regard to some of the numerous tribes of northern Negro-land, who frequent the English colony of Sierra Leone. In the skull of the more improved and civilized nations among the woolly-haired blacks of Africa, there is comparatively slight deviation from the form which may be looked upon as the common type of the human head. We are assured, for example, by M. Golberry, that the Ioloffs, whose colour is a deep transparent black, and who have woolly hair, are robust and well made, and have regular features. Their countenances, he says, are ingenuous, and inspire confidence: they are honest, hospitable, generous, and faithful. The women are mild, very pretty, well made, and of agreeable manners. On the other side of the equinoctial line, the Congo Negroes, as Pigafetta declares, have not thick lips or ugly features; except in colour they are very like the Portuguese. Kafirs in South Africa frequently resemble Europeans, as many late travellers have declared. It has been the opinion of many that the Kafirs ought to be separated from the Negroes as a distinct branch of the human family. This has been proved to be an error. In the conformation of the skull, which is the leading character, the Kafirs associate themselves with the great majority of woolly African nations.[1]

---

[1] Prichard's Physical History of Mankind, vol. i. pp. 247–249.

THE NEGROES.

THE Negroes inhabit Africa from the southern margin of the Sahara as far as the territory of the Hottentots and Bushmen, and from the Atlantic to the Indian Ocean, although the extreme east of their domain has been wrested from them by intrusive Hamites and Semites. Most negroes have high and narrow skulls. According to Welcker the average percentage of width begins at 68 and rises to 78. The variations are so great that, among eighteen heads from Equatorial Africa, Barnard Davis found no less than four brachycephals. In the majority dolichocephalism is combined with a prominence of the upper jaw and an oblique position of the teeth, yet there are whole nations which are purely mesognathous. It is to be regretted that in the opinion of certain mistaken ethnologists, the negro was the ideal of every thing barbarous and beast-like. They endeavoured to deny him any capability of improvement, and even disputed his position as a man. The negro was said to have an oval skull, a flat forehead, snout-like jaws, swollen lips, a broad flat nose, short crimped hair, falsely called wool, long arms, meagre thighs, calfless legs, highly elongated heels, and flat feet. No single tribe, however, possesses all these deformities. The colour of the skin passes through every gradation, from ebony black, as in the Joloffers, to the light tint of the mulattoes, as in the Wakilema, and Barth even describes copper-coloured negroes in Marghi. As to the skull in many tribes, as in the above mentioned Joloffers, the jaws are not prominent, and the lips are not swollen. In some tribes the nose is pointed, straight, or hooked; even " Grecian profiles " are spoken of, and travellers say with surprise that they cannot perceive anything of the so-called negro type among the negroes.

According to Paul Broca, the upper limbs of the negro are comparatively much shorter than the lower, and therefore less ape-like than in Europeans, and, although in the length of the femur the negro may approximate to the proportions of the ape, he differs from them by the shortness of the humerus more than is the case with Europeans. Undoubtedly narrow and more or less high skulls are prevalent among the negroes. But the only persistent character which can be adduced as common to all is greater or less darkness of skin, that is to say, yellow, copper-red, olive, or dark brown, passing into ebony black. The colour is always browner than that of Southern Europe. The hair is generally short, elliptic in section, often split longitudinally, and much crimped. That of the negroes of South Africa, especially of the Kaffirs and Betshuans, is matted into tufts, although not in the same degree as that of the Hottentots. The hair is black, and in old age white, but there are also negroes with red hair, red eye-brows, and eye-lashes, and among the Monbuttoo, on the Uelle, Schweinfurth even discovered negroes with ashy fair hair. Hair on the body and beards exist, though not abundantly; whiskers are rare although not quite unknown.

The negroes form but a single race, for the predominant as well as the constant characters recur in Southern as well as in Central Africa, and it was therefore a mistake to separate the Bantu negroes into a peculiar race. But, according to language, the South Africans can well be separated, as a great family, from the Soudan negroes.[1]

THE RELATION OF PHYSICAL CHARACTER TO CLIMATE.

WE shall now find, on comparing these several departments with each other, that marked differences of physical character, and particularly of complexion, distinguished the human races which respectively inhabit them, and that these differences are successive or by gradations.

---

[1] Peschel, The Races of Man, pp. 462–464.

First, Among the people of level countries within the Mediterranean region, including Spaniards, Italians, Greeks, Moors, and the Mediterranean islanders, black hair with dark eyes is almost universal, scarcely one person in some hundreds presenting an exception to this remark : with this colour of the hair and eyes is conjoined a complexion of brownish white, which the French call the colour of brunettes. We must observe, that throughout all the zones into which we have divided the European region, similar complexions to this of the Mediterranean countries are occasionally seen. The qualities, indeed, of climate are not so diverse, but that even the same plants are found sporadically in the North of Europe as in the Alps and Pyrenees. But if we make a comparison between the prevalent colours of great numbers, we can easily trace a succession of shades or of different hues.

Secondly, In the southernmost of the three zones, to the northward of the Pyreno-Alpine line, namely, in the latitude of France, the prevalent colour of the hair is a chestnut-brown, to which the complexion and the colour of the eyes bear a certain relation.

Thirdly, In the northern parts of Germany, England, in Denmark, Finland, and a great part of Russia, the xanthous variety, strongly marked, is prevalent. The Danes have always been known as a people of florid complexion, blue eyes, and yellow hair. The Hollanders were termed by Silius Italicus, "Auricomi Batavi," the golden-haired Batavians; and Linnæus has defined the Finns as a tribe distinguished by "capillis flavis prolixis."

Fourthly, In the northern division we find the Norwegians and Swedes to be generally tall, white-haired men, with light gray eyes, characters so frequent to the northward of the Baltic, that Linnæus has specified them in a definition of the inhabitants of Swedish Gothland. We have thus to the northward of Mount Atlas, four well-marked varieties of human complexion succeeding each other, and in exact accordance with the gradations of latitude and of climate from south to north. The people are thus far nearly white in the colour of their skin ; but in the more southerly of the three regions above defined, with a mixture of brown, or of the complexion of brunettes, or such as we term swarthy or sallow persons.

Fifthly, In the next region, to the southward of Atlas, the native inhabitants are the "gentes sub fusci coloris" of Leo, and the immigrant Arabs in the same country are, as we have seen by abundant testimonies, of a similar light brown hue, but varying between that and a perfect black.

Sixthly, With the tropic and the latitude of the Senegal, begins the region of predominant and almost universal black, and this continues, if we confine ourselves to the low and plain countries, through all inter-tropical Africa.

Seventhly, Beyond this is the country of copper-coloured and red people, who, in Kafirland, are the majority, while in inter-tropical Africa there are but few such tribes, and those in countries of mountainous elevation.

Lastly, Towards the Cape are the tawny Hottentots, scarcely darker than the Mongoles, whom they resemble in many other particulars besides colour.

It has long been well known, that as travellers ascend mountains, in whatever region, they find the vegetation at every successive level altering its character, and assuming a more northern aspect, thus indicating that the state of the atmosphere, temperature, and physical agencies in general, assimilate as we approach alpine regions, to the peculiarities locally connected with high latitudes. If therefore, complexions and other bodily qualities belonging to races of men depend upon climate and external conditions, we should expect to find them varying in reference to elevation of surface, and if they should be found actually to undergo such variations, this will be a strong argument that these external characters do, in fact, depend upon local conditions. Now, if we inquire respecting the physical characters of the tribes inhabiting high tracts within either of the regions above marked out, we shall find that they coincide with those which prevail in the level or low parts of more northern tracts. The Swiss, in the high mountains above the plains of Lombardy, have sandy or brown hair. What a contrast presents itself to the traveller who descends into the Milanese, where the peasants have black hair and eyes, with strongly-marked Italian and almost Oriental features. In the higher parts of the Biscayan country, instead of the swarthy complexion and black hair of the Castilians, the natives have a fair complexion with light-blue eyes and flaxen or auburn hair. And in Atlantica, while the Berbers of the plains are of brown complexion with black hair, we have seen that the Shuluh mountaineers are fair, and that the inhabitants of the high tracts of Mons Aurasius are completely xanthous, having red or yellow hair and blue eyes, which fancifully, and without the shadow of any proof, they have been conjectured to have derived from the Vandal troops of Genseric.

Even in the inter-tropical region, high elevations of surface, as they produce a cooler climate, seem to occasion the appearance of light complexions. In the high parts of Senegambia, which front the Atlantic, and are cooled by winds from the Western Ocean, where, in fact, the temperature is known to be moderate and even cool at times, the light copper-coloured Frelahs are found surrounded on every side by Negro nations inhabiting lower districts; and nearly in the same parallel, but at the opposite side of Africa, are the high plains of Enarea and Kaffa, where the inhabitants are said to be fairer than the natives of southern Europe. The Galla and the Abyssinians themselves are, in proportion to the elevation of the country inhabited by them, fairer than the natives of low countries; and lest an exception should be taken to a comparison of straight-haired races with woolly Negroes or Shungalla, they bear the same comparison with the Danakil, Hazorta, and the Bishari tribes, resembling them in their hair and features, who inhabit the low tracts between the mountains of Tigre and the shores of the Red Sea, and who are equally or nearly as black as Negroes.

We may find occasion to observe that an equally decided relation exists between local conditions and the existence of other characters of human races in Africa. Those races who have the Negro character in an exaggerated degree, and who may be said to approach to deformity in person — the ugliest blacks with depressed foreheads, flat noses, crooked legs — are in many instances inhabitants of low countries, often of swampy tracts near the sea-coast, where many of them, as the Papels, have scarcely any other means of subsistence than shell fish, and the accidental gifts of the sea. In many places similar Negro tribes occupy thick forests in the hollows beneath high chains of mountains, the summits of which are inhabited by Abyssinian or Ethiopian races. The high table-lands of Africa are chiefly, as far as they are known, the abode or the wandering places of tribes of this character, or of nations who, like the Kafirs, recede very considerably from the Negro type. The Mandingos are, indeed, a Negro race inhabiting a high region; but they have neither the depressed forehead nor the projecting features considered as characteristic of the Negro race.[1]

CHAPTER VII.

CITIES OF AFRICA.

Carthage. The foundation of this celebrated city is ascribed to Elissa, a Tyrian princess, better known as Dido; it may therefore be fixed at the year of the world 3158; when Joash was king of Judah; 98 years before the building of Rome, and 846

---

[1] Prichard, vol. ii pp. 334–338.

years before Christ. The king of Tyre, father of the famous Jezebel, called in Scripture Ethbaal, was her great-grandfather. She married her near relation Acerbas, also called Sicharbas, or Sichæus, an extremely rich prince; Pygmalion, king of Tyre, was her brother. Pygmalion put Sichæus to death in order that he might have an opportunity to seize his immense treasures; but Dido eluded her brother's cruel avarice, by secretly conveying away her deceased husband's possessions. With a large train of followers she left her country, and after wandering some time, landed on the coast of the Mediterranean, in Africa; and located her settlement at the bottom of the gulf, on a peninsula, near the spot where Tunis now stands. Many of the neighboring people, allured by the prospect of gain, repaired thither to sell to those foreigners the necessaries of life; and soon became incorporated with them. The people thus gathered from different places soon grew very numerous. And the citizens of Utica, an African city about fifteen miles distant, considering them as their countrymen, as descended from the same common stock, advised them to build a city where they had settled. The other natives of the country, from their natural esteem and respect for strangers, likewise encouraged them to the same object. Thus all things conspiring with Dido's views, she built her city, which was appointed to pay an annual tribute to the Africans for the ground it stood upon, and called it Carthage — a name that in the Phœnician and Hebrew languages, [which have a great affinity,] signifies the "New City." It is said that in digging the foundation, a horse's head was found; which was thought to be a good omen, and a presage of the future warlike genius of that people. Carthage had the same language and national character as its parent state — Tyre. It became at length, particularly at the period of the Punic War, one of the most splendid cities in the world; and had under its dominion 300 cities bordering upon the Mediterranean. From the small beginning we have described, Carthage increased till her population numbered 700,000; and the number of her temples and other public buildings was immense. Her dominion was not long confined to Africa. Her ambitious inhabitants extended their conquest into Europe, by invading Sardinia, seizing a great part of Sicily, and subduing almost all of Spain. Having sent powerful colonies everywhere, they enjoyed the empire of the seas for more than six hundred years; and formed a State which was able to dispute pre-eminence with the greatest empire of the world, by their wealth, their commerce, their numerous armies, their formidable fleets, and above all by the courage and ability of their commanders; and she extended her commerce over every part of the known world. A colony of Phœnicians or Ethiopians, known in Scripture as Canaanites, settled in Carthage. The Carthaginians settled in Spain and Portugal. The first inhabitants of Spain were the Celtæ, a people of Gaul; after them the Phœnicians possessed themselves of the most southern parts of the country, and may well be supposed to have been the first civilizers of this kingdom, and the founders of the most ancient cities. After these, followed the Grecians; then the Carthaginians.

Portugal was anciently called Lusitania, and inhabited by tribes of wandering people, till it became subject to the Carthaginians and Phœnicians, who were dispossessed by the Romans 250 years before Christ. (ROLLIN.)

The Carthaginians were masters of all the coast which lies on the Mediterranean, and all the country as far as the river Iberus. Their dominions, at the time when Hannibal the Great set out for Italy, all the coast of Africa from the Aræ Phileanorum, by the great Syrtis, to the pillars of Hercules was subject to the Carthaginians, who had maintained three great wars against the Romans. But the Romans finally prevailed by carrying the war into Africa, and the last Punic war terminated with the overthrow of Carthage. (NEPOS, *in Vita Annibalis*, liv.)

The celebrated Cyrene was a very powerful city, situated on the Mediterranean, towards the greater Syrtis, in Africa, and had been built by Battus, the Lacedæmonian. (ROLLIN.)

Cyrene. — (Acts xi. 20.)   A province and city of Libya.   There was anciently a Phœnician colony called Cyrenaica, or "Libya, about Cyrene."   (Acts ii. 10.)

Cyrene. — A country west of Egypt, and the birthplace of Callimachus the poet, Eratosthenes the historian, and Simon who bore the Saviour's cross.   Many Jews from hence were at the Pentecost, and were converted under Peter's sermon (Acts ii.).   The region is now under the Turkish power, and has become almost a desert.   It is now called Cairoan.   Some of the Cyrenians were among the earliest Christians (Acts xi. 20) ; and one of them, it is supposed, was a preacher at Antioch (Acts xiii. 1).   We find also, that among the most violent opposers of Christianity were the Cyrenians, who had a synagogue at Jerusalem, as had those of many other nations.   It is said there were four hundred and eighty synagogues in Jerusalem.

Lybia, or Libya (Acts ii. 10), was anciently, among the Greeks, a general name for Africa ; but properly it embraced only so much of Africa as lay west of Egypt, on the southern coast of the Mediterranean.   Profane geographers call it Libya Cyrenaica, because Cyrene was its capital.   It was the country of the Lubims (2 Chron. xii. 3), or Lehabims, of the Old Testament, from which it is supposed to have derived its name.

The ancient city of Cyrene is now called Cyreune, Cairoan, or Cayran, and lies in the dominion of Tripoli.   This district of the earth has lately occasioned much interest among Italian and French geographers.   Great numbers of . Jews resided here (Matt. xxvii. 32).

Libya, a part of Africa, bordering on Egypt, famous for its armed chariots and horses (2 Chron. xvi. 8).

Ophir, the son of Joktan, gave name to a country in Africa, famous for gold, which was renowned even in the time of Job (Job xxii. 24, xxviii. 16) ; and from the time of David to the time of Jehoshaphat the Hebrews traded with it, and Uzziah revived this trade when he made himself master of Elath, a noted port on the Red Sea.   In Solomon's time, the Hebrew fleet took up three years in their voyage to Ophir, and brought home gold, apes, peacocks, spices, ivory, ebony, and almug-trees (1 Kings ix. 28, x. 11, xxii. 48 , 2 Chron. ix. 10).

Tarshish (Isa. xxiii. 1), or Tharsish (1 Kings x. 22).   It is supposed that some place of this name existed on the eastern coast of Africa, or among the southern ports of Asia, with which the ships of Hiram and Solomon traded in gold and silver, ivory, and apes and peacocks (2 Chron. ix. 21).   It is said that once in every three years these ships completed a voyage, and brought home their merchandise.   Hence, it is inferred, the place with which they traded must have been distant from Judea.

The vessels given by Hiram to Solomon, and those built by Jehoshaphat, to go to Tarshish, were all launched at Eziongeber, at the northern extremity of the eastern gulf of the Red Sea, now called the Gulf of Ahaba (2 Chron. xx. 36).   The name of Tarshish was from one of the sons of Javan (Gen. x. 4).

Phut (Gen. x. 6), or Put (Nah. iii. 9), was the third son of Ham ; and his descendants, sometimes called Libyans, are supposed to be the Mauritanians, or Moors of modern times.   They served the Egyptians and Tyrians as soldiers (Jer. xlvi. 9 ; Ezek. xxvii. 10, xxx. 5, xxxviii. 5).

Pul.   A district in Africa, thought by Bochart to be an island in the Nile, not far from Syene (Isa. lxvi. 19).

Seba (Isa. xliii. 3).   A peninsular district of African Ethiopia, deriving its name from the eldest son of Cush (Gen. x. 7), who is supposed to have been the progenitor of the Ethiopians.   It is called Seba by the Hebrews.

CITIES OF ETHIOPIA.

Ethiopian is a name derived from the " Land of Ethiopia," the first settled country before the flood. " The second river that went out of Eden, to water the garden, or earth, was Gihon; the same that encompasseth the whole land, or country, of *Ethiopia* " (Gen. ii. 13). Here Adam and his posterity built their tents and tilled the ground (Gen. iii. 23, 24).

The first city was Enoch, built before the flood, in the land of Nod, on the east of Eden, — a country now called Arabia. Cain, the son of Adam, went out of Eden, and dwelt in the land of Nod. We suppose, according to an ancient custom, he married his sister; and she bare Enoch. And Cain built a city, and called the name of the city after the name of his son, Enoch (Gen. iv. 16, 17). We know there must have been more than Cain and his son Enoch in the land of Nod, to build a city, but who were they? . . . (MALCOM'S *Bible Dictionary*.)

The first great city described in ancient and sacred history was built by the Cushites, or Ethiopians. They surrounded it with walls, which, according to Rollin, were eighty-seven feet in thickness, three hundred and fifty feet in height, and four hundred and eighty furlongs in circumference. And even this stupendous work they shortly after eclipsed by another, of which Diodorus says, " Never did any city come up to the greatness and magnificence of this."

It is a fact well attested by history, that the Ethiopians once bore sway, not only in all Africa, but over almost all Asia; and it is said that even two continents could not afford field enough for the expansion of their energies.

" They found their way into Europe, and built a city on the western coast of Spain, called by them Iberian Ethiopia." " And," says a distinguished writer, " wherever they went, they were rewarded for their *wisdom*."

THE TOWER OF BABEL. — Nimrod, the son of Cush, an Ethiopian, attempted to build the Tower of Babel (Gen. x. 8-10, xi. 4-9). One hundred and two years after the flood, in the land of Shinar — an extensive and fertile plain, lying between Mesopotamia on the west and Persia on the east, and watered by the Euphrates, — mankind being all of one language, one color, and one religion, — they agree to erect a tower of prodigious extent and height. Their design was not to secure themselves against a second deluge, or they would have built their tower on a high mountain; but to get themselves a famous character, and to prevent their dispersion by the erection of a monument which should be visible from a great distance. No quarries being found in that alluvial soil, they made bricks for stone, and used slime for mortar. Their haughty and rebellious attempt displeased the Lord; and after they had worked, it is said, twenty-two years, he confounded their language. This effectually stopped the building, procured it the name of *Babel*, or *Confusion*, and obliged some of the offspring of Noah to disperse themselves and replenish the world. The tower of Babel was in sight from the great city of Babylon. Nimrod was a hunter and monarch of vast ambition. When he rose to be king of Babylon he re-peopled Babel, which had been desolate since the confusion of tongues; but did not dare to attempt the finishing of the tower. The Scriptures inform us, he became "mighty upon earth; " but the extent of his conquests is not known. (MALCOM'S *Bible Dictionary*.)

The private houses, in most of the ancient cities, were simple in external appearance; but exhibited, in the interior, all the splendor and elegance of refined luxury. The floors were of marble; alabaster and gilding were displayed on every side. In every great house there were several fountains, playing in magnificent basins. The smallest house had three pipes, — one for the kitchen, another for the garden, and a third for washing. The same magnificence was displayed in the mosques, churches, and coffee-houses. The environs presented, at all seasons of the year, a pleasing verdure, and contained extensive series of gardens and villas.

THE GREAT AND SPLENDID CITY OF BABYLON. — This city was founded by Nimrod, about 2,247 years B.C., in the land of Shinar, or Chaldea, and made the capital of his kingdom. It was probably an inconsiderable place, until it was enlarged and embellished by Semiramis; it then became the most magnificent city in the world, surpassing even Nineveh in glory. The circumference of both these cities was the same; but the walls which surrounded Babylon were twice as broad as the walls of Nineveh, and having a hundred brass gates. The city of Babylon stood on the river Euphrates, by which it was divided into two parts, eastern and western; and these were connected by a cedar bridge of wonderful construction, uniting the two divisions. Quays of beautiful marble adorned the banks of the river; and on one bank stood the magnificent Temple of Belus, and on the other the Queen's Palace. These two edifices were connected by a passage under the bed of the river. This city was at least forty-five miles in circumference; and would, of course, include eight cities as large as London and its appendages. It was laid out in six hundred and twenty-five squares, formed by the intersection of twenty-five streets at right angles. The walls, which were of brick, were three hundred and fifty feet high, and eighty-seven feet broad. A trench surrounded the city, the sides of which were lined with brick and waterproof cement. This city was famous for its hanging gardens, constructed by one of its kings, to please his queen. She was a Persian, and was desirous of seeing meadows on mountains, as in her own country. She prevailed on him to raise artificial gardens, adorned with meadows and trees. For this purpose, vaulted arches were raised from the ground, one above another, to an almost inconceivable height, and of a magnificence and strength sufficient to support the vast weight of the whole garden. Babylon was a great commercial city, and traded to all parts of the earth then known, in all kinds of merchandise; and she likewise traded in slaves, and the souls of men. For her sins she has been blotted from existence, — even her location is a matter of supposition. Great was Babylon of old; in merchandise did she trade, and in souls. For her sins she thus became blotted from the sight of men.

THE ETHIOPIAN KINGS OF EGYPT.

1. *Menes* was the first king of Egypt. We have accounts of but one of his successors — Timans, during the first period, a space of more than two centuries.

2. *Shishak* was king of Ethiopia, and doubtless of Egypt. After his death

3. *Zerah* the son of Judah became king of Ethiopia, and made himself master of Egypt and Libya; and intending to add Judea to his dominions made war upon Asa king of Judea. His army consisted of a million of men, and three hundred chariots of war (2 Chron. xiv. 9).

4. *Sabachus*, an Ethiopian, king of Ethiopia, being encouraged by an oracle, entered Egypt with a numerous army, and possessed himself of the country. He reigned with great clemency and justice. It is believed, that this Sabachus was the same with Solomon, whose aid was implored by Hosea king of Israel, against Salmanaser king of Assyria.

5. *Sethon* reigned fourteen years. He is the same with Sabachus, or Savechus the son of Sabacan or Saul the Ethiopian who reigned so long over Egypt.

6. *Tharaca*, an Ethiopian, joined Sethon, with an Ethiopian army to relieve Jerusalem. After the death of Sethon, who had filled the Egyptian throne fourteen years, Tharaca ascended the throne and reigned eight years over Egypt.

7. *Sesach* or Shishak was the king of Egypt to whom Jeroboam fled to avoid

death at the hands of king Solomon. Jeroboam was entertained till the death of Solomon, when he returned to Judea and was made king of Israel. (2 Chron. xi. and xii.)

This Sesach, in the fifth year of the reign of Rehoboam marched against Jerusalem, because the Jews had transgressed against the Lord. He came with twelve hundred chariots of war, and sixty thousand horses. He had brought numberless multitudes of people, who were all Libyans, Troglodytes, and Ethiopians. He seized upon all the strongest cities of Judah, and advanced as far as Jerusalem. Then the king, and the princes of Israel, having humbled themselves, and implored the protection of the God of Israel, he told them, by his prophet Shemaiah, that, because they humbled themselves, he would not utterly destroy them, as they had deserved; but that they should be the servants of Sesach; in order *that they might know* the difference of *his service, and the service of the kingdoms of the country.* Sesach retired from Jerusalem, after having plundered the treasures of the house of the Lord, and of the king's house; he carried off every thing with him, *and even also the three hundred shields of gold which Solomon had made.*

The following are the kings of Egypt mentioned in Scripture by the common appellation of Pharaoh : —

8. *Psammetichus.* — As this prince owed his preservation to the Ionians and Carians, he settled them in Egypt, from which all foreigners hitherto had been excluded; and, by assigning them sufficient lands and fixed revenues, he made them forget their native country. By his order, Egyptian children were put under their care to learn the Greek tongue; and on this occasion, and by this means, the Egyptians began to have a correspondence with the Greeks; and, from that era, the Egyptian history, which till then had been intermixed with pompous fables, by the artifice of the priests, begins, according to Herodotus, to speak with greater truth and certainty.

As soon as Psammetichus was settled on the throne, he engaged in a war against the king of Assyria, on account of the limits of the two empires. This war was of long continuance. Ever since Syria had been conquered by the Assyrians, Palestine, being the only country that separated the two kingdoms, was the subject of continual discord : as afterwards it was between the Ptolemies and the Seleucidæ. They were perpetually contending for it, and it was alternately won by the stronger. Psammetichus, seeing himself the peaceable possessor of all Egypt, and having restored the ancient form of government, thought it high time for him to look to his frontiers, and to secure them against the Assyrian, his neighbour, whose power increased daily. For this purpose he entered Palestine at the head of an army.

Perhaps we are to refer to the beginning of this war, an incident related by Diodorus; that the Egyptians, provoked to see the Greeks posted on the right wing by the king himself in preference to them, quitted the service, being upwards of two hundred thousand men, and retired into Ethiopia, where they met with an advantageous settlement.

Be this as it will, Psammetichus entered Palestine, where his career was stopped by Azotus, one of the principal cities of the country, which gave him so much trouble, that he was forced to besiege it twenty-nine years before he could take it. This is the longest siege mentioned in ancient history. Psammetichus died in the 24th year of the reign of Josiah king of Judah; and was succeeded by his son Nechoa or Necho — in Scriptures frequently called Pharaoh Necho.

9. *Nechao* or *Pharaoh-Necho* reigned sixteen years king of Egypt, (2 Chron. xxxv. 20,) whose expeditions are often mentioned in profane history.

The Babylonians and Medes having destroyed Nineveh, and with it the empire of the Assyrians, were thereby become so formidable, that they drew upon themselves the jealousy of all their neighbours. Nechao, alarmed at the danger, advanced to the Euphrates, at the head of a powerful army, in order to check their progress. Josiah, king of Judah, so famous for his uncommon piety, observing that he took his route through Judea, resolved to oppose his passage. With this view he raised all the forces of his kingdom, and posted himself in the valley of Megiddo (a city on this side of Jordan, belonging to the tribe of Manasseh, and called Magdolus by Herodotus). Nechao informed him by a herald, that his enterprise was not designed against him; that he had other enemies in view, and that he had undertaken this war in the name of God, who was with him; that for this reason he advised Josiah not to concern himself with this war for fear it otherwise should turn to his disadvantage. However, Josiah was not moved by these reasons; he was sensible that the bare march of so powerful an army through Judea would entirely ruin it. And besides, he feared that the victor, after the defeat of the Babylonians, would fall upon him and dispossess him of part of his dominions. He therefore marched to engage Nechao; and was not only overthrown by him, but unfortunately received a wound of which he died at Jerusalem, whither he had ordered himself to be carried.

Nechao, animated by this victory, continued his march and advanced towards the Euphrates. He defeated the Babylonians; took Carchemish, a large city in that country; and securing to himself the possession of it by a strong garrison, returned to his own kingdom after having been absent three months.

Being informed in his march homeward, that Jehoaz had caused himself to be proclaimed king at Jerusalem, without first asking his consent, he commanded him to meet him at Riblah in Syria. The unhappy prince was no sooner arrived there than he was put in chains by Nechao's order, and sent prisoner to Egypt, where he died. From thence, pursuing his march, he came to Jerusalem, where he gave the sceptre to Eliakim (called by him Jehoiakim), another of Josiah's sons, in the room of his brother; and imposed an annual tribute on the land, of a hundred talents of silver, and one talent of gold. This being done, he returned in triumph to Egypt.

Herodotus, mentioning this king's expedition, and the victory gained by him at Magdolus, (as he calls it,) says that he afterwards took the city Cadytis, which he represents as situated in the mountains of Palestine, and equal in extent to Sardis, the capital at that time not only of Lydia, but of all Asia Minor. This description can suit only Jerusalem, which was situated in the manner above described, and was then the only city in those parts that could be compared to Sardis. It appears besides, from Scripture, that Nechao, after his victory, made himself master of this capital of Judea; for he was there in person, when he gave the crown to Jehoiakim. The very name Cadytis, which in Hebrew, signifies the holy, points clearly to the city of Jerusalem, as is proved by the learned dean Prideaux.

10. *Psammis.* — His reign was but of six years' duration, and history has left us nothing memorable concerning him, except that he made an expedition into Ethiopia.

11. *Apries.* — In Scripture he is called Pharaoh-Hophra; and, succeeding his father Psammis, reigned twenty-five years.

During the first year of his reign, he was as happy as any of his predecessors. He carried his arms into Cyprus; besieged the city of Sidon by sea and land; took it, and made himself master of all Phœnicia and Palestine.

So rapid a success elated his heart to a prodigious degree, and, as Herodotus informs us, swelled him with so much pride and infatuation, that he boasted it was not in the power of the gods themselves to dethrone him; so great was the idea he had formed to himself of the firm establishment of his own power. It was with a view to these arrogant conceits, that Ezekiel put the vain and impious words following into his mouth: *My river is mine own, and I have made it for myself.* But the true God proved to him afterwards that he had a master, and that he was a mere man; and he had threatened him long before, by his prophets, with all the calamities he was resolved to bring upon him, in order to punish him for his pride.

12. *Amasis.* — After the death of Apries, Amasis became peaceable possessor of Egypt, and reigned over it forty years. He was, according to Plato, a native of the city of Sais.

As he was but of mean extraction, he met with no respect, and was contemned by his subjects in the beginning of his reign. He was not insensible of this; but nevertheless thought it his interest to subdue their tempers by an artful carriage, and to win their affection by gentleness and reason. He had a golden cistern, in which himself, and those persons who were admitted to his table, used to wash their feet; he melted it down, and had it cast into a statue, and then exposed the new god to public worship. The people hastened in crowds to pay their adorations to the statue. The king, having assembled the people, informed them of the vile uses to which this statue had once been put, which nevertheless was now the object of their religious prostrations : the application was easy, and had the desired success; the people thenceforward paid the king all the respect that is due to majesty.

He always used to devote the whole morning to public affairs, in order to receive petitions, give audience, pronounce sentences, and hold his councils : the rest of the day was given to pleasure; and as Amasis, in hours of diversion, was extremely gay, and seemed to carry his mirth beyond due bounds, his courtiers took the liberty to represent to him the unsuitableness of such a behaviour; when he answered that it was impossible for the mind to be always serious and intent upon business, as for a bow to continue always bent.

It was this king who obliged the inhabitants of every town to enter their names in a book kept by the magistrates for that purpose, with their profession and manner of living. Solon inserted this custom among his laws.

He built many magnificent temples, especially at Sais the place of his birth. Herodotus admired especially a chapel there, formed of one single stone, and which was twenty-one cubits in front, fourteen in depth, and eight in height; its dimensions within were not quite so large : it had been brought from Elephantina, and two thousand men were employed three years in conveying it along the Nile.

Amasis had a great esteem for the Greeks. He granted them large privileges; and permitted such of them as were desirous of settling in Egypt to live in the city of Naucratis, so famous for its harbour. When the rebuilding of the temple of Delphi, which had been burnt, was debated on, and the expense was computed at three hundred talents, Amasis furnished the Delphians with a very considerable sum towards discharging their quota, which was the fourth part of the whole charge.

He made an alliance with the Cyrenians, and married a wife from among them.

He is the only king of Egypt who conquered the island of Cyprus, and made it tributary. Under his reign Pythagoras came into Egypt, being recommended to that monarch by the famous Polycrates, tyrant of Samos, who had contracted a friendship with Amasis, and will be mentioned hereafter. Pythagoras, during his stay in Egypt, was initiated in all the mysteries of the country, and instructed by the priests in whatever was most abstruse and important in their religion. It was here he imbibed his doctrine of the metempsychosis, or transmigration of souls.

In the expedition in which Cyrus conquered so great a part of the world, Egypt doubtless was subdued, like the rest of the provinces; and Xenophon positively declares this in the beginning of his Cyropædia, or institution of that prince. Probably, after that the forty years of desolation, which had been foretold by the prophet, were expired, Egypt beginning gradually to recover itself, Amasis shook off the yoke, and recovered his liberty.

Accordingly we find, that one of the first cares of Cambyses, the son of Cyrus, after he had ascended the throne, was to carry his arms into Egypt. On his arrival there, Amasis was just dead, and succeeded by his son Psammetus.

13. *Rameses Miamun,* according to Archbishop Usher, was the name of this king,

who is called Pharaoh in Scripture. He reigned sixty-six years, and oppressed the Israelites in a most grievous manner. *He set over them taskmasters, to afflict them with their burdens, and they built for Pharaoh treasure cities, Pithon and Raamses. And the Egyptians made the children of Israel serve with rigour, and they made their lives bitter with hard bondage, in mortar and in brick, and in all manner of service in the field ; all their service wherein they made them serve, was with rigour.* This king had two sons, Amenophis and Busiris.

14. *Amenophis*, the eldest, succeeded him. He was the Pharaoh under whose reign the Israelites departed out of Egypt, and who was drowned in his passage through the Red Sea. Archbishop Usher says, that Amenophis left two sons, one called Sesothis, or Sesostris, and the other Armais. The Greeks call him Belus, and his two sons, Egyptus and Danaus.

15. *Sesostris* was not only one of the most powerful kings of Egypt, but one of the greatest conquerors that antiquity boasts of. He was at an advanced age sent by his father against the Arabians, in order that, by fighting with them, he might acquire military knowledge. Here the young prince learned to bear hunger and thirst, and subdued a nation which till then had never been conquered. The youth educated with him, attended him in all his campaigns.

Accustomed by this conquest to martial toils he was next sent by his father to try his fortune westward. He invaded Libya, and subdued the greatest part of that vast continent.

His army consisted of six hundred thousand foot, and twenty thousand horse, besides twenty thousand armed chariots.

He invaded Ethiopia, and obliged the nations of it to furnish him annually with a certain quantity of ebony, ivory, and gold.

He had fitted out a fleet of four hundred sail, and ordering it to sail to the Red Sea, made himself master of the isles and cities lying on the coast of that sea. After having spread desolation through the world for nine years, he returned, laden with the spoils of the vanquished nations. A hundred famous temples, raised as so many monuments of gratitude to the tutelar gods of all the cities, were the first, as well as the most illustrious testimonies of his victories.

16. *Pheron* succeeded Sesostris in his kingdom, but not in his glory. He probably reigned fifty years.

17. *Proteus* was son of Memphis, and according to Herodotus, must have succeeded the first — since Proteus lived at the time of the siege of Troy, which, according to Usher, was taken An. Mun. 2820.

18. *Rhampsinitus* who was richer than any of his predecessors, built a treasury. Till the reign of this king, there had been some shadow at least of justice and moderation in Egypt; but, in the two following reigns, violence and cruelty usurped their place.

19, 20. Cheops and Cephrenus, reigned in all one hundred and six years. Cheops reigned fifty years, and his brother Cephrenus fifty-six years after him. They kept the temples closed during the whole time of their long reign; and forbid the offerings of sacrifice under the severest penalties. They oppressed their subjects.

21. *Mycerinus* the son of Cheops, reigned but seven years. He opened the temples; restored the sacrifices; and did all in his power to comfort his subjects, and make them forget their past miseries.

22. *Asychis* one of the kings of Egypt. He valued himself for having surpassed all his predecessors, by building a pyramid of brick, more magnificent, than any hitherto seen.

23. *Busiris*, built the famous city of Thebes, and made it the seat of his empire. This prince is not to be confounded with Busirus, so infamous for his cruelties.

24. *Osymandyas*, raised many magnificent edifices, in which were exhibited sculptures and paintings of exquisite beauty.

25. *Uchoreus,* one of the successors of Osymandyas, built the city of Memphis. This city was 150 furlongs, or more than seven leagues in circumference, and stood at the point of the Delta, in that part where the Nile divides itself into several branches or streams. A city so advantageously situated, and so strongly fortified, became soon the usual residence of the Egyptian kings.

26. *Thethmosis* or *Amosis,* having expelled the Shepherd kings, reigned in Lower Egypt.[1]

CHAPTER VIII.

AFRICAN LANGUAGES.

In the language of the Kafirs, for example, not only the cases but the numbers and genders of nouns are formed entirely by prefixes, analogous to articles. The prefixes vary according to number, gender and case, while the nouns remain unaltered except by a merely euphonic change of the initial letters. Thus, in Coptic, from *sheri,* a son, comes the plural *neu-sheri,* the sons; from *sori,* accusation, *hau-sori,* accusations. Analogous to this we have in the Kafir *ama* marking the plural, as *amakosah* the plural of *kosah, amahashe* the plural of *ihashe, insana* the plural of *usana.* The Kafir has a great variety of similar prefixes; they are equally numerous in the language of Kongo, in which, as in the Coptic and the Kafir, the genders, numbers, and cases of nouns are almost solely distinguished by similar prefixes.

" The Kafir language is distinguished by one peculiarity which immediately strikes a student whose views of language have been formed upon the examples afforded by the inflected languages of ancient and modern Europe. With the exception of a change of termination in the ablative case of the noun, and five changes of which the verb is susceptible in its principal tenses, the whole business of declension, conjugation, &c., is carried on by prefixes, and by the changes which take place in the initial letters or syllables of words subjected to grammatical government."[2]

Resources are not yet in existence for instituting a general comparison of the languages of Africa. Many years will probably elapse before it will be possible to produce such an analysis of these languages, investigated in their grammatical structure, as it is desirable to possess, or even to compare them by extensive collections of well-arranged vocabularies, after the manner of Klaproth's Asia Polyglotta. Sufficient data however are extant, and I trust that I have adduced evidence to render it extremely probable that a principle of analogy in structure prevails extensively among the native idioms of Africa. They are probably allied, not in the manner or degree in which Semitic or Indo-European idioms resemble each other, but by strong analogies in their general principles of structure, which may be compared to those discoverable between the individual members of two other great classes of languages, by no means connected among themselves by what is called family relation. I allude to the monosyllabic and the polysynthetic languages, the former prevalent in Eastern Asia, the latter throughout the vast regions of the New World. If we have sufficient evidence for constituting such a class of dialects under the title of African languages, we have likewise reason — and it is equal in degree — for associating in this class the language of the ancient Egyptians.[3]

That the written *Abyssinian* language, which we call *Ethiopick,* is a dialect of old *Chaldean,* and sister of *Arabick* and *Hebrew;* we know with certainty, not only from the great multitude of identical words, but (which is a far stronger proof) from

---

[1] Rollin, vol. i. pp. 129-147.   [2] Kafir Grammar, p. 3.   [3] Prichard, vol. ii. pp. 216, 217.

the similar grammatical arrangement of the several idioms : we know at the same time, that it is written like all the *Indian* characters, from the left hand to the right, and that the vowels are annexed, as in Devanagari, to the consonants; with which they form a syllabick system extremely clear and convenient, but disposed in a less artificial order than the system of letters now exhibited in the *Sanscrit* grammars; whence it may justly be inferred, that the order contrived by PANINI or his disciples is comparatively modern; and I have no doubt, from a cursory examination of many old inscriptions on pillars and in caves, which have obligingly been sent to me from all parts of India, that the *Nagari* and *Ethiopean* letters had at first a similar form. It has long been my opinion, that the *Abyssinians* of the *Arabian* stock, having no symbols of their own to represent articulate sounds, borrowed those of the black pagans, whom the *Greeks* call *Troglodytes*, from their primeval habitations in natural caverns, or in mountains excavated by their own labour : they were probably the first inhabitants of *Africa*, where they became in time the builders of magnificent cities, the founders of seminaries for the advancement of science and philosophy, and the inventors (if they were not rather the importers) of symbolical characters. I believe on the whole, that the *Ethiops* of *Meroe* were the same people with the first *Egyptians*, and consequently, as it might easily be shown, with the original *Hindus*. To the ardent and intrepid MR. BRUCE, whose travels are to my taste, uniformally agreeable and satisfactory, though he thinks very differently from me on the language and genius of the Arabs, we are indebted for more important, and, I believe, more accurate information concerning the nations established near the *Nile*, from its fountains to its mouths, than all *Europe* united could before have supplied; but, since he has not been at the pains to compare the seven languages, of which he has exhibited a specimen, and since I have not leisure to make the comparison, I must be satisfied with observing, on his authority, that the dialects of the *Gafots* and the *Gallas*, the *Agows* of both races, and the *Falashas*, who must originally have used a *Chaldean* idiom, were never preserved in writing, and the *Amharick* only in modern times : they must, therefore, have been for ages in fluctuation, and can lead, perhaps, to no certain conclusion as to the origin of the several tribes who anciently spoke them. It is very remarkable, as MR. BRUCE and MR. BRYANT have proved, that the *Greeks* gave the appellation of *Indians* both to the southern nations of *Africk* and to the people, among whom we now live ; nor is it less observable, that, according to EPHORUS, quoted by STRABO, they called all the southern nations in the world *Ethiopians*, thus using *Indian* and *Ethiop* as convertible terms : but we must leave the gymnosophists of Ethiopia, who seemed to have professed the doctrines of BUDDHA, and enter the great *Indian* ocean, of which their *Asiatick* and *African* brethren were probably the first navigators.[1]

SHERBRO MISSION–DISTRICT, WESTERN AFRICA.

Western Africa is one of the most difficult mission-fields in the entire heathen world. The low condition of the people, civilly, socially, and religiously, and the deadly climate to foreigners, make it indeed a hard field to cultivate. I am fully prepared to indorse what Rev. F. Fletcher, in charge of Wesleyan District, Gold Coast, wrote a few months ago in the following language : " The Lord's work in western Africa is as wonderful as it is deadly. In the last forty years more than 120 missioaries have fallen victims to that climate ; but to-day the converts to Christianity number at least 30,000, many of whom are true Christians. In this district we have 6,000

---

[1] Asiatic Researches, vol. iii. pp. 4, 5.

church-members; and though they are poor, last year they gave over 5,000 dollars for evangelistic and educational work.

"*Sherbro Mission* now has four stations and chapels and over forty appointments, 112 church-members, 164 seekers of religion, 75 acres of clear land, with carpenter, blacksmith, and tailor shops, in and upon which, twenty-five boys are taught to labor, and where eleven girls are taught to do all ordinary house work and sewing, with its four day and Sunday-schools, 212 in the former and more than that number in the latter, and with an influence for good that now reaches the whole Sherbro tribe, embracing a country at least fifty miles square and containing about 15,000 people. The seed sown is taking deep root there, and the harvest is rapidly ripening, when thousands of souls will be garnered for heaven. Surely we ought to thank God for past success and resolve to do much more for that needy country in the future.

"We now have Revs. Gomer, Wilberforce, Evans, and their wives, all excellent missionaries, from America; then Revs. Sawyer, Hero, Pratt, and their wives, Mrs. Lucy Caulker, and other native laborers, all of whom are doing us good service. With these six ordained ministers, and twice that number of teachers and helpers, who are devoting all their time to the mission, the work is going forward gloriously. Still, there should be new stations opened and more laborers sent out immediately."[1]

Part II.

SLAVERY IN THE COLONIES.

CHAPTER XV.

CONDITION OF SLAVES IN MASSACHUSETTS.

THE following memorandum in Judge Sewall's letter-book was called forth by Samuel Smith, murderer of his Negro slave at Sandwich. It illustrates the deplorable condition of servants at that time in Massachusetts, and shows Judge Sewall to have been a man of great humanity.

"The poorest Boys and Girls in this Province, such as are of the lowest Condition; whether they be English, or Indians, or Ethiopians: They have the same Right to Religion and Life, that the Richest Heirs have.

"And they who go about to deprive them of this Right, they attempt the bombarding of HEAVEN, and the Shells they throw, will fall down upon their own heads.

"Mr Justice Davenport, Sir, upon your desire, I have sent you these *Quotations*, and my *own Sentiments*. I pray GOD, the Giver and Guardian of Life, to give his gracious Direction to you, and the other Justices; and take leave, who am your brother and most humble servant,

"SAMUEL SEWALL.
"BOSTON, July 20, 1719.

"I inclosed also the *selling of Joseph*, and my Extract out of the *Athenian Oracle*.
"To Addington Davenport, Esq., etc., going to Judge Sam'l. Smith of Sandwitch, for killing his Negro."[2]

---

[1] Twenty-fifth Annual Report, United Brethren, 1881.
[2] Slavery in Mass., pp. 96, 97.

Petition of Slaves in Boston.

On the 23d of June, 1773, the following petition was presented to the General Court of Massachusetts, which was read, and referred to the next session: —

PETITION OF SLAVES IN BOSTON.

PROVINCE OF MASSACHUSETTS BAY.

To His Excellency, Thomas Hutchinson, Esq., Governor: —

"To the Honorable, His Majesty's Council, and to the Honorable House of Representatives, in general court assembled at Boston, the 6th day of January, 1773: — The humble petition of many slaves living in the town of Boston, and other towns in the province, is this, namely: —

That Your Excellency and Honors, and the Honorable the Representatives, would be pleased to take their unhappy state and condition under your wise and just consideration.

We desire to bless God, who loves mankind, who sent his Son to die for their salvation, and who is no respecter of persons, that he hath lately put it into the hearts of multitudes, on both sides of the water, to bear our burthens, some of whom 'are men of great note and influence, who have pleaded our cause with arguments, which we hope will have their weight with this Honorable Court.

We presume not to dictate to Your Excellency and Honors, being willing to rest our cause on your humanity and justice, yet would beg leave to say a word or two on the subject.

Although some of the negroes are vicious, (who, doubtless, may be punished and restrained by the same laws which are in force against others of the King's subjects,) there are many others of a quite different character, and who, if made free, would soon be able, as well as willing, to bear a part in the public charges. Many of them, of good natural parts, are discreet, sober, honest and industrious; and may it not be said of many, that they are virtuous and religious, although their condition is in itself so unfriendly to religion, and every moral virtue, except *patience?* How many of that number have there been and now are, in this province, who had every day of their lives embittered with this most intolerable reflection, that, let their behavior be what it will, neither they nor their children, to all generations, shall ever be able to do or to possess and enjoy any thing — no, not even *life itself* — but in a manner as the *beasts* that perish!

We have no property! we have no wives! we have no children! we have no city! no country! But we have a Father in heaven, and we are determined, as far as his grace shall enable us, and as far as our degraded condition and contemptuous life will admit, to keep all his commandments; especially will we be obedient to our masters, so long as God, in his sovereign providence, shall *suffer* us to be holden in bondage.

It would be impudent, if not presumptuous, in us to suggest to Your Excellency and Honors, any law or laws proper to be made in relation to our unhappy state, which although our greatest unhappiness, is not our *fault;* and this gives us great encouragement to pray and hope for such relief as is consistent with your wisdom, justice and goodness.

We think ourselves very happy, that we may thus address the great and general court of this province, which great and good court is to us the best judge, under God, of what is wise, just and good.

We humbly beg leave to add but this one thing more: we pray for such relief only, which by no possibility can ever be productive of the least wrong or injury to our masters, but to us will be as life from the dead.[1]

---

[1] Nell, pp. 39–41.

CHAPTER XIII.

THE COLONY OF NEW YORK.

1693, August 21st. — All Indians, Negroes, and others not "listed in the militia," are ordered to work on the fortification for repairing the same, to be under the command of the captains of the wards they inhabit. And £100 to be raised for the fortifications.

1722, February 20th. — A law passed by the common council of New York, "restraining slaves, negroes, and Indians from gaming with moneys." If found gaming with any sort of money, "copper pennies, copper halfpence, or copper farthings," they shall be publickly whipped at the publick whipping-post of this city, at the discretion of the mayor, recorder, and aldermen, or any one of them, unless the owner pay to the church-wardens for the poor, 3s.

1731, November 18th. — If more than three negro, mulatto, or Indian slaves assemble on Sunday and play or make noise, (or at any other time at any place from their master's service,) they are to be publickly whipped fifteen lashes at the publick whipping-post.

NEW YORK.

NEGRO slavery, a favorite measure with England, was rapidly extending its baneful influence in the colonies. The American Register, of 1769, gives the number of negroes brought in slavery from the coast of Africa, between Cape Blanco and the river Congo, by different nations in one year, thus: Great Britain, 53,100; British Americans, 6,300; France, 23,520; Holland, 11,300; Portugal, 1,700; Denmark, 1,200; in all, 104,100, bought by barter for European and Indian manufacturers, — £15 sterling being the average price given for each negro. Thus we see that more than one-half of the wretches who were kidnapped, or torn by force from their homes by the agents of European merchants (for such those who supply the market must be considered), were sacrificed to the cupidity of the merchants of Great Britain: the traffic encouraged by the government at the same time that the boast is sounded through the world, that the moment a slave touches the sacred soil, governed by those who encourage the slave-makers, and inhabited by those who revel in the profits derived from murder, he is free. Somerset, the negro, is liberated by the court of king's bench, in 1772, and the world is filled with the fame of English justice and humanity! James Grahame tells us that Somerset's case was not the first in which the judges of Great Britain counteracted in one or two cases the practical inhumanity of the government and the people: he says, that in 1762, his grandfather, Thomas Grahame, judge of the admiralty court of Glasgow, liberated a negro slave imported into Scotland.

It was in vain that the colonists of America protested against the practice of slave dealing. The governors appointed by England were instructed to encourage it; and when the assemblies enacted laws to prohibit the inhuman traffic, they were annulled by the vetoes of the governors. With such encouragement, the reckless and avaricious among the colonists engaged in the trade; and the slaves were purchased when brought to the colonies by those who were blind to the evil, or preferred present ease or profit to all future good. Paley, the moralist, thought the American Revolution was designed by Providence, to put an end to the slave-trade, and to show that a nation encouraging it was not fit to be intrusted with the government of extensive colonies. But the planter of the Southern States have discovered, since made free by that revolution, that slavery is no evil; and better moralists than Paley, that the increase of slaves, and their extension over new regions, is the duty of every good democrat. The men who lived in 1773, to whom America owes her liberty, did not think so.

Although resistance to the English policy of increasing the number of negro slaves in America agitated many minds in the colonies, opposition to the system of taxation was the principal source of action; and this opposition now centered in a determination to baffle the designs of Great Britain in respect to the duties on tea. Seventeen millions of pounds of tea were now accumulated in the warehouses of the East-India Company. The government was determined, for reasons I have before given, to assist this mercantile company, as well as the African merchants, at the expense of the colonists of America. The East-India Company were now authorized to export their tea free of all duty. Thus the venders being enabled to offer it cheaper than hitherto to the colonists, it was expected that it would find a welcome market. But the Americans saw the ultimate intent of the whole scheme, and their disgust towards the mother country was proportionably increased.

INDEX.

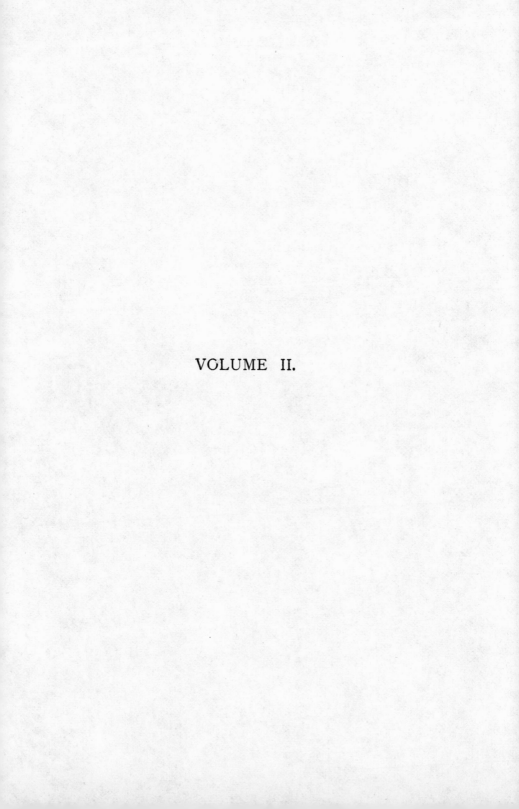

VOLUME II.

HISTORY

OF THE

NEGRO RACE IN AMERICA

FROM 1619 TO 1880

NEGROES AS SLAVES, AS SOLDIERS, AND AS CITIZENS

TOGETHER WITH

A PRELIMINARY CONSIDERATION OF THE UNITY OF THE HUMAN
FAMILY, AN HISTORICAL SKETCH OF AFRICA, AND AN
ACCOUNT OF THE NEGRO GOVERNMENTS OF
SIERRA LEONE AND LIBERIA

BY

GEORGE W. WILLIAMS

FIRST COLORED MEMBER OF THE OHIO LEGISLATURE, AND LATE JUDGE ADVOCATE OF THE
GRAND ARMY OF THE REPUBLIC OF OHIO, ETC.

IN TWO VOLUMES

VOLUME II

1800 TO 1880

NEW YORK

G. P. PUTNAM'S SONS

27 AND 29 WEST 23D STREET

1883

NOTE.

THIS second volume brings the HISTORY OF THE NEGRO RACE IN
AMERICA from 1800 down to 1880. It consists of six parts and
twenty-nine chapters. Few memories can cover this eventful
period of American history. Commencing its career with the Republic,
slavery grew with its growth and strengthened with its strength. The
dark spectre kept pace and company with liberty until separated by the
sword. Beginning with the struggle for restriction or extension of
slavery, I have striven to record, in the spirit of honest and impartial
historical inquiry, all the events of this period belonging properly to my
subject. The development and decay of anti-slavery sentiment at the
South; the pious efforts of the good Quakers to ameliorate the condition of the slaves; the service of Negroes as soldiers and sailors; the
anti-slavery agitation movement; the insurrections of slaves; the national legislation on the slavery question; the John Brown movement;
the war for the Union; the valorous conduct of Negro soldiers; the
emancipation proclamations; the reconstruction of the late Confederate
States; the errors of reconstruction; the results of emancipation; vital,
prison, labor, educational, financial, and social statistics; the exodus—
cause and effect; and a sober prophecy of the future,—are all faithfully
recorded.

After seven years I am loath to part with the saddest task ever
committed to human hands! I have tracked my bleeding countrymen
through the widely scattered documents of American history; I have
listened to their groans, their clanking chains, and melting prayers, until
the woes of a race and the agonies of centuries seem to crowd upon my
soul as a bitter reality. Many pages of this history have been blistered
with my tears; and, although having lived but a little more than a
generation, my mind feels as if it were cycles old.

The long spectral hand on the clock of American history points to
the completion of the second decade since the American slave became
an American citizen. How wondrous have been his strides, how marvellous his achievements! Twenty years ago we were in the midst of a

iii

great war for the extinction of slavery ; in this anniversary week I complete my task, record the results of that struggle. I modestly strive to lift the Negro race to its pedestal in American history. I raise this post to indicate the progress of humanity ; to instruct the present, to inform the future. I commit this work to the considerate judgment of my fellow-citizens of every race, "with malice toward none, and charity for all."

GEO. W. WILLIAMS.

HOFFMAN HOUSE, NEW YORK CITY, Dec. 28, 1882.

CONTENTS.

Part 4.

CONSERVATIVE ERA—NEGROES IN THE ARMY AND NAVY.

CHAPTER I.

RESTRICTION AND EXTENSION.

1800–1825.

CHAPTER II.

NEGRO TROOPS IN THE WAR OF 1812.

CHAPTER III.

NEGROES IN THE NAVY.

Part 5.

ANTI-SLAVERY AGITATION.

CHAPTER IV.

RETROSPECTION AND REFLECTION.

1825–1850.

CHAPTER V.

ANTI-SLAVERY METHODS.

CHAPTER VI.

ANTI-SLAVERY EFFORTS OF FREE NEGROES.

CHAPTER VII.

NEGRO INSURRECTIONS.

CHAPTER VIII.

THE "AMISTAD" CAPTIVES.

𝔓𝔞𝔯𝔱 6.

THE PERIOD OF PREPARATION.

CHAPTER IX.

NORTHERN SYMPATHY AND SOUTHERN SUBTERFUGES.

1850–1860.

CHAPTER X.

THE "BLACK LAWS" OF "BORDER STATES."

CHAPTER XI.

THE NORTHERN NEGROES.

CHAPTER XII.

NEGRO SCHOOL LAWS.

1619–1860.

CHAPTER XIII.

JOHN BROWN—HERO AND MARTYR.

𝕻art 7.

THE NEGRO IN THE WAR FOR THE UNION.

CHAPTER XIV.

DEFINITION OF THE WAR ISSUE.

CHAPTER XV.

" A WHITE MAN'S WAR."

CHAPTER XVI.

THE NEGRO ON FATIGUE DUTY.

CHAPTER XVII.

THE EMANCIPATION PROCLAMATIONS.

CHAPTER XVIII.

EMPLOYMENT OF NEGROES AS SOLDIERS.

CHAPTER XIX.

NEGROES AS SOLDIERS.

CHAPTER XX.

CAPTURE AND TREATMENT OF NEGRO SOLDIERS.

Part 8.

THE FIRST DECADE OF FREEDOM.

CHAPTER XXI.

RECONSTRUCTION — MISCONSTRUCTION.

1865–1875.

CHAPTER XXII.

THE RESULTS OF EMANCIPATION.

CHAPTER XXIII.

REPRESENTATIVE COLORED MEN.

CHAPTER XXIV.

THE AFRICAN METHODIST EPISCOPAL CHURCH.

CHAPTER XXV.

THE METHODIST EPISCOPAL CHURCH.

CHAPTER XXVI.

THE COLORED BAPTISTS OF AMERICA.

𝔓art 9.

THE DECLINE OF NEGRO GOVERNMENTS.

CHAPTER XXVII.

REACTION, PERIL, AND PACIFICATION.

1875–1880.

HISTORY OF THE NEGRO RACE IN AMERICA.

Part 4.

CONSERVATIVE ERA—NEGROES IN THE ARMY AND NAVY.

CHAPTER I.

RESTRICTION AND EXTENSION.

1800–1825.

COMMENCEMENT OF THE NINETEENTH CENTURY. — SLAVE POPULATION OF 1800. — MEMORIAL PRESENTED TO CONGRESS CALLING ATTENTION TO THE SLAVE-TRADE. TO THE COAST OF GUINEA. — GEORGIA CEDES THE TERRITORY LYING WEST OF HER TO BECOME A STATE. — OHIO ADOPTS A STATE CONSTITUTION. — WILLIAM HENRY HARRISON APPOINTED GOVERNOR OF THE TERRITORY OF INDIANA. — AN ACT OF CONGRESS PROHIBITING THE IMPORTATION OF SLAVES INTO THE UNITED STATES OR TERRITORIES. — SLAVE POPULATION OF 1810. — MISSISSIPPI APPLIES FOR ADMISSION INTO THE UNION WITH A SLAVE CONSTITUTION. — CONGRESS BESIEGED BY MEMORIALS URGING MORE SPECIFIC LEGISLATION AGAINST THE SLAVE-TRADE. — PREMIUM OFFERED TO THE INFORMER OF EVERY ILLEGALLY IMPORTED AFRICAN SEIZED WITHIN THE UNITED STATES. — CIRCULAR LETTERS SENT TO THE NAVAL OFFICERS ON THE SEACOAST OF THE SLAVE-HOLDING STATES. — PRESIDENT MONROE'S MESSAGE TO CONGRESS ON THE QUESTION OF SLAVERY. — PETITION PRESENTED BY THE MISSOURI DELEGATES FOR THE ADMISSION OF THAT STATE INTO THE UNION. — THE ORGANIZATION OF THE ARKANSAS TERRITORY. — RESOLUTIONS PASSED FOR THE RESTRICTION OF SLAVERY IN NEW STATES. — THE MISSOURI CONTROVERSY. — THE ORGANIZATION OF THE ANTI-SLAVERY SOCIETIES. — AN ACT FOR THE GRADUAL ABOLITION OF SLAVERY IN NEW JERSEY. — ITS PROVISIONS. — THE ATTITUDE OF THE NORTHERN PRESS ON THE SLAVERY QUESTION. — SLAVE POPULATION OF 1820. — ANTI-SLAVERY SENTIMENT AT THE NORTH.

THE nineteenth century opened auspiciously for the cause of the Negro. Although slavery had ceased to exist in Massachusetts and Vermont, the census of 1800 showed that the slave population in the other States was steadily on the increase. In the total population of 5,305,925, there were 893,041 slaves. The subjoined table exhibits the number of slaves in each of the slave-holding States in the year 1800.

CENSUS OF 1800—SLAVE POPULATION.

District of Columbia	3,244
Connecticut	951
Delaware	6,153
Georgia	59,404
Indiana Territory	135
Kentucky	40,343
Maryland	105,635
Mississippi Territory	3,489
New Jersey	12,422
New Hampshire	8
New York	20,343
North Carolina	133,296
Pennsylvania	1,706
Rhode Island	381
South Carolina	146,151
Tennessee	13,584
Virginia	345,796
Aggregate	893,041

On the 2d of January, 1800, a number of Colored citizens of the city and county of Philadelphia presented a memorial to Congress, through the delegate from that city, Mr. Waln, calling attention to the slave-trade to the coast of Guinea. The memorial charged that the slave-trade was clandestinely carried on from various ports of the United States contrary to law; that under this wicked practice free Colored men were often seized and sold as slaves; and that the fugitive-slave law of 1793 subjected them to great inconvenience and severe persecutions. The memorialists did not request Congress to transcend their authority respecting the slave-trade, nor to emancipate the slaves, but only to prepare the way, so that, at an early period, the oppressed might go free.

Upon a motion by Mr. Waln for the reference of the memorial to the Committee on the Slave-trade, Rutledge, Harper, Lee, Randolph, and other Southern members, made speeches against such a reference. They maintained that the petition requested Congress to take action on a question over which they had no control. Waln, Thacher, Smilie, Dana, and Gallatin contended that there were portions of the petition that came within the jurisdiction of the Constitution, and, therefore, ought to be received and acted upon. Mr. Rutledge demanded the yeas and nays; but in such a spirit as put Mr. Waln on his guard, so he withdrew his motion, and submitted another one by which such parts of the memorial as came within the jurisdiction of Congress should be referred. Mr. Rutledge raised a point of order on the motion of the gentleman from Pennsylvania that a "part" of the memorial could not be referred, but was promptly overruled. Mr. Gray, of Virginia, moved to amend by adding a declaratory clause that the portions of the memorial, not referred, inviting Congress to exercise authority not delegated, "have a tendency to create disquiet and jealousy, and ought, therefore, to receive the pointed disapprobation of this House." After some discussion, it was finally agreed to strike out the last clause and insert the following: "ought therefore to receive no encouragement or countenance from this House." The call of the roll resulted in the adoption of the amendment, with but one vote in the negative by Mr. Thacher, of Maine, an uncompromising enemy of slavery. The committee to whom the memorial was referred brought in a bill during the session prohibiting American ships from supplying slaves from the United States to foreign markets.

On the 2d of April, 1802, Georgia ceded the territory lying west of her present limits, now embracing the States of Alabama and Mississippi. Among the conditions she exacted was the following:

"That the territory thus ceded shall become a State, and be admitted into the Union as soon as it shall contain sixty thousand free inhabitants, or at an earlier period, if Congress shall think it expedient, on the same conditions and restrictions, with the same privileges, and in the same manner, as provided in the ordinance of Congress of the 13th day of July, 1787, for the government of the western territory of the United States: which ordinance shall, in all its parts, extend to the territory contained in the present act of cession, the article only excepted which forbids slavery."

The demand was acceded to, and, as the world knows, Alabama and Mississippi became the most cruel slave States in the United States.

Ohio adopted a State constitution in 1802-3, and the residue of the territory not included in the State as it is now, was designated as Indiana Territory. William Henry Harrison was appointed governor. One of the earliest moves of the government of the new territory was to secure a modification of the ordinance of 1787 by which slavery or involuntary servitude was prohibited in the territory northwest of the Ohio River. It was ordered by a convention presided over by Gen. Harrison in 1802–3, that a memorial be sent to Congress urging a restriction of the ordinance of 1787. It was referred to a select committee, with John Randolph as chairman. On the 2d of March, 1803, he made a report by the unanimous request of his committee, and the portion referring to slavery was as follows :

" The rapid population of the State of Ohio sufficiently evinces, in the opinion of your committee, that the labor of slaves is not necessary to promote the growth and settlement of colonies in that region. That this labor—demonstrably the dearest of any—can only be employed in the cultivation of products more valuable than any known to that quarter of the United States ; that the committee deem it highly dangerous and inexpedient to impair a provision wisely calculated to promote the happiness and prosperity of the northwestern country, and to give strength and security to that extensive frontier. In the salutary operations of this sagacious and benevolent restraint, it is believed that the inhabitants of Indiana will, at no very distant day, find ample remuneration for a temporary privation of labor and of emigration."

After discussing the subject-matter embodied in the memorial from the territory of Indiana, the committee presented eight resolves, one of which related to the subject of slavery, and was as follows:

" *Resolved*, That it is inexpedient to suspend, for a limited time, the operation of the sixth article of the compact between the original States and the people and the States west of the river Ohio."

Congress was about to close its session, and, therefore, there was no action taken upon this report. At the next session it went into the hands of a new committee whose chairman was Cæsar Rodney, of Delaware, who had just been elected to Congress. On the 17th of February, 1804, Mr. Rodney made the following report :

"That taking into their consideration the facts stated in the said memorial and petition, they are induced to believe that a qualified suspension, for a limited time, of the sixth article of compact between the original States and the people and States west of the river Ohio, might be productive of benefit and advantage to said territory."

After discussing other matters contained in the Indiana petition, the committee says, in reference to slavery :

" That the sixth article of the ordinance of 1787, which prohibited
slavery within the said territory, be suspended in a qualified manner
for ten years, so as to permit the introduction of slaves born within the
United States, from any of the individual States : *provided*, that such
individual State does not permit the importation of slaves from foreign
countries ; *and* provided *further*, that the descendants of all such slaves
shall, if males, be free at the age of twenty-five years, and, if female, at
the age of twenty-one years."

The House did not take up and act upon this report, and so
the matter passed for the time being. But the original memorial,
with several petitions of like import, came before Congress in
1805–6. They were referred to a select committee, and on the
14th of February, 1806, Mr. Garnett, of Virginia, the chairman,
made the following favorable report :

" That, having attentively considered the facts stated in the said
petitions and memorials, they are of opinion that a qualified suspension
for a limited time, of the sixth article of compact between the original
States and the people and States west of the river Ohio, would be beneficial to the people of the Indiana Territory. The suspension of this
article is an object almost universally desired in that Territory.
"It appears to your committee to be a question entirely different
from that between Slavery and Freedom ; inasmuch as it would merely
occasion the removal of persons, already slaves, from one part of the
country to another. The good effects of this suspension, in the present
instance, would be to accelerate the population of that Territory, hitherto
retarded by the operation of that article of compact, as slave-holders emigrating into the Western country might then indulge any preference
which they might feel for a settlement in the Indiana Territory, instead
of seeking, as they are now compelled to do, settlements in other States
or countries permitting the introduction of slaves. The condition of
the slaves themselves would be much ameliorated by it, as it is evident,
from experience, that the more they are separated and diffused, the
more care and attention are bestowed on them by their masters—each
proprietor having it in his power to increase their comforts and conveniences, in proportion to the smallness of their numbers. The dangers,
too (if any are to be apprehended), from too large a black population
existing in any one section of country, would certainly be very much
diminished, if not entirely removed. But whether dangers are to be

feared from this source or not, it is certainly an obvious dictate of sound policy to guard against them, as far as possible. If this danger does exist, or there is any cause to apprehend it, and our Western brethren are not only willing but desirous to aid us in taking precautions against it, would it not be wise to accept their assistance ?

"We should benefit ourselves, without injuring them, as their population must always so far exceed any black population which can ever exist in that country, as to render the idea of danger from that source chimerical."

After a lengthy discussion of matters embodied in the Indiana memorial, the committee recommended the following resolve on the question of slavery:

"*Resolved*, That the sixth article of the ordinance of 1787, which prohibits slavery within the Indiana Territory, be suspended for ten years, so as to permit the introduction of slaves born within the United States, from any of the individual States."

The report and resolves were made the special order for the following Monday, but were never called up.

At the opening of the next session, Gen. Harrison presented another letter, accompanied by several resolves passed by the Legislative Council and House of Representatives, urging the passage of a measure restricting the ordinance of 1787. The letter and enclosures were received on the 21st of January, 1807, and referred to the following select committee: Parke, of Indiana, chairman; Alston, North Carolina; Masters, New York; Morrow, Ohio; Rhea, Tennessee; Sandford, Kentucky; Trigg, Virginia.

On the 12th of February, 1807, the chairman, Mr. Parke, made the following report in favor of the request of the memorialists [the *third*]. It was unanimous.

"The resolutions of the Legislative Council and House of Representatives of the Indiana Territory relate to a suspension, for the term of ten years, of the sixth article of compact between the United States and the Territories and States northwest of the river Ohio, passed the 13th July, 1787. That article declares that there shall be neither Slavery nor involuntary servitude in the said Territory.

"The suspension of the said article would operate an immediate and essential benefit to the Territory, as emigration to it will be inconsiderable for many years, except from those States where Slavery is tolerated.

" And although it is not considered expedient to force the population of the Territory, yet it is desirable to connect its scattered settlements, and, in admitted political rights, to place it on an equal footing with the different States. From the interior situation of the Territory, it is not believed that slaves could ever become so numerous as to endanger the internal peace or future prosperity of the country. The current of emigration flowing to the Western country, the Territories should all be opened to their introduction. The abstract question of Liberty and Slavery is not involved in the proposed measure, as Slavery now exists to a considerable extent in different parts of the Union ; it would not augment the number of slaves, but merely authorize the removal to Indiana of such as are held in bondage in the United States. If Slavery is an evil, means ought to be devised to render it least dangerous to the community, and by which the hapless situation of the slaves would be most ameliorated ; and to accomplish these objects, no measure would be so effectual as the one proposed. The Committee, therefore, respectfully submit to the House the following resolution :

" *Resolved*, That it is expedient to suspend, from and after the 1st day of January, 1808, the sixth article of compact between the United States and the Territories and States northwest of the Ohio, passed the 13th day of July, 1787, for the term of ten years."

Like its predecessor this report was made a special order, but was never taken up.

On the 7th of November, 1807, the President laid a letter from Gen. Harrison [probably the one already referred to], and the resolves of his Legislature, before Congress, and that body referred them to a select committee consisting of Franklin, of North Carolina; Ketchel, of New Jersey; and Tiffin, of Ohio.

On the 13th of November, Mr. Franklin made the following adverse report :

" The Legislative Council and House of Representatives, in their resolutions, express their sense of the propriety of introducing Slavery into their Territory, and solicit the Congress of the United States to suspend, for a given number of years, the sixth article of compact, in the ordinance for the government of the Territory northwest of the Ohio, passed the 13th day of July, 1787. That article declares : 'There shall be neither Slavery nor involuntary servitude within the said Territory.'

" The citizens of Clark County, in their remonstrance, express their sense of the impropriety of the measure, and solicit the Congress of the United States not to act on the subject, so as to permit the introduction of slaves into the Territory ; at least, until their population shall entitle them to form a constitution and State government.

"Your Committee, after duly considering the matter, respectfully submit the following resolution :

"*Resolved*, That it is not expedient at this time to suspend the sixth article of compact for the government of the Territory of the United States northwest of the river Ohio."

Thus ended in defeat the stubborn effort to secure a restriction of the ordinance of 1787, and the admission of slavery into the Territory lying west of the Ohio and Mississippi rivers, now comprising the States of Ohio, Indiana, Illinois, Michigan, and Wisconsin.

In his message to Congress at the commencement of the session of 1806–7, President Jefferson suggested to that body the wisdom of abolishing the African slave-trade. He said in this connection :

"I congratulate you, fellow-citizens, on the approach of the period at which you may interpose your authority, constitutionally, to withdraw the citizens of the United States from all further participation in those violations of human rights which have so long been continued on the unoffending inhabitants of Africa, and which the morality, the reputation, and the best interest of our country have long been eager to proscribe."

This portion of the message was referred to a select committee ; and in due time they reported a bill "to prohibit the importation or bringing of slaves into the United States or the territories thereof after the 31st day of December, 1807."

Mr. Early, of Georgia, the chairman of the committee, inserted a clause into the bill requiring that all slaves illegally imported "should be forfeited and sold for life for the benefit of the United States." A long debate ensued and was conducted with fiery earnestness from beginning to end. It was urged in support of the above regulation, that nothing else could be done but to sell them ; that it would never do to release them in the States where they might be captured, poor, ignorant, and dangerous. It was said by the opponents of the measure, that Congress could not regulate the matter, as the States had the reserved authority to have slavery, and were, therefore, competent to say who should be free and who bond. It was suggested, farther along in the debate, that Congress might order such slaves into such States as prohibited slavery, where they could be bound out for a term of years. After a great many able speeches the House refused to strike out the forfeiture clause by a vote of sixty-three to thirty-six. When the act was called up for final passage, it was amended by inserting a clause imposing a fine of $20,000, upon all persons concerned in fitting out a vessel for the slave-trade; and likewise a fine of $5,000, and forfeiture of the vessel, for taking on board any Negro or Mulatto, or any person of color, in any foreign port with the intention of selling them in the United States.

During these efforts at restriction the slave population was growing daily. The census of 1810 showed that within a decade the slave population had sprung from 893,041, in 1800, to 1,191,364,—an increase of 33 per cent. The following table exhibits this remarkable fact:

CENSUS OF 1810.—SLAVE POPULATION.

District of Columbia	5,395
Rhode Island	108
Connecticut	310
Pennsylvania	795
Delaware	4,177
New Jersey	10,851
New York	15,017
Louisiana	34,660
Tennessee	44,535
Kentucky	80,561
Georgia	105,218
Maryland	111,502
North Carolina	168,824
South Carolina	196,365
Virginia	392,518
Mississippi Territory	17,088
Indiana Territory	237
Louisiana Territory	3,011
Illinois Territory	168
Michigan Territory	24

On the 10th of December, 1817, Mississippi applied for admission into the Union with a slave constitution. The provisions relating to slavery dispensed with grand juries in the indictment of slaves, and trial by jury was allowed only in trial of capital cases.

During the session of 1817–8, Congress was besieged by a large number of memorials praying for more specific legislation against the slave-trade. During the session the old fugitive-slave act was amended so as to make it more effective, and passed by a vote of eighty-four to sixty-nine. In the Senate, with several amendments, and heated debate, it passed by a vote of seventeen to thirteen ; but upon being returned to the House for concurrence, the Northern members had heard from their constituents, and the bill was tabled, and its friends were powerless to get it up.

In 1818-9, Congress passed an act offering a premium of fifty dollars to the informer of every illegally imported African seized within the United States, and twenty-five dollars for those taken at sea. The President was authorized to have such slaves removed beyond the limits of the United States, and to appoint agents on the West Coast of Africa to superintend their reception. An effort was made to punish slave-trading with death. It passed the House, but was struck out in the Senate.

On the 12th of January, 1819, the Secretary of the Navy transmitted to the Speaker of the House of Representatives copies of circular letters that had been sent to the naval officers on the various stations along the sea-coast of the slave-holding States. The following letter is a fair sample of the remainder : [1]

"Navy Department, January 22, 1811.

"Sir :—I hear, not without great concern, that the law prohibiting the importation of slaves has been violated in frequent instances, near St. Mary's, since the gun-boats have been withdrawn from that station.

"We are bound by law, by the obligations of humanity and sound policy, to use our most strenuous efforts to restrain this disgraceful traffic, and to bring those who shall be found engaged in it to those forfeitures and punishments which are by law prescribed for such offences.

"Hasten the equipment of the gun-boats which, by my letter of the 24th ultimo, you were directed to equip, and as soon as they shall be ready, despatch them to St. Mary's with orders to their commanders to use all practicable diligence in enforcing the law prohibiting the importation of slaves, passed March 2, 1807, entitled ' An Act to prohibit the importation of slaves into any port or place within the jurisdiction of the United States from and after the 1st day of January, 1808.'

---

[1] I have in my possession large numbers of official orders and letters on the suppression of the slave-trade, but the space appropriated to this history precludes their publication. There are, however, some important documents in the appendix to this volume.

The whole of this law, but especially the 7th section, requires your particular attention ; that section declares, that *any* ship or vessel which shall be found in any river, port, bay, or harbor, or on the high seas, within the jurisdictional limits of the United States, or hovering on the coast thereof, having on board any negro, mulatto, or person of color, for the purpose of selling them as slaves, or with intent to land the same in any port or place within the jurisdiction of the United States, contrary to the prohibition of the act, shall, together with her tackle, apparel, and furniture, and the goods and effects which shall be found on board the same, be forfeited and may be seized, prosecuted, and condemned in any court of the United States having jurisdiction thereof.

"It further authorizes the President of the United States to cause any of the armed vessels of the United States to be manned and employed to cruise on any part of the coast of the United States, or territories thereof, and to instruct and direct the commanders to seize, take, and bring into any port of the United States, all such ships or vessels ; and, moreover, to seize, take, and bring into any port of the United States, all ships or vessels *of the United States, wherever found on the high seas*, contravening the provisions of the act, to be proceeded against according to law.

" You will, therefore, consider yourself hereby especially instructed and required, and you will instruct and require all officers placed under your command, to seize, take, and bring into port, *any vessel of whatever nature*, found in any river, port, bay, or harbor, or on the high seas, within the juisdictional limits of the United States, or hovering on the coast thereof, having on board any negro, mulatto, or person of color, for the purpose of selling them as slaves, or with intent to land the same, contrary to law ; and, moreover, to seize, take, and bring into port, all ships or vessels *of the United States*, wheresoever found on the high seas or elsewhere, contravening the provisions of the law. Vessels thus to be seized, may be brought into *any* port of the United States ; and when brought into port, must, without delay, be reported to the district-attorney of the United States residing in the district in which such port may be, who will institute such further proceedings as law and justice require.

" Every person found on board of such vessels must be taken especial care of. The negroes, mulattoes, or persons of color, are to be delivered to such persons as the respective States may appoint to receive the same. The commanders and crews of such vessels will be held under the prosecutions of the district-attorneys, to answer the pains and penalties prescribed by law for their respective offences. Whenever negroes, mulattoes, or persons of color shall be delivered to the persons appointed to receive the same, duplicate receipts must be taken therefore, and if no person shall be appointed by the respective States to receive them, they must be delivered ' to the overseers of the poor of the port or place where such ship or vessel may be brought or found,' and an account of your proceedings, together with the number and descriptive list of such negroes, mulattoes, or persons of color, must be immediately transmitted to the governor or chief magistrate of the State. You will communicate to me, minutely, all your proceedings.

" I am, sir, respectfully, etc.

PAUL HAMILTON.

"H. G. CAMPBELL, *Commanding Naval Officer,*
  Charleston, S. C."

On the 17th of December, 1819, President Monroe sent the following message to Congress on the subject of the slave-trade :

" MESSAGE.

" *To the Senate and House of Representatives of the United States :*

"Some doubt being entertained respecting the true intent and meaning of the act of the last session, entitled 'An Act in addition to the Acts prohibiting the slave-trade,' as to the duties of the agents, to be appointed on the coast of Africa, I think it proper to state the interpretation which has been given of the act, and the measures adopted to carry it into effect, that Congress may, should it be deemed advisable, amend the same, before further proceeding is had under it.

" The obligation to instruct the commanders of all our armed vessels to seize and bring into port all ships or vessels of the United States, wheresoever found, having on board any negro, mulatto, or person of color, in violation of former acts for the suppression of the slave-trade, being imperative, was executed without delay. No seizures have yet been made, but, as they were contemplated by the law, and might be presumed, it seemed proper to make the necessary regulations applicable to such seizures for carrying the several provisions of the act into effect.

" It is enjoined on the executive to cause all negroes, mulattoes, or persons of color, who may be taken under the act, to be removed to Africa. It is the obvious import of the law, that none of the persons thus taken should remain within the United States ; and no place other than the coast of Africa being designated, their removal or delivery, whether carried from the United States or landed immediately from the vessels in which they were taken, was supposed to be confined to that coast. No settlement or station being specified, the whole coast was thought to be left open for the selection of a proper place, at which the persons thus taken should be delivered. The executive is authorized to appoint one or more agents, residing there, to receive such persons ; and one hundred thousand dollars are appropriated for the general purposes of the law.

"On due consideration of the several sections of the act, and of its humane policy, it was supposed to be the intention of Congress, that all the persons above described, who might be taken under it, and landed in Africa, should be aided in their return to their former homes, or in their establishment at or near the place where landed. Some shelter and food would be necessary for them there, as soon as landed, let their subsequent disposition be what it might. Should they be landed without such provision having been previously made, they might perish. It was supposed, by the authority given to the executive to appoint agents residing on that coast, that they should provide such shelter and food, and perform the other beneficent and charitable offices contemplated by the act. The coast of Africa having been little explored, and no persons residing there who possessed the requisite qualifications to entitle them to the trust being known to the executive, to none such could it be committed. It was believed that citizens only, who would go hence, well instructed in the views of their government, and zealous to give them effect, would be competent to these duties, and that it was not the intention of the law to preclude their appointment. It was obvious that the longer these persons should be detained in the United States in the hands of the marshals, the greater would be the expense, and that for the same term would the main purpose of the law be suspended. It seemed, therefore, to be incumbent on me to make the necessary arrangements for carrying this act into effect in Africa, in time to meet the delivery of any persons who might be taken by the public vessels, and landed there under it.

"On this view of the policy and sanctions of the law, it has been decided to send a public ship to the coast of Africa with two such agents, who will take with them tools and other implements necessary for the purposes above mentioned. To each of these agents a small salary has been allowed—fifteen hundred dollars to the principal, and twelve hundred to the other. All our public agents on the coast of Africa receive salaries for their services, and it was understood that none of our citizens possessing the requisite qualifications would accept these trusts, by which they would be confined to parts the least frequented and civilized, without a reasonable compensation. Such allowance, therefore, seemed to be indispensable to the execution of the act. It is intended, also, to subject a portion of the sum appropriated, to the order of the principal agent, for the special· objects above stated, amounting in the whole, including the salaries of the agents for one year, to rather less than one third of the appropriation. Special instructions will be given to these agents, defining, in precise terms, their duties in regard to the persons thus delivered to them ; the disbursement of the money by the principal agent ; and his accountability for the same. They will also have power to select the most suitable place on the coast of Africa, at which all persons who may be taken under this act shall be delivered to them, with an express injunction to exercise no power founded on the principle of colonization, or other power than that of performing the benevolent offices above recited, by the permission and sanction of the existing government under which they may establish themselves. Orders will be given to the commander of the public ship in which they will sail, to cruise along the coast, to give the more complete effect to the principal object of the act.

" JAMES MONROE.

"WASHINGTON, December, 17, 1819."

In March, 1818, the delegate from Missouri presented petitions from the inhabitants of that territory, praying to be admitted into the Union as a State. They were referred to a select committee, and a bill was reported for the admission of Missouri as a State on equal footing with the other States. The bill was read twice, when it was sent to the Committee of the Whole, where it was permitted to remain during the entire session. During the next session, on the 13th of February, 1819, the House went into the Committee of the Whole with Gen. Smith, of Maryland, in the chair. The committee had two sittings during which they discussed the bill. Gen. Tallmadge, of New York, offered the following amendment directed against the life of the clause admitting slavery :

"And provided that the introduction of slavery, or involuntary servitude, be prohibited, except for the punishment of crimes whereof the party has been duly convicted, and that all children born within the said State, after the admission thereof into the Union, shall be declared free at the age of twenty-five years."

A long and an able discussion followed, in which the authority of the government to prohibit slavery under new State governments was affirmed and denied. On coming out of the Committee of the Whole, the yeas and nays were demanded on the amendment prohibiting the introduction of slavery into Missouri, and resulted as follows : yeas, 87,—only one vote from the

South, Delaware; nays, 76,—ten votes from Northern States. Upon the latter clause of the amendment—" and that all children of slaves, born within the said State, after the admission thereof into the Union, shall be declared free at the age of twenty-five years": yeas, 82,—one vote from Maryland; nays, 78,—fourteen from Northern States. And thus the entire amendment of Gen. Tallmadge was sustained, and being reported to the House, passed by a vote 98 to 56.

The bill reached the Senate on the 17th of February, and after its second reading was referred to a select committee. On the 22d of February, the chairman, Mr. Tait, of Georgia, reported the bill back with amendments, striking out the Tallmadge restriction clauses. The House went into the Committee of the Whole on the 27th of February, to consider the bill, when Mr. Wilson, of New Jersey, moved to postpone the further consideration of the bill until the 5th of March. It was rejected. The committee then began to vote upon the recommendations of the select committee. Upon striking out the House amendment, providing that all the children of slaves born within said State should be free, etc., it was carried by a vote of 27 to 7, eleven Northern Senators voting to strike out. The seven votes against striking out were all from free States.

Upon the clause prohibiting servitude except for crimes, etc., 22 votes were cast for striking out,—five being from Northern States; against striking out, 16,—and they were all from Northern States.

Thus amended, the bill was ordered to be engrossed, and on the 2d of March—the last day but one of the session—was read a third time and passed. It was returned to the House, where the amendments were read, when Mr. Tallmadge moved that the bill be indefinitely postponed. His motion was rejected by a vote of: yeas, 69; nays, 74. But upon a motion to concur in the Senate amendments, the House refused to concur: yeas, 76; nays, 78. The Senate adhered to their amendments, and the House adhered to their disagreement by a vote of 76 to 66; and thus the bill fell between the two Houses and was lost.

The southern portion of the territory of Missouri, which was not included within the limits of the proposed State, was organized as a separate territory, under the designation of the Arkansas Territory. After considerable debate, and several attempts to insert an amendment for the restriction of slavery, the bill creating the territory of Arkansas passed without any reference to slavery, and thus the territory was left open to slavery, and also the State some years later.

The Congressional discussion of the slavery question aroused the anti-slavery sentiment of the North, which found expression in large and earnest meetings, in pungent editorials, and numerous memorials. At Trenton, New York, Philadelphia, Boston, and other places, the indignation against slavery was great. On December 3, 1819, a large meeting was held in the State House at Boston, when a resolution was adopted to memorialize Congress on the subject of "restraining the increase of slavery in *new States* to be admitted into the Union." The memorial was drawn by Daniel Webster, and signed by himself, George Blake, Josiah Quincy, James T. Austin, and others. The New York Legislature passed resolutions against the extension of slavery into the territories and new States; and requested the Congressmen and instructed the Senators from that State not to vote for the admission of any State into the Union, except such State should pledge itself to unqualified restriction in the letter and spirit of the ordinance of 1787. These resolutions were signed on January 17, 1820.

On the 24th of January the New Jersey Legislature followed in the same strain, with six pertinent resolves, a copy of which the governor was requested to forward " to each of the senators and representatives of this State, in the Congress of the United States."

Pennsylvania had taken action on the 11th of December, 1819; but the resolves were not signed by Gov. William Findlay until the 16th of the month. The Legislature was composed of fifty-four Democrats and twenty Whigs, and yet there was not a dissenting vote cast.

Two Southern States passed resolutions,—Delaware and Kentucky: the first in favor of restriction, the last opposed to restriction.

The effort to secure the admission of Missouri with a slave constitution was not dead, but only sleeping. The bill was called up as a special order on the 24th of January, 1820. It occupied most of the time of the House from the 25th of January till the 19th of February, when a bill came from the Senate providing for the admission of Maine into the Union, but containing a rider authorizing the people of Missouri to adopt a State constitution, etc., without restrictions respecting slavery. The bill providing for the admission of Maine had passed the House during the early days of the session, and now returned to the House for concurrence in the rider. The debate on the bill and amendments had occupied much of the time of the Senate. In the Judiciary Committee on the 16th of February, the question was taken on amendments to the Maine admission bill, authorizing Missouri to form a State constitution, making no mention of slavery: and twenty-three votes were cast against restriction,—three from Northern States; twenty-one in favor of restriction,—but only two from the South.

Mr. Thomas offered a resolution reaffirming the doctrine of the sixth article of the ordinance of 1787, and declaring its applicability to all that territory ceded to the United States by France, under the general designation of Louisiana, which lies north of thirty-six degrees and thirty minutes north latitude, etc. But on the following day he withdrew his original amendment, and submitted the following:

"*And be it further enacted*, That in all the territory ceded by France to the United States, under the name of Louisiana, which lies north of thirty-six degrees thirty minutes, north latitude, excepting only such part thereof as is included within the limits of the State contemplated by this act, slavery and involuntary servitude, otherwise than in the punishment of crime whereof the party shall have been duly convicted, shall be and is hereby forever prohibited. Provided always, that any person escaping into the same, from where labor or service is lawfully claimed in any State or territory of the United States, such fugitive may be lawfully reclaimed and conveyed to the person claiming his or her labor or service as aforesaid."

Mr. Trimble, of Ohio, offered a substitute, but it was rejected. The question recurring upon the passage of the amendment of Mr. Thomas, excluding slavery from all the territory north and west of Missouri, it was carried by a vote of 34 to 20.

Thus amended, the bill was ordered to engrossment by a vote of 24 to 20. On the 18th of February the bill passed, and this was its condition when it came to the House. By a vote of 93 to 72 the House agreed not to leave the Missouri question on the Maine bill as a rider; but immediately thereafter struck out the Thomas Senate amendment by a vote of 159 to 18. The House disagreed to the remaining Senate amendments, striking out the clause restricting slavery in Missouri by a vote of 102 to 68.

Thus rejected, the bill was returned to the Senate shorn of its amendments.   After four days of debate in the Senate it was decided not to recede from the attachment of the Missouri subject to the Maine bill; not to recede from the amendment prohibiting slavery west of Missouri, and north of 36° 30′ north latitude, and insisted upon the remaining amendments without division.

When the bill was returned to the House a motion was made to insist upon its disagreement to all but section nine of the Senate amendments, and was carried by a vote of 97 to 76.

The Senate asked for a committee of conference upon differences between the two Houses, which was cheerfully granted by the House.   On the 2d of March, Mr. Holmes, of Massachusetts, as chairman, made the following report:

." 1. The Senate should give up the combination of Missouri in the same bill with Maine.

" 2. The House should abandon the attempt to restrict Slavery in Missouri.

" 3. Both Houses should agree to pass the Senate's separate Missouri bill, with Mr. Thomas's restriction or compromising proviso, excluding Slavery from all territory north and west of Missouri.

" The report having been read,

" The first and most important question was put, viz. :

"Will the House concur with the Senate in so much of the said amendments as proposes to strike from the fourth section of the [Missouri] bill the provision prohibiting Slavery or involuntary servitude in the contemplated State, otherwise than in the punishment of·crimes ?"

The vote resulted as follows: For giving up restriction on Missouri, yeas, 90; against giving up restriction of slavery in Missouri, 87.

Mr. Taylor, of New York, offered an amendment to include Arkansas Territory under the prohibition of slavery in the territory west and north of Missouri, but his amendment was cut off by a call for the previous question.   Then the House concurred in the Senate amendment excluding forever slavery from the territory west and north of Missouri by a vote of 134 to 42 !   And on the following day the bill admitting Maine into the Union was passed without opposition.

Thus the Northern delegates in Congress were whipped into

line, and thus did the South gain her point in the extension of slavery in violation of the sacred compact between the States contained in the ordinance of 1787.

But the struggle was opened afresh when Missouri presented herself for admission on the 16th of November, 1820. The constitution of this new State, adopted by her people on the 19th of July, 1820, contained the following resolutions which greatly angered the Northern members, who so keenly felt the defeat and humiliation they had suffered so recently:

" The General Assembly shall have no power to pass laws, first, for the emancipation of Slaves without the consent of their owners, or without paying them, before such emancipation, a full equivalent for such slaves so emancipated ; and second, to prevent *bona-fide* emigrants to this State, or actual settlers therein, from bringing from any of the United States, or from any of their Territories, such persons as may there be deemed to be Slaves, so long as any persons of the same description are allowed to be held as Slaves by the laws of this State. . . . "It shall be their duty, as soon as may be, to pass such laws as may be necessary,

" First, to prevent free negroes and mulattoes from coming to, and settling in, this State, under any pretext whatever."

Upon the motion to admit the State the vote stood : yeas, 79 ; nays, 93. Upon a second attempt to admit her, with the understanding that the resolution just quoted should be expunged, the vote was worse than before, standing : yeas, 6 ; nays, 146 !

The House now rested, until a joint resolve, admitting her with but a vague and ineffective qualification, came down from the Senate, where it was passed by a vote of 26 to 18—six Senators from Free States in the affirmative. Mr. Clay, who had resigned in the recess, and been succeeded, as Speaker, by John W. Taylor, of New York, now appeared as the leader of the Missouri admissionists, and proposed terms of compromise, which were twice voted down by the Northern members, aided by John Randolph and three others from the South, who would have Missouri admitted without condition or qualification. At last, Mr. Clay proposed a joint committee on this subject, to be chosen by ballot—which the House agreed to by a vote of 101 to 55 ; and Mr. Clay became its chairman. By this committee it was agreed, that a solemn pledge should be required of the Legislature of Missouri, that the constitution of that State should not be construed to authorize the passage of any act, and that no act should be passed " by which any of the citizens of either of the States should be excluded from the enjoyment of the privileges and immunities to which they are entitled under the Constitution of the United States." The joint resolution, amended by the addition of this proviso, passed the House by 86 yeas to 82 nays; the Senate concurred (Feb. 27, 1821) by 26 yeas to 15 nays— (all Northern but Macon, of N. C.). Missouri complied with the condition, and became an accepted member of the Union. Thus closed the last stage of the fierce Missouri controversy, which for a time seemed to threaten—as so many other controversies have harmlessly threatened—the existence of the Union.

By this time there was scarcely a State in the North but that had organized anti-slavery, or abolition, societies. Pennsylvania boasted of a society that was accomplishing a great work. Where it was impossible to secure freedom for the enslaved, religious training was imparted, and many excellent efforts made for the amelioration of the condition of the Negroes, bond and free. A society for promoting the "*Abolition of Slavery*" was formed at Trenton, New Jersey, on the 2d of March, 1786. It adopted an elaborate constitution, which was amended on the 26th of November, 1788. It did an effective work throughout the State; embraced in its membership some of the ablest men of the State; and changed public sentiment for the better by the methods it adopted and the literature it circulated. On the 15th of February, 1804, it secured the passage of the following Act for the gradual emancipation of the slaves in the State:

"AN ACT FOR THE GRADUAL ABOLITION OF SLAVERY.

"SECTION 1. *Be it enacted by the Council and General Assembly of this State, and it is hereby enacted by the authority of the same,* That every child born of a slave within this State, after the fourth day of July next, shall be free; but shall remain the servant of the owner of his or her mother, and the executors, administrators, or assigns of such owner, in the same manner as if such child had been bound to service by the trustees or overseers of the poor, and shall continue in such service, if a male, until the age of twenty-five years, and if a female, until the age of twenty-one years.

"2. *And be it enacted,* That every person being an inhabitant of this State, who shall be entitled to the service of a child born as aforesaid, after the said fourth day of July next, shall within nine months after the birth of such child, cause to be delivered to the clerk of the county whereof such person shall be an inhabitant, a certificate in writing, containing the name and station of such person, and the name, age, and sex of the child so born ; which certificate, whether the same be delivered before or after the said nine months, shall be by the said clerk recorded in a book to be by him provided for that purpose ; and such record thereof shall be good evidence of the age of such child ; and the clerk of such county shall receive from said person twelve cents for every child so registered ; and if any person shall neglect to deliver such certificate to the said clerk within said nine months, such person shall forfeit and pay for every such offence, five dollars, and the further sum of one dollar for every month such person shall neglect to deliver the same, to be sued for and recovered by any person who will sue for the same, the one half to the use of such prosecutor, and the residue to the use of the poor of the township in which such delinquent shall reside.

" 3. *And be it enacted,* That the person enitled to the service of any child born as aforesaid, may, nevertheless, within one year after the birth of such child, elect to abandon such right ; in which case a notification of such abandonment, under the hand of such person, shall be filed with the clerk of the township, or where there may be a county poor-house established, then with the clerk of the board of trustees of said poor-house of the county in which such person shall reside ; but every child so abandoned shall be maintained by such person until such child arrives to the age of one year, and thereafter shall be considered as a pauper of such township or county, and liable to be bound out by the trustees or overseers of the poor in the same manner as other poor children are directed to be bound out, until, if a male, the age of twenty-five, and if a female, the age of twenty-one ; and such child, while such pauper, until it shall be bound out, shall be maintained by the trustees or overseers of the poor of such county or township, as the case may be, at the expense of this State ; and for that purpose the director of the board of chosen freeholders of the county is hereby required, from time to time, to draw his warrant on the treasurer in favor of such trustees or overseers for the amount of such expense, not exceeding the rate of three dollars per month ; provided the accounts for the same be first certified and approved by such board of trustees, or the town committee of such township ; and every person who shall omit to notify such abandonment as aforesaid, shall be considered as having elected to retain the service of such child, and be liable for its maintenance until the period to which its servitude is limited as aforesaid.

" A. Passed at Trenton, Feb. 15, 1804."

The public journals of the larger Northern cities began to

take a lively interest in the paramount question of the day, which, without doubt, was the slavery question. Gradual emancipation was doing an excellent work in nearly all the Northern States, as may be seen by the census of 1820. When the entire slave population was footed up it showed an increase of 30 per cent. during the previous ten years, but when examined by States it was found to be on the decrease in all the Northern or free States, except Illinois. The slave population of Virginia had increased only 8 per cent.; North Carolina 21 per cent.; South Carolina 31 per cent.; Tennessee 79 per cent.; Mississippi 92 per cent.; and Louisiana 99 per cent. The slave population by States was as follows:

CENSUS OF 1820—SLAVE POPULATION.

Alabama	41,879
District of Columbia	6,377
Connecticut	97
Delaware	4,509
Georgia	149,654
Illinois	917
Indiana	190
Kentucky	126,732
Louisiana	69,064
Maryland	107,397
Mississippi	32,814
Missouri	10,222
New Jersey	7,557
New York	10,088
North Carolina	205,017
Pennsylvania	211
Rhode Island	48
South Carolina	258,475
Tennessee	80,107
Virginia	425,153
Arkansas Territory	1,617
Aggregate	1,538,125

The anti-slavery sentiment of the Northern States was growing, but no organization with a great leader at its head had yet announced its platform or unfurled its banner in a holy war for the emancipation of the Bondmen of the Free Republic of North America.

CHAPTER II.

NEGRO TROOPS IN THE WAR OF 1812.

EMPLOYMENT OF NEGROES AS SOLDIERS IN THE WAR OF 1812. — THE NEW YORK LEGISLATURE AUTHORIZES THE ENLISTMENT OF A REGIMENT OF COLORED SOLDIERS. — GEN. ANDREW JACKSON'S PROCLAMATION TO THE FREE COLORED INHABITANTS OF LOUISIANA CALLING THEM TO ARMS. — STIRRING ADDRESS TO THE COLORED TROOPS THE SUNDAY BEFORE THE BATTLE OF NEW ORLEANS. — GEN. JACKSON ANTICIPATES THE VALOR OF HIS COLORED SOLDIERS. — TERMS OF PEACE AT THE CLOSE OF THE WAR BY THE COMMISSIONERS AT GHENT. — NEGROES PLACED AS CHATTEL PROPERTY. — THEIR VALOR IN WAR SECURES THEM NO IMMUNITY IN PEACE.

WHEN the war-clouds gathered in 1812, there was no time wasted in discussing whether it would be prudent to arm the Negro, nor was there a doubt expressed as to his valor. His brilliant achievements in the war of the Revolution, his power of endurance, and martial enthusiasm, were the golden threads of glory that bound his memory to the victorious cause of the American Republic. A lack of troops and an imperiled cause led to the admission of Negroes into the American army during the war of the Revolution. But it was the Negro's eminent fitness for military service that made him a place under the United States flag during the war in Louisiana. The entire country had confidence in the Negro's patriotism and effectiveness as a soldier. White men were willing to see Negroes go into the army because it reduced their chances of being sent forth to the tented field and dangerous bivouac.

New York did not hesitate to offer a practical endorsement of the prevalent opinion that Negroes were both competent and worthy to fight the battles of the Nation. Accordingly, the following Act was passed authorizing the organization of two regiments of Negroes.

"AN ACT TO AUTHORIZE THE RAISING OF TWO REGIMENTS OF MEN OF COLOR; PASSED OCT. 24, 1814.

" SECT. I. *Be it enacted* by the people of the State of New York, represented in Senate and Assembly, That the Governor of the State be, and he is hereby, authorized to raise, by voluntary enlistment, two regiments of free men of color, for the defence of the State for three years, unless sooner discharged.

"SECT. 2. *And be it further enacted,* That each of the said regiments shall consist of one thousand and eighty able-bodied men ; and the said regiments shall be formed into a brigade, or be organized in such manner, and shall be employed in such service, as the Governor of the State of New York shall deem best adapted to defend the said State.

"SECT. 3. *And be it further enacted,* That all the commissioned officers of the said regiments and brigade shall be white men ; and the Governor of the State of New York shall be, and he is hereby, authorized to commission, by brevet, all the officers of the said regiments and brigade, who shall hold their respective commissions until the council of appointment shall have appointed the officers of the said regiments and brigade, in pursuance of the Constitution and laws of the said State.

"SECT. 4. *And be it further enacted,* That the commissioned officers of the said regiments and brigade shall receive the same pay, rations, forage, and allowances, as officers of the same grade in the army of the United States ; and the non-commissioned officers, musicians, and privates of the said regiments shall receive the same pay, rations, clothing, and allowances, as the non-commissioned officers, musicians, and privates of the army of the United States ; and the sum of twenty-five dollars shall be paid to each of the said non-commissioned officers, musicians, and privates, at the time of enlistment, in lieu of all other bounty.

"SECT. 5. *And be it further enacted,* That the troops to be raised as aforesaid may be transferred into the service of the United States, if the Government of the United States shall agree to pay and subsist them, and to refund to this State the moneys expended by this State in clothing and arming them ; and, until such transfer shall be made, may be ordered into the service of the United States in lieu of an equal number of militia, whenever the militia of the State of New York shall be ordered into the service of the United States.

"SECT. 6. *And be it further enacted,* That it shall be lawful for any able-bodied slave, with the written assent of his master or mistress, to enlist into the said corps ; and the master or mistress of such slave shall be entitled to the pay and bounty allowed him for his service ; and, further, that the said slave, at the time of receiving his discharge, shall be deemed and adjudged to have been legally manumitted from that time, and his said master or mistress shall not thenceforward be liable for his maintenance.

"SECT. 7. *And be it further enacted,* That every such enrolled person, who shall have become free by manumission or otherwise, if he shall thereafter become indigent, shall be deemed to be settled in the town in which the person who manumitted him was settled at the time of such manumission, or in such other town where he shall have gained a settlement subsequent to his discharge from the said service ; and the former owner or owners of such manumitted person, and his legal representatives, shall be exonerated from his maintenance, any law to the contrary hereof notwithstanding.

"Sect. 8. *And be it further enacted*, That, when the troops to be raised as aforesaid shall be in the service of the United States, they shall be subject to the rules and articles which have been or may be hereafter established by the By-laws of the United States for the government of the army of the United States ; that, when the said troops shall be in the service of the State of New York, they shall be subject to the same rules and regulations ; and the Governor of the said State shall be, and he is hereby, authorized and directed to exercise all the power and authority which, by the said rules and articles, are required to be exercised by the President of the United States." [1]

Gen. Andrew Jackson believed in the fighting capacity of the Negro, as evidenced by the subjoined proclamation :

"Headquarters of 7th Military District,
                "Mobile, September 21, 1814.

"To the Free Colored Inhabitants of Louisiana :

"Through a mistaken policy you have heretofore been deprived of a participation in the glorious struggle for national rights in which our country is engaged. This no longer shall exist.

"As sons of freedom, you are now called upon to defend our most inestimable blessing. As Americans, your country looks with confidence to her adopted children for a valorous support, as a faithful return for the advantages enjoyed under her mild and equitable government. As fathers, husbands, and brothers, you are summoned to rally around the standard of the eagle, to defend all which is dear in existence.

"Your country, although calling for your exertions, does not wish you to engage in her cause without amply remunerating you for the services rendered. Your intelligent minds are not to be led away by false representations. Your love of honor would cause you to despise the man who should attempt to deceive you. In the sincerity of a soldier and the language of truth I address you.

"To every noble-hearted, generous freeman of color, volunteering to serve during the present contest with Great Britain, and no longer, there

---

[1] Laws of the State of New York, passed at the Thirty-eighth Session of the Legislature, chap. xviii.

will be paid the same bounty in money and lands, now received by the white soldiers of the United States, viz.: one hundred and twenty-four dollars in money, and one hundred and sixty acres of land. The non-commissioned officers and privates will also be entitled to the same monthly pay and daily rations, and clothes, furnished to any American soldier.

"On enrolling yourselves in companies, the major-general commanding will select officers for your government from your white fellow-citizens. Your non-commissioned officers will be appointed from among yourselves.

"Due regard will be paid to the feelings of freemen and soldiers. You will not, by being associated with white men in the same corps, be exposed to improper comparisons or unjust sarcasm. As a distinct, independent battalion or regiment, pursuing the path of glory, you will, undivided, receive the applause and gratitude of your countrymen.

"To assure you of the sincerity of my intentions, and my anxiety to engage your invaluable services to our country, I have communicated my wishes to the Governor of Louisiana, who is fully informed as to the manner of enrollment, and will give you every necessary information on the subject of this address.

"ANDREW JACKSON, *Major-General Commanding.*" [1]

Just before the battle of New Orleans, General Jackson reviewed his troops, white and black, on Sunday, December 18, 1814. At the close of the review his Adjutant-General, Edward Livingston, rode to the head of the column, and read in rich and sonorous tones the following address:

"TO THE MEN OF COLOR.—Soldiers ! From the shores of Mobile I collected you to arms ; I invited you to share in the perils and to divide the glory of your white countrymen. I expected much from you, for I was not uninformed of those qualities which must render you so formidable to an invading foe. I knew that you could endure hunger and thirst and all the hardships of war. I knew that you loved the land of your nativity, and that, like ourselves, you had to defend all that is most dear to man. But you surpass my hopes. I have found in you, united to these qualities, that noble enthusiasm which impels to great deeds.

"Soldiers ! The President of the United States shall be informed of your conduct on the present occasion ; and the voice of the representatives of the American nation shall applaud your valor, as your general now praises your ardor. The enemy is near. His sails cover the lakes.

---

[1] Niles's Register, vol. vii. p. 205.

But the brave are united ; and if he finds us contending among ourselves, it will be for the prize of valor, and fame, its noblest reward." [1]

But in this war, as in the Revolutionary struggle, the commissioners who concluded the terms of peace, armed with ample and authentic evidence of the Negro's valorous services, placed him among chattel property.

And in no State in the South were the laws more rigidly enforced against Negroes, both free and slave, than in Louisiana. The efficient service of the Louisiana Negro troops in the war of 1812 was applauded on two continents at the time, but the noise of the slave marts soon silenced the praise of the " Black heroes of the battle of New Orleans."

---

[1] Niles's Register, vol. vii. pp. 345, 346.

CHAPTER III.

NEGROES IN THE NAVY.

No Proscription against Negroes as Sailors. — They are carried upon the Rolls in the Navy without Regard to their Nationality. — Their Treatment as Sailors. — Commodore Perry's Letter to Commodore Chauncey in Regard to the Men sent him. — Commodore Chauncey's Spirited Reply. — The Heroism of the Negro set forth in the Picture of Perry's Victory on Lake Erie. — Extract of a Letter from Nathaniel Shaler, Commander of a Private Vessel. — He cites several Instances of the Heroic Conduct of Negro Sailors.

IT is rather a remarkable fact of history that Negroes were carried upon the rolls of the navy without reference to their nationality. About one tenth of the crews of the fleet that sailed to the Upper Lakes to co-operate with Col. Croghan at Mackinac, in 1814, were Negroes. Dr. Parsons says:—

" In 1816, I was surgeon of the ' Java,' under Commodore Perry. The white and colored seamen messed together. About one in six or eight were colored.

" In 1819, I was surgeon of the ' Guerrière,' under Commodore Macdonough ; and the proportion of blacks was about the same in her crew. There seemed to be an entire absence of prejudice against the blacks as messmates among the crew. What I have said applies to the crews of the other ships that sailed in squadrons." [1]

This ample and reliable testimony as to the treatment of Negroes as sailors, puts to rest all doubts as to their status in the United States navy.

In the summer of 1813, Captain (afterwards Commodore) Perry wrote a letter to Commodore Chauncey in which he complained that an indifferent lot of men had been sent him. The following is the letter that he wrote.

" Sir :—I have this moment received, by express, the enclosed letter from General Harrison. If I had officers and men—and I have no

---

[1] Livermore, pp. 159, 160.

doubt you will send them—I could fight the enemy, and proceed up the lake ; but, having no one to command the 'Niagara,' and only one commissioned lieutenant and two acting lieutenants, whatever my wishes may be, going out is out of the question. The men that came by Mr. Champlin are a motley set—blacks, soldiers, and boys. I cannot think you saw them after they were selected. I am, however, pleased to see any thing in the shape of a man." [1]

Commodore Chauncey replied in the following sharp letter, in which he gave Captain Perry to understand that the color of the skin had nothing to do with a man's qualifications for the navy :

"Sir :—I have been duly honored with your letters of the twenty-third and twenty-sixth ultimo, and notice your anxiety for men and officers. I am equally anxious to furnish you ; and no time shall be lost in sending officers and men to you as soon as the public service will allow me to send them from this lake. I regret that you are not pleased with the men sent you by Messrs. Champlin and Forrest ; for, to my knowledge, a part of them are not surpassed by any seamen we have in the fleet ; and I have yet to learn that the color of the skin, or the cut and trimmings of the coat, can affect a man's qualifications or usefulness. I have nearly fifty blacks on board of this ship, and many cf them are among my best men ; and those people you call soldiers have been to sea from two to seventeen years ; and I presume that you will find them as good and useful as any men on board of your vessel ; at least, if I can judge by comparison ; for those which we have on board of this ship are attentive and obedient, and, as far as I can judge, many of them excellent seamen : at any rate, the men sent to Lake Erie have been selected with a view of sending a fair proportion of petty officers and seamen ; and, I presume, upon examination it will be found that they are equal to those upon this lake." [2]

Perry was not long in discovering that the Negroes whom Commodore Chauncey had sent him were competent, faithful, and brave ; and his former prejudice did not prevent him from speaking their praise.

"Perry speaks highly of the bravery and good conduct of the negroes, who formed a considerable part of his crew. They seemed to be absolutely insensible to danger. When Captain Barclay came on board the 'Niagara,' and beheld the sickly and party-colored beings

---

[1] Mackenzie's Life of Perry, vol. i. pp. 165, 166.
[2] Mackenzie's Life of Perry, vol. i. pp. 186, 187.

around him, an expression of chagrin escaped him at having been conquered by such men.   The fresh-water service had very much impaired
the health of the sailors, and crowded the sick-list with patients.'[1]

These brave Negro sailors served faithfully through all the
battles on the Lakes, and in the battle of Lake Erie rendered
most effective service.   Once more the artist has rescued from
oblivion the heroism of the Negroes; for in the East Senate
stairway of the Capitol at Washington, and in the rotunda of
the Capitol at Columbus, in the celebrated picture of Perry's
Victory on Lake Erie, a Negro sailor has a place among the immortalized crew.

The following testimony to the bravery of Colored sailors is
of the highest character.

"EXTRACT OF A LETTER FROM NATHANIEL SHALER, COMMANDER OF
THE PRIVATE-ARMED SCHOONER 'GOV. TOMPKINS,' TO HIS AGENT
IN NEW YORK, DATED—

"AT SEA, Jan. 1, 1813.

.   .   .   .

"Before I could get our light sails in, and almost before I could turn
round, I was under the guns, not of a transport, but of a large *frigate!*
and not more than a quarter of a mile from her. . . . Her first
broadside killed two men, and wounded six others. . . . My officers
conducted themselves in a way that would have done honor to a more
permanent service. . . . The name of one of my poor fellows who
was killed ought to be registered in the book of fame, and remembered
with reverence as long as bravery is considered a virtue.   He was a
black man, by the name of John Johnson.   A twenty-four-pound shot
struck him in the hip, and took away all the lower part of his body.   In
this state, the poor brave fellow lay on the deck, and several times exclaimed to his shipmates : '*Fire away, my boys ; no haul a color down.*'
The other was also a black man, by the name of John Davis, and was
struck in much the same way.   He fell near me, and several times requested to be thrown overboard, saying he was only in the way of
others.

"When America has such tars, she has little to fear from the tyrants
of the ocean."[2]

After praise of such a nature and from such a source, eulogy
is superfluous.

---

[1] Analectic Magazine, vol. iii. p. 255.
[2] Niles's Weekly Register, Saturday, Feb. 26, 1814.

𝔓𝔞𝔯𝔱 5.

ANTI-SLAVERY AGITATION.

CHAPTER IV.

RETROSPECTION AND REFLECTION.

1825–1850.

THE SECURITY OF THE INSTITUTION OF SLAVERY AT THE SOUTH. — THE RIGHT TO HOLD SLAVES QUESTIONED. — RAPID INCREASE OF THE SLAVE POPULATION. — ANTI-SLAVERY SPEECHES IN THE LEGISLATURE OF VIRGINIA. — THE QUAKERS OF MARYLAND AND DELAWARE EMANCIPATE THEIR SLAVES. — THE EVIL EFFECT OF SLAVERY UPON SOCIETY. — THE CONSCIENCE AND HEART OF THE SOUTH DID NOT RESPOND TO THE VOICE OF REASON OR DICTATES OF HUMANITY.

A N awful silence succeeded the stormy struggle that ended in the violation of the ordinance of 1787. It was now time for reflection. The Southern statesmen had proven themselves the masters of the situation. The institution of slavery was secured to them, with many collateral political advantages. And, in addition to this, they had secured the inoculation of the free territory beyond the Mississippi and Ohio rivers with the virus of Negro-slavery.

If the mother-country had forced slavery upon her colonial dependencies in North America, and if it were difficult and inconvenient to part with slave-labor, who were now responsible for the extension of the slave area? Southern men, of course. What principle or human law was strong enough to support an institution of such cruel proportions? The old law of European pagans born of bloody and destroying wars? No; for it was now the nineteenth century. Abstract law? Certainly not; for law is the perfection of reason—it always tends to conform thereto—and that which is not reason is not law. Well did Justinian write: " Live honestly, hurt nobody, and render to every one his just dues." The law of nations? Verily not; for it is a system of rules deducible from reason and natural justice, and established by universal consent, to regulate the conduct and mutual intercourse between independent States. The Declaration of Independence? Far from it; because the prologue of that incomparable instrument recites: " *We hold these truths to be self-evident—that all* MEN *are created equal ; that they are endowed by their Creator with certain unalienable Rights ; that among these are life, liberty, and the pursuit of happiness; that, to secure these rights, governments are instituted among men, deriving their just powers from the consent of the governed.*" And the peerless George Bancroft has added : " The heart of Jefferson in writing the Declaration, and of Congress in adopting it, beat for all humanity; the assertion of right was made for all mankind and all coming generations, without any exception whatever; for the proposition which admits of exceptions can never be self-evident." There was but one authority for slavery left, and that was the Bible.

Many slave-holders thought deeply on the question of their right to hold slaves. A disturbed conscience cried aloud for a "Thus saith the Lord," and the pulpit was charged with the task of quieting the general disquietude. The divine origin of slavery was heard from a thousand pulpits. God, who never writes a poor hand, had written upon the brow of every Negro, the word "*Slave*"; slavery was their normal condition, and the white man was God's agent in the United States to carry out the prophecy of Noah respecting the descendants of Ham; while St. Paul had sent Onesimus back to his owner, and had written, "Servants, obey your masters."

But apologetic preaching did not seem to silence the gnawing of a guilty conscience. Upon the battle-fields of two great wars; in the army and in the navy, the Negroes had demonstrated their worth and manhood. They had stood with the undrilled minute-men along the dusty roads leading from Lexington and Concord to Boston, against the skilled redcoats of boastful Britain. They were among the faithful little band that held Bunker Hill against overwhelming odds; at Long Island, Newport, and Monmouth, they had held their ground against the stubborn columns of the Ministerial army. They had journeyed with the Pilgrim Fathers through eight years of despair and hope, of defeat and victory; had shared their sufferings and divided their glory. These recollections made difficult an unqualified acceptance of the doctrine of the divine nature of perpetual slavery. Reason downed sophistry, and human sympathy shamed prejudice. And against prejudice, custom, and political power, the thinking men of the South launched their best thoughts. Jefferson said: "The hour of emancipation is advancing in the march of time. It will come, and whether brought on by the generous energy of our own minds, or by the bloody process of St. Domingo, excited and conducted by the power of our present enemy [Great Britain], if once stationed permanently within our country and offering asylum and arms to the oppressed [Negro], is a leaf in our history *not yet turned over*." These words, written to Edward Coles, in August, 1814, were still ample food for the profound meditation of the slave-holders. In his "Notes on Virginia" Mr. Jefferson had written the following words: "*Indeed, I tremble for my country when I reflect that God is just; that His justice cannot sleep forever.* That, considering numbers, nature, and natural means, only a revolution of the wheel of fortune, an exchange of situation, is among possible events. That it may become probable by *supernatural interference. The Almighty has no attribute which can take side with us in such a contest.*" [1]

The eloquence of Patrick Henry and the logic and philosophy of Madison and Jefferson rang in the ears of the people of the slave-holding States, and they paused to think. In forty years the Negro population of Virginia had increased 186 per cent.— from 1790 to 1830,—while the white had increased only 51 per cent. The rapid increase of the slave population winged the fancy and produced horrid dreams of insurrection; while the pronounced opposition of the Northern people to slavery seemed to proclaim the weakness of the government and the approach of its dissolution. In 1832, Thomas Jefferson Randolph, a grandson of Thomas Jefferson, lifted up his voice in the Legislature of Virginia against the institution of slavery.

Said Mr. Jefferson :—" There is one circumstance to which we are to look as inevitable in the fulness of time—*a dissolution of this Union.* God grant it may not happen in our time or that of our children ; but, sir, it must come sooner or later, and when it does come, border war follows it, as certain as the night follows the day. An enemy upon

---

[1] Jefferson's Writings, vol. viii, p. 404.

your frontier offering arms and asylum to this population, tampering with it in your bosom, when your citizens shall march to repel the invader, their families butchered and their homes desolated in the rear, the spear will fall from the warrior's grasp ; his heart may be of steel, but it must quail. Suppose an invasion in part with *black troops*, speaking the same language, of the same nation, burning with enthusiasm for the liberation of their race ; if they are not crushed the moment they put foot upon your soil, they roll forward, an hourly swelling mass ; your energies are paralyzed, your power is gone ; the morasses of the lowlands, the fastnesses of the mountains, cannot save your wives and children from destruction. Sir, we cannot war with these disadvantages ; *peace, ignoble, abject peace,—peace upon any conditions that an enemy may offer, must be accepted.* Are we, then, prepared to barter the liberty of our children for slaves for them ? . . . Sir, it is a practice, and an increasing practice in parts of Virginia to *rear slaves for market.* How can an honorable mind, a patriot and a lover of his country, bear to see this ancient Dominion, rendered illustrious by the noble devotion and patriotism of her sons in the cause of liberty, converted into one grand managerie, where men are to be reared for market like oxen for the shambles. Is this better, is it not worse, than the *Slave-Trade,* that trade which enlisted the labor of the *good and the wise of every creed and every clime to abolish it ?* "

Mr. P. A. Bolling said :—

" Mr. Speaker, it is vain for gentlemen to deny the fact, the feelings of society are fast becoming adversed to slavery. The moral causes which produce that feeling are on the march, and will on *until the groans of slavery are heard no more in this else happy country.* Look over this world's wide page—see the rapid progress of liberal feelings—see the shackles falling from nations who have long writhed under the galling yoke of slavery. Liberty is going over the whole earth—hand-in-hand with Christianity. The ancient temples of slavery, rendered venerable alone by their antiquity, are crumbling into dust. Ancient prejudices are flying before the light of truth—are dissipated by its rays, as the idle vapor by the bright sun. The noble sentiment of Burns :

> ' Then let us pray that come it may,
>   As come it will for a' that,
>   That man to man, the warld o'er,
>   Shall brothers be for a' that '—

is rapidly spreading. The day-star of human liberty has risen above the dark horizon of slavery, and will continue its bright career, until it smiles alike on all men."

Mr. C. J. Faulkner said :—

"Sir, I am gratified that no gentleman has yet risen in this hall, the advocate of slavery. * * * Let me compare the condition of the slave-holding portion of this commonwealth, barren, desolate, and scarred, as it were, by the avenging hand of Heaven, with the descriptions which we have of this same country from those who first broke its virgin soil. To what is this change ascribable? Alone to the withering, blasting effects of slavery. If this does not satisfy him, let me request him to extend his travels to the Northern States of this Union, and beg him to contrast the happiness and contentment which prevail throughout that country—the busy and cheerful sound of industry, the rapid and swelling growth of their population, their means and institutions of education, their skill and proficiency in the useful arts, their enterprise and public spirit, the monuments of their commercial and manufacturing industry, and, above all, their devoted attachment to the government from which they derive their protection, with the division, discontent, indolence, and poverty of the Southern country. To what, sir, is all this ascribable? 'T is to that *vice* in the organization of society by which one half of its inhabitants are arrayed in interest and feeling against the other half ; to that unfortunate state of society in which free men regard labor as disgraceful, and slaves shrink from it as a burden tyrannically imposed upon them. ' *To that condition of things in which half a million of your population can feel no sympathy with the society in the prosperity of which they are forbidden to participate, and no attachment to a government at whose hands they receive nothing but injustice.*' In the language of the wise, prophetic Jefferson, ' you must approach this subject, YOU MUST ADOPT SOME PLAN OF EMANCIPA-TION, OR WORSE WILL FOLLOW.' "

In Maryland and Delaware the Quakers were rapidly emancipating their slaves, and the strong reaction that had set in among the thoughtful men of the South began to threaten the institution. Men felt that it was a curse to the slave, and poisoned the best white society of the slave-holding States. As early as 1781, Mr. Jefferson, with his keen, philosophical insight, beheld with alarm the demoralizing tendency of slavery. "The whole commerce," says Mr. Jefferson, "between master and slave is a perpetual exercise of the most boisterous passions ; the most unrelenting despotism on the one part, and degrading submission on the other. Our children see this, and learn to imitate it—for man is an imitative animal. This quality is the germ of all education in him. From his cradle to his grave he is learning to do what he sees others do. If a parent could find no motive, either in his philanthropy or his self-love, for restraining the intemperance of passion toward his slave, it should always be a sufficient one that his child is present. But generally, it is not sufficient. The parent storms; the child looks on, catches the lineaments of wrath, puts on the same airs in the circle of smaller slaves, gives a loose tongue to the worst of passions, and, thus nursed, educated, and daily exercised in tyranny, cannot but be stamped with odious peculiarities. The man must be a prodigy who can retain his manners and morals undepraved by such circumstances. And with what execration should the statesman be loaded, who, permitting one half the citizens thus to trample on the rights of the other, transforms those into despots and these into enemies, destroys the morals of the one part, and the *amor patriæ* of the other!"[1]

And what was true in Virginia, as coming under the observation of Mr. Jefferson, was true in all the other States where slavery existed. And indeed it was difficult to tell whether the slave or master was injured the more. The ignorance of the former veiled from him the terrible evils of his condition, while the intelligence of the latter revealed to him, in detail, the baleful effects of the institution upon all who came within its area. It was at war with social order; it contracted the sublime ideas of national unity; it made men sectional, licentious, profligate, cruel,—and selfishness paled the holy fires of patriotism.

But notwithstanding the profound reflection of the greatest minds in the South, and the philosophic prophecies of Jefferson, the conscience and heart of the South did not respond to the dictates of humanity. Cotton and cupidity led captive the reason of the South, and, once more joined to their idols, the slave-holders no longer heard the voice of prudence or justice in the slave marts of their " section."

---

[1] Jefferson's Writings, vol. viii. p. 403.

CHAPTER V.

ANTI-SLAVERY METHODS.

THE ANTIQUITY OF ANTI-SLAVERY SENTIMENT. — BENJAMIN LUNDY'S OPPOSITION TO SLAVERY IN
THE SOUTH AND AT THE NORTH. — HE ESTABLISHES THE "GENIUS OF UNIVERSAL EMAN-
CIPATION." — HIS GREAT SACRIFICES AND MARVELLOUS WORK IN THE CAUSE OF EMANCIPA-
TION. — WILLIAM LLOYD GARRISON EDITS A PAPER AT BENNINGTON, VERMONT. — HE PENS A
PETITION TO CONGRESS FOR THE ABOLITION OF SLAVERY IN THE DISTRICT OF COLUMBIA. —
GARRISON THE PEERLESS LEADER OF THE ANTI-SLAVERY AGITATION. — EXTRACT FROM A SPEECH
DELIVERED BY DANIEL O'CONNELL AT CORK, IRELAND. — INCREASE OF ANTI-SLAVERY SOCIE-
TIES IN THE COUNTRY. — CHARLES SUMNER DELIVERS A SPEECH ON THE "ANTI-SLAVERY DUTIES
OF THE WHIG PARTY." — MARKED EVENTS OF 1846. — SUMNER THE LEADER OF THE POLITI-
CAL PARTY. — HETERODOX ANTI-SLAVERY PARTY. — ITS SENTIMENTS. — HORACE GREELEY THE
LEADER OF THE ECONOMIC ANTI-SLAVERY PARTY. — THE AGGRESSIVE ANTI-SLAVERY PARTY. —
ITS LEADERS. — THE COLONIZATION ANTI-SLAVERY SOCIETY. — AMERICAN COLONIZATION SOCIETY.
— MANUMITTED NEGROES COLONIZE ON THE WEST COAST OF AFRICA. — A BILL ESTABLISHING
A LINE OF MAIL STEAMERS TO THE COAST OF AFRICA. — IT PROVIDES FOR THE SUPPRESSION OF
THE SLAVE-TRADE, PROMOTION OF COMMERCE, AND THE COLONIZATION OF FREE NEGROES. —
EXTRACTS FROM THE PRESS WARMLY URGING THE PASSAGE OF THE BILL. — THE UNDERGROUND
RAILROAD ORGANIZATION. — ITS EFFICIENCY IN FREEING SLAVES. — ANTI-SLAVERY LITERATURE.
— IT EXPOSES THE TRUE CHARACTER OF SLAVERY. — "UNCLE TOM'S CABIN," BY HARRIET
BEECHER STOWE, PLEADED THE CAUSE OF THE SLAVE IN TWENTY DIFFERENT LANGUAGES. —
THE INFLUENCE OF "IMPENDING CRISIS."

ANTI-SLAVERY sentiment is as old as the human family.
It antedates the Bible; it was eloquent in the days of
our Saviour; it preached the Gospel of Humanity in the
palaces of the Cæsars and Antonies; its arguments shook the
thrones of Europe during the Mediæval ages. And when the
doctrine of property in man was driven out of Europe as an exile,
and found a home in this New World in the West, the ancient
and time-honored anti-slavery sentiment combined all that was
good in brain, heart, and civilization, and hurled itself, with
righteous indignation, against the institution of slavery, the perfected curse of the ages! And how wonderful that God should
have committed the task of blotting out this terrible curse to
Americans! And what "vessels of honor" they were whom the
dear Lord chose "to proclaim liberty to the captives, and the
opening of the prison to them that are bound!" Statesmen like
Franklin, Rush, Hamilton, and Jay; divines like Hopkins, Ed
wards, and Stiles; philanthropists like Woolman, Lay, and

Benezet! And the good Quakers—God bless them!—or *Friends*, which has so much tender meaning in it, did much to hasten the morning of freedom. In the poor Negro slave they saw Christ " an hungered," and they gave Him meat ; "thirsty," and they gave Him drink ; "a stranger," and they took Him in ; " naked," and they clothed Him ; " sick," and they visited Him ; " in prison," and they came unto Him. Verily they knew their " *neighbor.*"

They began their work of philanthropy as early as 1780. In Maryland,[1] Pennsylvania, and New Jersey the Friends emancipated all their slaves. At a single monthly meeting in Pennsylvania eleven hundred slaves were set at liberty. Nearly every Northern State had its anti-slavery society. They were charged with the humane task of ameliorating the condition of the Negro, and scattering modest literary documents that breathed the spirit of Christian love.

But the first apostle of *Abolition Agitation* was Benjamin Lundy. He was the John Baptist to the new era that was to witness the doing away of the law of bondage and the ushering in of the dispensation of universal brotherhood. He raised his voice against slave-keeping in Virginia, Ohio, Tennessee, and Maryland. In 1821 he established an anti-slavery paper called " The Genius of Universal Emancipation," which he successively published in Philadelphia, Baltimore, and Washington City,—and frequently *en route* during the tours he took through the country, wherever he could find a press. Once he made a tour of the free States, like another Apostle Paul, stirring up the love of the brethren for those who were in bonds, lecturing, obtaining subscribers, writing editorials, getting them printed where he could, stopping by the wayside to read his " proof," and directing and mailing his papers at the nearest post-office. Then, packing up his " column-rules," type, " heading," and " directing-book," he would journey on, a lone, solitary " Friend." He said in 1830:—

" I have, within the period above mentioned (ten years), sacrificed several thousands of dollars of my own hard earnings ; I have travelled

---

[1] In the Library of the New York Historical Society there is " An Oration Upon the Moral and Political Evil of Slavery. Delivered at a Public Meeting of the Maryland Society for Promoting the Abolition of Slavery and the Relief of Free Negroes and Others Unlawfully Held in Bondage, Baltimore, July 4, 1791. By George Buchanan, M.D., Member of the American Philosophical Society. Baltimore : Printed by Phillip Edwards, MDCCXCIII."

upwards of five thousand miles on foot and more than twenty thousand in other ways ; have visited nineteen States of this Union, and held more than two hundred public meetings ; have performed two voyages to the West Indies, by which means the emancipation of a considerable number of slaves has been effected, and I hope the way paved for the enfranchisement of many more."

He was a slight-built, wiry figure ; but inflamed by a holy zeal for the cause of the oppressed, he was almost unconscious of the vast amount of work he was accomplishing. As a Quaker his methods were moderate. His journalistic voice was not a whirlwind nor the fire, but the still, small voice of persuasiveness. Though it was published in a slave mart, his paper, a monthly, was regarded as perfectly harmless. But away up in Vermont there was being edited, at Bennington, a paper called "The Journal of the Times." It was started chiefly to advocate the claims of John Quincy Adams to the Presidency, but much space was devoted to the subject of anti-slavery. The young editor of the above-named journal had had experience with several other papers previous to this—"The Free Press," of Newburyport, Mass., and "The National Philanthropist," of Boston. "The Genuis of Universal Emancipation," was among the exchanges of "The Journal of the Times," and its sentiments greatly enthused the heart of the Vermont editor, who, under God, was destined to become the indefatigable leader of the Anti-slavery Movement in America, *William Lloyd Garrison!* To his advocacy of "temperance and peace" young Garrison added another excellent principle, intense hatred of slavery. He penned a petition for the abolition of slavery in the District of Columbia, which he sent to all the postmasters in Vermont, beseeching them to secure signatures. As the postmasters of those days paid no postage for their letters, many names were secured. The petition created a genuine sensation in Congress. The "Journal of Commerce" about this time said:

"It appears from an article in 'The Journal of the Times,' a newspaper of some promise, just established in Bennington, Vt., that a petition to Congress for the abolition of slavery in the District of Columbia is about to be put in circulation in that State.

"The idea is an excellent one, and we hope it will meet with success. That Congress has a right to abolish slavery in that District seems reasonable, though we fear it will meet with some opposition, so

very sensitive are the slave-holding community to every movement relating to the abolition of slavery. At the same time, it would furnish to
the world a beautiful pledge of their sincerity if they would unite with
the non-slave-holding States, and by a unanimous vote proclaim freedom
to every soul within sight of the capital of this free government. We
could then say, and the world would then admit our pretence, that the
voice of the nation is against slavery, and throw back upon Great Britain that disgrace which is of right and justice her exclusive property."

Charmed by the originality, boldness, and humanity of Garrison, the meek little Quaker went to Boston by stage ; and then,
with staff in hand, walked to Bennington, Vt., to see the young
man whose great heart-throbs for the slave he had felt in "The
Journal of the Times." There, in the Green Mountains of Vermont, swept by the free air, and mantled by the pure snow,' the
meek Quaker communed with the strict Baptist, and they both
took sweet counsel together. The bright torch that Garrison
had held up to the people in Vermont was to be transferred to
the people of Baltimore, who were " sitting in darkness." So,
as a result of this conference, Garrison agreed to join Lundy in
conducting "The Genius of Universal Emancipation." Accordingly, in September, 1829, Garrison took the principal charge of
the Journal, enlarged it, and issued it as a weekly. Lundy was to
travel, lecture, and solicit subscribers in its interest, and contribute to its editorial columns as he could from time to time.

Both men were equally against slavery : Lundy for gradual
emancipation and *colonization ;* but Garrison for *immediate and
unconditional emancipation.* Garrison said of this difference :
"But I was n't much help to him, for he had been all for gradual
emancipation, and as soon as I began to look into the matter, I
became convinced that immediate abolition was the doctrine to
be preached, and I scattered his subscribers like pigeons."

But the good " Friend " contemplated the destructive zeal
of his young helper with the complacency so characteristic of his
class, standing by his doctrine that every one should follow " his
own light." But it was not long before Garrison made a bold
attack upon one of the vilest features of the slave-trade, which
put an end to his paper, and resulted in his arrest, trial for libel,
conviction, and imprisonment. The story runs as follows :

" A certain ship, the 'Francis Todd,' from Newburyport, came to
Baltimore and took in a load of slaves for the New Orleans market.

All the harrowing cruelties and separations which attend the rending asunder of families and the sale of slaves, were enacted under the eyes of the youthful philanthropist, and in a burning article he denounced the inter-State slave-trade as piracy, and piracy of an aggravated and cruel kind, inasmuch as those born and educated in civilized and Christianized society have more sensibility to feel the evils thus inflicted than imbruted savages. He denounced the owners of the ship and all the parties in no measured terms, and expressed his determination to 'cover with thick infamy all who were engaged in the transaction.'"

Then, to be sure, the sleeping tiger was roused, for there was a vigor and power in the young editor's eloquence that quite dissipated the good-natured contempt which had hitherto hung round the paper. He was indicted for libel, found guilty, of course, condemned, imprisoned in the cell of a man who had been hanged for murder. His mother at this time was not living, but her heroic, undaunted spirit still survived in her son, who took the baptism of persecution and obloquy not merely with patience, but with the joy which strong spirits feel in endurance. He wrote sonnets on the walls of his prison, and by his cheerful and engaging manners made friends of his jailer and family, who did every thing to render his situation as comfortable as possible. Some considerable effort was made for his release, and much interest was excited in various quarters for him.[1]

Finally, the benevolent Arthur Tappan came forward and paid the exorbitant fine imposed upon Garrison, and he went forth a more inveterate foe of slavery. This incident gave the world one of the greatest reformers since Martin Luther. Without money, social influence, or friends, Garrison lifted again the standard of liberty. He began a lecture tour in which God taught him the magnitude of his work. Everywhere mouths were sealed and public halls closed against him. At length, on January 1, 1831, he issued the first number of "The Liberator," which he continued to edit for thirty-five years, and discontinued it only when every slave in America was free! His methods of assailing the modern Goliath of slavery were thus tersely put :

" I determined, at every hazard, to lift up the standard of emancipation in the eyes of the nation, within sight of Bunker Hill, and in the birthplace of liberty. That standard is now unfurled ; and long may it

---

[1] Men of our Times, pp. 162, 163.

float, unhurt by the spoilations of time or the missiles of a desperate foe ; yea, till every chain be broken, and every bondman set free ! Let Southern oppressors tremble ; let their secret abettors tremble ; let all the enemies of the persecuted Black tremble. Assenting to the self-evident truths maintained in the American Declaration of Independence, —'that all men are created equal, and endowed by their Creator with certain inalienable rights, among which are life, liberty, and the pursuit of happiness,' I shall strenuously contend for the immediate enfranchisement of our slave population.

"I am aware that many object to the severity of my language ; but is there not cause for severity ? I will be as harsh as truth, and as uncompromising as justice. On this subject I do not wish to think, or speak, or write with moderation. No ! No ! Tell a man whose house is on fire to give a moderate alarm ; tell him to moderately rescue his wife from the hands of the ravisher ; tell the mother to gradually extricate her babe from the fire into which it has fallen ; but urge me not to use moderation in a cause like the present ! I am in earnest. I will not equivocate—I will not excuse—I will not retreat a single inch. AND I WILL BE HEARD. The apathy of the people is enough to make every statue leap from its pedestal, and to hasten the resurrection of the dead.

"It is pretended that I am retarding the cause of emancipation by the coarseness of my invective and the precipitancy of my measures. The charge is not true. On this question, my influence, humble as it is, is felt at this moment to a considerable extent ; and it shall be felt in coming years—not perniciously, but beneficially,—not as a curse, but as a blessing ; and POSTERITY WILL BEAR TESTIMONY THAT I WAS RIGHT. I desire to thank God that He enables me to disregard 'the fear of man which bringeth a snare,' and to speak truth in its simplicity and power ; and I here close with this dedication :

> "Oppression ! I have seen thee, face to face,
> And met thy cruel eye and cloudy brow ;
> By thy soul-withering glance I fear not now—
> For dread to prouder feelings doth give place,
> Of deep abhorrence ! Scorning the disgrace
> Of slavish knees that at thy footstool bow,
> I also kneel—but with far other vow
> Do hail thee and thy herd of hirelings base ;
> I swear, while life-blood warms my throbbing veins,
> Still to oppose and thwart, with heart and hand,
> Thy brutalizing sway—till Afric's chains
> Are burst, and Freedom rules the rescued land,
> Trampling Oppression and his iron rod ;
> Such is the vow I take—so help me, God ! "

There never was a grander declaration of war against slavery. There never was a more intrepid leader than William Lloyd Garrison. Words more prophetic were never uttered by human voice. His paper did indeed make "Southern oppression tremble," while its high resolves and sublime sentiments found a response in the hearts of many people. It is pleasant to record that this first impression of "The Liberator" brought a list of twenty-five subscribers from Philadelphia, backed by $50 in cash, sent by James Forten, a Colored man!

One year from the day he issued the first number of his paper, William Lloyd Garrison, at the head of eleven others, organized *The American Anti-Slavery Society.* It has been indicated already that he was in favor of immediate emancipation; but, in addition to that principle, he took the ground that slavery was supported by the Constitution; that it was "a covenant with death and an agreement with hell"; that as a Christian it was his duty to obey God rather than man; that his conscience was paramount to the Constitution, and, therefore, his duty was to work outside of the Constitution for the destruction of slavery. Thus did Garrison establish the first Anti-slavery Society in this country to adopt aggressive measures and demand immediate and unconditional emancipation. It is not claimed that his methods were original. Daniel O'Connell was perhaps the greatest *agitator* of the present century. In a speech delivered at Cork, he said :—

"I speak of liberty in commendation. Patriotism is a virtue, but it can be selfish. Give me the great and immortal Bolivar, the savior and regenerator of his country. He found her a province, and he has made her a nation. His first act was to give freedom to the slaves upon his own estate. (Hear, hear.) In Colombia, all castes and all colors are free and unshackled. But how I like to contrast him with the far-famed Northern heroes ! George Washington ! That great and enlightened character—the soldier and the statesman—had but one blot upon his character. He had slaves, and he gave them liberty when he wanted them no longer. (Loud cheers.) Let America, in the fulness of her pride wave on high her banner of freedom and its blazing stars. I point to her, and say : There is one foul blot upon it : you have negro slavery. They may compare their struggles for freedom to Marathon and Leuctra, and point to the rifleman with his gun, amidst her woods and forests, shouting for liberty and America. In the midst of their laughter and their pride, I point them to the negro children screaming for the mother from whose bosom they have been torn.

America, it is a foul stain upon your character ! (Cheers.) This conduct kept up by men who had themselves to struggle for freedom, is
doubly unjust. Let them hoist the flag of liberty, with the whip and
rack on one side, and the star of freedom upon the other. The Americans are a sensitive people ; in fifty-four years they have increased their
population from three millions to twenty millions ; they have many
glories that surround them, but their beams are partly shorn, for they
have slaves. (Cheers.) Their hearts do not beat so strong for liberty
as mine. . . . I will call for justice, in the name of the living God,
and I shall find an echo in the breast of every human being. (Cheers.)" [1]

But while Garrison's method of agitation was not original, it
was new to this country. He spoke as one having authority, and
his fiery earnestness warmed the frozen feeling of the Northern
people, and startled the entire South. One year from the formation of the society above alluded to (December 4, 5, and 6,
1833), a *National Anti-Slavery Convention* was held in Philadelphia, with sixty delegates from ten States! In 1836 there were
250 auxiliary anti-slavery societies in thirteen States ; and eighteen months later they had increased to 1,006. Money came
to these societies from every direction, and the good work had
been fairly started.

William Lloyd Garrison created a party, and it will be known
in history as the *Garrisonian Party.*

While Mr. Garrison had taken the position that slavery was
constitutional, there were those who held the other view, that
slavery was unconstitutional, and, therefore, upon constitutional
grounds should be abolished.

The Whig party was the nearest to the anti-slavery society
of any of the political organizations of the time. It had promised, in convention assembled, " to promote all constitutional
measures for the overthrow of slavery, and to oppose at all times,
with uncompromising zeal and firmness, any further addition of
slave-holding States to this Union, out of whatever territory
formed.[2] But the party never got beyond this. Charles Sumner
was a member of the Whig party, but was greatly disturbed
about its indifference on the question of slavery. In 1846 he delivered a speech before the Whig convention of Massachusetts
on " *The Anti-Slavery Duties of the Whig Party.*" He declared

---

[1] Speech delivered at the Annual Meeting of the Cork Anti-Slavery Society, 1829.
[2] Sumner's Works, vol. i. p. 336.

his positive opposition to slavery; said that he intended to attack
the institution on constitutional grounds; that slavery was not a
"covenant with death or an agreement with hell"; that he intended to do his work for the slave inside of the Constitution.
He said:—

"There is in the Constitution no compromise on the subject of
slavery of a character not to be reached legally and constitutionally,
which is the only way in which I propose to reach it. Wherever power
and jurisdiction are secured to Congress, they may unquestionably be
exercised in conformity with the Constitution. And even in matters
beyond existing powers and jurisdiction there is a constitutional mode
of action. The Constitution contains an article pointing out how at
any time amendments may be made thereto. This is an important
article, giving to the Constitution a progressive character, and allowing
it to be moulded to suit new exigencies and new conditions of feeling.
The wise framers of this instrument did not treat the country as a Chinese foot, never to grow after its infancy, but anticipated the changes
incident to its growth."

He proposed to the Whigs as their rallying watchword, the
"REPEAL OF SLAVERY UNDER THE CONSTITUTION AND LAWS
OF THE FEDERAL GOVERNMENT." Discussing the methods, he
continued :—

"The time has passed when this can be opposed on constitutional
grounds. It will not be questioned by any competent authority that
Congress may by express legislation abolish slavery, first, in the District
of Columbia; second, in the territories, if there should be any; third,
that it may abolish the slave-trade on the high seas between the States;
fourth, that it may refuse to admit any new State with a constitution
sanctioning slavery. Nor can it be doubted that the people of the free
States may, in the manner pointed out by the Constitution, proceed to
its amendment."

Thus did Charles Sumner lay down a platform for a *Political
Abolition Party*, and of such a party he became the laurelled
champion and leader.

The year 1846 was marked by the most bitter political discussion; Garrison the *Agitator*, the Mexican war, and other issues
had greatly exercised the people. At a meeting held in Tremont Temple, Boston, on the 5th of November, 1846, Mr. Sumner took occasion to give his reasons for bolting the nominee of

the Whig party for Congress, Mr. Winthrop.[1] Mr. Sumner said that he had never heard Mr. Winthrop's voice raised for the slave; and that, judging from the past, he never expected to hear it. " Will he oppose," asked Mr. Sumner, " at all times, without compromise, any further addition of slave-holding States? Here, again, if we judge him by the past, he is wanting. None can forget that in 1845, on the 4th of July, a day ever sacred to memories of freedom, in a speech at Faneuil Hall, he volunteered, in advance of any other Northern Whig, to receive Texas with a welcome into the family of States, although on that very day she was preparing a constitution placing slavery beyond the reach of Legislative change."[2]

Here, then, was another party created—a *Political Abolition Party*—for the suppression of slavery.

In 1848, Mr. Sumner left the Whig party, and gave his magnificent energies and splendid talents to the organization of the *Free-Soil Party*, upon the principles he had failed to educate the Whigs to accept.

Charles Sumner was in the United States Senate, where " his words were clothed with the majesty of Massachusetts." The young lawyer who had upbraided Winthrop for his indifference respecting the slave, and opposed the Mexican war, was consistent in the Senate, and in harmony with his early love for humanity. He closed his great speech on FREEDOM NATIONAL, SLAVERY SECTIONAL, in the following incisive language:—

" At the risk of repetition, but for the sake of clearness, review now this argument, and gather it together. Considering that slavery is of such an offensive character that it can find sanction only in positive law, and that it has no such ' positive ' sanction in the Constitution ; that the Constitution, according to its Preamble, was ordained to ' establish justice,' and ' secure the blessings of liberty ' ; that in the convention which framed it, and also elsewhere at the time, it was declared not to ' sanction ' ; that according to the Declaration of Independence, and the address of the Continental Congress, the nation was dedicated to 'Liberty' and the 'rights of human nature'; that according to the principles of common law, the Constitution must be interpreted openly, actively, and

---

[1] At the election that took place on the 9th of November, 1846, the vote stood as follows: Winthrop (Whig), 5,980 ; Howe (Anti-Slavery), 1,334 ; Homer (Democrat), 1, 688 ; Whiton (Independent), 331. The number of tickets in the field indicated the state of public feeling.

[2] Sumner's Works, vol. I. p. 337.

perpetually for Freedom ; that according to the decision of the Supreme Court, it acts upon slaves, *not as property*, but as *persons* ; that at the first organization of the national government under Washington, slavery had no national favor, existed nowhere on the national territory, beneath the national flag, but was openly condemned by the nation, the Church, the colleges, and literature of the times ; and finally, that according to an amendment of the Constitution, the national government can only exercise powers delegated to it, among which there is none to support slavery ;—considering these things, sir, it is impossible to avoid the single conclusion that slavery is in no respect a national institution, and that the Constitution nowhere upholds property in man."

This speech set men in the North to thinking. Sumner was now the acknowledged leader of the only political party in the country that had a wholesome anti-slavery plank in its platform.

Daniel Webster and the Whig party were in their grave. After the Democratic Convention had met and adjourned without mentioning Webster, a Northern farmer exclaimed when he had read the news, " *The South never pay their slaves !* "

During all these years of agitation and struggle, the pulpit of New England maintained an unbroken silence on the slavery question. Doctor Lyman Beecher was the acknowledged leader of the orthodox pulpit. Dr. William E. Channing was the champion of Unitarianism and the leader of the heterodox pulpit. Dr. Beecher was fond of controversy, enjoyed a battle of words upon every thing but the slavery question. He proclaimed the doctrine of " *immediate repentance* "; was earnest in his entreaties to men to quit their "cups" at *once;* but on the slavery question was a slow coach. He was for *gradual* emancipation. He frowned not a little upon the vigorous editorials in "The Liberator." He regarded Mr. Garrison as a hot-head; "having zeal, but not according to knowledge." Abolitionism received no encouragement from this venerable divine.

Dr. Channing was a gentle, pure-hearted, and humane sort of a man. He dreaded controversy, and shunned the agitation and agitators of anti-slavery.

The lesser lights followed the example of these bright stars in the churches.

But all could not keep silent,—for slavery needed apologists in the North. Stewart, of Andover; Alexander, of Princeton; Fisk, of Wilberham, and many other leading ministers endeavored to prove the *Divine Origin and Biblical Authority of Slavery.*

The silence of the pulpit drove out many anti-slavery men who, up to this time, had been hoping for aid from this quarter. Many went out of the Church temporarily, hoping that the scales would drop from the eyes of the preachers ere long; but others never returned—were driven to infidelity and bitter hatred of the Christian Church. Dr. Albert Barnes said: "That there was no power out of the Church that would sustain slavery an hour if it were not sustained in it."

Among the leaders of the HETERODOX ANTI-SLAVERY PARTY —those who attacked the reticency, silent acquiescence, or act of support the Church gave slavery,—were Parker Pillsbury, James G. Birney, Stephen S. Foster, and Samuel Brooke. The platform of this party was clearly defined by Mr. Pillsbury :—

"That slavery finds its surest and sternest defence in the prevailing religion of the country, is no longer questionable. Let it be driven from the Church, with the burning seal of its reprobation and execration stamped on its iron brow, and its fate is fixed forever. Only while its horrors are baptized and sanctified in the name of Christianity, can it maintain an existence.

"The Anti-Slavery movement has unmasked the character of the American Church. *Our religion has been found at war with the interests of humanity and the laws of God.* And it is more than time the world was awakened to its unhallowed influence on the hopes and happiness of man, while it makes itself the palladium of the foulest iniquity ever perpetrated in the sight of heaven."

This was a bold movement, but it was doubtless a sword that was as dangerous to those who essayed to handle it, as to the Church whose destruction it was intended to effect. The doctrine that was to sustain and inspire this party can be briefly stated in a sentence: THE FATHERHOOD OF GOD, AND THE BROTHERHOOD OF MAN.

Once outside the orthodox church, Theodore Parker gave himself wholly to this idea. He preached the "*Gospel of Humanity*"; and, standing upon a broad platform, preaching a broad doctrine, bound by no ecclesiastical law, his claims to a place in the history of his county, and in the gratitude of his countrymen can be fairly audited when his work for the emancipation of evangelical churches from the thraldom of slavery is

---

[1] Church As It Is, etc., Introduction.

considered. He did more in his day to rupture the organic and sympathetic relation existing between the Northern and Southern churches, and, thereby, hasten the struggle between the sections for the extension or extinction of domestic slavery, than any other man in America. The men who found themselves on the outside of the Church gathered about Parker, and applauded his invective and endorsed his arraignment of the churches that had placed their hands upon their mouths, and their mouths in the dust, before the slave power. He touched a chord in the human heart, and it yielded rich music. He educated the pew until an occasional voice broke the long silence respecting the bondman of the land. First, the ministers were not so urgent in their invitations to Southern ministers to occupy their pulpits. This coldness was followed by feeble prayer and moderate speech on behalf of those who were bound. And the churches themselves began to feel that they were "an offence" to the world. Every note of sympathy that fell from the pulpit was amplified into a grand chorus of pity for the slave. And thus the leaven of human sympathy hid in the orthodox church of New England, leavened the whole body until a thousand pulpits were ablaze with a righteous condemnation of the wrongs of the slaves. Even Dr. Channing came to the conclusion that something should be " So done as not to put in jeopardy the peace of the slave-holding States!" [1]

THE ECONOMIC ANTI-SLAVERY PARTY was headed by the industrious and indomitable Horace Greeley. His claim to the feelings of humanity should never be disputed ; but as a practical man who sought to solve the riddle of every-day life he placed his practical views in the foreground. As a political economist he reasoned that slave labor was degrading to free labor ; that free labor was better than slave labor, and, therefore, he most earnestly desired its abolition. Wherever you turn in his writings this idea gives the edge to all his arguments concerning slavery. " But slavery," wrote Mr. Greeley, " primarily considered, has still another aspect—that of a natural relation of simplicity to cunning, of ignorance to knowledge, of weakness to power. Thomas Carlyle, before his melancholy decline and fall into devil-worship, truly observed, that the capital mistake of Rob Roy was his failure to comprehend that it was cheaper

---

[1] Channing's Works, vol. ii. p. 10, sq.

to buy the beef he required in the Grassmarket at Glasgow than to obtain it without price, by harrying the lowland farms. So the first man whoever imbibed or conceived the fatal delusion that it was more advantageous to him, or to any human being, to procure whatever his necessities or his appetites required by address and scheming than by honest work—by the unrequited rather than the fairly and faithfully recompensed toil of his fellow-preachers—was, in essence and in heart, a slave-holder, and only awaited opportunity to become one in deed and practice. . . . It is none the less true, however, that ancient civilization, in its various national developments, was habitually corrupted, debauched, and ultimately ruined by slavery, which rendered labor dishonorable, and divided society horizontally into a small caste of the wealthy, educated, refined, and independent, and a vast hungry, sensual, thriftless, and worthless populace; rendered impossible the preservation of republican liberty and of legalized equality, even among the nominally free. Diogenes, with his lantern, might have vainly looked, through many a long day, among the followers of Marius, or Catiline, or Cæsar, for a specimen of the poor but virtuous and self-respecting Roman citizen of the days of Cincinnatus, or even of Regulus."[1]

But Mr. Greeley's philosophy was as destructive as his logic was defective. He wished the slave free, not because he loved him; but because of the deep concern he had for the welfare of the free, white working-men of America. He was willing the Negro should be free, but never suggested any plan of relief for his social condition, or prescribed for his spiritual and intellectual health. He handled the entire Negro problem with the icy fingers of the philosopher, and always applied the flinty logic of abstract political economy. He was an *anti-slavery* advocate, but not an *abolitionist*. He was opposed to slavery, as a system at war with the social and commercial prosperity of the nation; but so far as the humanity of the question, in reaching out after the slave as an injured member of society, was concerned, he was silent.

The aggressive anti-slavery party had its birth in the pugnacious brains of E. P. Lovejoy, James G. Birney, Cassius M. Clay, and John Brown. All of the anti-slavery parties had

---

[1] American Conflict, vol. i. pp. 25, 26.

taught the doctrine of *non-resistance;* that if "thy enemy smite thee on thy cheek, turn the other also." But there were a few men who believed they were possessed of sacred rights, and that it was their duty to defend them, even with their lives. It was not a popular doctrine ; and yet a conscientious few practised it with sublime courage whenever occasion required. In 1836 James G. Birney, editor of *The Philanthropist*, published at Cincinnati, Ohio, defended his press, as best he could, against a mob, who finally destroyed it. And on the 7th of November, 1837, the Rev. Mr. Lovejoy sealed the sacred doctrine of the liberty of the press with his precious blood in the defence of his printing-press at Alton, Illinois. Cassius M. Clay went armed, and insisted upon his right to freely and peaceably discuss the cause of anti-slavery.

But these men only laid down a great, fundamental truth ; it was given to John Brown to write the lesson upon the hearts of the American people, so that they were enabled, a few years later, to practise the doctrine of *resistance*, and preserve the *Nation* against the bloody aggressions of the Southern Confederacy.

THE COLONIZATION ANTI-SLAVERY SOCIETY ante-dated any of the other organizations. Benjamin Lundy was one of the earliest advocates of colonization. The object of colonizationists was to transport to Liberia, on the West Coast of Africa, all manumitted slaves. Only *free* Negroes were to be colonized. It was claimed by the advocates of the scheme that this was the only hope of the free Negro ; that the proscription everywhere directed against his social and intellectual endeavors cramped and lamed him in the race of life ; that in Liberia he could build his own government, schools, and business ; and there would be nothing to hinder him in his ambition for the highest places in Church or State. Moreover, they claimed that the free Negro owed something to his benighted brethren who were still in pagan darkness ; that a free Negro government on the West Coast of Africa could exert a missionary influence upon the natives, and thus the evangelization of Africa could be effected by the free Negro himself.[1]

---

[1] The following were the objects of the Colonization Society :

" 1st. To rescue the free colored people of the United States from their political and social disadvantages.

" 2d. To place them in a country where they may enjoy the benefits of free government, with all the blessings which it brings in its train.

To this method Henry Clay, of Kentucky, Horace Mann, of Massachusetts ; Rev. Howard Malcom, of Pennsylvania : Rev. R. R. Gurley, of New York ; and many other persons of distinction, gave their endorsement and assistance. The American Colonization Society was organized in 1817. Its earliest supporters were from the Southern and Middle States. A fair idea can be had of the character of the men who sustained the cause of colonization by an examination of the following list of officers elected in March, 1834.

"*President.*—JAMES MADISON, of Virginia.

"*Vice-Presidents.*—Chief-Justice MARSHALL ; General LAFAYETTE, of France ; Hon. WM. H. CRAWFORD, of Georgia ; Hon. HENRY CLAY, of Lexington, Kentucky; Hon. JOHN C. HERBERT, of Maryland; ROBERT RALSTON, Esq., of Philadelphia ; Gen. JOHN MASON, of Georgetown, D. C. ; SAMUEL BAYARD, Esq., of New Jersey ; ISAAC McKIM, Esq., of Maryland ; Gen. JOHN HARTWELL COCKE, of Virginia ; Rt. Rev. Bishop WHITE, of Pennsylvania ; Hon. DANIEL WEBSTER, of Boston ; Hon. CHARLES F. MERCER, of Virginia ; JEREMIAH DAY, D.D., of Yale College ; Hon. RICHARD RUSH, of Pennsylvania ; Bishop Mc-KENDREE ; PHILIP E. THOMAS, Esq., of Maryland ; Dr. THOMAS C. JAMES, of Philadelphia ; Hon. JOHN COTTON SMITH, of Connecticut ; Hon. THEODORE FRELINGHUYSEN, of New Jersey ; Hon. LOUIS McLANE, of Washington City ; GERRIT SMITH, of New York ; J. H. M'CLURE, Esq., of New Jersey ; Gen. ALEXANDER MACOMB, of Washington City ; MOSES ALLEN, Esq., of New York ; Gen. WALTER JONES, of Washington City ; F. S. KEY, Esq., of Georgetown, D. C. ; SAMUEL H. SMITH, Esq., of Washington City ; JOSEPH GALES, Jr., Esq., of Washington City ; Rt. Rev. WM. MEADE, D.D., Assistant Bishop of Virginia ; Hon. ALEXANDER PORTER, of Louisiana ; JOHN McDONOUGH, Esq., of Louisiana ; Hon. SAMUEL L. SOUTHARD, of New Jersey.

"*Managers.*—Rev. JAMES LAURIE, D.D. ; Gen. WALTER JONES ; FRANCIS S. KEY ; Rev. WM. HALEY ; JOHN UNDERWOOD ; WILLIAM W. SEATON ; WALTER LOWRIE · Dr. PHINEAS BRADLEY ; Dr. THOMAS SEWALL.

"*Secretaries.*—Rev. RALPH R. GURLEY, WILLIAM H. MACFARLAND.

"*Treasurer.*—JOSEPH GALES, Senior.

"*Recorder.*—PHILLIP R. FENDALL."

"3d. To spread civilization, sound morals, and true religion through the continent of Africa.

"4. To arrest and destroy the slave-trade.

"5. To afford slave-owners who wish, or are willing, to liberate their slaves an asylum for their reception."

The Colonization Society was never able to secure the sym-
'pathy of the various anti-slavery societies of the country; and
was unable to gain the confidence of the Colored people to any
great extent. But it had the advantage of being in harmony
with what little humane sentiment there was at the South. It
did not attempt to agitate. It only sought to colonize on the
West Coast of Africa all Negroes who could secure legal manumission. Nearly all the Southern States had laws upon their
statute-books requiring all emancipated slaves to leave the State.
The question as to where they should go was supposed to be
answered by the Colonization Society. It had much influence
with Congress, and did not hesitate to use it. A Mr. Joseph
Bryan, of Alabama, petitioned Congress for the establishment
" of a line of Mail Steam-ships to the Western Coast of Africa,"
in the summer of 1850. The Committee on Naval Affairs reported favorably the following bill:

"A Bill to Establish a Line of War Steamers to the
Coast of Africa. [Report No. 438.]

" *In the House of Representatives, August 1, 1850. Read twice, and committed to the Committee of the whole House on the State of the Union.*

" Mr. F. P. Stanton, from the Committee on Naval Affairs, reported
the following bill :—A bill to establish a line of war steamers to the
coast of Africa, for the suppression of the slave-trade, and the promotion of commerce and colonization :

SEC. I *'Be it enacted* by the Senate and House of Representatives
of the United States of America, in Congress assembled, That it shall
be the duty of the Secretary of the Navy, immediately after the passage
of this act, to enter into contract with Joseph Bryan, of Alabama, and
George Nicholas Saunders, of New York, and their associates, for the
building, equipment, and maintenance of three steam-ships to run
between the United States and the coast of Africa, upon the following
terms and conditions, to wit :

"The said ships to be each of not less than four thousand tons burden, to be so constructed as to be convertible, at the least possible
expense, into war steamers of the first class, and to be built and
equipped in accordance with plans to be submitted to and approved by
the Secretary of the Navy, and under the superintendence of an officer
to be appointed by him , two of said ships to be finished and ready for
sea in two and a half years, and the other within three years after the
date of the contract, and the whole to be kept up by alterations, re-

pairs, or additions, to be approved by the Secretary of the Navy, so as to be fully equal to the exigencies of the service and the faithful performance of the contract. The said Secretary, at all times, to exercise such control over said ships as may not be inconsistent with the provisions of this act, and especially to have the power to direct, at the expense of the Government, such changes in the machinery and internal arrangements of the ships as he may at any time deem advisable.

"Each of said ships to be commanded by an officer of the Navy, who with four Passed Midshipmen to act as watch officers, and any mail agents who may be sent by the Government, shall be accommodated and provided for in a manner suitable to their rank, at the expense of the contractors. Each of said ships, if required by the Secretary, shall receive two guns of heavy calibre, and the men from the United States Navy necessary to serve them, who shall be provided for as aforesaid. In the event of war the Government to have the right to take any or all of said ships for its own exclusive use on payment of the value thereof ; such value not exceeding the cost, to be ascertained by appraisers chosen by the Secretary of the Navy and the contractors.

"Each of said ships to make four voyages per annum ; one shall leave New Orleans every three months ; one shall leave Baltimore every three months, touching at Norfolk and Charleston ; and one shall leave New York every three months, touching at Savannah ; all having liberty to touch at any of the West India Islands ; and to proceed thence to Liberia, touching at any of the islands or ports on the coast of Africa ; thence to Gibraltar, carrying the Mediterranean mails ; thence to Cadiz, or some other Spanish port to be designated by the Secretary of the Navy ; thence to Lisbon ; thence to Brest, or some other French port to be designated as above ; thence to London, and back to the place of departure, bringing and carrying the mails to and from said ports.

"The said contractors shall further agree to carry to Liberia so many emigrants being free persons of color, and not exceeding twenty-five hundred for each voyage, as the American Colonization Society may require, upon the payment by said Society of ten dollars for each emigrant over twelve years of age, and five dollars for each one under that age , these sums, respectively, to include all charges for baggage of emigrants and the daily supply of sailors' rations. The contractors, also, to carry, bring back, and accommodate, free from charge, all necessary agents of the said Society.

"The Secretary of the Navy shall further stipulate to advance to said contractors, as the building of said ships shall progress, two thirds of the amount expended thereon ; such advances to be made in the bonds of the United States, payable thirty years after date, and bearing five per cent. interest, and not to exceed six hundred thousand dollars for each ship. And the said contractors shall stipulate to repay the said advances in equal annual instalments, with interest from the date of the completion of said ships until the termination of the contract, which shall continue fifteen years from the commencement of the service. The Secretary of the Navy to require ample security for the faithful performance of the contract, and to reserve a lien upon the ships for the sum advanced. The Government to pay said contractors forty thousand dollars for each trip, or four hundred and eighty thousand dollars per annum.

"SEC. 2. *And be it further enacted*, That the President of the United States shall cause to be issued the bonds of the United States, as the same may, from time to time, be required by the Secretary of the Navy to carry out the contract aforesaid."

Public sentiment, North and South, was greatly in favor of the measure. T. J. Durant, Esq., of New Orleans, in an elaborate letter addressed to the "Commercial Bulletin" of New Orleans, under date of September 12, 1850, answered objections, and warmly urged the passage of the bill. The Chaplain of the U. S. Senate, Rev. R. R. Gurley, wrote a letter on the 10th of October, 1850, to George N. Saunders, Esq., urging the measure as of paramount importance to both America and Africa. The press of the country generally endorsed the bill, and commented upon the general good to follow in numerous editorials. A scheme of such gigantic proportions poorly set forth the profound thought that harassed the public mind in regard to the crime of keeping men in slavery. A few extracts from the papers will suffice to show how the matter was regarded.

EXTRACTS FROM THE PRESS.

"The Report of the Naval Committee to the House of Representatives in favor of the establishment of a line of mail steam-ships to the Western Coast of Africa, and thence via the Mediterranean to London, has been received by the public press throughout the Union with the warmest expressions of approbation. The Whig, Democratic, and neutral papers of the North and South, in the slave-holding and non-slaveholding States, with a very few exceptions, appear to vie with each other in pressing its consideration upon the public attention. This earnest and almost unanimous support of the measure by the organs of public opinion, without respect to party or section, shows the deep hold which the objects it proposes to effect have upon the public favor. Those objects are to promote the emigration of free persons of color from this country to Liberia; also to increase the steam navy, and to extend the commerce of the United States,—all, it will be almost universally conceded, desirable objects. The desirableness of the objects being admitted, the question is, does the mode proposed for promoting them recommend itself to the sanction of Congress? We are forced to the conclusion that it does. We are aware that while all agree as to the expediency of increasing our steam navy—some are in favor of the Government's building its own steam-ships, and others advocate the encouragement of lines of steam-packets, to be established by private enterprise under the auspices of Government. . . .

" The considerations, however, which in our opinion should commend this measure to the favorable attention of Congress are so obvious, and have been so clearly and strongly presented in the report of the committee, that we need not here repeat them. If the voice of the press, of all sections and of all parties, be any indication of popular opinion, we are free to say, that it would be difficult for Congress to pass a measure which would be received with more *general* satisfaction by the people of the United States." [1]

" AFRICAN STEAM-LINES.—The entertainment by the Government of Great Britain of a project for the establishment of a powerful line of steam-vessels between that country and the African coast, ostensibly for the conveyance of a monthly mail, and the more effectual checking of the slave-traffic, is strong proof, we think, of the value that the commerce between the two countries is capable of becoming. It may, in addition, be regarded as corroborative of the justness of the position taken by the advocates of a mail-steamer line between this country and Africa. We are by no means disposed to look invidiously on the enterprising spirit exhibited abroad for securing a closer connection with a country, the great mercantile wealth of which is yet, comparatively speaking, untouched. This spirit should have on us no other than a stimulating effect. Besides, for years, if not ages, to come, the trade with Africa can admit of no very close competition. The promised vastness of this trade, whilst excluding all idea of monopoly, must continue to excite the new enterprise by its unlimited rewards. It is unnecessary that we should exhibit statistics to show her how largely England has been benefited by persevering though frequently interrupted communication with the interior parts of that great continent; nor to make plain how, with better knowledge and more ready means of access, mercantile risks will be lessened and mercantile profits enlarged. It will be remembered that the Congressional committee to

---

[1] The Republic, Sept. 11, 1850.

whom the question of establishing mail steamers between this country and Africa was referred, adverted in their report to the aid its adoption would afford in the consummation of the plans .of the Colonization Society. On the intimate relation between the one and the other, it was supposed that a good part of the required success was dependent. It is something singular that the colored race—those in reality most interested in the future destinies of Africa—should be so lightly affected by the evidences continually being presented in favor of colonization. He will do a service to this country as well as Africa who shall do any thing to open the eyes of the colored race to the advantages of emigration to the fertile and, to them, congenial shores of Africa." [1]

" AFRICA AND STEAM-SHIPS.—If but a single line of steam-ships is to be authorized this Session—and the state and prospects of the finances must counsel frugality and caution,—we think a line to Africa fairly entitled to the preference. · That continent on its western side is comparatively proximate and accessible ; it is filled with inhabitants who need the articles we can abundantly fabricate, and it is the ancestral soil of more than three millions of our people—of a race on whose account we are deeply debtors to justice and to heaven.. That race is more plastic and less conservative than the Chinese ; their soil produces in spontaneous profusion many articles which are to us comforts and luxuries, while nearly every thing we produce is in eager demand among its inhabitants, if they can but find the wherewithal to pay for them. Instead of being a detriment and a depression to our own manufacturing and mechanical industry, as the trade induced by our costly steam-ship lines to Liverpool, Bremen, and Havre mainly is, all the commerce with Africa which a more intimate communication with her would secure, would be advantageous to every department of American labor. Her surplus products are so diverse from ours, that no collision of interests between her producers and ours could ever be realized, while millions' worth of her tropical products which will not endure the slow and capricious transportation which is now their only recourse, would come to us in good order by steam-ships, and richly reward the labor of the gatherers and the enterprise of the importers.

" But the social and moral aspects of this subject are still more important. We are now expending life and treasure, in concert with other nations, to suppress the African slave-trade, and it is now generally conceded that such suppression can never be effected by the means hitherto relied on. The colonization of the Slave Coast, with direct reference to its Christianization and civilization, is the only sure means of putting an end to this inhuman traffic. And this colonization, all who are interested in the work seem heartily to agree, would

---

[1] National Intelligencer, October 23, 1850.

be immensely accelerated by the establishment of a line of African steam-ships. Liberia, now practically distant as Buenos Ayres, would, by such a line, be brought as near us as Bremen, and the ports regularly visited by our steamers could not fail rapidly to assume importance as centres of commerce and of increasing intelligence and industry." [1]

"THE COLONY OF LIBERIA AND ITS PROSPECTUS.—By every arrival from Liberia we learn that the colony of free negroes from the United States is progressing at a rate truly astonishing, and that before many years it promises to be a strong and powerful republic. The experiment of self-government has been completely successful ; the educational interests of the inhabitants are duly cared for ; civilization is making great headway among the aborigines ; and, by means of Liberia, there is a very flattering prospect of the slave-trade on the coast of Africa being entirely destroyed. Governor Roberts, a very intelligent colored man, of mixed blood, goes even so far as to say that Liberia is destined to rival the United States, and that both republics, by a unity of action, can civilize and Christianize the world, and especially benighted Africa. We are pleased to hear such good accounts from Liberia, and we shall always be pleased to hear of its success, and of the progress and welfare of its inhabitants. Founded, as it has been, by American philanthropists, and peopled by our emancipated slaves, the United States will ever watch its progress with interest, and aid and assist it as far as it possibly can." [2]

But notwithstanding the apparent favor the cause of colonization received from the press, it was an impractical, impossible, wild, and visionary scheme that could not be carried to the extent its projectors designed. It lost strength yearly, until all were convinced that the Negro would be emancipated here and remain here ; that it was as impossible to colonize a race of people as to colonize the sun, moon, and stars.

THE UNDERGROUND RAILROAD organization was perhaps one of the most useful auxiliaries the cause of agitation had. It could scarcely be called an organization. Unlike the other societies, it did not print its reports.[3] Like good Samaritans, its conductors did not ask passengers their creed ; but wherever they found human beings wounded in body and mind by slavery,

---

[1] Tribune, December 25, 1850.   [2] Herald, December, 17, 1850.

[3] It is to be regretted that William Still, the author of the U. G. R. R., failed to give any account of its origin, organization, workings, or the number of persons helped to freedom. It is an interesting narrative of many cases, but is shorn of that minuteness of detail so indispensable to authentic historical memorials.

they gave them passage to the "Inn" of Freedom on Canadian soil.

In a sense, the Underground Railroad was a secret organization. This was necessary, as the fugitive-slave law gave the master the right to pursue his slave when "fleeing from labor and service in one State into another," and apprehend him by due process of Federal law. The men who managed this road felt that they should obey God rather than man; that the slave's right to his freedom was greater than any law the nation could make through its representatives. So the Underground Railroad was made up of a company of godly men who stretched themselves across the land, from the borders of the sunny slave States to the snow-white shores of Canada. When men came up out of the hell of slavery gasping for a breath of free air, these good friends sheltered and fed them; and then hastened them off in the stillness of the night, with the everlasting stars as their ministers, toward Canada. The fugitives would be turned over to another conductor, who would conceal them until nightfall, when he would load his living freight into a covered conveyance, and drive all night to reach the next "station"; and so on until the fugitives found themselves free and safe under the English flag in Canada.

This was the safety-valve to the institution of slavery. As soon as leaders arose among the slaves, refusing to endure the yoke, they came North. Had they remained, the direful scenes of St. Domingo would have been enacted, and the hot, vengeful breath of massacre would have swept the South as a tornado, and blanched the cheek of the civilized world.

ANTI-SLAVERY LITERATURE wrought mightily for God in its field.[1] Frederick Douglass's book, "My Bondage and My Freedom"; Bishop Loguen's, "As a Slave and As a Freeman"; Autobiography of a Fugitive Negro," by the Rev. Samuel Ringgold Ward; "Twenty-two Years a Slave, and Forty Years a Freeman," by the Rev. Austin Stewart; "Narrative of Solomon Northup," "Walker's Appeal,"—all by eminent Negroes, exposed the true character of slavery, informed the public mind, stimulated healthy thought, and touched the heart of two continents with a sympathy almost divine.

But the uncounted millions of anti-slavery tracts, pamphlets,

---

[1] Judge Stroud, William Goodell, Wendell Phillips, William Jay, and hundreds of other white men contributed to the anti-slavery literature of the period.

journals, and addresses of the entire period of agitation were little more than a paper wad compared with the solid shot "Uncle Tom's Cabin" was to slavery. Written in vigorous English, in scintillating, perspicuous style; adorned with gorgeous imagery, bristling with living "*facts*"; going to the lowest depths, mounting to the greatest altitudes, moving with panoramic grandeur, picturing humanity forlorn and outraged; giving forth the shrillest, most *despairing* cries of the afflicted, and the sublimest strains of Christian faith; the struggle of innocent, defenceless womanhood, the subdued sorrow of chattel-babyhood, the yearnings of fettered manhood, and the piteous sobs of helpless old age,—made Mrs. Harriet Beecher Stowe's "Uncle Tom's Cabin" the magnifying wonder of enlightened Christendom! It pleaded the cause of the slave in twenty different languages; it engrossed the thought of philosophers, and touched the heart of youth with a strange pity for the slave. It covered audiences with the sunlight of laughter, wrapt them in sorrow, and veiled them in tears. It illustrated the power of the Gospel of Love, the gentleness of Negro character, and the powers and possibilities of the race. It was God's message to a people who had refused to listen to his anti-slavery prophets and priests; and its sad, wierd, and heart-touching descriptions and dialogues restored the milk of human kindness to a million hearts that had grown callous in an age of self-seeking and robbery of the poor.

In a political and sectional sense, the "Impending Crisis," by Helper, exerted a wide influence for good. It was read by merchants and politicians.

Diverse and manifold as were the methods of the friends of universal freedom, and sometimes apparently conflicting, under God no honest effort to rid the Negro and the country of the curse of slavery was lost. All these agencies, running along different lines, converged at a common centre, and aimed at a common end—the ultimate extinction of the foreign and domestic slave-trade.

CHAPTER. VI.

ANTI-SLAVERY EFFORTS OF FREE NEGROES.

INTELLIGENT INTEREST OF FREE NEGROES IN THE AGITATION MOVEMENT. — " FIRST ANNUAL CON-
VENTION OF THE PEOPLE OF COLOR" HELD AT PHILADELPHIA. — REPORT OF THE COMMITTEE
ON THE ESTABLISHMENT OF A COLLEGE FOR YOUNG MEN OF COLOR. — PROVISIONAL COMMITTEE
APPOINTED IN EACH CITY. — CONVENTIONAL ADDRESS. — SECOND CONVENTION HELD AT BENE-
ZET HALL, PHILADELPHIA. — RESOLUTIONS OF THE MEETING. — CONVENTIONAL ADDRESS. —
THE MASSACHUSETTS GENERAL COLORED ASSOCIATION. — CONVENTION OF ANTI-SLAVERY WOMEN
OF AMERICA AT NEW YORK. — PREJUDICE AGAINST ADMITTING NEGROES INTO WHITE SOCIE-
TIES. — COLORED ORATORS. — THEIR ELOQUENT PLEAS FOR THEIR ENSLAVED RACE.

THE free Negroes throughout the Northern States were not
passive during the agitation movement. They took a
lively interest in the cause that had for its ultimate end
the freedom of the slave. They did not comfort themselves
with the consciousness that *they* were free; but thought of *their
brethren* who were bound, and sympathized with them.

" *The First Annual Convention of the People of Color*" was held
in Philadelphia from the 6th to the 11th of June, 1831. Its sessions
were held "in the brick Wesleyan Church, Lombard Street,"
"pursuant to public notice, . . . signed by Dr. Belfast Burton
and William Whipper." The following delegates were present:

Philadelphia—John Bowers, Dr. Belfast Burton, James Cornish,
Junius C. Morel, William Whipper.
New York—Rev. Wm. Miller, Henry Sipkins, Thos. L. Jennings,
Wm. Hamilton, James Pennington.
Maryland—Rev. Abner Coker, Robert Cowley.
Delaware—Abraham D. Shad, Rev. Peter Gardiner.
Virginia—Wm. Duncan.

The following officers were chosen :

President—John Bowers.
Vice-Presidents—Abraham D. Shad, William Duncan.
Secretary—William Whipper.
Assistant Secretary—Thos. L. Jennings.

The first concern of this convention was the condition of that class which it directly represented—the "free persons of color" in the United States. A committee, consisting of Messrs. Morel, Shad, Duncan, Cowley, Sipkins, and Jennings, made the following report on the condition of the free persons of color in the United States:

"*Brethren ana Fellow-Citizens :*

"We, the Committee of Inquiry, would suggest to the Convention the propriety of adopting the following resolutions, viz. :

"*Resolved,* That, in the opinion of this Convention, it is highly necessary that the different societies engaged in the *Canadian Settlement* be earnestly requested to persevere in their praiseworthy and philanthropic undertaking ; firmly believing that, at a future period, their labors will be crowned with success.

" The Committee would also recommend this Convention to call on the free people of color to assemble *annually* by delegation at such place as may be designated as suitable.

" They would also respectfully submit to your wisdom the necessity of your deliberate reflection on the dissolute, intemperate, and ignorant condition of a large portion of the colored population of the United States.   They would not, however, refer to their unfortunate circumstances to add degradation to objects already degraded and miserable ; nor, with some others, improperly class the virtuous of our color with the abandoned, but with the most sympathizing and heartfelt commiseration, show our sense of obligation as the true guardians of our interests, by giving wholesome advice and good counsel.

" The Committee consider it as highly important that the Convention recommend the necessity of creating a general fund, to be denominated the CONVENTIONAL FUND, for the purpose of advancing the objects of this and future conventions, as the public good may require.

" They would further recommend, that the Declaration of Independence and the Constitution of the United States be read in our Conventions ; believing, that the truths contained in the former are incontrovertible, and that the latter guarantees in letter and spirit to every free-man born in this country, all the rights and immunities of citizenship.

"Your Committee with regret have witnessed the many oppressive, unjust, and unconstitutional laws which have been enacted in the different parts of the Union against the free people of color, and they would call upon this Convention, as possessing the rights of freemen, to recommend to the people, through their delegation, the propriety of memorializing the proper authorities, whenever they may feel themselves aggrieved, or their rights invaded, by any cruel or oppressive laws.

"And your Committee would further report, that, in their opinion, *Education, Temperance, and Economy* are best calculated to promote the elevation of mankind to a proper rank and standing among men, as they enable him to discharge all those duties enjoined on him by his Creator. We would, therefore, respectfully request an early attention to those virtues among our brethren who have a desire to be useful.

"And lastly, your Committee view with unfeigned regret, and respectfully submit to the wisdom of this Convention, the operations and misrepresentations of the American Colonization Society in these United States.

"We feel sorrowful to see such an immense and wanton waste of lives and property, not doubting the benevolent feelings of some individuals engaged in that cause. But we cannot for a moment doubt, but that the cause of many of our unconstitutional, unchristian, and unheard-of sufferings emanate from that unhallowed source ; and we would call on Christians of every denomination firmly to resist it." [1]

The convention was in session for several days. It attracted public attention on account of the intelligence, order, and excellent judgment which prevailed. ·It deeply touched the young white men who had, but a few months previous, enlisted under the broad banner Wm. Lloyd Garrison had given to the breeze. They called to see Colored men conduct a convention. The Rev. S. S. Jocelyn, of New Haven, Connecticut ; Arthur Tappan, of New York ; Benjamin Lundy, of Washington, D. C. ; William Lloyd Garrison, of Boston, Massachusetts ; Thomas Shipley and Charles Pierce, of Philadelphia, visited the convention and were cordially received. Messrs. Jocelyn, Tappan, and Garrison were invited to address the convention, They delivered stirring addresses, and especially urged the necessity of establishing a college for the education of "Young Men of Color." At the suggestion of the speaker the convention appointed a committee with whom the speaker conferred. The report of the committee was as follows :

"That a plan had been submitted to them by the above-named gentlemen, for the liberal education of Young Men of Color, on the Manual-Labor System, all of which they respectfully submit to the consideration of the Convention, are as follow :

"The plan proposed is, that a College be established at New Haven, Conn., as soon as $20,000 are obtained, and to be on the Manual-Labor

---

The Minutes, in possession of the author.

System, by which, in connection with a scientific education, they may also obtain a useful Mechanical or Agricultural profession ; and (they further report, having received information) that a benevolent individual has offered to subscribe one thousand dollars toward this object, provided that a farther sum of nineteen thousand dollars can be obtained in one year.

"After an interesting discussion, the above report was unanimously adopted ; one of the inquiries by the Convention was in regard to the place of location. On interrogating the gentlemen why New Haven should be the place of location, they gave the following as their reasons :—

"1st.   The site is healthy and beautiful.

"2d.   Its inhabitants are friendly, pious, generous, and humane.

"3d.   Its laws are salutary and protecting to all, without regard to complexion.

"4th.   Boarding is cheap and provisions are good.

"5th.   The situation is as central as any other that can be obtained. with the same advantages.

"6th.   The town of New Haven carries on an extensive West India trade, and many of the wealthy colored residents in the Islands, would, no doubt, send their sons there to be educated, and thus a fresh tie of friendship would be formed, which might be productive of much real good in the end.

"And last, though not the least, the literary and scientific character of New Haven, renders it a very desirable place for the location of the college."

The report of the Committee was received and adopted. The Rev. Samuel E. Cornish was appointed general agent to solicit funds, and Arthur Tappan was selected as treasurer. A Provisional Committee was appointed in each city, as follows :

"*Boston*—Rev. Hosea Easton, Robert Roberts, James G. Barbadoes, and Rev. Samuel Snowden.

"*New York*—Rev. Peter Williams, Boston Cromwell, Philip Bell, Thomas Downing, Peter Voglesang.

"*Philadelphia*—Joseph Cassey, Robert Douglass, Sr., James Forten, Richard Howell, Robert Purvis.

"*Baltimore*—Thomas Green, James P. Walker, Samuel G. Mathews, Isaac Whipper, Samuel Hiner.

"*New Haven*—Biars Stanley, John Creed, Alexander C. Luca.

"*Brooklyn, L. I.*—Jacob Deyes, Henry Thomson, Willis Jones.

"*Wilmington, Del.*—Rev. Peter Spencer, Jacob Morgan, William S. Thomas.

"*Albany*—Benjamin Latimore, Captain Schuyler, Captain Francis March.

"*Washington, D. C.*—William Jackson, Arthur Waring, Isaac Carey.

"*Lancaster, Pa.*—Charles Butler and Jared Grey.

"*Carlisle, Pa.*—John Peck and Rowland G. Roberts.

"*Chambersburg, Pa.*—Dennis Berry.

"*Pittsburgh*—John B. Vashon, Lewis Gardiner, Abraham Lewis.

"*Newark, N. J.*—Peter Petitt, Charles Anderson, Adam Ray.

"*Trenton*—Samson Peters, Leonard Scott."

The proceedings of the convention were characterized by a deep solemnity and a lively sense of the gravity of the situation. The delegates were of the ablest Colored men in the country, and were conversant with the wants of their people. The subjoined address shows that the committee that prepared it had a thorough knowledge of the public sentiment of America on the subject of race prejudice.

"CONVENTIONAL ADDRESS.

"*Respected Brethren and Fellow-Citizens :*

"Our attention has been called to investigate the political standing of our brethren wherever dispersed, but more particularly the situation of those in this great Republic.

"Abroad, we have been cheered with pleasant views of humanity, and the steady, firm, and uncompromising march of equal liberty to the human family. Despotism, tyranny, and injustice have had to retreat, in order to make way for the unalienable rights of man. Truth has conquered prejudice, and mankind are about to rise in the majesty and splendor of their native dignity.

"The cause of general emancipation is gaining powerful and able friends abroad. Britain and Denmark have performed such deeds as will immortalize them for their humanity, in the breasts of the philanthropists of the present day ; whilst, as a just tribute to their virtues, after-ages will yet erect unperishable monuments to their memory. (Would to God we could say thus of our own native soil !)

"And it is only when we look to our own native land, to the birth-place of our *fathers*, to the land for whose prosperity their blood and our sweat have been shed and cruelly extorted, that the Convention has had cause to hang its head and blush. Laws, as cruel in themselves as they were unconstitutional and unjust, have in many places been enacted against our poor unfriended and unoffending brethren ; laws, (without a shadow of provocation on our part,) at whose bare recital the very savage draws him up for fear of the contagion,—looks noble, and prides himself because he bears not the name of a Christian.

"But the Convention would not wish to dwell long on this subject, as it is one that is too sensibly felt to need description.

"We would wish to turn you from this scene with an eye of pity, and a breast glowing with mercy, praying that the recording angel may drop a tear, which shall obliterate forever the remembrance of so foul a stain upon the national escutcheon of this great Republic.

"This spirit of persecution was the cause of our Convention. It was that first induced us to seek an asylum in the Canadas ; and the Convention feels happy to report to its brethren, that our efforts to establish a settlement in that province have not been made in vain. Our prospects are cheering ; our friends and funds are daily increasing ; wonders have been performed far exceeding our most sanguine expectations ; already have our brethren purchased eight hundred acres of land—and two thousand of them have left the soil of their birth, crossed the lines, and laid the foundation for a structure which promises to prove an asylum for the colored population of these United States. They have erected two hundred log-houses, and have five hundred acres under cultivation.

"And now it is to your fostering care the Convention appeals, and we appeal to you as to men and brethren, yet to enlarge their borders.

"We therefore ask of you, brethren,—we ask of you, philanthropists of every color and of every kindred,—to assist us in this undertaking. We look to a kind Providence and to you to say whether our desires shall be realized and our labors crowned with success.

"The Convention has done its duty, and it now remains for you, brethren, to do yours. Various obstacles have been thrown in our way by those opposed to the elevation of the human species ; but, thanks to an all-wise Providence, his goodness has as yet cleared the way, and our advance has been slow but steady. The only thing now wanted, is an accumulation of funds, in order to enable us to make a purchase agreeable to the direction of the first Convention ; and, to effect that purpose, the Convention has recommended, to the different Societies engaged in that cause, to preserve and prosecute their designs with double energy ; and we would earnestly recommend to every colored man (who feels the weight of his degradation), to consider himself in duty bound to contribute his mite toward this great object. We would say to all, that the prosperity of the rising generation mainly depends upon our active exertions.

"Yes, it is with us to say whether they shall assume a rank and standing among the nations of the earth, as men and freemen, or whether they shall still be prized and held at market-price. Oh, then, by a brother's love, and by all that makes man dear to man, awake in time !

Be wise! Be free! Endeavor to walk with circumspection; be obedient to the laws of our common country; honor and respect its lawmakers and law-givers; and, through all, let us not forget to respect ourselves.

"During the deliberations of this Convention, we had the favor of advising and consulting with some of our most eminent and tried philanthropists—men of unblemished character and of acknowledged rank and standing. Our sufferings have excited their sympathy; our ignorance appealed to their humanity; and, brethren, we feel that gratitude is due to a kind and benevolent Creator, that our excitement and appeal have neither been in vain. A plan has been proposed to the Convention for the erection of a college for the instruction of young men of color, on the manual-labor system, by which the children of the poor may receive a regular classical education, as well as those of their more opulent brethren, and the charge will be so regulated as to put it within the reach of all. In support of this plan, a benevolent individual has offered the sum of one thousand dollars, provided that we can obtain subscriptions to the amount of nineteen thousand dollars in one year.

"The Convention has viewed the plan with considerable interest, and, after mature deliberation, on a candid investigation, feels strictly justified in recommending the same to the liberal patronage of our brethren, and respectfully solicits the aid of those philanthropists who feel an interest in sending light, knowledge, and truth to all of the human species.

"To the friends of general education, we do believe that our appeal will not be in vain. For the present ignorant and degraded condition of many of our brethren in these United States (which has been a subject of much concern to the Convention) can excite no astonishment (although used by our enemies to show our inferiority in the scale of human beings); for, what opportunities have they possessed for mental cultivation or improvement? Mere ignorance, however, in a people divested of the means of acquiring information by books, or an extensive connection with the world, is no just criterion of their intellectual incapacity; and it had been actually seen, in various remarkable instances, that the degradation of the mind and character, which has been too hastily imputed to a people kept, as we are, at a distance from those sources of knowledge which abound in civilized and enlightened communities, has resulted from no other causes than our unhappy situation and circumstances.

"True philanthropy disdains to adopt those prejudices against any people which have no better foundation than accidental diversities of color, and refuses to determine without substantial evidence and incontestible fact as the basis of her judgment. And it is in order to remove these prejudices, which are the actual causes of our ignorance, that we have appealed to our friends in support of the contemplated institution.

" The Convention has not been unmindful of the operations of the American Colonization Society, and it would respectfully suggest to that august body of learning, talent, and worth, that, in our humble opinion, strengthened, too, by the ópinions of eminent men in this country, as well as in Europe, that they are pursuing the direct road to perpetuate slavery, with all its unchristianlike concomitants, in this boasted land of freedom ; and, as citizens and men whose best blood is sapped to gain popularity for that institution, we would, in the most feeling manner, beg of them to desist ; or, if we must be sacrificed to their philanthropy, we would rather die at home.   Many of our fathers, and some of us, have fought and bled for the liberty, independence, and peace which you now enjoy ; and, surely, it would be ungenerous and unfeeling in you to deny us an humble and quiet grave in that country which gave us birth !

" In conclusion, the Convention would remind our brethren that knowledge is power, and to that end, we call on you to sustain and support, by all honorable, energetic, and necessary means, those presses which are devoted to our instruction and elevation, to foster and encourage the mechanical arts and sciences among our brethren, to encourage simplicity, neatness, temperance, and economy in our habits, taking due care always to give the preference to the production of freemen wherever it can be had.   Of the utility of a General Fund, the Convention believes there can exist but one sentiment, and that is for a speedy establishment of the same.   Finally, we trust our brethren will pay due care to take such measures as will ensure a general and equal representation in the next Convention.

[Signed]   " BELFAST BURTON,
                                         " JUNIUS C. MOREL,
                                         " WILLIAM WHIPPER,
                                                 " *Publishing Committee.*"

Encouraged by the good results that followed the first convention, another one was called, and assembled in Philadelphia, at Benezet Hall, Seventh Street, June 4, 1832.   The following delegates were admitted to seats in the convention :

PENNSYLVANIA.

Pittsburgh—John B. Vashon.
Philadelphia—John Bowers, William Whipper, J. C. Morel, Benjamin Paschal, F. A. Hinton.
Carlisle—John Peck.
Lewistown, Miffin County—Samuel Johnson.

NEW YORK.

New York City—William Hamilton, Thomas L. Jennings, Henry Sipkins, Philip A. Bell.

Brooklyn—James Pennington.

DELAWARE.

Wilmington—Joseph Burton, Jacob Morgan, Abm. D. Shad, William Johnson, Peter Gardiner.

MARYLAND.

Baltimore—Samuel Elliott, Robert Cowley, Samuel Hiner.

NEW JERSEY.

Gloucester—Thomas D. Coxsin, Thomas Banks.

Trenton—Aaron Roberts.

MASSACHUSETTS.

Boston—Hosea Easton.

New Bedford—Nathan Johnson.

CONNECTICUT,

Hartford—Paul Drayton.

New Haven—Scipio C. Augustus.

RHODE ISLAND.

Providence—Ichabod Northrop.

On the following day the convention adjourned to the "First African Presbyterian Church." The following report was adopted :

" *Resolved,* That in the opinion of this Committee, the plan suggested by the first General Convention, of purchasing land or lands in Upper Canada, for the avowed object of forming a settlement in that province, for such colored persons as may choose to emigrate there, still merits and deserves our united support and exertions ; and further, that the appearances of the times, in this our native land, demand an immediate action on that subject. Adopted.

" *Resolved,* That in the opinion of this committee, we still solemnly and sincerely protest against any interference, on the part of the American Colonization Society, with the free colored population in these United States, so long as they shall countenance or endeavor to use coercive measures (either directly or indirectly) to colonize us in any place which is not the object of our choice. And we ask of them respectfully, as men and as Christians, to cease their unhallowed persecutions of a people already sufficiently oppressed, or if, as they profess to have our welfare and prosperity at heart, to assist us in the object of our choice.

" *Resolved*, That this committee would recommend to the members of this Convention, to discountenance, by all just means in their power, any emigration to Liberia or Hayti, believing them only calculated to distract and divide the whole colored family."

In accordance with a resolution of the previous day the Rev. R. R. Gurley, Secretary of the American Colonization Society, was invited to address the convention. He endeavored to offer an acceptable explanation of the Society, and to advocate its principles. But the Colored people, almost to a man, were opposed to colonization; and most of the anti-slavery societies regarded colonization as impracticable and hurtful to the cause of emancipation. William Lloyd Garrison happened to be present, and followed Gurley in a speech that destroyed the hopes of the friends of colonization, and greatly delighted the convention.

While the Colored people opposed colonization they regarded Canada as a proper place to go. They felt that as citizens they had the right to decide where to go, and, when they got ready, to go on their own account. Canada had furnished an asylum to their flying, travel-soiled, foot-sore, and needy brethren,—was not so very far away, and, therefore, it was preferred to the West Coast of Africa. The committee having under consideration this subject, made the following comprehensive report :

" *Resolved*, That the members of this Convention take into consideration the propriety of effecting the purchase of lands in the province of Upper Canada, as an asylum for those of our bretheren who may be compelled to remove from these United States, beg leave, most respectfully to report :

" That, after due consideration, they believe the resolution embraces three distinct inquiries for the consideration of this Convention, which should be duly weighed before they can adopt the sentiments contained in the above-named resolution. Therefore, your Committee conceive the resolution premature, and now proceed to state the enquiries separately.

" *First*.—Is it proper for the Free people of color in this country, under existing circumstances, to remove to any distant territory beyond these United States ?

" *Secondly*.—Does Upper Canada possess superior advantages and conveniences to those held out in these United States or elsewhere ?

" *Thirdly.*—Is there any certainty that the people of color will be compelled by oppressive legislative enactments to abandon the land of their birth for a home in a distant region ?

"Your Committee, before examining those enquiries, would most respectfully take a retrospective view of the object for which the Convention was first associated, and the causes which have actuated their deliberations.

" The expulsory laws of Ohio, in 1829, which drove our people to seek a new home in Upper Canada, and their impoverished situation afterward, excited a. general burst of sympathy for their situation, by the wise and good, over the whole country. This awakened public feeling on their behalf, and numerous meetings were called to raise funds to alleviate their present miseries. The bright prospects that then appeared to dawn on the new settlement, awakened our people to the precariousness of their situations, and, in order more fully to be prepared for future exigencies, and to extend the system of benevolence still further to those who should remove to Upper Canada, a circular was issued by five individuals, viz.:—the Rev. Richard Allen, Cyrus Black, Junius C. Morel, Benjamin Pascal, and James C. Cornish, in behalf of the citizens of Philadelphia, calling a convention of the colored delegates from the several States, to meet on the 20th day of September, 1830, to devise plans and means for the establishment of a colony in Upper Canada, under the patronage of the general Convention, then called.

" That Convention met, pursuant to public notice, and recommended the formation of a parent society, to be established, with auxiliaries in the different towns where they had been represented in *general* convention, for the purpose of raising moneys to defray the object of purchasing a colony in the province of Upper Canada, for those who should hereafter wish to emigrate thither, and that immediately after its organization, a corresponding agent should be appointed to reside at or near the intended purchase.

" Our then limited knowledge of the manners, customs, and privileges, and rights of aliens in Upper Canada, together with the climate, soil, and productions thereof, rendered it necessary to send out agents to examine the same, who returned with a favorable report, except that citizens of these United States could not purchase lands in Upper Canada, and legally transfer the same to other individuals.

"The Convention resolved to reassemble on the first Monday in June, 1831, during which time the order of the Convention had been carried into operation, relative to establishing Societies for the promotion of said object ; and the sum and total of their proceedings were, that the Convention recommended to the colored people generally, when persecuted as were our brethren in Ohio, to seek an Asylum in

Upper Canada.   During which time, information having been received that a part of the white inhabitants of said province had, through prejudice and the fear of being overburthened with an ejected population, petitioned the provincial parliament to prohibit the general influx of colored population from entering their limits, which threw some consternation on the prospect.   The Convention did not wholly abandon the subject, but turned its attention more to the elevation of our people in this, our native home.

" The recent occurrences at the South have swelled the tide of prejudice until it has almost revolutionized public sentiment, which has given birth to severe legislative enactments in some of the States, and almost ruined our interests and prospects in others, in which, in the opinion of your Committee, our situation is more precarious than it has been at any other period since the Declaration of Independence.

" The events of the past year have been more fruitful in persecution, and have presented more inducements than any other period of the history of our country, for the men of color to fly from the graves of their fathers, and seek new homes in a land where the roaring billows of prejudice are less injurious to their rights and privileges.

" Your Committee would now approach the present Convention and examine the resolution under consideration, beginning with the first interrogatory, viz. : Is it proper for the Free people of color in this country, under existing circumstances, to remove to any distant territory beyond the United States ?

" If we admit the first interrogatory to be true, as it is the exact spirit of the language of this resolution, now under consideration, it is altogether unnecessary for us to make further preparation for either our moral, intellectual, or political advancement in this our own, our native land.

" Your Committee also believe that if this Convention shall adopt a resolution that will, as soon as means can be obtained, remove our colored population to the province of Upper Canada, the best and brightest prospect of the philanthropists who are laboring for our elevation in this country will be thwarted, and they will be brought to the conclusion that the great object which actuated their labors would now be removed, and they might now rest from their labors and have the painful feeling of transmitting to future generations, that an oppressed people, in the land of their birth, supported by the genuine philanthropists of the age, amidsts friends, companions, and their natural attachments, a genial clime, a fruitful soil,—amidst the rays of as proud institutions as ever graced the most favored spot that has ever received the glorious rays of a meridian sun,—have abandoned their homes on account of their persecutions, for a home almost similarly precarious, for an abiding-place among strangers !

"Your Committee further believe that any express plan to colonize our people beyond the limits of these United States, tends to weaken the situation of those who are left behind, without any peculiar advantage to those who emigrate. But it must be admitted, that the rigid oppression abroad in the land is such, that a *part* of our suffering brethren cannot live under it, and that the compulsory laws and the inducements held out by the American Colonization Society are such as will cause them to alienate all their natural attachments to their homes, and accept of the only mode left open, which is to remove to a distant country to receive those rights and privileges of which they have been deprived. And as this Convention is associated for the purpose of recommending to our people the best mode of alleviating their present miseries,

"Therefore, your Committee would, most respectfully, recommend to the general Convention, now assembled, to exercise the most vigorous means to collect monies through their auxiliaries, or otherwise, to be applied in such manner, as will advance the interests, and contribute to the wants of the free colored population of this country generally.

"Your Committee would now most respectfully approach the *second inquiry*, viz. :—Does Upper Canada possess superior advantages and conveniences to those held out in the United States or elsewhere ?

"Your Committee, without summing up the advantages and disadvantages of other situations, would, most respectfully answer in the affirmative. At least they are willing to assert that the advantage is much in favor of those who are obliged to leave their present homes. For your more particular information on that subject we would, most respectfully, refer you to the interesting account given by our real and indefatigable friend, Benjamin Lundy, in a late number of the "Genius of Universal Emancipation." *Vide* "Genius of Universal Emancipation," No. 10, vol. 12.

"From the history there laid down, your Committee would, most respectfully, request the Convention to aid, so far as in their power lies, those who are obliged to seek an asylum in the province of Upper Canada ; and, in order that they may more effectually carry their views into operation, they would respectfully request them to appoint an Agent in Upper Canada, to receive such funds as may be there transmitted for their use.

"Your Committee have now arrived at the *third* and last inquiry, viz. :—Is there any certainty that we, as a people, will be compelled to leave this our native land, for a home in a distant region ? To this inquiry your Committee are unable to answer ; it belongs to the fruitful events of time to determine. The mistaken policy of some of the friends of our improvement, that the same could be effected on the shore of Africa, has raised the tide of our calamity until it has overflowed the valleys of peace and tranquillity—the dark clouds of prejudice have rained persecution—the oppressor and the oppressed have suffered together—and we have yet been protected by that Almighty arm, who holds in his hands the destinies of nations, and whose presence is a royal safeguard, should we place the utmost reliance on his wisdom and power.

"Your Committee, while they rejoice at the noble object for which the Convention was first associated, have been unable to come to any conclusive evidence that lands can be purchased by this Convention and legally transferred to individuals, residents of said colony, so long as the present laws exist.   But, while they deem it inexpedient for the Convention to purchase lands in Upper Canada for the purpose of erecting a colony thereon, do again, most respectfully, hope that they will exercise the same laudable exertions to collect funds for the comfort and happiness of our people there situated, and those who may hereafter emigrate, and pursue the same judicious measures in the appropriation of said funds, as they would in procuring a tract of land, as expressed by the resolution.

"Your Committee, after examining the various circumstances connected with our situation as a people, have come, unanimously, to the conclusion* to recommend to this Convention to adopt the following resolution, as the best mode of alleviating the miseries of our oppressed brethren :

"*Resolved,* That this Convention recommend the establishment of a Society, or Agent, in Upper Canada, for the purpose of purchasing lands and contributing to the wants of our people generally, who may be, by oppressive legislative enactments, obliged to flee from these United States and take up residence within her borders.   And that this Convention will employ its auxiliary societies, and such other means as may lie in its power, for the purpose of raising monies, and remit the same for the purpose of aiding the proposed object.

[Signed]   "Robert Cowley,   Benj. Paschal, ⎫
           "John Peck,   Thos. D. Coxsin, ⎬ *Committee.*"
           "Wm. Hamilton,   J. C. Morel,   ⎪
           "Wm. Whipper,   ⎭

This convention's work was carefully done, its plans were laid upon a broader scale, and the Colored people, beholding its proceedings, took heart, and went forward with zeal and courage seeking to increase their intelligence and wealth, and improve their social condition.   In their address the convention did not fail to give the Colonization Society a parting shot.

"CONVENTIONAL ADDRESS.

" *To the Free Colored Inhabitants of these United States :*

"FELLOW-CITIZENS : We have again been permitted to associate in our representative character, from the different sections of this Union, to pour into one common stream, the afflictions, the prayers, and sympathies of our oppressed people ; the axis of time has brought around this glorious, annual event. And we are again brought to rejoice that the wisdom of Divine Providence has protected us during a year whose autumnal harvest has been a reign of terror and persecution, and whose winter has almost frozen the streams of humanity by its frigid legislation. It is under the influence of times and feelings like these, that we now address you. Of a people situated as we are, little can be said, except that it becomes our duty strictly to watch those causes that operate against our interests and privileges ; and to guard against whatever measures that will either lower us in the scale of being, or perpetuate our degradation in the eyes of the civilized world.

" The effects of Slavery on the bond and Colonization on the free. Of the first we shall say but little, but will here repeat the language of a high-minded Virginian in the Legislature of that State, on the recent discussion of the slave question before that honorable body, who declared, that man could not hold property in man, and that the master held no right to the slave, either by a law of nature or a patentee from God, but by the will of society ; which we declare to be an unjust usurpation of the rights and privileges of men.

" But how beautiful must the prospect be to the philanthropist, to view us, the children of persecution, grown to manhood, associating in our delegated character to devise plans and means for our moral elevation, and attracting the attention of the wise and good over the whole country, who are anxiously watching our deliberations.

"We have here to inform you, that we have patiently listened to the able and eloquent arguments produced by the Rev. R. R. Gurley, Secretary of the American Colonization Society, in behalf of the doings of said Society, and Wm. Lloyd Garrison, Esq., in opposition to its action.

" A more favorable opportunity to arrive at truth seldom has been witnessed, but while we admire the distinguished piety and Christian feelings with which he so solemnly portrayed the docrines of that institution, we do now *assert*, that the result of the same has tended more deeply to rivet our solid conviction, that the doctrines of said Society are at enmity with the principles and precepts of religion, humanity, and justice, and should be regarded by every man of color in these United States as an evil, for magnitude, unexcelled, and whose doctrines aim at the entire extinction of the free colored population and the riveting of slavery.

"We might here repeat our protest against that institution, but it is unnecessary ; your views and sentiments have long since gone to the world ; the wings of the wind have borne your disapprobation to that institution. Time itself cannot erase it. You have dated your opposition from its beginning, and your views are strengthened by time and circumstances, and they hold the uppermost seat in your affections. We have not been unmindful of the compulsory laws which caused our brethren in Ohio to seek new homes in a distant land, there to share and suffer all the inconveniences of exiles in an uncultivated region ; which has led us to admire the benevolent feelings of a rival government in its liberal protection to strangers ; which has induced us to recommend to you, to exercise your best endeavors, to collect monies to secure the purchase of lands in the Canadas, for those who may by oppressive legislative enactments be obliged to move thither.

"In contributing to our brethren that aid which will secure them a refuge in a storm, we would not wish to be understood as possessing any inclination to remove, nor in the least to impoverish, that noble sentiment which we rejoice in exclaiming—

"This is *our* own,
Our native land.

"All that we have done, humanity dictated it ; neither inclination nor alienated feelings to our country prescribed it, but that power which is above all other considerations, viz. : the law of necessity.

"We yet anticipate in the moral strength of this nation, a final redemption from those evils that have been illegitimately entailed on us as a people. We yet expect, by due exertions on our part, together with the aid of the benevolent philanthropists of our country, to acquire a moral and intellectual strength that will unshaft the calumnious darts of our adversaries, and present to the world a general character that they will feel bound to respect and admire.

"It will be seen by a reference to our proceedings, that we have again recommended the further prosecution of the contemplated college, proposed by the last Convention, to be established at New Haven, under the rules and regulations then established. A place for its location will be selected in a climate and neighborhood where the inhabitants are less prejudiced to our rights and privileges. The proceedings of the citizens of New Haven, with regard to the erection of the college, were a disgrace to them, and cast a stigma on the reputed fame of New England and the country. We are unwilling that the character of the whole country should sink by the proceedings of a few. We are determined to present to another portion of the country not far distant, and at no very remote period, the opportunity of gaining for them the character of a truly philanthropic spirit, and of retrieving the character of the country, by the disreputable proceedings of New Haven. We must have colleges and high-schools on the manual-labor system, where our youth may be instructed in all the arts of civilized life. If we ever expect to see the influence of prejudice decrease, and ourselves respected, it must be by the blessings of an enlightened education. It must be by being in possession of that classical knowledge which promotes genius, and causes man to soar up to those high intellectual enjoyments and acquirements, which place him in a situation to shed upon a country and a people that scientific grandeur which is imperishable by time, and drowns in oblivion's cup their moral degradation. Those who think that our primary schools are capable of effecting this, are a century behind the age when to have proved a question in the rule of three was considered a higher attainment than solving the most difficult problem in Euclid is now. They might have at that time performed what some people expect of them now, in the then barren state of science; but they are now no longer capable of reflecting brilliancy on our national character, which will elevate us from our present situation. If we wish to be respected, we must build our moral character on a base as broad and high as the nation itself; our country and our character require it; we have performed all the duties from the menial to the soldier,—our fathers shed their blood in the great struggle for independence. In the late war between Great Britain and the United States, a proclamation was issued to the free colored inhabitants of Louisiana, September 21, 1814, inviting them to take up arms in defence of their country, by Gen. Andrew Jackson. And in order that you may have an idea of the manner in which they acquitted themselves on that perilous occasion, we will refer you to the proclamation of Thomas Butler, Aid-de-Camp.

"You there see that your country expects much from you, and that you have much to call you into action, morally, religiously, and scientifically. Prepare yourselves to occupy the several stations to which the wisdom of your country may promote you. We have been told in this Convention, by the Secretary of the American Colonization Society, that there are causes which forbid our advancement in this country, which no humanity, no legislation, and no religion can control. Believe it not. Is not humanity susceptible of all the tender feelings of benevolence? Is not legislation supreme—and is not religion virtuous? Our oppressed situation arises from their opposite causes. There is an awakening spirit in our people to promote their elevation, which speaks volumes in their behalf. We anticipated at the close of the last Convention, a larger representation and an increased number of delegates; we were not deceived, the number has been tenfold. And we have a right to expect that future Conventions will be increased by a geometrical ratio, until we shall present a body not inferior in numbers to our State Legislatures, and the *phenomenon* of an *oppressed people*, deprived of the rights of citizenship, in the midst of an elightened nation, devising plans and measures for their personal and mental elevation, by *moral suasion alone.*

"In recommending you a path to pursue for our present good and future elevation, we have taken into consideration the circumstances of the free colored population, so far as it was possible to ascertain their views and sentiments, hoping that at a future Convention, you will all come ably represented, and that your wishes and views may receive that deliberation and attention for which this body is particularly associated.

"Finally, before taking our leave, we would admonish you, by all that you hold dear, beware of that bewitching evil, that bane of society, that curse of the world, that fell destroyer of the best prospects and the last hope of civilized man,—INTEMPERANCE.

"Be righteous, be honest, be just, be economical, be prudent, offend not the laws of your country,—in a word, live in that purity of life, by both precept and example,—live in the constant pursuit of that moral and intellectual strength which will invigorate your understandings and render you illustrious in the eyes of civilized nations, when they will assert that all that illustrious worth which was once possessed by the Egyptians, and slept for ages, has now arisen in their descendents, the inhabitants of the New World."

Excellent as was the work of these conventions of men of color, they nevertheless became the magazines from which the pro-slavery element secured dangerous ammunition with which to attack the anti-slavery movement. The white anti-slavery societies were charged with harboring a spirit of race prejudice ; with inconsistency, in that while seeking freedom for the Negro by means of agitation, separate efforts were put forth by the white and black anti-slavery people of the North. And this had its due effect. Massachusetts and other States had abolition societies composed entirely of persons of Color. "*The Massachusetts General Colored Association*" organized in the early days of the agitation movement. It had among its leading men the most intelligent and public-spirited Colored citizens of Boston. James G. Barbadoes, Coffin Pitts, John E. Scarlett, the Eastons, Hosea and Joshua ; Wm. C. Nell, Thomas Cole, Thomas Dalton, Frederick Brimley, Walker Lewis, and John T. Hilton were a few of "the faithful." In January, 1833, the following communication was sent to the white anti-slavery society of New England.

" BOSTON, January 15, 1833.

" *To the Board of Managers of the New-England Anti-Slavery Society :*

" The Massachusetts General Colored Association, cordially approving the objects and principles of the New-England Anti-Slavery Society, would respectfully communicate their desire to become auxiliary thereto. They have accordingly chosen one of their members to attend the annual meeting of the Society as their delegate (Mr. JOSHUA EASTON, of North Bridgewater), and solicit his acceptance in that capacity.

" THOMAS DALTON, *President,*
" WILLIAM C. NELL, *Vice-President.*
" JAMES G. BARBADOES, *Secretary.*"

The request was granted, but a few hints among friends on the outside, sufficed to demonstrate the folly and hurtfulness of anti-slavery societies composed exclusively of men of color. Within the next two years Colored organizations perished, and their members took their place in the white societies. Such Colored men as John B. Vashon and Robert Purvis, of Pennsylvania; David Ruggles and Philip A. Bell, of New York; and Charles Lenox Remond and Wm. Wells Brown, of Massachusetts, were soon seen as orators and presiding officers in the different anti-slavery societies of the free States. Frederick Douglass, the Rev. Samuel Ringgold Ward, James McCune Smith, M.D.; James W. C. Pennington, D.D. ; Henry Highland Garnett, D.D. ; Alexander Crummell, D.D.; and other Colored men were eloquent, earnest, and effective in their denunciation of the institution that enslaved their brethren. In England and in Europe a corps of intelligent Colored orators was kept busy painting, to interested audiences, the cruelties and iniquities of American slavery. By association and sympathy these Colored orators took on the polish of Anglo-Saxon scholarship. Of the influence of the American Anti-slavery Society upon the Colored man, Maria Weston Chapman once said, it is " church and university, high school and common school, to all who need real instruction and true religion. Of it what a throng of authors, editors, lawyers, orators, and accomplished gentlemen of color have taken their degree ! It has equally implanted hopes and aspirations, noble thoughts, and sublime purposes, in the hearts of both races. It has prepared the white man for the freedom of the black man, and it has made the black man scorn the thought of enslavement, as does a white man, as far as its influence has ex-

tended. *Strengthen that noble influence!*   Before its organization, the country only saw here and there in slavery some ' faithful Cudjoe or Dinah,' whose strong natures blossomed even in
bondage, like a fine plant beneath a heavy stone.   Now, under
the elevating and cherishing influence of the American Anti-
slavery Society, the colored race, like the white, furnishes Corin-
thian capitals for the noblest temples.   Aroused by the American
Anti-slavery Society, the very white men who had forgotten and
denied the claim of the black man to the rights of humanity,
now thunder that claim at every gate, from cottage to capitol,
from school-house to university, from the railroad carriage to the
house of God.   He has a place at their firesides, a place in their
hearts—the man whom they once cruelly hated for his color. So
feeling, they *cannot* send him to Coventry with a horn-book in
his hand, and call it *instruction!*   They inspire him to climb to
their side by a visible, acted gospel of freedom.   Thus, instead
of bowing to prejudice, they conquer it."

In January, 1836, Rev. Mr. Follen offered the following resolution in a meeting of the New England Anti-slavery Society:

"*Resolved*, That we consider the Anti-slavery cause the cause of
philanthropy, with regard to which all human beings, white men and
colored men, citizens and foreigners, men and women, have the same
duties and the same rights."

In support of his resolution, he said:

" We have been advised, if we really wished to benefit the slave and
the colored race generally, not unnecessarily to shock the feelings,
though they were but prejudices, of the white people, by admitting colored persons to our Anti-slavery meetings and societies. We have been
told that many who would otherwise act in unison with us were kept
away by our disregard of the feelings of the community in this respect.
. . . But what, I would ask, is the great, the single object of all our
meetings and societies?   Have we any other object than to impress
upon the community this one principle, that the *colored man is a man?*
And, on the other hand, is not the prejudice which would have us exclude colored people from our meetings and societies the same which,
in our Southern States, dooms them to perpetual bondage?"

In May, 1837, the *Anti-slavery Women of America* met in
convention in New York.   In a circular issued by the authority
of the convention, and signed by Mary S. Parker, President,

Angelina E. Grimkie, Secretary, another attack was made upon proscription in anti-slavery societies. There was a Colored lady named Sarah Douglass on the Central Committee. The following paragraphs from the circular are specimens sufficient to show the character of the circular; and the poetry at the end, written by a Colored member, Miss Sarah Forten, justified the hopes of her white sisters concerning the race:

"Those Societies that reject colored members, or seek to avoid them, have never been active or efficient. The blessing of God does not rest upon them, because they 'keep back a part of the price of the land,'—they do not lay *all* at the apostle's feet.

"The abandonment of prejudice is required of us as a proof of our sincerity and consistency. How can we ask our Southern brethren to make sacrifices, if we are not even willing to encounter inconveniences? First cast the beam from thine own eye, then wilt thou see clearly to cast it from his eye.

> "We are thy sisters. God has truly said
> That of one blood the nations He has made.
> O Christian woman! in a Christian land,
> Canst thou unblushing read this great command?
> Suffer the wrongs which wring our inmost heart,
> To draw one throb of pity on thy part?
> Our Skins may differ, but from thee we claim
> A sister's privilege and a sister's name."

Every barrier was now broken down inside of anti-slavery organizations; and having conquered the prejudice that crippled their work, they enjoyed greater freedom in the prosecution of their labors.

The Colored orators wrought a wonderful change in public sentiment. In the inland white communities throughout the Northern States Negroes were few, and the majority of them were servants; some of them indolent and vicious. From these few the moral and intellectual photograph of the entire race was taken. So it was meet that Negro orators of refinement should go from town to town. The North needed arousing and educating on the anti-slavery question, and no class did more practical work in this direction than the little company of orators, with the peerless Douglass at its head, that pleaded the cause of their brethren in the flesh before the cultivated audiences of New England, the Middle and Western States,—yea, even in the capital cities of conservative Europe.

CHAPTER VII.

NEGRO INSURRECTIONS.

THE NEGRO NOT SO DOCILE AS SUPPOSED. — THE REASON WHY HE WAS KEPT IN BONDAGE. — NEGROES POSSESSED COURAGE BUT LACKED LEADERS. — INSURRECTION OF SLAVES. — GEN. GABRIEL AS A LEADER. — NEGRO INSURRECTION PLANNED IN SOUTH CAROLINA. — EVILS OF SLAVERY REVEALED. — THE "NAT. TURNER" INSURRECTION IN SOUTH HAMPTON COUNTY, VIRGINIA. — THE WHITES ARM THEMSELVES TO REPEL THE INSURRECTIONISTS. — CAPTURE AND TRIAL OF "NAT. TURNER." — HIS EXECUTION. — EFFECT OF THE INSURRECTION UPON SLAVES AND SLAVE-HOLDERS.

THE supposed docility of the American Negro was counted among the reasons why it was thought he could never gain his freedom on this continent.   But this was a misinterpretation of his real character.   Besides, it was next to impossible to learn the history of the Negro during the years of his enslavement at the South. The question was often asked : Why don't the Negroes rise at the South and exterminate their enslavers ?   Negatively, not because they lacked the courage, but because they lacked leaders [as has been stated already, they sought the North and their freedom through the Underground R. R.] to organize them.   But notwithstanding this great disadvantage the Negroes *did* rise on several different occasions, and did effective work.

"Three times, at intervals of thirty years, has a wave of unutterable terror swept across the Old Dominion, bringing thoughts of agony to every Virginian master, and of vague hope to every Virginian slave. Each time has one man's name become a spell of dismay and a symbol of deliverance. Each time has that name eclipsed its predecessor, while recalling it for a moment to fresher memory ; John Brown revived the story of Nat. Turner, as in his day Nat. Turner recalled the vaster schemes of Gabriel." [1]

Mention has been made of the insurrection of slaves in South Carolina in the last century.   Upon the very threshold of the

---

[1] Atlantic Monthly, vol. x. p. 337.

nineteenth century, "General Gabriel" made the master-class of
Virginia quail with mortal dread. He was a man of more than
ordinary intelligence; and his plans were worthy of greater success. The following newspaper paragraph reveals the condition
of the minds of Virginians respecting the Negroes:

"For the week past, we have been under momentary expectation
of a rising among the negroes, who have assembled to the number of
nine hundred or a thousand, and threatened to massacre all the whites.
They are armed with desperate weapons, and secrete themselves in the
woods. God only knows our fate; we have strong guards every night
under arms."

The above was communicated to the "United States Gazette,"
printed in Philadelphia, under date of September 8, 1800, by a
Virginia correspondent. The people felt that they were sleeping
over a magazine. The movement of Gabriel was to have taken
place on Saturday, September 1st. The rendezvous of the Negro
troops was a brook, about six miles from Richmond. The force
was to comprise eleven hundred men, divided into three divisions. Richmond—then a town of eight thousand inhabitants
—was the point of attack, which was to be effected under cover
of night. The right wing was to fall suddenly upon the penitentiary, lately improvised into an arsenal; the left wing was to
seize the powder-house; and, thus equipped and supplied with the
munitions of war, the two columns were to assign the hard fighting to the third column. This column was to have possession
of all the guns, swords, knives, and other weapons of modern
warfare. It was to strike a sharp blow by entering the town
from both ends, while the other two columns, armed with shovels, picks, clubs, etc., were to act as a reserve. The white troops
were scarce, and the situation, plans, etc., of the Negroes were
admirable.

". . . the penitentiary held several thousand stand of arms;
the powder-house was well-stocked; the capitol contained the State
treasury; the mills would give them bread; the control of the bridge
across James River would keep off enemies from beyond. Thus secured and provided, they planned to issue proclamations summoning to
their standard 'their fellow-negroes and the friends of humanity
throughout the continent.' In a week, it was estimated, they would
have fifty thousand men on their side, with which force they could easily

possess themselves of other towns ; and, indeed, a slave named John Scott—possibly the dangerous possessor of ten dollars—was already appointed to head the attack on Petersburg.   But in case of final failure, the project included a retreat to the mountains, with their newfound property.   John Brown was therefore anticipated by Gabriel sixty years before, in believing the Virginia mountains to have been ' created, from the foundation of the world, as a place of refuge for fugitive slaves.' " [1]

The plot failed, but everybody, and the newspapers also, said the plan was well conceived.

In 1822 another Negro insurrection was planned in Charleston, S. C.   The leader of this affair was Denmark Vesey.[2]   This plot for an insurrection extended for forty-five or fifty miles around Charleston, and intrusted its secrets to thousands.   Denmark Vesey, assisted by several other intelligent and trusty Negroes, had conceived the idea of slaughtering the whites in and about Charleston, and thus securing liberty for the blacks.   A recruiting committee was formed, and every slave enlisted was sworn to secrecy.   Household servants were rarely trusted. Talkative and intemperate slaves were not enlisted.   Women were excluded from the affair that they might take care of the children.   Peter Poyas, it was said, had enlisted six hundred without assistance.   There were various opinions respecting the number enlisted.   Some put it at hundreds, others thousands ; one witness at the trial said there were nine thousand, another six thousand.   But no white person ever succeeded in gaining the confidence of the black conspirators.   Never was a plot so carefully guarded for so long a time.

" During the excitement and the trial of the supposed conspirators, rumor proclaimed all, and doubtless more than all, the horrors of the plot.   The city was to be fired in every quarter, the arsenal in the immediate vicinity was to be broken open, and the arms distributed to the insurgents, and an universal massacre of the white inhabitants to take place.   Nor did there seem to be any doubt in the mind of the people that such would actually have been the result, had not the plot fortunately been detected before the time appointed for the outbreak. It was believed, as a matter of course, that every black in the city would join in the insurrection, and that, if the original design had been at-

---

[1] Atlantic Monthly, vol. x. p. 339.
[2] Atlantic Monthly, vol. vii. pp. 728, 744.

tempted, and the city taken by surprise, the negroes would have achieved a complete and easy victory. Nor does it seem at all impossible that such might have been or yet may be the case, if any well-arranged and resolute rising should take place." [1]

This bold plot failed because a Negro named William Paul began to make enlistments without authority. He revealed the secret to a household servant, just the very man he should have left to the skilful manipulations of Peter Poyas or Denmark Vesey. As an evidence of the perfection of the plot it should be stated that after a month of official investigation only fifteen out of the thousands had been apprehended!

" The leaders of this attempt at insurrection died as bravely as they had lived; and it is one of the marvels of the remarkable affair, that none of this class divulged any of their secrets to the court. The men who did the talking were those who knew but little."

The effect was to reveal the evils of slavery, to stir men to thought, and to hasten the day of freedom.

"Nat." Turner combined the lamb and lion. He was a Christian and a *man*. He was conscious that he was a man and not a "thing"; therefore, driven by religious fanaticism, he undertook a difficult and bloody task. Nathaniel Turner was born in Southampton County, Virginia, October 2, 1800. His master was one Benjamin Turner, a very wealthy and aristocratic man. He owned many slaves, and was a cruel and exacting master. Young "Nat." was born of slave parents, and carried to his grave many of the superstitions and traits of his father and mother. The former was a preacher; the latter a "mother in Israel." Both were unlettered, but, nevertheless, very pious people. The mother began when Nat. was quite young to teach him that he was born, like Moses, to be the deliverer of his race. She would sing to him snatches of wild, rapturous songs, and repeat portions of prophecy she had learned from the preachers of those times. Nat. listened with reverence and awe, and believed every thing his mother said. He imbibed the deep religious character of his parents, and soon manifested a desire to preach. He was solemnly set apart to "the Gospel Ministry" by his father, the Church, and visiting preachers. He was quite low in stature, dark, and had the genuine African features. His eyes

---

[1] Atlantic Monthly, vol. vii. p. 737.

were small, but sharp, and gleamed like fire when he was talking about his "mission," or preaching from some prophetic passage of Scripture. It is said that he never laughed. He was a dreamy sort of a man, and avoided the crowd. Like Moses, he lived in the solitudes of the mountains and brooded over the condition of his people. There was something grand to him in the rugged scenery that nature had surrounded him with. He believed that he was a prophet, a leader raised up by God to burst the bolts of the prison-house and set the oppressed free. The thunder, the hail, the storm-cloud, the air, the earth, the stars, at which he would sit and gaze half the night, all spake the language of the God of the oppressed. He was seldom seen in a large company, and never drank a drop of ardent spirits. Like John the Baptist, when he had delivered his message, he would retire to the fastness of the mountain, or seek the desert, where he could meditate upon his great work.

At length he declared that God spake to him. He began to dream dreams and to see visions. His grandmother, a very old and superstitious person, encouraged him in his dreaming. But, notwithstanding, he believed that he had communion with God, and saw the most remarkable visions, he denounced in the severest terms the familiar practices among slaves, known as "conjuring," "gufering," and fortune-telling. The people regarded him with mixed feelings of fear and reverence. He preached with great power and authority. He loved the prophecies, and drew his illustrations from nature. He presented God as the "*All-Powerful*"; he regarded him as a great "*Warrior.*" His master soon discovered that Nat. was the acknowledged leader among the slaves, and that his fame as "prophet" and "leader" was spreading throughout the State. The poor slaves on distant plantations regarded the name of Nat. Turner as very little removed from that of God. Though having never seen him, yet they believed in him as the man under whose lead they would some time march out of the land of bondage. His influence was equally great among the preachers, while many white people honored and feared him. His master thought it necessary to the safety of his property, to hire Nat. out to a most violent and cruel man. Perhaps he thought to have him "broke." If so, he was mistaken. Nat. Turner was the last slave to submit to an insult given by a white man. His new master could do nothing with him. He ran off, and spent thirty

days in the swamps—but returned. He was upbraided by some
of his fellow-slaves for not seeking, as he certainly could have
done, "the land of the free." He answered by saying, that a
voice said to him : " Return to your earthly master ; for he who
knoweth his Master's will and doeth it not, shall be beaten with
many stripes." It was no direction to submit to an earthly
master, but to return to him in order to carry out the will of his
Heavenly Master. He related some of the visions he saw during
his absence. "About that time I had a vision, and saw white
spirits and black spirits engaged in battle ; and the sun was
darkened, the thunder rolled in the heavens, and blood flowed in
streams ; and I heard a voice saying : ' Such is your luck, such are
you called on to see ; and let it come, rough or smooth, you
must surely bear it.' " It was not long after this when he saw
another vision. He says a spirit appeared unto him and spake
as follows : " The serpent is loosened, and Christ has laid down
the yoke he has borne for the sins of men ; and you must take
it up and fight against the serpent, for the time is fast approaching when the first shall be last, and the last shall be first." These
visions and many others enthused Nat., and led him to believe
that the time was near when the Blacks would be " first " and
the whites " last."

The plot for a general uprising was laid in the month of
February, 1831. He had seen the last vision. He says : " I was
told I should arise and prepare myself, and slay my enemies with
their own weapons." He was now prepared to arrange the details of his plot. He appointed a meeting, to which he invited
four trusted friends, Sam. Edwards, Hark Travis, Henry Porter,
and Nelson Williams. A wild and desolate glen was chosen as
the place of meeting, and night the time when they could perfect their plans without being molested by the whites. They
brought with them provisions, and ate while they debated among
themselves the methods by which to carry out their plan of blood
and death. The main difficulty that confronted them was how
to get arms. Nat. remembered that a spirit had instructed him
to " slay my enemies with their own weapons," so they decided
to follow these instructions. After they had decided upon a
plan, " the prophet Nat." arose, and, like a great general, made a
speech to his small but brave force. " Friends and brothers,"
said he, " we are to commence a great work to-night ! Our race
is to be delivered from slavery, and God has appointed us as the

men to do his bidding; and let us be worthy of our calling. I am told to slay all the whites we encounter, without regard to age or sex. We have no arms or ammunition, but we will find these in the houses of our oppressors; and, as we go on, others can join us. Remember, we do not go forth for the sake of blood and carnage; but it is necessary that, in the commencement of this revolution, all the whites we meet should die, until we have an army strong enough to carry on the war upon a Christian basis. Remember that ours is not a war for robbery, nor to satisfy our passions; it is a *struggle for freedom.* Ours must be deeds, not words. Then let 's away to the scene of action!"

The blow was struck on the night of the 21st of August, 1831, in Southampton County, near Jerusalem Court-House. The latter place is about seventy miles from Richmond. Not only Southampton County but old Virginia reeled under the blow administered by the heavy hand of Nat. Turner. On their way to the first house they were to attack, that of a planter by the name of Joseph Travis, they were joined by a slave belonging to a neighboring plantation. We can find only one name for him, "Will." He was the slave of a cruel master, who had sold his wife to the "nigger traders." He was nearly six feet in height, well developed, and the most powerful and athletic man in the county. He was marked with an ugly scar, extending from his right eye to the extremity of the chin. He hated his master, hated slavery, and was glad of an opportunity to wreak his vengeance upon the whites. He armed himself with a sharp broad-axe, under whose cruel blade many a white man fell. Nat.'s speech gives us a very clear idea of the scope and spirit of his plan. We quote from his confession at the time of the trial, and will let him tell the story of this terrible insurrection.

"On returning to the house, Hark went to the door with an axe, for the purpose of breaking it open, as we knew we were strong enough to murder the family should they be awakened by the noise; but, reflecting that it might create an alarm in the neighborhood, we determined to enter the house secretly, and murder them whilst sleeping. Hark got a ladder and set it against the chimney, on which I ascended, and, hoisting a window, entered and came down stairs, unbarred the doors, and removed the guns from their places. It was then observed that I must spill the first blood, on which, armed with a hatchet and accompanied by Will., I entered my master's chamber. It being dark, I could not give a death-blow. The hatchet glanced from his head; he sprang from his bed and called his wife. It was his last word. Will. laid him dead with a blow of his axe."

After they had taken the lives of this family, they went from plantation to plantation, dealing death-blows to every white man, woman, or child they found. They visited vengeance upon every white household they came to. The excitement spread rapidly, and the whites arose and armed themselves in order to repel these insurrectionists.

" The first news concerning the affair was in the shape of a letter from Col. Trezvant, which reached Richmond Tuesday morning, too late for the columns of the (Richmond) " Enquirer," which was a tri-weekly. The letter was written on the 21st of August, and lacked definiteness, which gave rise to doubts in reference to the 'insurrection.' It was first sent to Petersburgh, and was then immediately dispatched to the Mayor of Richmond.

" Arms and ammunition were dispatched in wagons to the county of Southampton. The four volunteer companies of Petersburgh, the dragoons and Lafayette artillery company of Richmond, one volunteer company from Norfolk and one from Portsmouth, and the regiments of Southampton and Sussex, were at once ordered out. The cavalry and infantry took up their line of march on Tuesday evening, while the artillery embarked on the steamer ' Norfolk,' and landed at Smithfield. . . . A member of the Richmond dragoons, writing from Petersburgh, under date of the 23d, after careful examination, thought that ' about two hundred and fifty negroes from a camp-meeting about the Dismal Swamp had murdered about sixty persons, none of them families much known.' " [1]

Will., the revengeful slave, proved himself the most destructive and cruel of Nat.'s followers. A hand to hand battle came. The whites were well armed, and by the force of their superior numbers overcame the army of the " Prophet,"—five men. Will. would not surrender. He laid three white men dead at his feet, when he fell mortally wounded. His last words were : " Bury my axe with me," believing that in the next world he would need it for a similar purpose. Nat. fought with great valor and skill with a short sword, and finding it useless to continue the struggle, escaped with some of his followers to the swamps, where he defied the vigilance of the military and the patient watching of the

---

[1] Richmond Enquirer, August 26, 1831.

citizens for more than two months. He was finally compelled to surrender. When the Court asked: "Guilty or not guilty?" he pleaded: "Not guilty." He was sustained during his trial by his unfaltering faith in God. Like Joan of Arc, he "heard the spirits," the "voices," and believed that God had "sent him to free His people."

In the impression of the "Enquirer" of the 30th of August, 1831, the first editorial, or leader, is under the caption of THE BANDITTE. The editor says:

"They remind one of a parcel of blood-thirsty wolves rushing down from the Alps; or, rather like a former incursion of the Indians upon the white settlements. Nothing is spared: neither age nor sex respected—the helplessness of women and children pleads in vain for mercy . . . The case of Nat. Turner warns us. No black-man ought to be permitted to turn a Preacher through the country. The law must be enforced—or the tragedy of Southampton appeals to us in vain."[1]

A remarkable prophecy was made by Nat. The trial was hurried, and, like a handle on a pitcher, was on one side only. He was sentenced to die on the gallows. He received the announcement with stoic indifference, and was executed at Jerusalem, the county seat of Southampton, in April, 1831. He died like a man, bravely, calmly; looking into eternity, made radiant by a faith that had never faltered. He prophesied that on the day of his execution the sun would be darkened, and other evidences of divine disapprobation would be seen. The sheriff was much impressed by Nat.'s predictions, and consequently refused to have any thing to do with the hanging. No Colored man could be secured to cut the rope that held the trap. An old white man, degraded by drink and other vices, was engaged to act as executioner, and was brought forty miles. Whether it was a fulfilment of Nat.'s prophecy or not, the sun was hidden behind angry clouds, the thunder rolled, the lightning flashed, and the most terrific storm visited that county ever known. All this, in connection with Nat.'s predictions, made a wonderful impression upon the minds of the Colored people, and not a few white persons were frightened, and regretted the death of the "Prophet."

The results of this uprising, led by a lone man—he was alone,

---

[1] Richmond Enquirer, August 26 and 30, 1831.

and yet he was not alone,—are apparent when we consider that fifty-seven whites and seventy-three Blacks were killed and many were wounded.

The first reliable list of the victims of the "tragedy" was written on the 24th of August, 1831.

" List of the dead that have been buried :—At Mrs. Whiteheads', 7 ; Mrs. Waller's, 13 ; Mr. Williams', 3 ; Mr. Barrows', 2 ; Mr. Vaughn's, 5 ; Mrs. Turner's, 3 ; Mr. Travis's, 5 ; Mr. J. Williams', 5 ; Mr. Reice's, 4 ; Names unknown, 10 ; Total, 57."

Then there was a feeling of unrest among the slaves and a fear among the whites throughout the State. Even the proceedings of the trial of Nat. were suppressed for fear of evil consequences among the slaves. But now all are free, and the ex-planters will not gnash their teeth at this revelation. Nat. Turner's insurrection, like all other insurrections led by oppressed people, lacked detail and method. History records but one successful uprising—San Domingo has the honor. Even France failed in 1789, and in 1848. There is always a zeal for freedom, but not according to knowledge. No stone marks the resting-place of this martyr to freedom, this great religious fanatic, this Black John Brown. And yet he has a prouder and more durable monument than was ever erected of stone or brass. The image of Nat. Turner is carved on the fleshy tablets of four million hearts. His history has been kept from the Colored people at the South, but the women have handed the tradition to their children, and the " Prophet Nat." is still marching on.

Of the character of this remarkable man, Mr. Gray, the gentleman to whom he made his confession, had the following to say :—

" It has been said that he was ignorant and cowardly, and that his object was to murder and rob, for the purpose of obtaining money to make his escape. It is notorious that he was never known to have a dollar in his life, to swear an oath, or drink a drop of spirits. As to his ignorance, he certainly never had the advantages of education ; but he can read and write, and for natural intelligence and quickness of apprehension, is surpassed by few men I have ever seen. As to his being a coward, his reason, as given, for not resisting Mr. Phipps, shows the decision of his character. When he saw Mr. Phipps present his gun, he said he knew it was impossible for him to escape, as the woods were full of men ; he therefore thought it was better for him to surrender, and trust to fortune for his escape.

"He is a complete fanatic, or plays his part most admirably. On other subjects he possesses an uncommon share of intelligence, with a mind capable of attaining any thing, but warped and perverted by the influence of early impressions. He is below the ordinary stature, though strong and active, having the true negro face, every feature of which is strongly marked. I shall not attempt to describe the effect of his narrative, as told and commented on by himself, in the condemned hole of the prison : the calm, deliberate composure with which he spoke of his late deeds and intentions ; the expression of his fiend-like face, when excited by enthusiasm ; still bearing the stains of the blood of helpless innocence about him, clothed with rags and covered with chains, yet daring to raise his manacled hands to Heaven, with a spirit soaring above the attributes of man. I looked on him, and the blood curdled in my veins."

In the "Richmond Enquirer," of September 2, 1831, appeared the following : "It is reported that a map was found, and said to have been drawn by Nat. Turner, with *polk-berry juice*, which was a description of the county of Southampton."

The influence of this bloody insurrection spread beyond the Old Dominion, and for years afterward, in nearly every Southern State the whites lived in a state of dread. To every dealer in flesh and blood the "Nat. Turner Insurrection" was a stroke of poetic justice.

CHAPTER VIII.

THE "AMISTAD" CAPTIVES.

THE SPANISH SLAVER "AMISTAD" SAILS FROM HAVANA, CUBA, FOR PORTO PRINCIPE. — FIFTY-FOUR NATIVE AFRICANS ON BOARD. — JOSEPH CINQUEZ, THE SON OF AN AFRICAN PRINCE. — THE "AMISTAD" CAPTURED AND TAKEN INTO NEW LONDON, CONN. — TRIAL AND RELEASE OF THE SLAVES. — TOUR THROUGH THE UNITED STATES. — RETURN TO THEIR NATIVE COUNTRY IN COMPANY WITH MISSIONARIES. — THE ANTI-SLAVERY CAUSE BENEFITED BY THEIR STAY IN THE UNITED STATES. — THEIR APPRECIATION OF CHRISTIAN CIVILIZATION.

ON the 28th of June, 1839, the " Amistad," a Spanish slaver (schooner), with Captain Ramon Ferrer in command, sailed from Havana, Cuba, for Porto Principe, a place in the island of Cuba, about 100 leagues distant.   The passengers were Don Pedro Montes and Jose Ruiz, with fifty-four Africans just from their native country, Lemboko, as slaves.   Among the slaves was one man, called in Spanish, Joseph Cinquez,[1] said to be the son of an African prince.   He was possessed of wonderful natural abilities, and was endowed with all the elements of an intelligent and intrepid leader.   The treatment these captives received was very cruel. They were chained down between the decks—space not more than four feet—by their wrists and ankles ; forced to eat rice, sick or well, and whipped upon the slightest provocation.   On the fifth night out, Cinquez chose a few trusty companions of his misfortunes, and made a successful attack upon the officers and crew.   The captain and cook struck down, two sailors put ashore, the Negroes were in full possession of the vessel.   Montes was compelled, under pain of death, to navigate the vessel to Africa. He steered eastwardly during the daytime, but at night put about hoping to touch the American shore.   Thus the vessel wandered until it was cited off of the coast of the United States during the month of August.   It was described as a " long, low, black schooner."   Notice was sent to all the collectors of the ports along the Atlantic Coast, and a steamer and several revenue

---

[1] Sometimes written Cinque.

cutters were dispatched after her. Finally, on the 26th of August, 1839, Lieut. Gedney, U. S. Navy, captured the "Amistad," and took her into New London, Connecticut.

The two Spaniards and a Creole cabin boy were examined before Judge Andrew T. Judson, of the United States Court, who, without examining the Negroes, bound them over to be tried as pirates. The poor Africans were cast into the prison at New London. Public curiosity was at a high pitch; and for a long time the "*Amistad captives*" occupied a large place in public attention. The Africans proved to be natives of the Mendi country, and quite intelligent. The romantic story of their sufferings and meanderings was given to the country through a competent interpreter; and many Christian hearts turned toward them in their lonely captivity in a strange land. The trial was continued several months. During this time the anti-slavery friends provided instruction for the Africans. Their minds were active and receptive. They soon learned to read, write, and do sums in arithmetic. They cultivated a garden of some fifteen acres, and proved themselves an intelligent and industrious people.

The final decision of the court was that the "Amistad captives" were not slaves, but freemen, and, as such, were entitled to their liberty. The good and liberal Lewis Tappan had taken a lively interest in these people from the first, and now that they were released from prison, felt that they should be sent back to their native shores and a mission started amongst their countrymen. Accordingly he took charge of them and appeared before the public in a number of cities of New England. An admission fee of fifty cents was required at the door, and the proceeds were devoted to leasing a vessel to take them home. Large audiences greeted them everywhere, and the impression they made was of the highest order. Mr. Tappan would state the desire of the people to return to their native land, appeal to the philanthropic to aid them, and then call upon the people to read the Scriptures, sing songs in their own language, and then in the English. Cinquez would then deliver an account of their capture, the horrors of the voyage, how he succeeded in getting his manacles off, how he aided his brethren to loose their fetters, how he invited them to follow him in an attempt to gain their liberty, the attack, and their rescue, etc., etc. He was a man of magnificent physique, commanding presence, graceful manners, and effective oratory. His speeches were delivered in Mendi, and translated into English by an interpreter.

"It is impossible," wrote Mr. Tappan from Boston, "to describe the novel and deeply interesting manner in which he acquitted himself. The subject of his speech was similar to that of his countrymen who had spoken in English ; but he related more minutely and graphically the occurrences on board the "Amistad." The easy manner of Cinquez, his natural, graceful, and energetic action, the rapidity of his utterance, and the remarkable and various expressions of his countenance, excited admiration and applause. He was pronounced a powerful natural orator, and one born to sway the minds of his fellow-men. Should he be converted and become a preacher of the cross in Africa what delightful results may be anticipated ! "

A little fellow called Kali, only eleven years of age, pleased the audience everywhere he went by his ability not only to spell any word in the Gospels, but sentences, without blundering. For example, he would spell out a sentence like the following sentence, naming each letter and syllable, and recapitulating as he went along, until he pronounced the whole sentence : " Blessed are the meek, for they shall inherit the earth."

Of their doings in Philadelphia, Mr. Joseph Sturge wrote :

"On this occasion, a very crowded and miscellaneous assembly collected to see and hear the Mendians, although the admission had been fixed as high as half a dollar, with the view of raising a fund to carry them to their native country. Fifteen of them were present, including one little boy and three girls. Cinque, their chief, spoke with great fluency in his native language ; and his action and manner were very animated and graceful. Not much of his speech was translated, yet he greatly-interested his audience. The little boy could speak our language with facility ; and each of them read, without hesitation, one or two verses in the New Testament. It was impossible for any one to go away with the impression, that in native intellect these people were inferior to the whites. The information which I privately received from their tutor, and others who had full opportunities of appreciating their capacities and attainments, fully confirmed my own very favorable impressions."

But all the while their sad hearts were turning toward their home and the dear ones so far away. One of them eloquently declared : " If Merica men offer me as much gold as fill this cap full up, and give me houses, land, and every ting, so dat I stay in this country, I say: 'No! no! I want to see my father, my mother, my brother, my sister.'" Nothing could have been more tender and expressive. They were willing to endure any hardships short of life that they might once more see their own, their native land. The religious instruction they had enjoyed made a wonderful impression on their minds. One of them said: "We owe every thing to God; he keeps us alive, and makes us free. When we go to home to Mendi we tell our brethren about God, Jesus Christ, and heaven." Another one was asked: "What is faith?" and replied: "Believing in Jesus Christ, and trusting in him." Reverting to the murder of the captain and cook of the "Amistad," one of the Africans said that if it were to be done over again he would pray for rather than kill them. Cinquez, hearing this, smiled and shook his head. When asked if he would not pray for them, said: "Yes, I would pray for 'em, an' kill 'em too."

These captives were returned to their native country in the fall of 1841, accompanied by five missionaries. Their objective point was Sierra Leone, from which place the British Government assisted them to their homes. Their stay in the United States did the anti-slavery cause great good. Here were poor, naked, savage pagans, unable to speak English, in less than three years able to speak the English language and appreciate the blessings of a Christian civilization.

𝔓art 6.

THE PERIOD OF PREPARATION.

CHAPTER IX.

NORTHERN SYMPATHY AND SOUTHERN SUBTERFUGES.

1850–1860.

VIOLENT TREATMENT OF ANTI-SLAVERY ORATORS. — THE SOUTH MISINTERPRETS THE MOBOCRATIC SPIRIT OF THE NORTH. — THE "GARRISONIANS" AND "CALHOUNITES." — SLAVE POPULATION OF 1830-1850. — THE THIRTY-FIRST CONGRESS. — MOTION FOR THE ADMISSION OF NEW MEXICO AND CALIFORNIA. — THE DEMOCRATIC AND WHIG PARTIES ON THE TREATMENT OF THE SLAVE QUESTION. — CONVENTION OF THE DEMOCRATIC PARTY AT BALTIMORE, MARYLAND. — NOMINATION OF FRANKLIN PIERCE FOR PRESIDENT. — WHIG PARTY CONVENTION. — NOMINATION OF GEN. WINFIELD SCOTT FOR THE PRESIDENCY BY THE WHIGS. — MR. PIERCE ELECTED PRESIDENT IN 1853. — A BILL INTRODUCED TO REPEAL THE "MISSOURI COMPROMISE." — SPEECH BY STEPHEN A. DOUGLASS. — MR. CHASE'S REPLY. — AN ACT TO ORGANIZE THE TERRITORIES OF KANSAS AND NEBRASKA. — STATE MILITIA IN THE SOUTH MAKE PREPARATIONS FOR WAR. — PRESIDENT BUCHANAN IN SYMPATHY WITH THE SOUTH.

THE arguments of anti-slavery orators were answered everywhere throughout the free States by rotten eggs, clubs, and missiles. The public journals, as a rule, were unfriendly and intolerant. Even Boston could contemplate, with unruffled composure, a mob of her most " reputable citizens " dragging Mr. Garrison through the streets with a halter about his neck. Public meetings were broken up by pro-slavery mobs; owners of public halls required a moneyed guarantee against the destruction of their property, when such halls were used for anti-slavery meetings. Colored schools were broken up, the teachers driven away, and the pupils maltreated.

The mobocratic demonstrations in the Northern States were the thermometer of public feeling upon the subject of slavery. The South was, therefore, emboldened ; for the political leaders in that section thought they saw a light from the distance that encouraged them to entertain the belief and indulge the hope that their present sectional institution could be made national. Southerners thought slavery would grow in the cold climate of the North, excited into a lively existence by the warmth of a generous sympathy. But the South misinterpreted the real motive that inspired opposition to anti-slavery agitation in the North. The violent opposition came from the mercantile class and foreign element who believed that the agitation of the slavery question was a practical disturbance of their business affairs. The next class, more moderate in opposition to agitation, believed slavery constitutional, and, therefore, argued that anti-slavery orators were traitors to the government. The third class, conservative, did not take sides, because of the unpopularity of agitation on the one hand, and because of an harassing conscience on the other.

There were two classes of men who were seeking the dissolution of the Union. The Garrisonians sought this end in the hope of forming another Union *without* slavery.

In an address delivered by Wm. Lloyd Garrison, July 20, 1860, at the Framingham celebration, he declares:

"Our object is the abolition of slavery *throughout the land;* and whether in the prosecution of our object this party goes up or the other party goes down, it is nothing to us. We cannot alter our course one hair's breadth, nor accept a compromise of our principles for the hearty adoption of our principles. I am for *meddling with slavery everywhere — attacking it by night and by day, in season and out of season* (no, it can never be out of season)—in order to *effect its overthrow.* (Loud applause.) Higher yet will be my cry. Upward and onward ! No union with slave-holders ! Down with this slave-holding government ! Let this 'covenant with death and agreement with hell' be annulled ! *Let there be a free, independent, Northern republic,* and *the speedy abolition of slavery* will inevitably follow ! (Loud applause.) So I am laboring to dissolve this blood-stained Union as a work of paramount importance. Our mission is to regenerate public opinion."

The Calhounites sought the dissolution of the Union in order that another Union might be formed *with* slavery as its chief corner-stone. Inspired by this hope and misguided by the apparent sympathy of the North, Southern statesmen began *preparations to dissolve the Union of the United States.*

During these years of agitation and discussion, although the foreign slave-trade had been suppressed, the slave population increased at a wonderful ratio.

CENSUS OF 1830.—SLAVE POPULATION.

District of Columbia	6,119
Delaware	3,292
Florida	15,501
Georgia	217,531
Illinois	747
Kentucky	165,213
Louisiana	109,588
Maryland	102,994
Alabama	117,549
Mississippi	65,659
Missouri	25,091
New Jersey	2,254
North Carolina	245,601
South Carolina	315,401
Tennessee	141,603
Virginia	469,757
Arkansas	4,576
Aggregate	2,008,476

Now, this was the year the agitation movement began. Instead of the slave population decreasing during the first decade of anti-slavery discussion and work, it really increased 478,412![1]

CENSUS OF 1840.—SLAVE POPULATION.

Alabama	253,532
Arkansas	19,935
District of Columbia	4,694
Delaware	2,605
Florida	25,717
Georgia	280,944
Illinois	331
Kentucky	182,258
Louisiana	168,452
Maryland	89,737
Mississippi	195,211
Missouri	58,240
New Jersey	674
New York	4

[1] There were nearly 500 slaves held in Northern States not placed in this census.

CENSUS OF 1840.—SLAVE POPULATION.—(*Continued.*)

Pennsylvania	64
North Carolina	245,817
South Carolina	327,038
Tennessee	183,059
Virginia	449,087
Aggregate	2,487,399

During the next decade the slave population swept forward to an increase of 716,858. The entire population of slaves was 3,204,313; 2,957,657 were unmixed Africans, and 246,656 were Mulattoes. The free Colored population amounted to 434,495, of whom 275,400 were unmixed, and 159,095 mixed or Mulatto. The total number of families owning slaves in 1850 was 347,525.

CENSUS OF 1850.—SLAVE POPULATION.

Alabama	342,844
Arkansas	47,100
District of Columbia	3,687
Delaware	2,290
Florida	39,310
Georgia	381,682
Kentucky	210,981
Louisiana	244,809
Maryland	90,368
Mississippi	309,878
Missouri	87,422
New Jersey	236
North Carolina	288,548
South Carolina	384,984
Tennessee	239,459
Texas	58,161
Virginia	472,528
Utah Territory	26
Total	3,204,313

The Thirty-first Congress was three weeks attempting an organization, and at last effected it by the election of a Southerner to the Speakership, the Hon. Howell Cobb, of Georgia. President Zachary Taylor had called the attention of Congress to the admission of California and New Mexico into the Union, in his message to that body upon its assembling. On the 4th of January, 1850, Gen. Sam. Houston, United States Senator from Texas, submitted the following proposition to the Senate:

"WHEREAS, The Congress of the United States, possessing only a delegated authority, has no power over the subject of negro slavery within the limits of the United States, either to prohibit or to interfere with it in the States, territories, or districts, where, by municipal law, it now exists, or to establish it in any State or territory where it does not exist; but as an assurance and guarantee to promote harmony, quiet apprehension, and remove sectional prejudice, which by possibility might impair or weaken love and devotion to the Union in any part of the country, it is hereby

"*Resolved*, That, as the people in territories have the same inherent rights of self-government as the people in the States, if, in the exercise of such inherent rights, the people in the newly acquired territories, by the annexation of Texas and the acquisition of California and New Mexico, south of the parallel of thirty-six degrees and thirty minutes of north latitude, extending to the Pacific Ocean, shall establish negro slavery in the formation of their State governments, it shall be deemed no objection to their admission as a State or States into the Union, in accordance with the Constitution of the United States."

On the 29th of January, Henry Clay, of Kentucky, submitted to the United States Senate the following propositions looking toward an amicable adjustment of the entire slavery question:

"1. *Resolved*, That California, with suitable boundaries, ought, upon her application, to be admitted as one of the States of this Union, without the imposition by Congress of any restriction in respect to the exclusion or introduction of slavery within those boundaries.

"2. *Resolved*, That as slavery does not exist by law, and is not likely to be introduced into any of the territory acquired by the United States from the republic of Mexico, it is inexpedient for Congress to provide by law either for its introduction into, or exclusion from, any part of the said territory; and that appropriate territorial governments ought to be established by Congress in all the said territory not assigned as within the boundaries of the proposed State of California, without the adoption of any restriction or condition on the subject of slavery.

"3. *Resolved*, That the western boundary of the State of Texas ought to be fixed on the Rio del Norte, commencing one marine league from its mouth, and running up that river to the southern line of New Mexico, thence with that line eastwardly, and so continuing in the same direction to the line as established between the United States and Spain, excluding any portion of New Mexico, whether lying on the east or west of that river.

" 4. *Resolved,* That it be proposed to the State of Texas, that the United States will provide for the payment of all that portion of the legitimate and *bona-fide* public debt of that State contracted prior to its annexation to the United States, and for which the duties on foreign imports were pledged by the said State to its creditors, not exceeding the sum of ———— dollars, in consideration of the said duties so pledged having been no longer applicable to that object after the said annexation, but having thenceforward become payable to the United States ; and upon the condition, also, that the said State of Texas shall, by some solemn and authentic act of her Legislature, or of a convention, relinquish to the United States any claim which she has to any part of New Mexico.

" 5. *Resolved,* That it is inexpedient to abolish slavery in the District of Columbia whilst that institution continues to exist in the State of Maryland, without the consent of that State, without the consent of the people of the District, and without just compensation to the owners of slaves within the District.

" 6. *But Resolved,* That it is expedient to prohibit within the District, the slave-trade in slaves brought into it from States or places beyond the limits of the District, either to be sold therein as merchandise, or to be transported to other markets without the District of Columbia.

" 7. *Resolved,* That more effectual provision ought to be made by law, according to the requirement of the Constitution, for the restitution and delivery of persons bound to service or labor in any State, who may escape into any other State or territory in the Union. And

" 8. *Resolved,* That Congress has no power to prohibit or obstruct the trade in slaves between the slave-holding States, but that the admission or exclusion of slaves brought from one into another of them, depends exclusively upon their own particular laws."

Senator Bell, of Tennessee, offered a series of resolutions on the same question on the 28th of February, containing nine resolves. As usual, on all propositions respecting slavery, the debate was protracted, earnest, and able. The Clay resolutions attracted most attention. Jefferson Davis, of Mississippi, said:

" Sir, we are called upon to receive this as a measure of compromise ! As a measure in which we of the minority are to receive nothing. A measure of compromise ! I look upon it as but a modest mode of taking that, the claim to which has been more boldly asserted by others ; and, that I may be understood upon this question, and that my position may go forth to the country in the same columns that convey the sentiments of the Senator from Kentucky, I here assert, that never will I take less than the Missouri compromise line extended to the Pacific Ocean, with the specific recognition of the right to hold slaves in the territory below that line ; and that, before such territories are admitted into the Union as States, slaves may be taken there from any of the United States at the option of the owners. I can never consent to give additional power to a majority to commit further aggressions upon the minority in this Union, and will never consent to any proposition which will have such a tendency, without a full guaranty or counteracting measure is connected with it."

A number of very able speeches were made on the resolutions of Mr. Clay, but the most characteristic one—the one most thoroughly representing the sentiment of the South—was made by John C. Calhoun. He said :

" The Union was in danger. The cause of this danger was the discontent at the South. And what was the cause of this discontent ? It was found in the belief which prevailed among them that they could not, consistently with honor and safety, remain in the Union. And what had caused this belief ? One of the causes was the long-continued agitation of the slave question at the North, and the many aggressions they had made on the rights of the South. But the primary cause was in the fact, that the equilibrium between the two sections at the time of the adoption of the Constitution had been destroyed. The first of the series of acts by which this had been done, was the ordinance of 1787, by which the South had been excluded from all the northwestern region. The next was the Missouri compromise, excluding them from all the Louisiana territory north of thirty-six degrees thirty minutes, except the State of Missouri,—in all 1,238,025 square miles, leaving to the South the southern portion of the original Louisiana territory, with Florida, to which had since been added the territory acquired with Texas,—making in all but 609,023 miles. And now the North was endeavoring to appropriate to herself the territory recently acquired from Mexico, adding 526,078 miles to the territory from which the South was, if possible, to be excluded. Another cause of the destruction of this equilibrium was our system of revenue (the tariff), the duties falling mainly upon the Southern portion of the Union, as being the greatest exporting States, while more than a due proportion of the revenue had been disbursed at the North.

" But while these measures were destroying the equilibrium between the two sections, the action of the government was leading to a radical change in its character. It was maintained that the government itself had the right to decide, in the last resort, as to the extent of its powers, and to resort to force to maintain the power it claimed. The doctrines of General Jackson's proclamation, subsequently asserted and maintained by Mr. Madison, the leading framer and expounder of the Constitution, were the doctrines which, if carried out, would change the character of the government from a federal republic, as it came from the hands of its framers, into a great national consolidated democracy."

Mr. Calhoun also spoke of the anti-slavery agitation, which, if not arrested, would destroy the Union; and he passed a censure upon Congress for receiving abolition petitions. Had Congress in the beginning adopted the course which he had advocated, which was to refuse to take jurisdiction, by the united voice of all parties, the agitation would have been prevented. He charged the North with false professions of devotion to the Union, and with having violated the Constitution. Acts had been passed in Northern States to set aside and annul the clause of the slavery question, with the avowed purpose of abolishing slavery in the States, which was another violation of the Constitution. And during the fifteen years of this agitation, in not a single instance had the people of the North denounced these agitators. How then could their professions of devotion to the Union be sincere?

Mr. Calhoun disapproved both the plan of Mr. Clay and that of President Taylor, as incapable of saving the Union. He would pass by the former without remark, as Mr. Clay had been replied to by several Senators. The Executive plan could not save the Union, because it could not satisfy the South that it could safely or honorably remain in the Union. It was a modification of the Wilmot proviso, proposing to effect the same object, the exclusion of the South from the new territory. The Executive proviso was more objectionable than the Wilmot. Both inflicted a dangerous wound upon the Constitution, by depriving the Southern States of equal rights as joint partners in these territories; but the former inflicted others equally great. It claimed for the inhabitants the right to legislate for the territories, which belonged to Congress. The assumption of this right was utterly unfounded, unconstitutional, and without example. Under this assumed right, the people of California had formed a constitution and a State government, and appointed Senators and Representatives. If the people as adventurers had conquered the territory and established their independence, the sovereignty of the country would have been vested in them. In that case they would have had the right to form a State government, and afterward they might have applied to Congress for admission into the Union. But the United States had conquered and acquired California; therefore, to them belonged the sovereignty and the powers of government over the territory. Michigan was the first case of departure from the uniform rule of acting. Hers, however, was a slight departure from established usage. The ordinance of 1787 secured to her the right of becoming a State when she should have 60,000 inhabitants. Congress delayed taking the census. The people became impatient ; and after her population had increased to twice that number, they formed a constitution without waiting for the taking of the census ; and Congress waived the omission, as there was no doubt of the requisite number of inhabitants. In other cases there had existed territorial governments.

Having shown how the Union could not be saved, he then proceeded to answer the question how it could be saved. There was but one way certain. Justice must be done to the South, by a full and final settlement of all the questions at issue. The North must concede to the South an equal right to the acquired territory, and fulfil the stipulations respecting fugitive slaves ; must cease to agitate the slave question, and join in an amendment of the Constitution, restoring to the South the power she possessed of protecting herself, before the equilibrium between the two sections had been destroyed by the action of the government.

Here was a clear statement of the position and feelings of the South respecting slavery. The ordinance of 1787 and the Missouri compromise of 1820 " were destroying the equilibrium between the *two sections !* " And the anti-slavery agitation, " if not arrested, would destroy the Union ! " The sophistry of Calhoun sought a reasonable excuse for the South to dissolve the Union. In a speech of his, written during a spell of sickness, and read by Mr. Mason, of Virginia, he referred to Washington as " the illustrious Southerner." When it was read in the Senate Mr. Cass said :

" Our Washington—the Washington of our whole country—receives in this Senate the epithet of ' Southerner,' as if that great man, whose distinguished characteristic was his attachment to his country, and his whole country, who was so well known, and who, more than any one, deprecated all sectional feeling and all sectional action, loved Georgia better than he loved New Hampshire, because he happened to be born on the southern bank of the Potomac. I repeat, sir, that I heard with great pain that expression from the distinguished Senator from South Carolina."

There was certainly no ground for reasonable complaint on the part of the South. From the convention that framed the

Federal Constitution, through all Congressional struggle, and in national politics as well, the South had secured nearly all measures asked for. And the discussion in Congress at this time was intended to divert attention from the real object of the South. Another fugitive-slave law was demanded by the South, and the Northern members voted them the right to hunt slaves upon free soil. The law passed, and was approved on the 18th of September, 1850.

It was difficult to choose between the Democratic and Whig parties by reading the planks in their platforms referring to the subject of slavery. On the 1st of June, 1852, the Democratic Convention, at Baltimore, Maryland, nominated Franklin Pierce, of New Hampshire, for the Presidency, on the forty-ninth ballot. This plank defined the position of that party on the question of slavery.

"That Congress has no power under the Constitution to interfere with or control the domestic institutions of the several States, and that such States are the sole and proper judges of every thing appertaining to their own affairs, not prohibited by the Constitution ; that all efforts of the abolitionists, or others, made to induce Congress to interfere with questions of slavery, or to take incipient steps in relation thereto, are calculated to lead to the most alarming and dangerous consequences ; and that all such efforts have an inevitable tendency to diminish the happiness of the people, and endanger the stability and permanency of the Union, and ought not to be countenanced by any friend of our political institutions.

"That the foregoing proposition covers, and was intended to embrace, the whole subject of slavery agitation in Congress ; and therefore the Democratic party of the Union, standing on this national platform, will abide by and adhere to a faithful execution of the acts known as the compromise measures settled by the last Congress—the act for reclaiming fugitives from service or labor included ; which act being designed to carry out an express provision of the Constitution, can not with fidelity thereto be repealed, nor so changed as to destroy or impair its efficiency.

"That the Democratic party will resist all attempts at renewing, in Congress or out of it, the agitation of the slavery question, under whatever shape or color the attempt may be made."

The Whig party, at the same city, in convention assembled, on the 16th of June, 1852, nominated Gen. Winfield Scott, for the Presidency, on the fifty-third ballot. The Whig party declared its position on the slavery question as follows:

" That the series of acts of the Thirty-first Congress—the act known as the fugitive-slave law included—are received and acquiesced in by the Whig party of the United States, as a settlement in principle and substance of the dangerous and exciting question which they embrace ; and so far as they are concerned, we will maintain them and insist on their strict enforcement, until time and experience shall demonstrate the necessity of further legislation, to guard against the evasion of the laws on the one hand, and the abuse of their powers on the other, not impairing their present efficiency ; and we deprecate all agitation of the question thus settled, as dangerous to our peace ; and will discountenance all efforts to continue or renew such agitation whenever, wherever, or however the attempt may be made ; and we will maintain this system as essential to the nationality of the Whig party of the Union."

The political contest ended in the autumn in favor of Mr. Pierce. The public journals in many parts of the country thought the end of the " slavery question " had come, and that as the Whigs were determined to " discountenance all efforts to continue or renew " the agitation of the subject, there was no fear of sectional strife.

In his inaugural address, March 4, 1853, President Pierce said:

" I believe that involuntary servitude is recognized by the Constitution. I believe that the States where it exists are entitled to efficient remedies to enforce the constitutional provisions. I hold that the compromise measures of 1850 are strictly constitutional, and to be unhesitatingly carried into effect. And now, I fervently hope that the question is at rest," etc.

In the month of December, upon the assembling of Congress, the President, in his message to that body, again referred to slavery as " a subject which had been set at rest by the deliberate judgment of the people." But on the 15th of December, nine days after the message of the President had been received by Congress, Mr. Dodge, of Iowa, submitted to the Senate a bill to organize the territory of Nebraska, which was referred to the Committee on Territories. After some discussion in the committee, it was finally reported back to the Senate by Mr. Douglass, of Illinois, with amendments. The report was elaborate, and raised considerable doubt as to whether the amendments did not repeal the Missouri compromise. A special report was made on the 4th of January, 1854, so amending the bill as to remove all doubt ; and, contemplating the opening of all the vast territory secured forever to freedom, startled the nation from the "repose" it had apparently taken from agitation on the slavery question, and opened an interminable controversy.

On the 16th of January, Mr. Dixon, of Kentucky, gave notice that he would introduce a bill clearly repealing the Missouri compromise. The first champion of the repeal of the compromise of 1820 was a Northern Senator, Stephen A. Douglass, of Illinois. He hung a massive argument—excelling rather in quantity than in quality—upon the following propositions:

"From these provisions, it is apparent that the compromise measures of 1850 affirm, and rest upon, the following propositions:

"*First.*—That all questions pertaining to slavery in the territories, and the new States to be formed therefrom, are to be left to the decision of the people residing therein, by their appropriate representatives, to be chosen by them for that purpose.

"*Second.*—That 'all cases involving title to slaves,' and 'questions of personal freedom,' are to be referred to the adjudication of the local tribunals, with the right of appeal to the Supreme Court of the United States.

"*Third.*—That the provision of the Constitution of the United States in respect to fugitives from service, is to be carried into faithful execution in all 'the original territories,' the same as in the States.

"The substitute for the bill which your committee have prepared, and which is commended to the favorable action of the Senate, proposes to carry these propositions and principles into practical operation, in the precise language of the compromise measures of 1850."

Mr. Douglass said:

"The legal effect of this bill, if passed, was neither to legislate slavery into nor out of these territories, but to leave the people to do as they pleased. And why should any man, North or South, object to this principle? It was by the operation of this principle, and not by any dictation from the Federal government, that slavery had been abolished in half of the twelve States in which it existed at the time of the adoption of the Constitution."

On the 3d of February, Mr. Chase, of Ohio, moved to amend by striking out the words, "was superseded by the principles of the legislation of 1850, commonly called the compromise measures, and," so that the clause would read: "That the Constitution, and all laws of the United States which are not locally in-

applicable, shall have the same force and effect within the said
territory of Nebraska as elsewhere within the United States, except the eighth section of the act preparatory to the admission
of Missouri into the Union, approved March 6, 1820, which is
hereby declared inoperative."

Mr. Chase then proceeded to reply to Mr. Douglass. He
called attention to that part of the President's message which
referred to the "repose" of the subject of slavery, and then said:

"The agreement of the two old political parties, thus referred to by
the Chief Magistrate of the country, was complete, and a large majority
of the American people seemed to acquiesce in the legislation of which
he spoke. A few of us, indeed, doubted the accuracy of these statements, and the permanency of this repose. We never believed that the
acts of 1850 would prove to be a permanent adjustment of the slavery
question. But, sir, we only represented a small, though vigorous and
growing party in the country. Our number was small in Congress. By
some we were regarded as visionaries, by some as factionists; while almost
all agreed in pronouncing us mistaken. And so, sir, the country was at
peace. As the eye swept the entire circumference of the horizon and
upward to mid-heaven, not a cloud appeared; to common observation
there was no mist or stain upon the clearness of the sky. But suddenly
all is changed; rattling thunder breaks from the cloudless firmament.
The storm bursts forth in fury. And now we find ourselves in the
midst of an agitation, the end and issue of which no man can foresee.

"Now, sir, who is responsible for this renewal of strife and controversy? Not we, for we have introduced no question of territorial
slavery into Congress; not we, who are denounced as agitators and
factionists. No, sir; the quietists and the finalists have become agitators; they who told us that all agitation was quieted, and that the
resolutions of the political conventions put a final period to the
discussion of slavery. This will not escape the observation of the
country. It is *slavery* that renews the strife. It is slavery that again
wants room. It is slavery with its insatiate demand for more slave territory and more slave States. And what does slavery ask for now?
Why, sir, it demands that a time-honored and sacred compact shall be
rescinded—a compact which has endured through a whole generation
—a compact which has been universally regarded as inviolable, North
and South—a compact, the constitutionality of which few have doubted,
and by which all have consented to abide."

But notwithstanding the able and eloquent speech of Mr.
Chase, his amendment only received thirteen votes. The debate

went on until the 3d of March, when the bill was placed upon its passage, and even then the discussion went on. When the vote was finally taken, the bill passed by a vote of 37 yeas to 14 nays. The bill went to the House, where it was made a substitute to a bill already introduced, and passed by a vote of 113 yeas to 100 nays as follows:

" Representatives from free States in favor of the bill, 44.
" Representatives from slave States in favor of the bill, 69.
—113.
" Representatives from free States against the bill, 91.
" Representatives from slave States against the bill, 9.
—100."

And thus, approved by the President, the measure became a law under the title of " *An Act to Organize the Territories of Kansas and Nebraska.*"

Congress had violated the sublimest principles of law, had broken faith with the people; had opened a wide door to slavery; had blotted from the map of the United States the last asylum where the oppressed might seek protection; had put the country in a way to be reddened with a fratricidal war, and made our flag a flaunting lie in the eyes of the civilized world. There was nothing to be done now but to let the leaven of sectional malice work, that had been hurled into the slavery discussions in Congress. The bloodless war of words was now transferred to the territory of Kansas, where a conflict of political parties, election frauds, and assassination did their hateful work.

The South began to put her State militia upon a war footing, and to make every preparation for battle. The Administration of President Buchanan was in the interest of the South from beginning to end. He refused to give Gov. John W. Geary, of Kansas, the military support the " *border ruffians*" made necessary; allowed the public debt to increase, our precious coin to go abroad, our treasury to become depleted, our navy to go to the distant ports of China and Japan, our army to our extremest frontiers, the music of our industries to cease; and the faith of a loyal people in the perpetuity of the republic was allowed to faint amid the din of mobs and the threats of secession.

CHAPTER X.

THE "BLACK LAWS" OF "BORDER STATES."

STRINGENT LAWS ENACTED AGAINST FREE NEGROES AND MULATTOES. — FUGITIVE-SLAVE LAW
RESPECTED IN OHIO. — A LAW TO PREVENT KIDNAPPING. — THE FIRST CONSTITUTION OF
OHIO. — HISTORY OF THE DRED SCOTT CASE. — JUDGE TANEY'S OPINION IN THIS CASE. — OHIO
CONSTITUTION OF 1851 DENIED FREE NEGROES THE RIGHT TO VOTE. — THE ESTABLISHMENT OF
COLORED SCHOOLS. — LAW IN INDIANA TERRITORY IN REFERENCE TO EXECUTIONS. — AN ACT
FOR THE INTRODUCTION OF NEGROES AND MULATTOES INTO THE TERRITORY. — FIRST CONSTI-
TUTION OF INDIANA. — THE ILLINOIS CONSTITUTION OF 1818. — CRIMINAL CODE ENACTED. — ILLI-
NOIS LEGISLATURE PASSES AN ACT TO PREVENT THE EMIGRATION OF FREE NEGROES INTO THE
STATE. — FREE NEGROES OF THE NORTHERN STATES ENDURE RESTRICTION AND PROSCRIPTION.

A LTHOUGH slavery was excluded from all the new States northwest of the Ohio River, the free Negro was but little better off in Ohio, Indiana, and Illinois than in any of the Southern States. From the earliest moment of the organic existence of the border free States, severe laws were enacted against free Negroes and Mulattoes. At the second session of the first Legislature of the State of Ohio, "*An Act to Regulate Black and Mulatto Persons*" [1] was passed.

Sec. 1. That no black or mulatto person shall be permitted to settle or reside in this State "without a certificate of his or her actual freedom."

2. Resident blacks and mulattoes to have their names recorded, etc. (Amended in 1834, Jan. 5 1, Curwen, 126.) *Proviso*, "That nothing in this act contained shall bar the lawful claim to any black or mulatto person."

3. Residents prohibited from hiring black or mulatto persons not having a certificate.

4. Forbids, under penalty, to "harbor or secrete any black or mulatto person the property of any person whatever," or to "hinder or prevent the lawful owner or owners from re-taking," etc.

5. Black or mulatto persons coming to reside in the State with a legal certificate, to record the same.

---

[1] 1, Chase, p. 393, sects. 1–7.

6. "That in case any person or persons, his or their agent or agents, claiming any black or mulatto person or persons that now are or hereafter may be in this State, may apply, upon making satisfactory proof that such black or mulatto person or persons are the property of him or her who applies, to any associate judge or justice of the peace within the State, the associate judge or justice is hereby empowered and required, by his precept, to direct the sheriff or constable to arrest such black or mulatto person or persons, and deliver the same, in the county or township where such officers shall reside, to the claimant or claimants, or his or their agent or agents, for which service the sheriff or constable shall receive such compensation as he is entitled to receive in other cases for similar services."

7. " That any person or persons who shall attempt to remove or shall remove from this State, or who shall aid and assist in removing, contrary to the provisions of this act, any black or mulatto person or persons, without first proving, as herein before directed, that he, she, or they is or are legally entitled so to do, shall, on conviction thereof before any court having cognizance of the same, forfeit and pay the sum of one thousand dollars, one half to the use of the informer and the other half to the use of the State, to be recovered by the action of debt *quitam* or indictment, and shall moreover be liable to the action of the party injured "

So here upon free soil, under a State government that did not recognize slavery in its constitution, the Negro was compelled to produce a certificate of freedom. Thus the fugitive-slave law was recognized, but at the same time an unlawful removal of free Negroes from the State was forbidden.

At the session of 1806–7, " *An Act to Amend the Act Entitled ' an Act Regulating Black and Mulatto Persons,'* " was passed amending the old law. The first act simply required " a certificate of freedom " ; the amended law required Negroes and Mulattoes intending to settle in Ohio to give a bond not to become a charge upon the county in which they settled. Section four reads as follows:

" 4. That no black or mulatto person or persons shall hereafter be permitted to be sworn or give evidence in any court of record or elsewhere in this State, in any cause depending or matter of controversy where either party to the sale is a white person, or in any prosecution which shall be instituted in behalf of this State, against any white person." [1]

---

[1] 1, Chase, p. 555.

But this law did not apply to persons a shade nearer white than Mulatto [the seven-eighths law].[1] Their testimony was admissible, while that of Negroes and Mulattoes was not admitted against them. In Jordan *vs.* Smith [1846], 14, Ohio, p. 199: " A black person sued by a white, may make affidavit to a plea so as to put the plaintiff to proof."

Attention has been called to the fact that the fugitive-slave law was respected in Ohio. In 1818–19, a law was passed to prevent the unlawful kidnapping of free Negroes, which, in its preamble, recites the provisions of the law of Congress, passed February 12, 1793, respecting fugitives from service and labor.[2] And in 1839 the Legislature passed another act relating to " fugitives from labor," etc., paving the way by the following recital :

" WHEREAS, The second section of the fourth article of the Constitution of the United States declares that ' no person' [etc., reciting it] ; and whereas the laws now in force within the State of Ohio are wholly inadequate to the protection pledged by this provision of the Constitution to the Southern States of this Union ; and whereas it is the duty of those who reap the largest measure of benefits conferred by the Constitution to recognize to their full extent the obligations which that instrument imposes ; and whereas it is the deliberate conviction of this General Assembly that the Constitution can only be sustained as it was framed by a spirit of just compromise ; therefore."

Sec. 1. Authorizes judges of courts of record, " or any justice of the peace, or the mayor of any city or town corporate," on application, etc., of claimant, to bring the fugitive before a judge within the county where the warrant was issued, or before some State judge with certain cautions as to proving the official character of the officer issuing the warrrant ; gives the form of warrant, directing the fugitive to be brought before, etc., " to be be dealt with as the law directs."[3]

J. Peck, Esq. [9, Ohio, p. 212], refers to the laws of 1818–19, and 1830–31, as a recognition by the State of Ohio of the power of Congress to pass the act of 1793, though that the act was not specially mentioned.

The first constitution of Ohio [1802] restricted the right of suffrage to " all white male inhabitants." " In all elections, all white male inhabitants above the age of twenty-one years, hav-

---

[1] Jeffries *vs.* Ankeny, 11, Ohio, p. 375.　　[2] 2, Chase L., p. 1052.
[3] Curwen, p. 533.

ing resided in the State one year next preceding the election, and who have paid or are charged with a State or county tax, shall enjoy the right of an elector," etc.[1] This was repeated in the Bill of Rights adopted in 1851.[2]

Article iv., Section 2, of the Constitution of the United States says : "The citizens of each State shall be entitled to all privileges and immunities of citizens in the several States." The question as to whether free Negroes were included in the above was discussed at great length in the Dred Scott case, where Chief-Justice Taney took the ground that a Negro was not a citizen under the fourth article of the Constitution. But the fourth article of the Articles of Confederation [1778] recognized free Negroes as citizens. It is given here :

"ART. 4.—The better to secure and perpetuate mutual friendship and intercourse among the people of the different States in this Union, the free inhabitants of each of these States—paupers, vagabonds, and fugitives from justice excepted—shall be entitled to all privileges and immunities of free citizens in the several States ; and the people of each State shall have free ingress and regress to and from any other State, and shall enjoy therein all the privileges of trade and commerce, sub-ject to the same duties, impositions, and restrictions as the inhabitants thereof, respectively ; provided that such restrictions shall not extend so far as to prevent the removal of property imported into any State, from any other State, of which the owner is an inhabitant ; provided, also, that no imposition, duty, or restriction shall be laid by any State on the property of the United States, or either of them."[3]

By this it is evident that "paupers, vagabonds, and fugitives from justice" were the only persons excluded from the right of citizenship. The following is the history of the Dred Scott case:

"In the year 1834, the plaintiff was a negro slave belonging to Dr. Emerson, who was a surgeon in the army of the United States. In that year, 1834, said Dr. Emerson took the plaintiff from the State of Mis-souri to the military post at Rock Island, in the State of Illinois, and held him there as a slave until the month of April or May, 1836. At the time last mentioned, said Dr. Emerson removed the plaintiff from said military post at Rock Island to the military post at Fort Snelling, situate on the west bank of the Mississippi River, in the territory known as Upper Louisiana, acquired by the United States of France,

---

[1] Revised Statutes of Ohio, vol. i. p. 60.   [2] Ibid., p. 111.

[3] Elliot's Debates, vol. i. p. 79.

and situate north of the latitude of thirty-six degrees thirty minutes north, and north of the State of Missouri. Said Dr. Emerson held the plaintiff in slavery at said Fort Snelling, from said last-mentioned date until the year 1838.

"In the year 1835, Harriet, who is named in the second count of the plaintiff's declaration, was the negro slave of Major Taliaferro, who belonged to the army of the United States. In that year, 1835, said Major Taliaferro took said Harriet to said Fort Snelling, a military post, situated as herein before stated, and kept her there as a slave until the year 1836, and then sold and delivered her as a slave at said Fort Snelling unto the said Dr. Emerson herein before named. Said Dr. Emerson held said Harriet in slavery at said Fort Snelling until the year 1838.

"In the year 1836, the plaintiff and said Harriet at said Fort Snelling, with the consent of said Dr. Emerson, who then claimed to be their master and owner, intermarried, and took each other for husband and wife. Eliza and Lizzie, named in the third count of the plaintiff's declaration, are the fruit of that marriage. Eliza is about fourteen years old, and was born on board the steamboat 'Gipsey,' north of the north line of the State of Missouri, and upon the river Mississippi. Lizzie is about seven years old, and was born in the State of Missouri, at the military post called Jefferson Barracks.

"In the year 1838, said Dr. Emerson removed the plaintiff and said Harriet and their said daughter Eliza from said Fort Snelling to the State of Missouri, where they have ever since resided.

"Before the commencement of this suit, said Dr. Emerson sold and conveyed the plaintiff, said Harriet, Eliza, and Lizzie to the defendant, as slaves, and the defendant has ever since claimed to hold them and each of them as slaves.

"At the time mentioned in the plaintiff's declaration, the defendant, claiming to be owner as aforesaid, laid his hands upon said plaintiff, Harriet, Eliza, and Lizzie, and imprisoned them, doing in this respect, however, no more than what he might lawfully do if they were of right his slaves at such times.

.   .   .   .

"It is agreed that Dred Scott brought suit for his freedom in the Circuit Court of St. Louis County; that there was a verdict and judgment in his favor; that on a writ of error to the Supreme Court the judgment below was reversed, and the same remanded to the Circuit Court, where it has been continued to await the decision of this case.

"In May, 1854, the cause went before a jury, who found the following verdict, viz. : 'As to the first issue joined in this case, we of the jury find the defendant not guilty; and as to the issue secondly above joined, we of the jury find that before and at the time when, etc., in the first count mentioned, the said Dred Scott was a negro slave, the lawful property of the defendant ; and as to the issue thirdly above joined, we, the jury, find that before and at the time when, etc., in the second and third counts mentioned, the said Harriet, wife of said Dred Scott, and Eliza and Lizzie, the daughters of the said Dred Scott, were negro slaves, the lawful property of the defendant.'

"Whereupon, the court gave judgment for the defendant.

"After an ineffectual motion for a new trial, the plaintiff filed the following bill of exceptions.

"On the trial of this cause by the jury, the plaintiff, to maintain the issues on his part, read to the jury the following agreed statement of facts (see agreement above). No further testimony was given to the jury by either party. Thereupon the plaintiff moved the court to give to the jury the following instructions, viz. :

" ' That, upon the facts agreed to by the parties, they ought to find for the plaintiff.' The court refused to give such instruction to the jury, and the plaintiff, to such refusal, then and there duly excepted.

The court then gave the following instruction to the jury, on motion of the defendant :

" ' The jury are instructed, that upon the facts in this case, the law is with the defendant.' The plaintiff excepted to this instruction.

"Upon these exceptions, the case came up to the Supreme Court, December term, 1856." [1]

Judge Taney gave the following opinion :

"The question is simply this : Can a negro, whose ancestors were imported into this country and sold as slaves, become a member of the political community formed and brought into existence by the Constitution of the United States, and as such become entitled to all the rights and privileges and immunities guaranteed by that instrument to the citizen ? One of which rights is the privilege of suing in a court of the United States in the cases specified in the Constitution.

"It will be observed that the plea applies to that class of persons only whose ancestors were negroes of the African race, and imported into this country, and sold and held as slaves. The only matter in issue before the court, therefore, is, whether the descendants of such slaves, when they shall be emancipated, or who are born of parents who had become free before their birth, are citizens of a State, in the sense in which the word citizen is used in the Constitution of the United States. And this being the only matter in dispute on the pleadings, the

---

[1] Sanford's Dred Scott Case, pp. 397-399.

court must be understood as speaking in this opinion of that class only, that is, of those persons who are the descendants of Africans who were imported into this country and sold as slaves.

· · · · · · · ·

"We proceed to examine the case as presented by the pleadings.

"The words 'people of the United States' and 'citizens' are synonymous terms, and mean the same thing. They both describe the political body who, according to our republican institutions, form the sovereignty, and who hold the power and conduct the government through their representatives. They are what we familiarly call the 'sovereign people, and every citizen is one of this people, and a constituent member of this sovereignty. The question before us is, whether the class of persons described in the plea in abatement compose a portion of this people, and are constituent members of this sovereignty. We think they are not, and that they are not included, and were not intended to be included, under the word 'citizen' in the Constitution, and can therefore claim none of the rights and privileges which that instrument provides for and secures to citizens of the United States. On the contrary, they were at that time considered as a subordinate [405] and inferior class of beings, who had been subjugated by the dominant race, and, whether emancipated or not, yet remained subject to their authority, and had no rights or privileges but such as those who held the power and the government might choose to grant them.

"It is not the province of the court to decide upon the justice or injustice, the policy or impolicy, of these laws. . . .

"In discussing this question, we must not confound the rights of citizenship which a State may confer within its own limits, and the rights of citizenship as a member of the Union. It does not by any means follow, because he has all the rights and privileges of a citizen of a State, that he must be a citizen of the United States. He may have all of the rights and privileges of the citizen of a State, and yet not be entitled to the rights and privileges of a citizen of any other State. For, previous to the adoption of the Constitution of the United States, every State had the undoubted right to confer on whomsoever it pleased the character of citizen, and to endow him with all its rights. But this character of course was confined to the boundaries of the State, and gave him no rights or privileges in other States beyond those secured to him by the laws of nations and the comity of States. Nor have the several States surrendered the power of conferring these rights and privileges by adopting the Constitution of the United States. Each State may still confer them upon an alien, or any one it thinks proper, or upon any class or description of persons; yet he would not be a citizen in the sense in which that word is used in the Constitution of the

United States, nor entitled to sue as such in one of its courts, nor to the privileges and immunities of a citizen in the other States. The rights which he would acquire would be restricted to the State which gave them. The Constitution has conferred on Congress the right to establish an uniform rule of naturalization, and this right is evidently exclusive, and has always been held by this court to be so. Consequently no State, since the adoption of the Constitution, can, by naturalizing an alien, invest him with the rights and privileges secured to a citizen of a State under the Federal Government, although, so far as the State alone was concerned, he would undoubtedly be entitled to the rights of a citizen, and clothed with all the [406] rights and immunities which the Constitution and laws of the State attached to that character.

"It is very clear, therefore, that no State can, by any act or law of its own, passed since the adoption of the Constitution, introduce a new member into the political community created by the Constitution of the United States. It cannot make him a member of this community by making him a member of its own. And, for the same reason, it cannot introduce any person or description of persons who were not intended to be embraced in this new political family, which the Constitution brought into existence, but were intended to be excluded from it.

"The question then arises, whether the provisions of the Constitution, in relation to the personal rights and privileges to which the citizen of a State should be entitled, embraced the negro African race, at that time in this country, or who might afterwards be imported, who had then or should afterwards be made free in any State ; and to put it in the power of a single State to make him a citizen of the United States, and indue him with the full rights of citizenship in every other State without their consent. Does the Constitution of the United States act upon him whenever he shall be made free under the laws of a State, and raised there to the rank of a citizen, and immediately clothe him with all the privileges of a citizen in every other State and in its own courts ?

"The court think the affirmative of these propositions cannot be maintained. And if it cannot, the plaintiff in error could not be a citizen of the State of Missouri, within the meaning of the Constitution of the United States, and, consequently, was not entitled to sue in its courts." [1]

This decision of the Supreme Court on the plea in abatement that the plaintiff (a Negro, Dred Scott) was not a citizen in the sense of the word in Article iii, Sec. 2 of the Constitution, was

---

[1] Howard's Reports, vol. xix. pp. 403–405, sq.

based upon an erroneous idea respecting the location of the word *citizen* in the instrument. The premise of the court was wrong, and hence the feebleness of the reasoning and the false conclusions. Article iii, Section 2 of the Constitution, extends judicial power to all cases, in law and equity, "between citizens of different States, between citizens of the same State," etc. But Article iv, Section 2, declares that "citizens of each State shall be entitled to all privileges and immunities of citizens in the several States." The plea in abatement was brought under Article iii, but all the judges, except Justice McLean, built their decision upon the word *citizen* as it stood in Article iv.

By the constitution of Ohio, adopted in 1851, free Negroes were not only denied the right to vote, but were excluded from the militia service. This law was not repealed until 1878.

Neither the constitution of 1802, nor that of 1851, discriminated against free Negroes in matters of education ; but separate schools have been maintained in Ohio from the beginning down to the present time, by special acts of the Legislature.

In the territory of Indiana there were quite a number of Negroes from the beginning of the century. Some were slaves. In 1806, the first Legislature, at its second session, passed a law in reference to *executions*, as follows:

"Sec. 7. And whereas doubts have arisen whether the time of service of negroes and mulattoes, bound to service in this territory, may be sold on execution against the master, *Be it therefore enacted* that the time of service of such negroes or mulattoes may be sold on execution against the master, in the same manner as personal estate, immediately from which sale the said negroes or mulattoes shall serve the purchaser or purchasers for the residue of their time of service ; and the said purchasers and negroes and mulattoes shall have the same remedies against each other as by the laws of the territory are mutually given them in the several cases therein mentioned, and the purchasers shall be obliged to fulfil to the said servants the contracts they made with the masters, as expressed in the indenture or agreement of servitude, and shall, for want of such contract, be obliged to give him or them their freedom due at the end of the time of service, as expressed in the second section of the law of the territory, entitled ' Law concerning servants,' adopted the twenty-second day of September, eighteen hundred and three. This act shall commence and be in force from and after the first day of February next." [1]

---

[1] Hurd, vol ii. p. 123.

This was bold legislation ; but it was not all. Negroes were required to carry passes, as in the slave States. And on the 17th of September, 1807, "*An Act for the Introduction of Negroes and Mulattoes into*" the territory was passed.

"Sec. 1.   That it shall and may be lawful for any person being the owner or possessor of any negroes or mulattoes of and above the age of fifteen years, and owning service and labor as slaves in any of the States or territories of the United States, or for any citizens of the said States or territories purchasing the same to bring the said negroes and mulattoes into this territory.

"Sec. 2.   The owners or possessors of any negroes or mulattoes as aforesaid, and bringing the same into this territory, shall, within thirty days after such removal, go with the same before the clerk of Court of Common Pleas of proper county, and in presence of said clerk the said owner or possessor shall determine and agree to, and with his or her negro or mulatto, upon the term of years which the said negro or mulatto will and shall serve his or her said owner or possessor, and the clerk shall make a record.

"Sec. 3.   If any negro or mulatto removed into this territory as aforesaid shall refuse to serve his or her owner as aforesaid, it shall and may be lawful for such person, within sixty days thereafter, to remove the said negro or mulatto to any place [to] which by the laws of the United States or territory from whence such owner or possessor may [have come] or shall be authorized to remove the same. (As quoted in Phœbe v. Jay, Breese, Ill. R., 208.)

"Sec. 4.   An owner failing to act as required in the preceding sections should forfeit all claim and right to the service of such negro or mulatto.

"Sec. 5.   Declares that any person removing into this territory and being the owner or possessor of any negro or mulatto as aforesaid, under the age of fifteen years, or if any person shall hereafter acquire a property in any negro or mulatto under the age aforesaid, and who shall bring them into this territory, it shall and may be lawful for such person, owner, or possessor to hold the said negro to service or labor— the males until they arrive at the age of thirty-five, and females until they arrive at the age of thirty-two years.

"Sec. 6.   Provides that any person removing any negro or mulatto into this territory under the authority of the preceding sections, it shall be incumbent on such person, within thirty days thereafter, to register the name and age of such negro or mulatto with the clerk of the Court of Common Pleas for the proper county.

"Sec. 7.   Requires new registry on removal to another county."

" Secs. 8, 9. Penalties by fine for breach of this act.

" Sec. 10. Clerk to take security that negro be not chargeable when his term expires.

" Sec. 12. Fees.

" Sec. 13. That the children born in said territory of a parent of color owning service or labor, by *indenture* according to law, should serve the master or mistress of such parent—the males until the age of thirty, and the females until the age of twenty-eight years. (As quoted in Boon v. Juliet, 1836, 1, Scammon, 258.)

" Sec. 14. That an act respecting apprentices misused by their master or mistress should apply to such children. (See the statute cited in Rankin v. Lydia, 2, A. K. Marshall's Ky., 467 ; and in Jarrot v. Jarrot, 2, Gilman, 19.) This act was repealed in 1810." [1]

Under the first constitution of Indiana, adopted in 1816, Negroes were not debarred from the elective franchise. In Article i, Section 1, of the Bill of Rights, this remarkable language occurs: " That all men are born equally free and independent, and have certain natural, inherent, and unalienable rights," etc. But the very next year the primal rights of the Negro as a citizen were struck down by the following : " No negro, mulatto, or Indian shall be a witness, except in pleas of the State against negroes, mulattoes, or Indians, or in civil cases where negroes, mulattoes, or Indians alone shall be parties." [2]

In 1819 [March 22d], an execution law was passed by which the time of service of Negroes could be sold on execution against the master, in the same manner as personal estate. From the time of the sale, such Negroes or Mulattoes were compelled to serve the buyer until the expiration of the term of service. [3]

In 1831, an act regulating free Negroes and Mulattoes, servants and slaves, declared :

" Sec. 1. Negroes and mulattoes emigrating into the State shall give bond, etc.

" Sec. 2. In failure of this, such negro, etc., may be hired out and the proceeds applied to his benefit, or removed from the State under the poor law.

" Sec. 3. Penalty for committing such without authority.

" Sec. 4. Penalty for harboring such who have not given bond.

" Sec. 5. That the right of any persons to pass through this State,

---

[1] Terr. laws 1807-8, p. 423.   [2] Laws of 1817, ch. 3, sec. 52.
[3] See Hurd, vol. ii. p. 129.

with his, her, or their negroes or mulattoes, servant or servants, when emigrating or travelling to any other State or territory or country, making no unnecessary delay, is hereby declared and secured." [1]

In 1851 the new constitution limited the right of franchise to "white male citizens of the United States." "No negro or mulatto shall have the right of suffrage."

"Art. xii., Sec. 1.   The militia shall consist of all able-bodied white male persons, between, etc.

"Art. xiii., Sec. 1.   No negro or mulatto shall come into, or settle in the State after the adoption of this Constitution.

"Sec. 2.   All contracts made with any negro or mulatto coming into the State contrary to the foregoing section shall be void ; and any person who shall employ such negro or mulatto or encourage him to remain in the State shall be fined not less than ten, nor more than five hundred dollars.

"Sec. 3.   All fines which may be collected for a violation of the provisions of this article, or of any law hereafter passed for the purpose of carrying the same into execution, shall be set apart and appropriated for the colonization of such negroes and mulattoes and their descendants as may be in the State at the adoption of this Constitution and may be willing to emigrate.

"Sec. 4.   The General Assembly shall pass laws to carry out the provisions of this article."

Other severe laws were enacted calculated to modify and limit the rights of free persons of color.

The first constitution of the State of Illinois, adopted in 1818, limited the [Art. ii, Sec. 27] elective franchise to "free white" persons.   Article v, Sec. 1, exempted "negroes, mulattoes, and Indians" from service in the militia.   In March, 1819, "*An Act Respecting Free Negroes, Mulattoes, Servants, and Slaves*" passed. Sec. 1 required Negro and Mulatto persons coming into the State to produce a certificate of freedom.   Sec. 2 required them to register their family as well as themselves.   Sec. 3 required persons bringing slaves into the State, for the purpose of emancipating them, to give bonds.   Passes were required of Colored people, and many other hard exactions.   The bill above referred to contained twenty-five sections. [2]

---

[1] Revised Laws of Indiana, 1838.
[2] Session Laws, 1819, p. 354.   R. S., 1833, p. 466.

On the 6th of January, 1827, a criminal code was enacted for offences committed by Negroes and servants, which contained many cruel features. On the 2d of February a law was passed declaring that all Negroes, Mulattoes, and Indians were incompetent to be witnesses in any court against a white person; and that a person having one fourth part Negro blood shall be adjudged a Mulatto. This law was re-enacted in 1845.[1] In 1853, February 12th, the Legislature of Illinois passed *"An Act to Prevent the Immigration of Free Negroes into this State."*

"Secs. 1, 2. Fine and imprisonment for bringing slave, for any purpose, into the State. *Proviso:* ' That this shall not be construed so as to affect persons or slaves, *bona fide*, travelling through this State from and to any other State in the United States.'

" Sec. 3. Misdemeanor for negro or mulatto, bond or free, to come with intention of residing.

"Sec. 4. Such may be prosecuted and fined or sold, for time, for fine and costs.

" Secs. 5, 6, 7. If such do not afterwards remove, increased fine and like proceedings, etc., etc. Appeal allowed to the circuit.

" Sec. 8. If claimed as fugitive slave, after being thus arrested, a justice of the peace, ' after hearing the evidence, and being satisfied that the person or persons claiming said negro or mulatto is or are the owner or owners of and entitled to the custody of said negro or mulatto, in accordance with the laws of the United States passed upon this subject,' shall give the owner a certificate, after his paying the costs and the negro's unpaid fine, ' and the said owner or agent so claiming shall have a right to take and remove said slave out of the State.'

" Sec. 9. Punishment of justice for nonfeasance, and of witness falsely accusing negro."[2]

While slavery had no legal, constitutional existence in the three border States, there were, in fact, quite a number of slaves within their jurisdiction during the first generation of their existence. And the free people of Color were, *first*, denied the right of citizenship; *second*, excluded from the militia service; *third*, ruled out of the courts whenever their testimony was offered against a white person; *fourth*, could not come into the free border States without producing a certificate of freedom; and, *fifth*, were annoyed by many little, mean laws in the exercise of the few rights they were suffered to enjoy. A full

---

[1] R. S., 1845, p. 154.   [2] Rev. St. of 1856, p. 780.

description of the infamous "*Black Code*" of these States would occupy too much space, and, therefore, the dark subject must be dismissed. Posterity shall know, however, how patiently the free Negroes of the Northern States endured the restrictions and proscriptions which law and public sentiment threw across their social and political pathway!

CHAPTER XI.

THE NORTHERN NEGROES.

Nominal Rights of Negroes in the Slave States. — Fugitive Slaves seek Refuge in Canada. — Negroes petition against Taxation without Representation. — A Law preventing Negroes from other States from settling in Massachusetts. — Notice to Blacks, Indians, and Mulattoes, warning them to leave the Commonwealth. — The Rights and Privileges of the Negro restricted. — Colored Men turn their Attention to the Education of their own Race. — John V. De Grasse, the first Colored Man admitted to the Massachusetts Medical Society. — Prominent Colored Men of New York and Philadelphia. — The Organization of the African Methodist Episcopal and Colored Baptist Churches. — Colored Men distinguish themselves in the Pulpit. — Report to the Ohio Anti-slavery Society of Colored People in Cincinnati in 1835. — Many purchase their Freedom. — Henry Boyd, the Mechanic and Builder. — He becomes a Successful Manufacturer in Cincinnati. — Samuel T. Wilcox, the Grocer. — His Success in Business in Cincinnati. — Ball and Thomas, the Photographers. — Colored People of Cincinnati evince a Desire to take Care of themselves. — Lydia P. Mott establishes a Home for Colored Orphans. — The Organization effected in 1844. — Its Success. — Formation of a Colored Military Company called "The Attucks Guards." — Emigration of Negroes to Liberia. — The Colored People live down much Prejudice.

IN 1850 there were 238,187 free Negroes in the slave States. Their freedom was merely nominal. They were despised beneath the slaves, and were watched with suspicious eyes, and disliked by their brethren in bondage.

In 1850 there were 196,016 free Negroes in the Northern States. Their increase came from [chiefly] two sources, viz.: births and emancipated persons from the South. Fugitive slaves generally went to Canada, for in addition to being in danger of arrest under the fugitive-slave law, none of the State governments in the North sympathized with escaped Negroes. The Negroes in the free States were denied the rights of citizenship, and were left to the most destroying ignorance. In 1780, some free Negroes, of the town of Dartmouth, petitioned the General Court of Massachusetts for relief from taxation, because they were denied the privileges and duties of citizenship. The petition set forth the hardships free Negroes were obliged to endure, even in Massachusetts, and was in itself a proof of the fitness of the petitioners for the duties of citizenship.

" *To the Honorable Council and House of Representatives, in General Court Assembled, for the State of Massachusetts Bay, in New England :*

" The petition of several poor negroes and mulattoes, who are inhabitants of the town of Dartmouth, humbly showeth :

" That we being chiefly of the African extract, and by reason of long bondage and hard slavery, we have been deprived of enjoying the profits of our labor or the advantage of inheriting estates from our parents, as our neighbors the white people do, having some of us not long enjoyed our own freedom ; yet of late, contrary to the invariable custom and practice of the country, we have been, and now are, taxed both in our polls and that small pittance of estate which, through much hard labor and industry, we have got together to sustain ourselves and families withall. We apprehend it, therefore, to be hard usage, and will doubtless (if continued) reduce us to a state of beggary, whereby we shall become a burthen to others, if not timely prevented by the interposition of your justice and power.

" Your petitioners further show, that we apprehend ourselves to be aggrieved, in that, while we are not allowed the privilege of freemen of the State, having no vote or influence in the election of those that tax us, yet many of our color (as is well known) have cheerfully entered the field of battle in the defence of the common cause, and that (as we conceive) against a similar exertion of power (in regard to taxation) too well known to need a recital in this place.

" We most humble request, therefore, that you would take our unhappy case into your serious consideration, and, in your wisdom and power, grant us relief from taxation, while under our present depressed circumstances ; and your poor petitioners, as in duty bound, shall ever pray, etc.

> " JOHN CUFFE,
> " ADVENTUR CHILD,
> " PAUL CUFFE,
> " SAMUEL GRAY, [his x mark.]
> " PERO HOWLAND, [his x mark.]
> " PERO RUSSELL, [his x mark.]
> " PERO COGGESHALL.

" Dated at Dartmouth, the 10th of February, 1780.
" Memorandum in the handwriting of John Cuffe :

" This is the copy of the petition which we did deliver unto the Honorable Council and House, for relief from taxation in the days of our distress. But we received none.   JOHN CUFFE." [1]

---

[1] This is inserted in this volume as the more appropriate place.

Not discouraged at the failure that attended the above petition, the indefatigable Paul Cuffe, addressed the following to the selectmen of his town the next year.

"A REQUEST.

" *To the Selectmen of the Town of Dartmouth, Greeting :*

We, the subscribers, your humble petitioners, desire that you would, in your capacity, put a stroke in your next warrant for calling a town meeting, so that it may legally be laid before said town, by way of vote, to know the mind of said town, whether all free negroes and mulattoes shall have the same privileges in this said Town of Dartmouth as the white people have, respecting places of profit, choosing of officers, and the like, together with all other privileges in all cases that shall or may happen or be brought in this our said Town of Dartmouth. We, your petitioners, as in duty bound, shall ever pray,

[Signed.]   "JOHN CUFFE,

"PAUL CUFFE,

" Dated at Dartmouth, the 22d of the 4th mo., 1781."

As early as 1788 Massachusetts passed a law requiring all Negroes who were not citizens, to leave the Commonwealth within two months from the date of the publication of the law. It has been said, upon good authority, that this law was drawn by several of the ablest lawyers in the Bay State, and was intended to keep out all Negroes from the South who, being emancipated, might desire to settle there. It became a law on the 26th of March, 1788, and instead of becoming a dead letter, was published and enforced in post-haste. The following section is the portion of the act pertinent to this inquiry.

"V. *Be it further enacted by the authority aforesaid* [the Senate and House of Representatives in General Court assembled], that no person being an African or Negro, other than a subject of the Emperor of Morocco, or a citizen of some one of the United States (to be evidenced by a certificate from the Secretary of the State of which he shall be a citizen), shall tarry within this Commonwealth, for a longer time than two months, and upon complaint made to any Justice of the Peace within this Commonwealth, that any such person has been within the same more than two months, the said Justice shall order the said person to depart out of this Commonwealth, and in case that the said African or Negro shall not depart as aforesaid, any Justice of the

Peace within this Commonwealth, upon complaint and proof made that such person has continued within this Commonwealth ten days after notice given him or her to depart as aforesaid, shall commit the said person to any house of correction within the county, there to be kept to hard labor, agreeable to the rules and orders of the said house, until the Sessions of the Peace, next to be holden within and for the said county ; and the master of the said house of correction is hereby required and directed to transmit an attested copy of the warrant of commitment to the said Court on the first day of their said session, and if upon trial at the said Court, it shall be made to appear that the said person has thus continued within the Commonwealth, contrary to the tenor of this act, he or she shall be whipped not exceeding ten stripes, and ordered to depart out of this Commonwealth within ten days ; and if he or she shall not so depart, the same process shall be had and punishment inflicted, and so *toties quoties.*" [1]

The following notice, with the subjoined names, shows that the cruel law was enforced.

NOTICE TO BLACKS.

The Officers of Police having made return to the Subscriber of the names of the following persons, who are Africans or Negroes, not subjects of the Emperor of *Morocco* nor citizens of the *United States*, the same are hereby warned and directed to depart out of this Commonwealth before the 10th day of October next, as they would avoid the pains and penalties of the law in that case provided, which was passed by the Legislature, March 26, 1788.

CHARLES BULFINCH,
Superintendent.

By Order and Direction of the Selectmen.

Portsmouth—Prince Patterson, Eliza Cotton, Flora Nash.

Rhode Island—Thomas Nichols and Philis Nichols, Hannah Champlin, Plato Alderson, Raney Scott, Jack Jeffers, Thomas Gardner, Julius Holden, Violet Freeman, Cuffy Buffum, Sylvia Gardner, Hagar Blackburn, Dolly Peach, Polly Gardner, Sally Alexander, Philis Taylor.

Providence—Dinah Miller, Salvia Hendrick, Rhode Allen, Nancy Hall, Richard Freeman, Elizabeth Freeman, Nancy Gardner, Margaret Harrison.

Connecticut—Bristol Morandy, John Cooper, Scipio Kent, Margaret Russell, Phoebe Seamore, Phoebe Johnson, Jack Billings.

---

[1] Slavery in Massachusetts, pp. 228, 229.

New London—John Denny, Thomas Burdine, Hannah Burdine.

New York—Sally Evens, Sally Freeman, Cæsar West and Hannah West, Thomas Peterson, Thomas Santon, Henry Sanderson, Henry Wilson, Robert Willet, Edward Cole, Mary Atkins, Polly Brown, Amey Spalding, John Johnson, Rebecca Johnson, George Homes, Prince Kilsbury, Abraham Fitch, Joseph Hicks, Abraham Francis, Elizabeth Francis, Sally Williams, William Williams, Rachel Pewinck, David Dove, Esther Dove, Peter Bayle, Thomas Bostick, Katy Bostick, Prince Hayes, Margaret Bean, Nancy Hamik, Samuel Benjamin, Peggy Ocamum, Primus Hutchinson. .

Philadelphia—Mary Smith, Richard Allen, Simon Jeffers, Samuel Posey, Peter Francies, Prince Wales, Elizabeth Branch, Peter Gust, William Brown, Butterfield Scotland, Clarissa Scotland, Cuffy Cummings, John Gardner, Sally Gardner, Fortune Gorden, Samuel Stevens.

Baltimore—Peter Larkin and Jenny Larkin, Stepney Johnson, Anne Melville.

Virginia—James Scott, John Evens, Jane Jackson, Cuffey Cook, Oliver Nash, Robert Woodson, Thomas Thompson.

North Carolina—James Jurden, Polly Johnson, Janus Crage.

South Carolina—Anthony George, Peter Cane.

Halifax—Catherine Gould, Charlotte Gould, Cato Small, Philis Cole, Richard M'Coy.

West Indies—James Morfut and Hannah his wife, Mary Davis, George Powell, Peter Lewis, Charles Sharp, Peter Hendrick, William Shoppo and Mary Shoppo, Isaac Johnson, John Pearce, Charles Esings, Peter Branch, Newell Symonds, Rosanna Symonds, Peter George, Lewis Victor, Lewis Sylvester, John Laco, Thomas Foster, Peter Jesemy, Rebecca Jesemy, David Bartlet, Thomas Grant, Joseph Lewis, Hamet Lewis, John Harrison, Mary Brown, Boston Alexander.

Cape François—Casme Francisco and Nancy his wife, Mary Fraceway.

Aux Cayes—Susannah Ross.

Port-au-Prince—John Short.

Jamaica—Charlotte Morris, John Robinson.

Bermuda—Thomas Williams.

New Providence—Henry Taylor.

Liverpool—John Mumford.

Africa—Francis Thompson, John Brown, Mary Joseph, James Melvile, Samuel Bean, Hamlet Earl, Cato Gardner, Charles Mitchel, Sophia Mitchel, Samuel Frazier, Samuel Blackburn, Timothy Philips, Joseph Ocamum.

France—Joseph ———.

Isle of France—Joseph Lovering.

LIST OF INDIANS AND MULATTOES.

The following persons from several of the United States, being people of colour, commonly called Mulattoes, are presumed to come within the intention of the same law, and are accordingly warned and directed to depart out of the Commonwealth before the 10th day of October next.

Rhode Island—Peter Badger, Kelurah Allen, Waley Green, Silvia Babcock.

Providence—Polly Adams, Paul Jones.

Connecticut—John Brown, Polly Holland, John Way and Nancy Way, Peter Virginia, Leville Steward, Lucinda Orange, Anna Sprague, Britton Doras, Amos Willis, Frank Francies.

New London—Hannah Potter.

New York—Jacob and Nelly Cummings, James and Rebecca Smith, Judith Chew, John Schumagger, Thomas Willouby, Peggy Willouby, John Reading, Mary Reading, Charles Brown, John Miles, Hannah Williams, Betsy Harris, Douglass Brown, Susannah Foster, Thomas Burros, Mary Thomson, James and Freelove Buck, Lucy Glapcion, Lucy Lewis, Eliza Williams, Diana Bayle, Cæsar and Sylvia Caton, —— Thompson, William Guin.

Albany—Elone Virginia, Abijah Reed and Lydia Reed, Abijah Reed, Jr., Rebecca Reed and Betsy Reed.

New Jersey—Stephen Boadley, Hannah Victor.

Philadelphia—Polly Boadley, James Long, Hannah Murray, Jeremiah Green, Nancy Principeso, David Johnson, George Jackson William Coak, Moses Long.

Maryland—Nancy Gust.

Baltimore—John Clark, Sally Johnson.

Virginia—Sally Hacker, Richard and John Johnson, Thomas Stewart, Anthony Paine, Mary Burk, William Hacker, Polly Losours, Betsy Guin, Lucy Brown.

Africa—Nancy Doras.[1]

The constitutions of nearly all the States, statutes, or public sentiment drove the Negro from the ballot-box, excused him from the militia, and excluded him from the courts. Although born on the soil, a soldier in two wars, an industrious, law-abiding *person*, the Negro, nevertheless, was not regarded as a member of political society. He was taxed, but enjoyed no representation; was governed by laws, and yet had no voice in making the laws.

---

[1] Massachusetts Mercury, vol. xvi. No. 22, Sept. 16, 1780.

The doors of nearly all the schools of the entire North were shut in his face; and the few separate schools accorded him were given grudgingly. They were usually held in the lecture-room of some Colored church edifice, or thrust off to one side in a portion of the city or town toward which aristocratic ambition would never turn. These schools were generally poorly equipped; and the teachers were either Colored persons whose opportunities of securing an education had been poor, or white persons whose mental qualifications would not encourage them to make an honest living among their own race; there were noble exceptions.

A deeply rooted prejudice shut the Negro out from the trades. He could not acquire the art of setting type, civil engineering, building machinery, house carpentering, or any of the trades. The schools of medicine, law, and theology were not open to him; and even if he secured admission into some gentleman's office, or instruction from some divine, the future gave him no promise. The white wings of hope were broken in an ineffectual attempt to move against the bitter winds of persecution, under the dark sky of hate and proscription. Corporations, churches, theatres, and political parties made the Negro a subject of official action. If a Negro travelled by stage coach, it was among the baggage in the "boot," or on top with the driver. If he were favored with a ride on a street car, it was in a separate car marked, "*This car for Colored people.*" If he journeyed any distance by rail, he was assigned to the "Jim Crow" car, or "smoker," where himself and family were subjected to inconvenience, insult, and the society of the lowest class of white rowdies. If he were hungry and weary at the end of the journey, there was "no room for him in the inn," and, like his Master, was assigned a place among the cattle. If he were so fortunate as to get into a hotel as a servant, bearing the baggage of his master, he slept in the garret, and took his meals in the kitchen. It mattered not who the Colored man was—whether it was Langston, the lawyer, McCune Smith, the physician, or Douglass, the orator—he found no hotel that would give him accommodations. And forsooth, if some host had the temerity to admit a Negro to his dining-room, a dozen white guests would leave the hotel rather than submit to the "*outrage!*"

The places of amusements in all the large cities in the North excluded the Negro; and when he did gain admission, he was shown to the gallery, where he could enjoy peanut-hulls, boot-blacks, and " black-legs." Occasionally the side door of a college was put ajar for some invincible Negro. But this was a per-formance of very rare occurrence ; and the instances are easily remembered.

When courts and parties, corporations and companies had re-fused to accord the Negro the rights that were his due as a man, he carried his case to the highest earthly court, the Christian Church. He felt sure of sympathy and succor from this source. The Church had stood through the centuries as a refuge for the unfortunate and afflicted. But, alas! the Church shrank from the Negro as if he had been a reptile. If he gained admission it was to the " Negro pew " in the " organ loft." If he secured the precious " emblems of the broken body and shed blood " of his Divine Master, it was after the " white folks " were through. If the cause of the Negro were mentioned in the prayer or ser-mon, it was in the indistinct whisper of the moral coward who occupied the sacred desk. And when the fight was on at fever heat, when it was popular to plead the cause of the slave and demand the rights of the free Negro, the Church was the last organization in the country to take a position on the question ; and even then, her " moderation was known to all men."

If the Negro had suffered from neglect only, had been left to solve the riddle of his anomalous existence without further embarrassment, it would have been well. But no, it was not so. Studied insolence jostled Colored men and women from the streets of the larger cities ; mobocratic violence broke up assem-blages and churches of Colored people; and malice sought them in the quiet of their homes—outraged and slew them in cold blood. Thus with the past as a haunting, bitter recollection, the present filled with fear and disaster, and the future a shapeless horror, think ye life was sweet to the Negro? Bitter? Bitter as death? Ay, bitter as hell!

Driven down from the lofty summit of laudable ambitions into the sultry plains of domestic drudgery and menial toil, nearly every ray of hope had perished upon the strained vision of the Negro. The only thing young Colored men could aspire to was the position of a waiter, the avocation of a barber, the place of a house-servant or groom, and teach or preach to their own people with little or no qualifications. Denied the opportu-nities and facilities of securing an education, they were upbraided by the press and pulpit, in private gatherings and public meetings, for their ignorance, which was enforced by a narrow and contracted public prejudice.

But "none of these things moved" the Negro. Undismayed he bowed to his herculean task with a complacency and courage worthy of any race or age of the world's history. The small encouragement that came to him from the conscientious minority of white men and women was as refreshing as the cool ocean breeze at even-tide to the feverish brow of a travel-soiled pilgrim. The Negro found it necessary to exert *himself*, to lift himself out of his social, mental, and political dilemma by the straps of his boots. Colored men turned their attention to the education of themselves and their children. Schools were begun, churches organized, and work of general improvement and self-culture entered into with alacrity and enthusiasm. Boston had among its teachers the scholarly Thomas Paul; among its clergymen Leonard A. Grimes and John T. Raymond; among its lawyers Robert Morris and E. G. Walker; among its business men J. B. Smith and Coffin Pitts; among its physicians John R. Rock and John V. DeGrasse; among its authors Brown and Nell; and among its orators Remond and Hilton. Robert Morris was admitted to the bar in Boston, on Thursday, June 27, 1850, at a meeting of the members of the Suffolk County Bar. The record is as follows:

"*Resolved*, That ROBERT MORRIS, Esq., be recommended for admittance to practice as a Counsellor and Attorney of the Circuit and District Courts of the United States.

"(Signed)　ELLIS GRAY LORING, *Chairman.*
"CHAS. THEO. RUSSELL, *Secretary.*"

John V. DeGrasse, M.D., an eminent physician of Boston was perhaps the most accomplished Colored gentleman in New England between 1850–1860. The following notice appeared in a Boston journal in August, 1854:

"On the 24th of August, 1854, Mr. DeGrasse was admitted in due form a member of the 'Massachusetts Medical Society.' It is the first instance of such honor being conferred upon a colored man in this State, at least, and probably in the country; and therefore it deserves particular notice, both because the means by which he has reached this distinction are creditable to his own intelligence and perseverance, and because others of his class may be stimulated to seek an elevation which has hitherto been supposed unattainable by men of color. The Doctor is a native of New York City, where he was born in June, 1825, and where he spent his time in private and public schools till 1840. He then entered the Oneida Institute, Beriah Green, President, and spent one year ; but as Latin was not taught there, he left and entered the Clinton Seminary, where he remained two years, intending to enter college in the fall of 1843. He was turned from this purpose, however, by the persuasions of a friend in France, and after spending two years in a college in that country, he returned to New York in November, 1845, and commenced the study of medicine with Dr. Samuel R. Childs, of that city. There he spent two years in patient and diligent study, and then two more in attending the medical lectures of Bowdoin College, Me. Leaving that institution with honor in May, 1849, he went again to Europe in the autumn of that year, and spent considerable time in the hospitals of Paris, travelling, at intervals, through parts of France, England, Italy, and Switzerland. Returning home in the ship ' Samuel Fox,' in the capacity of surgeon, he was married in August, 1852, and since that time he has practised medicine in Boston. Earning a good reputation here by his diligence and skill, he was admitted a member of the Medical Society, as above stated. Many of our most respectable physicians visit and advise with him whenever counsel is required. The Boston medical profession, it must be acknowledged, has done itself honor in thus discarding the law of caste, and generously acknowledging real merit, without regard to the hue of the skin.''

The Colored population of New York was equal to the great emergency that required them to put forth their personal exertions. Dr. Henry Highland Garnet, Dr. Charles B. Ray, and the Rev. Peter Williams in the pulpit ; Charles L. Reason and William Peterson as teachers ; James McCune Smith and Philip A. White as physicians and chemists ; James Williams and Jacob Day among business' men, did much to elevate the Negro in self-respect and self-support.

Philadelphia early ranked among her foremost leaders of the Colored people, William Whipper, Stephen Smith, Robert Purvis, William Still, Frederick A. Hinton, and Joseph Cassey. From an inquiry instituted in 1837, it was ascertained that out of the 18,768 Colored people in Philadelphia, 250 had paid for their freedom the aggregate sum of $79,612, and that the real and personal property owned by them was near $1,500,000. There were returns of several chartered benevolent societies for the purpose of affording mutual aid in sickness and distress, and there were sixteen houses of public worship, with over 4,000 communicants. And in Western Pennsylvania there were John Peck, John B. Vashon, Geo. Gardner, and Lewis Woodson. Every State in the North seemed to produce Colored men of marked ability to whom God committed a great work. Their examples of patient fortitude, industry, and frugality, and their determined efforts to obtain knowledge and build up character, stimulated the youth of the Negro race to greater exertions in the upward direction.

The African Methodist Episcopal Church was organized as early as 1816. Its churches grew and its ministry increased in numbers, intelligence, and piety, until it became the most powerful organization of Colored men on the continent. The influence of this organization upon the Colored race in America was excellent. It brought the people together, not only in religious sympathy, but by the ties of a common interest in all affairs of their race and condition. The men in the organization who possessed the power of speech, who had talents to develop, and an ambition to serve their race, found this church a wide field of usefulness.

The Colored Baptists were organized before the Methodists, [in Virginia,] but their organization has always lacked strength. The form of government, being purely Democratic, was adapted to a people of larger intelligence and possessed of greater capacity for self-government. But, notwithstanding this fact, the "independent" order of Colored Baptists gave the members and clergymen of the denomination exalted ideas of government, and abiding confidence in the capacity of the Negro for self-government. No organization of Colored people in America has produced such able men as the Colored Baptist Church.

In Ohio, Illinois, Indiana, and Michigan, Colored men distinguished themselves in the pulpit, in the forum, in business, and letters. William Howard Day, of Cleveland, during this period [1850–1860] Librarian of the Cleveland Library and editor of a newspaper; John Mercer Langston, of Oberlin; John Liverpool and John I. Gaines, of Cincinnati, Ohio, were good men and true. What they did for their race was done worthily and well. At the Ohio Anti-Slavery Convention, held at Putnam on the 22d, 23d, and 24th of April, 1835, the committee on the condition of the "people of Color," made the following report from Cincinnati:

The number of Colored people in Cincinnati is about 2,500. As illustrating their general condition, we will give the statistics of one or two small districts. The families in each were visited from house to house, taking them all as far as we went :

Number of families in one of these districts	26
" of individuals	125
" of heads of families	49
" of heads of families who are professors of religion .	19
" of children at school	20
" of *heads of families* who have been slaves	39
" of individuals who have been slaves	95
Time since they obtained their freedom, from 1 to 15 years ; average, 7 years.	
Number of individuals who have purchased themselves	23
Whole amount paid for themselves	$9,112
Number of fathers and mothers still in slavery	9
" of children	18
" of brothers and sisters	98
" of newspapers taken	0
" of heads of familles who can read	2

EMPLOYMENT OF HEADS OF FAMILIES.

Common laborers and porters	7
Dealers in second-hand clothing	1
Hucksters	1
Carpenters	2
Shoe-blacks	6
Cooks and waiters	11
Washer-women	18

Five of these women purchased themselves from slavery. One paid four hundred dollars for herself, and has since bought a house and lot worth six hundred dollars. All this she has done by washing.

Another individual had bargained for his wife and two children. Their master agreed to take four hundred and twenty dollars for them. He succeeded at length in raising the money, which he carried to their owner. "I shall charge you thirty dollars more than when you was here before," said the planter, "for your wife is in a family-way, and you may pay thirty dollars for that or not take her, just as you please."

"And so," said he (patting the head of a little son, three years old, who hung upon his knee), "I had to pay thirty dollars for this little fellow six months before he was born."

Number of families in another district 63
" of individuals 258
" of heads of families 106
" . of families who are professors of religion ᷍ . 16
" of heads of families at school 53
" of newspapers taken 7
Amount of property in real estate $9,850
Number of *individuals* who have been slaves . . . 108
" of *heads of families* who have been slaves . . 69
Age at which they obtained their freedom, from 3 months to
    60 years ; average, 33 years.
Time since they obtained their freedom, from 4 weeks to 27
    years ; average, 9 years.
Number of heads of families who have purchased themselves, 36
Whole amount paid for themselves . . . ·. $21,515.00
Average price $597.64
Number of children which the same families have already
    purchased 14
Whole amount paid for these children $2,425.75
Average price $173.27
Total amount paid for these parents and children . $23,940.75
Number of parents still in slavery 16
" of husbands or wives 7
" of children 35
" of brothers and sisters 144

These districts were visited without the least reference to their being exhibited separately. If they give a fair specimen of the whole population (and we believe that to be a fact), then we have the following results : 1,129 of the Colored population of Cincinnati have been in slavery ; 476 have purchased themselves, at the total expense of $215,522.04, averaging for each, $452.77 ; 163 parents are still in slavery, 68 husbands and wives, 346 children, 1,579 brothers and sisters.

There are a large number in the city who are now working out their own freedom—their free papers being retained as security. One man of our acquaintance has just given his master seven notes of one hundred dollars each, one of which he intends to pay every year, till he has paid them all ; his master promises then to give him his free papers. After paying for himself, he intends to buy his wife and then his chil-

dren. Others are buying their husbands or wives, and others again
their parents or children. To show that on this subject they have
sympathies like other people, we will state a single fact. A young man,
after purchasing himself, earned three hundred dollars. This sum he
supposed was sufficient to purchase his aged mother, a widow, whom
he had left in slavery five years before, in Virginia. Hearing that she
was for sale, he started immediately to purchase her. But, after travelling five hundred miles, and offering all his money, he was refused.
Not because she was not for sale, nor because he did not offer her full
value. She had four sons and daughters with her, and the planter
thought he could do better to keep the family together and send them
all down the river. In vain the affectionate son pleaded for his mother.
The planter's heart was steel. He would not sell her, and with a
heavy heart the young man returned to Cincinnati. He has since
heard that they were sold in the New Orleans market "*in lots to suit
purchasers.*"

Cincinnati produced quite a number of business men among
her Colored population.

HENRY BOYD

was born in the State of Kentucky, on the 14th day of May,
1802. He received some instruction in reading and writing.
He was bound out to a gentleman, from whom he learned the
cabinet-making trade. He developed at quite an early age a
genius for working in all kinds of wood—could make any thing
in the business. He came to Ohio in 1826, and located in Cincinnati. He was a fine-looking man of twenty-four years, and a
master mechanic. He expected to secure employment in some
of the cabinet shops in the city. Accordingly, he applied at
several, but as often as he applied he was refused employment
on the ground of complexional prejudice. In some instances the
proprietor was willing that a Colored man should work for him,
but the white mechanics would not work by the side of a Colored
man. In other cases it was quite different. The proprietors
would not entertain the idea of securing the services of a "Black
mechanic." So it was for weeks that Mr. Boyd sought an opportunity to use his skill in the direction of his genius and training; but he sought in vain. Disappointed, though not disheartened, he turned to the work of a stevedore, which he did for four
months. At the expiration of this time he found employment
with a house-builder. Within six months from the time he be-

gan work as a builder he had so thoroughly mastered the trade
that he quit working as a journeyman, formed a co-partnership
with a white man, and went into business. The gentleman with
whom he joined his fortunes was a mechanic of excellent abilities, and acknowledged the superior fitness of Boyd for the
business.

As a builder he succeeded first-rate for four years. But his
color was against him. His white partner would make the contracts, secure the jobs, and then Boyd would come forward when
the work was to be done. He had an abundance of work, and
always finished it to the entire satisfaction of his patrons. It is
impossible to estimate just how many houses he built, but the
number is not small. He had made a beginning, and secured
some capital. He did not like the builder's trade, and only entered it at the first from necessity—as a stepping-stone to his
own trade, for which he had a great deal of enthusiasm. In
1836, ten years after his arrival in Cincinnati, he engaged in the
manufacture of bedsteads. For six years he carried on this business—found a ready market and liberal pay. He brought to his
business some of the oldest buyers in the bedstead line, and had
a trade that kept him busy at all seasons of the year. His very
excellent business habits won for him many friends, and through
their solicitations he enlarged his business by manufacturing all
kinds of furniture. He put up a building on the corner of Eighth
Street and Broadway, where he carried on his manufacturing from
1836 till 1859, a period of twenty-three years. His business required
four large buildings and a force of skilful workmen, never less
than twenty, frequently fifty. He used the most approved machinery and paid excellent wages.

His manufactory presented, perhaps, what was never seen in
this country before or since. His workmen represented almost
all the leading races. There were Negroes, Americans, Irishmen,
Scotchmen, Englishmen, Frenchmen, and men of other nationalities. And they did n't bite each other! Their relations were
pleasant.

He was burned out three times, but he rebuilt and went ahead.
He was doing such an extensive business that some thought it
advisable to destroy his buildings. His losses were very heavy,
yet he kept right on, and kept up his business for some time;
but finally had to yield at the last fire, when he had no insurance.

He invented a machine to turn the rails of a bed, but being a Colored man he could not take out a patent. He, therefore, had one taken out in the name of a white gentleman. "The Boyd bedstead" sold throughout the United States then, and was popular for many years after he quit the business.

He has been engaged in several different businesses since he quit manufacturing, and for the last nine years has been in the employ of the city.

SAMUEL T. WILCOX.

In 1850 Samuel T. Wilcox decided to embark in some business venture in Cincinnati. Accordingly he built a store on the northeast corner of Broadway and Fifth streets. He at once occupied it as a grocer. In those days fancy groceries were not kept. But Mr. Wilcox opened a new era in the business. He introduced fancy articles, such as all varieties of canned fruit, choice liquors, cigars, first quality of hams, all kinds of dried fruit, the best brands of sugars, molasses, and fine soaps. He made a specialty of these, and succeeded admirably.

His trade was divided between two classes—the finest river packets and the best families of the city. His customers were the very *best families*—people of wealth and high standing. And perhaps no grocer of his times in Cincinnati did so large a business as Samuel T. Wilcox.

His business increased rapidly until he did about $140,000 *of trade per year !* This continued for six years, when his social habits were not favorable to permanent success. He had been sole owner of the business up to this time. He sold out one half of the store to Charles Roxboro, Sr.; thus the firm name became "Wilcox & Roxboro." The latter gentleman was energetic and business-like in his habits. He cast his courage and marvellous tact against the high tide of business disaster that came sweeping along in the last days of the firm. He resorted to every honorable and safe expedient in order to avert failure. But the handwriting was upon the wall. He failed. Wilcox had begun business with $25,000 cash. He had accumulated $60,000 in real estate, and had transacted $140,000 of business in a single year! He failed because his life was immoral, his habits extravagant, and his attention to business indifferent.

ALEX. S. THOMAS.

This gentleman came to Cincinnati in 1852, where he made the acquaintance of a Colored gentleman of intelligence, J. P. Ball, who was in the daguerrian business at Nos. 28 and 30 West Fourth Street. Mr. Thomas became affianced to Miss Elizabeth Ball, sister of J. P. Ball; and after they were married, Mr. Thomas accepted the position of reception clerk for his brother-in-law. He filled this position with credit and honor for the space of one year. It was now 1853. Daguerrotypes were all the " rage." Photography was unknown. Mr. Ball had an excellent run of custom, and was making money rapidly.

As operator, Mr. Ball soon discovered that Mr. Thomas was a man of quick perception, thorough, and entirely trustworthy. He soon became familiar with the instrument, and in 1854 began to " operate." He continued at the instrument during the remainder of the time he spent at 28 West Fourth Street. He shortly acquired the skill of an old and well-trained operator; and his success in this department of the business added greatly to the already well-established reputation of the gallery.

Mr. Thomas was not satisfied with being a successful clerk and first-class operator. He wanted to go into business for himself. Accordingly he opened a gallery at No. 120 West Fourth Street, near the "Commercial," under the firm name of " Ball & Thomas." The rooms were handsomely fitted up, and the building leased for five years.

In May, 1860, a severe tornado passed over the city, destroying much property and several lives. The roof of the Commercial [Potter's Building] was carried away; part passed over the gallery of Ball & Thomas, while part went through the operating room, and some fragments of timber, etc., penetrated a saloon in the rear of the photographic gallery, and killed a child and a woman. The gallery was a complete wreck, the instruments, chemicals, scenery, cases, pictures, carpets, furniture, and every thing else, were ruined. This was in the early days of the firm. All their available capital had been converted into stock, used in fitting up the gallery. Ball & Thomas were young men— they were Colored men, and were financially ruined. Apparently their business was at an end. But they were artists; and many white families in Cincinnati recognized them as such. Their white friends came to the rescue. The gallery was fitted up again most elaborately, and was known as "the finest photographic gallery west of the Alleghany Mountains."

This marked a distinct era in the history of the firm, and many persons often remarked that the luckiest moment in their history was when the roof of the Commercial building sat down upon them. For years the best families of the city patronized the famous firm of Ball & Thomas. They had more business than they could attend to at times, and consequently had to engage extra help. These were years of unprecedented success. One hundred dollars a day was small money then. The firm became quite wealthy. After spending fifteen years at 120 they returned to 30 West Fourth Street, where they remained until May, 1874.

Photographers move considerable, and it is seldom that men in this business remain in one street or building as long as Ball & Thomas. They passed twenty-one of the best years of the firm in Fourth Street. This is both a compliment to the public and themselves. It shows, on the one hand, that Colored men can conduct business like white men, and, on the other hand, if Colored men have ability to carry on any kind of business, white people will patronize them.

The old stand at 30 West Fourth Street was fitted up anew, and business began with all the wonted zeal and desire to please the public which characterized the firm in former years. The rooms were at once elegant and capacious. Their motto was to do the best work at the cheapest rates. · But as in all other businesses, so in photographic art, there was competition. And rather than do poor work at the low rates of competitors, they decided to remove to another locality. Accordingly, in May, 1874, they moved into No. 146 West Fifth Street. The building was leased for a term of years. It was in no wise adapted to the photographic business. The walls were cut out, doors made, stairs changed, skylight put in, chemical rooms constructed, gas-fixtures put in, papering, painting, and graining done, carpets and new furniture ordered. It cost the firm more than $2,800 to enter this new stand.

The first year at the new stand was characterized by liberal custom and excellent work. The old customers who were delighted with the work done at 30 West Fourth Street, were convinced that the firm had redoubled its artistic zeal, and was determined to outdo the palmy days of Fourth Street. The business, which at this time was in a flourishing condition, was destined to suffer an interruption in the death of Thomas Carroll

Ball, the senior member of the firm. It was at a time when the trade demanded the energies of both gentlemen. But Death never tarries to consider the far-reach of results or the wishes of the friends of his subject. The business continued. Ball Thomas, the son of Mr. A. S. Thomas, who had grown up under the faithful tuition of his father, now became a successful retouching artist. For the last two years Mr. Thomas has conducted the business alone. He is now doing business at 166 West Fifth Street, and it is said that he is doing a good business.

The Colored people of Cincinnati evinced not only an anxiety to take care of themselves, but took steps early toward securing a home for the orphans in their midst.

In *ante-bellum* days there was no provision made for Colored paupers or Colored orphans. Where individual sympathy or charity did not intervene, they were left to die in the midst of squalid poverty, and were cast into the common ditch, without having medical aid or ministerial consolation. There was not simply studious neglect, but a strong prohibition against their entrance into institutions sustained by the county and State for white persons not more fortunate than they. At one time a good Quaker was superintendent of the county poorhouse. His heart was touched with kindest sympathy for the uncared-for Colored paupers in Cincinnati. He acted the part of a true Samaritan, and gave them separate quarters in the institution of which he was the official head. This fact came to the public ear, and the trustees of the poorhouse, in accordance with their own convictions and in compliance with the complexional prejudices of the community, discharged the Quaker for this breach of the law. The Colored paupers were turned out of this lazar-house on the Sabbath. The time to perpetuate this crime against humanity was indeed significant—on the Lord's day. The God of the poor and His followers beheld the streets of Christian Cincinnati filled with the maimed, halt, sick, and poor, who were denied the common fare accorded the white paupers! There was no sentiment in those days, either in the pulpit or press, to raise its voice against this act of cruelty and shame.

Lydia P. Mott, an eminent member of the Society of Friends and an able leader of a conscientious few, espoused the cause of the motherless, fatherless, and homeless Colored children of this community. She attracted the attention and won the confidence of the few Abolitionists of this city. She determined to establish a home for these little wanderers, and immediately set to work at a plan. The late Salmon P. Chase was then quite young, a man of brilliant abilities and of anti-slavery sentiments. He joined himself to the humane movement of Lydia P. Mott, with the following persons: Christian Donaldson, James Pullan, William Donaldson, Robert Buchanan, John Liverpool, Richard Phillips, John Woodson, Charles Satchell, Wm. W. Watson, William Darnes, Michael Clark, A. M. Sumner, Reuben P. Graham, Louis P. Brux, Sarah B. McLain, Mrs. Eustis, Mrs. Dr. Stanton, Mrs. Hannah Cooper, Mrs. Mary Jane Gordon, Mrs. Susan Miller, Mrs. Rebecca Darnes, Mrs. Charlotte Armstrong, Mrs. Eliza Clark, Mrs. Ruth Ellen Watson, and others. Six of the gentlemen and four of the ladies were white. Only six of this noble company are living at this time.

The organization was effected in 1844, and the act of incorporation was drawn up by Salmon P. Chase. It was chartered in February, 1845, the passage of the act having been assured through the personal influence of Mr. Chase upon the members of the Legislature.

The first Board of Trustees under the charter were William Donaldson, John Woodson, Richard Phillips, Christian Donaldson, Reuben P. Graham, Richard Pullan, Charles Satchell, Louis P. Brux, and John Liverpool. But one is alive—Richard Pullan.

The first building the Trustees secured as an asylum was on Ninth Street, between Plum and Elm. They paid a rental of $12.50 per month. The building was owned by Mr. Nicholas Longworth, but the ground was leased by him from Judge Burnet. The Trustees ultimately purchased the building for $1,500; and in 1851 the ground also was purchased of Mr. Groesbeck for $4,400 in cash.

During the three or four years following, the institution had quite an indifferent career. The money requisite to run it was not forthcoming. The children were poorly fed and clothed, and many times there was no money in the treasury at all. The Trustees were discouraged, and it seemed that the asylum would have to be closed. But just at this time that venerable Abolitionist and underground railroader, Levi Coffin, with his excellent wife, "Aunt Kitty," came to the rescue. He took charge of the institution as superintendent, and his wife assumed the duties of matron. Through their exertions and adroit management they succeeded in enlisting the sympathy of many benevolent folk, and secured the support of many true friends.

It was now 1866. The asylum building presented a forlorn aspect. It was far from being a comfortable shelter for the children. But a lack of funds forbade the Trustees from having it repaired. They began to look about for a more desirable and comfortable building. During the closing year of the Rebellion a large number of freedmen sought the shelter of our large Northern cities. Cincinnati received her share of them, and acted nobly toward them. The government authorities built a hospital for freedmen in a very desirable locality in Avondale. At this time (1866), the building, which was very capacious, was not occupied. The Trustees secured a change in the charter, permitting them, by consent of the subscribers, to sell the Ninth Street property, and purchase the hospital building and the accompanying six acres in Avondale. The Ninth Street property brought $9,000; the purchase in Avondale, refitting, etc., cost $11,000, incurring a debt of $2,000.

During the first twenty-two years of the institution much good was accomplished. Hundreds of children—orphans and friendless children—found shelter in the asylum, which existed only through the almost superhuman efforts of the intelligent Colored persons in the community, and the unstinted charity of many generous white persons. The asylum has been pervaded with a healthy religious atmosphere; and many of its inmates have gone forth to the world giving large promise of usefulness. An occasional letter from former inmates often proves that much good has been done; and that some of these children, without the kindly influence and care of the asylum, instead of occupying places of usefulness and trust in society, might have drifted into vagrancy and crime.

Amidst the struggle for temporal welfare, the Colored people of Cincinnati were not unmindful of the interests and destinies of the Union. A military company was formed, bearing the name of *Attucks Guards*. On the 25th of July, 1855, an association of ladies presented a flag to the company. The address, on the part of the ladies, was delivered by Miss Mary A. Darnes. Among many excellent things, she said:

"Should the love of liberty and your country ever demand your services, may you, in imitation of that noble patriot whose name you bear, promptly respond to the call, and fight to the last for the great and noble principles of liberty and justice, to the glory of your fathers and the land of your birth.

"The time is not far distant when the *slave must be free ;* if not by moral and intellectual means, it must be done by the sword. Remember, gentlemen, should duty call, it will be yours to obey, and strike to the last for freedom or the grave.

"But God forbid that you should be called upon to witness our peaceful homes involved in war. May our eyes never behold this flag in any conflict ; let the quiet breeze ever play among its folds, and the fullest peace dwell among you !"

While the great majority of the Colored people in the country were bowing themselves cheerfully to the dreadful task of living among wolves, some of the race were willing to brave the perils of the sea, and find a new home on the West Coast of Africa. Between the years of 1850–1856, 9,502 Negroes went to Liberia, of whom 3,676 had been born free. In 1850, there were 1,467 manumitted, while 1,011 ran away from their masters.

Notwithstanding the many disadvantages under which the free Negroes of the North had to labor, they accomplished a great deal. In an incredibly short time they built schools, planted churches, established newspapers ; had their representatives in law, medicine, and theology before the world as the marvel of the centuries. Shut out from every influence calculated to incite them to a higher life, and provoke them to better works, nevertheless, the Colored people were enabled to live down much prejudice, and gained the support and sympathy of noble men and women of the Anglo-Saxon race.

CHAPTER XII.

NEGRO SCHOOL LAWS.

1619–1860.

THE POSSIBILITIES OF THE HUMAN INTELLECT. — IGNORANCE FAVORABLE TO SLAVERY. — AN ACT BY THE LEGISLATURE OF ALABAMA IMPOSING A PENALTY ON ANY ONE INSTRUCTING A COLORED PERSON. — EDUCATIONAL PRIVILEGES OF THE CREOLES IN THE CITY OF MOBILE. — PREJUDICE AGAINST COLORED SCHOOLS IN CONNECTICUT. — THE ATTEMPT OF MISS PRUDENCE CRANDALL TO ADMIT COLORED GIRLS INTO HER SCHOOL AT CANTERBURY. — THE INDIGNATION OF THE CITIZENS AT THIS ATTEMPT TO MIX THE RACES IN EDUCATION. — THE LEGISLATURE OF CON-NECTICUT PASSES A LAW ABOLISHING THE SCHOOL. — THE BUILDING ASSAULTED BY A MOB. — MISS CRANDALL ARRESTED AND IMPRISONED FOR TEACHING COLORED CHILDREN AGAINST THE LAW. — GREAT EXCITEMENT. — THE LAW FINALLY REPEALED. — AN ACT BY THE LEGISLATURE OF DELAWARE TAXING PERSONS WHO BROUGHT INTO, OR SOLD SLAVES OUT OF, THE STATE. — UNDER ACT OF 1829 MONEY RECEIVED FOR THE SALE OF SLAVES IN FLORIDA WAS ADDED TO THE SCHOOL FUND IN THAT STATE. — GEORGIA PROHIBITS THE EDUCATION OF COLORED PER-SONS UNDER HEAVY PENALTY. — ILLINOIS ESTABLISHES SEPARATE SCHOOLS FOR COLORED CHIL-DREN. — THE "FREE MISSION INSTITUTE" AT QUINCY, ILLINOIS, DESTROYED BY A MISSOURI MOB. — NUMEROUS AND CRUEL SLAVE LAWS IN KENTUCKY RETARD THE EDUCATION OF THE NEGROES. — AN ACT PASSED IN LOUISIANA PREVENTING THE NEGROES IN ANY WAY FROM BEING INSTRUCTED. — MAINE GIVES EQUAL SCHOOL PRIVILEGES TO WHITES AND BLACKS. — ST. FRANCIS ACADEMY FOR COLORED GIRLS FOUNDED IN BALTIMORE IN 1831. — THE WELLS SCHOOL. — THE FIRST SCHOOL FOR COLORED CHILDREN ESTABLISHED IN BOSTON BY INTELLI-GENT COLORED MEN IN 1798. — A SCHOOL-HOUSE FOR THE COLORED CHILDREN BUILT AND PAID FOR OUT OF A FUND LEFT BY ABIEL SMITH FOR THAT PURPOSE. — JOHN B. RUSSWORM ONE OF THE TEACHERS AND 'AFTERWARD GOVERNOR OF THE COLONY OF CAPE PALMAS, LIBERIA. — FIRST PRIMARY SCHOOL FOR COLORED CHILDREN ESTABLISHED IN 1820. — MISSOURI PASSES STRINGENT LAWS AGAINST THE INSTRUCTION OF NEGROES. — NEW YORK PROVIDES FOR THE EDUCATION OF NEGROES. — ELIAS NEAU OPENS A SCHOOL IN NEW YORK CITY FOR NEGRO SLAVES IN 1704. — "NEW YORK AFRICAN FREE SCHOOL" IN 1786. — VISIT OF LAFAY-ETTE TO THE AFRICAN SCHOOLS IN 1824. — HIS ADDRESS. — PUBLIC SCHOOLS FOR·COLORED CHILDREN IN NEW YORK. — COLORED SCHOOLS IN OHIO. — "CINCINNATI HIGH SCHOOL" FOR COLORED YOUTHS FOUNDED IN 1844. — OBERLIN COLLEGE OPENS ITS DOORS TO COLORED STU-DENTS. — THE ESTABLISHMENT OF COLORED SCHOOLS IN PENNSYLVANIA BY ANTHONY BENEZET IN 1750. — HIS WILL. — "INSTITUTE FOR COLORED YOUTHS" ESTABLISHED IN 1837. — "AVERY COLLEGE," AT ALLEGHENY CITY, PENNSYLVANIA, FOUNDED IN 1849. — ASHMUN INSTITUTE, OR LINCOLN UNIVERSITY, FOUNDED IN OCTOBER, 1856. — SOUTH CAROLINA TAKES DEFINITE ACTION AGAINST THE EDUCATION OR PROMOTION OF THE COLORED RACE IN 1800-1803-1834. — TENNESSEE MAKES NO DISCRIMINATION AGAINST COLOR IN THE SCHOOL LAW OF 1840. — LITTLE OPPORTU-NITY AFFORDED IN VIRGINIA FOR THE COLORED MAN TO BE ENLIGHTENED. — STRINGENT LAWS ENACTED. — HISTORY OF SCHOOLS FOR THE COLORED POPULATION IN THE DISTRICT OF COLUMBIA.

THE institution of American slavery needed protection from the day of its birth to the day of its death. Whips, thumb-screws, and manacles of iron were far less helpful to it than the thraldom of the intellects of its hapless victims. "Created a little lower than the angels," "crowned with glory and honor," armed with authority " over every living creature," man was intended by his Maker to rule the world through his intellect. The homogeneousness of the crude faculties of man has been quite generally admitted throughout the world ; while even scientists, differing widely in many other things, have united in ascribing to the human mind everywhere certain possibilities. But one class of men have dissented from this view—the slave-holders of all ages. A justification of slavery has been sought in the alleged belief of the inferiority of the persons enslaved ; while the broad truism of the possibilities of the human mind was confessed in all legislation that sought to prevent slaves from acquiring knowledge. So the slave-holder asserted his belief in the mental inferiority of the Negro, and then advertised his lack of faith in his assertion by making laws to prevent the Negro intellect from receiving those truths which would render him valueless as a slave, but equal to the duties of a freeman.

ALABAMA

had an act in 1832 which declared that " Any person or persons who shall attempt to teach any free person of color or slave to spell, read, or write, shall, upon conviction thereof by indictment, be fined in a sum not less than $250, nor more than $500." This act also prohibited with severe penalties, by flogging, " any free negro or person of color" from being in company with any slaves without written permission from the owner or overseer of such slaves ; it also prohibited the assembling of more than five male slaves at any place off the plantation to which they belonged ; but nothing in the act was to be considered as forbidding attendance at places of public worship held by white persons. No slave or free person of color was permitted to " preach, exhort, or harangue any slave or slaves, or free persons of color, except in the presence of five respectable slave-holders, or unless the person preaching was licensed by some regular body of professing Christians in the neighborhood, to whose society or church the negroes addressed properly belonged."

In 1833, the mayor and aldermen of the city of Mobile were authorized by an act of the Legislature to grant licenses to such persons as they deemed suitable to give instruction to the children of free Colored Creoles. This applied only to those who resided in the city of Mobile and county of Baldwin. The instruction was to be given at brief periods, and the children had to secure a certificate from the mayor and aldermen. The ground of this action was the treaty between France and the United States in 1803, by which the rights and privileges of citizens had been secured to the Creoles residing in the above places at the time of the treaty.

ARKANSAS,

so far as her laws appear, did not prohibit the education of Negroes; but a study of her laws leaves the impression that the Negroes there were practically denied the right of instruction.

CONNECTICUT

never legislated against educating Colored persons, but the prejudice was so strong that it amounted to the same thing. The intolerant spirit of the whites drove the Colored people of Hartford to request a separate school in 1830. Prejudice was so great against the presence of a Colored school in a community of white people, that a school, established by a very worthy white lady, was mobbed and then legislated out of existence.

"In the summer of 1832, Miss Prudence Crandall, an excellent, well-educated Quaker young lady, who had gained considerable reputation as a teacher in the neighboring town of Plainfield, purchased, at the solicitation of a number of families in the village of Canterbury, Connecticut, a commodious house in that village, for the purpose of establishing a boarding and day school for young ladies, in order that they might receive instruction in higher branches than were taught in the public district school. Her school was well conducted, but was interrupted early in 1833 in this wise : Not far from the village a worthy colored man was living, by the name of Harris, the owner of a good farm, and in comfortable circumstances. His daughter Sarah, a bright girl, seventeen years of age, had passed with credit through the public school of the district in which she lived, and was anxious to acquire a better education, to qualify herself to become a teacher of the colored people. She applied to Miss Crandall for admission to her school. Miss Crandall hesitated, for prudential reasons, to admit a colored person among her pupils ; but Sarah was a young lady of pleasing appearance and manners, well known to many of Miss Crandall's present pupils, having been their classmate in the district school, and was, moreover, a virtuous, pious girl, and a member of the church in Canterbury. No objection could be made to her admission, except on acount of her complexion, and Miss Crandall decided to receive her as a pupil.

No objection was made by the other pupils, but in a few days the parents of some of them called on Miss Crandall and remonstrated ; and although Miss Crandall pressed upon their consideration thé eager desire of Sarah for knowledge and culture, and the good use she wished to make of her education, her excellent character, and her being an accepted member of the same Christian church tó which they belonged, they were too much prejudiced to listeñ to any arguments—'they would not have it said that their daughters went to school with a nigger girl.' It was urged that if Sarah was not dismissed, the white pupils would be withdrawn ; but although the fond hopes of success for an institution which she had established at the risk óf all her property, and by incurring a debt of several hundred dollars, seemed to be doomed to disappointment, she decided not to yield to thę demand for the dismissal of Sarah ; and on the 2d day of March, 1833, she advertised in the 'Liberator' that on the first Monday in April her school would be open for 'young ladies and little misses of color.' Her determination having become known, a fierce indignation was kindled and fanned by prominent people of the village and pervaded the town. In this juncture, the Rev. Samuel J. May, of the neighboring town of Brooklyn, addressed her a letter of sympathy, expressing his readiness to assist her to the extent of his power, and was present at the town meeting held on the 9th of March, called for the express purpose of devising and adopting such measures as 'would effectually avert the nuisance or speedily abate it if it should be brought into the village.'

"The friends of Miss Crandall were authorized by her to state to the moderator of thé town meeting that she would give up her house, which was one of the most conspicuous in the village, and not wholly paid for, if those who were opposed to her school being there would take the property off her hands at the price for which she had purchased it, and which was deemed a reasonable one, and allow her time to procure another house in a more retired part of the town.

"The town meeting was held in the meeting-house, which, though capable of holding a thousand people, was crowded throughout to its utmost capacity. After the warning for the meeting had been read, resolutions were introduced in which were set forth the disgrace and damage that would be brought upon the town if a school for colored girls should be set up there, protesting emphatically against the impending evil, and appointing the civil authority and select-men a committee to wait upon 'the person contemplating the establishment of said school, and persuade her, if possible, to abandon the project.'

"The resolutions were advocated by Rufus Adams, Esq., and Hon. Andrew T. Judson, who was then the most prominent man of the town, and a leading politician in the State, and much talked of as the Democratic candidate for governor, and was a representative in Congress from 1835 to 1839, when he was elected judge of the United States District Court, which position he held until his death in 1853, adjudicating, among other causes, the libel of the ' Amistad ' and the fifty-four Africans on board. After his address on this occasion, Mr. May, in company with Mr. Arnold Buffum, a lecturing agent of the New England Anti-Slavery Society, applied for permission to 'speak in behalf of Miss Crandall, but their application was violently opposed, and the resolutions being adopted, the meeting was declared, by the moderator, adjourned.

" Mr. May at once stepped upon the seat where he had been sitting, and rapidly vindicated Miss Crandall, replying to some of the misstatements as to her purposes and the character of her expected pupils, when he gave way to Mr. Buffum, who had spoken scarcely five minutes before the trustees of the church ordered the house to be vacated and the doors to be shut. There was then no alternative but to yield.

" Two days afterward Mr. Judson called on Mr. May, with whom he had been on terms of a pleasant acquaintance, not to say of friendship, and expressed regret that he had applied certain epithets to him ; and went on to speak of the disastrous effect on the village from the establishment of ' a school for nigger girls.' Mr. May replied that his purpose was, if he had been allowed to do so, to state at the town meeting Miss Crandall's proposition to sell her house in the village at its fair valuation, and retire to some other part of the town. To this Mr. Judson replied : ' Mr. May, we are not merely opposed to the establishment of that school in Canterbury, we mean there shall not be such a school set up anywhere in the State.'

" Mr. Judson continued, declaring that the colored people could never rise from their menial condition in our country, and ought not to be permitted to rise here ; that they were an inferior race and should not be recognized as the equals of the whites ; that they should be sent back to Africa, and improve themselves there, and civilize and Christianize the natives. To this Mr. May replied that there never would be fewer colored people in this country than there were then ; that it was unjust to drive them out of the country ; that we must accord to them their rights or incur the loss of our own ; that education was the primal, fundamental right of all the children of men ; and that Connecticut was the last place where this should be denied.

" The conversation was continued in a similar strain, in the course of which Mr. Judson declared with warmth : ' That nigger school shall never be allowed in Canterbury, nor in any town of this State ' ; and he avowed his determination to secure the passage of a law by the Legislature then in session, forbidding the institution of such a school in any part of the State.

" Undismayed by the opposition and the threatened violence of her neighbors, Miss Crandall received, early in April, fifteen or twenty colored young ladies and misses from Philadelphia, New York, Providence, and Boston, and the annoyances of her persecutors at once commenced : all accommodations at the stores in Canterbury being denied her, her pupils being insulted whenever they appeared on the streets, the doors and door-steps of her house being besmeared, and her well filled with filth ; under all of which, both she and her pupils remained firm. Among other means used to intimidate, an attempt was made to drive away those innocent girls by a process under the obsolete vagrant law, which provided that the select-men of any town might warn any person, not an inhabitant of the State, to depart forthwith, demanding $1.67 for every week he or she remained after receiving such warning ; and in case the fine was not paid and the person did not depart before the expiration of ten days after being sentenced, *then he or she should be whipped on the naked body, not exceeding ten stripes.*

" A warrant to that effect was actually served upon Eliza Ann Hammond, a fine girl from Providence, aged seventeen years ; but it was finally abandoned, and another method was resorted to, most disgraceful to the State as well as the town. Foiled in their attempts to frighten away Miss Crandall's pupils by their proceedings under the obsolete ' pauper and vagrant law,' Mr. Judson and those who acted with him pressed upon the Legislature, then in session, a demand for the enactment of a law which should enable them to accomplish their purpose ; and in that bad purpose they succeeded, by securing the following enactment, on the 24th of May, 1833, known as the ' *black law.'*

" ' Whereas, attempts have been made to establish literary institutions in this State for the instruction of colored persons belonging to other States and countries, which would tend to the great increase of the colored population of the State, and thereby to the injury of the people : therefore,

" ' *Be it enacted, etc.,* That no person shall set up or establish in this State any school, academy, or other literary institution for the instruction or education of colored persons, who are not inhabitants of this State, or harbor or board, for the purpose of attending or being taught or instructed in any such school, academy, or literary institution, any colored person who is not an inhabitant of any town in this State, without the consent in writing, first obtained, of a majority of the civil authority, and also of the select-men of the town in which such school, academy, or literary institution is situated,' etc.

" ' And each and every person who shall knowingly do any act forbidden as aforesaid, or shall be aiding or assisting therein, shall for the first offense forfeit and pay to the treasurer of this State a fine of $100, and for the second offense $200, and so double for every offense of which he or she shall be convicted ; and all informing officers are required to make due presentment of all breaches of this act.'

" On the receipt of the tidings of the passage of this law, the people of Canterbury were wild with exultation ; the bells were rung and a cannon was fired to manifest the joy. On the 27th of June, Miss Crandall was arrested and arraigned before Justices Adams and Bacon, two of those who had been the earnest opponents of her enterprise ; and the result being predetermined, the trial was of course brief, and Miss Crandall was 'committed' to take her trial at the next session of the Supreme Court at Brooklyn, in August. A messenger was at once dispatched by the party opposed to Miss Crandall to Brooklyn, to inform Mr. May, as her friend, of the result of the trial, stating that she was in the hands of the sheriff, and would be put in jail unless he or some of her friends would 'give bonds' for her in a certain sum."

The denouement may be related most appropriately in the language of Mr. May :

" I calmly told the messenger that there were gentlemen enough in Canterbury whose bond for that amount would be as good or better than mine, and I should leave it for them to do Miss Crandall that favor. 'But,' said the young man, 'are you not her friend ?' 'Certainly,' I replied, 'too sincerely her friend to give relief to her enemies in their present embarrassment, and I trust you will not find any one of her friends, or the patrons of her school, who will step forward to help them any more than myself.' 'But, sir,' he cried, 'do you mean to allow her to be put in jail ?' 'Most certainly,' was my answer, 'if her persecutors are unwise enough to let such an outrage be committed.' He turned from me in blank surprise, and hurried back to tell Mr. Judson and the justices of his ill success.

" A few days before, when I first heard of the passage of the law, I had visited Miss Crandall with my friend, Mr. George W. Benson, and advised with her as to the course she and her friends ought to pursue when she should be brought to trial. She appreciated at once and fully the importance of leaving her persecutors to show to the world how base they were, and how atrocious was the law they had induced the Legislature to enact—a law, by the force of which a woman might be fined and imprisoned as a felon in the State of Connecticut for giving instruction to colored girls. She agreed that it would be best for us to leave her in the hands of those with whom the law originated, hoping that, in their madness, they would show forth all their hideous features.

" Mr. Benson and I, therefore, went diligently around to all who he knew were friendly to Miss Crandall and her school, and counselled

them by no means to give bonds to keep her from imprisonment, because nothing would expose so fully to the public the egregious wickedness of the law and the virulence of her persecutors as the fact that
they had thrust her into jail.

"When I found that her resolution was equal to the trial which
seemed to be impending, that she was ready to brave and to bear
meekly the worst treatment that her enemies would venture to subject
her to, I made all the arrangements for her comfort that were practicable in our prison. It fortunately happened that the most suitable
room, unoccupied, was the one in which a man named Watkins had recently been confined for the murder of his wife, and out of which he
had been taken and executed. This circumstance we foresaw would
add not a little to the public detestation of the *black law*. The jailer,
at my request, readily put the room in as nice order as was possible,
and permitted me to substitute for the bedstead and mattrass on which
the murderer had slept, fresh and clean ones from my own house and
Mr. Benson's.

"About 2 o'clock, P.M., another messenger came to inform me that
the sheriff was on the way from Canterbury to the jail with Miss Crandall, and would imprison her unless her friends would give the required
bail. Although in sympathy with Miss Crandall's persecutors, he saw
clearly the disgrace that was about to be brought upon the State, and
begged me and Mr. Benson to avert it. Of course we refused. I
went to the jailer's house and met Miss Crandall on her arrival. We
stepped aside. I said : ' If now you hesitate—if you dread the gloomy
place so much as to wish to be saved from it, I will give bonds for
you even now.' ' Oh, no,' she promptly replied, ' I am only afraid they
will not put me in jail. Their evident hesitation and embarrassment
show plainly how much they deprecated the effect of this part of their
folly, and therefore I am the more anxious that they should be exposed,
if not caught in their own wicked devices.

"We therefore returned with her to the sheriff and the company
that surrounded him, to await his final act. He was ashamed to do it.
He knew it would cover the persecutors of Miss Crandall and the
State of Connecticut with disgrace. He conferred with several about
him, and delayed yet longer. Two gentlemen came and remonstrated
with me in not very seemly terms : ' It would be a —— shame, an
eternal disgrace to the State, to have her put into jail—into the very
room that Watkins had last occupied.'

" ' Certainly, gentlemen,' I replied, ' and this you may prevent if
you please.'

" ' Oh ! ' they cried, ' we are not her friends ; we are not in favor of
her school ; we don't want any more —— niggers coming among us. It
is your place to stand by Miss Crandall and help her now. You and

your —— abolition brethren have encouraged her to bring this nuisance into Canterbury, and it is —— mean in you to desert her now.'

"I rejoined : 'She knows we have not deserted her, and do not intend to desert her. The law which her persecutors have persuaded our legislators to enact is an infamous one, worthy of the dark ages. It would be just as bad as it is whether we would give bonds for her or not. But the people generally will not so soon realize how bad, how wicked, how cruel a law it is unless we suffer her persecutors to inflict upon her all the penalties it prescribes. She is willing to bear them for the sake of the cause she has so nobly espoused. If you see fit to keep her from imprisonment in the cell of a murderer for having proffered the blessings of a good education to those who in our country need it most, you may do so ; *we shall not.*'

"They turned from us in great wrath, words falling from their lips which I shall not repeat.

"The sun had descended nearly to the horizon ; the shadows of night were beginning to fall around us. The sheriff could defer the dark deed no longer. With no little emotion, and with words of earnest deprecation, he gave that excellent, heroic, Christian young lady into the hands of the jailer, and she was led into the cell of Watkins. So soon as I had heard the bolts of her prison door turned in the lock, and saw the key taken out, I bowed and said : 'The deed is done, completely done. It cannot be recalled. It has passed into the history of our nation and our age.' I went away with my steadfast friend, George W. Benson, assured that the legislators of the State had been guilty of a most unrighteous act, and that Miss Crandall's persecutors had also committed a great blunder ; that they all would have much more reason to be ashamed of her imprisonment than she or her friends could ever have.

"The next day we gave the required bonds. Miss Crandall was released from the cell of the murderer, returned home, and quietly resumed the duties of her school until she should be summoned as a culprit into court, there to be tried by the infamous '*Black Law of Connecticut.*' And, as we expected, so soon as the evil tidings could be carried in that day, before Professor Morse had given to Rumor her telegraphic wings, it was known all over the country and the civilized world, that an excellent young lady had been imprisoned as a criminal—yes, put into a murderer's cell—in the State of Connecticut, for opening a school for the instruction of colored girls. The comments that were made upon the deed in almost all the newspapers were far from grateful to the feelings of her persecutors. Even many who, under the same circumstances, would probably have acted as badly as Messrs. A. T. Judson & Co., denounced their procedure as 'un-Christian, inhuman, anti-Democratic, base, mean.'

"On the 23d of August, 1833, the first trial of Miss Crandall was had in Brooklyn, the seat of the county of Windham, Hon. Joseph Eaton presiding at the county court.

"The prosecution was conducted by Hon. A. T. Judson, Jonathan A. Welch, Esq., and I. Bulkley, Esq. Miss Crandall's counsel was Hon. Calvin Goddard, Hon. W. W. Elsworth, and Henry Strong, Esq.

"The judge, somewhat timidly, gave it as his opinion 'that the law was constitutional and obligatory on the people of the State.'

"The jury, after an absence of several hours, returned into court, not having agreed upon a verdict. They were instructed and sent out again, and again a third time, in vain ; they stated to the judge that there was no probability that they could ever agree. Seven were for conviction and five for acquittal, so they were discharged.

"The second trial was on the 3d of October, before Judge Daggett of the Supreme Court, who was a strenuous advocate of the black law. His influence with the jury was overpowering, insisting in an elaborate and able charge that the law was constitutional, and, without much hesitation, the verdict was given against Miss Crandall. Her counsel at once filed a bill of exceptions, and took an appeal to the Court of Errors, which was granted. Before that, the highest legal tribunal in the State, the cause was argued on the 22d of July, 1834. Both the Hon. W. W. Elsworth and the Hon. Calvin Goddard argued with great ability and eloquence against the constitutionality of the black law. The Hon. A. T. Judson and Hon. C. F. Cleaveland said all they could to prove such a law consistent with the *Magna Charta* of our republic. The court reserved a decision for some future time ; and that decision was never given, it being evaded by the court finding such defects in the information prepared by the State's attorney that it ought to be quashed.

"Soon after this, an attempt was made to set the house of Miss Crandall on fire, but without effect. The question of her duty to risk the lives of her pupils against this mode of attack was then considered, and upon consultation with friends it was concluded to hold on and bear a little longer, with the hope that this atrocity of attempting to fire the house, and thus expose the lives and property of her neighbors, would frighten the instigators of the persecution, and cause some restraint on the 'baser sort.' But a few nights afterward, about 12 o'clock, being the night of the 9th of September, her house was assaulted by a number of persons with heavy clubs and iron bars, and windows were dashed to pieces. Mr. May was summoned the next morning, and after consultation it was determined that the school should be abandoned."

Mr. May thus concluded his account of this event, and of the enterprise :

"The pupils were called together and I was requested to announce to them our decision. Never before had I felt so deeply sensible of the cruelty of the persecution which had been carried on for eighteen months in that New England village, against a family of defenseless females. Twenty harmless, well-behaved girls, whose only offense against the peace of the community was that they had come together there to obtain useful knowledge and moral culture, were to be told that they had better go away, because, forsooth, the house in which they dwelt would not be protected by the guardians of the town, the conservators of the peace, the officers of justice, the men of influence in the village where it was situated. The words almost blistered my lips. My bosom glowed with indignation. I felt ashamed of Canterbury, ashamed of Connecticut, ashamed of my country, ashamed of my color." [1]

Thus ended the generous, disinterested, philanthropic Christian enterprise of Prudence Crandall, but the law under which her enterprise was defeated was repealed in 1838.

It is to be regretted that Connecticut earned such an unenviable place in history as this. It seems strange, indeed, that such an occurrence could take place in the nineteenth century in a free State in a republic in North America! But such is "the truth of history."

DELAWARE

never passed any law against the instruction of Negroes, but in 1833 passed an act taxing every person who sold a slave out of the State, or brought one into the State, five dollars, which went into a school fund for the education of *white children alone*. In 1852, the Revised Statutes provided for the taxation of all the property of the State for the support of the schools for *white children* alone. So, by implication, Delaware prohibited the education of Colored children.

In 1840, the Friends formed the African School Association in Wilmington; and under its management two excellent schools, for boys and girls, were established.

FLORIDA.

On the 28th of December, 1848, an act was passed providing "for the establishment of common schools." The right to vote at district meetings was conferred upon every person whose property was liable to taxation for school purposes; but only white children were allowed school privileges.

---

[1] Recollections of the Anti-Slavery Conflict, by Rev. Samuel J. May.

In the same year an act was passed providing that the school funds should consist of "the proceeds of the school lands," and of all estates, real or personal, escheating to the State, and "the proceeds of all property found on the coast or shores of the State." In 1850 the counties were authorized to provide, by taxation, not more than four dollars for each child within their limits of the proper school age. In the same year the amount received from the sale of any slave, under the act of 1829, was required to be added to the school fund. The common school law was revised in 1853, and the county commissioners were authorized to add from the county treasury any sum they thought proper for the support of common schools.[1]

GEORGIA

passed a law in 1770 (copied from S. C. Statutes, passed in 1740), fixing a fine of £20 for teaching a slave to read or write. In 1829 the Legislature enacted the following law :

"If any slave, negro, or free person of color, or any white person, shall teach any other slave, negro, or free person of color to read or write either written or printed characters, the said free person of color or slave shall be punished by fine and whipping, or fine or whipping, at the discretion of the court ; and if a white person so offend, he, she, or they shall be punished with a fine not exceeding $500, and imprisonment in the common jail at the discretion of the court."

In 1833 the above law was consolidated into a penal code. A penalty of $100 was provided against persons who employed any slave or free person of Color to set type or perform any other labor about a printing-office requiring a knowledge of reading or writing. During the same year an ordinance was passed in the city of Savannah, "that if any person shall teach or cause to be taught any slave or free person of color to read or write within the city, or who shall keep a school for that purpose, he or she shall be fined in a sum not exceeding $100 for each and every such offense; and if the offender be a slave or free person of color, he or she may also be whipped, not exceeding thirty-nine lashes."

In the summer of 1850 a series of articles by Mr. F. C. Adams appeared in one of the papers of Savannah, advocating the education of the Negroes as a means of increasing their value and

---

[1] Barnard, p. 337.

of attaching them to their masters. The subject was afterward taken up in the Agricultural Convention which met at Macon in September of the same year. The matter was again brought up in September, 1851, in the Agricultural Convention, and after being debated, a resolution was passed that a petition be presented to the Legislature for a law granting permission to educate the slaves. The petition was presented to the Legislature, and Mr. Harlston introduced a bill in the winter of 1852, which was discussed and passed in the lower House, to repeal the old law, and to grant to the masters the privilege of educating their slaves. The bill was lost in the senate by two or three votes.[1]

ILLINOIS'

school laws contain the word "white" from beginning to end. There is no prohibition against the education of Colored persons; but there being no mention of them, is evidence that they were purposely omitted. Separate schools were established for Colored children before the war, and a few white schools opened their doors to them. The Free Mission Institute at Quincy was destroyed by a mob from Missouri in *ante-bellum* days, because Colored persons were admitted to the classes.

INDIANA

denied the right of suffrage to her Negro population in the constitution of 1851. No provision was made for the education of the Negro children. And the cruelty of the laws that drove the Negro from the State, and pursued him while in it, gave the poor people no hope of peaceful habitation, much less of education.

KENTUCKY

never put herself on record against the education of Negroes. By an act passed in 1830, all the inhabitants of each school district were taxed to support a common-school system. The property of Colored persons was included, but they could not vote or enjoy the privileges of the schools. And the slave laws were so numerous and cruel that there was no opportunity left the bondmen in this State to acquire any knowledge of books even secretly.

---

[1] Barnard, p. 339.

LOUISIANA

passed an act in 1830, forbidding free Negroes to enter the State. It provided also, that whoever should "write, print, publish, or distribute any thing having a tendency to produce discontent among the free colored population, or insubordination among the slaves," should, on conviction thereof, be imprisoned "*at hard labor for life, or suffer death*, at the discretion of the court." And whoever used language calculated to produce discontent among the free or slave population, or was "instrumental in bringing into the State any paper, book, or pamphlet having such tendency," was to "suffer imprisonment at hard labor, not less than three years nor more than twenty-one years, or death, at the discretion of the court." "All persons," continues the act, "who shall teach, or permit, or cause to be taught, any slave to read or write, shall be imprisoned not less than one month nor more than twelve months."

In 1847, a system of common schools for "the education of white youth was established." It was provided that "one mill on the dollar, upon the *ad valorem* amount of the general list of taxable property," should be levied for the support of the schools.

MAINE

gave the elective franchise and ample school privileges to all her citizens, without regard to race or color, by her constitution of 1820.

MARYLAND

always restricted the right of suffrage to her "white male inhabitants," and, therefore, always refused to make any provisions for the education of her Negro population. There is nothing upon her statute-books prohibiting the instruction of Negroes, but the law that designates her schools for "white children" is sufficient proof that Negro children were purposely omitted and excluded from the benefits of the schools.

St. Frances Academy for Colored girls was founded in connection with the Oblate Sisters of Providence Convent, in Baltimore, June 5, 1829, under the hearty approbation of the Most Rev. James Whitfield, D.D., the Archbishop of Baltimore at that time, and receiving the sanction of the Holy See, October 2, 1831. The convent originated with the French Fathers, who came to Baltimore from San Domingo as refugees, in the time of the revolution in that island in the latter years of last century. There were many Colored Catholic refugees who came to Baltimore during that period, and the French Fathers soon opened schools there for the benefit of the refugees and other Colored people. The Colored women who formed the original society which founded the convent and seminary, were from San Domingo, though they had, some of them, certainly, been educated in France. The schools which preceded the organization of the convent were greatly favored by Most Rev. Ambrose Marechal, D.D., who was a French Father, and Archbishop of Baltimore from 1817 to 1828, Archbishop Whitfield being his successor. The Sisters of Providence is the name of a religious society of Colored women who renounced the world to consecrate themselves to the Christian education of Colored girls. The following extract from the announcement which, under the caption of " Prospectus of a School for Colored Girls under the Direction of the Sisters of Providence," appeared in the columns of the "Daily National Intelligencer," October 25, 1831, shows the spirit in which the school originated, and at the same time shadows forth the predominating ideas pertaining to the province of the race at that period.

The prospectus says :

" The object of this institute is one of great importance, greater, indeed, than might at first appear to those who would only glance at the advantages which it is calculated to directly impart to the leading portion of the human race, and through it to society at large. In fact, these girls will either become mothers of families or household servants. In the first case the solid virtues, the religious and moral principles which they may have acquired in this school will be carefully transferred as a legacy to their children. Instances of the happy influence which the example of virtuous parents has on the remotest lineage in this humble and naturally dutiful class of society are numerous. As to such as are to be employed as servants, they will be intrusted with domestic concerns and the care of young children. How important, then, it will be that these girls shall have imbibed religious principles, and have been trained up in habits of modesty, honesty, and integrity." [1]

The Wells School, established by a Colored man by the name of Nelson Wells, in 1835, gave instruction to free children of

---

[1] Barnard, pp. 205, 206.

color. It was managed by a board of trustees who applied the income of $7,000 (the amount left by Mr. Wells) to the support of the school. It accomplished much good.

MASSACHUSETTS.

A separate school for Colored children was established in Boston, in 1798, and was held in the house of a reputable Colored man named Primus Hall. The teacher was one Elisha Sylvester, whose salary was paid by the parents of the children whom he taught. In 1800 sixty-six Colored citizens presented a petition to the School Committee of Boston, praying that a school might be established for their benefit. A sub-committee, to whom the petition had been referred, reported in favor of granting the prayer, but it was voted down at the next town meeting. However, the school taught by Mr. Sylvester did not perish. Two young gentlemen from Harvard University, Messrs. Brown and Williams, continued the school until 1806. During this year the Colored Baptists built a church edifice in Belknap Street, and fitted up the lower room for a school for Colored children. From the house of Primus Hall the little school was moved to its new quarters in the Belknap Street church. Here it was continued until 1835, when a school-house for Colored children was erected and paid for out of a fund left for the purpose by Abiel Smith, and was subsequently called "Smith School-house." The authorities of Boston were induced to give $200.00 as an annual appropriation, and the parents of the children in attendance paid 12½ cents per week. The school-house was dedicated with appropriate exercises, Hon. William Minot delivering the dedicatory address.

The African school in Belknap Street was under the control of the school committee from 1812 to 1821, and from 1821 was under the charge of a special sub-committee. Among the teachers was John B. Russworm, from 1821 to 1824, who entered Bowdoin College in the latter year, and afterward became governor of the colony of Cape Palmas in Southern Liberia.

The first primary school for Colored children in Boston was established in 1820, two or three of which were subsequently kept until 1855, when they were discontinued as separate schools, in accordance with the general law passed by the Legislature in

that year, which provided that, " in determining the qualifications of scholars to be admitted into any public school, or any
district school in this commonwealth, no distinction shall be
made on account of the race, color, or religious opinions of the
applicant or scholar." "Any child, who, on account of his race,
color, or religious opinions should be excluded from any public
or district school, if otherwise qualified," might recover damages
in an action of *tort*, brought in the name of the child in any
court of competent jurisdiction, against the city or town in which
the school was located.[1]

MISSISSIPPI

passed an act in 1823 providing against the meeting together of
slaves, free Negroes, or Mulattoes above the number of five.
They were not allowed to meet at any public house in the night ;
or at any house, for teaching, reading, or writing, in the day or
night. The penalty for the violation of this law was whipping,
" not exceeding thirty-nine " lashes.

In 1831 an act was passed making it " unlawful for any slave,
free negro, or mulatto to preach the Gospel," upon pain of receiving thirty-nine lashes upon the naked back of the presumptuous preacher. If a Negro received written permission from
his master he might preach to the Negroes in his immediate
neighborhood, providing six respectable white men, owners of
slaves, were present.

In 1846, and again in 1848, school laws were enacted, but
in both instances schools and education were prescribed for
" white youth between the ages of six and twenty years."

MISSOURI

ordered all free persons of color to move out of the State in
1845. In 1847 an act was passed providing that " no person shall
keep or teach any school for the instruction of negroes or mulattoes in reading or writing in this State."

NEW YORK

had the courage and patriotism, in 1777, to extend the right of
suffrage to every male inhabitant of full age. But by the revised
constitution, in 1821, this liberal provision was abridged so that

---

[1] Barnard, p. 357.

" no man of color, unless he shall have been for three years a citizen of this State, and for one year next preceding any election, shall be seized and possessed of a freehold estate of $250 over and above all debts and encumbrances charged thereon, and shall have been actually rated and paid a tax thereon, shall be entitled to vote at any such election. And no person of color shall be subject to direct taxation unless he shall be seized and possessed of such real estate as aforesaid." In 1846, and again in 1850, a Constitutional amendment conferring equal privileges upon the Negroes, was voted down by large majorities.

A school for Negro slaves was opened in the city of New York in 1704 by Elias Neau, a native of France, and a catechist of the "Society for the Propagation of the Gospel in Foreign Parts." After a long imprisonment for his public profession of faith as a Protestant, he founded an asylum in New York. His sympathies were awakened by the condition of the Negroes in slavery in that city, who numbered about 1,500 at that time. The difficulties of holding any intercourse with them seemed almost insurmountable. At first he could only visit them from house to house, after his day's toil was over; afterward he was permitted to gather them together in a room in his own house for a short time in the evening. As the result of his instructions at the end of four years, in 1708, the ordinary number under his instruction was 200. Many were judged worthy to receive the sacrament at the hands of Mr. Vesey, the rector of Trinity Church, some of whom became regular and devout communicants, remarkable for their orderly and blameless lives.

But soon after this time some Negroes of the Carmantee and Pappa tribes formed a plot for setting fire to the city and murdering the English on a certain night. The work was commenced but checked, and after a short struggle the English subdued the Negroes. Immediately a loud and angry clamor arose against Elias Neau, his accusers saying that his school was the cause of the murderous attempt. He denied the charge in vain; and so furious were the people that, for a time, his life was in danger. The evidence, however, at the trial proved that the Negroes most deeply engaged in this plot were those whose masters were most opposed to any means for their instruction. Yet the offence of a few was charged upon the race, and even the provincial government lent its authority to make the burden of Neau the heavier. The common council passed an order forbidding

Negroes "to appear in the streets after sunset, without lanthorns or candles"; and as they could not procure these, the result was to break up the labors of Neau. But at this juncture Governor Hunter interposed, and went to visit the school of Neau, accompanied by several officers of rank and by the society's missionaries, and he was so well pleased that he gave his full approval to the work, and in a public proclamation called upon the clergy of the province to exhort their congregations to extend their approva also. Vesey, the good rector of Trinity Church, had long watched the labors of Neau and witnessed the progress of his scholars, as well as assisted him in them; and finally the governor, the council, mayor, recorder, and two chief justices of New York joined in declaring that Neau "in a very eminent degree deserved the countenance, favor, and protection of the society." He therefore continued his labors until 1722, when, "amid the unaffected sorrow of his negro scholars and the friends who honored him for their sake, he was removed by death."

The work was then continued by "Huddlestone, then schoolmaster in New York"; and he was succeeded by Rev. Mr. Wetmore, who removed in 1726 to Rye; whereupon the Rev. Mr. Colgan was appointed to assist the rector of Trinity Church, and to carry on the instruction of the Negroes. A few years afterward Thomas Noxon assisted Mr. Colgan, and their joint success was very satisfactory. Rev. R. Charlton, who had been engaged in similar labor at New Windsor, was called to New York in 1732, where he followed up the work successfully for fifteen years, and was succeeded by Rev. Samuel Auchmuty. Upon the death of Thomas Noxon, in 1741, Mr. Hildreth took his place, who, in 1764, wrote that "not a single black admitted by him to the holy communion had turned out badly, or in any way disgraced his profession." Both Auchmuty and Hildreth received valuable support from Mr. Barclay, who, upon the death of Mr. Vesey, in 1746, had been appointed to the rectory of Trinity Church.

The frequent kidnapping of free persons of color excited public alarm and resulted in the formation of "The New York Society for Promoting the Manumission of Slaves, and Protecting such of them as have been or may be Liberated." These are the names of the gentlemen who organized the society, and became the board of trustees of the "*New York African Free School*":

Melancthon Smith, Jno. Bleeker, James Cogswell, Lawrence Embree, Thomas Burling, Willett Leaman, Jno. Lawrence, Jacob Leaman, White Mattock, Mathew Clarkson, Nathaniel Lawrence, Jno. Murray, Jr.

Their school, located in Cliff Street, between Beekman and Ferry, was opened in 1786, taught by Cornelius Davis, attended by about forty pupils of both sexes, and appears, from their book of minutes, to have been satisfactorily conducted. In the year 1791 a female teacher was added to instruct the girls in needle-work, the expected advantages of which measure were soon realized and highly gratifying to the society. In 1808 the society was incorporated, and in the preamble it is recorded that "a free school for the education of such persons as have been liberated from bondage, that they may hereafter become useful members of the community," has been established. It may be proper here to remark that the good cause in which the friends of this school were engaged, was far from being a popular one. The prejudices of a large portion of the community were against it; the means in the hands of the trustees were often very inadequate, and many seasons of discouragement were witnessed; but they were met by men who, trusting in the Divine support, were resolved neither to relax their exertions nor to retire from the field.

Through the space of about twenty years they struggled on; the number of scholars varying from forty to sixty, until the year 1809, when the Lancasterian, or monitorial, system of instruction was introduced (this being the second school in the United States to adopt the plan), under a new teacher, E. J. Cox, and a very favorable change was produced, the number of pupils, and the efficiency of their instruction being largely increased.

Soon after this, however, in January, 1814, their school-house was destroyed by fire, which checked the progress of the school for a time, as no room could be obtained large enough to accommodate the whole number of pupils. A small room in Doyer Street was temporarily hired, to keep the school together till further arrangements could be made, and an appeal was made to the liberality of the citizens and to the corporation of the city, which resulted in obtaining from the latter a grant of two lots of ground in William Street, on which to build a new school-house; and in January, 1815, a commodious brick building, to accommo-

date 200 pupils, was finished on this lot, and the school was resumed with fresh vigor and increasing interest.   In a few months
the room became so crowded that it was found necessary to engage a separate room, next to the school, to accommodate such
of the pupils as were to be taught sewing.   This branch had been
for many years discontinued, but was now resumed under the
direction of Miss Lucy Turpen, a young lady whose amiable disposition and faithful discharge of her duties rendered her greatly
esteemed both by her pupils and the trustees.   This young
lady, after serving the board for several years, removed with
her parents to Ohio, and her place was supplied by Miss Mary
Lincrum, who was succeeded by Miss Eliza J. Cox, and the latter
by Miss Mary Ann Cox, and she by Miss Carolina Roe, under each
of whom the school continued to sustain a high character for
order and usefulness.

The school in William Street increasing in numbers, another
building was found necessary, and was built on a lot of ground
50 by 100 feet square, on Mulberry Street, between Grand and
Hester streets, to accommodate five hundred pupils, and was
completed and occupied, with C. C. Andrews for teacher, in May,
1820.

General Lafayette visited this school September 10, 1824, an
abridged account of which is copied from the "Commercial Ad-
vertiser" of that date:

Visit of Lafayette to the African School in 1824.

"At 1 o'clock the general, with the company invited for the occasion, visited the African free school, on Mulberry Street.   This school
embraces about 500 scholars ; about 450 were present on this occasion,
and they are certainly the best disciplined and most interesting school
of children we have ever witnessed.   As the general was conducted to
a seat, Mr. Ketchum adverted to the fact that as long ago as 1788 the
general had been elected a member of the institution (Manumission Society) at the same time with Granville Sharp and Thomas Clarkson,
of England.   The general perfectly remembered the circumstances, and
mentioned particularly the letter he had received on that occasion from
the Hon. John Jay, then president of the society.   One of the pupils,
Master James M. Smith, aged eleven years, then stepped forward and
gracefully delivered the following address :

"'GENERAL LAFAYETTE :   In behalf of myself and fellow-school-
mates may I be permitted to express our sincere and respectful grati-

tude to you for the condescension you have manifested this day in visiting this institution, which is one of the noblest specimens of New York philanthropy. Here, sir, you behold hundreds of the poor children of Africa sharing with those of a lighter hue in the blessings of education ; and while it will be our pleasure to remember the great deeds you have done for America, it will be our delight also to cherish the memory of General Lafayette as a friend to African emancipation, and as a member of this institution.'

" To which the general replied, in his own characteristic style, ' I thank you, my dear child.'

"Several of the pupils underwent short examinations, and one of them explained the use of the globes and answered many questions in geography."

PUBLIC SCHOOLS FOR COLORED CHILDREN.

These schools continued to flourish under the same management, and with an attendance varying from 600 in 1824 to 862 in 1832, in the latter part of which year the Manumission Society, whose schools were not in part supported by the public fund, applied to the Public School Society for a committee of conference to effect a union. It was felt by the trustees that on many accounts it was better that the two sets of schools should remain separate, but, fearing further diversion of the school fund, it was desirable that the number of societies participating should be as small as possible, and arrangements were accordingly made for a transfer of the schools and property of the elder society. After some delay, in consequence of legislative action being found necessary to give a title to their real estate, on the 2d of May, 1834, the transfer was effected, all their schools and school property passing into the hands of the New York Public School Society, at an appraised valuation of $12,130.22.

The aggregate register of these schools at the time of the transfer was nearly 1,400, with an average attendance of about one half that number. They were placed in charge of a committee with powers similar to the committee on primary schools, but their administration was not satisfactory, and it was soon found that the schools had greatly diminished in numbers, efficiency, and usefulness. A committee of inquiry was appointed, and reported that, in consequence of the great anti-slavery riots and attacks on Colored people, many families had removed from the city, and of those that remained many kept their children at home ; they knew the Manumission Society as their special friends.

but knew nothing of the Public School Society; the reduction of all the schools but one to the grade of primary had given great offence; also the discharge of teachers long employed, and the discontinuance of rewards, and·taking home of spelling books; strong prejudices had grown up against the Public School Society. The committee recommended a prompt assimilation of the Colored schools to the white; the establishment of two or more upper schools in a new building; a normal school for Colored monitors; and the appointment of a Colored man as school agent, at $150 ·a year. The school on Mulberry Street at this time, 1835, was designated Colored Grammar School No. 1. A. Libolt was principal, and registered 317 pupils; there were also six primaries, located in different parts of the city, with an aggregate attendance of 925 pupils.

In 1836 a new school building was completed in Laurens Street, opened with 210 pupils, R. F. Wake (colored), principal, and was designated Colored Grammar School No. 2. Other means were taken to improve the schools, and to induce the Colored people to patronize them; the principal of No. 1, Mr. Libolt, was replaced by Mr. John Peterson, colored, a sufficient assurance of whose ability and success we have in the fact that he has been continued in the position ever since. A "Society for the Promotion of Education among Colored Children" was organized, and established two additional schools, one in Thomas Street, and one in Centre, and a marked improvement was manifest; but it required a long time to restore the confidence and interest felt before the transfer, and even up to 1848 the aggregate attendance in all the Colored schools was only 1,375 pupils.

In the winter of 1852 the first evening schools for Colored pupils were opened; one for males and one for females, and were attended by 379 pupils. In the year 1853 the Colored schools, with all the schools and school property of the Public School Society, were transferred to the "Board of Education of the City and County of New York," and still further improvements were made in them; a normal school for Colored teachers was established, with Mr. John Peterson, principal, and the schools were graded in the same manner as those for white children. Colored Grammar School No. 3, was opened at 78 West Fortieth Street, Miss Caroline W. Simpson, principal, and in the ensuing year three others were added; No. 4 in One Hundred and Twentieth Street (Harlem), Miss Nancy Thompson, principal;

No. 5, at 101 Hudson Street, P. W. Williams, principal; and No. 6, at 1,167 Broadway, Prince Leveridge, principal. Grammar Schools Nos. 2, 3, and 4, had primary departments attached, and there were also at this time three separate primary schools, and the aggregate attendance in all was 2,047. Since then the attendance in these schools has not varied much from these figures. The schools themselves have been altered and modified from time to time, as their necessity seemed to indicate; though under the general mangement of the Board of Education, they have been in the care of the school officers of the wards in which they are located, and while in some cases they received the proper attention, in others they were either wholly, or in part, neglected. A recent act has placed them directly in charge of the Board of Education, who have appointed a special committee to look after their interests, and measures are being taken by them which will give this class of schools every opportunity and convenience possessed by any other, and, it is hoped, will also improve the grade of its scholarship.[1]

NORTH CAROLINA

suffered her free persons of color to maintain schools until 1835, when they were abolished by law. During the period referred to, the Colored schools were taught by white teachers, but after 1835 the few teachers who taught Colored children in private houses were Colored persons. The public-school system of North Carolina provided that no descendant from Negro ancestors, to the fourth generation inclusive, should enjoy the benefit thereof.

OHIO.

The first schools for Colored children in Ohio were established at Cincinnati in 1820, by Colored men. These schools were not kept up regularly. A white gentleman named Wing, who taught a night school near the corner of Vine and Sixth Streets, admitted Colored pupils into his school. Owen T. B. Nickens, a public-spirited and intelligent Colored man, did much to establish schools for the Colored people.

In 1835 a school for Colored children was opened in the Baptist Church on Western Row. It was taught at different periods by Messrs. Barbour, E. Fairchild, W. Robinson, and Augustus

[1] Barnard, pp. 364–366.

Wattles; and by the following-named ladies : Misses Bishop, Matthews, Lowe, and Mrs. Merrell.   Although excellent teachers as well as upright ladies and gentlemen, they were subjected to great persecutions. They were unable to secure board, because the spirit of the whites would not countenance the teachers of Negro schools, and they spelled the word with two g's.   And at times the teachers were compelled to close the school on account of the violence of the populace. The salaries of the teachers were paid partly by an educational society of white philanthropists, and partly by such Colored persons as had means. Of the latter class were John Woodson, John Liverpool, Baker Jones, Dinnis Hill, Joseph Fowler, and William O'Hara

In 1844, the Rev. Hiram S. Gilmore, founded the "Cincinnati High School" for Colored youth.   Mr. Gilmore was a man rich in sentiments of humanity, and endowed plenteously with executive ability and this world's goods. All these he consecrated to the elevation and education of the Colored people.

This school-house was located at the east end of Harrison Street, and was in every sense a model building, comprising five rooms, a chapel, a gymnasium, and spacious grounds.   The pupils increased yearly, and the character of the school made many friends for the cause. The following persons taught in this school : Joseph H. Moore, Thomas L. Boucher, David P. Lowe, Dr. A. L. Childs, and W. F. Colburn. Dr. Childs became principal of the school in 1848.

In 1849, the Legislature passed an act establishing schools for Colored children, to be maintained at the public expense. In 1850, a board of Colored trustees was elected, teachers employed, and buildings hired. The schools were put in operation. The law of 1849 provided that so much of the funds belonging to the city of Cincinnati as would fall to the Colored youth, by a *per capita* division, should be held subject to the order of the Colored trustees. But their order was not honored by the city treasurer, upon the ground that under the constitution of the State only electors could hold office ; that Colored men were not electors, and, therefore, could not hold office. After three months the Colored schools were closed, and the teachers went out without their salaries.

John I. Gaines, an intelligent and fearless Colored leader, made a statement of the case to a public meeting of the Colored people of Cincinnati, and urged the employment of counsel to try the case in the courts. Money was raised, and Flamen Ball, Sr., was secured to make an application for *mandamus*. The case was finally carried to the Supreme Court and won by the Colored people.

In 1851, the schools were opened again ; but the rooms were small and wretchedly appointed, and the trustees unable to provide better ones. Without notice the Colored trustees were deposed. The management of the Colored schools was vested in a board of trustees and school visitors, who were also in charge of the schools for the white children. This board, under a new law, had authority to appoint six Colored men who were to manage the Colored schools with the exception of the school fund. This greatly angered the leading Colored men, and, therefore, they refused to endorse this new management.

The law was altered in 1856, giving the Colored people the· right to elect, by ballot, their own trustees.

In 1858, Nicholas Longworth built the first school-house for the Colored people, and gave them the building on a lease of fourteen years, in which time they were to pay for it—$14,000. In 1859, a large building was erected on Court Street.

Oberlin College opened its doors to Colored students from the moment of its existence in 1833, and they have never been closed at any time since. It was here that the incomparable Finney, with the fierceness of John Baptist, the gentleness of John the Evangelist, the logic of Paul, and the eloquence of Isaiah, pleaded the cause of the American slave, and gave instruction to all who sat at his feet regardless of color or race. George B. Vashon, William Howard Day, John Mercer Langston, and many other Colored men graduated from Oberlin College before any of the other leading colleges of the country had consented to give Colored men a classical education.

PENNSYLVANIA.

Anthony Benezet established, in 1750, the first school for Colored people in this State, and taught it himself without money and without price. He solicited funds for the erection of a school-house for the Colored children, and of their intellectual capacities said : " I can with truth and sincerity declare that I have found among the negroes as great variety of talents as among a like number of whites, and I am bold to assert that the notion entertained by some, that the blacks are inferior in their capacity, is a vulgar prejudice, founded on the pride or ignorance of their lordly masters, who have kept their slaves at such a distance as to be unable to form a right judgment of them."

He died on the 3d of May, 1784, universally beloved and sincerely mourned, especially by the Negro population of Pennsylvania, for whose education he had done so much. The following clause in his will illustrates his character in respect to public instruction :

" I give my above said house and lot, or ground-rent proceeding from it, and the rest and residue of my estate which shall remain undisposed of after my wife's decease, both real and personal, to the public school of Philadelphia, founded by charter, and to their successors forever, in trust, that they shall sell my house and lot on perpetual ground-rent forever, if the same be not already sold by my executors, as before mentioned, and that as speedily as may be they receive and take as much of my personal estate as may be remaining, and therewith purchase a yearly ground-rent, or ground-rents, and with the income of such ground-rent proceeding from the sale of my real estate, hire and employ a religious-minded person, or persons, to teach a number of negro, mulatto, or Indian children to read, write, arithmetic, plain accounts, needle-work, etc. And it is my particular desire, founded on the experience I have had in that service, that in the choice of such tutors, special care may be had to prefer an industrious, careful person of true piety, who may be or become suitably qualified, who would undertake the service from a principle of charity, to one more highly learned, not equally disposed ; this I desire may be carefully attended to, sensible that from the number of pupils of all ages, the irregularity of attendance their situation subjects them to will not admit of that particular inspection in their improvement usual in other schools, but that the real well-doing of the scholars will very much depend upon the master making a special conscience of doing his duty ; and shall likewise defray such other necessary expense as may occur in that service ; and as the said remaining income of my estate, after my wife's decease, will not be sufficient to defray the whole expense necessary for the support of such a school, it is my request that the overseers of the said public school shall join in the care and expense of such school, or schools, for the education of negro, mulatto, or Indian children, with any committee which may be appointed by the monthly meetings of Friends in Philadelphia, or with any other body of benevolent persons who may join in raising money and employing it for the education and care of such children ; my desire being that as such a school is now set up, it may be forever. maintained in this city."

Just before his death he addressed the following note to the " overseers of the school for the instruction of the black people."

" My friend, Joseph Clark, having frequently observed to me his desire, in case of my inability of continuing the care of the negro school, of succeeding me in that service, notwithstanding he now has a more advantageous school, by the desire of doing good to the black people makes him overlook these pecuniary advantages, I much wish the overseers of the school would take his desires under their peculiar notice and give him such due encouragement as may be proper, it being a matter of the greatest consequence to that school that the master be a person who makes it a principle to do his duty."

The noble friends were early in the field as the champions of education for the Negroes. It was Anthony Benezet, who, on the 26th of January, 1770, secured the appointment of a committee by the monthly meeting of the Friends, " to consider on the instruction of negro and mulatto children in reading, writing, and other useful learning suitable to their capacity and circumstances." On the 30th of May, 1770, a special committee of Friends sought to employ an instructor " to teach, not more at one time than thirty children, in the first rudiments of school learning and in sewing and knitting." Moles Paterson was first employed at a salary of £80 a year, and an additional sum of £11 for one half of the rent of his dwelling-house. Instruction was free to the poor ; but those who were able to pay were required to do so " at the rate of 10s. a quarter for those who write, and 7s. 6d. for others."

In 1784, William Waring was placed in charge of the larger children, at a salary of £100; and Sarah Dougherty, of the younger children and girls, in teaching spelling, reading, sewing, etc., at a salary of £50. In 1787, aid was received from David Barclay, of London, in behalf of a committee for managing a donation for the relief of Friends in America; and the sum of £500 was thus obtained, which, with the fund derived from the estate of Benezet, and £300 from Thomas Shirley, a Colored man, was appropriated to the erection of a school-house. In 1819 a committee of "women Friends," to have exclusive charge of the admission of girls and the general superintendence of the girls' school, was associated with the overseers in the charge of the school. In 1830, in order to relieve the day school of some of the male adults who had been in the habit of attending, an evening school for the purpose of instructing such persons gratuitously was opened, and has been continued to the present time. In 1844, a lot was secured on Locust Street, extending along Shield's Alley, now Aurora Street, on which a new house was erected in 1847, the expense of which was paid for in part from the proceeds of the sale of a lot bequeathed by John Pemberton. Additional accommodations were made to this building, from time to time, as room was demanded by new classes of pupils.

In 1849, a statistical return of the condition of the people of color in the city and districts of Philadelphia shows that there were then one grammar school, with 463 pupils; two public primary schools, with 339 ; and an infant school, under the charge of the Pennsylvania Abolition Society, of 70 pupils, in Clifton Street; a ragged and a moral-reform school, with 81 pupils. In West Philadelphia there was also a public school, with 67 pupils ; and, in all, there were about 20 private schools, with 300 pupils ; making an aggregate of more than 1,300 children receiving an education.

In 1859, according to Bacon's " Statistics of the Colored People of Philadelphia," there were 1,031 Colored children in public schools, 748 in charity schools of various kinds, 211 in benevolent and reformatory schools, and 331 in private schools, making an aggregate of 2,321 pupils ; besides four evening schools, one for adult males, one for females, and one for young apprentices. There were 19 Sunday-schools connected with the congregations of the Colored people, and conducted by their own teachers, containing 1,667 pupils, and four Sunday-schools gathered as mission schools by members of white congregations, with 215 pupils. There was also a " Public Library and Reading-room " connected with the "Institute for Colored Youth," established in 1853, having about 1,300 volumes ; besides three other small libraries in different parts of the city. The same pamphlet shows that there were 1,700 of the Colored population engaged in different trades and occupations, representing every department of industry.[1]

---

[1] Barnard, pp. 377, 378.

In 1794, the Pennsylvania Abolition Society established a school for children of the people of color, and in 1809 erected a school building at a cost of four thousand dollars, which they designated as "Clarkson Hall," in 1815. In 1813, a board of education was organized consisting of thirteen persons, with a visiting committee of three, whose duty it was to visit the schools once each week. In 1818, the school board, in their report, speak very kindly and encouragingly of the Clarkson Schools, which, they say, "furnish a decided refutation of the charge that the mental endowments of the descendants of Africa are inferior to those possessed by their white brethren. We can assert, without fear of contradiction, that the pupils of this seminary will sustain a fair comparison with those of any other institution in which the same elementary branches are taught."

In 1820, an effort was made to have the authorities of the white schools provide for the education of the Colored children as well as the whites, because the laws of the State required the education of all the youth. The comptrollers of the public schools confessed that the law provided for the education of "poor and indigent children," and that it extended to those of persons of color. Accordingly, in 1822, a school for the education of indigent persons of color of both sexes, was opened in Lombard Street, Philadelphia. In 1841, a primary school was opened in the same building. In 1833, the "Unclassified School" in Coates Street, and at frequent intervals after this several schools of the same grade, were started in West Philadelphia.

In 1837, by the will of Richard Humphreys, who died in 1832, an "Institute for Colored Youth" was started. The sum of ten thousand dollars was devised to certain trustees who were to pay it over to some society that might be disposed to establish a school for the education of the "descendants of the African race in school learning in the various branches of the mechanic arts and trade, and in agriculture." Thirty members of the society of Friends formed themselves into an association for the purpose of carrying out the wishes and plans of Mr. Humphreys. In the preamble of the constitution they adopted, their ideas and plans were thus set forth:

"We believe that the most successful method of elevating the moral and intellectual character of the descendants of Africa, as well as of improving their social condition, is to extend to them the benefits of a good education, and to instruct them in the knowledge of some useful trade or business, whereby they may be enabled to obtain a comfortable livelihood by their own industry ; and through these means to prepare them for fulfilling the various duties of domestic and social life with reputation and fidelity, as good citizens and pious men."

In order to carry out the feature of agricultural and mechanic arts, the association purchased a farm in Bristol township, Philadelphia County, in 1839, where boys of the Colored race were taught farming, shoemaking, and other useful trades. The incorporation of the institution was secured in 1842, and in 1844 another friend dying—Jonathan Zane—added a handsome sum to the treasury, which, with several small legacies, made $18,000 for this enterprise. But in 1846 the work came to a standstill ; the farm with its equipments was sold, and for six years very little was done, except through a night school.

In 1851, a lot for a school building was purchased on Lombard Street, and a building erected, and the school opened in the autumn of 1852, for boys, under the care of Charles L. Reason, an accomplished young Colored teacher from New York. A girls' school was opened the same year, and, under Mr. Reason's excellent instruction, many worthy and competent teachers and leaders of the Negro race came forth.

Avery College, at Allegheny City, was founded by the Rev. Charles Avery, a native of New York, but for the greater part of a long and useful life adorned by the noblest virtues, a resident of Pennyslvania. By will he left $300,000 for the christianization of the African race ; $150,000 to be used in Africa, and $150,000 in America. He left $25,000 as an endowment fund for Avery College.

At a stated meeting during the session of the Presbytery at New Castle, Pa., October 5, 1853, it was resolved that " there shall be established within our bounds, and under our supervision, an institution, to be called the Ashum Institute, for the scientific, classical, and theological education of colored youth of the male sex."

Accordingly, J. M. Dickey, A. Hamilton, R. P. Dubois, ministers ; and Samuel J. Dickey and John M. Kelton, ruling elders, were appointed a committee to perfect the idea. They were to solicit and receive funds, secure a charter from the State of Pennsylvania, and erect suitable buildings for the institute. On the 14th of November, 1853, they purchased thirty acres of land at the cost of $1,250. At the session of the Legislature in 1854, a charter was granted establishing "at or near a place called Hinsonville, in the county of Chester, an institution of learning for the scientific, classical, and theological education of colored youth of the male sex, by the name and style of Ashum Institute." The trustees were John M. Dickey, Alfred Hamilton, Robert P. Dubois, James Latta, John B. Spottswood, James M. Crowell, Samuel J. Dickey, John M. Kelton, and William Wilson.

By the provisions of the charter the trustees were empowered "to procure the endowment of the institute, not exceeding the sum of $100,000; to confer such literary degrees and academic honors as are usually granted by colleges"; and it was required that "the institute shall be open to the admission of colored pupils of the male sex, of all religious denominations, who exhibit a fair moral character, and are willing to yield a ready obedience to the general regulations prescribed for the conduct of the pupils and the government of the institute."

The institute was formally dedicated on the 31st of December, 1856. It is now known as Lincoln University.

RHODE ISLAND

conferred the right of elective franchise upon her Colored citizens by her constitution in 1843, and ever since equal privileges have been afforded them. In 1828 the Colored people of Providence petitioned for a separate school, but it was finally abolished by an act of the Legislature.

SOUTH CAROLINA

took the lead in legislating against the instruction of the Colored race, as she subsequently took the lead in seceding from the Union. In 1740, while yet a British province, the Legislature passed the following law:

"Whereas the having of slaves taught to write, or suffering them to be employed in writing, may be attended with inconveniences, *Be it enacted*, That all and every person and persons whatsoever, who shall hereafter teach, or cause any slave or slaves to be taught, or shall use or employ any slave as a scribe in any manner of writing whatever, hereafter taught to write, every such person or persons shall for every such offense forfeit the sum of £100 current money."

In 1800 the State Assembly passed an act, embracing free Colored people as well as slaves in its shameful provisions, enacting "that assemblies of slaves, free negroes, mulattoes, and mestizoes, whether composed of all or any such description of persons, or of all or any of the same and a proportion of white persons, met together for the purpose of *mental* instruction in a confined or secret place, or with the gates or doors of such place barred, bolted, or locked, so as to prevent the free ingress to and from the same," are declared to be unlawful meetings; the officers dispersing such unlawful assemblages being authorized to "inflict such corporal punishment, not exceeding twenty lashes, upon such slaves, free negroes, mulattoes, and mestizoes, as they may judge necessary for deterring them from the like unlawful assemblage in future." Another section of the same act declares, "that it shall not be lawful for any number of slaves, free negroes, mulattoes, or mestizoes, even in company with white persons, to meet together and assemble for the purpose of mental instruction or religious worship before the rising of the sun or after the going down of the same." This section was so oppressive, that in 1803, in answer to petitions from certain religious societies, an amending act was passed forbidding any person before 9 o'clock in the evening "to break into a place of meeting wherever shall be assembled the members of any religious society of the State, provided a majority of them shall be white persons, or other to disturb their devotions unless a warrant has been procured from a magistrate, if at the time of the meeting there should be a magistrate within three miles of the place; if not, the act of 1800 is to remain in full force."

On the 17th of December, 1834, definite action was taken against the education of free Colored persons as well as slaves. The first section is given:

"SECTION 1. If any person shall hereafter teach any slave to read or write, or shall aid or assist in teaching any slave to read or write, or cause or procure any slave to be taught to read or write, such person, if a free white person, upon conviction thereof shall, for each and every offense against this act, be fined not exceeding $100 and imprisonment not more than six months; or, if a free person of color, shall be whipped not exceeding fifty lashes, and fined not exceeding $50, at the discretion of the court of magistrates and freeholders before which such free person of color is tried; and if a slave, to he whipped, at the discretion of the court, not exceeding fifty lashes, the informer to be entitled to one-half the fine and to be a competent witness. And if any free person of color or slave shall keep any school or other place of instruction for teaching any slave or free person of color to read or write, such free person of color or slave shall be liable to the same fine, imprisonment, and corporal punishment as by this act are imposed and inflicted on free persons of color and slaves for teaching slaves to write."

The second section forbids, under pain of severe penalties, the employment of any Colored persons as " clerks or salesmen in or about any shop, store, or house used for trading."

TENNESSEE

passed a law in 1838 establishing a system of common schools by which the scholars were designated as " white children over the age of six years and under sixteen." In 1840 an act was passed in which no discrimination against color appeared. It simply provided that "all children between the ages of six and twenty-one years shall have the privilege of attending the public schools." And while there was never afterward any law prohibiting the education of Colored children, the schools were used exclusively by the whites.

TEXAS

never put any legislation on her statute-books withholding the blessings of the schools from the Negro, for the reason, doubtless, that she banished all free persons of color, and worked her slaves so hard that they had no hunger for books when night came.

VIRGINIA,

under Sir William Berkeley, was not a strong patron of education for the masses. For the slave there was little opportunity to learn, as he was only allowed part of Saturday to rest, and kept under the closest surveillance on the Sabbath day. The free persons of color were regarded with suspicion, and little chance was given them to cultivate their minds.

On the 2d of March, 1819, an act was passed prohibiting " all meetings or assemblages of slaves, or free negroes, or mulattoes, mixing and associating with such slaves, at any meeting-house or houses, or any other place or places, in the night, or at any school or schools for teaching them reading and writing either in the day or night." But notwithstanding this law, schools for free persons of color were kept up until the Nat. Turner insurrection in 1831, when, on the 7th of April following, the subjoined act was passed:

"Sec. 4. *And be it enacted,* That all meetings of free negroes or mulattoes at any school-house, church, meeting-house, or other place, for teaching them reading or writing, either in the day or night, under whatsoever pretext, shall be deemed and considered an unlawful assembly ; and any justice of the county or corporation wherein such assemblage shall be, either from his own knowledge, or on the information of others of such unlawful assemblage or meeting, shall issue his warrant directed to any sworn officer or officers, authorizing him or them to enter the house or houses where such unlawful assemblage or meeting may be, for the purpose of apprehending or dispersing such free negroes or mulattoes, and to inflict corporal, punishment on the offender or offenders, at the discretion of any justice of the peace, not exceeding 20 lashes.

"Sec. 5. *And be it enacted,* That if any person or persons assemble with free negroes or mulattoes at any school-house, church, meeting-house, or other place, for the purpose of instructing such free negroes or mulattoes to read or write, such persons or persons shall, on conviction thereof, be fined in a sum not exceeding $50, and, moreover, may be imprisoned, at the discretion of a jury, not exceeding two months.

"Sec. 6. *And be it enacted,* That if any white person, for pay or compensation, shall assemble with any slaves for the purpose of teaching, and shall teach any slave to read or write, such person, or any white person or persons contracting with such teacher so to act, who shall offend as aforesaid, shall, for each offense, be fined, at the discretion of a jury, in a sum not less than $10, nor exceeding $100, to be recovered on an information or indictment."

This law was rigidly enforced, and in 1851, Mrs. Margaret Douglass, a white lady from South Carolina, was cast into the Norfolk jail for violating its provisions.

West Virginia was not admitted into the Union until 1863. Wisconsin, Vermont, New Hampshire, and New Jersey did not prohibit the education of their Colored children.

THE DISTRICT OF COLUMBIA

presents a more pleasing and instructive field for the examination of the curious student of history.

In 1807, the first school-house for the use of Colored pupils was erected in Washington, D. C., by three Colored men, named George Bell, Nicholas Franklin, and Moses Liverpool. Not one of this trio of Negro educators knew a letter of the alphabet; but having lived as slaves in Virginia, they had learned to appreciate the opinion that learning was of great price. They secured a white teacher, named Lowe, and put their school in operation.

At this time the entire population of free persons amounted to 494 souls. After a brief period the school subsided, but was reorganized again in 1818. The announcement of the opening of the school was printed in the "National Intelligencer" on the 29th of August, 1818.

"A School,

Founded by an association of free people of color, of the city of Washington, called the 'Resolute Beneficial Society,' situate near the Eastern Public School and the dwelling of Mrs. Fenwick, is now open for the reception of children of free people of color and others, that ladies or gentlemen may think proper to send to be instructed in reading, writing, arithmetic, English grammar, or other branches of education apposite to their capacities, by a steady, active, and experienced teacher, whose attention is wholly devoted to the purposes described. It is presumed that free colored families will embrace the advantages thus presented to them, either by subscribing to the funds of the society, or by sending their children to the school. An improvement of the intellect and morals of colored youth being the objects of this institution, the patronage of benevolent ladies and gentlemen, by donation or subscription, is humbly solicited in aid of the fund, the demands thereon being heavy and the means at present much too limited. For the satisfaction of the public, the constitution and articles of association are printed and published. And to avoid disagreeable occurrences, no writings are to be done by the teacher for a slave, neither directly nor indirectly, to serve the purpose of a slave on any account whatever. Further particulars may be known by applying to any of the undersigned officers.

"WILLIAM COSTIN, *President.*
"GEORGE HICKS, *Vice-President.*
"JAMES HARRIS, *Secretary.*
"GEORGE BELL, *Treasurer.*
"ARCHIBALD JOHNSON, *Marshal.*
"FRED. LEWIS, *Chairman of the Committee.*
"ISAAC JOHNSON, }
"SCIPIO BEENS, } *Committee.*

" N. B.—An evening school will commence on the premises on the first Monday of October, and continue throughout the season.

" ☞ The managers of Sunday-schools in the eastern district are thus most dutifully informed that on Sabbath-days the school-house belonging to this society, if required for the tuition of colored youth, will be uniformly at their service.

August 29, 3t."

This school was first taught by a Mr. Pierpont, of Massachusetts, a relative of the poet, and after several years was succeeded by a Colored man named John Adams, the first teacher of his race in the District of Columbia. The average attendance of this school was about sixty-five or seventy.

MR. HENRY POTTER'S SCHOOL.

The third school for Colored children in Washington was established by Mr. Henry Potter, an Englishman, who opened his school about 1809, in a brick building which then stood on the southeast corner of F and Seventh streets, opposite the block where the post-office building now stands. He continued there for several years and had a large school, moving subsequently to what was then known as Clark's Row on Thirteenth Street, west, between G and H streets, north.

MRS. HALL'S SCHOOL.

During this period Mrs. Anne Maria Hall started a school on Capitol Hill, between the old Capitol and Carroll Row, on First Street, east. After continuing there with a full school for some ten years, she moved to a building which stood on what is now the vacant portion of the Casparis House lot on A Street, close to the Capitol. Some years later she went to the First Bethel Church, and after a year or two she moved to a house still standing on E Street, north, between Eleventh and Twelfth, west, and there taught many years. She was a Colored woman from Prince George's County, Maryland, and had a respectable education, which she obtained at schools with white children in Alexandria. Her husband died early, leaving her with children to support, and she betook herself to the work of a teacher, which she loved, and in which, for not less than twenty-five years, she met with uniform success. Her schools were all quite large, and the many who remember her as their teacher speak of her with great respect.

MRS. MARY BILLING'S SCHOOL.

Of the early teachers of Colored schools in this district there is no one whose name is mentioned with more gratitude and respect by the intelligent Colored residents than that of Mrs. Mary Billing, who established the first Colored school that was gathered in Georgetown. She was an English woman ; her husband, Joseph Billing, a cabinet-maker, coming from England in 1800, settled with his family that year in Washington, and dying in 1807, left his wife with three children. She was well educated, a capable and good woman, and immediately commenced teaching to support her family. At first, it is believed, she was connected with the Corporation School of Georgetown. It was while in a white school certainly that her attention was arrested by the wants of the Colored children, whom she was accustomed to receive into her schools, till the opposition became so marked that she decided to make her school exclusively Colored. She was a woman of strong religious convictions, and being English, with none of the ideas peculiar to slave society, when she saw the peculiar destitution of the Colored children in the community around her, she resolved to give her life to the class who seemed most to need her services. She established a Colored school about 1810, in a brick house still standing on Dunbarton Street, opposite the Methodist church, between Congress and High streets, remaining there till the winter of 1820–'21, when she came to Washington and opened a school in the house on H Street, near the Foundry Church, then owned by Daniel Jones, a Colored man, and still owned and occupied by a member of that family. She died in 1826, in the fiftieth year of her age. She continued her school till failing health, a year or so before her death, compelled its relinquishment. Her school was always large, it being patronized in Georgetown as well as afterward by the best Colored families of Washington, many of whom sent their children to her from Capitol Hill and the vicinity of the Navy Yard. Most of the better-educated Colored men and women now living, who were school children in her time, received the best portion of their education from her, and they all speak of her with a deep and tender sense of obligation. Henry Potter succeeded her in the Georgetown school, and after him Mr. Shay, an Englishman, who subsequently came to Washington and for many years had a large Colored school in a brick building known as the Round Tops, in the western part of the

city, near the Circle, and still later removing to the old Western
Academy building, corner of I and Seventeenth streets. He was
there till about 1830, when he was convicted of assisting a slave
to his freedom, and sent a term to the penitentiary. Mrs. Billing
had a night school in which she was greatly assisted by Mr. Monroe, a government clerk and a Presbyterian elder, whose devout
and benevolent character is still remembered in the churches.
Mrs. Billing had scholars from Bladensburg and the surrounding
country, who came into Georgetown and boarded with her and
with others. About the time when Mrs. Billing relinquished her
school in 1822 or 1823, what may be properly called

THE SMOTHERS SCHOOL-HOUSE,

was built by Henry Smothers on the corner of Fourteenth and
H streets, not far from the Treasury building. Smothers had a
small dwelling-house on this corner, and built his school-
house on the rear of the same lot. He had been long a pupil of
Mrs. Billing, and had subsequently taught a school on Washington Street, opposite the Union Hotel in Georgetown. He
opened his school in Washington in the old corporation school-
house, built in 1806, but some years before this period abandoned
as a public school-house. It was known as the Western Academy, and is still standing and used as a school-house on the corner of I and Nineteenth streets, west. When his school-house on
Fourteenth and H streets was finished, his school went into the
new quarters. This school was very large, numbering always
more than a hundred and often as high as a hundred and fifty
scholars. He taught here about two years, and was succeeded
by John W. Prout about the year 1825. Prout was a man of
ability. In 1831, May 4, there was a meeting, says the "National
Intelligencer" of that date, of "the colored citizens, large and
very respectable, in the African Methodist Episcopal Church," to
consider the question of emigrating to Liberia. John W. Prout was
chosen to preside over the assemblage, and the article in the "Intelligencer" represents him as making "a speech of decided force
and well adapted to the occasion, in support of a set of resolutions which he had drafted, and which set forth views adverse to
leaving the soil that had given them birth, their true and verita-
ble home, *without the benefits of education.*" The school under
Prout was governed by a board of trustees and was organized as

A FREE SCHOOL,

and so continued two or three years. The number of scholars was very large, averaging a hundred and fifty. Mrs. Anne Maria Hall was the assistant teacher. It relied mainly for support upon subscription, twelve and a half cents a month only being expected from each pupil, and this amount was not compulsory. The school was free to all Colored children, without money or price, and so continued two or three years, when failing of voluntary pecuniary support (it never wanted scholars), it became a regular tuition school. The school under Mr. Prout was called the "Columbian Institute," the name being suggested by John McLeod, the famous Irish school-master, who was a warm friend of this institution after visiting and commending the scholars and teachers, and who named his new building, in 1835, the Columbian Academy. The days of thick darkness to the Colored people were approaching. The Nat. Turner insurrection in Southampton County, Virginia, which occurred in August, 1831, spread terror everywhere in slave communities In this district, immediately upon that terrible occurrence, the Colored children, who had in very large numbers been received into the Sabbath-schools in the white churches, were all turned out of those schools. This event, though seeming to be a fiery affliction, proved a blessing in disguise. It aroused the energies of the Colored people, taught them self-reliance, and they organized forthwith Sabbath-schools of their own. It was in the Smothers school-house that they formed their first Sunday-school, about the year 1832, and here they continued their very large school for several years, the Fifteenth Street Presbyterian Church ultimately springing from the school organization. It is important to state in this connection that

THE SUNDAY—SCHOOL,

always an extremely important means of education for Colored people in the days of slavery, was emphatically so in the gloomy times now upon them. It was the Sabbath-school that taught the great mass of the free people of color about all the school knowledge that was allowed them in those days, and hence the consternation which came upon them when they found themselves excluded from the schools of the white churches. Lindsay Muse, who has been the messenger for eighteen Secretaries of the Navy, successively, during fifty-four years, from 1828 to the present time, John Brown, Benjamin M. McCoy, Mr. Smallwood, Mrs. Charlotte Norris, afterward wife of Rev. Eli Nugent, and Siby McCoy, are the only survivors of the resolute little band of Colored men and women who gathered with and guided that Sunday-school. They had, in the successor of Mr. Prout, a man after their own heart,

JOHN F. COOK,

who came into charge of this school in August, 1834, about eight years after his aunt, Alethia Tanner, had purchased his freedom. He learned the shoemaker's trade in his boyhood, and worked diligently, after the purchase of his freedom, to make some return to his aunt for the purchase-money. About the time of his becoming of age, he dislocated his shoulder, which compelled him to seek other employment, and in 1831, the year of his majority, he obtained the place of assistant messenger in the Land Office. Hon. John Wilson, now Third Auditor of the Treasury, was the messenger, and was Cook's firm friend till the day of his death. Cook had been a short time at school under the instruction of Smothers and Prout, but when he entered the Land Office his education was at most only the ability to stumble along a little in a primary reading-book. He, however, now gave himself in all his leisure moments, early and late, to study. Mr. Wilson remembers his indefatigable application, and affirms that it was a matter of astonishment at the time, and that he has seen nothing in all his observations to surpass and scarcely to equal it. He was soon able to write a good hand, and was employed with his pen in clerical work by the sanction of the commissioner, Elisha Hayward, who was much attached to him. Cook was now beginning to look forward to the life of a teacher, which, with the ministry, was the only work not menial in its nature then open to an educated Colored man. At the end of three years he resigned his place in the Land Office, and entered upon the work which he laid down only with his life. It was then that he gave himself wholly to study and the business of education, working with all his might; his school numbering quite a hundred scholars in the winter and a hundred and fifty in the summer. He had been in his work one year when the storm which had been, for some years, under the discussion of the slavery question, gathering over the country at large, burst upon this district.

THE SNOW RIOT,

or "Snow storm," as it has been commonly called, which occurred in September, 1835, is an event that stands vividly in the
memory of all Colored people who lived in this community at
that time. Benjamin Snow, a smart Colored man, keeping a
restaurant on the corner of Pennsylvania Avenue and Sixth
Street, was reported to have made some remark of a bravado
kind derogatory to the wives of white mechanics; whereupon this
class, or those assuming to represent them, made a descent upon
his establishment, destroying all his effects. Snow himself, who
denied using the offensive language, with difficulty escaped unharmed, through the management of white friends, taking refuge
in Canada, where he still resides. The military was promptly
called to the rescue, at the head of which was General Walter
Jones, the eminent lawyer, who characterized the rioters, greatly
to their indignation, as "a set of ragamuffins," and his action was
thoroughly sanctioned by the city authorities.

At the same time, also, there was a fierce excitement among
the mechanics at the Navy Yard, growing out of the fact that a
large quantity of copper bolts being missed from the yard and
found to have been carried out in the dinner-pails by the hands,
the commandant had forbid eating dinners in the yard. This
order was interpreted as an insult to the white mechanics, and
threats were made of an assault on the yard, which was put in a
thorough state of defence by the commandant. The rioters
swept through the city, ransacking the houses of the prominent
Colored men and women, ostensibly in search of anti-slavery
papers and documents, the most of the gang impelled undoubtedly by hostility to the Negro race and by motives of plunder.
Nearly all the Colored school-houses were partially demolished
and the furniture totally destroyed, and in several cases they
were completely ruined. Some private houses were also torn
down or burnt. The Colored schools were nearly all broken up,
and it was with the greatest difficulty that the Colored churches
were saved from destruction, as their Sabbath-schools were regarded, and correctly regarded, as the means through which the
Colored people, at that time, procured much of their education.

The rioters sought, especially, for John F. Cook, who, however, had seasonably taken from the stable the horse of his
friend, Mr. Hayward, the Commissioner of the Land Office, an
anti-slavery man, and fled precipitately from the city. They

marched to his school-house, destroyed all the books and furniture, and partially destroyed the building. Mrs. Smothers, who owned both the school-house and the dwelling adjoining the lots, was sick in her house at the time, but an alderman, Mr. Edward Dyer, with great courage and nobleness of spirit, stood between the house and the mob for her protection, declaring that he would defend her house from molestation with all the means he could command. They left the house unharmed, and it is still standing on the premises. Mr. Cook went to Columbia, Pennsylvania, opened a school there, and did not venture back to his home till the autumn of 1836. At the time the riot broke out, General Jackson was absent in Virginia. He returned in the midst of the tumult, and immediately issuing orders in his bold, uncompromising manner to the authorities to see the laws respected at all events, the violence was promptly subdued. It was, nevertheless, a very dark time for the Colored people. The timid class did not for a year or two dare to send their children to school, and the whole mass of the Colored people dwelt in fear day and night. In August, 1836, Mr. Cook returned from Pennsylvania and reopened his school, which under him had, in 1834, received the name of

UNION SEMINARY.

During his year's absence he was in charge of a free Colored public school in Columbia, Lancaster County, Pennsylvania, which he surrendered to the care of Benjamin M. McCoy when he came back to his home, Mr. McCoy going there to fill out his engagement.

He resumed his work with broad and elevated ideas of his business. This is clearly seen in the plan of his institution, embraced in the printed annual announcements and programmes of his annual exhibitions, copies of which have been preserved. The course of study embraced three years, and there was a male and a female department, Miss Catharine Costin at one period being in charge of the female department. Mr. Seaton, of the " National Intelligencer," among other leading and enlightened citizens and public men, used to visit his school from year to year, and watch its admirable working with deep and lively interest. Cook was at this period not only watching over his very large school, ranging from 100 to 150 or more pupils, but was active in the formation of the " First Colored Presbyterian

Church of Washington," which was organized in November, 1841, by Rev. John C. Smith, D.D., and worshipped in this school-house. He was now also giving deep study to the preparation for the ministry, upon which, in fact, as a licentiate of the African Methodist Episcopal Church, he had already in some degree entered. At a regular meeting of " The presbytery of the District of Columbia," held in Alexandria, May 3, 1842, this church, now commonly called the Fifteenth Street Presbyterian Church, was formally received under the care of that presbytery, the first and still the only Colored Presbyterian church in the district. Mr. Cook was elected the first pastor July 13, 1843, and preached his trial sermon before ordination on the evening of that day in the Fourth Presbyterian Church (Dr. J. C. Smith's) in the city, in the presence of a large congregation. This sermon is remembered as a manly production, delivered with great dignity and force, and deeply imbued with the spirit of his work. He was ordained in the Fifteenth Street Church the next evening, and continued to serve the church with eminent success till his death in 1855. Rev. John C. Smith, D.D., who had preached his ordination sermon, and been his devoted friend and counsellor for nearly twenty years, preached his funeral sermon, selecting as his text, " There was a man sent from God whose name was John." There were present white as well as Colored clergymen of no less than five denominations, many of the oldest and most respectable citizens, and a vast concourse of all classes white and Colored. " The Fifteenth Street Church," in the words of Dr. Smith in relation to them and their first pastor, " is now a large and flourishing congregation of spiritually-minded people. They have been educated in the truth and the principles of our holy religion, and in the new, present state of things the men of this church are trusted, relied on as those who fear God and keep His commandments. The church is the monument to John F. Cook, the first pastor, who was faithful in all his house, a workman who labored night and day for years, and has entered into his reward. ' Blessed are the dead who die in the Lord.' ' They rest from their labors, and their works do follow them.' "

In 1841, when he entered, in a preliminary and informal way, upon the pastorate of the Fifteenth Street Church, he seems to have attempted to turn his seminary into a high school, limited to twenty-five or thirty pupils, exclusively for the more advanced scholars of both sexes; and his plan of studies to that end, as seen in his prospectus, evinces broad and elevated views—a desire to aid in lifting his race to higher things in education than they had yet attempted. His plans were not put into execution, in the matter of a high school, being frustrated by the circumstances that there were so few good schools in the city for the Colored people, at that period, that his old patrons would not allow him to shut off the multitude of primary scholars which were depending upon his school. His seminary, however, continued to maintain its high standard, and had an average attendance of quite 100 year after year, till he surrendered up his work in death.

He raised up a large family and educated them well. The oldest of the sons, John and George, were educated at Oberlin College. The other three, being young, were in school when the father died. John and George, it will be seen, succeeded their father as teachers, continuing in the business down to the present year. Of the two daughters, the elder was a teacher till married in 1866, and the other is now a teacher in the public schools of the city. One son served through the war as sergeant in the Fortieth Colored Regiment, and another served in the navy.

At the death of the father, March 21, 1855, the school fell into the hands of the son, John F. Cook, who continued it till May, 1857, when it passed to a younger son, George F. T. Cook, who moved it from its old home, the Smothers House, to the basement of the Presbyterian Church, in the spring of 1858, and maintained it till July, 1859. John F. Cook, jr., who had erected a new school-house on Sixteenth Street, in 1862, again gathered the school which the tempests of the war had dispersed, and continued it till June, 1867, when the new order of things had opened ample school facilities throughout the city, and the teacher was called to other duties. Thus ended the school which had been first gathered by Smothers nearly forty-five years before, and which, in that long period, had been continually maintained with seldom less than one hundred pupils, and for the most part with one hundred and fifty, the only suspensions being in the year of the Snow riot, and in the two years which ushered in the war.

The Smothers House, after the Cook school was removed in 1858, was occupied for two years by a *free Catholic school*, supported by "The St. Vincent de Paul Society," a benevolent organization of Colored people. It was a very large school with two departments, the boys under David Brown, and the girls under Eliza Anne Cook, and averaging over one hundred and fifty scholars. When this school was transferred to another house, Rev. Chauncey Leonard, a Colored Baptist clergyman, now pastor of a church in Washington, and Nannie Waugh opened a school there, in 1861, that became as large as that which had preceded it in the same place. This school was broken up in 1862 by the destruction of the building at the hands of the incendiaries, who, even at that time, were inspired with all their accustomed vindictiveness toward· the Colored people. But this was their last heathenish jubilee, and from the ashes of many burnings imperishable liberty has sprung forth.

About the time that Smothers built his school-house, in 1823,

LOUISA PARKE COSTIN'S SCHOOL

was established in her father's house on Capitol Hill, on A Street, south, under the shadow of the Capitol. This Costin family came from Mount Vernon immediately after the death of Martha Washington, in 1802. The father, William Costin, who died suddenly in his bed, May 31, 1842, was for twenty-four years messenger for the Bank of Washington in this city. His death was noticed at length in the columns of the "National Intelligencer" in more than one communication at the time. The obituary notice, written under the suggestions of the bank officers who had previously passed a resolution expressing their respect for his memory, and appropriating fifty dollars toward the funeral expenses, says: "It is due to the deceased to say that his colored skin covered a benevolent heart"; concluding with this language: "The deceased raised respectably a large family of children of his own, and, in the exercise of the purest benevolence, took into his family and supported four orphan children. The tears of the orphan will moisten his grave, and his memory will be dear to all those—a numerous class—who have experienced his kindness"; and adding these lines:

> " Honor and shame from *no condition* rise ;
> Act well your part—there all the honor lies."

John Quincy Adams, also, a few days afterward, in a discussion of the wrongs of slavery, alluded to the deceased in these words, " The late William Costin, though he was not white, was as much respected as any man in the district, and the large concourse of citizens that attended his remains to the grave, as well white as black, was an evidence of the manner in which he was estimated by the citizens of Washington." His portrait, taken by the direction of the bank authorities, still hangs in the directors' room, and it may also be seen in the houses of more than one of the old and prominent residents of the city.

William Costin's mother, Ann Dandridge, was the daughter of a half-breed (Indian and Colored), her grandfather being a Cherokee chief, and her reputed father was the father of Martha Dandridge, afterward Mrs. Custis, who, in 1759, was married to General Washington. These daughters, Ann and Martha, grew up together on the ancestral plantations. William-Costin's reputed father was white, and belonged to a prominent family in Virginia, but the mother, after his birth, married one of the Mount Vernon slaves by the name of Costin, and the son took the name of William Costin. His mother, being of Indian descent, made him, under the laws of Virginia, a free-born man. In 1800 he married Philadelphia Judge (his cousin), one of Martha Washington's slaves, at Mount Vernon, where both were born in 1780. The wife was given by Martha Washington at her decease to her granddaughter, Eliza Parke Custis, who was the wife of Thomas Law, of Washington. Soon after William Costin and his wife came to Washington, the wife's freedom was secured on kind and easy terms, and the children were all born free. This is the account which William Costin and his wife and his mother, Ann Dandridge, always gave of their ancestry, and they were persons of great precision in all matters of family history, as well as of the most marked scrupulousness in their statements. Their seven children, five daughters and two sons, went to school with the white children on Capitol Hill, to Mrs. Maria Haley and other teachers. The two younger daughters, Martha and Frances, finished their education at the Colored convent in Baltimore. Louisa Parke and Ann had passed their school days before the convent was founded. Louisa Parke Costin opened her school at nineteen years of age, continuing it with much success till her sudden death in 1831, the year in which her mother also died. When Martha returned from the convent seminary, a year or so later, she reopened the school, continuing it till about 1839. This school, which was maintained some fifteen years, was always very full. The three surviving sisters own and reside in the house which their father built about 1812. One of these sisters married Richard Henry Fisk, a Colored man of good education, who died in California, and she now has charge of the Senate ladies' reception-room. Ann Costin was for several years in the family of Major Lewis (at Woodlawn, Mount Vernon), the nephew of Washington. Mrs. Lewis (Eleanor Custis) was the granddaughter of Martha Washington. This school was not molested by the mob of 1835, and it was always under the care of a well-bred and well-educated teacher.

THE WESLEYAN SEMINARY.

While Martha Costin was teaching, James Enoch Ambush, a Colored man, had also a large school in the basement of the Israel Bethel Church, on Capitol Hill, for a while, commencing there in April, 1833, and continuing in various places till 1843, when he built a school-house on E Street, south, near Tenth, island, and established what was known as "The Wesleyan Seminary," and which was successfully maintained for thirty-two years, till the close of August, 1865. The school-house still stands, a comfortable one-story wooden structure, with the sign "Wesleyan Seminary" over the door, as it has been there for twenty-five years. This was the only Colored school on the island of any account for many years, and in its humble way it accomplished a great amount of good. For some years Mr. Ambush had given much study to botanic medicine, and since closing his school he has become a botanic physician. He is a man of fine sense, and without school advantages, has acquired a respectable education.

FIRST SEMINARY FOR COLORED GIRLS.

The first seminary in the District of Columbia for Colored girls was established in Georgetown, in 1827, under the special auspices of Father Vanlomen, a benevolent and devout Catholic priest, then pastor of the Holy Trinity Church, who not only gave this interesting enterprise his hand and his heart, but for several years himself taught a school of Colored boys three days in a week, near the Georgetown college gate, in a small frame house, which was afterward famous as the residence of the broken-hearted widow of Commodore Decatur. This female seminary was under the care of Maria Becraft, who was the most remarkable Colored young woman of her time in the district, and, perhaps, of any time. Her father, William Becraft, born while his mother, a free woman, was the housekeeper of Charles Carroll, of Carrollton, always had the kindest attentions of this great man, and there are now pictures, more than a century and a half old, and other valuable relics from the Carroll family in the possession of the Becraft family, in Georgetown, which Charles Carroll, of Carrollton, in his last days presented to William Becraft as family keepsakes. William Becraft lived in Georgetown sixty-four years, coming there when eighteen years of age. He was for many years chief steward of Union Hotel, and a remarkable man, respected and honored by everybody. When he died, the press of the district noticed, in a most prominent manner, his life and character. From one of the extended obituary notices, marked with heavy black lines, the following paragraph is copied :

" He was among the last surviving representatives of the old school of well-bred, confidential, and intelligent domestics, and was widely known at home and abroad from his connection, in the capacity of steward for a long series of years, and probably from its origin, and until a recent date, with the Union Hotel, Georgetown, with whose guests, for successive generations, his benevolent and venerable aspect, dignified and obliging manners, and moral excellence, rendered him a general favorite."

Maria Becraft was marked, from her childhood, for her uncommon intelligence and refinement, and for her extraordinary piety. She was born in 1805, and first went to school for a year to Henry Potter, in Washington, about 1812; afterward attending Mrs. Billing's school constantly till 1820. She then, at the age of fifteen, opened a school for girls in Dunbarton Street, in Georgetown, and gave herself to the work, which she loved, with the greatest assiduity, and with uniform success. In 1827, when she was twenty-two years of age, her remarkable beauty and elevation of character so much impressed Father Vanlomen, the good priest, that he took it in hand to give her a higher style of school in which to work for her sex and race, to the education of which she had now fully consecrated herself. Her school was accordingly transferred to a larger building, which still stands on Fayette Street, opposite the convent, and there she opened a boarding and day school for Colored girls, which she continued with great success till August, 1831, when she surrendered her little seminary into the care of one of the girls that she had trained, and in October of that year joined the convent at Baltimore as a Sister of Providence, where she was the leading teacher till she died, in December, 1833, a great loss to that young institution, which was contemplating this noble young woman as its future Mother Superior. Her seminary in Georgetown averaged from thirty to thirty-five pupils, and there are those living who remember the troop of girls, dressed uniformly, which was wont to follow in procession their pious and refined teacher to devotions on the Sabbath at Holy Trinity Church. The school comprised girls from the best Colored families of Georgetown, Washington, Alexandria, and surrounding country. The sisters of the Georgetown convent were the admirers of Miss Becraft, gave her instruction, and extended to her most heartfelt aid and approbation in all her noble work, as they were in those days wont to do in behalf of the aspiring Colored girls who sought for education, withholding themselves from such work only when a depraved and degenerate public sentiment upon the subject of educating the Colored people had compelled them to a more rigid line of demarcation between the races. Ellen Simonds and others conducted the school a few years, but with the loss of its original teacher it began to fail, and finally became extinct. Maria Becraft is remembered, wherever she was known, as a woman of the rarest sweetness and exaltation of Christian life, graceful and attractive in person and manners, gifted, well-educated, and wholly devoted to doing good. Her name as a Sister of Providence was Sister Aloyons.

MISS MYRTILLA MINER'S SEMINARY

for Colored girls was initiated in Washington. This philanthropic woman was born in Brookfield, Madison County, New York, in 1815. Her parents were farmers, with small resources for the support of a large family. The children were obliged to work, and the small advantages of a common school were all the educational privileges furnished to them. Hop-raising was a feature in their farming, and this daughter was accustomed to work in the autumn, picking the hops. She was of a delicate physical organization, and suffered exceedingly all her life with spinal troubles. Being a girl of extraordinary intellectual activity, her place at home chafed her spirit. She was restless, dissatisfied with her lot, looked higher than her father, dissented from his ideas of woman's education, and, in her desperation, when about twenty-three years old, wrote to Mr. Seward, then recently elected Governor of her State, asking him if he could show her how it was possible for a woman in her circumstances to become a scholar; receiving from him the reply that he could not, but hoped a better day was coming, wherein woman might have a chance to be and to do to the extent of her abilities. Hearing at this time of a school at Clinton, Oneida County, New York, for young women, on the manual-labor system, she decided to go there; but her health being such as to make manual labor impossible at the time, she wrote to the principal of the Clover Street Seminary, Rochester, New York, who generously received her, taking her notes for the school bills, to be paid after completing her education. Grateful for this noble act, she afterward sent her younger sister there to be educated, for her own associate as a teacher; and the death of this talented sister, when about to graduate and come as her assistant in Washington, fell upon her with crushing force. In the Rochester school, with Myrtilla Miner, were two free Colored girls, and this association was the first circumstance to turn her thoughts to the work to which she gave her life. From Rochester she went to Mississippi, as a teacher of planters' daughters, and it was what she was compelled to see, in this situation, of the dreadful practices and conditions of slavery, that filled her soul with a pity for the Colored race, and a detestation of the system that bound them, which held possession of her to the last day of her life. She remained there several years, till her indignant utterances, which she would not withhold, compelled her employer, fearful of the results, to part reluctantly with a teacher whom he valued. She came home broken down with sickness, caused by the harassing sights and sounds that she had witnessed in plantation life, and while in this condition she made a solemn vow that whatever of life remained to her should be given to the work of ameliorating the condition of the Colored people. Here her great work begins. She made up her mind to do something for the education of free Colored girls, with the idea that through the influence of educated Colored women she could lay the solid foundations for the disenthrallment of their race. She selected the district for the field of her efforts, because it was the common property of the nation, and because the laws of the district

gave her the right to educate *free* Colored children, and she
attempted to teach none others. She opened her plan to
many of the leading friends of freedom, in an extensive correspondence, but found especially, at this time, a wise and
warm encourager and counsellor in her scheme, in William
R. Smith, a Friend, of Farmington, near Rochester, New York,
in whose family she was now a private teacher. Her correspondents generally gave her but little encouragement, but wished
her God-speed in what she should dare in the good cause.
One Friend wrote her from Philadelphia; entering warmly
into her scheme, but advised her to wait till funds could be
collected. "I do not want the wealth of Crœsus," was her
reply ; and the Friend sent her $100, and with this capital, in
the autumn of 1851, she came to Washington to establish a
Normal School for the education of Colored girls, having associated with her Miss Anna Inman, an accomplished and benevolent
lady of the Society of Friends, from Southfield, Rhode Island,
who, however, after teaching a class of Colored girls in French,
in the house of Jonathan Jones, on the island, through the winter, returned to New England. In the autumn of 1851 Miss
Miner commenced her remarkable work here in a small room,
about fourteen feet square, in the frame house then, as now,
owned and occupied by Edward C. Younger, a Colored man, as
his dwelling, on Eleventh Street, near New York Avenue. With
but two or three girls to open the school, she soon had a room-
ful, and to secure larger accommodation, moved, after a couple of
months, to a house on F Street, north, between Eighteenth and
Nineteenth streets, west, near the houses then occupied by
William T. Carroll and Charles H. Winder. This house furnished
her a very comfortable room for her school, which was composed
of well-behaved girls from the best Colored families of the district. The persecution of those neighbors, however, compelled
her to leave, as the Colored family who occupied the house was
threatened with conflagration, and after one month her little
school found a more unmolested home in the dwelling-house of
a German family on K Street, near the western market. After
tarrying a few months here, she moved to L Street, into a room
in the building known as "The Two Sisters," then occupied by
a white family. She now saw that the success of her school
demanded a school-house, and in reconnoitring the ground she
found a spot suiting her ideas as to size and locality, with a

house on it, and in the market at a low price. She raised the money, secured the spot, and thither, in the summer of 1851, she moved her school, where for seven years she was destined to prosecute, with the most unparalleled energy and conspicuous success, her remarkable enterprise. This lot, comprising an entire square of three acres, between Nineteenth and Twentieth streets, west, N and O streets, north, and New Hampshire Avenue, selected under the guidance of Miss Miner, the contract being perfected through the agency of Sayles J. Bowen, Thomas Williamson, and Allen M. Gangewer, was originally conveyed in trust to Thomas Williamson and Samuel Rhodes, of the Society of Friends, in Philadelphia. It was purchased of the executors of the will of John Taylor, for $4,000, the deed being executed June 8, 1853, the estimated value of the property now being not less than $30,000. The money was mainly contributed by Friends, in Philadelphia, New York, and New England. Catharine Morris, a Friend, of Philadelphia, was a liberal benefactor of the enterprise, advancing Miss Miner $2,000, with which to complete the purchase of the lot, the most, if not all, of which sum, it is believed, she ultimately gave to the institution; and Harriet Beecher Stowe was another generous friend, who gave her money and her heart to the support of the brave woman who had been willing to go forth alone at the call of duty. Mr. Rhodes, some years editor of the "Friends' Quarterly Review," died several years ago, near Philadelphia. Mr. Williamson, a conveyancer in that city, and father of Passmore Williamson, is still living, but some years ago declined the place of trustee. The board, at the date of the act of incorporation, consisted of Benjamin Tatham, a Friend, of New York City, Mrs. Nancy M. Johnson, of Washington, and Myrtilla Miner, and the transfer of the property to the incorporated body was made a few weeks prior to Miss Miner's death. This real estate, together with a fund of $4,000 in government stocks, is now in the hands of a corporate body, under act of Congress approved March 3, 1863, and is styled "The Institution for the Education of Colored Youth in the District of Columbia." The officers of the corporation at this time are John C. Underwood, president; Francis G. Shaw, treasurer; George E. Baker, secretary; who, with Nancy M. Johnson, S. J. Bowen, Henry Addison, and Rachel Howland, constitute the executive committee. The purpose of the purchase of this property is declared, in a paper signed by Mr.

Williamson and Mr. Rhodes, dated Philadelphia, June 8, 1858, to have been " *especially for the education of colored girls.*"

This paper also declares that " the grounds were purchased at the special instance of Myrtilla Miner," and that " the contributions by which the original price of said lot, and also the cost of the subsequent improvements thereof, were procured chiefly by her instrumentality and labors." The idea of Miss Miner in planting a school here was to train up a class of Colored girls, in the midst of slave institutions, who should show forth in their culture and capabilities, to the country and to mankind, that the race was fit for something higher than the degradation which rested upon them. The amazing energy with which this frail woman prosecuted her work is well known to those who took knowledge of her career. She visited the Colored people of her district from house to house, and breathed a new life into them pertaining to the education of their daughters. Her correspondence with the philanthropic men and women of the North was immense. She importuned Congressmen, and the men who shaped public sentiment through the columns of the press, to come into her school and see her girls, and was ceaseless in her activities day and night, in every direction, to build up, in dignity and refinement, her seminary, and to force its merits upon public attention.

The buildings upon the lot when purchased—a small frame dwelling of two stories, not more than twenty-five by thirty-five feet in dimensions, with three small cabins on the other side of the premises—served for the seminary and the homes of the teacher and her assistant. The most aspiring and decently bred Colored girls of the district were gathered into the school; and the very best Colored teachers in the schools of the district at the present time, are among those who owe their education to this self-sacrificing teacher and her school. Mrs. Means, aunt of the wife of General Pierce, then President of the United States, attracted by the enthusiasm of this wonderful person, often visited her in the midst of her work, with the kindest feelings; and the fact that the carriage from the Presidential mansion was in this way frequently seen at the door of this humble institution, did much to protect it from the hatred with which it was surrounded.

Mr. Seward and his family were very often seen at the school, both Mrs. Seward and her daughter Fanny being constant visitors;

the latter, a young girl at the time, often spending a whole day there. Many other Congressmen of large and generous instincts, some of them of pro-slavery party relations, went out there, all confessing their admiration of the resolute woman and her school, and this kept evil men in abeyance.

The opposition to the school throughout the district was strong and very general, among the old as well as the young. Even Walter Lenox, who, as mayor, when the school was first started, gave the teacher assurances of favor in her work, came out in 1857, following the prevailing current of depraved public sentiment and feeding its tide, in an elaborate article in the "National Intelligencer," under his own signature; assailed the school in open and direct language, urging against it that it was raising the standard of education among the Colored population, and distinctly declaring that the white population of the district would not be just to themselves to permit the continuance of an institution which had the temerity to extend to the Colored people "a degree of instruction so far beyond their social and political condition, which condition must continue," the article goes on to say, "in this and every other slave-holding community." This article, though fraught with extreme ideas, and to the last degree proscriptive and inflammatory, neither stirred any open violence, nor deterred the courageous woman in the slightest degree from her work. When madmen went to her school-room threatening her with personal violence, she laughed them to shame; and when they threatened to burn her house, she told them that they could not stop her in that way, as another house, better than the old, would immediately rise from its ashes.

The house was set on fire in the spring of 1860, when Miss Miner was asleep in the second story, alone, in the night-time, but the smell of the smoke awakened her in time to save the building and herself from the flames, which were extinguished. The school-girls, also, were constantly at the mercy of coarse and insulting boys along the streets, who would often gather in gangs before the gate to pursue and terrify these inoffensive children, who were striving to gather wisdom and understanding in their little sanctuary. The police took no cognizance of such brutality in those days. But their dauntless teacher, uncompromising, conscientious, and self-possessed in her aggressive work, in no manner turned from her course by this persecution, was, on the other hand, stimulated thereby to higher vigilance and energy in her great undertaking. The course of instruction in the school was indeed of a higher order than had hitherto been opened to the Colored people of the district, as was denounced against the school by Walter Lenox, in his newspaper attack. Lectures upon scientific and literary subjects were given by professional and literary gentlemen, who were friends to the cause. The spacious grounds afforded to each pupil an ample space for a flower bed, which she was enjoined to cultivate with her own hands and to thoroughly study. And an excellent library, a collection of paintings and engravings, the leading magazines and choice newspapers, were gathered and secured for the humble home of learning, which was all the while filled with students, the most of whom were bright, ambitious girls, composing a female Colored school, which, in dignity and usefulness, has had no equal in the district since that day. It was her custom to gather in her vacations and journeys not only money, but every thing else that would be of use in her school, and in this way she not only collected books, but maps, globes, philosophical, and chemical, and mathematical apparatus, and a great variety of things to aid in her instruction in illustrating all branches of knowledge. This collection was stored in the school building during the war, and was damaged by neglect, plundered by soldiers, and what remains is not of much value. The elegant sofa-bedstead which she used during all her years in the seminary, and which would be an interesting possession for the seminary, was sold, with her other personal effects, to Dr. Carrie Brown (Mrs. Winslow), of Washington, one of her bosom friends, who stood at her pillow when she died.

Her plan embraced the erection of spacious structures, upon the site which had been most admirably chosen, complete in all their appointments for the full accommodation of a school of one hundred and fifty boarding scholars. The seminary was to be a female college, endowed with all the powers and professorships belonging to a first-class college for the other sex. She did not contemplate its springing up into such proportions, like a mushroom, in a single night, but it was her ambition that the institution should one day attain that rank. In the midst of her anxious, incessant labors, her physical system began so sensibly to fail, that in the summer of 1858, under the counsel of the friends of herself and her cause, she went North to seek health, and, as usual in all her journeys, to beg for her seminary, leaving her girls in the care of Emily Howland, a noble young woman, who came down here for the love of the cause, without money and without price, from the vicinity of Auburn, New York. In the autumn, Miss Miner returned to her school; Miss Howland still continuing with her through the winter, a companion in her trials, aiding her in her duties, and consenting to take charge of the school again in the summer of 1859, while Miss Miner was on another journey for funds and health. In the autumn of that year, after returning from her journey, which was not very successful, she determined to suspend the school, and to go forth into the country with a most persistent appeal for money to erect a seminary building, as she had found it impossible to get a house of any character started with the means already in her hands. She could get no woman, whom she deemed fit to take her work, willing to continue her school, and in the spring of 1860, leasing the premises, she went North on her errand. In the ensuing year she traversed many States, but the shadow of the Rebellion was on her path, and she gathered neither much money nor much strength. The war came, and in October, 1862, hoping, but vainly, for health from a sea-voyage and from the Pacific climate, she sailed from New York to California. When about to return, in 1866, with vivacity of body and spirit, she was thrown from a carriage in a fearful manner; blighting all the high hopes of resuming her school under the glowing auspices she had anticipated, as she saw the Rebellion and the hated system tumbling to pieces. She arrived in New York, in August of that year, in a most shattered condition of body, though with the fullest confidence that she should speedily be well and at her work in Washington. In the first days of December she went to Washington in a dying condition, still resolute to resume her work; was carried to the residence of her tried friend, Mrs. Nancy M. Johnson; and on the tenth of that month, surrounded by the friends who had stood with her in other days, she put off her wasted and wearied body in the city which had witnessed her trials and her triumphs, and her remains slumber in Oak Hill Cemetery.

Her seminary engaged her thoughts to the last day of her life. She said in her last hours that she had come back here to resume her work, and could not leave it thus unfinished. No marble marks the resting-place of this truly wonderful woman, but her memory is certainly held precious in the hearts of her throngs of pupils, in the hearts of the Colored people of this district, and of all who took knowledge of her life, and who reverenced the cause in which she offered herself a willing sacrifice. Her assistants in the school were Helen Moore, of Washington ; Margaret Clapp, Amanda Weaver, and Anna H. Searing, of New York State, and two of her pupils, Matilda Jones, of Washington, and Emma Brown, of Georgetown, both of whom subsequently, through the influence of Miss Miner and Miss Howland, finished their education at Oberlin, and have since been most superior teachers in Washington. Most of the assistant teachers from the North were from families connected with the Society of Friends, and it has been seen that the bulk of the money came from that society. The sketch would be incomplete without a special tribute to Lydia B. Mann, sister of Horace Mann, who came here in the fall of 1856, from the Colored Female Orphan Asylum of Providence, R. I., of which she was then, as she continues to be, the admirable superintendent, and, as a pure labor of love, took care of the school in the most superior manner through the autumn and winter, while Miss Miner was North recruiting her strength and pleading for contributions. It was no holiday duty to go into that school, live in that building, and work alone with head and hands, as was done by all those refined and educated women who stood from time to time in that humble, persecuted seminary. Miss Mann is gratefully remembered by her pupils here and their friends.

Mention should also be made of Emily Howland, who stood by Miss Miner in her darkest days, and whose whole heart was with her in all her work. She is a woman of the largest and most self-sacrificing purposes, who has been and still is giving her best years, all her powers, talents, learning, refinement, wealth, and personal toil, to the education and elevation of the Colored race. While here she adopted, and subsequently educated in the best manner, one of Miss Miner's pupils, and assisted several others of her smart girls in completing their education at Oberlin. During the war she was teaching contrabands in the hospital and the camp, and is now engaged in planting a colony of Colored people in Virginia with homes and a school-house of their own.

A seminary, such as was embraced in the plan of Miss Miner, is exceedingly demanded by the interest of Colored female education in the District of Columbia and the country at large, and any scheme by which the foundations that she laid so well may become the seat of such a school, would be heartily approved by all enlightened friends of the Colored race. The trustees of the Miner property, not insensible of their responsibilities, have been carefully watching for the moment when action on their part would seem to be justified. They have repeatedly met in regard to the matter, but, in their counsels, hitherto, have deemed it wise to wait further developments. They are now about to hold another meeting, it is understood, and it is to be devoutly hoped that some plan will be adopted by which a school of a high order may be, in due time, opened for Colored girls in this district, who exceedingly need the refining, womanly training of such a school.

The original corporators of Miss Miner's institution were Henry Addison, John C. Underwood, George C. Abbott, William H. Channing, Nancy M. Johnson, and Myrtilla Miner. The objects, as expressed in the charter, "are to educate and improve the moral and intellectual condition of such of the colored youth of the nation as may be placed under its care and influence."

MARY WORMLEY'S SCHOOL.

In 1830, William Wormley built a school-house for his sister Mary, near the corner of Vermont Avenue and I Street, where the restaurant establishment owned and occupied by his brother, James Wormley, now stands. He had educated his sister expressly for a teacher, at great expense, at the Colored Female Seminary in Philadelphia, then in charge of Miss Sarah Douglass, an accomplished Colored lady, who is still a teacher of note in the Philadelphia Colored High School. William Wormley was at that time a man of wealth. His livery-stable, which occupied the place where the Owen House now stands, was one of the largest and best in the city. Miss Wormley had just brought her school into full and successful operation when her health broke down, and she lived scarcely two years. Mr. Calvert, an English gentleman, still living in the first ward, taught a class of Colored scholars in this house for a time, and James Wormley was one of the class. In the autumn of 1834, William Thomas Lee opened a school in the same place, and it was in a flourishing condition in the fall of 1835, when the Snow mob dispersed it, sacking the school-house, and partially destroying it by fire. William Wormley was at that time one of the most enterprising and influential Colored men of Washington, and was the original agent of the "Liberator" newspaper for this district. The mob being determined to lay hold of him and Lee, they fled from the city to save their lives, returning when General Jackson, coming back from Virginia a few days after the outbreak, gave notice that the fugitives should be protected. The persecution of William Wormley was so violent and persistent, that his health and spirits sank under its effects, his business was broken up, and he died a poor man, scarcely owning a shelter for his dying couch. The school-house was repaired after the riot, and occupied for a time by Margaret Thompson's school, and still stands in the rear of James Wormley's restaurant.

BENJAMIN M'COY'S, AND OTHER SCHOOLS.

. About this time another school was opened in Georgetown, by Nancy Grant, a sister of Mrs. William Becraft, a well-educated Colored woman. She was teaching as early as 1828, and had a useful school for several years. Mr. Nuthall, an Englishman, was teaching in Georgetown during this period, and as late as 1833 he went to Alexandria and opened a school in that city. William Syphax, among others now resident in Washington, attended his school in Alexandria about 1833. He was a man of ability, well educated, and one of the best teachers of his time in the district. His school in Georgetown was at first in Dunbarton Street, and afterward on Montgomery.

The old maxim, that "the blood of the martyrs is the seed of the Church," seems to find its illustration in this history. There is no period in the annals of the country in which the fires of persecution against the education of the Colored race burned more fiercely in this district, and the country at large, than in the five years from 1831 to 1836, and it was during this period that a larger number of respectable Colored schools were established than in any other five years prior to the war. In 1833, the same year in which Ambush's school was started, Benjamin M. McCoy, a Colored man, opened a school in the northern part of the city, on L Street, between Third and Fourth streets, west. In 1834 he moved to Massachusetts Avenue, continuing his school there till he went to Lancaster County, Pennsylvania, in the autumn of 1836, to finish the engagement of Rev. John F. Cook, who came back to Washington at that time and re-opened his school. The school at Lancaster was a free public Colored school, and Mr. McCoy was solicited to continue another year; but declining, came back, and in 1837 opened a school in the basement of Asbury Church, which, in that room and in the house adjoining, he maintained with great success for the ensuing twelve years. Mr. McCoy was a pupil of Mrs. Billing and Henry Smothers; is a man of good sense, and his school gave a respectable rudimental education to multitudes, who remember him as a teacher with great respect. He is now a messenger in the Treasury Department. In 1833, a school was established by Fanny Hampton, in the western part of the city, on the northwest corner.of K and Nineteenth streets. It was a large school, and was continued till about 1842, the teacher dying soon afterward. She was half-sister of Lindsay Muse. Margaret Thompson succeeded her, and had a flourishing school of some forty scholars on Twenty-sixth Street, near the avenue, for several years, about 1846. She subsequently became the wife of Charles H. Middleton, and assisted in his school for a brief time. About 1830, Robert Brown commenced a small school, and continued it at intervals for many years till his death. As early as 1833, there was a school opened in a private house in the rear of Franklin Row, near the location of the new Franklin School building. It was taught by a white man, Mr. Talbot, and continued a year or two. Mrs. George Ford, a white teacher, a native of Virginia, kept a Colored school in a brick house still standing on New Jersey Avenue, between K and L streets. She taught there many years, and as early, perhaps, as half a century ago.

DR. JOHN H. FLEET'S SCHOOL

was opened, in 1836, on New York Avenue, in a school-house which stood nearly on the spot now occupied by the Richards buildings at the corner of New York Avenue and Fourteenth Street. It had been previously used for a white school, taught by Mrs. McDaniel, and was subsequently again so used. Dr. Fleet was a native of Georgetown, and was greatly assisted in his education by the late Judge James Morsell, of that city, who was not only kind to this family, but was always regarded by the Colored people of the district as their firm friend and protector. John H. Fleet, with his brothers and sisters, went to the Georgetown Lancasterian School, with the white children, for a long period, in their earlier school days, and subsequently to other white schools. He was also for a time a pupil of Smothers and Prout. He was possessed of a brilliant and strong intellect, inherited from his father, who was a white man of distinguished abilities. He studied medicine in Washington, in the office of Dr. Thomas Henderson, who had resigned as assistant surgeon in the army, and was a practising physician of eminence in Washington. He also attended medical lectures at the old medical college, corner of Tenth and E streets. It was his intention at that time to go to Liberia, and his professional education was conducted under the auspices of the Colonization Society. This, with the influence of Judge Morsell, gave him privileges never extended here to any other Colored man. He decided, however, not to go to Liberia, and in 1836 opened his school. He was a refined and polished gentleman, and conceded to be the foremost Colored man in culture, in intellectual force, and general influence in this district at that time. His school-house on New York Avenue was burned by an incendiary about 1843, and his flourishing and excellent school was thus ended. For a time he subsequently taught music, in which he was very proficient; but about 1846 he opened a school on School-house Hill, in the Hobbrook Military School building, near the corner of N Street, north, and Twenty-third Street, west, and had a large school there till about 1851, when he relinquished the business, giving his attention henceforth exclusively to music, and with eminent success. He died in 1861. His school was very large and of a superior character.

CHARLES H. MIDDLETON'S SCHOOL

was started in the same section of the city, in a school-house which then stood near the corner of Twenty-second Street, west, and I, north, and which had been used by Henry Hardy for a white school. Though both Fleet's and Johnson's schools were in full tide of success in that vicinity, he gathered a good school, and when his two competitors retired—as they both did about this time,—his school absorbed a large portion of their patronage, and was thronged. In 1852, he went temporarily with his school to Sixteenth Street, and thence to the basement of Union Bethel Church on M Street, near Sixteenth, in which, during the administration of President Pierce, he had an exceedingly large and excellent school, at the same period when Miss Miner was prosecuting her signal work. Mr. Middleton, now a messenger in the Navy Department, a native of Savannah, Ga., is free-born, and received his very good education in schools in that city, sometimes with white and sometimes with Colored children. When he commenced his school he had just returned from the Mexican war, and his enterprise is especially worthy of being made prominent, not only because. of his high style as a teacher, but also because it is associated with

THE FIRST MOVEMENT FOR A FREE COLORED PUBLIC SCHOOL.

This movement originated with a city officer, Jesse E. Dow, who, in 1848 and 1849, was a leading and influential member of the common council. He encouraged Mr. Middleton to start his school, by assuring him that he would give all his influence to the establishment of free schools for Colored as well as for white children, and that he had great confidence that the council would be brought to give at least some encouragement to the enterprise. In 1850 Mr. Dow was named among the candidates for the mayoralty; and when his views in this regard were assailed by his opponents, he did not hesitate to boldly avow his opinions, and to declare that he wished no support for any office which demanded of him any modification of these convictions. The workmen fail, but the work succeeds. The name of Jesse E. Dow merits conspicuous record in this history for this bold and magnanimous action. Mr. Middleton received great assistance in building up his school from Rev. Mr. Wayman, then pastor of the Bethel Church, and afterward promoted to the bishopric. The school was surrendered finally to Rev. J. V. B. Morgan, the succeeding pastor of the church, who conducted the school as a part of the means of his livelihood.

ALEXANDER CORNISH AND OTHERS.

In the eastern section of the city, about 1840, Alexander Cornish had a school several years in his own house on D Street, south, between Third and Fourth, east, with an average of forty scholars. He was succeeded, about 1846, by Richard Stokes, who was a native of Chester County, Pa. His school, averaging one hundred and fifty scholars, was kept in the Israel Bethel Church, near the Capitol, and was continued for about six years. In 1840, there was a school opened by Margaret Hill in Georgetown, near Miss English's seminary. She taught a very good school for several years.

ALEXANDER HAYS'S SCHOOL

was started on Ninth Street, west, near New York Avenue. Mr. Hays was born in 1802, and belonged originally to the Fowler family in Maryland. When a boy he served for a time at the Washington Navy Yard, in the family of Captain Dove, of the navy, the father of Dr. Dove, of Washington, and it was in that family that he learned to read. Michael Tabbs had a school at that time at the Navy Yard, which he taught in the afternoons *under a large tree*, which stood near the old Masonic Hall. The Colored children used to meet him there in large numbers daily, and while attending this singular school, Hays was at the same time taught by Mrs. Dove, with her children. This was half a century ago. In 1826, Hays went to live in the family of R. S. Coxe, the eminent Washington lawyer, who soon purchased him, paying Fowler $300 for him. Mr. Coxe did this at the express solicitation of Hays, and seventeen years after he gave him his freedom—in 1843. While living with Mr. Coxe he had married Matilda Davis, the daughter of John Davis, who served as steward many years in the family of Mr. Seaton, of the " National Intelligencer." The wedding was at Mr. Seaton's residence, and Mr. Coxe and family were present on the occasion. In 1836, he bought the house and lot which they still own and occupy, and in 1842, the year before he was free, Hays made his last payment, and the place was conveyed to his wife. She was a free woman, and had opened a school in the house in 1841. Hays had many privileges while with Mr. Coxe, and with the proceeds of his wife's school they paid the purchase-money ($550) and interest in seven years. Mr. Hays was taught reading, writing, and arithmetic by Mr. Coxe, his wife, and daughters, while a slave in their family. When the Colored people were driven from the churches, in the years of the mobs, Mrs. Coxe organized a large Colored Sabbath-school in her own parlor, and maintained it for a long period, with the cooperation of Mr. Coxe and the daughters. Mr. Hays was a member of this school. He also attended day schools, when his work would allow of it. This was the education with which, in 1845, he ventured to take his wife's school in charge. He is a man of good-sense, and his school flourished. He put up an addition to his house, in order to make room for his increasing school, which was continued down to 1857—sixteen years from its opening. He had also a night school and taught music, and these two features of his school he has revived since the war. This school contained from thirty-five to forty-five pupils. Rev. Dr. Samson, Mr. Seaton, and Mr. Coxe often visited his school and encouraged him in his excellent work. Thomas Tabbs used also to come into his school and give him aid and advice, as also did John McLeod.

MR. AND MRS. FLETCHER'S SCHOOL

was opened about 1854, in the building in which Middleton first taught, on I, near Twenty-second Street. Mr. Fletcher was an Englishman, a well-educated gentleman, and a thorough teacher. He was induced to open the school by the importunities of some aspiring Colored young men in that part of the city, who desired first-rate instruction. He soon became the object of persecution, though he was a man of courtesy and excellent character. His school-house was finally set on fire and consumed, with all its books and furniture; but the school took, as its asylum, the basement of the John Wesley Church. The churches which they had been forced to build in the days of the mobs, when they were driven from the white churches which they had aided in building, proved of immense service to them in their subsequent struggles. Mrs. Fletcher kept a variety store, which was destroyed about the time the school was opened. She then became an assistant in her husband's school, which numbered over one hundred and fifty pupils. In 1858, they were driven from the city, as persecution at that time was particularly violent against all white persons who instructed the Colored people. This school was conducted with great thoroughness, and had two departments, Mrs. Fletcher, who was an accomplished person, having charge of the girls in a separate room.

ELIZA ANNE COOK,

a niece of Rev. John F. Cook, and one of his pupils, who has been teaching for about fifteen years, should be mentioned. She attended Miss Miner's school for a time, and was afterward at the Baltimore convent two years. She opened a school in her mother's house, and subsequently built a small school-house on the same lot, Sixteenth Street, between K and L streets. With the exception of three years, during which she was teaching in the free Catholic school opened in the Smothers school-house in 1859, and one year in the female school in charge of the Colored sisters, she has maintained her own private school from 1854 down to the present time, her number at some periods being above sixty, but usually not more than twenty-five or thirty.

MISS WASHINGTON'S SCHOOL.

In 1857, Annie E. Washington opened a select primary school in her mother's house, on K Street, between Seventeenth and Eighteenth streets, west. The mother, a widow woman, was a laundress, and by her own labor has given her children good advantages, though she had no such advantages herself. This daughter was educated chiefly under Rev. John F. Cook and Miss Miner, with whom she was a favorite scholar. Her older sister was educated at the Baltimore convent. Annie E. Washington is a woman of native refinement, and has an excellent aptitude for teaching, as well as a good education. Her schools have always been conducted with system and superior judgment, giving universal satisfaction, the number of her pupils being limited only by the size of her room. In 1858, she moved to the basement of the Baptist Church, corner of Nineteenth and I streets, to secure larger accommodations, and there she had a school of more than sixty scholars for several years.

A FREE CATHOLIC COLORED SCHOOL.

A free school was established in 1858, and maintained by the St. Vincent de Paul Society, an association of Colored Catholics, in connection with St. Matthew's Church. It was organized under the direction of Father Walter, and kept in the Smothers school-house for two years, and was subsequently for one season maintained on a smaller scale in a house on L Street, between Twelfth and Thirteenth streets, west, till the association failed to give it the requisite pecuniary support after the war broke out. This school has already been mentioned.

OTHER SCHOOLS.

In 1843, Elizabeth Smith commenced a school for small children on the island in Washington, and subsequently taught on Capitol Hill. In 1860, she was the assistant of Rev. Wm. H. Hunter, who had a large school in Zion Wesley Church, Georgetown, of which he was the pastor. She afterward took the school into her own charge for a period, and taught among the contrabands in various places during the war.

About 1850, Isabella Briscoe opened a school on Montgomery Street, near Mount Zion Church, Georgetown. She was well educated, and one of the best Colored teachers in the district before the Rebellion. Her school was always well patronized, and she continued teaching in the district up to 1868.

Charlotte Beams had a large school for a number of years, as early as 1850, in a building next to Galbraith Chapel, I Street, north, between Fourth and Fifth, west. It was exclusively a girls' school in its later years. The teacher was a pupil of Enoch Ambush, who assisted her in establishing her school.

A year or two later, Rev. James Shorter had a large school in the Israel Bethel Church, and Miss Jackson taught another good school on Capitol Hill about the same time. The above-mentioned were all Colored teachers.

Among the excellent schools broken up at the opening of the war, was that of Mrs. Charlotte Gordon, Colored, on Eighth Street, in the northern section of the city. It was in successful operation several years, and the number in attendance sometimes reached one hundred and fifty. Mrs. Gordon was assisted by her daughter.

In 1841, David Brown commenced teaching on D Street, south, between First and Second streets, island, and continued in the business till 1858, at which period he was placed in charge of the large Catholic free school in the Smothers house, as has been stated.[1]

Here is a picture that every Negro in the country may contemplate with satisfaction and pride. In the stronghold of slavery, under the shadow of the legalized institution of slavery, within earshot of the slave-auctioneer's hammer, amid distressing circumstances, poverty, and proscription, three unlettered ex-slaves, upon the threshold of the nineteenth century, sowed the seed of education for the Negro race in the District of Columbia, from which an abundant harvest has been gathered, and will be gathered till the end of time!

What the Negro has done to educate himself, the trials and hateful laws that have hampered him during the long period anterior to 1860, cannot fail to awaken feelings of regret and admiration among the people of both sections and two continents.

---

[1] Report of the Commissioner of Education for 1871.

CHAPTER XIII.

JOHN BROWN—HERO AND MARTYR.

JOHN BROWN'S APPEARANCE IN KANSAS. — HE DENOUNCES SLAVERY IN A POLITICAL MEETING AT OSAWATOMIE. — MRS. STEARNS'S PERSONAL RECOLLECTION OF JOHN BROWN. — KANSAS INFESTED BY BORDER RUFFIANS. — THE BATTLE OF HARPER'S FERRY. — THE DEFEAT AND CAPTURE OF CAPTAIN JOHN BROWN. — HIS LAST LETTER WRITTEN TO MRS. STEARNS. — HIS TRIAL AND EXECUTION. — HIS INFLUENCE UPON THE SLAVERY QUESTION AT THE NORTH. — HIS PLACE IN HISTORY.

ON the 9th of May, 1800, at Torrington, Connecticut, was born a man who lived for two generations, but accomplished the work of two centuries. That man was John Brown, who ranks among the world's greatest heroes. Greater than Peter the Hermit, who believed himself commissioned of God to redeem the Holy Sepulchre from the hands of infidels; greater than Joanna Southcote, who deemed herself big with the promised Shiloh; greater than Ignatius Loyola, who thought the Son of Man appeared to him, bearing His cross upon His shoulders, and bestowed upon him a Latin commission of wonderful significance; greater than Oliver Cromwell, the great Republican Protector; and greater than John Hampden,—he deserves to rank with William of Orange.

John Brown was nearly six feet high, slim, wiry, dark in complexion, sharp in feature, dark hair sprinkled with gray, eyes a dark gray and penetrating, with a countenance that betokened frankness, honesty, and firmness. His brow was prominent, the centre of the forehead flat, the upper part retreating, which, in conjunction with his slightly Roman nose, gave him an interesting appearance. The crown of his head was remarkably high, in the regions of the phrenological organs of firmness, conscientiousness, self-esteem, indicating a stern will, unswerving integrity, and marvellous self-possession. He walked rapidly with a firm and elastic tread. He was somewhat like John Baptist, taciturn in habits, usually wrapped in meditation. He was rather meteoric in his movements, appearing suddenly and unexpectedly at this place, and then disappearing in the same mysterious manner.

When Kansas lay bleeding at the feet of border ruffians; when Congress gave the free-State settlers no protection, but was rather trying to drag the territory into the Union with a slave constitution,—without noise or bluster John Brown dropped down into Osage County. He was not a member of the Republican party; but rather hated its reticency. When it cried Halt! he gave the command *Forward, march!* He was not in sympathy with any of the parties, political or anti-slavery. All were too conservative to suit him. So, as a political orphan he went into Kansas, organized and led a new party that swore eternal death to slavery. The first time he appeared in a political meeting in Kansas, at Osawatomie, the politicians were trimming their speeches and shaping their resolutions to please each political faction. John Brown took the floor and made a speech that threw the convention into consternation. He denounced slavery as the curse of the ages; affirmed the manhood of the slave; dealt "middle men" terrible blows; and said he could "see no use in talking." "Talk," he continued, "is a national institution; but it does no good for the slave." He thought it an excuse very well adapted for weak men with tender consciences. Most men who were afraid to fight, and too honest to be silent, deceived themselves that they discharged their duties to the slave by denouncing in fiery words the oppressor. His ideas of duty were far different; the slaves, in his eyes, were prisoners of war; their tyrants, as he held, had taken up the sword, and must perish by it. This was his view of the great question of slavery.

The widow of the late Major George L. Stearns gives the following personal recollections of John Brown, in a bright and entertaining style. Mrs. Stearns's noble husband was very intimately related to the "old hero," and what Mrs. Stearns writes is of great value.

"The passage of the Fugitive-Slave Bill in 1850, followed by the virtual repeal of the Missouri Compromise, under the name of the Kansas Nebraska Act, in 1854, alarmed all sane people for the safety of republican institutions; and the excitement reached a white heat when, on the 22d of May, 1856, Charles Sumner was murderously assaulted in the Senate chamber by Preston S. Brooks, of South Carolina, for words spoken in debate: the celebrated speech of the 19th and 20th of May, known as 'The Crime Against Kansas.' That same week the town of Lawrence in the territory of Kansas was sacked and burned in the interest of the slave power. The atrocities committed by the 'Border Ruffians' upon the free-State settlers sent a thrill of terror through all law-abiding communities. In Boston the citizens gathered in Faneuil Hall to consider what could be done, and a committee was chosen, with Dr. S. G. Howe as chairman, for the relief of Kansas, called the 'Kansas Relief Committee.' After some $18,000 or $20,000 had been collected, chiefly in Boston, and forwarded to Kansas, the interest flagged, and Mr. Stearns, who had been working with that committee, saw the need of more energetic action ; so one day he went to Dr. Howe, and told him he was ready to give *all* his time, and much of his money, to push forward the work. Dr. Howe seeing that here was the man for the hour, immediately resigned, and Mr. Stearns was chosen unanimously chairman of the 'Massachusetts State Kansas Commit- tee,' which took the place of the one first organized. In the light of subsequent history it is difficult to believe the apathy and blindness which failed to recognize the significance of this attack upon Kansas by the slave-holding power. Only faithful watchmen in their high towers could see that it was the first battle-ground between the two conflicting systems of freedom and slavery, which was finally to culmi- nate in the war of the Rebellion. 'Working day and night with- out haste or rest,' failing in no effort to rouse and stimulate the com- munity, still Mr. Stearns found that a vitalizing interest was wanting. When Gov. Reeder was driven in disguise from the territory, he wrote to him to come to Boston and address the people. He organized a mass-meeting for him in Tremont Temple, and for a few days the story he related stimulated to a livelier activity the more conservative people, who were inclined to think the reports of the free-State men much exaggerated. Soon, however, things settled back into the old sluggish way ; so that for three consecutive committee meetings the chairman was the only person who presented himself at the appointed time and place. Nothing daunted, he turned to the country towns, and at the end of five months he had raised by his personal exertions, and through his agents, the sum of $48,000. Women formed societies all over the State, for making and furnishing clothing, and various sup- plies, which resulted in an addition of some $20,000 or $30,000 more. In January, 1867, this species of work was stopped, by advices from Kansas that no more contributions were needed, except for *defense.* At this juncture Mr. Stearns wrote to John Brown, that if he would come to Boston and consult with the friends of freedom he would pay his expenses. They had never met, but 'Osawatomie Brown' had become a cherished household name during the anxious summer of 1856.[1] Arriving in Boston, they were introduced to each other in the

---

[1] This was in the last days of 1856.

street by a Kansas man, who chanced to be with Mr. Stearns on his way to the committee rooms in Nilis's Block, School Street. Captain Brown made a profound impression on all who came within the sphere of his moral magnetism. Emerson called him 'the most ideal of men, for he wanted to put all his ideas into action.' His absolute superiority to all selfish aims and narrowing pride of opinion touched an answering chord in the self-devotion of Mr. Stearns. A little anecdote illustrates the modest estimate of the work he had in hand. After several efforts to bring together certain friends to meet Captain Brown at his home in Medford, he found that Sunday was the only day that would serve their several convenience, and being a little uncertain how it might strike his ideas of religious propriety, he prefaced his invitation with something like an apology. With characteristic promptness came the reply : 'Mr. Stearns, I have a little ewe-lamb that I want to pull out of the ditch, and the Sabbath will be as good a day as any to do it.'

" It was this occasion which furnished to literature one of the most charming bits of autobiography. Our oldest son, Harry, a lad of eleven years, was an observant listener, and drank eagerly every word that was said of the cruel wrongs in Kansas, and of slavery everywhere. When the gentlemen rose to go, he privately asked his father if he might be allowed to give all his spending money to John Brown. Leave being granted, he bounded away, and returning with his small treasure, said : 'Captain Brown, will you buy something with this money for those poor people in Kansas, and some time will you write to me and tell me *what sort of a little boy* you were ?' 'Yes, my son, I will, and God bless you for your kind heart !' The autobiography has been printed many times, but never before with the key which unlocked it.

" It may not be out of place to describe the impression he made upon the writer on this first visit. When I entered the parlor, he was sitting near the hearth, where glowed a bright open fire. He rose to greet me, stepping forward with such an erect, military bearing ; such fine courtesy of demeanor and grave earnestness, that he seemed to my instant thought some old Cromwellian hero suddenly dropped down before me ; a suggestion which was presently strengthened by his saying [proceeding with the conversation my entrance had interrupted] : 'Gentlemen, I consider the Golden Rule and the Declaration of Independence one and inseparable ; and it is better that a whole generation of men, women, and children should be swept away, than that this crime of slavery should exist one day longer.' These words were uttered like rifle balls ; in such emphatic tones and manner that our little Carl, not three years old, remembered it in manhood as one of his earliest recollections. The child stood perfectly still, in the middle of the room, gazing with his beautiful eyes on this new sort of man, until his absorption arrested the attention of Captain Brown, who soon coaxed him to his knee, tho' the look of awe and childlike wonder remained. His dress was of some dark brown stuff, quite coarse, but its exactness and neatness produced a singular air of refinement. At dinner, he declined all dainties, saying that he was unaccustomed to luxuries, even to partaking of butter.

" The 'friends of freedom' with whom Mr. Stearns had invited John Brown to consult, were profoundly impressed with his sagacity, integrity, and devotion ; notably among these were R. W. Emerson, Theodore Parker, H. D. Thoreau, A. Bronson Alcott, F. B. Sanborn, Dr. S. G. Howe, Col. T. W. Higginson, Gov. Andrew, and others. In February (1857) he appeared before a committee of the State Legislature, to urge that Massachusetts should make an appropriation in money in aid of those persons who had settled in Kansas from her own soil. The speech is printed in Redpath's ' Life.' He obtained at this time, from the Massachusetts State Kansas Committee,[1] some two hundred Sharp's rifles, with which to arm one hundred mounted men for the defense of Kansas, who could also be of service to the peculiar property of Missouri. In those dark days of slave-holding supremacy, the friends of freedom felt justified in aiding the flight of its victims to free soil whenever and wherever opportunity offered. The Fugitive-Slave Law was powerless before the law written on the enlightened consciences of those devoted men and women. These rifles had been forwarded previously to the National Committee at Chicago, for the defense of Kansas, but for some unexplained reasons had never proceeded farther than Tabor, in the State of Iowa. Later on, Mr. Stearns, in his individual capacity, authorized Captain Brown to purchase two hundred revolvers from the Massachusetts Arms Company, and paid for them from his private funds, thirteen or fifteen hundred dollars. During the summer of 1857 he united with Mr. Amos A. Lawrence and others in paying off the mortgage held by Mr. Gerritt Smith on his house and farm at North Elba, N. Y., he paying two hundred and sixty dollars. It would be difficult to state the entire amount of money Mr. Stearns put into the hands of John Brown for Anti-Slavery purposes and his own subsistence. He kept no account of what he gave. In April or May, 1857, he gave him a check for no less a sum than seven thousand dollars. Early in 1858, Hon. Henry Wilson wrote to Dr. S. G. Howe that he had learned John Brown was suspected of the intention of using those arms in other ways than for the *defense* of Kansas ; and by order of the committee, Mr. Stearns wrote (under date May 14, 1858) to Brown not to use them for any other purpose, and to hold them subject to his order, as chairman of said committee. When the operations of the Massachusetts State Kan-

---

[1] The committee also authorized him to draw on their treasurer, Patrick L. Jackson, for $500.

sas Committee virtually ceased, in June or July, 1858, it happened that this committee were some four thousand dollars in debt to Mr. Stearns, for advances of money from time to time to keep the organization in existence ; and it was voted to make over to the chairman these two hundred Sharp's rifles as part payment of the committee's indebtedness. They were of small account to Mr. Stearns. He knew them to be in good hands, and troubled himself no further about them, either the rifles or the revolvers ; although keeping up from time to time a correspondence with his friend upon the all-engrossing subject.

"In February of 1859, John Brown was in Boston, and talked with some of his friends about the feasibility of entrenching himself, with a little band of men, in the mountains of Virginia, familiar to him from having surveyed them as engineer in earlier life. His plan was to open communication with the slaves of neighboring-plantations, collect them together, and send them off in squads, as he had done in Missouri, 'without snapping a gun.' Mr. Stearns had so much more faith in John Brown's opposition to *Slavery*, than in any theories he advanced of the *modus operandi*, that they produced much less impression on his mind than upon some others gifted with more genius for details. *From first to last, he believed in John Brown.* His plans, or theories, might be feasible, or they might not. If the glorious old man wanted money to try his plans, he should have it. His plans might fail ; probably would, but *he* could never be a failure. There he stood, unconquerable, in the panoply of divine Justice. Both of these men were of the martyr type. No thought or consideration for themselves, for *history*, or the estimation of others, ever entered into their calculations. It was the service of *Truth* and *Right* which brought them together, and in that service they were ready to die.

"In the words of an eminent writer[1]: 'A common spirit made these two men recognize each other at first sight ; and the power of both lay in that inability to weigh difficulties against duty, that instant step of thought to deed, which makes individuals fully possessed by the idea of the age, the turning-points of its destiny ; hands in the right place for touching the match to the train it has laid, or for leading the public will to the heart of its moral need. They knew each other as minute-men on the same watch ; as men to be found *in* the breach, before others knew where it was ; they were one in pity, one in indignation, one in moral enthusiasm, burning beneath features set to patient self-control ; one in simplicity, though of widely different culture ; one in religious inspiration, though at the poles of religious thought. The old frontiersman came from his wilderness toils and agonies to find

---

[1] Samuel Johnson, the accomplished Oriental scholar and devoted friend of the slave.

within the merchant's mansion of art and taste by the side of Bunker Hill, a perfect sympathy: the reverence of children, tender interest in his broken household, free access to a rich man's resources, and even a valor kindred with his own.'

"The attack upon Harper's Ferry was a 'side issue,' to quote the words of John Brown, Jr., and a departure from his father's original plan. It certainly took all his friends by surprise. In his letter of Nov. 15, 1859 (while in prison), to his old schoolmaster, the Rev. H. L. Vaill, are these words: 'I am not as yet, in the *main*, at all disappointed. I have been a good deal disappointed as it regards *myself* in not keeping up to my own plans; but I now feel entirely reconciled to that even: for God's plan was infinitely better, *no doubt*, or I should have kept my own. Had Samson kept to his determination of not telling Delilah wherein his great strength lay, he would probably have never overturned the house. *I did not tell Delilah;* but I was induced to act very *contrary to my better judgment.*' [1]

*　　*　　*　　*　　*　　*　　*　　*

"It is idle to endeavor to explain, by any methods of the *understanding*, any rules of worldly wisdom, or prudence, this influx of the Divine Will, which has made John Brown already an ideal character. 'The wind bloweth where it listeth, and we hear the sound thereof; but know not whence it cometh, or whither it goeth.' So is every one that is born of the Spirit. Man works in the midst of laws which execute themselves, more especially, if by virtue of obedience he has lost sight of all selfish aims, and perceives that Truth and Right alone can claim allegiance. Emerson says: 'Divine intelligence carries on its administration by good men; that great men are they who see that the spiritual are greater than any material forces; and that really there never was any thing great accomplished but under religious impulse.'

"The deadly *Atheism* of Slavery was rolling its car of Juggernaut all over the beautiful Republic, and one pure soul was inspired to confront it by a practical interpretation of the Golden Rule.

"That Virginia would hang John Brown was a foregone conclusion. The Moloch of Slavery would have nothing less. His friends exerted themselves to secure the best counsel which could be induced to undertake the *formality* of a defense, foremost among whom was Mr. Stearns. A well-organized plan was made to rescue him, conducted by a brave man from Kansas, Col. James Montgomery, but a message came from the prisoner, that he should not feel at liberty to walk out, if the doors were left open; a sense of honor to his jailer (Captain Acvis) forbidding any thing of the kind.

---

[1] The italics are his.

"Not a litttle anxiety was felt lest certain of his adherents might be summoned as witnesses, whose testimony would lessen the chances of acquittal, and possibly involve their own lives. John A. Andrew (afterward Gov. Andrew) gave it as his opinion, after an exhaustive search of the records, that Virginia would have no right to summon these persons from Massachusetts, but subsequently changed his opinion, and urged Mr. Stearns to take passage to Europe, sending him home one day to pack his valise. The advice was opposed to his instincts, but he considered that his wife should have a voice in the matter, who decided, 'midst many tears and prayers, that if slavery required another victim, he must be ready.

"With Dr. Howe it was quite different. He became possessed with a dread that threatened to overwhelm his reason. He was in delicate health, and constitutionally subject to violent attacks of nervous headache. One day he came to Medford and insisted that Mr. Stearns should accompany him to Canada, urging that if he remained here he should be insane, and that Mr. Stearns of all his friends was the only one who would be at all satisfactory to him. This request, or rather demand, Mr. Stearns promptly declined. How well I remember his agitation, walking up and down the room, and finally entreating Mr. Stearns for 'friendship's sake' to go and take care of him. I can recall no instance of such self-abnegation in my husband's self-denying career. He did not *stoop* to an *explanation*, even when Dr. Howe declared in his presence, some months later, "that he never did any thing in his life he so much wished to take back." I had hoped that Dr. Howe would himself have spared *me* from making this contribution to the truth of history.

"On the 2d of December, Mr. Stearns yearned for the solitude of his own soul, in communion of spirit, with the friend who, on that day, would 'make the gallows glorious like the Cross'; and he left Dr. Howe and took the train for Niagara Falls. There, sitting alone beside the mighty rush of water, he solemnly consecrated his remaining life, his fortune, and all that was most dear, to the *cause* in whose service John Brown had died.

"How well and faithfully he kept his vow, may partly be seen in his subsequent efforts in recruiting the colored troops at a vital moment in the terrible war of the Rebellion which so swiftly followed the sublime apotheosis of 'Old John Brown.'"[1]

That John Brown intended to free the slaves, and nothing more, the record shows clearly. His move on Harper's Ferry

---

[1] The above account of Capt. Brown was prepared for us by the widow of the late Major Geo. L. Stearns. It is printed as written, and breathes a beautiful spirit of love and tender remembrance for the two heroes mentioned.

was well planned, and had all the parties interested done their part the work would have been done well. As to the rectitude of his intentions he gives the world this leaf of history :

"And now, gentlemen, let me press this one thing on your minds. You all know how dear life is to you, and how dear your lives are to your friends : and in remembering that, consider that the lives of others are as dear to them as yours are to you. Do not, therefore, take the life of any one if you can possibly avoid it ; but if. it is necessary to take life in order to save your own, then make sure work of it."—John Brown, before the battle at Harper's Ferry.

"I never did intend murder, or treason, or the destruction of property, or to excite or incite slaves to rebellion, or to make insurrection. The design on my part was to free the slaves."—John Brown, after the battle at Harper's Ferry.

Distance lends enchantment to the view. What the world condemns to-day is applauded to-morrow.

We must have a "fair count" on the history of yesterday and last year. The events chronicled yesterday, when the imagination was wrought upon by exciting circumstances, need revision to-day.

The bitter words spoken this morning reproach at eventide the smarting conscience. And the judgments prematurely formed, and the conclusions rapidly reached, may be rectified and repaired in the light of departed years and enlarged knowledge.

John Brown is rapidly settling down to his proper place in history, and "the madman" has been transformed into a "saint." When Brown struck his first blow for freedom, at the head of his little band of liberators, it was almost the universal judgment of both Americans and foreigners that he was a "fanatic." It seemed the very soul of weakness and arrogance for John Brown to attempt to do so great a work with so small a force. Men reached a decision with the outer and surface facts. But many of the most important and historically trustworthy truths bearing upon the motive, object, and import of that "bold move," have been hidden from the public view, either by prejudice or fear.

Some people have thought John Brown—"*The Hero of Harper's Ferry*"—a hot-headed, blood-thirsty brigand ; they animadverted against the precipitancy of his measures, and the severity of his invectives ; said that he was lacking in courage and deficient in judgment ; that he retarded rather than accelerated the cause he championed. But this was the verdict of other times, not the judgment of to-day.

John Brown said to a personal friend during his stay in Kansas: "Young men must learn to wait. Patience is the hardest lesson to learn. I have waited for twenty years to accomplish my purpose." These are not the words of a mere visionary idealist, but the mature language of a practical and judicious leader, a leader than whom the world has never seen a greater. By greatness is meant deep convictions of duty, a sense of the Infinite, "a strong hold on truth," a "conscience void of offence toward God and man," to which the appeals of the innocent and helpless are more potential than the voices of angry thunder or destructive artillery. Such a man was John Brown. He was strong in his moral and mental nature, as well as in his physical nature. He was born to lead ; and he led, and made himself the pro-martyr of a cause rapidly perfecting. All through his boyhood days he felt himself lifted and quickened by great ideas and sublime purposes. He had flowing in his veins the blood of his great ancestor, Peter Brown, who came over in the "Mayflower"; and the following inscription appears upon a marble monument in the graveyard at Canton Centre, New York: "In memory of Captain John Brown, who died in the Revolutionary army, at New York, September 3, 1776. He was of the fourth generation, in regular descent, from Peter Brown, one of the Pilgrim Fathers, who landed from the 'Mayflower,' at Plymouth, Massachusetts, December 22, 1620." This is the best commentary on his inherent love of absolute liberty, his marvellous courage and transcendent military genius. For years he elaborated and perfected his plans, working upon the public sentiment of his day by the most praiseworthy means. He bent and bowed the most obdurate conservatism of his day, and rallied to his standards the most eminent men, the strongest intellects in the North. His ethics and religion were as broad as the universe, and beneficent in their wide ramification. And it was upon his "religion of humanity," that embraced our entire species, that he proceeded with his herculean task of striking off the chains of the enslaved. Few, very few of his most intimate friends knew his plans—the plan of freeing the slaves. Many knew his great faith, his exalted sentiments, his ideas of liberty, in their crudity ; but to a faithful few only did he reveal his stupendous plans in their entirety.

Hon. Frederick Douglass and Colonel Richard J. Hinton, knew more of Brown's real purposes than any other persons, with the exception of J. H. Kagi, Osborn Anderson, Owen Brown, Richard Realf, and George B. Gill.

"Of men born of woman," there is not a greater than John Brown. He was the forerunner of Lincoln, the great apostle of freedom.

One year before he went to Harper's Ferry, a friend met Brown in Kansas [in June, 1858], and learned that during the previous month he had brought almost all of his plans to perfection ; and that the day and hour were fixed to strike the blow. One year before, a convention had met, on the 8th of May, 1858, at Chatham, Canada. At this convention a provisional constitution and ordinances were drafted and adopted, with the following officers : Commander-in-Chief, John Brown ; Secretary of War, J. H. Kagi ; Members of Congress, Alfred M. Ellsworth, Osborn Anderson ; Treasurer, Owen Brown ; Secretary of the Treasury, Geo. B. Gill ; Secretary of State, Richard Realf.

John Brown made his appearance in Ohio and Canada in the spring of 1859. He wrote letters, made speeches, collected funds for his little army, and made final arrangements with his Northern allies, etc. He purchased a small farm, about six miles from Harper's Ferry, on the Maryland side, and made it his ordnance depot. He had 102 Sharp's rifles, 68 pistols, 55 bayonets, 12 artillery swords, 483 pikes, 150 broken handles of pikes, 16 picks, 40 shovels, besides quite a number of other appurtenances of war. This was in July. He intended to make all of his arrangements during the summer of 1859, and meet his men in the Alleghanies in the fall of the same year.

The apparent rashness of the John Brown movement may be mitigated somewhat by the fact that he failed to carry out his original plan. During the summer of 1859 he instructed his Northern soldiers and sympathizers to be ready for the attack on the night of the 24th of October, 1859. But while at Baltimore, in September, he got the impression that there was conspiracy in his camp, and in order to preclude its consummation, suddenly, without sending the news to his friends at the North, determined to strike the first blow on the night of the 17th of October. The news of his battle and his bold stand against the united forces of Virginia and Maryland swept across the country as the wild storm comes down the mountain side. Friend and foe were alike astonished and alarmed. The enemies of the cause he represented, when they recovered from their surprise, laughed their little laugh of scorn, and eased their feelings by referring to him as the "madman." Friends faltered, and, while they did not question his earnestness, doubted his judgment. "Why," they asked, "should he act with such palpable rashness, and thereby render more difficult and impossible the emancipation of the slaves?" They claimed that the blow he struck, instead of severing, only the more tightly riveted, the chains upon the helpless and hapless Blacks. But in the face of subsequent history we think his surviving friends will change their views. There is no proof that his fears were not well grounded; that a conspiracy was in progress. And who can tell whether a larger force would have been more effective, or the night of the 24th more opportune? May it not be believed that the good old man was right, and that Harper's Ferry was just the place, and the 17th of October just the time to strike for freedom, and make the rock-ribbed mountains of Virginia to tremble at the presence of a "master!"—the king of freedom?

He was made a prisoner on the 19th of October, 1859, and remained until the 7th of November without a change of clothing or medical aid. Forty-two days from the time of his imprisonment he expiated his crime upon the scaffold—a crime against slave-holding, timorous Virginia, for bringing liberty to the oppressed. He was a man, and there was nothing that interested man which was foreign to his nature. He had gone into Virginia to save life, not to destroy it. The sighs and groans of the oppressed had entered into his soul.

He had heard the Macedonian cry to come over and help them. He went, and it cost him his life, but he gave it freely.

Captain Acvis, the jailer, said: "He was the gamest man I ever saw." And Mr. Valandingham, at that time a member of Congress from Ohio, and who examined him in court, said in a speech afterward.

"It is in vain to underrate either the man or the conspiracy. Captain John Brown is as brave and resolute a man as ever headed an insurrection, and, in a good cause, and with a sufficient force, would have been a consummate partisan commander. He has coolness, daring, persistency, stoic faith and patience, and a firmness of will and purpose unconquerable! He is the farthest possible remove from the ordinary ruffian, fanatic, or madman."

No friend, howsoever ardent in his love, could have woven a chaplet more worthy than the one placed upon the brow of the old hero by his most embittered foe. A truer estimate of John Brown cannot be had.

South Carolina, Missouri, and Kentucky sent a rope to hang him, but, the first two lacking strength, Kentucky had the everlasting disgrace of furnishing the rope to strangle the noblest man that ever lived in any age.

The last letter he ever wrote was written to Mrs. Geo. L. Stearns, and she shall give its history :

This letter requires the history which attaches to it, and illustrates the consideration which the brave martyr had for those in any way connected with him. It was written on a half sheet of paper, the exact size of the pages of a book into which he carefully inserted it, and tied up in a handkerchief with other books and papers, which he asked his jailer (Mr. Avis) to be allowed to go with his body to North Elba, and which Mrs. Brown took with her from the Charlestown prison. Her statement to me about it is this : She had been at home some two weeks, had looked over the contents of the handkerchief many times, when one day in turning the leaves of that particular book, she came upon this letter, on which she said she found two or three blistered spots, the only *tear drops* she had seen among his papers. They are now yellow with time. On the back of the half sheet was written : " Please mail this to her," which she did, and so it reached my hand ; seeming as if from the world to which his spirit had fled. It quite overwhelmed my husband. Presently he said : " See, dear, how careful the old man has been, he would not even direct it with your name to go from Virginia to Boston through the post-offices ; and altho' it contains no message to me, one of those '*farewells !*' is intended for me, and also the ' Love to *All* who love their neighbors.' "

" CHARLESTOWN, JEFFERSON CO VA. 29th Nov. 1859.

" MRS. GEORGE L. STEARNS
" Boston, Mass.

"My Dear Friend :—No letter I have received since my imprisonment here, has given me more satisfaction, or comfort, than yours of the 8th inst. I am quite cheerful : and never more happy. Have only time to write you a word. May God forever reward you *and all yours.*

"*My love to* ALL who love their neighbors. I have asked to be *spared* from having any *mock, or hypocritical prayers made over me* when I am publicly *murdered ;* and that my only *religious attendents* be

poor little, dirty, ragged, bareheaded and barefooted, Slave Boys ; and Girls,
led by some old *gray-headed slave Mother.*

     " Farewell. Farewell.

       " Your Friend,

        " JOHN BROWN." [1]

The man who hung him, Governor Wise, lived to see the plans
of Brown completed and his most cherished hopes fulfilled. He
heard the warning shot fired at Sumter, saw Richmond fall, the
war end in victory to the party of John Brown; saw the slave-
pen converted into the school-house, and the four millions Brown
fought and died for, elevated to the honors of citizenship. And
at last he has entered the grave, where his memory will perish
with his body, while the soul and fame of John Brown go marching down the centuries!

Galileo, Copernicus, Newton, and John Brown have to wait
the calmer judgments of future generations. These men believed that God sent them to do a certain work—to reveal a
hidden truth ; to pour light into the minds of benighted and
superstitious men. They completed their work ; they did nobly
and well, then bowed to rest—

  "With patriarchs of the infant world—with kings,
   The powerful of the earth,"

while generation after generation studies their handwriting
on the wall of time and interprets their thoughts. Despised, persecuted, and unappreciated while in the flesh, they are honored
after death, and enrolled among earth's good and great, her wise
and brave. The shock Brown gave the walls of the slave institution was felt from its centre to its utmost limits. It was the
entering wedge ; it laid bare the accursed institution, and taught
good men everywhere to hate it with a perfect hatred. Slavery
received its death wound at the hands of a " lonely old man."
When he smote Virginia, the non-resistants, the anti-slavery men,
learned a lesson. They saw what was necessary to the accomplishment of their work, and were now ready for the " worst."
He rebuked the conservatism of the North, and gave an example of adherence to duty, devotion to truth, and fealty to God
and man that make the mere " professor" to tremble with
shame. " John Brown's body lies mouldering in the clay," but
his immortal name will be pronounced with blessings in all lands
and by all people till the end of time.

---

[1] This letter is printed for the first time, with Mrs. Stearns's consent.

𝕻art 7.

THE NEGRO IN THE WAR FOR THE UNION.

CHAPTER XIV.

DEFINITION OF THE WAR ISSUE.

INCREASE OF SLAVE POPULATION IN SLAVE-HOLDING STATES FROM 1850–1860. — PRODUCTS OF SLAVE LABOR. — BASIS OF SOUTHERN REPRESENTATION. — SIX SECEDING STATES ORGANIZE A NEW GOVERNMENT. — CONSTITUTION OF THE CONFEDERATE GOVERNMENT. — SPEECH BY ALEXANDER H. STEPHENS. — MR. LINCOLN IN FAVOR OF GRADUAL EMANCIPATION. — HE IS ELECTED PRESIDENT OF THE UNITED STATES. — THE ISSUE OF THE WAR BETWEEN THE STATES.

IN 1860 there were, in the fifteen slave-holding States, 12,240,-000 souls, of whom 8,039,000 were whites, 251,000 free persons of color, and 3,950,000 were slaves. The gain of the entire population of the slave-holding States, from 1850–1860, was 2,627,-000, equal to 27.33 per cent. The slave population had increased 749,931, or 23.44 per cent., not including the slaves in the District of Columbia, where they had lost 5.02 slaves during the decade. The nineteen non-slave-holding States and the seven territories, including the District of Columbia, contained 19,203,-008 souls, of whom 18,920,771 were whites, 237,283 free persons of color, and 41,725 civilized Indians. The actual increase of this population was 5,624,101, or 41.24 per cent. During the same period—1850–1860—the total population of free persons of color in the United States increased from 434,449 to 487,970, or at the rate of 12.33 per cent., annual increase of above 1 per cent. In 1850 the Mulattoes were 11.15 per cent., regarding the United States as one aggregate, and in 1860 were 13.25 per cent., of the entire Colored population.

TOTAL COLORED POPULATION OF THE UNITED STATES.

Colored.	Numbers.		Proportions.	
	1850.	1860.	1850.	1860.
Blacks	3,233,057	3,853,478	88.85	86.75
Mulattoes	405,751	588,352	11.15	13.25
Total Colored . . .	3,638,808	4,441,830	100.00	100.00

So, in ten years, from 1850–1860, the increase of blacks above the current deaths was 620,421, or more than one half of a million, while the corresponding increase of Mulattoes was 182,601. Estimating the deaths to have been 22.4 per cent. during the same period, or one in 40 annually, the total births of Blacks in ten years was about 1,345,000, and the total births of Mulattoes about 273,000. Thus it appears, in the prevailing order, that of every 100 births of Colored, about 17 were Mulattoes, and 83 Blacks, indicating a ratio of nearly 1 to 5.

There were:

Deaf and dumb slaves	531
Blind	1,387
Insane	327
Idiotic	1,182
Total	3,427

There were 400,000 slaves in the towns and cities of the South, and 2,804,313 in the country. The products of slave labor in 1850 were as follows:

SLAVE LABOR PRODUCTS IN 1850.

Cotton	$98,603,720
Tobacco	13,982,686
Cane sugar	12,378,850
Hemp	5,000,000
Rice	4,000,000
Molasses	2,540,179
	$136,505,435

There were 347,525 slave-holders against 5,873,893 non-slave-holders in the slave States. The representation in Congress was as follows:

Northern representatives based on white population . . 142
Northern representatives based on Colored population . 2
Southern representatives based on white population . . 68
Southern representatives based on free Colored population 2
Southern representatives based on slave population . . 20
    Ratio of representation for 1853 . . . 93,420

The South owned 16,652 churches, valued at $22,142,085; the North owned 21,357 churches, valued at $65,167,586. The South printed annually 92,165,919 copies of papers and periodicals; the North printed annually 334,146,081 copies of papers and periodicals. The South owned, other than private, 722 libraries, containing 742,794 volumes; the North owned, other than private, 14,902 libraries, containing 3,882,217 volumes.

In sentiment, motive, and civilization the two "Sections" were as far apart as the poles. New England, Puritan, Round-head civilization could not fellowship the Cavaliers of the South. There were not only two sections and two political parties in the United States;—there were two antagonistic governmental ideas. John C. Calhoun and Alexander H. Stephens, of the South, represented the idea of the separate and individual sovereignty of each of the States; while William H. Seward and Abraham Lincoln, of the North, represented the idea of the centralization of governmental authority, so far as it was necessary to secure uniformity of the laws, and the supremacy of the Federal Constitution. On the 25th of October, 1858, in a speech delivered in Rochester, N. Y., William H. Seward said:

"Our country is a theatre which exhibits, in full operation, two radically different political systems: the one resting on the basis of servile or slave labor; the other on the basis of voluntary labor of freemen.

  .   .   .   .

"The two systems are at once perceived to be incongruous. They never have permanently existed together in one country, and they never can.

  .   .   "These antagonistic systems are continually coming in closer contact, and collision ensues.

"Shall I tell you what this collision means? It is an irrepressible conflict between opposing and enduring forces, and it means that the

United States must, and will, sooner or later, become entirely a slave-holding nation, or entirely a free labor nation. Either the cotton and rice fields of South Carolina, and the sugar plantations of Louisiana, will ultimately be tilled by free-labor, and Charleston and New Orleans become marts for legitimate merchandise alone, or else the rye fields and wheat fields of Massachusetts and New York must again be surrendered by their farmers to the slave culture and to the production of slaves, and Boston and New York become once more markets for trade in the bodies and souls of men."

Upon the eve of the great Rebellion, Mr. Seward said in the United States Senate:

"A free Republican government like this, notwithstanding all its constitutional checks, cannot long resist and counteract the progress of society.

"Free labor has at last apprehended its rights and its destiny, and is organizing itself to assume the government of the 'Republic. It will henceforth meet you boldly and resolutely here (Washington); it will meet you everywhere, in the territories and out of them, wherever you may go to extend slavery. It has driven you back in California and in Kansas; it will invade you soon in Delaware, Maryland, Virginia, Missouri, and Texas. It will meet you in Arizona, in Central America, and even in Cuba.

"You may, indeed, get a start under or near the tropics, and seem safe for a time, but it will be only a short time. Even there you will found States only for free labor, or to maintain and occupy. The interest of the whole race demands the ultimate emancipation of all men. Whether that consummation shall be allowed to take effect, with needful and wise precautions against sudden change and disaster, or be hurried on by violence, is all that remains for you to decide. The white man needs this continent to labor upon. His head is clear, his arm is strong, and his necessities are fixed.

"It is for yourselves, and not for us, to decide how long and through what further mortifications and disasters the contest shall be protracted before Freedom shall enjoy her already assured triumph.

"You may refuse to yield it now, and for a short period, but your refusal will only animate the friends of freedom with the courage and the resolution, and produce the union among them, which alone is necessary on their part to attain the position itself, simultaneously with the impending overthrow of the existing Federal Administration and the constitution of a new and more independent Congress."

Mr. Lincoln said during a discussion of the impending crisis:

"I believe this government cannot endure permanently, half slave and half free. I do not expect the Union to be dissolved; I do not expect the house to fall, but I do expect that it will cease to be divided. It will become all one thing, or all the other. Either the opponents of slavery will arrest the further spread of it, and place it where the public mind shall rest in the belief that it is in the course of ultimate extinction, or its advocates will push it forward until it shall become alike lawful in all the States, old as well as new, North as well as South.

"I have always hated slavery as much as any Abolitionist. I have always been an old-line Whig. I have always hated it, and I always believed it in a course of ultimate extinction. If I were in Congress, and a vote should come up on a question whether slavery should be prohibited in a new territory, in spite of the Dred Scott decision I would vote that it should."

Notwithstanding the confident tone of Mr. Lincoln's statement that he did "not expect the house to fall," it *did* fall, and great was the fall thereof!

On Saturday, 9th of February, 1861, six seceding States met at Montgomery, Alabama, and organized an independent government. The ordinances of secession were passed by the States as follows:

STATE.	DATE.	YEAS.	NAYS.
South Carolina	Dec. 20, 1860	169	——
Mississippi	Jan. 9, 1861	84	15
Alabama	Jan. 11, 1861	61	39
Florida	Jan. 11 1861	62	7
Georgia	Jan. 19, 1861	228	89
Louisiana	Jan. 25, 1861	113	17

The following delegates presented their credentials and were admitted and represented their respective States:

ALABAMA.—R. W. Walker, R. H. Smith, J. L. M. Curry, W. P. Chilton, S. F. Hale Colon, J. McRae, John Gill Shorter, David P. Lewis, Thomas Fearn.

FLORIDA.—James B. Owens, J. Patten Anderson, Jackson Morton (not present).

GEORGIA.—Robert Toombs, Howell Cobb, F. S. Bartow, M. J. Crawford, E. A. Nisbet, B. H. Hill, A. R. Wright, Thomas R. Cobb, A. H. Kenan, A. H. Stephens.

LOUISIANA.—John Perkins, Jr., A. Declonet, Charles M. Conrad, D. F. Kenner, G. E. Sparrow, Henry Marshall.

MISSISSIPPI.—W. P. Harris, Walter Brooke, N. S. Wilson, A. M. Clayton, W. S. Barry, J. T. Harrison.

SOUTH CAROLINA.—R. B. Rhett, R. W. Barnwell, L. M. Keitt, James Chestnut, Jr., C. G. Memminger, W. Porcher Miles, Thomas J. Withers, W. W. Boyce.

A president and vice-president were chosen by unanimous vote. President—Honorable Jefferson Davis, of Mississippi. Vice-President—Honorable Alexander H. Stephens, of Georgia. The following gentlemen composed the Cabinet :

Secretary of State, Robert Toombs ; Secretary of Treasury, C. G. Memminger ; Secretary of Interior (Vacancy) ; Secretary of War, L. P. Walker ; Secretary of Navy, John Perkins, Jr. ; Post-master-General, H. T. Ebett ; Attorney-General, J. P. Benjamin.

The Constitution of the Confederate Government did not differ so very radically from the Federal Constitution. The following were the chief points :

" 1. The importation of African negroes from any foreign country other than the slave-holding States of the Confederate States is hereby forbidden, and Congress is required to pass such laws as shall effectually prevent the same.

" 2. Congress shall also have power to prohibit the introduction of slaves from any State not a member of this Confederacy.

" The Congress shall have power :

" 1. To lay and collect taxes, duties, imposts, and excises, for revenue necessary to pay the debts and carry on the government of the Confederacy, and all duties, imposts, and excises shall be uniform throughout the Confederacy.

" A slave in one State escaping to another shall be delivered, upon the claim of the party to whom said slave may belong, by the Executive authority of the State in which such slave may be found ; and in any case of abduction or forcible rescue, full compensation, including the value of slave, and all costs and expense, shall be made to the party by the State in which such abduction or rescue shall take place.

" 2. The government hereby instituted shall take immediate steps for the settlement of all matters between the States forming it and their late confederates of the United States in relation to the public property and public debt at the time of their withdrawal from them ; these States hereby declaring it to be their wish and earnest desire to adjust everything pertaining to the common property, common liabilities, and common obligations of that Union, upon principles of right, justice, equity, and good faith."

At first blush it would appear that the new government had not been erected upon the slave question; that it had gone as far as the Federal Government to suppress the foreign slave-trade; and that nobler and sublimer ideas and motives had inspired and animated the Southern people in their movement for a new government. But the men who wrote the Confederate platform knew what they were about. They knew that to avoid the charge that would certainly be made against them, of having seceded in order to make slavery a national institution, they must be careful not to exhibit such intentions in their Constitution. But that the South seceded on account of the slavery question, there can be no historical doubt whatever. Jefferson Davis, President, so-called, of the Confederate Government, said in his Message, April 29, 1861 :

" When the several States delegated certain powers to the United States Congress, a large portion of the laboring population consisted of African slaves, imported into the colonies by the mother-country. In twelve out of the thirteen States, negro slavery existed ; and the right of property in slaves was protected by law. This property was recognized in the Constitution ; and provision was made against its loss by the escape of the slave.

"The increase in the number of slaves by further importation from Africa was also secured by a clause forbidding Congress to prohibit the slave-trade anterior to a certain date ; and in no clause can there be found any delegation of power to the Congress, authorizing it in any manner to legislate to the prejudice, detriment, or discouragement of the owners of that species of property, or excluding it from the protection of the Government.

" The climate and soil of the Northern States soon proved unpropitious to the continuance of slave labor ; whilst the converse was the case at the South. Under the unrestricted free intercourse between the two sections, the Northern States consulted their own interest, by selling their slaves to the South, and prohibiting slavery within their limits. The South were willing purchasers of a property suitable to their wants, and paid the price of the acquisition without harboring a suspicion that their quiet possession was to be disturbed by those who were inhibited not only by want of constitutional authority, but by good faith as vendors, from disquieting a title emanating from themselves.

" As soon, however, as the Northern States that prohibited African slavery within their limits had reached a number sufficient to give their representation a controlling voice in the Congress, a persistent and organized system of hostile measures against the rights of the owner's of slaves in the Southern States was inaugurated, and gradually extended. A continuous series of measures was devised and prosecuted for the purpose of rendering insecure the tenure of property in slaves.

.　　.　　.　　.　　.　　.　　.　　.　　.

"With interests of such overwhelming magnitude imperilled, the people of the Southern States were driven by the conduct of the North to the adoption of some course of action to avoid the danger with which they were openly menaced. With this view, the Legislatures of the several States invited the people to select delegates to conventions to be held for the purpose of determining for themselves what measures were best adapted to meet so alarming a crisis in their history." [1]

Alexander H. Stephens, Vice-President, as he was called, said, in a speech delivered at Savannah, Georgia, 21st of March, 1861 :

"The new Constitution has put at rest *forever* all the agitating questions relating to our peculiar institution,—African slavery as it exists amongst us, the proper *status* of the negro in our form of civilization. *This was the immediate cause of the late rupture and present revolution.* JEFFERSON, in his forecast, had anticipated this, as the 'rock upon which the old Union would split.' He was right. What was conjecture with him is now a realized fact. But whether he fully comprehended the great truth upon which that great rock *stood* and *stands*, may be doubted. *The prevailing ideas entertained by him and most of the leading statesmen at the time of the formation of the old Constitution, were, that the enslavement of the African was in violation of the laws of nature ; that it was wrong in principle, socially, morally, and politically.* It was an evil they knew not well how to deal with ; but the general opinion of the men of that day was, that, somehow or other in the order of Providence, the institution would be evanescent, and pass away. This idea, though not incorporated in the Constitution, was the prevailing idea at the time. The Constitution, it is true, secured every essential guarantee to the institution while it should last ; and hence no argument can be justly used against the constitutional guarantees thus secured, because of the common sentiment of the day. *Those ideas, however, were fundamentally wrong. They rested upon the assumption of the equlity of races. This was an error.* It was a sandy foundation ; and the idea of a government built upon it,—when the 'storm came and the wind blew, it *fell.*'

---

[1] National Intelligencer, Tuesday, May 7, 1861.

"*Our new government is founded upon exactly the opposite ideas. Its foundations are laid, its corner-stone rests, upon the great truth, that the negro is not equal to the white man ; that slavery, subordination to the superior race, is his natural and normal condition. This, our new government, is the first, in the history of the world, based upon this great physical, philosophical, and moral truth.* This truth has been slow in the process of its development, like all other truths in the various departments of science. It has been so even amongst us. Many who hear me, perhaps, can recollect well that this truth was not generally admitted, even within their day." [1]

Now, then, what was the real issue between the Confederate States and the United States? Why, it was extension of slavery by the former, and the restriction of slavery by the latter. To put the issue as it was understood by Northern men—in poetic language, it was "*The Union as it is.*" While the South, at length, through its leaders, acknowledged that slavery was their issue, the North, standing upon the last analysis of the Free-Soil idea of resistance to the further inoculation of free territory with the virus of slavery, refused to recognize slavery as an issue. But what did the battle cry of the loyal North, "*The Union as it is,*" mean? A Union half free and half slave ; a dual government, if not in fact, certainly in the brains and hearts of the people ; two civilizations at eternal and inevitable war with each other ; a Union with the canker-worm of slavery in it, impairing its strength every year and threatening its life ; a Union in which two hostile ideas of political economy were at work, and where unpaid slave labor was inimical to the interests of the free workingmen. And it should not be forgotten that the Republican party acknowledged the right of Southerns to hunt slaves in the free States, and to return such slaves, under the fugitive-slave law, to their masters. Mr. Lincoln was not an Abolitionist, as many people think. His position on the question was clearly stated in the answers he gave to a number of questions put to him by Judge Douglass in the latter part of the summer of 1858. Mr. Lincoln said :

"Having said this much, I will take up the judge's interrogatories as I find them printed in the Chicago 'Times,' and answer them *seriatim*. In order that there may be no mistake about it, I have copied

---

[1] National Intelligencer, Tuesday, April, 2, 1861.

the interrogatories in writing, and also my answers to them. The first one of these interrogatories is in these words :

" Question 1. ' I desire to know whether Lincoln to-day stands, as he did in 1854, in favor of the unconditional repeal of the Fugitive-Slave Law ? '

" Answer. I do not now, nor ever did, stand in favor of the unconditional repeal of the Fugitive-Slave Law.

" Q. 2. ' I desire him to answer whether he stands pledged to-day, as he did in 1854, against the admission of any more slave States into the Union, even if the people want them ? '

" A. I do not now, nor ever did, stand pledged against the admission of any more slave States into the Union.

" Q. 3. ' I want to know whether he stands pledged against the admission of a new State into the Union with such a constitution as the people of that State may see fit to make.'

" Q. 4. ' I want to know whether he stands to-day pledged to the abolition of slavery in the District of Columbia ? '

" A. I do not stand to-day pledged to the abolition of slavery in the District of Columbia.

" Q. 5. ' I desire him to answer whether he stands pledged to the prohibition of the slave-trade between the different States ? '

" A. I do not stand pledged to the prohibition of the slave-trade between the different States.

" Q. 6. ' I desire to know whether he stands pledged to prohibit slavery in all the territories of the United States, north as well as south of the Missouri Compromise line ? '

" A. I am impliedly, if not expressly, pledged to a belief in the *right* and *duty* of Congress to prohibit slavery in all the United States territories. [Great applause.]

" Q. 7. ' I desire him to answer whether he is opposed to the acquisition of any new territory unless slavery is first prohibited therein ? '

" A. I am not generally opposed to honest acquisition of territory ; and, in any given case, I would or would not oppose such acquisition, accordingly as I might think such acquisition would or would not agitate the slavery question among ourselves.

" Now, my friends, it will be perceived upon an examination of these questions and answers, that so far I have only answered that I was not *pledged* to this, that, or the other. The judge has not framed his interrogatories to ask me any thing more than this, and I have answered in strict accordance with the interrogatories, and have answered truly that I am not *pledged* at all upon any of the points to which I have answered. But I am not disposed to hang upon the exact form of his interrogatories. I am rather disposed to take up at least some of these questions, and state what I really think upon them.

"As to the first one, in regard to the Fugitive-Slave Law, I have never hesitated to say, and I do not now hesitate to say, that I think, under the Constitution of the United States, the people of the Southern States are entitled to a congressional slave law. Having said that, I have had nothing to say in regard to the existing Fugitive-Slave Law, further than that I think it should have been framed so as to be free from some of the objections that pertain to it, without lessening its efficiency. And inasmuch as we are not now in an agitation in regard to an alteration or modification of that law, I would not be the man to introduce it as a new subject of agitation upon the general question of slavery.

"In regard to the other question, of whether I am pledged to the admission of any more slave States into the Union, I state to you very frankly that I would be exceedingly sorry ever to be put in a position of having to pass upon that question. I should be exceedingly glad to know that there would never be another slave State admitted into the Union ; but I must add, that if slavery shall be kept out of the territories during the territorial existence of any one given territory, and then the people shall, having a fair chance and a clear field, when they come to adopt the constitution, do such an extraordinary thing as to adopt a slave constitution, uninfluenced by the actual presence of the institution among them, I see no alternative, if we own the country, but to admit them into the Union. [Applause.]

"The third interrogatory is answered by the answer to the second, it being, as I conceive, the same as the second.

"The fourth one is in regard to the abolition of slavery in the District of Columbia. In relation to that I have my mind very distinctly made up. I should be exceedingly glad to see slavery abolished in the District of Columbia. I believe that Congress possesses the constitutional power to abolish it. Yet, as a member of Congress, I should not, with my present views, be in favor of *endeavoring* to abolish slavery in the District of Columbia, unless it would be upon these conditions : *First*, that the abolition should be gradual ; *second*, that it should be on a vote of the majority of qualified voters in the district ; and, *third*, that compensation should be made to unwilling owners. With these three conditions I confess I would be exceedingly glad to see Congress abolish slavery in the District of Columbia, and, in the language of Henry Clay, ' sweep from our capital that foul blot upon our nation.'

"In regard to the fifth interrogatory, I must say here that, as to the question of the abolition of the slave-trade between the different States, I can truly answer, as I have, that I am *pledged* to nothing about it. It is a subject to which I have not given that mature consideration that would make me feel authorized to state a position so as to hold myself entirely bound by it. In other words, that question has never been prominently enough before me to induce me to investigate whether we really have the constitutional power to do it. I could investigate it, if I had sufficient time, to bring myself to a conclusion upon that subject; but I have not done so, and I say so frankly to you here, and to Judge Douglass. I must say, however, that if I should be of opinion that Congress does possess the constitutional power to abolish slave-trading among the different States, I should still not be in favor of the exercise of that power unless upon some conservative principle as I conceive it, akin to what I have said in relation to the abolition of slavery in the District of Columbia.

"My answer as to whether I desire that slavery should be prohibited in all territories of the United States, is full and explicit within itself, and cannot be made clearer by any comments of mine. So, I suppose, in regard to the question whether I am opposed to the acquisition of any more territory unless slavery is first prohibited therein, my answer is such that I could add nothing by way of illustration, or making myself better understood, than the answer which I have placed in writing.

"Now, in all this the judge has me, and he has me on the record. I suppose he had flattered himself that I was really entertaining one set of opinions for one place, and another set for another place—that I was afraid to say at one place what I uttered at another. What I am saying here I suppose I say to a vast audience as strongly tending to abolitionism as any audience in the State of Illinois, and I believe I am saying that which, if it would be offensive to any persons and render them enemies to myself, would be offensive to persons in this audience." [1]

Here, then, is the position of Mr. Lincoln set forth with deliberation and care. He was opposed to any coercive measures in settling the slavery question; he was for gradual emancipation; and for admitting States into the Union with a slave constitution. Within twenty-four months, without a change of views, he was nominated for and elected to the Presidency of the United States.

With no disposition to interfere with the institution of slavery, Mr. Lincoln found himself chief magistrate of a great *nation* in the midst of a great rebellion. And in his inaugural address on the 4th of March, 1861, he referred to the question of slavery again in a manner too clear to admit of misconception, affirming his previous views:

---

[1] Barrett, pp. 177–180.

"There is much controversy about the delivering up of fugitives from service or labor. The clause I now read is as plainly written in the Constitution as any other of its provisions :

"'No person held to service or labor in one State under the laws thereof, escaping into another, shall, in consequence of any law or regulation therein, be discharged from such service or labor, but shall be delivered up on claim of the party to whom such service or labor may be due.'

"It is scarcely questioned that this provision was intended by those who made it for the reclaiming of what we call fugitive slaves ; and the intention of the lawgiver is the law.

"All members of Congress swear their support to the whole Constitution—to this provision as well as any other. To the proposition, then, that slaves whose cases come within the terms of this clause 'shall be delivered up,' their oaths are unanimous. Now, if they would make the effort in good temper, could they not, with nearly equal unanimity, frame and pass a law by means of which to keep good that unanimous oath ?

"There is some difference of opinion whether this clause should be enforced by National or by State authority; but surely that difference is not a very material one. If the slave is to be surrendered, it can be of but little consequence to him or to others by which authority it is done ; and should any one, in any case, be content that this oath shall go unkept on a merely unsubstantial controversy as to how it shall be kept ?"

So the issues were joined in war. The South aggressively, offensively sought the extension and perpetuation of slavery. The North passively, defensively stood ready to protect her free territory, but not to interfere with slavery. And there was no day during the first two years of the war when the North would not have cheerfully granted the slave institution an indefinite lease of *legal* existence upon the condition that the war should cease.

CHAPTER XV.

" A WHITE MAN'S WAR."

The First Call for Troops. — Rendition of Fugitive Slaves by the Army. — Col. Tyler's Address to the People of Virginia. — General Isaac R. Sherwood's Account of an Attempt to secure a Fugitive Slave in his Charge. — Col. Steedman refuses to have his Camp searched for Fugitive Slaves, by Order from Gen. Fry. — Letter from Gen. Buell in Defence of the Rebels in the South. — Orders issued by Generals Hooker, Williams, and Others, in Regard to harboring Fugitive Slaves in Union Camps. — Observation concerning Slavery from the " Army of the Potomac." — Gen. Butler's Letter to Gen. Winfield Scott. — It is answered by the Secretary of War. — Horace Greeley's Letter to the President. — President Lincoln's Reply. — Gen. John C. Fremont, Commander of the Union Army in Missouri, issues a Proclamation emancipating Slaves in his District. — It is disapproved by the President. — Emancipation Proclamation by Gen. Hunter. — It is rescinded by the President. — Slavery and Union joined in a Desperate Struggle.

WHEN the war clouds broke over the country and hostilities began, the North counted the Negro on the outside of the issue. The Federal Government planted itself upon the policy of the "defence of the free States,"—pursued a defensive rather than an offensive policy. And, whenever the Negro was mentioned, the leaders of the political parties and the Union army declared that it was "*a white man's war.*"

The first call for three months' troops indicated that the authorities at Washington felt confident that the "trouble" would not last long. The call was issued on the 15th of April, 1861, and provided for the raising of 75,000 troops. It was charged by the President that certain States had been guilty of forming " combinations too powerful to be suppressed by the ordinary course of judicial proceedings," and then he proceeded to state :

" The details for this object will be immediately communicated to the State authorities through the War Department. I appeal to all loyal citizens to favor, facilitate, and aid this effort to maintain the honor, the integrity, and the existence of our National Union, and the perpetuity of popular government, and to redress wrongs already long enough endured. I deem it proper to say that the first service assigned to the forces hereby called forth, will probably be to repossess the forts, places, and property which have been seized from the Union ; and in every event the utmost care will be observed, consistently with the objects aforesaid, to avoid any devastation, any destruction of, or interference with, property, or any disturbance of peaceful citizens of any part of the country ; and I hereby command the persons composing the combinations aforesaid, to disperse and retire peaceably to their respective abodes within twenty days from this date." [1]

There was scarcely a city in the North, from New York to San Francisco, whose Colored residents did not speedily offer their services to the States to aid in suppressing the Rebellion. But everywhere as promptly were their services declined. The Colored people of the Northern States were patriotic and enthusiastic ; but their interest was declared insolence. And being often rebuked for their loyalty, they subsided into silence to bide a change of public sentiment.

The almost unanimous voice of the press and pulpit was against a recognition of the Negro as the cause of the war. Like a man in the last stages of consumption who insists that he has only a bad cold, so the entire North urged that slavery was not the cause of the war: it was a little local misunderstanding. But the death of the gallant Col. Elmer E. Elsworth palsied the tongues of mere talkers ;' and in the tragic silence that followed, great, brave, and true men began to think.

Not a pulpit in all the land had spoken a word for the slave. The clergy stood dumb before the dreadful issue. But one man was found, like David of old, who, gathering his smooth pebble of fact from the brook of God's eternal truth, boldly met the boastful and erroneous public sentiment of the hour. That man was the Rev. Justin D. Fulton, a Baptist minister of Albany, New York. He was chosen to preach the funeral sermon of Col. Elsworth, and performed that duty on Sunday, May 26, 1861. Speaking of slavery, the reverend gentleman said :

" Shall this magazine of danger be permitted to remain ? *We must answer this question. If we say no, it is no !* Slavery is a curse to the North. It impoverishes the South, and demoralizes both. It is the parent of treason, the seedling of tyranny, and the fountain-source of all the ills that have infected our life as a people, being the central cause of all our conflicts of the past and the war of to-day. What

---

[1] Rebellion Recs., vol. i. Doc., p. 63.

reason have we for permitting it to remain ? God does not want it, for His truth gives freedom. The South does not need it, for it is the chain fastened to her limb that fetters her progress. Morality, patriotism, and humanity alike protest against it.

"The South fights for slavery, for the despotism which it represents, for the ignoring the rights of labor, and for reducing to slavery or to serfdom all whose hands are hardened by toil.

"Why not make the issue at once, which shall inspire every man that shoulders his musket with a noble purpose? Our soldiers need to be reminded that this government was consecrated to freedom by those who first built here the altars of worship, and planted on the shore of the Western Continent the tree of liberty, whose fruit to-day fills the garners of national hope. . . . I would not forget that I am a messenger of the Prince of Peace. My motives for throwing out these suggestions are three-fold : 1. Because I believe God wants us to be actuated by motives not one whit less philanthropic than the giving of freedom to four million of people. 2. I confess to a sympathy for and faith in the slave, and cherish the belief that if freed, the war would become comparatively bloodless, and that as a people we should enter on the discharge of higher duties and a more enlarged prosperity. 3. The war would hasten to a close, and the end secured would then form a brilliant dawn to a career of prosperity unsurpassed in the annals of mankind."[1]

Brave, prophetic words ! But a thousand vituperative editors sprang at Mr. Fulton's utterances, and as snapping curs, growled at and shook every sentence. He stood his ground. He took no step backward. When notice was kindly sent him that a committee would wait on him to treat him to a coat of tar and feathers, against the entreaties of anxious friends, he sent word that he would give them a warm reception. When the best citizens of Albany said the draft could not be enforced without bloody resistance, the Rev. Mr. Fulton exclaimed : "If the floodgates of blood are to be opened, we will not shoot down the poor and ignorant, but the swaggering and insolent men whose hearts are not in this war ! "

The "Atlas and Argus," in an editorial on *Ill-Timed Pulpit Abolitionism,* denounced Rev. Mr. Fulton in bitterest terms ; while the "Evening Standard" and "Journal" both declared that the views of the preacher were as a fire-brand thrown into the magazine of public sentiment.

---

[1] Albany Atlas and Argus, May 27, 1861.

Everywhere throughout the North the Negro was counted as on the outside. Everywhere it was merely "a war for the Union," which was half free and half slave.

When the Union army got into the field at the South it was confronted by a difficult question. What should be done with the Negroes who sought the Union lines for protection from their masters? The sentiment of the press, Congress, and the people of the North generally, was against interference with the slave, either by the civil or military authorities. And during the first years of the war the army became a band of slave-catchers. Slave-holders and sheriffs from the Southern States were permitted to hunt fugitive slaves under the Union flag and within the lines of Federal camps. On the 22d of June, 1861, the following paragraph appeared in the "Baltimore American":

"Two free negroes, belonging to Frederick, Md., who concealed themselves in the cars which conveyed the Rhode Island regiment to Washington from this city, were returned that morning by command of Colonel Burnside, who *supposed them to be slaves.* The negroes were accompanied by a sergeant of the regiment, who lodged them in jail."

On the 4th of July, 1861, Col. Tyler, of the 7th Ohio regiment, delivered an address to the people of Virginia; a portion of which is sufficient to show the feeling that prevailed among army officers on the slavery question:

"To you, fellow-citizens of West Virginia—many of whom I have so long and favorably known,—I come to aid and protect. [The grammar is defective.]

"I have no selfish ambition to gratify, no personal motives to actuate. I am here to protect you in person and property—to aid you in the execution of the law, in the maintenance of peace and order, in the defence of the Constitution and the Union, and in the extermination of our common foe. As our enemies have belied our mission, and represented us as a band of Abolitionists, I desire to assure you that the relation of master and servant as recognized in your State shall be respected. Your authority over that species of property shall not in the least be interfered with. To this end I assure you that those under my command have peremptory orders to take up and hold any negroes found running about the camp without passes from their masters."

When a few copies had been struck off, a lieutenant in Captain G. W. Shurtleff's company handed him one. He waited upon the colonel, and told him, that it was not true that the troops had been ordered to arrest fugitive slaves. The colonel threatened to place Captain Shurtleff in arrest, when he exclaimed: "I 'll never be a slave-catcher, so help me God!" There were few men in the army at this time who sympathized with such a noble declaration, and, therefore, Captain Shurtleff found himself in a very small minority.

The following account of an attempt to secure a fugitive slave from General Isaac R. Sherwood has its historical value. General Sherwood was as noble a *man* as he was a brave and intelligent soldier. He obeyed the still small voice in his soul and won a victory for humanity:

"In the February and March of 1863, I was a major in command of 111th O. V. I. regiment. I had a servant, as indicated by army regulations, in charge of my private horse. He was from Frankfort, Ky., the property of a Baptist clergyman. When the troops passed through Frankfort, in the fall of 1862, he left his master, and followed the army. He came to me at Bowling Green, and I hired him to take care of my horse. He was a lad about fifteen years old, named *Alfred Jackson.*

"At this time, Brig.-Gen. Boyle, or Boyd (I think Boyle), was in command of the District of Kentucky, and had issued his general order, that fugitive slaves should be delivered up. Brig.-Gen. H. M. Judah was in command of Post of Bowling Green, also of our brigade, there stationed.

"The owner of Alfred Jackson found out his whereabouts, and sent a U. S. marshal to Bowling Green to get him. Said marshal came to my headquarters under a pretence to see my very fine saddle-horse, but really to identify Alfred Jackson. The horse was brought out by Alfred Jackson. The marshal went to Brig.-Gen. Judah's headquarters and got a written order addressed to me, describing the lad and ordering me to deliver the boy. This order was delivered to me by Col. Sterling, of Gen. Judah's staff, in person. I refused to obey it. I sent word to Gen. Judah that he could have my sword, but while I commanded that regiment no fugitive slave should ever be delivered to his master. The officer made my compliments to Gen. Judah as aforesaid, and I was placed under arrest for disobedience to orders, and my sword taken from me.

"In a few days the command was ordered to move to Glasgow, Ky., and Gen. Judah, not desiring to trust the regiment in command of a captain, I was temporarily restored to command, pending the meeting of a court-martial to try my case. When the command moved I took Alfred Jackson along. After we reached Glasgow, Ky., Gen. Judah sent for me, and said if I would then deliver up Alfred Jackson he would restore me to command. The United States marshal was present. This I again refused to do.

" The same day, I sent an ambulance out of the lines, with Alfred Jackson tucked under the seat, in charge of a man going North, and I gave him money to get to Hillsdale, Michigan, where he went, and where he resided and grew up to be a good man and a citizen. I called the attention of Hon. James M. Ashley (then Member of Congress) to the matter, and under instructions from Secretary Stanton, Gen. Boyle's order was revoked, and I never delivered a fugitive, nor was I ever tried."

In Mississippi, in 1862, Col. James B. Steedman (afterward major-general) refused to honor an order of Gen. Fry, delivered by the man who wanted the slave in Steedman's camp. Col. Steedman read the order and told the bearer that he was a rebel; that he could not search *his* camp ; and that he would give him just ten minutes to get out of the camp, or he would riddle him with bullets. When Gen. Fry asked for an explanation of his refusal to allow his camp to be searched, Col. Steedman said he would never consent to have his camp searched by a *rebel ;* that he would use every bayonet in his regiment to protect the Negro slave who had come to him for protection ; and that he was sustained by the Articles of War, which had been amended about that time.

Again, in the late summer of 1863, at Tuscumbia, Tennessee, Gen. Fry rode into Col. Steedman's camp to secure the return of the slaves of an old lady whom he had known before the war. Col. Steedman said he did not know that any slaves were in his camp; and that if they were there they should not be taken except they were willing to go. Gen. Fry was a Christian gentleman of a high Southern type, and combined with his loyalty to the Union an abiding faith in "the sacredness of slave property." Whether he ever recovered from the malady, history saith not.

The great majority of regular army officers were in sympathy with the idea of protecting slave property. Gen. T. W. Sherman, occupying the defences of Port Royal, in October, 1861, issued the following proclamation to the people of South Carolina:

" In obedience to the orders of the President of these United States of America, I have landed on your shores with a small force of

National troops. The dictates of a duty which, under the Constitution, I owe to a great sovereign State, and to a proud and hospitable people, among whom I have passed some of the pleasantest days of my life, prompt me to proclaim that we have come among you with no feelings of personal animosity ; no desire to harm your citizens, destroy your property, or interfere with any of your lawful rights, or your social and local institutions, beyond what the causes herein briefly alluded to may render unavoidable." [1]

This proclamation sounds as if the general were a firm believer in State sovereignty; and that he was possessed with a feeling that he had landed in some strange land, among a people of different civilization and peculiar institutions.

On the 13th of November, 1861, Major-Gen. John A. Dix, upon taking possession of the counties of Accomac and Northampton, Va., issued the following proclamation :

"The military forces of the United States are about to enter your counties as a part of the Union. They will go among you as friends, and with the earnest hope that they may not, by your own acts, be compelled to become your enemies. They will invade no right of person or property. On the contrary, your laws, your institutions, your usages, will be scrupulously respected. There need be no fear that the quietude of any fireside will be disturbed, unless the disturbance is caused by yourselves.

"Special directions have been given not to interfere with the condition of any person held to domestic servitude ; and, in order that there may be no ground for mistake or pretext for misrepresentation, commanders of regiments or corps have been instructed not to permit such persons to come within their lines." [2]

Gen. Halleck, while in command of the Union forces in Missouri, issued his " Order No. 3." as follows :

"It has been represented that important information, respecting the number and condition of our forces, is conveyed to the enemy by means of fugitive slaves who are admitted within our lines. In order to remedy this evil, it is directed that no such person be hereafter permitted to enter the lines of any camp, or of any forces on the march, and that any now within such lines be immediately excluded therefrom."

---

[1] Greeley, vol. ii. p. 240.
[2] Rebellion Records, vol. iii. Doc. p. 376.

On the 23d of February, 1862, in " Order No. 13," he referred to the slave question as follows :

" It does not belong to the military to decide upon the relation of master and slave. Such questions must be settled by the civil courts. No fugitive slaves will, therefore, be admitted within our lines or camps, except when specially ordered by the general commanding."

On the 18th of February, 1862, Major-Gen. A. E. Burnside issued a proclamation in which he said to the people :

" The Government asks only that its authority may be recognized ; and we repeat, in no manner or way does it desire to interfere with your laws, constitutionally established, your institutions of any kind whatever, your property of any sort, or your usages in any respect."

The following letter from Gen. Buell shows how deeply attached he was to the " constitutional guaranties" accorded to the rebels of the South :

" HEADQUARTERS DEPARTMENT OF THE OHIO,
    " NASHVILLE, March 6, 1862.

"*Dear Sir :* I have the honor to receive your communication of the 1st instant, on the subject of fugitive slaves in the camps of the army.

"It has come to my knowledge that slaves sometimes make their way improperly into our lines ; and in some instances they may be enticed there ; but I think the number has been magnified by report. Several applications have been made to me by persons whose servants have been found in our camps ; and in every instance that I know of the master has recovered his servant and taken him away.

"I need hardly remind you that there will always be found some lawless and mischievous person in every army ; but I assure you that the mass of this army is law-abiding, and that it is neither its disposition nor its policy to violate law or the rights of individuals in any particular. With great respect, your obedient servant,

"D. C. BUELL,
" *Brig.-Gen. Commanding Department.*
" Hon. J. R. UNDERWOOD, *Chairman Military Committee,*
    " Frankfort, Ky."

So "in every instance" the master had recovered his slave when found in Gen. Buell's camp !

On the 26th of March, 1862, Gen. Joseph Hooker, commanding the " Upper Potomac," issued the following order :

" *To Brigade and Regimental Commanders of this Division :*

"Messrs. Nally, Gray, Dunnington, Dent, Adams, Speake, Price, Posey, and Cobey, citizens of Maryland, have negroes supposed to be with some of the regiments of this division. The brigadier-general commanding directs that they be permitted to visit all the camps of his command, in search of their property ; and if found, that they be allowed to take possession of the same, without any interference whatever. Should any obstacle be thrown in their way by any officer or soldier in the division, he will be at once reported by the regimental commander to these headquarters."

In the spring of 1862, Gen. Thos. Williams, in the Department of the Gulf, issued the following order [1] :

"In consequence of the demoralizing and disorganizing tendencies to the troops of harboring runaway negroes, it is hereby ordered that the respective commanders of the camps and garrisons of the several regiments, 2d brigade, turn all such fugitives in their camps or garrisons out beyond the limits of their respective guards and sentinels.
"By order of
"Brig.-Gen. T. WILLIAMS." [2]

In a letter dated "Headquarters Army of the Potomac, July 7, 1862," Major-Gen. Geo. B. McClellan made the following observations concerning slavery :

"This Rebellion has assumed the character of a war ; as such it should be regarded ; and it should be conducted upon the highest principles known to Christian civilization. It should not be a war looking to the subjugation of the people of any State, in any event. It should not be at all a war upon populations, but against armed forces and political organizations. Neither confiscation of property, political executions of persons, territorial organization of States, nor forcible abolition of slavery should be contemplated for a moment."

But the drift of the sentiment of the army was in the direction of compromise with the slavery question. Nearly every statesman at Washington—in the White House and in the Congress—and nearly every officer in the army regarded the Negro question as purely political and not military. That it was a problem hard of solution no one could doubt. Hundreds of loyal

---

[1] I have quite a large number of such orders, but the above will suffice.
[2] Greeley, vol. ii. p. 246.

Negroes, upon the orders of general officers, were turned away from the Union lines, while those who had gotten on the inside were driven forth to the cruel vengeance of rebel masters. Who could solve the problem? Major-Gen. Benjamin F. Butler banished the politician, and became the loyal, patriotic *soldier !* In the month of May, 1861, during the time Gen. Butler commanded the Union forces at Fortress Monroe, three slaves made good their escape into his lines. They stated that they were owned by Col. Mallory, of the Confederate forces in the front; that he was about to send them to the North Carolina seaboard to work on rebel fortifications; and that the fortifications were intended to bar that coast against the Union arms. Having heard this statement, Gen. Butler, viewing the matter from a purely military stand-point, exclaimed: "These men are *contraband* of war; set them at work." Here was a solution of the entire problem; here was a blow delivered at the backbone of the Rebellion. He claimed no right to act as a politician, but acting as a loyal-hearted, clear-headed *soldier*, he coined a word and hurled a shaft at the enemy that struck him in a part as vulnerable as the heel of Achilles. In his letter to the Lieut.-Gen. of the Army, Winfield Scott, 27th of May, 1861, he said:

"Since I wrote my last, the question in regard to slave property is becoming one of very serious magnitude. The inhabitants of Virginia are using their negroes in the batteries, and are preparing to send their women and children South. The escapes from them are very numerous, and a squad has come in this morning, and my pickets are bringing in their women and children. Of course these can not be dealt with upon the theory on which I designed to treat the services of able-bodied men and women who might come within my lines, and of which I gave you a detailed account in my last dispatch.

"I am in the utmost doubt what to do with this species of property. Up to this time I have had come within my lines men and women, with their children,—entire families,—each family belonging to the same owner. I have therefore determined to employ—as I can do very profitably—the able-bodied persons in the party, issuing proper food for the support of all ; charging against their services the expense of care and sustenance of the non-laborers ; keeping a strict and accurate account, as well of the services as of the expenditures ; having the worth of the services and the cost of the expenditures determined by a board of survey hereafter to be detailed. I know of no other manner in which to dispose of this subject and the questions connected therewith. As a matter of property, to the insurgents it will be of very great moment—the number that I now have amounting, as I am informed, to what in good times would be of the value of $60,000.

"Twelve of these negroes, I am informed, have escaped from the erection of the batteries on Sewell's Point, which fired upon my expedition as it passed by out of range. As a means of offense, therefore, in the enemy's hands, these negroes, when able-bodied, are of great importance. Without them the batteries could not have been erected ; at least, for many weeks. As a military question it would seem to be a measure of necessity, and deprives their masters of their services.

"How can this be done ? As a political question, and a question of humanity, can I receive the services of a father and a mother and not take the children ? Of the humanitarian aspect, I have no doubt ; of the political one, I have no right to judge. I therefore submit all this to your better judgment, and, as these questions have a political aspect, I have ventured—and I trust I am not wrong in so doing—to duplicate the parts of my dispatch relating to this subject, and forward them to the Secretary of War.

" Your obedient servant,

"Lt.-General SCOTT."[1]   "BENJ. F. BUTLER.

The letter of Gen. Butler was laid before the Secretary of War, who answered it as follows :

"SIR : Your action in respect to the negroes who came within your lines, from the service of the rebels, is approved. The Department is sensible of the embarrassments which must surround officers conducting military operations in a State, by the laws of which slavery is sanctioned. The Government can not recognize the rejection by any State of its Federal obligations, resting upon itself. Among these Federal obligations, however, no one can be more important than that of suppressing and dispersing any combination of the former for the purpose of overthrowing its whole constitutional authority. While, therefore, you will permit no interference, by persons under your command, with the relations of persons held to service under the laws of any State, you will, on the other hand, so long as any State within which your military operations are conducted remains under the control of such armed combinations, refrain from surrendering to alleged masters any persons who come within your lines. You will employ such persons in the services to which they will be best adapted ; keeping an account of the labor by them performed, of the value of it, and the expenses of their maintenance. The question of their final disposition will be reserved for future determination.

"SIMON CAMERON, *Secretary of War.*

"To Maj.-Gen. BUTLER.

---

[1] Greeley, vol. ii. p. 238.

In an account of the life and services of Capt. Grier Talmadge, the " Times" correspondent says:

" To the deceased, who was conservative in his views and actions, belongs the credit of first enunciating the 'contraband' idea as subsequently applied in the practical treatment of the slaves of rebels, Early in the spring of 1861, Flag-Officer Pendergrast, in command of the frigate 'Cumberland,' then the vessel blockading the Roads, restored to their owners certain slaves that had escaped from Norfolk. Shortly after, the Flag-Officer, Gen. Butler, Capt. Talmadge, and the writer chanced to meet in the ramparts of the fortress, when Capt. T. took occasion, warmly, but respectfully, to dissent from the policy of the act, and proceeded to advance some arguments in support of his views. Turning to Gen. Butler, who had just assumed command of this department, he said : 'General, it is a question you will have to decide, and that, too, very soon ; for in less than twenty-four hours deserting slaves will commence swarming to your lines. The rebels are employing their slaves in thousands in constructing batteries all around us. And, in my judgment, in view of this fact, not only slaves who take refuge within our lines are contrabands, but I hold it as much our duty to seize and capture those employed, or intended to be employed, in constructing batteries, as it is to destroy the arsenals or any other warmaking element of the rebels, or to capture and destroy the batteries themselves.' Within two days after this conversation, Gen. Butler has the question practically presented to him, as predicted, and he solved it by applying the views advanced by the deceased." [1]

The conservative policy of Congress, the cringing attitude of the Government at Washington, the reverses on the Potomac, the disaster of Bull Run, the apologetic tone of the Northern press, the expulsion of slaves from the Union lines, and the conduct of "Copperheads" in the North—who crawled upon their stomachs, snapping and biting at the heels of Union men and Union measures,—bred a spirit of unrest and mob violence. It was not enough that the service of free Negroes was declined; they were now hunted out and persecuted by mobs and other agents of the disloyal element at the North. Like a man sick unto death the Government insisted that it only had a slight cold, and that it would be better soon. The President was no better informed as to the nature of the war than other conservative Republicans. On the 19th of August, 1862, Horace Greeley

---

[1] New York Times.

addressed an open letter to the President, known as "The Prayer of Twenty Millions," of which the following are specimen passages :

"On the face of this wide earth, Mr. President, there is not one disinterested, determined, intelligent champion of the Union cause who does not feel that all attempts to put down the Rebellion, and at the same time uphold its inciting cause, are preposterous and futile—that the Rebellion, if crushed out to-morrow, would be renewed within a year if slavery were left in full vigor—that army officers, who remain to this day devoted to slavery, can at best be but half-way loyal to the Union—and that every hour of deference to slavery is an hour of added and deepened peril to the Union. I appeal to the testimony of your Embassadors in Europe. It is freely at your service, not mine. Ask them to tell you candidly whether the seeming subserviency of your policy to the slave-holding, slavery-upholding interest, is not the perplexity, the despair, of statesmen of all parties ; and be admonished by the general answer !

"I close, as I began, with the statement that what an immense majority of the loyal millions of your countrymen require of you is a frank, declared, unqualified, ungrudging execution of the laws of the land, more especially of the Confiscation Act. That Act gives freedom to the slaves of rebels coming within our lines, or whom those lines may at any time inclose,—we ask you to render it due obedience by publicly requiring all your subordinates to recognize and obey it. The rebels are everywhere using the late anti-negro riots in the North—as they have long used your officers' treatment of negroes in the South— to convince the slaves that they have nothing to hope from a Union success—that we mean in that case to sell them into a bitter bondage to defray the cost of the war. Let them impress this as a truth on the great mass of their ignorant and credulous bondmen, and the Union will never be restored—never. We can not conquer ten millions of people united in solid phalanx against us, powerfully aided by Northern sympathizers and European allies. We must have scouts, guides, spies, cooks, teamsters, diggers, and choppers, from the blacks of the South—whether we allow them to fight for us or not—or we shall be baffled and repelled. As one of the millions who would gladly have avoided this struggle at any sacrifice but that of principle and honor, but who now feel that the triumph of the Union is indispensable not only to the existence of our country, but to the well-being of mankind, I entreat you to render a hearty and unequivocal obedience to the law of the land.

"Yours,

"HORACE GREELEY."[1]

---

[1] Greeley, vol. ii. pp. 249, 250.

It was an open letter. Mr. Greeley had evidently lost sight of his economic theories as applied to slavery in the abstract, and now, as a practical philosopher, caught hold of the question by the handle. Mr. Lincoln replied within a few days, but was still joined to his abstract theories of constitutional law. He loved the Union, and all he should do for the slave should be done to help the Union, not the slave. He was not desirous of saving or destroying slavery. But certainly he had spoken more wisely than he knew when he had asserted, a few years before, that "a nation half free and half slave, could not long exist." That was an indestructible truth. Had he adhered to that doctrine the way would have been easier. In every thing he consulted the Constitution. His letter is interesting reading.

"EXECUTIVE MANSION, WASHINGTON, }
"August 22, 1862. }

"Hon. HORACE GREELEY:

"*Dear Sir:* I have just read yours of the 19th instant, addressed to myself through the New York Tribune.

"If there be in it any statements or assumptions of fact which I may know to be erroneous, I do not now and here controvert them.

"If there be any inferences which I may believe to be falsely drawn, I do not now and here argue against them.

"If there be perceptible in it an impatient and dictatorial tone, I waive it in deference to an old friend whose heart I have always supposed to be right.

"As to the policy 'I seem to be pursuing,' as you say, I have not meant to leave any one in doubt. I would save the Union. I would save it in the shortest way under the Constitution.

"The sooner the national authority can be restored, the nearer the Union will be the Union as it was.

"If there be those who would not save the Union unless they could at the same time save slavery, I do not agree with them.

"If there be those who would not save the Union unless they could at the same time destroy slavery, I do not agree with them.

"*My paramount object is to save the Union, and not either to save or destroy slavery.*

"If I could save the Union without freeing any slave, I would do it; if I could save it by freeing all the slaves, I would do it; and if I could do it by freeing some and leaving others alone, I would also do that.

"What I do about slavery and the Colored race, I do because I believe it helps to save this Union; and what I forbear, I forbear because I do not believe it would help to save the Union.

" I shall do less'whenever I shall believe what I am doing hurts the cause ; and I shall do more whenever I believe doing more will help the cause.

" I shall try to correct errors when shown to be errors ; and I shall adopt new views so fast as they shall appear to be true views.

" I have here stated my purpose according to my views of official duty ; and I intend no modification of my oft-expressed personal wish that all men everywhere could be free.

" Yours,

" A. LINCOLN." [1]

But there were few men among the general officers of the army who either reached the conclusion by their own judgment, or were aided by the action of General Butler, that it was their duty to confiscate *all the property* of the enemy. Acting upon the plainest principle of military law, Major-General John C. Fremont, commanding the Department of the Missouri, or the Union forces in that State, issued the following proclamation :

" HEADQUARTERS OF THE WESTERN DEP'T,
"ST. LOUIS, August 31st.

"Circumstances, in my judgment, of sufficient urgency, render it necessary that the Commanding General of this Department should assume the administrative power of the State. Its disorganized condition, the helplessness of the civil authority, the total insecurity of life, and the devastation of property by bands of murderers and marauders, who infest nearly every county in the State, and avail themselves of the public misfortunes and the vicinity of a hostile force to gratify private and neighborhood vengeance, and who find an enemy wherever they find plunder, finally demand the severest measures to repress the daily increasing crimes and outrages which are driving off the inhabitants and ruining the State. In this condition, the public safety and the success of our arms require unity of purpose, without let or hindrance to the prompt administration of affairs.

" In order, therefore, to suppress disorders, to maintain, as far as now practicable, the public peace, and to give security and protection to the persons and property of loyal citizens, I do hereby extend and declare established martial law throughout the State of Missouri. The lines of the army of occupation in this State are, for the present, declared to extend from Leavenworth, by way of the posts of Jefferson-City, Rolla, and Ironton, to Cape Girardeau, on the Mississippi River.

---

[1] Greeley, vol. ii. p. 250.

All persons who shall be taken with arms in their hands, within these lines, shall be tried by Court Martial, and, if found guilty, will be shot. The property, real and personal, of all persons in the State of Missouri who shall take up arms against the United States, or shall be directly proven to have taken active part with their enemies in the field, is declared to be confiscated to the public use ; and their slaves, if any they have, are hereby declared free men.

"All persons who shall be proven to have destroyed, after the publication of this order, railroad tracks, bridges, or telegraphs, shall suffer the extreme penalty of the law.

"All persons engaged in treasonable correspondence, in giving or procuring aid to the enemies of the United States, in disturbing the public tranquillity by creating and circulating false reports or incendiary documents, are in their own interest warned that they are exposing themselves.

"All persons who have been led away from their allegiance are required to return to their homes forthwith ; any such absence, without sufficient cause, will be held to be presumptive evidence against them.

"The object of this declaration is to place in the hands of the military authorities the power to give instantaneous effect to existing laws, and to supply such deficiencies as the conditions of war demand. But it is not intended to suspend the ordinary tribunals of the country, where the law will be administered by the civil officers in the usual manner and with their customary authority, while the same can be peaceably exercised.

"The Commanding General will labor vigilantly for the public welfare, and, in his efforts for their safety, hopes to obtain not only the acquiescence, but the active support, of the people of the country.

"J. C. FREMONT, *Major-Gen. Com.*"[1]

This magnificent order thrilled the loyal hearts of the North with joy; but the President, still halting and hesitating, requested a modification of the order so far as it related to the liberation of slaves. This Gen. Fremont declined to do unless ordered to do so by his superior. Accordingly the President wrote him as follows:

"WASHINGTON, D. C., Sept. 11, 1861.

"Major-Gen. JOHN C. FREMONT :

"*Sir :*—Yours of the 8th, in answer to mine of the 2d inst., is just received. Assured that you, upon the ground, could better judge of the necessities of your position than I could at this distance, on seeing

---

[1] Greeley, vol. i. p. 585.

your proclamation of August 30th, I perceived no general objection to it; the particular clause, however, in relation to the confiscation of property and the liberation of slaves, appeared to me to be objectionable in its non-conformity to the Act of Congress, passed the 6th of last August, upon the same subjects; and hence I wrote you, expressing my wish that that clause should be modified accordingly. Your answer, just received, expresses the preference on your part that I should make an open order for the modification, which I very cheerfully do. It is, therefore, ordered that the said clause of said proclamation be so modified, held, and construed, as to conform with, and not to transcend, the provisions on the same subject contained in the Act of Congress entitled 'An Act to Confiscate Property Used for Insurrectionary Purposes,' approved August 6, 1861; and that the said act be published at length with this order.

"Your obedient servant,

"A. LINCOLN."[1]

Gen. Fremont's removal followed speedily. He was in advance of the slow coach at Washington, and was sent where he could do no harm to the enemy of the country, by emancipating Negroes. It seems as if there were nothing else left for Gen. Fremont to do but to free the slaves in his military district. They were the bone and sinew of Confederate resistance. It was to weaken the enemy that the general struck down this peculiar species of property, upon which the enemy of the country relied so entirely.

Major-Gen. David Hunter assumed command at Hilton Head, South Carolina, on the 31st of March, 1862. On the 9th of May he issued the following "General Order:"

"HEADQUARTERS DEP'T OF THE SOUTH,
"HILTON HEAD, S. C., May 9, 1862.

"*General Order*, No. 11.

"The three States of Georgia, Florida, and South Carolina, comprising the Military Department of the South, having deliberately declared themselves no longer under the United States of America, and having taken up arms against the United States, it becomes a military necessity to declare them under martial law.

"This was accordingly done on the 25th day of April, 1862. Slavery and martial law in a free country are altogether incompatible. The persons in these States—Georgia, Florida, and South Carolina—heretofore held as slaves, are therefore declared forever free."[2]

---

[1] Greeley, vol. ii. pp. 239, 240.

[2] Greeley, vol. ii. p. 246.

But the President, in ten days after its publication, rescinded the order of General Hunter, in the following Proclamation :

"*And whereas,* The same [Hunter's proclamation] is producing some excitement and misunderstanding, therefore, I, Abraham Lincoln, President of the United States, proclaim and declare that the Government of the United States had no knowledge or belief of an intention on the part of Gen. Hunter to issue such a proclamation, nor has it yet any authentic information that the document is genuine : and, further, that neither Gen. Hunter nor any other commander or person have been authorized by the Government of the United States to make proclamation declaring the slaves of any State free ; and that the supposed proclamation now in question, whether genuine or false, is altogether void, so far as respects such declaration. I further make known that, whether it be competent for me, as Commander-in-Chief of the Army and Navy, to declare the slaves of any State or States free ; and whether at any time, or in any case, it shall have become a necessity indispensable to the maintenance of the Government to exercise such supposed power, are questions which, under my responsibility, I reserve to myself, and which I cannot feel justified in leaving to the decision of commanders in the field.

"Those are totally different questions from those of police regulations in armies or in camps.

"On the sixth day of March last, by a special Message, I recommended to Congress the adoption of a joint resolution, to be substantially as follows :

"'*Resolved,* That the United States ought to coöperate with any State which may adopt gradual abolishment of slavery, giving to such State pecuniary aid, to be used by such State in its discretion, to compensate for the inconveniences, public and private, produced by such change of system.'

"The resolution, in the language above quoted, was adopted by large majorities in both branches of Congress, and now stands an authentic, definite, and solemn proposal of the nation to the States and people most interested in the subject-matter. To the people of these States now I mostly appeal. I do not argue—I beseech you to make the arguments for yourselves. You cannot, if you would, be blind to the signs of the times.

"I beg of you a calm and enlarged consideration of them, ranging, if it may be, far above partisan and personal politics.

"This proposal makes common cause for a common object, casting no reproaches upon any. It acts not the Pharisee. The change it contemplates would come gently as the dews of Heaven, not rending or wrecking any thing. Will you not embrace it ? So much good has not been done by one effort in all past time. as, in the Providence of God, it is now your high privilege to do. May the vast future not have to lament that you have neglected it!

" In witness whereof I have hereunto set `my hand and caused the seal of the United States to be hereunto affixed.

" Done at the city of Washington this 19th day of May, in the year of our Lord 1862, and of the independence of the United States the eighty-sixth.

" (Signed)   ABRAHAM LINCOLN.

" By the President :

" W. H. SEWARD, *Secretary of State."*

The conservative policy of the President greatly discouraged the friends of the Union, who felt that a vigorous prosecution of the war was the only hope of the nation. Slavery and the Union had joined in a terrible struggle for the supremacy. Both could not exist. Our treasury was empty; our bonds depreciated; our credit poor; our industries languishing; and the channels of commerce were choked. European governments were growing impatient at the dilatory policy of our nation; and every day we were losing sympathy and friends. Our armies were being repulsed and routed; and Columbia's war eagles were wearily flapping their pinions in the blood-dampened dust of a nerveless nation. But the Negro was still on the outside,—it was "a white man's war."

CHAPTER XVI.

THE NEGRO ON FATIGUE DUTY.

Negroes employed as Teamsters and in the Quartermaster's Department. — General Mercer's Order to the Slave-holders issued from Savannah. — He receives Orders from the Secretary of War to impress a Number of Negroes to build Fortifications. — The Negro proves himself Industrious and earns Promotion.

THE light began to break through the dark cloud of prejudice in the minds of the friends of the Union. If a Negro were useful in building rebel fortifications, why not in casting up defences for the Union army? Succeeding Gen. Butler in command at Fortress Monroe, on the 14th of October, 1861, Major-Gen. Wool issued an order, directing that "all colored persons called contrabands," employed by officers or others within his command, must be furnished with subsistence by their employers, and paid, if males, not less than four dollars per month, and that "all able-bodied colored persons, not employed as aforesaid," will be immediately put to work in the Engineer's or the Quartermaster's Department. On the 1st of November, Gen. Wool directed that the compensation of "contrabands" working for the government should be five to ten dollars per month, with soldier's rations. These Negroes rendered valuable service in the sphere they were called upon to fill.

In the Western army, Gen. James B. Steedman was the first man to suggest the idea of employing Negroes as teamsters. He saw that every Negro who drove a team of mules gave to the army one more white soldier with a musket in his hands; and so with the sympathy and approval of the gallant Gen. Geo. H. Thomas, Gen. Steedman put eighty Negroes into uniforms, and turned them over to an experienced white "wagon-master." The Negroes made excellent teamsters, and the plan was adopted quite generally.

In September, 1862, an order from Washington directed the employment of fifty thousand Negro laborers in the Quartermaster's Department, under Generals Hunter and Saxton! This showed that the authorities at Washington had begun to get their eyes open on this question. "And while speaking of the negroes," wrote a "Times" correspondent, in 1862, from Hilton Head, "let me present a few statistics obtained from an official source, respecting the success which has crowned the experiment of employing them as free paid laborers upon the plantations. The population of the Division (including Port Royal, St. Helena and Ladies' islands, with the smaller ones thereto adjacent, but excluding Hilton Head and its surroundings) is as follows:

"Effective 3,817
"Non-effective . . . . . : . 3,110

"Total 6,927

"The number of acres under cultivation on the same islands, is:

"Of Corn 6,444
"Of Cotton 3,384
"Of Potatoes 1,407

"A little calculation will show that the negroes have raised enough corn and potatoes to support themselves, besides a crop of cotton (now ripe) somewhat smaller than in former years, but still of very considerable value to the Government."[1]

Gen. Mercer issued the following order at Savannah, Georgia, which shows that the rebels did not despise the fatigue services of Negroes:

"C. S. ENGINEER'S OFFICE, }
"SAVANNAH, GA., Aug. 1, 1863. }

"The Brigadier-General Commanding desires to inform the slaveholders of Georgia that he has received authority from the Secretary of War to impress a number of negroes sufficient to construct such additional fortifications as are necessary for the defence of Savannah.

"He desires, if possible, to avoid the necessity of impressment, and therefore urges the owners of slave property to volunteer the services of their negroes. He believes that, while the planters of South Carolina are sending their slaves by thousands to aid the defence of Charleston, the slave-holders of Georgia will not be backward in contributing in the same patriotic manner to the defence of their own seaport, which has so far resisted successfully all the attacks of the enemy at Fort McAllister and other points.

"Remember, citizens of Georgia, that on the successful defence of Georgia depends the security of the interior of your State, where so

---

[1] Times, Sept. 4, 1862.

much of value both to yourselves and to the Confederacy at large is concentrated. It is best to meet the enemy at the threshold, and to hurl back the first wave of invasion. Once the breach is made, all the horrors of war must desolate your now peaceful and quiet homes. Let no man deceive himself. If Savannah falls the fault will be yours, and your own neglect will have brought the sword to your hearth-stones.

"The Brigadier-General Commanding, therefore, calls on all the slave-holders of Eastern, Southern, and Southwestern Georgia, but especially those in the neighborhood of Savannah, to send him immediately one fifth of their able-bodied male slaves, for whom transportation will be furnished and wages paid at the rate of twenty-five dollars per month, the Government to be responsible for the value of such Negroes as may be killed by the enemy, or may in any manner fall into his hands. By order of

"Brig.-Gen. MERCER, *Commanding.*

"JOHN MCCRADY,
"*Captain and Chief Engineer, State of Georgia.*" [1]

Negroes built most of the fortifications and earth-works for Gen. Grant in front of Vicksburg. The works in and about Nashville were cast up by the strong arm and willing hand of the loyal Blacks. Dutch Gap was dug by Negroes, and miles of earth-works, fortifications, and corduroy-roads were made by Negroes. They did fatigue duty in every department of the Union army. Wherever a Negro appeared with a shovel in his hand, a white soldier took his gun and returned to the ranks. There were 200,000 Negroes in the camps and employ of the Union armies, as servants, teamsters, cooks, and laborers. What a mighty host! Suppose the sentiment that early met the Negro on the picket lines and turned him back to the enemy had continued, 50,000 white soldiers would have been required in the Engineer's and Quartermaster's Department; while 25,000 white men would have been required for various other purposes, outside of the ranks of the army.

A narrow prejudice among some of the white troops, upon whose pedigree it would not be pleasant to dwell, met the Negro teamster, with a blue coat and buttons with eagles on them, with a growl. They disliked to see the Negro wearing a Union uniform;—it looked too much like equality.

But in his lowly station as a hewer of wood and a drawer of water, the Negro proved himself industrious, trustworthy, efficient, and cheerful. He earned promotion, and in due time secured it;

---

[1] Rebellion Recs., vol. vii. Doc. p. 479.

CHAPTER XVII.

THE EMANCIPATION PROCLAMATIONS.

CONGRESS PASSES AN ACT TO CONFISCATE PROPERTY USED FOR INSURRECTIONARY PURPOSES. — A
FRUITLESS APPEAL TO THE PRESIDENT TO ISSUE AN EMANCIPATION PROCLAMATION. — HE
THINKS THE TIME NOT YET COME FOR SUCH AN ACTION, BUT WITHIN A FEW WEEKS CHANGES
HIS OPINION AND ISSUES AN EMANCIPATION PROCLAMATION. — THE REBELS SHOW NO DISPOSI-
TION TO ACCEPT THE MILD TERMS OF THE PROCLAMATION. — MR. DAVIS GIVES ATTENTION TO
THE PROCLAMATION IN HIS THIRD ANNUAL MESSAGE. — SECOND EMANCIPATION PROCLAMATION
ISSUED BY PRESIDENT LINCOLN JANUARY 1, 1863. — THE PROCLAMATION IMPARTS NEW HOPE
TO THE NEGRO.

THE position taken by General Butler on the question of
receiving into the Federal lines the slaves of persons who
were in rebellion against the National Government, and
who were liable to be used in service against the government
by their owners, had its due influence in Washington. But all
the general officers did not share in the views of General Butler.
As many as twenty Union generals still had it in their minds
that it was the duty of the army "to catch run-away slaves";
and they afforded rebels every facility to search their camps.
They arrested fugitive Negroes and held them subject to the
order of their masters. Congress was not long in seeing the
suicidal tendency of such a policy, and on the 6th of August, 1861,
passed "An Act to Confiscate Property Used for Insurrectionary
Purposes." Notwithstanding this act, General McClellan and
other officers still clung to the obsolete doctrine of "the sacredness of slave property." His conduct finally called forth the
following letter from the Secretary of State:

"CONTRABANDS IN DISTRICT OF COLUMBIA.

"DEPARTMENT OF STATE,
"WASHINGTON CITY, December 4, 1861.

"*To Major-General George B. McClellan, Washington:*

"GENERAL: I am directed by the President to call your attention
to the following subject:

"Persons claimed to be held to service or labor under the laws of the State of Virginia, and actually employed in hostile service against the Government of the United States, frequently escape from the lines of the enemy's forces and are received within the lines of the Army of the Potomac. This Department understands that such persons, afterward coming into the city of Washington, are liable to be arrested by the city police, upon presumption, arising from color, that they are fugitives from service or labor.

"By the fourth section of the act of Congress, approved August 6, 1861, entitled 'An Act to Confiscate Property Used for Insurrectionary Purposes,' such hostile employment is made a full and sufficient answer to any further claim to service or labor. Persons thus employed and escaping are received into the military protection of the United States, and their arrest as fugitives from service or labor should be immediately followed by the military arrest of the parties making the seizure.

"Copies of this communication will be sent to the Mayor of the City of Washington and to the Marshal of the District of Columbia, that any collision between the civil and military authorities may be avoided.

"I am, General, your very obedient,

"WM. H. SEWARD."

It was now 1862. The dark war clouds were growing thicker. The Union army had won but few victories; our troops had to fight a tropical climate, the forces of nature, and an arrogant, jubilant, and victorious enemy. Autumn had come but nothing had been accomplished. The friends of the Union who favored a speedy and vigorous prosecution of the war, besieged the President with letters, memorials, and addresses to "*do something.*" But intrenched behind his "constitutional views" of how the war should be managed he heard all, but would not yield. On the 13th of September, 1862, a deputation of gentlemen, representing the various Protestant denominations of Chicago, called upon the President and urged him to adopt a vigorous policy of emancipation as the only way to save the Union; but he denied the request. He said:

"The subject is difficult, and good men do not agree. For instance: the other day, four gentlemen of standing and intelligence from New York called as a delegation on business connected with the war; but before leaving two of them earnestly besought me to proclaim general Emancipation; upon which the other two at once attacked them. You know also that the last session of Congress had a decided majority of anti-slavery men, yet they could not unite on this policy. And the

same is true of the religious people. Why, the Rebel soldiers are praying with a great deal more earnestness, I fear, than our own troops, and
expecting God to favor their side: for one of our soldiers, who had been
taken prisoner, told Senator Wilson a few days since that he met nothing so discouraging as the evident sincerity of those he was among in
their prayers. But we will talk over the merits of the case.

"What good would a proclamation of Emancipation from me do,
especially as we are now situated? I do not want to issue a document
that the whole world will see must necessarily be inoperative, like the
Pope's bull against the comet. Would my word free the slaves, when I
cannot even enforce the Constitution in the Rebel States? Is there a
single court, or magistrate, or individual, that would be influenced by
it there? And what reason is there to think it would have any greater
effect upon the slaves than the late law of Congress, which I approved,
and which offers protection and freedom to the slaves of rebel masters
who come within our lines? Yet I cannot learn that that law has
caused a single slave to come over to us. And, suppose they could be
induced by a proclamation of freedom from me to throw themselves
upon us, what should we do with them? How can we feed and care
for such a multitude? Gen. Butler wrote me a few days since that he
was issuing more rations to the slaves who have rushed to him than to
all the White troops under his command. They eat, and that is all;
though it is true Gen. Butler is feeding the Whites also by the thousand;
for it nearly amounts to a famine there. If, now, the pressure of the
war should call off our forces from New Orleans to defend some other
point, what is to prevent the masters from reducing the Blacks to
Slavery again; for I am told that whenever the rebels take any Black
prisoners, free or slave, they immediately auction them off! They did
so with those they took from a boat that was aground in the Tennessee
river a few days ago. And then I am very ungenerously attacked for
it! For instance, when, after the late battles at and near Bull Run, an
expedition went out from Washington, under a flag of truce, to bury
the dead and bring in the wounded, and the Rebels seized the Blacks
who went along to help, and sent them into Slavery, Horace Greeley said
in his paper that the Government would probably do nothing about it.
What *could* I do?

"Now, then, tell me, if you please, what possible result of good
would follow the issuing of such a proclamation as you desire? Understand: I raise no objection against it on legal or constitutional grounds;
for, as Commander-in-Chief of the army and navy in time of war, I suppose I have a right to take any measure which may best subdue the
enemy; nor do I urge objections of a moral nature, in view of possible
consequences of insurrection and massacre at the South. I view this
matter as a practical war measure, to be decided on according to the

advantages or disadvantages it may offer to the suppression of the Rebellion."

Not discouraged, the deputation urged in answer to his conservative views, that a policy of emancipation would strengthen the cause of the Union in Europe, and place the government upon high humane grounds, where it could boldly and confidently appeal to Almighty God in an honest attempt to save His poor children from the degrading curse of American slavery. But the President replied:

"I admit that Slavery is at the root of the Rebellion, or at least its *sine quâ non.* The ambition of politicians may have instigated them to act; they would have been impotent without Slavery as their instrument. I will also concede that Emancipation would help us in Europe, and convince them that we are incited by something more than ambition. I grant, further, that it would help somewhat at the North, though not so much, I fear, as you and those you represent imagine. Still, some additional strength would be added in that way to the war; and then, unquestionably, it would weaken the Rebels by drawing off their laborers, which is of great importance; but I am not so sure we could do much with the Blacks. If we were to arm them, I fear that in a few weeks the arms would be in the hands of the Rebels; and, indeed, thus far, we have not had arms enough to equip our White troops. I will mention another thing, though it meet only your scorn and contempt. There are fifty thousand bayonets in the Union army from the Border Slave States. It would be a serious matter if, in consequence of a proclamation such as you desire, they should go over to the Rebels. I do not think they all would—not so many, indeed, as a year ago, or as six months ago—not so many to-day as yesterday. Every day increases their Union feeling. They are also getting their pride enlisted, and want to beat the Rebels. Let me say one thing more: I think you should admit that we already have an important principle to rally and unite the people, in the fact thàt constitutional government is at stake. This is a fundamental idea, going down about as deep as anything."[1]

But there were millions of prayers ascending to the God of Battles daily that the President might have the courage and disposition to pursue a course required by the lamentable condition of the Union. And just nine days from the time he thought a proclamation not warranted and impracticable, he issued the following:

---

[1] Greeley, vol. ii. pp. 251, 252.

" I, ABRAHAM LINCOLN, President of the United States of America, and Commander-in-chief of the Army and Navy thereof, do hereby proclaim and declare that hereafter, as heretofore, the war will be prosecuted for the object of practically restoring the constitutional relation between the United States and each of the States, and the people thereof, in which States that relation is or may be suspended or disturbed.

" That it is my purpose, upon the next meeting of Congress, to again recommend the adoption of a practical measure tendering pecuniary aid to the free acceptance or rejection of all Slave States, so called, the people whereof may not then be in rebellion against the United States, and which States may then have voluntarily adopted, or thereafter may voluntarily adopt, immediate or gradual abolishment of Slavery within their respective limits ; and that the effort to colonize persons of African descent, with their consent, upon this continent or elsewhere, with the previously obtained consent of the governments existing there, will be continued.

That, on the first day of January, in the year of our Lord one thousand eight hundred and sixty-three, all persons held as slaves within any State, or designated part of the State, the people whereof shall then be in rebellion against the United States, shall be then, thenceforward, and forever free ; and the Executive Government of the United States, including the military and naval authority thereof, will recognize and maintain the freedom of such persons, and will do no act or acts to repress such persons, or any of them, in any efforts they may make for their actual freedom.

" That the Executive will, on the first day of January aforesaid, by proclamation, designate the States and parts of States, if any, in which the people thereof respectively shall then be in rebellion against the United States ; and the fact that any State, or the people thereof, shall on that day be in good faith represented in the Congress of the United States, by members chosen thereto at elections wherein a majority of the qualified voters of such State shall have participated, shall, in the absence of strong countervailing testimony, be deemed conclusive evidence that such State, and the people thereof, are not then in rebellion against the United States.

" That attention is hereby called to an act of Congress entitled 'An Act to make an additional Article of War,' approved March 13th, 1862 ; and which act is in the words and figures following :

" ' *Be it enacted by the Senate and House of Representatives of the United States of America in Congress assembled*, That hereafter the following shall be promulgated as an additional article of war for the government of the Army of the United States, and shall be obeyed and observed as such :

" ' SECTION I. All officers or persons in the military or naval service of the United States are prohibited from employing any of the forces under their respective commands for the purpose of returning fugitives from service or labor who may have escaped from any persons to whom such service or labor is claimed to be due ; and any officer who shall be found guilty of a court-martial of violating this article shall be dismissed from the service.

" ' SEC. 2. *And be it further enacted*, That this act shall take effect from and after its passage.'

" Also, to the ninth and tenth sections of an act entitled ' An Act to Suppress Insurrection, to Punish Treason and Rebellion, to Seize and Confiscate Property of Rebels, and for other Purposes, approved July 16, 1862 ; and which sections are in the words and figures following :

" ' SEC. 9. *And be it further enacted*, That all slaves of persons who shall hereafter be engaged in rebellion against the Government of the United States, or who shall in any way give aid or comfort thereto, escaping from such persons and taking refuge within the lines of the army ; and all slaves captured from such persons, or deserted by them and coming under the control of the Government of the United States ; and all slaves of such persons found *on* [or] being within any place occupied by Rebel forces and afterward occupied by forces of the United States, shall be deemed captives of war, and shall be forever free of their servitude, and not again held as slaves.

" ' SEC. 10. *And be it further enacted*, That no slave escaping into any State, Territory, or the District of Columbia, from any other State, shall be delivered up, or in any way impeded or hindered of his liberty, except for crime, or some offense against the laws, unless the person claiming said fugitive shall first make oath that the person to whom the labor or service of such fugitive is alleged to be due is his lawful owner, and has not borne arms against the United States in the present Rebellion, nor in any way given aid and comfort thereto ; and no person engaged in the military or naval service of the United States shall, under any pretense whatever, assume to decide on the validity of the claim of any person to the service or labor of any other person, or surrender up any such person to the claimant, on pain of being dismissed from the service.'

" And I do hereby enjoin upon and order all persons engaged in the military and naval service of the United States to observe, obey, and enforce, within their respective spheres of service, the act and sections above recited.

" And the Executive will in due time recommend that all citizens of the United States, who shall have remained loyal thereto throughout the Rebellion, shall (upon the restoration of the constitutional relation between the United States and their respective States and people, if that relation shall have been suspended or disturbed) be compensated for all losses by acts of the United States, including the loss of slaves.

"In witness whereof, I have hereunto set my hand and caused the seal of the United States to be affixed.

[L. S.] "Done at the City of Washington, this twenty-second day of September, in the year of our Lord one thousand eight hundred and sixty-two, and of the independence of the United States the eighty-seventh.

"ABRAHAM LINCOLN.

"By the President :

"WILLIAM H. SEWARD, *Secretary of State.*"

But why this change in the views of the President? History, thus far, is left to conjecture. It was hinted that our embassadors in Western Europe had apprised the State Department at Washington that an early recognition of the Southern Confederacy was possible, even probable. It was also stated that he was waiting for the issue at the battle of Antietam, which was fought on the 17th—five days before the proclamation was issued. But neither explanation stands in the light of the positive and explicit language of the President on the 13th of September. However, he issued the proclamation,—the Diving Being may have opened his eyes to see the angel that was to turn him aside from the destruction that awaited the Union that he sought to save with slavery preserved !

The sentiment of the people upon the wisdom of the proclamation was expressed in the October elections. New York, New Jersey, Pennsylvania, Ohio, Indiana, and Illinois went democratic; while the supporters of the Administration fell off in Michigan and other Western States. In the Congress of 1860 there were 78 Republicans and 37 Democrats ; in 1862 there were 57 Administration representatives, and 67 in the Opposition.

The army did not take kindly to the proclamation. It was charged that "the war for the Union was changed into a war for the Negro." Some officers resigned, while many others said that if they *thought* they were fighting to free the " niggers" they would resign. This sentiment was contagious. It found its way into the rank and file of the troops, and did no little harm. The following telegram shows that the rebels were angered not a little at the President:

" CHARLESTON, S. C., Oct. 13, 1862.

" Hon. WM. P. MILES, Richmond, Va. :

" Has the bill for the execution of Abolition prisoners, after January next, been passed ? Do it ; and England will be stirred into action. It is high time to proclaim the black flag after that period. Let the execution be with the garrote.

" (Signed) G. T. BEAUREGARD."

But the proclamation was a harmless measure. *First,* it declared that the object of the war was to restore "the constitutional relation between the United States and each of the States." After nearly two years of disastrous war Mr. Lincoln declares the object of the war. Certainly no loyal man had ever entertained any other idea than the one expressed in the proclamation. It was not a war on the part of the United States to destroy her children, nor to disturb her own constitutional, comprehensive unity. It must have been understood, then, from the commencement, that the war begun by the seceding States was waged on the part of the United States to preserve the *Union of the States,* and restore them to their " constitutional relation."

Second, the proclamation implored the slave States to accept (certainly in the spirit of compromise) a proposition from the United States to emancipate their slaves for a *pecuniary consideration,* and, by their gracious consent, assist in *colonizing* loyal Negroes in this country or in Africa !

Third, the measure proposed to free slaves of persons and States in rebellion against the lawful authority of the United States Government on the first day of January, 1863. Nothing more difficult could have been undertaken than to free *only* the slaves of persons and States in *actual* rebellion against the Government of the United States. Persons in *actual* rebellion would be *most* likely to have immediate oversight of this species of their property; and the owners of slaves in the States in *actual* rebellion against the United States Government would doubtless be as thoroughly prepared to take care of slave property as the muskets in their rebellious hands.

Fourth, this emancipation proclamation (?) proposed to pay out of the United States Treasury,—for all slaves of loyal masters lost in a rebellion begun by slave-holders and carried on by slave-holders !

Under the condition of affairs no emancipation proclamation was necessary. Treason against the United States is "levying war against them," or "adhering to their enemies, giving them aid and comfort." The rebel States were guilty of treason; and from the moment Sumter was fired upon, every slave in the Confederate States was *ipso facto* free!

But it was an occasion for rejoicing. The President had taken a step in the right direction, and, thank God! he never retraced it.

A severe winter had set in. The rebels had shown the kind-hearted President no disposition to accept the mild terms of his proclamation. On the contrary, it was received with gnashing of teeth and bitter imprecations. On the 12th of January, 1863, the titular President of the Confederate States, in his third Annual Message, gave attention to the proclamation of the President of the United States. Mr. Davis said:

"It has established a state of things which can lead to but one of three possible consequences—the extermination of the slaves, the exile of the whole white population of the Confederacy, or absolute and total separation of these States from the United States. This proclamation is also an authentic statement by the Government of the United States of its inability to subjugate the South by force of arms, and, as such, must be accepted by neutral nations, which can no longer find any justification in withholding our just claims to formal recognition. It is also, in effect, an intimation to the people of the North that they must prepare to submit to a separation now become inevitable; for that people are too acute not to understand that a restitution of the Union has been rendered forever impossible by the adoption of a measure which, from its very nature, neither admits of retraction nor can coexist with union.

. . . .

"We may well leave it to the instincts of that common humanity which a beneficent Creator has implanted in the breasts of our fellow-men of all countries to pass judgment on a measure by which several millions of human beings of an inferior race—peaceful and contented laborers in their sphere—are doomed to extermination, while at the same time they are encouraged to a general assassination of their masters by the insidious recommendation to abstain from violence unless in necessary self-defense. Our own detestation of those who have attempted the most execrable measures recorded in the history of guilty man is tempered by profound contempt for the impotent rage which it discloses. So far as regards the action of this Government on such criminals as may attempt its execution, I confine myself to informing you that I shall—unless in your wisdom you deem some other course more expedient—deliver to the several State authorities all commissioned officers of the United States that may hereafter be captured by our forces in any of the States embraced in the proclamation, that they may be dealt with in accordance with the laws of those States providing for the punishment of criminals engaged in exciting servile insurrection. The enlisted soldiers I shall continue to treat as unwilling instruments in the commission of these crimes, and shall direct their discharge and return to their homes on the proper and usual parole."

And although the President and his supporters had not reaped the blessings their hopes had sown, they were, nevertheless, not without hope. For when the sober second thought of the nation took the place of prejudice and undue excitement, the proclamation had more friends. And so, in keeping with his promise, the President issued the following proclamation on the first of January, 1863.

" *Whereas,* on the 22d day of September, in the year of our Lord 1862, a proclamation was issued by the President of the United States, containing, among other things, the following, to wit:

" ' That on the 1st day of January, in the year of our Lord 1863, all persons held as slaves within any State or designated part of a State, the people whereof shall then be in rebellion against the United States, shall be then, thenceforward, and forever free ; and the Executive Government of the United States, including the military and naval authority thereof, will recognize and maintain the freedom of such persons, and will do no act or acts to repress such persons, or any of them, in any efforts they may make for their actual freedom.

" ' That the Executive will, on the first day of January aforesaid, by proclamation, designate the States and parts of States, if any, in which the people thereof respectively shall then be in rebellion against the United States ; and the fact that any State, or the people thereof, shall on that day be in good faith represented in the Congress of the United States, by members chosen thereto at elections wherein a majority of the qualified voters of such State shall have participated, shall, in the absence of strong countervailing testimony, be deemed conclusive evidence that such State, and the people thereof, are not then in rebellion against the United States.'

" Now, therefore, I, ABRAHAM LINCOLN, President of the United States, by virtue of the power in me vested as Commander-in-Chief of the Army and Navy of the United States in time of actual armed rebellion against the authority and Government of the United States, and as a fit and necessary war measure for suppressing said rebellion, do, on this first day of January, in the year of our Lord one thousand eight hundred and sixty-three, and in accordance with my purpose so to do, publicly proclaimed for the full period of one hundred days from the day first above mentioned, order and designate as the States and parts of States wherein the people thereof respectively are this day in rebellion against the United States, the following, to wit :

"Arkansas, Texas, Louisiana (except the parishes of St. Bernard, Plaquemine, Jefferson, St. John, St. Charles, St. James, Ascension, Assumption, Terre Bonne, Lafourche, St. Mary, St. Martin, and Orleans, including the city of New Orleans), Mississippi, Alabama, Florida, Georgia, South Carolina, North Carolina, and Virginia (except the forty-eight counties designated as West Virginia, and also the counties of Berkeley, Accomac, Northampton, Elizabeth City, York, Princess Anne, and Norfolk, including the cities of Norfolk and Portsmouth), and which excepted parts are, for the present, left precisely as if this proclamation were not issued.

"And, by virtue of the power and for the purpose aforesaid, I do order and declare that all persons held as slaves within said designated States and parts of States, are and henceforward shall be free ; and that the Executive Government of the United States, including the military and naval authorities thereof, will recognize and maintain the freedom of said persons.

"And I hereby enjoin upon the people so declared to be free, to abstain from all violence, unless in necessary self-defense ; and I recommend to them that, in all cases when allowed, they labor faithfully for reasonable wages.

"And I further declare and make known that such persons, of suitable condition, will be received into the armed service of the United States to garrison forts, positions, stations, and other places, and to man vessels of all sorts in said service.

"And upon this act, sincerely believed to be an act of justice, warranted by the Constitution upon military necessity, I invoke the considerate judgment of mankind, and the gracious favor of Almighty God.

"In testimony whereof, I have hereunto set my name and caused the seal of the United States to be affixed.

"Done at the City of Washington, this 1st day of January, in the [L. S.]   year of our Lord 1863, and of the independence of the United States the 87th.

  "By the President :   ABRAHAM LINCOLN.
"WILLIAM H. SEWARD, *Secretary of State.*"

Even this proclamation—not a measure of humanity—to save the Union, not the slave—left slaves in many counties and States at the South. It was a war measure, pure and simple. It was a blow aimed at the most vulnerable part of the Confederacy. It was destroying its corner-stone, and the ponderous fabric was doomed to a speedy and complete destruction. It discovered that the strength of this Sampson of rebellion lay in its vast slave population. To the slave the proclamation came as the song of the rejoicing angels to the shepherds upon the plains of Bethlehem. It was like music at night, mellowed by the distance, that rouses slumbering hopes, gives wings to fancy, and peoples the brain with blissful thoughts. The notes of freedom came careering to them across the red, billowy waves of battle and thrilled their souls with ecstatic peace. Old men who, like Samuel the prophet, believing the ark of God in the hands of the Philistines, and were ready to give up the ghost, felt that it was just the time to begin to live. Husbands were transported with the thought of gathering to their bosoms the wife that had been sold to the " nigger traders "; mothers swooned under the tender touch of the thought of holding in loving embrace the children who pined for their care ; and young men and maidens could only " think thanksgiving and weep gladness."

The slave-holder saw in this proclamation the handwriting upon the walls of the institution of slavery. The brightness and revelry of his banqueting halls were to be succeeded by gloom and sorrow. His riches, consisting in human beings, were to disappear under the magic touch of the instrument of freedom. The chattel was to be transformed into a person, the person into a soldier, the soldier into a citizen—and thus the Negro slave, like the crawling caterpillar, was to leave his grovelling situation, and in new form, wing himself to the sublime heights of free American citizenship !

The Negroes had a marvellous facility of communicating news to each other. The proclamation, in spite of the precautions of the rebel authorities, took to itself wings. It came to the plantation of weary slaves as the glorious light of a new-born day. It flooded the hovels of slaves with its golden light and rich promise of " *forever free.*" Like St. Paul the poor slaves could exclaim :

" In stripes, in imprisonments, in tumults, in labors, in watchings, in fastings ; by pureness, by knowledge, by long-suffering, by kindness, by the Holy Ghost, by love unfeigned, by the word of truth, by the power of God, by the armor of righteousness on the right hand and on the left, by honor and dishonor, by evil report and good report ; as deceivers, and yet true ; as unknown, and yet well known ; as dying, and, behold, we live ; as chastened, and not killed ; as sorrowful, yet alway rejoicing ; as poor, yet making many rich ; as having nothing, and yet possessing all things."

And the significant name of Abraham—"father of the faithful "—was pronounced by the Negroes with blessings, and mingled in their songs of praise.

CHAPTER XVIII.

EMPLOYMENT OF NEGROES AS SOLDIERS.

The Question of the Employment of Negroes. — The Rebels take the First Step toward the Military Employment of Negroes. — Grand Review of the Rebel Troops at New Orleans. — General Hunter Arms the First Regiment of Loyal Negroes at the South. — Official Correspondence between the Secretary of War and General Hunter respecting the Enlistment of The Black Regiment. — The Enlistment of Five Negro Regiments authorized by the President. — The Policy of General Phelps in Regard to the Employment of Negroes as Soldiers in Louisiana. — A Second Call for Troops by the President. — An Attempt to amend the Army Appropriation Bill so as to prohibit the further Employment of Colored Troops. — Governor John A. Andrew, of Massachusetts, authorized by Secretary of War to organize Two Regiments of Colored Troops. — General Lorenzo Thomas is despatched to the Mississippi Valley to superintend the Enlistment of Negro Soldiers in the Spring of 1863. — An Order issued by the War Department in the Fall of 1863 for the Enlistment of Colored Troops. — The Union League Club of New York City. — Recruiting of Colored Troops in Pennsylvania. — George L. Stearns assigned Charge of the Recruiting of Colored Troops in the Department of the Cumberland. — Free Military School established at Philadelphia, Pennsylvania. — Endorsement of the School by Secretary Stanton. — The Organization of the School. — Official Table giving Number of Colored Troops in the Army. — The Character of Negro Troops. — Mr. Greeley's Editorial on "Negro Troops." — Letter from Judge Advocate Holt to the Secretary of War on the "Enlistment of Slaves." — The Negro Legally and Constitutionally a Soldier. — History records his Deeds of Patriotism.

A T no time during the first two years of the war was the President or the Congress willing to entertain the idea of employing Negroes as soldiers. It has been shown that the admission of loyal Negroes into the Union lines, and into the service of the Engineer's and Quartermaster's Department, had been resisted with great stubbornness by the men in the "chief places." There were, however, a few men, both in and out of the army, who secretly believed that the Negro was needed in the army, and that he possessed all the elements necessary to make an excellent soldier. Public sentiment was so strong against the employment of Negroes in the armed service that few men had the courage of conviction; few had the temerity to express their views publicly. In the summer of 1860,—before the election of Abraham Lincoln,—General J. Watts De Peyster, of New York, wrote an article for a Hudson paper, in which he advocated the arming of Negroes as soldiers, should the Southern States declare war against the Government of the United States. The article was reproduced in many other papers, pronounced a fire-brand, and General De Peyster severely denounced for his advice. But he stood his ground, and when the war did come he gave to his country's service three gallant sons; and from the first to the last was an efficient and enthusiastic supporter of the war for the Union.

The rebels took the first step in the direction of the military employment of Negroes as soldiers. Two weeks after the firing upon Sumter took place, the following note appeared in the "Charleston Mercury":

Several companies of the Third and Fourth Regiments of Georgia passed through Augusta for the expected scene of warfare—Virginia. Sixteen well-drilled companies of volunteers and one negro company, from Nashville, Tennessee, offered their services to the Confederate States." [1]

In the "Memphis Avalanche" and "Memphis Appeal of the 9th, 10th, and 11th of May, 1861, appeared the following notice:

"ATTENTION, VOLUNTEERS : Resolved by the Committee of Safety, that C. Deloach, D. R. Cook, and William B. Greenlaw be authorized to organize a volunteer company composed of our patriotic free men of color, of the city of Memphis, for the service of our common defence. All who have not enrolled their names will call at the office of W. B. Greenlaw & Co. "F. TITUS, *President.*

"F. W. FORSYTHE, *Secretary.*"

On the 9th of February, 1862, the rebel troops had a grand review, and the "Picayune," of New Orleans, contained the following paragraph :

"We must also pay a deserved compliment to the companies of free colored men, all very well drilled, and comfortably uniformed. Most of these companies, quite unaided by the administration, have supplied themselves with arms without regard to cost or trouble. One of these companies, commanded by the well-known veteran, Captain Jordan, was presented, a little before the parade, with a fine war-flag of the new style. This interesting ceremony took place at Mr. Cushing's store, on

---

[1] Charleston Mercury, April 30, 1861.

Camp, near Common Street. The presentation was made by Mr. Bigney, and Jordan made, on this occasion, one of his most felicitous speeches."

And on the 4th of February, 1862, the "Baltimore Traveller" contained the following paragraph :

"ARMING OF NEGROES AT RICHMOND.—Contrabands who have recently come within the Federal lines at Williamsport, report that all the able-bodied colored men in that vicinity are being taken to Richmond, formed into regiments, and armed for the defence of that city."

The following telegram was sent out:

"NEW ORLEANS, NOV. 23, 1861.

"Over twenty-eight thousand troops were reviewed to-day by Governor Moore, Major-General Lovell, and Brig.-General Ruggles. The line was over seven miles long. One regiment comprised fourteen hundred free colored men."

These are sufficient to show that from the earliest dawn of the war the rebel authorities did not frown upon the action of local authorities in placing arms into the hands of free Negroes. The President of the United States was still opposing any attempt on the part of the supporters of the war to constrain him to approve of the introduction of Negroes into the army. But the Secretary of War, the Hon. Simon Cameron, had sent an order to Brig.-Gen. T. W. Sherman, directing him to accept the services of all loyal persons who desired to aid in the suppression of the Rebellion in and about Port Royal. When Gen. David Hunter relieved Gen. Sherman, the latter turned over to him the instructions of the Secretary of War. There was no mention of color, nor was any class of persons mentioned save " loyal persons." Gen. Hunter was a gentleman of broad, liberal, and humane views, and seeing 'an opportunity open to employ Negroes as soldiers, in the spring of 1862 directed the organization of a regiment of blacks. He secured the best white officers for the regiment, and it soon obtained a fine condition of discipline. The news of a Union Negro regiment in South Carolina completely surprised the people at Washington. On the 9th of June, 1862, Mr. Wickliffe, of Kentucky, introduced in the National House of Representatives a resolution of inquiry, calling upon Gen. Hunter to explain to Congress his unprecedented conduct in arming Negroes to fight the battles of the Union. Mr. Stanton was now at the head of the War Department, and the following correspondence took place:

"GENERAL HUNTER'S NEGRO REGIMENT.

" OFFICIAL CORRESPONDENCE.

" WAR DEPARTMENT, June 14, 1862.

"Hon. G. A. Grow, Speaker of the House of Representatives :

" SIR : A resolution of the House of Representatives has been received, which passed the ninth instant, to the following effect:

" ' *Resolved*, That the Secretary of War be directed to inform this House if Gen. Hunter, of the Department of South Carolina, has organized a regiment of South Carolina volunteers for the defence of the Union, composed of black men (fugitive slaves), and appointed a Colonel and officers to command them.

" ' 2d. Was he authorized by the Department to organize and muster into the army of the United States, as soldiers, the fugitive or captive slaves?

" ' 3d. Has he been furnished with clothing, uniforms, etc., for such force ?

" ' 4th. Has he been furnished, by order of the Department of War, with arms to be placed in the hands of the slaves ?

" ' 5th. To report any orders given said Hunter, and correspondence between him and the Department.' "

" In answer to the foregoing resolution, I have the honor to inform the House :

" 1st. That this Department has no official information whether Gen. Hunter, of the Department of South Carolina, has or has not organized a regiment of South Carolina volunteers for the defence of the Union, composed of black men, fugitive slaves, and appointed the Colonel and other officers to command them. In order to ascertain whether he has done so or not, a copy of the House resolution has been transmitted to Gen. Hunter, with instructions to make immediate report thereon.

" 2d. Gen. Hunter was not authorized by the Department to organize and muster into the army of the United States the fugitive or captive slaves.

" 3d. Gen. Hunter, upon his requisition as Commander of the South, has been furnished with clothing and arms for the force under his command, without instructions as to how they should be used.

" 4th. He has not been furnished by order of the Department of War with arms to be placed within the hands of ' those slaves.'

" 5th.   In respect to so much of said resolution as directs the Secretary ' to report to the House ·my orders given said Hunter, and correspondence between him and the Department,' the President instructs me to answer that the report, at this time, of the orders given to and correspondence between Gen. Hunter and this Department would, in his opinion, be incompatible with the public welfare.

" Very respectfully, your obedient servant,

" EDWIN M. STANTON,

" *Secretary of War.*"

" WAR DEPARTMENT, }
" WASHINGTON, July 2, 1862. ¦

" SIR : On reference to the answer of this Department of the fourteenth ultimo to the resolution of the House of Representatives of the ninth of last month, calling for information respecting the organization by Gen. Hunter, of the Department of South Carolina, of a regiment of volunteers for the defence of the Union, composed of black men, fugitive slaves, etc., it will be seen that the resolution had been referred to that officer with instructions to make an immediate report thereon.   I have now the honor to transmit herewith the copy of a communication just received from Gen. Hunter, furnishing information as to his action touching the various matters indicated in the resolution.

" I have the honor to be, very respectfully, your obedient servant,

" EDWIN M. STANTON,

" *Secretary of War.*

" Hon. G. A. GROW,

" *Speaker of the House of Representatives.*"

" HEADQUARTERS DEPARTMENT OF THE SOUTH, }
" PORT ROYAL, S. C., June 23, 1862.   )

" Hon. EDWIN M. STANTON, *Secretary of War*, Washington.

" SIR : I have the honor to acknowledge the receipt of a communication from the Adjutant-General of the army, dated June thirteenth, 1862, requesting me to furnish you with the information necessary to answer certain resolutions introduced in the House of Representatives, June ninth, 1862, on motion of the Hon. Mr. Wickliffe, of Kentucky, their substance being to inquire :

" First.   Whether I had organized or was organizing a regiment of ' fugitive slaves ' in this department ?

" Second.   Whether any authority had been given to me from the War Department for such organization ? and

" Third.   Whether I had been furnished, by order of the War Department, with clothing, uniforms, arms, equipments, etc., for such a force ?

"Only having received the letter covering these inquiries at a late hour on Saturday night, I urge forward my answer in time for the steamer sailing to-day (Monday)—this haste preventing me from entering as minutely as I could wish upon many points of detail, such as the paramount importance of the subject calls for. But, in view of the near termination of the present session of Congress, and the widespread interest which must have been awakened by Mr. Wickliffe's resolutions, I prefer sending even this imperfect answer to waiting the period necessary for the collection of fuller and more comprehensive data.

"To the first question, therefore, I reply that no regiment of 'fugitive slaves' has been or is being organized in this department. There is, however, a fine regiment of persons whose late masters are 'fugitive rebels,'—men who everywhere fly before the appearance of the national flag, leaving their servants behind them to shift as best they can for themselves. So far, indeed, are the loyal persons composing this regiment from seeking to avoid the presence of their late owners, that they are now, one and all, working with remarkable industry to place themselves in a position to go in full and effective pursuit of their fugacious and traitorous proprietors.

"To the second question I have the honor to answer that the instructions given to Brig.-Gen. T. W. Sherman, by the Hon. Simon Cameron, late Secretary of War, and turned over to me by succession for my guidance, do distinctly authorize me to employ all loyal persons offering their services in defence of the Union and for the suppression of this rebellion in any manner I might see fit, or that the circumstances might call for. There is no restriction as to the character or color of the persons to be employed, or the nature of the employment, whether civil or military, in which their services should be used. I conclude, therefore, that I have been authorized to enlist 'fugitive slaves' as soldiers, could any such be found in this department. No such characters, however, have yet appeared within view of our most advanced pickets, the loyal slaves everywhere remaining on their plantations to welcome us, aid us, and supply us with food, labor, and information. It is the masters who have in every instance been the 'fugitives,' running away from loyal slaves as well as loyal soldiers, and whom we have only partially been able to see—chiefly their heads over ramparts, or, rifle in hand, dodging behind trees—in the extreme distance. In the absence of any 'fugitive-master law,' the deserted slaves would be wholly without remedy, had not the crime of treason given them the right to pursue, capture, and bring back those persons of whose protection they have been thus suddenly bereft.

"To the third interrogatory it is my painful duty to reply that I never have received any specific authority for issues of clothing, uniforms, arms, equipments, and so forth, to the troops in question—my general instructions from Mr. Cameron to employ them in any manner I might find necessary, and the military exigencies of the department and the country being my only, but, in my judgment, sufficient justification. Neither have I had any specific authority for supplying these persons with shovels, spades, and pickaxes when employing them as laborers, nor with boats and oars when using them as lightermen ; but these are not points included in Mr. Wickliffe's resolution. To me it seemed that liberty to employ men in any particular capacity implied with it liberty also to supply them with the necessary tools ; and acting upon this faith I have clothed, equipped, and armed the only loyal regiment yet raised in South Carolina.

"I must say, in vindication of my own conduct, that had it not been for the many other diversified and imperative claims on my time, a much more satisfactory result might have been hoped for ; and that in place of only one, as at present, at least five or six well-drilled, brave, and thoroughly acclimated regiments should by this time have been added to the loyal forces of the Union.

"The experiment of arming the blacks, so far as I have made it, has been a complete and even marvellous success. They are sober, docile, attentive, and enthusiastic, displaying great natural capacities for acquiring the duties of the soldier. They are eager beyond all things to take the field and be led into action ; and it is the unanimous opinion of the officers who have had charge of them, that in the peculiarities of this climate and country they will prove invaluable auxiliaries, fully equal to the similar regiments so long and successfully used by the British authorities in the West-India Islands.

"In conclusion, I would say it is my hope—there appearing no possibility of other reënforcements, owing to the exigencies of the campaign in the Peninsula—to have organized by the end of next fall, and to be able to present to the Government, from forty-eight to fifty thousand of these hardy and devoted soldiers.

"Trusting that this letter may form part of your answer to Mr. Wickliffe's resolutions, I have the honor to be, most respectfully, your very obedient servant,

"D. HUNTER,
"Major-General Commanding."

Mr. Wickliffe seemed to feel that he had received an exhaustive reply to his resolution of inquiry, but his colleague, Mr. Dunlap, offered the following resolution on the 3d of July, 1862, which was never acted upon:

"*Resolved*, That the sentiments contained in the paper read to this body yesterday, approving the arming of slaves, emanating from Major-

General David Hunter, clothed in discourteous language, are an indignity to the American Congress, an insult to the American people and our brave soldiers in arms ; for which sentiments, so uttered, he justly merits our condemnation and censure."

There was quite a flutter among the politicians in the rear, and many army officers felt that the United States uniform had been disgraced by being put upon "fugitive slaves."

Within a few weeks after the affair in Congress alluded to above, two United States Senators,[1] charmed with the bold idea of General Hunter, called upon the President to urge him to accept the services of two Negro regiments. The "New York Herald" of the 5th of August, 1862, gave an account of the interview under the caption of "*Important Decision of the President.*"

"The efforts of those who love the negro more than the Union to induce the President to swerve from his established policy are unavailing. He will neither be persuaded by promises nor intimidated by threats. To day he was called upon by two United States Senators and rather peremptorily requested to accept the services of two negro regiments. They were flatly and unequivocally rejected. The President did not appreciate the necessity of employing the negroes to fight the battles of the country and take the positions which the white men of the nation, the voters, and sons of patriotic sires, should be proud to occupy ; there were employments in which the negroes of rebel masters might well be engaged, but he was not willing to place them upon an equality with our volunteers, who had left home and family and lucrative occupations to defend the Union and the Constitution, while there were volunteers or militia enough in the loyal States to maintain the Government without resort to this expedient. If the loyal people were not satisfied with the policy he had adopted, he was willing to leave the administration to other hands. One of the Senators was impudent enough to tell the President he wished to God he would resign."[2]

But there the regiment was,—one thousand loyal and competent soldiers ; and there was no way out but for the government to father the regiment, and, therefore, on the 25th of August, 1862, the Secretary of War sent General Rufus Saxton the following order :

---

[1] They were, no doubt, from Massachusetts.
[2] New York Herald, Tuesday, August 5, 1862.

" 3. In view of the small force under your command, and the ina-bility of the Government at the present time to increase it, in order to guard the plantations and settlements occupied by the United States from invasion, and protect the inhabitants thereof from captivity and murder by the enemy, you are also authorized to arm, uniform, equip, and receive into the service of the United States, such number of Vol-unteers of African descent as you may deem expedient, not exceeding five thousand ; and may detail officers to instruct them in military drill, discipline, and duty, and to command them ; the persons so received into service, and their officers, to be entitled to and receive the same pay and rations as are allowed by law to Volunteers in the service.

" 4. You will occupy, if possible, all the islands and plantations here-tofore occupied by the Government, and secure and harvest the crops, and cultivate and improve the plantations.

" 5. The population of African descent, that cultivate the land and perform the labor of the Rebels, constitute a large share of their military strength, and enable the White masters to fill the Rebel armies, and wage a cruel and murderous war against the people of the Northern States. By reducing the laboring strength of the Rebels, their military power will be reduced. You are, therefore, authorized, by every means in your power, to withdraw from the enemy their laboring force and population, and to spare no effort, consistent with civilized warfare, to weaken, harass, and annoy them, and to establish the authority of the Government of the United States within your Department."

But public sentiment was growing with every passing day. The very presence of the Negro regiment at Port Royal con-verted the most pronounced enemies of Negro troops into friends and admirers. The newspaper correspondents filled their letters to the papers North with most extravagant praise of the Negro soldier; and the President was driven from his position of " *no negro soldiers.*"

The correspondent of the " Times," in a letter dated Sep-tember 4, 1862, wrote :

" There is little doubt that the next mail from the North will bring an order from the War Department recalling Major-Gen. Hunter to a field of greater activity. The Government had not lent him a hearty support in carrying out his policy of arming the blacks, by which alone he could make himself useful in this department to the National cause ; and, therefore, more than two months since he applied to be relieved, rather than sit supinely with folded hands when his military abilities might be found of service elsewhere. Now, however, I have reason to believe that Gen. Hunter's views upon the question of forming negro regiments, have been unreservedly adopted by the President, and the whole question has assumed such a different phase that Gen. Hunter almost regrets that he is to leave the department. The last mail brought the authorization of the President to *enlist* five negro regiments, each of a thousand negroes, to be armed and uniformed for the service of the United States, and also authorizes the enrollment of an additional 50,000 to be employed in the Quartermaster's Department nominally as laborers, but as they are to be organized into companies and uniformed, and a portion of their time is to be spent in drilling, it is easy to understand that the possibility of their being used as soldiers is not lost sight of. The exact time of commencing the work of enlisting the colored recruits, I am not able to state, but that it will be shortly, to my mind, there is not a shadow of doubt. The only way in which the men can be obtained is by the establishment of posts at various places upon the coast, where the negroes, assured of protection, will flock to us by thousands. Past experience and present information both go to prove this fact, and to establish these posts more men will be required ; therefore we may soon expect that the Government will be deriving positive advantages from this department which, heretofore, has been only negative of service, as the field of experiments and the testing of ideas. Gen. Saxton will go to Washington by the first steamer, for consultation with the President on the subject."

Just what one thing changed the President so suddenly upon the question of the employment of Negroes as soldiers was not known.

In Louisiana the Negroes were anxious to enlist in the service of the Union, and with this object in view thousands of them sought the Federal camps. Brig.-Gen. J. W. Phelps, commanding the forces at Carrolton, La., found his camps daily crowded with fugitives from slavery. What to do with them became a question of great moment. Gen. Phelps became convinced that it was impossible to subdue a great rebellion if slavery were to have the protection of Federal bayonets. He gave the Negroes who came to his camp protection ; and for this was reported to his superior officer, Gen. Butler. In a report to the latter officer's Adjutant-General, on June 16, 1862, he said :

"The enfranchisement of the people of Europe has been, and is still, going on, through the instrumentality of military service ; and by this means our slaves might be raised in the scale of civilization and prepared for freedom. Fifty regiments might be raised among them at once, which could be employed in this climate to preserve order, and thus prevent the necessity of retrenching our liberties, as we should do by a large army exclusively of Whites. For it is evident that a considerable army of Whites would give stringency to our Government ; while an army partly of Blacks would naturally operate in favor of freedom and against those influences which at present most endanger our liberties. At the end of five years, they could be sent to Africa, and their places filled with new enlistments."

Receiving no specific response to this overture, Gen. Phelps made a requisition of arms, clothing, etc., for "three regiments of Africans, which I propose to raise for the defense of this point"; adding:

"The location is swampy and unhealthy ; and our men are dying at the rate of two or three a day.

"The Southern loyalists are willing, as I understand, to furnish their share of the tax for the support of the war ; but they should also furnish their quota of men ; which they have not thus far done. An opportunity now offers of supplying the deficiency ; and it is not safe to neglect opportunities in war. I think that, with the proper facilities, I could raise the three regiments proposed in a short time. Without holding out any inducements, or offering any reward, I have now upward of 300 Africans organized into five companies, who are all willing and ready to show their devotion to our cause in any way that it may be put to the test. They are willing to submit to any thing rather than to slavery.

"Society, in the South, seems to be on the point of dissolution ; and the best way of preventing the African from becoming instrumental in a general state of anarchy, is to enlist him in the cause of the Republic. If we reject his services, any petty military chieftain, by offering him freedom, can have them for the purpose of robbery and plunder. It is for the interests of the South, as well as of the North, that the African should be permitted to offer his block for the temple of freedom. Sentiments unworthy of the man of the present day—worthy only of another Cain—could alone prevent such an offer from being accepted.

"I would recommend that the cadet graduates of the present year should be sent to South Carolina and this point, to organize and discipline our African levies ; and that the more promising non-commissioned officers and privates of the army be appointed as company officers to command them. Prompt and energetic efforts in this direction would probably accomplish more toward a speedy termination of the war, and an early restoration of peace and unity, than any other course which could be adopted." [1]

Gen. Butler advised Gen. Phelps to employ " contrabands" for mere fatigue duty, and charged him not to use them as soldiers. On the 31st of July, 1862, Gen. Phelps rejoined by informing Gen. Butler: " I am not willing to become the mere slave-driver you propose, having no qualifications that way," and immediately tendered his resignation.

Nothing could stay the mighty stream of fugitives that poured into the Union lines by day and by night. Nothing could cool the ardor of the loyal Negroes who so earnestly desired to share the perils and honors of the Federal army. There was but one course left and that was to call the Negroes to arms as Gen. Jackson had done nearly a half century before. Gen. Butler repented his action toward the gallant and intelligent Phelps, and on the 24th of August, 1862, appealed to the free Colored men of New Orleans to take up arms in defence of the Union. As in the War of 1812, they responded to the call with enthusiasm ; and in just two weeks one thousand Negroes were organized into a regiment. All the men and line officers were Colored ; the staff-officers were white. Another regiment was raised and officered like the first—only two white men in it ; while the third regiment was officered without regard to nationality. Two Colored batteries were raised, but all the officers were white because there were no Negroes found who understood that arm of the service.

The summer was gone, and Gen. McClellan, instead of " taking Richmond," had closed his campaign on the Peninsula most ingloriously. The President was compelled to make another call for troops—60,000. Conscription was unavoidable in many places, and prejudice against the military employment of Negroes began to decrease in proportion to the increase of the chances of white men to be drafted. On the 16th of July, 1862, Gen. Henry Wilson, United States Senator from Massachusetts, and Chairman of the Committee on Military Affairs, introduced a bill in the Senate amending the act of 1795, prescribing the manner of the calling forth of the militia to suppress insurrections, etc. Several amendments were offered, much debate was had, and finally it passed, amended, empowering the President to accept

---

[1] Greeley, vol. ii, pp. 517, 518.

" persons of African descent, for the purpose of constructing en-
trenchments or performing camp service, or *any* war service for
which they may be found competent." It was agreed, grudgingly, to free the slaves of rebels *only* who should faithfully serve
the country,—but *not* their wives and children ! The vote was 28
yeas to 9 nays.   It went to the House, where it was managed
by Mr. Stevens, of Pennsylvania, and upon a call of the previous
question was passed.   On the next day, July 17th, it received
the signature of the President, and became the law of the land.

On the 28th of January the Army Appropriation bill was
under consideration in the United States Senate. Garrett Davis,
of Kentucky, had opposed, by the most frantic and desperate
efforts, every attempt to use Negroes in any capacity to aid in
the suppression of the Rebellion.   Accordingly he offered the
following amendment to the Appropriation bill :

" *Provided*, That no part of the sums appropriated by this act shall be
disbursed for the pay, subsistence, or any other supplies, of any negro,
free or slave, in the armed military service of the United States."

It received 8 votes, with 28 against it.   Those who sustained
the amendment were all Democrats :
Messrs. Carlyle, G. Davis, Kennedy, Latham, Nesmith,
Powell, Turpie, and Wall.
The fight against the employment of Negroes as soldiers was
renewed.   On every occasion the opposition was led by a Kentucky representative !   On the 21st of December, 1863, during
the pendency of the Deficiency bill in the House, Mr. Harding,
of Kentucky, desired to amend it by inserting the following :

" *Provided*, That no part of the moneys aforesaid shall be applied to
the raising, arming, equipping, or paying of negro soldiers."

It was rejected : yeas, 41 ; nays, 105.   The yeas were :
Messrs. Ancona, Bliss, James S. Brown, Coffroth, Cox, Daw-
son, Dennison, Eden, Edgerton, Eldridge, Finck, Grider, Hall,
Harding, Harrington, Benjamin G. Harris, Charles M. Harris,
Philip Johnson, William Johnson, King, Knapp, Law, Long,
Marcy, McKinney, William H. Miller, James R. Morris, Mor-
rison, Noble, John O'Neill, Pendleton, Samuel J. Randall,
Rogers, Ross, Scott, Stiles, Strouse, Stuart, Chilton A. White,
Joseph W. White, Yeaman.

On the 26th of January, 1863, the Secretary of War authorized Gov. John A. Andrew, of Massachusetts, to raise two regiments of Negro troops to serve three years.   The order allowed
the governor to raise " volunteer companies of artillery for duty
in the forts of Massachusetts and elsewhere, and such companies
of infantry for the volunteer military service as he may find convenient, and may include persons of African descent, organized
into separate corps."

The Governor of Massachusetts immediately delegated authority to John W. M. Appleton to superintend the recruiting of
the 54th Massachusetts, the first regiment of free Colored men
raised at the North.   The regiment was filled by the 13th of
May, and ready to march to the front.   It had been arranged
that the regiment should pass through New York City on its way
to the scene of the war in South Carolina, but the Chief of
Police of New York suggested that the regiment would be subject to insult if it came.   The regiment was sent forth with the
blessings of Massachusetts and the prayers of its patriotic people.
It went by water to South Carolina.

While Massachusetts was engaged in recruiting Negro sol-
diers, Gen. Lorenzo Thomas, Adjutant-General of the United
States Army, was despatched from Washington to the Mississippi
Valley, where he inaugurated a system of recruiting service for
Negroes.   In a speech to the officers and men in the organization
of white troops, he said, on the 8th of April, 1863, at Lake
Providence, La.:

" You know full well—for you have been over this country—that
the Rebels have sent into the field all their available fighting men—
every man capable of bearing arms ; and you know they have kept
at home all their slaves for the raising of subsistence for their armies in
the field.   In this way they can bring to bear against us all the strength
of their so-called Confederate States ; while we at the North can only
send a portion of our fighting force, being compelled to leave behind
another portion to cultivate our fields and supply the wants of an immense army.   The Administration has determined to take from the
Rebels this source of supply—to take their negroes and compel them
to send back a portion of their whites to cultivate their deserted plantations—and very poor persons they would be to fill the place of the dark-
hued laborer.   They must do this, or their armies will starve.   *   *   *

" All of you will some day be on picket duty ; and I charge you all,
if any of this unfortunate race come within your lines, that you do not

turn them away, but receive them kindly and cordially. They are to be encouraged to come to us ; they are to be received with open arms ; they are to be fed and clothed ; they are to be armed."

On the 1st of May, 1863, Gen. Banks, in an order directing the recruiting of the "Corps d'Afrique," said :

" The prejudices or opinions of men are in no wise involved"; and "it is not established upon any dogma of equality, or other theory, but as a practical and sensible matter of business. The Government makes use of mules, horses, uneducated and educated White men, in the defense of its institutions. Why should not the negro contribute whatever is in his power for the cause in which he is as deeply interested as other men ? We may properly demand from him whatever service he can render," etc., etc.

In the autumn of 1863, Adjutant-General Thomas issued the following order respecting the military employment of Negroes as soldiers :

"ENLISTMENT OF COLORED TROOPS.

"GENERAL ORDERS, No. 329.

"WAR DEPARTMENT, ADJUTANT-GENERAL'S OFFICE, ⎱
"WASHINGTON, D. C., October 13, 1863. ⎰

" WHEREAS, The exigencies of the war require that colored troops be enlisted in the States of Maryland, Missouri, and Tennessee, it is

" ORDERED BY THE PRESIDENT, That the Chief of the Bureau for the Organization of Colored Troops shall establish recruiting stations at convenient places within said States, and give public notice thereof, and be governed by the following regulations :

" First.   None but able-bodied persons shall be enlisted.

" Second.   The State and county in which the enlistments are made shall be credited with the recruits enlisted.

" Third.   All persons enlisted into the military service shall forever thereafter be FREE.

" Fourth.   Free persons, and slaves with the written consent of their owners, and slaves belonging to those who have been engaged in or given aid or comfort to the rebellion, may now be enlisted—the owners who have not been engaged in or given aid to the rebellion being entitled to compensation as hereinafter provided.

" Fifth.   If within thirty days from the date of opening enlistments, notice thereof and of the recruiting stations being published, a sufficient number of the description of persons aforesaid to meet the exigencies of the service should not be enlisted, then enlistments may be made of slaves without requiring consent of their owners, but they may receive compensation as herein provided for owners offering their slaves for enlistment.

" Sixth. Any citizen of said States, who shall offer his or her slave for enlistment into the military service, shall, if such slave be accepted, receive from the recruiting officer a certificate thereof, and become entitled to compensation for the service of said slave, not exceeding the sum of three hundred dollars, upon filing a valid deed of manumission and of release, and making satisfactory proof of title. And the recruiting officer shall furnish to any claimant of descriptive list of any person enlisted and claimed under oath to be his or her slave, and allow any one claiming under oath that his or her slave has been enlisted without his or her consent, the privilege of inspecting the enlisted man for the purpose of identification.

"Seventh. A board of three persons shall be appointed by the President, to whom the rolls and recruiting lists shall be furnished for public information, and, on demand exhibited, to any person claiming that his or her slave has been enlisted against his or her will.

" Eighth. If a person shall within ten days after the filing of said rolls, make a claim for the service of any person so enlisted, the board shall proceed to examine the proof of title, and, if valid, shall award just compensation, not exceeding three hundred dollars for each slave enlisted belonging to the claimant, and upon the claimant filing a valid deed of manumission and release of service, the board shall give the claimant a certificate of the sum awarded, which on presentation shall be paid by the chief of the Bureau.

"Ninth. All enlistments of colored troops in the State of Maryland, otherwise than in accordance with these regulations, are forbidden.

" Tenth. No person who is or has been engaged in the rebellion against the Government of the United States, or who in any way has or shall give aid or comfort to the enemies of the Government, shall be permitted to present any claim or receive any compensation for the labor or service of any slave, and all claimants shall file with their claim an oath of allegiance to the United States. By order of the President.

"E. D. TOWNSEND,

"Assistant Adjutant-General."

This order was extended, on October 26th, to Delaware, at the personal request of Governor Cannon.

On the 12th of November, 1863, the Union League Club of New York City appointed a committee for the purpose of recruiting Colored troops. Col. George Bliss was made chairman and entered upon the work with energy and alacrity. On the 23d of November the committee addressed a letter to Horatio Seymour, Governor of New York, stating that as he had no authority to grant them permission to enlist a Negro regiment; and as the National Government was unwilling to grant such authority without the sympathy and assent of the State government, they would feel greatly obliged should his excellency grant the committee his official concurrence. Gov. Seymour assured the committee of his official inability to grant authority for the raising of Colored troops,—just what the committee had written him,—and referred them to the National Government, on the 27th of November. The committee applied to the authorities at Washington, and on the 5th of December, 1863, the Secretary of War granted them authority to raise the 20th Regiment of United States Colored Troops. Having secured the authority of the Government to begin their work, the committee wrote Gov. Seymour: " We express the hope 'that, so far as in your power, you will give to the movement your aid and countenance." The governor never found the time to answer the request of the committee !

The work was pushed forward with zeal and enthusiasm. The Colored men rallied to the call, and within two weeks from the time the committee called for Colored volunteers 1,000 men responded. By the 27th of January, 1864, a second regiment was full; and thus in forty-five days the Union League Club Committee on the Recruiting of Colored Regiments had raised 2,000 soldiers!

Out of 9,000 men of color, eligible by age—18 to 45 years—to go into the service, 2,300 enlisted in less than sixty days. There was no bounty held out to them as an incentive to enlist ; no protection promised to their families, nor to them should they fall into the hands of the enemy. But they were patriots! They were willing to endure any thing rather than the evils that would surely attend the triumph of the Confederacy. They went to the front under auspicious circumstances.

The 20th Regiment, under the command of Col. Bartram, landed at Thirty-Sixth Street, was headed by the police and the patriotic members of the Union League Club, and had a triumphal march through the city.

"The scene of yesterday," says a New York paper, "was one which marks an era of progress in the political and social history of New York. A thousand men with black skins and clad and equipped with the uniforms and arms of the United States Government, marched from their camp through the most aristocratic and busy streets, received a grand ovation at the hands of the wealthiest and most respectable ladies and gentlemen of New York, and then moved down Broadway to the steamer which bears them to their destination—all amid the enthusiastic cheers, the encouraging plaudits, the waving handkerchiefs, the showering bouquets and other approving manifestations of a hundred thousand of the most loyal of our people.

"In the month of July last the homes of these people were burned and pillaged by an infuriated political mob ; they and their families were hunted down and murdered in the public streets of this city ; and the force and majesty of the law were powerless to protect them. Seven brief months have passed, and a thousand of these despised and persecuted men march through the city in the garb of United States soldiers, in vindication of their own manhood, and with the approval of a countless multitude—in effect saving from inevitable and distasteful conscription the same number of those who hunted their persons and destroyed their homes during those days of humiliation and disgrace. This is noble vengeance—a vengeance taught by Him who commanded, 'Love them that hate you ; do good to them that persecute you.'"

The recruiting of Colored troops in Pennsylvania was carried on, perhaps, with more vigor, intelligence, and enthusiasm than in any of the other free States. A committee for the recruiting of men of color for the United States army was appointed at Philadelphia, with Thomas Webster as Chairman, Cadwalader Biddle, as Secretary, and S. A. Mercer, as Treasurer. This committee raised $33,388.00 for the recruiting of Colored regiments. The 54th and 55th Massachusetts regiments had cost about $60,000, but this committee agreed to raise three regiments at a cost of $10,000 per regiment.

The committee founded a camp, and named it "Camp William Penn," at Shelton Hill, near Philadelphia. On the 26th of June, 1863, the first squad of eighty men went into camp. On the 3d of February, 1864, the committee made the following statement, in reference to the raising of regiments :

"On the 24th July, 1863, the First (3d United States) regiment was full.

"On the 13th September, 1863, the Second (6th United States) regiment was full.

"On the 4th December, 1863, the Third (8th United States) regiment was full.

" On the 6th January, 1864, the Fourth (22d United States) regiment was full.

" On the 3d February, 1864, the Fifth (25th United States) regiment was full.

" August 13th, 1863, the Third United States regiment left Camp William Penn, and was in front of Fort Wagner when it surrendered.

" October 14th, 1863, the Sixth United States regiment left for Yorktown.

" January 16th, 1864, the Eighth United States regiment left for. Hilton Head.

" The 22d and 25th regiments are now at Camp William Penn, waiting orders from the Government."

The duty of recruiting "Colored troops" in the Department of the Cumberland was committed by Secretary Stanton to an able, honest, and patriotic man, Mr. George L. Stearns, of Massachusetts. Mr. Stearns had devoted his energies, wealth, and time to the cause of the slave during the holy anti-slavery agitation. He was a wealthy merchant of Boston; dwelt, with a noble wife and beautiful children, at Medford. He had been, from the commencement of the agitation, an ultra Abolitionist. He regarded slavery as a gigantic system of complicated evils, at war with all the known laws of civilized society; inimical to the fundamental principles of political economy; destructive to republican institutions; hateful in the sight of God, and ever abhorrent to all honest men. He hated slavery. He hated truckling, obsequious, cringing hypocrites. He put his feelings into vigorous English, and keyed his deeds and actions to the sublime notes of charity that filled his heart and adorned a long and eminently useful life. He gave shelter to the majestic and heroic John Brown. His door was—like the heavenly gates— ajar to every fugitive from slavery, and his fiery earnestness kindled the flagging zeal of many a conservative friend of God's poor.

Such a man was chosen to put muskets into the hands of the Negroes in the Department of the Cumberland. His rank was that of major, with the powers of an assistant adjutant-general. He took up his headquarters at Nashville, Tennessee. He carried into the discharge of the duties of his important office large executive ability, excellent judgment, and rare fidelity. He organized the best regiments that served in the Western army. When he had placed the work in excellent condition he committed it to the care of Capt. R. D. Mussey, who afterward was made the Colonel of the 100th U. S. Colored Troops.

The intense and unrelenting prejudice against the Negroes, and their ignorance of military tactics, made it necessary for the Government to provide suitable white commissioned officers. The prospect was pleasing to many young white men in the ranks; and ambition went far to irradicate prejudice against Negro soldiers. Nearly every white private and non-commissioned officer was expecting the lightning to strike him; *every* one expected to be promoted to be a commissioned officer, and, therefore, had no prejudice against the men they hoped to command as their *superior* officers. To prepare the large number of applicants for commissions in Colored regiments a "Free Military School" was established at No. 1210 Chestnut Street, Philadelphia, Pa. Secretary Stanton gave the school the following official endorsement in the spring of 1864.

"War Department, }
"Washington City, March 21, 1864. }

"Thomas Webster, Esq., *Chairman*,
    "1210 Chestnut Street, Philadelphia.

"Sir: The project of establishing a free Military School for the education of candidates for the position of commissioned officers in the Colored Troops, received the cordial approval of this Department. Sufficient success has already attended the workings of the institution to afford the promise of much usefulness hereafter in sending into the service a class of instructed and efficient officers.
    "Very respectfully,
        "Your obedient servant,
            "Edwin M. Stanton,
                "*Secretary of War.*"

In reply to a letter from Thomas Webster, Esq., Chairman, etc., of the Recruiting Committee, General Casey sent the following letter:

"Washington, D. C., March 7, 1864.

"Dear Sir: Yours of the 4th instant is received, and I have directed the Secretary of the Board to attend to your request.

"It gives me great pleasure to learn that your School is prospering, and I am also pleased to inform you that the Board of which I am President has not as yet rejected one of your candidates. I am gratified to see that the necessity of procuring competent officers for the armies of the Republic is beginning to be better appreciated by the public.

"I trust I shall never have occasion to regret my agency in suggesting the formation of your School, and I am sure the country owes your Committee much for the energy and judgment with which it has carried it out. The liberality which opens its doors to the young men of all the States is noble, and does honor to those citizens of Philadelphia from whom its support is principally derived.

"Truly yours,

"SILAS CASEY,

"*Major-General.*

"To THOMAS WEBSTER, ESQ., *Chairman,*

"1210 Chestnut Street, Philadelphia."

In reference to applicants the following letter was written by the Adjutant-General :

"GENERAL ORDERS, }
   "No. 125." }   "WAR DEPARTMENT,

"ADJUTANT-GEN.'S OFFICE,

"WASHINGTON, March 29, 1864.

"Furloughs, not to exceed thirty days in each case, to the non-commissioned officers and privates of the army who may desire to enter the Free Military School at Philadelphia, may be granted by the Commanders of Armies and Departments, when the character, conduct, and capacity of the applicants are such as to warrant their immediate and superior commanders in recommending them for commissioned appointments in the regiments of colored troops.

"By order of the Secretary of War.

"E. D. TOWNSEND,

"*Assistant Adjutant-General.*"

The organization of the school was as follows :

Chief Preceptor.

JOHN H. TAGGART

(Late Colonel 12th Regiment Pennsylvania Reserve Corps),

Professor of Infantry Tactics and Army Regulations.

Assistant Professors.

MILITARY STAFF.

ALBERT L. MAGILTON

(Graduate of West Point Military Academy, and late Colonel 4th
Regiment Pennsylvania Reserve Corps),
Professor of Infantry Tactics and Army Regulations.

LEVI FETTERS

(Late Captain 175th Pennsylvania Regiment),
Professor of Infantry Tactics and Army Regulations.

Student DANL. W. HERR

(Late 1st Lieutenant Co. E., 122d Pennsylvania Regiment),
Post Adjutant.

Student J. HALE SYPHER, of Pennsylvania,
Field Adjutant.

Student LOUIS M. TAFT. M.D.
(Graduate of University of Penn.),
Surgeon.

ACADEMIC STAFF.

JOHN P. BIRCH, A.M.,
A. E. ROGERSON, A.M.,
Professors of Mathematics, Geography, and History

Wm. L. WILSON,
Librarian and Phonographic Clerk.

Student CHARLES BENTRICK, Sr.,
Postmaster.

JAMES BUCHANAN (Colored),
Messenger.

Within less than six months 1,051 applicants had been examined ; 560 passed, and 491 were rejected.

Four regular classes were formed, and in addition to daily
recitations the students were required to drill twice every day.
The school performed excellent work ; and furnished for the service many brave and efficient officers.

By December, 1863, 100,000 Colored Troops were in the service. About 50,000 were armed by that time and in the field.

Everywhere they were winning golden laurels by their aptitude in drill, their patient performance of the duties of the camp,
and by their matchless courage in the deadly field.   The young
white officers who so cheerfully bore the odium of commanding
Colored Troops, and who so heroically faced the dangers of capture and cruel death, had no superiors in the army.   They had
the supreme satisfaction of commanding brave men to whom
they soon found themselves deeply attached.   It was a school in
which the noblest and purest patriot might feel himself honored
and inspired to the performance of deathless deeds of valor.

The following tables indicate the manner in which the work
was done.

*Analysis of Examination of Applicants for Command of Colored Troops,
before the Board at Washington, of which Major-General Silas
Casey is President, from the organization of the Board to March
29th, 1864, inclusive.*

Rank.	Number examined.	Number accepted and for what rank recommended.						Number rejected.
		Colonels.	Lieut.-Colonels.	Majors.	Captains.	1st Lieutenants.	2d Lieutenants.	
Colonels	4	—	—	2	—	—	—	2
Lieutenant-Colonels .	3	—	2	—	—	1	—	—
Majors	9	2	3	1	2	—	—	1
Captains . . .	68	3	7	8	20	5	3	22
1st Leutenants . . .	52	3	—	4	10	8	7	20
2d Lieutenants . .	24	—	—	—	9	2	3	10
Sergeants	505	—	1	—	62	75	133	234
Corporals	230	—	—	—	23	46	64	97
Privates	449	—	—	—	26	57	124	242
Civilians . . .	429	1	6	15	48	49	94	216
	1,773	9	19	30	200	243	428	844
Students of the Philadelphia Free Military School . .	94	2	4	6	28	25	25	4
	1,867	11	23	36	228	268	453	848

Analysis of the Examination to 31st March, 1864, of the Students of the Philadelphia Free Military School, before the Board of Examiners at Washington, for Applicants for Command of Colored Troops, Major-General Silas Casey, President.

Rank.	Number examined.	Number accepted and for what rank recommended.						Number rejected.
		Colonels.	Lieut.-Colonels.	Majors.	Captains.	1st Lieutenants	2d Lieutenants.	
Sergeants	14	—	1	—	3	3	6	1
Corporals . . .	8	—	—	—	2	4	2	—
Privates	33	1	—	1	9	11	10	1
Civilians [1] . . .	39	1	3	5	14	6	8	2
	94	2	4	6	28	24	26	4

The following official table gives the entire number of Colored Troops in the army from beginning to end.

STATES AND TERRITORIES.

Colored Troops furnished
1861–'65.

Connecticut	1,764
Maine	104
Massachusetts	3,966
New Hampshire	125
Rhode Island	1,837
Vermont	120
Total of New England States	7,916
New Jersey	1,185
New York	4,125
Pennsylvania	8,612
Total of Middle States	13,922

[1] Many of these had previously been in the three months', nine months', and three years' service, from which they had been honorably discharged.

STATES AND TERRITORIES.—(*Continued.*)

	Colored Troops furnished 1861–'65.
Colorado Ter.	95
Dakota Ter.	
Illinois	1,811
Indiana	1,537
Iowa	440
Kansas	2,080
Michigan	1,387
Minnesota	104
Nebraska Ter.	
New Mexico Ter.	
Ohio . . . . :	5,092
Wisconsin	165
Total, Western States and Territories . .	12,711
California	
Nevada	
Oregon	
Washington Ter.	
Delaware	954
Dist. Columbia	3,269
Kentucky	23,703
Maryland	8,718
Missouri	8,344
West Virginia	196
Total, Border States	45,184
Alabama	4,969
Arkansas	5,526
Florida	1,044
Georgia	
Louisiana	3,486
Mississippi	17,869
North Carolina	5,035
South Carolina	5,462
Tennessee	20,133
Texas	47
Virginia	
Total, Southern States	63,571

STATES AND TERRITORIES. — (*Continued.*)

	Colored Troops furnished 1861–'65.
Indian Nation	
Colored Troops [1]	
Grand Total	173,079
At Large	733
Not accounted for	5,083
Officers	7,122
Total	186,017

Notwithstanding the complete demonstration of fact that Negroes were required as United States soldiers, there were many opposers of the movement. Some of the best men and leading journals were very conservative on this question. An elaborate and cautious editorial in the "New York Times" of February 16, 1863, fairly exhibits the nervousness of the North on the subject of the military employment of the Negro

"USE OF NEGROES AS SOLDIERS.

"One branch of Congress has rejected a bill authorizing the enlistment of negro soldiers. Mr. Sumner declares his intention to persist in forcing the passage of such a law by offering it as an amendment to some other bill. Meantime the President, by laws already enacted, has full authority over the subject, and we can see no good object to be attained by forcing it into the discussions of Congress and adding it to the causes of dissension already existing in the country at large.

" A law of last Congress authorized the President to use the negroes as laborers or *otherwise*, as they can be made most useful in the work of quelling the rebellion. Under this authority, it is understood that he has decided to use them in certain cases as soldiers. Some of them are already employed in garrisoning Southern forts, on the Mississippi River, which whites cannot safely occupy on account of the climate. Governor Sprague has authority to raise negro regiments in Rhode Island, and has proclaimed his intention to lead them when raised in person, and Gov Andrew has received similar authority for the State of Massachusetts. We see, therefore, not the slightest necessity for any further legislation on this subject, and hope Mr. Sumner will consent that Congress may give its attention, during the short remainder of its session, to topics of pressing practical importance.

---

[1] This gives Colored Troops enlisted in the States in rebellion ; besides this, there were 92,576 Colored Troops (included with the white soldiers) in the quotas of the several States.

" Whether negroes shall or shall not be employed as soldiers, seems to us purely a question of expediency, and to be solved satisfactorily only by experiment. As to our *right* so to employ them, it seems absurd to question it for a moment. The most bigoted and inveterate stickler for the absolute divinity of slavery in the Southern States would scarcely insist that, as a matter of right, either constitutional or moral, we could not employ negroes as soldiers in the army. Whether they are, or are not, by nature, by law, or by usage, the equals of the white man, makes not the slightest difference in this respect. Even those at the North who are so terribly shocked at the prospect of their being thus employed, confine their objections to grounds of expediency. They urge :

" 1st. That the negroes will not fight. This, if true, is exclusive against their being used as soldiers. But we see no way of testing the question except by trying the experiment. It will take but a very short time and but very few battles to determine whether they have courage, steadiness, subjection to military discipline and the other qualities essential to good soldiership or not. If they have, this objection will fall, if not then beyond all question they will cease to be employed.

" 2d. It is said that the whites will not fight with them—that the prejudice against them is so strong that our own citizens will not enlist, or will quit the service, if compelled to fight by their side,—and that we shall thus lose two white soldiers for one black one that we gain. If this is true, they ought not to be employed. The object of using them is to strengthen our military force ; and if the project does not accomplish this, it is a failure. The question, moreover, is one of fact, not of theory. It matters nothing to say that it *ought* not to have this effect— that the prejudice is absurd and should not be consulted. The point is, not what men *ought* to do, but what they will *do*. We have to deal with human nature, with prejudice, with passion, with habits of thought and feeling, as well as with reason and sober judgment and the moral sense. Possibly the Government may have made a mistake in its estimate of the effect of this measure on the public mind. The use of negroes as soldiers may have a worse effect on the army and on the people than they have supposed.

" But this is a matter of opinion upon which men have differed. Very prominent and influential persons, Governors of States, Senators, popular Editors and others have predicted the best results from such a measure, while others have anticipated the worst. The President has resolved to try the experiment. If it works well, the country will be the gainer. If not, we have no doubt it will be abandoned. If the effect of using negroes as soldiers upon the army and the country, proves to be depressing and demoralizing, so as to weaken rather than strengthen our military operations, they will cease to be employed.

The President is a practical man, not at all disposed to sacrifice practical results to abstract theories.

" 3d. It is said we shall get no negroes—or not enough to prove of any service. In the free States very few will volunteer, and in the Slave States we can get but few, because the Rebels will push them Southward as fast as we advance upon them. This may be so. We confess we share, with many others, the opinion that it will.

" But we may as well wait patiently the short time required to settle the point. When we hear more definitely from Gov. Sprague's black battalions and Gov. Andrew's negro brigades, we shall know more accurately what to think of the measure as one for the Free States ; and when we hear further of the success of Gen. Banks and Gen. Saxton in enlisting them at the South, we can form a better judgment of the movement there. If we get very few or even none, the worst that can be said will be that the project is a failure ; and the demonstration that it is so will have dissipated another of the many delusions which dreamy people have cherished about this war.

" 4th. The use of negroes will exasperate the South ; and some of our Peace Democrats make that an objection to the measure. We presume it will ; but so will any other scheme we may adopt which is warlike and effective in its character and results. If that consideration is to govern us, we must follow Mr. Vallandingham's advice and stop the war entirely, or as Mr. McMasters puts it in his Newark speech, go 'for an immediate and *unconditional* peace.' We are not quite ready for *that* yet.

" The very best thing that can be done under existing circumstances, in our judgment, is to possess our souls in patience while *the experiment* is being tried. The problem will probably speedily solve itself—much more speedily than heated discussion or harsh criminations can solve it."

It did n't require a great deal of time for the Black troops to make a good impression ; and while the Congress, the press, and the people were being exercised over the probable out-come, the first regiment of ex-slaves ever equipped for the service was working a revolution in public sentiment. On the last day of January, 1863, the "New York Tribune" printed the following editorial on the subject :

" A disloyal minority in the House is factiously resisting the passage of the Steven's bill, authorizing the President to raise and equip 150,000 soldiers of African descent. Meanwhile, in the Department of the South a full regiment of blacks has been enlisted under Gen. Saxton ; is already uniformed and armed, and has been actively drilling for the last seven weeks. A letter which we printed on Wednesday from our Special Correspondent, who is usually well qualified to judge of its military proficiency, says of this regiment that no honest-minded, unprejudiced observer could come to any other conclusion than that it had attained a remarkable proficiency in the short period during which it had been drilled. We have in addition from an officer of the regiment, who is thoroughly informed as to its condition, a very interesting statement of its remarkable progress, and some valuable suggestions on the employment of negro troops in general.

" ' This regiment — the 1st South Carolina Volunteers, Colonel Thomas Wentworth Higginson—marched on the 17th for the first time through the streets of Beaufort. It was the remark of many bitterly pro-slavery officers that they looked "splendidly." They marched through by platoons, and returned by the flank ; the streets were filled with soldiers and citizens, but every man looked straight before him and carried himself steadily. How many white regiments do the same? One black soldier said : "We did n't see a thing in Beaufort ; ebery man hold his head straight up to de front, ebery step was worth a half dollar."

" ' Many agreed with what is my deliberate opinion,' writes this officer, 'that no regiment in this department can, even now, surpass this one. In marching in regimental line I have not seen it equalled. In the different modes of passing from line into column, and from column into line, in changing front, countermarching, forming divisions, and forming square, whether by the common methods, or by Casey's methods, it does itself the greatest credit. Nor have I yet discovered the slightest ground of inferiority to white troops.

" ' So far is it from being true that the blacks as material soldiers are inferior to white, that they are in some respects manifestly superior ; especially in aptness for drill, because of their imitativeness and love of music ; docility in discipline, when their confidence is once acquired ; and enthusiasm for the cause. *They* at least know what they are fighting for. They have also a *pride* as soldiers, which is not often found in our white regiments, where every private is only too apt to think himself specially qualified to supersede his officers. They are above all things faithful and trustworthy on duty from the start. In the best white regiments it has been found impossible to trust newly-enlisted troops with the countersign—they invariably betray it to their comrades. There has been but one such instance in this black regiment, and that was in the case of a mere boy, whose want of fidelity excited the greatest indignation among his comrades.

" ' Drunkenness, the bane of our army, does not *exist* among the black troops. There has not been *one* instance in the regiment. Enough. The only difficulty which threatened to become at all serious was that of absence without leave and overstaying passes, but this was checked by a few decided measures and has ceased entirely.

" ' When this regiment was first organized, some months ago, it had to encounter bitter hostility from the white troops at Port Royal, and there was great exultation when General Hunter found himself obliged to disband it. Since its reorganization this feeling seems to have almost disappeared. There is no complaint by the privates of insult or ill-treatment, formerly disgracefully common from their white comrades.

" ' It has been supposed that these black troops would prove fitter for garrison duty than active service in the field. No impression could be more mistaken. Their fidelity as sentinels adapts them especially, no doubt, to garrison duty ; but their natural place is in the advance. There is an inherent dash and fire about them which white troops of more sluggish Northern blood do not emulate, and their hearty enthusiasm shows itself in all ways. Such qualities are betrayed even in drill, as anybody may know who has witnessed the dull, mechanical way in which ordinary troops make a bayonet charge on the parade ground, and contrasts it with the spirit of those negro troops in the same movement. They are to be used, moreover, in a country which they know perfectly. Merely from their knowledge of wood-craft and water-craft, it would be a sheer waste of material to keep them in garrison. It is scarcely the knowledge which is at once indispensable and impossible to be acquired by our troops. See these men and it is easier to understand the material of which the famous Chasseurs d' Afrique are composed.'

" General Saxton, in a letter published yesterday, said : ' In no regiment have I ever seen duty performed with so much cheerfulness and alacrity. * * * In the organization of this regiment I have labored under difficulties which might have discouraged one who had less faith in the wisdom of the measure; but I am glad to report that the experiment is a complete success. My belief is that when we get a footing on the mainland regiments may be raised which will do more than any now in the service to put an end to this rebellion.'

"We are learning slowly, very slowly, in this war to use the means of success which lie ready to our hands. We have learnt at last that the negro is essential to our success, but we are still hesitating whether to allow him to do all he can or only a part.

" It will not take many such proofs as this black regiment now offers to convince us of the full value of our new allies. But we ought to go beyond that selfishness which regards only our own necessities and remember that the negro has a right to fight for his freedom, and that he will be all the more fit to enjoy his new destiny by helping to achieve it."

On the 28th of March, 1863, Mr. Greeley sent forth the following able and sensible editorial on the Negro as a soldier:

" Negro Troops.

" Facts are beginning to dispel prejudices. Enemies of the negro race, who have persistently denied the capacity and doubted the courage of the Blacks, are unanswerably confuted by the good conduct and gallant deeds of the men whom they persecute and slander. From many quarters come evidence of the swiftly approaching success which is to crown what is still by some persons deemed to be the experiment of arming whom the Proclamation of Freedom liberates.

" The 1st and 2d South Carolina Volunteers, under Colonels Higginson and Montgomery, have ascended the St. John's River in Florida as far as Jacksonville, and have re-occupied that important town which was once before taken and afterward abandoned by the Union forces. Many of the negroes composing these regiments had been slaves in this very place. Their memory of old wrongs, of the privations, outrages and tortures of Slavery, must here, if anywhere, have been fresh and vivid, and the passions which opportunity for just revenges stimulates even in white breasts, ought to have been roused more than in all other places on the spot where they had suffered.

" If, then, Jacksonville were to-day in ashes, and the ghastly spirit visions of ' *The World*' materialized into terrible realities, the negro haters would have no cause to be disappointed. ' *The World*' hailed the alleged repulse and massacre of the negroes and white officers—a report which it invented outright, in sheer malignity, in order to forestall public opinion by creating a belief in the failure of the expedition —would have changed into agonized shrieks over the outrages on its Southern brethren. The experiment of subjecting negroes to military rules and accustoming them to those amenities of civilized warfare which the rebels so uniformly practice would again have been declared to be a hopeless failure ; and for the hundredth time the Proclamation and the radicals who advised it would have been pilloried for public execration.

" Since, however, the contrary of all this is true, it may be presumed by a confiding public which does not read it that '*The World*' has honestly acknowledged the injustice of its slanders. It is unpleasant to disabuse a confiding public on any subject, but we who are sometimes obliged to look at that paper as a professional duty, regret to say that we have not discovered a single evidence of its repentance. The facts are, however, that Colonel Higginson's men landed quietly at Jacksonville, marched through its streets in perfect order, committed no outrages or excesses of any kind, and by the testimony of all witnesses conducted themselves with a military decorum and perfect discipline which is far from common among white regiments in similar circumstances. They have gone before this time still further into the interior, and will doubtless do good service in a direction where their presence has been least expected by the Rebels. In the only instance in which the white chivalry ventured to make a stand against them, the whites were defeated and driven off the field by the Blacks.

"The truth is that the fitness of negroes to be soldiers has long since, in this country and elsewhere, been amply demonstrated, and the success of Col. Higginson's Black Troops is no matter of surprise to any person tolerably well informed about the history of the race. If it were in any sense an experiment, the only thing to be tested was the obstinacy of our Saxon prejudice which denied the possibility of suc- cess, and did what it could to prevent it. But even Saxon prejudice must shortly yield to the logic of facts."

In the face of the fact that the United States Government had employed Negroes as soldiers to fight the battles of the Union, there were men of intelligence who held that it was all wrong in fact, in policy, and in point of law. And this opinion attained such proportions that the Secretary of War felt called upon to request the opinion of Judge Advocate Holt. It is given here.

ENLISTMENT OF SLAVES.

In a letter to Edwin M. Stanton, Secretary of War, dated Aug. 20, 1863, Judge Advocate Holt said : "The right of the Government to employ for the suppression of the rebellion persons of African De- scent held to service or labor under the local law, rests firmly on two grounds :

"First, as property. Both our organic law and the usages of our institutions under it recognize fully the authority of the Government to seize and apply to public use private property, on making compensation therefor. What the use may be to which it is to be applied does not enter into the question of the right to make the seizure, which is un- trammelled in its exercise, save by the single condition mentioned.

"Secondly, as persons. While those of African Descent held to service or labor in several of the States, occupy under the laws of such States, the status of property ; they occupy also under the Federal Government, the status of 'persons.' They are referred to so *nomine* in the Constitution of the United States, and it is not as property but as 'persons' that they are represented on the floor of Congress, and thus form a prominent constituent element alike in the organization and practical administration of the Government.

"The obligation of all persons—irrespective of creed or color—to bear arms, if physically capable of doing so, in defence of the Government under which they live and by which they are protected, is one that is universally acknowledged and enforced. Corresponding to this obligation is the duty resting on those charged with the administration of the Government, to employ such persons in the military service whenever the public safety may demand it. Congress realized both this obligation on the one hand, and this duty on the other when, by the 12th section of the Act of the 17th of July, 1862, it was enacted that 'the President be and is hereby authorized to receive into the service of the United States for the purpose of constructing intrenchments, or performing camp service or any other labor, or any military or naval service for which they may be found competent, persons of African Descent, and such persons shall be enrolled and organized under such regulations not inconsistent with the Constitution and the ·laws, as the President may prescribe.'

"The terms of this Act are without restriction and no distinction is made, or was intended to be made, between persons of African Descent held to service or labor or those not so held.

"The President is empowered to receive them all into the military service, and assign them such duty as they may be found competent to perform.

"The tenacious and brilliant valor displayed by troops of this race at Port Hudson, Milliken's Bend, and Fort Wagner, has sufficiently demonstrated to the President and to the country, the character of service of which they are capable. In the interpretation given to the Enrolment Act, free citizens of African Descent are treated as citizens of the United States, in the sense of the law, and are everywhere being drafted into the military service.

"In reference to the other class of persons of this race—those held to service or labor—the 12th section of the Act of July 17th is still in full force, and the President may in his discretion receive them into the army and assign them to such field of duty as he may deem them prepared to occupy. In view of the loyalty of this race, and of the obstinate courage which they have shown themselves to possess, they certainly constitute at this crisis in our history a most powerful and reliable arm of the public defence. Whether this arm shall now be exerted is not a·question of power or right, but purely of policy, to be determined by the estimate which may be entertained of the conflict in which we are engaged, and of the necessity that presses to bring this waste of blood and treasure to a close. A man precipitated into a struggle for his life on land or sea, instinctively and almost necessarily puts forth every energy with which he is endowed, and eagerly seizes upon every source of strength within his grasp ; and a nation battling for existence, that does not do the same, may well be regarded as neither wise nor obedient to that great law of self-preservation, from which are derived our most urgent and solemn duties. That there exists a prejudice against the employment of persons of African Descent is undeniable ; it is, however, rapidly giving way, and never had any foundation in reason or loyalty   It originated with and has been diligently nurtured by those in sympathy with the Rebellion, and its utterance at this moment is necessarily in the interests of treason.

" Should the President feel that the public interests require he shall exert the power with which he is clothed by the 12th section of the Act of the 17th of July, his action should be in subordination to the Constitutional principle which exacts that compensation shall be made for private property devoted to the public uses. A just compensation to loyal claimants to the service or labor of persons of African Descent enlisted in our army, would accord with the uniform practice of the Government and the genius of our institutions !

"Soldiers of this class, after having perilled their lives in the defence of the Republic, could not be re-enslaved without a national dishonor revolting and unendurable for all who are themselves to be free. The compensation made, therefore, should be such as entirely to exhaust the interest of claimants ; so that when soldiers of this class lay down their arms at the close of the war, they may at once enter into the enjoyment of that freedom symbolized by the flag which they have followed and defended."

The Negro was now a soldier, legally, " constitutionally." He had donned the uniform of an American soldier ; was entrusted with the honor and defence of his country, and had set before him liberty as his exceeding great reward. Rejected at first he was at last urged into the service—even *drafted !* He was charged with the solution of a great problem—his fitness, his valor. History shall record his deeds of patriotism, his marvellous achievements, his splendid triumphs.

CHAPTER XIX.

NEGROES AS SOLDIERS.

Justification of the Federal Government in the Employment of Slaves as Soldiers. — Trials of the Negro Soldier. — He undergoes Persecution from the White Northern Troops, and Barbarous Treatment from the Rebels. — Editorial of the "New York Times" on the Negro Soldier in Battle. — Report of the "Tribune" on the Gallant Exploits of the 1st South Carolina Volunteers. — Negro Troops in all the Departments. — Negro Soldiers in the Battle of Port Hudson. — Death of Captain André Callioux. — Death of Color-Sergeant Anselmas Planciancois. — An Account of the Battle of Port Hudson. — Official Report of Gen. Banks. — He applauds the Valor of the Colored Regiments at Port Hudson. — George H. Boker's Poem on "The Black Regiment." — Battle of Milliken's Bend, June, 1863. — Description of the Battle. — Memorable Events of July, 1863. — Battle on Morris Island. — Bravery of Sergeant Carney. — An Account of the 54th Massachusetts Regiment by Edward L. Pierce to Governor Andrew. — Death of Col. Shaw. — Colored Troops in the Army of the Potomac. — Battle of Petersburg. — Table showing the Losses at Nashville. — Adjt.-Gen. Thomas on Negro Soldiers. — An Extract from the "New York Tribune," in Behalf of the Soldierly Qualities of the Negroes. — Letter received by Col. Darling from Mr. Aden and Col. Foster praising the Eminent Qualifications of the Negro for Military Life. — History records their Deeds of Valor in the Preservation of the Union.

ALL history, ancient and modern, Pagan and Christian, justified the conduct of the Federal Government in the employment of slaves as soldiers. Greece had tried the experiment; and at the battle of Marathon there were two regiments of heavy infantry composed of slaves. The beleaguered city of Rome offered freedom to her slaves who should volunteer as soldiers; and at the battle of Cannae a regiment of Roman slaves made Hannibal's cohorts reel before their unequalled courage. When Abraham heard of the loss of his stock, he armed his slaves, pursued the enemy, and regained his possessions. Negro officers as well as soldiers had shared the perils and glories of the campaigns of Napoleon Bonaparte; and even the royal guard at the Court of Imperial France had been mounted with black soldiers. In two wars in North America Negro soldiers had followed the fortunes of military life, and won the applause of white patriots on two continents. So then all history furnished a precedent for the guidance of the United States Government in the Civil War in America.

But there were several aggravating questions which had to be referred to the future. In both wars in this country the Negro had fought a foreign foe—an enemy representing a Christian civilization. He had a sense of security in going to battle with the colonial fathers ; for their sacred battle-songs gave him purpose and courage. And, again, the Negro knew that the English soldier had never disgraced the uniform of Hampden or Wellington by practising the cruelties of uncivilized warfare upon helpless prisoners. In the Rebellion it was altogether different. Here was a war between the States of one Union. Here was a war between two sections differing in civilization. Here was a war all about the *Negro ;* a war that was to declare him forever bond, or forever free. Now, in such a war the Negro appeared in battle against his master. For two hundred and forty-three years the Negro had been learning the lesson of obedience and obsequious submission to the white man. The system of slavery under which he had languished had destroyed the family relation, the source of all virtue, self-respect, and moral growth. The tendency of slavery was to destroy the confidence of the slave in his ability and resources, and to disqualify him for those relations where the noblest passion of mankind is to be exercised in an intelligent manner—*amor patriæ.*

Negro soldiers were required by an act of Congress to fight for the Union at a salary of $10 per month, with $3 deducted for clothing—leaving them only $7 per month as their actual pay. White soldiers received $13 per month and clothing.[1]

The Negro soldiers had to run the gauntlet of the persecuting hate of white Northern troops, and, if captured, endure the most barbarous treatment of the rebels, without a protest on the part of the Government—for at least nearly a year. Hooted at, jeered, and stoned in the streets of Northern cities as they marched to the front to fight for the Union ; scoffed at and abused by white troops under the flag of a common country, there was little of a consoling or inspiring nature in the experience of Negro soldiers.

---

[1] This was remedied at length, after the 54th Massachusetts Infantry had refused pay for a year, unless the regiment could be treated as other regiments. Major Sturges, Agent for the State of Massachusetts, made up the difference between $7 and $13 to disabled and discharged soldiers of this regiment, until the 15th June, 1864, when the Government came to its senses respecting this great injustice to its gallant soldiers.

"But none of these things" moved the Negro soldier. His qualifications for the profession of arms were ample and admirable. To begin with, the Negro soldier was a patriot of the highest order. No race of people in the world are more thoroughly domestic, have such tender attachments to home and friends as the Negro race. And when his soul was quickened with the sublime idea of liberty for himself and kindred—that his home and country were to be rid of the triple curse of slavery—his enthusiasm was boundless. His enthusiasm was not mere animal excitement. No white soldier who marched to the music of the Union possessed a more lofty conception of the sacredness of the war for the Union than the Negro. The intensity of his desires, the sincerity of his prayers, and the sublimity of his faith during the long and starless night of his bondage made the Negro a poet, after a fashion. To him there was poetry in our flag—the red, white, and blue. Our national odes and airs found a response in his soul, and inspired him to the performance of heroic deeds. He was always seeing something "sublime," "glorious," "beautiful," "grand," and "wonderful" in war. There was poetry in the swinging, measured tread of companies and regiments in drill or battle ; and dress parade always found the Negro soldier in the height of his glory. His love of harmonious sounds, his musical faculty, and delight of show aided him in the performance of the most difficult manœuvres. His imitativeness gave him facility in handling his musket and sabre ; and his love of domestic animals, and natural strength made him a graceful cavalryman and an efficient artilleryman.

The lessons of obedience the Negro had learned so thoroughly as a slave were turned to good account as a soldier. He obeyed orders to the letter. He never used his discretion ; he added nothing to, he subtracted nothing from, his orders ; he made no attempt at reading between the lines ; he did not interpret—he *obeyed.* Used to outdoor life, with excellent hearing, wonderful eyesight, and great vigilance, he was a model picket. Heard every sound, observed every moving thing, and was quick to shoot, and of steady aim. He was possessed of exceptionally good teeth, and, therefore, could bite his cartridge and hard tack. He had been trained to long periods of labor, poor food, and miserable quarters, and therefore, could endure extreme fatigue and great exposure.

His docility of nature, patient endurance, and hopeful disposition enabled him to endure long marches, severe hardships, and painful wounds. His joyous, boisterous songs on the march and in the camp; his victorious shout in battle, and his merry laughter in camp proclaimed him the insoluble enigma of military life. He never was discouraged; *melancholia* had no abiding place in his nature.

But how did the Negro meet his master in battle? How did he stand fire? On the 31st of July, 1863, the " New York Times," editorially answered these questions as follows :

" Negro soldiers have now been in battle at Port Hudson and at Milliken's Bend in Louisiana ; at Helena in Arkansas, at Morris Island in South Carolina, and at or near Fort Gibson in the Indian Territory. In two of these instances they assaulted fortified positions and led the assault ; in two they fought on the defensive, and in one they attacked rebel infantry. In all of them they acted in conjunction with white troops and under command of white officers. In some instances they acted with distinguished bravery, and in all they acted as well as could be expected of raw troops.

" Some of these negroes were from the cotton States, others from New England States, and others from the slave States of the Northwest. Those who fought at Port Hudson were from New Orleans ; those who fought at Battery Wagner were from Boston ; those who fought at Helena and Young's Point were from the river counties of Arkansas, Mississippi, and Tennessee. Those who fought in the Indian Territory were from Missouri."

This is warm praise from a journal of the high, though conservative, character of the "Times." Warmer praise and more unqualified praise of the Negro soldier's fighting qualities could not be given. And it was made after a careful weighing of all the facts and evidence supplied from careful and reliable correspondents. But more specific evidence was being furnished on every hand. The 1st South Carolina Volunteers—the first regiment of Negroes enlisted during the war,—commanded by Col. Thomas Wentworth Higginson, was the first Black regiment of its character under the fire of the enemy. The regiment covered itself with glory during an expedition upon the St. John's River in Florida. The " Times " gave the following editorial notice of the expedition at the time, based upon the official report of the colonel and a letter from its special correspondent:

"THE NEGROES IN BATTLE.

"Colonel Higginson, of the 1st S. C. Volunteers, furnishes an entertaining official report of the exploits of his black regiment in Florida. He seems to think it necessary to put his case strongly, and in rather exalted language, as well as in such a way as to convince the public that negroes will fight. In this expedition, his battalion was repeatedly under fire—had rebel cavalry, infantry, and, says he, 'even artillery' arranged against them, yet in every instance came off with unblemished honor and undisputed triumph. His men made the most urgent appeals to him to be allowed to press the flying enemy. They exhibited the most fiery energy beyond anything of which Colonel Higginson ever read, unless it may be in the case of the French Zouaves. He even says that 'it would have been madness to attempt with the bravest white troops what he successfully accomplished with black ones.' No wanton destruction was permitted, no personal outrages desired, during the expedition. The regiment, besides the victories which it achiéved, and the large amount of valuable property which it secured, obtained a cannon and a flag which the Colonel very properly asks permission for the regiment to retain. The officers and men desire to remain permanently in Florida, and obtain supplies of lumber, iron, etc., for the Government. The Colonel puts forth a very good sugggstion, to the effect that a 'chain of such posts would completely alter the whole aspect of the war in the seaboard slave States, and would accomplish what no accumulation of Northern regiments can so easily effect.' This is the very use for negro soldiers suggested in the Proclamation of the President. We have no doubt that the whole State of Florida might easily be held for the Government in this way, by a dozen negro regiments." [1]

On the 11th of February, 1863, the "Times" gave the following account of the exploits of this gallant regiment in the following explicit language:

"ACCOUNT OF A SUCCESSFUL EXPEDITION INTO GEORGIA AND FLORIDA WITH A FORCE OF FOUR HUNDRED AND SIXTY-TWO OFFICERS AND MEN OF THE 1ST SOUTH CAROLINA VOLUNTEERS.

"The bravery and good conduct of the regiment more than equalled the high anticipations of its commander. The men were repeatedly under fire,—were opposed by infantry, cavalry, and artillery,—fought on board a steamer exposed to heavy musketry fire from the banks of a

---

[1] Times, Feb. 10, 1863.

narrow river,—were tried in all ways, and came off invariably with honor and success. They brought away property to a large amount, capturing also a cannon and a flag, which the Colonel asks leave to keep for the regiment, and which he and they have fairly won.

"It will not need many such reports as this—and there have been several before it—to shake our inveterate Saxon prejudice against the capacity and courage of negro troops. Everybody knows that they were used in the Revolution, and in the last war with Great Britain fought side by side with white troops, and won equal praises from Washington and Jackson. It is shown also that black sailors employed on our men-of-war, are valued by their commanders, and are on equal terms with their white comrades. If on the sea, why not on the land? No officer who has commanded black troops has yet reported against them. They are tried in the most unfavorable and difficult circumstances, but never fail. When shall we learn to use the full strength of the formidable ally who is only waiting for a summons to rally under the flag of the Union? Colonel Higginson says: 'No officer in this regiment now doubts that the successful prosecution of this war lies in the unlimited employment of black troops.' The remark is true in a military sense, and it has a still deeper political significance.

"When General Hunter has scattered 50,000 muskets among the negroes of the Carolinas, and General Butler has organized the 100,000 or 200,000 blacks for whom he may perhaps shortly carry arms to New Orleans, the possibility of restoring the Union as it was, with slavery again its dormant power, will be seen to have finally passed away. The negro is indeed the key to success."[1]

So here, in the Department of the South, where General Hunter had displayed such admirable military judgment, first, in emancipating the slave, and second, in arming them; here where the white Union soldiers and their officers had felt themselves insulted; and where the President had disarmed the 1st regiment of ex-slaves and removed the officer who had organized it, a few companies of Negro troops had fought rebel infantry, cavalry, artillery, and guerillas, and put them all to flight. They had invaded the enemy's country, made prisoners, and captured arms and flags; and without committing a single depredation. Prejudice gave room to praise, and the exclusive, distant spirit of white soldiers was converted into the warm and close admiration of comradeship. The most sanguine expectations and high opin-

---

[1] *Times*, Feb. 11, 1863.

ions of the advocates of Negro soldiers were more than realized, while the prejudice of Negro haters was disarmed by the flinty logic and imperishable glory of Negro soldiership.[1]

Every Department had its Negro troops by this time; and everywhere the Negro was solving the problem of his military existence. At Port Hudson in May, 1863, he proved himself worthy of his uniform and the object of the most extravagant eulogies from the lips of men who were, but a few months before the battle, opposed to Negro soldiers. Mention has been made in another chapter of the Colored regiment raised in New Orleans under General Butler. After remaining in camp from the 7th of September, 1862, until May, 1863, they were quite efficient in the use of their arms. The 1st Louisiana regiment was ordered to report to General Dwight. The regiment was at Baton Rouge. Its commanding officer, Colonel Stafford [white], was under arrest when the regiment was about ready to go to the front.

The line officers assembled at his quarters to assure him that the regiment would do its duty in the day of battle, and to tender their regrets that he could not lead them on the field. At this moment the color-guard marched up to receive the regimental flags. Colonel Stafford stepped into his tent and returned with the flags. He made a speech full of patriotism and feeling, and concluded by saying : " *Color-guard, protect, defend, die for, but do not surrender these flags !* " Sergeant Planciancois said : " Colonel, I will bring back these colors to you in honor, or report to God the reason why ! " Noble words these, and brave ! And no more fitting epitaph could mark the resting-place of a hero who has laid down his life in defence of human liberty ! A king might well covet these sublime words of the dauntless Planciancois !

PORT HUDSON.

It was a question of grave doubt among white troops as to the fighting qualities of Negro soldiers. There were various doubts expressed by the officers on both sides of the line. The Confederates greeted the news that " niggers " were to meet them in battle with derision, and treated the whole matter as a huge joke. The Federal soldiers were filled with amazement and fear as to the issue.

---

[1] For the official report of Colonel Higginson and the war correspondent, see Rebellion Records, vol. vii. Document, pp. 176–178.

It was the determination of the commanding officer at Port Hudson to assign this Negro regiment to a post of honor and danger. The regiment marched all night before the battle of Port Hudson, and arrived at one Dr. Chambers's sugar house on the 27th of May, 1863. It was just 5 A. M. when the regiment stacked arms. Orders were given to rest and breakfast in one hour. The heat was intense and the dust thick, and so thoroughly fatigued were the men that many sank in their tracks and slept soundly.

Arrangements were made for a field hospital, and the drum corps instructed where to carry the wounded. Officers' call was beaten at 5:30, when they received instructions and encouragement. "Fall in" was sounded at 6 o'clock, and soon thereafter the regiment was on the march. The sun was now shining in his full strength upon the field where a great battle was to be fought. The enemy was in his stronghold, and his forts were crowned with angry and destructive guns. The hour to charge had come. It was 7 o'clock. There was a feeling of anxiety among the white troops as they watched the movements of these Blacks in blue. The latter were anxious for the fray. At last the command came, "Forward, double-quick, march!" and on they went over the field of death. Not a musket was heard until the command was within four hundred yards of the enemy's works, when a blistering fire was opened upon the left wing of the regiment. Unfortunately Companies A, B, C, D, and E wheeled suddenly by the left flank. Some confusion followed, but was soon over. A shell—the first that fell on the line—killed and wounded about twelve men. The regiment came to a right about, and fell back for a few hundred yards, wheeled by companies, and faced the enemy again with the coolness and military precision of an old regiment on parade. The enemy was busy at work now. Grape, canister, shell, and musketry made the air hideous with their noise. A masked battery commanded a bluff, and the guns could be depressed sufficiently to sweep the entire field over which the regiment must charge. It must be remembered that this regiment occupied the extreme right of the charging line. The masked battery worked upon the left wing. A three-gun battery was situated in the centre, while a half dozen large pieces shelled the right, and enfiladed the regiment front and rear every time it charged the battery on the bluff. A bayou ran under the bluff, immediately in front of the guns. It was too deep to be forded by men. These brave Colored soldiers made six desperate charges with indifferent success, because

> " Cannon to right of them,
> Cannon to left of them,
> Cannon in front of them
>   Volleyed and thundered ;
> Stormed at with shot and shell."

The men behaved splendidly. As their ranks were thinned by shot and grape, they closed up into place, and kept a good line. But no matter what high soldierly qualities these men were endowed with, no matter how faithfully they obeyed the oft-repeated order to " charge," it was both a moral and physical impossibility for these men to cross the deep bayou that flowed at their feet—already crimson with patriots' blood—and capture the battery on the bluff. Colonel Nelson, who commanded this black brigade, despatched an orderly to General Dwight, informing him that it was not in the nature of things for his men to accomplish any thing by further charges. " Tell Colonel Nelson," said General Dwight, " I shall consider that he has accomplished nothing unless he takes those guns." This last order of General Dwight's will go into history as a cruel and unnecessary act. He must have known that three regiments of infantry, torn and shattered by about fifteen or twenty heavy guns, with an impassable bayou encircling the bluff, could accomplish nothing by charging. But the men, what could they do?

> " Theirs not to make reply,
> Theirs not to reason why,
> Theirs but to do and die."

Death of Captain Andre Callioux.

Again the order to charge was given, and the men, worked up to a feeling of desperation on account of repeated failures, raised a cry and made another charge. The ground was covered with dead and wounded. Trees were felled by shell and solid shot; and at one time a company was covered with the branches of a falling tree. Captain Callioux was in command of Company E, the color company. He was first wounded in the left arm—the limb being broken above the elbow. He ran to the front of his company, waving his sword and crying, " Follow me." But when within about fifty yards of the enemy he was struck by a shell and fell dead in front of his company.

Many Greeks fell defending the pass at Thermopylæ against the Persian army, but history has made peculiarly conspicuous Leonidas and his four hundred Spartans. In a not distant future, when a calm and truthful history of the battle of Port Hudson is written, notwithstanding many men fought and died there, the heroism of the "Black Captain," the accomplished gentleman and fearless soldier, Andre Callioux, and his faithful followers, will make a most fascinating picture for future generations to look upon and study.

DEATH OF COLOR-SERGEANT ANSELMAS PLANCIANCOIS.

" Colonel, I will bring back these colors to you in honor, or report to God the reason why." It was now past 11 A.M., May 27, 1863. The men were struggling in front of the bluff. The brave Callioux was lying lifeless upon the field, that was now slippery with gore and crimson with blood. The enemy was directing his shell and shot at the flags of the First Regiment. A shell, about a six-pounder, struck the flag-staff, cut it in two, and carried away part of the head of Planciancois. He fell, and the flag covered him as a canopy of glory, and drank of the crimson tide that flowed from his mutilated head. Corporal Heath caught up the flag, but no sooner had he shouldered the dear old banner than a musket ball went crashing through his head and scattered his brains upon the flag, and he, still clinging to it, fell dead upon the body of Sergeant Planciancois. Another corporal caught up the banner and bore it through the fight with pride.

This was the last charge—the seventh ; and what was left of this gallant Black brigade came back from the hell into which they had plunged with so much daring and forgetfulness seven times.

They did not capture the battery on the bluff it's true, but they convinced the white soldiers on both sides that they were both willing and able to help fight the battles of the Union. And if any person doubts the abilities of the Negro as a soldier, let him talk with General Banks, as we have, and hear " his golden eloquence on the black brigade at Port Hudson."

A few days after the battle a " New York Times " corre spondent sent the following account to that journal :

"Battle of Port Hudson.

" In an account of the Battle of Port Hudson, the ' Times'' correspondent says : ' Hearing the firing apparently more fierce and continuous to the right than anywhere else, I hurried in that direction, past the sugar house of Colonel Chambers, where I had slept, and advanced to near the pontoon bridge across the Big Sandy Bayou, which the negro regiments had erected, and where they were fighting most desperately. I had seen these brave and hitherto despised fellows the day before as I rode along the lines, and I had seen General Banks acknowledge their respectful salute as he would have done that of any white troops ; but still the question was—with too many,—" Will they fight ? " The black race was, on this eventful day, to be put to the test, and the question to be settled—now and forever,—whether or not they are entitled to assert their right to manhood. Nobly, indeed, have they acquitted themselves, and proudly may every colored man hereafter hold up his head, and point to the record of those who fell on that bloody field.

" ' General Dwight, at least, must have had the idea, not only that they were men, but something *more than men,* from the terrific test to which he put their valor. Before any impression had been made upon the earthworks of the enemy, and in full face of the batteries belching forth their 62 pounders, these devoted people rushed forward to encounter grape, canister, shell, and musketry, with no artillery but two small howitzers—that seemed mere pop-guns to their adversaries—and no reserve whatever.

" ' Their force consisted of the 1st. Louisiana Native Guards (with colored field-officers) under Lieut.-Colonel Bassett, and the 3d Louisiana Native Guards, Colonel Nelson (with white field-officers), the whole under command of the latter officer.

" ' On going into action they were 1,080 strong, and formed into four lines, Lieut.-Colonel Bassett, 1st Louisiana, forming the first line, and Lieut.-Colonel Henry Finnegas the second. When ordered to charge up the works, they did so with the skill and nerve of old veterans, (black people, be it remembered who had never been in action before,) but the fire from the rebel guns was so terrible upon the unprotected masses, that the first few shots mowed them down like grass and so continued.

" ' Colonel Bassett being driven back, Colonel Finnegas took his place, and his men being similarly cut to pieces, Lieut.-Colonel Bassett reformed and recommenced ; and thus these brave people went in, from morning until 3:30 p. m., under the most hideous carnage that men ever had to withstand, and that very few white ones would have had nerve to encounter, even if ordered to. During this time, they rallied, and *were ordered to make six distinct charges,* losing thirty-seven killed, and one hundred and fifty-five wounded, and one hundred and sixteen missing, —the majority, if not all, of these being, in all probability, now lying dead on the gory field, and without the rites of sepulture ; for when, by flag of truce, our forces in other directions were permitted to reclaim their dead, the benefit, through some neglect, was not extended to these black regiments.

" ' The deeds of heroism performed by these colored men were such as the proudest white men might emulate. Their colors are torn to pieces by shot, and literally bespattered by blood and brains. The color-sergeant of the 1st. La., on being mortally wounded, hugged the colors to his breast, when a struggle ensued between the two color-corporals on each side of him, as to who should have the honor of bearing the sacred standard, and during this generous contention one was seriously wounded. One black lieutenant actually mounted the enemy's works three or four times, and in one charge the assaulting party came within fifty paces of them. Indeed, if only ordinarily supported by artillery and reserve, no one can convince us that they would not have opened a passage through the enemy's works.

" ' Capt. Callioux of the 1st. La., a man so black that he actually prided himself upon his blackness, died the death of a hero, leading on his men in the thickest of the fight. One poor wounded fellow came along with his arm shattered by a shell, and jauntily swinging it with the other, as he said to a friend of mine : " Massa, guess I can fight no more." I was with one of the captains, looking after the wounded going in the rear of the hospital, when we met one limping along toward the front. On being asked where he was going, he said : " I been shot bad in the leg, captain, and dey want me to go to de hospital, but I guess I can gib 'em some more yet." I could go on filling your columns with startling facts of this kind, but I hope I have told enough to prove that we can hereafter rely upon black arms as well as white in crushing this iniernal rebellion. I long ago told you there was an army of 250,000 men ready to leap forward in defence of freedom at the first call. You know where to find them and what they are worth.

" ' Although repulsed in an attempt which—situated as things were— was all but impossible, these regiments, though badly cut up, are still on hand, and burning with a passion ten times hotter from their fierce baptism of blood. Who knows but that it is a black hand which shall first plant the standard of the Republic upon the doomed ramparts of Port Hudson ? " [1]

The official report of Gen. Banks is given in full. It shows the disposition of the troops, and applauds the valor of the Colored regiments.

---

[1] New York Times, June 13, 1863.

"HEADQUARTERS ARMY OF THE GULF, }
"BEFORE PORT HUDSON, May 30, 1863. }

" *Major-General H. W. Halleck, General-in-Chief, Washington.*

"GENERAL :—Leaving Sommesport on the Atchafalaya, where my command was at the date of my last dispatch, I landed at Bayou Sara at two o'clock on the morning of the 21st.

"A portion of the infantry were transported in steamers, and the balance of the infantry, artillery, cavalry, and wagon-train moving down on the west bank of the river, and from this to Bayou Sara.

"On the 23d a junction was effected with the advance of Major-General Augur and Brigadier-General Sherman, our line occupying the Bayou Sara road at a distance five miles from Port Hudson.

"Major-General Augur had an encounter with a portion of the enemy on the Bayou Sara road in the direction of Baton Rouge, which resulted in the repulse of the enemy, with heavy loss.

"On the 25th the enemy was compelled to abandon his first line of works.

"General Weitzel's brigade, which had covered our rear in the march from Alexandria, joined us on the 26th, and on the morning of the 27th a general assault was made upon the fortifications.

"The artillery opened fire between 5 and 6 o'clock, which was continued with animation during the day. At 10 o'clock Weitzel's brigade, with the division of General Grover, reduced to about two brigades, and the division of General Emory, temporarily reduced by detachments to about a brigade, under command of Colonel Paine, with two regiments of colored troops, made an assault upon the right of the enemy's works, crossing Sandy Creek, and driving them through the woods to their fortifications.

"The fight lasted on this line until 4 o'clock, and was very severely contested. On the left, the infantry did not come up until later in the day ; but at 2 o'clock an assault was opened on the centre and left of centre by the divisions under Major-General Augur and Brigadier-General Sherman.

"The enemy was driven into his works, and our troops moved up to the fortifications, holding the opposite sides of the parapet with the enemy on the right. Our troops still hold their position on the left. After dark the main body, being exposed to a flank fire, withdrew to a belt of woods, the skirmishers remaining close upon the fortifications.

"In the assault of the 27th, the behavior of the officers and men was most gallant, and left nothing to be desired. Our limited acquaintance of the ground and the character of the works, which were almost hid-

den from our observation until the moment of approach, alone prevented
the capture of the post.

"On the extreme right of our line I posted the first and third regiments of negro troops. The First regiment of Louisiana Engineers,
composed exclusively of colored men, excepting the officers, was also engaged in the operations of the day. The position occupied by these
troops was one of importance, and called for the utmost steadiness and
bravery in those to whom it was confided.

"It gives me pleasure to report that they answered every expectation. Their conduct was heroic. No troops could be more determined
or more daring. They made, during the day, three charges upon the
batteries of the enemy, suffering very heavy losses, and holding their
position at nightfall with the other troops on the right of our line. The
highest commendation is bestowed upon them by all the officers in command on the right. Whatever doubt may have existed before as to the
efficiency of organizations of this character, the history of this day proves
conclusively to those who were in a condition to observe the conduct of
these regiments, that the Government will find in this class of troops
effective supporters and defenders.

"The severe test to which they were subjected, and the determined
manner in which they encountered the enemy, leave upon my mind no
doubt of their ultimate success. They require only good officers, commands of limited numbers, and careful discipline, to make them excellent soldiers.

"Our losses from the 23d to this date, in killed, wounded, and
missing, are nearly 1,000, including, I deeply regret to say, some of
the ablest officers of the corps. I am unable yet to report them in
detail.

"I have the honor to be, with much respect

"Your obedient servant,

"N. P. BANKS,
"*Major-General Commanding.*"

The effect of this battle upon the country can scarcely be described. Glowing accounts of the charge of the Black Regiments appeared in nearly all the leading journals of the North.
The hearts of orators and poets were stirred to elegant utterance. The friends of the Negro were encouraged, and their
number multiplied. The Colored people themselves were jubilant. Mr. George H. Boker, of Philadelphia, the poet friend of
the Negro, wrote the following elegant verses on the gallant
charge of the 1st Louisiana:

THE BLACK REGIMENT.

MAY 27, 1863.

BY GEORGE H. BOKER.

———

Dark as the clouds of even,
Ranked in the western heaven,
Waiting the breath that lifts
All the dread mass, and drifts
Tempest and falling brand
Over a ruined land ;—
So still and orderly,
Arm to arm, knee to knee,
Waiting the great event,
Stands the black regiment.

Down the long dusky line
Teeth gleam and eyeballs shine ;
And the bright bayonet,
Bristling and firmly set,
Flashed with a purpose grand,
Long ere the sharp command
Of the fierce rolling drum
Told them their time had come,
Told them what work was sent
For the black regiment.

" Now," the flag-sergeant cried,
" Though death and hell betide,
Let the whole nation see
If we are fit to be
Free in this land ; or bound
Down, like the whining hound—
Bound with red stripes of pain
In our old chains again ! "
Oh ! what a shout there went
From the black regiment !

" Charge ! " Trump and drum awoke,
Onward the bondmen broke ;
Bayonet and sabre-stroke
Vainly opposed their rush.

Through the wild battle's crush,
With but one thought aflush,
Driving their lords like chaff,
In the guns' mouths they laugh ;
Or at the slippery brands
Leaping with open hands,
Down they tear man and horse,
Down in their awful course ;
Trampling with bloody heel
Over the crashing steel,
All their eyes forward bent,
Rushed the black regiment.

" Freedom ! " their battle-cry—
" Freedom ! or leave to die ! "
Ah ! and they meant the word,
Not as with us 't is heard,
Not a mere party-shout :
They gave their spirits out ·
Trusted the end to God,
And on the gory sod
Rolled in triumphant blood.
Glad to strike one free blow,
Whether for weal or woe ;
Glad to breathe one free breath,
Though on the lips of death.
Praying—alas ! in vain !—
That they might fall again,
So they could once more see
That burst to liberty !
This was what "freedom" lent
To the black regiment.

Hundreds on hundreds fell ;
But they are resting well ;
Scourges and shackles strong
Never shall do them wrong.
Oh, to the living few,
Soldiers, be just and true !
Hail them as comrades tried ;
Fight with them side by side ;
Never, in field or tent,
Scorn the black regiment !

The battle of Milliken's Bend was fought on the 6th of June, 1863. The troops at this point were under the command of Brig.-Gen. E. S. Dennis. The force consisted of the 23d Iowa, 160 men; 9th La., 500; 11th La., 600; 1st Miss., 150; total, 1,410. Gen. Dennis's report places the number of his troops at 1,061; but evidently a clerical error crept into the report. Of the force engaged, 1,250 were Colored, composing the 9th and 11th Louisiana and the 1st Mississippi. The attacking force comprised six Confederate regiments—about 3,000 men,— under the command of Gen. Henry McCulloch. This force, coming from the interior of Louisiana, by the way of Richmond, struck the 9th Louisiana and two companies of Federal cavalry, and drove them within sight of the earthworks at the Bend. It was now nightfall, and the enemy rested, hoping and believing himself able to annihilate the Union forces on the morrow.

During the night a steamboat passed the Bend, and Gen. Dennis availed himself of the opportunity of sending to Admiral Porter for assistance. The gun-boats, "Choctaw" and "Lexington" were despatched to Milliken's Bend from Helena. As the "Choctaw" was coming in sight, at 3 o'clock in the morning, the rebels made their first charge on the Federal earthworks, filling the air with their vociferous cries: "*No quarter!*" to Negroes and their officers. The Negro troops had just been recruited, and hence knew little or nothing of the manual or use of arms. But the desperation with which they fought has no equal in the annals of modern wars. The enemy charged the works with desperate fury, but were checked by a deadly fire deliberately delivered by the troops within. The enemy fell back and charged the flanks of the Union columns, and, by an enfilading fire, drove them back toward the river, where they sought the protection of the gun-boats. The "Choctaw" opened a broadside upon the exulting foe, and caused him to beat a hasty retreat. The Negro troops were ordered to charge, and it was reported by a "Tribune" correspondent that many of the Union troops were killed before the gun-boats could be signalled to "*cease firing.*" The following description of the battle was given by an eye-witness of the affair, and a gentleman of exalted character:

"My informant states that a force of about one thousand negroes and two hundred men of the Twenty-third Iowa, belonging to the Second brigade, Carr's division (the Twenty-third Iowa had been up the river with prisoners, and was on its way back to this place), was surprised in camp by a rebel force of about two thousand men. The first intimation that the commanding officer received was from one of the black men, who went into the colonel's tent and said : ' Massa, the secesh are in camp.' The colonel ordered him to have the men load their guns at once. He instantly replied : ' We have done did dat now, massa.' Before the colonel was ready, the men were in line, ready for action. As before stated, the rebels drove our force toward the gun-boats, taking colored men prisoners and murdering them. This so enraged them that they rallied and charged the enemy more heroically and desperately than has been recorded during the war. It was a genuine bayonet charge, a hand-to-hand fight, that has never occurred to any extent during this prolonged conflict. Upon both sides men were killed with the butts of muskets. White and black men were lying side by side, pierced by bayonets, and in some instances transfixed to the earth. In one instance, two men, one white and the other black, were found dead, side by side, each having the other's bayonet through his body. If facts prove to be what they are now represented, this engagement of Sunday morning will be recorded as the most desperate of this war. Broken limbs, broken heads, the mangling of bodies, all prove that it was a contest between enraged men : on the one side from hatred to a race ; and on the other, desire for self-preservation, revenge for past grievances and the inhuman murder of their comrades. One brave man took his former master prisoner, and brought him into camp with great gusto. A rebel prisoner made a particular request, that *his own* negroes should not be placed over him as a guard. Dame Fortune is capricious ! His request was *not* granted. Their mode of warfare does not entitle them to any privileges. If any are granted, it is from magnanimity to a fellow-foe.

" The rebels lost five cannon, two hundred men killed, four hundred to five hundred wounded, and about two hundred prisoners. Our loss is reported to be one hundred killed and five hundred wounded ; but few were white men." [1]

Mr. G. G. Edwards, who was in the fight, wrote, on the 13th of June :

" Tauntingly it has been said that negroes won't fight. Who say it, and who but a dastard and a brute will dare to say it, when the battle of Milliken's Bend finds its place among the heroic deeds of this war? This battle has significance. It demonstrates the fact that the freed slaves will fight."

---

[1] Rebellion Records, vol. vii. Doc. p. 15.

The month of July, 1863, was memorable. Gen. Mead had driven Lee from Gettysburg, Grant had captured Vicksburg, Banks had captured Port Hudson, and Gillmore had begun his operations on Morris Island. On the 13th of July the New York Draft Riot broke out. The Democratic press had advised the people that they were to be called upon to fight the battles of the "Niggers" and "Abolitionists"; while Gov. Seymour "*requested*" the rioters to await the return of his adjutant-general whom he had despatched to Washington to have the President suspend the draft. The speech was either cowardly or treasonous. It meant, when read between the lines, it is unjust for the Government to draft you men; I will try and get the Government to rescind its order, and until *then* you are respectfully requested to suspend your violent acts against *property*. But the riot went on. When the troops under Gen. Wool took charge of the city, thirteen rioters were killed, eighteen wounded, and twenty-four made prisoners. The rioters rose ostensibly to resist the draft, but there were three objects before them: robbery, the destruction of the property of the rich sympathizers with the Union, and the assassination of Colored persons wherever found. They burned the Colored Orphans' Asylum, hung Colored men to lamp posts, and destroyed the property of this class of citizens with impunity.

During these tragic events in New York a gallant Negro regiment was preparing to lead an assault upon the rebel Fort Wagner on Morris Island, South Carolina. On the morning of the 16th of July, 1863, the 54th Massachusetts—first Colored regiment from the North—was compelled to fall back upon Gen. Terry from before a strong and fresh rebel force from Georgia. This was on James Island. The 54th was doing picket duty, and these early visitors thought to find Terry asleep; but instead found him awaiting their coming with all the vigilance of an old soldier. And in addition to the compliment his troops paid the enemy, the gunboats "Pawnee," "Huron," "Marblehead," "John Adams," and "Mayflower" paid their warmest respects to the intruders. They soon withdrew, having sustained a loss of 200, while Gen. Terry's loss was only about 100. It had been arranged to concentrate the Union forces on Morris Island, open a bombardment upon Fort Wagner, and then charge and take it on the 18th. The troops on James Island were put in motion to form a junction with the forces already upon Morris

Island. The march of the 54th Mass., began on the night of the 16th and continued until the afternoon of the 18th. Through ugly marshes, over swollen streams, and broken dykes—through darkness and rain, the regiment made its way to Morris Island where it arrived at 6 A. M. of the 18th of July. The bombardment of Wagner was to have opened at daylight of this day; but a terrific storm sweeping over land and sea prevented. It was 12:30 P.M. when the thunder of siege guns, batteries, and gunboats announced the opening of the dance of death. A semi-circle of batteries, stretching across the island for a half mile, sent their messages of destruction into Wagner, while the fleet of iron vessels battered down the works of the haughty and impregnable little fort. All the afternoon one hundred great guns thundered at the gates of Wagner. Toward the evening the bombardment began to slacken until a death-like stillness ensued. To close this part of the dreadful programme Nature lifted her hoarse and threatening voice, and a severe thunder-storm broke over the scene. Darkness was coming on. The brave Black regiment had reached Gen. Strong's headquarters fatigued, hungry, and damp. No time could be allowed for refreshments. Col. Shaw and Gen. Strong addressed the regiment in eloquent, inspiring language. Line of battle was formed in three brigades. The first was led by Gen. Strong, consisting of the 54th Massachusetts (Colored), Colonel Robert Gould Shaw; the 6th Connecticut, Col. Chatfield; the 48th New York, Col. Barton; the 3d New Hampshire, Col. Jackson; the 76th Pennsylvania, Col. Strawbridge; and the 9th Maine. The 54th was the only regiment of Colored men in the brigade, and to it was assigned the post of honor and danger in the front of the attacking column. The shadows of night were gathering thick and fast. Gen. Strong took his position, and the order to charge was given. On the brave Negro regiment swept amid the shot and shell of Sumter, Cumming's Point, and Wagner. Within a few minutes the troops had double-quicked a half mile; and but few had suffered from the heavy guns; but suddenly a terrific fire of small arms was opened upon the 54th. But with matchless courage the regiment dashed on over the trenches and up the side of the fort, upon the top of which Sergt. Wm. H. Carney planted the colors of the regiment. But the howitzers in the bastions raked the ditch, and hand-grenades from the parapet tore the brave men as they climbed the battle-scarred face of the fort. Here waves the flag of a Northern Negro regiment ; and here its brave, beautiful, talented young colonel, Robert Gould Shaw, was saluted by death and kissed by immortality ! Gen. Strong received a mortal wound, while Col. Chatfield and many other heroic officers yielded a full measure of devotion to the cause of the Union. Three other colonels were wounded,—Barton, Green, and Jackson. The shattered brigade staggered back into line under the command of Major Plympton, of the 3d New Hampshire, while the noble 54th retired in care of Lieutenant Francis L. Higginson. The second brigade, composed of the 7th New Hampshire, Col. H. S. Putnam ; 62d Ohio, Col. Steele; 67th Ohio, Col. Vorhees; and the 100th New York, under Col. Danby, was led against the fort, by Col. Putnam, who was killed in the assault. So this brigade was compelled to retire. One thousand and five hundred (1,500) men were thrown away in this fight, but one fact was clearly established, that Negroes could and would fight as bravely as white men. The following letter, addressed to the Military Secretary of Gov. Andrew, of Massachusetts, narrates an instance of heroism in a Negro soldier which deserves to go into history:

" HEADQUARTERS 54TH MASSACHUSETTS VOLS., ⎱
" MORRIS ISLAND, S. C., Oct. 15, 1863. ⎰

" COLONEL : I have the honor to forward you the following letter, received a few days since from Sergeant W. H. Carney, Company C, of this regiment. Mention has before been made of his heroic conduct in preserving the American flag and bearing it from the field, in the assault on Fort Wagner on the 18th of July last, but that you may have the history complete, I send a simple statement of the facts as I have obtained them from him, and an officer who was an eye-witness :

" When the Sergeant arrived to within about one hundred yards of the fort—he was with the first battalion, which was in the advance of the storming column—he received the regimental colors, pressed forward to the front rank, near the Colonel, who was leading the men over the ditch. He says, as they ascended the wall of the fort, the ranks were full, but as soon as they reached the top, 'they melted away' before the enemy's fire 'almost instantly.' He received a severe wound in the thigh, but fell only upon his knees. He planted the flag upon the parapet, lay down on the outer slope, that he might get as much shelter as possible ; there he remained for over half an hour, till the 2d brigade came up. He kept the colors flying until the second conflict was ended. When our forces retired he followed, creeping on one knee, still holding up the flag. It was thus that Sergeant Carney came from the field, having held the emblem of liberty over the walls of Fort Wagner during the sanguinary conflict of the two brigades, and having reeeived two very severe wounds, one in the thigh and one in the head. Still he refused to give up his sacred trust until he found an officer of his regiment.

" When he entered the field hospital, where his wounded comrades were being brought in, they cheered him and the colors. Though nearly exhausted with the loss of blood, he said : ' Boys, the old flag never touched the ground.'

" Of him as a man and soldier, I can speak in the highest term of praise.

" I have the honor to be, Colonel, very respectfully,

" Your most obedient servant,

" M. S. LITTLEFIELD,

" *Col. Comd'g 54th Reg't Mass. Vols.*

" Col. A. G. BROWN, Jr., *Military Secretary to his Excellency John A. Andrew, Mass.*"

It was natural that Massachusetts should feel a deep interest in her Negro regiment : for it was an experiment ; and the fair name of the Old Bay State had been committed to its keeping. Edward L. Pierce gave the following account of the regiment to Gov. John A. Andrew :

" BEAUFORT, July *22,* 1863.

" MY DEAR SIR : You will probably receive an official report of the losses in the Fifty-fourth Massachusetts by the mail which leaves to-morrow, but perhaps a word from me may not be unwelcome. I saw the officers and men on James Island on the thirteenth instant, and on Saturday last saw them at Brigadier-General Strong's tent, as they passed on at six or half-past six in the evening to Fort Wagner, which is some two miles beyond. I had been the guest of General Strong, who commanded the advance since Tuesday. Colonel Shaw had become attached to General Strong at St. Helena, where he was under him, and the regard was mutual. When the troops left St. Helena they were separated, the Fifty-fourth going to James Island. While it was there, General Strong received a letter from Colonel Shaw, in which the desire was expressed for the transfer of the Fifty-fourth to General Strong's brigade. So when the troops were brought away from James Island, General Strong took this regiment into his command. It left James Island on Thursday, July sixteenth, at nine P. M., and marched to Cole's Island, which they reached at four o'clock on Friday morning, marching all night, most of the way in single file. over swampy and muddy ground. There they remained during the day, with hard-tack and coffee for their fare, and this only what was left in their haversacks ; not a regular ration. From eleven o'clock of Friday evening until four o'clock of Saturday they were being put on the transport, the General Hunter, in a boat which took about fifty at a time. There they breakfasted on the same fare, and had no other food before entering into the assault on Fort Wagner in the evening.

"The General Hunter left Cole's Island for Folly Island at six A.M., and the troops landed at the Pawnee Landing about half-past nine A.M., and thence marched to the point opposite Morris Island, reaching there about two o'clock in the afternoon. They were transported in a steamer across the inlet, and at five P.M. began their march for Fort Wagner. They reached Brigadier-General Strong's quarters, about midway on the island, about six or half-past six, where they halted for five minutes. I saw them here, and they looked worn and weary.

"General Strong expressed a great desire to give them food and stimulants, but it was too late, as they were to lead the charge. They had been without tents during the pelting rains of Thursday and Friday nights. General Strong had been impressed with the high character of the regiment and its officers, and he wished to assign them the post where the most severe work was to be done, and the highest honor was to be won. I had been his guest for some days, and knew how he regarded them. The march across Folly and Morris Islands was over a very sandy road, and was very wearisome. The regiment went through the centre of the island, and not along the beach where the marching was easier. When they had come within about one thousand six hundred yards of Fort Wagner, they halted and formed in line of battle— the Colonel leading the right and the Lieutenant-Colonel the left wing. They then marched four hundred yards further on and halted again. There was little firing from the enemy at this point, one solid shot falling between the wings, and another falling to the right, but no musketry.

"At this point the regiment, together with the next supporting regiments, the Sixth Connecticut, Ninth Maine, and others, remained half an hour. The regiment was addressed by General Strong and Colonel Shaw. Then at half-past seven or a quarter before eight o'clock the order for the charge was given. The regiment advanced at quick time, changed to double-quick when at some distance on. The intervening distance between the place where the line was formed and the Fort was run over in a few minutes. When within one or two hundred yards of the Fort, a terrific fire of grape and musketry was poured upon them along the entire line, and with deadly results. It tore the ranks to pieces and disconcerted some. They rallied again, went through the ditch, in which were some three feet of water, and then up the parapet. They raised the flag on the parapet, where it remained for a few minutes. Here they melted away before the enemy's fire, their bodies falling down the slope and into the ditch. Others will give a more detailed and accurate account of what occurred during the rest of the conflict.

"Colonel Shaw reached the parapet, leading his men, and was probably killed. Adjutant James saw him fall. Private Thomas Burgess, of Company I, told me that he was close to Colonel Shaw ; that he waved his sword and cried out : 'Onward, boys !' and, as he did so, fell. Burgess fell, wounded, at the same time. In a minute or two, as he rose to crawl away, he tried to pull Colonel Shaw along, taking hold of his feet, which were near his own head, but there appeared to be no life in him. There is a report, however, that Colonel Shaw is wounded and a prisoner, and that it was so stated to the officers who bore a flag of truce from us, but I cannot find it well authenticated. It is most likely that this noble youth has given his life to his country and to mankind. Brigadier-General Strong (himself a kindred spirit) said of him to-day, in a message to his parents : 'I had but little opportunity to be with him, but I already loved him. No man ever went more gallantly into battle. None knew but to love him.' I parted with Colonel Shaw between six and seven, Saturday evening, as he rode forward to his regiment, and he gave me the private letters and papers he had with him, to be delivered to his father. Of the other officers, Lieutenant-Colonel Hallowell is severely wounded in the groin ; Adjutant James has a wound from a grape-shot in his ankle, and a flesh-wound in his side from a glancing ball or piece of shell. Captain Pope has had a musket-ball extracted from his shoulder. Captain Appleton is wounded in the thumb, and also has a contusion on his right breast from a hand-grenade. Captain Willard has a wound in the leg, and is doing well. Captain Jones was wounded in the right shoulder. The ball went through and he is doing well. Lieutenant Homans wounded by a ball from a smooth-bore musket entering the left side, which has been extracted from the back. He is doing well.

"The above-named officers are at Beaufort, all but the last arriving there on Sunday evening, whither they were taken from Morris Island to Pawnee Landing, in the Alice Price, and thence to Beaufort in the Cosmopolitan, which is specially fitted up for hospital service and is provided with skilful surgeons under the direction of Dr. Bontecou. They are now tenderly cared for with an adequate corps of surgeons and nurses, and provided with a plentiful supply of ice, beef and chicken broth, and stimulants. Lieutenant Smith was left at the hospital tent on Morris Island. Captain Emilio and Lieutenants Grace, Appleton, Johnston, Reed, Howard, Dexter, Jennison, and Emerson, were not wounded and are doing duty. Lieutenants Jewett and

Tucker were slightly wounded and are doing duty also. Lieut. Pratt was wounded and came in from the field on the following day. Captains Russell and Simpkins are missing. The Quartermaster and Surgeon are safe and are with the regiment.

"Dr. Stone remained on the Alice Price during Saturday night, caring for the wounded until she left Morris Island, and then returned to look after those who were left behind. The Assistant Surgeon was at the camp on St. Helena Island, attending to duty there. Lieutenant Littlefield was also in charge of the camp at St. Helena. Lieutenant Higginson was on Folly Island with a detail of eighty men. Captain Bridge and Lieutenant Walton are sick and were at Beaufort or vicinity. Captain Partridge has returned from the North, but not in time to participate in the action.

"Of the privates and non-commissioned officers I send you a list of one hundred and forty-four who are now in the Beaufort hospitals. A few others died on the boats or since their arrival here. There may be others at the Hilton Head Hospital; and others are doubtless on Morris Island; but I have no names or statistics relative to them. Those in Beaufort are well attended to—just as well as the white soldiers, the attentions of the surgeons and nurses being supplemented by those of the colored people here, who have shown a great interest in them. The men of the regiment are very patient, and where their condition at all permits them, are cheerful. They express their readiness to meet the enemy again, and they keep asking if Wagner is yet taken. Could any one from the North see these brave fellows as they lie here, his prejudice against them, if he had any, would all pass away. They grieve greatly at the loss of Colonel Shaw, who seems to have acquired a strong hold on their affections. They are attached to their other officers, and admire General Strong, whose courage was so conspicuous to all. I asked General Strong if he had any testimony in relation to the regiment to be communicated to you. These are his precise words, and I give them to you as I noted them at the time:

" 'The Fifty-fourth did well and nobly, only the fall of Colonel Shaw prevented them from entering the Fort. They moved up as gallantly as any troops could, and with their enthusiasm they deserve a better fate.' The regiment could not have been under a better officer than Colonel Shaw. He is one of the bravest and most genuine men. His soldiers loved him like a brother, and go where you would through the camps you would hear them speak of him with enthusiasm and affection. His wound is severe, and there are some apprehensions as to his being able to recover from it. Since I found him at the hospital tent on Morris Island, about half-past nine o'clock on Saturday, I have been all the time attending to him or the officers of the Fifty-fourth, both on the boats and here. Nobler spirits it has never been my fortune to be with. General Strong, as he lay on the stretcher in the tent, was grieving all the while for the poor fellows who lay uncared for on the battle-field, and the officers of the Fifty-fourth have had nothing to say of their own misfortunes, but have mourned constantly for the hero who led them to the charge from which he did not return. I remember well the beautiful day when the flags were presented at Readville, and you told the regiment that your reputation was to be identified with its fame. It was a day of festivity and cheer. I walk now in these hospitals and see mutilated forms with every variety of wound, and it seems all a dream. But well has the regiment sustained the hope which you indulged, and justified the identity of fame which you trusted to it.

"I ought to add in relation to the fight on James Island, on July sixteenth, in which the regiment lost fifty men, driving back the rebels, and saving, as it is stated, three companies of the Tenth Connecticut, that General Terry, who was in command on that Island, said to Adjutant James :

"'Tell your Colonel that I am exceedingly pleased with the conduct of your regiment. They have done all they could do.'

"Yours truly,

"EDWARD L. PIERCE." [1]

The Negro in the Mississippi Valley, and in the Department of the South had won an excellent reputation as a soldier. In the spring of 1864 Colored Troops made their *début* in the army of the Potomac. In the battles at Wilson's Wharf, Petersburg, Deep Bottom, Chapin's Farm, Fair Oaks, Hatcher's Run, Farmville, and many other battles, these soldiers won for themselves lasting glory and golden opinions from the officers and men of the white organizations. On the 24th of May, 1864, Gen. Fitz-Hugh Lee called at Wilson's Wharf to pay his respects to two Negro regiments under the command of Gen. Wild. But the chivalry of the South were compelled to retire before the destructive fire of Negro soldiers. A "Tribune" correspondent who witnessed the engagement gave the following account the next day :

"At first the fight raged fiercely on the left. The woods were riddled with bullets; the dead and wounded of the rebels were taken away from this part of the field, but I am informed by one accustomed to judge, and who went over the field to-day, that from the pools of

---

[1] Rebellion Recs., vol. vii. Doc., p. 215, 216.

blood and other evidences the loss must have been severe. Finding that the left could not be broken, Fitz-Hugh Lee hurled his chivalry—dismounted of course—upon the right. Steadily they came on, through obstructions, through slashing, past abattis without wavering. Here *one* of the advantages of colored troops was made apparent. They obeyed orders, and bided their time. When well tangled in the abattis the death-warrant, 'Fire,' went forth. Southern chivalry quailed before Northern balls, though fired by negro hands. Volley after volley was rained upon the superior by the inferior race, and the chivalry broke and tried to run."

On the 8th of June Gen. Gillmore, at the head of 3,500 troops, crossed the Appomattox, and moved on Petersburg by turnpike from the north. Gen. Kautz, with about 1,500 cavalry, was to charge the city from the south, or southwest; and two gun-boats and a battery were to bombard Fort Clinton, defending the approach up the river. Gillmore was somewhat dismayed at the formidable appearance of the enemy, and, thinking himself authorized to use. his own discretion, did not make an attack. On the 10th of June, Gen. Kautz advanced without meeting any serious resistance until within a mile and one half of the city, drove in the pickets and actually entered the city! Gillmore had attracted considerable attention on account of the display he made of his forces; but when he declined to fight, the rebels turned upon Kautz and drove him out of the city.

Gen. Grant had taken up his headquarters at Bermuda Hundreds, whence he directed Gen. Butler to despatch Gen. W. F. Smith's corps against Petersburg. The rebel general, A. P. Hill, commanding the rear of Lee's army, was now on the south front of Richmond. Gen. Smith moved on toward Petersburg, and at noon of the 15th of June, 1864, his advance felt the outposts of the enemy's defence about two and one half miles from the river. Here again the Negro soldier's fighting qualities were to be tested in the presence of our white troops. Gen. Hinks commanded a brigade of Negro soldiers. This brigade was to open the battle and receive the fresh fire of the enemy. Gen. Hinks—a most gallant soldier—took his place and gave the order to charge the rebel lines. Here, under a clear Virginia sky, in full view of the Union white troops, the Black brigade swept across the field in magnificent line. The rebels received them with siege gun, musket, and bayonet, but they never wavered. In a short time they had carried a line of rifle-pits,

driven the enemy out in confusion, and captured two large guns.
It was a supreme moment; all that was needed was the order,
" On to Petersburg," and the city could have been taken by the
force there was in reserve for the Black brigade. But he who
doubts is damned, and he who dallies is a dastard. Gen. Smith
hesitated. Another assault was not ordered until near sundown,
when the troops cleared another line of rifle-pits, made three
hundred prisoners, and captured sixteen guns, sustaining a loss
of only six hundred. The night was clear and balmy; there was
nothing to hinder the battle from being carried on ; but Gen. Smith
halted for the night—a fatal halt. During the night the enemy
was reënforced by the flower of Lee's army, and when the sunlight of the next morning fell upon the battle field it revealed an
almost new army,—a desperate and determined enemy. Then
it seems that Gens. Meade and Hancock did not know that
Petersburg was to be attacked. Hancock's corps had lingered
in the rear of the entire army, and did not reach the front until
dusk. Why Gen. Smith delayed the assault until evening was
not known. Even Gen. Grant, in his report of the battle, said:
" Smith, for some reason that I have never been able to satisfactorily understand, did not get ready to assault the enemy's main
lines until near sundown." But whatever the reason was, his
conduct cost many a noble life and the postponement of the end
of the war.

On the 16th of June, 1864, Gens. Burnside and Warren came
up. The 18th corps, under Gen. Smith, occupied the right of
the Federal lines, with its right touching the Appomattox River.
Gens. Hancock, Burnside, and Warren stretched away to the extreme left, which was covered by Kautz's cavalry. After a consultation with Gen. Grant, Gen. Meade ordered a general attack
all along the lines, and at 6 P.M. on the 16th of June, the battle of Petersburg was opened again. Once more a division
of Black troops was hurled into the fires of battle, and once
more proved that the Negro was equal to all the sudden
and startling changes of war. The splendid fighting of these
troops awakened the kindliest feelings for them among the white
troops, justified the Government in employing them, stirred the
North to unbounded enthusiasm, and made the rebel army feel
that the Negro was the equal of the Confederate soldier under all
circumstances. Secretary Stanton was in a state of ecstasy over
the behavior of the Colored troops at Petersburg, an unusual
thing for him. In his despatch on this battle, he said:

" The hardest fighting was done by the black troops. The forts they stormed were the worst of all. After the affair was over Gen. Smith went to thank them, and tell them he was proud of their courage and dash. He says they cannot be exceeded as soldiers, and that hereafter he will send them in a difficult place as readily as the best white troops." [1]

The "Tribune" correspondent wrote on the day of the battle :

" The charge upon the advanced works was made in splendid style; and as the 'dusky warriors' stood shouting upon the parapet, Gen. Smith decided that 'they would do,' and sent word to storm the first redoubt. Steadily these troops moved on, led by officers whose unostentatious bravery is worthy of emulation. With a shout and rousing cheers they dashed at the redoubt. Grape and canister were hurled at them by the infuriated rebels. They grinned and pushed on, and with a yell that told the Southern chivalry their doom, rolled irresistibly over and into the work. The guns were speedily turned upon those of our 'misguided brethren,' who forgot that discretion was the better part of valor. Another redoubt was carried in the same splendid style, and the negroes have established a reputation that they will surely maintain.

" Officers on Gen. Hancock's staff, as they rode by the redoubt, surrounded by a moat with water in it, over which these negroes charged, admitted that its capture was a most gallant affair. The negroes bear their wounds quite as pluckily as the white soldiers."

Here the Colored Troops remained, skirmishing, fighting, building earthworks, and making ready for the next assault upon Petersburg, which was to take place on the 30th proximo. In the actions of the 18th, 21st, 23d, 24th, 25th, and 28th of June, the Colored Troops had shared a distinguished part. The following letter on the conduct of the Colored Troops before Petersburg, written by an officer who participated in all the actions around that city, is worth its space it gold :

" IN THE FIELD, NEAR PETERSBURG, VIRGINIA,
" June 27, 1864.

" The problem is solved. The negro is a man, a soldier, a hero. Knowing of your laudable interest in the colored troops, but particularly those raised under the immediate auspices of the Supervisory

---

[1] *Herald,* June 18, 1864.

Committee, I have thought it proper that I should let you know how they acquitted themselves in the late actions in front of Petersburg, of which you have already received newspaper accounts. If you remember, in my conversations upon the character of these troops, I carefully avoided saying anything about their fighting qualities till I could have an opportunity of trying them.

"That opportunity came on the fifteenth instant, and since, and I am now prepared to say that I never, since the beginning of this war, saw troops fight better, more bravely, and with more determination and enthusiasm. Our division, commanded by General Hinks, took the advance on the morning of the fifteenth instant, arrived in front of the enemy's works about nine o'clock A.M., formed line, charged them, and took them most handsomely. Our regiment was the first in the enemy's works, having better ground to charge over than some of the others, and the only gun that was taken on this first line was taken by our men. The color-sergeant of our regiment planted his colors on the works of the enemy, a rod in advance of any officer or man in the regiment. The effect of the colors being thus in advance of the line, so as to be seen by all, was truly inspiring to our men, and to a corresponding degree dispiriting to the enemy. We pushed on two and a half miles further, till we came in full view of the main defences of Petersburg. We formed line at about two o'clock P.M., reconnoitred and skirmished the whole afternoon, and were constantly subject to the shells of the enemy's artillery. At sunset we charged these strong works and carried them. Major Cook took one with the left wing of our regiment as skirmishers, by getting under the guns, and then preventing their gunners from using their pieces, while he gained the rear of the redoubt, where there was no defence but the infantry, which, classically speaking, 'skedaddled.' We charged across what appeared to be an almost impassable ravine, with the right wing all the time subject to a hot fire of grape and canister, until we got so far under the guns as to be sheltered, when the enemy took to their rifle-pits as infantrymen. Our brave fellows went steadily through the swamp, and up the side of a hill, at an angle of almost fifty degrees, rendered nearly impassable by fallen timber. . Here again our color-sergeant was conspicuous in keeping far ahead of the most advanced, hanging on to the side of the hill, till he would turn about and wave the stars and stripes at his advancing comrades ; then steadily advancing again, under the fire of the enemy, till he could almost have reached their rifle-pits with his flagstaff. How he kept from being killed I do not know, unless it can be attributed to the fact that the party advancing up the side of the hill always has the advantage of those who hold the crest. It was in this way that we got such decided advantage over the enemy at South Mountain. We took, in these two redoubts, four more guns, making, in all, five for our regiment, two redoubts, and part of a rifle-pit as our day's work. The Fifth, Sixth, and Seventh United States colored troops advanced against works more to the left. The Fourth United States colored troops took one more redoubt, and the enemy abandoned the other. In these two we got two more guns, which made, in all, seven. The Sixth regiment did not get up in time, unfortunately, to have much of the sport, as it had been previously formed in the second line. We left forty-three men wounded and eleven killed in the ravine, over which our men charged the last time. Our loss in the whole day's operations was one hundred and forty-three, including six officers, one of whom was killed. Sir, there is no underrating the good conduct of these fellows during these charges ; with but a few exceptions, they all went in as old soldiers, but with more enthusiasm.. I am delighted that our first action resulted in a decided victory.

" The commendations we have received from the Army of the Potomac, including its general officers, are truly gratifying. Hancock's corps arrived just in time to relieve us (we being out of ammunition), before the rebels were reinforced and attempted to retake these strong works and commanding positions, without which they could not hold Petersburg one hour, if it were a part of Grant's plan to advance against it on the right here.

" General Smith speaks in the highest terms of the day's work, as you have doubtless seen, and he assured me, in person, that our division should have the guns we took as trophies of honor. He is also making his word good in saying that he could hereafter trust colored troops in the most responsible positions. Colonel Ames, of the Sixth United States colored troops, and our regiment, have just been relieved in the front, where we served our tour of forty-eight hours in turn with the other troops of the corps. While out, we were subjected to some of the severest shelling I have ever seen, Malvern Hill not excepted. The enemy got twenty guns in position during the night, and opened on us yesterday morning at daylight. Our men stood it, behind their works, of course, as well as any of the white troops. Our men, unfortunately, owing to the irregular features of ground, took no prisoners. Sir, we can bayonet the enemy to terms on this matter of treating colored soldiers as prisoners of war far sooner than the authorities at Washington can bring him to it by negotiation. This I am morally persuaded of. I know, further, that the enemy won't fight us if he can help it. I am sure that the same number of white troops could not have taken those works on the evening of the fifteenth ; prisoners that we took told me so. I mean prisoners who came in after the abandonment of the fort, because they could not get away. They excuse themselves on the ground of pride ; as one of them said to me : ' D——d if men educated as we have been will fight with niggers, and your government ought not to expect it.' The real fact is, the rebels will not stand against our colored soldiers when there is any chance of their being taken prisoners, for they are conscious of what they justly deserve. Our men went into these works after they were taken, yelling ' Fort Pillow ! ' The enemy well knows what this means, and I will venture the assertion, that that piece of infernal brutality enforced by them there has cost the enemy already two men for every one they so inhumanly murdered." [1]

The 9th corps, under Burnside, containing a splendid brigade of Colored Troops, had finally pushed its way up to one hundred and fifty yards of the enemy's works. In the immediate front a small fort projected out quite a distance beyond the main line of the enemy's works. It was decided to place a mine under this fort and destroy it. Just in the rear of the 9th corps was a ravine, which furnished a safe and unobserved starting-point for the mine. It was pushed forward with great speed and care. When the point was reached directly under the fort, chambers were made to the right and left, and then packed with powder or other combustibles. It was understood from the commencement that the Colored Troops were to have the post of honor again, and charge after the mine should be sprung. The inspecting officer having made a thorough examination of the entire works reported to Gen. Burnside that the " Black Division was the fittest for this perilous service." But Gen. Grant was not of the same opinion. Right on the eve of the great event he directed the three white commanders of divisions to *draw lots*—who should *not* go into the crater! The lot fell to the poorest officer, for a dashing, brilliant movement, in the entire army, Gen. Ledlie.

The mine was to be fired at 3:30 A.M., on the morning of the 30th of July, 1864. The match was applied, but the train did not work. Lieut. Jacob Douty and Sergt. Henry Rees, of the 48th Pennsylvania, entered the gallery, removed the hindering cause, and at 4:45 A.M. the match was applied and the explosion took place. The fort was lifted into the air and came down a mass of ruins, burying 300 men. Instead of a fort there was a yawning chasm, 150 feet long, 25 feet wide, and about 25 or 30 feet deep. At the same moment all the guns of the Union forces opened from one end of their line to the other. It was verily a judgment morn. Confusion reigned among the Confederates. The enemy fled in disorder from his works. The way to Petersburg was

---

[1] Rebellion Recs., vol. xi. Doc. pp. 580, 581.

open, unobstructed for several hours; all the Federal troops had to do was to go into the city at a trail arms without firing a gun. Gen. Ledlie was not equal to the situation. He tried to mass his division in the mouth of the crater. The 10th New Hampshire went timidly into line, and when moved forward broke into the shape of a letter V, and confusion indescribable followed. Gens. Potter and Wilcox tried to support Ledlie, but the latter division had halted after they had entered the crater, although the enemy had not recovered from the shock. Gen. Potter, by *some* means, got his division out of the crater and gallantly led a charge toward the crest, but so few followed him that he was compelled to retire. After all had been lost, after the rebels had regained their composure, Gen. Burnside was *suffered* to send in his " Black Division." It charged in splendid order to the right of the crater toward the crest, but was hurled back into the crater by a destructive fire from batteries and muskets. But they rallied and charged the enemy again and again until nightfall; exhausted and reduced in numbers, they fell back into the friendly darkness to rest. The Union loss was 4,400 killed, wounded, and captured. Again the Negro had honored his country and covered himself with glory. Managed differently, with the Black Division as the charging force, Petersburg would have fallen, the war would have ended before the autumn, and thousands of lives would have been saved. But a great sacrifice had to be laid upon the cruel altar of race prejudice.

In the battles around Nashville about 8,000 or 10,000 Colored Troops took part, and rendered efficient aid. Here the Colored Troops, all of them recruited from slave States, stormed fortified positions of the enemy with the bayonet through open fields, and behaved like veterans under the most destructive fire. In his report of the battle of Nashville, Major-Gen. James B. Steedman said:

" The larger portion of these losses, amounting in the aggregate to fully twenty-five per cent. of the men under my command who were taken into action, it will be observed, fell upon the Colored Troops. The severe loss of this part of my troops was in the brilliant charge on the enemy's works on Overton Hill on Friday afternoon. I was unable to discover that *color* made any difference in the fighting of my troops. All, white and black, nobly did their duty as soldiers, and evinced cheerfulness and resolution, such as I have never seen excelled in any campaign of the war in which I have borne a part." [1]

---

[1] Rebellion Recs., vol. xi. Doc., p. 89.

The following table shows the losses in this action :

	Killed		Wounded		Missing		Total		
	Officers	Men	Officers	Men	Officers	Men	Officers	Men	
Fourteenth U. S. Colored Infantry		4		41		20		65	⎫ Organized as the First Colored Brigade, Colonel T. J. Morgan, commanding.
Forty-fourth " " "	1	2		27	2	49	3	78	
Sixteenth " " "		1		2				3	
Eighteenth " " "		1		5		3		9	
Seventeenth " " "	2	14	4	64			6	78	⎭
Twelfth " " "	3	10	3	99			6	109	⎫ Organized as the Second Colored Brigade, Col. C. K. Thompson, commanding.
Thirteenth " " "	4	51	4	161		1	8	213	
One Hundredth " " "		12	5	116			5	128	⎭
Eighteenth Ohio Infantry	2	9	2	38		9	4	56	⎫ Included in the Provisional Division, A. C., Brigadier-General Cruft, commanding.
Sixty-eighth Indiana Infantry		1		7				8	
Provisional Division, A. C.	1	19	3	74		33	4	126	⎭
Twentieth Indiana Battery			2	6			2	6	} Captain Osborn.
Aggregate	13	124	23	640	2	115	38	879	
Total								917	

At the battle of Appomattox a division of picked Colored Troops (Gen. Birney[1]) accomplished some most desperate and brilliant fighting, and received the praise of the white troops who acted as their support.

From the day the Government put arms into the hands of Negro soldiers to the last hour of the Slave-holders' Rebellion they rendered effective aid in surpressing the rebellion and in saving the Union. They fought a twofold battle—conquered the prejudices and fears of the white people of the North and the swaggering insolence and lofty confidence of the South.

As to the efficiency of Negroes as soldiers abundant testimony awaits the hand of the historian. The following letter speaks for itself.

ADJ.-GEN. THOMAS ON NEGRO SOLDIERS.

"War Dep't, Adj.-General's Office,
"Washington, May 30, 1864.

"Hon. H. Wilson :

"Dear Sir : On several occasions when on the Mississippi River, I contemplated writing to you respecting the colored troops and to suggest that, as they have been fully tested as soldiers, their pay should be raised to that of white troops, and I desire now to give my testimony in their behalf. You are aware that I have been engaged in the organization of freedmen for over a year, and have necessarily been thrown in constant contact with them.

"The negro in a state of slavery is brought up by the master, from early childhood, to strict obedience and to obey implicitly the dictates of the white man, and they are thus led to believe that, they are an inferior race. Now, when organized into troops, they carry this habit of obedience with them, and their officers being entirely white men, 'the negroes promptly obey their orders.

"A regiment is thus rapidly brought into a state of discipline. They are a religious people—another high quality for making good soldiers. They are a musical people, and thus readily learn to march and accurately perform their manœuvres. They take pride in being elevated as soldiers, and keep themselves, as their camp grounds, neat and clean. This I know from special inspection, two of my staff-officers being constantly on inspecting duty. They have proved a most important addi-

---

[1] I remember now, as I was in the battle of Appomattox Court House, that Gen. Birney was relieved just after the battle of Farmville, because he refused to march his division in the rear of all the white troops. It was doubtless Gen. Foster who led the Colored Troops in the action at Appomattox.

tion to our forces, enabling the Generals in active operations to take a large force of white troops into the field ; and now brigades of blacks are placed with the whites. The forts erected at the important points on the river are nearly all garrisoned by blacks—artillery regiments raised for the purpose,—say at Paducah and Columbus, Kentucky, Memphis, Tennessee, Vicksburg and Natchez, Mississippi and most of the works around New Orleans.

" Experience proves that they manage heavy guns very well. Their fighting qualities have also been fully tested a number of times, and I am yet to hear of the first case where they did not fully stand up to their work. I passed over the ground where the 1st Louisiana made the gallant charge at Port Hudson, by far the stronger part of the rebel works. The wonder is that so many have made their escape. At Milliken's Bend where I had three incomplete regiments,—one without arms until the day previous to the attack,—greatly superior numbers of the rebels charged furiously up to the very breastworks. The negroes met the enemy on the ramparts, and both sides freely used the bayonet —a most rare occurrence in warfare, as one of the other party gives way before coming in contact with the steel. The rebels were defeated with heavy loss. The bridge at Moscow, on the line of railroad from Memphis to Corinth, was defended by one small regiment of blacks. A cavalry attack of three times their number was made, the blacks defeating them in three charges made by the Rebels.

" They fought them hours till our cavalry came up, when the defeat was made complete, many of the dead being left on the field.

" A cavalry force of three hundred and fifty attacked three hundred rebel cavalry near the Big Black with signal success, a number of prisoners being taken and marched to Vicksburg. Forrest attacked Paducah with 7,500 men. The garrison was between 500 and 600, nearly 400 being colored troops recently raised. What troops could have done better ? So, too, they fought well at Fort Pillow till overpowered by greatly superior numbers.

" The above enumerated cases seem to me sufficient to demonstrate the value of the colored troops.

" I have the honor to be, very respectfully,

" Your obedient servant,

" L. Thomas, *Adj.-General.*

In regard to the conduct of the Colored Troops at Petersburg, a correspondent to the " Boston Journal " gave the following account from the lips of Gen. Smith :

" A few days ago I sat in the tent of Gen. W. F. Smith, commander of the 18th Corps, and heard his narration of the manner in which

Gen. Hinks' division of colored troops stood the fire and charged upon the Rebel works east of Petersburg on the 16th of June. There were thirteen guns pouring a constant fire of shot and shell upon those troops, enfilading the line, cutting it lengthwise and crosswise, 'Yet they stood unmoved for *six hours*. Not a man flinched. [These are the words of the General.] It was as severe a test as I ever saw. But they stood it, and when my arrangements were completed for charging the works, they moved with the steadiness of veterans to the attack. I expected that they would fall back, or be cut to pieces; but when I saw them move over the field, gain the works and capture the guns, I was astounded. They lost between 500 and 600 in doing it. There is material in the negroes to make the best troops in the world, if they are properly trained.'

"These are the words of one of the ablest commanders and engineers in the service. A graduate of West Point, who, earlier in the war, had the prejudices which were held by many other men against the negro. He has changed his views. He is convinced, and honorably follows his convictions, as do all men who are not stone blind or perversely wilful."[1]

Gen. Blunt in a letter to a friend speaks of the valor of Colored Troops at the battle of Honey Springs. He says:

"The negroes (1st colored regiment) were too much for the enemy, and let me here say that I never saw such fighting as was done by that negro regiment. They fought like veterans, with a coolness and valor that is unsurpassed. They preserved their line perfect throughout the whole engagement, and although in the hottest of the fight, they never once faltered. Too much praise cannot be awarded them for their gallantry. The question that negroes will fight is settled, besides they make better soldiers in every respect, than any troops I have ever had under my command."[2]

The following from the Washington correspondent of the "New York Tribune" is of particular value:

"In speaking of the soldierly qualities of our colored troops, I do not refer specially to their noble action in the perilous edge of battle; that is settled, but to their docility and their patience of labor and suffering in the camp and on the march.

"I have before me a private letter from a friend, now Major in one of the Pennsylvania colored regiments, a portion of which I think the

---

[1] Tribune, July 26, 1864.   [2] Tribune, August 19, 1863.

public should find in your columns. He says in speaking of service in his regiment : ' I am delighted with it. I find that these colored men learn every thing that pertains to the duties of a soldier much faster than any white soldiers I have ever seen. The reason is apparent,— not that they are smarter than white men, but they feel promoted ; they feel as though their whole sphere of life was advanced and enlarged. They are willing, obedient, and cheerful ; move with agility, and *are full of music,* which is almost a *sine qua non* to soldierly bearing.'

" Soon after the letter of which the above is an extract was written, the regiment was ordered to the field from which the Major writes again : ' The more I know and see of these negro regiments, the more I am delighted with the whole enterprise. It is truly delightful to command a regiment officered as these are. In all my experience I have never known a better class of officers. . . . I have charge of the school of non-commissioned officers here. I drill them once a day and have them recite from the oral instructions given them the day before. I find them more anxious to learn their duties and more ready to perform them when they know them than any set of non-commissioned officers I ever saw. . . . There is no discount on these fellows at all. Give me a thousand such men as compose this regiment and I desire no stronger battalion to lead against an enemy that is at once their oppressors and traitors to my, and my soldiers' country.'

" This testimony is worth a chapter of speculation. The Major alludes to one fact above, moreover, to which the public attention has not been often directed—the excellent and able men who are in command of our colored troops. They are generally men of heart—men of opinions—men whose generous impulses have not been chilled in ' the cold shade of West Point.'

" The officer from whose letter I have quoted was a volunteer in the ranks of a Pennsylvania regiment from the day of the attack on Sumter until August, 1862. His bravery, his devotion to the principles of freedom, his zeal in the holy cause of his country through all the campaigns of the calamitous McClellan, won the regard and attention of our loyal Governor Curtin, who, with rare good sense and discrimination, took him from the ranks and made him first, Lieut.-Colonel, and then Colonel of a regiment in the nine months' service. He carried himself through all in such a manner as fully justified the Governor's confidence, and has stepped now into a position where his patriotic zeal can concentrate the valor of these untutored free men in defense of our imperrilled country. So long as these brave colored men are officered by gallant, high-hearted, slave-hating men, we can never despair of the Republic." [1]

---

[1] New York Tribune, Nov. 14, 1863.

Mr. D. Aden in a letter to Col. Darling, dated Norfolk, Va., Feb. 22, 1864, said :

"During the expedition last October to Charles City Court House, on the Peninsula, the colored troops marched steadily through storm and mud ; and on coming up with the enemy, behaved as bravely under fire as veterans. An officer of the 1st N. Y. Mounted Rifles—a most bitter opponent and reviler of colored troops—who was engaged in this affair, volunteered the statement that they had fought bravely, and, in his own language, more expressive than elegant, were 'bully boys'— which coming from such a source, might be regarded as the highest praise.

"During the recent advance toward Richmond to liberate the Union prisoners, the 4th, 5th, and 9th regiments formed part of the expedition and behaved splendidly. They marched thirty miles in ten hours, and an unusually small number straggled on the route."

Col. John A. Foster of the 175th New York, in January, 1864, wrote to Col. Darling as follows :

"While before Port Hudson, during the siege of that place, I was acting on Col. Gooding's staff, prior to the arrival of my regiment at that place. On the assault of May 27, 1863, Col. Gooding was ordered to proceed to the extreme right of our lines and oversee the charge of the two regiments constituting the negro-brigade, and I accompanied him.

"We witnessed them in line of battle, under a very heavy fire of musketry, and siege and field pieces. There was a deep gully or bayou before them, which they could not cross nor ford in the presence of the enemy, and hence an assault was wholly impracticable. Yet they made five several attempts to swim and cross it, preparatory to an assault on the enemy's works ; and in this, too, in fair view of the enemy, and at short musket range. Added to this, the nature of the enemy's works was such that it allowed an enfilading fire. Success was impossible ; yet they behaved as cool as if veterans, and when ordered to retire, marched off as if on parade. I feel satisfied that, if the position of the bayou had been known and the assault made a quarter of a mile to the left of where it was, the place would have been taken by this negro brigade on that day.

"On that day I witnessed the attack made by the divisions of Generals Grover and Paine, and can truly say I saw no steadier fighting by those daring men than did the negroes in this their first fight.

"On the second assault, June 14th, in the assault made by Gen. Paine's division, our loss was very great in wounded, and, as there was a want of ambulance men, I ordered about a hundred negroes, who were standing idle and unharmed, to take the stretchers and carry the wounded from the field. Under a most severe fire of musketry, grape, and canister, they performed this duty with unflinching courage and nonchalance. They suffered severely in this duty both in killed and wounded ; yet not a man faltered. These men had just been recruited, and were not even partially disciplined. But I next saw the negroes (engineers) working in these trenches, under a heavy fire of the enemy. They worked faithfully, and wholly regardless of exposure to the enemy's fire."

Mr. Cadwallader in his despatch concerning the battle of Spottsylvania, dated May 18th, says:

" It is a subject of considerable merriment in camp that a charge of the famous Hampton Legion, the flower of Southern chivalry, was repulsed by the Colored Troops of General Ferrero's command." [1]

These are but a *few* of the tributes that brave and true white men cheerfully gave to the valor and loyalty of Colored Troops during the war. No officer, whose privilege it was to command or observe the conduct of these troops, has ever hesitated to give a full and cheerful endorsement of their worth as men, their loyalty as Americans, and their eminent qualifications for the duties and dangers of military life. No history of the war has ever been written, no history of the war ever can be written, without mentioning the patience, endurance, fortitude, and heroism of the Negro soldiers who prayed, wept, fought, bled, and died for the preservation of the Union of the United States of America !

---

[1] New York Herald, May 20, 1864.

CHAPTER XX.

CAPTURE AND TREATMENT OF NEGRO SOLDIERS.

THE MILITARY EMPLOYMENT OF NEGROES DISTASTEFUL TO THE REBEL AUTHORITIES. — THE CONFEDERATES THE FIRST TO EMPLOY NEGROES AS SOLDIERS. — JEFFERSON DAVIS REFERS TO THE SUBJECT IN HIS MESSAGE, AND THE CONFEDERATE CONGRESS ORDERS ALL NEGROES CAPTURED TO BE TURNED OVER TO THE STATE AUTHORITIES, AND RAISES THE "BLACK FLAG" UPON WHITE OFFICERS COMMANDING NEGRO SOLDIERS. — THE NEW YORK PRESS CALLS UPON THE GOVERNMENT TO PROTECT ITS NEGRO SOLDIERS. — SECRETARY STANTON'S ACTION. — THE PRESIDENT'S ORDER. — CORRESPONDENCE BETWEEN GEN. PECK AND GEN. PICKETT IN REGARD TO THE KILLING OF A COLORED MAN AFTER HE HAD SURRENDERED AT THE BATTLE OF NEWBERN. — SOUTHERN PRESS ON THE CAPTURE AND TREATMENT OF NEGRO SOLDIERS. — THE REBELS REFUSE TO EXCHANGE NEGRO SOLDIERS CAPTURED ON MORRIS AND JAMES ISLANDS ON ACCOUNT OF THE ORDER OF THE CONFEDERATE CONGRESS WHICH REQUIRED THEM TO BE TURNED OVER TO THE AUTHORITIES OF THE SEVERAL STATES. — JEFFERSON DAVIS ISSUES A PROCLAMATION OUTLAWING GEN. B. F. BUTLER. — HE IS TO BE HUNG WITHOUT TRIAL BY ANY CONFEDERATE OFFICER WHO MAY CAPTURE HIM. — THE BATTLE OF FORT PILLOW. — THE GALLANT DEFENCE BY THE LITTLE BAND OF UNION TROOPS. — IT REFUSES TO CAPITULATE AND IS ASSAULTED AND CAPTURED BY AN OVERWHELMING FORCE. — THE UNION TROOPS BUTCHERED IN COLD BLOOD. — THE WOUNDED ARE CARRIED INTO HOUSES WHICH ARE FIRED AND BURNED WITH THEIR HELPLESS VICTIMS. — MEN ARE NAILED TO THE OUTSIDE OF BUILDINGS THROUGH THEIR HANDS AND FEET AND BURNT ALIVE. — THE WOUNDED AND DYING ARE BRAINED WHERE THEY LAY IN THEIR EBBING BLOOD. — THE OUTRAGES ARE RENEWED IN THE MORNING — DEAD AND LIVING FIND A COMMON SEPULCHRE IN THE TRENCH. — GENERAL CHALMERS ORDERS THE KILLING OF A NEGRO CHILD. — TESTIMONY OF THE FEW UNION SOLDIERS WHO WERE ENABLED TO CRAWL OUT OF THE GILT EDGE, FIRE PROOF HELL AT PILLOW. — THEY GIVE A SICKENING ACCOUNT OF THE MASSACRE BEFORE THE SENATE COMMITTEE ON THE CONDUCT OF THE WAR. — GEN. FORREST'S FUTILE ATTEMPT TO DESTROY THE RECORD OF HIS FOUL CRIME. — FORT PILLOW MASSACRE WITHOUT A PARALLEL IN HISTORY.

THE appearance of Negroes as soldiers in the armies of the United States seriously offended the Southern view of "the eternal fitness of things." No action on the part of the Federal Government was so abhorrent to the rebel army. It called forth a bitter wail from Jefferson Davis, on the 12th of January, 1863, and soon after the Confederate Congress elevated its olfactory organ and handled the subject with a pair of tongs. After a long discussion the following was passed:

"*Resolved, by the Congress of the Confederate States of America,* In response to the message of the President, transmitted to Congress at the commencement of the present session, That, in the opinion of Congress, the commissioned officers of the enemy ought *not* to be delivered to the authorities of the respective States, as suggested in the said message, but all captives taken by the Confederate forces ought to be dealt with and disposed of by the Confederate Government.

" SEC. 2. That, in the judgment of Congress, the proclamations of the President of the United States, dated respectively September 22, 1862, and January 1, 1863, and the other measures of the Government of the United States and of its authorities, commanders, and forces, designed or tending to emancipate slaves in the Confederate States, or to abduct such slaves, or to incite them to insurrection, or to employ negroes in war against the Confederate States, or to overthrow the institution of African Slavery, and bring on a servile war in these States, would, if successful, produce atrocious consequences, and they are inconsistent with the spirit of those usages which, in modern warfare, prevail among civilized nations ; they may, therefore, be properly and lawfully repressed by retaliation.

" SEC. 3. That in every case wherein, during the present war, any violation of the laws or usages of war among civilized nations shall be, or has been, done and perpetrated by those acting under the authority of the Government of the United States, on the persons or property of citizens of the Confederate States, or of those under the protection or in the land or naval service of the Confederate States, or of any State of the Confederacy, the President of the Confederate States is hereby authorized to cause full and ample retaliation to be made for every such violation, in such manner and to such extent as he may think proper.

" SEC. 4. That every white person, being a commissioned officer, or acting as such, who, during the present war, shall command negroes or mulattoes in arms against the Confederate States, or who shall arm, train, organize, or prepare negroes or mulattoes for military service against the Confederate States, or who shall voluntarily aid negroes or mulattoes in any military enterprise, attack, or conflict in such service, shall be deemed as inciting servile insurrection, and shall, if captured, be put to death, or be otherwise punished at the discretion of the court.

" SEC. 5. Every person, being a commissioned officer, or acting as such in the service of the enemy, who shall, during the present war, excite, attempt to excite, or cause to be excited, a servile insurrection, or who shall incite, or cause to be incited, a slave or rebel, shall, if captured, be put to death, or be otherwise punished at the discretion of the court.

" SEC. 6. Every person charged with an offence punishable under the preceding resolutions shall, during the present war, be tried before the military court attached to the army or corps by the troops of which he shall have been captured, or by such other military court as the

President may direct, and in such manner and under such regulations as the President shall prescribe ; and, after conviction, the President may commute the punishment in such manner and on such terms as he may deem proper.

"SEC. 7. All negroes and mulattoes who shall be engaged in war, or be taken in arms against the Confederate States, or shall give aid or comfort to the enemies of the Confederate States, shall, when captured in the Confederate States, be delivered to the authorities of the State or States in which they shall be captured, to be dealt with according to the present or future laws of such State or States."

This document stands alone among the resolves of the civilized governments of all Christendom. White persons acting as commissioned officers in organizations of Colored Troops were to "be put to death!" And all Negroes and Mulattoes taken in arms against the Confederate Government were to be turned over to the authorities—civil, of course—of the States in which they should be captured, to be dealt with according to the present or future laws of such States! Now, what were the laws of the Southern States respecting Negroes in arms against white people? The most cruel death. And fearing some of those States had modified their cruel slave Code, the States were granted the right to pass *ex post facto* laws in order to give the cold-blooded murder of captured Negro soldiers the semblance of law,—and by a *civil law* too. Colored soldiers and their officers had been butchered before this in South Carolina, Mississippi, Louisiana, and Florida, notwithstanding the rebels were the first to arm Negroes, as has been already shown. If the Confederates had a right to arm Negroes and include them in their armies, why could not the Federal Government pursue the same policy? But the Rebel Government had determined upon a barbarous policy in dealing with captured Negro soldiers,—and barbarous as that policy was, the rebel soldiers exceeded its cruel provisions tenfold. Their treatment of Negroes was perfectly fiendish.

But what was the attitude of the Federal Government? Silence, until the butcheries of its gallant defenders had sickened the civilized world, and until the Christian governments of Europe frowned upon the inhuman indifference of the Government that would *force* its slaves to fight its battles and then allow them to be tortured to death in the name of "*State laws!*" Even the most conservative papers of the North began to feel that some policy ought to be adopted whereby the lives of Colored soldiers could be protected against the inhuman treatment bestowed upon them when captured by the rebels. In the spring of 1863, the " Tribune," referring to this subject, said, editorially :

" The Government has sent Adj.-General Thomas to the West with full authority to arm and organize the negroes for service against the Rebels. They are to be employed to protect the navigation of the Mississippi and other rivers against guerrillas, and as garrisons at fortified posts, and are evidently destined for all varieties of military duty. Seven thousand soldiers who listened to this announcement at Fort Curtis received it with satisfaction and applause. Gen. Thomas, heretofore known as opposed to this and all similar measures, urged in his address that the Blacks should be treated with kindness ; declared his belief in their capacity, and informed the officers of the army that no one would be permitted to oppose or in any way interfere with this policy of the Government.

" It is not directly stated, but may be inferred from the Despatch, that the negroes are not to be encouraged to enlist, but are to be drafted. At all events, the policy of the Government to employ Black Troops in active service is definitely established, and it becomes—as indeed it has been for months—a very serious question what steps are to be taken for their protection. The Proclamation of Jefferson Davis remains unrevoked. By it he threatened death or slavery to every negro taken in arms, and to their white officers the same fate. What is the response of our Government? Hitherto, silence. The number of negroes in its service has already increased ; in South Carolina they have already been mustered into regiments by a sweeping conscription, and now in the West apparently the same policy is adopted and rigorously enforced.

" Does the Government mean that the men are to be exposed not merely to the chances of battle, but to the doom which the unanswered Proclamation of the Rebel President threatens ?

" Every black soldier now marches to battle with a halter about his neck. The simple question is : Shall we protect and insure the ordinary treatment of a prisoner of war ? Under it, every negro yet captured has suffered death or been sent back to the hell of slavery from which he had escaped. The bloody massacre of black prisoners at Murfreesboro, brooked, so far as the public knows, no retaliation at Washington. The black servants captured at Galveston—free men and citizens of Massachusetts—were sold into slavery and remained there. In every instance in which they have had the opportunity, the rebels have enforced their barbarous proclamation. How much longer are they to be suffered to do it without remonstrance ?

" Gen. Hunter—at this moment in the field,—General Butler, and hundreds of other white officers are included in this Proclamation, or were previously outlawed and adjudged a felon's death. Delay remonstrance much longer, and retaliation must supersede it. If the Government wishes to be spared the necessity of retaliating, it has only to *say* that it will retaliate—to declare by proclamation or general order that all its soldiers who may be captured must receive from the Rebels the treatment to which, as prisoners of war, they are, by the usages of war, entitled. The Government can know no distinction of color under its flag. The moment a soldier shoulders a musket he is invested with every military right which belongs to a white soldier. He is at least and above all things entitled to the safeguards which surround his white comrades.

"It is not possible to suppose the Government means to withhold them; we only urge that the wisest, safest, and humanest, as well as the most honorable policy, is at once to announce its purpose." [1]

The able article just quoted had a wholesome effect upon many thoughtful men at the South, and brought the blush to the cheek of the nation. A few of the Southern journals agreed with Mr. Greeley that the resolves of the Confederate Congress were unjustifiable; that the Congress had no right to say what color the Union soldiers should be; and that such action would damage their cause in the calm and humane judgment of all Europe. But the Confederate Congress was unmoved and unmovable upon this subject.

Three Colored men had been captured in Stone River on the gun-boat "Isaac Smith." They were free men; but, notwithstanding this, they were placed in close confinement and treated like felons. Upon the facts reaching the ear of the Government, Secretary Stanton took three South Carolina prisoners and had them subjected to the same treatment, and the facts telegraphed to the Rebel authorities. Commenting upon the question of the treatment of captured Colored soldiers the "Richmond Examiner" said:

"It is not merely the pretension of a regular Government affecting to deal with 'Rebels,' but it is a deadly stab which they are aiming at our institutions themselves—because they know that, it we were insane enough to yield this point, to treat Black men as the equals of White, and insurgent slaves as equivalent to our brave soldiers, the very foundation of Slavery would be fatally wounded."

---

[1] New York Tribune, April 14, 1863.

Shortly after this occurrence an exchange of prisoners took place in front of Charleston. The rebels returned only white prisoners. When upbraided by the Union officers for not exchanging Negroes the reply came that under the resolutions of the Confederate Congress they could not deliver up any Negro soldiers. This fact stirred the heart of the North, and caused the Government to act. The following order was issued by the President :

"EXECUTIVE MANSION,
"WASHINGTON, July 30, 1863.

"It is the duty of every Government to give protection to its citizens, of whatever class, color, or condition, and especially to those who are duly organized as soldiers in the public service. The law of nations, and the usages and customs of war, as carried on by civilized powers, permit no distinction as to color in the treatment of prisoners of war as public enemies. To sell or enslave any captured person, on account of his color, and for no offense against the laws of war, is a relapse into barbarism, and a crime against the civilization of the age.

"The Government of the United States will give the same protection to all its soldiers ; and if the enemy shall sell or enslave any one because of his color, the offense shall be punished by retaliation upon the enemy's prisoners in our possession.

"It is therefore ordered that, for every soldier of the United States killed in violation of the laws of war, a Rebel soldier shall be executed ; and for every one enslaved by the enemy or sold into Slavery, a Rebel soldier shall be placed at hard labor on public works, and continued at such labor until the other shall be released and receive the treatment due to a prisoner of war.

"ABRAHAM LINCOLN.

"By order of the Secretary of War.
"E. D. TOWNSEND, *Assistant Adjutant-General.*"

In the early spring of 1864, there was a great deal said in the Southern journals and much action had in the rebel army respecting the capture and treatment of Negro soldiers. The "Richmond Examiner" contained an account of the battle of Newbern, North Carolina, in which the writer seemed to gloat over the fact that a captured Negro had been hung after he had surrendered. It came to the knowledge of Gen. Peck, commanding the army of the District of North Carolina, when the following correspondence took place :

" Headquarters of the Army and District of ⎫
    " North Carolina, Newbern, North ⎬
        " Carolina, Feb. 11, 1864. ⎭

" Major-General Pickett, *Department of Virginia and North Carolina,*
        " *Confederate Army, Petersburg.*

"General : I have the honor to inclose a slip cut from the Richmond 'Examiner,' February eighth, 1864. It is styled 'The Advance on Newbern,' and appears to have been extracted from the Petersburg 'Register,' a paper published in the city where your headquarters are located.

"Your attention is particularly invited to that paragraph which states 'that Colonel Shaw was shot dead by a negro soldier from the other side of the river, which he was spanning with a pontoon bridge, and that 'the negro was watched, followed, taken, and hanged after the action at Thomasville.'

"'The Advance on Newbern.—The Petersburg "Register gives the following additional facts of the advance on Newbern : Our army, according to the report of passengers arriving from Weldon, has fallen back to a point sixteen miles west of Newbern. The reason assigned for this retrograde movement was that Newbern could not be taken by us without a loss on our part which would find no equivalent in its capture, as the place was stronger than we had anticipated. Yet, in spite of this, we are sure that the expedition will result in good to our cause. Our forces are in a situation to get large supplies from a country still abundant, to prevent raids on points westward, and keep tories in check, and hang them when caught.

"' From a private, who was one of the guard that brought the batch of prisoners through, we learn that Colonel Shaw was shot dead by a negro soldier from the other side of the river, which he was spanning with a pontoon bridge. The negro was watched, followed, taken, and hanged after the action at Thomasville. It is stated that when our troops entered Thomasville, a number of the enemy took shelter in the houses and fired upon them. The Yankees were ordered to surrender, but refused, whereupon our men set fire to the houses, and their occupants got, bodily, a taste in this world of the flames eternal.'

" The Government of the United States has wisely seen fit to enlist many thousand colored citizens to aid in putting down the rebellion, and has placed them on the same footing in all respects as her white troops.

.   .   .   .

"Believing that this atrocity has been perpetrated without your knowledge, and that you will take prompt steps to disavow this violation of the usages of war, and to bring the offenders to justice, I shall refrain from executing a rebel soldier until I learn your action in the premises.

"I am, very respectfully, your obedient servant,

"JOHN J. PECK,
"*Major-General.*"

REPLY OF GENERAL PICKETT.

"HEADQUARTERS OF THE DEPARTMENT OF NORTH }
"CAROLINA, PETERSBURG, VIRGINIA, February 16, 1864. }

"Major-General JOHN J. PECK, U. S. A., *Commanding at Newbern :*

"GENERAL : Your communication of the eleventh of February is received. I have the honor to state in reply, that the paragraph from a newspaper inclosed therein, is not only without foundation in fact, but so ridiculous that I should scarcely have supposed it worthy of consideration ; but I would respectfully inform you that had I caught *any negro,* who had killed either officer, soldier, or citizen of the Confederate States, I should have caused him to be immediately executed.

"To your threat expressed in the following extract from your communication, namely : 'Believing that this atrocity has been perpetrated without your knowledge, and that you will take prompt steps to disavow this violation of the usages of war, and to bring the offenders to justice, I shall refrain from executing a rebel soldier until I learn of your action in the premises,' I have merely to say that I have in my hands and subject to my orders, captured in the recent operations in this department, some four hundred and fifty officers and men of the United States army, and for every man you hang I will hang ten of the United States army.

"I am, General, very respectfully, your obedient servant,

"J. E. PICKETT,
"*Major-General Commanding.*" [1]

As already indicated, some of the Southern journals did not endorse the extreme hardships and cruelties to which the rebels subjected the captured Colored men. During the month of July, 1863, quite a number of Colored soldiers had fallen into the hands of the enemy on Morris and James islands. The rebels did not only refuse to exchange them as prisoners of war, but treated them most cruelly.

On this very important subject, in reply to some strictures of

---

[1] Rebellion Recs., vol. viii. Doc. pp. 418, 419.

the Charleston " Mercury" (made under *misapprehension*), the Chief of Staff of General Beauregard addressed to that journal the following letter:

" HEADQUARTERS, DEPARTMENT OF S. C., GA., AND FLA.,
" CHARLESTON, S. C., August 12, 1863.

"Colonel R. B. RHETT, Jr., *Editor of* 'Mercury':

" In the ' Mercury ' of this date you appear to have written under a misapprehension of the facts connected with the present *status* of the negroes captured in arms on Morris and James Islands, which permit me to state as follows :

" The Proclamation of the President, dated December twenty-fourth, 1862, directed that all negro slaves captured in arms should be at once delivered over to the executive authorities of the respective States to which they belong, to be dealt with according to the laws of said States.

" An informal application was made by the State authorities for the negroes captured in this vicinity ; but as none of them, it appeared, had been slaves of citizens of South Carolina, they were not turned over to the civil authority, for at the moment there was no official information at these headquarters of the Act of Congress by which ' all negroes and mulattoes, who shall be engaged in war, or be taken in arms against the confederate States, or shall give aid or comfort to the enemies of the confederate States,' were directed to be turned over to the authorities of ' State or States in which they shall be captured, to be dealt with according to the present or future laws of such State or States.'

" On the twenty-first of July, however, the Commanding General telegraphed to the Secretary of War for instructions as to the disposition to be made of the negroes captured on Morris and James Islands, and on the twenty-second received a reply that they must be turned over to the State authorities, by virtue of the joint resolutions of Congress in question.

" Accordingly, on the twenty-ninth July, as soon as a copy of the resolution or act was received, his Excellency Governor Bonham was informed that the negroes captured were held subject to his orders, to be dealt with according to the laws of South Carolina.

" On the same day (twenty-ninth July) Governor Bonham requested that they should be retained in military custody until he could make arrangements to dispose of them ; and in that custody they still remain, awaiting the orders of the State authorities.

" Respectfully, your obedient servant,
" THOMAS JORDAN,
" *Chief of Staff*."

The Proclamation of Jefferson Davis, referred to in the second paragraph of Mr. Jordan's letter, had declared Gen. Butler "a felon, an outlaw, and an enemy of mankind." It recited his hanging of Mumford ; the neglect of the Federal Government to explain or disapprove the act ; the imprisonment of non-combatants ; Butler's woman order ; his sequestration of estates in Western Louisiana ; and the inciting to insurrection and arming of slaves. Mr. Davis directed any Confederate officer who should capture Gen. Butler to hang him immediately and without trial. Mr. Davis's proclamation is given here, as history is bound to hold him personally responsible for the cruelties practised upon Negro soldiers captured by the rebels from that time till the close of the war.

"First. That all commissioned officers in the command of said Benjamin F. Butler be declared not entitled to be considered as soldiers engaged in honorable warfare, but as robbers and criminals, deserving death ; and that they and each of them be, whenever captured, reserved for execution.

"Second. That the private soldiers and non-commissioned officers in the army of said Butler be considered as only the instruments used for the commission of crimes perpetrated by his orders, and not as free agents ; that they, therefore, be treated, when captured as prisoners of war, with kindness and humanity, and be sent home on the usual parole that they will in no manner aid or serve the United States in any capacity during the continuance of this war, unless duly exchanged.

"Third. That all negro slaves captured in arms be at once delivered over to the executive authorities of the respective States to which they belong, to be dealt with according to the laws of said States.

"Fourth. That the like orders be executed in all cases with respect to all commissioned officers of the United States, when found serving in company with said slaves in insurrection against the authorities of the different States of this Confederacy.

"[Signed and sealed at Richmond, Dec. 23, 1862.]

"JEFFERSON DAVIS."

The ghastly horrors of Fort Pillow stand alone in the wide field of war cruelties. The affair demands great fortitude in the historian who would truthfully give a narrative of such bloody, sickening detail.

On the 18th of April, 1864, Gen. N. B. Forrest, commanding a corps of Confederate cavalry, appeared before Fort Pillow, situ-

ated about forty miles above Memphis, Tennessee, and demanded its surrender. It was held by Major L. F. Booth, with
a garrison of 557 men, 262 of whom were Colored soldiers of the
6th U. S. Heavy Artillery; the other troops were white, under
Major Bradford of the 13th Tennessee Cavalry. The garrison
was mounted with six guns. From before sunrise until nine A.M.
the Union troops had held an outer line of intrenchments; but
upon the death of Major Booth Major Bradford retired his force
into the fort. It was situated upon a high bluff on the Mississippi River, flanked by two ravines with sheer declivities and partially timbered. The gun-boat "New Era" was to have coöper-
ated with the fort, but on account of the extreme height of the
bluff, was unable to do much. The fighting continued until
about two o'clock in the afternoon, when the firing slackened on
both sides to allow the guns to cool off. The "New Era,"
nearly out of shell, backed into the river to clean her guns.
During this lull Gen. Forrest sent a flag of truce demanding the
unconditional surrender of the fort. A consultation of the Federal officers was held, and a request made for twenty minutes to
consult the officers of the gun-boat. Gen. Forrest refused to
grant this, saying that he only demanded the surrender of the
fort and not the gun-boat. He demanded an immediate surrender, which was promptly declined by Major Bradford. During
the time these negotiations were going on, Forrest's men were
stealing horses, plundering the buildings in front of the fort, and
closing in upon the fort through the ravines, which was unsol-
dierly and cowardly to say the least. Upon receiving the refusal
of Major Booth to capitulate, Forrest gave a signal and his troops
made a frantic charge upon the fort. It was received gallantly
and resisted stubbornly, but there was no use of fighting. In ten
minutes the enemy, assaulting the fort in the centre, and striking
it on the flanks, swept in. The Federal troops surrendered;
but an indiscriminate massacre followed. Men were shot down
in their tracks; pinioned to the ground with bayonet and sabre. Some were clubbed to death while dying of wounds;
others were made to get down upon their knees, in which condition they were shot to death. Some were burned alive, having been fastened into the buildings, while still others were
nailed against the houses, tortured, and then burned to a crisp.
A little Colored boy only eight years old was lifted to the
horse of a rebel who intended taking him along with him, when

Gen. Forrest meeting the soldier ordered him to put the. child down and shoot him. The soldier remonstrated, but the stern and cruel order was repeated, emphasized with an oath, and backed with a threat that endangered the soldier's life, so he put the child on the ground and shot him dead! From three o'clock in the afternoon until the merciful darkness came and threw the sable wings of night over the carnival of death, the slaughter continued. The. stars looked down in pity upon the dead—ah! they were beyond the barbarous touch of the rebel fiends—and the dying; and the angels found a spectacle worthy of their tears. And when the morning looked down upon the battle-field, it was not to find it peaceful in death and the human hyenas gone. Alas! those who had survived the wounds of the day before were set upon again and brained or shot to death.

The Committee on the Conduct and Expenditures of the War gave this " Horrible Massacre " an investigation. They examined such of the Union soldiers as escaped from death at Fort Pillow and were sent to the Mound City Hospital, Illinois. The following extracts from the testimony given before the Committee, the Hons. Ben. F. Wade and D. W. Gooch, give something of an idea of this the most cruel and. inhuman affair in the history of the civilized world.

Manuel Nichols (Colored), private, Company B, Sixth United States Heavy Artillery, sworn and examined.

By Mr. Gooch:

Question. Were you in the late fight at Fort Pillow ?
Answer. Yes, sir.
Q. Were you wounded there ?
A. Yes, sir.
Q. When ?
A. I was wounded once about a half an hour before we gave up.
Q. Did they do any thing to you after you surrendered ?
A. Yes, sir ; they shot me in the head under my left ear, and the morning after the fight they shot me again in the right arm. When they came up and killed the wounded ones, I saw some four or five coming down the hill. I said to one of our boys : " Anderson, I expect if those fellows come here they will kill us." I was lying on my right side, leaning on my elbow. One of the black soldiers went into the house where the white soldiers were. I asked him if there was any water in there, and he said yes ; I wanted some, and took a stick and tried to get to the house. I did not get to the house. Some of them

came along, and saw a little boy belonging to Company D. One of them had his musket on his shoulder, and shot the boy down. He said : " All you damned niggers come out of the house ; I am going to shoot you." Some of the white soldiers said : " Boys, it is only death anyhow ; if you don't go out they will come in and carry you out." My strength seemed to come to me as if I had never been shot, and I jumped up and ran down the hill. I met one of them coming up the hill ; he said : " Stop ! " but I kept on running. As I jumped over the hill, he shot me through the right arm.

Q. How many did you see them kill after they had surrendered ?

A. After I surrendered I did not go down the hill. A man shot me under the ear, and I fell down and said to myself : " If he don't shoot me any more this won't hurt me." One of their officers came along and hallooed : " Forrest says no quarter ! no quarter ! " and the next one hallooed : " Black flag ! black flag ! "

Q. What did they do then ?

A. They kept on shooting. I could hear them down the hill.

Q. Did you see them bury any body ?

A. Yes, sir ; they carried me around right to the corner of the Fort, and I saw them pitch men in there.

Q. Was there any alive ?

A. I did not see them bury any body alive.

Q. How near to you was the man who shot you under the ear ?

A. Right close to my head. When I was shot in the side, a man turned me over, and took my pocket-knife and pocket-book. I had some of these brass things that looked like cents. They said : " Here 's some money ; here 's some money." I said to myself : " You got fooled that time."

Major Williams (Colored), private, Company B, Sixth United States Heavy Artillery, sworn and examined.

By the Chairman :

Q. Where were you raised ?

A. In Tennessee and North Mississippi.

Q. Where did you enlist ?

A. In Memphis.

Q. Who was your captain ?

A. Captain Lamburg.

Q. Were you in the fight at Fort Pillow ?

A. Yes, sir.

Q. Was your captain with you ?

A. No, sir ; I think he was at Memphis.

Q. Who commanded your company?

A. Lieutenant Hunter and Sergeant Fox were all the officers we had.

Q. What did you see done there?

A. We fought them right hard during the battle, and killed some of them. After a time they sent in a flag of truce. They said afterward that they did it to make us stop firing until their reinforcements could come up. They said that they never could have got in if they had not done that; that we had whipped them; that they had never seen such a fight.

Q. Did you see the flag of truce?

A. Yes, sir.

Q. What did they do when the flag of truce was in?

A. They kept coming up nearer, so that they could charge quick. A heap of them came up after we stopped firing.

Q. When did you surrender?

A. I did not surrender until they all ran.

Q. Were you wounded then?

A. Yes, sir; after the surrender.

Q. At what time of day was that?

A. They told me it was about half after one o'clock, I was wounded. Immediately we retreated.

Q. Did you have any arms in your hands when they shot you?

A. No, sir; I was an artillery man, and had no arms.

Q. Did you see the man who shot you?

A. No, sir.

Q. Did you hear him say any thing?

A. No, sir; I heard nothing. He shot me, and I was bleeding pretty free, and I thought to myself: "I will make out it was a dead shot, and maybe I will not get another."

Q. Did you see any others shot?

A. No, sir.

Q. Was there any thing said about giving quarter?

A. Major Bradford brought in a black flag, which meant no quarter. I heard some of the rebel officers say: "You damned rascals, if you had not fought us so hard, but had stopped when we sent in a flag of truce, we would not have done any thing to you." I heard one of the officers say: "Kill all the niggers"; another one said: "No; Forrest says take them and carry them with him to wait upon him and cook for him, and put them in jail and send them to their masters." Still they kept on shooting. They shot at me after that, but did not hit me; a rebel officer shot at me. He took aim at my side; at the crack of his pistol I fell. He went on and said: "There's another dead nigger."

Q. Was there any one shot in the hospital that day?

A. Not that I know of. I think they all came away and made a raft and floated across the mouth of the creek and got into a flat bottom.

Q. Did you see any buildings burned?

A. I stayed in the woods all day Wednesday. I was there Thursday and looked at the buildings. I saw a great deal left that they did not have a chance to burn up. I saw a white man burned up who was nailed up against the house.

Q. A private or an officer?

A. An officer; I think it was a lieutenant in the Tennessee cavalry.

Q. How was he nailed?

A. Through his hands and feet right against the house.

Q. Was his body burned?

A. Yes, sir; burned all over—I looked at him good.

Q. When did you see that?

A. On the Thursday after the battle.

Q. Where was the man?

A. Right in front of the Fort.

Jacob Thompson (Colored), sworn and examined.
By Mr. Gooch:

Q. Were you a soldier at Fort Pillow?

A. No, sir; I was not a soldier; but I went up in the Fort and fought with the rest. I was shot in the hand and the head.

Q. When were you shot?

A. After I surrendered.

Q. How many times were you shot?

A. I was shot but once; but I threw my hand up, and the shot went through my hand and my head.

Q. Who shot you?

A. A private.

Q. What did he say?

A. He said: " God damn you, I will shoot you, old friend."

Q. Did you see anybody else shot?

A. Yes, sir; they just called them out like dogs, and shot them down. I reckon they shot about fifty, white and black, right there. They nailed some black sergeants to the logs, and set the logs on fire.

Q. When did you see that?

A. When I went there in the morning I saw them; they were burning all together.

Q. Did they kill them before they burned them?

A. No, sir; they nailed them to the logs; drove the nails right through their hands.

Q. How many did you see in that condition?

A. Some four or five; I saw two white men burned.

Q. Was there any one else there who saw that?

A. I reckon there was; I could not tell who.

Q. When was it that you saw them?

A. I saw them in the morning after the fight; some of them were burned almost in two. I could tell they were white men, because they were whiter than the colored men.

Q. Did you notice how they were nailed?

A. I saw one nailed to the side of a house; he looked like he was nailed right through his wrist. I was trying then to get to the boat when I saw it.

Q. Did you see them kill any white men?

A. They killed some eight or nine there. I reckon they killed more than twenty after it was all over; called them out from under the hill, and shot them down. They would call out a white man and shoot him down, and call out a colored man and shoot him down; do it just as fast as they could make their guns go off.

Q. Did you see any rebel officers about there when this was going on?

A. Yes, sir; old Forrest was one.

Q. Did you know Forrest?

A. Yes, sir; he was a little bit of a man. I had seen him before at Jackson.

Ransom Anderson (Colored), Company B, Sixth United States Heavy Artillery, sworn and examined.
By Mr. Gooch:

Q. Where were you raised?

A. In Mississippi.

Q. Were you a slave?

A. Yes, sir.

Q. Where did you enlist?

A. At Corinth.

Q. Were you in the fight at Fort Pillow?

A. Yes, sir.

Q: Describe what you saw done there.

A. Most all the men that were killed on our side were killed after the fight was over. They called them out and shot them down. Then they put some in the houses and shut them up, and then burned the houses.

Q. Did you see them burn?

A. Yes, sir.

Q. Were any of them alive?

A. Yes, sir; they were wounded, and could not walk. They put them in the houses, and then burned the houses down.

Q. Do you know they were in there?

A. Yes, sir; I went and looked in there.

Q. Do you know they were in there when the house was burned?

A. Yes, sir; I heard them hallooing there when the houses were burning.

Q. Are you sure they were wounded men, and not dead men, when they were put in there?

A. Yes, sir; they told them they were going to have the doctor see them, and then put them in there and shut them up, and burned them.

Q. Who set the house on fire?

A. I saw a rebel soldier take some grass and lay it by the door, and set it on fire. The door was pine plank, and it caught easy.

Q. Was the door fastened up?

A. Yes, sir; it was barred with one of those wide bolts.

James Walls, sworn and examined.
By Mr. Gooch:

Q. To what company did you belong?

A. To Company E, Thirteenth Tennessee Cavalry.

Q. Under what officers did you serve?

A. I was under Major Bradford and Captain Potter.

Q. Were you in the fight at Fort Pillow?

A. Yes, sir.

Q. State what you saw there of the fight, and what was done after the place was captured.

A. We fought them for some six or eight hours in the Fort, and when they charged our men scattered and ran under the hill; some turned back and surrendered, and were shot. After the flag of truce came in I went down to get some water. As I was coming back I turned sick, and laid down behind a log. The secesh charged, and after they came over I saw one go a good ways ahead of the others. One of our men made to him and threw down his arms. The bullets were flying so thick there I thought I could not live there, so I threw down my arms and surrendered. He did not shoot me then, but as I turned around he or some other one shot me in the back

Q. Did they say any thing while they were shooting?

A. All I heard was : " Shoot him, shoot him ! " " Yonder he goes ! " " Kill him, kill him ! " That is about all I heard.

Q. How many do you suppose you saw shot after they surrendered ?

A. I did not see but two or three shot around me. One of the boys of our company, named Taylor, ran up there, and I saw him shot and fall. Then another was shot just before me, like—shot down after he threw down his arms.

Q. Those were white men ?

A. Yes, sir. I saw them make lots of niggers stand up, and then they shot them down like hogs. The next morning I was lying around there waiting for the boat to come up. The secesh would be prying around there, and would come to a nigger, and say : " You ain't dead, are you ? " They would not say any thing ; and then the secesh would get down off their horses, prick them in their sides, and say : " Damn you, you ain't dead ; get up." Then they would make them get up on their knees, when they would shoot them down like hogs.

Q. Did you see any rebel officers about while this shooting was going on ?

A. I do not know as I saw any officers about when they were shooting the negroes. A captain came to me a few minutes after I was shot ; he was close by me when I was shot.

Q Did he try to stop the shooting ?

A. I did not hear a word of their trying to stop it. After they were shot down, he told them not to shoot them any more. I begged him not to let them shoot me again, and he said they would not. One man, after he was shot down, was shot again. After I was shot down, the man I surrendered to went around the tree I was against and shot a man, and then came around to me again and wanted my pocket-book. I handed it up to him, and he saw my watch-chain and made a grasp at it, and got the watch and about half the chain. He took an old Barlow knife I had in my pocket. It was not worth five cents ; was of no account at all, only to cut tobacco with.

Lieutenant McJ. Leming, sworn and examined.
By Mr. Gooch :

Q. Were you in the fight at Fort Pillow ?

A. Yes, sir.

Q. What is your rank and position ?

A. I am a First Lieutenant and Adjutant of the Thirteenth Tennessee Cavalry. A short time previous to the fight I was Post-Adjutant at

Fort Pillow, and during most of the engagement I was acting as Post-Adjutant. After Major Booth was killed, Major Bradford was in command. The pickets were driven in just before sunrise, which was the first intimation we had that the enemy were approaching. I repaired to the Fort, and found that Major Booth was shelling the rebels as they came up toward the outer intrenchments. They kept up a steady fire by sharp-shooters behind trees and logs and high knolls. The Major thought at one time they were planting some artillery, or looking for places to plant it. They began to draw nearer and nearer, up to the time our men were all drawn into the Fort. Two companies of the Thirteenth Tennessee Cavalry were ordered out as sharp-shooters, but were finally ordered in. We were pressed on all sides.

I think Major Booth fell not later than nine o'clock. His Adjutant, who was then acting Post-Adjutant, fell near the same time. Major Bradford then took the command, and I acted as Post-Adjutant. Previous to this, Major Booth had ordered some buildings in front of the Fort to be destroyed, as the enemy's sharp-shooters were endeavoring to get possession of them. There were four rows of buildings, but only the row nearest the fort was destroyed ; the sharp-shooters gained possession of the others before they could be destroyed. The fight continued, one almost unceasing fire all the time, until about three o'clock. They threw some shells, but they did not do much damage with their shells.

I think it was about three o'clock that a flag of truce approached. I went out, accompanied by Captain Young, the Provost-Marshal of the post. There was another officer, I think, but I do not recollect now particularly who it was, and some four mounted men. The rebels announced that they had a communication from General Forrest. One of their officers there, I think, from his dress, was a colonel. I received the communication, and they said they would wait for an answer. As near as I remember, the communication was as follows :

"HEADQUARTERS CONFEDERATE CAVALRY, }
"NEAR FORT PILLOW, April 12, 1864. }

"As your gallant defence of the Fort has entitled you to the treatment of brave men [or something to that effect], I now demand an unconditional surrender of your force, at the same time assuring you that they will be treated as prisoners of war. I have received a fresh supply of ammunition, and can easily take your position.

"N. B. FORREST.

"Major L. F. BOOTH,
    "*Commanding United States Forces.*"

I took this message back to the Fort. Major Bradford replied that he desired an hour for consultation and consideration with his officers and the officers of the gun-boat. I took out this communication to them, and they carried it back to General Forrest. In a few minutes another flag of truce appeared, and I went out to meet it. Some one said, when they handed the communication to me: "That gives you twenty minutes to surrender; I am General Forrest." I took it back. The substance of it was: "Twenty minutes will be given you to take your men outside of the Fort. If in that time they are not out, I will immediately proceed to assault your works," or something of that kind. To this Major Bradford replied: "I will not surrender." I took it out in a sealed envelope, and gave it to him. The general opened it and read it. Nothing was said; we simply saluted, and they went their way, and I returned back into the Fort.

Almost instantly the firing began again. We mistrusted, while this flag of truce was going on, that they were taking horses out at a camp we had. It was mentioned to them, the last time that this and other movements excited our suspicion, that they were moving their troops. They said that they had noticed it themselves, and had it stopped; that it was unintentional on their part, and that it should not be repeated.

It was not long after the last flag of truce had retired, that they made their grand charge. We kept them back for several minutes. What was called ———— brigade or battalion attacked the centre of the Fort where several companies of colored troops were stationed. They finally gave way, and, before we could fill up the breach, the enemy got inside the Fort, and then they came in on the other two sides, and had complete possession of the Fort. In the mean time nearly all the officers had been killed, especially of the colored troops, and there was no one hardly to guide the men. They fought bravely indeed until that time. I do not think the men who broke had a commissioned officer over them. They fought with the most determined bravery, until the enemy gained possession of the Fort. They kept shooting all the time. The negroes ran down the hill toward the river, but the rebels kept shooting them as they were running; shot some again after they had fallen; robbed and plundered them. After every thing was all gone, after we had given up the Fort entirely, the guns thrown away and the firing on our part stopped, they still kept up their murderous fire, more especially on the colored troops, I thought, although the white troops suffered a great deal. I know the colored troops had a great deal the worst of it. I saw several shot after they were wounded; as they were crawling around, the secesh would step out and blow their brains out.

About this time they shot me. It must have been four or half-past four o'clock. I saw there was no chance at all, and threw down my sabre. A man took deliberate aim at me, but a short distance from me, certainly not more than fifteen paces, and shot me.

Q. With a musket or pistol ?

A. I think it was a carbine ; it may have been a musket, but my impression is, that it was a carbine. Soon after I was shot I was robbed. A secesh soldier came along, and wanted to know if I had any greenbacks. I gave him my pocket-book. I had about a hundred dollars, I think, more or less, and a gold watch and gold chain. They took every thing in the way of valuables that I had. I saw them robbing others. That seemed to be the general way they served the wounded, so far as regards those who fell in my vicinity. Some of the colored troops jumped into the river, but were shot as fast as they were seen. One poor fellow was shot as he reached the bank of the river. They ran down and hauled him out. He got on his hands and knees, and was crawling along, when a secesh soldier put his revolver to his head, and blew his brains out. It was about the same thing all along, until dark that night.

I was very weak, but I finally found a rebel who belonged to a society that I am a member of (the Masons), and he got two of our colored soldiers to assist me up the hill, and he brought me some water. At that time it was about dusk. He carried me up just to the edge of the Fort, and laid me down. There seemed to be quite a number of dead collected there. They were throwing them into the outside trench, and I heard them talking about burying them there. I heard one of them say : " There is a man who is not quite dead yet." They buried a number there ; I do not know how many.

I was carried that night to a sort of little shanty that the rebels had occupied during the day with their sharp-shooters. I received no medical attention that night at all. The next morning early I heard the report of cannon down the river. It was the gun-boat 28 coming up from Memphis ; she was shelling the rebels along the shore as she came up. The rebels immediately ordered the burning of all the buildings, and ordered the two buildings where the wounded were to be fired. Some one called to the officer who gave the order, and said there were wounded in them. The building I was in began to catch fire. I prevailed upon one of our soldiers who had not been hurt much to draw me out, and I think others got the rest out. They drew us down a little way, in a sort of gully, and we lay there in the hot sun without water or any thing.

About this time a squad of rebels came around, it would seem for the purpose of murdering what negroes they could find. They began to shoot the wounded negroes all around there, interspersed with the whites. I was lying a little way from a wounded negro, when a secesh soldier came up to him, and said : " What in hell are you doing here ? " The colored soldier said he wanted to get on the gun-boat. The secesh soldier said : " You want to fight us again, do you ? Damn you, I 'll teach you," and drew up his gun and shot him dead.

Another negro was standing up erect a little way from me—he did not seem to be hurt much. The rebel loaded his gun again immediately. The negro begged of him not to shoot him, but he drew up his gun and took deliberate aim at his head. The gun snapped, but he fixed it again, and then killed him. I saw this. I heard them shooting all around there—I suppose killing them

By the Chairman :

Q. Do you know of any rebel officers going on board our gun-boat after she came up ?

A. I don't know about the gun-boat, but I saw some of them on board the " Platte Valley," after I had been carried on her. They came on board, and I think went into drink with some of our officers. I think one of the rebel officers was General Chalmers.

Q. Do you know what officers of ours drank with them ?

A. I do not.

Q. You know that they did go on board the " Platte Valley " and drink with some of our officers ?

A. I did not see them drinking at the time, but I have no doubt they did ; that was my impression from all I saw, and I thought our officers might have been in better business.

Q. Were our officers treating these rebel officers with attention ?

A. They seemed to be ; I did not see much of it, as they passed along by me.

Q. Do you know whether or not the conduct of the privates, in murdering our soldiers after they had surrendered, seemed to have the approval of their officers ?

A. I did not see much of their officers, especially during the worst of those outrages ; they seemed to be back.

Q. Did you observe any effort on the part of their officers to suppress the murders?

A. No, sir ; I did not see any where I was first carried ; just about dusk, all at once several shots were fired just outside. The cry was : " They are shooting the darkey soldiers." I heard an officer ride up and say : " Stop that firing ; arrest that man." I suppose it was a rebel officer, but I do not know. It was reported to me, at the time, that several darkeys were shot then. An officer who stood by me, a prisoner, said that they had been shooting them, but that the general had had it stopped.

Q. Do you know of any of our men in the hospital being murdered?

A. I do not.

Q. Do you know any thing of the fate of your Quartermaster, Lieutenant Akerstrom?

A. He was one of the officers who went with me to meet the flag of truce the last time. I do not know what became of him; that was about the last I saw of him. I heard that he was nailed to a board and burned, and I have very good reason for believing that was the case, although I did not see it. The First Lieutenant of Company D of my regiment says that he has an affidavit to that effect of a man who saw it.

Francis A. Alexander, sworn and examined.
By the Chairman:

Q. To what company and regiment do you belong?
A. Company C, Thirteenth Tennessee Cavalry.
Q. Were you at Fort Pillow at the fight there?
A. Yes, sir.
Q. Who commanded your regiment?
A. Major Bradford commanded the regiment, and Lieutenant Logan commanded our company.
Q. By what troops was the Fort attacked?
A. Forrest was in command. I saw him.
Q. Did you know Forrest?
A. I saw him there, and they all said it was Forrest. Their own men said so.
Q. By what troops was the charge made
A. They are Alabamians and Texans.
Q. Did you see any thing of a flag of truce?
A. Yes, sir.
Q. State what was done while the flag of truce was in.
A. When the flag of truce came up our officers went out and held a consultation, and it went back. They came in again with a flag of truce; and while they were consulting the second time, their troops were coming up a gap or hollow, where we could have cut them to pieces. They tried it before, but could not do it. I saw them come up there while the flag of truce was in the second time.
Q. That gave them an advantage?
A. Yes, sir.
Q. Were you wounded there?
A. Not in the Fort. I was wounded after I left the Fort, and was going down the hill.
Q. Was that before or after the Fort was taken?
A. It was afterward.
Q. Did you have any arms in your hand at the time they shot you?
A. No, sir; I threw my gun away, and started down the hill, and got about twenty yards, when I was shot through the calf of the leg.

Q. Did they shoot you more than once?

A. No, sir; they shot at me, but did not hit me more than once.

Q. Did they say why they shot you after you had surrendered?

A. They said afterward they intended to kill us all for being there with their niggers.

Q. Were any rebel officers there at the time this shooting was going on?

A. Yes, sir.

Q. Did they try to stop it?

A. One or two of them did.

Q. What did the rest of them do?

A. They kept shouting and hallooing at the men to give no quarter. I heard that cry very frequent.

Q. Was it the officers that said that?

A. I think it was. I think it was them, the way they were going on. When our boys were taken prisoners, if anybody came up who knew them, they shot them down. As soon as ever they recognized them, wherever it was, they shot them.

Q. After they had taken them prisoners?

A. Yes, sir.

Q. Did you know any thing about their shooting men in the hospitals?

A. I know of their shooting negroes in there. I don't know about white men.

Q. Wounded negro men?

A. Yes, sir.

Q. Who did that?

A. Some of their troops. I don't know which of them. The next morning I saw several black people shot that were wounded, and some that were not wounded. One was going down the hill before me, and the officer made him come back up the hill; and after I got in the boat I heard them shooting them.

Q. You say you saw them shoot negroes in the hospital the next morning?

A. Yes, sir; wounded negroes who could not get along; one with his leg broke. They came there the next day and shot him.

John F. Ray, sworn and examined.
By Mr. Gooch:

Q. To what company and regiment do you belong?

A. Company B, Thirteenth Tennessee Cavalry.

Q. Were you at Fort Pillow when it was attacked?

A. Yes, sir.

Q. At what time were you wounded?

A. I was wounded about two o'clock, after the rebels got in the breastworks.

Q. Was it before or after you had surrendered?

A. It was after I threw down my gun, as they all started to run.

Q. Will you state what you saw there?

A. After I surrendered they shot down a great many white fellows right close to me—ten or twelve, I suppose—and a great many negroes, too.

Q. How long did they keep shooting our men after they surrendered?

A. I heard guns away after dark shooting all that evening, somewhere; they kept up a regular fire for a long time, and then I heard the guns once in a while.

Q. Did you see any one shot the next day?

A. I did not; I was in a house, and could not get up at all.

Q. Do you know what became of the Quartermaster of your regiment, Lieutenant Akerstrom?

A. He was shot by the side of me.

Q. Was he killed?

A. I thought so at the time; he fell on his face. He was shot in the forehead, and I thought he was killed. I heard afterward he was not.

Q. Did you notice any thing that took place while the flag of truce was in?

A. I saw the rebels slipping up and getting in the ditch along our breastworks.

Q. How near did they come up?

A. They were right at us; right across from the breastworks. I asked them what they were slipping up there for. They made answer that they knew their business.

Q. Are you sure this was done while the flag of truce was in?

A. Yes, sir. There was no firing; we could see all around; we could see them moving up all around in large force.

Q. Was any thing said about it except what you said to the rebels?

A I heard all our boys talking about it. I heard some of our officers remark, as they saw it coming, that the white flag was a bad thing; that they were slipping on us. I believe it was Lieutenant Akerstrom that I heard say it was against the rules of war for them to come up in that way.

Q. To whom did he say that?

A. To those fellows coming up; they had officers with them.

Q. Was Lieutenant Akerstrom shot before or after he had surrendered?

A. About two minutes after the flag of truce went back, during the action.

Q. Do you think of any thing else to state? If so, go on and state it.

A. I saw a rebel lieutenant take a little negro [1] boy up on the horse behind him ; and then I heard General Chalmers—I think it must have been—tell him to " Take that negro down and shoot him," or " Take him and shoot him," and he passed him down and shot him.

Q. How large was the boy?

A. He was not more than eight years old. I heard the lieutenant tell the other that the negro was not in the service ; that he was nothing but a child ; that he was pressed and brought in there. The other one said : " Damn the difference ; take him down and shoot him, or I will shoot him." I think it must have been General Chalmers. He was a smallish man ; he had on a long gray coat, with a star on his coat.[2]

The country and the world stood aghast. The first account of this human butchery was too much for credence : after a while the truth began to dawn upon the country ; and at last the people admitted that in a Christian land like America a deed so foul—blacker than hell itself!—had actually been perpetrated. The patience of the North and the Union army gave way to bitterest imprecations ; the exultation and applause of the South and Confederate army were succeeded by serious thoughts and sad reflections. But it is the duty of impartial history to record that this bloody, sickening affair was not endorsed by all the rebels.

In a letter dated Okalona, Mississippi, June 14, 1864, to the " Atlanta Appeal," a rebel gives this endorsement of Forrest's conduct at Fort Pillow :

" You have heard that our soldiers buried negroes alive at Fort Pillow. This is true. At the first fire after Forrest's men scaled the walls, many of the negroes threw down their arms and fell as if they were dead. They perished in the pretence, and could only be restored at

---

[1] Gen. Chalmers has denied, with vehemence, that he ever did any cruel act at Fort Pillow, but the record is against him. Soldiers under brave, intelligent, and humane officers could never be guilty of such cruel and unchristian conduct as these rebels at Pillow. Gen. Chalmers is responsible. As an illustration of the gentle and forgiving spirit of the Negro, it should be recorded here that many supported the candidacy of Gen. Chalmers for Congress, and voted for him at the recent election in Mississippi.

[2] See Report of Committee on Conduct of War.

the point of the bayonet. To resuscitate some of them, more terrified than the rest, they were rolled into the trenches made as receptacles for the fallen. Vitality was not restored till breathing was obstructed, and then the resurrection began. On these facts is based the pretext for the crimes committed by Sturgis, Grierson, and their followers. You must remember, too, that in the extremity of their terror, or for other reasons, the Yankees and negroes in Fort Pillow neglected to haul down their flag. In truth, relying upon their gun-boats, the officers expected to annihilate our forces after we had entered the fortifications. They did not intend to surrender.

" A terrible retribution, in any event, has befallen the ignorant, deluded Africans."

Gen. Forrest was a cold-blooded murderer; a fiend in human form. But as the grave has opened long since to receive him; and as the cause he represented has perished from the earth, it is enough to let the record stand without comment, and God grant without malice! It is the duty of history to record that there is to be found no apologist for cruelties that rebels inflicted upon brave but helpless Black soldiers during the war for the extirpation of slavery. The Confederate conduct at Pillow must remain a foul stain upon the name of the men who fought to perpetuate human slavery in North America, but failed.

Part 8.

THE FIRST DECADE OF FREEDOM.

CHAPTER XXI.

RECONSTRUCTION [1]—MISCONSTRUCTION.

1865–1875.

THE WAR OVER, PEACE RESTORED, AND THE NATION CLEANSED OF A PLAGUE. — SLAVERY GIVES PLACE TO A LONG TRAIN OF EVENTS. — UNSETTLED CONDITION OF AFFAIRS AT THE SOUTH. — THE ABSENCE OF LEGAL CIVIL GOVERNMENT NECESSITATES THE ESTABLISHMENT OF PROVISIONAL MILITARY GOVERNMENT. — AN ACT ESTABLISHING A BUREAU FOR REFUGEES AND ABANDONED LANDS. — CONGRESSIONAL METHODS FOR THE RECONSTRUCTION OF THE SOUTH. — GEN. U. S. GRANT CARRIES THESE STATES IN 1868 AND 1872. — BOTH BRANCHES OF THE LEGISLATURES IN ALL THE SOUTHERN STATES CONTAIN NEGRO MEMBERS. — THE ERRORS OF RECONSTRUCTION CHARGEABLE TO BOTH SECTIONS OF THE COUNTRY.

APPOMATTOX had taken her place in history; and the echo of the triumph of Federal arms was heard in ·the palaces of Europe. The United States Government had survived the shock of the embattled arms of a gigantic Rebellion; had melted the manacles of four million slaves in the fires of civil war; had made four million bondmen freemen; had wiped slavery from the map of North America; had demonstrated the truth that the Constitution is the supreme law of the land; and that the United States is a NATION, not a league.

The brazen-mouthed, shotted cannon were voiceless; a million muskets and swords hung upon the dusty walls of silent arsenals; and war ceased from the proud altitudes of the mountains of Virginia to where the majestic Atlantic washes the shores of the Carolinas. A million soldiers in blue melted

---

[1] I am preparing a History of the Reconstruction of the Late Confederate States, 1865–1880. Hence I shall not enter into a thorough treatment of the subject in this work. It will follow this work, and comprise two volumes.

quietly into the modest garb of citizens. The myriad hum of busy shuttles, clanking machinery, and whirling wheels proclaimed the day of peace. Families and communities were restored and bound together by the indissoluble, golden ties of domestic charities. The war was over; peace had been restored; and the nation was cleansed of a plague.

But what was to be done with the millions of Negroes at the South? The war had made them free. That was all. They could leave the plantation. They had the right of locomotion; were property no longer. But what a spectacle! Here were four million human beings without clothing, shelter, homes, and, alas! most of them without names. The galling harness of slavery had been cut off of their weary bodies, and like a worn-out beast of burden they stood in their tracks scarcely able to go anywhere. Like men coming from long confinement in a dark dungeon, the first rays of freedom blinded their expectant eyes. They were almost delirious with joy. The hopes and fears, the joys and sorrows, the pain and waiting, the prayers and tears of the cruel years of slavery gave place to a long train of events that swept them out into the rapid current of a life totally different from the checkered career whence they had just emerged. It required time, patience, and extraordinary wisdom on the part of the Government to solve the problem of this people's existence—of this "Nation born in a day." Their joy was too full, their peace too profound, and their thanksgiving too sincere to attract their attention at once to the vulgar affairs of daily life. One fervent, beautiful psalm of praise rose from every Negro hut in the South, and swelled in majestic sweetness until the nation became one mighty temple canopied by the stars and stripes, and the Constitution as the common altar before whose undimmed lights a ransomed race humbly bowed.

The emancipated Negroes had no ability, certainly no disposition, to reason concerning the changes and disasters which had overtaken their former masters. The white people of the South were divided into three classes. *First*, those who felt that defeat was intolerable, and a residence in this country incongenial. They sought the service of the Imperial cause in war-begrimed Mexico; they went to Cuba, Australia, Egypt, and to Europe. *Second*, those who returned to their homes after the "affair at Appomattox," and sitting down under the portentous clouds of defeat, refused to take any part in the rehabilitation of their States. *Third*, those who accepted the situation and stood ready to aid in the work of reconstruction.

In the unsettled condition of affairs at the close of hostilities, as there was no legal State governments at the South, necessity and prudence suggested the temporary policy of dividing the South into military districts. A provisional military government in the conquered States was to pursue a pacific, protective, helpful policy. The people of both races were to be fed and clothed. Schools were to be established; agriculture and industry encouraged. Courts were to be established of competent jurisdiction to hear and decide cases among the people. Such a government while military in name was patriarchal in spirit. As early as the spring of 1865, before the war was over, an act was passed by Congress providing for the destitute of the South.

"An Act to Establish a Bureau for the Relief of Freedmen and Refugees.

"*Be it enacted by the Senate and House of Representatives of the United States of America in Congress assembled*, That there is hereby established in the War Department, to continue during the present war of rebellion, and for one year thereafter, a Bureau of Refugees, Freedmen, and Abandoned Lands, to which shall be committed, as hereinafter provided, the supervision and management of all abandoned lands, and the control of all subjects relating to refugees and freedmen from rebel States, or from any district of country within the territory embraced in the operations of the army, under such rules and regulations as may be prescribed by the head of the bureau and approved by the President. The said bureau shall be under the management and control of a commissioner, to be appointed by the President, by and with the advice and consent of the Senate, whose compensation shall be three thousand dollars per annum, and such number of clerks as may be assigned to him by the Secretary of War, not exceeding one chief clerk, two of the fourth class, two of the third class, three of the second class, and five of the first class. And the commissioner and all persons appointed under this act shall, before entering upon their duties, take the oath of office prescribed in an act entitled, 'An act to prescribe an oath of office, and for other purposes,' approved July 2, 1862. And the commissioners and the chief clerk shall, before entering upon their duties, give bonds to the Treasurer of the United States, the former in the sum of fifty thousand dollars, and the latter in the sum of ten thousand dollars, conditioned for the faithful discharge of their duties respectively, with securities to be approved as sufficient by the attorney general. which bonds shall be filed in the office of the First Comptroller of the Treasury, to be by him put in suit for the benefit of any injured party, upon any breach of the conditions thereof.

"SEC. 2. *And be it further enacted*, That the Secretary of War may direct such issues of provisions, clothing, and fuel as he may deem needful for the immediate and temporary shelter and supply of destitute and suffering refugees and freedmen, and their wives and children, under such rules and regulations as he may direct.

"SEC. 3. *And be it further enacted*, That the President may, by and with the advice and consent of the Senate, appoint an assistant commissioner for each of the States declared to be in insurrection, not exceeding ten in number, who shall, under the direction of the commissioner, aid in the execution of the provisions of this act, and he shall give a bond to the Treasurer of the United States in the sum of twenty thousand dollars, in the form and manner prescribed in the first section of this act. Each of said assistant commissioners shall receive an annual salary of two thousand and five hundred. dollars, in full compensation for all his services. And any military officer may be detailed and assigned to duty under this act without increase of pay or allowances. The commissioner shall, before the commencement of each regular session of Congress, make full report of his proceedings, with exhibits of the state of his accounts, to the President, who shall communicate the same to Congress, and shall also make special reports whenever required to do so by the President, or either house of Congress. And the assistant commissioners shall make quarterly reports of their proceedings to the commissioner, and also such other special reports as from time to time may be required.

"SEC. 4. *And be it further enacted*, That the commissioner, under the direction of the President, shall have authority to set apart for the use of loyal refugees and freedmen such tracts of land, within the insurrectionary States, as shall have been abandoned, or to which the United States shall have acquired title by confiscation, or sale, or otherwise. And to every male citizen, whether refugee or freedman, as aforesaid, there shall be assigned not more than forty acres of such land, and the person to whom it is so assigned shall be protected in the use and enjoyment of the land for the term of three years, at an annual rent not exceeding six per centum upon the value of said land as it was appraised by the State authorities in the year 1860, for the purpose of taxation, and in case no such appraisal can be found, then the rental shall be based upon the estimated value of the land in said year, to be ascertained in such manner as the commissioner may, by regulation, prescribe. At the end of said term, or at any time during said term, the occupants of any parcels so assigned may purchase the land and receive such title thereto as the United States can convey, upon paying therefor the value of the land, as ascertained and fixed for the purpose of determining the annual rent as aforesaid.

"SEC. 5.   *And be it further enacted,* That all acts and parts of acts inconsistent with the provisions of this act are hereby repealed.

" ROBERT C. SCHENCK,	HENRY WILSON,
" GEORGE S. BOUTWELL,	JAMES HARLAN,
" JAMES S. ROLLINS,	W. T. WILLEY,
" *Managers on part of House.*	*Managers on part of Senate.*"

To have subjected the late rebellious States to military rule for a stated term of years, say a decade or a generation, would have given force to the hasty statement of rebels and their sympathizers in the courts of Europe.   It was charged that the United States Government fought to subjugate the Confederate States.   The United States did not " begin it," and did not intend, at any time, to lay the mailed hand of military power against the throat of the rights of loyal citizens or loyal States. The *sine qua non* of reconstruction was *loyalty to the Federal Government.*   But while this idea was next to the heart of the Government, the sudden and horrible taking off of Abraham Lincoln discovered many master-builders, who built not well or wisely.   The early education of Andrew Johnson was not in line with the work of reconstruction.   His sympathies were with the South in spite of his position and circumstances.   The friends of his early political life were more potent than the friends of a sound, sensible, and loyal policy upon which to build the shattered governments of the South.   And by indicating and advocating a policy at variance with the logical events of the war, he was guilty of a political crime, and did the entire nation an irreparable injury.

Congress seemed to be unequal to the task of perfecting a proper plan for reconstructing the Southern States.   To couple general amnesty to the rebels with suffrage to the Negroes was a most fatal policy.   It has been shown that there was but one class of white men in the South friendly to reconstruction,—numerically, small; and mentally, weak.   But it was thought best to do this.   To a triple element Congress committed the work of reconstruction.   The " *Scalawag,*" the " *Carpet-bagger,*" and the *Negro.* Who were this trio?   The scalawag was the native white man who made up the middle class of the South ; the planter above, the Negro below.   And between this upper and nether millstone he was destined to be ground to powder, under the old regime. A "nigger-driver," without schools, social position, or money, he was "the poor white trash" of the South. He was loyal during the war, because in the triumph of the Confederacy, with slavery as its corner-stone, he saw no hope for his condition. Those of them who fought under the rebel flag were unwilling conscripts. They had no qualifications for governing—except that they were *loyal;* and this was of no more use to them in this great work, than *piety* in the pulpit when the preacher cannot repeat the Lord's prayer without biting his tongue. The carpet-baggers ran all the way from "good to middling." Some went South with fair ability and good morals, where they lost the latter article and never found it; while many more went South to get all they could and keep all they got. The Negro could boast of numerical strength only. The scalawag managed the Negro, the latter did the voting, while the carpet-bagger held the offices. And when there were "more stalls than horses" the Negroes and scalawags occasionally got an office.

The rebels were still in a swoon.

The States were reconstructed, after a manner, and the governments went forward.

In 1868 Gen. U. S. Grant carried these States. It was like the handle on a jug, all on one side. The rebels took no part; but after a while a gigantic Ku Klux conspiracy was discovered. This organization sought to obstruct the courts, harass the Negroes, and cripple local governments. It spread terror through the South and made a political graveyard of startling dimensions. The writ of *habeas corpus* was suspended; arrests made, trials and convictions secured, and the penitentiary at Albany, New York, crowded with the enemies of law and order. A subsidence followed, and the scalawag-carpetbag-Negro governments began a fresh existence.

In 1872 Gen. Grant carried the Southern States again, meeting with but little resistance. In Louisiana, Mississippi, and South Carolina there were Negro lieutenant-governors. The Negroes were learning rapidly the lesson of rotation in office, and demanded recognition. Alabama, Georgia, Florida, Louisiana, Mississippi, and South Carolina, were represented, in part, by Negroes in the National House of Representatives, and Mississippi in the Senate as well. Both branches of the Legislatures of all the Southern States contained Negro members; while many of the most important and lucrative offices in the States were held by Negroes.

The wine cup, the gaming-table, and the parlors of strange women charmed many of these men to the neglect of important public duties.   The bonded indebtedness of these States began to increase, the State paper to depreciate, the burden of taxation to grow intolerable, bad laws to find their way into the statute-books, interest in education and industry to decline, the farm Negroes to grow idle and gravitate to the infectious skirts of large cities, and the whole South went from bad to worse.

The hand of revenge reached for the shot-gun, and before its deadly presence white leaders were intimidated, driven out, or destroyed.   Before 1875 came, the white element in the Republican party at the South was reduced to a mere shadow of its former self.   Thus abandoned, the Negro needed the presence of the United States army while he voted, held office, and drew his salary.   But even the army lacked the power to inject life into the collapsed governments at the South.

The mistake of reconstruction was twofold: on the part of the Federal Government, in committing the destinies of the Southern States to hands so feeble; and on the part of the South, in that its best men, instead of taking a lively interest in rebuilding the governments they had torn down, allowed them to be constructed with untempered mortar.   Neither the South nor the Government could say: "Thou canst not say I did it: shake not thy gory locks at me."   Both were culpable, and both have suffered the pangs of remorse.

CHAPTER XXII.

THE RESULTS OF EMANCIPATION.

The Apparent Idleness of the Negro Sporadic rather than Generic. — He quietly settles down to Work. — The Government makes Ample Provisions for his Educational and Social Improvement. — The Marvellous Progress made by the People of the South in Education. — Earliest School for Freedmen at Fortress Monroe in 1861. — The Richmond Institute for Colored Youth. — The Unlimited Desire of the Negroes to obtain an Education. — General Order organizing a "Bureau of Refugees, Freedmen, and Abandoned Lands." — Gen. O. O. Howard appointed Commissioner of the Bureau. — Report of all the Receipts and Expenditures of the Freedmen's Bureau from 1865-1867. — An Act incorporating the Freedman's Bank and Trust Company. — The Business of the Company as shown from 1866-1871. — Financial Statement by the Trustees for 1872. — Failure of the Bank. — The Social and Financial Condition of the Colored People in the South. — The Negro rarely receives Justice in Southern Courts. — Treatment of Negroes as Convicts in Southern Prisons. — Increase of the Colored People from 1790-1880. — Negroes susceptible of the Highest Civilization.

SURELY some good did come out of Nazareth. The poor, deluded, misguided, confiding Negro finished his long holiday at last, and turning from the dream of "forty acres and a mule," settled down to the stubborn realities of his new life of duties, responsibilities, and privileges. His idleness was sporadic, not generic,—it was simply reaction. He had worked faithfully, incessantly for two centuries and a half; had enriched the South with the sweat of his brow; and in two wars had baptized the soil with his patriotic blood. And when the year of jubilee came he enjoyed himself right royally.

This disposition to frolic on the part of the Negro gave rise to grave concern among his friends, and was promptly accepted as conclusive proof of his unfitness for the duties of a freeman by his enemies. But he soon dispelled the fears of his friends and disarmed the prejudices of his foes.

As already shown there was no provision made for the education of the Negro before the war; every thing had been done to keep him in ignorance. To emancipate 4,000,000 of slaves and absorb them into the political life of the government without detriment to both was indeed a formidable undertaking.

Republics gain their strength and perpetuity from the self-governing force in the people ; and in order to be self-governing a people must be educated. Moreover, all good laws that are cheerfully obeyed are but the emphatic expression of public sentiment. Where the great majority of the people are kept in ignorance the tendency is toward the production of two other classes, aristocrats and political " Herders." The former seek to get as far from " the common herd " as possible, while the latter bid off the rights of the poor and ignorant to the highest bidder.

It was quite appropriate for the Government to make speedy provision for plying the mass of ignorant Negroes with school influences. And the liberality of the provision was equalled by the eagerness of the Negroes to learn. Nor should history fail to record that the establishment of schools for freedmen by the Government was the noblest, most sensible act it could have done. What the Negroes have accomplished through these schools is the marvel of the age.

On the 20th of May, 1865, Major-Gen. O. O. Howard was appointed Commissioner of the Freedmen's Bureau. He gave great attention to the subject of education ; and after planting schools for the freedmen throughout a great portion of the South, in 1870—five years after the work was begun—he made a report. It was full of interest. In five years there were 4,239 schools established, 9,307 teachers employed, and 247,333 pupils instructed. In 1868 the average attendance was 89,396 ; but in 1870 it was 91,398, or 79¾ per cent. of the total number enrolled. The emancipated people sustained 1,324 schools themselves, and owned 592 school buildings. The Freedmen's Bureau furnished 654 buildings for school purposes. The wonderful progress they made from year to year, in scholarship, may be fairly judged by the following, corresponding with the half year in 1869 :

	JULY, 1869.	JULY, 1870.
Advanced readers . . .	43,746	43,540
Geography	36,992	39,321
Arithmetic	51,172	52,417
Writing	53,606	58,034
Higher branches	7,627	9,690

There were 74 high and normal schools, with 8,147 students ; and 61 industrial schools, with 1,750 students in attendance. In doing this great work—for buildings, repairs, teachers, etc.,—$1,002,896.07 was expended. Of this sum the *freedmen raised* $200,000.00! This was conclusive proof that emancipation was no mistake. Slavery was a twofold cross of woe to the land. It did not only degrade the slave, but it blunted the sensibilities, and, by its terrible weight, carried down under the slimy rocks of society some of the best white people in the South. Like a cankerous malady its venom has touched almost every side of American life.

The white race is in a constant and almost overpowering relation to the other races upon this continent. It is the duty of this great totality of intellectual life and force, to supply adequate facilities for the education of the less intelligent and less fortunate. Of every ten thousand (10,000) inhabitants there are:

	WHITE.	COLORED.	CHINESE.	INDIANS.
In the States . .	8,711	1,269	15	5
In the Territories .	8,711	1,017	158	114
In the whole Union	8,711	1,266	16	7

When we turn our attention to the Southern States, we shall find that the white people are in excess of the Colored as follows:

	MAJORITY.
Alabama	45,874
Arkansas	239,946
Delaware	79,427
Florida	4,368
Georgia	93,774
Kentucky	876,442
Maryland	430,106
Missouri	1,485,075
North Carolina	286,820
Tennessee	613,788
Texas	311,225
Virginia	199,248
West Virginia	406,043

while the Colored people are in excess in only three States, having over the whites the following majorities:

	MAJORITY.
Louisiana	2,145
South Carolina	126,147
Mississippi	61,305

This leaves the whites in these sixteen States in a majority of 4,882,539, over the Colored people. There are more than two whites to every Colored in the entire population in these States.

Group the States and territories into three geographical classes, and designate them as Northern, Pacific, and Southern. The first may comprise all the "free States," where slavery never existed; put in the second the three Pacific States and all the territories, except the District of Columbia; and in the third gather all the "slave States" and the District. Now then, in the Northern class, out of every 14 persons who can neither read nor write, 13 are white. In the Pacific class, out of every 23 who can neither read nor write, 20 are white. In the Southern class, out of every 42 who can neither read nor write, 15 are white. Thus it can be seen that the white illiterates of the United States outnumber those of all the other races together. It might be profitable to the gentlemen who, upon every convenient occasion, rail about "the deplorable ignorance of the blacks," to look up this question a little! [1]

The Colored people have made wonderful progress in educational matters since the war. Take a few States for examples of what they are doing. In Georgia, in 1860, there were 458,540 slaves. In 1870 there were 87 private schools, 79 teachers with 3,021 pupils. Of other schools, more public in character, there were 221, with an attendance of 11,443 pupils. In 1876 the Colored school population of this State was 48,643, with 879 schools; and with 55,268 pupils in public and private schools in 1877.

In South Carolina, in 1874, there were 63,415 Colored children attending the public schools; in 1876 there were 70,802, or an increase of 7,387.

In Virginia, in 1870, there were 39,000 Colored pupils in the schools, which were few in number. In 1874 there were 54,941 pupils; in 1876 there were 62,178, or a gain of 7,237. In 1874 there were 539 teachers; in 1876 there were 636, or an increase of 97. In 1874 there were 1,064 schools for Colored youth; in 1876 there were 1,181, or an increase of 117.

In the District of Columbia, in 1871, there were 4,986 Colored children in 69 schools, with 71 teachers. In 1876, of Colored schools in the District, 62 were primary, 13 grammar, and 1 high, with an enrolment of 5,454.

---

[1] For an account of this problem, see the Appendix to this volume.

The following statistics exhibit the wonderful progress the Colored people of the South have made during the brief period of their freedom in the department of education. These tables come as near showing the extent, the miraculous magnitude of the work, as is possible.

COMPARATIVE STATISTICS OF EDUCATION AT THE SOUTH.

Table showing comparative population and enrolment of the White and Colored races in the public schools of the recent slave States, with total annual expenditure for the same in 1879.

States.	White.			Colored.			Total expenditure for both races. a
	School population.	Enrolment.	Percentage of the school population enrolled.	School population.	Enrolment.	Percentage of the school population enrolled.	
Alabama	214,098	106,950	50	162,551	67,635	42	$377,033
Arkansas	b174,253	b39,063	22	b62,348	b13,986	22	205,449
Delaware	31,849	23,830	75	3,800	2,842	75	223,638
Florida	c40,606	bc18,169	45	c42,001	bc18,795	45	c134,880
Georgia	c236,319	147,192	62	c197,125	79,435	40	465,748
Kentucky	d476,870	e208,500	48	d62,973	e19,107	30	e1,130,000
Louisiana	c141,130	44,052	31	c133,276	34,476	26	529,065
Maryland	f213,669	138,029	65	f63,591	27,457	43	1,551,558
Mississippi	156,434	105,957	68	205,936	111,796	54	641,548
Missouri	663,135	428,992	65	39,018	20,790	53	3,069,454
North Carolina	271,348	153,534	57	154,841	85,215	55	337,541
South Carolina	e83,813	58,368	70	e144,315	64,095	44	319,320
Tennessee	388,355	208,858	54	126,288	55,829	44	710,652
Texas	b160,482	c111,048	69	b47,842	c35,896	75	837,913
Virginia	280,849	72,306	26	202,852	35,768	18	570,389
West Virginia	198,844	132,751	67	7,279	3,775	52	709,071
District of Columbia . . .	c26,426	16,085	61	c12,374	9,045	73	368,343
Total	3,758,480	2,013,684	. . . . .	1 668,410	685,942	. . . . .	12,181,602

a In Delaware and Kentucky the school tax collected from Colored citizens is the only State appropriation for the support of Colored schools ; in Maryland there is a biennial appropriation by the Legislature ; in the District of Columbia one third of the school moneys is set apart for Colored public schools ; and in the other States mentioned above the school moneys are divided in proportion to the school population without regard to race.

b Estimated by the Bureau.   *c* In 1878.

d For whites the school age is 6-20; for Colored, 6-16.   *e* In 1877.   *f* Census of 1870.

Statistics of institutions for the instruction of the Colored race for 1879.

Name and class of institution.	Location.	Religious denomination.	Instructors.	Students
NORMAL SCHOOLS.				
Rust Normal Institute	Huntsville, Ala.	Meth.	3	235
State Normal School for Colored Students	Huntsville, Ala.		2	51
Lincoln Normal University	Marion, Ala.		a5	a225
Emerson Institute	Mobile, Ala.	Cong.	6	240
Alabama Baptist Normal and Theological School	Selma, Ala.	Bapt.	6	250
Normal department of Talladega College	Talladega, Ala.	Cong.	6	95
State Normal School for Colored Students	Pine Bluff, Ark.		4	
Normal department of Atlanta University	Atlanta, Ga.	Cong.		a176
Haven Normal School	Waynesboro', Ga.	Meth.		72
Normal department of Berea College	Berea, Ky.	Cong.	(b)	125
Normal department of New Orleans University	New Orleans, La.	Meth.		(b)
Normal department of Straight University	New Orleans, La.	Cong.	(b)	91
Peabody Normal School	New Orleans, La.		a2	a35
Baltimore Normal School for Colored Pupils	Baltimore, Md.		4	190
Centenary Biblical Institute	Baltimore, Md.	M. E.	a5	a75
Natchez Seminary	Natchez, Miss.	Bapt.	4	46
Tougaloo University and Normal School	Tougaloo, Miss.	Cong.	6	96
Lincoln Institute	Jefferson, Mo.		6	139
State Normal School for Colored Students	Fayetteville, N. C.		3	93
Bennett Seminary	Greensboro', N. C.	Meth.	3	125
Lumberton Normal School	Lumberton, N. C.		2	51
St. Augustine's Normal School	Raleigh, N C.	P. E.	4	81
Shaw University	Raleigh, N. C.	Bapt.	5	192
Institute for Colored Youth	Philadelphia, Pa.	Friends .		300
Avery Normal Institute	Charleston, S. C.	Cong.	8	322
Normal department of Brainerd Institute	Chester, S. C.	Presb.	3	50
Claflin University, normal department	Orangeburg, S. C.	M. E.	3	167
Fairfield Normal Institute	Winnsboro', S. C.	Presb.		390.
The Warner Institute	Jonesborough, Tenn.		c4	c149
Knoxville College	Knoxville, Tenn.	Presb.	13	240
Freedman s Normal Institute	Maryville, Tenn.	Friends.	a4	a229
Le Moyne Normal Institute	Memphis, Tenn.	Cong.		a200
Central Tennessee College, normal department	Nashville, Tenn.	M. E.	a7	
Nashville Normal and Theological Institute	Nashville, Tenn.	Bapt.	3	114
Normal department of Fisk University	Nashville, Tenn.	Cong.	6	231
Tillotson Collegiate and Normal Institute	Austin, Tex.		5	215
State Normal School of Texas for Colored Students	Prairie View, Tex.		3	158
Hampton Normal and Agricultural Institute.d	Hampton, Va.	Cong.	e28	49
St. Stephen's Normal School	Petersburg, Va.	P. E.	8	e320
Miner Normal School	Washington, D. C.		5	240
Normal department of Howard University	Washington, D. C.	Non-sect.	2	19
Normal department of Wayland Seminary	Washington, D. C.	Bapt.	(f)	95
				(f)
Total			181	6,171
INSTITUTIONS FOR SECONDARY INSTRUCTION.				
Trinity School	Athens, Ala.	Cong.	2	162
Dadeville Seminary	Dadeville, Ala.	M. E.		
Lowery's Industrial Academy	Huntsville, Ala.			
Swayne School	Montgomery, Ala.	Cong.	6	470
Burrell School	Selma, Ala.	Cong.	5	448
Talladega College	Talladega, Ala.	Cong.	12	212
Walden Seminary	Little Rock, Ark.	M. E.		
Cookman Institute	Jacksonville, Fla.	M. E.	a5	a140
Clark University	Atlanta, Ga.	M. E.	5	167
Storrs School	Atlanta, Ga.	Cong.	5	528

a In 1878.   *b* Included in university and college reports.   *c* For two years.

d In addition to the aid given by the American Missionary Association, this institute is aided from the income of Virginia's agricultural college land fund.

e For all departments.   *f* Reported under schools of theology.

Statistics of institutions for the instruction of the Colored race for 1879.—
Continued.

Name and class of institution.	Location.	Religious denomination.	Instructors.	Students.
INSTITUTIONS FOR SECONDARY INSTRUCTION. —Continued.				
Howard Normal Institute	Cuthbert, Ga. . .	Cong. .	3	66
La Grange Seminary	La Grange, Ga. .	M. E. .	4	140
Lewis High School	Macon, Ga. . . .	Cong. .	2	110
Beach Institute	Savannah, Ga. . .	Cong. .	6	338
St. Augustine's School	Savannah, Ga. .	P. E. .	...	...
Day School for Colored Children . .	New Orleans, La. . .	R. C. .	...	80
St. Augustine's School	New Orleans, La. .	R. C. .	3	60
St. Mary's School for Colored Girls .	New Orleans, La. . .	R. C. .	...	60
St. Francis's Academy	Baltimore, Md. . .	R. C. .	...	50
Meridian Academy	Meridian, Miss. . .	M. E. .	...	...
Natchez Seminary	Natchez, Miss. . .	Bapt. .	4	45
Scotia Seminary	Concord, N. C. . .	Presb. .	8	152
St. Augustine's School	New Berne, N. C. .	P. E. .	...	...
Estey Seminary	Raleigh, N. C. . .	Bapt. .	...	...
Washington School	Raleigh, N. C. . .	Cong. .	3	149
St. Barnabas School	Wilmington, N. C. .	P. E. .	...	*a*100
Williston Academy and Normal School . .	Wilmington, N. C. .	Cong. .	*a*6	*a*126
Albany Enterprise Academy . .	Albany, Ohio . .	Non-sect.	4	64
Polytechnic and Industrial Institute .	Bluffton, S. C. . .	Non-sect.	8	265
High School for Colored Pupils . .	Charleston. S. C. . .	P. E. .	...	...
Wallingford Academy	Charleston, S. C. .	Presb. .	6	261
Brainerd Institute	Chester, S. C. . .	Presb. .	5	300
Benedict Institute	Columbia, S. C. . .	Bapt. .	4	142
Brewer Normal School	Greenwood, S. C. . .	Cong. .	*a*1	*a*58
West Tennessee Preparatory School	Mason, Tenn. . .	Meth. .	2	76
Canfield School	Memphis, Tenn. . .	P. E. .	...	...
West Texas Conference Seminary . .	Austin, Tex. . .	M. E. .	...	...
Wiley University	Marshall, Tex. . .	M. E. .	*a*3	*a*123
Thyne Institute	Chase City, Va. . .	U. Presb. .	3	213
Richmond Institute	Richmond, Va. . .	Bapt. .	3	92
St. Philip's Church School . . .	Richmond, Va. . .	P. E. .	2	100
St. Mary's School	Washington, D. C. .	P. E. .	...	...
Total	. . . . . .	. . . .	120	5,297
UNIVERSITIES AND COLLEGES.				
Atlanta University	Atlanta, Ga. . .	Cong. .	*ab*13	*a*71
Berea College	Berea, Ky. . .	Cong. .	*b*12	*b*180
Leland University	New.Orleans, La. .	Bapt. .	*a*6	*ac*91
New Orleans University	New Orleans, La. . .	M. E. .	5	92
Straight University	New Orleans, La. .	Cong. .	*b*11	*d*260
Shaw University	Holly Springs, Miss. .	M. E. .	6	273
Alcorn University	Rodney, Miss. .	Non-sect. .	10	180
Biddle University	Charlotte, N. C. . .	Presb. .	9	151
Wilberforce University	Wilberforce, Ohio .	M. E. .	15	*b*150
Lincoln University	Lincoln University, Pa. .	Presb. .	*a*9	*a*74
Claflin University and College of Agriculture	Orangeburg, S. C. .	M. E. .	10	165
Central Tennessee College	Nashville, Tenn. .	M. E. .	13	139
Fisk University	Nashville, Tenn. . .	Cong. .	13	74
Agricultural and Mechanical College .	Hempstead, Tex. .	. . . .	...	...
Hampton Normal and Agricultural Institute	Hampton, Va. . .	Cong. .	(*e*)	(*e*)
Howard University *f*	Washington, D. C. . .	Non-sect.	5	*f* 33
Total	. . . . . .	. . . .	137	1,933

a In 1878.   *b* For all departments.   *c* These are preparatory.
d Normal students are here reckoned as preparatory.   *e* Reported with normal schools.
f This institution is open to both races, and the figures given are known to include some vhites.

Statistics of institutions for the instruction of the Colored race for 1879.—
Continued.

Name and class of institution.	Location.	Religious de-nomination.	Instructors.	Students.
SCHOOLS OF THEOLOGY.				
Alabama Baptist Normal and Theological School	Selma, Ala.	Bapt.	1	...
Theological department of Talladega College	Talladega, Ala.	Cong.	2	14
Institute for the Education of Colored Ministers	Tuscaloosa, Ala.	Presb.	...	...
Atlanta Baptist Seminary	Atlanta, Ga.	Bapt.	3	113
Theological department of Leland University	New Orleans, La.	Bapt.	a2	a55
Thomson Biblical Institute (New Orleans University)	New Orleans, La.	M. E.	a1	a16
Theological department of Straight University	New Orleans, La.	Cong.	1	21
Centenary Biblical Institute	Baltimore, Md.	Meth.	a6	a29
Theological department of Shaw Univers'y	Holly Springs, Miss.	Meth.	a2	a17
Natchez Seminary	Natchez, Miss.	Bapt.	2	31
Theological department of Biddle University	Charlotte, N. C.	Presb.	4	8
Bennett Seminary	Greensboro', N. C.	Meth.	2	6
Theological department of Shaw Univers'y	Raleigh, N. C.	Bapt.	2	59
Theological Seminary of Wilberforce University	Wilberforce, Ohio	M. E.	7	16
Theological department of Lincoln University	Lincoln University, Pa.	Presb.	a7	a22
Baker Theological Institute (Claflin University)	Orangeburg, S. C.	Meth.	2	28
Nashville Normal and Theological Institute	Nashville, Tenn.	Bapt.	6	50
Theological course in Fisk University	Nashville, Tenn.	Cong.	a2	a12
Theological department of Central Tennessee College	Nashville, Tenn.	M. E.	4	45
Richmond Institute	Richmond, Va.	Bapt.	10	86
Theological department of Howard University	Washington, D. C.	Non-sect.	4	50
Wayland Seminary	Washington, D. C.	Bapt.	b9	b84
Total			79	762
SCHOOLS OF LAW.				
Law department of Straight University	New Orleans, La.		a4	a28
Law department of Shaw University	Holly Springs, Miss.		a1	a6
Law department of Howard University	Washington, D. C.		3	8
Total			8	42
SCHOOLS OF MEDICINE.				
Medical department of New Orleans University	New Orleans. La.		a5	a8
Medical department of Shaw University	Holly Springs, Miss.		a1	a4
Meharry medical department of Central Tennessee College	Nashville, Tenn.		9	22
Medical department of Howard Univers'y	Washington, D. C.		8	65
Total.			23	99
SCHOOLS FOR THE DEAF AND. DUMB AND THE BLIND.				
Institution for the Colored Blind and Deaf-Mutes	Baltimore, Md.		1	30
North Carolina Institution for the Deaf and Dumb and the Blind (Colored department)	Raleigh, N. C.		ab15	a60
Total			16	120

a In 1878.   *b* For all departments.

Summary of statistics of institutions for the instruction of the Colored race for 1879.

States.	Public schools.		Normal schools.			Institutions for secondary instruction.		
	School population.	Enrolment.	Schools.	Teachers.	Pupils.	Schools.	Teachers.	Pupils.
Alabama	162,551	67,635	6	28	1,096	6	25	1,292
Arkansas	62,348	13,986	1	4	72	1	....	......
Delaware	3,800	2,842	....	....	.....	....	....	......
Florida	42,001	18,795	....	....	.....	1	5	140
Georgia	197,125	79,435	2	....	301	7	25	1,349
Kentucky	62,973	19,107	1	....	.....	....	....	......
Louisiana	133,276	34,476	3	2	126	3	3	200
Maryland	63,591	27,457	2	9	265	1	....	5?
Mississippi	205,936	111,796	2	10	142	2	4	45
Missouri	39,018	20,790	1	6	139	....	....	......
North Carolina	154,841	85,215	5	17	542	6	17	527
Ohio	....	....	....	....	.....	1	4	64
Pennsylvania	....	....	1	....	300	....	....	......
South Carolina	144,315	64,095	4	14	929	6	24	1,026
Tennessee	126,288	55,829	7	42	1,378	2	2	76
Texas	47,842	35,896	2	6	207	2	2	123
Virginia	202,852	35,768	2	36	560	3	8	405
West Virginia	7,279	3,775	....	....	.....	....	....	......
District of Columbia	12,374	9,045	3	7	114	1	....	......
Total	1,668,410	685,942	42	181	6,171	42	120	5,297

Summary of statistics of institutions for the instruction of the Colored race for 1879.—Continued.

States.	Universities and colleges.			Schools of theology.			Schools of law.		
	Schools.	Teachers.	Pupils.	Schools.	Teachers.	Pupils.	Schools.	Teachers.	Pupils.
Alabama	....	....	.....	3	3	14	....	....	....
Georgia	1	13	71	1	3	113	....	....	....
Kentucky	1	12	180	....	....	....	....	....	....
Louisiana	3	22	443	3	4	92	1	4	28
Maryland	....	....	.....	1	5	29	....	....	....
Mississippi	2	16	453	2	4	48	1	1	6
North Carolina	1	9	151	3	8	73	....	....	....
Ohio	1	15	150	1	7	16	....	....	....
Pennsylvania	1	9	74	1	7	22	....	....	....
South Carolina	1	10	165	1	2	28	....	....	....
Tennessee	2	26	213	3	12	107	....	....	....
Texas	1	....	.....	....	....	....	....	....	....
Virginia	1	....	.....	1	10	86	....	....	....
District of Columbia	1	5	33	2	13	134	1	3	8
Total	16	137	1,933	22	79	762	3	8	42

Summary of statistics of institutions for the instruction of the Colored race for 1879.—Continued.

States.	Schools of medicine.			Schools for the deaf and dumb and the blind.		
	Schools.	Teachers.	Pupils.	Schools.	Teachers.	Pupils.
Louisiana	1	5	8	....	....	....
Maryland	....	....	....	1	1	30
Mississippi	1	1	4	....	....	....
North Carolina	....	....	....	1	15	90
Tennessee	1	9	22	....	....	....
District of Columbia	1	8	65	....	....	....
Total	4	23	99	2	16	120

Table showing the number of schools for the Colored race and enrolment in them by institutions without reference to States.

Class of institutions.	Schools.	Enrolment.
Public schools	a14,341	a685,942
Normal schools	42	6,171
Institutions for secondary instruction	42	5,297
Universities and colleges	16	1,933
Schools of theology	22	762
Schools of law	3	42
Schools of medicine	4	99
Schools for the deaf and dumb and the blind	2	120
Total	14,472	700,366

a To these should be added 417 schools, having an enrolment of 20,487 in reporting free States, making total number of Colored public schools 14,758, and total enrolment in them 706,429; this makes the total number of schools, as far as reported, 14,889, and total number of the Colored race under instruction in them 720,853. The Colored public schools of those States in which no separate reports are made, however, are not included; and the Colored pupils in white schools cannot be enumerated.

Virginia has done more intelligent and effective educational work than any other State in the South. The Hon. W. H. Ruffner has no equal in America as a superintendent of public instruction. He is the Horace Mann of the South.

It appears from the reports of the Freedmen's Bureau that the earliest school for freedmen was opened by the American Missionary Association at Fortress Monroe, September, 1861; and before the close of the war, Hampton and Norfolk were leading points where educational operations were conducted; but after the cessation of hostilities, teachers were sent from Northern States, and schools for freedmen were opened in all parts of the State.

The Colored normal school at Richmond, and the one at Hampton, were commenced in 1867 and 1868. Captain C. S. Schaeffer, Bureau officer at Christiansburg, commenced his remarkable efforts about the same time in Montgomery County.

School superintendents for each State were appointed by the Freedmen's Bureau, July 12, 1865, and a general superintendent, or "Inspector of Schools," was appointed in September, 1865. These superintendents were instructed "to work as much as possible in conjunction with State officers, who may have had school matters in charge, and to take cognizance of all that was being done to educate refugees and freedmen." In 1866 an act of Congress was passed enlarging the powers of the Bureau, and partially consolidating all the societies and agencies engaged in educational work among the freedmen. In this bill $521,000 were appropriated for carrying on the work, to which was to be added forfeitures of property owned by the Confederate Government. Up to January 1, 1868, over a million of dollars was expended for school purposes among the freedmen. In Virginia 12,450 pupils are reported for 1867. Mr. Manly, the Virginia superintendent, reports the following statistics for the year 1867-8 : Schools, 230 ; teachers, 290 ; pupils enrolled, 14,300 ; in average attendance, 10,320 ; the cost as follows :

From Charity	$78,766
From the Freedmen	10,789
From the Bureau	42,844
Total Cost	$132,399

The amount raised from freedmen was in the form of small tuition fees of from ten to fifty cents a month—a system approved by Mr. Manly.

In the final report to the Freedmen's Bureau, made July 1, 1870, the Virginia statistics are : Schools, 344 ; teachers, 412 ; pupils, 18,234 ; the average attendance, 78 per cent. This year the freedmen paid $12,286.50 for tuition. Mr. C. S. Schaeffer and Mr. Samuel H. Jones, who remained in Virginia as teachers—the former still at Christiansburg, and the latter, until very lately, at Danville—both acted as assistants to Mr. Manly. A considerable number of school-houses were built in Virginia by the Bureau, including the splendid normal and high school building in Richmond, erected and equipped at a cost of $25,000, and afterward turned over to the city. After the conclusion of his superintendency, Mr. Manly continued for several years to do valuable service as principal of this school.

"The Freedmen's Bureau ceased its educational operations in the summer of 1870, and in the autumn of that year our State public schools were opened. So that, counting from the beginning of the mission school at Hampton in 1861, there has been an unbroken succession of schools for freedmen in one region for nineteen years ; and at a number of leading points in the State—such as Norfolk, Richmond, Petersburg, Danville, Charlottesville, Christiansburg, etc.—an unbroken line of schools for fourteen years and upwards. These efforts, however, of the Federal Government toward educating the rising generation of Colored people, could not have been designed as any thing more than an experiment, intended first to test and then to stimulate the appetite of those people for learning. And in this view they were entirely successful in both particulars ; for the children flocked to the schools, attended well, made good progress in knowledge, and paid a surprising amount of money for tuition.

"But, considered as a serious attempt to educate the children of the freedmen, the movement was wholly inadequate, even when contrasted with the operations of our imperfect State system. The largest number enrolled in the schools supported by the combined efforts of the Bureau, the charitable societies, and the tuition fees, was 18,234, in 1870. The next year we had in our public schools considerably over double this number, and an annual increase ever since, always excepting those two dark years (*tenebricosus* and *tenebricosissimus*), 1878 and 1879." [1]

"Two institutions for the education of the Colored race, founded before the beginning of our school system, are still in successful operation, but remain independent of our school system. One of them has some connection with the State by reason of the receipt of one-third of the proceeds of the Congressional land-grant for education. I refer to the well-known Hampton Normal and Agricultural Institute, and the Richmond Colored Institute. Nothing need be said in reference to the Hampton School, except that its numbers and usefulness are constantly increasing under the continued superintendence of the indomitable Gen. Armstrong. Its reports, which are published every year as State documents in connection with the Report of this department, are so accessible to all, that I will only repeat here the testimony often given,

---

[1] See the annual reports of the Superintendent of Public Instruction for Virginia. There were more than 18,234 Colored children in the schools of this State in 1870.

that in my opinion this is the most valuable of all the schools opened on this Continent for Colored people. Its most direct benefit is in furnishing to our State schools a much-needed annual contribution of teachers ; and teachers so good and acceptable that the demand for them is always much greater than the supply.

"The Richmond Institute has more of a theological intent, but it also sends out many good teachers. As a school it has prospered steadily under the excellent management of the Rev. C. H. Corey, D.D.; and it will soon be accommodated in a large new and handsome building. Both these institutions receive their support chiefly from the North." [1]

It will be seen that the tables we give refer only to the work done in educating the Negro in the Southern States. Much has been done in the Northern States, but in quite a different manner. The work of education for the Negro at the South had to begin at the bottom. There were no schools at all for this people ; and hence the work began with the alphabet. And there could be no classification of the scholars. All the way from six to sixty the pupils ranged in age ; and even some who had given slavery a century of their existence—mothers and fathers in Israel—crowded the schools established for their race. Some ministers of the Gospel after a half century of preaching entered school to learn how to spell out the names of the twelve Apostles. Old women who had lived out their threescore years and ten prayed that they might live to spell out the Lord's prayer, while the modest request of many departing patriarchs was that they might recognize the Lord's name in print. The sacrifices they made for themselves and children challenged the admiration of even their former owners.

The unlettered Negroes of the South carried into the school-room an inborn love of music, an excellent memory, and a good taste for the elegant—almost grandiloquent—in speech, gorgeous in imagery, and energetic in narration ; their apostrophe and simile were wonderful. Geography and history furnished great attractions, and they developed ability to master them. In mathematics they did not do so well, on account of the lack of training to think consecutively and methodically. It is a mistake to believe this a mental infirmity of the race ; for a very large number of the students in college at the present time do as well in mathematics, geometry, trigonometry, mensuration, and conic

---

[1] Annual Report of the Hon. W. H. Ruffner, for 1874.

sections as the white students of the same age ; and some of them excel in mathematics.

The majority of the Colored students in the Southern schools qualify themselves to teach and preach ; while the remainder go to law and medicine. Few educated Colored men ever return to agricultural life. There are two reasons for this : First, reaction. There is an erroneous idea among some of these young men that labor is dishonorable ; that an educated man should never work with his hands. Second, some of them believe that a profession gives a man consequence. Such silly ideas should be abandoned —they must be abandoned ! There is a great demand for educated farmers and laborers. It requires an intelligent man to conduct a farm successfully, to sell the products of his labor, and to buy the necessaries of life. No profession can furnish a man with brains, or provide him a garment of respectability. Every man must furnish brains and tact to make his calling and election sure in this world, as well as by faith in the world to come. Unfortunately there has been but little opportunity for Colored men or boys to get employment at the trades : but prejudice is gradually giving way to reason and common-sense ; and the day is not distant when the Negro will have a free field in this country, and will then be responsible for what he is not that is good. The need of the hour is a varied employment for the Negro race on this continent. There is more need of educated mechanics, civil engineers, surveyors, printers, artificers, inventors, architects, builders, merchants, and bankers than there is demand for lawyers, physicians, or clergymen. Waiters, barbers, porters, bootblacks, hack-drivers, grooms, and private valets find but little time for the expansion of their intellects. These places are not dishonorable ; but what we say is, *there is room at the top !* An industrial school, something like Cooper Institute, situated between New York and Philadelphia, where Colored boys and girls could learn the trades that race prejudice denies them now, would be the grandest institution of modern times. It matters not how many million dollars are given toward the education of the Negro ; so long as he is deprived of the privilege of learning and plying the trades and mechanic arts his education will injure rather than help him.[1] We would rather see a Negro boy build an engine than take the highest prize in Yale or Harvard.

---

[1] For an account of the John F. Slater Bequest of $1,000.000 for the education of the freedmen, see the Appendix to this volume.

It is quite difficult to get at a clear idea of what has been done in the Northern States toward the education of the Colored people. In nearly all the States on the borders of the Ohio and Mississippi rivers " Colored schools " still exist ; and in many instances are kept alive through the spirit of the self-seeking of a few Colored persons who draw salaries in lieu of their continuance. They should be abolished, and will be, as surely as heat follows light and the rising of the sun. In the New England, Middle, and extreme Western States, with the exception of Kansas, separate schools do not exist. The doors of all colleges, founded and conducted by the white people in the North, are open to the Colored people who desire to avail themselves of an academic education. At the present time there are one hundred and sixty-nine Colored students in seventy white colleges in the Northern States ; and the presidents say they are doing well.

The Bureau of Refugees, Freedmen, and Abandoned Lands was established in the spring of 1865 to meet the state of affairs incident upon the closing scenes of the great civil war. The Act creating the Bureau was approved and became a law on the 3d of March, 1865. The Bureau was to be under the management of the War Department, and its officers were liable for the property placed in their hands under the revised regulations of the army. In May, 1865, the following order was issued from the War Department appointing Major-Gen. O. O. Howard Commissioner of the Bureau :

" [GENERAL ORDERS NO. 91.]

" WAR DEPARTMENT, ADJUTANT GENERAL'S OFFICE, }
" WASHINGTON, May 12, 1865.   }

" Order Organizing Bureau of Refugees, Freedmen, and Abandoned
" Lands.

" I. By the direction of the President, Major General O. O. Howard is assigned to duty in the War Department as Commissioner of the Bureau of Refugees, Freedmen, and Abandoned Lands, under the act of Congress entitled 'An act to establish a bureau for the relief of freedmen and refugees,' to perform the duties and exercise all the rights, authority, and jurisdiction vested by the act of Congress in such Commissioner. General Howard will enter at once upon the duties of Commissioner specified in said act.

" II. The Quartermaster General will, without delay, assign and furnish suitable quarters and apartments for the said bureau.

"III. The Adjutant General will assign to the said bureau the number of competent clerks authorized by the act of Congress.

"By order of the President of the United States :

"E. D. Townsend,
"Assistant Adjutant General."

Gen. Howard entered upon the discharge of the vast, varied, and complicated duties of his office with his characteristic zeal, intelligence, and high Christian integrity. Hospitals were founded for the care of the sick, infirm, blind, deaf, and dumb. Rations were issued, clothing distributed, and lands apportioned to the needy and worthy.

From May 30, 1865, to November 20, 1865, inclusive, this Bureau furnished transportation for 1,946 freedmen, and issued to this class of persons in ten States, 1,030,100 rations.

"Congress, when it created the bureau, made no appropriation to defray its expenses ; it has, however, received funds from miscellaneous sources, as the following report will show :

"In several of the States, Virginia, North and South Carolina, Georgia, Louisiana, Mississippi, Tennessee, Kentucky, Arkansas, Missouri, and the District of Columbia, the interests of the freedmen were under the control of military officers assigned by the War Department previous to the organization of this bureau. Their accounts became naturally absorbed in the accounts of the bureau, and the following report embraces all the receipts and expenditures in all States now under control of the bureau since January 1, 1865 : "

RECEIPTS.

Amount on hand January 1, 1865, and received since, to October 31, 1865 :

From freedmen's fund	$466,028 35
From retained bounties	115,236 49
For clothing, fuel, and subsistence	7,704 21
Farms	76,709 12
From rents of buildings	56,012 42
From rents of lands	125,521 00
From Quartermaster's department	12,200 00
From conscript fund	13,498 11
From schools (tax and tuition)	34,486 58
Total received	907,396 28

EXPENDITURES.

Freedmen's fund	$8,009 14
Clothing, fuel, and subsistence . . .	75,504 05
Farms	40,069 71
Household furniture	2,904 90
Rents of buildings	11,470 88
Labor (by freedmen and other employés) .	237,097 62
Repairs of buildings	19,518 46
Contingent expenses	46,328 07
Rents of lands	300 00
Internal revenue	1,379 86
Conscript fund	6,515 37
Transportation	1,445 51
Schools	27,819 60
Total expended	478,363 17

RECAPITULATION.

Total amount received . . .	$907,396 28
Total amount expended	478,363 17
Balance on hand October 31, 1865 . .	429,033 11
Deduct the amount held as retained bounties.	115,236 49
Balance on hand October 31, 1865, available to meet liabilities	313,796 62.[1]

It was the policy of the Government to help the freedmen on to their feet ; to give them a start in the race of self-support and manhood. They received such assistance as was given them with thankful hearts, and were not long in placing themselves upon a safe foundation for their new existence. Out of a population of 350,000 in North Carolina only 5,000 were receiving aid from the Government in the fall of 1865. Each month witnessed a wonderful reduction of the rations issued to the freedmen. In the month of August, 1865, Gen. C. B. Fisk had reduced the number of freedmen receiving rations from 3,785 to 2,984, in Kentucky. In the same month, in Mississippi, Gen. Samuel Thomas, of the 64th U. S. C. I., had reduced the number of persons receiving rations to 669. In his report for 1865, Gen. Thomas said:

---

[1] See report of the Commissioner.

" The freedmen working land assigned them at Davis's Bend, Camp Hawley, near Vicksburg, De Soto Point, opposite, and at Washington, near Natchez, are all doing well. These crops are maturing fast; as harvest time approaches, I reduce the number of rations issued and compel them to rely on their own resources. At least 10,000 bales of cotton will be raised by these people, who are conducting cotton crops on their own account. Besides this cotton, they have gardens and corn enough to furnish bread for their families and food for their stock till harvest time returns. * * * A more industrious, energetic body of citizens does not exist than can be seen at the colonies now."

Speaking of the industry of the freed people Gen. Thomas added: "I have lately visited a large portion of the State, and find it in much better condition than I expected. In the eastern part fine crops of grain are growing; the negroes are at home working quietly; they have contracted with their old masters at fair wages; all seem to accept the change without a shock."

From June 1, 1865, to September 1, 1866, the Freedmen's Bureau issued to the freed people of the South 8,904,451½ rations, and was able to make the following financial showing of the Refugees' and Freedmen's fund. From November 1, 1865, to October 1, 1866, the receipts and expenditures were as follows:

Amount on hand November 1, 1865 . . $313,796 62

Received from various sources, as follows :

Freedmen's fund	$367,659 93
Clothing, fuel, and subsistence . .	2,074 55
Farms (sales of crops)	109,709 98
Rent of buildings	48,560 87
Rent of lands	113,641 78
Conscript funds	140 95
Transportation	1,053 50
Schools (taxes)	64,145 86

Total on hand and received . . $1,020,784 04

EXPENDITURES.

Freedmen's fund	$7,411 32
Clothing, fuel, and subsistence . .	13,870 93
Farms (fencing, seeds, tools, etc.) . .	7,210 66
Labor (by freedmen and other employés)	426,918 12
Rent of buildings (offices, etc.) . .	50,186 61
Repairs of buildings	1,957 47

EXPENDITURES.—(*Continued.*)

Contingent expenses	74,295 77
Rent of lands (restored)	9,260 58
Quartermaster's department . . .	11 26
Internal revenue (tax on salaries) . .	7,965 22
Conscript fund	1,664 01
Transportation	22,387 01
Schools	115,261 56
Total expended	**$738,400 52**
Balance on hand October 1, 1866 .	**$282,383 52**

In September, 1866, the Bureau had on hand:

RECAPITULATION.

Balance on hand of freedmen's fund .	$282,383 52
Balance of District destitute fund .	18,328 67
Balance of appropriation . . .	6,856,259 30
Total	**$7,156,971 49**

Estimated amount due subsistence department	$297,000 00
Transportation reported unpaid . .	26,015 94
Transportation estimated due . . .	20,000 00
Estimated amount due medical department	100,000 00
Estimated amount due quartermaster's department	200,000 00
	$643,015 94
Total balance for all purposes of expenditures	**$6,513,955 55**

But the estimate of Gen. Howard for funds to run the Bureau for the fiscal year commencing July 1, 1867, only called for the sum of three million eight hundred and thirty-six thousand and three hundred dollars, as follows:

Salaries of assistant commissioners, sub-assistants, and agents	$147,500
Salaries of clerks	82,800
Stationery and printing	63,000
Quarters and fuel	200,000

Subsistence stores	1,500,000
Medical department	500,000
Transportation	800,000
School superintendents	25,000
Buildings for schools and asylums, including construction, rental, and repairs .	500,000
Telegraphing and postage	18,000
	$3,836,300

This showed that the freed people were rapidly becoming self-sustaining, and that the aid rendered by the Government was used to a good purpose.

Soon after Colored Troops were mustered into the service of the Government a question arose as to some safe method by which these troops might save their pay against the days of peace and personal effort. The noble and wise Gen. Saxton answered the question and met the need of the hour by establishing a Military Savings Bank at Beaufort, South Carolina. Soldiers under his command were thus enabled to husband their funds. Gen. Butler followed in this good work, and established a similar one at Norfolk, Virginia. These banks did an excellent work, and so favorably impressed many of the friends of the Negro that a plan for a Freedman's Savings Bank and Trust Company was at once projected. Before the spring campaign of 1865 opened up, the plan was presented to Congress; a bill introduced creating such a bank, was passed and signed by President Lincoln on the 3d of March. The following is the Act:

"AN ACT TO INCORPORATE THE FREEDMAN'S SAVINGS AND TRUST "COMPANY.

"*Be it enacted by the Senate and House of Representatives of the United States of America in Congress assembled:* That Peter Cooper, WilliamC. Bryant, A. A. Low, S. B. Chittenden, Charles H. Marshall, William A. Booth, Gerrit Smith, William A. Hall, William Allen, John Jay, Abraham Baldwin, A. S. Barnes, Hiram Barney, Seth B. Hunt, Samuel Holmes, Charles Collins, R. R. Graves, Walter S. Griffith, A. H. Wallis, D. S. Gregory, J. W. Alvord, George Whipple, A. S. Hatch, Walter T. Hatch, E. A. Lambert, W. G. Lambert, Roe Lockwood, R. H. Manning, R. W. Ropes, Albert Woodruff, and Thomas Denny, of New York ; John M. Forbes, William Claflin, S. G. Howe, George L. Stearns, Edward Atkinson, A. A. Lawrence, and John M. S. Williams, of Massachusetts ; Edward Harris and Thomas Davis, of Rhode Island ; Stephen Colwell, J. Wheaton Smith, Francis E. Cope, Thomas Webster, B. S. Hunt, and Henry Samuel, of Pennsylvania ; Edward Harwood, Adam Poe, Levi Coffin, J. M. Walden, of Ohio, and their successors, are constituted a body corporate in the City of Washington, in the District of Columbia, by the name of the FREEDMAN'S SAVINGS AND TRUST COMPANY, and by that name may sue and be sued in any court of the United States.

"SEC. 2. *And be it further enacted,* That the persons named in the first section of this act shall be the first Trustees of the Corporation, and all vacancies by death, resignation, or otherwise, in the office of Trustee shall be filled by the Board, by ballot, without unnecessary delay, and at least ten votes shall be necessary for the election of any Trustee. The Trustees shall hold a regular meeting, at least once in each month, to receive reports of their officers on the affairs of the Corporation, and to transact such business as may be necessary ; and any Trustee omitting to attend the regular meetings of the Board for six months in succession, may thereupon be considered as having vacated his place, and a successor may be elected to fill the same.

"SEC. 3. *And be it further enacted,* That the business of the Corporation shall be managed and directed by the Board of Trustees, who shall elect from their number a President and two Vice-Presidents, and may appoint such other officers as they may see fit ; nine of the Trustees, of whom the President or one of the Vice-Presidents shall be one, shall form a quorum for the transaction of business at any regular or adjourned meeting of the Board of Trustees ; and the affirmative vote of at least seven members of the Board shall be requisite in making any order for, or authorizing the investment of, any moneys, or the sale or transfer of any stock or securities belonging to the Corporation, or the appointment of any officer receiving any salary therefrom.

"SEC. 4. *And be it further enacted,* That the Board of Trustees of the Corporation shall have power, from time to time, to make and establish such By-Laws and regulations as they shall judge proper with regard to the elections of officers and their respective functions, and generally for the management of the affairs of the Corporation, provided such By-Laws and regulations are not repugnant to this act, or to the Constitution or laws of the United States.

"SEC. 5. *And be it further enacted,* That the general business and object of the Corporation hereby created shall be, to receive on deposit such sums of money as may, from time to time, be offered therefor, by or on behalf of persons heretofore held in slavery in the United States, or their descendants, and investing the same in the stocks, bonds, Treasury notes, or other securities of the United States.

" Sec. 6. *And be it further enacted,* That it shall be the duty of the Trustees of the Corporation to invest, as soon as practicable, in the securities named in the next preceding section, all sums received by them beyond an available fund, not exceeding one third of the total amount of deposits with the Corporation, at the discretion of the Trustees, which available funds may be kept by the Trustees, to meet current payments of the Corporation, and may by them be left on deposit, at interest or otherwise, or in such available form as the Trustees may direct.

" Sec. 7. *And be it further enacted,* That the Corporation may, under such regulations as the Board of Trustees shall, from time to time, prescribe, receive any deposit hereby authorized to be received, upon such trusts and for such purposes, not contrary to the laws of the United States, as may be indicated in writing by the depositor, such writing to be subscribed by the depositor and acknowledged or proved before any officer in the civil or military service of the United States, the certificate of which acknowledgment or proof shall be endorsed on the writing ; and the writing, so acknowledged or proved, shall accompany such deposit and be filed among the papers of the Corporation, and be carefully preserved therein, and may be read in evidence in any court or before any judicial officer of the United States, without further proof ; and the certificate of acknowledgment or proof shall be *prima facie* evidence only of the due execution of such writing.

" Sec. 8. *And be it further enacted,* That all sums received on deposit shall be repaid to such depositor when required, at such time, with such interest, not exceeding seven per centum per annum, and under such regulations as the Board of Trustees shall, from time to time, prescribe, which regulations shall be posted up in some conspicuous place in the room where the business of the Corporation shall be transacted, but shall not be altered so as to affect any deposit previously made.

" Sec. 9. *And be it further enacted,* That all trusts upon which, and all purposes for which any deposit shall be made, and which shall be indicated in the writing to accompany such deposit, shall be faithfully performed by the Corporation, unless the performing of the same is rendered impossible.

" Sec. 10. *And be it further enacted,* That when any depositor shall die, the funds remaining on deposit with the Corporation to his credit, and all accumulations thereof, shall belong and be paid to the personal representatives of such depositor, in case he shall have left a last will and testament, and in default of a last will and testament, or of any person qualifying under a last will and testament, competent to act as executor, the Corporation shall be entitled, in respect to the funds so remaining on deposit to the credit of any such depositor, to adminis-

tration thereon in preference to all other persons, and letters or administration shall be granted to the Corporation accordingly in the
manner prescribed by law in respect to granting of letters of administration, with the will annexed, and in cases of intestacy.

"SEC. 11. *And be it further enacted*, That in the case of the death
of any depositor, whose deposit shall not be held upon any trust created
pursuant to the provisions hereinbefore contained, or where it may
prove impossible to execute such trust, it shall be the duty of the Corporation to make diligent efforts to ascertain and discover whether
such deceased depositor has left a husband, wife, or children, surviving,
and the Corporation shall keep a record of the efforts so made, and of
the results thereof ; and in case no person lawfully entitled thereto shall
be discovered, or shall appear, or claim the funds remaining to the
credit of such depositor before the expiration of two years from the
death of such depositor, it shall be lawful for the Corporation to hold
and invest such funds as a separate trust fund, to be applied, with the
accumulations thereof, to the education and improvement of persons
heretofore held in slavery, or their descendants, being inhabitants of
the United States, in such manner and through such agencies as the
Board of Trustees shall deem best calculated to effect that object ;
Provided, That if any depositor be not heard from within five years
from the date of his last deposit, the Trustees shall advertise the same
in some paper of general circulation in the State where the principal
office of the Company is established, and also in the State where the
depositor was last heard from ; and if, within two years thereafter, such
depositor shall not appear, nor a husband, wife, or child of such depositor, to claim his deposits, they shall be used by the Board of Trustees
as hereinbefore provided for in this section.

"SEC. 12. *And be it further enacted*, That no President, Vice-
President, Trustee, officer, or servant of the Corporation shall, directly
or indirectly, borrow the funds of the Corporation or its deposits, or in
any manner use the same, or any part thereof, except to pay necessary
expenses, under the direction of the Board of Trustees. All certificates
or other evidences of deposit made by the proper officers shall be as
binding on the Corporation as if they were made under their common
seal. It shall be the duty of the Trustees to regulate the rate of interest
allowed to the depositors, so that they shall receive, as nearly as may be,
a rateable proportion of all the profits of the Corporation, after deducting all necessary expenses ; *Provided, however*, That the Trustees may
allow to depositors to the amount of five hundred dollars or upward
one per centum less than the amount allowed others ; *And provided, also*,
Whenever it shall appear that, after the payment of the usual interest
to depositors, there is in the possession of the Corporation an excess of
profits over the liabilities amounting to ten per centum upon the de-

posits, such excess shall be invested for the security of the depositors in the Corporation ; and thereafter, at each annual examination of the affairs of the Corporation, any surplus over and above such ten per centum shall, in addition to the usual interest, be divided rateably among the depositors, in such manner as the Board of Trustees shall direct.

"SEC. 13. *And be it further enacted,* That whenever any deposits shall be made by any minor, the Trustees of the Corporation may, at their discretion, pay to such depositor such sum as may be due to him, although no guardian shall have been appointed for such minor, or the guardian of such minor shall not have authorized the drawing of the same ; and the check, receipt, or acquittance of such minor shall be as valid as if the same were executed by a guardian of such minor, or the minor were of full age, if such deposit was made personally by such minor. And whenever any deposits shall have been made by married women, the Trustees may repay the same on their own receipts.

"SEC. 14. *And be it further enacted,* That the Trustees shall not directly or indirectly receive any payment or emolument for their services as such, except the President and Vice-President.

"SEC. 15. *And be it further enacted,* That the President, Vice-President, and subordinate officers and agents of the Corporation, shall respectively give such security for their fidelity and good conduct as the Board of Trustees may, from time to time, require, and the Board shall fix the salaries of such officers and agents.

"SEC. 16. *And be it further enacted,* That the books of the Corporation shall, at all times during the hours of business, be open for inspection and examination to such persons as Congress shall designate or appoint.

"Approved March 3, 1865."

Eleven of these banks were established in 1865, nine in 1866, three in 1868, one in 1869, and the remainder in 1870, after the charter had been amended as follows :

"AN ACT TO AMEND AN ACT ENTITLED 'AN ACT TO INCORPORATE THE FREEDMAN'S SAVINGS AND TRUST COMPANY,' APPROVED MARCH THIRD, EIGHTEEN HUNDRED AND SIXTY-FIVE.

"*Be it enacted by the Senate and House of Representatives of the United States of America in Congress assembled,* That the fifth section of the Act entitled 'An Act to Incorporate the Freedman's Savings and Trust Company,' approved March third, eighteen hundred and sixty-five, be, and the same is hereby, amended by adding thereto at the end

thereof the words following : 'and to the extent of one half in bonds
or notes, secured by mortgage on real estate in double the value of the
loan ; and the corporation is also authorized hereby to hold and improve the real estate now owned by it in the city of Washington, to wit :
the west half of lot number three ; all of lots four, five, six, seven, and
the south half of lot number eight, in square number two hundred and
twenty-one, as laid out and recorded in the original plats or plan of said
city : *Provided,* That said corporation shall not use the principal of any
deposits made with it for the purpose of such improvement.'

"SEC. 2. *And be it further enacted,* That Congress shall have the
right to alter or repeal this amendment at any time.

"Approved May 6, 1870."

The company was organized on the 16th of May, 1865, and
the trustees made their first report on the 8th of June, 1865.
Deposits up to this date were $700, besides $7,956.38 transferred from the Military Savings Bank at Norfolk, Virginia, on
the 3d of June. On the 1st of August the first branch office was
opened at Washington, D. C., and on the 1st of September it had
a balance due its depositors of $843.84

Other branches were opened during the year at Louisville,
Richmond, Nashville, Wilmington, Huntsville, Memphis, Mobile,
and Vicksburg. December 14, 1865, the Military Bank at Beaufort, organized October 16, 1865, was, by order of General Saxton,
transferred to this company, with its balance of $170,000. At
the end of the first year, March 1, 1866, fourteen branch offices
had been opened, and the balance due depositors was $199,-
283.42.

The total deposits made by freedmen in them, from their establishment up to July 1, 1870, was $16,960,336, of which over
$2,000,000 still remained on deposit. The total amount of de-
posits in the Richmond branch up to that date was $318,913, and
the balance undrawn $84,537. The average amount deposited
by the various depositors was nearly $284. So far as the facts
were obtained, it appeared that about seventy per cent. of the
money drawn from these banks was invested in real estate and in
business.

By the financial statement of the banking company, for
August, 1871, it appears that in the thirty-four banks then in operation the deposits made during that month, which was considered " dull," amounted to $882,806.67, and that the total
amount to the credit of the depositors was $3,058,232.81. In the

Richmond branch, the deposits for that month were $17,790.60, and the total amount due depositors was $123,733.75 ; all of which was to the credit of Colored people, except $6,929.19. A branch shortly before had been established in Lynchburg, which showed a balance due depositors of $7,382.83.

The following table shows the business of the company for the years 1866–1871 :

Table Showing the Relative Business of the Company for Each Fiscal Year.

For year ending March 1.	Total amount of deposits.	Total amount of drafts.	Balance due depositors.
1866 . .	$305,167 00	$105,883 58	$199,283 42
1867 . .	1,624,853 33	1,258,515 00	366,338 33
1868 . .	3,582,378 36	2,944,079 36	638,299 00
1869 . .	7.257,798 63	6,184,333 32	1,073,465 31
1870 . .	12,605,781 95	10,948,775 20	1,657,006 75
1871 . .	19,952,647 36	17,497,111 25	2,455,836 11

For year ending March 1.	Deposits each year.	Drafts each year.	Gain each year.
1866 . .	$305,167 00	$105,883 58	$199,283 42
1867 . .	1,319,686 33	1,152,631 42	167,054 91
1868 . .	1,957,525 03	1,685,564 36	271,960 67
1869 . .	3,675,420 27	3,240,253 96	435,166 31
1870 . .	5,347,983 32	4,764,441 88	583,341 44
1871 . .	7,347,165 41	6,548,336 05	798,829 36

The total amount of deposits received from the organization of the company to October 1, 1871—six years from the opening of the first branch—was . . $25,977,435 48
Total drafts during the same period were . . . 22,850,926 47

Leaving due depositors October 1, 1871 . . . . 3,126,509 01
The *total assets* of company on same day amounted to . 3,157,206 17

The interest paid during this time amounted to . . 180,565 35

In 1872 the trustees made the following interesting statement:

THE FREEDMAN'S SAVINGS AND TRUST COMPANY.

FINANCIAL STATEMENT FOR THE MONTH OF AUGUST, 1872.

BRANCHES.	Deposits for the month.	Drafts for the month.	Total amount of Deposits.	Total amount of Drafts.	Balance due Depositors.
Atlanta, Georgia . . .	$9,419 68	$11,242 30	$245,200 27	$223,020 17	$22,180 10
Augusta, Georgia . .	10,771 99	9,217 94	367,653 16	284,406 14	83,247 02
Baltimore, Maryland . .	29,755 52	18,644 57	1,278,042 32	996,371 98	281,670 34
Beaufort, South Carolina,	189,600 74	184,924 40	2,993,873 30	2,944,441 88	49,431 42
Charleston, South Carolina,	67,668 83	84,464 53	3,100,641 65	2,795,176 24	305,465 41
Columbus, Mississippi .	2,426 15	4,364 34	132,036 46	121,776 67	10,259 79
Columbia, Tennessee .	2,552 55	2,086 05	34,088 97	15,738 76	18,350 21
Huntsville, Alabama .	7,343 50	10,127 61	416,617 72	364,382 51	52,235 21
Jacksonville, Florida . .	67,292 09	57,307 54	3,312,424 55	3,234,445 72	77,978 83
Lexington, Kentucky .	14,383 85	11,221 13	238,680 22	188,308 76	50,371 46
Little Rock, Arkansas .	7,871 27	9,506 37	172,392 10	154,914 42	17,477 68
Louisville, Kentucky .	18,311 01	17,535 74	1,057,587 71	914,504 61	143,083 10
Lynchburg, Virginia . .	3,104 48	1,242 56	36,880 98	18,354 87	18,526 11
Macon, Georgia . .	6,808 98	7,061 52	197,050 01	156,308 75	40,741 26
Memphis, Tennessee .	20,045 40	27,197 06	970,096 09	840,218 91	129,877 18
Mobile, Alabama . .	11,136 05	18,645 62	1,039,097 05	933,424 30	105,672 75
Montgomery, Alabama .	8,522 90	8,679 60	238,106 08	213,861 71	24,244 37
Natchez, Mississippi .	25,548 53	15,005 17	649,256 70	612,985 74	36,270 96
Nashville, Tennessee .	15,731 46	17,098 58	739,691 88	625,166 40	114,525 48
New Berne, North Carolina,	38,113 83	37,775 73	1,057,688 32	1,001,645 74	56,042 58
New Orleans, Louisiana .	193,145 48	207,878 53	2,393,584 08	2,171,056 95	222,527 13
New York, New York .	133,209 58	74,461 61	1,673,249 36	1,227,449 57	445,799 79
Norfolk, Virginia . .	16,771 88	17,757 38	1,048,762 05	916,047 59	132,714 46
Philadelphia, Pennsylvania,	11,451 12	9,887 49	357,924 89	278,641 10	79,283 79
Raleigh, North Carolina .	5,663 28	4,660 18	231,685 82	202,032 44	29,653 38
Richmond, Virginia . .	64,112 51	53,900 72	1,082,152 71	912,933 45	169,219 26
Savannah, Georgia .	30,951 23	27,066 33	1,031,173 38	893,321 30	137,852 02
Shreveport, Louisiana .	20,688 72	21,105 59	299,428 39	264,707 78	34,720 61
St. Louis, Missouri .	26,323 93	20,599 02	615,876 74	526,490 86	89,385 88
Tallahassee, Florida .	4,589 45	4,526 75	361,614 57	329,618 33	31,996 24
Vicksburg, Mississippi .	61,691 73	60,068 28	2,962,235 58	2,823,700 87	138,534 71
Washington, Dist. Colum'a,	323,555 79	296.321 26	7,438,918 17	6,406,092 39	1,032,825 78
Wilmington, N'th Carolina,	10,714 10	12,632 65	457,360 75	407,512 51	49,848 24
Alexandria, Virginia	1,929 91	685 80	14,091 77	1,626 35	12,465 42
	$1,461,207 52	$1,364,899 95	$38,245,163 80	$34,000,685 77	$4,244,478 03

Total amount of deposits for the month $1,461,207 56
Total amount of drafts for the month 1,364,899 95

Gain for the month 96,307 61

Total amount of deposits $38,245,163 80
Total amount of drafts 34,000,685 77

Total amount due depositors $4,244,478 03

This first experiment of the new citizen in saving his funds was working admirably. Each report was more cheering than the preceding one. The deposits were generally made by day laborers, house servants, farmers, mechanics, and washerwomen. Two facts were established, viz.: that the Negroes of the South were working; and that they were saving their earnings. Northern as well as Southern whites were agreeably surprised.

But bad management doomed the institution to irreparable ruin. The charter was violated in the establishment of branch banks; "persons who were never held in bondage and their descendants" were allowed to deposit funds in the bank; money was loaned upon valueless securities and meaningless collaterals, and in the fall of 1873, having been kept open for a long time on money borrowed on collateral securities belonging to its customers, the bank failed!

During the brief period of its existence about $57,000,000 had been deposited. The liabilities of the institution at the time of the failure, as corrected to date, were $3,037,483, of which $73,774.34 were special deposits and preferred claims. The number of open accounts at the time of the failure were 62,000. The *nominal* assets at the time of the failure were $2,693,095.20. And in the almost interminable list of over-drafts amounting to $55,567.63, there appeared but one solitary surety!

On the 20th of June, 1874, Congress passed an act permitting the very men who had destroyed the bank to nominate three Commissioners, who, upon the approval of the Secretary of the Treasury, should wind up the affairs of this insolvent institution. Section 7 of the Act reads as follows:

"SEC. 7. That whenever it shall be deemed advisable by the trustees of said corporation to close up its entire business, then they shall select three competent men, not connected with the previous management of the institution and approved by the Secretary of the Treasury, to be known and styled commissioners, whose duty it shall be to take charge of all the property and effects of said Freedman's Savings and Trust Company, close up the principal and subordinate branches, collect from the branches all the deposits they have on hand, and proceed to collect all sums due said company, and dispose of all the property owned by said company, as speedily as the interests of the corporation require, and to distribute the proceeds among the creditors pro rata, according to their respective amounts; they shall make a pro rata dividend whenever they have funds enough to pay twenty per centum of the claims of depositors. Said commissioners, before they proceed to act, shall execute a joint bond to the United States, with good sureties, in the penal sum of one hundred thousand dollars, conditioned for the faithful discharge of their duties as commissioners aforesaid, and shall take an oath to faithfully and honestly perform their duties as such, which bonds shall be executed in presence of the Secretary of the Treasury, be approved by him, and by him safely kept; and whenever said trustees shall file with the Secretary of the Treasury a certified copy of the order appointing said commissioners, and they shall have executed the bonds and taken the oath aforesaid, then said commisioners shall be invested with the legal title to all of said property of said company, for the purposes of this act, and shall have full power and authority to sell the same, and make deeds of conveyance to any and all of the real estate sold by them to the purchasers. Said commissioners may employ such agents as are necessary to assist them in closing up said company, and pay them a reasonable compensation for their services out of the funds of said company ; and the said commissioners shall retain out of said funds a reasonable compensation for their trouble, to be fixed by the Secretary of the Treasury and the Comptroller of the Currency, and not exceeding three thousand dollars each per annum. Said commissioners shall deposit all sums collected by them in the Treasury of the United States until they make a pro rata distribution of the same."

There are several legal questions that history would like to ask. 1. Did not the trustees of the Freedman's Savings Bank and Trust Company violate their charter in establishing branch banks ? 2. Were not the trustees personally liable for receiving deposits from persons who were neither " heretofore held in slavery " nor the descendants of such persons? 3. Were not persons " heretofore held in slavery" and " their descendants " preferred creditors? 4. Had Congress the authority to go outside of the Federal bankruptcy laws and create such special machinery for the settlement of a collapsed bank? This matter may come before Congress in a new shape some time in the future.

The three commissioners, at a salary of $3,000 per annum, were charged with the settlement of the affairs of the bank. They were Jno. A. J. Creswell, Robert Purvis, and R. H. T. Leipold. Mr. Creswell was retained by the United States before the Alabama Claims Commission at a salary of $10,000 per annum ; while Mr. Leipold was a lawyer with considerable practice. But neither one of these gentlemen ever entered a court on behalf of the company. In a little more than five years they used up out of the assets of the company, $40,000 for their salaries ; paid for salaries to agents, $64,000, and $31,000 for attorneys' fees, aggregating $135,000—nearly one half of the amount distributed among depositors for the same length of time.

The more the commissioners examined, the greater the liabilities of the company grew. On the 1st of October, 1875, a dividend of 20 per cent. was declared; on the 1st of February, 1878, a dividend of 10 per cent. was declared; on the 21st of August, 1880, they declared another dividend of 10 per cent.; and on the 14th of April, 1881, a circular was sent out as a crumb of comfort to the anxious, defrauded, and outraged depositors. It is not enough for history to pronounce the failure of this bank an irreparable calamity to the Colored people of the South; it should be branded as a *crime !* There was no more necessity for the failure of this bank than for the failure of the United States Treasury. Its management was criminal; and Congress should yet seek out and punish the guilty; and the depositors should be indemnified out of the United States Treasury. Justice and equity demand it.

The failure of the Freedman's Bank worked great mischief among the Colored people in the South. But hardy, persistent, earnest, and hopeful, they turned again to the work of making and saving money. They have been more prudent than their circumstances, in some instances, would seem to warrant. In Georgia the Colored people have made wonderful progress in business matters.

Polls.	No. of Acres of Land.	Value of Land.	City or Town Property.	Amount of Money and Solvent Debts of all Kinds.	Household and Kitchen Furniture.
88,522	541,199	$1,348,758	$1,094,435	$73,253	$448,713

Horses, Mules, Hogs, Sheep, and Cattle.	Plantation and Mechanical Tools.	Value of all other Property, not before Enumerated, except Annual Crops, Provisions, etc.	Aggregate Value of Whole Property.	Total Amount of Tax Assessed on Polls and Property.
$1,704,230	$143,258	$369,751	$5,182,398	$106,660.39

Increase in number of acres since return of 1878 39,309
Increase in wealth since return of 1878 . . . . . $57,523

In Alabama, Florida, Louisiana, North and South Carolina, and in Maryland, Colored men have possessed themselves of excellent farms and moderate fortunes. In Baltimore a company of Colored men own a ship dock, and transact a large business. Some of the largest orange plantations in Florida are owned by Colored men. On most of the plantations, and in many of the large towns and cities Colored mechanics are quite numerous. The Montgomeries who own the plantation, once the property of Jefferson Davis, extending for miles along the Mississippi, are probably the best business men in the South. In Louisiana, P. P. Deslonde, A. Dubuclet, Hon. T. T. Allain, and State Senator Young are men who, although taking a lively interest in politics, have accumulated property and saved it.

There is nothing vicious in the character of the Southern Negro. He is gentle, affectionate, and faithful. If it has appeared, through false figures, that he is a criminal, there is room for satisfactory explanation. In 1870, out of a population, of persons of color, in all the States and Territories, of 4,880,009, there were only 9,400 who were receiving aid on the 1st of June, 1870; and only 8,056 in all the prisons of America. Nine tenths of these were South, and could neither read nor write.

During the Rebellion, when every white male from fifteen to seventy was out fighting to sustain the Confederacy—when the Southern Government was robbing the cradle and the grave for soldiers—the wives and children of the Confederates were committed to the care and keeping of their slaves. And what is the verdict of history? That these women were outraged and their children brained? No! But that during all those years of painful anxiety, of hope and fear, of fiery trial and severe privation, those faithful Negroes toiled, not only to support the wives and children of the men who were fighting to make slavery national and perpetual, but fed the entire rebel army, and never laid the weight of a finger upon the head of any of the women or children entrusted to their care! To this virtue of fidelity to their worst enemies they added still another, loyalty to the Union flag and escaping Union soldiers. All night long they would direct the lonely, famishing, fainting, and almost delirious Union soldier in a safe way, and then when the night and morning met they would point their pilgrim friends to the North Star, hide them and feed them during the day, and then return to the plantation to care for the loved ones of the men who starved Union soldiers and hunted them down with bloodhounds! This is the brightest gem that history can place upon the brow of the Negro; and in conferring it there is no one found to object.

Since the war the crime among Colored people is to be accounted for upon two grounds, viz.: ignorance, and a combination of circumstances over which they had no control. It was one thing for the Negro to understand the cruel laws of slavery, but when he found himself a freeman he was not able to know what was an infraction of the law. They did not know what in law constituted a *tort*, or a civil action from a sled. The violent passions pampered in slavery, the destruction of the home, the promiscuous mingling of the sexes, a conscience enfeebled by disuse, made them easy transgressors. The Negro is not a criminal generically; he is an accidental criminal. The judiciary and juries of the South are responsible for the alarming prison statistics which stand against the Negro. It takes generations for men to overcome their prejudices. With a white judge and a white jury a Negro is guilty the moment he makes his appearance in court. It is seldom that a Negro can get judgment against a white person under the most favorable circumstances. The Negroes who appear in courts are of the poorer and more ignorant class. They have no funds with which to employ counsel, and have but few intelligent lawyers to come to their rescue. In cases of theft, especially of poultry, pigs, sheep, fruit, etc., it is next to impossible to convince a white judge or jury that the defendant is not guilty. They reason that because the half-fed, overworked slave appropriated articles of food, as a freeman the Negro was not changed. They ascribed a general habit, growing out of trying circumstances, to the Negro as a slave that he soon learned to regard as morally wrong when a freeman.

But the most effective agency in filling Southern prisons with Negroes has been, and is, the chain-gang system—the farming out of convict labor. Just as great railway, oil, and telegraph companies in the North have been capable of controlling legislation, so the corporations at the South which take the prisoners of the State off of the hands of the Government, and then speculate upon the labor of the prisoners, are able to control both court and jury. It has been the practice, and is now, in some of the Southern States, to pronounce long sentences upon able-bodied young Colored men, whose offences, in a Northern court, could not be visited with more than a few months' confinement and a trifling fine. The object in giving Negro men a long term of years, is to make sure the tenure of the soulless corporations upon the convicts whose unhappy lot it is to fall into their iron grasp. In some of the Southern States a strong and healthy Negro convict brings thirty-seven cents a day to the State, while he earns a dollar for the corporations above his expenses. The convicts are cruelly treated—especially in Georgia and Kentucky;—their food is poor, their quarters miserable, and their morals next to the brute creation. In many of these camps men and women are compelled to sleep in the same bunks together, with chains upon their limbs, in a promiscuous manner too sickening and disgusting to mention. When a prisoner escapes he is hunted down by fiery dogs and cruel guards; and often the poor prisoner is torn to pieces by the dogs or beaten to death by the guards. No system of slavery was ever equal in its cruel and dehumanizing details to this convict system, which, taking advantage of race prejudice on the one hand and race ignorance on the other, with cupidity and avarice as its chief characteristics, has done more to curse the South than all things else since the war.

It was predicted by persons hostile to the rights and citizenship of the Negro, that a condition of freedom would not be in harmony with his character; that it would destroy him, and that he would destroy the country and party which tried to make him agree to a state of independent life; that having been used to the "kind treatment" (?) of his master he would find himself unequal to the responsibilities of freedom; and that his migratory disposition would lead him into a climate too cold for him, where he would be welcomed to an inhospitable grave.

It is true that a great many Negroes died during the first years of their new life. The joy of emancipation and the excitement that disturbed business swept the Negroes into the large cities. Like the shepherds who left their flocks on the plains and went into Bethlehem to see the promised redemption, these people sought the centres of excitement. The large cities were overrun with them. The demand for unskilled labor was not great. From mere spectators they became idlers, helpless and offensive to industrious society. Ignorant of sanitary laws, imprudent in their daily living, changing from the pure air and plain diet of farm life to the poisonous atmosphere and rich, fateful food of the city, many fell victims to the sudden change from bondage to freedom, from darkness to light, and from the flesh-pots, garlic, and onions of their Egyptian bondage to the milk and honey of the Canaan of their deliverance.

But this was in accordance with an immutable law of nature. Every year a large number of .birds perish in an attempt to change their home ; every spring-time many flowers die at their birth. The law of the survival of the fittest is impartial and inexorable. The Creator said centuries ago "the soul that sinneth shall surely die," and the law has remained until the present time. Those who sinned ignorantly or knowingly died the death ; but those who obeyed the laws of health, of man, and of God, lived to be useful members of society.

But this was the exception to the rule. The Negro race in America is not dying out. The charge is false. The wish was father to the thought, while no doubt many honest people have been misled by false figures. Nearly all white communities at the South had more than enough of physicians ; and science and culture were summoned to the aid of the white mother in the hour of childbirth. The record of births was preserved with pride and official accuracy ; and thus there was a record upon which to calculate the increase. But, on the contary, among the Negroes there were no physicians and no record of births. The venerable system of midwifery prevailed. In burying their dead, however, this people were compelled to obtain a burial permit from the Board of Health. Thus the statistics were all on one side—all deaths and no births. Looking at these statistics it did seem that the race was dying out. But the Government steps in and takes the census every decade, and, thereby, the world is enabled, upon reliable figures, to estimate the increase or decrease of the Colored race. The subjoined table exhibits the increase of the Colored people for nine decades.

	Year.	Colored.	Colored gain per cent.	
1st census.	1790	757,208		
2d "	1800	1,002,037	32.3	1st decade.
3d "	1810	1,377,808	37.5	2d "
4th "	1820	1,771,656	28.6	3d "
5th "	1830	2,328,642	31.5	4th "
6th "	1840	2,873,648	23.4	5th "
7th "	1850	3,638,808	26.6	6th "
8th "	1860	4,441,830	22.1	7th "
9th "	1870	4,880,009	9.9[1]	8th "
10th "	1880	6,580,793	34.8	9th "

[1] There is no disguising the fact that the ninth census was incorrect. No doubt it was the worst we have ever had.

So here is a remarkable fact, that from 757,208 in 1790 the Negro race has grown to be 6,580,793 in 1880! The theory that the race was dying out under the influences of civilization at a greater ratio than under the annihilating influences of slavery was at war with common-sense and the efficient laws of Christian society. Emancipation has taken the mother from field-work to house-work. The slave hut has been supplanted by a pleasant house ; the mud floor is done away with ; and now, with carpets on the floor, pictures on the wall, a better quality of food properly prepared, the influence of books and papers, and the blessings of a preached Gospel, the Negro mother is more prolific, and the mortality of her children reduced to a minimum. The Negro is not dying out. On the contrary he has shown the greatest recuperative powers, and against the white population of the United States as it stands to-day—if it were not fed by European immigrants,—within the next hundred years the Negroes would outnumber the whites 12,000,000! Or at an increase of 33⅓ per cent. the Negro population in 1980 would be 117,000,000! providing the ratio of increase continues the same between the races.

And in addition to the fact that the Negro, like the Irishman, is prolific, is able to reproduce his species, it should be recorded that the Negro intellect is growing and expanding at a wonderful rate. The children of ten and twelve years of age are more apt to-day than those of the same age ten years ago. And the children of the next generation will have no superiors in any of the schools of the country.

CHAPTER XXIII.

REPRESENTATIVE COLORED MEN.

Thirteenth Amendment to the Constitution. — The Legal Destruction of Slavery and a Constitutional Prohibition. — Fifteenth Amendment granting Manhood Suffrage to the American Negro. — President Grant's Special Message upon the Subject. — Universal Rejoicing among the Colored People. — The Negro in the United States Senate and House of Representatives. — The Negro in the Diplomatic Service of the Country. — Frederick Douglass. — His Birth, Enslavement, Escape to the North, and Life as a Freeman. — Becomes an Anti-slavery Orator. — Goes to Great Britain. — Returns to America. — Establishes the "North Star." — His Eloquence, Influence, and Brilliant Career. — Richard Theodore Greener. — His Early Life, Education, and Successful Literary Career. — John P. Green. — His Early Struggles to obtain an Education. — A Successful Orator, Lawyer, and Useful Legislator. — Other Representative Colored Men. — Representative Colored Women.

THE Government could not escape the logic of the position it took when it made the Negro a soldier, and invoked his aid in putting down the slave-holders' Rebellion. As a soldier he stood in line of promotion: the Government destroyed the Confederacy when it placed muskets in the hands of the slaves; and at the close of the war had to legally render slavery forever impossible in the United States. The bloody deduction of the great struggle had to be made a living, legal verity in the Constitution, and hence the Thirteenth Amendment.

" ARTICLE XIII.

" Section 1. Neither slavery nor involuntary servitude, except as a punishment for crime whereof the party shall have been duly convicted, shall exist within the United States, or any place subject to their jurisdiction.

" Section 2. Congress shall have power to enforce this article by appropriate legislation."

This was the consummation of the ordinance of 1787, carried to its last analysis, applied in its broadest sense. It drove the last nail in the coffin of slavery, and blighted the fondest hope of the friends of secession.

But there was need for another amendment to the Constitution conferring upon the Colored people manhood suffrage. On the 27th of February, 1869, the Congress passed a resolution recommending the Fifteenth Amendment for ratification by the Legislatures of the several States. On the 30th of March, 1870, President U. S. Grant sent a special message to Congress, calling the attention of that body to the proclamation of the Secretary of State in reference to the ratification of the Amendment by twenty-nine of the States.

SPECIAL MESSAGE OF PRESIDENT GRANT ON RATIFICATION OF THE FIFTEENTH AMENDMENT.

" *To the Senate and House of Representatives :*

"It is unusual to notify the two houses of Congress, by message, of the promulgation, by proclamation of the Secretary of State, of the ratification of a constitutional amendment. In view, however, of the vast importance of the XVth Amendment to the Constitution, this day declared a part of that revered instrument, I deem a departure from the usual custom justifiable. A measure which makes at once four millions of people voters, who were heretofore declared by the highest tribunal in the land not citizens of the United States, nor eligible to become so, (with the assertion that, 'at the time of the Declaration of Independence, the opinion was fixed and universal in the civilized portion of the white race, regarded as an axiom in morals as well as in politics, that black men had no rights which the white man was bound to respect,') is indeed a measure of grander importance than any other one act of the kind from the foundation of our free government to the present day.

"Institutions like ours, in which all power is derived directly from the people, must depend mainly upon their intelligence, patriotism, and industry. I call the attention, therefore, of the newly-enfranchised race to the importance of their striving in every honorable manner to make themselves worthy of their new privilege. To the race more favored heretofore by our laws I would say, withold no legal privilege of advancement to the new citizen. The framers of our Constitution firmly believed that a republican government could not endure without intelligence and education generally diffused among the people. The 'Father of his Country,' in his farewell address, uses this language: 'Promote, then, as a matter of primary importance, institutions for the general diffusion of knowledge. In proportion as the structure of the government gives force to public opinion, it is essential that public opinion should be enlightened.' In his first annual message to Congress the same views are forcibly presented, and are again urged in his eighth message.

"I repeat that the adoption of the XVth Amendment to the Constitution completes the greatest civil change and constitutes the most important event that has occurred since the nation came into life. The change will be beneficial in proportion to the heed that is given to the urgent recommendations of Washington. If these recommendations were important then, with a population of but a few millions, how much more important now, with a population of forty millions, and increasing in a rapid ratio.

"I would therefore call upon Congress to take all the means within their constitutional powers to promote and encourage popular education throughout the country ; and upon the people everywhere to see to it that all who possess and exercise political rights shall have the opportunity to acquire the knowledge which will make their share in the government a blessing and not a danger. By such means only can the benefits contemplated by this amendment to the Constitution be secured.

"U. S. GRANT.

"EXECUTIVE MANSION, March 30, 1870."

CERTIFICATE OF MR. SECRETARY FISH RESPECTING THE RATIFICATION OF THE XVTH AMENDMENT TO THE CONSTITUTION, MARCH 30, 1870.

"HAMILTON FISH, SECRETARY OF STATE OF THE UNITED STATES.

" *To all to whom these presents may come, greeting :*

" Know ye that the Congress of the United States, on or about the 27th day of February, in the year 1869, passed a resolution in the words and figures following, to wit :

" A RESOLUTION proposing an amendment to the Constitution of the United States.

" *Resolved by the Senate and House of Representatives of the United States of America in Congress assembled,* (*two-thirds of both houses concurring.*) That the following article be proposed to the legislatures of the several States as an amendment to the Constitution of the United States, which, when ratified by three-fourths of said legislatures, shall be valid as part of the Constitution, namely :

" ARTICLE XV.

" SECTION 1. The right of citizens of the United States to vote shall not be denied or abridged by the United States, or by any State, on account of race, color, or previous condition of servitude.

" SEC. 2. The Congress shall have power to enforce this article by appropriate legislation.

" And, further, that it appears, from official documents on file in this department, that the amendment to the Constitution of the United States, proposed as aforesaid, has been ratified by the legislatures of the States of North Carolina, West Virginia, Massachusetts, Wisconsin, Maine, Louisiana, Michigan, South Carolina, Pennsylvania, Arkansas, Connecticut, Florida, Illinois, Indiana, New York, New Hampshire, Nevada, Vermont, Virginia, Alabama, Missouri, Mississippi, Ohio, Iowa, Kansas, Minnesota, Rhode Island, Nebraska, and Texas ; in all, twenty-nine States.

" And, further, that the States whose legislatures have so ratified the said proposed amendment constitute three-fourths of the whole number of States in the United States.

" And, further, that it appears, from an official document on file in this department, that the legislature of the State of New York has since passed resolutions claiming to withdraw the said ratification of the said amendment which had been made by the legislature of that State, and of which official notice had been filed in this department.

" And, further, that it appears, from an official document on file in this department, that the legislature of Georgia has by resolution ratified the said proposed amendment.

" Now, therefore, be it known that I, Hamilton Fish, Secretary of State of the United States, by virtue and in pursuance of the 2d section of the act of Congress, approved the 20th day of April, 1818, entitled " An act to provide for the publication of the laws of the United States, and for other purposes," do hereby certify, that the amendment aforesaid has become valid, to all intents and purposes, as part of the Constitution of the United States.

" In testimony whereof, I have hereunto set my hand and caused the seal of the Department of State to be affixed.

" Done at the city of Washington, this 30th day of March, in the year of our Lord, 1870, and of the independence of the

[SEAL.]   United States, the ninety-fourth.
                                          " HAMILTON FISH."

The Emancipation Proclamation itself did not call forth such genuine and wide-spread rejoicing as the message of President Grant. The event was celebrated by the Colored people in all the larger cities North and South. Processions, orations, music and dancing proclaimed the unbounded joy of the new citizen. In Philadelphia Frederick Douglass, Bishop Jabez P. Campbell, I. C. Weass, and others delivered eloquent addresses to enthusiastic audiences. Mr. Douglass deeply wounded the religious feelings of his race by declaring : " I shall not dwell in any hackneyed cant by thanking God for this deliverance which has been wrought out through our common humanity." A hundred pulpits, a hundred trenchant pens sprang at the declaration with fiery indignation ; and it was some years before the bold orator was able to make himself tolerable to his people. There was little of the spirit of tolerance among the Colored people at the time, and upon such an occasion the remark was regarded as imprudent, to say the least.

A new era was opened up before the Colored people. They were now for the first time in possession of their full political rights. On the 25th of February, 1870, Hiram R. Revels took his seat as United States Senator from Mississippi. On the 9th of January, 1861, Mississippi passed her ordinance of secession, and Jefferson Davis resigned his seat as United States Senator. Within a brief decade a civil war had raged for four and a half years ; and after the seceding Mississippi had passed through the refining fires of battle and had been purged of slavery, she sent to succeed the arch traitor a *Negro*,[1] a representative of the race that Mr. Davis intended to be the corner-stone of his new government ! ![2] It was God's work, and marvellous in the eyes of the world. But this was not all. Just one year from the day and hour Senator Revels took his seat in the United States Senate, on the 24th of February, 1871, Jefferson F. Long, a *Negro*, was sworn in as a member of the House of Representatives from Georgia, the State of Alexander H. Stephens, the Vice-President of the Confederate States ! ! And then, as if to add glory to glory, the American Government despatched E. D. Bassett, a Colored man from Pennsylvania, as Minister Resident and Consul-General to Hayti ! And with almost the same stroke of his pen, President Grant sent J. Milton Turner, a Colored man from Missouri, as Resident Minister and Consul-General to Liberia ! Mr. Bassett came from Philadelphia where the Declaration of Independence was written and proclaimed, and where the noble Dr. Franklin had stood against the slavery compromises of the Constitution ! Philadelphia, then, the birthplace of American Independence, had the honor of furnishing the first

---

[1] Hiram R. Revels was the successor of Mr. Jefferson Davis. He was a Methodist preacher from Mississippi. It was our privilege to be present in the Senate when he was sworn in and took his seat.

[2] This idea had been put forth in a speech by Alexander H. Stephens just after he had been chosen Vice-President of the Confederate States.

Negro who was to illustrate the lofty sentiment of the equality of *all* men before the law. And the republic that Mr. Bassett went to had won diplomatic relations with all the civilized powers of the earth through the matchless valor and splendid statesmanship of Toussaint L'Ouverture. This was a black republic that had a history and a name among the peoples of the world.

Mr. Turner went from Missouri, the first State to violate the ordinance of 1787, and to establish slavery "northwest of the Ohio" River. He went to a republic on the West Coast of Africa that had been built by the industry, intelligence, and piety of Negroes who had flown from the accursed influences of American slavery. The slave-ships had disappeared from the coast, and commercial fleets from all lands came to trade with the citizens of a free republic whose ministers were welcomed in every court of Europe, and whose official acts were clothed with the authority and majesty of "*the Republic of Liberia !*"

In this same period Frederick Douglass was made a Presidential Elector for the State of New York; and thus helped cast the vote of that great commonwealth for U. S. Grant as President, in 1872. In the chief city of this State the first Federal Congress met, and on the first day of its first session spent the entire time in discussing the slavery question. Through the streets of this same city Mr. Douglass had to skulk and hide from slave-catchers on his way from the hell of slavery to the land of freedom. In this city, a few years later, he was hounded by a pro-slavery mob,—but at last he represented the popular will of its noblest citizens when they had chosen him to act for them in the Electoral College.

Born a slave, some time during the present century, on the eastern shore, Maryland, in the county of Talbot, and in the district of Tuckahoe, Frederick Douglass was destined by nature and God to be a giant in the great moral agitation for the extinction of slavery and the redemption of his race. He came of two extremes—representative Negro and representative Saxon. Tall, large-boned, colossal frame, compact head, broad, expressive face adorned with small brown, mischievous eyes, nose slightly Grecian, chin square set, and thin lips, Frederick Douglass would attract attention upon the streets of any city in Europe or America. His life as a slave was studded with painful experiences. Early separation from his mother, neglect, and then cruel treatment gave to the holy cause of freedom one of its ablest champions, and to slavery one of its most invincible opponents.

Transferred from Talbot County to Baltimore, Maryland, where he spent seven years, Mr. Douglass began to extend the horizon of his intellectual vision, and to come face to face with the hideous monster of slavery in the moments of reflection upon his condition in contrast with that of a fairer race about him. Inadvertently his mistress began to teach him characters of letters; but she was stopped by the advice of her husband, because it was thought inimical to the interest of the master to teach his slave. But having lighted the taper of knowledge in the mind of the slave boy, it was forever beyond human power to put it out. The incidents and surroundings of young Douglass peopled his brain with ideas, gave wings to his thoughts and order to his reasoning. The word of reproof, the angry look, and the precautions to prevent him from acquiring knowledge rankled in his young heart and covered his moral sky with thick clouds of despair. He reasoned himself right out of slavery, and ran away and went North.

David Ruggles, a Colored gentleman of intelligence, took charge of Mr. Douglass in New York, and sent him to New Bedford, Massachusetts. Having married in New York a free Colored woman from Baltimore named " Anna," he was ready now to enter upon the duties of the new life as a freeman. He found in one Nathan Johnson, an intelligent and industrious Colored man of New Bedford, a warm friend, who advanced him a sum of money to redeem baggage held for fare, and gave him the name which he has since rendered illustrious.

The intellectual growth of Mr. Douglass from this on was almost phenomenal. He devoured knowledge with avidity, and retained and utilized all he got. He used information as good business men use money. He made every idea bear interest; and now setting the music of his soul to the words he acquired, he soon earned a reputation as a gifted conversationalist and an impressive orator.

In the summer of 1841 an anti-slavery convention was held at Nantucket, Massachusetts, under the direction of William Lloyd Garrison. Mr. Douglass had attended several meetings in New Bedford, where he had listened to a defence of his race and a denunciation of its oppressors. And when he heard of the forthcoming convention at Nantucket he resolved to take a little respite from the hard work he was performing in a brass foundry, and attend. Previous to this he had felt the warm heart of Mr. Garrison beating for the slave through the columns of the " Liberator "; had received a copy each week for a long time, had mastered its matchless arguments against slavery, and was, therefore, possessed with an idea of the anti-slavery cause. At Nantucket he was sought out of the vast audience and requested by William C. Coffin, of New Bedford, where he had heard the fervid eloquence of the young man as an exhorter in the Colored Methodist Church, to make a speech. The hesitancy and diffidence of Mr. Douglàss were overcome by the importunate invitation to speak. He spoke: and from that hour a new sphere opened to him ; from that hour he began to exert an influence against slavery which for a generation was second only to that of Mr. Garrison. He was engaged as an agent of the Anti-Slavery Society led by Mr. Garrison. He was taken in charge by George Foster, and in his company made a lecturing tour of the eastern tier of counties in the old Bay State. The meetings were announced a few days ahead of the lecturer. He was advertised as a " fugitive slave," as " a chattel," as " a thing " that could talk and give an interesting account of the cruelties of slavery. As a narrator he had few equals among the most polished white gentlemen of all New England. His white friends were charmed by the lucidity and succinctness of his account of his life as a slave, and always insisted upon his narrative. But he was more than a narrator, more than a story-teller ; he was an orator, and in dealing with the problem of slavery proved himself to be a thinker. The old story of his bondage became stale to him. His friends' advice to keep on telling the same story could no longer be complied with ; and dashing out of the beaten path of narration he began a career as an orator that has had no parallel on this continent. He found no adequate satisfaction in relating the experiences of a slave ; his soul burned with a holy indignation against the institution of slavery. Having increased his vocabulary of words and his information concerning the purposes and plans of the Anti-Slavery Society, he was prepared to make an assault upon slavery. Instead of being the pupil of the anti-slavery friends who had furnished him a great opportunity, his close reasoning, blighting irony, merciless invective, and matchless eloquence made him the peer of any anti-slavery orator of his times. His appearance on the anti-slavery platform was sudden. He appeared as a new star of magnificent magnitude and surpassing beauty. All eyes were turned toward the "fugitive slave orator." His eloquence so astounded the people that few would believe he had ever felt the cruel touch of the lash. Moreover, he had withheld from the public, the State and place of his nativity and the circumstances of his escape. He had done this purposely for prudential reasons. In those days there was no protection that protected a fugitive slave against the slave-catcher assisted by the United States courts. To reveal his master's name and recount the exciting circumstances under which he had made his escape from bondage, Mr. Douglass felt was but to invite the slave-hounds to Massachusetts and endanger his liberty. But there were many good friends hard by who were ready to pay the market value of Mr. Douglass if a price were placed upon his flesh and blood. They urged him, therefore, to write out an account of his life as a slave,—to be specific ; and to boldly mention names of places and persons. In 1845 a pamphlet written by Mr. Douglass, embodying the experiences of a "fugitive slave," was published by the Anti-Slavery Society. It breathed a fiery zeal into the apathy of the North, and drew the fire of the Southern press and people. For safety his friends sent him abroad. During the voyage, in accepting an invitation to deliver a lecture on slavery, he gave offence to some pro-slavery men who desired very much to feed his body to the inhabitants of the deep. But a resolute captain and a few friends were able to reduce the wrath of the Southerners to a minimum. The occurrence on shipboard duly found its way into the public journals of London ; and the Southern gentlemen in an attempt to justify their conduct in a card drew upon themselves the wrath of the United Kingdom of Great Britain, and gave Mr. Douglass an advertisement such as he could never have secured otherwise.

Mr. Douglass spent nearly two years in Europe lecturing and writing in the cause of anti-slavery. He made a profound impression and helped the anti-slavery cause amazingly.

During his absence he wrote an occasional letter to the editor of the "Liberator," and the first is, for composition, vigorous English, symbols of thought, similes, and irony, superior to any letter he ever wrote before or since. It bore date of January 1, 1846.

" MY DEAR FRIEND GARRISON : Up to this time I have given no direct expression of the views, feelings, and opinions which I have formed, respecting the character and condition of the people of this land. I have refrained thus, purposely. I wish to speak advisedly, and in order to do this, I have waited till, I trust, experience has brought my opinions to an intelligent maturity. I have been thus careful, not because I think what I say will have much effect in shaping the opinions of the world, but because whatever of influence I may possess, whether little or much, I wish it to go in the right direction, and according to truth. I hardly need say that, in speaking of Ireland, I shall be influenced by no prejudices in favor of America. I think my circumstances all forbid that. I have no end to serve, no creed to uphold, no government to defend ; and as to nation, I belong to none. I have no protection at home, or resting-place abroad. The land of my birth welcomes me to her shores only as a slave, and spurns with contempt the idea of treating me differently ; so that I am an outcast from the society of my childhood, and an outlaw in the land of my birth. 'I am a stranger with thee, and a sojourner, as all my fathers were.' That men should be patriotic, is to me perfectly natural ; and as a philo- sophical fact, I am able to give it an *intellectual* recognition. But no further can I go. If ever I had any patriotism, or any capacity for the feeling, it was whipped out of me long since, by the lash of the American soul-drivers.

" In thinking of America, I sometimes find myself admiring her bright blue sky, her grand old woods, her fertile fields, her beautiful rivers, her mighty lakes, and star-crowned mountains. But my rapture is soon checked, my joy is soon turned to mourning. When I remember that all is cursed with the infernal spirit of slave-holding, robbery, and wrong ; when I remember that with the waters of her noblest rivers, the tears of my brethren are borne to the ocean, disregarded and forgotten, and that her most fertile fields drink daily of the warm blood of my outraged sisters, I am filled with unutterable loathing, and led to reproach myself that any thing could fall from my lips in praise of such a land. America will not allow her children to love her. She seems bent on compelling those who would be her warmest friends, to be her worst enemies. May God give her repentance, before it is too late, is the ardent prayer of my heart. I will continue to pray, labor, and wait, believing that she cannot always be insensible to the dictates of justice, or deaf to the voice of humanity.

" My opportunities for learning the character and condition of the people of this land have been very great. I have travelled almost from the Hill of Howth to the Giant's Causeway, and from the Giant's Cause- way to Cape Clear. During these travels, I have met with much in the character and condition of the people to approve, and much to condemn ; much that has thrilled me with pleasure, and very much that has filled me with pain. I will not, in this letter, attempt to give any description of those scenes which have given me pain. This I will do hereafter. I have enough, and more than your subscribers will be disposed to read at one time, of the bright side of the picture. I can truly say, I have spent some of the happiest moments of my life since landing in this country. I seem to have undergone a transformation. I live a new life. The warm and generous coöperation extended to me by the friends of my despised race ; the prompt and liberal manner with which the press has rendered me its aid ; the glorious enthusiasm with which thousands have flocked to hear the cruel wrongs of my down-trodden and long-enslaved fellow-countrymen portrayed ; the deep sympathy for the slave, and the strong abhorrence of the slave-holder, everywhere evinced ; the cordiality with which members and ministers of various religious bodies, and of various shades of religious opinion, have embraced me, and lent me their aid ; the kind hospitality constantly proffered me by persons of the highest rank in society ; the spirit of freedom that seems to animate all with whom I come in contact, and the entire absence of every thing that looked like prejudice against me, on account of the color of my skin—contrasted so strongly with my long and bitter experience in the United States, that I look with wonder and amazement on the transition. In the southern part of the United States, I was a slave, thought of and spoken of as property ; in the language of the LAW, '*held, taken, reputed, and adjudged to be a chattel in the hands of my owners and possessors, and their executors, administrators, and assigns, to all intents, constructions, and purposes whatsoever.*' (Brev. Digest, 224.) In the northern states, a fugitive slave, liable to be hunted at any moment like a felon, and to be hurled into the terrible jaws of slavery—doomed by an inveterate prejudice against color to insult and outrage on every hand, (Massachussetts out of the question)—denied the privileges and courtesies common to others in the use of the most humble means of conveyance—shut out from the cabins of steamboats—refused admission to respectable hotels—caricatured, scorned, scoffed, mocked, and maltreated with impunity by any one, (no matter how black his heart,) so he has a white skin. But now behold the change ! Eleven days and a half gone, and I have crossed three thousand miles of the perilous deep. Instead of a democratic government, I am under a monarchical government. Instead of the bright, blue sky of America, I am covered with the soft, grey fog of the Emerald Isle. I breathe, and lo ! the chattel becomes a man. I gaze around in vain for one who will question my equal humanity, claim me as his slave, or offer me an insult. I employ a cab—I am seated beside white people—I reach the hotel—I enter the same door—I am shown into the same parlor—I dine at the same table—and no one is offended.

No delicate nose grows deformed in my presence. I find no difficulty here in obtaining admission into any place of worship, instruction, or amusement, on equal terms with people as white as any I ever saw in the United States. I meet nothing to remind me of my complexion. I find myself regarded and treated at every turn with the kindness and deference paid to white people. When I go to church, I am met by no upturned nose and scornful lip to tell me, '*We don't allow niggers in here!*'

"I remember, about two years ago, there was in Boston, near the south-west corner of Boston Common, a menagerie. I had long desired to see such a collection as I understood was being exhibited there. Never having had an opportunity while a slave, I resolved to seize this, my first, since my escape. I went, and as I approached the entrance to gain admission, I was met and told by the door-keeper, in a harsh and contemptuous tone, '*We don't allow niggers in here!*' I also remember attending a revival meeting in the Rev. Henry Jackson's meeting-house, at New Bedford, and going up the broad aisle to find a seat, I was met by a good deacon, who told me, in a pious tone, '*We don't allow niggers in here!*' Soon after my arrival in New Bedford, from the South, I had a strong desire to attend the Lyceum, but was told, '*They don't allow niggers in here!*' While passing from New York to Boston, on the steamer 'Massachusetts,' on the night of the 9th of December, 1843, when chilled almost through with the cold, I went into the cabin to get a little warm. I was soon touched upon the shoulder, and told, '*We don't allow niggers in here!*' On arriving in Boston, from an anti-slavery tour, hungry and tired, I went into an eating-house, near my friend, Mr. Campbell's, to get some refreshments. I was met by a lad in a white apron, '*We don't allow niggers in here!*' A week or two before leaving the United States, I had a meeting appointed at Weymouth, the home of that glorious band of true abolitionists, the Weston family, and others. On attempting to take a seat in the omnibus to that place, I was told by the driver (and I never shall forget his fiendish hate), '*I don't allow niggers in here!*' Thank heaven for the respite I now enjoy! I had been in Dublin but a few days, when a gentleman of great respectability kindly offered to conduct me through all the public buildings of that beautiful city; and a little afterward, I found myself dining with the lord mayor of Dublin. What a pity there was not some American democratic christian at the door of his splendid mansion, to bark out at my approach, '*They don't allow niggers in here!*' The truth is, the people here know nothing of the republican negro hate prevalent in our glorious land. They measure and esteem men according to their moral and intellectual worth, and not according to the color of their skin. Whatever may be said of the aristocracies here, there is none based on the color of a man's skin.

This species of aristocracy belongs preëminently to 'the land of the free, and the home of the brave.' I have never found it abroad, in any but Americans. It sticks to them wherever they go. They find it almost as hard to get rid of, as to get rid of their skins.

"The second day after my arrival at Liverpool, in company with my friend, Buffum, and several other friends, I went to Eaton Hall, the residence of the Marquis of Westminster, one of the most splendid buildings in England. On approaching the door, I found several of our American passengers, who came out with us in the 'Cambria,' waiting for admission, as but one party was allowed in the house at a time. We all had to wait till the company within came out. And of all the faces, expressive of chagrin, those of the Americans were preëminent. They looked as sour as vinegar, and as bitter as gall, when they found I was to be admitted on equal terms with themselves. When the door was opened, I walked in, on an equal footing with my white fellow-citizens, and from all I could see, I had as much attention paid me by the servants that showed us through the house, as any with a paler skin. As I walked through the building, the statuary did not fall down, the pictures did not leap from their places, the doors did not refuse to open, and the servants did not say, '*We don't allow niggers in here.*'

"A happy new-year to you, and all the friends of freedom."

During the time of his visit in Europe a few friends, under the inspiration of one Mrs. Henry Richardson, raised money, purchased Mr. Douglass, and placed his freedom papers in his hands. The documents are of quaint historic value.

"The following is a copy of these curious papers, both of my transfer from Thomas to Hugh Auld, and from Hugh to myself :

"Know all men by these Presents, That I, Thomas Auld, of Talbot county, and state of Maryland, for and in consideration of the sum of one hundred dollars, current money, to me paid by Hugh Auld, of the city of Baltimore, in the said state, at and before the sealing and delivery of these presents, the receipt whereof, I, the said Thomas Auld, do hereby acknowledge, have granted, bargained, and sold, and by these presents do grant, bargain, and sell unto the said Hugh Auld, his executors, administrators, and assigns, ONE NEGRO MAN, by the name of FREDERICK BAILY, or DOUGLASS, as he calls himself—he is now about twenty-eight years of age—to have and to hold the said negro man for life. And I, the said Thomas Auld, for myself, my heirs, executors, and administrators, all and singular, the said FREDERICK BAILY, *alias* DOUGLASS, unto the said Hugh Auld, his executors, administrators, and assigns, against me, the said Thomas Auld, my executors, and administrators, and against all and every other person or persons whatsoever, shall and will warrant and forever defend by these presents. In witness whereof, I set my hand and seal, this thirteenth day of November, eighteen hundred and forty-six. THOMAS AULD.

" Signed, sealed, and delivered in presence of Wrightson Jones.
" JOHN C. LEAS."

" The authenticity of this bill of sale is attested by N. Harrington, a justice of the peace of the state of Maryland, and for the county of Talbot, dated same day as above.

" To all whom it may concern : Be it known, that I, Hugh Auld, of the city of Baltimore, in Baltimore county, in the state of Maryland, for divers good causes and considerations, me thereunto moving, have released from slavery, liberated, manumitted, and set free, and by these presents do hereby release from slavery, liberate, manumit, and set free, MY NEGRO MAN, named FREDERICK BAILY, otherwise called DOUGLASS, being of the age of twenty-eight years, or thereabouts, and able to work and gain a sufficient livelihood and maintenance ; and him the said negro man, named FREDERICK BAILY, otherwise called FREDERICK DOUGLASS, I do declare to be henceforth free, manumitted, and discharged from all manner of servitude to me, my executors, and administrators forever.

" In witness whereof, I, the said Hugh Auld, have hereunto set my hand and seal, the fifth of December, in the year one thousand eight hundred and forty-six. HUGH AULD.

" Sealed and delivered in presence of T. Hanson Belt.
" JAMES N. S. T. WRIGHT."

Mr. Douglass had returned to America, but the truths he proclaimed in England, Ireland, and Scotland echoed adown their mountains, and reverberated among their hills. The Church of Scotland and the press of England were distressed with the problem of slavery. The public conscience had been touched, and there was " no rest for the wicked." Mr. Douglass had received his name—Douglass—from Nathan Johnson, of New Bedford, Massachusetts, because he had just been reading about the virtuous Douglass in the works of Sir Walter Scott. How wonderful then, in the light of a few years, that a fugitive slave from America, bearing one of the most powerful names in Scotland should lean against the pillars of the *Free Church of Scotland*, and meet and vanquish its brightest and ablest teachers (the friends of slavery, unfortunately), Doctors Cunningham and Candlish !

It will be remembered that Mr. Garrison had built his school upon the fundamental idea that slavery was constitutional; and that in order to secure the overthrow of the institution he was compelled to do his work outside of the Constitution ; and to effect the good desired, the Union should be dissolved. With these views Mr. Douglass had coincided at first, and into the ranks of this party he had entered. But upon his return from England he changed his residence and views about the same time, and established his home and a newspaper in Rochester, New York State. Mr. Douglass gave his reasons for leaving the Garrisonian party as follows:

" About four years ago, upon a reconsideration of the whole subject, I became convinced that there was no necessity for dissolving the ' union between the northern and southern states ' ; that to seek this dissolution was no part of my duty as an abolitionist ; that to abstain from voting, was to refuse to exercise a legitimate and powerful means for abolishing slavery ; and that the constitution of the United States not only contained no guarantees in favor of slavery, but, on the contrary, it is, in its letter and spirit, an anti-slavery instrument, demanding the abolition of slavery as a condition of its own existence, as the supreme law of the land." [1]

It was charged by some persons that for financial reasons Mr. Douglass changed his views and residence ; that the Garrisonians were poor; but that Gerrit Smith was rich; and that he assisted Mr. Douglass in establishing the " North Star," a weekly paper. But Mr. Douglass was a man of boldness of thought and independence of character; and whatever the motives were which led him away from his early friends he at least deserved credit for possessing the courage necessary to such a change. But Mr. Douglass was not the only anti-slavery man who imagined that the Constitution was an anti-slavery instrument. This was the error of Charles Sumner. Slavery was as legal as the right of the Government to coin money. As has been shown already, it was recognized and protected by law when the British sceptre ruled the colonies ; it was recognized by all the courts during the Confederacy ; it was acknowledged as a legal fact by the Treaty of Paris of 1782, and of Ghent in 1814; the gentlemen who framed the Constitution fixed the basis of representation in Congress upon three fifths of the slaves ; and gave the owners of

---

[1] My Bondage and My Freedom, p. 396.

slaves a fugitive slave law, at the birth of the nation, by which to hunt their slaves in all the States and Territories of North America. But Mr. Douglass lived long enough to see that he was wrong and Mr. Garrison right ; that the dissolution of the Union was the only way to free his race. In his way he did his part as faithfully and as honestly as any of his brethren in either one of the anti-slavery parties.

Having established a reputation as an orator in England and America ; and having lifted over the tangled path of his fugitive brethren the unerring, friendly " North Star," he now turned his attention to debating. It was a matter of regret that two such powerful and accomplished orators as Frederick Douglass and Samuel Ringgold Ward should have taken up so much precious time in splitting hairs on the constitutionality or unconstitutionality of slavery. Perhaps it did good. It certainly did the men good. It was an education to them, and exciting to their audiences. Mr. Douglass's forte was in oratory ; in exposing the hideousness of slavery and the wrongs of his race. Mr. Ward— a *protégé* of Gerrit Smith's—was scholarly, thoughtful, logical, and eloquent. Mr. Douglass was generally worsted in debate, but always triumphant in oratory. A careful study of Mr. Douglass's speeches from the time he began his career as a public speaker down to the present time reveals wonderful progress in their grammatical and synthetical structure. He grew all the time. On the 12th of May, 1846, he delivered a speech at Finsbury Chapel, Moorfields, England, from which the following is extracted :

' All the slaveholder asks of me is silence. He does not ask me to go abroad and preach *in favor* of slavery ; he does not ask any one to do that. He would not say that slavery is a good thing, but the best under the circumstances. The slaveholders want total darkness on the subject. They want the hatchway shut down, that the monster may crawl in his den of darkness, crushing human hopes and happiness, destroying the bondman at will, and having no one to reprove or rebuke him. Slavery shrinks from the light ; it hateth the light, neither cometh to the light, lest its deeds should be reproved. To tear off the mask from this abominable system, to expose it to the light of heaven, aye, to the heat of the sun, that it may burn and wither it out of existence, is my object in coming to this country. I want the slaveholder surrounded, as by a wall of anti-slavery fire, so that he may see the condemnation of himself and his system glaring down in letters of light. I want him to feel that he has no sympathy in England, Scotland, or Ireland ; that he has none in Canada, none in Mexico, none among the poor wild Indians ; that the voice of the civilized, aye, and savage world is against him. I would have condemnation blaze down upon him in every direction, till, stunned and overwhelmed with shame and confusion, he is compelled to let go the grasp he holds upon the persons of his victims, and restore them to their long-lost rights."

This was in 1846. On the 5th of July, 1852, at Rochester, New York, he, perhaps, made the most effective speech of his life. The poet Sheridan has written : " Eloquence consists in the man, the subject, and the occasion." . None of these conditions were wanting. There was the man, the incomparable Douglass ; the wrongs of slavery was his subject ; and the occasion was the 4th of July.

" FELLOW-CITIZENS :—Pardon me, and allow me to ask, why am I called upon to speak here to-day ? What have I, or those I represent, to do with your national independence ? Are the great principles of political freedom and of natural justice embodied in that Declaration of Independence, extended to us ? and am I, therefore, called upon to bring our humble offering to the national altar, and to confess the benefits, and express devout gratitude for the blessings resulting from your independence to us ?

" Would to God, both for your sakes and ours, that an affirmative answer could be truthfully returned to these questions ! Then would my task be light, and my burden easy and delightful. For who is there so cold, that a nation's sympathy could not warm him ? Who so obdurate and dead to the claims of gratitude, that would not thankfully acknowledge such priceless benefits ? Who so stolid and selfish, that would not give his voice to swell the hallelujahs of a nation's jubilee, when the chains of servitude had been torn from his limbs ? I am not that man. In a case like that, the dumb might eloquently speak, and the ' lame man leap as an hart.'

" But, such is not the state of the case. I say it with a sad sense of the disparity between us. I am not included within the pale of this glorious anniversary ! Your high independence only reveals the immeasurable distance between us. The blessings in which you this day rejoice, are not enjoyed in common. The rich inheritance of justice, liberty, prosperity, and independence, bequeathed by your fathers, is shared by you, not by me. The sunlight that brought life and healing to you, has brought stripes and death to me. This Fourth of July is *yours*, not *mine*. *You* may rejoice, *I* must mourn. To drag a man in fetters into the grand illuminated temple of liberty, and call upon him to join you in joyous anthems, were inhuman mockery and sacrilegious irony. Do you mean, citizens, to mock me, by asking me to speak to-day ? If so, there is a parallel to your conduct. And let me warn you that it is dangerous to copy the example of a nation whose crimes, towering up to heaven, were thrown down by the breath of the Almighty, burying that nation in irrecoverable ruin ! I can to-day take up the plaintive lament of a peeled and woe-smitten people.

" ' By the rivers of Babylon, there we sat down, yea, we wept, when we remembered Zion. We hanged our harps upon the willows in the midst thereof. For there they that carried us away captive required of us a song ; and they that wasted us required of us mirth, saying, Sing us one of the songs of Zion. How shall we sing the Lord's song in a strange land ? If I forget thee, O Jerusalem, let my right hand forget her cunning. If I do not remember thee, let my tongue cleave to the roof of my mouth.'

" Fellow-citizens, above your national, tumultuous joy, I hear the mournful wail of millions, whose chains, heavy and grievous yesterday, are to-day rendered more intolerable by the jubilant shouts that reach them. If I do forget, if I do not faithfully remember those bleeding children of sorrow this day, ' may my right hand forget her cunning, and may my tongue cleave to the roof of my mouth ! ' To forget them, to pass lightly over their wrongs, and to chime in with the popular theme, would be treason most scandalous and shocking, and would make me a reproach before God and the world. My subject, then, fellow-citizens, is AMERICAN SLAVERY. I shall see this day and its popular characteristics from the slave's point of view. Standing there, identified with the American bondman, making his wrongs mine, I do not hesitate to declare, with all my soul, that the character and conduct of this nation never looked blacker to me than on this Fourth of July. Whether we turn to the declarations of the past, or to the professions of the present, the conduct of the nation seems equally hideous and revolting. America is false to the past, false to the present, and solemnly binds herself to be false to the future. Standing with God and the crushed and bleeding slave on this occasion, I will, in the name of humanity which is outraged, in the name of liberty which is fettered, in the name of the Constitution and the Bible, which are disregarded and trampled upon, dare to call in question and to denounce, with all the emphasis I can command, every thing that serves to perpetuate slavery—the great sin and shame of America ! ' I will not equivocate ; I will not excuse ' ; I will use the severest language I can command ; and yet not one word shall escape me that any man, whose judgment is not blinded by prejudice, or who is not at heart a slaveholder, shall not confess to be right and just."

His speech in England was labored, heavy, and some portions of it ambitious. But here are measured sentences, graceful transitions, truth made forcible, and the oratory refined. Thus he went on from good to better, until the managers of leading lecture-courses of the land felt that the season would not be a success without Frederick Douglass. He began to venture into deeper water ; to expound problems not exactly in line with the only theme that he was complete master of. His attempts at wit usually missed fire. He could not be funny. He was in earnest from the first moment the light broke into his mind in Baltimore. He was rarely eloquent except when denouncing slavery. He was not at his best in abstract thought : too much logic dampened his enthusiasm ; and an attempt at elaborate preparation weakened his discourse. He was majestic when speaking of the insults he had received or the wrongs his race were suffering. Martin Luther said during the religious struggle in Germany for freedom of thought : "Sorrow has pressed many sweet songs out of me." It was the sorrows of the child-heart of Douglass the chattel, and the sorrows of the great man-heart of Douglass the human being, that gave the world such remarkable eloquence. There were but two chords in his soul that could yield a rich sound, viz.: sorrow and indignation. Sorrow for the helpless slave, and indignation against the heartless master, made him grand, majestic, and eloquent beyond comparison.

Although he was going constantly he saved his means, and raised a family of two girls—one dying in her teens, an affliction he took deeply to heart—and three boys. When the war was on at high tide, and Colored soldiers required, he gave all he had, three stalwart boys, while he made it very uncomfortable for the Copperheads at home. At the close of the war he moved to Washington and became deeply interested in the practical work of reconstruction. He was appointed one of the Commissioners to visit San Domingo, when General Grant recommended its annexation to the United States ; was a trustee of Howard University and of the Freedman's Savings Bank and Trust Company. Unfortunately he accepted the presidency of the latter institution after nearly all the thieves had got through with it, and was its official head when the crash and ruin came.

Mr. Douglass's home [1] life has been pure and elevated. He

---

[1] While this history is passing through the press, the sad intelligence comes of the death, after a painful illness, of his beloved wife. All through her life she was justly proud of her husband and children ; and she leaves a precious memory.

has done well by his boys; and has aided many young men to places of usefulness and profit. He strangely and violently opposed the exodus of his race from the South, and thereby incurred the opposition of the Northern press and the anathemas of the Colored people. It was not just the thing, men said—white and black,—for a man who had been a slave in the South, and had come North to find a market for his labor, to oppose his brethren in their flight from economic slavery and the shot-gun policy of the South. His efforts to state and justify his position before the Colored people of New York were received with an impatient air and tolerated even for the time with ill grace. Before the Social Science Congress at Saratoga, New York, he met Richard T. Greener, a young Colored man, in a discussion of this subject. But Mr. Greener, a son of Harvard College, with a keen and merciless logic, cut right through the sophistries of Mr. Douglass; and although the latter gentleman threw bouquets at the audience, and indulged in the most exquisite word-painting, he was compelled to leave the field a vanquished disputant.

President Hayes appointed Mr. Douglass United States Marshall for the District of Columbia, an office which he held until President Garfield made him Recorder of Deeds for the same district. He has accumulated a comfortable little fortune, has published three books, edited two newspapers, passed through a checkered and busy life; and to-day, full of honors and years, he stands confessedly as the first man of his race in North America. Not that he is the greatest in every sense; but considering "the depths from whence he came," the work he has accomplished, the character untarnished, — his memory and character, like the granite shaft, will have an enduring and undying place in the gratitude of humanity throughout the world.

Among the representative young men of color in the United States—and now, happily in the process of time, their name is legion—Richard Theodore Greener has undisputed standing. He was born in Pennsylvania in 1844, but spent most of his life in Massachusetts. His father and grandfather were men of unusual intelligence, social energy, and public spirit. Richard T. early manifested an eagerness to learn and a capacity to retain and utilize. He enjoyed better surroundings in childhood than the average Colored child a generation ago; and always accustomed to hear the English correctly spoken, he had in himself all the required conditions to acquire a thorough education. Having obtained a start in the common schools, he turned to Oberlin College, Lorain County, Ohio, — at that time an institution toward which the Colored people of the country were very partial, and whose anti-slavery professors they loved with wonderful tenderness. For some of these professors, in the *Oberlin-Wellington Rescue Case*, had preferred imprisonment in preference to obedience to the unholy fugitive-slave law. The years of 1862–3 were spent at Oberlin, and Mr. Greener showed himself an excellent student. His ambition was to excel in every thing. Not exactly satisfied with the course of studies at Oberlin, he went to Phillips Academy, Andover, Massachusetts. This institution was a feeder for Harvard, and using uniform text-books he was placed in line and harmony with the course of studies to be pursued at Cambridge. He entered Harvard College in the autumn of 1865, and graduated with high honors in 1870.[1] He was the first of his race to enter this famous university, and while there did himself credit, and honored the race from which he sprang. All his performances were creditable. He won a second prize for reading aloud in his freshman year; in his sophomore year he won the first prize for the Boylston Declamation, notwithstanding members of the junior and senior classes contested. During his junior year he did not contest, preferring to tutor two of the competitors who were successful. In his senior year he won the two highest prizes, viz: the First Bowdoin for a Dissertation on " The Tenures of Land in Ireland," and the " Boylston Prize for Oratory."

The entrance, achievements, and graduation of Mr. Greener received the thoughtful and grateful attention of the press of Europe and America; while what he did was a stimulating example to the young men of his race in the United States.

At the time of his graduation there was a great demand for and a wide-spread need of educated Colored men as teachers. The Institute for Colored Youth, in Philadelphia, had been but recently deprived of its principal, Prof. E. D. Bassett, who had been sent as Resident Minister and Consul-General to the Re-

---

[1] Mr. Greener was turned back one year upon the ground of alleged imperfection in mathematics ; but it was done in support of an old theory, long since exploded, that the Negro has no capacity for the solution of mathematical problems. We know this to be the case. But the charming nature and natural pluck of young Greener brought him out at last without a blemish in any of his studies.

public of Hayti. Mr. Greener was called to take the chair vacated by Mr. Bassett. He was principal of this institution from Sept., 1870, to Dec., 1872. From Philadelphia he was called to fill a similar position in Sumner High School, at Washington, D. C. He did not remain long in Washington. His fame as an educator had grown until he was celebrated as a teacher throughout the country. He was offered and accepted the Chair of Metaphysics and Logic in the University of South Carolina, situate at Columbia. He remained here until 1877, when the Hampton Government found no virtue in a Negro as a teacher in an institution of the fame and standing of this university. In 1877 he was made Dean of the Law Department of Howard University, Washington, D. C., and held the position until 1880. He graduated from the Law School of the University of South Carolina, and has practised in Washington since his residence there. In addition to his work as teacher, lawyer, and orator, Prof. Greener was associate editor of the *New National Era* at Washington, D. C., and his editorial *Young Men to the Front*, gave him a reputation as a progressive and aggressive leader which he has sustained ever since with marked ability.

As a political speaker he began while in college, in 1868, and has continued down to the present time. He is a pleasant speaker, and acceptable and efficient in a campaign. As an orator and writer he excels. His early style was burdened, like that of the late Charles Sumner, with a too-abundant classical illustration and quotation ; but during the last five years his illustrations are drawn largely from the English classics and history. His ablest effort at oratory was his oration on *Charles Sumner, the Idealist, Statesman, and Scholar*. It was by all odds the finest effort of its kind delivered in this country. It was eminently fitting that a representative of the race toward whose elevation Mr. Sumner contributed his splendid talents, and a graduate from the same College that honored Sumner, and from the State that gave him birth and opportunity, should give the true analysis of his noble life and spotless character.

In the " National Quarterly Review " for July, 1880, Prof. Greener replied to an article from the pen of Mr. James Parton on *Antipathy to the Negro*, published in the " North American Review." Prof. Greener's theme was *The Intellectual Position of the Negro*. The following paragraphs give a fair idea of the style of Mr. Greener :

"The writer himself appears not to feel such an antipathy to us that it must need find expression ; for his liberality is well known to those who have read his writings for the past fifteen years. Nor is there any apparent ground for its appearance because of any new or startling exhibitions of *antipathia* against us noticeable at the present time. No argument was needed to prove that there has been an unreasonable and unreasoning prejudice against negroes as a class, a long-existing antipathy, seemingly ineradicable, sometimes dying out it would appear, and then bursting forth afresh from no apparent cause. If Mr. Parton means to assert that such prejudice is ineradicable, or is increasing, or is even rapidly passing away, then is his venture insufficient, because it fails to support either of these views. It does not even attempt to show that the supposed antipathy is general, for the author expressly, and, we think, very properly, relegates its exercise to those whom he calls the most ignorant—the 'meanest' of mankind.

"If his intention was to attack a senseless antipathy, hold it up to ridicule, show its absurdity, analyze its constituent parts, and suggest some easy and safe way for Americans to rid themselves of unchristian and un-American prejudices, then has he again conspicuously failed to carry out such purpose. He asserts the existence of antipathies, but only by inference does he discourage their maintenance, although on other topics he is rather outspoken whenever he cares to express his own convictions.

"On this question Mr. Parton is, to say the least, vacillating, because he fails to exhibit any platform upon which we may combat those who support early prejudices and justify their continuance from the mere fact of their existence. We never expect Mr. Gayarré and Mr. Henry Watterson to look calmly and dispassionately at these questions from the negro's point of view. The one gives us the old argument of De Bow's *Review*, and the other deals out the *ex parte* views of the present leaders of the South. The one line of argument has been answered over and over again by the old anti-slavery leaders ; the pungent generalizations of the latter, the present generation of negroes can answer whenever the opportunity is afforded them.

"But Mr. Parton was born in a cooler and calmer atmosphere, where men are accustomed to give a reason for the faith that is in them, and hence it is necessary, in opening any discussion such as he had provoked, that he should assign some ground of opposition or support— Christian, Pagan, utilitarian, constitutional, optimist, or pessimist.

"The very apparent friendliness of his intentions makes even a legitimate conclusion from him seem mere conjecture, likely to be successfully controverted by any subtle thinker and opponent. No definite conclusion is, indeed, reached with regard to the first query (Jefferson's fourteenth) with which Mr. Parton opens his article : Whether the white and black races can live together on this continent as equals. He lets us see at the close, incidentally only, what his opinion is, and it inclines to the negative. But throughout the article he is in the anomalous and dubious position of one who opens a discussion which he cannot end, and the logical result of whose own opinion he dares not boldly state. The illustrations of the early opinions of Madison and Jefferson only show how permanent a factor the negro is in American history and polity, and how utterly futile are all attempts at his expatriation. Following Mr. Parton's advice, the negro has always prudently abstained from putting 'himself against inexorable facts.' He is careful, however, to make sure of two things,—that the alleged facts are verities and that they are inexorable. Prejudice we acknowledge as a fact; but we know that it is neither an ineradicable nor an inexorable one. We find fault with Mr. Parton because he starts a trail on antipathy, evidently purposeless, and fails to track it down either systematically or persistently, but branches off, *desipere in loco*, to talk loosely of 'physical antipathy,' meaning what we usually term natural antipathy; and at last, emerging from the 'brush,' where he has been hopelessly beating about from Pliny to Mrs. Kemble, he gains a partial 'open' once more by asserting a truism—that it is the 'ignorance of a despised class' (the lack of knowledge we have of them) which nourishes these 'insensate antipathies.' Here we are at one with Mr. Parton. Those who know us most intimately, who have associated with us in the nursery, at school, in college, in trade, in the tenderer and confidential relations of life, in health, in sickness, and in death, as trusted guides, as brave soldiers, as magnanimous enemies, as educated and respected men and women, give up all senseless antipathies, and feel ashamed to confess they ever cherished any prejudice against a race whose record is as unsullied as that of any in the land."

The following passages from a most brilliant speech at the Dinner of the Harvard Club of New York, exhibit a pure, perspicuous, and charming style:

"What Sir John Coleridge in his 'Life of Keble' says of the traditions and influences of Oxford, each son of Harvard must feel is true also of Cambridge. The traditions, the patriotic record, and the scholarly attainments of her alumni are the pride of the College. Her contribution to letters, to statesmanship, and to active business life, will keep her memory perennially green. Not one of the humblest of her children, who has felt the touch of her pure spirit, or enjoyed the benefits of her culture, can fail to remember what she expects of her sons wherever they may be: to stand fast for good government, to maintain the right, to uphold honesty and character, to be, if nothing else, good citizens, and to perform, to the extent of their ability, every duty assumed or imposed upon them,—democratic in their aristocracy, catholic in their liberality, impartial in judgment, and uncompromising in their convictions of duty. [Cheers and applause.]

"Harvard's impartiality was not demonstrated solely by my admission to the College. In 1770, when Crispus Attucks died a patriot martyr on State Street, she answered the rising spirit of independence and liberty by abolishing all distinctions founded upon color, blood, and rank. Since that day, there has been but one test for all. Ability, character, and merit,—these are the sole passports to her favor. [Applause.]

"When, in my adopted State, I stood on the battered ramparts of Wagner, and recalled the fair-haired son of Harvard who died there with his brave black troops of Massachusetts,—

> " ' him who, deadly hurt, agen
> Flashed on afore the charge's thunder,
> Tippin' with fire the bolt of men,
> Thet rived the Rebel line asunder,'—

I thanked God, with patriotic pleasure, that the first contingent of negro troops from the North should have been led to death and fame by an alumnus of Harvard ; and I remembered, with additional pride of race and college, that the first regiment of black troops raised on South Carolina soil were taught to drill, to fight, to plough, and to read by a brave, eloquent, and scholarly descendant of the Puritans and of Harvard, Thomas Wentworth Higginson. [Great applause and cheers.]

"Is it strange, then, brothers, that I there resolved for myself to maintain the standard of the College, so far as I was able, in public and in private life ? I am honored by the invitation to be present here tonight. Around me I see faces I have not looked upon for a decade. Many are the intimacies of the College, the society, the buskin, and the oar which they bring up, from classmates and college friends. I miss, as all Harvard men must miss to-night, the venerable and kindly figure of Andrew Preston Peabody, the student's friend, the consoler of the plucked, the encourager of the strong, Mæcenas's benign almoner, the felicitous exponent of Harvard's Congregational Unitarianism. I miss, too, another of high scholarship, of rare poetic taste, of broad liberality —my personal friend, Elbridge Jefferson Cutler, loved alike by students and his fellow-members of the Faculty for his conscientious performance of duty and his genial nature.

"Mr. President and brothers, my time is up. I give you 'Fair Harvard,' the exemplar, the prototype of that ideal America, of which the greatest American poet has written,—

" ' Thou, taught by Fate to know Jehovah's plan,
Thet man's devices can't unmake a man,
An' whose free latch-string never was drawed in
Against the poorest child of Adam's kin.'

"[Great applause.]"

Prof. Greener rendered legal services in the case of Cadet Whittaker at West Point, and in the trial at New York City, where, as associate counsel with ex-Gov. Chamberlain,—an able lawyer and a magnificent orator,—he developed ability and industry as an attorney, and earned the gratitude of his race.

Prof. Greener entered Harvard as a member of the Baptist Church ; but the transcendentalism and rationalism of the place quite swept him from his spiritual moorings. In a recent address before a literary society in Washington, D. C., he is represented to have maintained that Mohammedanism was better for the indigenous races of Africa than Christianity, Dr. John William Draper made a similar mistake in his " *Conflict between Religion and Science !* " The learned doctor should have written " Conflict between the Church and Science." Religion is not and never was at war with science. Prof. Greener should have written, " Mohammedanism better for the Africans than Snake Worship." This brilliant young man cannot afford to attempt to exalt Mohammedanism above the cross of our dear Redeemer, and expect to have leadership in the Negro race in America. Nor can he support the detestable ideas and execrable philosophy of Senator John P. Jones, which seek to shut out the Chinaman from free America. The Negro must stand by the weak in a fight like this, remembering the pit from which he was dug. But Prof. Greener is young as well as talented ; and seeing his mistake, will place himself in harmony with not only the rights of his race, but those of humanity everywhere.

Blanche K. Bruce was born a slave on a plantation in Prince Edward County, Virginia, March 1, 1841, and in the very month and week of the anniversary of his birth he was sworn in as United States Senator from Mississippi. Reared a slave there was nothing in his early life of an unusual nature. He secured his freedom at the end of the war, and immediately sought the opportunities and privileges that would, if properly used, fit him for his new life as a man and a citizen. He went to Oberlin College where, in the Preparatory Department, he applied himself to his studies, attached himself to his classmates by charming personal manners, and gentlemanly deportment. He realized that there were many splendid opportunities awaiting young men of color at the South; and that profitable positions were going begging.

Mr. Bruce made his appearance in Mississippi at an opportune moment. The State was just undergoing a process of reconstruction. He appeared at the capital, Jackson, with seventy-five cents in his pocket; was a stranger to every person in the city. He mingled in the great throng, joined in the discussions that took place by little knots of politicians, made every man his friend to whom he talked, and when the State Senate was organized secured the position of Sergeant-at-arms. He attracted the attention of Gov. Alcorn, who appointed him a member of his staff with the rank of colonel. Col. Bruce was not merely Sergeant-at-arms of the Senate, but was a power behind that body. His intelligence, his knowledge of the character of the legislation needed for the people of Mississippi, and the excellent impression he made upon the members, gave him great power in suggesting and influencing legislation.

The sheriffs of Mississippi were not elected in those days; and the Governor had to look a good ways to find the proper men for such positions. His faith in Col. Bruce as a man and an officer led him to select him to be sheriff of Bolivar County. Col. Bruce discharged the delicate duties of his office with eminent ability, and attained a popularity very remarkable under the circumstances.

During this time, while other politicians were dropping their money at the gaming-table and in the wine cup, Col. Bruce was saving his funds, and after purchasing a splendid farm at Floraville, on the Mississippi River, he made cautious and profitable investments in property and bonds. His executive ability was marvellous, and his successful management of his own business and that of the people of the county made him friends among all classes and in both political parties. He was appointed tax-collector for his county, a position that was calculated to tax the most accomplished financier and business man in the State. But Col. Bruce took to the position rare abilities, and managed his office with such matchless skill, that when the term of Henry R. Pease expired, he was chosen United States Senator from Mississippi on the third of February, 1875, for the constitutional term of six years. He took his seat on the 4th of March, 1875.

He did nothing in the line of oratory while in the Senate. That was not his forte. He was an excellent worker, a faithful committee-man, and finally was chairman of the Committee on the Freedman's Savings Bank, etc. Mr. Bruce was chairman of the Committee on Mississippi Levees, where he performed good work. He presided over the Senate with dignity several times. To the charge that he was a "silent Senator," it may be observed that it was infinitely better that he remained silent, than in breaking the silence to exhibit a mental feebleness in attempting to handle problems to which most of the Senators had given years of patient study. His conduct was admirable; his discretion wise; his service faithful, and his influence upon the honorable Senate and the country at large beneficial to himself and helpful to his race.

In the convention of the Republican party at Chicago, in 1880, he was a candidate for Vice-President. In the spring of 1881, after the close of his senatorial career the President nominated him to be Register of the United States Treasury, and the nomination was confirmed without reference, after a complimentary speech from his associate, Senator L. Q. C. Lamar. He has appeared as a political speaker on several occasions. As nature did not intend him for this work, his efforts appear to be the products of hard labor, but nevertheless excellent; his estimable and scholarly wife (*née* Miss Wilson, of Cleveland, Ohio) has been a great blessing to him;—a good wife and a helpful companion. From a penniless slave he has risen to the position of writing his name upon the currency of the country. Register Bruce is a genial gentleman, a fast friend, and an able officer.

John Mercer Langston was born a slave in Virginia; is a graduate of Oberlin College and Theological Institution, and as a lawyer, college president, foreign minister, and politician, has exerted a wide influence for the good of his race. As Secretary of the Board of Health for the District of Columbia, and as President of the Howard University, he displayed remarkable executive ability and sound business judgment. He is one of the bravest of the brave in public matters, and his influence upon young Colored men has been wide-spread and admirable. He is now serving as Resident Minister and Consul-General to Hayti; and ranks among the best diplomats of our Government.

In Massachusetts, Charles L. Mitchell, George L. Ruffin, John J. Smith, J. B. Smith, and Wm. J. Walker have been members of the Legislature. In Illinois, a Colored man has held a position in the Board of Commissioners for Cook County—Chicago ; and one has been sent to the Legislature. In Ohio, two Colored men have been members of the Legislature, one from Cincinnati and the other from Cleveland. Gov. Charles Foster was the first Executive in any of the Northern States to appoint a Colored man to a responsible position ; and in this, as in nearly every other thing, Ohio has taken the lead. The present member (John P. Green) of the Legislature of Ohio representing Cuyahoga County, is a young man of excellent abilities both as a lawyer and as an orator. John P. Green was born at New Berne, North Carolina, April 2, 1845, of free parents. His father died in 1850, and his widow was left to small resources in raising her family. But being an excellent seamstress she did very well for her five-year-old son, while she had an infant in her arms.

In 1857 Mrs. Green moved to Ohio and located at Cleveland. Her son John was now able and willing to assist his mother some ; and so as an errand-boy he hired himself out for $4 per month. He obtained about a year and one half of instruction in the common schools, and did well. In 1862 he became a waiter in a hotel, and spent every leisure moment in study. He succeeded in learning something of Latin and Algebra, without a teacher.

Mr. Green had acquired an excellent style of composition, and to secure funds with which to complete his education, he wrote and published a pamphlet containing *Essays on Miscellaneous Subjects*, by a self-educated Colored youth. He sold about 1,500 copies in Ohio, Pennsylvania, and New York, and then entered the Cleveland Central High School. He completed a four years' classical course in two years, two terms, and two months. He graduated at the head of a class of twenty-three. He entered the law office of Judge Jesse P. Bishop, and in 1870 graduated from the Cleveland Law School. He turned his face Southward, and having settled in South Carolina, began the practice of law, which was attended with great success. But the climate was not agreeable to his health, and in 1872 he returned to the scenes of his early toils and struggles. He became a practising attorney in Cleveland, and in the spring of 1873 was elected a justice of the peace for Cuyahoga County by a majority of 3,000 votes. He served three terms as a justice, and in eight years of service as such decided more than 12,000 cases. As a justice he has had no equal for many years. In 1877 he was nominated for the Legislature, but was defeated by sixty-two votes. In 1881 he was again before the people for the Legislature, and was elected by a handsome majority.

Mr. Green is rather a remarkable young man; and with good health and a fair field he is bound to make a success. He will bear comparison with any of his associates in the Legislature; and, as a clear, impressive speaker, has few equals in that body.

There are yet at least one hundred representative men of color worthy of the places they hold in the respect and confidence of their race and the country. Their number is rapidly increasing; and ere many years there will be no lack of representative Colored men.[1]

Colored women had fewer privileges of education before the war, and indeed since the war, than the men of their race, yet, nevertheless, many of these women have shown themselves capable and useful.

FRANCES ELLEN HARPER

was born in Baltimore, Maryland, in 1825. She was not permitted to enjoy the blessings of early educational training, but in after-years proved herself to be a woman of most remarkable intellectual powers. She applied herself to study, most assiduously; and when she had reached woman's estate was well educated.

She developed early a fondness for poetry, which she has since cultivated; and some of her efforts are not without merit. She excels as an essayist and lecturer. She has been heard upon many of the leading lecture platforms of the country; and her efforts to elevate her sisters have been crowned with most signal success.

MARY ANN SHADD CAREY,

of Delaware, but more recently of Washington, D. C., as a lecturer, writer, and school teacher, has done and is doing a great deal for the educational and social advancement of the Colored people.

FANNY M. JACKSON—

at present Mrs. Fanny M. Jackson Coppin—was born in the District of Columbia, in 1837. Though left an orphan when

---

[1] Biography is quite a different thing from history; and the Colored men who may imagine themselves neglected ought to remember that this is a *History of the Negro Race.* We have mentioned these men as representative of several classes.

quite a child, Mrs. Sarah Clark, her aunt, took charge of her, and gave her a first-class education. She prosecuted the gentlemen's course in Oberlin College, and graduated with high honors.

Deeply impressed with the need of educated teachers for the schools of her race, she accepted a position at once in the Institute for Colored Youth, at Philadelphia, Pa. And here for many years she has taught with eminent success, and exerted a pure and womanly influence upon all the students that have come into her classes.

Without doubt she is the most thoroughly competent and successful of the Colored women teachers of her time. And her example of race pride, industry, enthusiasm, and nobility of character will remain the inheritance and inspiration of the pupils of the school she helped make the pride of the Colored people of Pennsylvania.

LOUISE DE MORTIE,

of Norfolk, Virginia, was born of free parents in that place, in 1833, but being denied the privileges of education, turned her face toward Massachusetts.

In 1853 she took up her residence in Boston. She immediately began to avail herself of all the opportunities of education. A most beautiful girl, possessed of a sweet disposition and a remarkable memory, she won a host of friends, and took high standing as a pupil.

In 1862 she began a most remarkable career as a public reader. An elocutionist by nature, she added the refinement of the art; and with her handsome presence, engaging manners, and richly-toned voice, she took high rank in her profession. Just as she was attracting public attention by her genius, she learned of the destitution that was wasting the Colored orphans of New Orleans. Thither she hastened in the spirit of Christian love; and there she labored with an intelligence and zeal which made her a heroine among her people. In 1867 she raised sufficient funds to build an asylum for the Colored orphans of New Orleans. But just then the yellow fever overtook her in her work of mercy, and she fell a victim to its deadly touch on the 10th of October, 1867, saying so touchingly, " I belong to God, our Father," as she expired.

Although cut off in the morning of a useful life, she is of blessed memory among those for whose improvement and elevation she gave the strength of a brilliant mind and the warmth of a genuine Christian heart.

MISS CHARLOTTE L. FORTUNE—

now the wife of the young and gifted clergyman, Rev. Frank J. Grimke,—is a native of Pennsylvania. She comes of one of the best Colored families of the State. She went to Salem, Massachusetts, in 1854, where she began a course of studies in the " Higginson High School." She proved to be a student of more than usual application, and although a member of a class of white youths, Miss Fortune was awarded the honor of writing the Parting Hymn for the class. It was sung at the last examination, and was warmly praised by all who heard it.

Miss Fortune became a contributor to the columns of the "Anti-Slavery Standard" and "Atlantic Monthly." She wrote both prose and poetry, and did admirably in each.

EDMONIA LEWIS,

the Negro sculptress, is in herself a great prophecy of the possibilities of her sisters in America. Of lowly birth, left an orphan when quite young, unable to obtain a liberal education, she nevertheless determined to be somebody and do something.

Some years ago, while yet in humble circumstances, she visited Boston. Upon seeing a statue of Benjamin Franklin she stood transfixed before it. It stirred the latent genius within the untutored child, and produced an emotion she had never felt before. " I, too, can make a stone man," she said. Almost instinctively, she turned to that great Apostle of Human Liberty, Wm. Lloyd Garrison, and asked his advice. The kindhearted agitator gave her a note to Mr. Brackett, the Boston sculptor. He received her kindly, heard her express the desire and ambition of her heart, and then giving her a model of a human foot and some clay, said: " Go home and make that. If there is any thing in you it will come out." She tried, but her teacher broke up her work and told her to try again. And so she did, and triumphed.

Since then, this ambitious Negro girl has won a position as an artist, a studio in Rome, and a place in the admiration of the lovers of art on two continents. She has produced many meritorious works of art, the most noteworthy being *Hagar in the Wilderness ;* a group of the *Madonna with the Infant Christ and two adoring Angels ; Forever Free ; Hiawatha's Wooing ;* a bust of *Longfellow, the Poet ;* a bust of *John Brown ;* and a medallion portrait of *Wendell Phillips.* The *Madonna* was purchased by the Marquis of Bute, Disraeli's Lothair.

She has been well received in Rome, and her studio has become an object of interest to travellers from all countries.

Of late many intelligent young Colored women have risen to take their places in society, and as wives and mothers are doing much to elevate the tone of the race and its homes. Great care must be given to the education of the Colored women of America; for virtuous, intelligent, educated, cultured, and pious wives and mothers are the hope of the Negro race. Without them educated Colored men and the miraculous results of emancipation will go for nothing.

CHAPTER XXIV.

THE AFRICAN METHODIST EPISCOPAL CHURCH.

Its Origin, Growth, Organization, and Excellent Influence. — Its Publishing House, Periodicals, and Papers. — Its Numerical and Financial Strength. — Its Missionary and Educational Spirit. — Wilberforce University.

THE African Methodist Episcopal Church of America has exerted a wider and better influence upon the Negro race than any other organization created and managed by Negroes. The hateful and hurtful spirit of caste and race prejudice in the Protestant Church during and after the American Revolution drove the Negroes out. The Rev. Richard Allen, of Philadelphia, Pennsylvania, was the founder of the African Methodist Episcopal Church. He gathered a few Christians in his private dwelling, during the year 1816, and organized a church and named it "*Bethel.*" Its first General Conference was held in Philadelphia during the same year with the following representation:

Rev. Richard Allen, Jacob Tapsico, Clayton Durham, James Champion, and Thomas Webster, of Philadelphia, Pennsylvania; Daniel Coker, Richard Williams, Henry Harden, Stephen Hill, Edward Williamson, and Nicholas Gailliard, of Baltimore, Maryland; Peter Spencer, of Wilmington, Delaware; Jacob Marsh, Edward Jackson, and William Andrew, of Attleborough, Pennsylvania; Peter Cuff, of Salem, New Jersey.

The minutes of the Conference of 1817 were lost, but in 1818 there were seven itinerants: Baltimore Conference—Rev. Daniel Coker, Richard Williams, and Rev. Charles Pierce; Philadelphia Conference—Bishop Allen, Rev. William Paul Quinn, Jacob Tapsico, and Rev. Clayton Durham.

The Church grew mightily, increasing in favor with God and man. The zeal of its ministers was wonderful, and the spirit of missions and consecration to the work wrought miracles for the cause. In 1826 the strength of the Church was as follows:

Bishops 2
Annual conferences 2
Itinerant preachers 17
Stations 2
Circuits 10
Missions 5
Total number of members 7,927
Amount of salary for travelling preachers . $1,054.50
Amount of incidental expenses . . . $97.25

The grand total amount of money raised in 1826 for all purposes was $1,151.75. In 1836 there were:

Bishops 3
Conferences 4
Travelling preachers 27
Stations 7
Circuits . . . . . - . . . 18
Missions 2
Churches 86
Probable value of church property . . $43,000.00
Total salary of pastors $1,126.29
Amount raised for general purposes . . $259.59

Total amount of money raised in 1836 for all purposes, $1,385.88. The total number of members in 1836 was 7,594. This was a decrease of 333 members, and is to be accounted for in the numerous sales of slaves in the Baltimore Conference, as the decrease was in that conference. In 1846 there were:

Bishops 4
Annual conferences 6
Travelling preachers 40
Stations 16
Circuits and missions 25
Churches 198
Probable value of church property . . $90,000.00
Total amount raised to support ministers . $6,267.43½
Amount raised for general purposes . . $963.59½

The grand total amount of money raised in 1846 for all purposes was $7,231.03.

There were supported in the Church in 1846 three educational societies and three missionary societies.

In 1866 there were :

Annual conferences.	10
Bishops	4
Travelling preachers	185
Stations	50
Circuits	39
Missions	96
Churches	285
Probable value of church property	$823,000.00
Number of Sunday-school teachers and officers,	21,000
" " volumes in libraries	17,818
" " members	50,000

The amount of money expended to assist the widows and orphans was $5,000. The amount paid this year for the support of the pastors was $83,593. The amount expended for Sunday-school work was $3,000.

The receipts of the Church in 1876 were as follows :

Amount of contingent money raised	$2,976 85
Amount raised for the support of pastors .	201,984 06
Amount raised for the support of presiding elders	23,896 66
Amount of Dollar Money for general educational purposes, etc. .	28,009 97
Amount raised to support Sunday-schools for the year 1876 .	17,415 33
Amount raised for the missionary society,	3,782 72
Amount raised in one year for building churches	169,558 60
Total amount raised for all purposes,	$447,624 19

STATISTICS OF MEMBERS.

Ministers.

Number of bishops .	6
" " travelling preachers .	1,418
" " local preachers	3,168
" " exhorters .	2,546
Total ministerial force in 1876	7,138
Ministerial force in 1816 .	8
Ministerial gain in 60 years	7,130

Members and Probationers.

Number of members 172,806
" " probationers 33,525

Total number of members and probationers 206,331

SUMMARY OF MEMBERS.

Total number of ministers 7,138
Total number of members and probationers . 206,331

Grand total membership . . . 213,469

CHURCH PROPERTY.

Number of churches 1,833
" " parsonages 218

VALUE OF CHURCH PROPERTY.

Value of churches $3,064,911 00
" " parsonages 138,800 00

Total value of church property . $3,203,711 00

ANNUAL CONFERENCES.

Number of annual conferences 25

SUNDAY-SCHOOLS.

Number of Sunday-schools 2,309
" " superintendents 2,458
" " teachers and officers . . 8,085
" " pupils 87,453
" " volumes in libraries . . . 129,066

MISSIONARY SOCIETIES.

Number of parent home and foreign societies . 11
" " annual conference societies . . 24
" " local societies 250

WILBERFORCE UNIVERSITY IN 1876.

Number of students enrolled—males . . . 375
" " " " —females . . 225
" " professors—males 3
" " " —females 7

The total receipts of Wilberforce University for the year was $4,547.89.

The assets of Wilberforce University in 1876 were as follows:

Endowment notes	$18,000 00
College property	39,000 00
Bequest of Chief-Justice Chase . . .	10,000 00
Nine semi-annual and annual notes . .	900 00
Bills receivable	125 00
Horse, wagon, etc.	200 00
Cash in bank	1,000 00
Total assets	$69,225 00

The liabilities were only $2,973.42, leaving the handsome amount of $66,251.58 of assets over the liabilities of the institution.

The General Conference of 1880 met in St. Louis, Mo., on the third day of May. The following are some of the facts, as we glean from the reports:

The Financial Secretary, Rev. J. C. Embry, reported that for the fiscal year ending April 24, 1880, he had received $32,336.31 for general purposes alone, and in the four years from April 24, 1876, to April 24, 1880, he had received $99,999.42 for the general expenses of the Church.

The General Business Manager, Dr. H. M. Turner, reported the receipts in the Book Concern to be $50,133.76. This was the largest amount of business ever reported by the Concern.

The receipts of the two departments were $150,133.18. The total amount raised in 1826 was $1,151.75. The gain since that time has been $148,981.43.

RECEIPTS.

Amount of contingent money . . .	$27,897 36
" " dollar money . . .	33,400 00
" " missionary money . . .	25,248 08
" " ladies' mite missionary money	2,296 06
" for Sunday-school purposes .	115,694 40
" " pastors' support . . .	1,282,465 16
" " pastors' travelling expenses .	36,608 16
" " presiding elders' travelling exps.	7,338 20
" " presiding elders' support . .	106,817 20
	$1,637,764 62

RECEIPTS.—(*Continued.*)

Amount brought up . . .	$1,637,764	62
Amount for educational purposes . .	6,125	46
" " building and repairing churches	596,824	48
" " charitable and benevolent purposes	20,937	02
Total annual collection . . .	$2,261,651	58
The amount for four years . . .	9,046,606	24
The General Business Manager's report .	51,000	00
Grand total for four years . .	$9,097,606	24

STATISTICS OF MEMBERS.

Travelling Preachers.

Number of bishops	9
" " general officers	4
" " travelling licentiates	434
" " travelling elders	445
" " travelling deacons	940
Total number of travelling preachers . .	1,832

Local Preachers.

Number of superannuated preachers . . .	21
" " local preachers and exhorters . .	7,719
" " " elders	42
" " " deacons	146
Total number of local preachers . .	7,928

Members and Probationers.

Number of members	306,044
" " probationers	85,000
Total number of members and probationers,	391,044

SUMMARY OF MEMBERS.

Total number of travelling preachers . .	1,832
" " " local preachers . . .	7,928
" " " members and probationers .	391,044
Grand total membership . . .	400,804

SUNDAY-SCHOOLS.

Number of Sunday-schools 2,345
"   " teachers and officers . . . 15,454
"   " pupils 154,549
"   " volumes in library . . . 193,358

CHURCH PROPERTY.

Number of school-houses 88
"   " churches 2,051
"   " parsonages 395

VALUE OF CHURCH PROPERTY.

Value of school-houses $26,400 00
"   " churches 2,884,251 00
"   " parsonages 162,603 20
                                            ———————
Total value of church property . $3,073,254 20

PAPER.

Number of subscriptions to "Christian Recorder" 5,380

In 1818 a publishing department was added to the work of the Church. But its efficiency was impaired on account of the great mass of its members being in slave States or the District of Columbia, where the laws prohibited them from attending school, and deprived them of reading books or papers. In 1817 the Rev. Richard Allen published a book of discipline; and shortly after this a Church hymn-book was published also. Beyond this there was but little done in this department until 1841, when the New York Conference passed a resolution providing for the publication of a monthly magazine. But the lack of funds compelled the projectors to issue it as a quarterly. For nearly eight years this magazine exerted an excellent influence upon the ministers and members of the Church. Its coming was looked forward to with a strange interest. It contained the news in each of the conferences; its editorials breathed a spirit of love and fellowship; and thus the members were brought to a knowledge of the character of the work being accomplished.

At length the prosperity of the magazine seemed to justify the publication of a weekly paper. Accordingly a weekly journal, named the "Christian Herald," made its appearance and ran its course for the space of four years. In 1852, by order of the General Conference, the paper was enlarged and issued as the "Christian Recorder," which has continued to be published up to the present time In addition to this a "Child's Recorder" is published as a monthly. About 50,000 copies of both are issued every month.

The managers and editors in this department have been:

From 1818 to 1826—Right-Reverened Richard Allen, First Bishop of the A. M. E. Church, served in the capacity of Bishop and General Book Steward.

From 1826 to 1835—Rev. Jos. M. Corr. He was the first regularly appointed General Book Steward, and served until October, 1836, at which time he died.

From 1835 to 1848—Rev. Geo. Hogarth.

From 1848 to 1852—Rev. Augustus R. Green.

From 1852 to 1854—Rev. M. M. Clark, Editor; Rev. W. T. Catto, General Book Steward, and Rev. W. H. Jones, Travelling Agent.

From 1854 to 1860—Rev. J. P. Campbell (now Bishop) served in the capacity of General Book Steward and Editor.

From 1860 to 1868—Rev. Elisha Weaver served the most of the time as both Manager and Editor.

From 1868 to 1869—Rev. Joshua Woodlin, Manager, and Rev. B. T. Tanner, Editor. During the year 1869 Rev. Joshua Woodlin resigned.

From 1869 to 1871—Rev. A. L. Stanford served until above date, when he also resigned, and Dr. B. T. Tanner was left to act in the capacity of Editor and Manager until May, 1872.

From 1872 to 1876—Rev. W. H. Hunter, Business Manager, and Rev. B. T. Tanner reappointed Editor.

From 1876 to 1880—Rev. H. M. Turner, Business Manager, and Rev. B. T. Tanner again reappointed Editor.

1880—Rev. Theo. Gould, Business Manager, and Rev. B. T. Tanner was for the fourth term appointed Editor.

In addition to the work done here on the field, this Church has been blessed with a true missionary spirit. It has pushed its work into "the regions beyond." In 1844 *The Parent Home and Foreign Missionary Society* was organized by the General Conference. Its first corresponding secretary was appointed in 1864, John M. Brown, Washington, D.C.; 1865 to 1868, John M. Brown; 1868 to 1872, James A. Handay, Baltimore, Maryland; 1872, Rev. W. J. Gaines, Macon, Georgia; 1873, Rev. T. G.

Stewart, Philadelphia, Pennsylvania; 1874 to 1876, Rev. G. W. Brodie; 1876 to 1878, Rev. Richard H. Cain, Columbia, S. C.; 1878 to 1881, Rev. James M. Townsend, Richmond, Indiana.

The following is the last report of the present missionary secretary:

RECAPITULATION.

Receipts.

Collected for general work (including $300 from the W. M. M Society)	$2,630	35
Collected on the field in Hayti . . .	1,221	54
Women's Mite Society (in addition to the above $300)	364	31
Collected for domestic missions . . .	3,743	87
Total receipts	$7,960	07

Expenditures.

Total expended on salaries, travelling expenses, printing, etc.	$7,773	10
Balance in Women's M. M. treasury . .	48	97
Balance in general treasury	138	00
	$7,960	07

Respectfully submitted,

JAMES M. TOWNSEND.

The work of education has been fostered and pushed forward by this Church. Wilberforce University is owned and managed by the Church, and is doing a noble work for both sexes. More than one thousand students have received instruction in this institution, and some of the ablest preachers in the denomination are proud of Wilberforce as their *Alma Mater.* The following gentlemen constitute the faculty:

WILBERFORCE UNIVERSITY.

FACULTY.

REV. B. F. LEE, B.D., *President,*
Professor of Intellectual and Moral Philosophy and Systematic Theology.

Professor of Ecclesiastical History, Homiletics, and Pastoral Theology.

J. P. SHORTER, A.B.,
Professor of Mathematics and Secretary of the Faculty.

W. S. SCARBOROUGH, A.M.,
Professor of Latin and Greek.

ROSWELL F. HOWARD, A.B., B.L.,
Professor of Law.

Hon. JOHN LITTLE,
Professor of Law.

Mrs. S. C. BIERCE,
*Principal of Normal Department, Instructor in French, and
Natural Sciences.*

Mrs. ALICE M. ADAMS,
Lady Principal, Matron, and Instructor in Academic Department.

Miss GUSSIE E. CLARK,
Teacher of Instrumental Music.

ASSISTANT TEACHERS.

CARRIE E. FERGUSON,
Teacher of Penmanship.

D. M. ASHBY,
G. S. LEWIS,
Teachers of Arithmetic.

ANNA H. JONES,
Teacher of Reading.

Rev. T. H. JACKSON, D.D.,
General Agent.

In the summer of 1856 the Cincinnati Conference of the Methodist Episcopal Church decided to establish in that place a university for the education of Colored youth. Its Board of Trustees consisted of twenty white and four Colored men. Mr. Alfred J. Anderson, Rev. Lewis Woodson, Mr. Ishmael Keith, and Bishop Payne were the Colored members. Among the former were State Senator M. D. Gatch and the late Salmon P. Chase. It was dedicated in October, 1856, when the Rev. M. P. Gaddis took charge. He held the position of Principal for one year, when he was succeeded by Professor J. R. Parker, who worked faithfully and successfully until 1859. Rev. R. T. Rust, D.D., became President upon the retirement of Mr. Parker, and accomplished a noble work. He raised the educational standard of the school, attracted to its support and halls friends and pupils, and gained the confidence of educators and laymen within the outside of his denomination. Unfortunately, his faithful labors were most abruptly terminated by the war of the Rebellion. The college doors were closed in 1862 for want of funds; the main friends of the institution having cast their lot with the Confederate States. It should be remembered that up to this time this college was in the hands of the white Methodist Church. The Colored Methodists bought the land and buildings on the 10th of March, 1863, for the sum of $10,000. The land consisted of fifty-two acres, with an abundance of timber, fine springs, and a commodious college building with a dozen beautiful cottages. And the growth of the institution under the management of Colored men is a credit to their Church and race.

Bishop D. H. Payne, D.D., was elected to the presidency of the university, which position he has filled with rare fidelity and ability for the last thirteen years. In 1876 Rev. B. F. Lee, a former graduate of the college, was elected to occupy the presidential chair. It was not a position to be sought after since it had been filled for thirteen years by the senior bishop of the Church, but Mr. Lee was the choice of his official brethren and so was elected. President Lee is a native of New Jersey. He is about the medium height, well knit, of light complexion, dark hair and beard of the same color that covers a face handsomely moulded. He is plainly a man of excellent traits of character; he is somewhat bald and has a finely-cut head, broad and massive. He moves quickly, and impresses one as a man who is armed with a large amount of executive tact. His face is of a thoughtful cast, and does not change much when he laughs. There were many difficulties to hinder his administration when he took charge, but he surmounted them all. Under his administration the institution has grown financially and numerically.

The following report shows the financial condition of the college at the present time.

RECEIPTS.

June 20, 1880.

Balance in Treasury,	Avery Fund	.	$10,000 00
" "	Rust Prize Fund	.	100 00
" "	cash	.	63 82
Total balance	. . . .	.	$10,163 82

RECEIPTS.—(*Continued.*)

Balance		$10,163 82
Received from Financial Secretary	200 00	
" " tuition . .	1,604 49	
" " dormitories .	525 80	
" " Unitarian Association	600 00	
Received from loans . .	100 00	
Received from interest from Avery Fund	800 00	
Received from interest from Rust Fund	8 00	
Received from General Agent .	150 00	
" " contributions .	232 00	
" " Philadelphia Conference	52 95	
Received from Illinois Conference	30 00	
" " bequest of John Pfaff	602 08	
Received from miscellaneous .	407 64	
		$5,312 96
Total receipts		$15,476 78

EXPENDITURES.

To salaries	$3,166 15
" building and grounds	243 25
" furnishing building	177 37
" notes paid with interest	285 86
" lectures	600 00
" fuel	116 64
" Powers' Fund interest	114 90
" incidental	296 17
" insurance	219 00
" miscellaneous	144 21

Total expenditures		$5,363 55
Balance in bank—Avery Fund securities	$10,000 00	
Balance in bank—Rust Fund securities	100 00	
Balance in bank—cash . .	13 23	
		$10,113 23
		$15,476 78

STATEMENT OF CASH RECEIPTS, FROM 1865 TO 1881.

1865 to 1866	$ 10,677 82
1866 to 1867	6,717 88
1867 to 1868	9,000 00
1868 to 1869	5,403 83
1869 to 1870	9,498 24
1870 to 1871	28,672 22
1871 to 1872	7,270 31
1872 to 1873	4,452 30
1873 to 1874	6,129 77
1874 to 1875	4,962 50
1875 to 1876	7,805 36
1876 to 1877	13,757 66
1877 to 1878	14,429 15
1878 to 1879	4,944 37
1879 to 1880	6,942 98
1880 to 1881	5,312 96
Total	$145,977 35

The following-named persons are the bishops of the Church : James A. Shorter, Daniel A. Payne, A. W. Wayman, J. P. Campbell, John M. Brown, T. M. D. Ward, H. M. Turner, William F. Dickerson, and R. H. Cain.

The African Methodist Episcopal Church will remain through the years to come as the best proof of the Negro's ability to maintain himself in an advanced state of civilization. Commencing with nothing—save an unfaltering faith in God,—this Church has grown to magnificent proportions. Her name has gone to the ends of the earth. In the Ecumenical Council of the Methodists in London, 1881, its representatives made a splendid impression ; and their addresses and papers took high rank.

This Church has taught the Negro how to govern and how to submit to government. It has kept its membership under the influence of wholesome discipline, and for its beneficent influence upon the morals of the race, it deserves the praise and thanks of mankind.[1]

---

[1] We have to thank the Rev. B. W. Arnett, B.D., the Financial Secretary, for the valuable statistics used in this chapter. He is an intelligent, energetic, and faithful minister of the Gospel, and a credit to his Church and race.

CHAPTER XXV.

THE METHODIST EPISCOPAL CHURCH.

Founding of the M. E. Church of America in 1768. — Negro Servants and Slaves among the First Contributors to the Erection of the First Chapel in New York. — The Rev. Harry Hosier the First Negro Preacher in the M. E. Church in America. — His Remarkable Eloquence as a Pulpit Orator. — Early Prohibition against Slave-holding in the M. E. Church. — Strength of the Churches and Sunday-schools of the Colored Members in the M. E. Church. — The Rev. Marshall W. Taylor, D.D. — His Ancestors. — His Early Life and Struggles for an Education. — He teaches School in Kentucky. — His Experiences as a Teacher. — Is ordained to the Gospel Ministry and becomes a Preacher and Missionary Teacher. — His Settlement as Pastor in Indiana and Ohio. — Is given the Title of Doctor of Divinity by the Tennessee College. — His Influence as a Leader, and his Standing as a Preacher.

PHILLIP EMBURY, Barbara Heck, and Capt. Thomas Webb were the germ from which, in the good providence of God, has sprung the Methodist Episcopal Church in the United States of America. The first chapel was erected upon leased ground on John Street, New York City, in 1768. The ground was purchased in 1770. Subscriptions were asked and received from all classes of people for the building, from the mayor of the city down to African female servants known only by their Christian names. Here the Colored people became first identified with American Methodism. From this stock have sprung all who have been subsequently connected with it. Meetings were held, prior to the erection of John Street Church, in the private residence of Mrs. Heck, and in a rigging-loft, sixty by eighteen feet, in William Street, which was rented in 1767. Here Capt. Webb and Mr. Embury preached thrice a week to large audiences. The original design to erect a chapel must be credited to Mrs. Heck, the foundress of American Methodism. Mr. Richard Owen, a convert of Robert Strawbridge, the founder of Methodism in Baltimore, was the first native Methodist preacher on the continent. The first American Annual Conference was held in Philadelphia, Pa., twenty-nine years after Mr. Wesley held his first conference in England, with ten members, precisely the same number there were in his. They were Thos. Rankin, President ; Richard Boardman, Joseph Pilmoor, Francis Asbury, Richard Wright, George Shadford, Thomas Webb, John King, Abraham Whiteworth, and Joseph Yearbry. It began Wednesday the 14th and closed Friday the 16th of July, 1773. All the members were foreigners, and in the Revolution many of them were subject to unjust suspicions of sympathy with England, in consequence of this fact alone. The aggregate statistical returns for this conference showed 1,160, which was much less than Mr. Rankin supposed to be the strength of Methodism in America.

On the 2d of September, 1784, Rev. Thomas Coke, D.D., LL.D., a presbyter in the Church of England, was ordained by John Wesley, A.M., Superintendent or Bishop of the Methodist Societies in America. He was charged with a commission to organize them into an Episcopal Church, and to ordain Mr. Francis Asbury an Associate Bishop. He sailed for America at 10 o'clock A. M., September 18th, and landed at New York, Wednesday, November 3, 1784. Mr. Coke at once set out on a tour of observation, accompanied by Harry Hosier, Mr. Asbury's travelling servant, a Colored minister. Hosier was one of the notable characters of that day. He was the first American Negro preacher of the M. E. Church in the United States. In 1780 Mr. Asbury alluded to him as a companion, suitable to preach to the Colored people. Dr. Rush, allowing for his illiteracy—for he could not read—pronounced him the greatest orator in America. He was small in stature and very black ; but he had eyes of remarkable brilliancy and keenness ; and singular readiness and aptness of speech. He travelled extensively with Asbury, Coke, and Whiteworth. He afterward travelled through New England. He excelled all the whites in popularity as a preacher ; sharing with them in their public services, not only in Colored but also in white congregations. When they were sick or otherwise disabled they could trust the pulpit to Harry without fear of unfavorably disappointing the people. Mr. Asbury acknowledges that the best way to obtain a large congregation was to announce that Harry would preach. The multitude preferred him to the Bishop himself. Though he withstood for years the temptations of extraordinary popularity, he fell, nevertheless, by the indulgent hospitalities which were lavished upon him. He became temporarily the victim of wine ; but possessed

moral strength enough to recover himself. Self-abased and con-
trite, he started one evening down the neck below Southwark,
Philadelphia, determined to remain till his backslidings were
healed. Under a tree he wrestled in prayer into the watches of
the night. Before the morning God restored to him the joys of
His salvation. Thenceforward he continued faithful. He resumed his public labors. In the year 1810 he died in Philadelphia. " Making a good end," he was borne to the grave by a
great procession of both Colored and white admirers, who
buried him as a hero—one overcome, but finally victorious.

It is said that on one occasion, in Wilmington, Del., where
Methodism was long unpopular, a number of the citizens, who
did not ordinarily attend Methodist preaching, came together to
hear Bishop Asbury. Old Asbury Chapel was, at that time, so
full that they could not get in. They stood outside to hear the
Bishop, as they supposed ; but in reality they heard Harry.
Before they left the place, they complimented the speaker by
saying : "If all Methodist preachers could preach like the
Bishop we should like to be constant hearers." Some one
present replied : " That was not the Bishop, but his servant."
This only raised the Bishop higher in their estimation, as their
conclusion was, if such be the servant what must the master be?
The truth was, that Harry was a more popular speaker than
Asbury, or almost any one else in his day.[1]

So we find in the very inception of Methodism in the United
States the Colored people were conspicuously represented in its
membership, contributing both money, labor, and eloquence to
its grand success.

The great founder of Methodism was an inveterate foe of
human slavery, which he pronounced "the sum of all villainies,"
and in this particular the Methodist societies in their earliest
times reflected his sentiments. The early preachers were especially hostile to slavery. In 1784 it was considered and declared
to be contrary to the Golden Law of God, as well as every principle of the Revolution. They required every Methodist to
execute and record, within twelve months after notice by the
preacher, a legal instrument emancipating all slaves in his possession at specified ages. Any person who should not concur in
this requirement had liberty to leave the Church within one year;
otherwise the preacher was to exclude him. No person holding

---

[1] Stevens's Hist. of M. E. Church, pp. 174, 175 ; also Lednum, p. 282.

slaves could be admitted to membership, or to the Lord's Supper, until he complied with this law. But it was to be applied only where the law of the State permitted.[1] These rules provoked great hostility, and were suspended within six months.

The Church had, however, put the stamp of condemnation upon it. And ever in a more or less active but always consistent manner opposed it, until its final extirpation was accomplished, though not until the Church had been several times divided in favor of and against it.

The Methodist Episcopal Church in the United States of America was organized in what is historically known as the Christmas Conference, which convened in Baltimore at ten o'clock Friday morning, December 24, 1784, Bishop Thomas Coke, presiding. Rev. Francis Asbury was there consecrated a bishop. In 1786 a resolution emphatically enjoining it upon the preachers to leave nothing undone for the spiritual benefit and salvation of the Colored people was adopted. The Church is a limited Episcopacy. The bishops are elected by the General Conference. They fix the appointments of all the preachers, but the conference arranges their duration. The bishops hold office during good behavior. The General Conference is the Legislative, and the bishops, presiding elders, pastors, annual, district, and quarterly conferences, with the leaders' and stewards' meetings, and the general and local trustees, are the Executive Department. The ministerial orders are two: elder and deacon. The offices of the ministry and rank are in the order named,—bishop, sub-bishop, pastor, and sub-pastors. The ministry are classified as Effective, Supernumerary, Superannuate, and Local. The property of each congregation is deeded in trust for them to a Board of Local Trustees, who may sell, buy, or improve it for the use of said congregation. The stewards are officers whose labors are partly temporal and partly spiritual. They are entrusted with the raising of supplies, benevolence, and the support of the ministry. Exhorters are prayer-meeting leaders and general helpers in the work of the circuits.

Methodism began in a college and has been a great patron of education. It has been largely devoted to the educational and religious culture of the Colored people in the South and in

---

[1] And there was not a single State where this rule could be applied. Slavery ruled the land.

Africa. There are sixteen conferences of Colored members in the M. E. Church—fifteen in the United States and one in Liberia. For the Liberian Conference two Colored bishops have been consecrated, viz.: Francis Burns and ex-President Thomas Wright Roberts, both deceased. The present bishops are all white, one of whom annually visits Africa. The same is true of conferences in Germany, Switzerland, Sweden, Denmark, Norway, India, China, and Japan. The agency by which the Church prosecutes this work is the Missionary, Church Extension, Freedmen's Aid, Education, and Sunday-school Union societies. Books and periodicals are amply supplied by its own publishing house, which is the largest religious publishing house in the world.

In the sixteen conferences there are 225,000 members, 200,000 Sunday-school scholars, 3,500 day scholars, one medical, three law, and seven theological colleges, and twelve seminaries. There is $500,000 in school and $2,000,000 in church and parsonage property owned by the Colored membership! The Colored members elect their own representatives to the General Conference, and are fully represented in all the work of the Church.

At the present time the Rev. Marshall W. Taylor, D. D., and the Rev. Wm. M. Butler are the most prominent men in the Church. Marshall William Boyd (alias) Taylor was born July 1, 1846, at Lexington, Fayette County, Kentucky, of poor, uneducated, but respectable parents. He was the fourth in a family of five children, three of whom were boys, viz.: George Summers, Francis Asbury, and himself; and two girls, Mary Ellen and Mary Cathrine. He is of Scotch-Irish and Indian descent on his father's side. Hon. Samuel Boyd, of New York; Joseph Boyd, of Virginia; and Lieut.-Gov. Boyd, of Kentucky, were blood-relations of his, and all descended from the "Clan Boyd" of Scotland. His mother was of African and Arabian stock. His grandmother, on his mother's side, Phillis Ann, was brought from Madagascar when a little girl, and became the slave of Mr. Alexander Black, a Kentucky farmer, who at his death willed his slaves free. His mother, Nancy Ann, thus obtained her freedom, and by the terms of the will she was put to the millinery trade, which she fully mastered, and meantime obtained an elementary knowledge of reading, writing, and arithmetic. She married Albert Summers, and bore to him two children, viz., George Summers and Mary Catharine. He ran away to prevent being sold, and she afterward married Samuel Boyd, to whom she bore three children, viz., Francis Asbury, Marshall William, and Mary Ellen. His father, Samuel, was the son of Hon. Samuel Boyd, of New York. He was noted for his independence of character; was a valuable but unruly slave. He was allowed an opportunity to purchase his freedom, and this he began to do, and had paid $250, three fourths of the price, when his master sold him to Tennessee. He promptly ran away from his new master, but unwilling to forsake his family, went back to Kentucky. His master pursued and overtook him at Lexington, where he had stopped. He refused to go back to Tennessee, and once more was permitted to select a master, and finally to again contract for his freedom, which he this time succeeded in obtaining. In consequence of his mother's emancipation, Marshall was free when he first saw the light of day. By occupation his father was a hemp-breaker, rope-maker, and farmer. The last he elected to follow after he was free. He employed his boys as farmers, but his mother strenuously opposed it, wishing better opportunities than could be thus afforded for their education. She at length succeeded in carrying her point.

In religion his father at first inclined to the Baptists, of which Church he became a deacon in the congregation of Rev. Mr. Ferrill, of Pleasant Green Church, Lexington. Later he became dissatisfied with the Baptists, and united with the African Methodists at Frankfort, Ky. He finally went back to the Baptist Church and died in that faith.

Marshall's mother, and all her people, so far as known, were Methodists. His early training and first and only religious impressions were Methodistic, which Church, after his conversion, he joined. His father had no knowledge of letters, so that all his home instruction came from his mother. Her text-books were the Bible, Methodist Catechism, and Webster's Elementary Spelling Book. And in these young Marshall became very proficient. He afterward attended school daily to Rev. John Tibbs, an African Methodist preacher, who came from Cincinnati to Lexington to teach free children and such of the slaves as would be permitted to attend. Some masters granted this permission, but the greater number refused it. Finally, some "*poor white*" fellows, unable to own slaves themselves, mobbed the teacher, rode him on a rail, tarred, feathered, and drove him from town. They were called black Indians. It was impossible to secure another teacher in Lexington for a day school, but Mr. George Perry, an intelligent free Colored man, had the courage to teach Sunday-school, in the Branch Methodist Church. It is now called Asbury M. E. Church. Marshall attended, as did his mother and brothers. In 1854 the family moved to Louisville, looking for a school. Finding none there, they continued their journey about fifty miles above there on the Ohio River, and landed at Ghent, a little village in Carroll County, Ky., opposite Vevey, Indiana. They indulged a hope that the children would be allowed to attend the public schools at Vevey, but they were doomed in this expectation. They spent two years at Ghent. Marshall and his brother obtained instruction during this period from the little white children who attended school, after hours, using " an old hay loft back of a Mr. Sanders's Tavern " for a recitation-room, and paying their teachers with cakes and candies bought with odd pennies gathered here and there.

On the 1st of August, 1856, there was an Emancipation celebration at Dayton, Ohio. Frederick Douglass was advertised to speak, and other eminent Abolitionists were expected to participate. Marshall's mother attended it. Soon after her return several slaves mysteriously disappeared from the vicinity of Ghent. Among them was a very valuable family belonging to Esquire Craig, of the village. Suspicion fastened on the old lady who had been off among the "Abolitionists." She was indicted by the Grand Jury, and thirty-six men filed into her cabin, and while she lay sick in bed, read the indictment to her. They ordered her to leave the place. She refused to go, claimed her innocence, but to no purpose. " They chased Francis with guns and dogs on the public streets in daylight; shaddowed the cabin and gave unmistakable evidence of a diabolical purpose." She soon after returned to Louisville.

Young Marshall became a messenger in the law firm of J. B. Kincaid and John W. Barr. Here his chances were good, both of these gentlemen aiding him in his studies. He did his work after school hours at the office, and attended a school which was kept in the "Centre Street Colored Methodist Church," until it closed.

Rev. Henry Henderson, a Colored Methodist preacher, now opened a school in Centre Street, and Marshall was duly enrolled among his pupils. On his retirement, Mrs. Elizabeth Cumings, a highly cultured and pious lady, taught a private school on Grayson, between Sixth and Seventh streets. He now went to her. She died soon after, when he was sent to a Mr. William H. Gibson, who had already opened a school on Seventh, between Jefferson and Green streets, in an old carpenter shop. Here he continued until 1861.

In 1866 Mr. Taylor opened a Freedmen's School at Hardinsburg, Breckenridge Co., Ky. This was in an old church, the property of the M. E. Church South. It had been donated for church purposes by George Blanford. If used otherwise it was to revert to the donor. A Negro school was obnoxious to the community. His was the first there had ever been in the village, and notwithstanding the white people had long since abandoned the property to the Colored people this question was now raised in order to break up the school. It did not succeed, as they easily proved that the original intent of the donor was not violated, since Colored people still used the property as a church. Failing in this the school was tormented by ruffians. Pepper was rolled up in cotton, set on fire, and hurled into the room to set every one coughing. Finally threats of personal violence were made if he did not leave, but Mr. Taylor armed himself, defied the enemies of freedom, and stayed. At last, on Christmas evening, Dec. 25, 1867, the house was blown up with powder. The arrangement was to set off the blast with a slow match so as to catch the house full of people, there being a school exhibition that night. The explosion took place at 11:30 P.M., but owing to the excitement occasioned by the novelty of such a thing as a "Negro School Exhibition," the crowd had gathered much earlier than announced. The programme was completed before 11 P.M., and by this accident the school and teacher were saved. The old wreck still remains a monument to color prejudice.

By the aid of the Freedmen's Bureau another school-house was soon built, and the school proceeded. This was followed by a meeting-house. The white people, whose sentiments were now rapidly turning, subscribed liberally toward it.

In 1868 an educational convention was held at Owensboro, in Davies Co., Ky., of which Mr. Taylor was elected president. He soon after wrote a manual for Colored schools, which was generally used in that section. In 1869 he attended the first Colored political convention ever held in Kentucky, at Major Hall in Frankfort. He was one of the Educational Committee, and submitted a report. This year he was also a member of a convention at Jackson Street Church, Louisville, which inaugurated the movement for the Lexington M. E. Conference. He was licensed as a local preacher this year by Rev. Hanson Tolbert at Hardinsburg, and was assisted in the study of theology by Rev. R. G. Gardiner, J. H. Lennin, and Dr. R. S. Rust. He went to Arkansas as a missionary teacher and preacher at the call of Rev. W. J. Gladwin, and remained there one year. He organized several societies of the Church, taught school at Midway, Forrest City, and Wittsburg: took part in the political campaign of that year; and was nominated, but declined to run, for Representative from Saint Frances County.

He preached in Texas, Indian Territory, and Missouri; was put in peril by the Ku Klux at Hot Springs; took the chills and returned to Ky., in 1871. He was then appointed to the Litchfield Circuit, Southwestern Kentucky. In 1872 he united with the Lexington Conference of M. E. Church on trial. He was ordained a deacon by Bishop Levi Scott at Maysville, Ky., and sent to Coke Chapel, Louisville, Ky., and Wesley Chapel, Jeffersonville, Indiana. He remained in this charge three years, during which time he published the monthly "Kentucky Methodist," and wrote extensively for the press. He was elected assistant secretary, editor of the printed minutes of the conference, and finally secretary. In 1875 he was sent as pastor to Indianapolis, Ind. He was ordained elder by Bishop Wiley at Lexington in 1876, and returned to Indianapolis. He took an active part in the political campaign of 1876, and was sent to Union Chapel, Cincinnati, 1877–8. In 1879 the faculty of Central Tennessee College, at Nashville, Tennessee, conferred upon him the title and credentials of a Doctor of Divinity. He wrote the life of Rev. Geo. W. Downing.

In 1879 Dr. Taylor was appointed Presiding Elder of the Ohio District, Lexington Conference. In 1880 he was sent as fraternal delegate from the M. E. to the A. M. E. General Conference at St. Louis; he having been previously elected lay delegate to the General Conference of the M. E. Church in Brooklyn, New York, in 1879. He was the youngest member of that body. Upon his motion fraternal representatives were sent to the various Colored denominations of Methodists. He was appointed in 1881 as a delegate from the M. E. Church to the Ecumenical Conference at London, England. He was the caucus nominee of the Colored delegates to the General Conference in Cincinnati in 1880 for bishop. He was always opposed to caste discriminations in

Church, State, or society. He has opposed Colored conferences and a Colored bishop as tending to perpetuate discriminations. He does not oppose the election of Colored men, but wishes that every honor may fall upon them because of merit and not on account of their color. He has become famous as an eloquent preacher, safe teacher, ready speaker, and earnest worker; always aiming to do the greatest good to the greatest number. Certainly the Methodist Episcopal Church has reason to be proud of Marshall W. Taylor.

In this Church there are many other worthy and able Colored preachers. The relations they sustain to the eloquent, scholarly, and pious white clergymen of the denomination are pleasant and beneficial. It is an education. And the fact that the best pulpits of white men are opened to the Colored preachers is a prophecy that race antagonisms in the Christian Church, so tenacious and harmful, are to perish speedily.

CHAPTER XXVI.

THE COLORED BAPTISTS OF AMERICA.

THE COLORED BAPTISTS AN INTELLIGENT AND USEFUL PEOPLE. — THEIR LEADING MINISTERS IN MISSOURI, OHIO, AND IN NEW ENGLAND. — THE BIRTH, EARLY LIFE, AND EDUCATION OF DUKE WILLIAM ANDERSON. — AS FARMER, TEACHER, PREACHER, AND MISSIONARY. — HIS INFLUENCE IN THE WEST. — GOES SOUTH AT THE CLOSE OF THE WAR. — TEACHES IN A THEOLOGICAL INSTITUTE AT NASHVILLE, TENNESSEE. — CALLED TO WASHINGTON. — PASTOR OF 19TH STREET BAPTIST CHURCH. — HE OCCUPIES VARIOUS POSITIONS OF TRUST. — BUILDS A NEW CHURCH. — HIS LAST REVIVAL. — HIS SICKNESS AND DEATH. — HIS FUNERAL AND THE GENERAL SORROW AT HIS LOSS. — LEONARD ANDREW GRIMES, OF BOSTON, MASSACHUSETTS. — HIS PIETY, FAITHFULNESS AND PUBLIC INFLUENCE FOR GOOD, — THE COMPLETION OF HIS CHURCH. — HIS LAST DAYS AND SUDDEN DEATH. — GENERAL SORROW. — RESOLUTIONS BY THE BAPTIST MINISTERS OF BOSTON. — A GREAT AND GOOD MAN GONE.

THE Baptist Church has always been a purely democratic institution. With no bishops or head-men, except such as derive their authority from the consent of the governed, this Church has been truly independent and self-governing in its spirit. Its only Head is Christ, and its teachers such as are willing to take " the Word of God as the Man of their Counsel." From the time of the introduction of the Baptist Church into North America down to the present time, the Colored people have formed a considerable part of its membership. The generous, impartial, and genuine Christian spirit of Roger Williams had a tendency, at the beginning, to keep out of the Church the spirit of race prejudice. But the growth of slavery carried with it, as a logical result, the idea that the slave's presence in the Christian Church was a rebuke to the system. For conscience' sake the slave was excluded, and to oblige the feelings of those who transferred the spirit of social caste from gilded drawing-rooms to cushioned pews, even the free Negro was conducted to the organ-loft.

The simplicity of the Negro led him to the faith of the Baptist Church; but being denied fellowship in the white congregations, he was compelled to provide churches for himself. In Virginia, Georgia, Tennessee, Kentucky, and Mississippi the

Colored Baptists were numerous. In the other States the Methodists and Catholics were numerous. There were few ministers of note at the South; but New England, the Middle States, and the West produced some very able Baptist preachers. The Rev. Richard Anderson, of St. Louis, Missouri, was a man of exalted piety, consummate ability, and of almost boundless influence in the West. He was the pastor of a large church, and did much to mould and direct the interests of his people throughout Missouri. He was deeply revered by his own people, and highly respected by the whites. When he died, the entire city of St. Louis was plunged into profound mourning, and over three hundred carriages—many belonging to the wealthiest families in the city—followed his body to the place of interment.

In Ohio the Rev. Charles Satchell, the Rev. David Nickens, the Rev. W. P. Newman, the Rev. James Poindexter, and the Rev. H. L. Simpson were the leading clergymen in the Colored Baptist churches. Cincinnati has had for the last half century excellent Baptist churches, and an intelligent and able ministry. There are several associations embracing many live churches.

In Kentucky the Colored Baptists are very numerous, and own much valuable property; but Virginia seems to have more Baptists among its great population of Colored people than any other State in the South. There are a dozen or more in Richmond, including the one presided over by the famous John Jasper. One of them has, it is said, three thousand members (?). But the District of Columbia has more Colored churches for its area and population than any other place in the United States. There are at least twenty-five Baptist churches in the District, and some of them have interesting histories. The Nineteenth Street Baptist Church is as an intelligent a society of Christian people of color as there is to be found in any city in the country. Its pulpit has always been occupied by the ablest ministers in the country. The Revs. Sampson White, Samuel W. Madden, and Duke W. Anderson were men of education and marked ability. And there is little doubt but what Duke W. Anderson was the ablest, most distinguished clergyman of color in the United States. And for his work's sake he deserves well of history.

Duke William Anderson was born April 10, 1812, in the vicinity of Lawrenceville, Lawrence County, in the State of Illinois, of a Negro mother by a white father. His father, lately from North

Carolina, fell under Gen. Harrison fighting the Indians. Like so many other great men he was born in an obscure place—a wigwam. At the time of his father's death he was quite a young baby. He was now left to the care of a mother who, in many respects, was like her husband, bold and courageous for the truth, and yet as gentle as a child. It is peculiarly trying and difficult for a mother who has all the comforts of modern city life, to train and educate her boys for the duties of life ; and if so, how much more trying and difficult must it have been for a mother on the North-western frontiers, seventy years ago, to train her boys?

Destitute of home and its comforts, without friends or money ; no farm, school, or church, Mrs. Anderson began to train her two boys, John Anderson and D. W. Anderson. Of the former, little or nothing is known, save that he was the only brother of D. W. Anderson.

True to the instincts of her motherly heart, Mrs. Anderson was determined to remain upon the spot purchased and consecrated by the blood of her lamented husband. She could not divorce herself from the approximate idea and object of her husband's life and death. He had turned from the comforts of a happy home ; had chosen hardships rather than ease that he might realize the dream of his youth, and the object of his manly endeavors—the right of suffrage to all. Her children could not build their play-house of Shakespeare, Milton, Dryden, or Southey. All the instruction Duke William obtained came from his mother. She was very large and healthy. Her complexion was of perfect black. She was possessed of excellent judgment, patience, and industry. She stored the young mind of her boy with useful agricultural knowledge, of which she possessed a large amount.

An education does not consist in acquiring lessons, obtaining a simple, abstract, objective knowledge of certain sciences. It is more than this. It consists, also, in being able to apply and use rightly a given amount of knowledge. And though D. W. Anderson was never permitted to enter college, yet, what he got he got thoroughly, and used at the proper time to the best advantage.

Nature was his best teacher. While yet a very young boy he was awed by her splendors, and attracted by the complicated workings of her manifold laws. He began to study the innumerable mysteries which met him in every direction. He heard

God in the rippling water, in the angry tempest, in the sighing wind, and in the troops of stars which God marshals upon the plains of heaven. In the study of nature he exulted. He sat in her velvet lap, sported by her limpid waters, acquainted himself perfectly with her seasons, and knew the coming and going of every star.

God was training this man for the great mission which he afterward so faithfully performed. No soul that was ever filled with such grand and humane ideas as was that of Duke William Anderson can be crushed. He knew no boundaries for his soul, —except God on one side and the whole universe on the other. He was as free in thought and feeling as the air he inhaled, or the birds in the bright sky over his head. His soul had for many years communed with the God of nature; had been taught by the mighty workings of truth, feeling, and genius within, and by the world without, that he was not to be confined to earth forever, but that beyond the deep blue sky, into which he so much longed to peer, there dwelt the Creator of all things, and there the home of the good! Like the "wise men of the East," —knowing no other God but the God of nature,—his primitive ideas of religion were naturally based upon nature. In that wild and barren territory nature was impressive, desolate, and awful. The earth, air, and sky incited him to thought and stimulated his imagination. Every appearance, every phenomenon—the storm, the thunder,—speak the prophecies of God. He was filled with great thoughts and driven by grand ideas.

It is difficult to compute the value of the mother to the child. It is the mother who loves, because she has suffered. And this seems to be the great law of love. Not a triumph in art, literature, or jurisprudence—from the story of Homer to the odes of Horace, from the times of Bacon and Leibnitz to the days of Tyndall and Morse—that has not been obtained by toil and suffering! The mother of Anderson, having suffered so much in her loneliness and want, knew how to train her boy,—the joy of her life. And he in return knew how to appreciate a mother's love. He remembered that to her he owed every thing,—his life, his health, and his early training. He remembered that in childhood she had often, around their little camp-fire, enchanted his youthful mind by the romance of the sufferings and trials of herself and husband. And now finding himself a young man he was determined to change the course of their life.

No work so thoroughly develops the body and mind, and is so conducive to health, as farming; and, perhaps, none so inde- pendent. Anderson was naturally healthy and strong, so that farming agreed with him. By this he made a comfortable living, and soon demonstrated to his aged mother that she had not la- bored in vain, nor spent her strength for naught.

For a number of years he farmed. His motto was "excel- sior" in whatever he engaged, and in farming he realized success.

As the father of Duke William Anderson had fallen under the U. S. flag, it became the duty of the Government to care for his widow and orphans. Accordingly, Duke William was sent to an Illinois school where he received the rudiments of a Western education. A Western education did not consist in reading poe- try, or in examining Hebrew roots, but in reading, writing, spell- ing, arithmetic, geography, and history. There were no soft seats, no beautifully frescoed walls, dotted with costly maps, or studded with beautiful pictures; not a school with a dozen beautiful rooms, heated by hot air. In those days a Western school-house was erected by the side of some public highway, remote from the town. It was constructed of logs,—not of the logs that have lost their roughness by going through the saw-mill, but logs cut by the axe of the hardy frontiersman. The axe was the only tool needed to fit the timber for the building. The building was about twelve feet in height, and about sixteen by twenty. The cracks were often left open, and sometimes closed by chips and mud. The floor was made of split logs with the flat side up. At one end of the building was a fireplace and chimney occupying the whole end of the house. At each end of the fireplace were laid two large stones upon which to rest the ends of the logs of wood, under all of which were laid closely large pieces of flat stones covered with an inch or two of mud. At the other end of the building was a door. It was constructed of thinly split pieces of logs held together by pieces of hickory withes which crossed each end of the door. This door was hung upon wooden hinges, one part of which, instead of being fastened to the door by screws, was fastened by little wooden pegs. The step at the door was a short piece of log flattened a little on the top and braced on the under side by small stones and pieces of chips. The roof was made of long pieces of split timber, the flat side out and the edges smoothed by the axe in order to make them lie snugly.

Such was the school-house in which D. W. Anderson was educated. And it may be that the plain school in which he was educated loaned him that modesty, plainness, and unostentatious air, which were among the many remarkable traits in his character. The circumstances and society by which boys are surrounded help to mould their character and determine their future. To a healthy and vigorous body was coupled a clear and active mind. He loved knowledge, and was willing to buy it at any price—willing to make any sacrifice. He was an industrious student, and possessed great power of penetration and acquisition. And every thing he read he remembered. The greatest difficulty with students is that they fail to apply themselves. A man may have the ability to accomplish a given amount of work and yet that work can never be accomplished except by the severest effort. It is one thing to possess a negative power, but it is quite another thing to possess a positive power. In this world we are set over against all external laws and forces. We are to assume the offensive. We are to climb up to the stars by microscopes. We are to measure this earth by our mathematics. We are to penetrate its depths and lift to the sun its costly treasures. We are to acquaint ourselves with the workings of the manifold laws which lie about us. If we would know ourselves, understand our relation to God, we must see after the requisite knowledge. Suppose that Duke William Anderson had despaired of ever receiving an education; sat down by the way in life and said: "There is no use of troubling myself, I cannot get what I desire. I am destined to be ignorant and weak all the days of my life; and if there is any good thing for me it will come to me. I will sit here and wait." Would the world ever have known of Anderson? His life would have shed no perfume; his name would have been unknown and his grave would have been forgotten.

But it was that courage which never knows defeat, it was that devotion that never wavers, it was that assiduity, and it was that patience that is certain to triumph, which bore him on to a glorious end, as a summer wind bears up a silver cloud. At the age of seventeen he began to teach school. What Colored man would have essayed to teach school on the frontiers fifty years ago? But D. W. Anderson was born to rule. He was of commanding presence, full of confidence and earnestness. He entered upon his new duties full of hope and joy. This was something new.

There was a great deal of difference between handling the hoe and the pen. He found that there was a great difference between the farm and the school-house. But he was one of those boys who do every thing with all their might, and he was at once at home, and soon became master of his new situation.

Three laborious years were occupied in teaching. And they were years of profit to teacher as well as to pupil. He labored hard to be thorough ; and he greatly improved and finished his own education during his teaching.

About this time young Anderson met, courted, and married Miss Ruth Ann Lucas.

Anderson soon made all necessary arrangements, and the nuptial ceremony was solemnized by the village parson on the 30th of September, 1830. With his bride he now settled down at home. For some years he lived the life of a farmer. His mother was riveted to the spot where her devoted husband fell at the hands of a besotted Indian. But her son was of a progressive spirit. He longed to leave the old home for one more comfortable. How strange that the old should sit by the grave of the past, while the young never weary of chasing some vague fancy !

He bought a tract of land, cleared it, and opened up a farm. He planted a large orchard ; became the owner of seven horses and all the implements necessary to farming.

By his own industry and perseverance he had now acquired a neat little home ; on his farm he raised enough produce for the consumption of his family, and still there was a large quantity left for the market. Apples, potatoes, wheat, corn, and other commodities brought him handsome returns.

On this farm were born five children, four of whom lived to adult age. The oldest child, Luther Morgan, was born October 10, 1831. The second child, Mary Catharine, was born in 1833. The third, George Washington, was born in 1835. The fourth, Elizabeth, was born in 1837. And the fifth and last child was born on the night of September 4, 1839, when, also, the mother and child died.

This sad event filled a hitherto happy home with gloom, and bowed a strong heart with grief. Anderson was a man possessed of a very tender nature, though he was manly and resolute. His heart was fixed upon his wife, and this sad providence smote him heavily.

During all these years, from his youth up, he had been very

profane. He knew no Sabbath, worshipped no God, and was himself the highest law. He was filled with a grand religious sentiment, and only needed the grace of God to bring it out, and the love of God to show him where he stood.

The object of his youthful affection was gone. The faithful woman who had walked for nineteen years by his side was no more; her eyes were closed to mortal things, and she had ceased to be. He followed her body to the grave, and there dropped a silent tear for her to whom he had given his heart. It was the first funeral of any one related to him, and its lessons were sharply cut into his heart.

He returned to a desolate home, where the sad faces of motherless children told that one whom they loved, and who had made home happy, was gone.

His mind now turned to religious matters. He began to think of the home beyond, of Jesus, who died for sinners, and wondered if he would ever be able to see the loved one beyond the tide of death. As he dreamed of immortality, longed for heaven, and wondered if Jesus were his Saviour, he was filled with a deep sense of sin. He felt more deeply a sense of sin. He felt more and more that he was unworthy of the Saviour's love; and if he had his just dues, he would be "assigned a portion among the lost."

For a long time he was bowed down under the weight of his sins, and at length he found peace through the blood of Christ. He was renewed. The avaricious man became liberal, the implacable enemy became the forgiving friend, and the man of cursing a man of prayer. But it was impossible for him to cease to grieve; so he thought he would sell the farm and seek another home. The farm was sold, the horses and tools, and every thing converted into money. The children were bound out, and all arrangements were perfected to seek another home.

He paid a visit to Alton, Illinois, where he spent two or three years. In those days Alton was the city *par excellence* of Illinois, and toward it flowed the tide of emigration. So favorably was he impressed with Alton, that he was determined to make it his home. Accordingly, he began to make preparations for moving the children. In the meanwhile he formed the acquaintance of a widow lady in Alton with whom he became very much pleased. She was a tall, handsome-looking yellow woman, of cultivated manners, and of pleasing address. Anderson's wife had been dead three or four years.

It was now August 17, 1842, and the hand and heart of Anderson were offered Mrs. Mary Jane Ragens and accepted. With his new companion he now returned to the scenes of his early days and to the four children who joyfully awaited his return. He had made up his mind to settle in Alton. He and his new companion began to prepare for the journey. The family now consisted of the four children of Anderson and two children of his wife, making a family of six besides the two heads.

During the time that intervened between the death of his first wife and his engagement to the second, he taught school in Vincennes, Indiana, Alton and Brookton, Illinois. The old home stood upon the Wabash River, and was quite upon the line that divided the two States,—Indiana and Illinois. His own children went to his school, and were carried across the river on his back. On the other bank stood the log school-house of which he was principal.

In those days it was a matter of some comment to see a Colored man who dared write his name or tell his age, but to see one who was actually a schoolmaster was the marvel of the times. His teaching was a matter of comment in Vincennes, but Vincennes was only a little country town. But to go to Alton,—that city of great fame, then,—and teach school, was an undertaking that required strong nerves. D. W. Anderson had them. He never allowed himself to think that he was any person other than a man and citizen clothed with all civil rights and armed with God-given prerogatives. And so commanding was he, that a man who stood in his presence instantly felt him a superior. Moreover, the heated feeling and public sentiment which, on the night of November 7, 1837, wrested from the hand of God,—to whom alone vengeance belongeth,—a life, were not yet abated. Lovejoy, a peaceable citizen, had been deprived of free speech and struck down by the knife of the assassin ; and could it be expected that a Negro would be spared ? The times were exciting and dangerous, and yet Anderson was determined to take his place and work on in the path of duty, never wincing, but leaving the results with God.

Before in his quiet home and farm life, nature was his peculiar study. He had studied man in studying himself, but in the city of Alton he could study men. He loved to walk through its long streets, watch its hurrying pedestrians, and learn the manifold manifestations of city life.

Having been converted just after the death of his first wife, but never having connected himself with any church, he now joined the A. M. E. Church of Alton. His views from the first were Baptistic, but circumstances placed him among the Methodists. The elder in charge was the powerful preacher, the successful revivalist, and the eminently pious man, Rev. Shadrack Stewart. Some misunderstanding arose between the minister in charge and some of the members, which resulted in the withdrawal of the pastor, Rev. S. Stewart, Anderson and family, and quite a number of the leading members. Minister and all connected themselves with the Baptists. Anderson used often to say to his family: " *That move placed me at home.*" He was indeed at home, and stayed there until he was called to his heavenly rest! He loved very much to study the Bible, and to meditate upon its great truths. The more he studied it the clearer duty seemed and the deeper and purer his love grew for that beneficent Being whom he owned as Lord and King.

It was now 1843. He felt that it was his duty to enter the Gospel ministry. Naturally a modest man, he shrank somewhat from this voice of God; but finally, in 1844, submitted to ordination. He was ordained by the Rev. John Anderson, father of the late Richard Anderson, of St. Louis, or by the Rev. John Livingston, of Illinois, though it is a matter of some doubt as to who was present at his ordination.

He now moved to Upper Alton, and pitched his tent under the shadow of Shurtleff College. His aim was always to excel. He had absorbed every thing that had come within his reach, and now he had placed himself where he could rub against " *College men.*"

Some men have to study a great deal to get a very little; they lack the power of mental absorption, and, consequently, have to wade far out into the river of knowledge in order to feel the benefits of the invigorating waters. Not so with Anderson; he was an indefatigable student. He was always willing to be taught by any person who was able to impart knowledge. Every new word that saluted his ear was forced into his service; never mechanically, but always in its proper place. If he learned a word to-day, to-morrow he would use it in its grammatical relation to a sentence. He had no time for vacation; no mental cessation, but it was one unceasing struggle for knowledge. And no doubt his approximate relation to Shurtleff College helped to impart a certain healthy tone and solidity to his style as a writer and preacher which were ever strikingly manifest.

In a short time he moved out from Alton about twelve miles to the town of Woodburn, Madison County, where he remained for a year, during which time he taught school and preached occasionally. In 1845 he bought an eighty-acre farm on Wood River, about five miles from Alton. He moved his family on the farm, and began to make improvements. After the farm had been put in good working condition, it was not hard for Luther, the eldest child, to manage it. It might seem strange to the boys of to-day, who are dwarfed by cities and cramped by a false civilization, to know that Luther, a boy of fourteen, could follow the plow and swing the cradle. But, nevertheless, his father could trust most of the work of the farm to these young hands.

Duke William Anderson was a civilizer and a reformer. Wherever he placed his foot there were thrift and improvement. He never was satisfied with himself, or that which he did. He always felt when he had done a thing that he could have done it *better*. He never preached a sermon but what he felt that he ought to preach the next one *better*. In his great brain were the insatiable powers of civilization. He was prompt, rapid, decisive, and sagacious, working up to his ideal standard. It was not his object to simply improve and help himself; he was far from such selfishness. The basis of his reformatory and benevolent operations was as broad as humanity and as solid as granite. He never entered a community without the deep feeling that it should be made better, and never lived in one except his warm heart and willing hand went forth to minister to and sympathize with all who were in need.

He felt keenly the bitter prejudice which pervaded the community from which he had just moved, and was sensible of the weakness of the few free Colored citizens who lived in that portion of the State. Wood River was a healthy place to live; and the land was cheap and rich. He was not shut up to any selfish motives, but was planning for the good of his people. He knew that "in union there is strength," and if he could get a number of families to move on Wood River he could form a settlement, and thus bring the people together in religion and politics, in feeling and sentiment.

This plan was no idle dream. In due time he gave notice,

and offered inducements; to the people to come. And they came from every section ; and in a few years it had grown to be a large and prosperous settlement.

Duke William Anderson was the central figure in this community. His colossal form, his clear mind, and excellent judgment, placed him at the head of educational and religious matters. He was parson, schoolmaster, and justice. All questions of theology were submitted to his judgment, from which there was no appeal. All social and political feuds were placed before him, and his advice would heal the severest schisms and restore the most perfect harmony.

He now threw his great soul into the work of organization. He was filled with a grand idea. He felt that the purity and intelligence of the community depended upon their knowledge of the Bible and the preaching of the Gospel. It was a grand idea, though he had to work upon a small scale. It was this idea that made the Israelites victorious ; and Anderson was determined to impress upon this community this primal truth. He knew that in knowledge only is there safety, and in science alone can certainty be found. Before this idea every thing must bow, and around it were to cluster, not only the hopes of that little community, but the prayers of four million bondmen. He was confident that in God he would triumph, and in Him was his trust.

The work was begun in the family circle. One evening it would be at brother Anderson's house, and the next evening at another brother's house, and so on until the meetings had gone around the whole community. A deep work of grace was in progress. The whole community felt the pervading influence of the Spirit, and large results followed. Anderson was wrought upon powerfully. He felt to reconsecrate himself to the Master, and live a more faithful life. This feeling manifested itself in the lives of those who were professors of religion, and the ungodly were anxious about their salvation.

From a very few believers the company of the redeemed had largely increased. One house would not accommodate them, and it became necessary for them to hold their meetings outdoors. It became very evident that this company of believers ought to be organized into a church, and a pastor placed over them. Duke William Anderson was the man to do this work, and, seeing the necessity of it, he immediately organized a Baptist church.

He was a man who never desired to escape difficult **duties**— rather, he always was on hand when hard burdens were to be borne. He approached duty as something that, though at the time hard, brought peace in the end. He loved the approbation of conscience, and never sought to turn away from her teachings.

It is a task seldom, if ever, coveted by the ministers of to-day, to attempt the building of a church edifice, though wealth, art, and all modern facilities await their beck.

And one can easily imagine what a formidable task it must have been to attempt the building of a church thirty years ago. He organized a church out of those who had accepted the Gospel. And the next work was the building of a house of worship. He put his great hand to this work, and in a short time the house was completed and his people worshipping under their own vine and fig-tree.

The house was unique, spacious, and comfortable, all in keeping with the plain people and their unpretentious pastor.

There is a great deal in discipline, and Anderson knew it. Before the organization of his church the people had been placed under no discipline or charged with any special work. But now their leader began the work of church discipline and practical preaching. The feeling that every person was his own man, independent and free, under the preaching of Anderson, gave way to the feeling that they were members of one body, and Christ the head of that body. The unity of the church was preached with great earnestness, and followed by large results. It soon became evident that Duke William Anderson was no ordinary man, and his fame began to spread. He had sought no publicity, but in secret had toiled on in the path of duty.

During his labors in building a meeting-house and organizing a church he had relinquished his hold upon the school; but now as the church was erected and he had more time, he was against his will urged into the school-room again. In the school-room he was as faithful as he was in the pulpit. He sought, with marvellous earnestness, to do with all his might that which was committed to his hands; and all his labors were performed as if they were being performed for himself.

He was at this time pastor of a church, teacher of a school, and owner of an eighty acre farm. If he were going to slight any work, it would not be that of another, but his own. He watched the growth of his little church with an apostolical eye, and nipped every false doctrine in the bud. His excellent knowledge of human nature facilitated his work in the church. He knew every man, woman, and child. He made himself familiar with their circumstances and wants, and always placed himself in complete sympathy with any and all of their circumstances. He consequently won the confidence, love, and esteem of his people. In his school he was watchful and patient. He studied character, and classified his pupils; and was thereby enabled to deal with each pupil as he knew their temperament demanded. Some children are tender, affectionate, and obedient; while others are coarse, ugly, and insubordinate. Some need only to have the wrong pointed out, while others need the rod to convince them of bad conduct. And happy is that teacher who does not attempt to open every child's heart with the same key, or punish each with the same rod.

If there is one quality more than another that the minister needs, it is downright earnestness—perfect sympathy with those to whom he preaches. What does it amount to if a man preach unless he feels what he preaches? Certainly no one can be moved or edified. But Anderson was not a cold, lifeless man. He loved to preach, though he felt a deep sense of unfitness. And it can be truly said of his little church, as was said of the early church: "And believers were the more added to the Lord, multitudes both of men and women."

It was seen by the prophetic eye of Anderson that an association would be the means of bringing the people together. Accordingly he went to work to organize an association that would take into its arms all the feeble communities or churches that had no pastor. In due time all arrangements were perfected, and a call issued for the neighboring churches to send their pastor and two delegates to sit in council with the Salem Baptist Church on Wood River, to consider the propriety of calling into existence such an organization. After the usual preliminary services, Rev. D. W. Anderson stated the object of the meeting, and urged the immediate action of the council in the matter. After the usual amount of debate incident to such an occasion, the proper steps were taken for the organization of an association to be called the "*Wood River Baptist Association*," with Rev. Duke W. Anderson as its first Moderator, to meet on Wood River annually. What a triumph! that day was the proudest of his life! He had spoken to the poor disheartened Baptists for fifty miles around, who were cold and indifferent to the Master's cause: "Awake! and stand upon your feet! Come with me to help the Lord against the mighty! Let us organize for the conflict. There is much to do; so, let us be about our Master's work." The call sent forth breathed new life into the people, and was the signal for united effort in the cause of the Lord.

It was not enough that an association was formed, it was not enough that a few churches were represented in that association; but it must do definite work. It must organize where organization was needed; it must send out missionaries into the destitute places, and give the Gospel to the poor. Thus Anderson reasoned; and the association heard him. Gradually the Wood River Association grew and extended its workings throughout the entire State of Illinois.

It was evident that the associational gatherings were growing so large that it was impossible to accommodate them. He advised the people to build quarters sufficient to accommodate all. Accordingly two or three rows of small houses were erected for the people to live in each year during the time the association was in session. People now came yearly from every part of the State. The great distances did not detain them. Like the Jews who returned to Jerusalem every year to attend the feast, they were glad when the time came to rest from their accustomed duties and journey toward Wood River. It was a delightful gathering. Brother ministers met and compared notes; while young men and maidens gently ministered at the tables, and led the prayer-meetings.

They enjoyed those meetings. There were no conventionalities or forms to check the spirit of Christian love. There was perfect liberty. There were no strangers; for they were the children of one common father. They were as one family, and had all things in common. The utmost order and harmony characterized their gatherings. Not a cross word escaped a single lip. Not a rude act, on the part of the boys, could be seen. Boys, in those days, had the profoundest respect for their seniors, and held a minister of the Gospel in all the simplicity of a boy's esteem.

In the morning of the first day of their meeting the association was called to order by the "*Moderator*," and opened with prayer and a hymn. Then, after the usual business, a sermon was preached. In the afternoon a doctrinal sermon was preached and discussed ; and in the evening a missionary sermon was delivered.

Like the Apostle Paul he could say to the ministers of his day, that he had labored more abundantly than they all. He worked with his hands and preached the Gospel, esteeming it an honor. The church over which he presided had grown to one hundred and fifty active members, besides a large and attentive congregation. This church had been gathered through his incomparable assiduity. He had come into their midst with a heart glowing with the love of God. He had shown himself an excellent farmer, faithful teacher, and consistent Christian. He had led one hundred and fifty souls to Christ. That was not all. In the pulpit he had taught them the fundamental principles of Christianity, and demonstrated those principles in his daily life. His royal manhood towered high over the community, until he became to the whole people a perfect measure of every thing that is lovely and of good report.

He had every thing just as he could wish. He was proprietor of an eighty-acre farm, pastor of a flourishing church, schoolmaster of the community, enthroned in the affections of the people for whose well-being he had worked for seven years,—he might have remained the unrivalled and undisputed king of Woodburn community. But considerations rising high above his mere personal interests, led him to make a great sacrifice in selling his farm, severing his relation as pastor and teacher with a people whom he loved dearly, and who regarded him with a sort of superstitious reverence. The object of the change was that he might move to Quincy, Ill., where he might give his children a thorough education. He secured a scholarship in Knox College for his eldest son, Luther Morgan Anderson, and permission for him to attend. He put his son George W., and daughter, Elizabeth Anderson, to study in the Missionary Institute near Quincy. He now gave his time to farming, preaching, missionary service, and underground railroad work. His son, George W., says, concerning Missionary Institute : "At Missionary Institute the atmosphere was more mild, but such was the continued pressure by the slave-holding border of Mo., offering large rewards for the heads of the Institution, as well for those who were known to be connected with the underground railroad, that the Institution after having done much good went down."

The years of his residence at Quincy were full of public excitement, peril, and strife. He was a spirited, progressive, and representative man. This was the time of the Illinois Prohibition Law, making it a criminal offence to aid or encourage a runaway slave. The slavery question was being sharply discussed in all quarters, and began to color and modify the politics of the day. Anderson was a sharp, ready, and formidable debater, and was the most prominent Colored man in that section of the country. He was gifted in the use of good English, had an easy flow of language, was master of the most galling satire, quick in repartee, prompt to see a weak point and use it to the best advantage. He was a pungent and racy writer, and for a number of years contributed many able articles to the "Quincy Whig." He never spared slavery. In the pulpit, in the public prints, and in private, he fought manfully against the nefarious traffic in human flesh.

Dangerous as was the position he took he felt himself on the side of truth, humanity, and God, and consequently felt that no harm could reach him. At this time, to the duties of farmer, pastor, and contributor he added the severe and perilous duty of a missionary. He canvassed the State, preaching and lecturing against slavery. Often he was confronted by a mob who defied him, bantered him, but he always spoke. He was in every sense the child of nature, endowed with herculean strength, very tall, with a face beaming with benevolence and intelligence. He appeared at his best when opposed, and was enabled by his commanding presence, his phenomenal voice, and burning eloquence to quiet and win the most obstreperous mob.

It was quite easy for a man to be carried away by the irresistible enthusiasm of the excited multitude, and think the rising of the animal spirits the impulses of his better nature. But, for a man to be moved from within, to feel the irresistible power of truth, to feel that except he obeys the voice of his better nature he is arraigned by conscience—though the whole world without is against him, such a man is a hero, deserving of the gratitude and praise of the world.

There were heroes in the days of Anderson, and he was worthy of the high place he held among them. He was possessed of genius of the highest order. He appreciated the times in which he lived. He was equal to the work of his generation, and did not shrink from any work howsoever perilous. He worked between the sluggish conservatism of the anti-slavery element on the one hand, and the violent, mobocratic slave element on the other. Hence, the school of religious and political sentiment to which he belonged had few disciples and encountered many hardships. It was a desperate struggle between an ignorant, self-seeking majority and an intelligent, self-sacrificing minority. It often appears that vice has more votaries than virtue, that might is greater than right, and that wrong has the right of way. But in the light of reason, history, and philosophy, we see the divinity of truth and the mortality of error. We look down upon the great spiritual conflict going on in this world—in society and government,—and seeing the mutations of fortune we think we see truth worsted, and sound the funeral requiem of our fondest hopes, our most cherished ideals.

But the mills of the gods grind slowly, but they grind exceedingly fine. Time rewards the virtuous and patient. It was faith in God, united with a superior hope, that gave him strength in the darkest hours of the "irrepressible conflict."

He was a faithful and indefatigable worker; and the State Missionary Society honored him by thrice choosing him as State Missionary. About this time he became an active member of the "Underground Railroad." His presence, bearing, and high character carried conviction. He made men feel his superiority. He was, consequently, a safe counsellor and a successful manager. He was soon elevated to an official position, which he filled with honor and satisfaction. Many slaves were helped to their freedom by his efforts and advice. He was bold, yet discreet; wise without pedantry; humble without religious affectation; firm without harshness; kind without weakness.

The conflict between slavery and freedom grew hotter and hotter; and the spirit of intolerance became more general. Anderson had proven himself an able defender of human freedom and a formidable enemy to slavery. But it *seemed* as if his efforts in the great aggregate of good were unavailing. His high hopes of educating his children were blasted in the burning of Missionary Institute by a mob from Missouri. It was evident that the slave power would leave no stone unturned in order to accomplish their cowardly and inhuman designs. It was not enough to destroy the only school where all races could be educated together, to disturb the meetings of the few anti-slavery men who dared to discuss a question that they believed involved the golden rule and hence the well-being of the oppressed,—they put a price on his head. He was to be hung to the first tree if caught upon the sacred soil of Missouri. He was secretly, though closely watched. One of his sons writes: " He took a deep interest in the Underground Railroad in connection with a Mr. Turner and Vandorn of Quincy, and a Mr. Hunter and Payne of Missionary Institute. These gentlemen, I believe, with the exception of Mr. Payne, are alive and extensively known in the North."

He was not lacking in the qualities of moral or physical bravery. He could not be bought or bullied. He was unmovable when he felt he was right. The bitterest assaults of his enemies only drove him nearer his ideas, not from them. He might have lived and died in Quincy if he had not greatly desired the education of his children, who were denied such privileges in the destruction of the institute.

At this time intelligent, to say nothing of educated, ministers were few and far between. St. Louis was blessed with an excellent minister in the person of the Rev. Richard Anderson. He was a man of some education, fine manners, good judgment, and deep piety; beloved and respected by all classes both in and out of the church, white and black. The Rev. Galusha Anderson, D.D., who pronounced the funeral sermon over the remains of Richard Anderson, says he had the largest funeral St. Louis ever witnessed. His servant, who had been an attendant upon the ministrations of Richard Anderson, said mournfully, when asked by the doctor if they missed him : " Ah, sir, he led us as by a spider web ! " Richard Anderson saw Duke William Anderson and loved him. He saw in the young man high traits of character, and in his rare gifts auguries of a splendid career. He saw the danger he lived in, the hopeless condition of public sentiment, and advised him to accept the pastoral charge of the Baptist church in Buffalo, N. Y., where also he could educate his children.

Buffalo was an anti-slavery stronghold. The late Gerrit Smith was chief of the party in that section of New York. By his vast wealth, his high personal character, his deeply-rooted convictions, his wide-spread and consistent opposition to slavery, he was the most conspicuous character in the State, and made many converts to the anti-slavery cause. Buffalo was the centre of anti-slavery operations. Many conventions and conferences were held there. It was only twenty-four miles to the Canadian boundaries, hence it was the last and most convenient station of the U. G. R. R.

It was now about 1854–1855. The anti-slavery sentiment was a recognized and felt power in the politics of the Nation. Anderson appeared in Buffalo just in time to participate in the debates that were rendering that city important. He took the pastoral charge of the Baptist church and high standing as a leader. He remained here quite two years or more, during which time he used the pulpit and the press as the vehicles of his invectives against slavery. He did not have to go to men, they went to him. He was a great moral magnet, and attracted the best men of the city. The white clergy recognized in him the qualities of a preacher and leader worthy of their admiration and recognition. The Rev. Charles Dennison and other white brethren invited him to their pulpits, where he displayed preaching ability worthy of the intelligent audiences that listened to his eloquent discourses.

His stay in Buffalo was salutary. By his industry and usefulness he became widely known and highly respected. And when he accepted a call from the Groghan Street Baptist Church, of Detroit, Michigan, his Buffalo friends were conscious that in his departure from them they sustained a very great loss.

It was now the latter part of 1857. The anti-slavery conflict was at its zenith. This controversy, as do all moral controversies, had brought forth many able men; had furnished abundant material for satire and rhetoric. This era presented a large and brilliant galaxy of Colored orators. There were Frederick Douglass—confessedly the historic Negro of America,—Charles L. Remond, Charles L. Reason, William Wells Brown, Henry Highland Garnett, Martin R. Delany, James W. C. Pennington, Robert Purvis, Phillip A. Bell, Charles B. Ray, George T. Downing, George B. Vashon, William C. Nell, Samuel A. Neale, William Whipper, Ebenezer D. Bassett, William Howard Day, William Still, Jermain W. Loguen, Leonard A. Grimes, John Sella Martin, and many others. Duke William Anderson belonged to the same school of orators.

The church at Detroit had been under the pastoral charge of the Rev. William Troy, who had accepted the pulpit of the Baptist church in Windsor, Canada West, and started to England to solicit funds to complete a beautiful edifice already in process of erection. At this time John Sella Martin had obtained considerable notoriety as an orator. He had canvassed the Western States in the interest of the anti-slavery cause, and was now residing in Detroit. He was baptized and ordained by Brethren Anderson and Troy, and took charge of the church at Buffalo.

Detroit lies in a salubrious atmosphere, upon Detroit River, not far from Lake Erie ; and at this time was not lacking in a high social and moral atmosphere. The field was the most congenial he had yet labored in. He found an excellent church-membership, an intelligent and progressive people. He was heartily welcomed and highly appreciated. He entered into the work with zeal, and imparted an enthusiasm to the people. He developed new elements of strength in the church. He attracted a large, cultivated audience, and held them to the last day he remained in the city. His audience was not exclusively Colored : some of the best white families were regular attendants upon his preaching ; and they contributed liberally to his support. Detroit had never seen the peer of Duke William Anderson in the pulpit. He did not simply attract large congregations on the Sabbath, but had a warm place in the affections of all classes, and a personal moral influence, which added much to the spirituality of the church. In every church, thus far, he had been blessed with a revival of religion, and souls had been added as " seals to his ministry." Detroit was no exception to the rule. Under his leadership, through his preaching and pastoral visitations the church was aroused, and the result a revival. Many were added to the church.

It was now the spring of 1858. John Brown, the proto-martyr of freedom, by his heroism, daring, intrepid perseverance, inspired,—swallowed with one great idea, had stirred all Kansas and Missouri to fear, and carried off eleven slaves to Canada and set them free. He had established his headquarters at Chatham, Canada West, and begun the work of organization preparatory to striking the blow at Harper's Ferry. Brown held his first convention at Chatham—only a few hours' ride from Detroit—on May 8, 1858, at 10 o'clock A.M. The convention was composed of some very able men. The following-named gentlemen composed the convention : Wm. Charles Monroe, President of the Convention ; G. J. Reynolds, J. C. Grant, A. J. Smith, James M. Jones, Geo. B. Gill, M. F. Bailey, Wm. Lambert, C. W. Moffitt, John J. Jackson, J. Anderson, Alfred Whipple, James M. Bue,

Wm. H. Leeman, Alfred M. Ellsworth, John E. Cook, Stewart Taylor, James W. Purnell, Geo. Akin, Stephen Detlin, Thomas Hickinson, John Cannet, Robinson Alexander, Richard Realf, Thomas F. Cary, Thomas W. Stringer, Richard Richardson, J. T. Parsons, Thos. M. Kinnard, Martin R. Delany, Robert Van-rankin, Charles H. Tidd, John A. Thomas, C. Whipple, J. D. Shad, Robert Newman, Owen Brown, John Brown, J. H. Harris, Charles Smith, Simon Fislin, Isaac Hotley, James Smith. Signed, J. H. Kagi. The following is the list of officers elected:

Commander-in-chief, John Brown; Secretary of War, J. H. Kagi; Members of Congress, Alfred M. Ellsworth, Osborn Anderson; Treasurer, Owen Brown; Secretary of Treasury, Geo. B. Gill; Secretary of State, Richard Realf.

The reader will see that two Andersons are mentioned, J. Anderson and Osborn Anderson. [Who these gentlemen are, the author does not know, nor has he any means of knowing.]

Rev. D. W. Anderson's ministry in Detroit was a success both in and out of the pulpit, both among his parishioners and among those of the world.

His wife was in every sense a pastor's wife. She bore for him the largest sympathy in his work; and cheered him with her prayers and presence in every good cause. She was intelligent and pious, loved by the church, honored by society. She found pleasure in visiting the sick, helping the poor, comforting the sorrowful, and in instructing the erring in ways of peace.

It is almost impossible to compute the value of a pastor's wife who appreciates the work of saving souls. If she is a good woman her influence is unbounded. Every person loves her, every person looks up to her. There are so many little things that she can do, if not beyond the province of the pastor, often out of range of his influence. Mrs. Anderson was all that could be hoped as a pastor's wife. She was of medium size, in complexion light, rather reserved in her manners, affable in address, very sensitive in her physical and mental constitution. Much of Anderson's service in Detroit must go to the account of his sainted wife. And it may not be irrelevant to remark that every minister of Christ's influence and success is perceptibly modified by his wife—much depends upon her!

Eighteen years of happy wedded life had passed. It was the autumn of 1860. Mrs. Anderson's health was failing. Her presence was missed from the church, from society, and at last on the 23d of October, 1860, she died.

On the 18th of March, 1861, he married again, Mrs. Eliza Julia Shad, of Chatham, Canada. He turned his attention to farming for a while, in order to regain his health.

At the close of the war he went South and taught in a theological institution at Nashville. Soon after he began his work here he received and accepted a call from the 19th Street Baptist Church of Washington, D. C. Washington was in a vile condition at the close of the war. Its streets were mud holes; its inhabitants crowded and jammed by the troops and curious Negroes from the plantations. Society was in a critical condition. There was great need of a leader for the Colored people. D. W. Anderson was that man. He entered upon his work with zeal and intelligence. He carried into the pulpit rare abilities, and into the parish work a genial, kindly nature which early gave him a place in the affections and confidence of his flock.

As a preacher he was a marvel. He generally selected his text early in the week. He studied its exegesis, made the plan of the sermon, and then began to choose his illustrations and fill in. On Sunday he would rise in his pulpit, a man six feet two and a half inches, and in a rich, clear, deliberate voice commence an extemporaneous discourse. His presence was majestic. With a massive head, much like that of John Adams, a strong brown eye that flashed as he moved on in his discourse, a voice sweet and well modulated, but at times rising to tones of thunder, graceful, ornate, forcible, and dramatic, he was the peer of any clergyman in Washington, and of Negroes there were none his equal.

He showed himself a power in the social life of his people by being himself a living epistle. He encouraged the young, and set every one who knew him an example of fidelity and efficiency in the smaller matters of life.

His early experiences were now in demand. The entire community recognized in him the elements of magnificent leadership. He was in great demand in every direction. He was elected a Trustee of the Howard University, of the Freedman's Saving Bank and Trust Company, Commissioner of Washington Asylum, Sept. 3d, 1871, and Justice of the Peace, 8th of April, 1869, and 9th of April, 1872. The vast amount of work he did on the outside did not impair his usefulness as a pastor or his faithfulness as a minister of the Gospel. On the contrary he gathered ammunition and experience from every direction. He made every thing help him in his preparation for the pulpit. His deep spiritual life, his nearness to the Master gave him power with men. No winter passed without a revival of grace and the conversion of scores of sinners. Thus the work continued until the house was both too small and unsafe. Plans were drawn and steps taken to build a new church edifice.

On the first Sunday in March, 1871, the old house of worship, on the corner of Nineteenth and I streets was abandoned, and the congregation went to worship in the Stevens School building. The corner-stone of the new building was laid on the 5th of April, 1871, and the new edifice dedicated on the 19th of November, 1871, five months after the work had begun. The dedicatory exercises were as follows:

At eleven o'clock precisely, Rev. D. W. Anderson, pastor in charge, announced that the hour for the religious exercises to commence had arrived, and he took pleasure in introducing his predecessor, Rev. Samuel W. Madden, of Alexandria, Va., who gave out the 934th hymn, which was sung with considerable fervor and spirit, the entire congregation rising and participating; after which, Rev. Jas. A. Handy, read from the 6th chapter, 2d Chronicles, and also addressed the throne of grace.

" Lift up your heads, ye eternal gates" was admirably rendered by the choir, when the following letter was read from the President:

" EXECUTIVE MANSION, }
" WASHINGTON, Nov. 18, 1871. }

" To Rev. D. W. ANDERSON, No. 1971 I Street,

" SIR : The President directs me to say that your note of the 8th inst., inviting him to be present at the dedication of your church, was mislaid during his absence from the city, and was not brought to his notice till to-day. He regrets that his engagements will not admit of his attendance at the time you mention. He congratulates your congregation upon the completion of so handsome a place of worship, and hopes that its dedication may prove an occasion of deep interest to all who share in a desire to promote the spread of the Christian religion.

" I am, sir, your obedient servant,
" HORACE PORTER, *Secretary.*"

Rev. Henry Williams, of Petersburg, Va., who was announced to preach the dedicatory sermon, selected the following words: "And he was afraid, and said : How dreadful is this place! this is none other but the house of God, and this is the gate of heaven."

Prominent among those present who had been invited by Rev. Mr. Anderson, were His Excellency Governor H. D. Cooke, Hon. N. P. Chipman, Delegate to Congress; A. L. Sturtevant, Esq., Chief of Stationery Bureau, Treasury Department; Ed. Young, Esq., Chief of the Bureau of Statistics; Hon. A. K. Browne, Col. Wm. A. Cook, Dr. A. T. Augusta, and Wm. H. Thompson, Esq., of Philadelphia. While, seated around the altar, were Rev. Leonard A. Grimes, of Boston; Rev. Samuel. W Madden, of Alexandria, Va.; Rev. Geo. W. Goins, of Philadelphia; Rev. Jas. A. Handy, Washington; and Rev. Wm. Troy, Richmond, Va. At three o'clock, Rev. Leonard A. Grimes officiated and delivered an eloquent sermon.

A work of grace followed the dedication of the church; and from month to month souls were converted. On the 21st of January, 1873, he wrote the following letter to a Baptist minister residing in Chicago:

"1921 I Street, WASHINGTON, D. C., Jan. 21, 1873.

"REV. R. DEBAPTIST:

"DEAR BROTHER: I write to inform you of a wonderful outpouring of the Spirit of God in the 19th Street Baptist Church of which I am pastor. Without any especial effort, up to the last few days, there have been one to five converted every month, for the past seven years, in the congregation. This led too many to think that that was enough. At our watch-meeting I asked how many there were who would come to the front pews and kneel before God as a token to Christians to pray for them, and ten came. We had no other meeting until my weekly lecture, the first Thursday night in January after it. I saw a great feeling and called again; and there came twenty-two. The brethren and sisters decided to hold meeting the next night, and there came thirty-two who were converted. Now, at this date, Monday night, 20th, there came forward 'ninety-seven'; and there were over a hundred on their knees praying. Twenty-two found peace in believing last night.

"We are all well. Pray for us. Write soon.

"Yours ever,

"D. W. ANDERSON."

He was taken sick on the 7th of February, 1873, and after a painful illness of eleven days, he fell asleep on the 17th of February, full of years and honors, and was gathered to the fathers. On the Monday evening, just before he died, he told his wife, daughter, and a small company of friends who surrounded his death-bed: "It 's all well," and then, at 7:30 P.M., quietly "fell on sleep."

The news of his death cast gloom into thousands of hearts, and evoked eulogies and letters of condolence never before bestowed upon a Negro. His death was to the members of his church in the nature of a personal bereavement. The various interests to which he had loaned the enlightening influence of his judgment and the beneficence of his presence mourned his loss, and expressed their grief in appropriate resolutions. His life and character formed a fitting theme for the leading pulpits ; and the Baptist denomination, the Negro race, and the nation sincerely mourned the loss of a great preacher, an able leader, and a pure patriot.

At the request of many people of both races and political parties, his body was placed in state in the church for twenty-four hours, and thousands of people, rich and poor, black and white, sorrowfully gazed upon the face of the illustrious dead. The funeral services were held on the 20th of February, and his obsequies were the largest Washington had ever seen, except those of the late Abraham Lincoln. The church was crowded to suffocation, and the streets for many squares were filled with solemn mourners. Thus a great man had fallen. The officers of the Freedman's Bank passed the following resolutions, which were forwarded with the accompanying letter from the president :

"OFFICE OF THE FREEDMAN'S SAVINGS AND TRUST }
"COMPANY, WASHINGTON, D. C., Feb. 20th, 1873. }

"At a meeting of the Board of Trustees of the Freedman's Savings and Trust Company, held this date, the following resolutions were adopted :

"1st. *Resolved*, That in the death of the Rev. D. W. Anderson, Trustee and Vice-President of this Company, we sustain the loss of a most excellent Christian man, and an officer of highest integrity. In all his relations to us he was an endeared associate, and an honored, intelligent, co-worker : ever firm in purpose and faithful to those for whom he labored. Our long intercourse with him impressed us with the increasing value of his services to the church of which he was pastor, and to *this institution*.

"We also hereby express our sincere sympathy with his immediate friends, and especially his afflicted family.

"2d. *Resolved*, That, as an added expression of our esteem, this Board will attend and take part in his funeral services, *as a body*.

"3d. *Resolved*, That these resolutions be spread upon our Records, and that a copy of the same be transmitted to his family."

" Principal Office,
" Freedman's Savings and Trust Company,
" Washington, D. C., Feb. 21, '73.

" To Mrs. D. W. Anderson.

"*My Dear Sister:* Allow me to transmit to you the enclosed copy of resolutions passed by the Board of Trustees of the F. S. and T. Comp., *with* the sincerest assurances of my *personal* sympathy.

" Very respectfully, yours, etc.,

" I. W. Alvord, *President.*"

The Board of the Commissioners of the Washington Asylum passed the following resolutions of condolence :

" Whereas, it has pleased Divine Providence to remove from this life the Rev. D. W. Anderson, late President of this Board : therefore,

" *Be it resolved,* That in his death we have lost an honorable and faithful associate, a genial and kind-hearted friend, whom we delighted to honor and respect for his many virtues and sterling worth. In him the poor have lost a sympathizing friend ; the criminal an even dispenser of Justice, and the Government one of its most efficient officers.

" *Resolved,* That we tender our most sincere sympathy to his bereaved family, and condole with them in this sad dispensation of Divine Providence.

" *Resolved,* That the resolutions be entered upon the Journal of proceedings of this Board, and a copy sent to the family of the lamented deceased.

" A. B. Bohrer,

" *Sec. B. C. W. Asylum.*

" Mrs. D. W. Anderson,
" Present."

The Young People's Christian Association, which he had founded, have spread the following resolutions of respect upon their minutes :

" *Whereas,* It has pleased the Supreme Ruler and Architect of the Universe to remove from our Association our beloved and estimable brother and Corresponding Secretary D. W. Anderson, whose Christian life was a beacon light, for all associated with him to follow, being humble, patient, forbearing, and forgiving, Therefore,

" *Resolved,* That in his death we have lost an humble and true Christian, possessing the same prominent characteristics which distinguished the Saviour of Mankind, doing good whenever he believed he was serving his Heavenly Master, administering to the poor, feeding the hungry, clothing the naked, binding up the wounds of those offended, and laboring zealously for the salvation of souls, but while we feel the severe stroke of death that has stricken down one of our best members, we bow humbly to the will of Divine Providence, 'who doeth all things well,' believing that He has summoned our brother to dwell with Him in peace and happiness and to join the Army that is continually singing praises to Him who rules both the Heavens and the earth, so we cheerfully bow and acknowledge that our loss is his eternal gain.

"*Resolved*, That we tender to his bereaved family our sincere and Christian sympathy in this their hour of bereavement, and pray that He who has promised to be a Husband to the Widow, and a Father to the Fatherless, may keep and protect them.

"*Resolved*, That a copy of these resolutions be engrossed and sent to the family of our deceased brother, and that the same be entered upon the records of the Association."

And the church testified their love and sorrow in the following beautiful resolves:

"Baptist Church,
"Corner of 19th & I Streets,
"Washington, D. C., Feb. 28, 1873.

"*Whereas*, It has pleased the Almighty God, the Supreme Ruler of the universe to remove from us our much esteemed and beloved Pastor,

"Reverend D. W. Anderson,
"therefore, be it,

"*Resolved*, That we deeply deplore and lament the loss of so great and noble a pioneer in the cause of Christ, one who, like Christ, although scorned, traduced and ill-treated by enemies, went forward and labored in and out of his church for the promotion of the work of his Father in Heaven.

"*Resolved*, that as a Church we feel the severe stroke that has summoned from us our dearly beloved Pastor; but knowing that our loss is his eternal gain, we cheerfully submit to the will and order of that God who does all things well, that God who controls the destinies of nations, kingdoms, and empires, that God who 'moves in mysterious ways his wonders to perform.'

"*Resolved*, That we will endeavor by the assistance of our heavenly Master to live up to the teachings and examples set by our shepherd, thereby believing that when we are summoned to appear at the bar of God we will meet our Pastor in that grand Church above where 'sickness, pain, sorrow, or death is feared and felt no more,' 'where congregations ne'er break up, and Sabbath hath no end,' where 'we will sing hosannas to our heavenly King, where we will meet to part no more forever.'

"*Resolved*, That we, the Church, extend to the bereaved family our heartfelt sympathies, and that a copy of these resolutions be sent to them, and also entered on the Church journal.

"LINDSEY MUSE, *Moderator.*

"DAVID WARNER, *Clerk.*"

The Mite Society of his church erected a monument to his memory in *Harmony Cemetery*, bearing the following inscriptions:

"The Christian Mite Society of the 19th Street Baptist Church render this tribute to the memory of their beloved pastor. We shall go to him, but he shall not return to us.

"Rev. D. W. ANDERSON,

"Born April 10th, 1812. Died Feb. 17th, 1873.

"'I have finished the work which thou gavest me to do.'

"He was ordained in 1844, and after a ministry of 21 years settled with the 19th Street Baptist Church of Washington, D. C., where he fell asleep in the midst of a great revival.

"For the cause of education, the welfare of the poor, the promotion of humanity, liberty, and the conversion of the world.

"He labored faithfully until the Master called him hence."

This beautiful life was studded with the noblest virtues. From obscurity and poverty Duke William Anderson had risen to fame and honors; and having spent a useful life, died in the midst of a great revival in the capital of the nation, holding more positions of trust than any other man, white or black; died with harness on, and left a name whose lustre will survive the corroding touch of time.

The Rev. James Poindexter, of Columbus, Ohio, and the Rev. Wallace Shelton, of Cincinnati, are now and have been for years the foremost Baptist ministers of Ohio. Both men came to Ohio more than a generation ago, and have proven themselves able ministers of Christ.

But of New England Baptist ministers Leonard Andrew Grimes is of most blessed memory.

It was some time during the year 1840, when disputings arose —about what is not known—within the membership of what was known as the "First Independent Baptist Church," of Boston, Mass., which resulted in the drawing out from the same of about forty members. This party was led by the Rev. Mr. Black, who had been, for some time, pastor of the church he now left. They secured a place of worship in Smith Court, off of Joy Street, where they continued for a considerable space of time. It was not long, however, after they began to worship in their new home, before their highly esteemed and venerable leader was stricken down with disease, from which he subsequently died.

This little band was now without a leader, and was, consequently, speedily rent by a schism within its own circle. But in the nucleus that finally became the Twelfth Baptist Church, there were faithful men and women who believed in the integrity of their cause, and, therefore, stood firm. They believed that " He who was for them was greater than all they who were against them." Though few in number, they felt that "one shall chase a thousand, and two shall put ten thousand to flight," was a very pertinent passage when applied to themselves. And those who have been blessed to see that little " company of believers " grow to be an exceedingly large and prosperous church of Christ must be persuaded that God alone gave "the increase."

For a long time this little company struggled on without a leader. They were called upon to walk through many discouraging scenes, and to humble themselves under the remorseless hand of poverty. Unable to secure, permanently, the services of a clergyman, they were driven to the necessity of obtaining whomsoever they could when the Sabbath came. And what a blessed thing it was for them that they were placed under the severe discipline of want! It taught them humility and faith—lessons often so hard to acquire. They bore their trials heroically, and esteemed it great joy to be counted worthy to suffer for Christ. When one Sabbath was ended they knew not whom the Lord would send the next; and yet they never suffered for the " Word of God." For He who careth for the lilies of the field, and bears up the falling sparrow, fed them with the " bread of life," and gave them to drink of the waters of salvation. " Unto the poor the Gospel was preached."

After a few years of pain and waiting, after the watching and praying, the hoping and fearing, God seemed pleased to hear the prayers of this lonely band, and gave them a leader. It was whispered in the community that a very intelligent and useful man, by the name of " Grimes," of New Bedford, could be retained as their leader. After some deliberation upon the matter, they chose one of their number to pay a visit to " Brother Leonard

A. Grimes, of New Bedford," and on behalf of the company worshipping in "an upper room," on Belknap Street—now Joy Street—Boston, extended him an invitation to come and spend a Sabbath with them. In accordance with their request he paid them a visit. Impressed with the dignity of his bearing, and the earnestness of his manner, the company was unanimous in an invitation, inviting "the young preacher" to return and remain with them for "three months."

The invitation was accepted with alacrity, and the work begun with a zeal worthy of the subsequent life of "the beloved pastor of the Twelfth Baptist Church." Brother L. A. Grimes had been driven North on account of his friendly and humane relations to the oppressed. He had been incarcerated by the laws of slave-holding Virginia, for wresting from her hand, and piloting into the land of freedom, those whom slavery had marked as her children—or, rather, her "*goods.*" A soul like his was too grand to live in such an atmosphere. In keeping the golden rule, he had insulted the laws of the institution under whose merciless sway thousands of human beings were groaning. He would live no longer where his convictions of duty were to be subordinated to, and palliated by, the penurious and cruel teaching of the slave institution. So, after having been robbed of his property, he left, in company with his family, for the fair shores of New England. He had sought no distinction, but had settled down to a quiet life in New Bedford. But a man of his worth could not stay in the quiet walks of life ; he was born to lead, and heard God call him to the work his soul loved.

His quiet, unpretentious ministry of "three months" shadowed forth the loving, gentle, yet vigorous and successful ministry of a quarter of a century ; a ministry so like the Master's, not confined to sect or nationality, limited only by the wants of humanity and the great heart-love that went gushing out to friend and foe. Those who were so happy as to sit under his ministry for the "three months" were quite unwilling to be separated from one whose ministry had so greatly comforted and built them up. In the young preacher they had found a leader of excellent judgment, a pastor of tender sympathies, and a father who loved them with all the strength of true manly affection, How could they retain him? They were poor. How could they release him? They loved him. After much prayer and pleading, Brother Grimes was secured as their leader, with a salary at the rate of $100 per annum. He returned to New Bedford and moved his family to Boston. His salary barely paid his rent; but by working with his hands, as Paul did, and through the industry of his wife, he was enabled to get along.

During all this time this little company of believers was without "church organization." At length a council was called and their prayer for organization presented. After the procedure common to such councils, it was voted that this company of Christian men and women be organized as the "Twelfth Baptist Church." The church consisted of twenty-three members.

On the evening of the 24th of November, 1848, occurred the services of the recognition of the church, and the ordination of Rev. L. A. Grimes as its pastor. The order of exercises was as follows:

Reading of Scriptures and prayer, by the Rev. Edmund Kelley; sermon, by the Rev. J. Banvard, subject: "The way of salvation," from Acts xvi, 17: "The same followed Paul and us, and cried, saying, These men are the servants of the most high God, which show unto us the way of salvation"; hand of fellowship to the church, by the Rev. T. F. Caldicott; prayer of recognition and ordination, by the Rev. John Blain; charge to the candidate, by the Rev. Nathaniel Colver; address to the church, by the Rev. Rollin H. Neale; concluding prayer, by the Rev. Sereno Howe; benediction, by the pastor, Rev. Leonard A. Grimes.

The exercises were of a very pleasant nature, and of great interest to the humble little church that assembled to enjoy them. It was an occasion of no small moment that published to the world the "Twelfth Baptist Church," and sent upon a mission of love and mercy, Leonard Andrew Grimes! It was an occasion that has brought great strength to the Colored people of Boston, yea, of the country! It was the opening of a door; it was the loosening of chains, the beginning of a ministry that was to stretch over a period of twenty-five years, carrying peace and blessing to men in every station. And may we not, with propriety, halt upon the threshold of our gratitude, and thank that wise Being who gave him, a blessing to the church a friend to humanity?

Happy, thrice happy, was the little church that had wedded itself for life to one who had laid himself upon the altar of their common cause. These relations and manifold responsibilities were not hastily or rashly assumed. The little church felt keenly its poverty and weakness, while its new pastor knew that the road to prosperity lay through fields of toil and up heights of difficulty. Before him was no dark future, for the light of an extraordinary faith scattered the darkness as he advanced to duty. What man of intelligence, without capital or social influence, would have undertaken so discouraging a project as that to which Leonard A. Grimes unconditionally brought the sanctified zeal of a loving heart? To him it was purely a matter of duty, and it was this thought that urged him on with his almost superhuman burdens.

But to return to the "upper chamber," and take one more look at the happy little church. It was not the pastor's object to begin at once to perfect plans to secure a place more desirable to worship in than their present little room. His heart longed for that enlargement of soul secured by a nearness to the divine Master. His heart yearned after those who were enemies to the "*cross of Christ.*" His first prayer was: "O Lord, revive thy work!" and it was not offered in vain. A season of prayer was instituted for the outpouring of the Spirit. The pastor led the way to the throne of grace in a fervent and all-embracing prayer. A spirit of prayer fell upon his people. Every heart trembled in tenderest sympathy for those who were strangers to the "covenant of mercy"; every eye was dampened with tears of gratitude and love; every tongue was ready to exclaim with Watts :—

> " 'T was the same love that spread the feast,
> That sweetly forced us in ;
> Else we had still refused to taste,
> And perished in our sin."

The church had reached that point in feeling where the blessing is sure. They heard the coming of the chariot, and felt the saving power of the Lord in their midst. It was a glorious revival. There were more converted than there were members in the church. Oh, what joy, what peace, what comfort in the Holy Ghost was there in that "upper chamber"! What tongue or pen can describe the scene in that room when over thirty souls were gathered into the fold! A pastor's *first* revival! What rejoicing! The gathering of his first children in the Lord! Ask Paul what conscious pride he took in those who were his " epistles," his " fruit in the Gospel," his " children " in Christ

Jesus. It lifted Brother Grimes up to the heights of Pisgah in his rejoicing, and laid him low at the cross in his humility. " The Lord had done great things for him, whereof he was glad"; And they " did eat their meat with gladness and singleness of heart, praising God, and having favor with all the people. And the Lord added to the church daily such as should be saved."

The rooms in which they began now proved too small for their rapidly increasing membership. They agreed to have a building of their own. It was now the latter part of 1848. The business eye of the pastor fell upon a lot on Southac Street; and in the early part of 1849 the trustees purchased it. Preparations for building were at once begun. It seemed a large undertaking for a body of Christians so humble in circumstances, so weak in numbers. But faith and works were the *genii* that turned the tide of prosperity in their favor. They decided that the ground and edifice should not exceed in cost the sum of $10,000. The society proposed to raise two or three thousand within its own membership; three thousand by loan, and solicit the remainder from the Christian public. Previous to this period the public knew little or nothing of this society. Brother Grimes had come to Boston almost an entire stranger, and had now to undertake the severe task of presenting the interests of a society so obscure and of so recent date. But he believed in his cause, and knew that success would come. He had known Dr. Neale in Washington City, during his early ministry; they were boys together. They met. It was a pleasant meeting. The Rev. Mr. Neale vouched for him before the public. It was not particularly necessary, for Brother Grimes carried a recommendation in his face: it was written all over with veracity and benevolence.

Joyfully and successfully he hurried on his mission. He made friends of the enemies of evangelical religion, and gathered a host of admirers around him. The public saw in him not only the zealous pastor of an humble little church, but the true friend of humanity. The public ear was secured; his prayer was answered in the munificent gifts that came in from every direction. Every person seemed anxious to contribute something to this noble object.

It was a beautiful morning! The sun never shone brighter, nor the air smelled sweeter or purer than on that memorable first day of August, 1850 The first persons to usher themselves into the street that morning were the happy members of the " *Twelfth*

Baptist Church." Every face told of the inward joy and peace of thankful hearts. Those who had toiled long through the days of the church's "small things," felt that their long-cherished hopes were beginning to bud.

Long before the appointed hour the members and friends of the church began to gather to participate in the "laying of the corner-stone of the Twelfth Baptist Church." It was a sweet, solemn occasion.

"Rev. Drs. Sharp, Neale and Colver, together with the pastor of the church, officiated on the occasion. The usual documents were deposited with the stone, and the customary proceedings gone through with, in a solemn and impressive manner."

The occasion lent an enthusiasm for the work hitherto unknown. They were emboldened. The future looked bright, and on every hand the times were propitious. Gradually the walls of the edifice grew heavenward, and the building began to take on a pleasing phase. At length the walls had reached their proper height, and the roof crowned all. Their sky was never brighter. It is true a "little speck of cloud" was seen in the distance ; but they were as unsuspicious as children. The cloud approached gradually, and, as it approached, took on its terrible characteristics. It paused a while ; it trembled. Then there was a death-like silence in the air, and in a moment it vomited forth its forked lightning, and rolled its thunder along the sky. It was the explosion of a Southern shell over a Northern camp, that was lighted by the torch of ambition in the hands of fallen Webster. It was the culmination of slave-holding Virginia's wrath. It was invading the virgin territory of liberty-loving Massachusetts. It was hunting the fugitive on free soil, and tearing him from the very embrace of sweet freedom.

When the time came to enlist Colored soldiers, Leonard A. Grimes was as untiring in his vigilance as any friend of the Fifty-fourth Regiment of Massachusetts volunteers, while the members of his church were either joining or aiding the regiment. So highly were the services of Brother Grimes prized that the chaplaincy of the regiment was not only tendered him, but urged upon him ; but the multifarious duties of his calling forbade his going with the regiment he loved and revered.

The ladies of his congregation were busy with their needles, thus aiding the cause of the Union ; and no church threw its doors open more readily to patriotic meetings than the Twelfth

Baptist Church. And during those dark days of the Union, when all seemed hopeless, when our armies were weak and small, the prayers of a faithful pastor and pious people ascended day and night, and did much to strengthen the doubting.

The fugitive-slave law and civil war had done much to weaken the church financially and numerically. Many who fled from the fugitive-slave law had not returned ; the young men had entered the service of the country, while many others were absent from the city under various circumstances. But notwithstanding all these facts, God blessed the church—even in war times,—and many were converted.

The struggle was now ended. "The Boys in Blue" came home in triumph. The father separated from child, the husband from wife, could now meet again. Those who were driven before the wrath of an impious and cruel edict could now return to the fold without fear. What a happy occasion it was for the whole church ! The reunion of a family long separated ; the gathering of dispersed disciples. The occasion brought such an undistinguishable throng of fancies—such joy, such hope, such blessed fellowship—as no pen can describe.

At the commencement of the Rebellion the church numbered about 246 ; and at the close of the Rebellion it numbered about 300, notwithstanding the discouraging circumstances under which she labored. The revivals that followed brought many into the church, and the heart of the pastor was greatly encouraged.

At first it was thought that the entire cost of the land and building would not exceed $10,000 ; but the whole cost, from the time they began to build until the close of the war, was $14,044.09. In 1861 the indebtedness of the church was $2,967.62 ; at the close of the war it was about $2,000.

During all these years of financial struggle the church had ever paid her notes with promptness and without difficulty. And now that the war was over, freedom granted to the enslaved, and the public again breathing easy, the little church, not weary of well-doing, again began the work of removing the remaining debt. The public was sought only in the most extreme necessity. The ladies held sewing circles, and made with the needle fancy articles to be sold in a festival, while the members of the church were contributing articles of wearing apparel, or offering their services at the sale tables. The proceeds were given to the society to pay its debts ; and it was no mean gift.

From 1865 to 1871 the church grew rapidly. Revivals were of frequent occurrence; and many from the South, learning of the good name of Rev. Mr. Grimes, sought his church when coming to Boston. But it was apparent that their once commodious home was now too small. The pastor saw this need, and began to take the proper steps to meet it. It was at length decided that the church should undergo repairs; and the pastor was armed with the proper papers to carry forward this work. The gallery that was situated in the east end of the church was used chiefly by the choir and an instrument. In making repairs it was thought wise to remove the organ from the gallery, and put in seats, and thereby accommodate a larger number of people. Then, the old pulpit took up a great deal of room, and by putting in a new pulpit of less dimensions, more room could be secured for pews. This was done, with the addition of a baptistry, the lack of which for nearly twenty-five years had driven them, in all kinds of weather, to Charles River. Every thing, from the basement up, underwent repairs. The pews were painted and furnished with book-racks. The floors were repaired, and covered with beautiful carpet; while the walls and ceilings were richly clothed with fresco, by the hands of skilful workmen. In the centre of the ceiling was an excellent ventilator, from which was suspended a very unique chandelier, with twelve beautiful globes, that were calculated to dispense their mellow light upon the worshippers below. But to crown all this expensive work and exceeding beauty thus bestowed upon the house, was the beautiful organ that adorned the southwest corner of the church, just to the pastor's right when in the pulpit. It was secured for the sum of two thousand five hundred dollars. All was accomplished. The old house of worship was now entirely refitted. No heart was happier than the pastor's the day the church was reopened.[1] The new and elegant organ sent forth its loud peals of music in obedience to the masterly touch of the "*faithful one*," who for more than twelve years was never absent from her post of duty, and whom none knew but to love and honor.

What supreme satisfaction there is in the accomplishment of a work that comprehends, not the interests of an individual, but the interests of the greatest number of human beings! The

---

[1] It was our good fortune to be present. We remember distinctly his happy face, his words of gratitude and thanks. And as we looked around every face wore an expression of complete satisfaction.

labors of Rev. Mr. Grimes were bestowed upon those whom he loved. He had toiled for his church as a father does to support his family. And no pastor, perhaps, was ever more paternal to his flock than Leonard A. Grimes. He was a man wondrously full of loving-kindness,—a lover of mankind.

It has been the rule rather than the exception, for a long time, for churches to carry heavy debts; and when a church is free from debt, it certainly furnishes a cause for great rejoicing. It was so with the Twelfth Baptist Church. For a long time— more than twenty years—the church had been before the public as an object of charity. For more than twenty years the people had struggled heroically amid all of the storms that gathered around them. Sometimes they expected to see "*the red flag*" upon their house of worship, but the flag was never raised.

The debts of the church had all been removed. The house was absolutely free from every encumbrance; the people owned their church.

But the little church of twenty-three had become the large church of six hundred. The once commodious house was now too small for the communicants of the church. The pastor began to look around for a place to build, and considered the matter of enlarging the present house of worship. He had expended the strength of his manhood in the service of his church; he had built one house, and had never denied the public his service. It would seem natural that a man whose life had been so stormy, yea, so full of toil and care, would seek in advanced age the rest and quiet so much desired at that stage of life. But it was not so with Brother Grimes. He was willing to begin another life-time work, and with all the freshness of desire and energy of young manhood.

It was now the latter part of the winter of 1873. A revival had been for a long time, and was still, in progress. Converts were coming into the church rapidly. The heart of the pastor was never fuller of love than during the revival. He seemed to be in agony for sinners to be saved. He impatiently paced the aisles, and held private and personal interviews with the impenitent. He disliked to leave the church at the close of the services. He remained often in the vestibule, watching for an opportunity to say a word for the Saviour. Brother C. G. Swan, who preached for him once, said: " I never beheld a more heavenly face; it seemed as if his soul were ripe for heaven."

Those who saw him in the pulpit the last Sabbath he spent on earth—March 9, 1874—will not soon forget the earnestness and impressiveness of his manner. On Wednesday, March 12th, he left the scene of his labors to discharge a duty nearest to his heart. He took $100 from his poor church, as a gift to the *Home Mission Society*, that was to be used in the *Freedman's Fund*.

On Friday evening, March 14th, he reached home just in time to breathe his last in the arms of his faithful, though anxious wife. Thus he fell asleep in the path of duty, in the midst of a mighty work.

The news of his death spread rapidly, and cast a shadow of grief over the entire community. The people mourned him.

The morning papers gave full account and notice of his death. The following is one of the many notices that were given:

"DEATH OF AN ESTEEMED CLERGYMAN.

" The Rev. L. A. Grimes, the well-known and universally esteemed colored clergyman, died very suddenly last evening, at his residence on Everett Avenue, East Somerville. He had just returned from New York, where he had been to attend the meeting of the *Baptist Board of Home Missions*, of which he was a member. He had walked to his home from the cars, and died within fifteen minutes after his arrival. The physicians pronounce it a case of apoplexy. Mr. Grimes was pastor of the Twelfth Baptist Church, on Phillips Street, in this city. During the twenty-six years of his ministry in Boston he had won the confidence and regard, not only of his own sect, but of the entire community. His labors for the good of his oppressed race attracted public attention to him more than twenty years ago, and this interest manifested itself in the generous contributions of Unitarians, Episcopalians, and Universalists in aid of his church. During the thirty-four dark days of the infamous Fugitive-Slave Law, and the excitements occasioned by slave hunts in Boston, Mr. Grimes had a ' level head,' and did much to keep down riotous outbreaks from those who then were told that they had no rights that white men were bound to respect. Fortunate, indeed, will be the church of the deceased, if his successor, like him, shall be able to keep them together, and lead them in righteous ways for a quarter of a century."

On the following Monday morning, at the ministers' meeting, appropriate remarks were made, and resolutions drawn up. The following appeared in the daily papers:

" BAPTIST MINISTERS' MEETING.

"The Monday morning meeting of the Baptist ministers of Boston and vicinity was held at ten o'clock, Monday, as is the weekly custom. After the devotional exercises, the committee to prepare resolutions on the death of the late Rev. Leonard Andrew Grimes made their report to the meeting. Pending the acceptance of the report remarks eulogizing the deceased were made by Rev. R. H. Neale, D.D., and others. The resolutions, which were thereupon given a place upon the records of the meeting, are as follows : In the death of Leonard Andrew Grimes, for twenty-seven years the pastor of the Twelfth Baptist Church of Boston, the city in which he lived, the race for which he labored have sustained an irreparable loss. The *confrère* of Daniel Sharp, Baron Stow, Phineas Stow, Nathaniel Colver, Rev. Mr. Graves of the 'Reflector,' he was one whose coming might always be welcomed with the exclamation of our Saviour concerning Nathaniel : 'Behold an Israelite indeed in whom there is no guile.' His last efforts were put forth for his race. He carried to the Board of the American Baptist Home Mission Society, of which he had been for many years an honored member, a large contribution from his church, to help on Christ's work among the Freedmen, and, on returning from New York, stopped at New Bedford to comfort a broken-hearted mother, whose little child was dying, and then came to the city, and in fifteen minutes after crossing the threshold of his home passed on to God.

"His death affected the ministry and churches as when ' a standard-bearer fainteth.' His familiar face was ever welcome. His resolute bearing, his unswerving fidelity to Christ, to truth, to the church at large, and his own denomination in particular, and his life-long service as a philanthropist, his devotion to the interests of the negro, to whom he was linked by ties of consanguinity and of sympathy, made him a felt power for good in our State and in our entire country. No man among us was more sincerely respected or more truly loved. His departure, while it came none too soon for the tired warrior, impoverishes us with the withdrawal of an all-embracing love, and leaves God's poor to suffer to an extent it is impossible to describe.

"*Resolved*, That the death of this good minister of Jesus Christ imposes heavy responsibilities upon his surviving brethren. The interests of the race of which he was an honored representative are imperilled. Their noble champion has gone up higher ; but no waiting Elisha saw the ascent, and cried, 'My father, my father, the chariot of Israel and the horsemen thereof ' ; so who can hope to wear his mantle and continue his work ?

"*Resolved*, That we tender to his afflicted widow, and to the church he had so long and faithfully served, this poor expression of our sympathy, and this truthful evidence of our love.

" *Resolved*, That the good of his race, just passing from the morning of emancipation into the noonday radiance of a liberty of which they have dreamed, and for which they have prayed, demands that a permanent record be made of this noble man of God."

The ministers' meeting adjourned after the reading of the foregoing resolutions, to attend the funeral services, which were to take place in Charles Street Church. At an early hour in the morning the body was placed in front of the altar in the church of the deceased, where it lay in state all the forenoon, and where appropriate services were conducted by Drs. Cheney, Fulton, and others. Thousands, of every grade and hue, thronged the church to have a last fond look at the face so full of sunlight in life, and so peaceful in death.

At one o'clock the remains were removed to Charles Street Church, where the funeral services were conducted with a feeling of solemnity and impressiveness worthy of the sad occasion. The addresses of Drs. Neale and Fulton were full of tenderness and grief. Both of these gentlemen were, for many years, the intimate friends of the deceased. They were all associated together in a noble work for a number of years, and there were no hearts so sad as those of Brothers Neale and Fulton. Clergymen of every denomination were present, and the congregation contained men and women from all the walks of life. The funeral was considered one of the largest that ever took place in Boston.

On the following Sabbath quite a number of the Boston pulpits gave appropriate discourses upon the " Life and Character of the late L. A. Grimes." The most noticeable were those delivered by Rev. R. N. Neale, D.D., Rev. Justin D. Fulton, D.D., and Rev. Henry A. Cook.

Within the last decade quite a number of educated Colored Baptist clergymen have come into active work in the denomination. The old-time preaching is becoming distasteful to the people. The increasing intelligence of the congregations is an unmistakable warning to the preachers that a higher standard of preaching is demanded ; that the pew is becoming as intelligent as the pulpit. The outlook is very encouraging. However, the danger of the hour is, that too many Negro churches may be organized. We have the quantity ; let us *have* the *quality* now.

Part 9.

THE DECLINE OF NEGRO GOVERNMENTS.

CHAPTER XXVII.

REACTION, PERIL, AND PACIFICATION.

1875–1880.

THE BEGINNING OF THE END OF THE REPUBLICAN GOVERNMENTS AT THE SOUTH. — SOUTHERN ELEC-
TION METHODS AND NORTHERN SYMPATHY. — GEN. GRANT NOT RESPONSIBLE FOR THE DECLINE
AND LOSS OF THE REPUBLICAN STATE GOVERNMENTS AT THE SOUTH. — A PARTY WITHOUT A
LIVE ISSUE. — SOUTHERN WAR CLAIMS. — THE CAMPAIGN OF 1876. — REPUBLICAN LETHARGY
AND DEMOCRATIC ACTIVITY. — DOUBTFUL RESULTS. — THE ELECTORAL COUNT IN CONGRESS. —
GEN. GARFIELD AND CONGRESSMEN FOSTER AND HALE TO THE FRONT AS LEADERS. — PEACE-
FUL RESULTS. — PRESIDENT HAYES'S SOUTHERN POLICY. — ITS FAILURE. — THE IDEAS OF THE
HON. CHARLES FOSTER ON THE TREATMENT OF THE SOUTHERN PROBLEM. — "NOTHING BUT
LEAVES" FROM CONCILIATION. — A NEW POLICY DEMANDED BY THE REPUBLICAN PARTY. —
A REMARKABLE SPEECH BY THE HON. CHARLES FOSTER AT UPPER SANDUSKY, OHIO. — HE
CALLS FOR A SOLID NORTH AGAINST A SOLID SOUTH. — HE SOUNDS THE KEY-NOTE FOR
THE NORTH AND THE NATION RESPONDS. — THE DECAY AND DEATH OF THE NEGRO GOVERN-
MENTS AT THE SOUTH INEVITABLE. — THE NEGRO MUST TURN HIS ATTENTION TO EDUCATION,
THE ACCUMULATION OF PROPERTY AND EXPERIENCE. — HE WILL RETURN TO POLITICS WHEN
HE SHALL BE EQUAL TO THE DIFFICULT DUTIES OF CITIZENSHIP.

FROM 1868 to 1872 the Southern States had been held by the Republican party, with but a few exceptions, without much effort. The friends of the Negro began to congratulate themselves that the Southern problem had been solved. Every Legislature in the South had among its members quite a fair representation of Colored men. Among the State officers there was a good sprinkling of them ; and in some of the States there were Negroes as Lieut.-Governors. Congress had opened its doors to a dozen Negroes ; and the consular and diplomatic service had employed a number of them in foreign parts. And so with such evidences of political prosperity before their eyes the friends of the Negro at the North regarded his " calling and election sure."

In 1873 a great financial panic came to the business and monetary affairs of the country. It was the logic of an inflated currency, wild and visionary enterprises, bad investments, and prodigal living. Banks tottered and fell, large business houses suspended, and financial ruin ran riot. Northern attention was diverted from Southern politics to the " destruction that seemed to waste at noon-day." Taking advantage of this the South seized the shot-gun and wrote on her banners : *"We must carry these States, peaceably if we can ; forcibly if we must."* An organized, deliberate policy of political intimidation assumed the task of ridding the South of Negro government. The first step was in the direction of intimidating the white leaders of the Republican organizations ; and the next was to deny employment to all intelligent and influential Colored Republicans. Thus from time to time the leaders of the Republican party were reduced to a very small number. Without leaders the rank and file of the party were harmless and helpless in State and National campaigns. This state of affairs seemed to justify the presence of troops at the polls on election days. Under an Act of Congress " the President was empowered to use the army to suppress domestic violence, prevent bloodshed," and to protect the Negroes in the constitutional exercise of the rights conferred upon them by the Constitution. This movement was met by the most determined opposition from the South, aided by the sympathy of the Northern press, Democratic platforms, and a considerable element in the Republican party. •

In 1874 the condition of affairs in the South was such as to alarm the friends of stable, constitutional government everywhere. The city of New Orleans was in a state of siege. Streets were blockaded with State troops and White Line leagues, and an open battle was fought. The Republican State government fell before the insurgents, and a new government was established *vi et armis.* Troops were sent to New Orleans by the President, and the lawful government was restored. The Liberal movement in the North, which had resulted in the defeat of the Republican tickets in Indiana, Ohio, New York, New Jersey, Connecticut, and even in Massachusetts, greatly encouraged the Bourbon Democrats of the South, and excited them to the verge of the most open and cruel conduct toward the white and black Republicans in their midst.

A large number of Northern Legislatures passed resolutions

condemning the action of the President in sending troops into the South, although he did it in accordance with law. Many active and influential Republicans, displeased with the action of the Republican governments at the South, and the conduct of the Forty-third Congress, demanded the destruction of the Republican party. The Liberal movement had started in 1872. Its leaders thought the time had come for a new party, and counselled the country accordingly.

The Forty-fourth Congress was organized by the Democrats. The Cabinet Ministers were divided on the policy pursued toward the South. In the autumn of 1875 the shot-gun policy carried Mississippi; and from the 6th of July till the Republican government in that State went down into a bloody grave, there was an unbroken series of political murders.

President Grant was met by a Democratic Congress; a divided Cabinet : Zachariah Chandler and Edwards Pierrepont were in sympathy with him; Bristow and Jewell represented the Liberal sentiment. Then, the Republican party of the North, and many leading journals, were urging a change of policy toward the South. The great majority of Republicans wanted a change, not because they did not sympathize with the Negro governments, but because they saw some of the best men in the party withdrawing their support from the administration of Gen. Grant. There were other men who charged that the business failures in the country were occasioned by the financial policy of the Republican party, and in a spirit of desperation were ready to give their support to the Democracy.

It was charged by the enemies of Gen. Grant that when he was elected President he had a solid Republican South behind him ; that under his administration every thing had been lost; and that he was responsible for the political ruin which had overtaken the Republican party at the South. The charge was false. The errors of reconstruction under the administration of President Andrew Johnson, and the mistakes of the men who had striven to run the State governments at the South had to be counteracted by the administration of President Grant. This indeed was a difficult task. He did all he could under the Constitution; and when Congress endeavored to pass the Force Bill, the Hon. James G. Blaine, of Maine, made a speech against it in caucus. Mr. Blaine had a presidential ambition to serve, and esteemed his own promotion of greater moment than the

protection of the Colored voters of the South. And Mr. Blaine
never allowed an opportunity to pass in which he did not throw
every obstacle in the way of the success of the Grant administration. Mr. Blaine has never seen fit to explain his opposition to the Force Bill, which was intended to strengthen the
hands of the President in his efforts to protect the Negro voter
at the South.

When the National Republican Convention met at Cincinnati, Ohio, in the summer of 1876, there was still lacking a
definite policy for the South. Presidential candidates were
numerous, and the contest bitter. Gen. Rutherford B. Hayes,
at that time Governor of Ohio, was nominated as a compromise
candidate. There was no issue left the Republican party, as the
" bloody shirt ", had been rejected by the Liberals, and was
generally distasteful at the North. But the initial success of the
Democratic party South, and the loss of many Northern States
to the Republicans, had emboldened the South to expect national
success. But a too precipitous preparation for a raid upon the
United States Treasury for the payment of rebel war claims
threw the Republicans upon their guard, and, for the time being,
every other question was sunk into insignificance. So the insolence of the " Rebel Brigadier Congress," and the letter of
Samuel Jones Tilden, the Democratic candidate for the Presidency, on the question of the Southern war claims, gave the
Republican party a fighting chance. But there were a desperate
South and a splendid campaign organizer in Mr. Tilden to meet.
And with a shot-gun policy, tissue ballets, and intimidation at
the South, while a gigantic, bold, and matchless system of
fraudulent voting was pushed with vigor in the North, there
was little show of success for the Republican ticket. The contest on the part of the Republicans was spiritless. It was difficult to raise funds or excite enthusiasm. The Republican candidate had only a local reputation. He had been to Congress, but even those who had known that had forgotten it. A
modest, retiring man, Gov. Hayes was not widely known. The
old and tried leaders were not enthusiastic. Mr. Blaine had no
second choice. He was for himself or nobody. The Democrats
prosecuted their campaign with vigor, intelligence, and enthusiasm. They went " into the school districts," and their organization has never been equalled in America.

The result was doubtful. One thing, however, was sure:

the Negro governments of the South were now a thing of the past. Not a single State was left to the Republican party. Florida, Louisiana, and South Carolina were hanging by the slender thread of doubt, with the provisions of a returning board in favor of the Republican party. The returning boards were the creation of local law; their necessity having grown out of the peculiar methods employed by Democrats in carrying elections. These boards were empowered to receive and count the votes cast for presidential electors; and wherever it could be proven that intimidation and fraud had been used, the votes of such precincts, counties, etc., were to be thrown out. The three doubtful States named above were counted for the Republican presidential electors. Their work was carried before Congress. A high joint electoral commission was created by law, composed of the ablest men of the two parties in Congress, with the salt of judicial judgment thrown in. This commission examined the returns of the three doubtful States, and decided not to go behind the returns; and, according to a previous agreement, one branch of Congress ratifying, the candidate having the more votes was to be declared duly elected.

The country was in an unprecedented state of excitement; and even European governments felt the shock. The enemies of Republican government laughed their little laugh, and said that the end of the republic had come. British bankers brought out into the light Confederate bonds; while stocks in the United States went through an experience as variable as the weather in the Mississippi valley. The public press was intemperate in its utterances, and the political passions of the people were inflamed every hour. The national House of Representatives was a vast whirlpool of excitement,—or, rather it was an angry sea stirred to its depths, and lashing itself into aimless fury by day and by night. When the vote of a State was called, some Democrat would object, and the Senate, which was always present, would retire, and the House would then open a war of words running through hours and sometimes days. When the debate ended, or rather when the House had reached the end of its parliamentary halter, the Senate would again enter, the vote of the State would be counted, and the next one called. Thus the count proceeded through anxious days and weary nights. Business was suspended; and the bulletin boards of commercial 'changes were valueless so long as the bulletin boards of the newspapers contained "the latest news from Washington."

In this state of affairs there was need of statesmen at the head of the Republican minority in Congress. There were orators; but the demand was for men of judgment, energy, executive ability,—men in whom the Democrats had confidence, who could put a stop to filibustering, and secure a peaceful solution of a unique and dangerous problem.

These were forthcoming; the late President Garfield and Gov. Foster, then a member of Congress, with Kasson, Hale, and other members of Congress, were among those most active and effective in securing a peaceful result.

When the electoral fight was on, and the end seemed uncertain, these gentlemen stepped to the front and fairly won the reputation of statesmen. They saw that if the filibustering of the Democrats were brought to a close, it would have to be accomplished by the leaders in that party and on that side of the House. Accordingly they secured Fernando Wood, of New York, as the leader in opposition to filibustering, and John Young Brown, of Kentucky, as his lieutenant. The Republican policy was to allow the Democrats to lead and do the talking, while they should fall into line and vote when the proper time came. But Fernando Wood at the head of the Republicans as a leader, was a spectacle as strange and startling as Satan leading a prayer-meeting. It was too much for an orthodox, close-communion, hard-shell Republican like Martin I. Townsend!

On Thursday afternoon, the last day of the alarming scenes in Congress, nearly everybody had lost hope. There was no telling at what moment the government would be in anarchy. In the midst of the confusion, excitement, and threatening danger, the Hon. Charles Foster was the most imperturbable man in Congress. On Thursday afternoon Senator Hoar, a member of Congress from Massachusetts, saw Mr. Foster seated at his desk writing as quietly and composedly as if in his private office; he seemed perfectly oblivious to the angry storm which was raging about him. The cold-blooded, conservative New England Senator was as greatly amazed at the serenity of the clear-headed Western Congressman as he was distressed at the impending disaster. He went to Mr. Foster and talked very discouragingly respecting the situation. He said that the Senate was growing impatient at the dilatory conduct of the House, and would probably, at the earliest convenience, send a message to the House demanding that the latter open their doors and

admit the Senate to complete the count. Congressman Foster
stated to the Senator that the House was not in a temper to be
driven; that a resolution of the character of the one proposed
would hinder rather than help a peaceful solution of the vexatious count; and that if he would only possess his soul in patience, before the rising of another sun R. B. Hayes would be
peaceably and constitutionally declared the President of the
United States. And it was even as he said; for before four
o'clock the next morning the count was completed, and Hayes
declared the President of the United States for the Constitutional term of four years. This is given as one of the many
unwritten incidents that occurred during this angry, and, probably, most perilous controversy that ever threatened the life of
the American Republic.

A new policy for the South was now inevitable. From October 1876 till March 1877, President Grant had refused to recognize Chamberlain as Governor of South Carolina, or Packard as
Governor of Louisiana. He had simply preserved those governments *in statu quo*. He had heard all that could be said in favor
of the Republican side of the question, and seemed to believe
that it was now beyond his power to hold up the last of the
Negro governments with bayonets. He was right. It would
have been as vain to have attempted to galvanize those governments into existence as to have attempted the resuscitation
of a dead man by applying a galvanic battery. Governments
must have, not only the subjective elements of life, but the
powers of self-preservation. The Negro governments at the
South died for the want of these elements. It was a pity, too,
after the noble fight the Republican party of Louisiana and
South Carolina had made, and after they had secured their
electoral votes for Hayes, that their State officers who had been
chosen at the same time should have been abandoned to their
own frail governmental resources. But this was unavoidable.
Their governments could not have existed twenty-four hours
without the presence and aid of the United States army. And
this could not have been done in the face of the sentiment
against such use of the army which had grown to be nearly
unanimous throughout the country. If the Republicans could
have inaugurated their officers and administered their governments they would have received the applause of the administration at Washington and the God-speed of the Republican

party of the North; but the moment the United States troops were withdrawn the Negro governments melted into nothingness.

Every thing had been tried but pacification. The men who best understood the temper of that section knew it was incapable, as a whole, of receiving the olive branch in the spirit in which the North would tender it. But a policy of conciliation was demanded; the Northern journals asked it. An ex-Major-General of the Confederate Army was called to the Cabinet of President Hayes, and was given a portfolio where he could do more for the South than in any other place. Gen. Longstreet, a gallant Confederate soldier during the late war, was made Postmaster at Gainesville, Georgia, and afterward sent as Minister to Turkey. Col. Mosby, another Confederate soldier, or guerilla, was sent to China, and Col. Fitzsimmons was made Marshal of Georgia. It was the policy of the Hon. Charles Foster to have the President recognize young men at the South who had the pluck and ability to divide the Bourbon Democratic party of that section, and hasten the day of better feeling between the sections. But the President, either incapable of comprehending this idea, or jealous of the credit that the country had already bestowed upon him, blundered on in selecting men to represent his policy in the South who had no following, and were, therefore, valueless to his cause. His heart was right, but he put too much confidence in Southern statesmen.

The South showed no signs of improvement. White Republicans were intimidated, persecuted, and driven out. The black Republicans were allowed to vote, but the Democrats counted the votes and secured all the offices. The President was under the influence of Alex. H. Stephens, of Georgia, and Wade Hampton, of South Carolina. He expected much; but he received nothing. Instead of gratitude he received arrogance. The Southern leaders in Congress sought to deprive the Executive of his constitutional veto; to starve the army; and to protract the session of Congress. The North had invited its " erring brethren " back, and had killed the fatted calf, but were unwilling to allow the fellow to eat all the veal! The conduct of the South was growing more intolerable every day; and the President's barren policy was losing him supporters. He had not tied to any safe advisers. Hon. Charles Foster, Senator Stanley Matthews, and Gen. James A. Garfield could have piloted him through many dangerous places. But he shut himself up in his own abilities, and left his friends on the outside. The South had gulped down every thing that had been given it, and was asking for more. Every thing had been given except the honor of the cause that the Union army had fought for. To complete the task of conciliation it was only required that the nation destroy the monuments to its hero dead, and open the treasury to the payment of rebel war claims, and pension the men who were maimed in an attempt to shoot the government to death. To the credit of President Hayes let history record that he did not surrender his veto power to arrogant and disloyal Southern Congressmen. He became convinced at last that the South was incapable of appreciating his kindness, and was willing to change front. His policy was inevitable. It did great good. It united the Republican party against the South ; and a splendid cabinet, a clean administration, and the resumption of specie payments wrought wonders for the Republican party.

There was a ripe sentiment in the North in favor of " a change " of policy. The very men who had advocated pacification ; who had " flowers and tears for the Gray, and tears and flowers for the Blue " ; who wanted the grave of Judas equally honored with the grave of Jesus—the destroyer and the Saviour of the country placed in the same calendar,—were the first men to grow sick of the policy of pacification. But what policy to inaugurate was not clear to them.

In the summer of 1878 the Hon. Charles Foster returned to Ohio from Washington City. He had seen State governments in the North slip from the control of Republicans, because of the folly of the Hayes' policy of pacification toward the South. He had the good-sense to take in the situation. He saw that it was madness to attempt any longer to conciliate the South. He saw that the lamb and lion had lain down together, but that the lamb was on the inside of the lion. Brave, intelligent, and far-seeing, on the 1st of August, 1878, he gave the Republican party of the North a battle-cry that died away only amid the shouts of Republican State and National victories in 1880. This was all the North needed. A leader was demanded, and the Hon. Charles Foster sounded the key-note that met with a response in every loyal heart in the country. His idea was that as the South had not kept the faith ; had not accorded protection to the Negro voter ; had not broken up old Bourbon Democratic

organizations, it was the imperative duty of the North to meet
that section with a solid front. Hence his battle-cry : "*A Solid
North against a Solid South.*" The following is his famous
speech—pure gold :

" I happened to be one who thought and believed that the President's
Southern policy, as far as it related to the use of troops for the support
of State governments, was right. I sustained it upon the ground of
high principle, nevertheless it could have been sustained on the ground
of necessity. The President has extended to the people of the South
the hand of conciliation and friendship. He has shown a desire, probably contrary to the wishes of the great mass of his party, to bring
about, by the means of conciliation, better relations between the North
and South. In doing this he has alienated from him the great mass of
the leading and influential Republicans of the country. He had lost
their sympathy, and to a great degree their support. What has he received in return for these measures of conciliation and kindness ? How
have these measures been received by the South ? What advance can
we discover in them, of the recognition of the guarantees of the rights
of the Colored men under the Constitutional Amendments ? We see
Jeff. Davis making speeches as treasonable as those of 1861, and these
speeches endorsed and applauded by a great portion of their press and
people. We see also the declaration of Mr. Singleton, of Mississippi,
in answer to a question of mine on the floor of the House, declaring
that his paramount allegiance in peace and war was due to his State.

" No gentleman from the South, or even of the Democratic party, has
taken issue with him. We see also, all over the South, a disposition to
resist the execution of the United States laws, especially in the matter
of the collection of internal revenue. To-day there are four U. S.
officers under arrest by the authorities of the State of South Carolina,
in jail and bail refused, for an alleged crime in their State, while in fact
these officers were discharging their duty in executing the laws of the
United States in that State. Their State courts and their officers refused to obey the writs of the United States courts in the surrender of
these men to the United States authorities. No former act of this
treasonable State shows a more defiant attitude toward the U. S. Government, or a greater disposition to trample upon its authority. I trust
the Administration will, in this case, assert in the most vigorous manner
possible the authority of the United States Government for the rescue
and protection of these officers. I have no bloody shirt to wave. If
there is one man in this country, more than another, who desires peace
and quiet between the sections, I believe I am that man. Gentlemen
may philosophize over this question until they are gray, but you cannot

escape the discussion of this question so long as a Solid South menaces the peace of the country. A Solid Democratic South means the control of the country by the spirit and the men who sought its destruction.

"My own opinion is that there can be no peace—this question will not down, until the menace of the Solid South is withdrawn. I had hoped that the policy of President Hayes would lead to the assertion, by a very considerable portion of the South, of their antagonism to Bourbon Democracy.

"I confess to a degree of disappointment in this, though I think I see signs of a breaking up of the Solid South in the independent movement that seemed to be gaining a foothold in all sections of that country. But the effective way to aid these independent movements, this breaking up of the Solid South, is for the North to present itself united against the Solid South. A Solid South under the control of the Democratic party means the control of the party by this element. It means the repeal of the Constitutional Amendments, if not in form, in spirit. It means the payment of hundreds of rebel claims. It means the payment of pensions to rebel soldiers. It means the payment for slaves lost in the Rebellion. It means the abrogation of that provision of the Constitution which declares, that the citizens of one State shall have all the rights, privileges, and immunities of the citizens of other States.

"If my Democratic friends who seem to be anxious to bring about peace and quiet between the sections are sincere and desire to make their expressions effective, they should act with that party that presents a solid front, a United North, so long as we are menaced with the Solid South.

"If it could be understood in the South that they are to be met with a Solid North, I do not believe that the Solid South would exist in that condition a single year. They retain this position because they believe that they can have the support of a fragment of the North ; and thus with this fragment rule and control the country. I would have no fear of the control of the country by the Democratic party if it were made up of something like equal proportion from all sections of the country. I discuss this question, first, because I believe it the most important question at issue in the pending canvass. *I repeat that it is the imperative duty of the North to meet the Solid South with a united front."* [1]

This speech was delivered at Upper Sandusky, Wyandotte Co., Ohio. It thrilled the North, and put new life into the Republican party. It gave him the nomination for governor, and

---

[1] Cincinnati Commercial, Aug. 1, 1878.

from 23,000 Democratic majority he redeemed the State by a Republican majority of 17,000. A wave of enthusiasm swept the country. His battle-cry became the editorial of a thousand journals, and hundreds of orators found ammunition enough in his little speech of a hundred lines to keep up a campaign of two years' duration. It is a fact that history should not omit to record, that from the 1st of August, 1878, until the election of James A. Garfield to the presidency, there was no cessation to the campaign in the North.

But the securing of a Solid North did not restore the Negro governments at the South. The North had rallied to rebuke an insolent South ; to show the Democrats of that section that the United States Treasury should be protected, and that the honor of the nation *would* be maintained unsullied. If the South would not pay its honest debts there was every reason for believing that it would not pay the national debt. It was to be regretted that the Negro had been so unceremoniously removed from Southern politics. But such a result was inevitable. The Government gave him the statute-book when he ought to have had the spelling-book ; placed him in the Legislature when he ought to have been in the school-house. In the great revolution that followed the war, the heels were put where the brains ought to have been. An ignorant majority, without competent leaders, could not rule an intelligent Caucasian minority. Ignorance, vice, poverty, and superstition could not rule intelligence, experience, wealth, and organization. It was here that the " one could chase a thousand, and the two could put ten thousand to flight." The Negro governments were built on the shifting sands of the opinions of the men who reconstructed the South, and when the storm and rains of political contest came they fell because they were not built upon the granite foundation of intelligence and statesmanship.

It was an immutable and inexorable law which demanded the destruction of those governments. It was a law that knows no country, no nationality. Spain, Mexico, France, Turkey, Russia, and Egypt have felt its cruel touch to a greater or less degree. But a lesson was taught the Colored people that is invaluable. Let them rejoice that they are out of politics. Let white men rule. Let *them* enjoy a political life to the exclusion of business and education, and they too will sooner or later be driven out of their places by the same law that sent the Negro to the plantations and to the schools. And if the Negro is industrious, frugal, saving, diligent in labor, and laborious in study, there is another law that will quietly and peaceably, without a social or political shock, restore him to his normal relations in politics. He will be able to build his governments on a solid foundation, with the tempered mortar of experience and knowledge. This is inevitable. The Negro will return to politics in the South when he is qualified to govern ; will return to stay. He will be respected, courted and protected then. Then as a tax-payer, as well as a tax-gatherer, reading his own ballot, and choosing his own candidates, he will be equal to all the exigencies of American citizenship.

CHAPTER XXVIII.

THE EXODUS—CAUSE AND EFFECT.

The Negroes of the South delight in their Home so Long as it is Possible for them to remain. — The Policy of abridging their Rights Destructive to their Usefulness as Members of Society. — Political Intimidation, Murder, and Outrage disturb the Negroes. — The Plantation Credit System the Crime of the Century. — The Exodus not inspired by Politicians, but the Natural Outcome of the Barbarous Treatment bestowed upon the Negroes by the Whites. — The Unprecedented Sufferings of 60,000 Negroes fleeing from Southern Democratic Oppression. — Their Patient, Christian Endurance. — Their Industry, Morals, and Frugality. — The Correspondent of the "Chicago Inter-Ocean" sends Information to Senator Voorhees respecting the Refugees in Kansas. — The Position of Gov. St. John and the Faithful Labors of Mrs. Comstock. — The Results of the Exodus Beneficent. — The South must treat the Negro Better or lose his Labor.

THE exodus of the Negroes from Southern States forms one of the most interesting pages of the almost romantic history of the race. It required more than ordinary causes to drive the Negro from his home in the sunny South to a different climate and strange country. It was no caprice of his nature, nor even a nomadic feeling. During the entire period of the existence of the Republican governments at the South the Negroes remained there in a state of blissful contentment. And even after the fall of those governments they continued in a state of quiet industry. But there followed the decline of those governments a policy as hurtful to the South as it was cruel to the Negroes.

During the early years of reconstruction quite a number of Negroes began to invest in real estate and secure for themselves pleasant homes. Their possessions increased yearly, as can be seen by a reference to statistical reports. Some of the estates and homesteads of the oldest and most reputable white families, who had put every thing into the scales of Confederate rebellion, fell into the possession of ex-slaves. Such a spectacle was not only unpleasant, it was exasperating, to the whites. But so long as the Republican governments gave promise of success there was but little or no manifestation of displeasure on the part of the whites. Just as soon, however, as they became the masters of the situation, the property of many Negroes was seized, and sold upon the specious plea—"for delinquent taxes"; and the Negroes were driven from eligible places to the outskirts of the larger towns and cities. No Negro was allowed to live in the vicinity of white persons as tenants; and it became a social crime to sell property to Negroes in close proximity to the whites. In the rural districts, where Negroes had begun to secure small farms, this same cruel spirit was "the lion in their way." The spirit that sought to keep the Negro ignorant as a slave, now that he was at least nominally free, endeavored to deprive him of one of the necessary conditions of happy and useful citizenship: the possession of property, the aggregations of the results of honest labor. Nothing could have been more fatal to the growth of the Negro toward the perfect stature of free, intelligent, independent, and self-sustaining manhood and citizenship. The object and result of such a system can easily be judged. It was intended to keep the Negroes the laboring element after as well as before the war. The accomplishment of such a result would have been an argument in favor of the assertion of the South that the normal condition of the Negro was that of a serf; and that he did not possess the elements necessary to the life of a freeman. Thus would have perished the hopes, prayers, arguments and claims of the friends of the cause of universal, manhood suffrage.

Among the masses of laboring men the iniquitous, outrageous, thieving "*Plantation Credit System*" was a plague and a crime. Deprived of homes and property the Negroes were compelled to "work the crops on the shares." A plantation store was kept where the Negroes' credit was good for any article it contained. He got salt meat, corn meal, sugar, coffee, molasses, vinegar, tobacco, and coarse clothing for himself and family. An account was kept by "a young white man," and at the end of the season "a reckoning" was had. Unable to read or cipher, the poor, credulous, unsuspecting Negroes always found themselves in debt from $50 to $200! This necessitated another year's engagement; and so on for an indefinite period. There was nothing to encourage the Negroes; nothing to inspire them with hope for the future; nothing for their families but a languid, dead-eyed expectation that somehow a change *might* come. But the crime went on unrebuked by the men who were growing rich from this system of petty robbery of the poor. For the cheapest qualities of brown sugar, for which the laboring classes of the North pay 8 cents, the Negroes on the plantations were charged 11 and 13 cents a pound. Corn meal purchased at the North for 4 cents a quart, brought 9 and 10 cents at the plantation store. And thus for every article the Negroes purchased they were charged the most exorbitant prices.

There were two results which flowed from this system, viz.: robbing the families of these Negroes of the barest comforts of life, and destroying the confidence of the Negro in the blessings and benefits of freedom. No man—no race of men—could endure such blighting influences for any length of time.

Moreover the experiences of the Negroes in voting had not been extensive, and a sudden curtailing and abridgment of their rights was a shock to their confidence in the government under which they lived, and in the people by which they were surrounded. It was thought expedient to intimidate or destroy the more intelligent and determined Negroes; while the farm laborers were directed to refrain from voting the Republican ticket, or commanded to vote the Democratic ticket, or starve. There never was a more cruel system of slavery than this.

Writing under date of January 10, 1875, General P. H. Sheridan, then in command at New Orleans, says:

" Since the year 1866 nearly thirty-five hundred persons, a great majority of whom were colored men, have been killed and wounded in this State. In 1868 the official record shows that eighteen hundred and eighty-four were killed and wounded. From 1868 to the present time no official investigation had been made, and the civil authorities in all but a few cases have been unable to arrest, convict, or punish the perpetrators. Consequently there are no correct records to be consulted for information. There is ample evidence, however, to show that more than twelve hundred persons have been killed and wounded during this time on account of their political sentiments. Frightful massacres have occurred in the parishes of Bossier, Caddo, Catahoula, Saint Bernard, Grant, and Orleans."

He then proceeded to enumerate the political murders of Colored men in various parishes, and says:

" Human life in this State is held so cheaply that when men are killed on account of political opinions, the murderers are regarded rather as heroes than as criminals in the localities where they reside."

This brief summary is not by a politician, but by a distinguished soldier, who recounts the events which had occurred within his own military jurisdiction. Volumes of testimony have since been taken confirming in all respects General Sheridan's statement, and giving in detail the facts relating to such murders, and the times and circumstances of their occurrence. The results of the elections which immediately followed them disclose the motives and purposes of their perpetrators. These reports show that in the year 1867 a reign of terror prevailed over almost the entire State. In the parish of St. Landry there was a massacre of Colored·people which began on the 28th of September, 1868, and lasted from three to six days, during which time between three and four hundred of them were killed. " Thirteen captives were taken from the jail and shot, and a pile of twenty-five dead bodies were found burned in the woods." The result of this Democratic campaign in the parish was that the registered Republican majority of 1,071 was wholly obliterated, and at the election which followed a few weeks later, not a vote was cast for General Grant, while Seymour and Blair received 4,787.

In the parish of Bossier a similar massacre occurred between the 20th and 30th of September, 1868, which lasted from three to four days, during which time two hundred Negroes were killed. By the official registry of that year the Republican voters in Bossier Parish numbered 1,938, but at the ensuing election only *one* Republican vote was cast.

In the parish of Caddo, during the month of October, 1868, over forty Negroes were killed. The result of that massacre was that out of a Republican registered vote of 2,894 only *one* was cast for General Grant. Similar scenes were enacted throughout the State, varying in extent and atrocity according to the magnitude of the Republican majority to be overcome.

The total summing up of murders, maimings, and whippings which took place for political reasons in the months of September, October, and November, 1868, as shown by official sources, is over one thousand. The net political results achieved thereby may be succinctly stated as follows: The official registration for that year in twenty-eight parishes contained 47,923 names of Republican voters, but at the presidential election held a few weeks after the occurrence of these events but 5,360 Republican votes were cast, making the net Democratic gain from said transactions 42,563.

In nine of these parishes where the reign of terror was most prevalent, out of 11,604 registered Republican votes only nineteen were cast for General Grant. In seven of said parishes there were 7,253 registered Republican votes, but not one was cast at the ensuing election for the Republican ticket.

In the years succeeding 1868, when some restraint was imposed upon political lawlessness and a comparatively peaceful election was held, these same Republican parishes cast from 33,000 to 37,000 Republican votes, thus demonstrating the purpose and the effects of the reign of murder in 1868.

In 1876 the spirit of violence and persecution which, in parts of the State, had been partially restrained for a time, broke forth again with renewed fury. It was deemed necessary to carry that State for Tilden and Hendricks, and the policy which had proved so successful in 1868 was again invoked, and with like results. On the day of general election in 1876 there were in the State of Louisiana 92,996 registered white voters, and 115,310 Colored, making a Republican majority of the latter of 22,314. The number of white Republicans was far in excess of the number of Colored Democrats. It was, therefore, well known that if a fair election should be held the State would go Republican by from twenty-five to forty thousand majority. The policy adopted this time was to select a few of the largest Republican parishes and by terrorism and violence not only obliterate their Republican majorities, but also intimidate the Negroes in the other parishes. The sworn testimony found in our public documents and records at Washington shows that the same system of assassinations, whippings, burnings, and other acts of political persecution of Colored citizens, which had occurred in 1868, was again repeated in 1876, and with like results.

In fifteen parishes where 17,726 Republicans were registered in 1876 only 5,758 votes were cast for Hayes and Wheeler, and in one of them (East Feliciana) where there were 2,127 Republicans registered, but *one* Republican vote was cast. By some methods the Republican majority of the State was supposed to have been effectually suppressed and a Democratic victory assured. And because the legally constituted authorities of Louisiana, acting in conformity with law and justice, declined to count some of the parishes thus carried by violence and blood, the Democratic party, both North and South, has ever since complained that it was fraudulently deprived of the fruits of the victory thus achieved, and it now proposes to make this grievance the principal plank in the party platform[1] for the future.

The worm trampled upon so persistently at length turned over. There was nothing left to the Negro but to go out from the land of his oppression and task-masters.

The Exodus was not a political movement. It was not inspired from without. It was but the natural operation of a divine law that moved whole communities of Negroes to turn their faces toward the setting sun. When the Israelites went out of Egypt God commanded their women to borrow the finger-rings and ear-rings of the Egyptians. All had sandals on their feet, staves in their hand, and headed by a matchless leader. God went before them as a pillar of cloud by day and a pillar of fire by night. But when the Negroes began their exodus from the Egypt of their bondage they went out empty; without clothing, money, or leaders. They were willing to endure any hardships short of death to reach a land where, under their own vine and fig-tree, they could enjoy free speech, free schools, the privilege of an honest vote, and receive honest pay for honest work. And how forcibly they told why they left the South.

"Now, old Uncle Joe, what did you come for?"

"Oh, law! Missus, I follers my two boys an' the ole woman an' then 'pears like I wants a taste of votin' afore I dies, an' the ole man done wants no swamps to wade in afore he votes, 'kase he must be Republican, ye see."

"Well, old Aunty, give us the sympathetic side of the story; or, tell us what you think of leaving your old home."

"I done have no home nohow, if they shoots my ole man an' the boys, an' gives me no money for de washin." '

A bright woman of twenty-five years is asked her condition, when she answers: "I had n't much real trouble yet, like some of my neighbors who lost every thing. We had a lot an' a little house, an' some stock on the place. We sold all out 'kase we did n't dare to stay when votin' time came again. Some neighbors better off than we had been all broken up by a pack of "*night-riders*"—all in white,—who scared everybody to death, run the men off to the swamps before elections, run the stock off, an'

---

[1] See Senator Windom's speech on the Exodus, Monday, June 14, 1880; also the report of the Senate Committee having under consideration the investigation of the causes of the migration of the Colored people from the Southern to the Northern States.

set fire to their places. A poor woman might as well be killed and done with it."

In the early spring of 1879, the now famous Exodus of the Negroes from the South set in toward the Northern States.

" Many already have fled to the forest and lurk on its outskirts,
Waiting with anxious hearts the dubious fate of the morrow.
Arms have been taken from us, and warlike weapons of all kinds ;
Nothing is left but the blacksmith's sledge and the scythe of the mower."

The story of the emigration of a people has been often re-peated since the world began. The Israelites of old, with their wanderings of forty years, furnish the theme of an inspired poem as old as history itself. The dreadful tale of the Kalmuck Tartars, in 1770, fleeing from their enemies, the Russians, over the deso-late steppes of Asia in mid-winter; starting out six hundred thousand strong, men, women, and children, with their flocks and herds, and reaching the confines of China with only two hundred thousand left, formed an era in oriental annals, and made a com-bination from which new races of men have sprung. But still more appropriate to this occasion is the history of the Hugue-nots of France, driven by religious persecution to England and Ireland, where, under their influence, industries sprang up as the flowers of the field, and what was England's gain was irreparable loss to France.[1] The expulsion of the Acadians, a harmless and inoffensive people, from Nova Scotia, is another instance of the revenge that natural laws inflict upon tyranny and injustice. Next to the persecuted Pilgrims crossing a dreary ocean in mid-winter to the sterile coasts of a land of savages for freedom's sake, history hardly furnishes a more touching picture than that of forty thousand homeless, friendless, starving Negroes going to a land already consecrated with the blood of the martyrs to the cause of free soil and unrestricted liberty. It was grandly strange that these poor people, persecuted, beaten with many stripes, hungry, friendless, and without clothing or shelter, should instinctively seek a home in Kansas where John Brown had fought the first battle for liberty and the restriction of slavery! Some journeyed all the way from Texas to Kansas in teams, with great horned oxen, and little steers in front no larger than calves, bowing eagerly to the weary load. Worn and weary with a nine weeks' journey, the travellers strained their eyes toward the land

---

[1] Pamphlet on Exodus.—Anonymous.

of hope, blindly yet beautifully " trustin' de good Lord." Often they buried their dead as soon as they arrived, many dying on the hard floor of the hastily-built wooden barracks before beds could be provided, but praying all night long and saying touchingly : " Come, Lord Jesus. Come quickly. Come with dyin' grace in one hand and savin' love in the other." [1]

A relief association was organized at once. A dear, good, old Quaker lady, in her sixty-fourth year, a quarter of a century of which had been spent in relieving suffering humanity, came forward and offered her services free of charge. The association was organized as *The Kansas Freedmen's Relief Association.* Mrs. Comstock was just the person to manage the matter of raising funds and securing clothing. In Gov. J. P. St. John, Mrs. Comstock and the association found a warm-hearted Christian friend.

Notwithstanding the plain, world-known causes, the Hon. D. W. Voorhees, United States Senator from Indiana, introduced a resolution providing for the investigation of "*the causes of the migration of the Colored people from the Southern to the Northern States.*" It cost the Government thousands of dollars, but developed nothing save what the country had known for years, that the political cruelties and systematic robbery practised upon the Colored people in the South had forced them into a free country.

In one year those who had taken up a residence in Kansas had become self-sustaining. They took hold of the work with enthusiasm ; they proved themselves industrious and frugal.

The Relief Association at first supplied them with stoves, teams, and seed. In round numbers, in a little more than a year, $40,000 was used, and 500,000 pounds of clothing, bedding, etc. England contributed 50,000 pounds of goods and $8,000 in money; the chief givers being Mrs. Comstock's friends who knew her in her good work abroad. Much of the remainder had come in small sums, and from the Christian women of America. One third was furnished by the Society of Friends. Ohio gave more than any other State. The State and municipal funds of Kansas were not drawn upon at all, though much had come from private sources.

During the first year in Kansas the freedmen entered upon 20,000 acres of land, and plowed and fitted for grain-growing 3,000 acres. They built 300 cabins and dugouts, and accumulated $30,000. In 1878 Henry Carter, of Tennessee, set out

---

[1] The Congregationalist, Aug. 11, 1880.

from Topeka on foot·for Dunlap, sixty-five miles away; he carrying his tools, and his wife their bedclothes. In 1880 he had forty acres of land cleared and the first payment made, having earned his money on sheep ranches and elsewhere by daily labor. He has built a good stone cottage sixteen feet by ten, owns two cows, a horse, etc. In Topeka, where there were about 3,000 refugees, nearly all paupers when they came, all have found means in some way to make a living. These people have shown themselves worthy of aid. Mrs. Comstock has heard of only five or six cases of intoxication in nine months, and of no arrests for stealing. They do not want to settle where there is no church, and are all eager to have a Bible and to learn. Schools have been opened for the adults—the public schools of Kansas wisely making no distinction on account of color,—and also industrial schools, especially for women, who are quite ignorant of the ordinary duties of home life.

In the month of February, 1880, John M. Brown, Esq., General Superintendent of the Freedmen's Relief Association read an interesting report before the Association, from which the following extract is taken:

"The great exodus of Colored people from the South began about the 1st of February, 1879. By the 1st of April 1,300 refugees had gathered around Wyandotte, Ks. Many of them were in a suffering condition. It was then that the Kansas Relief Association came into existence for the purpose of helping the most needy among the refugees from the Southern States. Up to date about 60,000 refugees have come to the State of Kansas to live. Nearly 40,000 of them were in a destitute condition when they arrived, and have been helped by our association. We have received to date $68,000 for the relief of the refugees. About 5,000 of those who have come to Kansas have gone to other States to live, leaving about 55,000 yet in Kansas. About 30,000 of that number have settled in the country, some of them on lands of their own or rented lands; others have hired out to the farmers, leaving about 25,000 in and around the different cities and towns of Kansas. There has been great suffering among those remaining in and near the cities and towns this winter. It has been so cold that they could not find employment, and, if they did, they had to work for very low wages, because so many of them are looking for work that they are in each other's way.

"Most of those about the cities and towns are men with large families, widows, and very old people. The farmers want only able-bodied men and women for their work, and it is very hard for men with large families to get homes among the farmers. Kansas is a new State, and most farmers have small houses, and they cannot take large families to live with them. So, when the farmers call for help, they usually call for a man and his wife only, or for a single man or woman.

" Now, in order that men with large families may become owners of land, and be able to support their families, the K. F. R. Association, if they can secure the means, will purchase cheap lands, which can be bought at from $3 to $5 per acre, on long time, by making a small payment in cash. They will settle the refugees on those lands, letting each family have from twenty to forty acres, and not settling more than sixteen families in any one neighborhood, so that they can easily obtain work from the farmers in that section or near by. I do not think it best to settle too many of them in any one place, because it will make it hard for them to find employment.

" If our association can help them to build a small house, and have five acres of their land broken, the women and children can cultivate the five acres, and make enough to support their families, while the men are out at work by the day to earn money to meet the payments on their land as they come due. In this way many families can be helped to homes of their own, where they can become self-sustaining, educate their children, and be useful citizens to the State of Kansas.

"Money spent in this way will be much more profitable to them than so much old clothing and provisions. Then they will no longer be objects of charity or a burden to benevolent people."

The sad stories of this persecuted people had touched the hearts of the friends of humanity everywhere. Money and clothing came on every train, and as fast as the association could secure homes for the refugees they were distributed throughout the State.[1]

A special correspondent of the "Chicago Inter-Ocean" was despatched to Topeka to report the condition of things there, and to throw some light upon the great intellect of Senator Voorhees. He reported as follows:

"TOPEKA, KAN., April 9.—During the last few days I have, in obedience to your request, been taking notice of the exodus, as it may be

---

[1] We visited Kansas twice in 1880, and again in 1881. We conversed with Gov. St. John, Mr. John M. Brown, and other gentlemen related to and familiar with the matter of the Exodus, and found that those who at the first so violently opposed the coming of the Negroes had been pleased with their simplicity, patience, industry, and character. They were all doing well. The association had discontinued its work, and the people were settled in quiet homes.

studied here at the headquarters for relief among the refugees in Kansas. This is the third visit your correspondent has made to the ' promised land' of the dusky hosts who, fleeing from persecution and wrongs, have swarmed within its borders to the number of 25,000. In a letter written while here in December last the number then within the State was estimated at about 15,000, and since that date at least 12,000 more have come. In the 'barracks' to-day I found what seemed to be the same one hundred * * * who crowded about the stove that cold December day ; but they were not the same, of course, for their places have been filled many times with other hundreds, who have found their first welcome to Kansas in the rest, food, and warmth which the charity of the North has provided here. So efficient have the plan of relief and the machinery of distribution been made, that of the thousands who have passed through here, none have remained as a burden of expense to the association more than four or five days before places were found where their own labor could furnish them support.

"If that pure statesman of Indiana whose great heart was so filled with solicitude for the welfare of his colored brethren, that he asked Congress to appropriate thousands of dollars to ascertain why they moved from one State to another, will come here he will be rewarded by such a flood of light on the question as can never penetrate the recesses of his committee room in Washington. He need hardly propound an inquiry ; he had, indeed, best not let his great presence be known, for in the presence of Democracy the negro has learned to keep silence. But in search of the truth let him go to the file of over 3,000 letters in the Governor's office from negroes in the South, and read in them the homely but truthful tales of suffering, oppression, and wrongs. Let him note how real is their complaint, but how modest the boon they seek ; for in different words, sometimes in quaint and often in awkward phrases, the questions are always the same : Can we be free ? Can we have work, and can we have our rights in Kansas? Let him go next to the barracks and watch the tired, ragged, hungry, scared-looking negroes as they come by the dozens on every train. If he is not prompted by shame, then from caution necessary to the success of his errand, let him here conceal the fact that he is a Democrat, for these half-famished and terrified negroes have been fleeing from Democrats in the South, and in their ignorance they may not be able to comprehend the nice distinction between a Northern and Southern Democrat. If he will be content simply to listen as they talk among themselves, he will soon learn much that the laborious cross-examination of witnesses has failed to teach him. He may take note of the fact that fleeing from robbery, oppression, and murder, they come only with the plea for work and justice while they work. He may see reason to criticise what generally has been deemed by Southern Democrats at least, the unreasonable folly in a negro which prompts husband and wife to go only where they can go together, but he will find nothing to cause him to doubt the sincerity and good 'faith with which the negro grapples with the problem of his new life here. If he would learn more of this strength of resolution and the patience which they have brought to the search for a home in a free land, let him inquire concerning the lives of these refugees in Kansas. It may seem of significance and worthy of approving note to him, that as laborers they have been faithful and industrious ; that in no single case have they come back asking aid of the relief association nor become burdens in any way upon corporate or public charities ; that as citizens they are sober and law-abiding to such a degree that he would hardly be able to discover a single case of crime so far among them ; and, finally, that in those instances where they were able to purchase a little land and stock, they have made as good progress toward the acquirement of homes and property as have the average poor white immigrants to the State. He will first learn, then, from the refugees themselves something of the desperate nature of the causes that drove them from the South, and secondly, from their lives here, with what thrift, patience, and determination they have met the difficulties which they have encountered in their efforts to gain a foothold, and as men among men, in the land of equal rights. From the Hon. Milton Reynolds, President of the Auxiliary Relief Association at Parsons, I learn that the negroes who have come into the southern part of the State, mostly from Texas, are all either settled on small tracts of land or employed as laborers at from $8 to $12 per month, and are all doing well. Mr. Reynolds's testimony to this effect was positive and unqualified. To assist these refugees in Southern Kansas—over 3,000 in all—only $575 has been expended. From Judge R. W. Dawson, who was the Secretary of the association under the old management and during the early months of the movement, one year ago, when 6,000 refugees were distributed throughout the State and provided with homes at a cost of $5,000, I learned much of interest concerning the welfare and progress of this advance guard of the great exodus. Judge Dawson, although not connected now with the relief work, feels of course a great interest in the welfare of those to whose assistance he contributed much, and loses no opportunity for observation of their condition while travelling over the State. He says he knows of no case where one has come back to the association for aid, and that, as laborers and citizens, their conduct has been such as to win the approval of all classes. Four colonies have been established. State lands were bought by the association and given to the colonies with the understanding that, to secure their title, they must make the second and third payments on the land purchased on the one-third cash and two-thirds time payment plan. Two of the newest of these colonies are still receiving aid from the association, but the others are self-sustaining and will be able, it is thought, to make the small purchase payments on the land as they become due.

"If our inquiring Statesman is interested in observing in what spirit these refugees receive the aid which has made existence possible here during the cold winter months, he may be profited by spending a few days in looking about the city of Topeka. There are in Topeka alone over 3,000 refugees, and nearly all of them, paupers when they came, have found means in some way to make a living. In many cases it is a precarious subsistence that is gained, and in not a few cases among late arrivals he would find evidences of want and destitution, but, compared with this, he cannot but be struck with the small number of applicants to the Relief Association for aid. Only 213 rations were issued outside the barracks last week to the 3,000 refugees who came here only a few months since without money, and frequently without clothing, to undertake what seemed under the circumstances the desperate purpose of making a living.

"The dangers and difficulties which beset the refugees' departure from a land where even the right to emigrate is denied him are great. * * * He may learn (Mr. Voorhees), however, from copies of over 1,000 letters in the Governor's office, that Gov. St. John has never, in reply to their appeals, failed to warn them of the difficulties that would beset their way here, and has never extended them promise of other assistance than that implied in the equal rights which are guaranteed to every citizen of Kansas. Further than this, however surprising it may be to Mr. Voorhees' theory of the causes of the exodus, it is nevertheless a fact that this very association, which is charged with encouraging the exodus, has sent the Rev. W. O. Lynch, a colored man, to the South to warn the colored people that they must not come here expecting to be fed or to find homes already prepared, and to do all in his power to dissuade them from coming at all. Still they come, and why they come the country has determined long in advance of Mr. Voorhees' report. * * *

"While we have Mr. Voorhees here we would be glad to have him glance at a State document to be found upon Governor St. John's table, which bears the Great Seal and signature of Gov. O. M. Roberts, of the State of Texas. It is a requisition by the Governor of Texas upon the Governor of Kansas for the body of one Peter Womack, a colored man, who was indicted by the Grand Jury of Grimes County at the last November term for the felony of fraudulently disposing of ten bushels of corn. From further particulars we learn that this Peter Womack gave a mortgage early in the spring of 1879 upon his crop just planted to cover a debt of twenty dollars due the firm of Wilson and Howel. When Womack came to gather his crop, he yields to the importunities of another white creditor ten bushels of corn *to be applied* upon the debt. About this time this Peter Womack becomes influential in inducing a number of his colored neighbors in Grimes County to emigrate to Kansas. Undeterred by threats and despite the bull-dozing methods employed to cause him to remain a 'citizen' of Texas, Womack, with others, sick of a condition of citizenship which is nothing less than hopeless peonage, leaves stock and crops behind to seek a home in Kansas. His acts in inciting the movement of these black serfs are not forgotten, however, by the white chivalry of Grimes County. The evidence of this surrender on a debt of ten bushels of corn, mortgaged for another debt, is hunted up, presented to the Grand Jury of Grimes County, he is promptly indicted for a felony, and the great State of Texas rises in her majesty and demands a surrender of his body. The demand is in accordance with law, undoubtedly,—Texas law,—but if Texas would occasionally punish one of the white murderers who do not think it necessary to leave her borders, this pursuit of a negro for selling ten bushels of corn from a mortgaged crop would seem a more imposing exhibition of the power of the commonwealth to enforce its laws." [1]

The effect, or rather the results of the Exodus have been two-fold. It taught the Southern people that there was need of some effort to regain the confidence of the Negroes; that the Negro is the only laborer who can cultivate that section of the country; that the Negro can get on without the Southern people a great deal better than they can get on without Negro labor; that the severe political treatment and systematic robbery of the Negroes had not only driven them out, but had discouraged white people from settling or investing money at the South; that dissatisfied labor was against their interests; that it was the duty of business men in the South to take a firm stand for the protection of the Negroes, because every stroke of violence administered to the Negroes shocked and injured the business of that section; and that kind treatment of and protection for the Negroes would insure better work and greater financial prosperity. On the other hand, the Exodus benefited the Negroes who sought and found new homes in a new country; and it secured better treatment for those who remained behind. The Exodus was in line with a great law that governs nations. The Negro race must win by contact with the white race; by absorbing all that is good; by the inspiration of example. He must come in contact now not

---

[1] Chicago Inter-Ocean, April 15, 1880.

with a people who hate him, but with a people of industrious, sober, and honest habits; a people willing to encourage and instruct him in the duties of life. Race lines must be obliterated at the South, and the old theory of the natural inferiority of the Negro must give way to the demonstrations of Negro capacity. A new doctrine must supplant the old theories of pre-slavery days, and every man in the Republic must enjoy a citizenship as wide as the continent, and, like the coin of the Government, pass for his intrinsic value, and no more.

CHAPTER XXIX.

RETROSPECTION AND PROSPECTION.

The Three Grand Divisions of the Tribes of Africa. — Slave Markets of America supplied from the Diseased and Criminal Classes of African Society. — America robs Africa of 15,000,000 Souls in 360 Years. — Negro Power of Endurance. — His Wonderful Achievements as a Laborer, Soldier, and Student. — First in War, and First in Devotion to the Country. — His Idiosyncrasies. — Mrs. Stowe's Errors. — His Growing Love for Schools and Churches. — His General Improvement. — The Negro will endure to the End. — He is Capable for All the Duties of Citizenship. — Amalgamation will not obliterate the Race. — The American Negro will civilize Africa. — America will establish Steamship Communication with the Dark Continent. — Africa will yet be composed of States, and "Ethiopia shall soon stretch out her Hands unto God."

IT has been shown that the tribes of Africa are divisible into three classes: The tribes of the mountain districts, the tribes of the sandstone districts, and the tribes of the alluvial districts; those of the mountain districts most powerful, those of the sandstone districts less powerful, and those of the alluvial districts least powerful. The slave markets of America were supplied,[1] very largely, from two classes of Africans, viz.:

---

[1] From the year 1500 to 1860 the number of slaves imported from Africa were as follows:

	Number of Negroes imported into America per annum.	Total.
From 1500 to 1525	500	12,500
From 1525 to 1550	5,000	125,000
From 1550 to 1600	15,000	750,000
From 1600 to 1650	20,000	1,000,000
From 1650 to 1700	35,000	1,750,000
From 1700 to 1750	60,000	3,000,000
From 1750 to 1800	80,000	4,000,000
From 1800 to 1850	65,000	3,250,000
Total, 350 years		13,887,500
From 1850 to 1860, increase for decade . .		749,931
Total importation of Negro slaves into America during a period of 360 years		14,637,431
or about 15,000,000 in round numbers.		

The above figures are taken from Mr. Dunbar's Mexican Papers. The process by which he reaches his conclusions and secures his figures is rather remarkable.

the criminal class, and the refuse of African society, which has been preyed upon by local disease, decimated by wars waged by the more powerful tribes which have pushed down from the abundant supply that has poured over the terraces of the mountains for centuries. Nevertheless, some of the better class have found their way to this country. About 137 Negro tribes are represented in the United States.

For every slave landed safely in North America, there was one lost in procuring and bringing down to the coast, and in transportation. Thus in the period of 360 years, Africa was robbed of about 30,000,000 of souls! When it is remembered that the Negroes in America sprang from the criminal, diseased, and inferior classes of Africa, it is nothing short of a phenomenon that they were able to endure such a rigorous state of bondage. Under-fed and over-worked; poorly clad and miserably housed; with the family altar cast down, and intelligent men allowed to run over it as swine; and with the fountains of knowledge sealed by law against the thirstings of human souls for knowledge, the Negroes of America, nevertheless, have shown the most wonderful signs of recuperation, and the ability to rise, against every cruel act of man and the very forces of nature, to a manhood and intelligent citizenship that converts the cautious, impartial, and conservative spirit of history into eulogy! They have overcome the obstacles in the path of the physical civilization of North America; they have earned billions of dollars for a profligate people; they have made good laborers, efficient sailors, and peerless soldiers. In three wars they won the crown of heroes by steady, intrepid valor; and in peace have shown themselves the friends of stable government. During the war for the Union, 186,017[1] Colored men enlisted in the service of the nation, *and participated in* 249 *battles.* From 1866 to 1873, besides the money saved in other banking houses, they deposited in the Freedmen's Banks at the South $53,000,000! From 1866 to 1875 there were seven Negroes as Lieutenant-Governors of Southern States; two served in the United States Senate, and thirteen in the United States House of Representatives. There have been five Negroes appointed as Foreign Ministers. There have been ten Negro members of Northern Legislatures; and in the Government Departments at Washington there are 620 Negroes

---

[1] This includes the officers, most of whom were white men.

employed. Starting without schools this remarkable people have now 14,889 schools, with an attendance of 720,853 pupils! And this does not include the children of color who attend the white schools of the Northern States ; and as far as it is possible to get the statistics, there are at present 169 Colored students attending white colleges in the Northern States.

The first blood shed in the Revolution was that of a Negro, Crispus Attucks, on the 5th of March, 1770. The first blood shed in the war for the Union was that of a Negro, Nicholas Biddle, a member of the very first company that passed through Baltimore in April, 1861 ; while the first Negro killed in the war was named *John Brown !* The first Union regiment of Negro troops raised during the Rebellion, was raised in the State that was first to secede from the Union, South Carolina. Its colonel was a Massachusetts man, and a graduate of Harvard College. The first action in which Negro troops participated was in South Carolina. The first regiment of Northern Negro troops fought its first battle in South Carolina, at Fort Wagner, where it immortalized itself. The first Negro troops recruited in the Mississippi Valley were recruited by a Massachusetts officer, Gen. B. F. Butler ; while their first fighting here was directed by another Massachusetts officer, Gen. N. P. Banks. The first recognition of Negro troops by the Confederate army was in December, 1863, when Major John C. Calhoun, a grandson of the South Carolina statesman of that name, bore a flag of truce, which was received by Major Trowbridge of the First South Carolina Colored Regiment. The first regiment to enter Petersburg was composed of Negroes; while the first troops to enter the Confederate capital at Richmond were Gen. Godfry Weitzel's two divisions of Negroes. The last guns fired at Lee's army at Appomattox were in the hands of Negro soldiers. And when the last expiring effort of treason had, through foul conspiracy, laid our beloved President low in death, a Negro regiment guarded his remains, and marched in the stately procession which bore the illustrious dead from the White House. And on the 15th of May, 1865, at Palmetto Ranch, Texas, the 62d Regiment of Colored Troops fired the last volley of the war !

Several attempts have been made to define the racial characteristics of the Negro, but they have not been attended with success.

Mrs. Harriet Beecher Stowe has written more and written

better about the American Negro than any other person during the present century. She has given laboriously and minutely wrought pictures of plantation life. She has held up to the gaze of the world portraitures comic and serio-comic, which for the gorgeousness and awfulness of their drapery will perish only with the language in which they are painted.

But Mrs. Stowe's great characters are marred by some glaring imperfections. "Uncle Tom" is too goodish, too lamb-like, too obsequious. He is a child of full growth, yet lacks the elements of an enlarged manhood. His mind is feeble, body strong—too strong for the conspicuous absence of spirit and passion.

"Dred" is the divinest character of the times—is prophet, preacher, and saint. He is *so* grand. He is eloquent beyond compare, and as familiar with the Bible as if he were its author. And every hero Mrs. Stowe takes in charge must make up his mind to get religion, lots of it too, and then prepare to die. There is a terrible fatality among her leading characters.

Mrs. Stowe has given but one side of Negro character, and that side is terribly exaggerated. But all strong natures like hers are given to exaggeration. Wendell Phillips never tells the truth, and yet he always tells the truth. He is a man of strong convictions, and always pronounces his conviction strongly. He has a poetical nature, is a word-painter, and, therefore, indulges in the license of the poet and painter. Mrs. Stowe belongs to this school of writers. The lamb and lion are united in the Negro character. Mrs. Stowe's mistake consists in ascribing to the Negro a peculiarly religious character and disposition. Here is detected the mistake. The Negro is not, as she supposes, the most religious being in the world. He has more religion and has less religion than any other of the races, in one sense. And yet, divorced from the circumstances by which he has been surrounded in this country, he is not so very religious. Mrs. Stowe seizes upon a characteristic that belongs to mankind wherever mankind is enslaved, and gently binds it about the neck of the Negro. All races of men become religious when oppressed. Frederick the Great was an infidel when with his friend Voltaire, but when suffering the reverses of war in Silesia he could write very pious letters to his "favorite sister." This is true in national character when traced to its last analysis. Men pray while they are down in life, but curse when up. And of necessity the religion of a bond people is not always healthy. There is an involuntary turning to a divine helper; a sort of religious superstition, that believes all things, hopes all things, and is patient. The soul of such a people is surcharged with an almost incredulous amount of poetry, song, and rude but grand eloquence. And when the songs that cheered and lighted many a heavy heart in the starless night of bondage shall have been rescued and purified by the art of music, the hymnology of this century will be greatly indebted to this much-abused people. So, under this religious garb, woven by the cruel experiences consequent upon slavery, the lion slumbers in the Negro.

Every year since the close of the Rebellion the Negro has been taking on better and purer traits of character. Possessed of an impressible nature, a discriminating sense of the beautiful, and a deep, pure taste for music, his progress has been phenomenal. Strong in his attachments, gentle in manners, confiding, hopeful, enduring in affection, and benevolent to a fault, there is no limit to the outcome of his character.

Like the oscillations of the pendulum of a clock the Negro is swinging from an extreme religious fanaticism to an extreme rationalism. But he will finally take his position upon a solid religious basis; and to his "faith" will add virtue, knowledge, and good works. Everywhere under good influences he has made a good citizen. No issue in the State has been foreign to him. He has proven his patriotism and his fondness for this land to which he was dragged in chains, and in his obedience to its laws and devotion to its principles has stood second to none. His home promises much good. His whole life seems to have undergone a radical change. He has shown a disposition and delight in the education of his children; and the constantly growing demand for competent teachers and educated preachers shows that he has outgrown his old ideas concerning education and religion. From an insatiable desire for gewgaws he has turned to a practice of the precepts of economy. From the state of semi-civilization in which he cared only for the comforts of the present, his desires and wants have swept outward and upward into the years to come and toward the Mysterious Future. He has learned the difficult lesson that "man shall not live by bread alone," and has shown himself delighted with a keen sense of intellectual hunger. One hundred weekly newspapers, conducted by Negroes, are feeding the mind of the race, binding communities together by the cords of common interests and racial sympathy; while the works of twenty Negro authors · lend inspiration and purpose to every honest effort at self-improvement.

The fiery trials of the young Colored men who gained admission to West Point, and the noble conduct of the four regiments of black troops in the severe service of the frontiers have strengthened the hopes of a nation in the final outcome of the American Negro.

But what of the future? Can the Negro endure the sharp competition of American civilization? Can he keep his position against the tendencies to amalgamation? Since it has been proven that the Negro is not dying out, but on the contrary possesses the powers of reproduction to a remarkable degree, a new source of danger has been discovered. It is said that the Negro will perish, will be absorbed by the dominant race ere long; that where races are crossed the inferior race suffers; and that mixed races lack the power to reproduce their species; and that hence the disappearance of the Negro is but a question of time. Mr. Joseph C. G. Kennedy, superintendent of the Federal Census during the war, took the following view of this question:

" That an unfavorable moral condition has existed and continues among the free Colored, be the cause what it may, notwithstanding the great number of excellent people included in that population, no one can for a moment doubt who will consider that with them an element exists which is to some extent positive, and that is the fact of there being more than half as many mulattoes as blacks, forming, as they do, 36¼ per cent. of the whole Colored population, and they are maternally descendants of the Colored race, as it is well known that no appreciable amount of this admixture is the result of marriage between white and black, or the progeny of white mothers—a fact showing that whatever deterioration may be the consequence of this alloyage, is incurred by the Colored race. Where such a proportion of the mixed race exists, it may reasonably be inferred that the barriers to license are not more insuperable among those of the same color. That corruption of morals progresses with greater admixture of races, and that the product of vice stimulates the propensity to immorality, is as evident to observation as it is natural to circumstances. These developments of the census, to a good degree, explain the slow progress of the free Colored population in the Northern States, and indicate, with unerring certainty, the gradual extinction of that people the more rapidly as,

---

[1] Thus far the Negro has not gone, as an author, beyond mere narration. But we may soon expect a poet, a novelist, a composer, and a philosophical writer.

whether free or slave, they become diffused among the dominant race. There are, however, other causes, although in themselves not sufficient to account for the great excess of deaths over births, as is found to occur in some Northern cities, and these are such as are incident to incongenial climate and a condition involving all the exposures and hardships which accompany a people of lower caste. As but two censuses have been taken which discriminate between the blacks and mulattoes, it is not yet so easy to determine how far the admixture of the races affects their vital power ; but the developments already made would indicate that the mingling of the races is more unfavorable to vitality, than a condition of slavery, which practically ignores marriage to the exclusion of the admixture of races, has proved, for among the slaves the natural increase has been as high as three per cent. per annum, and ever more than two per cent., while the proportion of mulattoes at the present period reaches but 10.41 per cent. in the slave population. Among the free Colored in the Southern States, the admixture of races appears to have progressed at a somewhat less ratio than at the North, and we can only account for the greater proportionate number of mulattoes in the North by the longer period of their freedom in the midst of the dominant and more numerous race, and the supposition of more mulattoes than blacks having escaped or been manumitted from slavery."

Whatever merit this view possessed before the war of the Rebellion, it is obsolete under the present organization of society. The environments of the Negro, the downward tendencies of his social life, and the exposed state in which slave laws left him, have all perished. In addition to his aptitude for study and capacity for improvement, he is now under the protecting and restraining influences of congenial climate; and pure sociological laws will impart to his offspring the power of reproduction and the ability to maintain an excellent social footing with the other races of the world. The learned M. A. DeQuatrefages says, concerning this question :

None of the eminent men with whom I regret to differ take any account of the influence of the action of the surroundings. I believe that the conditions of the surroundings play as important a part in the crossing of races as they do in other matters. They may sometimes favor, sometimes restrict, sometimes prevent, the establishment of a mixed race. This simple consideration accounts for many apparently contradictory facts. Etwick and Long have affirmed that in Jamaica the mulattoes hold out only because they are constantly recruited by the marriage of whites with negresses. But in San Domingo, in the

Dominican Republic, there are, we may say, no whites, and the population consists of two thirds mulattoes and one third negroes. The numbers of the mulattoes are there well kept up by themselves without the introduction of fresh blood. In respect to fertility, different instances of crossing between individuals of the two same races may give different results, according to the place where they are effected. I believe it is unnecessary to insist and show that the physical and physiological faculties of children born of mixed unions ought to present analogous facts.

"In my view the aggregation of physical conditions does not in itself alone constitute the environment. Social and moral conditions have an equal part in it. Here, again, it is easy to establish, in the results of crossings, differences which have no other cause than differences in these conditions. It is true that mongrels, born and grown up in the midst of the hatred of the inferior race and the contempt of the superior race, are liable to merit the reproaches which are commonly attached to them. On the other hand, if real marriages take place between the races, and their offspring are placed upon a footing of equality with the mass of the population, they are quite able to reach the general level, and sometimes to display superior qualities.

"All of my studies on this question have brought me to the conclusion that the mixture of races has in the past had a great part in the constitution of a large number of actual populations. It is also clear to me that its part in the future will not be less considerable. The movement of expansion, to which I have just called attention, has not slackened since the days of Cortez and Pizarro, but has become more extended and general. The perfection of the means of communication has given it new activity. The people of mixed blood already constitute a considerable part of the population of certain states, and their number is large enough to entitle them to be taken notice of in the population of the whole world.

.   .   .   .

"These facts show that man is everywhere the same, and that his passions and instincts are independent of the differences that distinguish the human groups. The reason of it is that these differences, however accentuated they may seem to us, are essentially morphological, but do not in any way touch the wholly physiological power of reproduction." [1]

Race prejudice is bound to give way before the potent influences of character, education, and wealth. And these are necessary to the growth of the race. Without wealth there can be no

---

[1] Revue Scientifique, Paris.

leisure, without leisure there can be no thought, and without thought there can be no progress. The future work of the Negro is twofold : subjective and objective. Years will be devoted to his own education and improvement here in America. He will sound the depths of education, accumulate wealth, and then turn his attention to the civilization of Africa. The United States will yet establish a line of steamships between this country and the Dark Continent. Touching at the Grain Coast, the Ivory Coast, and the Gold Coast, America will carry the African missionaries, Bibles, papers, improved machinery, instead of rum and chains. And Africa, in return, will send America indigo, palm-oil, ivory, gold, diamonds, costly wood, and her richest treasures, instead of slaves. Tribes will be converted to Christianity ; cities will rise, states will be founded ; geography and science will enrich and enlarge their discoveries ; and a telegraph cable binding the heart of Africa to the ear of the civilized world, every throb of joy or sorrow will pulsate again in millions of souls. In the interpretation of *History* the plans of God must be discerned, *"For a thousand years in Thy sight are but as yesterday when it is passed, and as a watch in the night."*

THE END.

APPENDIX.

Part 5.

ANTI-SLAVERY AGITATION.

CHAPTER VI.

WALKER'S APPEAL.

One of the most remarkable papers written by a Negro during the Anti-Slavery Agitation Movement was the Appeal of David Walker, of Boston, Massachusetts. He was a shopkeeper and dealer in second-hand clothes. He was born in Wilmington, North Carolina, September 28, 1785, of a free mother by a slave father. When quite young he said: "If I remain in this bloody land, I will not live long. As true as God reigns, I will be avenged for the sorrow which my people have suffered. This is not the place for me—no, no. I must leave this part of the country. It will be a great trial for me to live on the same soil where so many men are in slavery ; certainly I cannot remain where I must hear their chains continually, and where I must encounter the insults of their hypocritical enslavers. Go, I must!"

He went to Boston, Massachusetts, where he took up his residence. He applied himself to study, and in 1827, capable of reading and writing, he began business in Brattle Street. He was possessed of a rather reflective and penetrating mind. And before Mr. William Lloyd Garrison unfurled his flag for the Agitation Movement, David Walker wrote and published his Appeal in 1829. It was circulated widely, and touched and stirred the South as no other pamphlet had ever done. Three editions were published. The feeling at the South was intense. The following correspondence shows how deeply agitated the South was by Walker's Appeal. The editor of the *Boston Courier* observed : "It will be recollected that some time in December last [1829] Gov. Giles sent a message to the Legislature of Virginia complaining of an attempt to circulate in the city of Richmond a seditious pamphlet, said to have been sent there from Boston. We find in the *Richmond Enquirer* of the 18th inst. [February, 1830] the following Message from the Governor, enclosing a correspondence which unravels all the mystery which has hitherto enveloped the transaction."

EXECUTIVE DEPARTMENT, Feb. 16th, 1830.

SIR: In compliance with the advice of the Executive Council, I do myself the honor of transmitting herewith the copy of a letter from the Honorable Harrison Gray Otis, Mayor of Boston, conveying the copy of a letter from him addressed to the Mayor of Savannah, in answer to one received by him from that gentleman respecting a seditious pamphlet written by a person of color in Boston, and circulated by him in other parts of the United States.

Very respectfully, your obd't serv't,

WM. B. GILES.

The Hon. LINN BANKS, *Speaker of the House of Delegates.*

To his Excellency, the Governor of Virginia :

SIR: Perceiving that a pamphlet published in this city has been a subject of animadversion and uneasiness in Virginia as well as in Georgia, I have presumed that it might not be amiss to apprize you of the sentiments and feelings of the city authorities in this place respecting it, and for that purpose I beg leave to send you a copy of my answer to a letter from the Mayor of Savannah, addressed to me on that subject. You may be assured that your good people cannot hold in more absolute detestation the sentiments of the writer than do the people of this city, and, as I verily believe, the mass of the New England population. The only difference is, that the insignificance of the writer, the extravagance of his sanguinary fanaticism tending to disgust all persons of common humanity with his object, and the very partial circulation of this book, prevent the affair from being a subject of excitement and hardly of serious attention.

I have reason to believe that the book is disapproved of by the decent portion even of the free colored population in this place, and it would be a cause of deep regret to me, and I believe to all my well-disposed fellow-citizens, if a publication of this character, and emanating from such a source, should be thought to be countenanced by any of their number.

I have the honor to be respectfully, your obedient servant,
BOSTON, Feb. 10, 1830.   H. G. OTIS, *Mayor of the City of Boston.*

To the Mayor of Savannah:

SIR: Indisposition has prevented an earlier reply to your favor of the 12th December. A few days before the receipt of it, the *pamphlet* had been put into my hands by one of the Board of Aldermen of this city, who received it from an individual, it not having been circulated here. I perused it carefully, in order to ascertain whether the writer had made himself amenable to our laws; but notwithstanding the extremely bad and inflammatory tendency of the publication, he does not seem to have violated any of these laws. It is written by a free black man, whose true name it bears. He is a shopkeeper and dealer in old clothes, and in a conversation which I authorized a young friend of mine to hold with him, he openly avows the sentiments of the book and authorship. I also hear that he declares his intention to be, to circulate his pamphlets by mail, at his own expense, if he cannot otherwise effect his object.

You may be assured, sir, that a disposition would not be wanting on the part of the city authorities here, to avail themselves of any lawful means for preventing this attempt to throw firebrands into your country. We regard it with deep disapprobation and abhorrence. But, we have no power to control the purpose of the author, and without it we think that any public notice of him or his book, would make matters worse.

We have been determined, however, to publish a general caution to Captains and others, against exposing themselves to the consequences of transporting incendiary writings into your and the other Southern States.

I have the honor to be your obedient servant,
                                                        H. G. OTIS.

Part 6.

THE PERIOD OF PREPARATION.

CHAPTER XI.

LIST OF WORKS BY NEGRO AUTHORS.

"Olaudah Equiano or Gustavus Vassa." Autobiography: Boston, 1837.

"Light and Truth." Lewis (R. B.). Boston, 1844.

"Volume of Poems." Whitfield, (James M.). 1846.

'Volume of Poems." Payne, (Daniel A., D.D.). 1850.

"The Condition, Elevation, Emigration, and Destiny of the Colored People of the United States, Politically Considered." Delaney (Martin R.). Philadelphia, 1852.

"Principia of Ethnology: The Origin of Races and Color." Delaney (Martin R.).

"Narrative of the Life of an American Slave." London, 1847. "My Bondage and My Freedom." New York, 1855. "Life and Times." Hartford, Conn., 1882. Douglass (Frederick).

"Autobiography of a Fugitive Negro," etc. Ward (Rev. Samuel Ringgold). London, 1855.

"The Colored Patriots of the American Revolution." Nell (Wm. C). Boston, 1855.

"Narrative of Solomon Northup." New York, 1859. "Twenty-two Years a Slave, and Forty Years a Freeman." Rochester, 1861. Stewart (Rev. Austin).

"The Black Man." Boston, Mass., 1863. "The Negro in the Rebellion." Boston, 1867. "Clotelle." Boston, 1867. "The Rising Sun." Boston, 1874. "Sketches of Places and People Abroad." 1854. Brown (Wm. Wells, M.D.).

"An Apology for African Methodism." Tanner (Benj. T.). Baltimore, 1867.

"The Underground Railroad." Still (William). Philadelphia, 1872.

"The Colored Cadet at West Point." Flipper (H. O.), U. S. A. New York, 1877.

"Music and Some Highly Musical People." Trotter (James M.). Boston, 1878.

"My Recollections of African Methodism." Wayman (Bishop A. W.). Philadelphia, Pa., 1881.

"First Lessons in Greek." Scarborough (W. S., A.M.). New York, 1882.

"History of the Black Brigade." Clark (Peter H.)

" Uncle Tom's Story of His Life." From 1789 to 1879. Henson (Rev. Josiah). Boston.

" The Future of Africa." New York, 1862, Charles Scribner & Co.

" The Greatness of Christ," and other Sermons. Crummell (Rev. Alexander, D.D.). T. Whittaker, 2 and 3 Bible House, New York, 1882.

" Not a Man and Yet a Man." Whitman (A. A.).

" Mixed Races." Sampson (John P.). Hampton, Va., 1881.

" Poems." Wheatley (Phillis). London, England, 1773.

" As a Slave and as a Freeman." Loguen (Bishop, J. W.).

CHAPTER XIII.

THE JOHN BROWN MEN.

The subjoined correspondence was published in the *Republican*, J. K. Rukenbrod, editor, at Salem, Ohio, Wednesday, December 28, 1859. The beautiful spirit of self-sacrifice, the lofty devotion to the sublime principles of universal liberty, and the heroic welcome to the hour of martyrdom, invest these letters with intrinsic historic value.

LETTER FROM EDWIN COPPOCK TO HIS UNCLE JOSHUA COPPOCK.

CHARLESTON, VA., December 13, 1859.

MY DEAR UNCLE : I seat myself by the stand to write for the *last* time, to thee and thy family. Though far from home, and overtaken by misfortune, I have not forgotten you. Your generous hospitality toward me during my short stay with you last Spring is stamped indelibly upon my heart ; and also the generosity bestowed upon my poor brother, at the same time, who now wanders an outcast from his native land. But thank God he is free, and I am thankful it is I who have to suffer instead of him.

The time may come when he will remember me. And the time may come when he will still further remember the *cause in which I die.* Thank God the principles of the cause in which we were engaged *will not die with me and my brave comrades.* They will spread wider and wider, and gather strength with each hour that passes.

The voice of truth will echo through our land, bringing conviction to the erring, and adding numbers to *that glorious Army who will enlist under its banner.* The cause of everlasting truth and justice will go on " conquering and to conquer," until onr broad and beautiful land shall rest beneath the banner of freedom. I had hoped to live to see the dawn of that glorious day. I had hoped to live to see the principles of the Declaration of our Independence fully realized. I had hoped to see the dark stain of slavery blotted from our land, and the *libel* of our boasted freedom erased ; when we can say in truth that our beloved country is " the land of the free, and the home of the brave."—But this cannot be. I have heard my sentence passed, my doom is sealed. But two brief days between me and eternity. At the expiration of those two days, I shall stand upon the scaffold to take my last look at earthly scenes. But that scaffold has but little dread for me ; for I honestly believe I am innocent of any crime justifying such punishment.

But by the taking of my life, and the lives of my comrades, Virginia is but hastening on that glorious day, when the slave will rejoice in his freedom ; when he can say that *I too am a man,* and am groaning no more under the yoke of oppression. But I must now close. Accept this short scrawl as a remembrance of me. Remember me to my relatives and friends. And now Farewell. From thy nephew,

EDWIN COPPOCK.

P. S. I will say for I know it will be a satisfaction to all of you, that we are all kindly treated, and I hope the North will not fail to give Sheriff Campbell and Captain Avis due acknowledgment for their kind and noble actions.

E.

LETTER FROM EDWIN COPPOCK TO THOMAS WINN.

MY DEAR FRIEND THOMAS WINN: For thy love and sympathy, and for thy unwearied exertion in my behalf, accept my warmest thanks. I have no words to tell the gratitude and love I have for thee. And may God bless thee and thy family, for the love and kindness thee has always shown towards my family and me. And when life with thee is over, may we meet on that shore where there is no parting, is the farewell prayer of thy true Friend.

EDWIN COPPOCK.

THAT LETTER.

The following is the letter from Edwin Coppock, seized upon by the Virginia authorities as a pretence for not commuting his sentence. The offensive remark consisted alone wherein he spoke of the chivalry as " the enemy." There certainly is nothing in this communication that could justify a Government in taking the life of a man whom it otherwise considered not guilty of a capital crime, but whose greatest offence was that of being found, as Wise claimed, in bad company. We give the letter entire :

EDWIN COPPOCK TO MRS. BROWN.

CHARLESTON JAIL, VIRGINIA, November —, 1859.

MRS. JOHN BROWN—Dear Madam: I was very sorry that your request to see the rest of the prisoners was not complied with. Mrs Avis brought me a book whose pages are full of truth and beauty, entitled "Voice of the True-Hearted," which she told me was a present from you. For this dear token of remembrance, please accept my thanks.

My comrade, J. E. Cook, and myself, deeply sympathize with you in your sad bereavement. We were both acquainted with Anna and Martha. They were to us as sisters, and as brothers we sympathize with them in the dark hour of trial and affliction.

I was with your sons when they fell. Oliver lived but a few moments after he was shot. He spoke no word, but yielded calmly to his fate. Watson was shot at 10 o'clock on Monday morning, and died about 3 o'clock on Wednesday morning. He suffered much. Though mortally wounded at 10 o'clock, yet at 3 o'clock Monday afternoon he fought bravely against the men who charged on us. When the enemy were repulsed, and the excitement of the charge was over, he began to sink rapidly.

After we were taken prisoners, he was placed in the guard-house with me. He complained of the hardness of the bench on which he was lying. I begged hard for a bed for him, or even a blanket, but could obtain none for him. I took off my coat and placed it under him, and held his head in my lap, in which position he died without a groan or a struggle.

I have stated these facts thinking that they may afford to you, and to the bereaved widows they have left, a mournful consolation.

Give my love to Anna and Martha, with our last farewell.

Yours truly,

EDWIN COPPOCK.

COOK'S LAST LETTER TO HIS WIFE.

CHARLESTOWN JAIL, Dec. 16, 1859.

MY DEAR WIFE AND CHILD: For the last time I take my pen to address you—for the last time to speak to you through the tongue of the absent. I am about to leave you and this world forever. But do not give way to your grief. Look with the eyes of hope beyond the vale of life, and see the dawning of that brighter morrow that shall know no clouds or shadows in its sunny sky—that shall know no sunset. To that eternal day I trust, beloved, I am going now. For me there waits no far-off or uncertain future. I am only going from my camp on earth to a home in heaven; from the dark clouds of sin and grief, to the clear blue skies, the flowing fountains, and the eternal joys of that better and brighter land, whose only entrance is through the vale of death —whose only gateway is the tomb.

Oh, yes! think that I am only going home; going to meet my Saviour and my God; going to meet my comrades, and wait and watch for you. Each hour that passes, every tolling bell, proclaims this world is not our home. We are but pilgrims here, journeying to our Father's house. Some have a long and weary road to wander; shadowed o'er with doubts and fears, they often tire and faint upon life's roadside; yet, still all wearied, they must move along. Some make a more rapid journey, and complete their pilgrimage in the bright morn of life; they know no weariness upon their journey, no ills or cares of toil-worn age. I and my comrades here are among that number. Our pilgrimage is nearly ended; we can almost see our homes. A few more hours and we shall be there.

True, it is hard for me to leave my loving partner and my little one, lingering on the rugged road on which life's storms are bursting. But cheer up, my beloved ones; those storms will soon be over; through their last lingering shadows you will see the promised rainbow. It will whisper of a happy land where all storms are over. Will you not strive to meet me in that clime of unending sunshine? Oh! yes, I know you will; that you will also try to lead our child along that path of glory; that you will claim for him an entrance to that celestial city whose maker and builder is God. Teach him the way of truth and virtue. Tell him for what and how his father left him ere his lips could lisp my name. Pray for him. Remember that there is no golden gateway to the realms of pleasure here, but there is one for the redeemed in the land that lies starward. There I hope we may meet, when you have completed your pilgrimage on the road of life. Years will pass on and your journey will soon be ended. Live so that when from the verge of life you look back you may feel no vain regrets, no bitter anguish for mis-spent years. Look to God in all your troubles; cast yourself on Him when your heart is dark with the night of sorrow and heavy with the weight of woe. He will shed over you the bright sunshine of His love, and take away the burden from your heart.

.   .   .   .   .   .

And now farewell. May that all-wise and eternal God, who governs all things, be with you to guide and protect you through life, and bring us together in eternal joy beyond the grave. Farewell, fond partner of my heart and soul. Farewell, dear babe of our love. A last, long farewell, till we meet in heaven.

I remain, in life and death, your devoted husband,

JOHN E. COOK.

FUNERAL OF JOHN E. COOK.

The funeral of Capt. Cook took place at Brooklyn on the 20th, from the residence of Mrs. S. L. Harris. The services were conducted by the Rev. Mr. Caldicott, of the Lee Avenue Dutch Reformed Church, and at the Cypress Hills Cemetery by the Rev. Wm. H. Johnson. Of the body the day previous, the *Tribune* says:

Owing to the length of time that elapsed between the decease and the time the body was delivered into the charge of Dr. Holmes, the process of embalming has been somewhat difficult, and consequently the appearance of the remains is not so natural as it otherwise would have been.

Last evening the body was placed in an erect position, in order to allow the injected fluid to settle in the veins and arteries, so as to give to the face a more natural appearance. The swelling has entirely disappeared from the neck and face, and the decomposition which had set in had been checked. The remains will not be enshrouded until this morning, when they will be placed in the coffin, enclosed in a white merino robe with a satin collar, satin cord about the waist, and a black neckerchief about the neck.

Yesterday afternoon the father, sisters, and wife of the deceased were permitted to view the remains. His wife removed the breast-pin and a miniature of their child from about his neck, which she had placed there but a few days previous to his execution. She is but eighteen years of age, and has an infant four months old. She is from Harper's Ferry, Va., where she was married about seventeen months since. She, as well as the other relatives, was overwhelmed with sorrow, and it was some moments before they were sufficiently recovered to be enabled to leave the body. The refusal of the Consistories of the Lee Avenue and Fourth Reformed Dutch Churches to permit the services to be held in their edifices has given rise to the expression of much feeling, and many of the friends of the deceased infer that this refusal is made from a fear of censure on the part of some of the members of their congregations, in allowing a Christian burial to the remains.

In the little burial-ground at Oberlin, Lorain County, Ohio, there is a monument dedicated to the memory of three of the John Brown Men, as follows :

> L. S. Leary, died at Harper's Ferry, Oct. 20, 1859, aged 24 years.
> S. Green, died at Charlestown, Virginia, Dec. 2, 1850, aged 28 years.
> J. A. Copeland, died at Charlestown, Virginia, Dec. 2, 1859, aged 25 years.

The monument bears the following inscription :

These Colored citizens of Oberlin, the heroic associates of the Immortal John Brown, gave their lives for the Slave.

THE NEGRO ARTIST OF THE STATUE OF LIBERTY ON THE CAPITOL.

When the bronze castings were being completed at the foundry of Mr. Mills, near Bladensburg, his foreman, who had superintended the work from the beginning, and who was receiving eight dollars per day, struck, and demanded ten dollars, assuring Mr. M. that the advance must be granted him, as nobody in America, except himself, could complete the work. Mr. M. felt that the demand was exorbitant, and appealed in his dilemma to the slaves who were assisting in the moulding. ".I can do that well," said one of them, an intelligent and ingenious servant, who had been intimately engaged in the various processes. The striker was dismissed, and the negro, assisted occasionally by the finer skill of his master, took the striker's place as superintendent, and the work went on. The black master-builder lifted the ponderous, uncouth masses, and bolted them together, joint by joint, piece by piece, till they blended into the majestic "Freedom," who to-day lifts her head in the blue clouds above Washington, invoking a benediction upon the imperilled Republic !

Was there a prophecy in that moment when the slave became the artist, and with rare poetic justice, reconstructed the beautiful symbol of freedom for America ? [1]

Part 7.

THE NEGRO IN THE WAR FOR THE UNION.

CHAPTER XIX.

NEGROES AS SOLDIERS.

Gen. Benj. F. Butler commanded a number of Negro Troops at Fort Harrison. on the 29th Sept., 1864. After white troops had been driven back by the enemy, Gen. Butler ordered his Negro troops to storm the fortified position of the enemy at the point of the bayonet. The troops had to charge down a hill, ford a creek, and—preceded by axemen who had to cut away two lines of *abatis*—then carry the works held by infantry and artillery. They made one of the most brilliant charges of the war,

---

[1] Washington Correspondent of the New York Tribune, December 2, 1863.

with " Remember Fort Pillow " as their battle-cry, and carried the works in an incredibly short time.

Nearly a decade after this battle, Gen. Butler, then a member of Congress from Massachusetts, said, in a speech on the Civil Rights Bill of this affair :

" It became my painful duty to follow in the track of that charging column, and there, in a space not wider than the clerk's desk, and three hundred yards long, lay the dead bodies of five hundred and forty-three of my colored comrades, fallen in defence of their country, who had offered up their lives to uphold its flag and its honor, as a willing sacrifice ; and as I rode along among them, guiding my horse this way and that way, lest he should profane with his hoofs what seemed to me the sacred dead, and as I looked on their bronze faces upturned in the shining sun, as if in mute appeal against the wrongs of the country for which they had given their lives, whose flag had only been to them a flag of stripes, on which no star of glory had ever shone for them— feeling I had wronged them in the past, and believing what was the future of my country. to them—among my dead comrades there, I swore to myself a solemn oath—'May my right hand forget its cunning, and my tongue cleave to the roof of my mouth,' if I ever fail to defend the rights of those men who have given their blood for me and my country that day and for their race forever, and God helping me, I will keep that oath."

BATTLES IN WHICH COLORED TROOPS PARTICIPATED.

" Alliance," Steamer, Fla.
March 8, 1865.
U. S. C. T. 99th Inf.

Amite River, La.
March 18, 1865.
U. S. C. T. 77th Inf.

Appomattox Court House, Va.
April 9, 1865.
U. S. C. T. 41st Inf.

Arkansas River, Ark.
Dec. 18, 1864.
U. S. C. T. 54th Inf.

Ash Bayou, La.
Nov. 19, 1864.
U. S. C. T. 93d Inf.

Ashepoo River, S. C.
May 16, 1864.
U. S. C. T. 34th Inf.

Ashwood, Miss.
June 25, 1864.
U. S. C. T. 63d Inf.

Ashwood Landing, La.
May 1 and 4, 1864.
U. S. C. T. 64th Inf.

Athens, Ala.
Sept. 24, 1864.
U. S. C. T. 106th, 110th, and 111th Inf.

Barrancas, Fla.
July 22, 1864.
U. S. C. T. 82d Inf.

Baxter's Springs, Kan.
Oct. 6, 1863.
U. S. C. T. 83d (new) Inf.

Bayou Bidell, La.
Oct. 15, 1864.
U. S. C. T. 52d Inf.

Bayou Boeuf, Ark.
Dec. 13, 1863.
U. S. C. T. 3d Cav.

Bayou Mason, Miss.
July ——, 1864.
U. S. C. T. 66th Inf.

Bayou St. Louis, Miss.
Nov. 17, 1863.
U. S. C. T. 91st Inf.

Bayou Tensas, La.
Aug. 10, 1863.
U. S. C. T. 48th Inf.

Bayou Tensas, La.
July 30 and Aug. 26, 1864.
U. S. C. T. 66th Inf.

Bayou Tunica, La.
Nov. 9, 1863.
U. S. C. T. 73d Inf.

Bermuda Hundred, Va.
May 4, 1864.
U. S. C. T. 4th Inf.

Bermuda Hundred, Va.
May 20, 1864.
U. S. C. T. 1st Cav.

Bermuda Hundred, Va.
Aug. 24 and 25, 1864.
U. S. C. T. 7th Inf.

Bermuda Hundred, Va.
Nov. 30 and Dec. 4, 1864.
U. S. C. T. 19th Inf.

Bermuda Hundred, Va.
Dec. 1, 1864.
U. S. C. T. 39th Inf.

Bermuda Hundred, Va.
Dec. 13, 1864.
U. S. C. T. 23d Inf.

Berwick, La.
April 26, 1864.
U. S. C. T. 98th Inf.

Big Creek, Ark.
July 26, 1864.
U. S. C. T. Batt'ry E, 2d Lt. Art.; 60th Inf.

Big Springs, Ky.
Jan. ——, 1865.
U. S. C. T. 12th Hy. Art.

Black Creek, Fla.
July 27, 1864.
U. S. C. T. 35th Inf.

Black River, La.
Nov. 1, 1864.
U. S. C. T. 6th Hy. Art.

Bogg's Mills, Ark.
Jan. 24, 1864.
U. S. C. T. 11th (old) Inf.

Boyd's Station, Ala.
March 18, 1865.
U. S. C. T. 101st Inf.

Boykin's Mill, S. C.
April 18, 1865.
U. S. C. T. 54th (Mass.) Inf.

Bradford's Springs, S. C.
April 18, 1865.
U. S. C. T. 102d Inf.

Brawley Fork, Tenn.
March 25, 1865.
U. S. C. T. 17th Inf.

Brice's Cross Roads, Miss.
June 10, 1864.
U. S. C. T. Batt'y F, 2d Lt. Art.; 55th and 59th Inf.

Briggin Creek, S. C.
Feb. 25, 1865.
U. S. C. T. 55th (Mass.) Inf.

Bryant's Plantation, Fla.
Oct. 21, 1864.
U. S. C. T. 3d Inf.

Cabin Creek, Caddo Nation.
July 1 and 2, 1863.
U. S. C. T. 79th (new) Inf.

Cabin Creek, Caddo Nation.
Nov. 4, 1865.
U. S. C. T. 54th Inf.

Cabin Point, Va.
Aug. 5, 1864.
U. S. C. T. 1st Cav.

Camden, Ark.
April 24, 1864.
U. S. C. T. 57th Inf.

Camp Marengo, La.
Sept. 14, 1864.
U. S. C. T. 63d Inf.

Cedar Keys, Fla.
Feb. 16, 1865.
U. S. C. T. 2d Inf.

Chapin's Farm, Va,
Sept. 29 and 30, 1864.
U. S. C. T. 2d Cav.; 1st, 4th, 5th, 6th, 7th, 8th
9th, 22d, 29th (Conn.), 36th, 37th, and 38th Inf.

Chapin's Farm, Va,
Nov. 4, 1864.
U. S. C. T. 22d Inf.

Chattanooga, Tenn.
Feb. —, 1865.
U. S. C. T. 18th Inf.

" Chippewia," Steamer, Ark.
Feb. 17, 1865.
U. S. C. T. 83d (new) Inf.

" City Belle," Steamer, La.
May 3, 1864.
U. S. C. T. 73d Inf.

City Point, Va.
May 6, 1864.
U. S. C. T. 5th Inf.

City Point, Va.
June —, 1864.
U. S. C. T. Batt'y B, 2d Lt. Art.

Clarksville, Ark.
Jan. 18, 1865.
U. S. C. T. 79th (new) Inf.

Clinton, La.
Aug. 25, 1864.
U. S. C. T. 4th Cav.

Coleman's Plantation, Miss.
July 4, 1864.
U. S. C. T. 52d Inf.

Columbia, La.
Feb. 4, 1864.
U. S. C. T. 66th Inf.

Concordia Bayou, La.
Aug. 5, 1864.
U. S. C. T. 6th Hy. Art.

Cow Creek, Kan.
Nov. 14, 1864.
U. S. C. T. 54th Inf.

Cox's Bridge, N. C.
March 24, 1865.
U. S. C. T. 30th Inf.

Dallas, Ga.
May 31, 1864.
U. S. C. T. 40th Inf.

Dalton, Ga.
Aug. 15 and 16, 1864.
U. S. C. T. 14th Inf.

Darbytown Road, Va.
Oct. 13, 1864.
U. S. C. T. 7th, 8th, 9th, and 29th (Conn.) Inf.

Davis's Bend, La.
June 2 and 29, 1864.
U. S. C. T. 64th Inf.

Decatur, Tenn.
Aug. 18, 1864.
U. S. C. T. 1st Hy. Art.

Decatur, Ala.
Oct. 28 and 29, 1864.
U. S. C. T. 14th Inf.

Decatur, Ala.
Dec. 27 and 28, 1864.
U. S. C. T. 17th Inf.

Deep Bottom, Va.
Aug. 14 to 18, 1864.
U. S. C. T. 7th and 9th Inf.

Deep Bottom, Va.
Sept. 2 and 6, 1864.
U. S. C. T. 2d Cav.

Deep Bottom, Va.
Oct. 1, 1864.
U. S. C. T. 38th Inf.

Deep Bottom, Va.
Oct. 31, 1864.
U. S. C. T. 127th Inf.

Deveaux Neck, S. C.
Dec. 7, 8, and 9, 1864.
U. S. C. T. 32d, 34th, 55th (Mass.), and 102d
Inf.

Drury's Bluff, Va.
May 10, 16, and 20, 1864.
U. S. C. T. 2d Cav.

Dutch Gap, Va.
Aug. 24, 1864.
U. S. C. T. 22d Inf.

Dutch Gap, Va.
Sept. 7, 1864.
U. S. C. T. 4th Inf.

Dutch Gap, Va.
Nov. 17, 1864.
U. S. C. T. 36th Inf.

East Pascagoula, Miss.
April 9, 1863.
U. S. C. T. Cos. B. and C., 74th Inf.

Eastport, Miss.
Oct. 10, 1864.
U. S. C. T. 61st Inf.

Fair Oaks, Va.
Oct. 27 and 28, 1864.
U. S. C. T. 1st, 5th, 9th, 22d, 29th (Conn.), and
37th Inf.

Federal Point, N. C.
Feb. 11, 1865.
U. S. C. T. 39th Inf.

Fillmore, Va.
Oct. 4, 1864.
U. S. C. T. 1st Inf.

Floyd, La.
July —, 1864.
U. S. C. T. 51st Inf.

Fort Adams, La.
Oct. 5, 1864.
U. S. C. T. 3d Cav.

Fort Anderson, Ky.
March 25, 1864.
U. S. C. T. 8th Hy. Art.

Fort Blakely, Ala.
March 31 to April 9, 1865.
U. S. C. T. 47th, 48th, 50th, 51st, 68th, 73d, 76th,
82d, and 86th Inf.

Fort Brady, Va.
Jan. 24, 1865.
U. S. C. T. 118th Inf.

Fort Burnham, Va.
Dec. 10, 1864.
U. S. C. T. 41st Inf.

Fort Burnham, Va.
Jan. 24, 1865.
U. S. C. T. 7th Inf.

Fort Donelson Tenn.
Oct. 11, 1864.
U. S. C. T. 4th Hy. Art.

Fort Gaines, Ala.
Aug. 2 to 8, 1864.
U. S. C. T. 96th Inf.

Fort Gibson, Caddo Nation.
Sept. 16, 1864.
U. S. C. T. 79th (new) Inf.

Fort Gibson, Caddo Nation.
Sept., 1865.
U. S. C. T. 54th Inf.

Fort Jones, Ky.
Feb. 18, 1865.
U. S. C. T. 12th Hy. Art.

Fort Pillow, Tenn.
April 12, 1864.
U. S. C. T. Batt'y F, 2d Lt. Art.; 11th (new) Inf.

Fort Pocahontas, Va.
Aug., 1864.
U. S. C. T. 1st Cav.

Fort Smith, Ark.
Aug. 24, 1864.
U. S. C. T. 11th (old) Inf.

Fort Smith, Ark.
Dec. 24, 1864.
U. S. C. T. 83d (new) Inf.

Fort Taylor, Fla.
Aug. 21, 1864.
U. S. C. T. 2d Inf.

Fort Wagner, S. C.
July 18 and Sept. 6, 1863.
U. S. C. T. 54th (Mass.) Inf.

Fort Wagner, S. C.
Aug. 26, 1863.
U. S. C. T. 3d Inf.

Franklin, Miss.
Jan. 2, 1865.
U. S. C. T. 3d Cav.

Ghent, Ky.
Aug. 29, 1864.
U. S. C. T. 117th Inf.

Glasgow, Mo.
Oct. 15, 1864.
U. S. C. T. 62d Inf

Glasgow, Ky.
March 25, 1865.
U. S. C. T. 119th Inf.

Goodrich's Landing, La.
March 24 and July 16, 1864.
U. S. C. T. 66th Inf.

Grand Gulf, Miss.
July 16, 1864.
U. S. C. T. 53d Inf.

Gregory's Farm, S. C.
Dec. 5 and 9, 1864.
U. S. C. T. 26th Inf.

Hall Island, S. C.
Nov. 24, 1863.
U. S. C. T. 33d Inf.

Harrodsburg, Ky.
Oct. 21, 1864.
U. S. C. T. 5th Cav.

Hatcher's Run, Va.
Oct. 27 and 28, 1864.
U. S. C. T. 27th, 39th, 41st, 43d, and 45th Inf.

Haynes Bluff, Miss.
Feb. 3, 1864.
U. S. C. T. 53d Inf.

Haynes Bluff, Miss.
April, 1864.
U. S. C. T. 3d Cav.

Helena, Ark.
Aug. 2, 1864.
U. S. C. T. 64th Inf.

Henderson, Ky.
Sept. 25, 1864.
U. S. C. T. 118th Inf.

Holly Springs, Miss.
Aug. 28, 1864.
U. S. C. T. 11th (new) Inf.

Honey Hill, S. C.
Nov. 30, 1864.
U. S. C. T. 32d, 35th, 54th, and 55th (Mass.), and 102d Inf.

Honey Springs, Kan.
July 17, 1863.
U. S. C. T. 79th (new) Inf.

Hopkinsville, Va.
Dec. 12, 1864.
U. S. C. T. 5th Cav.

Horse-Head Creek, Ark.
Feb. 17, 1864.
U. S. C. T. 79th (new) Inf.

Indian Bay, Ark.
April 13, 1864.
U. S. C. T. 56th Inf.

Indiantown, N. C.
Dec. 18, 1863.
U. S. C. T. 36th Inf.

Indian Village, La.
Aug. 6, 1864.
U. S. C. T. 11th Hy. Art.

Island Mound, Mo.
Oct. 27 and 29, 1862.
U. S. C. T. 79th (new) Inf.

Island No. 76, Miss.
Jan. 20, 1864.
U. S. C. T. Batt'y E, 2d Lt. Art.

Issaquena County, Miss.
July 10 and Aug. 17, 1864.
U. S. C. T. 66th Inf.

Jackson, La.
Aug. 3, 1863.
U. S. C. T. 73d, 75th, and 78th Inf.

Jackson, Miss.
July 5, 1864.
U. S. C. T. 3d Cav.

Jacksonville, Fla.
March 29, 1863.
U. S. C. T. 33d Inf.

Jacksonville, Fla.
May 1 and 23, 1864.
U. S. C. T. 7th Inf.

Jacksonville, Fla.
April 4, 1865.
U. S. C. T. 3d Inf.

James Island, S. C.
July 16, 1863.
U. S. C. T. 54th (Mass.) Inf.

James Island, S. C.
May 21, 1864.
U. S. C. T. 55th (Mass.) Inf.

James Island, S. C.
July 1 and 2, 1864.
U. S. C. T. 33d and 55th (Mass.) Inf.

James Island, S. C.
July 5 and 7, 1864.
U. S. C. T. 7th Inf.

James Island, S. C.
Feb. 10, 1865.
U. S. C. T. 55th (Mass.) Inf.

Jenkins's Ferry, Ark.
April 30, 1864.
U. S. C. T. 79th (new) and 83d (new) Inf.

Jenkins's Ferry, Ark.
May 4, 1864.
U. S. C. T. 83d (new) Inf.

John's Island, S. C.
July 5 and 7, 1864.
U. S. C. T. 26th Inf.

John's Island, S. C.
July 9, 1864.
U. S. C. T. 7th and 34th Inf.

Johnsonville, Tenn.
Sept. 25, 1864.
U. S. C. T. 13th Inf.

Jones's Bridge, Va.
June 23, 1864.
U. S. C. T. 28th Inf.

Joy's Ford, Ark.
Jan. 8, 1865.
U. S. C. T. 79th (new) Inf.

Lake Providence, La.
May 27, 1863.

Lawrence, Kan.
July 27, 1863.
U. S. C. T. 79th (new) Inf.

Little Rock, Ark.
April 26 and May 28, 1864.
U. S. C. T. 57th Inf.

Liverpool Heights, Miss.
Feb. 3, 1864.
U. S. C. T. 47th Inf.

" Lotus," Steamer, Kan.
Jan. 17, 1865.
U. S. C. T. 83d (new) Inf.

Madison Station, Ala.
Nov. 26, 1864.
U. S. C. T. 101st Inf.

Magnolia, Tenn.
Jan. 7, 1865
U. S. C. T. 15th Inf.

Mariana, Fla.
Sept. 27, 1864.
U. S. C. T. 82d Inf.

Marion, Va.
Dec. 18, 1864.
U. S. C. T. 6th Cav.

Marion County, Fla.
March 10, 1865.
U. S. C. T. 3d Inf.

McKay's Point, S. C.
Dec. 22, 1864.
U. S. C. T. 26th Inf.

Meffleton Lodge, Ark.
June 29, 1864.
U. S. C. T. 56th Inf.

Memphis, Tenn.
Aug. 21, 1864.
U. S. C. T. 61st Inf.

Milliken's Bend, La.
June 5, 6, and 7, 1863.
U. S. C. T. 5th Hy. Art. ; 49th and 51st Inf.

Milltown Bluff, S. C.
July 10, 1863.
U. S. C. T. 33d Inf.

Mitchell's Creek, Fla.
Dec. 17, 1864.
U. S. C. T. 82d Inf.

Morganzia, La.
May 18, 1864.
U. S. C. T. 73d Inf.

Morganzia, La.
Nov. 23, 1864.
U. S. C. T. 84th Inf.

Moscow, Tenn.
June 15, 1864.
U. S. C. T. 55th Inf.

Moscow Station, Tenn.
Dec. 4, 1863.
U. S. C. T. 61st Inf.

Mound Plantation, La.
June 29, 1863.
U. S. C. T. 46th Inf.

Mount Pleasant Landing, La.
May 15, 1864.
U. S. C. T. 67th Inf.

Mud Creek, Ala.
Jan. 5, 1865.
U. S. C. T. 106th Inf.

Murfreesboro', Tenn.
Dec. 24, 1864.
U. S. C. T. 12th Inf.

N. and N. W. R. R., Tenn.
Sept. 4, 1864.
U. S. C. T. 100th Inf.

Nashville, Tenn.
May 24, 1864.
U. S. C. T. 15th Inf.

Nashville, Tenn.
Lec. 2 and 21, 1864.
U. S. C. T. 44th Inf.

Nashville, Tenn.
Dec. 7, 1864.
U. S. C. T. 18th Inf.

Nashville, Tenn.
Dec. 15 and 16, 1864.
U. S. C. T. 12th, 13th, 14th, 17th, 18th, and 100th Inf.

Natchez, Miss.
Nov. 11, 1863.
U. S. C. T. 58th Inf.

Natchez, Miss.
April 25, 1864.
U. S. C. T. 98th Inf.

Natural Bridge, Fla.
March 6, 1865.
U. S. C. T. 2d and 99th Inf.

New Kent Court House, Va.
March 2, 1864.
U. S. C. T. 5th Inf.

New Market Heights, Va.
June 24, 1864.
U. S. C. T. 22d Inf.

Olustee, Fla.
Feb. 20, 1864.
U. S. C. T. 8th, 35th, and 54th (Mass.) Inf.

Owensboro', Ky.
Aug. 27, 1864.
U. S. C. T. 108th Inf.

Palmetto Ranch, Texas,
May 15, 1865.
U. S. C. T. 62d Inf.

Pass Manchas, La.
March 20, 1864.
U. S. C. T. 10th Hy. Art.

Petersburg, Va.
June 15, 1864, to April 2, 1865.
U. S. C. T. 5th (Mass.) Cav. ; 1st, 4th, 5th, 6th, 7th, 10th, 19th, 22d, 23d, 27th, 28th, 29th, 29th (Conn.), 30th, 31st, 36th, 39th, 41st, 43d, 45th, and 116th Inf.

Pierson's Farm, Va.
June 16, 1864.
U. S. C. T. 36th Inf.

Pine Barren Creek, Ala.
Dec. 17, 18, and 19, 1864.
U. S. C. T. 97th Inf.

Pine Barren Ford, Fla.
Dec. 17 and 18, 1864.
U. S. C. T. 82d Inf.

Pine Bluff, Ark.
July 2, 1864.
U. S. C. T. 64th Inf.

Pleasant Hill, La.
April 9, 1864.
U. S. C. T. 75th Inf.

Plymouth, N. C.
Nov. 26, 1863, and April 18, 1864.
U. S. C. T. 10th Inf.

Plymouth, N. C.
April 1, 1864.
U. S. C. T. 37th Inf.

Point Lookout, Va.
May 13, 1864.
U. S. C. T. 36th Inf.

Point of Rocks, Md.
June 9, 1864.
U. S. C. T. 2d Cav.

Point Pleasant, La.
June 25, 1864.
U. S. C. T. 64th Inf.

Poison Springs, Ark.
April 18, 1864.
U. S. C. T. 79th (new) Inf.

Port Hudson, La.
May 22 to July 8, 1863.
U. S. C. T. 73d, 75th, 78th, 79th (old), 80th 81st, 82d, and 95th Inf.

Powhatan, Va.
Jan. 25, 1865.
U. S. C. T. 1st Cav.

Prairie D'ann, Ark.
April 13, 1864.
U. S. C. T. 79th (new) and 83d (new) Inf.

Pulaski, Tenn.
May 13, 1864.
U. S. C. T. 111th Inf.

Raleigh, N. C
April 7, 1865.
U. S. C. T. 5th Inf.

Rector's Farm, Ark.
Dec. 19, 1864.
U. S. C. T. 83d (new) Inf.

Red River Expedition, La.
May —, 1864.
U. S. C. T. 92d Inf.

Richland, Tenn.
Sept. 26, 1864.
U. S. C. T. 111th Inf.

Richmond, Va.
Oct. 28 and 29, 1864.
U. S. C. T. 2d Cav.; 7th Inf.

Ripley, Miss.
June 7, 1864.
U. S. C. T. 55th Inf.

Roache's Plantation, Miss.
March 31, 1864.
U. S. C. T. 3d Cav.

Rolling Fork, Miss.
Nov. 22, 1864.
U. S. C. T. 3d Cav.

Roseville Creek, Ark.
March 20, 1864.
U. S. C. T. 79th (new) Inf.

Ross's Landing, Ark.
Feb. 14, 1864.
U. S. C. T. 51st Inf.

St. John's River, S. C.
May 23, 1864.
U. S. C. T. 35th Inf.

St. Stephen's, S. C.
March 1, 1865.
U. S. C. T. 55th (Mass.) Inf.

Saline River, Ark.
May 4, 1864.
U. S. C. T. 83d (new) Inf.

Saline River, Ark.
May —, 1865.
U. S. C. T. 54th Inf.

Salkehatchie, S. C.
Feb. 9, 1865.
U. S. C. T. 102d Inf.

Saltville, Va.
Oct. 2, 1864.
U. S. C. T. 5th and 6th Cav.

Saltville, Va.
Dec. 20, 1864.
U. S. C. T. 5th Cav.

Sand Mountain, Tenn.
Jan. 27, 1865.
U. S. C. T. 18th Inf.

Sandy Swamp, N. C.
Dec. 18, 1863.
U. S. C. T. 5th Inf.

Scottsboro', Ala.
Jan. 8, 1865.
U. S. C. T. 101st Inf.

Section 37, N. and N. W. R. R., Tenn.
Nov. 24, 1864.
U. S. C. T. 12th Inf.

Sherwood, Mo.
May 18, 1863.
U. S. C. T, 79th (new) Inf.

Simpsonville, Ky.
Jan. 25, 1865.
U. S. C. T. 5th Cav.

Smithfield, Va.
Aug. 30, 1864.
U. S. C. T. 1st. Cav.

Smithfield, Ky.
Jan. 5, 1865.
U. S. C. T. 6th Cav.

South Tunnel, Tenn.
Oct. 10, 1864.
U. S. C. T. 40th Inf.

Spanish Fort, Ala.
March 27 to April 8, 1865.
U. S. C. T. 68th Inf.

Suffolk, Va.
March 9, 1864.
U. S. C. T. 2d Cav.

Sugar Loaf Hill, N. C.
Jan. 19, 1865.
U. S. C. T. 6th Inf.

Sugar Loaf Hill, N. C.
Feb. 11, 1865.
U. S. C. T. 4th, 6th, and 30th Inf.

Sulphur Branch Trestle, Ala.
Sept. 25, 1864.
U. S. C. T. 111th Inf.

Swift's Creek, S. C.
April 19, 1865.
U. S. C. T. 102d Inf.

Taylorsville, Ky.
April 18, 1865.
U. S. C. T. 119th Inf.

Timber Hill, Caddo Nation.
Nov. 19, 1864.
U. S. C. T. 79th (new) Inf.

Town Creek, N. C.
Feb. 20, 1865.
U. S. C. T. 1st Inf.

Township, Fla.
Jan. 26, 1863.
U. S. C. T. 33d Inf.

Tupelo, Miss.
July 13, 14, and 15, 1864.
U. S. C. T. 59th, 61st, and 68th Inf

Vicksburg, Miss,
Aug. 27, 1863.
U. S. C. T. 5th Hy. Art.

Vicksburg, Miss.
Feb. 13, 1864.
U. S. C. T. 52d Inf.

Vicksburg, Miss
June 4, 1864.
U. S. C. T. 3d Cav.

Vicksburg, Miss.
July 4, 1864.
U. S. C. T. 48th Inf.

Vidalia, La.
July 22, 1864.
U. S. C. T. 6th Hy. Art.

Wallace's Ferry, Ark.
July 26, 1864,
U. S. C. T. 56th Inf.

Warsaw, N. C.
April 6, 1865.
U. S. C. T. 1st Inf.

Waterford, Miss.
Aug. 16 and 17, 1864.
U. S. C. T, 55th and 61st Inf.

Waterloo, La.
Oct. 20, 1864.
U. S. C. T. 75th Inf.

Waterproof, La.
Feb, 14, 1864.
U. S. C. T. 49th Inf.

Waterproof, La.
April 20, 1864
U. S. C. T. 63d Inf.

White Oak Road, Va.
March 31, 1865.
U. S. C. T. 29th Inf.

White River, Ark.
Oct. 22, 1864.
U. S. C. T. 53 Inf.

Williamsburg, Va.
March 4, 1864.
U. S. C. T. 6th Inf.

Wilmington, N. C.
Feb. 22, 1865.
U. S. C. T. 1st. Inf.

Wilson's Landing, Va.
June 11, 1864.
U. S. C. T. 1st Cav.

Wilson's Wharf, Va.
May 24, 1864.
U. S. C. T. Batt'y B, 2d Lt. Art.; 1st and 10th Inf.

Yazoo City, Miss.
March 5, 1864.
U. S. C. T. 3d Cav.; 47th Inf.

Yazoo City, Miss.
May 13, 1864.
U. S. C. T. 3d Cav.

Yazoo City, Miss.
March 15, 1865.
U. S. C. T. 3d Cav.

Yazoo Expedition, Miss.
Feb. 28, 1864.
U. S. C. T. 3d Cav.

CHAPTER XX.

HOISTING THE BLACK FLAG.—OFFICIAL CORRESPONDENCE AND REPORTS.

GENERAL S. D. LEE TO GENERAL COOPER.

HEADQUARTERS DEPARTMENT ALABAMA, MISSISSIPPI, AND }
EAST LOUISIANA, MERIDIAN, June 30, 1864. }

GENERAL: I have the honor to transmit copies of correspondence between General Washburn, U. S. A., General Forrest, and myself, which I consider very important, and should be laid before the Department. It will be my endeavor to avoid, as far as is consistent with my idea of the dignity of my position, resorting to such an extremity as the black flag; and the onus shall be with the Federal commander.

I would like that the onus be put where it properly belongs, before the public, should the extremity arise. The correspondence is not complete yet, and the Department will be informed of the result at the earliest practicable moment.

I am, General, yours respectfully,
S. D. LEE, *Lieutenant-General.*

General S. COOPER, *A. and I. G., Richmond, Va.*

GENERAL FORREST TO GENERAL WASHBURN.

HEADQUARTERS FORREST'S CAVALRY, }
IN THE FIELD, June 14, 1864. }

Major-General WASHBURN, *Commanding United States Forces, Memphis:*

GENERAL: I have the honor herewith to enclose copy of letter received from Brigadier-General Buford, commanding United States forces at Helena, Arkansas, addressed to Colonel E. W. Rucker, commanding Sixth Regiment of this command; also a letter from myself to General Buford, which I respectfully request you will read and forward to him.

There is a matter also to which I desire to call your attention, which, until now, I have not thought proper to make the subject of a communication. Recent events render it necessary,—in fact, demand it.

It has been reported to me that all the negro troops stationed in Memphis took an oath on their knees, in the presence of Major-General Hurlbut and other officers of your army, to avenge Fort Pillow, and that they would show my troops no quarter.

Again, I have it from indisputable authority that the troops under Brigadier-General Sturgis, on their recent march from Memphis, publicly and in various places proclaimed that no quarter would be shown my men. As his troops were moved into action on the eleventh, the officers commanding exhorted their men to remember Fort Pillow, and a large majority of the prisoners we have captured from that command have voluntarily stated that they expected us to murder them, otherwise they would have surrendered in a body rather than taken to the bushes after being run down and exhausted. The recent battle of Tishemingo Creek was far more bloody than it otherwise would have been but for the fact that your men evidently expected to be slaughtered when captured, and both sides acted as though neither felt safe in surrendering even when further resistance was useless. The prisoners captured by us say they felt condemned by the announcements, etc., of their own commanders, and expected no quarter. In all my operations since the war began, I have conducted the war on civilized principles, and desire still to do so, but it is due to my command that they should know the position you occupy and the policy you intend to pursue. I therefore respectfully ask whether my men in your hands are treated as other Confederate prisoners, also the course intended to be pursued in regard to those who may hereafter fall into your hands.

I have in my possession quite a number of wounded officers and men of General Sturgis's command, all of whom have been treated as well as we have been able to treat them, and are mostly in charge of a surgeon left at Ripley by General Sturgis to look after the wounded. Some of them are too severely wounded to be removed at present. I am willing to exchange them for any men of my command you may have, and as soon as they are able to be removed will give them safe escort through my lines in charge of the surgeon left with them.

I made such an arrangement with Major-General Hurlbut when he was in command of Memphis, and am willing to renew it, provided it is desired, as it would be better than to subject them to the long and fatiguing delay necessary to a regular exchange at City Point, Virginia.

I am, very respectfully, your obedient servant,

N. B. FORREST, *Major-General.*

GENERAL WASHBURN TO GENERAL LEE.

HEADQUARTERS DISTRICT OF WEST TENNESSEE, }
MEMPHIS, TENN., June 17, 1864. }

Major-General S. D. LEE, *Commanding Confederate Forces near Tupelo, Miss.:*

GENERAL: When I heard that the forces of Brigadier-General Sturgis had been driven back, and a portion of them probably captured, I felt considerable solicitude for the fate of the two colored regiments that formed a part of the command, until I was informed that the Confederate forces were commanded by you. When I learned that, I became satisfied that no atrocities would be committed upon those troops, but that they would receive the treatment which humanity as well as their gallant conduct demanded.

I regret to say that the hope that I entertained has been dispelled by facts which have recently come to my knowledge.

From statements that have been made to me by colored soldiers who were eye-witnesses, it would seem that the massacre at Fort Pillow had been reproduced at the late affair at Bryce's Cross-roads. The detail of the atrocities there committed I will not trouble you with. If true, and not disavowed, they must lead to consequences too fearful to contemplate. It is best that we should now have a fair understanding upon this question, of the treatment of this class of soldiers. If it is contemplated by the Confederate government to murder all colored troops that may by chance of war fall into their hands, as was the case at Fort Pillow, it is but fair that it should be freely and frankly avowed. Within the last six weeks I have, on two occasions, sent colored troops into the field from this point. In the expectation that the Confederate government would disavow the action of their commanding general at the Fort Pillow massacre, I have forborne to issue any instructions to the colored troops as to the course they should pursue toward Confederate soldiers. No disavowal on the part of the Confederate government having been made, but, on the contrary, laudations from the entire Southern press of the perpetrators of the massacre, I may safely presume that indiscriminate slaughter is to be the fate of colored troops that fall into your hands. But I am not willing to leave a matter of such grave import, and involving consequences so fearful, to inference, and I have therefore thought it proper to address you this, believing that you would be able to indicate the policy that the Confederate government intend to pursue hereafter on this question.

If it is intended to raise the black flag against that unfortunate race, they will cheerfully accept the issue. Up to this time no troops have fought more gallantly, and none have conducted themselves with greater propriety. They have fully vindicated their right (so long denied) to be treated as men.

I hope that I have been misinformed in regard to the treatment they have received at the battle of Bryce's Cross-roads, and that the accounts received result rather from the excited imaginations of the fugitives than from actual fact.

For the government of the colored troops under my command, I would thank you to inform me, with as little delay as possible, if it is your intention, or the intention of the Confederate government, to murder colored soldiers that may fall into your hands, or treat them as prisoners of war, and subject to be exchanged as other prisoners.

I am, General, respectfully, your obedient servant,

C. C. WASHBURN, *Major-General, Commanding.*

GENERAL WASHBURN TO GENERAL FORREST.

HEADQUARTERS DISTRICT OF WEST TENNESSEE, }
MEMPHIS, TENN., June 19, 1864. }

Major-General N. B. FORREST, *Commanding Confederate Forces:*

GENERAL: Your communication of the fourteenth instant is received. The letter to Brigadier-General Buford will be forwarded to him.

In regard to that part of your letter which relates to colored troops, I beg to say that I have already sent a communication on the subject to the officer in command of the Confederate forces at Tupelo.

Having understood that Major-General S. D. Lee was in command there, I directed my letter to him—a copy of it I enclose. You say in your letter that it has been reported to you that all the negro troops stationed in Memphis took an oath on their knees, in the presence of Major-General Hurlbut, and other officers of our army, to avenge Fort Pillow, and that they would show your troops no quarter.

I believe it is true that the colored troops did take such an oath, but not in the presence of General Hurlbut. From what I can learn, this act of theirs was not influenced by any white officer, but was the result of their own sense of what was due to themselves and their fellows who had been mercilessly slaughtered.

I have no doubt that they went into the field, as you allege, in the full belief that they would be murdered in case they fell into your hands. The affair at Fort Pillow fully justified that belief. I am not aware as to what they proclaimed on their late march, and it may be, as you say, that they declared that no quarter would be given to any of your men that might fall into their hands.

Your declaration that you have conducted the war, on all occasions, on civilized principles, cannot be accepted ; but I receive with satisfaction the intimation in your letter that the recent slaughter of colored troops at the battle of Tishemingo Creek resulted rather from the desperation with which they fought than a predetermined intention to give them no quarter.

You must have learned by this time that the attempt to intimidate the colored troops by indiscriminate slaughter has signally failed, and that, instead of a feeling of terror, you have aroused a spirit of courage and desperation that will not down at your bidding.

I am left in doubt, by your letter, as to the course you and the Confederate government intend to pursue hereafter in regard to colored troops, and I beg you to advise me, with as little delay as possible, as to your intentions.

If you intend to treat such of them as fall into your hands as prisoners of war, please so state ; if you do not so intend, but contemplate either their slaughter or their return to slavery, please state *that*, so that we may have no misunderstanding hereafter. If the former is your intention, I shall receive the announcement with pleasure, and shall explain the fact to the colored troops at once, and desire that they recall the oath they have taken ; if the *latter* is the case, then let the oath stand, and upon those who have aroused this spirit by their atrocities, and upon the government and people who sanction it, be the consequences.

In regard to your inquiry relating to prisoners of your command in our hands, I have to state that they have always received the treatment which a great and humane Government extends to its prisoners. What course will be pursued hereafter toward them must, of course, depend on circumstances that may arise. If your command, hereafter, does nothing which should properly exclude them from being treated as prisoners of war, they will be so treated.

I thank you for your offer to exchange wounded officers and men in your hands. If you will send them in, I will exchange man for man, so far as I have the ability to do so.

Before closing this letter, I wish to call your attention to one case of unparalleled outrage and murder that has been brought to my notice, and in regard to which the evidence is overwhelming.

Among the prisoners captured at Fort Pillow was Major Bradford, who had charge of the defence of the fort after the fall of Major Booth.

After being taken prisoner, he was started with other prisoners of war, in charge of Colonel Duckworth, for Jackson. At Brownsville they rested over night. The following morning two companies were detailed by Colonel Duckworth to proceed to Jackson with the prisoners.

After they had started, and proceeded a very short distance, five soldiers were recalled by Colonel Duckworth, and were conferred with by him ; they then rejoined the column, and after proceeding about five miles from Brownsville the column was halted, and Major Bradford taken about fifty yards from the roadside and deliberately shot by the five men who had been recalled by Colonel Duckworth, and his body left unburied upon the ground where he fell,

He now lies buried near the spot, and, if you desire, you can easily satisfy yourself of the truth of what I assert. I beg leave to say to you that this transaction hardly justifies your remark, that your operations have been conducted on civilized principles ; and until you take some steps to bring the perpetrators of this outrage to justice, the world will not fail to believe that it had your sanction.

I am, General, your obedient servant,

C. C. WASHBURN, *Major-General, Commanding.*

GENERAL FORREST TO GENERAL WASHBURN.

HEADQUARTERS FORREST'S CAVALRY, {
TUPELO, MISS., June 20, 1864. }

Major-General C. C. WASHBURN, *Commanding U. S. Forces, Memphis, Tenn.*

GENERAL : I have the honor to acknowledge the receipt (per flag of truce) of your letter of the seventeenth instant, addressed to Major-General S. D. Lee, or officer commanding Confederate forces near Tupelo. I have forwarded it to General Lee, with a copy of this letter.

I regard your letter as discourteous to the commanding officer of this department, and grossly insulting to myself.

You seek by implied threats to intimidate him, and assume the privilege of denouncing me as a murderer, and as guilty of the wholesale slaughter of the garrison at Fort Pillow, and found your assertion upon the *ex parte* testimony of (your friends) the enemies of myself and country. I shall not enter into the discussion, therefore, of any of the questions involved, nor undertake any refutation of the charges made by you against myself ; nevertheless, as a matter of personal privilege alone, I unhesitatingly say that they are unfounded and unwarranted by the facts. But whether those charges are true or false, they, with the question you ask, as to whether negro troops, when captured, will be recognized and treated as prisoners of war, subject to exchange, etc., are matters which the governments of the United States and Confederate States are to decide and adjust, not their subordinate officers. I regard captured negroes as I do other captured property, and not as captured soldiers ; but as to how regarded by my government, and the disposition which has been and will hereafter be made of them, I respectfully refer you, through the proper channel, to the authorities at Richmond. It is not the policy or the interest of the South to destroy the negro ; on the contrary to preserve and protect him, and all who have surrendered to us have received kind and humane treatment.

Since the war began I have captured many thousand Federal prisoners, and they, including the survivors of the " Fort Pillow Massacre," " black and white," are living witnesses of the fact that with my knowledge or consent, or by my order, not one of them has ever been insulted, or in any way maltreated.

You speak of your forbearance in not giving your negro troops instructions and orders as to the course they should pursue in regard to Confederate soldiers that might fall into their (your) hands, which clearly conveys to my mind two very distinct impressions. The first is, that in not giving them instructions and orders, you have left the matter entirely to the discretion of the negroes as to how they should dispose of prisoners. Second, an implied threat to give such orders as will lead to " consequences too fearful " for contemplation. In confirmation of the correctness of the first impression (which your language now fully develops), I refer most respectfully to my letter from the battle-field, Tishemingo Creek, and forwarded you by flag of truce on the fourteenth instant. As to the second impression, you seem disposed to take into your own hands the settlements which belong to, and can only be settled by, your government ; but if you are prepared to take upon yourself the responsibility of inaugurating a system of warfare contrary to civilized usages, the onus as well as the consequences will be chargeable to yourself.

Deprecating, as I should do, such a state of affairs; determined, as I am, not to be instrumental in bringing it about; feeling and knowing, as I do, that I have the approval of my government, my people, and my conscience as to the past, and with the firm belief that I will be sustained by them in my future policy, it is left with you to determine what that policy shall be, whether in accordance with the laws of civilized nations, or in violation of them.

I am, General, yours, very respectfully,
N. B. FORREST, *Major-General.*

GENERAL FORREST TO GENERAL WASHBURN.

HEADQUARTERS FORREST'S CAVALRY,
IN THE FIELD, June 23, 1864.

Major-General C. C. WASHBURN, *Commanding District of West Tennessee, Memphis, Tenn.* :

Your communication of the nineteenth inst. is received, in which you say "you are left in doubt as to the course the Confederate government intends to pursue hereafter in regard to colored troops."

Allow me to say that this is a subject upon which I did not and do not propose to enlighten you. It is a matter to be settled by our governments through their proper officers, and I respectfully refer you to them for a solution of your doubts.

You ask me to state whether "I contemplate either their slaughter or their return to slavery." I answer that I slaughter no man except in open warfare, and that my prisoners, both white and black, are turned over to my government to be dealt with as it may direct. My government is in possession of all the facts as regards my official conduct, and the operations of my command since I entered the service, and if you desire a proper discussion and decision, I refer you again to the President of the Confederate States. I would not have you understand, however, that in a matter of so much importance I am indisposed to place at your command and disposal any facts desired, when applied for in a manner becoming an officer holding your rank and position, for it is certainly desirable to every one occupying a public position to be placed right before the world, and there has been no time, since the capture of Fort Pillow, that I would not have furnished all the facts connected with its capture, had they been applied for properly, but now the matter rests with the two governments. I have, however, for your information, enclosed you copies of the official correspondence between the commanding officers at Fort Pillow and myself; also copies of a statement of Captain Young, the senior officer of that garrison, together with (sufficient) extracts from a report of the affair by my A. D. C., Captain Chas. W. Anderson, which I approve and endorse as correct.

As to the death of Major Bradford, I knew nothing of it until eight or ten days after it is said to have occurred.

On the thirteenth (the day after the capture of Fort Pillow) I went to Jackson, and the report I had of the affair was this : Major Bradford was, with other officers, sent to the headquarters of Colonel McCulloch, and all the prisoners were in charge of one of McCulloch's regiments. Bradford requested the privilege of attending the burial of his brother, which was granted, he giving his parole of honor to return. Instead of returning, he changed his clothing and started for Memphis. Some of my men were hunting deserters, and came on Bradford just as he had landed on the south bank of the Hatchie, and arrested him. When arrested, he claimed to be a Confederate soldier belonging to Bragg's army ; that he had been on furlough, and was then on his way to join his command.

As he could show no papers he was believed to be a deserter, and was taken to Covington, and not until he was recognized and spoken to by citizens did the guards know that he was Bradford.

He was sent by Colonel Duckworth, or taken by him, to Brownsville.

All of Chalmers's command went from Brownsville, *via* La Grange, and as all the other prisoners had been gone some time, and there was no chance for them to catch up and place Bradford with them, he was ordered by Colonel Duckworth or General Chalmers to be sent south to me at Jackson.

I knew nothing of the matter until eight or ten days afterwards I heard that his body was found near Brownsville. I understand that he attempted to escape and was shot. If he was improperly killed, nothing would afford me more pleasure than to punish the perpetrators to the full extent of the law, and to show you how I regard such transactions.

I can refer you to my demand on Major-General Hurlbut (no doubt upon file in your office) for the delivery to Confederate authorities of one Colonel Fielding Hurst and others of his regiment, who deliberately took out and killed seven Confederate soldiers, one of whom they left to die after cutting off his tongue, punching out his eyes, splitting his mouth on each side to his ears, and cutting off his privates. I have mentioned and given you these facts in order that you may have no further excuse or apology for referring to these matters in connection with myself, and to evince to you my determination to do all in my power to avoid the responsibility of causing the adoption of the policy which you have determined to press. In your letter you acknowledge the fact that the negro troops did take an oath on bended knees to show no quarters to my men, and you say further "you have no doubt they went to the battle-field expecting to be slaughtered," and admit, also, the probability of their having proclaimed on their march that no quarter would be shown us. Such being the case, why do you ask for the disavowal on the part of the commanding general of this department of the government, in regard to the loss of life at Tishemingo Creek? That your troops expected to be slaughtered, appears to me, after the oath they took, to be a very reasonable and natural expectation. Yet you who sent them out, knowing and now admitting that they had sworn to such a policy, are complaining of atrocities, and demanding acknowledgments and disavowals on the part of the very men you sent forth sworn to slay whenever in your power.

I will, in all candor and truth, say to you that I nad only neard these things, but did not believe them ; indeed, did not attach to them the importance they deserved, nor did I know of the threatened vengeance as proclaimed along the line of march until the contest was over. Had I and my men known it, as you admit it, the battle of Tishemingo Creek would have been noted as the bloodiest battle of the war. That you sanctioned this policy is plain, for you say now "that if the negro is treated as a prisoner of war, you will receive with pleasure the announcement, and will explain the facts to your colored troops, and *desire* (not *order*) that they recall the oath; but if they are to be either slaughtered or returned to slavery, let the oath stand." Your rank forbids a doubt as to the fact that you and every officer and man of your department are identified with the policy and responsible for it, and I shall not permit you, notwithstanding by your studied language in both your communications you seek to limit the operations of your unholy scheme, and visit its terrible consequences alone upon that ignorant, deluded, but unfortunate people, the negroes, whose destruction you are planning in order to accomplish ours. The negroes have our sympathy, and, so far as consistent with safety, we will spare them at the expense of those who are alone responsible for the inauguration of a worse than savage warfare.

Now, in conclusion, I demand a plain and unqualified answer to two questions, and then I have done with further correspondence with you on this subject. This matter must be settled. In battle and on the battle-field do you intend to slaughter my men who fall into your hands? If you do not intend so to do, will they be treated as prisoners of war?

I have over two thousand of Sturgis's command prisoners, and will hold every officer and private hostage until I receive your declarations, and am satisfied that you carry out in good faith the answers you make, and until I am assured that no Confederate soldier has been foully dealt with from the day of the battle of Tishemingo Creek to this time. It is not yet too late for you to retrace your steps and arrest the storm.

Relying, as I do, upon that Divine power which in wisdom disposes of all things; relying also upon the support and approval of my government and countrymen, and the unflinching bravery and endurance of my troops; and with a consciousness that I have done nothing to produce, but all in my power, consistent with honor and the personal safety of myself and command, to prevent it, I leave with you the responsibility of bringing about, to use your own language, " a state of affairs too fearful to contemplate."

I am, General, yours, very respectfully,
N. B. FORREST, *Major-General.*

OFFICIAL MEMORANDA.

CAHABA HOSPITAL, CAHABA, ALABAMA,
May 11, 1864.

Colonel H. C. DAVIS, *Commanding Post Cahaba:*

COLONEL: I herewith transmit you, as near as my memory serves me, according to promise, the demand made by Major-General Forrest, C. S. A., for the surrender of Fort Pillow, Tennessee.

Major BOOTH, *Commanding U. S. Forces, Fort Pillow, Tennessee:*

I have force sufficient to take your works by assault. I therefore demand an unconditional surrender of all your forces. Your heroic defence will entitle you to be treated as prisoners of war, but the surrender must be unconditional. I await your answer.
FORREST, *Major-General, Commanding.*

HEADQUARTERS UNITED STATES FORCES,
FORT PILLOW, TENNESSEE, April 12, 1864.

Major-General FORREST, *Commanding Confederate Forces:*

GENERAL: Your demand for the surrender of United States forces under my command received. I ask one hour for consultation with my officers and the commander of gunboat No. 7, at this place. I have the honor to be
Your obedient servant,
L. F. BOOTH, *Major, Commanding U. S. Forces, Fort Pillow.*

Major L. F. BOOTH. *Commanding United States Forces:*

I do not demand the surrender of the gunboat No. 7. I ask only for the surrender of Fort Pillow, with men and munitions of war. You have twenty minutes for consideration. At the expiration of that time, if you do not capitulate, I will assault your works.
Your obedient servant,
FORREST, *Major-General, Commanding.*

HEADQUARTERS UNITED STATES FORCES,
FORT PILLOW, TENNESSEE, April 12, 1864.

Major-General FORREST, *Commanding Confederate Forces:*

GENERAL: Your second demand for the surrender of my forces is received. Your demand will not be complied with.
Your obedient servant,
L. F. BOOTH, *Major, Commanding U. S. Forces, Fort Pillow.*

I give you the above for your own satisfaction from memory. I think it is true in substance My present condition would preclude the idea of this being an official statement.
I am, Colonel, your obedient servant,
JOHN T. YOUNG, *Captain, Company A, Twenty-fourth Mo. Inf. Vols.*

CAPTAIN J. T. YOUNG TO MAJOR-GENERAL FORREST.

CAHABA, ALABAMA, May 19, 1864.

Major-General FORREST, *C. S. A.:*

GENERAL: Your request, made through Judge P. T. Scroggs, that I should make a statement of the treatment of the Federal dead and wounded at Fort Pillow, has been made known to me. Details from Federal prisoners were made to collect the dead and wounded. The dead were buried by their surviving comrades. I saw no ill treatment of their wounded on the evening of the battle, or next morning. My friend, Lieutenant Leaming, Adjutant Thirteenth Tennessee

Cavalry, was left wounded in the sutler's store near the fort, also a lieutenant Sixth U. S. Artillery; both were alive next morning, and sent on board U. S. transport, among many other wounded. Among the wounded were some colored troops—I don't know how many.

Very respectfully, your obedient servant,

JNO. T. YOUNG, *Captain Twenty-fourth Missouri Volunteers.*

P. S.—I have examined a report said to be made by Captain Anderson (of) A. D. C. to Major-General Forrest, appendix to General Forrest's report, in regard to making disposition of Federal wounded left on the field at Fort Pillow, and think it is correct. I accompanied Captain Anderson, on the day succeeding the battle, to Fort Pillow, for the purpose above mentioned.

JOHN T. YOUNG, *Captain, Twenty-fourth Missouri Volunteers.*

A true copy.

SAMUEL DONALSON, *Lieutenant and A. D. C.*

Official,

HENRY B. LEE, *A.D.C.*

GENERAL WASHBURN TO GENERAL FORREST.

HEADQUARTERS DISTRICT OF WEST TENNESSEE, {
MEMPHIS, TENN., July 2, 1864. {

Major-General N. B. FORREST, *Commanding Confederate Forces, near Tupelo:*

GENERAL: Your communications of the twentieth and twenty-third ult. are received. Of the tone and temper of both I do not complain. The desperate fortunes of a bad cause excuse much irritation of temper, and I pass it by. Indeed, I received it as a favorable augury, and as evidence that you are not indifferent to the opinions of the civilized world.

In regard to the Fort Pillow affair, it is useless to prolong the discussion.

I shall forward your report, which you did me the favor to enclose, to my government, and you will receive the full benefit of it.

The record is now made up, and a candid world will judge of it. I beg leave to send you herewith a copy of the report of the Investigating Committee from the United States Congress on the affair. In regard to the treatment of Major Bradford, I refer you to the testimony contained in that report, from which you will see that he was not attempting to escape when shot. It will be easy to bring the perpetrators of the outrage to justice if you so desire.

I will add to what I have heretofore said, that I have it from responsible and truthful citizens of Brownsville, that when Major Bradford was started under an escort from your headquarters at Jackson, General Chalmers remarked that " he would never reach there."

You call attention, apparently as an offset to this affair of Major Bradford, to outrages said to have been committed by Colonel Fielding Hurst and others of his regiment (Sixth Tennessee Cavalry). The outrages, if committed as stated by you, are disgraceful and abhorrent to every brave and sensitive mind.

On receiving your letter I sent at once for Colonel Hurst, and read him the extract pertaining to him. He indignantly denies the charge against him, and until you furnish me the names of the parties murdered, and the time when, and the place where, the offence was committed, with the names of witnesses, it is impossible for me to act. When you do that, you may rest assured that I shall use every effort in my power to have the parties accused tried, and if found guilty, properly punished.

In regard to the treatment of colored soldiers, it is evidently useless to discuss the question further.

Your attempt to shift from yourself upon me the responsibility of the inauguration of a " worse than savage warfare," is too strained and far-fetched to require any response. The full and cumulative evidence contained in the Congressional Report I herewith forward, points to *you* as the person responsible for the barbarisms already committed.

It was *your* soldiers who, at Fort Pillow, raised the black flag, and while shooting, bayoneting, and otherwise maltreating the Federal prisoners in their hands, shouted to each other in the hearing of their victims that it was done by " Forrest's orders."

Thus far I cannot learn that you have made any disavowal of these barbarities.

Your letters to me inform me confidently that you have always treated our prisoners according to the rules of civilized warfare, but your disavowal of the Fort Pillow barbarities, if you intend to make any, should be full, clear, explicit, and published to the world.

The United States Government is, as it always has been, lenient and forbearing, and it is not yet too late for you to secure for yourself and your soldiers a continuance of the treatment due to honorable warriors, by a public disclaimer of barbarities already committed, and a vigorous effort to punish the wretches who committed them.

But I say to you now, clearly and unequivocally, that such measure of treatment as you mete out to Federal soldiers will be measured to you again.

If you give no quarter, you need expect none. If you observe the rules of civilized warfare, and treat our prisoners in accordance with the laws of war, your prisoners will be treated, as they ever have been, with kindness.

If you depart from these principles, you may expect such retaliation as the laws of war justify.

That you may know what the laws of war are, as understood by my Government, I beg leave to enclose a copy of General Orders No. 100 from the War Department Adjutant-General's Office, Washington, April twenty-four, 1863.

I have the honor to be, sir,

Very respectfully yours,

C. C. WASHBURN, *Major-General.*

GENERAL LEE TO GENERAL WASHBURN.

HEADQUARTERS DEPARTMENT ALABAMA, MISSISSIPPI, AND {
EAST LOUISIANA, MERIDIAN, June 28, 1864. {

Major-General C. C. WASHBURN, *Commanding Federal Forces at Memphis, Tennessee:*

GENERAL: I am in receipt of your letter of the seventeenth inst., and have also before me the reply of Major-General Forrest thereto. Though that reply is full, and approved by me, yet I deem it proper to communicate with you upon a subject so seriously affecting our future conduct and that of the troops under our respective commands.

Your communication is by no means respectful to me, and is by implication insulting to Major-General Forrest. This, however, is overlooked in consideration of the important character of its contents.

You assume as correct an exaggerated statement of the circumstances attending the capture of Fort Pillow, relying solely upon the evidence of those who would naturally give a distorted history of the affair.

No demand for an explanation has ever been made either by yourself or your government, a course which would certainly recommend itself to every one desirous of hearing truth; but, on the contrary, you seem to have been perfectly willing to allow your soldiers to labor under false impressions upon a subject involving such terrible consequences. Even the formality of parades and oaths have been resorted to for the purpose of inciting your colored troops to the perpetration of deeds which, you say, "will lead to consequences too fearful to contemplate."

As commanding officer of this Department I desire to make the following statement concerning the capture of Fort Pillow—a statement supported in a great measure by the evidence of one of your own officers captured at that place.

The version given by you and your government is untrue, and not sustained by the facts to the extent that you indicate.

The garrison was summoned in the usual manner, and its commanding officer assumed the responsibility of refusing to surrender after having been informed by General Forrest of his ability to take the fort, and of his fears as to what the result would be in case the demand was not complied with.

The assault was made under a heavy fire, and with considerable loss to the attacking party.

Your colors were never lowered, but retreated from the fort to the cover of the gunboats, with arms in their hands, and constantly using them.

This was true, particularly of your colored troops, who had been firmly convinced by your teachings of the certainty of their slaughter in case of capture. Even under these circumstances many of your men—white and black—were taken prisoners.

I respectfully refer you to history for numerous cases of indiscriminate slaughter, even under less aggravated circumstances.

It is generally conceded by all military precedents that where the issue has been fairly presented, and the ability displayed, fearful results are expected to follow a refusal to surrender.

The case under consideration is almost an extreme one.

You had a servile race armed against their masters, and in a country which had been desolated by almost unprecedented outrages.

I assert that our officers, with all these circumstances against them, endeavored to prevent the effusion of blood; and, as evidence of this, I refer you to the fact that both white and colored prisoners were taken, and are now in our hands.

As regards the battle of Tishemingo Creek, the statements of your negro witnesses are not to be relied on. In this panic they acted as might have been expected from their previous impressions. I do not think many of them were killed—they are yet wandering over the country, attempting to return to their masters.

With reference to the status of those captured at Tishemingo Creek and Fort Pillow, I will state that, unless otherwise ordered by my government, they will not be regarded as prisoners of war, but will be retained and humanely treated, subject to such future instructions as may be indicated.

Your letter contains many implied threats; these you can of course make, and you are fully entitled to any satisfaction that you may feel from having made them

It is my intention, and that also of my subordinates, to conduct this war upon civilized principles, provided you permit us to do so; and I take this occasion to state that we will not shrink from any responsibilities that your actions may force upon us.

We are engaged in a struggle for the protection of our homes and firesides, for the maintenance of our national existence and liberty; we have counted the cost and are prepared to go to any extremes; and although it is far from our wish to fight under the "black flag," still, if you drive us to it, we will accept the issue.

Your troops virtually fought under it at the battle of Tishemingo Creek, and the prisoners taken there state that they went into battle with the impression that they were to receive no quarter, and I suppose with the determination to give none.

I will further remark that if it is raised, so far as your soldiers are concerned, there can be no distinction, for the unfortunate people whom you pretend to be aiding are not considered entirely responsible for their acts, influenced as they are by the superior intellect of their white brothers.

I enclose for your consideration certain papers touching the Fort Pillow affair, which were procured from the writer after the exaggerated statements of your press were seen.

I am, General, very respectfully,
Your obedient servant,
S. D. LEE, *Lieutenant-General, Commanding.*

ENCLOSURE IN THE FOREGOING.

CAHABA, ALABAMA, May 16, 1864.

I was one of the bearers of the flag of truce, on the part of the United States authorities, at Fort Pillow. A majority of the officers of the garrison doubted whether General Forrest was present, and had the impression that it was a ruse to induce the surrender of the fort. At the second meeting of the flag of truce, General Forrest announced himself as being General Forrest; but the officers who accompanied the flag, being unacquainted with the General, doubted his word, and it was the opinion of the garrison, at the time of the assault, that General Forrest was not in the vicinity of the fort. The commanding officer refused to surrender. When the final assault was made, I was captured at my post, inside the works, and have been treated as a prisoner of war.

JOHN T. YOUNG, *Captain, Twenty-fourth Missouri Volunteers.*

F. W. UNDERHILL, *First Lieutenant, Cavalry.*

GENERAL WASHBURN TO GENERAL LEE.

HEADQUARTERS DISTRICT OF WEST TENNESSEE, }
MEMPHIS, TENNESSEE, July 3, 1864.   {

Lieutenant-General S D. LEE, *Conmanding Department Alabama, Mississippi and East Louisiana, C. S. A., Meridian, Miss.:*

GENERAL: Your letter of the twenty-eighth ult., in reply to mine of the seventeenth ult., is received.

The discourtesy which you profess to discover in my letter I utterly disclaim. Having already discussed at length, in a correspondence with Major-General Forrest, the Fort Pillow massacre, as well as the policy to be pursued in regard to colored troops, I do not regard it necessary to say more on those subjects. As you state that you fully approve of the letter sent by General Forrest to me, in answer to mine of the seventeenth ult., I am forced to presume that you fully approve of his action at Fort Pillow.

Your arguments in support of that action confirm such presumption. You state that the "version given by me and my government is not true, and not sustained by the facts to the extent I indicate." You furnish a statement of a certain Captain Young, who was captured at Fort Pillow, and is now a prisoner in your hands. How far the statement of a prisoner under duress and in the position of Captain Young should go to disprove the sworn testimony of the hundred eyewitnesses who had ample opportunity of seeing and knowing, I am willing that others shall judge.

In relying, as you do, upon this certificate of Captain Young, you confess that all better resources are at an end.

You are welcome to all the relief that that certificate is calculated to give you. Does he say that our soldiers were not inhumanly treated? No. Does he say that he was in a position to see in case they had been mistreated? No. He simply says that "he saw no ill-treatment of their wounded." If he was in a position to see and know what took place, it was easy for him to say so.

I yesterday sent to Major-General Forrest a copy of the report of the Congressional Investigating Committee, and I hope it may fall into your hands. You will find there the record of inhuman atrocities, to find a parallel for which you will search the page of history in vain. Men—white men and black men—were crucified and burned; others were hunted by bloodhounds; while others, in their anguish, were made the sport of men more cruel than the dogs by which they were hunted.

I have also sent to my government copies of General Forrest's reports, together with the certificate of Captain Young.

The record in the case is plainly made up, and I leave it. You justify and approve it, and appeal to history for precedents.

As I have said, history furnishes no parallel. True, there are instances where, after a long and protracted resistance, resulting in heavy loss to the assailing party, the garrison has been put to the sword, but I know of no such instance that did not bring dishonor upon the commander that ordered or suffered it.

There is no Englishman that would not gladly forget Badajos, nor a Frenchman that exults when Jaffa or the Caves of Dahra and Shelas are spoken of. The massacre of Glencoe, which the world has read of with horror, for nearly two hundred years, pales into insignificance before the truthful recital of Fort Pillow.

The desperate defence of the Alamo was the excuse for the slaughter of its brave survivors after its surrender, yet that act was received with just execration, and we are told by the historian that it led more than anything else to the independence of Texas.

At the battle of San Jacinto the Texans rushed into action with the war-cry, "Remember the Alamo," and carried all before them.

You will seek in vain for consultation in history, pursue the inquiry as far as you may.

Your desire to shift the responsibility of the Fort Pillow massacre, or to find excuses for it, is not strange. But the responsibility still remains where it belongs, and there it will remain.

In my last letter to General Forrest I stated that the treatment which Federal soldiers received would be their guide hereafter, and that if you give no quarter you need expect none. If you observe the rules of civilized warfare I shall rejoice at it, as no one can regret more than myself a resort to such measures as the laws of war justify towards an enemy that gives no quarter.

Your remark that our colored soldiers "will not be regarded as prisoners of war, but will be retained and humanely treated," indicating that you consider them as of more worth and importance than your own soldiers who are now in our hands, is certainly very complimentary to the colored troops, though but a tardy acknowledgment of their bravery and devotion as soldiers; but such fair words can neither do justice to the colored soldiers who were butchered at Fort Pillow after they had surrendered to their victors, nor relieve yourself, General Forrest, and the troops serving under you, from the fearful responsibility now resting upon you for those wanton and unparalleled barbarities.

I concur in your remarks that if the black flag is once raised, there can be no distinction so far as our soldiers are concerned. No distinction in this regard as to color is known to the laws of war, and you may rest assured that the outrages we complain of are felt by our white soldiers, no less than by our black ones, as insults to their common banner, the flag of the United States.

I will close by a reference to your statement that many of our colored soldiers "are yet wandering over the country attempting to return to their masters." If this remark is intended for a joke, it is acknowledged as a good one; but, if stated as a fact, permit me to correct your misapprehensions by informing you that most of them have returned to their respective commands, their search for their late "masters" having proved bootless; and I think I do not exaggerate in assuring you that there is not a colored soldier here who does not prefer the fate of his comrades at Fort Pillow to being returned to his "master."

I remain, General,
Yours, very respectfully,
C. C. WASHBURN, *Major-General.*

MEMPHIS, TENNESSEE, September 13, 1864.

Major-General C. C. WASHBURN, *Commanding District West Tennessee:*

GENERAL: I have the honor to address you in regard to certain papers forwarded you by Major-General Forrest, of the so-called Confederate army, signed by me under protest, whilst a prisoner of war at Cahaba, Alabama. I would first call your attention to the manner by which these papers were procured. About twenty-seventh April last, all Federal prisoners (except colored soldiers) were sent to Andersonville and Macon, Georgia, myself among the number. About ten days after my arrival at Macon prison, a Confederate captain, with two men as guard, came to that prison with an order for me to return to Cahaba. I appealed to the officer in command to know why I was taken from the other officers, but received no explanation. Many of my friends among the Federal officers who had been prisoners longer than myself felt uneasy at the proceedings, and advised me to make my escape going back, as it was likely a subject of retaliation. Consequently I felt considerable uneasiness of mind. On returning to Cahaba, being quite unwell, I was placed in hospital, under guard, with still no explanation from the military authorities. On the day following, I was informed by a sick Federal officer, also in hospital, that he had learned that I had been recognized by some Confederate as a deserter from the Confederate army, and that I was to be court-martialed and shot. The colored waiters about the hospital told me the same thing, and although I knew that the muster-rolls of my country would show that I had been in the volunteer service since first May, 1861, I still felt uneasy, having fresh in my mind Fort Pillow, and the summary manner the Confederate officers have of disposing of men on some occasions. With the above impressions on my mind, about three days after my return to Cahaba I was sent for by the Provost Marshal, and certain papers handed me, made out by General Forrest for my signature. Looking over the papers, I found that signing them would be an endorsement of General Forrest's official report of the Fort Pillow affair. I of course returned the papers, positively refusing to have anything to do with them. I was sent for again the same day, with request to sign other papers of the same tendency, but modified. I again refused to sign the papers, but sent General Forrest a statement, that although I considered some of the versions of the Fort Pillow affair, which I had read in their own papers, said to be copied from Federal papers, exaggerated, I also thought that his own official report was equally so in some particulars.

Here the matter rested about one week, when I was sent for by Colonel H. C. Davis, commander of post at Cahaba, who informed me that General Forrest had sent P. T. Scroggs to see me, and have a talk with me about the Fort Pillow fight. I found the judge very affable and rather disposed to flatter me; he said that General Forrest thought that I was a gentleman and a soldier, and that the General had sent him (the judge) down to see me and talk to me about the Fort Pillow fight; he then went on to tell over a great many things that were testified to before the Military Commission, which I was perfectly ignorant of, never having seen the testimony. He then produced papers which General Forrest wished me to sign. Upon examination, I found them about the same as those previously shown me, and refused again to sign them, but the Judge was very importunate, and finally prevailed on me to sign the papers you have in your possession, pledging himself that if I wished it they should only be seen by General Forrest himself, that they were not intended to be used by him as testimony, but merely for his own satisfaction.

I hope, General, that these papers signed by me, or rather extorted from me while under duress, will not be used by my government to my disparagement, for my only wish is now, after three years' service and over, to recruit my health, which has suffered badly by imprisonment, and *go in for the war.*

I have the honor to be, General,
Your obedient servant,
JOHN T. YOUNG, *Captain, Company A, Twenty-fourth Mo. Inf.*[1]

It should not be forgotten that the material part of Gen. Forrest's defence was extorted from Capt. John T. Young, an officer in the Union forces at Fort Pillow. He was sick and a prisoner in the hands of the rebels; and while in this condition he was compelled to sign the papers given above, which had been made out by Forrest himself. The last letter of the correspondence shows that Capt. Young did not want the papers used by the United States Government, because they were not true. Moreover, the despatches of Forrest to Major Bradford make no mention of retaliation. The despatches above are not true copies. For instance, he demanded the surrender of Paducah on the 25th of March, 1864, just before he took Fort Pillow, and this was his despatch:

H'DQU'RS FORREST'S CAVALRY CORPS, {
PADUCAH, March 25, 1864 }

To Col. HICKS, *Commanding Federal Forces at Paducah:*

Having a force amply sufficient to carry your works and reduce the place, in order to avoid the unnecessary effusion of blood, I demand the surrender of the fort and troops, with all the public stores. If you surrender, you shall be treated as prisoners of war; but, *if I have to storm your works, you may expect no quarter.*

N. B. FORREST, *Maj.-Gen. Com'ding.*

---

[1] Rebellion Records, vol. x. pp. 721-730.

And on the 19th of April, 1864, the next day after the massacre at Fort Pillow, Gen. Abe Buford demanded the surrender of Columbus, Kentucky, in the following despatch :

To the Commander of the United States Forces, Columbus, Ky.:

Fully capable of taking Columbus and its garrison by force, I desire to avoid shedding blood. I therefore demand the unconditional surrender of the forces under your command. Should you surrender, the negroes now in arms will be returned to their masters. Should I be compelled to take the place by force, *no quarter will be shown negro troops whatever ;* white troops will be treated as prisoners of war.

I am, sir, yours,
A. BUFORD, *Brig.-Gen.*

Now, as both Bradford and Booth were dead, it was impossible to learn just what language was used by Forrest in the despatches he sent them. But from the testimony given above, the explanation of Capt. Young and the language of the two despatches just quoted, addressed to the commander of the Union forces at Paducah and Columbus, Kentucky, history has made out a case against Gen. Forrest that no human being would covet.

𝔓art 8.

THE FIRST DECADE OF FREEDOM.

CHAPTER XXII.

AN EDUCATED AFRICAN.

Daniel Flickinger Wilberforce, a native African, and educated in America, presents a striking illustration of the capabilities of the Negro. He was born a pagan, and when brought in contact with the institutions of civilization he outstripped those whose earlier life had been impressed with the advantages of such surroundings. There was nothing in his blood, or in his early rearing, to develop him. He came from darkness himself as well as by his ancestry. Rev. Daniel K. Flickinger, D.D., has been secretary of the Home Frontier and Foreign Missionary Society for the past twenty-five years. He was the companion in Africa of George Thompson, and on one of his trips had a short association with Livingstone. Dr. Flickinger aided in establishing the United Brethren Mission on the Western Coast of Africa, and has had his heart in it for a quarter of a century. During that time he has made six trips to Africa to look after this mission ; returning from his last voyage in May, 1881. He has studied those people and found them apt in the schools as well as in the acquiring of American customs in tilling the soil and in the trades. During Dr. Flickinger's first visit to Africa in 1855, while at Good Hope Station, Mendi Mission, located on the eastern banks of Sherbro Island, latitude 7° north, and longitude 18° west, he employed a native to watch over him at night as he slept in his hammock, there being wild and dangerous tribes in the vicinity. To that man in that time was born a child. The father came to the missionaries the next day to tell them that his wife " done born picin" and wanted them to give it a name. Mr. Burton, the missionary in charge, suggested that of Daniel Flickinger, and it was taken. The missionaries had performed the usual marriage ceremony for as many as came within their reach, and broken up the former heathen customs in their immediate vicinity as far as possible, and this man was duly married. He took as his last name that of Wilberforce after the English philanthropist, who was dear to all Colored people, and from that time on this native and his family became attached to the mission, and were known by the name of Wilberforce. This man had children born in heathendom and under quite different circumstances.

Dr. Flickinger soon afterward sailed for America, and soon forgot that he had a namesake on the distant shore. He made other trips across the water, but failed to come in contact with the Wilberforce family. Sixteen years afterward, in 1871, he was in New York City shipping goods to the African missionaries. The boxes, labelled "Daniel K. Flickinger," were being loaded and unloaded at the American Mission Rooms in that city, and the doctor noticed that the colored porter boy was about half wild over something. He asked him if there was any thing wrong, but got no reply. The young porter kept rolling his eyes and acting half scared at the name on those boxes, and finally the doctor asked him his name, to which there came the prompt reply, Daniel Flickinger Wilberforce ! In his travels of a lifetime the missionary had often been surprised, but this bewildered him. A thunder-bolt could not have shocked him more. Then the two stood gazing at each other in perfect amazement, and neither able to tell how their names came to be so near alike. The boxes were forgotten. The boy soon had his relief and began laughing as few others could laugh, while the doctor was still unable to see through the mystery. He gave the young fellow two shillings and told him to proceed with the boxes. The doctor then began an investigation about the Mission Rooms, and found that this boy, just a short time before that, had been brought over on a merchant vessel to care for an invalid missionary lady during the voyage, that he had served a short time as bell-boy at a hotel, and that they had employed him in the Mission Rooms, but had promised to send him back on the next sail vessel. The doctor got his location in Africa and a complete chain of circumstances such as to convince him that this was the boy that was named after him in 1855. He told the authorities at the American Mission Rooms, to write to Africa and say that Dan. was well cared for over here, and for them to keep him till further advised. As soon as the doctor made his shipments to the missionaries he returned to Dayton and asked the Executive Committee of his Board if they would assist him in educating this African who had turned up in such a romantic manner. Consent was given, and young Wilberforce was shipped to Dayton. He was brought into Dr. Flickinger's office with the tag of an express company attached to his clothes—young, green, and, in fact, a raw recruit to the ranks of civilization. Seven years after that he bid adieu to his friends in that same office, to return to his people in Africa as a teacher, preacher, and physician. He was then one of the finest scholars of his age in this country. When he arrived at Dayton he of course had to have a private tutor. He was sixteen years old and had to start with the rudiments, but he was, at the beginning of the next school year, able to join classes on which he doubled right along. It requires a course of eight years to reach the High School, but in less than four years after his arrival in Dayton he passed the examination for admission to the High School of Dayton, Ohio, and was the first Colored pupil ever admitted to that school. Since then, other Colored pupils have annually been following his example. The course in the High School was four years, and the Board and teachers were very particularly averse to gaining time. Owing to Wilberforce's great aptness, that allowed him to go ahead of his class, he gained one year then and there, and took the honors of the class that started one year ahead of him. There were twenty-three members of that class. The Commencement was in the Opera-house at Dayton in 1878, and on that occasion the President of the Board said, without discredit to any others, he felt called upon to make special mention of young Wilberforce, which he did in a handsome manner. This was not all ; the Missionary Society wanted to send Wilberforce to Africa in September of that year, and as he went along they had him at other studies. He had become an excellent musician, both vocal and instrumental. He had been studying theology and read Hebrew well. He had also taken a course of reading in medicine, so that he might be of service to the bodies as well as the souls of his brethren. Marvellous as it may seem, all of this was done in so short a time, and from a state of savage life up to civilized life ; still it is true. And, besides, Wilberforce had been a reader of history and general literature, and was a writer of unusual merit. His progress has always and always will seem incredible, even to those who had personal knowledge of him during the time that he had this experience of seven years. He had a remarkable mind, was born a heathen, had no youthful advantages, and is to-day one of the best-informed and most thoroughly cultivated thinkers of his age. When he left Dayton in the summer of 1878, he was greatly missed. At the Colored United Brethren Church he was janitor, leader of a choir, organist, superintendent of the Sunday-school, and class leader, and when the pastor failed, Wilberforce also did the preaching. He was never proud. In the humble capacity of janitor he took excellent care of Dr. Flickinger's office, and was willing and ready to do anything. He was modest socially, but a favorite among his classmates, and not only respected but admired by all. He married a Dayton girl before he left for Africa, and has remained abroad since 1878, but he expects at no distant time to return to America to complete his professional studies. He belonged to the Sherbro tribe or people, and with them he is now laboring.

LAFAYETTE'S PLAN OF COLONIZATION.

Now, my dear General, that you are about to enjoy some repose, permit me to propose to you a scheme which may prove of great benefit to the black part of the human race. Let us unite in the purchase of a small estate, where we can attempt to free the negroes and employ them simply as farm laborers. Such an example set by you might be generally followed, and should we succeed in America I shall gladly consecrate a part of my time to introducing the custom into the Antilles. If this be a crude idea I prefer to be considered a fool in this way rather than be thought wise by an opposite conduct.[1]

5th February, 1783.

THE RESULTS OF EMANCIPATION.

As an evidence of the growing confidence in the eagerness for and capacity of the Negro to become an educated citizen, the handsome bequest of John F. Slater, Esq., for the education of the race stands forth as a conspicuous example. The Negroes of the South have acknowledged this munificent gift with that graceful gratitude so strikingly characteristic of them.

DRAFT OF AN ACT TO INCORPORATE THE TRUSTEES OF THE JOHN F. SLATER FUND.

Whereas, Messrs. RUTHERFORD B. HAYES, of Ohio ; MORRISON R. WAITE, of the District of Columbia ; WILLIAM E. DODGE, of New York ; PHILLIPS BROOKS, of Massachusetts ; DANIEL C. GILMAN, of Maryland ; JOHN A. STEWART, of New York ; ALFRED H. COLQUITT, of Georgia ; MORRIS K. JESUP, of New York ; JAMES P. BOYCE, of Kentucky ; and WILLIAM A. SLATER, of Connecticut, have, by their memorial, represented to the Senate and Assembly of this State that a letter has been received by them from JOHN F. SLATER, of Norwich, in the State of Connecticut, of which the following is a copy :

To Messrs. RUTHERFORD B. HAYES, of Ohio ; MORRISON R. WAITE, of the District of Columbia ; WILLIAM E. DODGE, of New York , PHILLIPS BROOKS, of Massachusetts ; DANIEL C. GILMAN, of Maryland ; JOHN A. STEWART, of New York ; ALFRED H. COLQUITT, of Georgia ; MORRIS K. JESUP, of New York ; JAMES P. BOYCE, of Kentucky ; and WILLIAM A. SLATER, of Connecticut :

GENTLEMEN.—It has pleased God to grant me prosperity in my business, and to put it into my power to apply to charitable uses a sum of money so considerable as to require the counsel of wise men for the administration of it.

It is my desire at this time to appropriate to such uses the sum of one million of dollars ($1,000,000 00) ; and I hereby invite you to procure a charter of incorporation under which a charitable fund may be held exempt from taxation, and under which you shall organize ; and I intend that the corporation, as soon as formed, shall receive this sum in trust to apply the income of it according to the instructions contained in this letter.

The general object which I desire to have exclusively pursued, is the uplifting of the lately emancipated population of the Southern States, and their posterity, by conferring on them the blessings of Christian education. The disabilities formerly suffered by these people, and their singular patience and fidelity in the great crisis of the nation, establish a just claim on the sympathy and good will of humane and patriotic men. I cannot but feel the compassion that is due in view of their prevailing ignorance which exists by no fault of their own

---

[1] Correspondence of American Revolution, vol. iii. p. 547.

But it is not only for their own sake, but also for the safety of our common country, in which they have been invested with equal political rights, that I am desirous to aid in providing them with the means of such education as shall tend to make them good men and good citizens—education in which the instruction of the mind in the common branches of secular learning shall be associated with training in just notions of duty toward God and man, in the light of the Holy Scriptures.

The means to be used in the prosecution of the general object above described, I leave to the discretion of the corporation ; only indicating, as lines of operation adapted to the present condition of things, the training of teachers from among the people requiring to be taught, if, in the opinion of the corporation, by such limited selection the purposes of the trust can be best accomplished ; and the encouragement of such institutions as are most effectually useful in promoting this training of teachers.

I am well aware that the work herein proposed is nothing new or untried. And it is no small part of my satisfaction in taking this share in it, that I hereby associate myself with some of the noblest enterprises of charity and humanity, and may hope to encourage the prayers and toils of faithful men and women who have labored and are still laboring in this cause.

I wish the corporation which you are invited to constitute, to consist at no time of more than twelve members, nor of less than nine members for a longer time than may be required for the convenient filling of vacancies, which I desire to be filled by the corporation, and, when found practicable, at its next meeting after the vacancy may occur.

I designate as the first President of the corporation the Honorable RUTHERFORD B. HAYES, of Ohio. I desire that it may have power to provide from the income of the fund, among other things, for expenses incurred by members in the fulfilment of this trust, and for the expenses of such officers and agents as it may appoint, and generally to do all such acts as may be necessary for carrying out the purposes of this trust. I desire, if it may be, that the corporation may have full liberty to invest its funds according to its own best discretion, without reference to, or restriction by, any laws or rules, legal or equitable, of any nature, regulating the mode of investment of trust funds ; only I wish that neither principal nor income be expended in land or buildings, for any other purpose than that of safe and productive investment for income. And I hereby discharge the corporation, and its individual members, so far as it is in my power so to do, of all responsibility, except for the faithful administration of this trust, according to their own honest understanding and best judgment. In particular, also, I wish to relieve them of any pretended claim on the part of any person, party, sect, institution, or locality, to benefactions from this fund, that may be put forward on any ground whatever ; as I wish every expenditure to be determined solely by the convictions of the corporation itself as to the most useful disposition of its gifts.

I desire that the doings of the corporation each year be printed and sent to each of the State Libraries in the United States, and to the Library of Congress.

In case the capital of the Fund should become impaired, I desire that a part of the income, not greater than one half, be invested, from year to year, until the capital be restored to its original amount.

I purposely leave to the corporation the largest liberty of making such changes in the methods of applying the income of the Fund as shall seem from time to time best adapted to accomplish the general object herein defined. But being warned by the history of such endowments that they sometimes tend to discourage rather than promote effort and self-reliance on the part of beneficiaries, or to inure to the advancement of learning instead of the dissemination of it ; or to become a convenience to the rich instead of a help to those who need help, I solemnly charge my Trustees to use their best wisdom in preventing any such defeat of the spirit of this trust ; so that my gift may continue to future generations to be a blessing to the poor.

If at any time after the lapse of thirty-three years from the date of this foundation it shall appear to the judgment of three fourths of the members of this corporation that, by reason of a change in social conditions, or by reason of adequate and equitable public provision for education, or by any other sufficient reason, there is no further serious need of this Fund in the form in which it is at first instituted, I authorize the corporation to apply the capital of the Fund to the establishment of foundations subsidiary to then already existing institutions of higher education, in such wise as to make the educational advantages of such institutions more freely accessible to poor students of the colored race.

It is my wish that this trust be administered in no partisan, sectional, or sectarian spirit, but in the interest of a generous patriotism and an enlightened Christian faith ; and that the corporation about to be formed, may continue to be constituted of men distinguished either by honorable success in business, or by services to literature, education, religion, or the State.

I am encouraged to the execution in this charitable foundation of a long-cherished purpose, by the eminent wisdom and success that has marked the conduct of the Peabody Education Fund in a field of operation not remote from that contemplated by this trust. I shall commit it to your hands, deeply conscious how insufficient is our best forecast to provide for the future that is known only to God ; but humbly hoping that the administration of it may be so guided by divine wisdom, as to be, in its turn, an encouragement to philanthropic enterprise on the part of others, and an enduring means of good to our beloved country and to our fellow-men.

I have the honor to be, Gentlemen, your friend and fellow-citizen,

JOHN F. SLATER.

NORWICH, CONN., March 4, 1882.

And whereas, said memorialists have further represented that they are ready to accept said trust and receive and administer said Fund, provided a charter of incorporation is granted by this State, as indicated in said letter ;

Now, therefore, for the purpose of giving full effect to the charitable intentions declared in said letter ;

The people of the State of New York, represented in Senate and Assembly, do enact as follows :

SEC 1. Rutherford B. Hayes, Morrison R. Waite, William E. Dodge, Phillips Brooks, Daniel C. Gilman, John A. Stewart, Alfred H. Colquitt, Morris K. Jesup, James P. Boyce, and William A. Slater, are hereby created a body politic and corporate by the name of THE TRUSTEES OF THE JOHN F. SLATER FUND, and by that name shall have perpetual succession ; said original corporators electing their associates and successors, from time to time, so that the whole number of corporators may be kept at not less than nine nor more than twelve.

Said corporation may hold and manage, invest and re-invest all property which may be given or transferred to it for the charitable purposes indicated in said letter, and shall, in so doing, and in appropriating the income accruing therefrom, conform to and be governed by the directions in said letter contained ; and such property and all investments and re-investments thereof, excepting real estate, shall, while owned by said corporation and held for the purposes of said trust, be exempt from taxation of any and every nature.

SEC. 2.   Rutherford B. Hayes, of Ohio, shall be the first President of the corporation, and it may elect such other officers and hold such meetings, whether within or without this State, from time to time, as its by-laws may authorize or prescribe.

SEC. 3.   Said corporation shall annually file with the Librarian of this State a printed report of its doings during the preceding year.

SEC. 4.   This act shall take effect immediately.

COLORED EMPLOYÉS IN WASHINGTON.

There are six hundred and twenty persons of color employed in the different departments of the Government at Washington, D. C., distributed as follows :

War Department	44
Treasury Department	342
Department of Justice	7
Department of State	20
Navy Department	40
Department of the Interior	106 men, 7 women
Post-Office Department	54
Total	620

NEWSPAPERS CONDUCTED BY COLORED MEN.

ALABAMA.

MOBILE.—*The Mobile Gazette ;* Phillip Joseph, Editor ; $2.00 per year ; office No. 36 Conti Street.

HUNTSVILLE.—*Huntsville Gazette ;* ——, Editor ; $1.50 per year ; Saturdays.

ARKANSAS.

HELENA.—*The Golden Epoch ;* H. W. Stewart.

LITTLE ROCK.—*Arkansas Mansion ;* Henry Simkens, Editor ; $1.50 a year.

CALIFORNIA.

SAN FRANCISCO.—*The Elevator ;* Phillip A. Bell, Editor.

DISTRICT OF COLUMBIA.

WASHINGTON CITY.—*People's Advocate*, established in 1876 ; J. W. Cromwell, Editor ; C. A. Lemar, Manager ; $1.50 a year.

WASHINGTON CITY.—*The Bee ;* W. C. Chase, Editor ; C. C. Stewart, Business Manager ; $2.00 per year ; Saturdays ; office, No. 1107 I Street, N. W.

FLORIDA.

PENSACOLA.—*The Journal of Progress ;* Matthews & Davidson, Editors and Proprietors ; $2.00 ; Saturdays.

KEY WEST.—*Key West News ;* J. Willis Menard, Editor ; weekly ; five columns ; price, $1.50 per annum.

GEORGIA.

ATLANTA.—*Weekly Defiance ;* W. H. Burnett, Editor.

AUGUSTA.—*The People's Defense ;* Smith, Nelson, & Co., Proprietors.

AUGUSTA.—*Georgia Baptist ;* Wm. J. White, Editor ; $2.00 per year ; office, No. 633 Ellis Street.

SAVANNAH.—*Savannah Echo ;* Hardin Bros. & Griffin, Proprietors ; $2.00 ; Saturdays.

ILLINOIS.

CHICAGO.—*The Conservator ;* Barnett, Clark, & Co., Editors and Proprietors ; $2.00 per year ; Saturdays ; 194 Clark Street.

CAIRO.—*The Three States ;* M. Gladding, Publisher ; Saturdays ; $1.50 per year ; 190 Commercial Avenue.

CAIRO.—*The Cairo Gazette ;* J. J. Bird, Editor ; Wednesdays and Saturdays ; $2.50 per year.

KANSAS.

TOPEKA — *Topeka Tribune ;* E. H. White.

KENTUCKY.

LOUISVILLE.— *The Bulletin ;* Adams Brothers ; $2.00 per year ; Saturdays ; 562 West Jefferson Street.

LOUISVILLE.— *The American Baptist ;* Wm. H. Stewart.

LOUISVILLE.—*Ohio Falls Express ;* Dr. H. Fitzbutler, Editor ; $1.50 per year ; Saturdays.

BOWLING GREEN.'—*Bowling Green Watchman ;* C. C. Strumm, Editor ; C. R. McDowell, Manager ; Saturdays ; $1.50 per year.

LOUISIANA.

NEW ORLEANS.—*Observer ;* Saturdays ; republican ; four pages ; size, 22 x 32 ; subscription, $2.00 ; established, 1878 ; G. T. Ruby, Editor and Publisher.

MASSACHUSETTS.

BOSTON.— *The Boston Leader ;* Howard L. Smith, Editor ; $1.50 per year ; office, No. 8 Boylston Street. Room 9.

MISSISSIPPI.

VERONA.— *The Banner of Liberty ;* J. B, Wilkins, Editor ; $1.50 per year.

GREENVILLE.— *The Baptist Signal ;* Rev. G. W. Gayles, Editor ; $1.00 per year.

JACKSON.—*People's Adviser.*

JACKSON.—*Mississippi Republican ;* Preston Hay, Editor ; $1.00 ; Saturdays.

MAYERSVILLE.—*Mayersville Spectator ;* W. E. Mollison, Editor ; D. T. Williamson, Publisher ; $1.50 per year ; Saturdays.

MISSOURI.

ST. LOUIS.— *Tribune ;* Sundays ; republican ; eight pages ; size, 26 x 40 ; subscription, $2 00 ; established, 1876 ; J. W. Wilson, Editor and Publisher ; circulation, I.

KANSAS CITY.— *The Kansas City Enterprise ;* D. V. A. Nero ; published every Wednesday and Saturday ; $2.00 per year ; office, No. 537 Main Street, Room No. 2.

NEW JERSEY.

TRENTON.—*The Sentinel ;* R. Henri Herbert, Editor ; Saturdays ; $1.25 per year ; No. 4 North Green Street.

NEW YORK.

NEW YORK CITY.—*Progressive American ;* Thursdays ; four pages ; size, 22 x 31 ; subscription, $2.00; established, 1871 ; John J. Freeman, Editor ; George A. Washington, Publisher ; circulation, J.; office, 125 W. 25th Street.

NEW YORK CITY.—*New York Globe ;* Geo. Parker & Co. ; T. Thos. Fortune, Editor ; office, No. 4 Cedar Street, Room 15.

BROOKLYN.— *The National Monitor ;* R. Rufus L. Perry, D.D.

NORTH CAROLINA.

GOLDSBOROUGH.— *The Carolina Enterprise ;* E. E. Smith, Editor ; $1.00 per year ; Saturday.

CHARLOTTE.—*Charlotte Messenger ;* W. H. Smith, Editor ; $1.50 per year.

WILSON.— *The Wilson News ;* Ward, Moore, & Hill, Editors ; $1 50 a year.

RALEIGH.—*Raleigh Banner ;* J. H. Williams.

WILMINGTON.—*Africo-American Presbyterian ;* D. J. Sanders.

OHIO.

CINCINNATI.— *The Afro-American* ; Clark, Johnson, and Jackson, Editors and Proprietors ; $1.50 per year ; Saturdays ; office, 172 Central Avenue.

CINCINNATI.— *The Weekly Review ; Review* Publishing Co. ; Chas. W. Bell, Editor ; $1.50 per year.

PENNSYLVANIA.

PHILADELPHIA.—*Christian Recorder;* Thursdays ; Methodist ; four pages ; size, 28 x 42 ; subscription, $2.00 ; established, 1862 ; Rev. Benj. T. Tanner, D.D., Editor ; Rev. Theo. Gould, Publisher ; circulation, G ; office, 631 Pine Street.

SOUTH CAROLINA.

CHARLESTON.— *The New Era;* Wm. Holloway, Business Manager ; $1.50 per year ; Saturdays ; democratic ; 196 Meeting Street.

CHARLESTON.— *The Palmetto Press;* Robert L. Smith, Editor ; $1.50 per year ; Saturdays.

TENNESSEE.

NASHVILLE.—*Knights of Wise Men ;* J. L. Brown, Editor ; office, No. 5 Cherry Street.

CHATTANOOGA.— *The Enterprise;* Rev. D. W. Hays.

TEXAS.

AUSTIN.— *The Austin Citizen ;* J. J. Hamilton & Co.

DALLAS.— *The Baptist Journal;* S. H. Smothers, Editor ; A. R. Greggs, Publisher.

DALLAS.—*Christian Preacher;* C. M. Wilmeth.

MARSHALL.— *The Christian Advocate ;* M. F. Jamison.

GALVESTON.—*Spectator;* Richard Nelson, Editor ; $1.50 per year.

PALESTINE.—*Colored American Journal;* monthly ; C. W. Porter, Editor.

VIRGINIA.

RICHMOND.—*Virginia Star;* Saturdays ; four pages ; size, 20 x 26 ; subscription, $2.00 ; established, 1876 ; R. M. Green, M.D., O. M. Stewart, and P. H. Woolfolk, Editors and Publishers ; circulation, K.

RICHMOND.—*Industrial Herald ;* John Oliver, Editor ; $1.00 per year.

PETERSBURGH.— *The Lancet;* Geo. F. Bragg, Jr., Manager ; $1.50 per year ; Saturdays.

WEST VIRGINIA.

WHEELING.— *The Weekly Times ;* Welcome, Buckner, & Co., Publishers ; Geo. W. Welcome, Editor ; 8 pages ; $1.00 per annum.

NEGROES IN NORTHERN COLLEGES.

In response to a circular sent out, seventy Northern Colleges sent information ; and in them are at present one hundred and sixty-nine Colored students. The exact number of graduates cannot be ascertained, as these colleges do not keep a record of the nationality of their students.

CHAPTER XXIII.

HENRY HIGHLAND GARNET, D.D.

The career of this man, who died at Monrovia, Liberia, Feb. 14, 1882, where he was the Minister of the United States, was extraordinary. Grandson of a native African, brought over in a slave-trader, himself born a slave, he was brought to Pennsylvania by his father, when he fled from slavery in 1824. Next we find him, at the age of seventeen, ridiculed for studying Greek and Latin ; then mobbed in a New Hampshire seminary ; then dragged from a street car in Utica ; then studying theology with Dr. Beman in Troy, N. Y. Soon he was settled as a minister ; afterward he travelled in Great Britain and on the Continent of Europe, and was sent by a Scottish Society as Presbyterian missionary to Jamaica, West Indies. He returned to New York, and was long the pastor of the Shiloh Presbyterian Church ; his house escaping the riots in 1863 " by the foresight of his daughter, who wrenched off the door plate." He was the first Colored man who ever spoke in public in the Capitol at

Washington, having preached there Sunday, Feb. 12, 1865. In 1881 he was appointed Minister to Liberia. Dr. Garnet was equal in ability to Frederick Douglass, and greatly his superior in learning, especially excelling in logic and terse statement. We heard him make a speech in 1865, which in force of reasoning, purity of language, and propriety of utterance, was not unworthy of comparison with a sermon of Bishop Thomson, or an address of George William Curtis. As he was "a full-blooded Negro," he was a standing and unanswerable proof that the race is capable of all that has distinguished MAN. How much of history and progress could be crowded in a memorial inscription for him! It might be something like this: Born a slave in the country to which his grandfather was stolen away, he competed, under the greatest disadvantages, with white men for the prizes of life; attaining the highest intellectual culture, and a corresponding moral elevation, his career commanded universal respect in Europe and America, wherever he was known. He died the Minister of the United States to a civilized nation in the land whence his barbaric ancestors were stolen. To God, who "hath made of one blood all nations of men for to dwell on all the face of the earth, and hath determined the times before appointed, and the bounds of their habitation" (Acts xvii : 26), be the glory: "How unsearchable are His judgments, and His ways past finding out!"

EBENEZER D. BASSETT.

One of the ablest diplomats the Negro race has produced is the Honorable Ebenezer D. Bassett, for nearly nine years the Resident Minister and Consul-General from the United States to Hayti. He was born and educated in the State of Connecticut, and for many years was the successful Principal of the Institute for Colored Youth at Philadelphia, Pennsylvania. As a classical scholar and for proficiency in the use of modern languages he has few equals among his race.

Returning to this country, after years of honorable service abroad, he was promoted by the Haytian Government to the position of Consul at New York City, and at present is serving the Republic of Hayti. As an evidence of the high esteem in which he was held as an officer the following documents attest:

(COPY.)

DEPARTMENT OF STATE,
WASHINGTON, October 5, 1877.

EBENEZER D. BASSETT, Esquire, etc., etc., etc.

SIR: I have to acknowledge the receipt of your despatch No. 529, of the 23d August last, tendering your resignation of the office of Minister Resident and Consul-General of the United States to Hayti, and to inform you that it is accepted.

I cannot allow this opportunity to pass without expressing to you the appreciation of the Department of the very satisfactory manner in which you have discharged the duties of the mission at Port au Prince during your term of office. This commendation of your services is the more especially merited, because at various times your duties have been of such a delicate nature as to have required the exercise of much tact and discretion.

I enclose herewith a letter addressed by the President of the United States to the President of Hayti, announcing your retirement from the mission at Port au Prince, together with an office copy of the same. You will transmit the latter to the Minister of Foreign Affairs, and make arrangements for the delivery of the original to the President when your successor shall present his credentials.

I am, sir, your obedient servant,
(Signed.)   F. W. SEWARD, *Acting Secretary.*

(TRANSLATION.)

BOISROND CANAL, *President of the Republic of Hayti,*
To His Excellency the President of the United States of America.

GREAT AND GOOD FRIEND: Mr. Ebenezer D. Bassett, who has resided here in the capacity of Minister of the United States, has placed in my hands the letter by which your Excellency has brought his mission to an end.

In taking leave of me in conformity with the wishes of your Excellency, he has renewed the assurance of the friendly sentiments which so happily exist on the part of the Government and the people of the United States toward the Government and the people of the Republic of Hayti.

I have not failed to request him to transmit to your Excellency, the expression of my great desire to maintain always the relations of the two Countries upon the footing of that cordial understanding.

It is for me a pleasing duty to acknowledge fully to your Excellency, the zeal and the intelligence with which Mr. Bassett has fulfilled here the high and delicate functions that had been entrusted to him.

I have, therefore, been happy to be able to testify to him publicly before his departure, in the name of my fellow-citizens, the esteem and sincere affection which his talents, his character, his private and public conduct have won for him, as well as the particular sentiments of friendship and gratitude I personally entertain for him.

I pray God that He may have your Excellency always in His Holy keeping.

Given at the National Palace of Port au Prince, the 29th day of November, 1877.

Your Good Friend,

(Signed)   BOISROND CANAL.

Countersigned.

(Signed.)   F. CARRIE, *Secretary of State.*

COLORED SENATORS AND CONGRESSMEN.

UNITED STATES SENATORS.

HIRAM R. REVELS, United States Senator from Mississippi, was born in Fayetteville, North Carolina, September 1, 1822 ; desiring to obtain an education, which was denied in his native State to those of African descent, he removed to Indiana ; spent some time at the Quaker Seminary in Union County ; entered the Methodist ministry ; afterward received further instructions at the Clarke County Seminary, when he became preacher, teacher, and lecturer among his people in the States of Indiana, Illinois, Ohio, and Missouri ; at the breaking out of the war, he was ministering at Baltimore ; he assisted in the organization of the first two Colored regiments in Maryland and Missouri ; during a portion of 1863 and 1864 he taught school in St. Louis, then went to Vicksburg, and assisted the provost marshal in managing the freedmen affairs ; followed on the heels of the army to Jackson ; organized churches, and lectured ; spent the next two years in Kansas and Missouri in preaching and lecturing on moral and religious subjects ; returned to Mississippi, and settled at Natchez ; was chosen presiding elder of the Methodist Church, and a member of the city council ; was elected a United States Senator from Mississippi as a Republican, serving from February 25, 1870, to March 3, 1871 ; was pastor of a Methodist Episcopal church at Holly Springs, Mississippi ; removed to Indiana, where he was pastor of the African Methodist Episcopal Church at Richmond.

BLANCHE K. BRUCE, United States Senator from Mississippi, was born in Prince Edward County, Virginia, March 1, 1841 ; as his parents were slaves, he received a limited education ; became a planter in Mississippi in 1869 ; was a member of the Mississippi Levee Board, and sheriff and tax-collector of Bolivar County from 1872 until his election to the United States Senate from Mississippi, February 3, 1875, as a Republican, to succeed Henry R. Pease, Republican, and took his seat March 4, 1875. His term of service expired March 3, 1881.

UNITED STATES CONGRESSMEN.

RICHARD H. CAIN was born in Greenbrier County, Virginia, April 12, 1825. His father removed to Ohio in 1831, and settled in Gallipolis. He had no education, except such as was afforded in Sabbath-school, until after his marriage ; entered the ministry at an early age ; became a student at Wilberforce University at Xenia, Ohio, in 1860, and remained there for one year ; removed, at the breaking out of the war, to Brooklyn, New York, where he was a pastor for four years ; was sent by his Church as a missionary to the freedmen in South Carolina ; was chosen a member of the Constitutional Convention of South Carolina ; was elected a member of the State Senate from Charleston, and served two years ; took charge of a republican newspaper in 1868 ; was elected a representative from South Carolina in the Forty-third Congress as a Republican, receiving 66,825 votes against 26,394 for Lewis E. Johnson, and was again elected to the Forty-fifth Congress as a Republican, receiving 21,385 votes against 16,074 votes for M. P. O'Connor, Democrat.

'ROBERT C. DE LARGE was born at Aiken, South Carolina, March 15, 1842 ; received such an education as was then attainable ; was a farmer ; was an agent of the Freedmen's Bureau from May, 1867, to April, 1868, when he was elected a member of the State Constitutional Convention ; was a member of the House of Representatives of the State Legislature in 1868, 1869, and 1870 ; was one of the State Commissioners of the Sinking Fund ; was elected in 1870 State Land Commissioner, and served until he was elected a representative from South Carolina in the Forty-second Congress as a Republican, receiving 16,686 votes, against 15,700 votes for C. C. Bowen, Independent Republican ; was appointed a trial justice, which office he held when he died at Charlestown, South Carolina, February 15, 1874.

ROBERT BROWN ELLIOTT was born at Boston, Massachusetts, August 11, 1842 ; received his primary education at private schools ; in 1853 entered High Holborn Academy in London, England ; in 1855 entered Eton College, England, and graduated in 1859 ; studied law, and practises his profession ; was a member of the State Constitutional Convention of South Carolina in 1868 ; was a member of the House of Representatives of South Carolina from July 6, 1868, to October 23, 1870 ; was appointed on the 25th of March, 1869, assistant adjutant-general, which position he held until he was elected a representative from South Carolina in the Forty-second Congress as a Republican, receiving 20,564 votes against 13,997 votes for J. E. Bacon, Democrat, serving from March 4, 1871, to 1873, when he resigned ; and was re-elected to the Forty-third Congress as a Republican, receiving 21,627 votes against 1,094 votes for W. H. McCan, Democrat, serving from December 1, 1873, to May, 1874, when he resigned, having been elected sheriff.

JERE HARALSON was born in Muscogee County, Georgia, April 1, 1846, the slave property of John Walker ; after Walker's death, was sold on the auction-block in the city of Columbus, and bought by J. W. Thompson, after whose death he became the property of J. Haralson, of Selma, and so remained until emancipated in 1865 ; received no education until after he was free, when he instructed himself ; was elected to the State House of Representatives of Alabama in 1870 ; was elected to the State Senate of Alabama in 1872 ; was elected a representative from Alabama in the Forty-fourth Congress as a Republican, receiving 19,551 votes against 16,953 votes for F. G. Bromberg, Democrat, serving from December 6, 1875, to .March 3, 1877 ; was defeated by the Republican candidate for the Forty-fifth Congress, receiving 8,675 votes against 9,685 votes for Charles L. Shelley, Democrat, and 7,236 votes for James T. Rapier, Republican.

JOHN R. LYNCH was born in Concordia Parish, Louisiana, September 10, 1847, a slave ; and he remained in slavery until emancipated by the results of the Rebellion, receiving no early education ; a purchaser of his mother carried her with her children to Natchez, where, when the Union troops took posession, he attended evening school for a few months, and he has since by private study acquired a good English education; he engaged in the business of photography at Natchez until 1869, when Governor Ames appointed him a justice of the peace ; he was elected a member of the State Legislature from Adams County, and re-elected in 1871, serving the last term as Speaker of the House ; was elected a representative from Mississippi in the Forty-third Congress as a Republican, receiving 15,391 votes against 8,430 votes for H. Cassidy, Sr., Democrat ; and was re-elected to the Forty-fourth Congress as a Republican (defeating Roderick Seals, Democrat), serving from December 1, 1873, to March 3, 1877.

CHARLES E. NASH was born at Opelousas, Louisiana; received a common-school education at New Orleans; was a bricklayer by trade; enlisted as private in the Eighty-third Regiment, United States Chasseurs d' Afrique, April 20, 1863, and was promoted until he became acting sergeant-major of the regiment; lost a leg at the storming of Fort Blakely, and was honorably discharged from the army May 30, 1865; was elected a representative from Louisiana in the Forty-fourth Congress as a Republican, receiving 13,156 votes against 12,085 votes for Joseph M. Moore, Democrat, serving from December 6, 1875, to March 3, 1877; was defeated as the Republican candidate for the Forty-fifth Congress, receiving 11,147 votes against 15,520 votes for Edward White Robertson, Democrat.

JOSEPH H. RAINEY was born at Georgetown, South Carolina (where both of his parents were slaves, but, by their industry, obtained their freedom), June 21, 1832; although debarred by law from attending school he acquired a good education, and further improved his mind by observation and travel; his father was a barber, and he followed that occupation at Charlestown till 1862, when, having been forced to work on the fortifications of the Confederates, he escaped to the West Indies, where he remained until the close of the war, when he returned to his native town; he was elected a delegate to the State Constitutional Convention of 1868, and was a member of the State Senate of South Carolina in 1870, resigning when elected a representative from South Carolina in the Forty-first Congress as a Republican (to fill the vacancy caused by the non-reception of B. F. Whittemore), by a majority of 17,193 votes over Dudley, Conservative; was re-elected to the Forty-second Congress, receiving 20,221 votes against 11,628 votes for C. W. Dudley, Democrat; was re-elected to the Forty-third Congress, receiving 19,765 votes, being all that were cast; was re-elected to the Forty-fourth Congress, receiving 14,370 votes against 13,563 votes for Samuel Lee, Republican; was re-elected to the Forty-fifth Congress, receiving 18,180 votes against 16,661 votes for J. S. Richardson, Democrat, serving from March 4, 1869.

ALONZO J. RANSIER was born at Charlestown, South Carolina, in January, 1834; was self-educated; was employed as shipping-clerk in 1850 by a leading merchant, who was tried for violation of law in "hiring a Colored clerk," and fined one cent with costs; was one of the foremost in the works of reconstruction in 1865; was a member of a convention of the friends of equal rights in October, 1865, at Charlestown, and was deputed to present the memorial there framed to Congress; was elected a member of the State Constitutional Convention of 1868; was elected a member of the House of Representatives in the State Legislature in 1869; was chosen chairman of the State Republican Central Committee, which position he held until 1872; was elected a presidential elector on the Grant and Colfax ticket in 1868; was elected lieutenant-governor of South Carolina in 1870 by a large majority; was president of the Southern States Convention at Columbia in 1871; was chosen a delegate to, and was a vice-president of, the Philadelphia Convention which nominated Grant and Wilson in 1872; and was elected a representative from South Carolina in the Forty-third Congress as a Republican, receiving 20,061 votes against 6,549 votes for W. Gurney, Independent Republican, serving from December 1, 1873, to March 3, 1875.

JAMES T. RAPIER was born in Florence, Alabama, in 1840; was educated in Canada; is a planter; was appointed a notary public by the governor of Alabama in 1866; was a member of the first Republican Convention held in Alabama, and was one of the committee that framed the platform of the party; represented Lauderdale County in the Constitutional Convention held at Montgomery in 1867; was nominated for secretary of State in 1870, but defeated with the rest of the ticket; was appointed assessor of internal revenue for the second collection-district of Alabama in 1871; was appointed State commissioner to the Vienna Exposition in 1873 by the governor of Alabama ; was elected a representative from Alabama in the Forty-third Congress as a Republican, receiving 19,100 votes against 16,000 votes for C. W. Oates, Democrat, serving from December 1, 1873, to March 3, 1875 ; and was defeated as the Republican candidate for the Forty-fourth Congress, receiving 19,124 votes against 20,180 votes for Jeremiah N. Williams, Democrat.

ROBERT SMALLS was born at Beaufort, South Carolina, April 5, 1839 ; being a slave, was debarred by statute from attending school, but educated himself with such limited advantages as he could secure ; removed to Charlestown in 1851 ; worked as a rigger, and led a seafaring life ; became connected in 1861 with " The Planter," a steamer plying in Charlestown harbor as a transport, which he took over Charlestown Bar in May, 1862, and delivered her and his services to the commander of the United States blockading squadron ; was appointed pilot in the United States navy, and served in that capacity on the monitor " Keokuk " in the attack on Fort Sumter ; served as pilot in the quartermaster's department, and was promoted as captain for gallant and meritorious conduct December 1, 1863, and placed in command of " The Planter," serving until she was put out of commission in 1866 ; was elected a member of the State Constitutional Convention of 1868 ; was elected a member of the State House of Representatives in 1868, and of the State Senate (to fill a vacancy) in 1870, and re-elected in 1872 ; and was elected a representative from South Carolina in the Forty-fourth Congress as a Republican, receiving 17,752 votes against 4,461 votes for J. P. M. Epping, Republican ; and was re-elected to the Forty-fifth Congress, receiving 19,954 votes against 18,516 votes for G. D. Tillman, Democrat, serving from December, 6, 1875, to March 3, 1877 ; and is now a member.

JOSIAH T. WALLS was born at Winchester, Virginia, December 30, 1842 ; received a common-school education ; was a planter ; was elected a member of the State Constitutional Convention in 1868 ; was elected a member of the State House of Representatives in 1868 ; was elected to the State Senate 1869–1872 ; claimed to have been elected a representative from the State-at-large to the Forty-second Congress as a Republican, but the election was contested by his competitor, Silas L. Niblack, who took the seat January 29, 1873 ; was re-elected for the State-at-large, receiving 17,503 votes against 15,881 votes for Niblack, Democrat ; and was re-elected to the Forty-fourth Congress, receiving 8,549 votes against 8,178 votes for Jesse J. Finley, Democrat.

BENJ. STERLING TURNER was born in Halifax County, North Carolina, March 17, 1825 ; was raised as a slave, and received no early education, because the laws of that State made it criminal to educate slaves ; removed to Alabama in 1830, and, by clandestine study, obtained a fair education ; became a dealer in general merchandise ; was elected tax-collector of Dallas County in 1867, and councilman of the city of Selma in 1869 ; was elected a representative from Alabama in the Forty-second Congress as a Republican, receiving 18,226 votes against 13,466 votes for S. J. Cumming, Democrat, serving from March 4, 1871, to March 3, 1873 ; was defeated as the Republican candidate for the Forty-third Congress, receiving 13,174 votes against 15,607 votes for F. G. Bromberg, Democrat and Liberal, and 7,024 votes for P. Joseph, Republican.

JEFFERSON F. LONG, Macon, Georgia.   Took his seat Feb. 24, 1871.

BUREAU OFFICER.

Honorable BLANCHE K. BRUCE, Register of the United States Treasury ; appointed by President James A. Garfield, 1881.

Hayti.—E. D. BASSETT, Pennsylvania, 1869–77.

Hayti.—JOHN M. LANGSTON, District of Columbia, Minister Resident and Consul-General to Hayti, 1877.

Liberia.—J. MILTON TURNER, Missouri.

Liberia.—JOHN H. SMYTH, North Carolina. Reappointed in 1882.

Liberia.—HENRY HIGHLAND GARNET, New York, Minister Resident and Consul-General to Liberia.

LIEUTENANT-GOVERNORS.

The following Colored men were Lieutenant-Governors during the years of reconstruction. At the head of them all for bravery, intelligence, and executive ability stands Governor Pinchback. One of the first men of his race to enter the army in 1862 as captain, when the conflict was over and his race free, he was the first Colored man in Louisiana to enter into the work of reconstruction. He has been and is a power in his State. He is true to his friends, but a terror to his enemies. A sketch of his life would read like a romance

Louisiana.	*South Carolina.*	*Mississippi.*
OSCAR J. DUNN,	ALONZO J. RANSIER,	ALEX. DAVIS.
P. B. S. PINCHBACK,	RICHARD H. GLEAVES,	
C. C. ANTOINE.		

INDEX.